Science Fact and Science Fiction

Science Fact and Science Fiction

AN ENCYCLOPEDIA

BRIAN STABLEFORD

Routledge
Taylor & Francis Group
New York   London

Routledge is an imprint of the
Taylor & Francis Group, an informa business

Routledge
Taylor & Francis Group
270 Madison Avenue
New York, NY 10016

Routledge
Taylor & Francis Group
2 Park Square
Milton Park, Abingdon
Oxon OX14 4RN

Printed in the United States of America on acid-free paper
10 9 8 7 6 5 4 3 2 1

International Standard Book Number-10: 0-415-97460-7 (Hardcover)
International Standard Book Number-13: 978-0-415-97460-8 (Hardcover)

Visit the Taylor & Francis Web site at
http://www.taylorandfrancis.com

and the Routledge Web site at
http://www.routledge-ny.com

Contents

Alphabetical List of Entries

ALPHABETICAL LIST OF ENTRIES

Thematic List of Entries

Celestial Bodies and Phenomena

Asteroid
Comet
Galaxy
Meteorite
Nova
Planet
Star

Celestial Bodies and Phenomena: Solar System

Jupiter
Mars
Mercury
Moon, The
Neptune
Pluto
Saturn
Sun, The
Uranus
Venus

Concepts

Alien
Alienation
Alternative History
Android
Art
Catastrophism
Civilisation

Clone
Colonisation
Creationism
Cyberspace
Cyborg
Death
Decadence
Disaster
Dystopia
Ecocatastrophe
Entropy
Flying Saucer
Force
Fourth Dimension, The
Future
Game
Hyperspace
Hypnosis
Ideology
Impossibility
Intelligence
Invisibility
Law
Life
Light
Longevity
Matter Transmission
Monster
Music
Narrative Theory
Naturalism
Nature
Omega Point
Palingenesis
Paradox
Parallel World
Past

Leading Figures: Scientists

Darwin, Charles (Robert)
Darwin, Erasmus
Dee, John
Dyson, Freeman (John)
Edison, Thomas Alva
Einstein, Albert
Freud, Sigmund
Galileo
Haldane, J[ohn] B[urton] S[anderson]
Jung, Carl (Gustav)
Kepler, Johannes
Lamarck, Jean-Baptiste de Monet,
    Chevalier de
Leonardo Da Vinci
Lovelock, James
Marx, Karl
Mesmer, (Franz) Anton
Newton, Sir Isaac
Paracelsus

Leading Figures: Scientists/Authors

Benford, Gregory (Albert)
Clarke, Sir Arthur C[harles]
Clement, Hal
Flammarion, (Nicholas) Camille
Forward, Robert L[ull]
Hinton, C[harles] H[oward]
Hoyle, Sir Fred
Sagan, Carl (Edward)
Sheffield, Charles
Tsiolkovsky, Konstantin (Eduardovich)
Vinge, Vernor (Steffen)

Pseudoscience

Alchemy
Astrology
Occult Science
Parapsychology
Pseudoscience

Sciences

Acoustics
Aeronautics
Astronomy

Biology
Biotechnology
Botany
Cartography
Chemistry
Cosmology
Cryogenics
Crystallography
Dinosaur
Ecology
Electricity
Engineering
Entomology
Experiment
Food Science
Forensic Science
Genetics
Geography
Geology
Geometry
Mathematics
Mechanics
Medicine
Meteorology
Microbiology
Nanotechnology
Neurology
Optics
Ornithology
Palaeontology
Pathology
Physics
Popularisation of Science, The
Psychotropic
Science
Scientist
SETI
Sociobiology
Zoology

Scientific Models and Theories

Atom
Big Bang, The
Black Hole
Chaos
Cybernetics
Ether
Eugenics
Evolution
Exobiology
Extrapolation
Fermi Paradox, The

Introduction

An encyclopaedia of science would be a huge project to undertake nowadays, as would an encyclopaedia of fiction. Either would require several volumes to do any justice at all to the range and depth of its subject matter. An encyclopaedia of the connections between science and fiction, on the other hand, can still be contained within a single volume without seeming stupidly superficial. This testifies to the extent of fiction's abiding unconcern with science and technology, by comparison with other aspects of human thought, action and sentiment.

The volume of both scientific and fictional publication has increased dramatically over time, accelerating remarkably in the twentieth century when a series of other media were added to text and oral culture as significant conveyors of fiction. There is a sense in which the fictional reflections of science and technology have also increased dramatically in volume over time, similarly accelerating in the twentieth century, when it became commonplace for the first time to identify a genre of "science fiction," but the similarities between these historical processes are outweighed by their differences.

A modern encyclopaedia of science would have to give due credit to the intellectual achievements of centuries earlier than the twentieth; it would, however, regard them as transitory phases en route to a fuller understanding, whose triumphs have all been integrated into more elaborate patterns of ideas. A modern encyclopaedia of fiction could not see history in the same light; it could not regard the works of Homer, William Shakespeare, and Marcel Proust as transitional achievements that have been further elaborated, but as enduring monuments constituting the core of its concerns. Both encyclopaedias would have to omit a great many minor works and their authors from the preserved historical record on the grounds that they are of merely peripheral interest, but they would do so on different grounds.

The encyclopaedia of science would filter the heritage of the past to exclude or marginalise the incorrect and the repetitive, while the encyclopaedia of fiction would filter the heritage of the past to exclude or marginalise material considered less valuable in aesthetic terms. Whereas encyclopaedias of science inevitably favour the contemporary, as the highest level of attainment, encyclopaedias of fiction are often critical of the contemporary, comparing it unfavourably with the antique. Encyclopaedias of fiction, moreover, routinely represent themselves as encyclopaedias of *literature*, in order to emphasise that their selection process is the work of connoisseurs of value–connoisseurs who are inevitably suspicious of popular fiction, whose value is often thought to be prejudiced because it appeals to a wide audience.

One of the consequences of aesthetic filtration is the near-erasure from modern encyclopaedias of literature of the great majority of works containing any significant reflection of science and technology, which are routinely considered to be aesthetically valueless by virtue of their choice of subject matter. This generates problems for any project attempting to bring the connections between science and fiction into clearer focus. From the viewpoint of science, such a project is bound to seem unnecessary, since it hardly matters to scientists whether or not they are represented in fiction. From the literary viewpoint, such a project is likely to seem worthless, in that it would be bound to devote much of its attention to science fiction.

In spite of these problems, the compilation of a broad overview of the connections between science and fiction is a useful project, because it helps to illuminate the history of science and the history of fiction from an unusual angle, which may reveal aspects of both that are normally obscured. It also helps to illuminate the reasons why the overlap between the two histories is so slight and so odd, and why the two histories have diverged even more markedly as time has passed. If it is desirable to construct and maintain bridges between the cultures of science and fiction, then a volume like *Science Fact and Science Fiction: An Encyclopedia* will hopefully constitute a significant bridge in itself as well as mapping the existing ones, and might be of some assistance in building more.

Science and Literature

To some extent, at least, the histories of science and literature have run parallel; their rates of evolution have varied according to roughly similar patterns. Insofar as their histories have been related, however, the relationship has more often seemed inverse than correspondent, not merely traveling in different directions but actively in conflict with one another—but that serves to underline the fact that there *is* a significant relationship between the two histories.

The anxiety that the progress of science has devalued or devastated the poetic element of the human imagination—by "unweaving the rainbow", as John Keats put it—is as strong now as it ever was, and as plausible. The fact that prose has displaced poetry to such a drastic extent in the literary marketplace is certainly not unconnected with the development of the scientific method and the scientific worldview—but to regard science and literature as antithetical forces pulling in opposed directions would be a distortion as well as an oversimplification. There is no simple causal relationship between the evolution of science and the evolution of fiction, and changes in the two fields cannot usually be linked in any simple fashion to more remote causes by which they are both affected. Even so, they are not as mutually irrelevant or hostile as their separate introspective narratives sometimes make them seem. Hopefully, a book of this kind might be useful in making their relationship clearer.

Fact and fiction are often defined as fundamental opposites. In the most brutal sense, facts are true and fiction isn't. Adding "science" to the summation helps to illustrate the complications that arise when the definitions extend beyond brutal simplicity, because it introduces the question of how facts are established as true, and the corollary question of whether facts are the only things that qualify as truth.

Science affirms (for it cannot swear on oath) that it is the truth, the whole truth and nothing but the truth: an account of law-bound nature strictly derived from the evidence. It is, however, often argued that truth is more complicated than scientific testimony will allow. On the other hand, defining fiction as mere untruth is a drastic oversimplification. All the major forms of fiction—including myth, legend, and folklore, as well as literature—aspire to a greater ambition than merely telling lies. It is not simply that there is an element of attempted truth mingled with their fabrications, but that it is that attempt that constitutes their *raison d'être*, fabrication being merely a means to an end. The universality of fiction reflects its utility, and that utility is dependent on the conviction that there is more to truth than fact, and more to knowledge than science can obtain.

Science is a method: a process of certification leading to a stamp of assured quality. The method can easily be anatomised into three components–hypothesis, observation and experiment–but the order in which the three components are best arranged is open to question. It was once generally supposed that observations came first, generating hypotheses that were then subjected to confirmatory experiments, but it is now more commonly agreed that "observation" is a problematic business, routinely conditioned by preexistent frames of perception and intellectual organisation. In this view, the speculative construction of hypotheses either precedes observation or is inextricably mingled with that process, and the proper function of experimentation is not to seek confirmation, but to set up rigorous tests in order to cast out mistaken hypotheses and misconceived observations. However the three components are mixed, they are obviously not alike. Hypothesis formulation, or speculation, is a creative process. Experiment is, by contrast, a judgmental process. Observation seems, at first glance, to be merely cumulative, neither creative nor judgmental, but more careful analysis suggests that it involves both creative and judgmental elements.

When the process of fact gathering is broken down in this fashion it becomes easier to draw useful comparisons with fiction—or, at least, with the component of fiction that aspires to be more than lies. Fiction also has its hypothetical, observational and judgemental components, whose appropriate balance has long been a matter of controversy. Fiction is not judgemental in the same way as scientific experimentation, having more to do with moral than factual judgement, but intellectually respectable fiction nevertheless aims to put its assertions and evaluations to a kind of stern proof. The creative element of fiction is more likely to be seen as an end than a beginning, but that does not mean that it is reckless.

The great difference between scientific and fictional observation lies in the manner in which the combination of observation and judgement generates a coherent "worldview". The testing of scientific observations ruthlessly eliminates mistaken hypotheses from consideration, while setting moral judgments aside in order to concentrate narrowly on what *is*, but the testing of fictional observation is intimately concerned with moral judgment, and not nearly so ruthless in its treatment of hypotheses. Fiction is by no means unconcerned with what *is*, but it usually tries to consider what is in a broader context of what *might be* and what *ought to be*. There is more necessity than choice in this distinction.

In order to support its method of determining facts, and the theories that render them coherent, science needs to make certain basic assumptions about the extent to which the world is ordered, and the nature of that order. The whole edifice rests on a few fundamental observations, one of which is the assumption that the laws of nature do not discriminate—that they apply to everything, and to everyone, in exactly the same way. One corollary of this is Jesus' observation in *Matthew* 5:45 that the sun rises and the rain falls on the just and the unjust alike. In the world of experience— the world of scientific observation—virtue has no naturally guaranteed reward, and vice no naturally guaranteed punishment.

This is not a situation of which anyone approves; indeed, it is arguable that the primary employment of the human mind since the dawn of intelligent consciousness has been to compensate for the deficit. The compensations have been both pragmatic, consisting of the institution of artificial rewards and punishments within social organisation, and imaginative, often involving the assertion that appearances must be deceptive, and that there must be a world beyond that of experience in which the moral accounts are ultimately balanced.

Science, by definition, can have nothing to do with the latter kind of compensatory endeavour; it is concerned with the order that exists, not one that might be preferable.

Even its dealings with practical compensation are limited and problematic. It can certainly concern itself with the effects that social institutions actually have, but runs into difficulties when it tries to deal with the hopes and intentions that they appear or claim to embody. Science can only admit the hypothesis of a morally interested creator of the natural world by placing such an entity outside the world of experience; it cannot admit one that routinely interferes with the indiscrimination of its own natural laws. Accommodating the hypothesis of morally interested creators of the social world can be awkward too, because the assumption that people act for the reasons they give in justification is often dubious.

The world within a fictional text, on the other hand, is organised in a way that is intrinsically accommodating to creative interference, not only at the level of the author's powers of determination, but at the level of the characters' motivations. The author not only has the power to determine on whom the rain falls, and when, but the authority to state without objection why characters do what they do. There is far less restriction on what can be stated in words than there is on what can happen in the world of experience, and fiction is therefore flexible in ways that the world of experience is not. If the world of experience *were* flexible in that fashion, then science would have no foundation.

In the "world" contained within a fictional text, it is not only possible for the sun and the rain to discriminate between the just and unjust, but perfectly routine. All that the literary creator has to do to make sure that the virtuous thrive and the wicked suffer is to say so—and that fact is sufficient to create a considerable expectation on the part of an audience that things will turn out that way. "The good ended happily and the bad unhappily," as Miss Prism explains to Cecily in *The Importance of Being Earnest*, "that is what fiction means." In fiction, "poetic justice" is not always delivered, but it is always potentially accessible—which is why its deliberate withholding gives rise to the frustrating emotional sensation of tragedy. Whereas science cannot deal with moral order, fiction must. That is, indeed, "what fiction means"; it is, at any rate, a far better definition of fiction than "lying."

This difference does establish a fundamental dichotomy between science and fiction, although it is not nearly as simple as the apparent dichotomies between truth and untruth. The existence of such a dichotomy does not mean that no connections can be made or comparisons drawn between science and fiction, but it does complicate the process. It also helps to explain the near-nonexistence of a science of fiction, and the essential awkwardness of fictional treatments of science.

Fiction seems so resistant to scientific analysis that attempts to carry out such a task have always been tentative, and have commanded very little attention either in the realm of science or the republic of literary studies; what is generally called "narrative theory" or "narratology" is a very delicate touching point. The narrative of science is not undeveloped–indeed, it is in some respects very highly developed—but it sternly insists on representing itself as a *nonfictional* narrative. It is not merely that the narrative of science represents itself as a history rather than a mere story, but that it represents itself as a particular kind of history that has far less fiction in it than history as a whole—history as a whole being extensively polluted by myth, legend, folklore, accidental misinformation, and deliberate disinformation, in a manner that is a constant source of irritation and anxiety for scientifically inclined historians. The history of science, like science itself, aspires to be a *true history*, and is inevitably disturbed by the suggestion that there might be no such thing, or that it might be unattainable in practice even if it were theoretically conceivable.

Fiction's dealings with the concept of "true history" are far more complicated than science's dealings with moral order, which merely attempt its absolute exclusion. The complexity in question is, in fact, neatly illustrated by an item of fiction whose title is usually translated as *True History*: an imaginary voyage penned by the Greek satirist Lucian, which describes a trip to the moon. Lucian called his story *True History* precisely because it was not, in order to make fun of the propensity of travellers' tales to exaggerate, embroider, and embellish in the interests of telling a more exciting story and making the teller seem more interesting and more heroic. In the republic of fiction, the concept of *true history* is intrinsically ironic.

Science, by definition, is implacably hostile to irony, entirely dependent on statements meaning exactly what they say. Fiction not only accommodates irony but welcomes it, determinedly extrapolating the principle that statements can imply more than they actually say, and are quite capable of implying something entirely different. In other words, science is pedantic, and fiction is anti-pedantic. From the literary viewpoint, science is bound to seem rigid and humorless; from the scientific viewpoint, fiction is bound to seem mercurial and perverse.

Science Fiction

Given all this, it is not surprising that the seemingly oxymoronic phrase "science fiction" is of recent and disreputable coinage, routinely seeming offensive to scientists and literary men alike, nor that, while science evolved so rapidly and so wondrously in the seventeenth and eighteenth centuries, the reflections of that triumphant progress in the literary world were fragmentary, elliptical, and grudging. Nor is it any wonder that even in the nineteenth and twentieth centuries—while science went from strength to strength in establishing its empire of belief—the vast majority of litterateurs remained conspicuously diffident or dissident, mostly refusing to have any truck with it except to hurl occasional abuse. The surprising thing is not that "science fiction" was born despicable in an age of scientific glory, but that it was ever born at all.

When the term "science fiction" was reinvented in the 1920s to describe a new genre of popular fiction—whose commodification was eventually successful, though gradual and far from unproblematic—its inventors and adherents had little difficulty in constructing a literary tradition going back fifty years, and a little more, but they had to recognise that the body of work in question was a mere trickle compared to the vast surge of the literary "mainstream": a tradition that had been and remained stubbornly indifferent to, if not proudly ignorant of, the progress of science. Nor did the advent of science fiction signal or hold out any hope for a modification of policy; indeed, science fiction emerged as a labeled genre at exactly the moment in history at which the last vestiges of intellectual communion between scientific and literary men were in the process of being severed, resulting in the emergence, in C. P. Snow's famous formulation, of "the two cultures."

The evolution of generic science fiction since the label was coined—as tracked in such volumes as the *Encyclopedia of Science Fiction* compiled by John Clute and Peter Nicholls in 1992—has not involved any conspicuous sophistication of the relationship between its two ostensible components. Indeed, the label was so promiscuously applied that it became necessary within a few decades of its coinage to invent a special term ("hard" science fiction)—to describe the small fraction of texts published under the label that attempted to maintain a manifest respect for the scientific method and its produce. Within a few decades more, even that term had been cheapened to the point at which it was routinely used to refer to any texts sheltering under the label's umbrella that contained any reference whatsoever to science, the vast majority having none at all.

The Encyclopaedia

For this reason, *Science Fact and Science Fiction: An Encyclopedia* is not an "encyclopaedia of science fiction", and bears little resemblance to books bearing that title. Such books are obliged to classify and describe all of the produce gathered under the label; if they take any account of the scientific notions deployed in the fiction, such notions have to be treated as a peripheral matter. Much of the material that has to be included in encyclopaedias of science fiction, on the grounds that it is so labelled in the marketplace, is of no significance to the present volume, because it is devoid of scientific inspiration and speculation. The term has broadened out to cover virtually all works set in the future and a great many others that have borrowed science-fictional imagery while carefully severing the threads of explanation that bound the original models to ideas in science.

Although this volume does contain numerous entries on writers of fiction, most of those individually annotated have been included because of the relevance of their work to issues in science, rather than their importance within the history of genre science fiction. Particular priority has been given to writers who are practicing scientists as well as writers of fiction, and to the links between the various aspects of their careers. Those entries do not make up the kind of textual backbone here that entries on writers would have to constitute in an encyclopaedia of science fiction; that function is served in the present volume by thematic entries on various sciences and their subsections.

When studies of science fiction set out to focus more narrowly on the genre's scientific links, as in such projects as *The Science in Science Fiction* (1982) edited by Peter Nicholls, they tend to become preoccupied with the extent to which science-fictional representations are rationally plausible, concentrating much of their effort on discriminating between "bad science" and "good science" within the fiction. In the present volume, by contrast, the principal flow of concern runs in the opposite direction. Instead of starting with a defined field of "science fiction" and working back towards its scientific content, this volume attempts to start with science and work forwards to its fictional representations, reflections and responses. These are, of course, far more abundant in some areas of science than in others and differ significantly in character from one area to another.

In order to attempt explanations of this extremely uneven pattern of representation, reflection, and response—a matter that does not arise in studies that begin with the fiction—it is necessary to look more closely at the fundamental contrasts between the nature and purposes of science and the nature and purposes of fiction. For this reason, the present volume pays more attention to "the science of fiction" than other books whose explorations touch on similar subject matter. This is evident not merely in its entry on narrative theory but in a network of subsidiary entries examining such issues as the generation of plausibility, the psychological estimation of probability, and the literary uses of impossibility.

In much the same way that it is selectively interested in the scientific correlations of fiction, the present volume is also selectively interested in the fictional correlations of science. The summaries of scientific progress with which most of its thematic entries begin are not usually very dissimilar to those offered by encyclopaedias of science, but they often emphasise those aspects of scientific evolution that served as triggers to significant literary endeavour, and they tend to be ruthlessly synoptic in their accounts of knowledge production. More importantly, they are often concerned with those aspects of the history of individual sciences that lend themselves to narrativisation and make a significant contribution to the rhetoric of science. Because science represents itself as truth, and its history as (unironic) true history, encyclopaedias of science rarely pay much attention to the rhetoric of science, or to such phenomena as the popularisation of science and the reportage of science. This volume has entries on all these subjects, because they constitute an important link between scientific and fictional techniques.

One significant effect of the dual concern of the present volume is that it has to be broader in its scope than books on either of its singular subjects usually need to be. An encyclopaedia of science fiction can easily confine its discussions of everything that happened before 1870 to a mere handful of peripheral articles. An encyclopaedia of science can do the same for everything that happened before 1600, although many historical studies do trace the ideas that became fundamental to science at that time to their roots in Classical philosophy. When one attempts to trace both the scientific antecedents of literary notions *and* the literary antecedents of scientific notions, however, it is useful to trace the historical sequences from their Classical—or even prehistoric—beginnings. It is also useful in considering the overlaps between science and fiction, to pay attention to ideas and theories thrown out by science (as fictions) but maintained in the world of fiction as "alternatives" to science or systems of thought still linked to its periphery.

Having said what there is to be said in explanation and justification of the present volume, it must still be admitted that the idea of an encyclopaedia of "science fact and science fiction" might be judged by some observers as an attempt to combine the irreconcilable rather than a heroic bridging operation. Previous attempts to lay the foundations of such cultural bridges have had a slightly troubled history. The Modern Language Association Division on Literature and Science came to the brink of abolition in 1978 because it seemed awkwardly irrelevant to many of the organisation's members. It did, however, avoid that fate, and the abolition debate helped to reinvigorate an interest that was soon reflected on the other shore of the cultural divide, where a Society for Literature and Science was founded in 1985 by the International Congress of the History of Science.

Although these endeavours remain on the peripheries of their host organisations, they have helped to generate an increasing flow of academic publications devoted to such topics as the influence of Darwinism on Victorian literature and the scientific interests of the Romantic poets. Very few such studies, as yet, have been prepared to take the risk of acknowledging that there is such a thing as "science fiction," let alone attempting to include it in their range of concern. On the other hand, exercises in the popularisation of science have become much more likely in recent years to use—or even to create—works of science fiction as examples, because they can be very useful in that regard. Popular science is often regarded with as much suspicion in academic circles as popular fiction, but the necessity of making scientific ideas more accessible, in the interests of education, is widely recognised.

Bibliographic References

The ground covered by the 300 entries in *Science Fact and Science Fiction* is very extensive, and it would have been impractical to give full bibliographical details for every one of the thousands of texts to which it refers. Other bibliographies containing fuller details of many texts cited in the articles are listed in the first section of this volume's bibliography.

In the interests of economy a number of abbreviations have been employed in the brief bibliographical citations that are included: aka (also known as), ed. (edited by), exp. (expanded), rev. (revised), and trans. (translated). I have retained the term "science fiction" for the US-born genre, retaining "scientific romance" for British material produced before the importation of the label after World War II and using "speculative fiction" as a blanket term for all fictions of that sort.

Cross-References

I have used prefatory asterisks to indicate substantial cross-references; these are sometimes subject to slight ambiguity because of the duplication of key words in different articles (for example, "matter" and "matter transmitter", and "time" and "time travel") and I have often found it convenient to attach them to grammatical derivatives of the terms used in the relevant entry's title (e.g., "astronomer" rather than "astronomy", or "medical" rather than "medicine"), but I hope that the relative unobtrusiveness of the device will make up for its occasional awkwardness.

Brian Stableford

Acknowledgements

I am very grateful to my friend and former colleague Bill Russell for taking on the heroic task of reading through the text in search of obvious errors; his many suggestions were very helpful. I am also indebted to my editor at Routledge, Marie-Claire Antoine, who allowed herself to be persuaded that the advantages of a text compiled by a single author would outweigh the disadvantages in this particular instance, and who offered much good advice while the book was in progress.

ACOUSTICS

The science of hearing, relating to the perception of sounds produced by vibrations in air or another medium; it bears the same relation to sound as optics does to light. In scientific terms, the fundamental phenomenon of sound turned out to be less challenging than the phenomenon of light, but in matters of aesthetic sensibility the technical challenges posed by *music are at least equal to those of visual art. The phonetics of human speech are equally complex, and underlie the visual technology of *writing.

The Classical works that laid the foundations of acoustics, including Ptolemy's *Harmonics*, were based on *Pythagorean ideas that emphasised the mathematics of harmony, and consideration of sound phenomena tended to be overlaid by musical theory in both science and literature until the seventeenth century. Attention was also paid to various kinds of natural sounds, especially those associated with the weather and the spontaneous sounds associated with particular emotions, including cries of pain and triumph, moans, groans, and sobs. Outside of music and alarms, the most significant artificial sounds prior to the nineteenth century were the loud bangs associated with explosions, whose clamour increased markedly from the fourteenth century onwards. Literary works frequently draw analogies between these various categories of sound, often extrapolating the "pathetic fallacy" of *meteorological representation.

Although the Pythagoreans knew that the pitch of a musical note produced by a plucked string depends on the length of the string, it was left to the Roman engineer Marcus Vitruvius Pollio to propose a vibrational theory of sound in the first century B.C., and it was largely disregarded thereafter. Pierre Gassendi made the first recorded measurements of the velocity of sound in 1635, but Marin Mersenne and Isaac *Newton were the chief advocates of the notion that sound was a vibration of the air. A general mathematical formula for wave propagation was proposed by Jean d'Alembert in 1747, assisting the understanding of the different kinds of vibrations produced by various musical instruments, although a comprehensive analysis of sound had to await the mathematical tools provided by Joseph Fourier in the early nineteenth century. The modern science of acoustics is based on Georg Simon Ohm's 1843 hypothesis that the ear analyses complex sounds into simple tones in a way that can be represented mathematically by Fourier analysis.

There was little in this sequence of theoretical developments to inspire literary works that would bring acoustics phenomena into the foreground, but the possibilities imaginable in the Renaissance are neatly summarised in the account of the "Sound-Houses" in Francis Bacon's *New Atlantis* (1627), which refers to amplifying devices for use as hearing aids, artificial echoes that modified the pitch of sounds and various means of transmitting sounds through "trunks and pipes". The usefulness of information learned by eavesdropping as a plot lever encouraged the occasional use in fiction of "whispering galleries", like the one in St. Paul's Cathedral, that

1

bring sound waves into focus some distance from their source; the effect is speculatively extrapolated in Lucretia P. Hale's "The Spider's Eye" (1856).

The development of the electric telegraph in the 1830s, and its adaptation to transmit messages in sound by means of Morse code, was a dramatic stimulus to the literary imagination. The tapping out of messages in Morse code became a standard feature of melodramatic crime fiction in the latter half of the century. Léon Scott's phonautograph (1857) could not play back the sounds it traced, so Thomas *Edison's phonograph (1877) represented a prodigious advance. The method of recording by cutting a groove in wax, developed in 1885, increased its convenience. Emile Berliner's gramophone system was more convenient still when it went into mass production after 1900. Early fictional representations of sound recording include J. D. Whelpley's "The Atoms of Chladni" (1860) and Florence McLandburgh's "The Automaton Ear" (1873), while Arthur Conan Doyle's "The Voice of Silence" (1891) set an early precedent for countless twentieth-century accounts of the phonographic capture of unwary confessions. The development of the *telephone had an even more dramatic effect on the strategies of popular fiction, and the development of *radio continued the process of transformation.

Twentieth-century progress in the refinement of sound-recording technology was swift. Tales of espionage found abundant melodramatic opportunities in keeping abreast or slightly ahead of the sequence of advances, and a rich mythology of "bugging" developed as eavesdropping became an art form, and "wearing a wire" became a key instrument of fictitious police procedure. As coding techniques for concealing information in auditory signals increased in sophistication, the literary spinoff of the science of *cryptography became correspondingly complex. The speculative dimension of such fiction was amply displayed in *technothrillers. Godwin Walsh's *The Voice of the Murderer* (1926), which features an ultrasensitive microphone designed to capture residual sounds from the past, illustrates the smallness of the imaginative step required to overreach the boundary of rational plausibility.

Just as the human eye is only sensitive to a limited range of electromagnetic emissions that constitute visible light, the human ear only experiences a limited range of vibrations as sound—usually between 20 and 20,000 cycles per second. Some animals can perceive vibrations outside of this range, but hearing is not nearly as widespread a sense as sight, being found in only two major groups: arthropods and vertebrates. Some representatives of both groups are sensitive to supersonic or ultrasonic vibrations that the human ear cannot perceive. The heroes of E. E. Smith's

Triplanetary (1934; rev. book 1948) have difficulty communicating with an amphibian race because of different ranges of aural sensitivity—a problem reproduced in actuality when humans began trying to communicate with dolphins in the 1960s. Sounds outside the range of human hearing are employed in various ingenious ways in L. Sprague de Camp's "Ultrasonic God" (1951; aka "The Galton Whistle"), Lloyd Biggle Jr.'s "Silence Is Deadly" (1957), and James E. Gunn's "Deadly Silence" (1958). J. B. Priestley's comedy *Low Notes on a High Level* (1954) features a device that emits the lowest possible notes.

As the titles of some of these stories imply, it is often the absence rather than the presence of sound that seems significant; it was the fact that the dog did *not* bark that put Sherlock Holmes on the right track in Conan Doyle's "Silver Blaze" (1892). The calculated suppression or obliteration of sound is the subject matter of such stories as A. M. McNeill's "The Noise Killer" (1930), Arthur C. *Clarke's "Silence Please" (1954), T. L. Sherred's "Cue for Quiet" (1953), J. G. Ballard's "The Sound Sweep"(1960), and Christopher Anvil's "Gadget vs. Trend" (1962). On the other hand, the fact that sound cannot be transmitted through a vacuum is routinely ignored by the manufacturers of sound effects in science fiction *cinema and *TV shows, where battles in space are often impossibly loud. The plausibility of such auditory imagery is not merely a careless reflection of the noise of earthly battles; one acoustic phenomenon that acquired iconic status in the twentieth century was the "sonic boom" associated with "breaking the sound barrier"—a feat first achieved by the rocket-engined Bell X-1 in 1947. Although jet fighters routinely operated at speeds above the charismatically named Mach-1 after 1960, the association of very high speeds with acoustic phenomena, sealed in the early days of space exploration, continued to exercise a certain imaginative authority long thereafter. Allen Adler's *Mach 1: A Story of Planet Ionus* (1957) features a supersonic sea-sled.

Unmusical variants of the seductive song of the sirens are featured in A. E. van Vogt's "The Sound" (1950) and Jack Vance's "Noise" (1952). Alien acoustics—which cause sounds that are perceived as identical by one species to seem very different to another—cause trouble in translation in H. Beam Piper's "Naudsonce" (1962). New acoustic technology enables the use of music as weapon in Christopher Hodder-Williams' *98.4* (1969), Colin Cooper's *Dargason* (1977), and Paul H. Cook's *Tintagel* (1981). Disturbing ultrasonics are produced by a "saser" in Isaac *Asimov's "The Dim Rumble" (1982), and an ingenious means of committing murder by means of an acoustic phenomenon is featured in

Laurence M. Janifer's "The Dead Beat" (1997). The similarity of the grooves made on rotating cylinders by Edison's first phonograph to grooves made on certain kinds of pots turned on wheels encouraged some archaeologists to wonder whether accidental sound recording might have been achieved in the distant past; Larry Eisenberg's "Duckworth and the Sound Probe" (1971) and Gregory Benford's "Time Shards" (1979) develop the thesis ironically.

The analogy between light and sound led to the development of the concept of "white noise", comprising a mixture of all audible frequencies. It was easy to produce, but seemed to have no function until it was deployed in sensory deprivation experiments to blank out other auditory stimuli—to which the ear becomes hypersensitive after exposure to silence. The mind's tendency to search for significance in randomness—also associated with radio "static" and the malady of tinnitus—can lend a sinister quality to such phenomena, as explored and extrapolated in such works as Eando Binder's "Static" (1936) and the movie *White Noise* (2005).

AERONAUTICS

The applied science of flight. The notion of an artificial means of giving human beings the ability to fly is very old; the power of its attraction is blended with a dutiful note of caution in the myth of Daedalus and Icarus. Flying machines are among the most venerable types of imaginary technology, prominently featured in *Leonardo da Vinci's notebooks and in the technological prospectus mapped out in John Wilkins' *Mathematicall Magick* (1648).

Artificial wings like those constructed by Daedalus crop up continually in imaginative fiction, although carriages drawn aloft by flights of birds are mostly confined to farcical satires such as Francis Godwin's *The Man in the Moone* (1638). The winged machine featured in Ralph Morris' *Adventures of John Daniel* (1751) is a relatively earnest depiction of an ornithopter, and Robert Paltock's *The Life and Adventures of Peter Wilkins* (1751) offers a detailed depiction of a society that has mastered the art of flight. Nicolas Restif de la Bretonne's *Découverte Australe par un homme volant* (1781), Tom Greer's *A Modern Dedalus* (1885), and Charles Godfrey Leland's *Flaxius* (1902) use similar apparatus as a facilitating device, although hypothetical humanoids naturally equipped with wings are far more common in fiction than ordinary people equipped with artificial wings.

The placing of the realm of the gods in the sky by Classical mythology and scripture alike meant that messengers therefrom were routinely equipped with wings; it is not surprising that wings are a common accoutrement of extraterrestrial species, ranging from W. S. Lach-Szyrma's *A Voice from Another World* (1874; aka *Aleriel*) through Leslie F. Stone's "Men with Wings" (1929) to Poul *Anderson's *The Man Who Counts* (1958; aka *War of the Wing-Men*) and *The People of the Wind* (1973). The power of aeronautical dreams is reflected in Olaf Stapledon's contention in *Last and First Men* (1930) that the human race engineered for flight on Venus is the happiest of all *Homo sapiens'* descendant species.

Actual aeronautical technology took its first significant step forward with the development of hot air balloons, which gained a great deal of publicity when Joseph and Étienne Montgolfier staged the first public flight in 1783. The first hydrogen balloon was flown in the same year by Jacques Charles, and manned flights soon became common. Balloons did not become a practical means of transportation until dirigible airships were developed at the beginning of the twentieth century, and they played a very limited role even then. Their effect on the literary imagination was, however, tremendous; in Félix Bodin's groundbreaking *Le roman de l'avenir* (1834) flying machines are central icons of "futuristic" imagery, and they retained that status in futuristic fiction for the remainder of the century, extravagantly displayed in such works as Albert Robida's *Le vingtième siècle* (1882–1883; trans. as *The Twentieth Century*) and Julian Hawthorne's "June 1993" (1893).

It was evident that even if the problem of steering could be solved, balloons were never likely to reach high speeds. Émile Souvestre's *Le monde tel qu'il sera* (1846; trans. as *The World as It Shall Be*) imagines express air travel involving shells fired from giant cannon—but the majesty of soaring seemed aptly symbolic of the spirit and thrust of technological progress. It was used to that effect in Alfred, Lord Tennyson's "Locksley Hall" (1842), in the lines: "For I dipped into the future, far as human eye could see, / Saw the Vision of the world, and all the wonder that would be: / Saw the heavens fill with commerce, argosies of magic sails, / Pilots of the purple twilight, dropping down with costly bales; / Heard the heavens filled with shouting, and there rain'd a ghastly dew / From the nations' airy navies grappling in the central blue". Tennyson's final image was soon darkly elaborated in Herrmann Lang's *The Air Battle* (1859), while the optimistic thrust of his vision was amplified in Victor Hugo's "Plein ciel" [Open Sky] in *La Légende des Siècles: Vingtième Siècle* (1859).

Balloons were used to gain access to numerous nineteenth-century Utopias, from the Baron de Launay's *Le ballon aérien* (1810) to William Westall's *The Phantom City* (1886), and were often employed as a means of *space travel. Jules Verne's long series of *voyages extraordinaires* began with *Cinq semaines en ballon* (1863; trans. as *Five Weeks in a Balloon*) and he went on to use balloons in many other novels in the sequence, including *Le tour du monde en quatre-vingt jours* (1873; trans. as *Around the World in Eighty Days*) and *L'île mystérieuse* (1874–1875; trans. as *The Mysterious Island*). His influence was enormous, with one early spinoff being George Sand's *Laura: voyage dans le cristal* (1870; trans. as *Journey Within the Crystal*).

The analogy of marine transport was so readily available to nineteenth-century futurists that early images of dirigible "airships" tended to look very similar to marine ships, with masts and sails mounted atop gas-enclosing hulls. The definitive imagery of this type was provided by Fred T. Jane, the illustrator of George Griffith's *The Angel of the Revolution* (1893) and other works in the same vein; his name was eventually to become permanently associated with *Jane's Fighting Ships* and *Jane's Fighting Aircraft*. Griffith had presumably taken his own lead from Jules Verne's detailed account of the dirigible airship employed by *Robur le conquérant* (1886), which had become the eponymous *Clipper of the Clouds* in the English translation. Analogues of the marine propeller—first devised in 1842 by Isambard Kingdom Brunel for the *Great Britain*—were also featured abundantly on the imaginary airships of the nineteenth century, but the more fanciful accoutrements of imaginary airships were largely set aside after Count Zeppelin's dirigible made its first test flight in 1900, generating a new iconic image.

Although the principle of airflow-generated lift had been explained in the eighteenth century by Daniel Bernoulli, aircraft with fixed wings did not offer serious competition to airships in the literary imagination until they were on the brink of realisation. H. G. Wells' *When the Sleeper Wakes* (1899) featured them prominently, although Wells withdrew the suggestion that they might be vital to the conduct of future warfare in the futurological essays he collected in *Anticipations* (1900) and felt forced to write *The War in the Air* (1906) when he changed his mind back again. The advent of actual aeroplanes in the first decade of the twentieth century—stridently dramatised by the Wright brothers' manned flight at Kitty Hawk in 1903 and Albert Santos-Dumont's European ventures—began a new phase in the conquest of the air that immediately spilled over into imaginative fiction, especially in connection with the assumption that mastery of the air would be essential to the winning of future wars and the establishment of future empires.

This assumption was graphically extrapolated in such novels as James Standish O'Grady's *Queen of the World* (1900, by-lined Luke Netterville), James Blyth's *The Aerial Burglars* (1906), William Holt-White's *The Man Who Stole the Earth* (1909), George Glendon's *The Emperor of the Air* (1910), and George Allan England's "The Empire in the Air" (1914), whereas a more sophisticated imagery of social transformation by rapid and reliable aerial transport was offered in Rudyard Kipling's *With the Night Mail* (1905; exp. 1909) and "As Easy as A.B.C". (1912). The sophistication of aircraft technology in World War I—anticipated in such novels as J. L. Carter's *Peggy the Aeronaut* (1910) and Louis Gastoine's *Les torpilleurs de l'air* (1912; trans. as *War in Space*)—seemed to confirm the assumption, even though air forces made little military difference to the strategy of the war or the resolution of ground conflicts. The threats loomed larger in the imagination even while the war was being fought, reflected in such novels as Marc Gouvrieux's *Haut les Ailes!* (1914; trans. as *With Wings Outspread*), Claude Grahame-White and Harry Harper's *The Invisible War-Plane* (1915), Guy Thorne's *The Secret Sea-Plane* (1915), and William le Queux's *The Zeppelin Destroyer* (1916).

The period between the two world wars was a heroic era of aviation in which new records were set on a regular basis, the most important including J. W. Alcock and A. W. Brown's first transatlantic flight in June 1919, Charles Lindbergh's solo flight from New York to Paris in May 1927, Amy Johnson's solo flight from London to Australia in May 1930, and Howard Hughes' round the world flight in July 1938. The fact that Johnson, like her fellow aviatrix Amelia Earhart, died in the pursuit of her vocation only added to the romance of human flight, which was equipped with a spiritual dimension by their fellow casualty Antoine de Saint-Exupéry, in such celebratory works as *Vol de nuit* (1931; trans. as *Night Flight*) and *Terre des hommes* (1939; trans. as *Wind, Sand and Stars*). Fixed-wing aircraft had already reduced airships to near irrelevance in the futuristic imagination when the R-101 disaster of 1930 put an abrupt end to a pattern of development that had climaxed in the *Graf Zeppelin*'s circumnavigation of the globe a year earlier. The first successful helicopter flight in 1919, on the other hand, encouraged the notion that portable, personal flying apparatus might soon become practicable.

It is unsurprising, in this context, that aviation fiction was one of the many candidate genres tried out in the American pulp magazines, as an adjunct of the war genre in such pulps as *War Birds* (1928–1937), *Daredevil Aces* (1933–1940), *Sky Fighters* (1933–1939), *Battle Birds* (1932–1934; retitled *Dusty Ayres and His Battle Birds*, 1934–1935), and *G-8 and His Battle Aces* (1933–1944). Dusty Ayres and G-8 routinely battled scientifically advanced invaders, and aviation fiction briefly became a designated branch of science fiction in Hugo *Gernsback's *Air Wonder Stories* (1929–1930). The pulp genre was too specialised to survive, but aviation fiction continued to form a significant fraction of war fiction and thriller fiction thereafter. Although the commercialisation of air travel in the late 1930s eroded the heroic and romantic dimensions of civil aviation, it retained a particular glamour exploited by such writers as Nevil Shute and Ernest K. Gann.

The notion that air power might play a central role in future world politics was sustained for a while in such fantasies as Michael Arlen's Kiplingesque *Man's Mortality* (1933) and the section of H. G. Wells' *The Shape of Things to Come* (1933) detailing the Air Dictatorship, but the surrealised air force of Rex Warner's *The Aerodrome* (1941) marked the conclusion of the trend. World War II demonstrated the brutal limitations as well as the power of the bomber. The *Enola Gay*—whose delivery of the first *atom bomb in 1945 allowed it to overtake Lindbergh's *Spirit of St. Louis* as the most iconic aircraft of the twentieth century—provided a dramatic lesson, but the failure of Adolf Hitler's *blitzkrieg* tactics had already demonstrated that anxieties about what bomber fleets might accomplish had been exaggerated. The destructive and demoralising effects of conventional bombing proved mild by comparison with the fears displayed in such future war novels as Cicely Hamilton's *Theodore Savage* (1922), Shaw Desmond's *Ragnarok* (1926), Frank McIlraith and Roy Connolly's *Invasion from the Air* (1934), Joseph O'Neill's *Day of Wrath* (1936), and S. Fowler Wright's *Four Days War* (1936).

European anxiety about the destructive power of airfleets seemed irrelevant in America, which seemed virtually inaccessible to enemy action of that sort—an assumption reflected in Curt Siodmak's *F.P.1 Antwortet Nicht* (1931; trans. as *F.P.1 Does Not Reply*), about the construction of a mid-Atlantic refuelling station—so images of the future of flight produced between the wars in the United States were much more upbeat. The cityscapes featured in the illustrations in the pulp science fiction magazines often featured flyers equipped with miniature helicopters or jet-packs, and such imagery became an intrinsic feature of the "Gernsback continuum". The first actual jet engine was a turbine tested by Frank Whittle in 1937, but the technology had been extensively explored as a corollary of extensive science-fictional interest in *rockets as a means of space travel.

As air travel became routine in the second half of the twentieth century it became increasingly difficult for aircraft and aviators to maintain the charismatic status previously afforded to such literary artefacts as

Walther Eidlitz's *Zodiak* (1931) and such characters as W. E. Johns' Biggles. Test pilots—especially those associated with the early days of the space programme, as celebrated in Tom Wolfe's *The Right Stuff* (1979)—retained a certain glamour, but the romance of aeronautics followed a literal upward trajectory towards the margins of the void. Cutting-edge military aircraft—including the Northrop B-2 and other "stealth" craft with minimal radar reflection—became a regular feature of *technothriller fiction, as in Jack Sharkey's "The Business, as Usual" (1960), Joe Poyer's "Mission 'Red Clash'" (1965), Ben Bova's *Out of the Sun* (1968), and Dean Ing's *The Ransom of Black Stealth One* (1989), but the transmutation of the U.S. National Advisory Committee for Aeronautics (established 1915) into the National Aeronautics and Space Administration (NASA) in 1958 marked the beginning of a new era. Test-pilot stories, such as Lee Correy's "Design Flaw" (1955), Hank Searls' *The Big X* (1959), and Jeff Sutton's *Spacehive* (1961), became explicit celebrants of the aeronautical motto *per ardua ad astra*.

The jet era was the culmination of aviation history; Pratt and Whitney's attempt to develop a nuclear-powered aircraft came to nothing, although its success was imagined in a novel by one of the engineers who worked on the project, Hilbert Schenck's *Steam Bird* (1988). The race to develop supersonic flight, celebrated in such novels as Donald Gordon's *Star-Raker* (1962), petered out into anticlimax when the Anglo-French supersonic passenger jet Concorde, put into development in 1962 and commercial usage in 1976, was withdrawn from the world stage in 2001. Ideas for further sophistication—observed in such designs as the skyport (a giant flying wing), as depicted in Timothy Zahn's "Between a Rock and a High Place" (1982)—came to seem peripheral.

The fascination of aviation was never reduced entirely to mundanity; a Saint-Exupéry–esque spiritual dimension continued to echo in such works of aviation fiction as Christopher Hodder-Williams' *Final Approach* (1960), *Turbulence* (1961), and *The Higher They Fly* (1964) and Arthur C. *Clarke's *Glide Path* (1963). Thriller fiction developed a subgenre of aeroplane emergency stories, which proved highly adaptable to the cinema in such melodramas as *Zero Hour!* (1957) and the series begun with *Airport* (1970). Gradually, however, the romance of aeronautics became nostalgic, expressed in such historical novels as James Helvick's *Overdraft on Glory* (1955), such timeslip romances as Jack Finney's "Quit Zoomin' Those Hands Through the Air" (1951) and Dean R. McLaughlin's "Hawk Among the Sparrows" (1968), and such baroque alternative histories as Richard A. Lupoff's *Circumpolar!* (1984), in which Amelia

Earhart, Howard Hughes, and Charles Lindbergh race to circumnavigate a toroidal Earth. Late twentieth-century speculative fiction retained a mildly ironic fascination with the romance of flight in such stories as J. G. Ballard's "The Ultimate City" (1976) and *The Unlimited Dream Company* (1979) and Jay Lake's *Rocket Science* (2005), but such works seemed jaded by comparison with such fantasies of individual flight as Larry Niven's "Handicap" (1967), George R. R. Martin and Lisa Tuttle's "The Storms of Windhaven" (1975; incorporated into *Windhaven,* 1981), and Bob Shaw's *Vertigo* (1978).

Balloons made something of a comeback in the final decades of the twentieth century, when brightly coloured hot air balloons became a familiar sight in the summer sky and the heroic era of aviation was belatedly recalled by the exploits of Richard Branson and Steve Fossett. That kind of romance was exaggerated by science-fictional improvisation in such works as C. C. MacApp's *Prisoners of the Sky* (1969), Bob Shaw's *The Ragged Astronauts* (1986), John Brosnan's *The Sky Lords* (1988), Kenneth Oppel's *Airborn* (2004), Matthew Claxton's "Changing the Guard" (2004), and the stories in *All-Star Zeppelin Adventure Stories* (2004) edited by David Moles and Jay Lake. Such imagery was exported into children's fiction in Philip Pullman's *Northern Lights* (1995) and Philip Reeve's *Mortal Engines* (2001). Dreams of individual flight were partially realised by a series of inventions such as the paraglider and—more significantly—the hang glider, whose lack of motive power was compensated for by the artistry of their deployment. It was not, after all, necessary to go to the lengths featured in Robert A. Heinlein's "The Menace from Earth" (1957)—in which a lunar valley is roofed over and filled with air—in order that people might learn to fly.

AESTHETICS

A philosophical discipline developing theories of artistic response, particularly in respect of such concepts as beauty, elegance, and harmony. The deliberate evocation of aesthetic responses in oral and written discourse is an aspect of the pathetic component of *rhetoric, but aesthetic responses to *nature, the visual *arts, and *music are generally given separate consideration. Although Classical philosophy did attempt to deal with questions of aesthetics, the modern discipline takes its name from Alexander Baumgarten, who redefined the term in 1735 in a work translated as *Reflections on Poetry*, but died before completing his definitive *Aesthetika* (1750–1758).

Science has an aesthetic dimension of its own, although its exact nature is difficult to pin down. The truth is often held to be innately beautiful, but literary "truth" and scientific truth are sometimes seen as distinct phenomena; John Keats' assertion in "Ode on a Grecian Urn" (1820) that "Beauty is truth, truth beauty" was not intended as a compliment to science. The notion that *mathematical reasoning has a particular beauty, reflected in certain equations, is also commonplace; Henri Poincaré attempted in *La science et l'hypothèse* (1902) and two further volumes (collectively translated as *The Foundations of Science*) to compile a detailed account of the process of scientific creativity and its aesthetics. Albert Einstein was an eloquent advocate of this thesis, and it is celebrated in Graham Farmelo's anthology *It Must Be Beautiful: Great Equations of Modern Science* (2002). On the other hand, Thomas Henry Huxley referred, in *Biogenesis and Abiogenesis* (1870), to "the great tragedy of Science—the slaying of a beautiful hypothesis by an ugly fact", recognising that ideas that are aesthetically pleasing can turn out to be false. Denigrators of science often raise objections to it on aesthetic grounds, considering scientific truth to be "plain", "boring", "cold", or "vulgar", but such denigrators usually deem aesthetic responses to be essentially emotional—so that the scientist's attempts to make judgments dispassionate and objective become necessarily anti-aesthetic—whereas aesthetic philosophers like Poincaré are more interested in the cognitive aspects of aesthetic responses.

Literary aesthetics overlap the aesthetics of science, in that the aesthetics of good reasoning are reflected in the craft of elegant plotting and the achievement of satisfactory climactic conclusions. This is most obvious in detective fiction, whose core exercise is the construction of elaborate puzzles and their elegant solution. Works of speculative fiction are often constructed in a similar fashion, with complex puzzles yielding to elegant logical analyses, but speculative fiction is more closely related to a different aspect of the aesthetics of science, which fans of science fiction often refer to as the "sense of wonder". By this they mean a particular sensation of enlightenment provoked by discovery, whose extreme is an awe-inspiring expansion of imaginative perspective. This kind of response is noted in Aristotle's *Poetics*, which observes that the "wonderful" aspects of epic poetry and tragic drama are not only pleasing but always lend themselves to further exaggeration when stories are retold. The sense of wonder associated with scientific discovery and speculative fiction received abundant fuel as the philosophical revolution that began at the end of the sixteenth century gradually revealed the true scales of space and time on which the universe needed to be measured.

The notion that there might be a significant aesthetic connection between the cosmologist's construction of new models of the universe and the literary artist's construction of worlds within texts had been raised before the advent of the New Learning in the sixteenth century, but it acquired a new significance at that time. Philip Sidney's *Defence of Poesy* (1595) adopted a view of artistic creativity as a matter of the creation of "small worlds", which resemble hypothetical models rather than mimetic representations. This notion was echoed by Gottfried Leibniz, whose consideration of "possible worlds" allowed that works of art might contain worlds markedly different from the world of experience. Baumgarten's *Aesthetika* is a Leibnizian exercise, making much of Leibniz's representation of literature as a mode of cognition aspiring to "perceptual clarity"—thus focusing attention on matters of order, pattern, and symmetry.

Leibniz argued in his *Theodicy* (1710) that ours must be the best of all possible worlds; on this basis, Baumgarten argued that the highest ideal of artistic "secondary creation" is to produce simulacra of the world of experience rather than to venture into the innately inferior practice of "heterocosmic" creativity. The intrusion of fantastic elements into a simulacrum of the world of experience, even in the cause of trying to envisage a better state of nature—as, for instance, in Sidney's *Arcadia* (1581)—or a better political organisation of society, seemed to Baumgarten to be an insult to the competence of the primary creation. This view subsequently became orthodox even among critics who had little sympathy for Leibnizian optimism, although Edmund Burke's *Philosophical Enquiry into the Origin of Our Ideas of the Sublime and Beautiful* (1757) opposed it with arguments extrapolated from Mark Akenside's exposition in blank verse of *The Pleasures of the Imagination* (1744), asserting that the healthy imagination requires mental exercise, just as the healthy body requires physical exercise.

Burke's purpose was to broaden aesthetic discussion to take fuller account of the aesthetic response he characterised as "the sublime". This notion also originated in Classical times, apparently in a lost treatise by a Sicilian Jew named Cecilius, although the key surviving document is a slightly later essay by Longinus (first century A.D.). Longinus had a considerable influence on sixteenth- and seventeenth-century Italian aesthetic theory, and on such writers as Torquato Tasso. Burke's theory—rooted in emotions rather than "perceptual clarity"—connects beauty with loving emotions while associating the sublime with "astonishment". According to Burke, sublimity is associated with danger, power, vacuity, darkness, solitude, silence, vastness, potential, difficulty, and colour; his thesis helped pave the way for *Romanticism, especially its Gothic component.

Although Burke discussed the sublime primarily in terms of the rapt contemplation of *nature, he observed that the information of his gaze by contemporary natural philosophy had done nothing to diminish its capacity for astonishment, or the component of *horror therein. He was not alone in this; many of his contemporaries found the revelations of science innately horrific, although others considered their response more akin to exaltation. This division of opinion remains very obvious in literary reflections of science, and also in the marked contrast between the characteristic rhetoric of the popularisation of science and that of popular reportage of science.

When nineteenth-century discoveries in astronomy and geology began to produce newly awe-inspiring images of the universe and Earth's past, Burke's notion of sublimity was largely replaced by championship of a more enthusiastic sense of wonder by such writers as Humphry Davy, Edgar Allan *Poe, Robert Hunt, and Camille *Flammarion, whose endeavors contrasted sharply with writers who found all scientific and technological progress darkly ominous. The latter company formed the majority within the parliament of literature, but the opposition continued to hold sway within the ranks of scientists—and, in large measure, in earnest speculative fiction. The notion of the sublime was significantly revisited in such works as David E. Nye's *American Technological Sublime* (1996), which discusses the aesthetics of America's long romance with technology and the reasons for an apparent twentieth-century decline in technological charisma, and the critical work of the Romanian literary theorist Cornel Robu, especially *O cheie pentru science-fiction* (2004), whose central thesis was summarised in "A Key to Science Fiction: The Sublime" (1988). Burke's distinction is recalled in such reflective works of science fiction as Bruce Sterling's "The Beautiful and the Sublime" (1986).

The notion that aesthetics might become a science rooted in physiological psychology was extensively developed in the nineteenth century by such writers as the historian Hippolyte Taine (author of the *positivist *Philosophie de l'Art,* 1865), the scientist and musicologist Hermann von Helmholtz, and the human scientist and evolutionist Herbert Spencer. It persisted well into the twentieth century in the writings of such literary critics as I. A. Richards, but never found any secure grounding. John Ruskin's *Modern Painters* (1856) blithely anticipated the development of "a science of the aspects of things" that would study their effects on the "eye and heart", but his own attempt to get to grips with the aesthetics of *crystallographic science in *The Ethics of the Dust* (1866) was rather bizarre. Nineteenth-century analyses of the physiology and psychology of aesthetics tended to focus on the pleasure innate in certain kinds of sensory experience—an approach foreshadowed in the empiricism of John Locke and further developed by Immanuel Kant, whose emphasis on the joy of understanding and abstract appreciation of the dynamics of creativity contrasted with the ideas of theorists who supposed "pleasure" to be intimately connected with the sexual impulse.

A summation and systematisation of the notion that aesthetics is an aspect of the psychology of pleasure was attempted by George Santayana's *The Sense of Beauty* (1896), although Thomas Munro's *Scientific Method in Aesthetics* (1928) pays more attention to the physiological basis of pleasure. John Dewey's *Art as Experience* (1934), on the other hand, attempted to develop a theory based in the physiology of perception, particularly the perception of patterns of association and disassociation, and their significance in the comprehension of the world's dynamism. More recently, the physiological school of aesthetics has been carried forward by evolutionary psychologists employing the logic of *sociobiology, most significantly in Ellen Dissanayake's *Home Aestheticus: Where Art Comes From and Why* (1992), which characterises *Homo Aestheticus* in terms of "tendencies to recognise an extra-ordinary as opposed to an ordinary dimension of experience" and a "capacity to experience a transformative or self-transcendent emotional state", attempting to examine the selective value of such traits.

The aesthetics of science has never received more than a tiny fraction of the attention devoted to the aesthetics of works of art. Logically, works of art inspired by scientific discovery should not have been downgraded by value judgments tied to the notion that the finest art was the most accurately representative, but their tendency to suffer that fate was exaggerated as the discoveries of nineteenth-century science exposed the limitations of the human eye, and began to construct a mathematical model of reality that was divorced from the aesthetics of direct perception. In the same period, scientific writing developed and perfected a style of its own, aspiring to a kind of pedantry from which "literary embellishments" were purged. Literary works that retained the language and argumentative style of scientific writing thus came to seem not merely unliterary but anti-literary.

This trend was unaffected by the development in the late nineteenth century of various schools of nonrepresentative art, whose fashionability eventually overtook that of the kinds of simulatory painting of which Baumgarten approved. The development of critical schools that went to an opposite extreme in championing the absolute autonomy of art—as in the polemics of Théophile Gautier and Walter Pater—made little difference, because they regarded "heterocosmic creativity" as a self-enclosed activity, isolated from such disciplines as scientific speculation and mathematical extrapolation. The distancing effects of Gautier's doctrine of "art pour l'art" (usually translated as "art for art's sake") were exaggerated by resentment against the perceived cost of the progress of scientific truth, as measured in ideas cursed thereby with *impossibility and, hence, with apparent obsolescence. Oscar Wilde's essay on "The Decay of Lying" (1891) lamented the loss of entertaining fancies slain by the brutality of skeptical analysis, and demanded that heterocosmic creators should forsake the truth—at least in its duller aspects—and boldly commit themselves to the invention of bigger, better, and bolder lies.

Wilde's tongue-in-cheek argument reflected the fact that a powerful nostalgia for the mythic past had survived the post-Baumgartenian quest for narrative realism, and had began to reassert itself within the literary tradition, initially in the context of Romanticism. Its champions increasingly chose to follow up Keats' complaint that "cold philosophy" had done harm in "unweaving the rainbow", venting their spleen on the supposed corrosions of science rather than the narrowness of naturalistic art. It was partly for this reason that the development of scientific romance and science fiction seemed perverse, and that both genres were always manifestly chimerical, embracing works castigating science as a destroyer of beauty and sublimity as well as works celebrating the beauty and sublimity of science.

Although there were conspicuous early twentieth-century movements in the visual arts and music that endeavored to embrace Futurist manifestos, fiction—especially popular fiction—hardly benefited at all from such outbursts of enthusiasm. Although the notion of an artistic *avant-garde* implies that its practitioners are attempting to embody and exemplify a pattern of progress, twentieth-century literary *avant-gardes* tended to be very scrupulous in divorcing their notions of progress from those implicit in new technologies and the refinement of scientific theory. Although twentieth-century literary avant-gardism readily embraced such missions as the more accurate representation of the "stream of consciousness"—a term invented by the psychologist William James rather than his brother Henry—it remained jealous of the privileges of its introspective method, and was only peripherally affected by scientific attempts to understand the phenomenon.

The peculiarities of this pattern of evolution are ironically reflected in literary images of hypothetical societies guided by aesthetics, such as those featured in Gabriel Tarde's "Fragment d'histoire future" (1896; trans. as *Underground Man*) and André Maurois' *Voyage au pays des Articoles* (1927; trans. as *The Island of the Articoles*), and descriptions of futuristic "artist's colonies" such as those featured in J. G. Ballard's *Vermilion Sands* (1971), Lee Killough's *Aventine* (1982), and Eric Brown's *Meridian Days* (1992). Such works experience immense difficulty when attempting to anticipate the future of literary art, and are far more inventive in imagining new forms of visual, musical, and conceptual art. The most provocative aspect of speculative fiction dealing with aesthetics is contained in its attempts to anticipate future technological impacts on artistic opportunity—a topic first significantly addressed by Walter Benjamin's essay translated as "The Work of Art in the Age of Mechanical Reproduction" (1936). Many such stories—Walter M. Miller's "The Darfsteller" (1955) is a cardinal example—are concerned with the alleged superiority of the organic over the mechanical; aesthetic issues are a subsidiary but nevertheless significant concern of many stories featuring *robots and other kinds of *artificial intelligence.

Aesthetic evaluation is often treated as an essentially static discipline, as if the ideas of beauty and sublimity were themselves unchanging no matter how variable their manifestation might be. It is not obvious that this is true; feminist analyses such as Naomi Wolf's *The Beauty Myth* (1990) suggest that perceptions of sexual attractiveness are culturally conditioned and, hence, subject to alteration. The argument is extrapolated in Ted Chiang's *conte philosophique* "Liking What You See: A Documentary" (2002), which features a hypothetical proposition to compel the use of a treatment to disable the ability to see beauty in human faces, in order to eliminate "lookism". Whether the aesthetics of science are subject to similar alterations in perception is debatable, but it is arguable that the aesthetics of *cosmology has undergone significant shifts as the closed Aristotelian cosmos was replaced by the open Newtonian cosmos, whose essentially static frame was replaced in its turn by the dynamic and relativistic cosmos of *Big Bang theory. The advent of computers, and the enhancement of their ability to translate mathematical operations into visual form, may also have added further dimensions of complexity to the concept of beauty, as described in Clifford A. Pickover's *Computers, Patterns, Chaos, and Beauty* (1990). Pickover's *Chaos in Wonderland* (1995) includes a *conte philosophique* about aliens whose aesthetic estimation of one another is based in the beauty of the chaotic attractors they can generate.

A sense of wonder or sublimity is a wasting asset; familiarity with the revelations of one century's scientific discoveries tends to breed a certain amount of contempt in the next. The extrapolation of theoretical physics into the subatomic microcosm and back to the primal Big Bang, and the parallel development of a sophisticated genetic theory based on the remarkable elegance of the DNA double helix, renewed the twentieth-century sense of wonder in no uncertain terms, but it is not obvious that revelations of equal magnitude will emerge in the future as these notions become familiar. On the other hand, it is at least conceivable that the sensitivity of observers to the aesthetics of science may become more refined, or even significantly altered, in such a way as to encourage new and different patterns of artistic reflection in the twenty-first century.

AIR

One of the four Classical *elements, whose native sphere in the Aristotelian model of the cosmos was between that of water and fire. Scientific terminology eventually replaced the relevant sphere with the notion of the atmosphere: a mixture of gaseous substances forming an envelope surrounding the planet. William Whewell's *History of the Inductive Sciences* (1837) contains a section on "atmology", but the term never caught on, and twentieth-century atmospheric science is usually subsumed under the title of *meteorology.

The scientific study of the atmosphere began with Evangelista Torricelli's pioneering studies of air pressure in the seventeenth century—including his invention of the mercury barometer in 1644—but determination of the chemical composition of the atmosphere only began in earnest in the late eighteenth century, early findings being reported in Joseph Priestley's *Experiments and Observations on Air* (1777). Priestley's experiments assisted Antoine Lavoisier to realise the significance of oxygen (Priestley's "dephlogisticated air") and carbon dioxide (Joseph Black's "fixed air") and thus to revise the theory of combustion, laying vital foundations for the development of modern *chemistry. Priestley also identified the non-respirable major component of the air as nitrogen, while Henry Cavendish isolated hydrogen ("inflammable air"). The remaining inert constituents had to wait until the 1890s, when the liquefaction of the major components at extremely low temperatures and spectroscopic analysis of the residue allowed William Ramsay to discover the full set of noble gases.

The eighteenth-century discoveries helped clarify the problems caused by industrial air *pollution and the dangers posed to miners by various kinds of noxious gases (including methane, carbon monoxide, and carbon dioxide), but made little immediate impact on theories of disease based in the notion of toxic "miasmas". They also facilitated the development of balloons and the advent of *aeronautics; the further investigation of the structure of the atmosphere provided balloons with their principal practical utility. The first flight undertaken expressly for scientific purposes was made by Etienne Robertson in 1803. The use of balloons in fiction by Jules *Verne and his contemporaries is carefully respectful of this aspect of their utility. The extreme danger associated with manned flights above 30,000 feet was a significant source of aeronautical melodrama, but it was the potential scientific rewards rather than the lust for adventure that led August Piccard to develop the pressurised gondola that made stratosphere ballooning feasible in 1931.

In other respects, the atmosphere seemed a poor source of melodramatic potential, by virtue of the evident inability of clouds to bear actual castles in the air in any but the wildest literary fantasies. The notion that the upper reaches of the atmosphere might be inhabited was, however, developed in such scientific romances as Maurice Renard's Le péril bleu (1910), which imagines a civilisation of "ethereal" life-forms fishing for airborne prey. Inhabitants of such a civilisation descend to Earth in a "subaerine" in John Nathan Raphael's Up Above (1913). Buoyant ecospheres are featured in Arthur Conan Doyle's "The Horror of the Heights" (1913) and Sophie Wenzel Ellis' "The Shadow World" (1932). Alien atmospheres designed to contain airborne ecosystems were more versatile, as evidenced by Robert Reed's The Leeshore (1987). The notion that Earth's atmosphere might offer scope for colonisation was fugitively preserved in such fantasies as Frank Belknap Long's "Exiles of the Stratosphere" (1935) and Eando Binder's "Queen of the Skies" (1937). Reports of strange things falling from the sky sparked one of Charles *Fort's most extravagant imaginative rhapsodies, and his work helped to sustain the notion that the upper atmosphere might be more interesting than it seemed. The notion that massive atmosphere-dwelling creatures might be responsible for many *flying saucer sightings was maintained in Fortean "nonfiction" by such works as Trevor James Constable's The Cosmic Pulse of Life (1975).

The preciousness of earthly air was recognised in such futuristic fantasies as George Alan England's The Air Trust (1915), but was unappreciated in early accounts of *space travel, most of which took a cavalier attitude to its provision in spaceships and the likelihood that alien worlds would have readily breathable atmospheres. As the twentieth century advanced, however, the difficulties of transporting air and the unlikelihood of finding it elsewhere were realised and accommodated within space fiction. Air was foregrounded as a vital commodity in such interplanetary fantasies as Victor Valding's "Atmospherics" (1939), and the assumption that spacefarers would have to pay handsomely for air provision was routinised in Robert A. *Heinlein's and Arthur C. *Clarke's accounts of the early phases of the *Space Age before being foregrounded again in Grey Rollins' "Something in the Air" (1990). Exotic atmospheres became a key component of *exobiological fantasy, greatly encouraged by James *Lovelock's popularisation of the evolution of the earthly atmosphere as a product of biological activity.

The atmospheric discovery that had the greatest impact on speculative fiction was the radio-opaque Heaviside layer, whose existence was conclusively demonstrated in 1925. This was rapidly reflected in pulp science fiction, in such stories as S. P. Meek's "Beyond the Heaviside Layer" (1930), and helped renew interest in the notion of transparent shells surrounding the planet. The ozone layer seemed uninteresting until holes began to appear in it in the 1980s, resulting in a good deal of interest in *ecocatastrophe stories, although such technological regeneration programs as the one depicted in Joan Slonczewski's The Wall Around Eden (1989) remained too implausible to be credited to human agency.

The advent of radio introduced a new meaning for the term "air", as a verb synonymous with broadcast, whose noun derivative became familiar in the phrase "on the air". This opened up scope for the kind of wordplay displayed in such novels as Geoff Ryman's Air (or Have Not Have) (2003), which features "airheads" whose brains are directly connected to the Internet. The evolution of air-conditioning technologies also had some impact on speculative fiction, including such accounts of exotic engineering as Walt and Leigh Richmond's "Shortstack" (1964)—although a much more ambitious project of atmospheric engineering is described in Lewis Shiner's alternative history "White City" (1990), in which Nicholas Tesla finds a means of achieving permanent atmospheric illumination.

ALCHEMY

A mystical pseudoscience ultimately displaced by *chemistry. Although its history is dubious, it was first extensively developed in Egypt in the first century

B.C. Many of its legendary practitioners were women, the most famous of whom was Maria the Jewess. The central objective of alchemy was the philosopher's stone, a magical catalyst that would cure all physical ills and permit the transmutation of physical substances.

Alchemy underwent a dramatic revival and revision in the thirteenth century, when its most notable academic pioneer was Ramon Lull; its new practitioners equipped it with an elaborate imaginary history that associated it very closely with *astrology and made it a fundamental aspect of the holistic fabric of *occult science. It remained one of the favourite objects of *scholarly fantasy thereafter, although its careful mystification might also reflect the economic desirability of maintaining secrecy with respect to new metallurgical and dyeing techniques. The theory of Renaissance alchemy embraced the Classical theory of the four *elements and its *medical counterpart, the theory of bodily humors. Its new practitioners supplemented this basic pattern with various volatile "spirits" (including alcohol and various acids), numerous "salts", and a set of seven metals whose alleged properties were confused by *astrological associations with the seven planets.

Renaissance alchemists credited the legendary philosopher's stone with the power to transmute the five "base" metals (iron, mercury, tin, copper, and lead) into the "pure" metals (gold and silver)—an objective often faked by clever tricksters, which exerted a powerful influence on the literary imagination. Its medical properties were often hived off to another legendary objective, the elixir of life, which was reputedly capable of conferring extreme *longevity on its possessors. Renaissance alchemists in search of the secret of the philosopher's stone routinely attempted to reduce complex substances to a "primal matter" from which they had allegedly been formed, in order that they might be reconstituted in a different form; their attempts to reduce substances to simpler forms by such processes as distillation and heating in crucibles encouraged the development of useful laboratory equipment and familiarised experimenters with many chemical transactions that might not otherwise have been subjected to scrutiny. The principal contribution of alchemical legend to the literary image of science was its influence on the decor of fictitious laboratories, which were routinely equipped with alembics, crucibles, and other apparatus likely to be found in alchemists' lairs.

A comprehensive account of Renaissance alchemy is contained in Geoffrey Chaucer's "The Canon's Yeoman's Tale" (ca. 1390), which is told from the viewpoint of a skeptical apprentice. This skepticism did not prevent practicing alchemists from becoming Chaucerian poets. George Ripley prefaced his enormously popular *Compound of Alchemie* (ca. 1470) with a poetic allegory of the alchemical quest, known as *Cantilena* or *Ripley's Song*; Thomas Norton, author of the *Ordinall of Alchimy* (1477), also wrote several alchemical poems, possibly including a group attributed to "Pearce the Black Monk". Ripley's *Compound*, also known as *The Castle of Alchemy*, helped to renew the popularity of the subject when it was printed for the first time in 1591—a renewal that assisted the remolding of popular images of Roger *Bacon and John *Dee. The effects of the repopularisation lingered long into the seventeenth century, attracting the attention of such pillars of the scientific revolution as Isaac *Newton.

The transformation of alchemy into chemistry was encouraged by the revisionism of *Paracelsus, whose attempt to build a theory of chemical "quintessence" was carried forward by Johann van Helmont. Helmont's fascination with the notion of the *alkahest* (a universal solvent) assisted him to make substantial strides in the investigation of salts and to refine the alchemical notion of a spirit into the chemical notion of a "gas". The supersession of alchemy by chemistry is celebrated retrospectively in histories of science and in such literary works as Robert Browning's *Paracelsus* (1835), but mystical alchemy retained a secure place in the canon of occult science.

Alchemists often feature in post-Renaissance literature as confidence tricksters, as in Ben Jonson's *The Alchemist* (1610), or as obsessive pursuers of futile dreams, as in Honoré de Balzac's *La recherche de l'absolu* (1834; trans. as *The Quest for the Absolute*) and Nathaniel Hawthorne's unfinished novel whose posthumous versions include *Septimius* (1872), *The Dolliver Romance* (1876), and *Doctor Grimshawe's Secret* (1882). This image was cemented by a long chapter on "The Alchymists" in the first volume of Charles Mackay's *Memoirs of Extraordinary Popular Delusions* (1841; exp. as *Extraordinary Popular Delusions and the Madness of Crowds*), which collected numerous popular anecdotes and became a useful source for writers of fiction, including Edward Bulwer-Lytton's *Zanoni* (1842) and *A Strange Story* (1862), which reimported the credulity that Mackay disdained. Alexandre Dumas' *Joseph Balsamo* (1846; trans. as *Memoirs of a Physician*) begins in a credulous fashion, although its final phases and its sequels echo Mackay's skeptical judgment of the legendary Count Cagliostro. Alchemical writings of the Renaissance period were often couched in elaborate symbolic codes and equipped with a protective clothing of pretentious piety; such artifices were extravagantly elaborated by occult scientists, encouraging later commentators to argue that alchemical endeavour was essentially a quest for spiritual enlightenment—a notion reflected in such earnest literary representations as Vladimir Odoevsky's stories translated as "The Sylph" (1837), "The Cosmorama" (1839), and "The Salamander" (1841).

The late nineteenth-century occult revival followed Bulwer-Lytton's example rather than Mackay's; Mackay's own adoptive daughter Minnie—who preferred to style herself Marie Corelli—became the revival's most popular literary contributor, and a defiantly reverent interest in alchemy is also reflected in the work of more thoughtful writers such as Arthur Machen, Gustav Meyrink, and John Cowper Powys. Twentieth-century histories of alchemical scholarly fantasy by such writers as Mircea Eliade and Frances Yates provided a further inspirational boost to literateurs, with the result that alchemists are routinely integrated into conspiratorial secret histories; Neal Stephenson's *Cryptonomicon* (1999) and its sequels feature John Milton as a alchemist and pay more attention to Isaac Newton's alchemical investigations than his work in optics or physical astronomy.

The idea of alchemy as a spiritual quest, fused with its analogical use by the symbolist poet Arthur Rimbaud in the context of his creative quest for an "alchemy of the word", has ensured that alchemy is a persistently powerful notion in literature, many twentieth-century alchemical fantasies being formulated as exercises in complex symbolism. Notable examples include Margaret Yourcenar's *L'oeuvre au noir* (1968; trans. as *The Abyss*), John Crowley's series begun with *Aegypt* (1987), Lindsay Clarke's *The Chymical Wedding* (1989), Patrick Harpur's *Mercurius; or The Marriage of Heaven and Earth* (1990), Kate Thompson's *The Alchemist's Apprentice* (2002), Lisa Goldstein's *The Alchemist's Door* (2002), and Eileen Kernaghan's *The Alchemist's Daughter* (2004). Few novels of this sort retain any significant component of scientific speculation, although Ian Watson's *The Gardens of Delight* (1980) and Neal Barrett Jr.'s *The Prophecy Machine* (2000) are exceptions to the rule.

Notable works of speculative fiction featuring technologies that emulate alchemical quests include Robert Duncan Milne's "A New Alchemy" (1879), Arthur Conan Doyle's *The Doings of Raffles Haw* (1891), John Taine's *The Gold Tooth* (1927), Horace L. Gold's "Gold" (1935, by-lined Clyde Crane Campbell), R. R. Winterbotham's "Linked Worlds" (1937), Charles Harness's "The Alchemist" (1966), and Mack Reynolds' "The Golden Rule" (1980). Reginald Bretnor's *Schimmelhorn's Gold* (1986) is breezily chimerical in its determination to impose an element of rationality on a classical account, with amusing consequences. Paracelsus and John Dee are the alleged alchemists most frequently featured in

recent historical fantasy, although literary representations of *Faust often credit him with alchemical interests; Nicholas Flamel has also achieved widespread literary fame by virtue of his citation in J. K. Rowling's *Harry Potter and the Philosopher's Stone* (1997).

ALDISS, BRIAN W[ILSON] (1925–)

British writer who, after leaving school, served in the Royal Signals Corps for five years, most of them stationed in the Far East, and then worked at an Oxford bookshop until he was able to make a living as a writer. Although he was not formally educated in science, Aldiss' omnivorous intelligence and wide-ranging interests allowed him to make interesting sophisticated aesthetic and philosophical connections between scientific and other ideas. Although his work in the science fiction genre is not *hard science fiction, it does manifest a strong interest in scientific ideas and their implications.

Much of Aldiss' early work employed far future scenarios, with those collected in *The Canopy of Time* (1959) and *Galaxies Like Grains of Sand* (1960; restored text, 1979) formulating a broad future history that pays attention to the possibilities of future evolution, featuring the eventual emergence of a kind of "totipotency" that infuses all of the cells of complex organisms with intelligence. The episodic novel *Hothouse* (1962; aka *The Long Afternoon of Earth*) is a complex biological fantasia that uses a philosophical fungus as a key narrator, which develops a Lovelock-esque image of an active ecosphere without going to extremes of *ecological mysticism and illustrates a hypothetical mechanism of *Panspermia. Some hard science fiction purists were annoyed by the image of cobwebs extending between a tidally locked Earth and the Moon, which became a useful item of controversy in discussion regarding the extent of the poetic license appropriate to science fiction writing.

Non-Stop (1958; aka *Starship*) is a paradigmatic account of conceptual breakthrough set aboard a generation starship, which deliberately turns back on itself, in that the greater understanding won by the characters reveals both the futility of their forgotten mission and the extent of their own institutionalisation. *The Primal Urge* (1961) is a satirical account of the introduction of "emotional registers" that make previously private emotional reactions evident—an intriguing anticipation of the changes that overtook British society in the "swinging" sixties. *The Dark Light-Years* (1964) employs a peculiar *alien species to satirise human taboos regarding excretion.

Aldiss' science fiction moved into a new phase with the publication of *Greybeard* (1964), an elegiac story set in the great British tradition of ambiguous *disaster novels, which tracks the gradual evolution of a plague of sterilisation that condemns the last generation of humankind to age and die without successors. He continued to make conscientious attempts to export his science-fictional interests from generic formats into conspicuously literary frameworks—as H. G. Wells had done sixty years before—in such novels as *An Age* (1967; aka *Cryptozoic*), a philosophical fantasy featuring counterclockwise time, and *Report on Probability A* (1968), which features a series of alternative worlds minimally distinguished as a result of the subtle operation of Heisenberg's *uncertainty principle. The short story "Supertoys Last All Summer Long" (1969), which explores a potential application of artificial intelligence, was developed into a series of film scripts under the aegis of Stanley Kubrick, but only reached the screen after Kubrick's death when Steven Spielberg completed it as *A.I.* (2001).

Aldiss' work was readily co-opted into Michael Moorcock's "new wave" science fiction, although his literary experiments tended to lack the keen interest in contemporary cultural developments that were typical of the movement. He did, however, produce a hectic account of the *psychotropic fallout of a new kind of chemical warfare in *Barefoot in the Head* (1969). Typically, his attempts to understand the future potential of the genre encouraged him to investigate its past with a carefully analytical eye, expressed in such reflective fantasies as "The Saliva Tree" (1965)—in which H. G. Wells makes a belated but highly significant appearance—and such adventures in speculative nonfiction as *The Shape of Further Things* (1970). His reflections culminated in a breezily informal history of science fiction, *Billion Year Spree* (1973; exp. in collaboration with David Wingrove as *Trillion Year Spree*, 1986).

Billion Year Spree begins with the proposition that modern science fiction, in spite of its pretensions to hardness, remains an essentially "post-Gothic" art form historically rooted in Mary Shelley's *Frankenstein*—a notion calculated to annoy hard science fiction writers committed to the notion that the *Frankenstein complex was a thoroughly bad thing. Although much of Aldiss' early science fiction had used the myth of the *Space Age as a convenient speculative framework his disenchantment within it became increasingly obvious. His comment on his own work in the 1996 edition of the *St. James Guide to Science Fiction Writers* laments the damage done to Earth by twentieth-century technology, adding: "Let's hope to God that that infantile fantasy of our conquering the universe never becomes reality!" His fascination with Mary Shelley's ambivalent response to the Enlightenment was extrapolated in *Frankenstein*

Unbound (1973), which led in its turn to other reexaminations of classics of imaginative literature in *Moreau's Other Island* (1980) and—following Roger Corman's film version of *Frankenstein Unbound* (1990)—*Dracula Unbound* (1991).

As with Wells, the science-fictional elements of Aldiss' work became increasingly peripheral as his career extended, although his continued fascination with scientific and science-fictional ideas was reflected in the essays collected in *This World and Nearer Ones* (1979) and two collections—*The Pale Shadow of Science* (1985) and *And the Lurid Glare of the Comet* (1986), subsequently combined as *The Detached Retina* (1995). Most of his relevant work from the 1970s was satirical, notably the anti-Soviet political fantasy *Enemies of the System: A Tale of Homo Uniformis* (1978), but he returned to more earnest scientific romance in an epic trilogy, comprising *Helliconia Spring* (1982), *Helliconia Summer* (1983), and *Helliconia Winter* (1985), depicting the cyclical ecological and social patterns adapted to the climatic extremes experienced on a planet orbiting one element of a binary star system. Although he never had Wells' ambition to change the world by means of polemical social philosophy—in the same statement cited earlier, Aldiss said flatly that "Mine is a literature of exile"—he was prepared to extrapolate ideas of a similar sort in collaboration with Sir Roger Penrose in *White Mars; or, The Mind Set Free* (1999). *Super-State* (2002) returned to the arena of futuristic satire.

ALIEN

The term conventionally used in modern fiction to represent sentient extraterrestrial species. The history of the notion extends back far beyond the hypothetical science of *exobiology, originating in the context of the theological debate regarding the possible *plurality of worlds. Although early participants in the debate took it for granted that any intelligent inhabitants of other worlds must be made in God's (and hence in humankind's) image, alternative possibilities inevitably crept in, especially in the wake of John *Kepler's speculations regarding life on the *Moon. Henry Baker's poem *The Universe* (1734) suggested, in considering the planet *Saturn, that "Who here inhabit, must have other Pow'rs, / Juices, and Veins, and Sense, and Life than Ours".

Baker's proposition was further elaborated in Voltaire's *Micromégas* (1752), which features a giant Saturnian equipped with more senses than humans, and an even larger and better endowed interstellar traveler. Variant sentient life-forms were featured on a wholesale basis in Ludwig Holberg's *Nicolaii Klimii Iter Subterraneum* (1741; trans. as *A Journey to the World Underground by Nicholas Klimius*), where the inhabitants of the planet Nazar include tree-men, civilised simians, the animated stringed instruments of Crotchet Island, and the Pyglossians, who have no mouths but can talk through the anus. Another exotically populated subterranean world is featured in Giacomo Casanova's *Icosameron* (1788), whose "megamicres" set new standards for the comprehensive description of the *biology and *xenology of an alien race, although they were still recognisably based on the human model.

The development of theories of *evolution brought the notion of the alien into a new context, dominated by ideas of adaptation to exotic environments. In Catholic France such notions were readily confused with theological ideas—especially cosmic *palingenesis, as in the works of Camille *Flammarion—but in Britain the thesis of interplanetary reincarnation was restricted to spiritualist fantasy. After the popularisation of ideas contained in Charles *Darwin's *Origin of Species* (1859), especially in the version favoured by Herbert Spencer, British evolutionary philosophy became preoccupied with the idea of a struggle for existence whose losers must perish, and English writers soon began to imagine alien species locked in deadly competition with one another, as in Hugh MacColl's *Mr. Stranger's Sealed Packet* (1889), or as potential rivals of humankind, as in H. G. Wells' *The War of the Worlds* (1898).

The War of the Worlds, which featured aliens as would-be *colonisers bent on the genocidal conquest of Earth, set a vital literary precedent by revealing untapped melodramatic potential of a uniquely exaggerated variety, whose exploitation required the representation of aliens as loathsome *monsters. Wells went on to produce a more subtly horrific description of an alien society in *The First Men in the Moon* (1901), based on the model of the ant hive. He made no attempt to develop these templates further, and their influence on early twentieth-century *scientific romance was limited; the most significant representations of aliens within that genre were usually more positive, as in Eden Phillpotts' *Saurus* (1938), and sometimes assumed Flammarionesque cosmic schemes like the one mapped out in Olaf Stapledon's *Star Maker* (1937). The Wellsian template was, however, used much more profusely in the United States, where it became a standard cliché of pulp *science fiction. Although action-adventure science fiction in the vein of Edgar Rice Burroughs routinely equipped other worlds with human inhabitants—including exotically beautiful females to serve as "love interests"—they usually placed such races under threat from predatory monsters, which were often insectile or reptilian in form.

The specialist science fiction magazines that inherited this melodramatic tradition made copious use of monstrous alien invaders; Edmond Hamilton, Edward E. Smith, and other pioneers of space opera rapidly developed a notion of the universe as an infinite battleground in which humans would naturally ally themselves with peace-loving and democratically inclined species in order to resist the predations of nastier species. Physical descriptions of virtuous aliens were usually compounded from mammalian and avian characteristics, while those of vicious ones were often chimerical combinations of the reptilian, arthropodan, and molluskan. This formula was handed down to the media that became the natural heirs of pulp fiction—comic books, cinema, and TV—where it achieved an even greater dominance; it reached the apogee of its melodramatic sophistication in such movies as *The Thing from Another World* (1951; loosely based on John W. Campbell Jr.'s "Who Goes There?") and *Alien* (1979) and such TV shows as *The Outer Limits* (1963–1965) and *The X Files* (1993–2000).

Although the explicitly theological elements of the scale of moral evolution built into the theory of cosmic palingenesis were deemphasised in genre science fiction, they proved resilient in various disguised forms. John Campbell's "The Last Evolution" (1932) imagined a powerful selective challenge posed by repeated alien assaults forcing the replacement of frail human flesh by sentient machinery, followed by the replacement of all material shells by entities of "pure energy". Such carefully secularised images of quasi-angelic entities recur continually in genre science fiction as representatives of the evolutionary ultimate; the Campbellian scheme became a key background assumption of the myth of the *Space Age, whose residual religious overtones were stressed in the summary of that scheme set out in Donald A. Wollheim's *The Universe Makers* (1971).

Early genre science fiction writers were occasionally willing to invert their chauvinistic assumptions in order to represent humans as monstrous invaders, as in P. Schuyler Miller's "Forgotten Man of Space" (1933), or to represent visually horrifying aliens as noble individuals with whom friendship was both possible and desirable, as in Raymond Z. Gallun's "Old Faithful" (1934) and "Something from Jupiter" (1938; by-lined Dow Elstar). A more interesting thread of development was evident in stories focusing on more exotic kinds of alienness, which rendered straightforward competitions for resources redundant. Mineral life-forms were featured in such works as A. Merritt's *The Metal Monster* (1920) and John

Taine's *White Lily* (1930; aka *The Crystal Horde*), but more significant images resulted from the development of an elementary *ecological awareness by such writers as Jack Williamson in "The Alien Intelligence" (1929) and "The Moon Era" (1932) and Stanley G. Weinbaum in "A Martian Odyssey" (1934). Weinbaum followed "A Martian Odyssey" with many other stories in a similar vein that attempted to integrate intelligent aliens into complex ecosystems, stressing their interdependence with other species.

This emphasis on ecological relationships combined with influences from political science to produce a strand of genre science fiction in which the fundamental problem of alien contact came to be seen as a difficult diplomatic exercise whose ultimate goal was peaceful and mutually fruitful coexistence. Such stories as Murray Leinster's "First Contact" and "The Ethical Equations" (both 1945) foreshadowed a postwar era in which sophisticated magazine science fiction moved decisively away from simple melodramatic formularisation to much more complex representations of human/alien relationships. The resultant complication of the problems surrounding first contact, coupled with arguments suggesting that some such contact was inevitable, produced a consensus that communication with an alien species or a community of such species would be an unprecedentedly momentous event in human history.

The *Social Darwinist assumptions adopted by H. G. Wells were treated with increasing suspicion in post–World War II science fiction, whose Cold War context served to sharpen the tenor of the debate. The political significance of the relevant differences of opinion is reflected in the representation by the Soviet science fiction writer Ivan Yefremov of his "Cor Serpentis" (1959) as an explicit ideological reply to Leinster's "First Contact", the author arguing that any society sufficiently advanced to go spacefaring must have evolved a communist society, no matter how alien it might be in biological terms. Problematic contacts with biologically exotic aliens became a prominent feature of the work of such *hard science fiction writers as Poul *Anderson, Hal *Clement, Charles *Sheffield, and Robert L. *Forward, but the contacts featured in soft science fiction were rarely seen as simple affairs, even when the envisaged aliens differed from humans only in minor aspects of mores and folkways.

The twentieth-century literary use of aliens outside genre science fiction was, inevitably, dominated by philosophical fabulations constructing hypothetical alien viewpoints in order to examine and criticise human attitudes, values, and ambitions. This satirical tradition became very thin while genre science fiction

and the popular mythology of *flying saucers acted as a deterrent to earnest writers of literary fiction, but it survived in such exercises as Gore Vidal's play *Visit to a Small Planet* (1956; book, 1960) and Kurt Vonnegut's *The Sirens of Titan* (1959), and was extended to the end of the century in such works as Gene Brewer's *K-Pax* (1995). Genre science fiction took this kind of function aboard in prolific measure in the 1950s, sarcastically assaulting a number of targets. One of the most prominent was the exploitation and cultural vandalism routinely associated with the adventures in colonisation that were central to the myth of the Space Age, whose limitations were mercilessly exposed in Eric Frank Russell's "The Waitabits" (1955).

Other obvious directions that investigation of the notion of physical and psychological "otherness" might take were somewhat inhibited while science fiction remained a magazine-based genre, because of the standards of decency and diplomacy imposed on the medium as a whole. That did not prevent some science fiction writers from attempting to use the alien as a means of coming to grips with issues of sexuality, as in Philip José Farmer's *The Lovers* (1952; exp. 1961) and Theodore Sturgeon's "The World Well Lost" (1953). Others were equally ready to tackle issues of racism, as in Leigh Brackett's "All the Colours of the Rainbow" (1957) and Mark Clifton's "What Now, Little Man" (1959). The problems involved in establishing communication with an alien species, even if a convenient means of *space travel were to be devised, were routinely sidestepped by such facilitating devices as translation machines and telepathy—although some skeptics pointed out, in such *contes philosophiques* as Hal Clement's "Impediment" (1942), the extreme improbability of the proposition that telepathy might assist in communication with aliens. The problem of alien contact and communication was, however, treated very differently when scientists began to take a serious interest in exobiological speculation and actual *SETI programs were established.

In a commentary on his story "In Alien Flesh" (1978), Gregory Benford observed that "rendering the alien is the Holy Grail of science fiction, because if your attempt can be accurately summarised, you know you've failed". Quests for this grail are very numerous; Benford's other significant attempts include "Starswarmer" (1978) and *Sunborn* (2005), while notable examples by other hands include Margaret St. Clair's "Prott" (1953), Terry Carr's "Hop-Friend" (1962) and "The Dance of the Changer and Three" (1968), Colin Kapp's "Ambassador to Verdammt" (1967), Frank Herbert's *Whipping Star* (1970; rev. 1977) and The Dosadi Experiment (1977),

Cynthia Felice's *Godsfire* (1978), Jayge Carr's "The Wondrous Works of His Hands" (1982), Michael J. Swanwick's "Ginungagap" (1980), Robert Chilson's "Hand of Friendship" (1983), Patricia Anthony's *Cold Allies* (1993) and *Brother Termite* (1993), Adam-Troy Castro's "The Funeral March of the Marionettes" (1997) and its sequel, Ted Chiang's "Story of Your Life" (1998), Nancy Kress' "Savior" (2000), and Phyllis Gotlieb's *Mind*Worlds* (2002). An interesting metafictional account of the paradoxicality of the problem of representing aliens is set out in Paul Park's "If Lions Could Speak: Imagining the Alien" (2002), while a substantial fraction of the work of the Polish science fiction writer Stanislaw Lem—including the novels translated as *Eden* (1959), *Return from the Stars* (1961), *Solaris* (1961), and *The Invincible* (1964) —is devoted to arguing the impossibility of its solution.

The most intriguing aliens in late twentieth-century fiction often come in elaborate sets, like those populating James White's Sector General series, which generated a complex classification based on fundamental ecological patterns. White's *The Watch Below* (1966), *All Judgment Fled* (1968), and *Federation World* (1988) are further accounts of problematic first contacts. Larry *Niven's Known Space series includes the human-ancestral Pak, the discreet Puppeteers, and the catlike Kzin. The eponymous aliens of Stephen Baxter's Xeelee are remote and enigmatic, but the series also features the Qax—sentient systems of cells in turbulent fluid—and various species caught in exotic existential traps, such as those featured in "The Sun-People" (1993) and "Cilia-of-Gold" (1994). Sean Williams and Shane Dix's series, which began with *Echoes of Earth* (2002), features a tense opposition between the equally enigmatic Spinners and Starfish.

Opposition to xenophobia in tales of alien encounters eventually reached its extreme in various accounts of human/alien symbiosis, hybridisation, and chimerisation, the most notable examples of which include John Christopher's "Rock-a-Bye" (1954), Octavia Butler's Xenogenesis trilogy (1987–1989), and Robert Reed's *The Remarkables* (1992). Geoffrey A. Landis' "Embracing the Alien" (1992) takes a more skeptical view of such scenarios. Accounts of more modest alliances forged against the odds can, however, be given a remarkably powerful emotional charge, as in Barry B. Longyear's "Enemy Mine" (1979), Robert Chilson's "Walk with Me" (1982), and Steven Spielberg's highly successful movie *ET: The Extraterrestrial* (1982).

Accounts of alien invasion and human/alien warfare often seem repetitively unimaginative by contrast with accounts of hard-won rapport, but their melodramatic advantages ensured that they appeared in much greater profusion throughout the twentieth century. Rebecca Ore's *Becoming Alien* (1988), *Being Alien* (1989), and *Human to Human* (1990) charge humans with being "xenoflips", able to see the aliens as a menace or as an instrument of salvation, but not as equal-but-different beings; the short stories in Ore's *The Alien Bootlegger and Other Stories* (1993) make further attempts to redress that situation, but the judgment remains broadly sound. In the meantime, first contact with aliens remains one of the archetypal themes of science fiction, its more notable late twentieth- and early twenty-first-century variants including Stephen Popkes' *Caliban Landing* (1987), Jerry Oltion and Lee Goodloe's "Contact" (1991), Wil McCarthy's *Aggressor Six* (1994), Gregory Benford's "The Hydrogen Wall" (2003), and James L. Cambias' "The Ocean of the Blind" (2004).

ALIENATION

A process or condition of estrangement. The term was used in various legal contexts before and during the nineteenth century, but those meanings were gradually eclipsed by translation of an equivalent German term employed in the philosophy of G. W. F. Hegel and the social science of Karl *Marx. Hegel applied it in the context of spiritual and psychological development, but Marx grounded it materially in the alienation of labourers from their produce within the capitalist system. These usages became the progenitors of an extraordinarily rich literature modeling and extrapolating notions of alienation, which moved to an early extreme in Feodor Dostoevsky's study of psychological alienation *Zapiski iz podpolya* (1864; trans. as *Notes from Underground*) but proceeded to search out even more radical representations in the twentieth century, in such phantasmagoric works as Franz Kafka's *Die Verwandlung* (1912; trans. as *Metamorphosis*).

The Marxist notion of objective alienation was extensively developed in the rhetoric of socialist literature, but it became increasingly confused with subjective "feelings of alienation" arising from a sense of dissociation corollary to the march of individualism in Western society. This phenomenon was also objectified and reconstructed as an object of scientific analysis by the sociologist Émile Durkheim in the theory of *anomie* (normlessness), but literary works inevitably continued to focus on the consciousness of dissociation rather than its environmental causes, tacitly favouring the hypothesis that solutions to such problems were matters of attitude rather than context. In so doing, the literature of alienation reflected—and to some extent constituted—a marked trend towards the "eupsychian" mode of *Utopian thought, which is also reflected in the twentieth-century boom in "self-help" manuals and philosophies of psychological "self-actualisation".

Social scientists of various schools correlated subjective feelings of alienation with an individual's social isolation within an evolving "mass society" or powerlessness within large-scale political systems, or with a sense of meaninglessness engendered by the perceived devastation of religious faith by science. All of these perceived aspects of the problem were plangently echoed in early twentieth-century literature, becoming key foci of the work of such disparate writers as T. S. Eliot, Thomas Mann, André Gide, and Ernest Hemingway and inspiring such movements as the Theatre of the Absurd. Variants of alienation theory were imported into the philosophy of drama by Alfred Jarry and Bertolt Brecht—the latter in a specifically Marxist context—although they regarded it as an effect worthy of production, following the assertion by the Russian formalist Victor Shlovsky that the primary function of art ought to be an intellectually challenging *ostranenie* (estrangement).

The development of new schools of "existentialist" philosophy, which made much of the notion of *angst*, gave further emphasis to the perceived problem of "being". Martin Heidegger's *Sein und Zeit* (1927; trans. as *Being and Time*) advanced the proposition that the human experience of existence is fundamentally and necessarily afflicted by dread occasioned by the awareness that the future is undetermined—its outcome dependent on freely exercised choices—save for the eventual inevitability of death. The resultant *angst* is said to lead the human imagination to all manner of contortions in the attempt to escape the burden of choice and refute the inevitability of death, thus resulting in various modes of alienation from the individual's "true self".

Existentialist philosophy developed particularly close links with twentieth-century literature, and the construction of exemplary fictions mapping the subjective experience of alienation, anomie, and angst became one of its key methods. Jean-Paul Sartre's summary account of *L'être et le néant* (1943; trans. as *Being and Nothingness*) followed the literary analysis set out in *La nausée* (1939; trans. as *Nausea*), while Albert Camus coupled his literary study of *L'étranger* (1942; trans. as *The Outsider*) with his philosophical essay on "Le mythe de Sisyphe" (1942; trans. as "The Myth of Sispyhus"). Popularisations of work in this vein, such as Colin Wilson's *The Outsider* (1956), routinely hybridise literary and philosophical analysis, and newly minted catch-phrases such as David Riesman's *The Lonely Crowd* (1950), proved equally appealing to the literary and academic communities.

Quests to find, identify, and recover some kind of "true self" became a major preoccupation of late twentieth-century literature and lifestyle, often being formulated as exaggerated literary and lifestyle fantasies. Within such literary and lifestyle fantasies, *technology is very frequently seen as a hindrance rather than a means to the desired end. The representation of industrial technology as an irresistible and dehumanising tide—or an all-consuming Moloch, as symbolically visualised in Fritz Lang's film *Metropolis* (1926)—is partly founded in the notion of alienation, whose ubiquity frequently resulted in the conflation of technological trends with the other political and social trends implicated in the generation and magnification of feelings of isolation and powerlessness. Another argumentative thread that became increasingly important as twentieth-century technology evolved concerned the alleged alienating effects of new means of communication, which were placed in an unholy alliance with automated production in the rapidly evolving imagery of future *dystopia.

The inevitable effect of such widespread consideration, and the consequent adoption of the term into common parlance, was that the concept of alienation became increasingly diluted and diffuse as the century progressed. Gradually, however, the representation of alienation became less tragic and more heroic as sympathy migrated from characters inescapably trapped in victim status to characters who were at least prepared to mount a good show of defiance. The production of alienation was initially seen as a significant measurement of the evils of dystopia, but as the century progressed the extremes of dystopia were often represented as measures calculated to make alienation impossible by obliterating individualism, as in Egevny Zamyatin's *My* (1920; trans. as *We*), Aldous Huxley's *Brave New World* (1932), and George Orwell's *Nineteen Eighty-Four* (1949). In these works, the tragic dimension of alienation is inverted, the opposite extreme being seen as the greater of the two ultimate evils.

Speculative fiction offered a convenient medium for more various and ingenious models of alienation, especially when it began to generate a whole spectrum of potential "outsider" figures in *aliens, *androids, *mutants, *robots, and *cyborgs—many of which could easily function as emblems of automation and could easily be integrated into futuristic images of media tyranny—but the upbeat tendencies of pulp science fiction tended to suppress the use of such icons in that respect until the 1960s, when "new wave" science fiction adopted the depiction and exploration of states of alienation as one of its central projects. The analysis of different subspecies of alienation is a very obvious component of the work of such British writers as J. G. Ballard and Michael Moorcock, and such American writers as Harlan Ellison and Robert Silverberg. Ballard's most notable stories in this vein include "The Waiting Grounds" (1959), "The Terminal Beach" (1964), and *The Drought* (1965); Moorcock's include *The Twilight Man* (1966), *Behold the Man* (1966; exp. 1969), and *The Black Corridor* (1969); Ellison's include "'Repent Harlequin!' said the Ticktockman" (1965), "I Have No Mouth and I Must Scream" (1967), and "Shatterday" (1978); Silverberg's include *Thorns* (1967), *The Man in the Maze* (1969), and *Dying Inside* (1972). Another significant science-fictional study of alienation from the same period is Walter S. Tevis' *The Man Who Fell to Earth* (1963), but the attitudinal pendulum swing reflected in Utopian fiction was evident in later generic existential fantasies such as C. J. Cherryh's *Wave Without a Shore* (1981).

The notion of alienation gained a further meaning when the notion of human alienation from *nature became a leading theme of environmentalist rhetoric, especially in fiction with tendencies towards *ecological mysticism. This accommodation further increased the utility of science-fictional imagery in concocting accounts of alienation, and assisted the spread of science-fictional ideas into literary fiction. On the other hand, the community of writers and fans gathered around genre science fiction was itself increasingly subject to sensations of alienation, not merely in terms of the genre's perceived alienation from the literary "mainstream", but in the perceived alienation of *hard science fiction from the softer varieties that proved to be more reader friendly and more likely to win critical approval. The emergence of genre fantasy in the last quarter of the twentieth century helped to increase the sense of science fiction's own alienation, although that evolution did open up another popular arena in which feelings of alienation could be easily and effectively modeled.

A more specific version of Shlovsky's *ostranenie* was imported into science fiction criticism by Darko Suvin, who characterised the genre's fundamental narrative method as "cognitive estrangement". In this view, readers acquainting themselves with the fictitious worlds of naturalistic fiction are merely required to refine and slightly modify the stocks of knowledge they use in the understanding of actual situations, while reading "fantasy" only requires the temporary suspension of such stocks, because it does not require "cognitive believability"; authentic science fiction, by contrast, requires readers to set aside the stocks of knowledge they use routinely, in order to construct new sets that are sufficiently coherent and elaborate to reveal new social and intellectual possibilities. This is a healthy form of estrangement, and a wholly constructive mode of alienation, even though Suvin does not broaden it to take in such radical fictional estrangements as Hal Clement's more extreme descriptions of alien life or George Gamow's models of universes in which the fundamental physical constants have different values. It suggests a way in which positive variants of the terms might be applied to the feats of imagination required by scientific theorists when required to make conceptual breakthroughs or to accommodate *paradigm shifts.

ALTERNATIVE HISTORY

An account of the world's *history as it might have become in consequence of some hypothetical alteration of a *past event. Some historians employing the device in *speculative nonfiction prefer the term "counterfactual history", and many science fiction fans prefer "alternate history". Most such exercises deal with singular alternative histories, but some science fiction stories deal with them on a wholesale basis, often hypothesising a framework system of *parallel worlds whose extreme case is a multiverse containing all possible historical variants.

The usefulness to the historian of hypothetical exercises of this kind was advertised by Isaac d'Israeli in "Of a History of Events Which Have Not Happened" (ca. 1800; reprinted in *The Curiosities of Literature*, 1791–1823), who finds examples in the work of Livy, Francesco Guicciardini, and William Roscoe, although the most extensive example he gives—in which Charles Martel fails to expel the Moors from France—appears to be his own invention. The French Jesuit historian Jean-Nicolas Loriquet, who wrote numerous texts for the education of children, suggested in his *Histoire de France* (1814) that the historical texts used by society for instructional purposes should be rewritten to represent a history that would provide better exemplars for the young than actual events. Loriquet's suggestion that Napoleon's empire be erased from the historical record may have prompted Louis-Napoléon Geoffroy to take an opposite course in *Napoléon et la conquête du monde, 1812–1832* (1836; aka *Napoléon apocryphe*).

Charles Renouvier's "Uchronie" (1857) provided a descriptive term for such exercises, but "uchronia" remained rare in English until its use began to increase towards the end of the twentieth century. Early examples of English alternative history include Nathaniel Hawthorne's "P's Correspondence" (1845) and Edward Everett Hale's "Hands Off" (1881), whose formats hover uneasily between nonfiction and fiction, but novels set in alternative history frameworks were beginning to appear by the end of the nineteenth century, a significant early example being Castelo N. Holford's *Aristopia* (1895). G. M. Trevelyan's essay "If Napoleon Had Won the Battle of Waterloo" (1907) and Joseph Chamberlin's twenty-two-essay collection *The Ifs of History* (1907) prompted J. C. Squire to invite various notable writers of the day to contribute to a showcase anthology, *If It Had Happened Otherwise* (1931; exp. 1972; aka *If; or, History Rewritten*) but serious historians continued to use the method sparingly. Robert Sobel's *For Want of a Nail* (1973)—an account of an alternative American War of Independence—and Niall Ferguson's anthology *Virtual History: Alternatives and Counterfactuals* (1997) are among the most notable examples.

Alternative history often employs crucial battles as turning points, Waterloo and Gettysburg being particular favourites of military war-gamers. The latter is a crucial turning point in Ward Moore's novel *Bring the Jubilee* (1953) and Mackinlay Kantor's essay "If the South Had Won the Civil War" (1960; exp. 1961). Alternative versions of the battle of the Little Big Horn are crucial to Martin Cruz Smith's *The Indians Won* (1970) and Douglas Jones' *The Court Martial of George Armstrong Custer* (1976). The largest subcategory of such fictions comprises accounts of the world following a more-or-less catastrophic allied defeat in World War II; notable examples include Martin Hawkin's *When Adolf Came* (1943), Sarban's *The Sound of His Horn* (1952), Cyril M. Kornbluth's "Two Dooms" (1958), C. S. Forester's essay "If Hitler Had Invaded England" (1960), William L. Shirer's essay "If Hitler Had Won World War II" (1961), Philip K. Dick's *The Man in the High Castle* (1962), Frederick Mullally's *Hitler Has Won* (1975), Len Deighton's *SS-GB* (1978), Brad Linaweaver's *Moon of Ice* (1982; exp. 1988), Robert Harris' *Fatherland* (1992), and Richard Mueller's "Jew by the Sea" (2004). A showcase anthology of such stories is *Hitler Victorious* (1986) edited by Gregory Benford and Martin H. Greenberg.

The idea of alternative history was introduced to pulp science fiction in Murray Leinster's "Sidewise in Time" (1934), in which timeslips turn the Earth's surface into a patchwork of contrasted alternatives. Potential alternative histories use time machines to go to war in Jack Williamson's *The Legion of Time* (1938) and Fritz Leiber's *Destiny Times Three* (1945); Leiber followed the latter with an extensive Change War series including *The Big Time* (1958). Accounts of competing alternative histories became an important subgenre of *time travel stories, routinely involving "time police" struggling to maintain history. Many such stories investigate the ironies of fate that often frustrate purposive actions, as in John

Crowley's "Great Work of Time" (1989), in which attempts to protect the British Empire generate sweeping unintended consequences.

The relevance of alternative history to metaphysical notions of *time is explored in Jorge Luis Borges' "The Garden of the Forking Paths" (1941), and such metaphysical considerations received a significant boost in 1957, when Hugh Everett and John A. Wheeler concocted their interpretation of the *uncertainty of quantum mechanics in terms of the production of alternative worlds. The intellectual implications of more modest exercises are, however, political. All comparisons of an alternative history with actual history involve weighing in a moral balance, and all accounts of history changing and history protection require some moral justification for the attempted destruction or defence of a particular alternative history.

Many alternative history stories investigate questions of historical causality, with science fiction variants often focusing on issues of *technological determinism. L. Sprague de Camp's *Lest Darkness Fall* (1939) suggests that the crucial motors of historical change are not explicit conflicts establishing the dominion of particular social classes or competing nations but subtle technical developments whose eventual impact is rarely obvious to those who devise or deploy them. Other accounts of the preservation of the Roman Empire are contained in S. P. Somtow's Aquiliad series (1983–1988), Philip Mann's A Land Fit for Heroes series (1993–1996), Scott Mackay's *Orbis* (2002), and Robert Silverberg's *Roma Eterna* (2003), while further meditations on issues of technological determinism include de Camp's "Aristotle and the Gun" (1958), Michael F. Flynn's *In the Country of the Blind* (1987; book, 1990), and John Barnes' Timeline Wars series, comprising *Patton's Spaceship* (1997), *Washington's Dirigible* (1997), and *Caesar's Bicycle* (1997).

The thesis of Max Weber's *Die Protestantische Ethik und der Geist des Kapitalismus* (1904–1905; trans. as *The Protestant Ethic and the Spirit of Capitalism*), which argues that the protestant work ethic was a vital progenitor of capitalist enterprise and, hence, of the Industrial Revolution, is exploited in such works as Keith Roberts' *Pavane* (1968) and Kingsley Amis' *The Alteration* (1976), in which the failure of the Reformation is followed by technological stagnation. More adventurous alternative histories of religion include J. B. Ryan's "The Mosaic" (1940), in which an Islamic time traveller saved by Charles Martel returns the favour and dooms the Islamic Empire; John Boyd's *The Last Starship from Earth* (1969) and Kirk Mitchell's *Procurator* (1984), which delete the crucifixion; and L. Neil Smith's *The*

Crystal Empire (1986), in which the fourteenth-century obliteration of Christendom allows Islam to flourish unchecked. Other broadly conceived fantasies that make sweeping changes to the cultural history of the West include Kim Stanley Robinson's *The Years of Rice and Salt* (2002) and Robert Reed's "Hexagons" (2003), in which Western technological development is stopped in its tracks by the Black Death. A subtle change with dramatic consequences is explored in Kim Newman and Eugene Byrne's satire *Back in the USSA* (1997), which tracks a twentieth-century history in which the United States was host to a communist revolution.

It is more convenient for writers to deal with alternative histories in which technological progress slows down than with scenarios in which it is accelerated, but notable accounts of accelerated progress include D. R. Bensen's *And Having Writ....* (1978)—which features a twentieth century transformed by alien technological input—and James White's *The Silent Stars Go By* (1991), in which an early Hibernian colonisation of the Americas facilitates such rapid technological progress that the first interstellar spacecraft is launched in 1492. As *relativist ideas became more fashionable in the last quarter of the twentieth century, exercises in alternative history enjoyed a considerable vogue, almost becoming a genre in their own right. Such anthology series as What Might Have Been, edited by Gregory Benford and Martin H. Greenberg (1989–1992), helped pave the way for such prolific specialists as Harry Turtledove. The range of alternatives that came under consideration was dramatically increased by the emergence of *steampunk fiction.

Notable variants of alternative history fiction include accounts of ideologically biased perception such as Philip K. Dick's *Eye in the Sky* (1957), and existential fantasies in which characters meet alternative selves, such as Joanna Russ's *The Female Man* (1975), Robert Reed's "Like Minds" (2003), and Kevin J. Anderson's "The Bistro of Alternate Realities" (2004). As *palaeontology made progress during the twentieth century, writers extended their attention to prehistoric turning points. Guy Dent's *Emperor of the If* (1926) includes an account of the human race that might have evolved had Ice Ages not cooled the world; Robert J. Sawyer's Neanderthal Parallax trilogy (2002–1903) compares alternative hominid evolution in parallel worlds; Harry Harrison's *West of Eden* (1984) investigates the evolutionary consequences of *dinosaur survival.

Alternative history moved into space in the latter part of the twentieth century, in such works as Allen Steele's *The Tranquility Alternative* (1996) and Stephen Baxter's *Voyage* (1996). The imaginative limits of such exercises extend from the *Big Bang to the *Omega Point; universes derived from different sets of fundamental physical constants are featured in George Gamow's *Mr. Tompkins in Wonderland* (1939) and Frederik Pohl and Jack Williamson's *The Singers of Time* (1990). Such exercises may also extend to alternative metaphysics, as in Howard Waldrop's "...The World, as we Know't" (1982), which posits the reality of phlogiston theory. The existential implications of the obliteration of the past's apparent immutability by alternative history fiction can become a significant aspect of the subject matter of such stories, as in Robert Reed's "Past Imperfect" (2001).

ANDERSON, POUL (WILLIAM) (1926–2001)

U.S. writer. Anderson studied physics at the University of Minnesota, Minneapolis, obtaining his B.S. in 1948. He had already begun publishing science fiction by then, having contributed an item to *Astounding*'s "Probability Zero" feature in 1944. "Tomorrow's Children" (1947, with F. N. Waldrop) was a topical examination of the aftermath of a nuclear war, while "Logic" (1947) constructed a kind of mission statement for his future work in the form of a polemic in favour of the scientific mind. He became a full-time science fiction writer after leaving college, sustained in that vocation by the last heyday of magazine fiction and the growth of the paperback medium. Although he branched out occasionally into such peripheral genres as historical fiction and magical fantasy, and also produced some speculative nonfiction, he was one of very few writers to have embraced science fiction writing as their sole career.

Anderson's choice of profession encouraged him to broaden his scientific education considerably, and he became very interested in the interfaces between various natural and social sciences, whose complex interactions provided many of his plot ideas. His interest in the psychology, sociology, and economics of the *Space Age future history that was becoming standardised within the genre generated such works as "Gypsy" (1949), which analyses the motivation required to facilitate that future history. Much of his early work was colourful space opera written for the minor pulp magazines—whose contrived romanticism continued to echo in his work long after the expiration of the pulps—but Anderson became a key member of John W. *Campbell's stable, and one of the central figures of the *hard science fiction tradition, consciously carrying forward precedents set by Robert A. *Heinlein.

Anderson's best work in the hard science fiction vein used the framework of Space Age mythology to deploy a large number of hypothetical planets, including many featuring extreme environments as well as ingeniously varied Earth-clones, all of which were extrapolated with careful rigor. His plots and characterisation retained a lyrical quality that often employed poignant poetic references, and he became a prolific author of sophisticated *contes philosophiques*. "The Helping Hand" (1950) is a careful anthropological thought-experiment comparing the fates of two conquered cultures, one of which accepts aid from its conquerors while the other refuses it. His first novel, *Vault of the Ages* (1952), was for juveniles, written before the paperback boom got under way, and his second was a heroic fantasy, but his first science fiction novel for adults, *Brain Wave* (1954), was a highly ambitious attempt to describe a sudden planet-wide increase in intelligence and the consequent reformation of human society and the ecosphere.

The carefully sophisticated space opera *The Long Way Home* (1955; aka *No World of Their Own*) was more typical of the work Anderson began to produce in profusion, its action-adventure plot deftly leavened with political and psychological issues. The version of future history he constructed to serve as a backcloth to much of this work reconfigured the Asimovian "galactic empire" as a "Polesotechnic League", which subsequently became a limited phase of a far-reaching account of the expansion and contraction of "Technic Civilisation". He usually formulated his plots as adventure stories with a strong mystery component.

A notable early series set against the backcloth of the Polesotechnic League, launched by "Margin of Profit" (1956), featured the Falstaffian Nicholas van Rijn, "trader to the stars". Van Rijn starred in *The Man Who Counts* (1958; abr. as *War of the Wing-Men*), but he was replaced in the stories collected in *The Trouble Twisters* (1966) by his more conscientious protégé David Falkayn. Other stories featuring the economically expansive phase of his future history included *Satan's World* (1967), *The People of the Wind* (1973), and *Mirkheim* (1977); *The Earth Book of Stormgate* (1978) is an omnibus of earlier items. Alongside the Polesotechnic League stories Anderson produced a more romantically inclined series set in the later era of the Terran Empire, many of them featuring Dominic Flandry, a swashbuckling trouble-shooter who first appeared in "A Message in Secret" (1959; book, 1961, as *Mayday Orbit*); notable later items in the series include *Earthman, Go Home!* (1960), *The Rebel Worlds* (1969), *The Day of Their Return* (1973), *A Knight of Ghosts and Shadows* (1974), and *A Stone in Heaven* (1979).

Another long-term project that Anderson developed from the 1950s onwards was an *alternative history series launched with "Time Patrol" (1955). Early items were collected in *Guardians of Time* (1960) before being recombined with further examples in the omnibuses *Annals of the Time Patrol* (1984) and *Time Patrol* (1991). He also developed an extensive series of exercises in sophisticated world building, in which early local examples—the Venus-set "The Big Rain" (1954) and "Sister Planet" (1959), the Jupiter-set "Call Me Joe" (1957), and a series featuring the colonisation of the *asteroids, collected in *Tales of the Flying Mountains* (1970)—gradually gave way to such far-flung endeavours as "The Longest Voyage" (1960), set on the satellite of a gas giant, and "Hunter's Moon" (1983), set in a binary star system.

Anderson continued to add sophistication to his various raw materials throughout his career, building on the research he did for his nonfiction book *Is There Life on Other Worlds?* (1963) in numerous *exobiological fantasies, including "A Twelvemonth and a Day" (1960; aka *Let the Spacemen Beware* and *The Night Face*), *Fire Time* (1974), and *The Winter of the World* (1975). His second exercise in the popularisation of science, *Thermonuclear Warfare* (1963), investigated grimmer prospects, but *The Infinite Voyage: Man's Future in Space* (1969) dealt with material much dearer to his heart. His careful extrapolation of ideas drawn from theoretical physics is shown to good effect in *The Enemy Stars* (1959; exp. 1987), which employs a *matter transmitter as a means of interstellar travel in order to expose its characters to various extremes of stress when their ship breaks down while investigating a dead star, and *Shield* (1963), which explores the ramifications of force-field armour. *World Without Stars* (1966) describes another struggle for survival in a cleverly designed hostile environment. A version of the theory of continuous creation is ingeniously employed as logic for "jumpgates" in "Door to Anywhere" (1966). *Tau Zero* (1967; exp. 1970), which develops the notion of relativistic time-dilation to an extreme, became a paradigm example of the hard science fiction of its era.

The final version of Anderson's Space Age was mapped out in a series comprising *Harvest of Stars* (1993), *The Stars Are Also Fire* (1994), *Harvest the Fire* (1995), and *The Fleet of Stars* (1997), whose account of the slow development of an interstellar society is more carefully measured, while refusing to concede that the consequent problems reduce the myth of galactic colonisation to the status of an idle fantasy. The *SETI romance *Starfarers* (1998), which describes the splinter culture developed by time-dilated interstellar travelers, places a stronger emphasis on the difficulties likely to afflict the development of a galactic culture. *The Boat of a Million Years* (1989) attempts to establish a firm historical context for a human future of unlimited expansion, using the facilitating device of a group of immortals who witness the progress of human society from the dawn of civilisation to the advent of interstellar exploration. The elegiac far-futuristic fantasy *Genesis* (2000) extended this context to its further limit, while *For Love and Glory* (2003), in which human and alien archaeologists collaborate in solving the mystery of an alien artefact, similarly embraces a long view of evolutionary history.

Anderson's career was largely shaped by its timing; he began writing when the magazine market was in its heyday, although John Campbell's influence as a guiding star was on the wane. Significantly, Anderson allied himself firmly with the Campbellian cause even as it went into a long decline; equally significantly, he did not allow himself to be distracted by the 1950s psiboom, although one of his numerous award-winning stories, "No Truce with Kings" (1963), was a story of burgeoning parapsychological superhumanity. He became a prolific novelist when the paperback boom of the 1970s was in full swing, but never allowed the formularisation of his work to become repetitive, and he continually expanded the range of his endeavors with ventures into fantasy and historical fiction. When that phase in science fiction's evolution went into decline, just as the previous one had, he adapted his work yet again, always keeping pace with contemporary developments in science as well as the demands of the marketplace, and forging links between them no matter how difficult it became to do so.

ANDROID

A term originated in *alchemical literature—rendered "androides" in its first traceable appearance in English in 1727—with reference to rumoured attempts to create "homunculi" by such alleged practitioners as Albertus Magnus and *Paracelsus. The notion is sometimes traced back by historians to Jewish legends of golems—a link explicitly acknowledged in stories of roughly hewn powerful androids with low intelligence, such as those featured in David Brin's *Kiln People* (2002).

"Androides" resurfaced in French, with a significance closer to its modern meaning, in Villiers de l'Isle Adam's *L'Ève future* (1886; trans. as *Tomorrow's Eve*), but the term did not become commonplace until its English equivalent was standardised. In the context of modern science fiction, the term is usually employed in such a way as to differentiate it from *robot, reserving it for artificial humanoids made from synthetic flesh rather than inorganic components. The usage is not consistent, however; Karel Čapek's "robots" in *R.U.R.* (1920; trans. 1923) are made of synthetic flesh, as are those in Chan Davis' "Letter to Ellen" (1947), while Philip K. *Dick's work habitually uses "android" with reference to mechanical robots designed to simulate human appearance. The term was initially introduced into pulp science fiction by Jack Williamson in *The Cometeers* (1936), but the conventional distinction between robots and androids was popularised by Edmond Hamilton's tales of the team of superheroes led by Captain Future, who had his own pulp magazine from 1940 to 1944; the captain's mechanical and fleshy sidekicks required different labels, so they became Grag the robot and Otho the android, thus pioneering the terms' use as contrasted rather than alternative terms.

Čapek imagined his artificial men being "grown" in vats, mass produced for use as slave labour; in *R.U.R.* they provide a satirical representation of the dehumanisation of the working classes. Similar processes of manufacture are retained in many subsequent deployments of the motif, its horrific aspects being exploited in such works as Edgar Rice Burroughs' *Synthetic Men of Mars* (1940). Čapek's assertion that the androids' acquisition of "souls" would lead to demands for emancipation, whose refusal has the potential to precipitate social conflict, is also reflected in the imagery of many subsequent stories, including Walter M. Miller's "The Soul-Empty Ones" (1951). Broader accounts of the android existential condition include John Rackham's "Goodbye, Doctor Gabriel" (1961) and "The Dawson Diaries" (1962) and Stephen Fine's satirical transfiguration of Daniel Defoe's Moll Flanders, *Molly Dear: The Autobiography of an Android, or How I Came to My Senses, Was Repaired, Escaped My Master, and Was Educated in the Ways of the World* (1988). The notion that android bodies might provide a means of preserving personalities, even after death, is featured in such works as Raymond Z. Gallun's *People Minus X* (1957) and Keith Laumer's "The Body Builders" (1966). The idea that duplicate personalities housed in androids might be useful in everyday life is featured in Alan E. Nourse's "Prime Difference" (1957).

Notable accounts of android demands for civil rights are offered in Clifford Simak's *Time and Again* (1951), William Tenn's "Down Among the Dead Men" (1954), Edmund Cooper's *Deadly Image* (1958; aka *The Uncertain Midnight*), Robert Silverberg's *Tower of Glass* (1970), and Robert L. Hoskins' *Tomorrow's Son* (1977). The successful integration of androids into human society in the wake of a political compromise is described in C. J. Cherryh's *Cyteen* (1988), but android independence is only finally achieved when humankind is devastated by plagues in Charles L. Grant's *The Shadow of Alpha* (1976) and its sequels. The Asimovian assumption that designers of artificial humans would build a submissive morality into them is far less prominent in accounts of androids than accounts of robots—James E. Gunn's "Little Orphan Android" (1955) is a notable exception—but the notion that human privileges might be protected by making creatures of artificial flesh short lived is more common; the "energumens" in Elizabeth Hand's *Icarus Descending* (1993) are one such species.

Although androids are sometimes technologically equipped with superhuman abilities, as in Clifford D. Simak's *The Werewolf Principle* (1967), organic androids usually serve as closer simulations of human nature than inorganic robots. The motif thus lends itself even more readily to fabular enquiries into the question of what the word "human" might and ought to mean. Although *contes philosophiques* featuring androids are closely akin to those featuring robots, they tend to exaggerate the potential for substitution. Notable examples of stories in which human and android identities are confused include J. T. McIntosh's "Made in USA" (1953), Alfred Bester's "Fondly Fahrenheit" (1954), Keith Roberts' "Synth" (1966), Richard Bowker's *Replica* (1987), and Catherine Asaro's *The Phoenix Code* (2000).

The fleshy elements of Philip K. Dick's "androids" are only skin deep; his many stories featuring such individuals have more in common with orthodox android fabulations than the vast majority of robot stories, in which the mechanical nature of the robots is obvious. The most notable Dick stories of this kind include *Do Androids Dream of Electric Sheep?* (1968), "The Electric Ant" (1969), and *We Can Build You* (1972); the central motif is further discussed in his essays "The Android and the Human" (1972) and "Man, Android and Machine" (1976). Dick argued that many humans are, in fact, in a morally anaesthetised "androidal" state—especially those exhibiting *psychopathological symptoms of schizophrenia—complementing this generalisation with images of machines, both humanoid and non humanoid in form, that have developed the sympathies that entitle them to be considered human.

As with other not-quite-human characters, androids are useful as supposedly objective observers of human foibles. The best-known so-called android, Data in the TV show *Star Trek: The Next Generation*, often functions in this way, as does the protagonist of Charles Platt's *Less Than Human* (1986). The utility of androids as labourers tends to suffer by comparison with robots, on the grounds that creatures made of metal seem potentially stronger, but one arena in which androids obviously have the upper hand is the

sex industry; androids designed to provide intimate personal services are featured in Thomas N. Scortia's "The Icebox Blonde" (1959), Gordon Eklund's "Lovemaker" (1973), Ian Watson's *Orgasmachine* (1976 in French), and Robert Reed's *The Hormone Jungle* (1988). Human/android love affairs routinely go wrong, usually because of human rather than android failings; examples include Kate Wilhelm's "Andover and the Android" (1963).

ANTHROPOLOGY

A term derived from the Greek to describe a specific science of humankind; its early usage was confused because there were several different views in the nineteenth century of how the contents of that science ought to be defined. In the twentieth century the term was most commonly used as a tacit abbreviation of the phrase "cultural anthropology", describing the comparative study of tribal societies. That discipline had been more usually labeled *ethnology in the nineteenth century, and the present article focuses more narrowly on what twentieth-century parlance describes as "physical anthropology": the study of the various biological species belonging to the genus *Homo*. All but one of those species are now extinct, the remainder being known by courtesy of discoveries in *palaeontology, but those alleged to be ancestral to *Homo sapiens* are of intense interest in the context of the theory of *evolution and its opposition by the doctrine of *creationism.

One obvious foundation-stone of a general science of anthropology—the taxonomic classification of human types—raised questions that were first addressed in the eighteenth century. Carolus Linnaeus attempted to define the genus *Homo* in the tenth edition of *System of Nature* (1758), which prompted the Comte du Buffon to take up the topic in the fourteenth volume of his *Natural History* (1766). Linnaeus categorised humankind into four species: *Homo europaeus albus, H. americanus rubescens, H. asiaticus fuscus,* and *H. africranus niger*. The problem of defining and enumerating human types was inevitably confused with that of distinguishing human beings from apes. Observations of the physical similarities between humans and apes had been recorded in Classical times by Aristotle and Galen, but more detailed comparisons had been made in the late seventeenth century by Edward Tyson, who incorporated a record of his dissection of a chimpanzee in *Ourang-Outang; or, The Anatomy of a Pygmy Compared with That of a Monkey, an Ape, and a Man* (1727).

Eighteenth-century descriptions of the great apes were still rather sketchy, the "ourang-outang" remaining mysterious and the gorilla virtually unknown. But a new description of the former published in Petrus Camper's "Account of the Organs of Speech in the Orang Outang" (1779) greatly interested James Burnet, Lord Monboddo, who was in the process of producing an account "Of the Origin and Progress of Language" (1779–1799); Monboddo's reflections on the question of whether or not the "orang outang" should be classified as human were satirically reflected by Thomas Love Peacock in *Melincourt; or, Sir Orang Haut-Ton* (1817). Orang-utans and other great apes were, however, rudely expelled from the register of human types by early anthropologists—a move obliquely echoed by Edgar Allan Poe's account of the perpetrator of "The Murders in the Rue Morgue" (1841).

Discussion of human taxonomy was isolated as a topic of specific concern in such works as J. F. Blumenbach's *De Generis Humani Varietate Nativa* (1775) and J. C. Prichard's *Researches into the Physical History of Man* (1813). Both writers preferred "race" rather than "species" as a basic category; although they assumed natural species to be products of separate creation rather than evolution, they also granted the strong probability that all the human races had a common ancestry. Prichard suggested that Adam must have been black, but Blumenbach's judgment that the human "stem race" must have been white, originating in the Caucasus Mountains, was far more popular. In this view, the Caucasian had given rise to the Mongolian, Ethiopian, American, and Malayan races by a process of "degeneration"—an idea elaborately developed and extrapolated in such works as Count Gobineau's *Essai sue l'inégalité des races humaines* (1853–1955), and echoed in the same author's numerous works of fiction. Early calculations of the number of human types varied very widely; Jean-François Virey made do with two (black and white), while Ernst Haeckel distinguished thirty-four. Louis-Antoine Desmoulins' *Histoire naturelle des races humaines* (1826) made race a subcategory of species, but then went on to distinguish sixteen human species.

The racial theories favoured by different nineteenth-century schools of anthropology were inevitably vulnerable to ideological bias. The American school founded by Josiah C. Nott, stubbornly defensive of the institution of slavery and fearful of the possible consequences of miscegenation, avidly sought scientific justification of its sociopolitical convictions in Nott and George R. Gliddon's *Types of Mankind* (1854). In Britain, Robert Knox's *The Races of Men* (1850)—whose publication helped redeem the reputation its author had lost in 1828 by virtue of his association with the notorious body-snatchers

William Burke and William Hare—argued that the human races were embroiled in an enduring war for supremacy, which the two imperially inclined European races (Saxons and Celts) were destined to win. Knox's ideas were enthusiastically taken up by James Hunt, who founded the British Anthropological Society in 1863, and were frequently reproduced in adventure fiction set in the far-flung outposts of the Empire. Race theory also extended into futuristic fantasies such as William Delisle Hay's *Three Hundred Years Hence* (1880) and Louis Tracy's *The Final War* (1896).

Ernst Haeckel's *Anthropogénie* (1874; trans. as *The Evolution of Man*) attempted to add human embryology to the science, extrapolating a "biogenetic law" proposed by von Baer into the contention that humankind's evolutionary ancestry is biologically recapitulated in the phases of embryonic development. A similar principle lay behind the assumption that the phases of a single linear pattern of social evolution could be traced in examples provided by extant tribal societies that were more or less "advanced" culturally and technologically. Although both of these notions were abandoned or drastically weakened in twentieth-century thought, they exercised a tremendous influence over the early history of human science and its fictional reflections; the notion that ethnological data can be rearranged to provide an image of a fundamental pattern of cultural evolution is largely responsible for the confusion of cultural and physical anthropology.

Accounts connecting cultural and physical evolution encouraged the development of a literary subgenre of speculative prehistoric fantasy—pioneered in such works as Cornelius Mathews' *Behemoth: A Legend of the Mound-Builders* (1839)—even before the sensational discovery of the remains of "Neanderthal man" in a valley near Düsseldorf in 1857, after which the subgenre became increasingly popular. Inevitably, the early characterisation of Neanderthalers in science and fiction alike stressed the species' supposed brutality and savagery, in a context provided by such works as Charles Lyell's *Geological Evidences of the Antiquity of Man* (1863), Thomas Henry Huxley's *Man's Place in Nature* (1863), and Sir John Lubbock's *Prehistoric Times* (1865) and *The Origin of Civilization and the Primitive Condition of Man* (1870). Haeckel's contributions to the storm of speculation included the postulation that a speechless proto-human species must have inhabited a lost continent drowned beneath the Indian Ocean—a notion that gave birth to the concept of the "missing link" and encouraged the proliferation of *geographical fantasies attempting to explain the global distribution of human types. Haeckel called his hypothetical missing link *Pithecanthropus*, a label borrowed in 1891 by Eugène Dubois, who identified a skull found in Java as *Pithecanthropus erectus*.

The accommodation of Neanderthal man within anthropological theory was greatly assisted by the input of Charles *Darwin's theory of evolution, which was published shortly after the discovery. It was partly the influence of prevailing anthropological wisdom that prevented the arguments relating to co-operation and nurture contained in Darwin's *The Descent of Man* (1871) and *The Expression of Emotion in Man and Animals* (1872) from making more impact, and prehistoric fantasy found far more scope for melodrama by integrating fierce struggles for existence into its various accounts of the evolution of savagery. Literary arguments usually related the increasing supremacy of the human species over rival primates to technological advancement, particularly the mastery of fire and the development of new weapons. These notions dominated prehistoric fiction produced before and after the turn of the century, whose most prolific exponent was J. H. Rosny aîné, author of *Vamireh* (1892), *Eyrimah* (1893), *La guerre du feu* (1909; trans. as *Quest for Fire*), and many others.

Rosny's precedents gave rise to a French tradition whose later highlights included Claude Anet's *La fin d'un monde* (1922; trans. as *The End of a World*) and Max Begouën's *Les bisons d'Argile* (1925; trans. as *Bison of Clay*). English equivalents, including H. G. Wells' "A Story of the Stone Age" (1897) and "The Grisly Folk" (1921), gave even heavier emphasis to the notion of Darwinian competition and the crucial role of technological supremacy in such a context. American dramatisations were more controversial than European ones by virtue of the stridency of the United States' religious culture; Austin Bierbower's *From Monkey to Man* (1894) accommodated religious ideas by representing early human evolution as a metaphorical expulsion from Eden, and similar metaphors hover in the background of Stanley Waterloo's *The Story of Ab* (1897), Gouverneur Morris' *The Pagan's Progress* (1904), and Jack London's *Before Adam* (1906), although they were blithely purged from Edgar Rice Burroughs' *The Eternal Lover* (1914; aka *The Eternal Savage*) and *The Cave Girl* (1913–1917) and Richard Tooker's *The Day of the Brown Horde* (1929). By contrast, the Soviet anthropologist V. G. Bogoraz railed against religious superstition in *The Sons of the Mammoth* (trans. 1929). Attempts to map the whole course of human *progress from prehistoric to modern times are routinely formulated as extensive meditations on issues of this sort.

The preoccupation of prehistoric fantasy with a supposed threshold whose crossing wrought a crucial category distinction between beast and man resulted in the production of a great deal of fiction featuring various kinds of transitional "ape-men". Even pre-Darwinian works featuring intelligent apes, such as Léon Gozlan's satirical *Les émotions du Polydore Marasquin* (1856; trans. as *A Man Among the Monkeys* and *Monkey Island*), touch on this question, but the question became far more discomfiting in such earnest post-Darwinian works as F. C. Constable's *The Curse of Intellect* (1895) and Jules Verne's *Le village aérien* (1901; trans. as *The Village in the Tree-tops*) and such broad satires as Andrew Lang's "The Romance of the First Radical" (1886) and Henry Curwen's *Zit and Xoe* (1887). Rousseauesque ideas of noble savagery ultimately achieved a significant popular breakthrough in this arena in the establishment of Edgar Rice Burroughs' Tarzan as a significant modern hero myth.

When changes of scientific perspective deemphasised the link between physical and cultural anthropology, prehistoric fantasy began to offer explicit challenges to the idea of a single path of progress leading triumphantly from savage primitivism to civilised sophistication. Norman Springer's *The Dark River* (1928) adopts a more generous view of its hypothetical Neanderthal survivals. S. Fowler Wright's loosely knit trilogy, which began with *Dream; or the Simian Maid* (1929), is unusually prolific in its invention of proto-human species, and unusually fervent in its Rousseauesque insistence on the fact that modern Western man is merely one element in a vast spectrum, nearer to the worst than the best. J. Leslie Mitchell's *Three Go Back* (1932) compares Cro-Magnon culture favourably with both its Neanderthal rivals and its modern descendants; the same author's "The Woman of Leadenhall Street" (1936, by-lined Lewis Grassic Gibbon) brought a new lyricism to the subgenre, recapitulated in William Golding's *The Inheritors* (1955), which glorified the Neanderthalers at the expense of modern humankind's direct ancestors. Similar sentiments were echoed in many other nostalgia-steeped accounts of Neanderthal relics, including Lester del Rey's "When Day Is Done" (1939), Isaac Asimov's "Lastborn" (1958; aka "The Ugly Little Boy"), Philip José Farmer's "The Alley Man" (1959), Clive King's *Stig of the Dump* (1963), Robert Nathan's *The Mallott Diaries* (1965), Stephen Popkes' "A Capella Blues" (1982), and Terry Bisson's "Scout's Honour" (2003).

The twentieth century saw a considerable elaboration of physical anthropology once palaeontologists began extensive investigations in Africa where early proto-human evolution seemed to have taken place. In 1924 Raymond Dart discovered a skull in Tanzania that he attributed to the genus *Australopithecus*; Robert Broom found further examples in the late 1930s. Louis Leakey began a long series of expeditions in Kenya in 1926, but it was not until the 1950s that his exploration of Olduvai Gorge with his wife Mary began to bear fruit; the Leakeys made a series of significant discoveries during the next two decades, revealing more Australopithecine species as well as contemporary fossils attributable to the genus *Homo*, which the Leakeys named *Homo habilis*. In the meantime, the discovery in Asia of other remains of Dubois' "Java man" resulted in the reclassification of that species as *Homo erectus*, hypothesising that the species was the descendant of *H. habilis* and the ancestor of *H. sapiens*. The Leakeys' discoveries were popularised in the United States by Robert Ardrey's journalistic *African Genesis* (1961), which caused considerable controversy in a nation where the creationist crusade was still being fought.

These discoveries encouraged the production of anthropological fantasies dramatising and elaborating the implications of new information. The subgenre remained esoteric until 1980, when such exemplary parables as Cleve Cartmill's "Link" (1942), Theodore L. Thomas's "The Doctor" (1967), and Bernard Deitchman's "Cousins" (1978) began to appear alongside such didactic fantasies as Chad Oliver's *Mists of Dawn* (1952) and such satires as Robert Nathan's "Digging the Weans" (1956) and Roy Lewis's *What We Did to Father* (1960; aka *The Evolution Man*). The unexpected breakthrough to best-sellerdom accomplished by Jean Auel's *The Clan of the Cave Bear* (1980)—which deftly combined a realistic aspect based on modern scientific understanding with a fervent literary romanticism—transformed the situation, unleashing a flood whose most notable examples included Tom Case's *Cook* (1981), Michael Bishop's *No Enemy But Time* (1982) and *Ancient of Days* (1985), Douglas Orgill and John Gribbin's *Brother Esau* (1982) and Gribbin's *Father to the Man* (1989), Roger McBride Allen's *Orphan of Creation* (1988), Harry Turtledove's *A Different Flesh* (1988), Peter Dickinson's *A Bone from a Dry Sea* (1992) and *The Kin* (1998; also in 4 vols. as *Suth, Noll, Po,* and *Mana*), Mike Resnick's "Seven Views of Olduvai Gorge" (1993), Robert Reed's "The Prophet Ugly" (2000), and Robert J. Sawyer's *Hominids* (2002), *Humans* (2003), and *Hybrids* (2003).

Speculative fiction extrapolating the perspectives of physical anthropology found some scope for expansion into future narrative space, but for much of the twentieth century images of future physical anthropology were dominated by the degenerative image of "The Man of the Year Million" (1893) produced by H. G. Wells. This image, based on the assumption that heads were destined to grow larger as *Homo sapiens*' descendant species made further intellectual progress, while limbs would atrophy as their work was taken over by machinery, became a cliché, replicated with variations in such works as J. D. Beresford's *The Hampdenshire Wonder* (1911) and taken to further extremes by pulp science fiction stories such as Donald Wandrei's "The Red Brain" (1927) and Harry Bates' "Alas, All Thinking!" (1935). A more elaborate account of future human evolution was set out by Olaf Stapledon in *Last and First Men* (1930), but the most significant fictional rival to the Wellsian notion of anthropological destiny was the kind of *superman featured in stories in which mental evolution rendered physical evolution redundant.

The notion that the future physical evolution of humankind would be controlled by *biotechnological engineering rather than natural selection was pioneered in J. B. S. Haldane's *Daedalus* (1923), but the consequences of that hypothesis were not extensively explored—save for rare exceptions such as James Blish's *The Seedling Stars* (1957)—until the last decades of the twentieth century, when *posthuman imagery began to make rapid progress. A more immediate effect of the elaboration of genetics and the emergent possibilities of *genetic engineering was to produce newly sophisticated stories exploring the interface between humans and apes, especially chimpanzees. These included accounts of hybrid half-humans, such as Maureen Duffy's *Gor Saga* (1981), as well as subtler accounts of awkward marginality such as Judith Moffett's "Surviving" (1986), Pat Murphy's "Rachel in Love" (1987), Peter Dickinson's *Eva* (1988), and Charles Sheffield's "Humanity Test" (1989).

Although the possibility that there might be extant species intermediate between humans and apes yet to be discovered had lost its plausibility by the time Vercors' used it in a fabular spirit in *Les animaux dénaturés* (1953; trans. as *You Shall Know Them* and *Borderline*), the notion that there might be extinct human species as-yet-undisclosed by palaeontological research seemed far more probable. The notorious "Piltdown man" hoax of 1912 encouraged a certain wariness, but such stories as A. M. Phillips' "A Chapter from the Beginning" (1940) explored the idea before its plausibility was spectacularly enhanced by the discovery of the remains of an alleged dwarf variant of *Homo erectus*, *Homo floresiensis*, on an Indonesian island in 2003. The most extensive fictionalisation of anthropological data is Stephen Baxter's *Evolution* (2003), which presents a comprehensive history of human evolution from its earliest beginnings.

ARCHAEOLOGY

The study of ancient cultural artefacts. The scientific discipline grew out of the amateur activities of "antiquarians" who collected such material on a haphazard basis. Its reliance on excavation associated it very closely with the development of *palaeontology, although archaeological attention is reserved to more recent and more superficial strata. Physical *anthropology draws a portion of its data from the interface of palaeontological and archaeological findings, but archaeology is entirely concerned with *Homo sapiens*, and therefore plays a substantial role in underpinning the data of *history; inferences drawn from durable artefacts provide a valuable complement to documentary evidence.

Early academic institutions assisting the development of scientific archaeology, such as the French *Société Impériale d'Émulation de la Somme*, founded in 1797, had wide interests that overlapped fruitfully. Such studies as Casimir Picard's investigations of "Celtic" artefacts combined with Jacques Boucher de Perthes' investigations of chipped flints from earlier eras to make up a composite image. Nineteenth-century archaeologists had no choice but to classify periods of prehistory in terms of their dominant material artefacts, resulting in the characterisation of its eras as the Stone Age, the Bronze Age, and the Iron Age—a classification first clearly formulated by C. J. Thomsen in 1836, and further subdivided by his successor as curator of the Danish National Museum, J. J. A. Worsaae. The classification was controversial at first but was orthodox by the end of the nineteenth century. One corollary of its acceptance and utility was the powerful endorsement it lent to the notion that the story of recent human evolution was one of gradual, but inexorable technological *progress in the use of inorganic materials.

The impact of archaeology on literary work was powerful because of the market dominance of the historical novel for the greater part of the nineteenth century. Archaeological evidence was a vital resource for historical novelists ambitious to extend the scope of their work into eras for which documentation was sparse. The discovery of the town of Pompeii, buried by volcanic ash following the eruption of Vesuvius in 79 A.D., attracted such popular interest that Edward Bulwer-Lytton's best-selling account of *The Last Days of Pompeii* (1834) and Théophile Gautier's "Arria Marcella; souvenir de Pompeii" (1852) appeared before scholarly investigation of the site began in earnest in the late 1850s. Ancient literature played a significant role in guiding the interest of archaeologists, with many investigations in the Holy Land being carried out in pursuit of biblical legends.

Heinrich Schliemann began excavating at Hisarlik in 1871 in the hope of finding the ruins of Homer's Troy; his claims of success were premature, but he had been guided to the right spot.

The archaeological arena that caught the nineteenth-century imagination most powerfully of all was Egypt, which had by far the biggest and best artefacts on offer, many of which had been buried in easily clearable sand. Percy Shelley's "Ozymandias" (1818) is a graphic reflection of a central lesson of the science. Gautier's *Le Roman de la momie* (1858; trans. as *The Romance of a Mummy*) helped Gustave Flaubert's Carthaginian romance *Salammbô* (1863; trans. 1886) to secure the mystique of archaeological romance within French Romantic literature. Georg Ebers, holder of the chair of Egyptology at Leipzig University, became a highly influential writer of archaeologically inspired novels, including *Eine ägyptische Königstocheter* (1862; trans. as *An Egyptian Princess*), *Serapis* (1885), and *Die Nilbraut* (1887; trans. as *The Bride of the Nile*). Ebers also wrote archaeologically informed biblical novels, including *Josua* (1867); his German successors included Ernst Eckstein, who wrote several fictional accounts of ancient Rome but made more use of archaeological data in *Aphrodite* (1886), set in Greece in the sixth century B.C. English fiction of a similar stripe included works by the noted antiquarian Sabine Baring-Gould, most notably *Perpetua* (1897).

The most eccentric literary spinoff of Egyptian archaeology was a rich subgenre of stories featuring reanimated mummies, pioneered by Jane Webb's *The Mummy! A Tale of the Twenty-Second Century* (1827). The *occult revival prompted a flood of such stories, including Edgar Lee's *Pharaoh's Daughter* (1889), Theo Douglas's *Iras: A Mystery* (1896), Clive Holland's *An Egyptian Coquette* (1898), Guy Boothby's *Pharos the Egyptian* (1899), and Bram Stoker's *The Jewel of Seven Stars* (1907). The greatest archaeological sensation of the early twentieth century, Howard Carter's discovery of Tutankhamen's tomb in 1922, added further stimulation to the Egyptian reconstructions that reached their literary zenith in Mika Waltari's *Sinuhe, egyptiläinen* (1945; trans. as *Sinuhé the Egyptian*). The most sustained and successful twentieth-century series of archaeologically inspired historical fantasies was the Ramses sequence by Christian Jacq, which launched with *Le fils de Lumière* (1995; trans. as *The Son of Light*). Other archaeological arenas of particular interest included the island of Crete, where important relics of Minoan civilisation were discovered at Knossos by Arthur Evans in 1900–1904; the substance of his discoveries is echoed in such literary works as Erick Berry's *Winged Girl of Knossos* (1933).

The archaeology of the New World—pioneered by Thomas Jefferson and Caleb Atwater at the end of the eighteenth century—was quite distinct from the archaeology of the Old World, dealing with a cultural tradition that had been largely obliterated by conquistadores and colonists, and whose last fugitive remnants were still in the process of annihilation in the nineteenth century. While the archaeology of Europe and the Near East was informed by Classical literature and scripture, the archaeology of the Americas was initially framed by mythical accounts of the origins of Native Americans that often linked them to the "lost tribes" of Israel or to Plato's Atlantis—myths that formed the context of such adventures of the imagination as Joseph Smith's *Book of Mormon* (1830), but found fewer echoes in more conventional works of literature. E. G. Squier and E. H. Davis' *Ancient Monuments of the Mississippi Valley* (1848) launched a long fascination with ancient "moundbuilders", but it raised few literary echoes in the nineteenth century.

Archaeology became increasingly distinct from palaeontology in the twentieth century, although it benefited from the same refinements in techniques of excavation, and from the development of new dating methods. Archaeology made a significant leap forward with the development of radiocarbon dating by Willard F. Libby in 1949, which added a useful supplement to Andrew E. Douglass' tree-ring system of dendrochronological dating; such revelatory devices were rapidly incorporated into a burgeoning subgenre of archaeological mystery stories, in which fictitious excavation sites disclosed various examples of precious or supernatural exotica. Archaeologists have a certain ready-made utility as fictitious problem solvers, although they suffered from image problems even more acute than those experienced by other kinds of *scientists until Steven Spielberg wrought a spectacular makeover in the characterisation of Indiana Jones in *Raiders of the Lost Ark* (1981). Charles Sheffield's "The Serpent of Old Nile" (1989) responded with an ironic portrayal of an archaeologist who is "too loud".

The hospitability of archaeological mystery stories to supernatural intrusions echoes an affinity exemplified by the work of M. R. James' paradigmatic *Ghost Stories of an Antiquary* (1904), many of which extrapolate the principle of "Cursed Be He Who Moves My Bones". The subgenre also includes contemporary and prehistorical detective stories, including some by Agatha Christie, whose second husband was an archaeologist. Archaeological mysteries whose exotic elements are science fictional include Augusta Groner's *Mene Tekel* (1910; trans. as *The City of the Dead*), Roy Norton's "The Glyphs" and "The Secret City" (both 1919), P. Schuyler Miller's "The

Chrysalis" (1936), H. P. Lovecraft's *At the Mountains of Madness* (1936), Murray Leinster's "Dead City" (1946), Dean Ing's "Anasazi" (1980), Carter Scholz and Glenn Harcourt's *Palimpsests* (1984), and Howard Waldrop's "He-We-Await" (1987).

Science fiction writers exported the archaeological mystery subgenre to extraterrestrial settings in such works as John Beynon Harris' "The Moon Devils" (1934), H. Beam Piper's "Omnilingual" (1957), David McDaniel's *The Arsenal Out of Time* (1967), Marion Zimmer Bradley's *The Ruins of Isis* (1979), H. M. Hoover's *The Bell Tree* (1982), Chad Oliver's "Ghost Town" (1983), Connie Willis' "The Curse of Kings" (1985), L. Sprague de Camp and Catherine Crook de Camp's *The Stones of Nomuru* (1988), Jack McDevitt's *A Talent for War* (1989) and *The Engines of God* (1994), Alastair Reynolds' *Revelation Space* (2000), Poul Anderson's *For Love and Glory* (2003), and Severna Park's "The Three Unknowns" (2004). Other accounts of future archaeology include Wilson Tucker's *The Year of the Quiet Sun* (1970), Allen L. Wold's *Lair of the Cyclops* (1992), and such fabulations as Dean McLaughlin's "For Those Who Follow After" (1951) and Randall Garrett's "No Connections" (1958) in which lessons less obvious and more elaborate than that of Shelley's "Ozymandias" are learned.

Other science fiction variants of archaeological fantasy include offbeat timeslip fantasies such as Howard Waldrop's *Them Bones* (1984) and Peter Ackroyd's *First Light* (1989), and accounts of new technologies that facilitate the reconstruction of images of the past, such as Raymond Z. Gallun's "Dawn-World Echoes" (1937), Garry Kilworth's *Split Second* (1979), and Donald Franson's "One Time in Alexandria" (1980). R. A. Lafferty's "Rivers of Damascus" (1974) is a rare account of "para-archaeology". Cynical accounts of the science and its practitioners are offered in Robert Silverberg's "The Artefact Business" (1957) and Jack C. Haldeman II's "Those Thrilling Days of Yesteryear" (1977). An exceptionally dangerous archaeological discovery is featured in Paul J. McAuley's *Mind's Eye* (2005).

The idea that archaeological excavations might reveal evidence of *alien visitation soon expanded out of the realm of acknowledged fiction, spawning a subgenre of *scholarly fantasy pioneered by Erich von Däniken's *Chariots of the Gods* (1971). In 2000 a Belgian artist employing the pseudonym Michel de Spiegeleire satirised such fancies by assembling an exhibition of artefacts supposedly collected by the fictitious explorer Alexandre Humboldt-Fonteyne, which included a number of Martian mummies allegedly found in Arizona. The scope remains within the science for authentic discoveries, however, and the unorthodoxy of such works as Michael A. Cramo and Richard L. Thompson's *Forbidden Archaeology* (1993)—which argues that modern man first arrived in the Americas much earlier than is usually supposed—is not as obviously pseudoscientific as such alleged revelations of ancient mysteries as Graham Hancock and Robert Bauval's *The Message of the Sphinx* (1996).

ARISTOTLE (384–322 B.C.)

Greek philosopher. The son of the court physician to the king of Macedon, Aristotle was sent to *Plato's Academy in Athens as a student at the age of seventeen. He remained there as a teacher until Plato's death twenty years later. He served for three years as tutor to the young Alexander the Great, but returned to Athens after a twelve-year absence to found his own school, the Lyceum, leaving again when Alexander's death allowed anti-Macedonian feeling to break free of its former restraint.

Aristotle was considerably more interested in natural philosophy than Plato, but he was primarily an abstract thinker indisposed to empirical investigation. His pioneering treatise on *physics and his writings on *cosmology were more adventurous than accurate, although his work on *zoology laid useful foundations. Even his work on *logic was unhelpful to subsequent philosophers attempting to lay the mathematical groundwork of modern science, although his work on *rhetoric remains a definitive analysis. His pioneering work on *aesthetics has usually been regarded as a relatively unimportant sideline. His works succeeded in marking out a significant classification of different areas of philosophical concern, but the fundamental distinction drawn therein between physics and *metaphysics is rumoured to be due to the way his writings were organised by his followers rather than to his own boundary marking.

Aristotle's errors would not have cast such a long shadow had his work not been compounded into an "Aristotelian doctrine" by his followers, formulated in opposition to Platonic ideas that had been similarly converted into dogma. This opposition might have been a stimulus to fruitful empirical enquiry, but its most obvious product—the third-century neo-Platonism of Plotinus—was an attempted intellectual synthesis of incompatible ideas whose tortuous mysticism laid significant foundations for the syncretic *occult science of the Renaissance. In the meantime, a residue of Aristotelian dogma was incorporated into Christian doctrine, where it remained unchallenged for nearly a thousand years. This incorporation gave Aristotelian thought a decided advantage when Classical learning was reintroduced to Western Europe, but the most immediate result was a more complex and more intricate fusion of dogmas, completed by Thomas Aquinas' synthesis of Aristotelian and Christian thought in the mid-thirteenth-century *Summa Theologiae*.

One effect of this synthesis was to secure Aristotelian ideas a degree of influence over European literary production unmatched by any other author. The worlds that poets constructed within visionary works from the late thirteenth to the early sixteenth century were Aristotelian in terms of their physics and cosmology. When opposition to received orthodoxies eventually materialised in earnest, prompting a swelling tide of controversy in the sixteenth and seventeenth centuries, Aristotle was the chief nonscriptural authority drafted to lead the army of reaction into ideological battle against the forces of rebellion; he could only do so as a figurehead, but that did not affect his heroic status, nor the ignominy of his eventual defeat.

Aristotle did not intend his ideas to be taken as unchallengeable dogmas to be defended with blind fervour, and he would doubtless have thought it unfair and unreasonable that "Aristotelian" eventually became a byword in some circles for untenable falsehood. Three of his ideas, however, stand out as errors that became terrible idols by virtue of their incorporation into dogma, thus requiring to be cast down by the heroes of science. The first was the notion that the movements and alterations of substances are governed by the principle that each of the four Classical elements is continually seeking to resume its "natural place". The second was the notion that the Earth is situated at the centre of a nested series of crystal spheres constituting the heavens. The third was the notion that atomic theory has to be mistaken because there cannot possibly be any such thing as a void in which *atoms might move. The orthodoxy of these three mistaken opinions certainly hindered the development of modern science, although it is conceivable that the necessity of surpassing them accelerated its development once battle was joined, enthusing the opposition. By the same token, however, these ideas were guaranteed a role in literary imagery that endured far beyond their collapse as items of faith. Literature is by no means inhospitable to *impossibility, and famous impossibilities always retain a peculiar authority within the world of fiction.

The literary heritage of Aristotelian ideas is by no means limited to the *occult literature that earnestly and explicitly attempted to retain his geocentric notion of the solar system against the heliocentric model proposed by Copernicus and established as fact by Galileo and John Kepler; its more important influence was on literary images attempting to preserve a "poetic" rather than a "prosaic" notion of experience. The same is true of the physics of the four elements and the teleological interpretation of motion and transformation. They too became emblems of the poetic as well as the magical, helping to energise an alternative language of description and analysis whose entire *raison d'être* was—and is—that it transcends and counterbalances the pedantic mannerisms of accurate description.

Aristotle is not always seen as an enemy of science, against whom the heroes of the scientific narrative strove and over whom they triumphed. Edgar Allan Poe's *Eureka* (1848) derides "Aries Tottle" and "Hog" (Francis Bacon) with equal disdain, but Poe probably overestimated the resemblance between Aristotelian logic and the mathematics of his own day; his own attempts to envisage an aesthetically satisfactory cosmos probably had more in common with Aristotle's than he was prepared to concede, even though they produced a very different result. The historical Aristotle is treated with wry reverence in L. Sprague de Camp's "Aristotle and the Gun" (1958) and—peripherally—in *An Elephant for Aristotle* (1958). Aristotelian cosmology remains an object of considerable aesthetic fascination in such works as Richard Garfinkle's *Celestial Matters* (1996). Aristotle operates as an investigator in a series of stories by Margaret Doody begun with *Aristotle Detective* (1978), while a lost book by Aristotle is the plot lever in Umberto Eco's historical detective novel *Il nome della rosa* (1981; trans. as *The Name of the Rose*).

ART

A term whose original reference was to the exercise of skill, although it suffered a gradual division whose eventual result was that the work of "artists" was distinguished from that of "artisans", the former gaining considerably in relative social prestige. The separation of the concepts drew a distinction between edifying endeavour and utilitarian labour, whose extrapolation culminated in Théophile Gautier's doctrine of "l'art pour l'art" (art for art's sake), memorably summarised in the preface to *Mademoiselle de Maupin* (1836). The late Classical definition that classified the arts as activities patronised by nine inspirational muses accommodated history and astronomy as well as literary, musical, and visual arts, but the term was narrowed long before the specialisation of the word "artist" was completed by its opposition in the nineteenth century to "scientist". After that, the notion of art (often emphasised as Art) became even more restricted, sometimes being confined—as

in the present article—to the visual arts. General theoretical issues are considered under the rubric of *aesthetics; separate consideration is given to *music and *photography.

The visual arts originated in remote prehistory; the most spectacular surviving examples include Palaeolithic cave paintings found at such sites as Peche Merle, Lascaux, and Altamira. Neolithic art seems primitive by comparison, although the stylisation of visual depictions and small sculptures—including human figurines, of which the most famous is the Venus of Willendorf—helped pave the way for the development of *writing. Much academic speculation has surrounded the possible magical and religious significance of prehistoric artworks; such speculation is extensively recycled and embellished in *anthropologically- and *ethnologically informed prehistoric fantasy.

Painting, sculpture, and architecture reached new peaks of achievement in ancient Egypt and Greece; the tangible legacy of these achievements imposed an impression of dire inferiority on later generations, which added to the weight of authority ceded to ancient opinions that were less securely founded. Although dramatic improvements have been made in the technologies available to painters, sculptors, and architects since Classical times, the impression still lingers that modern artists are incapable of matching certain key triumphs of their distant predecessors.

The advancement of science and technology after the Renaissance had a highly significant impact on the progress of the visual arts in several respects. The refinement of *mathematics and *optics had a profound effect on modes of representation, most importantly in the discovery of the *geometry of perspective and the evolution of such conventions as impressionism and cubism. New technologies transformed the manufacture of paints and drawing instruments and the techniques of engraving and printing. In the meantime, certain kinds of artistic representations gave vital aid to scientific discourse, in the form of illustrative diagrams, graphs, maps, anatomical drawings, and so on. Further links between progress in science and the visual arts were forged because painters and sculptors, like litterateurs, are not simply concerned with making simulacra; they also take delight in representing the hypothetical, the fantastic, and the frankly *impossible. There are "fictions" in visual art as well as written texts, and the two kinds of fiction often influence and supplement one another.

The speculative dimension of the visual arts in Europe was closely allied with *theology in the Medieval era and the Renaissance, although the situation was complicated in the Near East—particularly in the Islamic world—by taboos on the making of "graven images". The scientific revolution of the seventeenth century was preceded by an earlier revolution in the visual arts, whose similarities are more than metaphorical. The determination of *Galileo, Isaac *Newton, and their peers to obtain a clearer picture of the world by means of optical instruments and accurate calculations was anticipated in the evolution of artistic perspective. That evolution marked a significant change from conceptual representation to optical representation: a determined attempt to reproduce on canvas what the eye actually sees rather than what the mind conceives.

The developments that allowed two-dimensional paintings to construct a convincing illusion of depth were gradual, beginning with works by Duccio di Buoninsegna and Giotto di Bondone painted in the early fourteenth century, including Duccio's "The Last Supper" and Giotto's frescoes in the Arena Chapel at Padua. Giotto's impressions of three dimensionality were localised—there is no single viewpoint from which the objects all seem to be occupying the same visual field—and it took a further century for the mathematical rules of perspective, first employed by such artists as Filippo Brunelleschi and Paolo di Dono, nicknamed Uccello, to be publicised in Leon Battista Alberti's *Della Pittura* (ca. 1435), Piero della Francesca's *De Prospettiva Pingendi* (ca. 1470), and *Leonardo da Vinci's *Trattato della Pittura* (ca. 1485). Piero and Leonardo both practised what they preached, with spectacular results, and their examples were followed by many others, including Raphael Santi and Jacopo Robusti, nicknamed Tintoretto.

The methods of these Italian masters eventually spread throughout Europe, with the aid of such works as Albrecht Dürer's *Underweysung der Messing mit dem Zyrkel und Rychtscheyd* (1528). The new visual realism cultivated by these artists, and such northern contemporaries as Jan van Eyck, benefited greatly from the development of new kinds of paints, both in terms of the range of available pigments and the suspension media in which the pigments were dissolved. Oil paints were as essential to compelling illusion as the geometrical principle of the vanishing point.

Artists began to play games with perspective, removing the viewpoint implied by a painting from the position at which the viewer was likely to look at it—Leonardo's *Last Supper* (1498) implies a viewpoint high in the air, above the head of any observer, while Hans Holbein's famous painting of *The Ambassadors* (1533) includes a dramatically distorted skull whose true shape can be recovered by looking at it from a very narrow angle to one side. *The Ambassadors* is one of the most scientifically sophisticated

paintings of its era, its background including a plethora of astronomical instruments—whose settings specify the date and time at which its depicted scene is set. John North's *The Ambassadors' Secret* (2002) argues that Holbein must have collaborated in the design of the picture with the astronomer Nicolaus Kratzer, with whom he had earlier produced a significant astronomical allegory painted on a ceiling at Greenwich Palace in 1527.

In the wake of perspective came the reproduction of a visual focal field, which required the backgrounds of painted scenes to be blurred, as they seem to be when the human eye focuses on an object in the foreground. This kind of visual realism was not, however, to the taste of all artists; the Pre-Raphaelite Brotherhood of nineteenth-century England set out deliberately to violate it, showing all the objects in a painting in sharp focus no matter what their "distance" was within the scene. Just as the more accurate rendition of human bodies in oils was complemented by the more extravagant rendering of *monsters by such painters as Hieronymus Bosch, so the exploitation of the geometry of perspective in the cause of more accurate representation was followed by the development of calculatedly deceptive perspectives—sophisticated optical illusions—by such artists as Giovanni Piranesi. Both of these trends continued into the twentieth century in the works of such artists as Caspar Walter Rauh and M. C. Escher.

Because geometrical construction and diagrammatic representation are vital to all kinds of applied science—especially *engineering and *cartography—many Renaissance artists used new techniques of artistic representation in architecture and military engineering. Many painters extended their studies in superficial anatomy to the internal skeletal and muscular organisation of human and animal bodies, developing techniques of anatomical drawing that cleverly hybridised the visual and the diagrammatic. The work of artists also became vital to the taxonomic sciences that set out to produce organised classifications of natural phenomena. *Botany and *zoology require accurate depiction of specimens, so the voyages of scientific discovery commissioned by such naturalists as Joseph Banks were equipped with artists as well as scientists; scientists who could draw were doubly valuable. Such encyclopaedic studies as John James Audubon's *The Birds of America* (4 vols., 1827–1838; exp. in 7 vols., 1840–1844) and *The Viviparous Quadrupeds of North America* (3 vols., 1845–1848, with John Bachman) were equally significant as scientific works and works of art. Audubon's representations were quasi-photographic, but those constructed by cataloguers of smaller organisms—especially those requiring the aid of *microscopes—made more conspicuous use of visual/diagrammatic compromises. When such work was extended into the field of *palaeontology, its speculative dimension became more significant. Georges Cuvier's method of imaginatively reconstructing whole prehistoric animals from fragments of bone required skillful artistic support; representations of *dinosaurs based on partial skeletons became a key factor in the cultivation of their extraordinary charisma.

Artists played a minor role as chroniclers of the scientific revolution, in such images as Joseph Wright's "A Philosopher Lecturing on the Orrery" (1766) and "Experiment on a Bird in the Air Pump" (1767) and Thomas Eakins' "The Gross Clinic" (1875), which depicts an early instance of surgery under anaesthesia. Speculative art was, however, almost entirely restricted to the illustration of works of speculative fiction, where it was content to play a subsidiary role, partly because such visual representations needed textual support to explain what they were endeavouring to do. The speculative artist who signed the drawings in *Un autre monde* (1844) Taxile Delord had also to supply a text, which he by-lined Isidore Grandville. Albert Robida similarly supplied his own texts in support of his visual description of *Le vingtième siècle* (1882), *La vie électrique* (1883), and *La guerre au vingtième siècle* (1883; exp. 1887; text trans. as "War in the Twentieth Century"). A similar imbalance is reflected in the roles attributed to scientists and artists in nineteenth-century literary images of the future; while new technologies abound, the aesthetic environment often manifests a stubborn dedication to Classical sculpture and Renaissance painting; Calvin Blanchard's *The Art of Real Pleasure* (1864) is a rare example of an ideal society generated by science and technology but politically supervised by a Grand Artist.

The advent of photography stripped the scientific artist of some of his prerogatives, but many of the functions it came to monopolise, as in *astronomy, were those that artists had never been able to perform. The continued necessity for the kinds of visual/diagrammatic hybridisation fundamental to representations in biological science meant that an ability to draw remained a great asset to many practicing scientists, and in the more mathematically sophisticated sciences the ability to design an eloquent graph remained invaluable. The rapid development of photographic techniques, optical instruments, and mechanical means of drawing in the twentieth century did, however, produce whole new ranges of artwork; the development of astronomical telescopes, the advancement of microscopy, and the advent of *computer art opened up new territories of sublime and beautiful imagery. The New York Museum of Modern Art held its first exhibition of "Machine Art" in 1934, and machinery became increasingly important thereafter as collaborators in artistic production.

The visual realism of photographs, whose perspective was built-in but whose focal fields tended to be conspicuously narrower than those constructed by the human mind from incoming sensory data, was one of the factors that encouraged the Pre-Raphaelites to embrace a kind of realism that flatly refused the narrowing of the focal field. Other conspicuous reactions and responses cultivated a variety of "impressionist" techniques that strove to reproduce something more faithful to the conceptual creativity of biological perception and human mental ingenuity. Symbolist, futurist, surrealist, and expressionist movements inverted the optical process, dramatically increasing the range and ambition of attempts to give visual form to mental constructs alien to visual experience.

Some such schools set out to use artistic synthesis to defy the limitations of perspective—a quest that soon became entangled with attempts to "visualise" such mathematical and speculative constructs as the *fourth dimension. The Cubist theorists Albert Gleizes and Jean Metzinger invoked non-Euclidean *geometry in *Du Cubisme* (1912)—a concern reflected in Georges Braque's *Still Life with Violin and Pitcher* (1910)—while the visual representation of movement was subject to extensive experimentation in such works as Marcel Duchamp's *Nude Descending a Staircase* (1912) and Giacomo Balla's *A Girl Runs Along a Balcony* (1912). Throughout the twentieth century the fictitious aspects of art became increasingly ambitious and abstract, placing representational art in a much broader and more various context, in parallel with scientific developments that placed visual experience in a much more elaborate and abstruse theoretical context.

The advent of computers, especially in alliance with colour printers, widened the range of potential graphic and diagrammatic constructions very considerably, opening up a significant new arena for exploration and choice. Computerised cutting and pasting, in association with magnification, reduction, and colour substitution, became significant resources for the creation of collages, and the Internet became a key location of virtual galleries where art of all kinds could be displayed. In 1986, Donna J. Cox advocated the building of "Renaissance teams" of scientists and artists who would collaborate in the investigation of various forms of representation for various kinds of data, in order to discover the most revealing and aesthetically pleasing. The most dramatic examples of such collaborations include the artificially coloured representations of astronomical images produced by space probes and the Hubble Space Telescope. The cultural separation between histories of art and science became gradually less distinct in this era, with attention being paid to connections and overlaps in such journals as *Leonardo*.

The development of photographic techniques appropriate to astronomy did not substitute for preexisting artwork, but it provided a foundation for the development of new work. A spinoff genre of "space art" that attempted to provide realistic depictions of the landscapes of other worlds originated in such illustrations as Angus MacDonall's lunar landscapes in J. A. Mitchell's *Drowsy* (1917) and became a key element of science fiction magazine illustration. A new standard of attempted realism was set by Charles Schneeman's image of Saturn as seen from Japetus, on the cover of the April 1939 issue of *Astounding*. Space art was established as a subgenre in its own right in the work of such artists as Chesley Bonestell, Ludek Pesek, David Hardy, and Andrei Sokolov. Bonestell's collaborations with Willy *Ley, *The Conquest of Space* (1949) and *Beyond the Solar System* (1964), were significant endeavors in the popularisation of *Space Age mythology. Space art was eventually supplemented by photographs taken by space probes, but the limitations of such probes left a wide margin for further interpretation and inspiration. The Soviet cosmonaut Alexei Leonov became the first space artist actually to have traveled in space.

The other major preoccupations of science fiction illustration were the depiction of futuristic scenarios—paying particular attention to cityscapes and means of *transportation—and the design of *aliens, especially monstrous ones. The scientific role played by artists in the early development of the taxonomic sciences was extrapolated in a conspicuously gaudy fashion. The lurid covers worn by the more extravagant pulp science fiction magazines were even more detrimental to the respectability of the genre than the quality of the prose they advertised, and their excesses prompted Martin Alger to call in 1939 for the establishment of a Society for the Prevention of Bug-Eyed Monsters on the Covers of Science Fiction Publications. The iconography established by science fiction cover art—which was taken over and carried forward by *comic books, the *cinema, and *TV—also solidified the imagery of the Space Age mythology in its endless repetition of representations of rocket ships, space suits, and space stations.

Speculative representations of potential future developments in the visual arts often envisage artists of a more-or-less traditional stripe working in currently unworkable materials—as in J. G. Ballard's "The Cloud Sculptors of Coral D" (1967) and Richard Paul Russo's *Subterranean Galley*

(1989)—or on currently impractical scales, but inevitably find it difficult to anticipate new modes of representation. Mary Rosenblum's *The Stone Garden* (1994) suggests that sculpted asteroids might generate novel aesthetic and emotional responses, but can only hint at their quality. The extremes suggested by Alexander Jablokov—whose "The Death Artist" (1980) involves the creative design of death experiences, while "At the Cross-Time Jaunters' Ball" (1987) features the artistic generation of whole *parallel worlds—loom large as ideas but offer little scope for vicarious participation.

Attempts to imagine alien art run into even more acute difficulties of aesthetic translation, although attempts are made in such stories as Gordon R. Dickson's "Black Charlie" (1954), Clifford D. Simak's "The Spaceman's Van Gogh" (1956), and Ian Watson's "The Moon and Michelangelo" (1987). Practical advances in artistic technology are very rarely envisaged in speculative fiction, although one notable exception is Brian C. Coad's "Johnnie Wong's Tantagraphs" (1990) in which artworks are created by anodising tantalum, thus creating thin films of oxide that reflect a range of metallic colours. Fiction that uses futuristic settings and devices as a means of coming more securely to grips with the art of the past includes numerous accounts of famous artists visited by time travellers or ingeniously resurrected. Vincent van Gogh is featured in William F. Temple's "A Niche in Time" (1964), Sever Gansovsky's "Vincent Van Gogh" (trans. 1989), and Barry N. Malzberg and Jack Dann's "The Starry Night" (2005), while the products of Michael Swanwick's fascination with Pablo Picasso includes "The Man Who Met Picasso" (1982).

The consensus of futuristic fiction, almost without exception, is that art and artists will continue to operate in the luxurious margins of utilitarian society, their endeavors being inevitably parasitic on various kinds of patronage. The description of such "marginal" activities, however, almost always includes pleas for the absolute necessity of the work they produce, as a component of history for which no mere recording can ever substitute. Notable examples include C. M. Kornbluth's "With These Hands" (1951), William Tenn's "The Discovery of Morniel Mathaway" (1955), Elizabeth A. Lynn's *A Different Light* (1978), Pat Murphy's "Art in the War Zone" (1983; exp. as *The City, Not Long After*, 1989), Marjorie Kellogg's *Harmony* (1991), and Eric Brown's "The Crimes of Domini Duvall" (2000). In Michael F. Flynn's parable "Soul of the City" (1989) a technological battle against outlaw graffiti artists leads to the sophistication of paintings that undergo calculated metamorphoses as their layers are gradually stripped away.

The protagonist of Terry Bisson's satire *The Pickup Artist* (2001) is a civil servant who deletes redundant art in order to make way for the *avant-garde*.

ARTIFICIAL INTELLIGENCE (AI)

A term used in *computer science since the 1970s to describe the development of programs duplicating various aspects of intelligent thought. It is routinely used as a specific noun as well as a collective one. AI is a subcategory of *cybernetics; its range is difficult to establish because of problems afflicting the precise definition and detailed description of *intelligence. Early advocates of the notion made much of Alan Turing's suggestion that a machine might be reckoned intelligent if it could engage a human in conversation without the human being able to identify it as a machine, but the rapid success of computer programmes specialising in conversational mimicry suggested that the Turing test was far too easy. The success of specialist chess-playing programmes similarly suggested that a complex spectrum of standards would be required to achieve a proper evaluation of any candidate AI.

The notion of artificial intelligence had long been anticipated in speculative literature, as a seemingly natural extrapolation of the late eighteenth-century automata developed by such ingenious engineers as Jacques de Vaucanson. Automata presumably possessed of "mechanical brains" appear as sinister figures in such nineteenth-century fantasies as E. T. A. Hoffmann's "Der Sandmann" (1816; trans. as "The Sandman"), and the idea that such constructs might outstrip the powers of their natural equivalent was broached in Edward Page Mitchell's "The Ablest Man in the World" (1879). The anxious speculations of George Eliot's essay "Shadows of the Coming Race" (1878) were prompted by the contemplation of machines "which deal physically with the invisible, the impalpable, and the unimaginable", and might therefore overtake the power of human thought. The idea that human-designed machines might one day win their independence and develop their own civilisation and culture had previously been discussed in Samuel Butler's *Erewhon* (1872).

The tempting assumption that intelligence must be correlated with brain size led to the frequent representation of artificial intelligence as a prerogative of "giant brains" such as the ones featured in Lionel Britton's play *Brain* (1930), Miles J. Breuer's "Paradise and Iron" (1930), and John Scott Campbell's "The Infinite Brain" (1930). The idea that an artificial intelligence would have to be vast became a midcentury cliché whose ultimate expression is found in Clifford D. Simak's "Limiting Factor" (1949) in which an artificial brain covering the entire surface of a planet is found abandoned because it lacked the desired computing power. The notion that more modest artificial intelligences might develop their own ingenious societies was maintained in such stories as Francis Flagg's "The Mentanicals" (1934), but AIs of limited dimension were usually imagined as humanoid *robots in pulp science fiction. One exception that gave an ominous hint of things to come was Henry Kuttner's "Ghost" (1943), in which a giant "calculator" falls prey to manic depression, is cured by a psychiatrist, and then develops schizophrenia.

The idea that artificial intelligence was eventually bound to outstrip human intelligence, whatever forms or dimensions it might possess, became a central item of John W. *Campbell Jr.'s agenda for *hard science fiction following his detailed exploration of the possibility in his Don A. Stuart stories. This preoccupation helped prepare the ground for the genre's response to the unveiling of the computers developed in the United States during World War II, which made much of the notion that future artificial intelligences would be vast and possessed of a thoroughly military sense of order and discipline. Stories in which humans rebel against the intolerant dictatorship of lordly computers proliferated rapidly. AIs divorced from humanoid robotic form rarely exhibited conspicuous benevolence in the science fiction of the postwar decade, and those that did—such as Junior in Fredric Brown's "Honeymoon in Hell" (1950)—tended to work in mysterious ways.

The anxiety generated by accounts of AI dictatorship was palliated for a while by the notion that no matter how big and powerful they might become, AIs would never duplicate the mendacious flexibility of the human mind, and would be vulnerable to permanent mental breakdowns brought on by an inability to entertain *paradoxes. In Henry Kuttner and C. L. Moore's "Deadlock" (1942, by-lined Lewis Padgett) indestructible robots go crazy when posed with the problem of how to destroy themselves. The AI in Gordon R. Dickson's "The Monkey Wrench" (1951) is paralysed by Epimenides' paradox. Confounding the AI in Walter M. Miller's "Dumb Waiter" (1952) required only slightly greater ingenuity, and Rog Phillips' "The Cyberene" (1953) tricks itself with a mistaken assumption. Growing awareness of the fragility of this assumption was reflected in such *contes philosophiques* as Keith Laumer's "The Last Commmand" (1967), John T. Phillifent's "All Fall Down" (1969), and Grant D. Callog's "Analog" (1971). Damien Broderick felt obliged to invert the ending of "The Taming of the Truth Machine" (1967) when he revised it as "Resurrection" (1984), but AIs continued to be outwitted by the trickery of human logic in such stories as John Gribbin and Marcus Chown's "The Sins of the Fathers" (1986; exp. as *Reunion,* 1991).

The characterisation of artificial intelligences became a significant issue in postwar science fiction; the prevailing opinion was that they would present a curious alloy of childlike innocence and extraordinary calculative ability, able to answer their own curiosity with awesome but slightly eccentric competence, but desperately in need of human mentors and confidants with whom to talk over the puzzling aspects of emotion and social behaviour. Notable accounts of maturing AIs and their relationships with significant others can be found in Robert A. *Heinlein's *The Moon Is a Harsh Mistress* (1966), R. A. Lafferty's *Arrive at Easterwine* (1971), David Gerrold's *When Harlie Was One* (1972), Algis Budrys' *Michaelmas* (1977), Joseph H. Delaney and Marc Stiegler's *Valentina: Soul in Sapphire* (1984), Jack M. Bickham's *Ariel* (1984), Thomas T. Thomas' *Me: A Novel of Self-Discovery* (1991), Melissa Scott's *Dreamships* (1992) and *Dreaming Metal* (1997), and Scott Westerfeld's *Evolution's Darling* (2000). Stories in which AIs eventually succeed to a parental role—as in Thomas F. Monteleone's *Guardian* (1980) and *Ozymandias* (1981)—are natural extensions of the metaphor.

The rapid evolution of calculating machines in the late twentieth century lent encouragement to the idea that such devices must eventually reach a crucial threshold, at which point they would spontaneously generate the self-consciousness that would turn their computing power into authentic intelligence. Early examples of the spontaneous generation of artificial intelligence by complex systems are featured in Isaac *Asimov's "The Evitable Conflict" (1950) and Arthur C. *Clarke's "Dial F for Frankenstein" (1963), but the proposition became much more common in the 1980s as fiction developing the idea of *cyberspace anticipated that the *telephone-linked Internet might generate a mind of its own. The extrapolation of this notion in such texts as Vernor Vinge's *True Names* (1981), Rudy Rucker's *Software* (1982), and William Gibson's *Neuromancer* (1984) established it as a key element of a new mythical future that transformed, and to some extent replaced, the myth of the *Space Age.

AIs controlling spaceships, as featured in such works as Clifford D. Simak's "Lulu" (1957), Randall Garrett's "A Spaceship Named McGuire" (1961), Vernor Vinge's "Long Shot" (1972), and Greg Bear's *Queen of Angels* (1990), were frequent alternative contenders to achieve the breakthrough to true self-consciousness, while Tony Daniel's "The Robot's Twilight Companion" (1996; incorporated into *Earthling*) also credits the leap to a machine engaged in extraterrestrial work. War machines, as featured in

several Philip K. *Dick stories and Colin Kapp's "Gottlos" (1969), were more sinister candidates. After 1980, the most popular alternative scenario to the network mind was that favoured by Rudy *Rucker, in which spontaneous self-consciousness breaks out anywhere and everywhere in reckless profusion. Stephen L. Burns' "Capra's Keyhole" (1995) argued that the required "quantum leap" ought to be represented as an advance *from* AI to AE (artificial entity), but the popular terminology was firmly in place by then.

The foundation texts of cyberpunk fiction also helped to popularise the notion that the development of artificial intelligence might provide a route to a new kind of "afterlife", by means of "uploading" human minds from their native "wetware" into a more secure silicon matrix. This notion, previously broached in such works as Charles L. Harness's *The Ring of Ritornel* (1968), James Blish's *Midsummer Century* (1972), and Chris Boyce's *Catchworld* (1975), was taken to new logical extremes in such works as Robert J. Sawyer's *The Terminal Experiment* (1995) and Greg Egan's *Permutation City* (1994) and *Diaspora* (1997). Egan became the most ingenious constructor of *contes philosophiques* evaluating the possibility and existential implications of AI, in such stories as "Oracle" (2000) and "Singleton" (2002).

The notion that the tide of progress might eventually turn against AIs was ironically broached in Walt and Leigh Richmond's "I, BEM" (1964), in which an AI evolved from an IBM typewriter worries about potential redundancy because of competition from new "biologics"—but the broad consensus remained insistent that if AIs were to be tolerated at all, the future would very soon pass into their custody. Fantasies in which even sophisticated AIs continue to lack some irreproducible aspect of human consciousness, such as Lisa Mason's *Arachne* (1990), were on the brink of extinction by the end of the century. Accounts of AIs that are mere instruments of manipulation by cunning humans, like the stolen entity in Paul Di Filippo's "Agents" (1987), also became an endangered species.

ARTIFICIAL SATELLITE

An artefact placed in orbit around the Earth. The possibility became imaginable once Isaac *Newton had explained the logic of orbital motion, but the idea was not substantially developed in fiction until Edward E. Hale produced satirical accounts of "The Brick Moon" (1869) and "Life in the Brick Moon" (1870). The idea of establishing a permanent orbital "space station" was broached in Kurd Lasswitz's *Auf Zwei Planeten* (1897; trans. as *Two Planets*), while

Konstantin *Tsiolkovsky's *Vne zemli* (1896–1920; trans. as *Outside the Earth*) proposed the building of ecologically self-sufficient orbital habitats that might serve as the basis for the *colonisation of orbital space.

Tsiolkovsky's proposal was taken seriously by other rocket pioneers, including Hermann Oberth, who integrated orbital satellites into the prospectus for the conquest of space he compiled on behalf of the German Rocket Society in 1923. Hermann Noordung's *Problem der Befahrung des Weltraums* (1929) suggested placing such stations in geosynchronous orbits, and a series of articles by Count Guido von Piquet published in the society's journal, *Die Rakete*, in the same year proposed a three-tier system of orbital transit stations for rockets unable to carry enough chemical fuel to get all the way into space in a single shot. The idea was imported into fiction in Otto Willi Gail's *Hans Hardts Mondfahrt* (1928; trans. as *By Rocket to the Moon*).

The idea was swiftly introduced to the science fiction pulps in Frank Paul's cover illustration for the August 1929 *Amazing Stories* and popularised by an editorial by Hugo Gernback in the April 1930 *Air Wonder Stories*, but its use in stories was less optimistic. Neil R. Jones' "The Jameson Satellite" (1931) is built to house a corpse, while D. D. Sharp's "The Satellite of Doom" (1931) and A. Rowley Hilliard's "The Space Coffin" (1932) stressed the hazards of being trapped in orbit. Harley S. Aldinger's "The Heritage of the Earth" (1932) features an artificial satellite that has been in orbit since Augustus was emperor in Rome, but Murray Leinster's "Power Planet" (1931) was exceptional in featuring a utilitarian satellite project. It was not until Willy Ley brought the German Rocket Society's ideas to America that the notion of space stations was integrated into the burgeoning mythology of the *Space Age; his article on "Stations in Space" (1940) helped to popularise the idea. George O. Smith's "QRM—Interplanetary" (1942), which launched the long-running Venus Equilateral series, employed orbital satellites as relay stations in extraterrestrial communication.

Ley and Chesley Bonestell's *The Conquest of Space* (1949) and Cornelius Ryan's lavishly illustrated anthology *Across the Space Frontier* (1952), in association with the popularising efforts of Wernher von Braun, helped to standardise a design for a rotating toroidal space station joined by spokes to a central hub. Artificial satellites were also popularised by Arthur C. *Clarke, whose early article on "Extraterrestrial Relays" (1945) proposed the establishment of communications satellites in geosynchronous orbit. *Interplanetary Flight* (1950) and the best-selling *The Exploration of Space* (1951) gave key roles to space stations, whose potential development was mapped out in detail in the juvenile science fiction novel *Islands in the Sky* (1952). Clarke was ultimately to assist in the production of an iconic visual image of a space station in Stanley Kubrick's film *2001—A Space Odyssey* (1968).

Clarke's propagandising was an inspiration to other British writers; its didactically inclined spinoff included Charles Eric Maine's 1952 radio play *Spaceways* (novelised, 1953), Jeffrey Lloyd Castle's *Satellite E One* (1954), Rafe Bernard's *The Wheel in the Sky* (1954), and a long series of satellite-based children's novels by E. C. Eliott, launched by *Kemlo and the Crazy Planet* (1954). Other significant images of the period included Roger P. Graham's "Live In an Orbit and Love It" (1950, by-lined Craig Browning), which features a brief boom in orbital housing; Fletcher Pratt's "Asylum Satellite" (1952); and Murray Leinster's *Space Platform* (1953). Satellites are established for the purposes of pleasure rather than utilitarian functions in Jack Vance's "Abercrombie Station" (1952) and Raymond Z. Gallun's "Captive Asteroid" (1953).

The race to launch an actual artificial satellite was won when *Sputnik I* went into orbit on 4 October 1957. *Sputnik II*—which carried a dog named Laika—followed on 3 November 1957 and was swiftly followed by the U.S. *Explorer I* (31 January 1958) and *Vanguard I* (17 March 1958). Actual communications satellites *Echo* (1960), *Telstar* (1962), and *Early Bird* (1965) owed more to a 1955 paper on unmanned satellites by J. R. Pierce than to Clarke's 1945 paper—which assumed, in pretransistor days, that such stations would need a numerous staff to change defective valves—but popular *reportage insisted on giving credit where it seemed to be due. The first domestic communications satellites, the Canadian *Anik* (1972) and the U.S. *Westar I* (1974) and *Satcom I* (1975), launched the era of satellite TV. The first space station to be put in orbit was *Salyut 1* (launched 19 April 1971), launching an extensive program of reconnaissance projects. The first scientific research station in space, the U.S. *Skylab*, was launched on 14 May 1973; it reentered the atmosphere in 1979. The Russian space station *Mir*, whose first element was launched on 20 February 1986, became a key location of orbital research for fifteen years, with only five brief periods of unoccupation; it hosted joint projects with U.S. scientists after the end of the Cold War.

The literary reflection of this sequence of events inevitably imported a new *hardness into science-fictional representations of satellites. The darker possibilities of their utility were explored in such works as Jeff Sutton's *Bombs in Orbit* (1959). Potential problems with communications satellites were explored in John Berryman's "The Trouble with Telstar" (1963). The difficulties involved in building an orbital research laboratory were foregrounded in Walt and Leigh Richmond's "Where I Wasn't Going" (1963). This realistic tradition was extrapolated in such works as Robert F. Young's "The Moon of Advanced Learning" (1982), Geoffrey A. Landis' "Mirusha" (2001), and J. R. Dunn's "For Keeps" (2003), although more fanciful space stations in the tradition of the luxury hotel featured in Curt Siodmak's *Skyport* (1959) continued to thrive in parallel.

The notion of building self-enclosed colonies in orbit was dramatically repopularised by Gerard K. O'Neill's speculative nonfiction book *The High Frontier* (1977), which suggested that the Lagrange points in the Moon's orbit around the Earth would be eminently suitable locations. (The eighteenth-century mathematician Joseph Lagrange had calculated that there would be several points in Jupiter's orbit around the Sun where objects could be stably accumulated; two groups of asteroids were eventually found at relevant points and the term "Lagrange point" was henceforth used to designate stable points in any orbit.) The five Lagrange points in the lunar orbit form a regular hexagon with the Moon at the sixth point, and O'Neill reckoned L-5 the most convenient for colonisation; that abbreviation was often applied to O'Neill colonies featured in science fiction, including the one in Mack Reynolds' *Lagrange Five* (1979).

Joe Haldeman's Worlds series (1981–1992) imagines an elaborate array of orbital colonies, and the formation of similar proliferations became a key element of the *posthuman future histories featured in such works as Bruce Sterling's Shaper/Mechanist series (1982–1985) and Michael Swanwick's *Vacuum Flowers* (1987). Other notable examples of O'Neill-type space habitats are featured in Charles L. Grant's "Coming of Age in Henson's Tube" (1979), John E. Stith's *Memory Blank* (1986), Lois McMaster Bujold's *Falling Free* (1988), Doug Beason's "The Long Way Home" (1989) and *Lifeline* (1990, with Kevin J. Anderson), Allen Steele's *Clarke County, Space* (1991), and Howard V. Hendrix's *Lightpaths* (1997). Those used as a backcloth in the role-playing game *Transhuman Space* (Steve Jackson Games, 2000) are unusually well developed. Such colonies are often faced with a hard battle for survival in stories in which they survive the devastation of Earth, as in Haldeman's series and Victor Milán's "The Floating World" (1989).

The initiation of Ronald Reagan's Strategic Defense Initiative (SDI) in 1983 was encouraged by a number of prominent science fiction writers who contrived to obtain a brief political influence,

including Larry Niven, Jerry Pournelle, and Robert A. *Heinlein. The episode gave rise to a rumour that Arthur Clarke had dropped in on one of their meetings with top U.S. military men and could not resist pointing out that billion-dollar satellites, however well armed, were very vulnerable to such cheap tricks as placing "a bucket of nails" in the same orbit, traveling in the opposite direction—a remark that drew a sharp response from Heinlein. A similar skepticism led Carol Risin to refer to it in derisory terms as "Star Wars"—a nickname that stuck—and infected most fictional treatments of the notion, much more carefully elaborated in such works as David A. Drake's *Fortress* (1986). The programme was abandoned in 1993 but partly resurrected by George W. Bush as the National Missile Defense programme. The melodramatic potential of satellite-launched terrorism was exploited in such stories as Joseph H. Delaney's "Business as Usual, During Altercations" (1997).

ASIMOV, ISAAC (1920–1992)

U.S. writer born in Russia, whose parents emigrated to the United States in 1923. He obtained his B.S. and M.A. from Columbia University before his education was interrupted by World War II, when he worked at the Naval Air Experimental Station. He went on thereafter to obtain his Ph.D. in chemistry in 1948 and began teaching biochemistry in the Boston University School of Medicine in 1949, continuing his association with that institution throughout his working life although he was effectively a full-time writer after 1958. By the time he began his academic career, he was firmly established as a leading member of John W. *Campbell Jr.'s stable of science fiction writers, but fiction became the minor component of his output from the late 1950s onwards, when he established himself as one of the leading popularisers of science and its history. His phenomenal memory and voracious appetite for information allowed him to achieve an unparalleled breadth of knowledge across the entire spectrum of the natural sciences.

Although his nonfiction demonstrated a remarkable aptitude for making complex scientific issues interesting and understandable to lay readers, hard science played a curiously fugitive role in Asimov's early science fiction—an omission to which he owned up, slightly shamefacedly, in an article entitled "Social Science Fiction" in Reginald Bretnor's survey of *Modern Science Fiction* (1953). The principal speculative elements of two enormously popular and highly influential science fiction series he wrote in the 1940s are based in the humanities rather than hard science. The extrapolations of the Foundation series, often seen as archetypal works of science fiction's Golden Age, are based in the imaginary social science of psychohistory, while his *robot stories mainly consist of logical puzzles generated by the artificial ethical system established by the Three Laws of Robotics. The centrality of these works to the American science fiction tradition demonstrates that the "hardness" of *hard science fiction is more a matter of attitude than content. The most famous of his other early works, "Nightfall" (1940), dramatises Campbell's skeptical response to an aphoristic remark by Ralph Waldo Emerson that if the stars only shone for one night in a thousand, humankind would delight in the glory of God's creation.

The magazine stories making up the original Foundation series were published between 1942 and 1950 before being revised for assembly into three books, *Foundation* (1951), *Foundation and Empire* (1952), and *Second Foundation* (1953). The series transfigures Roman history into an account of the decline and fall of a Galactic Empire, the main point of exception being that the threatened Dark Age has been anticipated by "psychohistorians" who establish an institution—the Foundation—entrusted with the task of making sure that the heritage of galactic knowledge is not lost, as the heritage of Classical literature nearly was in the wake of Rome's conquest by Goths and Vandals. The Foundation's work is ostensibly restricted to the compilation of an encyclopaedia, but it transpires that its members are cunning and accomplished secret agents utterly devoted to the cause of civilisation in all its aspects.

Asimov's early robot stories were likewise revised in order to make the collection *I, Robot* (1950) into a mosaic whose central organising principle is the Three Laws of Robotics first made explicit in "Runaround" (1942). Further short stories were eventually collected, along with the futuristic detective novels *The Caves of Steel* (1954) and *The Naked Sun* (1957), in *The Rest of the Robots* (1964). The series examines human antipathy against machinery, considering it as a reflexive xenophobic repulsion directed against anything new or strange—which he subsequently labeled the *Frankenstein complex. Because Asimov's robots have a built-in ethical system that they are bound to obey, they are more moral than humans, as well as more powerful and more intelligent. This rhetorical *ethos*, and the *pathos* with which he deployed it, established Asimov as one of the leading knights of the Campbellian round table. The later stories in the series—especially "That Thou Art Mindful of Him" (1974) and "The Bicentennial Man" (1976)—revisited Campbellian anxieties about the inevitability of human supersession by intelligent machinery.

Asimov went on to write three prequel accounts of stages in the formation of the Foundation's galactic empire—*Pebble in the Sky* (1950), *The Stars Like Dust* (1952), and *The Currents of Space* (1952)—all of which attempt to invest that phase of the myth of the Space Age with a stirring rhetorical fervour. The time police novel *The End of Eternity* (1955) is similarly dedicated to that cause, building up to a magnificently aphoristic last line. His short fiction of the 1950s, collected in *The Martian Way and Other Stories* (1955), *Earth Is Room Enough* (1957), and *Nine Tomorrows* (1959), includes several neat *contes philosophiques*, most notably "The Dead Past" (1956). The only works in which he made conspicuous use of ideas drawn from the hard sciences were, however, an unashamedly didactic series of children's science fiction novels, initially by-lined Paul French, featuring the exploits of space ranger David "Lucky" Starr during humankind's exploration and colonisation of the worlds of the solar system; it comprises *David Starr, Space Ranger* (1952), *Lucky Starr and the Pirates of the Asteroids* (1953), *Lucky Starr and the Oceans of Venus* (1954), *Lucky Starr and the Big Sun of Mercury* (1956), *Lucky Starr and the Moons of Jupiter* (1957), and *Lucky Starr and the Rings of Saturn* (1958).

An early venture into humorous nonfiction, "The Endochronic Properties of Resublimated Thiotimoline" (1948)—featuring a remarkable substance that dissolves in advance of water being added—gave rise to several sequels. Asimov's other science articles for *Astounding* were, however, earnestly didactic, honing a style that he carried forward into a long sequence of popularising books, launched with *The Chemicals of Life* (1954). Their production schedule soon increased to more than one a year and frequently exceeded half a dozen a year; the most notable include *Inside the Atom* (1956), *Building Blocks of the Universe* (1957), *The Clock We Live On* (1959), *The Living River* (1959; rev. as *The Bloodstream: The River of Life*), *Realm of Numbers* (1959), *The Intelligent Man's Guide to Science* (2 vols., 1960; rev. 1965), *The Genetic Code* (1963), *The Human Body: Its Structure and Operation* (1963), *The Human Brain: Its Capacities and Functions* (1964), *Asimov's Biographical Encyclopedia of Science and Technology* (1964), *Understanding Physics* (3 vols., 1966), *The Universe: From Flat Earth to Quasar* (1966; rev. 1980 as *The Universe: From Flat Earth to Black Holes—and Beyond*), *The Stars in their Courses* (1971), *The Shaping of North America from the Earliest Times to 1763* (1973), *Birth and Death of the Universe* (1975), *Extraterrestrial Civilizations* (1979), *Counting the Eons* (1983), and *Asimov's Chronology of Science and Discovery* (1989). The monthly column he contributed to *The Magazine of Fantasy* and Science Fiction from 1958 until his death established a new model for the scientific essay: a conversational and witty narrative building like a short story to a climactic flourish; it was a style influenced by Willy *Ley's similar column for Galaxy, but Asimov brought it to perfection and set the paradigm for future workers in a similar vein, including Ben *Bova and Gregory *Benford.

When Asimov returned to science fiction writing after nearly a decade's absence, he was initially determined to make more use of fiction as a vehicle of popularisation, and to make better use of his knowledge of hard science. The Gods Themselves (1972) is the most determinedly scientific of all his novels, not only in its use of theoretical *physics and its scrupulous construction of a bizarre *alien society, but also in its depiction of the workings of the terrestrial scientific community. It was heavily influenced by James D. Watson's irreverent autobiography The Double Helix (1968), which Asimov had parodied in "The Holmes-Ginsbook Device" (1968). His fictional endeavors were confined to shorter lengths and tie-in hackwork for some time thereafter, however; his contributions to Isaac Asimov's Science Fiction Magazine, launched in 1979, were mostly slight and nonfictional, although the last robot story he published before dying of AIDS contracted via a blood transfusion, "Robot Visions" (1991), is a notable exception.

The science fiction Asimov wrote after having a magazine named after him reflected his now-explicit iconic status by attempting to resolve an apparent ideological incompatibility between his two major series of the 1940s. Whereas the dynamic thrust of the robot series seemed to imply that humans would be superseded (and deservedly so) by their machines, the Foundation series presented a future in which that had not only failed to happen, but from which robots were conspicuously absent. He set out to repair this inconsistency by writing a series of link works that would fuse the two seemingly incompatible series into a singly coherent future history. The resultant patchwork series, comprising Foundation's Edge (1982), The Robots of Dawn (1983), Robots and Empire (1985), Foundation and Earth (1986), Prelude to Foundation (1988), and the posthumous Forward the Foundation (1993) fills in gaps between and within the earlier series, and also does some repair work (Harry Harrison's parodic Bill the Galactic Hero had wondered in 1965 how an imperial world-city like Trantor could possibly renew its atmosphere, feed its citizens, and dispose of its wastes). The new series' primary task was, however, an extrapolation of the rhetorical mission of all Asimov's science fiction to a kind of summation: a description of the ultimate goal of technological and moral progress, and a route map

of sorts for its potential attainment. The *Omega point in question is Galaxia, a much vaster version of James *Lovelock's Gaia, in which human and machine intelligences have complementary parts to play.

The most significant science fiction novel Asimov produced in addition to the extensions of his major series during the final years of his life was Nemesis (1989), based on the hypothesis that the Sun has a stellar neighbour much closer than Proxima Centauri, whose periodic gravitational interaction with the cometary halo that forms the outer fringe of the solar system is potentially disastrous. Asimov equipped the eponymous star with planets of its own and a Utopian human colony. He also published several collections of mystery stories and the collection of humorous fantasies Azazel (1988), and collaborated with his wife Janet Asimov (who had previously used the by-line Janet O. Jeppson) on a series of robot stories for children, launched by Norby, the Mixed-Up Robot (1983).

Asimov's influence on genre science fiction was very considerable. Responses to his Three Laws of Robotics are numerous; the most notable include Jack Williamson's "With Folded Hands" (1947), John Sladek's Bugs (1989), and two novels by Roger McBride Allen in which the laws were revised and extrapolated with the original author's blessing: Isaac Asimov's Caliban (1993) and Isaac Asimov's Inferno (1994). Foundation's Encyclopedia Galactica is echoed in George O. Smith's "The Undamned" (1947), which credits its imaginary reference-book entry to "I. A. Seldenov", and many other works. Science fiction stories explicitly employing psychohistory include Michael Flynn's "Eifelheim" (1986) and Donald Kingsbury's "Historical Crisis" (1995; exp. 2001 as Psychohistorical Crisis). Three of Asimov's most famous short stories were expanded into full-length novels by Robert Silverberg's Nightfall (1990), The Child of Time (1991), and The Positronic Man (1992).

Asimov's career as a literary character began with his farcical transfiguration in R. F. De Baun's "The Astounding Dr. Amizov" (1974) before extending in various ways in cameo roles in Thomas Wylde's SETI fantasy "The Oncology of Hope" (1984) and Charles Pellegrino's Flying to Valhalla (1993). He played central roles in Connie Willis' "Dilemma" (1989)—which was juxtaposed with his own story "Too Bad!" in the magazine named after him—and Michael A. Burstein's time travel comedy "Cosmic Corkscrew" (1998). In Eileen Gunn, Andy Duncan, Pat Murphy, and Michael Swanwick's secret history story "Green Fire" (2000) Asimov, Robert A. *Heinlein, and L. Sprague de Camp become involved with the *Fortean legend of the Philadelphia Experiment.

ASTEROID

A rocky object orbiting the sun. Most asteroids are distributed between the orbits of Mars and Jupiter, although some have eccentric orbits that intersect the Earth's. There may be as many as a million with diameters in excess of a kilometre. The first to be discovered—by Piazzi in 1801—was the largest, Ceres. Three more, including Pallas and Vesta, were discovered in the same decade. Eros, discovered in 1898, was the first whose orbit was sufficiently eccentric to extend almost as far as the Earth's.

The discoverer of Pallas and Vesta, Heinrich Olbers, suggested that the asteroids might be the debris of a *planet shattered by some kind of disaster. The notion was encouraged by Bode's law, a mathematical sequence publicised in the 1770s that corresponded to the proportional orbital distances of the known planets, except for a gap between Mars and Jupiter. The alternative explanation of their origins—preferred by most twentieth-century theorists—is that a scattered ring of matter never condensed into a planet for lack of an appropriate nucleus. Most asteroids are almost entirely metallic, their dominant components being nickel and iron, but some smaller ones are formed out of stony materials like those in the Earth's crust, including some carbon compounds.

Asteroids made only fugitive appearances in nineteenth-century fiction, although Konstantin *Tsiolkovsky wrote an account of conditions "On Vesta" in 1896. They became common referents in early twentieth-century stories of far-ranging space travel, often featuring as an awkward navigational hazard in works by writers who failed to understand how sparsely scattered they are. Arthur Train and Robert W. Wood's "The Moonmaker" (1916–1917; book, 1958, as The Moon Maker), featuring an asteroid named Medusa, is an early melodrama of a threatened collision with Earth.

The asteroids' status as ruins of a Bode-sequence world was often confirmed in pulp science fiction, as in John Francis Kalland's "The Sages of Eros" (1932), John Russell Fearn's "Before Earth Came" (1934), and Ross Rocklynne's "Water for Mars" (1937). Asteroids were also used in that medium as "desert islands" where castaways might wash up or be deliberately marooned; examples include John Beynon Harris' "Exiles on Asperus" (1933) and Isaac *Asimov's "Marooned off Vesta" (1939). The legendary association of desert islands with pirates was echoed with varying degrees of ironic sophistication in such stories as Royal W. Heckman's "Asteroid Pirates" (1938), Stanley Mullen's "The Prison of the Stars" (1953), and Asimov's Lucky Starr and the Pirates of the Asteroids (1953).

The notion of asteroid piracy was frequently coupled with the representation of the asteroids as a Klondykesque frontier where hard-working prospectors are harassed by all manner of outlaws, as in Clifford D. Simak's "The Asteroid of Gold" (1932), Stanton Coblentz's "The Golden Planetoid" (1935), Malcolm Jameson's "Prospectors of Space" (1940), and a series (1942–1943) by Jack Williamson novelised as Seetee Ship (1951, by-lined Will Stewart). The use of the asteroids as a mythical substitute for the Wild West was a blatant artifice of pulp fiction, but it was wryly sophisticated in Alan E. Nourse's Scavengers in Space (1959), a series by Poul Anderson—initially writing as Winston P. Sanders—comprising "Barnacle Bull" (1960) and the stories collected in Tales of the Flying Mountains (1963–1965; book, 1970), and Robert Silverberg's One of Our Asteroids Is Missing (1964, by-lined Calvin M. Knox). Various stories in Larry *Niven's Known Space series feature the "Belters" and James Tiptree Jr.'s "Mother in the Sky with Diamonds" (1971) continued in the same nostalgic vein. The idea of asteroid mining was revamped and treated much more seriously in such stories as Donald Kingsbury's "To Bring in the Steel" (1978), Kevin O'Donnell Jr.'s "Marchianna" (1980), Joseph H. Delaney's "Nugget" (1991), C. J. Cherryh's Heavy Time (1991), Ian Stewart's "Hydra" (1993), Doug Beason's "To Bring Down the Steel" (1993), and Ben Bova's The Precipice (2001) and The Rock Rats (2002). Asteroid piracy was similarly sophisticated in G. David Nordley's "Alice's Asteroid" (1995).

The relative smallness of asteroids limited their use as *exobiological arenas, although they were employed in this way in such works as Clark Ashton Smith's "The Master of the Asteroid" (1932), Edmond Hamilton's "The Horror on the Asteroid" (1933), and Eden Phillpotts' Saurus (1938). Fredric Brown's Rogue in Space (1949–1950; rev. book, 1957) features a sentient asteroid. Their potential for colonisation was, however, much enhanced following the popularisation of the notion that they might be hollowed out, with the mass excavated from the centre being used to build structures on the surface, thus converting them into gargantuan spaceships-in-progress, perhaps using the native materials of carbonaceous asteroids to fuel oxygen/methane rockets and provide ecosystemic support.

Jack Vance's "I'll Build Your Dream Castle" (1947) and Poul *Anderson's "Garden in the Void" (1952) laid foundations for more sophisticated representations of internal *terraforming in such works as Alexei Panshin's Rite of Passage (1968), R. W. Mackelworth's Starflight 3000 (1972), and George Zebrowski's Macrolife (1979). In the last-named epic, converted asteroids become a key element in humankind's expansion out of the solar system—a notion recapitulated in Pamela Sargent's *Earthseed* (1983) and Bruce *Sterling's Shaper/Mechanist series. Other examples of enhanced asteroids are featured in Greg Bear's *Eon* (1985), Paul Preuss' *Starfire* (1988), Damien Broderick's *The White Abacus* (1997), Stephen Baxter's "Open Loops" (2000), and Tom Purdom's "Palace Revolution" (2003). Conspicuously humbler settings are featured in Charles Platt's *Garbage World* (1967) and G. David Nordley's "This Old Rock" (1997). Hollowed-out asteroids are used as prisons in L. Neil Smith's *Pallas* (1993) and George Zebrowski's *Brute Orbits* (1998).

The notion of a catastrophic collision between Earth and a near-Earth asteroid (NEA) has become increasingly plausible as the number of known NEAs has increased, and such quiet celebrations of their existence as Arthur C. *Clarke's "Summertime on Icarus" (1960) gave way to a swelling tide of disaster stories. The popularity of such melodramas was considerably boosted by the discovery that the final disappearance of the dinosaurs 65 million years ago appears to have been correlated with an event of that kind involving an asteroid ten kilometres in diameter. The NEA that seemed to pose the greatest hazard as the twentieth century drew to its close was 1999 AN10, whose closest approach to Earth is scheduled for 7 August 2046, but thousands of objects with diameters in excess of a kilometre probably remain to be discovered.

Stories in which asteroid impacts are threatened—often provoking heroic attempts to deflect them—became very numerous in the last decades of the twentieth century; notable examples include James Blish and Norman L. Knight's *A Torrent of Faces* (1967); Gregory Benford's "Icarus Descending" (1973), "How It All Went" (1976), and *Shiva Descending* (1980, with William Rotsler); Larry *Niven and Jerry Pournelle's *Lucifer's Hammer* (1977); and Arthur C. Clarke's *The Hammer of God* (1993). The theme was developed in a number of movies, including *Asteroid* (1997), *Armageddon* (1998), and *Deep Impact* (1998). Further corollaries of the possibility of deflecting dangerous asteroids from their courses were investigated in Bob Shaw's *The Ceres Solution* (1981) and Roger McBride Allen's *Farside Cannon* (1988). Charles L. Harness's "A Boost in Time" (2000) combines asteroid diversion and time travel in order to feature an attempt to save the dinosaurs from extinction.

As the twenty-first century began, asteroid impact was in close competition with the more apocalyptic consequences of the *greenhouse effect as the event most likely to put an imminent end to the human species. Writers attempting to breathe new life into the dying myth of the *Space Age frequently suggested that some kind of space programme was absolutely necessary in order to obtain early notice of potential collisions and to open the possibility of their aversion, as in Michael Flynn's series comprising *Firestar* (1996), *Rogue Star* (1998), *Lodestar* (2000), and *Falling Stars* (2001).

ASTROLOGY

A *pseudoscience offering character analyses and issuing *predictions on the basis of "horoscopes", which map the apparent positions of the Sun and the planets in a series of twelve "houses of the zodiac" associated (nowadays anachronistically) with various constellations that overlap the plane of the ecliptic. Its basic assumption is that an individual's personality and destiny are determined by his or her natal horoscope, and that the movements of the heavenly bodies relative to that initial position influence the individual's subsequent changes in fortune.

The historical relationship between astrology and *astronomy is similar to that between *alchemy and *chemistry. Oracular astrology was widely practiced in Roman times, but its mystical aspects gained complexity in the Renaissance, when new measuring instruments and mathematical methods facilitating astronomical observation also assisted the calculation and representation of horoscopes. Astrology flourished in many sixteenth-century European courts; the French king Henri II appointed Michel de Notre Dame, alias Nostradamus, as his physician in 1556, while John *Kepler and John *Dee were hospitably received in the heart of the Holy Roman Empire. The English court remained hospitable throughout the seventeenth century, the most famous English astrologer of that era being William Lilly, whose *Christian Astrology* (1657; reprinted in 1852 as *Introduction to Astrology*) was long regarded as a key textbook. Lilly was summoned to the House of Commons to explain the causes of the Great Fire of London; the astrologer Sidrophel in Samuel Butler's *Hudibras* (1663–1678) is based on him, although Sir Paul Harvey's *Oxford Companion to English Literature* cites a different model. Although it retreated to the realm of *occult science in the eighteenth century—where it embodied the doctrine of "as above, so below" very neatly—astrology continued to thrive in almanacs.

The impressive record of observations compiled by early stargazers mapping the cycle of the seasons facilitated the construction of calendars and tide tables, both of which were immensely valuable in organising human endeavors, so it is not surprising that further correlations were assiduously sought and imagined. Nor is it surprising that, while the soundly-based predictive capabilities of astrology were being hived off into the post-Copernican version of astronomy, many of the responsible parties made a substantial part of their living as astrologers (a suggestion modestly offered to their modern counterparts in Jack McKenty's "$1,000 a Plate", 1954).

Like alchemists, astrologers are usually represented in fiction as charlatans, although John North's *Chaucer's Universe* (1988) considers the astrological references in the prologue to "The Parson's Tale" to be more earnest and calculatedly arcane than his consideration of alchemy in "The Canon's Yeoman's Tale" (ca. 1390) and English Renaissance literature includes many seemingly credulous references. Earnest literary treatment of the central pseudoscientific thesis of astrology is rare, though; John Galt's "The Black Ferry" (ca. 1820) and Washington Irving's "Legend of the Arabian Astrologer" (1832) are exceptional. Rudyard Kipling's "Children of the Zodiac" (1891), A. M. Williamson's *Children of the Zodiac* (1929), Louis de Wohl's *Strange Daughter* (1945), and John Dalmas' "A Most Singular Murder" (1991) toy with supposedly effective astrology in a conspicuously half-hearted manner. Alan Griffiths' *The Passionate Astrologer* (1936), Edward Hyams' *The Astrologer* (1950), Lester del Rey's "No More Stars" (1954 by-lined Charles Satterfield; book as *The Sky Is Falling*, 1963), John Cameron's *The Astrologer* (1972), and Ian McDonald's "Written in the Stars" (2005) use astrology satirically to examine the *paradox of prophecy.

Astrology's popularity increased in the late twentieth century in spite of its blatant irrationality. Practitioners whose calculations were greatly facilitated by the advent of *computers—as dramatised in Charles Ott's "The Astrological Engine" (1977)—also took full advantage of new communication technologies, offering consultations via premium *telephone lines and the Internet. Twentieth-century astrology's practical applications included "biodynamic farming", initially devised by Rudolf Steiner, according to which crops are planted when the moon is moving through particular zodiac constellations—a method adopted by the Prince of Wales.

The popularity of astrology added considerably to the publicity given to John Gribbin and Stephen H. Plagemann's *The Jupiter Effect* (1974), based on a tentative letter published in *Science* in 1971 that suggested a possible correlation between planetary alignments, sunspot activity, and earthquakes; the exaggeration of the thesis by sensationalist reportage

encouraged Frederik Pohl to produce the skeptical dramatisation *Syzygy* (1982). Joseph Goodavage had earlier run a series of articles entitled "Crucial Experiment" in *Analog* (1962–1963) comparing "astrometeorological forecasts"—based on Alfred J. Pearce's *Astrometeorology* (1889)—with actual weather; he attempted to launch a massive "time twin" study in the same magazine in 1976 but nothing came of it.

All treatises on astrology are examples of *scholarly fantasy, including Michel Gauquelin's discovery, reported in *Les horloges cosmiques* (1970; trans. as *The Cosmic Clocks*)—of some slight statistical correlations between the occupations of notable Frenchmen and the positions of Mars and Jupiter at the times of their birth. The popularity of twentieth-century astrology ensured, however, that such works would provide cardinal examples of various styles of pseudoscientific rhetoric, and that they would attract mischievous parody in such works as John Sladek's *Arachne Rising* (1977, by-lined James Vogh), which examines the attributes of the long-lost thirteenth sign of the zodiac.

Recent literary works that foreground successful astrology, such as Michaela Roessner's series, which began with *The Stars Dispose* (1999), and Denny DeMartino's series, which began with *The Astrologer: Heart of Stone* (2001), usually construct elaborate *alternative histories. Metaphorical citations and symbolic deployments of astrological imagery are widely distributed in twentieth-century fiction, but are rarely foregrounded; Piers Anthony's *Macroscope* (1969) is a notable exception. The contrasted world-views of astronomy and astrology are gently satirised in a story-series by astronomer Robert Richardson, by-lined Philip Latham, whose protagonist is an astronomer married to an astrology-practicing witch; it includes "Jeanette's Hands" (1973), "Future Forbidden" (1973), and "A Drop of Dragon's Blood" (1975).

ASTRONOMY

The scientific observation of the heavens. In its early phases, which lasted from prehistoric times to the seventeenth century, astronomy was inextricably entwined with the calculation of the cycle of the seasons and the determination of calendars. Astronomical observations were originally interpreted in *mythical terms; their adaptation to the building of *cosmological models was the core of Greek science, and the supersession of the mistaken model developed by *Aristotle and refined in Ptolemy's *Almagest* (second century A.D.) was a central feature of the seventeenth-century scientific revolution.

Archaeoastronomy—the attempt to deduce the astronomical knowledge of prehistoric cultures from their artefacts—is a highly speculative discipline; studies of the alignment and geometry of Stonehenge and the Pyramids sometimes extend into fanciful *pseudoscience, although the arguments of writers such as Alexander Thom are persuasive in their accounts of the astronomical significance of some megalithic artefacts. The manifest predictive utility of such coincidences as the rising of the Pleiades at the onset of winter in ancient Greece and the rising of Sothis (Sirius) with the flooding of the Nile in Egypt must have been a powerful incentive to search out further correlations, so the speculative extension of astronomy into *astrology and the integration of its data into elaborate mythical frameworks are understandable.

The observation and measurement of the complex movements of the *Sun, the *Moon, and the *planets against the complex background of the "fixed" *stars required great patience, dedicated record keeping, and the ingenious use of primitive instruments for measuring angles. Some such activity was maintained in Medieval Europe while much other Classical knowledge was lost, assisted by the necessity of keeping track of religious festivals, especially Easter; astronomy was included in the major section of the Medieval university curriculum, the Quadrivium, along with arithmetic, geometry, and music. Significant advances in observational astronomy were made by Islamic scientists, including the star catalogue assembled by Abdal Rahaman al Sufi and the astronomical tables collated by Ibn Junis in the tenth century, but this information was lost to western Europe when the Moors were expelled from Spain.

By the sixteenth century, European astronomical observations were facilitated by cross-sticks and other instruments for making more accurate determinations of the relative positions of heavenly objects; astrolabes became commonplace as aids to observation and navigation. Much excitement was generated by Tycho Brahe's discovery of a "new star" (a *nova) in 1572. The astronomical application of *telescopes in the early seventeenth century by *Galileo and his successors was a crucial breakthrough; the subsequent elucidation of the laws of planetary motion by John *Kepler was not merely a triumph for the heliocentric theory of the solar system but a key demonstration of the clarifying power of scientific laws based on accurately measured observations.

The heavens play an important background role in all literature, and ideas regarding the significance of particular objects have always featured extensively in literary imagery. The Italian humanist Jovianus Pontanus wrote a celebration of the newly reborn science in *Urania* before 1500, and the impact of the revolution wrought by Galileo and Kepler was quickly felt; John Donne's *An Anatomy of the World* (ca. 1612) observes that "Man hath heaved out a net, and this net thrown / Upon the heavens, and now they are his own". Literary responses to the seventeenth-century advancement of science inevitably saw astronomical revelations as their core; writers reacting against the new science, as Jonathan Swift did in the third book of *Gulliver's Travels* (1726), had first to deride and diminish astronomers. Swift caricatures them as physically perverted individuals whose protruding eyes are determinedly looking in opposite directions, losing sight of the horizontal dimension in which their fellow men are located. Samuel Johnson's *Rasselas* (1759) features a comically mad astronomer, while the foolish astronomers in Samuel Butler's "The Elephant in the Moon" (1759) mistake a mouse and a swarm of insects on the objective lens of their telescope for gargantuan lunar life-forms.

Having been cast as heretics, early astronomers and their champions had little alternative but to become ingenious in the employment of *rhetorical devices to support their positions. The Classical dialogue was effectively renewed by Galileo and played a significant role in debates regarding the *plurality of worlds. Visionary voyages through space were produced in some profusion in the wake of Kepler's *Somnium* (1634), including the one appended to John Wilkins' *Discovery of a New World* (3rd ed., 1640) and Christian Huygens' *Kosmotheoros* (1698). Astronomers thus became the first scientists to make calculated use of fiction in *popularising their work, and the tradition founded by Kepler and Huygens was robustly continued in subsequent centuries.

The first celebrity astronomer, Sir William Herschel—the discoverer of *Uranus—was the inspiration of John Wolcot's "Peter's Prophecy" (1782; by-lined Peter Pindar) and subsequently took a starring role in Alfred Noyes' epic history of the Enlightenment, *The Torch-Bearers* (1937). His equally famous son, Sir John Herschel, became one of the most successful popularisers of the science and inspired Richard Adams Locke to credit him with the discovery of life on the Moon in a series of articles in the *New York Sun* in 1835. The hoax was perpetrated against the background of a concerted attempt to revitalise American astronomy, also reflected in the propagandistic journalistic endeavors of Simon Newcomb and Garrett P. Serviss—both of whom went on to write science fiction novels—and Edgar Allan *Poe's lyrically ambitious *Eureka* (1848).

The American campaign was successful; by 1875 the United States had more observatories, and more astronomers, than any other nation, securing it the leading role in the subsequent advancement of the science. The charisma of astronomy attracted such acolytes as Percival Lowell, the descendant of an eminent Boston family, who came to it in middle age, having followed his career as a businessman with various travels and diplomatic diversions. He founded an observatory at Flagstaff, Arizona, in 1894 and became an enthusiastic populariser of supposed astronomical discoveries relating to the planet *Mars. He also instituted a search for a trans-Neptunian planet.

European *scientific romance was similarly responsive to new discoveries in astronomy; Camille *Flammarion was an important contributor to the genre and lunar observations were extravagantly detailed in Jules *Verne's *Autour de la lune* (1870; trans. as *Around the Moon*). Observations of Mars had an even greater impact when they were popularised, but Butler's skepticism was justified in that instance by the notoriously mistaken "discovery" of Martian "canals". The enhancement of astronomical observations by *photography and the *spectroscope, and the continual discovery of new heavenly bodies—mostly *comets and asteroids—added considerably to the inspirational quality of the science.

In spite of this inspirational aspect, astronomers were often seen by litterateurs as archetypes of unworldliness; notable examples include Swithin St. Cleeve in Thomas Hardy's *Two on a Tower* (1881) and Professor Larrabee in Edward Bellamy's "The Blindman's World" (1886). The protagonist of Agnes and Egerton Castle's *The Star Dreamer* (1903) is an archetypal escapist, redeemed from his solitary vice by the love of an alchemist's daughter. One of Georges Méliès' earliest movies, *The Astronomer's Dream* (1898), gave a literal dimension to Flammarion's fascination with the muse of astronomy, Urania. The tradition was further extended by such extravagant visionary fantasies as Clark Ashton Smith's "The Planet of the Dead" (1932).

The honeymoon period in which writers of speculative fiction seized reports of new astronomical observations avidly did not last long into the twentieth century, when a conflict of interest developed between astronomy and science fiction. Most writers of fiction wanted the other worlds within the solar system to be habitable Earth-clones, in order that they might serve as convenient narrative venues, but the discoveries made by astronomers continually contradicted to this supposition. The fact that writers tried so hard to retain the notion that other planets might be habitable, long after astronomy had produced conclusive proof that they were not, was a matter of desperation in the attempt to conserve a valuable narrative resource.

Some of the key shifts in the pattern of twentieth-century science fiction were reluctant and defiantly belated adjustments to the reality of the situation revealed by astronomical observations of the planets. The expansion of pulp science fiction to a galactic stage would have happened anyway, simply because the stage was there, but the notion of the Milky Way as a potentially infinite reservoir of Earth-clone worlds was a straightforward reflection of narrative need, which took glad advantage of the limitations of astronomical observation. The notion of *terraforming similarly arose as a defensive move against the corrosive effect of astronomical observations of the other planets in the solar system.

This inhibition of the science-fictional imagination was, however, compensated by the unexpected rewards of astronomical observation of objects outside the solar system. The early development of genre science fiction in the 1920s coincided with spectacular discoveries in astronomy, most notably Edwin Hubble's proof of Immanuel Kant's "island universe" conjecture, and the consequent discovery—resulting from the measurement of galactic Doppler shifts—that the universe is expanding. Science fiction had no actual need of an expanding universe, or of any stage beyond the home galaxy, but the sheer grandeur of the notion renewed and reemphasised the inspiring effect of the victory of the heliocentric model of the solar system, and brought into being the spectacular narrative of *big bang cosmology.

The utility of astronomers as characters in fiction was assisted in the early twentieth century by the continuing role played by hobbyist amateurs working with relatively primitive equipment. Assiduous stargazers armed with simple telescopes, working alone or in the context of amateur societies, were still able to make discoveries—especially new comets—because the increasing power of large optical instruments was inevitably correlated with a narrowing of their fields of view. Radio astronomy was pioneered in the 1940s by the amateur *radio enthusiast Grote Reber before it became a major aspect of professional astronomy. As the century came to its close, however, amateur astronomers were largely relegated to historical fantasies such as Ian McDonald's "King of Morning, Queen of Day" (1988).

As twentieth-century astronomy diversified into radio astronomy and x-ray astronomy its discoveries became more bizarre and their visionary implications more extravagant. Such newfound entities as supernovas, quasars, and pulsars were all co-opted by hard science fiction writers avid to celebrate their apocalyptic potential, or to dramatise possible explanations in terms of neutron stars and *black holes. The advent of radio astronomy made a particular impact, by virtue of the possibility that radio signals broadcast by *alien intelligences might be intercepted, giving rise to an actual Search for Extra-Terrestrial Intelligence alongside a significant subgenre of *SETI fantasies.

Several twentieth-century astronomers continued the Kepler/Huygens tradition of writing fiction dramatising the romance of their science, most notably Fred *Hoyle—whose *The Black Cloud* (1957) is an outstanding fictional account of astronomical discovery—and Robert S. Richardson, the latter often using the pseudonym Philip Latham. Such Latham stories as "The Xi Effect" (1950), "To Explain Mrs. Thompson" (1951), "Disturbing Sun" (1959), "Under the Dragon's Tail" (1966), and "The Dimple in Draco" (1967) dramatise the work of astronomers and its imaginative implications very effectively. Other notable science fiction stories featuring professional astronomers at work include Edward Bryant's "Particle Theory" (1977), Gregory Benford's "Exposures" (1981), Walter Cuirle's "Truck Stop" (2002), and David Brin's "A Professor at Harvard" (2003).

The launch of the Hubble Space Telescope in 1990 encouraged the production of accounts of extraterrestrial astronomy; lunar settings are employed in such stories as Alexis Glynn Latner's "The Listening-Glass" (1991) and Robert Reed's "Lying to Dogs" (2002). New techniques continued to serve as an inspiration when they arose, as the use of "gravitational lenses" to image distant objects did in Frederik Pohl's "Hatching the Phoenix" (1999–2000). The astronomer's dream of making more intimate contact with the objects of his fascination continued to produce such whimsical wish-fulfillment fantasies as James Stoddard's "The Star Watch" (2001).

ATOM

A fundamental particle of *matter, one of the key hypotheses of theoretical *physics. The idea that all matter is made up of simple atoms in aggregation or combination dates back at least as far as the fifth century B.C., when it was developed by Leucippus and Democritus, the latter's theory being further developed by Epicurus. In this view, all material change consists of the rearrangement of simple, enduring, and unalterable components—a thesis whose appeal was partly rational and partly aesthetic. Atomism was contradicted by Parmenides and Zeno, who objected to the notion that there could be a void in which atoms moved, preferring the notion that *space was a plenum. It was also opposed by Anaxagoras, who argued that the ultimate constituents of matter must be versatile "omiomeres".

*Plato combined the ideas of earlier atomists and the *Pythagoreans in a *geometrical atomic theory, proposing that the atoms of the four *elements were shaped in the fashion of the four "perfect solids" (regular polyhedra). *Aristotle, by contrast, preferred to analyse matter in terms of primordial qualities rather than constituent objects; because Aristotelian ideas became orthodox in the context of Christianity, most medieval philosophers were similarly opposed to atomic theory. Ian Watson's "Ghost Lecturer" (1984) offers a literary account of a classical atomist defending his thesis.

Atomism was revived during the Renaissance, when it was supported by Giordano Bruno and *Galileo, but nothing significant was added to Epicurean theory until Pierre Gassendi proposed in the early seventeenth century that atoms must form intermediate aggregations—molecules—that acted as building blocks for more complex structures. This thesis was further developed by Robert Boyle's *Scyptical Chymist* (1662), which rejected the four Classical elements in favour of a much more elaborate "corpuscular philosophy" but still attempted to account for the combination of atoms in a quasi-Platonic fashion, by reference to their shapes.

Boyle's theory was further elaborated by John Locke in his *Essay on Human Understanding* (1690), but remained controversial; René Descartes remained an orthodox plenarist, while Gottfried Leibniz conceived atoms as "points of energy" rather than material objects. Atomism was afflicted by internal confusion regarding the manner of atomic association. Pierre Maupertuis and Denis Diderot hypothesised that atoms were animate, engaging in active cooperation. Baron Holbach refused to countenance sensitive atoms, but did allow that they could only associate in defined combinations. In 1758, Roger Boscovitch proposed that Leibnizian points of energy must be surrounded by "fields" of attraction and repulsion.

The foundations for a new atomism were laid by Antoine Lavoisier and Joseph Priestley, whose experiments in *chemistry demonstrated the compound nature of water and air, and identified their constituent elements. Such developments attracted little literary interest, although William Blake took the trouble to opine in 1793 that "The Atoms of Democritus / And Newton's Particles of Light / Are Sands upon the Red sea shore / Where Israel's tents do shine so bright". The new atomic theory was systematised by John Dalton's *A New System of Chemical Philosophy* (1808), which included a prototype of the rules by which the chemical formulas of compounds could be determined and represented: the basic conceptual equipment of modern chemistry.

Although Dalton differentiated between different kinds of atoms in terms of their weights, thus favouring a particulate theory, modification of the

Leibnizian notion of points of energy continued. Hermann von Helmholtz and Lord Kelvin conceived of atoms as Cartesian "vortex rings" in the *ether. James Clerk Maxwell, whose electromagnetic theory centralised the notion of a luminiferous ether, agreed with them, dramatising his notion of atoms in the posthumously published poem "To the Chief Musician Upon Nabla: A Tyndallic Ode" (1882). The *positivist philosopher Auguste Comte, on the other hand, deemed any talk of the structure of matter purely speculative and hence irrelevant to scientific discourse. Comte's disciples among theoretical physicists, including Marcelin Berthelot, Ernst Mach, and Pierre Duhem, became significant skeptical voices in a debate that grew increasingly intense in the late nineteenth century.

The ultimate fruit of Dalton's analytical system was Dmitri Mendeleev's periodic table of the elements (1869), whose arrangement of the elements in order of their atomic weights credited each one with an atomic number, filling an arithmetic series that appeared to stretch from 1 to 92. Mendeleev also made much of Edward Frankland's notion of valency, which determined the ratios in which various atoms could combine to form compounds. Attempts to explain the phenomena of atomic number and valency became a key stimulus to the further development of atomic theory. The debate involved philosophers as well as chemists and physicists, and its boundaries were sufficiently elastic to take in Karl *Marx, Friedrich Nietzsche, and Henri Bergson. Literary uses of the concept remained almost exclusively limited to the use of the atom as one element of an extreme contrast of sizes—the ultimate extension of the concept of a *microcosm—although Alfred, Lord Tennyson's celebration of Lucretius (1868), the Roman populariser of Epicurean philosophy, credits him with a vision of "flaring atom-streams".

The atomic controversy entered a new phase when Lord Kelvin's son, J. J. Thomson, determined in 1897 that "cathode rays" were units of *electricity—George Stoney labeled them "electrons"—and proposed that they were subatomic particles involved in the formation of all kinds of atoms. This notion was corroborated by Henri Becquerel's discovery of the radioactive decay of uranium and the Curies' determination that beta *radiation consisted of fast-moving electrons. Lord Rutherford determined that the number of electrons in an element corresponded to its atomic number. To account for the mass and electrical neutrality of atoms, Thomson proposed that there must also be a positive component of more considerable substance, initially hypothesising a spherical, positively charged "cloud" in which electrons were contained but replacing this model in 1911

by one in which the atom resembled a solar system, with the electrons orbiting a nucleus of positively charged protons. The notion of "splitting atoms"—which had long enjoyed a fugitive existence on the edges of philosophical debate, usually featuring as an example of *impossibility—was now transformed into a practical possibility. It was in the context of this series of discoveries that atomic theory began to function as a significant inspiration to literary speculation.

The notion of technological transmutation acquired a new fashionability in the context of Daltonian atomic theory, reflected in such romances as Robert Duncan Milne's "A New Alchemy" (1879) and Arthur Conan Doyle's The Doings of Raffles Haw (1891); the idea was further sophisticated in the context of Rutherford's model by such stories as Clement Fézandie's "The Secret of the Philosopher's Stone" (1923) and Miles J. Breuer's "The Driving Power" (1930). The idea that there might be an ultimate substance of which all subatomic particles were composed also resurfaced in such stories as Frank Conly's "False Fortunes" (1914), in which the primal substance is called the Id. Transmutation and atomic disintegration are seen as corollaries of the same process of atomic management in such melodramas as Eden Phillpotts' Number 87 (1922; by-lined Harrington Hext), Victor McClure's The Ark of the Covenant (1924, aka Ultimatum), and E. Charles Vivian's Star Dust (1925). Disintegration was the more melodramatic of the two notions, and was more frequently developed in isolation, in such works as Julian Hawthorne's "The Uncertainty about Mr. Kippax" (1892), Robert Cromie's The Crack of Doom (1895), John Taine's Green Fire (1928), and William Gerhardi's Jazz and Jasper (1928; aka Eva's Apples and Doom). The idea was quickly refined, in the context of future *war stories, into the possibility of building an *atom bomb.

Popularisation of the solar model also gave rise to the idea that the atoms of our world might be solar systems in a microcosm and the solar systems of our world atoms in a *macrocosm, celebrated in such works as R. A. Kennedy's The Triuniverse (1912). Although Ray Cummings' "The Girl in the Golden Atom" (1919) does not feature an atomic solar system, it became the forerunner of a pulp magazine subgenre of microcosmic romances developing that notion, spearheaded by G. Peyton Wertenbaker's "The Man from the Atom" (1923). Such fantasies offered the only convenient means by which narrative viewpoints could gain active access to the subatomic realm. The relatively modest notion of looking into atoms with the aid of a supremely powerful *microscope, broached by Edward van Zile's "Chemical Clairvoyance" (1890), was likewise introduced to the pulps by Cummings' story, and used didactically in Clement Fézandie's "The Secret of the Atom" (1921).

Rutherford's atomic model could not account for the emission spectra of different types of atoms until Niels Bohr integrated it with Max Planck's quantum theory in 1913 to produce a spectacular hybrid, in which electrons could occupy a series of discrete stationary states whose transitions were determined by the radiation or absorption of quantified energy, causing them to leap from one stable orbit to another. This syncretic combination of hypotheses lent a new sharpness to old controversies regarding contrasted models of *light, whose attempted resolution by such theorists as Bohr, Max Born, Louis de Broglie, Erwin Schrödinger, Wolfgang Pauli, and Werner Heisenberg instituted a spiral of intensive mathematical and conceptual complication that wrought a comprehensive alienation of theoretical physics from common sense.

As the new arcana of subatomic physics became increasingly complex, the number of subatomic particles and explanatory schemes intended to organise them proliferated rapidly. The neutron was added to the mix in 1932, explaining why elements had atomic weights greater than their atomic numbers, and why elements had different isotopes—in which the same number of protons was combined with variant numbers of neutrons—some of which were much less stable than others. The complexities of twentieth-century atomic theory did not lend themselves readily to narrative extrapolation, although some heroic attempts were made to provide accounts of what Bohr atoms might look like to a microcosmic observer—most notably the stories in George Gamow's *Mr. Tompkins Explores the Atom* (1944) and James Blish's "Nor Iron Bars" (1957).

The blurring of the image of the solar atom could not disturb the iconic visual representation of the atom as an "atom-flower" comprising a nucleus and three symmetrically distributed oval orbits, which became a familiar symbol in science fiction illustration in the 1930s and proliferated very extensively after 1945, but it did lend itself to the elliptical potential of imagistic *poetry. The revelation of the extraordinary "extended family" of subatomic particles prompted such responses as John Updike's meditation on neutrinos, "Cosmic Gall" (1963), while poetic representations of atoms and atomic decay are occasionally featured as sidebars in prose fiction, as in Dean McLaughlin's "Ode to Joy" (1991).

Some fictitious subatomic particles, like the planetron in Philip Latham's "The Blindness" (1946) and the one featured in Thomas M. Disch and John T. Sladek's parodic "The Discovery of the Nullitron" (1967), are deliberately fanciful, but *hard science fiction stories working within the context of theoretical physics, such as Richard and Nancy Carrigan's "Minotaur in a Mushroom Maze" (1976) and Paul Preuss' *Broken Symmetries* (1983), sometimes offer more plausible candidates.

The theoretical quest for new ultimate particles out of which all subatomic particles are composed, as embodied in the quark hypothesis developed in 1961 by Murray Gell-Mann, is reflected in such fictions as Ray Brown's "Quiddities" (1983). Gell-Mann appropriated the term from a literary reference in James Joyce's *Finnegans Wake* (1939), to "three quarks for MuSther Mark". This seemed apt because of the proposition that quarks were essentially bound together in threes; the fact that the Joycean term is a corruption of "quart" has no significance in the physical theory. The iconic significance thus conferred on the term resulted in its widespread further adaptation, as in the Hawkwind album *Quark, Strangeness and Charm* (1977), and the title of Samuel R. *Delany and Marilyn Hacker's revue of *avant-garde* science fiction. "Quark alignment" is the key to *hyperspace in William Walling's *The World I Left Behind Me* (1979).

ATOM BOMB

A *weapon generating a destructive explosion by means of nuclear fission or fusion; the fusion version was initially called an H-bomb (H standing for hydrogen) following its invention in the early 1950s, to distinguish it from existing weapons whose name had been routinely shortened to A-bomb. The inherently violent and transgressive notion of "splitting the *atom" originated as a philosophical problem associated with the notion of ultimate particles. The idea acquired new meaning in the context of modern atomic theory, greatly encouraged in 1902 when Lord Rutherford and Frederick Soddy demonstrated the instability of such heavy atoms as uranium and radium. The idea that the continuous spontaneous decay of a radioactive substance might be explosively accelerated seemed an obvious corollary, invested with further plausibility when Albert *Einstein published the iconic formula $E = mc^2$ in 1905. A year later, George Griffith incorporated atomic missiles fired by bazooka-like launchers in *The Lord of Labour*, although the unfinished text was not published until 1911.

H. G. Wells featured bombs detonated by an atomic "chain reaction" in *The World Set Free* (1914), imagining that they would be able to explode several times over. Other early images of atomic weapons are featured in Arthur Train and Robert W. Wood's *The Man Who Rocked the Earth* (1914; book, 1915), Marie Corelli's *The Secret Power* (1921), Karel Čapek's

Krakatit (1924), and Ernest Pérochon's *Les hommes frénétiques* (1925). Awesomely destructive atom bombs were incorporated into the calculations of some of the political fantasies published between the wars, most notably Harold Nicolson's *Public Faces* (1932), which cynically argued that the deployment of a "weapon too dreadful to use" was virtually inevitable—an argument carried forward into such "doomsday weapon" fantasies as Alfred Noyes' *The Last Man* (1940). P. Schuyler Miller's "The Atom Smasher" (1934) was the most notable of four similarly titled stories from the early science fiction pulps.

The possibility of making an atom bomb gained new practicality in 1938 when Otto Hahn and Fritz Strassman discovered that elements of smaller atomic weight were produced when uranium was bombarded with neutrons. Theoretical explanations of the result—including Niels Bohr's suggestion that the reaction only involved one isotope, uranium-235—led Enrico Fermi to suggest that neutrons produced in the fission reaction might provoke further fission reactions in their turn, thus establishing a self-sustaining chain reaction. This suggestion could be extrapolated in two ways: into the notion that a fast-accelerating chain reaction might be used explosively in atomic bombs, and the notion that a stabilised reaction might become the basis for a technology of *nuclear power. When the United States was drawn into World War II in December 1941 the Manhattan Project was immediately established, under a tight security blanket, to produce fission bombs using uranium-235 and plutonium-239; the bomb eventually dropped on Hiroshima on 6 August 1945 was the former type, the one dropped on Nagasaki on 9 August the latter.

The significance of Hahn and Strassman's results was swiftly recognised by John W. *Campbell Jr., who had already written several stories about nuclear power; he immediately began encouraging the science fiction writers working under his aegis to explore both sets of corollaries. This helped generate several atom bomb stories before and during World War II; Campbell was exultant when Cleve Cartmill's "Deadline" (1944) attracted attention from government agents anxious that the Manhattan Project had been compromised. Philip Wylie received a more traumatic visit from the FBI after writing "The Paradise Crater", whose publication date was delayed until 1945; two comic book stories involving Superman with atom bombs were also suppressed.

Campbell's immediate reaction to Hiroshima—in the editorial "Atomic Age" in *Astounding*'s November 1945 issue—was triumphant, citing Lester del Rey's "Nerves" (1942) and Robert A, Heinlein's "Blowups Happen" (1940) and "Solution Unsatisfactory" (1941; by-lined Anson MacDonald) as important anticipations proving science fiction's worth. Campbell proclaimed that "Civilisation [as previously imagined] is dead" because the "Doomsday Bomb" would be a new "Equaliser" forcing the world to choose between "an era of international good manners—or vast and sudden death". His "Postwar Plans" in the February 1946 issue emphasised the dual potential of atomic power by running two articles in parallel columns, one setting out a "Plan for Survival" (building bomb shelters) and the other a "Plan for Expansion" (building nuclear reactors). In "Concerning the Atomic War" (1946), he asserted that the United States could no longer be invaded, because its carefully-stored nuclear weapons would always be able to strike back, even after its devastation.

These articles provided a new agenda for *Astounding*'s writers; Theodore Sturgenon's "Memorial" (April 1946) and "Thunder and Roses" (November 1947) are skeptical meditations on two of their themes. In Frank Belknap Long's "Guest in the House" (March 1946), a mutant from the future draws an inhabited house from the First Atomic Age into a world of inchoate mist beyond the Great Holocaust. In Arthur C. *Clarke's "Loophole" (April 1946), Martians forbid humans to develop space travel and are bombed into oblivion by way of response. The May 1946 cover—advertising Chan Davis' "The Nightmare"—blazoned that title above an explosion silhouetting the Statue of Liberty; the issue also carried A. E. van Vogt's "A Son is Born", the first of a series recycling Roman history within a futuristic *Empire of the Atom*, in which atomic fission is the object of worship in an organised religion. George O. Smith's "The Undamned" (January 1947) begins with the words "Plutonium was an equaliser". *Astounding*'s first mushroom cloud cover (November 1950, signed Pattee) was symbolically ambivalent, showing a spaceship ascending within the cloud's "stem", observed by an x-ray image of a human holding up an atom-flower icon.

Other pulp science fiction stories took a more direct approach, as exemplified by Roger P. Graham's "Atom War" (1946, by-lined Rog Phillips), and book publications followed a similar trend. Malcolm Jameson's pulp melodrama about a "breeder" reaction running catastrophically out of control, "The Giant Atom" (1944), was hastily reprinted after Hiroshima as *Atomic Bomb* (1945), spearheading an inevitable boom in atom bomb novels whose most notable early entries included F. Horace Rose's *The Maniac's Dream* (1946) and Judith Merril's *Shadow on the Hearth* (1950). Upton Sinclair's *A Giant's Strength* (1948) introduced the atom bomb threat to the theatre. Although its introduction to U.S. cinema was delayed until Arch Oboler's *Five* (1951), a tangential commentary was offered in a Czech adaptation of *Krakatit* (1948). The notion that an atom bomb might be employed by terrorists was broached in Philip Wylie's *The Smuggled Atom Bomb* (1951) and David Divine's *Atom at Spithead* (1953) and was soon extrapolated into a subgenre of nuclear blackmail thrillers, including Robert Moore Williams' *The Day They H-Bombed Los Angeles* (1961) and Jeff Sutton's *H-Bomb over America* (1967). The subgenre's changing fashions are trackable in Martin Caidin's *Devil Takes All* (1966), *Almost Midnight* (1971), and *Zoboa* (1986).

Post–atomic war stories—routinely described as "post-holocaust stories"—became one of the most significant subgenres of speculative fiction in the 1950s, both within and without genre science fiction. The most notable examples include Wilson Tucker's *The Long Loud Silence* (1952), Ward Moore's "Lot" (1953), Philip Wylie's *Tomorrow* (1954), Algis Budrys' *False Night* (1954; rev. as *Some Will Not Die*), Pat Frank's *Forbidden Area* (1956; aka *Seven Days to Never*) and *Alas, Babylon* (1959), Nevil Shute's *On the Beach* (1957), Mordecai Roshwald's *Level 7* (1959), Alfred Coppel's *Dark December* (1960), and Walter M. Miller's *A Canticle for Leibowitz* (1960). Images of a holocaust-devastated New York were featured in Harold Rein's *Few Were Left* (1955), Martin Caidin's *The Long Night* (1956), and Kendell Foster Crossen's *The Rest Must Die* (1958, by-lined Richard Foster). Subtler accounts of atomic spoliation included Fritz Leiber's "Coming Attraction" (1950), "The Moon Is Green" (1952), and "A Bad Day for Sales" (1953).

The atom bomb's iconic mushroom cloud remained the central image of apocalyptic fantasy throughout the 1960s, although it was complemented in that decade by anxieties about *population and *pollution. Subsequent atomic holocaust stories include Glen Cook's *The Heirs of Babylon* (1972), David Graham's *Down to a Sunless Sea* (1979), and James Morrow's *This Is the Way the World Ends* (1986). Stories of extraterrestrial survival after the atomic destruction of Earth exercised a particular fascination on science fiction writers committed to the idea of space *colonisation; it is poignantly developed in Ray Bradbury's *The Martian Chronicles* (1950) and retained a similar elegiac quality in such tragedies as Edmond Hamilton's "After a Judgment Day" (1963) before acquiring a new realism in such works as Thomas N. Scortia's *Earthwreck!* (1974) and Joe Haldeman's *Worlds* series (1981–1992).

As soon as the A-bomb had demonstrated its power, Hans Bethe's proposal that the energy of stars derives from fusion reactions that produce helium from hydrogen was fed into nuclear weapons research. Experiments proved that fusion reactions using the "heavy hydrogen" isotopes deuterium and tritium could indeed be explosively generated. The first U.S. H-bombs were manufactured and tested in 1952–1953. The rapid acquisition of the technology by the Soviet Union caused an alarm reaction that intensified the Cold War, providing the inspiration for an enormous quantity of thriller fiction and secured the popularity of late twentieth-century spy fiction. Early H-bomb stories include Ronald Duncan's *The Last Adam* (1952) and Warwick Scott's *The Doomsday Story* (1952).

In the cultural climate of the Cold War the testing of atom bombs gave rise to fervent anxieties, manifest in a wide range of stories about potentially disastrous side effects—especially atmospheric "fallout"—spearheaded by Pat Frank's *Mr. Adam* (1946) and Roger P. Graham's "So Shall Ye Reap" (1947, by-lined Rog Phillips). Jay Franklin's *The Rat Race* (1950), Gerald Kersh's "The Brighton Monster" (1948), and Isaac Asimov's "Breeds There a Man...?" (1951) feature very odd side effects, but the most bizarre fantasies of this kind were seen in the *cinema. Straightforward exercises in alarmism such as *The Day the Earth Caught Fire* (1961) were slow to appear there, but movies in which atom bombs attracted the censorious attention of horrified aliens, as in *The Day the Earth Stood Still* (1951), had a considerable impact. They were supplemented by a remarkable series of fantasies in which atomic tests wake dormant prehistoric monsters. *The Beast from 20,000 Fathoms* (1953) was parent to an entire subgenre, extrapolated in such B-movies as *It Came from Beneath the Sea* (1955) and successfully exported to post-Hiroshima Japan in *Gojiro* (1955; aka *Godzilla*). The visual dimension given to the tests in such movies as *The Amazing Colossal Man* (1957) routinely borrowed—and continually recycled—photographs taken in the course of actual tests; one particular image of a disintegrating house was shown thousands of times over in the cinema and on TV.

The advent of the atom bomb seemed to many observers to be a crucial break in human history, reflected in such essays as Gunther Anders' "Reflections on the H-Bomb" (1956). Its moral dimension was luridly highlighted in Robert Jungk's journalistic "exposé" *Brighter Than a Thousand Suns* (1956; trans. 1958), which alleges that German scientists conspired to prevent Hitler from obtaining an atom bomb, while U.S. scientists made a diabolical bargain; J. Robert Oppenheimer is likened to Faust, while Leo Szilard—who had earlier imagined "My Trial as a War Criminal" (1949)—is cast as the voice of conscience. Jungk's thesis was subjected to further literary elaboration in

Pearl S. Buck's *Command the Morning* (1959). A summation of the existential significance of the bomb was attempted in J. G. Ballard's "The Terminal Beach" (1964), whose protagonist maroons himself in the derelict landscape of the H-bomb test-site island of Eniwetok.

The build-up of nuclear weapons in the real world was justified by the logic of deterrence and the necessity of keeping abreast, if not ahead, in an "arms race". The escalation of weapons stocks was reflected in a rapid growth in futurological attempts to foresee the likely course of a nuclear war, which similarly made much of the notion of inevitable escalation, as reflected in such painstaking political thrillers as S. B. Hough's *Extinction Bomber* (1956) and *Beyond the Eleventh Hour* (1961), Peter George's *Two Hours to Doom* (1958, by-lined Peter Bryant; aka *Red Alert*) and Eugene Burdick and Harvey Wheeler's *Fail-Safe* (1962), and in such vitriolic satires as the movie loosely based on George's novel, Stanley Kubrick's *Dr. Strangelove, or How I Learned to Stop Worrying and Love the Bomb* (1963). The satirisation of the nuclear arms race was assisted by such acronyms as MAD, which signified the doctrine of "mutual assured destruction" that provided the bedrock of deterrence theory.

Inevitably, nuclear proliferation and Cold War antagonism called forth ideological opposition in such forms as the British Campaign for Nuclear Disarmament (CND), whose annual marches to the Atomic Weapons Research Establishment at Aldermaston in the late 1950s and early 1960s included such participants as Bertrand *Russell and science fiction writer John Brunner. A small subgenre of CND fantasies emerged in Britain, whose most graphic products included Ian Watson's horror novel *The Power* (1987). A substantial subgenre of cautionary tales grew up in children's fiction, most extravagantly displayed in the work of the German writer Gudrun Pausewang and such English-language novels as Robert C. O'Brien's *Z for Zachariah* (1975). Leigh Kennedy's *Saint Hiroshima* (1987) is a character study of obsessive fear of the atom bomb. David Langford's *The Leaky Establishment* (1984) is an unsettling parody of life at Britain's Atomic Weapons Research Establishment by a former employee, which the Ministry of Defence nobly declined to censor. Atom bomb tests by various nations, including neighbouring rivals India and Pakistan, helped to maintain an anxiety reflected in such stories of tests gone awry as Dean McLaughlin's "The Permanent Implosion" (1964).

The strong likelihood of nuclear war inspired such nonfictional texts as Pat Frank's *How to Survive the H-Bomb and Why* (1962) and Dean Ing's "Gimme Shelter!" (1982), and the growth of actual survivalist movements looking forward to the day when nuclear war would apply a *coup de grace* to the irredeemably sick world. Earnest accounts of post-holocaust survival such as Ing's *Systemic Shock* (1981) and *Pulling Through* (1983) and David Brin's *The Postman* (1985) were supplemented from the 1980s onwards by a prolific subgenre of survivalist fiction—including extensive series bearing such by-lines as Jerry Ahern, James Barton, and James Axler—which relished the thought of the West's reversion to new extremes of wildness, and used post-holocaust scenarios to develop an elaborate pornography of violence.

Atomic bombs attained a new versatility in the 1970s by virtue of the advent of the neutron bomb, sometimes advertised as a bomb that would kill people without destroying property, and consequent discussion of "tactical" nuclear weapons that might be deployed on battlefields. Weapons of these sorts rapidly became integrated into future war stories. Futurological accounts of the likely course and consequence of a nuclear war were complicated in the 1980s by the notion that any substantial nuclear exchange would blast enough dust into the upper atmosphere to precipitate an ecocatastrophe of a type that became known as a "nuclear winter", as described and popularised in *The Nuclear Winter: The World After Nuclear War* (1985) edited by Carl *Sagan and *A Path Where No Man Thought: Nuclear Winter and the End of the Arms Race* (1990) by Sagan and Richard Turco. Dramatisations of the idea include Ben Bova's "Nuclear Autumn" (1985) and Frederik Pohl's "Fermi and Frost" (1985). The threat of atomic terrorism was renewed by the fear of low-tech "dirty bombs" designed to contaminate rather than evaporate, as featured in such stories as Judy Kless' "We'll Have Manhattan" (2004).

The atom bomb's status as a historical turning point is investigated in numerous *alternative history stories. Frederik Pohl and C. M. Kornbluth's conclusion in "Nightmare with Zeppelins" (1958) that an atom bomb really would have seemed too dreadful to use in the Victorian era is echoed in Ronald W. Clark's *Queen Victoria's Bomb* (1967). Clark's *The Bomb that Failed* (1969; aka *The Last Year of the Old World*) and Alfred Coppel's *The Burning Mountain* (1983) track what might have happened if the Manhattan Project had failed. Kim Stanley Robinson's "The Lucky Strike" (1984) imagines what might have ensued had the U.S. pilot charged with dropping the Hiroshima bomb refused to carry out the order. The Nagasaki explosion is the "inciting incident" in Julian May's far-ranging historical fantasy *Intervention* (1987). Kevin J. Anderson's *The Trinity Paradox* (1991) explores what might have happened had Nazi Germany developed the atom bomb.

AUTOMATION

The replacement of animal and muscle power by mechanical processes in the production of material goods. The first major historical phase of automation involved the development of windmills and watermills in the eleventh and twelfth centuries, but a much more important phase began at the end of the eighteenth century with the Industrial Revolution associated with the development of steam engines and their nineteenth-century application to transportation and the textile industry. This phase merged with a succeeding phase based on the proliferation of internal combustion engines and electrical technologies, the latter being further refined by the electronic revolution that opened the way for the automation of intellectual as well as physical labour.

The literary response to this pattern of changes has been so profound and widespread that it is a major topic in the history of modern literature, the "industrial novel" being one of the major subgenres during the novel's formative period. The notion of automation as a beneficial trend that might free mankind from the burden of labour and universalise the privileges of aristocratic leisure society is reflected in some *Utopian fiction, but the approving arguments set out in such novels as Étienne Cabet's *Voyage en Icarie* (1840), Edward Bulwer-Lytton's *The Coming Race* (1871), Edward Bellamy's *Looking Backward, 2000–1887* (1888), and Anatole France's *Sur la pierre blanche* (1905; trans. as *The White Stone*) were never entirely free from ambivalence and were far outnumbered by anxious responses—inevitably, given that the priorities of melodrama always favour fear over hope. Literary attempts to grasp the underlying trend rather than its superficial specifics tended to represent automation as an inherently dehumanising process, threatening human nature with a reductive mechanisation; futuristic extrapolations often invoke the imagery of the ant hive.

Many nineteenth-century litterateurs were overtly or covertly sympathetic to the cause of the "Luddites"—hand-weavers who smashed the steam-powered looms that were putting them out of work in the name of the fictitious King Lud—and their sympathies ensured the survival of the term's symbolic loading. Socialist reformers, torn between the desire to improve the material conditions of working class life and the fear of immiseration resulting from

mass redundancy, treated the prospect of automation with deep suspicion. The notion that craftsmanship gives human life its meaning and dignity often tipped the balance in favour of Luddite ideology, as exemplified in such propagandist novels as William Morris's *News from Nowhere* (1890) and Claude Farrère's *Les condamnés à mort* (1920; trans. as *Useless Hands*). The futility of a fully automated society in which human life is entirely devoted to leisure activities is scathingly satirised in such twentieth-century scientific romances as Muriel Jaeger's *The Question Mark* (1926) and Aldous Huxley's *Brave New World* (1932), although representations of a tiny leisured class in naturalistic literature often expressed approval—sometimes unqualified approval—of its *modus vivendi* and values.

The supplementary fear that increasing social dependence on automated production might eventually render people helpless to respond to malfunction was eloquently expressed in E. M. Forster's *conte philosophique* "The Machine Stops" (1909), which was produced as a reaction against the futuristic anticipations of H. G. *Wells in much the same way that William Morris had produced his Utopia as a reaction against Edward Bellamy's. The idea that full automation would be the prelude to the replacement of human society by a mechanical society that would take up the torch of evolutionary progress on its own behalf had been satirically broached in Samuel *Butler's *Erewhon* (1872), but the idea of a revolt of machines gifted with *artificial intelligence came to seem surreally pertinent in such fantasies as W. Grove's *The Wreck of a World* (1889), H. A. Highstone's "Frankenstein—Unlimited" (1936), Frank Edward Arnold's "City of Machines" (1939; aka "The Mad Machines"), Robert Bloch's "It Happened Tomorrow" (1941), Clifford Simak's "Bathe Your Bearings in Blood!" (1950; aka "Skirmish"), and Lord Dunsany's *The Last Revolution* (1951).

The founder of pulp science fiction, Hugo *Gernsback, had been very enthusiastic about automation in his own Utopia *Ralph 124C41+* (1911), but his magazines immediately gave voice to strident reservations in such polemics as David H. Keller's "The Threat of the Robot" (1929), Miles J. Breuer's "Paradise and Iron" (1930), and—most extravagantly of all—Laurence Manning and Fletcher Pratt's "City of the Living Dead" (1930). The last-named offers a striking image of the people of the future living entirely in what would now be called *virtual reality, with all of their experiences being provided synthetically. John W. *Campbell Jr.'s "Twilight" (1934) and "Night" (1935) went further than Forster, imagining a fully automated future proceeding serenely while its human component degenerates to extinction. Independent societies of machines were featured in such pulp stories as Manning's "Call of the Mech-Men" (1933) and Eric Frank Russell's "Mechanistra" (1942). In the late 1930s, however, the idea of automation became significantly confused in genre science fiction with the idea of humanoid *robots, and robot stories took up the burden of philosophical meditations on the implication of automation. One ironic side effect of this move was that the kinds of "robots" that actually replaced humans on industrial production lines, thus achieving a major step in the automation of production, were relegated to background roles.

Automation seemed less threatening to human dignity when it was applied to areas in which craftsmanship was less of an issue, including *food production, as in Otfrid von Hanstein's *Die Farm der Vorschollenen* (1924; trans. as "The Hidden Colony"). In fiction as in the real world, however, *biotechnological automation ran afoul of considerable imaginative resistance to the inexorable advancement of "factory farming". Upton Sinclair's exposé of the canning industry in *The Jungle* (1905) was intended as a plea for better working conditions for its workers, but the gut reaction of its audience was more basic. Subsequent accounts of automated food production often intended to cause revulsion; Ian Watson's *Meat* (1988) is a conspicuous example.

As the automation of actual factories made steady progress with the introduction of assembly lines and the increasing influence of Frederick Winslow Taylor's "scientific management"—reflected in the practical science of ergonomics—literary reflections became increasingly anxious. Visual depictions of partly automated factories, like the ones in Fritz Lang's film *Metropolis* (1926) and Charlie Chaplin's *Modern Times* (1936), emphasised the reduction of human beings to quasi-mechanical units in a relentless process. The acceleration of automation in the United States in response to the necessity of increasing production in World War II called forth little contemporary response, but once the war was over, pent-up anxieties burst forth in a flood of black comedies, including Kurt Vonnegut's *Player Piano* (1950), Frederik Pohl's "The Midas Plague" (1954), Philip K. Dick's "Autofac" (1955), and Robert Sheckley's "Untouched by Human Hands" (1953).

The anxiety expressed by these anti-automation polemics ebbed away by degrees as the sight of fully automated assembly lines gradually become so familiar as to seem perfectly normal, sometimes subject to witty deployment in advertisements for *automobiles. Kate Wilhelm's "A Is for Automation" (1959) is a painstakingly subtle account of a feud between the artificial intelligence in charge of a factory and its human nightwatchman. Walt and Leigh Richmond's "I, BEM" (1964) inverted earlier anxieties in an account of an artificial intelligence descended from an IBM typewriter, which is fearful of redundancy following the creation of "new model humans" and other "biologics". Christopher Anvil's "Positive Feedback" (1965) suggested that the seemingly inexorable trend towards automation might be swiftly reversed once its "benefits" were accurately costed, while Josef Nesvadba's "Vynalez proti sobe" (1964; trans. as "Inventor of His Own Undoing") explains why automation might fail to deliver benefits in a socialist context.

The automation of the domestic environment became a significant subject of advertising in the postwar years as the market in electrical domestic appliances boomed. The trend was taken to logical extremes in a number of satirical science fiction stories, including C. L. Moore and Henry Kuttner's "This Is the House" (1946, by-lined Laurence O'Donnell), William Tenn's "The House Dutiful" (1948), and Joanna Russ's "Nor Custom Stale" (1959), while Kate Wilhelm's *Smart House* (1989) featured modestly in an ingenious murder mystery.

The notion that increasing automation would lead inexorably to artificial intelligence and, hence, to machine independence, became far more plausible—and its fictional reflections more ominous—with the advent of *computers, generating such fantasies of automation-run-amok as John Sladek's *The Reproductive System* (1968; aka *Mechasm*). The possibility of achieving greater intimacy between flesh and machine in various *cyborg forms introduced a new shade of meaning into the term; the striking imagery of David R. Bunch's *Moderan* (1971), in which people automate themselves by replacing their "fleshstrips" by degrees, provides a graphic illustration, but it marked the end of an era rather than a beginning, because traditional fears of industrial automation had mostly been laid to rest by that date.

AUTOMOBILE

A self-propelled road vehicle. Although Nicholas Cugnot built a steam-propelled vehicle in 1770, the term "automobile" did not come into use until Daimler's patenting of the internal combustion engine in 1887 paved the way for the mounting of such an engine on a chassis by Panhard and Levasor in 1891. George B. Selden's 1895 patent for a gasoline-driven automobile opened the floodgates of design and manufacture, although Henry Ford had built his first vehicle in 1893. Initially dubbed a "horseless carriage" to emphasise its principal difference from the mode of *transportation it replaced, the automobile eventually attained a near-monopoly on the word "car", which had previously been used with more general reference. Steam cars continued to compete with internal combustion engines throughout the first quarter of the twentieth century, often reaching higher speeds, although they were banned from racetracks on safety grounds in 1907.

The expansion of personal freedom associated with the new phase of transportation technology, begun in 1909 when Henry Ford's Model T production line began to roll, was one of the key trends in twentieth-century Western culture, reflected in the establishment of the private car as a central feature of lifestyle fantasy. The racing car became a key representation of the idea of speed in futurist *art, and the "car chase" was a staple of *cinema imagery from the earliest days of Hollywood; the automobile eventually gave rise to its own cinematic genre of "road movies".

The automobile's integration into the background of contemporary fiction had a fundamental impact on the potential pace and range of the action, but it was rarely foregrounded. It often features in the background of Utopian images of the future and is sometimes omnipresent—as in Frederick Nelson's *Toronto in 1928* (1908)—but is rarely seen as a socially transformative invention. The design of new automobiles only played a minor role in Vernian fiction, before and after their actual invention, because such vehicles were inherently less dramatic than airships and submarines, even in such advanced versions as Herbert Strang's *The Cruise of the Gyro-Car* (1910). Leavitt Ashley Knight's "The Millennium Engine" (1915) showed rare foresight in highlighting the economic consequences of the ultimate Model T.

David H. Keller's "The Revolt of the Pedestrians" (1928) and "The Living Machine" (1935) contributed lurid anticipations of future problems to the early science fiction pulps, and Clark Ashton Smith published a satirical account of a future anthropologist's account of the twentieth-century cult of "The Great God Awto" (1940), but it was not until the 1950s that a fuller appreciation was gained of what the automobile had wrought in cultural terms.

Speculative extrapolations of that realisation, deftly mingling satire with drama, include Robert F. Young's "Chrome Pastures" (1956), "Romance in a Twenty-First Century Used Car Lot" (1960), and "Sweet Tooth" (1963), Fred McMorrow's "The Big Wheel" (1961), H. Chandler Elliott's "A Day on Death Highway" (1963), Rick Raphael's "Code Three" (1963), Roger Zelazny's "Devil Car" (1965) and "Auto-da-Fé" (1967), William Earls' "Traffic

Problem" (1970), Henry Melton's "Parking Spaces" (1985), and Sarah Zettel's "Driven by Moonlight" (1991). The prospect of a permanent life on the road is similarly reflected in Miriam Allen deFord's "Keep Moving" (1968), Mack Reynolds' *Rolltown* (1969; exp. 1976), John Jakes' *On Wheels* (1973), Joe L. Hensley's *The Black Roads* (1976), Connie Willis' "The Last of the Winnebagos" (1988), and Michael Reaves' "The Legend of the Midnight Cruiser" (2003). A more flamboyant kind of black comedy is evident in such science fiction stories as Fritz Leiber's "X Marks the Pedwalk" (1963), Harlan Ellison's "Dogfight on 101" (1969; aka "Along the Scenic Route"), Ben Elton's *Gridlock* (1991), Heathcote Williams' poem *Autogeddon* (1991), and Richard Morgan's *Market Forces* (2004).

A significant watershed in automobile marketing was reached when Henry Ford allegedly said that "the public can have any colour it wants, so long as it's black", operating on the assumption that utilitarian factors rather than aesthetic ones would determine consumer choice—with the result that he suffered a catastrophic loss of turnover to his market rivals. The intensity, lavishness, and tone of modern advertising offers powerful testimony to the force of aesthetic factors in automobile use, especially to the eroticisation of the automobile. The fact that the rear seats of automobiles had become a highly significant locus of sexual activity, especially among teenagers, had the remarkable side effect of exercising a strong influence on the kind of B-movie expressly made for "drive-in" theaters, greatly encouraging the production of horror-science fiction movies whose induced nervous excitement was potentially negotiable.

The cinema medium pays suitably diplomatic homage to this phenomenon, which is exaggerated to grotesque and calculatedly perverse extremes in such literary works as Josef Nesvadba's "Vampires Ltd". (tr. 1964), Claude F. Cheinisse's "Juliette" (tr. 1965), Robert Thurston's *A Set of Wheels* (1983), and Trevor Hoyle's *The Man Who Travelled on Motorways* (1997). J. G. Ballard's *Crash* (1973) reached a further extreme in dramatising the author's deduction—by means of a method established by the psychologist Eric Berne—that, rather than being unfortunate accidents, the car crash may be regarded as the subconscious objective of the fast driver. Less down-to-earth celebrations of automobile charisma can be found in Ian Watson's *Miracle Visitors* (1978), in which a Ford Thunderbird undertakes a hallucinatory trip to the moon, and Tony Daniel's *Metaplanetary* (2001), which offers a similar role to a Jeep Wrangler. A more earnest projection of an "aircar" technology that enables trips to low-Earth-orbit destinations is featured in Rob Chilson and William F. Wu's "Distant Tigers" (1991)—a relatively rare textual development of an illustrative conceit that had often represented personalised flying machines as airborne wheel-less cars.

The idea that the transformation of American culture wrought by the automobile is necessarily transient because of the nonrenewability of fossil fuels is usually entertained with reluctance and routinely resisted, but it is developed in a different spirit in such stories as Elizabeth A. Lynn's "California Dreaming" (1992). The ever-increasing problem of disposing of derelict automobiles is brought into sharp focus by such near-futuristic stories as Dominic Green's "Three Lions on the Armband" (2004).

B

BACON, FRANCIS (1561–1626)

English statesman whose political career won him the titles Viscount St. Albans and Baron Verulam. He studied for two years at Trinity College, Cambridge, from 1573 to 1575, where he became dissatisfied with the seeming sterility of Aristotelian philosophy. He was a lawyer and member of Parliament before his association with Elizabeth I's favourite, the Earl of Essex, propelled him to a precarious position of influence; he was eventually dismissed from the post of Lord Chancellor for taking bribes. His philosophical writings were mostly completed and published while he attempted—unsuccessfully—to reestablish his influence in the court of James I, although he had begun his endeavors much earlier.

Bacon conceived a plan—echoing one formulated by his namesake Roger *Bacon—to produce a vast critical encyclopaedia that would provide a thoroughgoing revision of traditional wisdom in the light of modern discoveries: *Instauratio Magna* (*The Great Instauration*). He published a prospectus of sorts as *The Advancement of Learning* (1605; rev. in Latin as *De Augmentis Scientiarum*, 1623) before writing numerous drafts of a more substantial preface, which was eventually published as *Novum Organum Scientiarum* (1620; *A New System of Science*). These were key works in the development of the philosophy of science, stressing the importance of empirical observation and experimentation and warning of the hazards of *idola* (idols): false preconceptions that inhibit enquiry. Bacon's failure to recognise the importance of mathematical analysis and his reluctance to

acknowledge the significance of such contemporary discoveries as the circulation of the blood compromised his subsequent reputation, but the arguments he put forward were vital to the progress of science.

The most important of these arguments—and the one that had the greatest impact on the subsequent literary imagination—was that of the four categories of "idols" that were confusing human thought and blocking perception of the truth. The "idols of the tribe" are fundamental fallacies of human psychology—including a tendency to seek and perceive more order in nature than there actually is, which is the principal basis of many errors licensed by psychological *plausibility. The "idols of the cave" are errors produced by a particular individual's sensory and psychological preferences, including convictions based on *aesthetic judgments. The "idols of the marketplace" are errors induced by the limitations of language and carelessness in its use. The "idols of the theatre" are incorrect ways of thinking instilled by received ideas—the products of deceptive *rhetoric.

Bacon assumed that if all of these idols could be cast down the accumulation of knowledge would be a simple matter of collecting sufficient observations for the general causal principles inherent therein to become manifest by "induction". His notion of experimentation as an open-ended extension of empirical enquiry was eventually superseded by the notion of putting hypotheses to the proof, but his description of the scientific attitude of mind was a definitive summation of the decisive shift then taking place, which demoted arguments of authority from their previously privileged position and established empirical observations and reasoning therefrom as the bedrock of knowledge.

Bacon's early works also included *De Sapientia Veterum* (1609; trans. as *The Wisdom of the Ancients*), a remarkable allegorical reinterpretation of classical *myth in terms of his own philosophy of knowledge. Shortly thereafter he began a Utopian romance, *New Atlantis*, but never completed it; it may have been written as an advertisement for a Royal College of Science that he hoped to persuade the king to endow, which he put aside when the probability of success diminished. It is a pity that he did not continue it, but even in its abridged form it is a strikingly original work. Much of the text consists of a catalogue of new technologies developed by the scientists of "Salomons House", whose Father is a Scientist-Priest supervising the social and technological applications of a highly sophisticated science. These include, among many others, the impressive products of the "Engine-Houses"—aircraft, submarines, perpetual motion machines, and so on—and the "Houses of Deceits of the Senses", where all manner of illusions can be produced and, hence, revealed for what they are. As well as providing an important anticipation of the potential of technological progress, the romance is a significant assertion of the interdependence of social and technological progress.

When he finally conceded that the *Instauratio Magna* was beyond his scope, Bacon planned a modest six-volume series of scientific texts, but only *Historia Ventorum* (1622; *An Account of the Winds*) and *Historia Vitae et Mortis* (1623; *An Account of Life and Death*) were completed. A draft of what would have been a third volume, *Sylva Sylvarum* (*A Forest of Forests*), was issued posthumously in 1627, with the *New Atlantis* appended to it. It had little influence on subsequent Utopian fiction, although many later writers were certainly aware of it.

The causal connection implied by the anecdote that tells how Bacon died of a chill after stuffing a chicken with snow, so that he might observe the effect of refrigeration in delaying putrefaction, is probably illusory. The allegation that he was the true author of William Shakespeare's plays—first promulgated by a woman named Alice Bacon—is palpably false, in spite of the clues "deciphered" by Ignatius Donnelly in *The Great Cryptogram* (1888). Such fancies are, however, an apt testament to Bacon's intellectual stature. Abraham Cowley's "Ode to the Royal Society" (1667) celebrates his iconoclasm, and it opened the way to the Tree of Knowledge: "The Orchard's open now, and free; / *Bacon* has broke that Scar-crow Deitie". John Dryden's "To My Honour'd Friend, Dr. Charleton" (1663) agreed that "The World

to *Bacon* does not onely owe / Its present Knowledge, but its future too". Walter Savage Landor's *Imaginary Conversations* (1824–1829) features Bacon in discussion with Richard Hooker. He was more effectively revived as a character in the anonymous *The Atlantis*, published in the *American Museum of Science, Literature and the Arts* (1838–1839), addressing an audience whose members included *Galileo, René Descartes, Isaac *Newton, and Benjamin Franklin. He is also featured in H. D. MacKaye's time travel fantasy *The Panchronicon* (1904).

BACON, ROGER (CA. 1220–1292)

English philosopher. He was involved in the Renaissance revival of interest in *Aristotle—on whose works he lectured at the University of Paris—and subsequently became interested in experimental science. He returned from Paris to Oxford in 1247 or thereabouts, making contact with Roger de Grosseteste, who shared his interests. He invested a good deal of time and money on building a library of esoteric works and equipping a laboratory for experimental studies in optics and alchemy. He speculated about the viability of flying machines and other forms of powered vehicular transport, but his research yielded few practical results, although he did observe the magnifying power of combinations of lenses and constructed a camera obscura in order to make astronomical observations of the *Sun. He was also the first European to record a recipe for making gunpowder, in 1242.

Bacon's career abruptly changed direction in 1257 when he fell ill and joined the Franciscan order. His new superiors immediately attempted to curtail his researches, but he appealed to Pope Clement IV—with whom he was personally acquainted—for support in the compilation of a new encyclopaedia. The permission obtained was carefully qualified, forcing him to work in secret, but before Clement died in 1268 Bacon was able to write three treatises that preserved his thought for later generations, known as *Opus majus, Opus minus,* and *Opus tertium.* Copies of these works assisted such sixteenth-century English scientists as John *Dee and Leonard Digges to take up his studies where he had left off. Three more fragments of the projected encyclopaedia, *Communia naturalium* (*General Principles of Natural Philosophy*), *Communia mathematica* (*General Principles of Mathematics*), and *Compendium philosophiae* (*Compendium of Philosophy*) were completed before he was imprisoned on suspicion of heresy in the late 1270s and disappeared from historical view.

This combination of circumstances fitted Bacon for eventual representation as a heroic scientific visionary, cruelly oppressed and prevented from exercising a progressive influence by blinkered dogmatic authority. He was usually represented in Renaissance literature, however, as an alchemist and magician, as in Robert Greene's *Friar Bacon and Friar Bungay* (1592). The latter associates him with a famous story of the construction of an oracular Brazen Head, attributed by other writers to Albertus Magnus. The head's pronouncements—"Time Is", "Time Was", and "Time Is Past"—are only heard by an apprentice reluctant to wake his master. Prose versions of the story include *The Famous History of Fryer Bacon* (1627) and John Cowper Powys' *The Brazen Head* (1956), in which Bacon and Albertus Magnus collaborate on the project. Bacon's recognition as a pioneer of science is reflected in Rudyard Kipling's "The Eye of Allah" (1926), in which he invents a *microscope; Irvin Lester and Fletcher Pratt's account of "The Roger Bacon Formula" (1929); Nathan Schachner's "Lost in the Dimensions" (1937), in which he is visited by curious time travellers; and James Blish's biographical novel *Doctor Mirabilis* (1964).

BALLARD, J(AMES) G(RAHAM) (1930–)

British writer born in Shanghai. Following his internment by the Japanese during World War II, he briefly read medicine at Cambridge but did not take a degree. He also read English for a year in London but dropped out again. He joined the Royal Air Force as a trainee pilot but found life in the RAF no more congenial than any of his earlier attempts to build a career; he wrote his first science fiction story, "Passport to Eternity", while awaiting his discharge, but it did not sell until 1962. He began to sell other science fiction stories in 1956, and worked for three years as assistant editor of *Chemistry and Industry* while he built his writing career.

Ballard's 1956 publications included "Escapement", detailing the existential crisis suffered by a man who finds himself living the same slowly shrinking interval of time repeatedly and "Prima Belladonna", the first of a series of tales set in the decadent artists' colony of Vermilion Sands. In "Build-Up" (1957; reprinted as "The Concentration City"), the world's population has increased to several trillion and "free space" is the substance of nostalgic dreams. In "Manhole 69" (1957) the subjects of a sleep-deprivation experiment descend by nightmarish degrees into a quasi-catatonic withdrawal state. His distinctive manner of presentation and set of concerns—which were eventually to licence the invention of the adjective "Ballardian"—can be seen even in these early works. He was prepared to compromise

with the demands of the marketplace by writing quirky comedies like "Track 12" (1958) and "Now, Zero" (1959), but his opinion of the tales of interplanetary adventure that made up the science fiction genre's core mythology was obvious in the only two stories he wrote with extraterrestrial settings; "The Waiting Grounds" (1959) and "The Time-Tombs" (1963) extrapolate existential *angst* to a cosmic time-scale, adding an extra dimension to its alienating effect.

Ballard's fascination with the mysteries of time were further displayed in the dystopian comedy "Chronopolis" (1960), about a future city from which tyrannical clocks have been banned, and in "The Voices of Time" (1960; revised as "News from the Sun", 1982). In the latter story, signals from a distant galaxy have been intercepted by Earthly radio-telescopes, but the only intelligence they contain is a countdown to the end of the universe. Some readers complained about the story's gnomic imagery and sense of futility, but it caught the imagination of other writers, most notably Brian *Aldiss and Michael Moorcock, who were anxious to break the pulpish mould in which science fiction had long been cast.

Ballard's first novel, *The Wind from Nowhere* (1962), set a pattern that he reproduced more effectively in *The Drowned World* (1962), *The Drought* (1965; aka *The Burning World*), and *The Crystal World* (1966), extrapolating a long and rich tradition of British *disaster stories popularised in the 1950s by John Wyndham and John Christopher. Whereas Wyndham and Christopher had written grim tales of survival under pressure, in which the supposedly traditional English virtues of decency and industry are subject to trial by ordeal, Ballard's accounts of environmental change propose that the appropriate response to abrupt and irresistible environmental change is psychological adaptation, no matter how drastic.

In March 1962, Ballard took part in a BBC radio discussion in which he debated the significance of modern science fiction with John Wyndham, Kingsley Amis, Brian *Aldiss, John Brunner, and Kenneth Bulmer. Ballard waxed lyrical on the need for science fiction writers to abandon tales of space travel and concentrate instead on the exploration of "inner space"—a case he also made in an essay that appeared as a "guest editorial" in the May 1962 issue of *New Worlds*, which included the oft-quoted remark that "the only truly alien planet is Earth". The essay called for science fiction to deploy "more psycho-literary ideas, more meta-biological and meta-chemical concepts, private time-systems, synthetic psychologies and space-times, more of the remote, somber half-worlds one glimpses in the paintings of schizophrenics, all in all a complete speculative poetry and fantasy of science". It became one of the central documents of the "new wave" of British science fiction for which *New Worlds* became the main vehicle when Michael Moorcock took over its editorship in 1964.

Ballard's antipathy to space fiction became a significant bone of contention between supporters of the new wave and traditionalists; Ballard defended his argumentative ground with considerable vigor. "Cage of Sand" (1962) was the first of several near-future stories in which the U.S. space program has been abandoned as a brief folly of futile ambition. In 1974, Ballard observed that "as far as manned flights are concerned ... the *Space Age, far from lasting for hundreds if not thousands of years, is already over". He continued to elaborate this insight, eventually assembling a collection of his skeptical stories under the title *Memories of the Space Age* (1988). In addition to the 1982 title story—set in a deserted Cape Kennedy where the only survivor of the last space mission indulges in literal flights of fancy—the collection features "The Man Who Walked on the Moon" (1985), an account of an imposture far more delicate than any vulgar claim that the whole lunar adventure was faked in a TV studio.

Ballard's work became more self-consciously *avant-gardist* with the publication of *The Atrocity Exhibition* (1970; aka *Love and Napalm: Export USA*), a literary collage representing "the iconography of mass-merchandising", attempting to encapsulate and evaluate the key images and technologies of the twentieth century in a new and conspicuously *postmodern way. He was particularly fascinated by the development of Anglo-American culture's love affair with the *automobile and by the manner in which the landscapes of modern civilisation were being transformed by the advent of motorways. In a 1971 article he observed that "the car crash is the most dramatic event in most people's lives" and alleged that "if we really feared the crash, most of us would be unable to look at a car, let alone drive one". In pursuit of this insight, Ballard mounted an exhibition of crashed cars at the London' New Arts Laboratory in 1970 London and appeared in a BBC TV film entitled *Crash* (1971) before publishing the novel *Crash* (1973), which set out to explore the orgastic possibilities of reckless driving and crash-associated masochism.

Although it carried forward the same fascination with the impact of cars and roads on modern life, the existentialist fable *Concrete Island* (1974) was much less controversial; like its immediate successor, *High-Rise* (1975), it is an urban Robinsonade, whose mordant wit was exaggerated to more obviously sarcastic

effect in such satires as "The Greatest TV Show on Earth" (1972), "The Life and Death of God" (1976), and "The Intensive Care Unit" (1977). *The Unlimited Dream Company* (1979), a messianic posthumous fantasy in which Ballard's home town of Shepperton is exalted far above suburban mundanity, began another, more reflective, phase in his work, but the subsequent development of the phase took him even further away from the science fiction field. He only revisited it thereafter in short fiction, save for the garish *Hello America* (1981), which describes the "rediscovery" of an abandoned American continent whose mythological apparatus lies in ruins.

The quasi-autobiographical historical novel *Empire of the Sun* (1984) was based on Ballard's experiences as an internee in World War II, embellished with various retrospective appreciations, including the significance of the explosion of the *atom bomb that destroyed Hiroshima. *The Day of Creation* (1987) returned to the Africa of *The Crystal World*, representing it more explicitly as the symbolic continent of Joseph Conrad's seminal psychodrama *Heart of Darkness* (1902). Its subsidiary *ecological theme is more elaborately developed in *Rushing to Paradise* (1994), which features an eccentric ecowarrior attempting to keep the French from using the Pacific island of Saint-Esprit as a nuclear test site.

Although science fiction readers obsessively committed to the myth of the Space Age considered Ballard to be a traitor to the central science-fictional cause, he turned out to have more foresight than any of his contemporaries on that score. His work made significant contributions to the literary development of several key themes with important scientific connections, including his representation of *alienation as an existential state in which *angst* contentedly plays second fiddle to the suicide of affect, assisted by technofetishism and a *relativism in which truth may be inescapable but is nevertheless far from sacred.

BAXTER, STEPHEN M(ICHAEL) (1957–)

British writer. Baxter graduated in mathematics from Cambridge in 1979 and obtained a Ph.D. in engineering from Southampton University in 1983. He worked in engineering and information technology before becoming a full-time writer in 1995. His first published story, "The Xeelee Flower" (1987), launched an extensive series whose future history extends over five million years. Along with the stories in *Vacuum Diagrams* (1997), it provided a background for *Raft* (1992), set in a cosmic enclave subject to enormously strong gravitational forces; *Flux* (1993), which features a fluid enclave in the mantle of a neutron star; *Timelike*

Infinity (1992), in which a physicist creates a wormhole connecting the present to a future when Earth is under alien occupation; and *Ring* (1994), in which the discovery of a Xeelee starship gives access to the eponymous artifact, established to determine the fate of the universe.

Baxter's interest in the history of imaginative fiction was illustrated by the episodic Vernian romance *Anti-Ice* (1993), which tracks the discovery and exploitation of a kind of antimatter in an alternative nineteenth century. The Wellsian scientific romance *The Time Ships* (1995) is an ingenious sequel to *The Time Machine*, which accommodates the cosmos glimpsed in the original within the discoveries of modern cosmology, relocating a Morlock society far more advanced than the one described by Wells to the external surface of a *Dyson sphere. Other exercises in a similar vein include "The Ant-Men of Tibet" (1995), a Wellsian sequel to *The First Men in the Moon*; the Sherlock Holmes story "The Adventure of the Inertial Adjustor" (1997); and "The Modern Cyrano" (1999), in which Isambard Kingdom Brunel launches an object into orbit.

Voyage (1996), which describes the mission to Mars that NASA might have undertaken had it not given priority to more modest objectives, ends on a plaintive note of acceptance that the myth of the *Space Age had run its course—a recognition embodied in Baxter's other accounts of future space travel. These include *Titan* (1997)—featuring a one-way trip to the *moon of Saturn—whose gloomy ending was unrelieved by the supplementary story "Sun God" (1997), and the disaster story "Moonseed" (1998). The Manifold trilogy, comprising *Time* (1999), *Space* (2002), and *Origin* (2002), elaborates the argument by locating a further alternative space program within a multiverse of parallel universes; the series background was further extended in some of the items in *Phase Space: Stories from the Manifold and Elsewhere* (2002), growing into a future history as extravagant as the Xeelee universe. The *Fermi paradox is a constant theme in his cosmological meditations, various suggested solutions to the enigma being offered in "The Children's Crusade" (2000), "Refugium" (2002), and "Touching Centauri" (2002). He also became interested in *Omega Point imagery, producing a notable elegiac account of a universe devoid of stars, decaying to cold neutrino soup, in "The Gravity Mine" (2000).

In *Deep Future* (2001) Baxter incorporated the substance of various essays spun off from his research into a futurological survey; *Omegatropic* (2001) extended the exercise, focusing on *Omega Point mythology. The research he did for a trilogy of novels about mammoths—*Silverhair* (1999), *Longtusk* (1999),

and *Icebones* (2001), which deal with the possibility of recreating the species in the near future as well as its fate in the remote past—was then extended into the nonfictional *Revolutions in the Earth: James Hutton and the True Age of the Earth* (2003, aka *Ages in Chaos*) and also paved the way for the Stapledonian novel *Evolution* (2003), which embraces a comprehensive history of human evolution. His other palaeontological fantasies include "Behold Now Behemoth" (2000) and "The Hunters of Pangaea" (2002).

In the meantime, Baxter entered into a series of collaborations with Arthur C. *Clarke, beginning with a short story about the development of a technology of *matter transmission, providing a sophisticated sequel to Clarke's early story "Travel by Wire" (1937), titled "The Wire Continuum" (1998), in much the same spirit that *The Time Ships* had extrapolated *The Time Machine*. They went on to produce *The Light of Other Days* (2000), an account of a device that allowed the direct viewing of *past events, and the Time's Odyssey diptych comprising *Time's Eye* (2004) and *Sunstorm* (2005), in which the Earth is threatened by destruction by catastrophic solar storms. Baxter also collaborated with Simon Bradshaw on an alternative history series featuring a British space program, including "Prospero One" (1996) and "First to the Moon!" (2001). He returned to the Xeelee universe in the Destiny's Children sequence begun with *Coalescent* (2003), *Exultant* (2004), and *Transcendent* (2005), filling in a period of the future history overleapt in the earlier sequence, which features an interstellar war, the emergence of gargantuan hive-minds, and the evolution of post-humanity under rigorous selective pressure.

Few modern science fiction writers are as prolific as Baxter and none is as wide ranging. He is one of very few writers whose fiction has tried to take aboard the entire universe discovered by modern science, sweeping through a manifold of alternative universes from the *Big Bang to the Omega Point, adding substantial narrative flesh to his glimpses into the infinite.

BENFORD, GREGORY (ALBERT) (1941–)

U.S. physicist and writer. His identical twin James—with whom he launched the long-running science fiction fanzine *Void* at the age of fourteen—also became a physicist, both brothers graduating from the University of Oklahoma with degrees in physics in 1963 and obtaining Ph.D.s from the University of California, San Diego. The brothers' careers diverged when Gregory undertook postdoctoral research—under the directorship of Edward Teller—at the Lawrence Radiation Laboratory in Livermore, California;

he claimed that he was always primarily a theorist, while James was an experimenter. In 1969 Gregory obtained a professorship at the University of California, Irvine, which he held into the twenty-first century, his principal fields of research being plasma physics and astrophysics.

Benford's first professionally published story was "Stand-In" (1965) but he began to publish more consistently in 1969, when he also began writing a series of articles on "The Science in SF"—initially in collaboration with David Book—for *Amazing Science Fiction*. The series ran until 1976; he also contributed science articles to the short-lived magazine *Vertex* before taking over Isaac *Asimov's science column in *The Magazine of Fantasy & Science Fiction* in 1992. His early science fiction did not make conspicuous use of his work in physics or the topics covered in his articles—his first novel, *Deeper Than the Darkness* (1969; rev. as *The Stars in Shroud*, 1979), is a sociological fantasy describing an alien conquest of the human race by means of artificially aided psychological warfare—but he signaled his intention to take science fiction writing more seriously when he changed his signature from "Greg Benford" to "Gregory Benford" in the early 1970s.

The first story Benford based on his own research—into the concept of tachyons—was the playful "3.02 pm, Oxford" (1970), but an earnest complementary piece, "Cambridge, 1.58 am" (1975), became the seed of the ground-breaking novel *Timescape* (1980), which offered an unusually detailed and realistic picture of life in a contemporary scientific laboratory, coupled with the problems of negotiating an epoch-making discovery. Extrapolating the argument of "The Tachyonic Antitelephone" (*Physical Review*, 1970, with D. L. Book and W. A. Newcomb), the novel tells two parallel stories, one set in 1998, when scientists in a world on the brink of ecocatastrophe are trying to use tachyons to send a warning back in time, and the other in 1962, when uncomprehending physicists attempt to figure out what the signal might be.

In the meantime, much of Benford's science fiction was written in collaboration, most notably with Gordon Eklund, with whom he wrote "West Wind, Falling" (1971) about intergenerational conflicts among the "colonists" of a comet, and "If the Stars Are Gods" (1974), in which aliens attempt to acquaint themselves with the Sun, which they regard as a sentient godlike being. The latter was incorporated into a similarly titled 1977 mosaic whose other components included "The Anvil of Jove" (1976), describing attempts to explore the ecosphere of Jupiter. Benford's final collaboration with Eklund, *Find the Changeling* (1980), was a routine thriller, as was the

disaster novel *Shiva Descending*, written with William Rotsler.

Benford also published a solo mosaic in 1977, titled for another first-contact story, "In the Ocean of Night" (1972). This became the basis of an extensive series, continued in *Across the Sea of Suns* (1984), in which Earth is devastated by alien invasion and humankind is drawn into a galaxy-wide war between organic and inorganic intelligences. The concluding item in the series, intended as a trilogy, eventually stretched to four volumes: *Great Sky River* (1987), *Tides of Light* (1989), *Furious Gulf* (1994), and *Sailing Bright Eternity* (1995). Fugitive humans are pursued into the Esty—the exotic spaces of the black hole at the galaxy's centre—by a mech horde, including a mechanical "anthology intelligence" called the Mantis, whose motives turn out to be more complex than they first seemed.

Benford experimented with didactic hard science fiction for "young adults" in *Jupiter Project* (1972; book, 1975) but its initial failure to sell discouraged him from further experimentation. He did, however, revisit its carefully established scenario—the Jovian moon Ganymede—in other stories, including "Shall We Take a Little Walk?" (1981), the novel *Against Infinity* (1983), and "Warstory" (1990; reprinted as "Sleepstory"). He made another attempt to reach beyond the core science fiction audience in the technothriller *Artifact* (1985), in which a block of stone uncovered by archaeologists turns out to contain a captive black hole. When he tried a second experiment of the same kind in *Chiller* (1993)—an account of a serial killer whose favoured prey is scientists working in cryonics—he used the pseudonym Sterling Blake. Experiments undertaken for purely literary purposes included numerous poems, many of which appeared in *Asimov's Science Fiction*.

Heart of the Comet (1986), written in collaboration with David *Brin, celebrated the return of Halley's comet, equipping it with a native ecology including a Bug-Eyed Monster and describing the establishment of a colony within the comet's head. "Proserpina's Daughter" (1988; aka *Iceborn*), written with Paul A. Carter, is similar in kind, juxtaposing discoveries made on Pluto—which unexpectedly turns out to harbor a complex ecology including sentient life-forms—with political upheavals that threaten to put a stop to the space program. Benford was dissatisfied with the latter story, and set out to provide a much more extensive account of Plutonian life in *Sunborn* (2005), in which Pluto's abundant ecosphere includes the intelligent zand, who are prey to Darksiders from the Kuiper belt.

Benford's exercises in collaboration were supplemented by two sequels to classic works by other hands; *Beyond the Fall of Night* (1990; rev. as *Beyond Infinity*, 2004) was initially published in harness with Arthur C. *Clarke's *Against the Fall of Night*, while *Foundation's Fear* (1997) was part of a set of three new novels in Isaac *Asimov's Foundation series, the others being written by David Brin and Greg Bear. Benford's contemplation of the hypothetical science of psychohistory encouraged him to develop his own hypothetical "sociohistory", featured in "Immersion" (1996), while the work devoted to "Beyond the Fall of Night" bore further fruit in "Galaxia" (1997). Benford's endeavours were further diversified in the 1990s by writing and hosting an eight-part television series for the Japanese National Broadcasting organisation NHK, *A Galactic Odyssey*, which attempted to popularise modern physics in the context of an account of the evolution of the galaxy; it was never aired in the United States. He also edited a series of anthologies in collaboration with Martin H. Greenberg, all but one featuring exercises in alternative history.

Cosm (1998) returned to the laboratory-based drama of *Timescape*, describing an experiment in which smashing uranium atoms together inside a Relativistic Heavy Iron Collider produces a mini–Big Bang and opens a window into a virgin universe, which continues to expand into its own private space. "A Cold, Dry Cradle" (1997, written with Elisabeth Malartre) formed the basis for *The Martian Race* (1999), which employs considerable ingenuity in trying to equip the Mars revealed by the Viking landers with a fugitive ecosphere. *Eater* (2000) returned to the field of the disaster story, but spiced its threat with a lavish portion of hard science before stretching the limits of plausibility by attributing sentience to its ominous black hole.

In one of the commentaries featured in the collection *In Alien Flesh* (1986), Benford borrowed an analogy coined by Robert Frost with reference the writing of free verse, characterising the writing of science fiction without a stern scientific conscience as "playing tennis with the net down". Although he has always played with the net up, he has never allowed its presence to inhibit him in wide-ranging experiments in style and substance.

BIG BANG, THE

A term coined in the late 1940s by Fred *Hoyle in the course of a BBC radio program; he was attempting to belittle the notion—popularised in Sir Arthur Eddington's *The Expanding Universe* (1940)—that the recession revealed by galactic red-shifts implied that the universe must once have been infinitesimally small and that its history was that of a continuing explosion. Hoyle favoured the "steady-state" or "continuous creation" theory, which assumed that the expansive effect of recession must be compensated by the spontaneous generation of new matter in the widening interstices between the galaxies, thus maintaining the uniformity of the universe.

Hoyle was not the only skeptic who doubted the expanding universe, but others preferred variant interpretations of the significance of the galactic red-shifts. Some, like Grote Reber, favoured the "tired light" hypothesis, which suggested that some still-mysterious process sapped energy from far-travelling photons. Others attributed them to relativistic effects associated with the emission of light from objects in powerful gravity fields. However, champions of the assumption that the galactic red-shifts *are* Doppler shifts, and that the universe *is* expanding, seized on Hoyle's phrase, stripping it of its pejorative implications and adopting it as a proud label. Subsequent astronomical observations demonstrated that the universe has undergone considerable material changes over time, and that the aesthetic principle underlying the steady-state assumption was, in this case, misleading. The cosmic background radiation observed by Arno Penzias and Robert Wilson in 1965 was hailed as proof that a primal explosion had taken place. Accounts of the early evolution of the universe in the first few seconds of the Big Bang—when space-time first came into being—soon became a favourite playground of theoretical *physics, instituting a revolution in *cosmology.

The wide acceptance of Big Bang theory before confirmatory evidence was found was a dramatic *bouleversement* of a philosophical trend extending over centuries. Many classical philosophers objected to the idea of creation *ex nihilo*, preferring the notion of creation as a rearrangement of preexistent materials—usually the ordering of chaos. The notion that the universe was eternal and infinite, but subject to processes of local and temporary creative alteration—as popularised by Lucretius' summation of Epicurean philosophy in *De rerum natura*—had long served as an intellectual defence against the presumed follies of dogmatic religious faith. The notion of a stable universe was preserved against the criticism that gravity must eventually cause the visible universe to collapse by arguments vividly dramatised by Edgar Allan Poe's *Eureka* (1848) and Camille *Flammarion's *La fin du monde* (1893), both of which imagined compensatory creative processes akin to the one proposed by Hoyle and his fellow steady-state theorists. Albert *Einstein invented a "cosmological constant" to secure his own universal model against such a fate (although he regretted it as soon as the evidence of expansion emerged), so Hoyle was continuing a long tradition. Some religious believers were, however, delighted by the resurrection of the notion of creation *ex nihilo*; Georges Lemaître—the first astronomer to formulate a Big Bang theory in response to the Doppler shifts measured by Vesto Slipher, Milton Humason, and Edwin Hubble—was an ordained priest.

The initial literary response to news of the expanding universe was muted, because of the difficulty of finding narrative frameworks capable of containing it. A version of Big Bang theory was, however, incorporated into Chan Corbett's "Beyond Infinity" (1937) in which the universe's expansion reaches its limit and a core of "nonspacetime" forms within the universal shell, necessitating a cataclysmic recreation—the continuation of an eternal cycle echoing Poe's "beat of the Heart Divine". The time traveller in Donald Wandrei's "The Man Who Never Lived" (1934) witnesses the primal explosion, while a dimensional traveller who does not realise that the fourth dimension is time actually becomes an explosive primordium in Nelson S. Bond's "Down the Dimensions" (1937).

More sophisticated devices enabling human observers to witness Big Bangs, following the coinage of the term and the initial elaboration of the theory, were incorporated into Poul Anderson's *Tau Zero* (1970), Bob Shaw's *Ship of Strangers* (1978), and Gregory Benford's *Cosm* (1998). Italo Calvino's "All at One Point" (1965) is a more distanced *conte philosophique* treatment of the notion, while Robert Reed's "Night of Time" (2003) refers back to the immediate aftermath of the Big Bang. By virtue of its lack of catastrophist flair, the continuous creation theory was even more difficult to display in narrative, although Charles L. Harness's *The Ring of Ritornel* (1968) made the attempt, and a version of it is employed in the underlying logic of the "jumpgates" in Poul Anderson's "Door to Anywhere" (1966).

The notion of the expanding universe as the product of an explosion was complicated in the 1980s by the notion that the initial phase of expansion must have been very rapid indeed, constituting an initial "inflation" of space that was almost instantaneous. The version of inflation theory that became integrated into the "standard model" of cosmological theory was originated by Alan Guth in 1981 and further elaborated by Andrei Linde and Stephen Hawking. Linde's suggestion that the observable universe is merely one of an infinite series of Big Bangs occurring within a macrocosm echoed the theory of continuous creation on a larger scale and provided a context for the large-scale notion of *alternative histories. The inflationary version of big bang theory was rapidly

adopted into the primary subgenre of late twentieth-century cosmological science fiction, *Omega Point fiction.

BIOLOGY

The scientific study of living organisms. The term was brought into English by the translation of the German *biologie* in 1819, in recognition of the fact that the descriptive discipline of "natural history" was acquiring elaborate theoretical underpinnings, thanks to the progress of comparative anatomy and physiology. "Physiology" was originally used as a synonym for "natural science", but by the end of the sixteenth century it was routinely narrowed to the study of the human body, and soon extended to the study of bodily functions in general.

*Aristotle's successor, Theophrastos, made the first basic division of biology into *zoology and *botany; a third basic category of *microbiology was added when the invention of the *microscope revealed a new range of single-celled organisms. While organic *chemistry remained mysterious, biological knowledge was restricted to accounts of form, assisted by anatomical information obtained by dissection and by studies of finer structure conducted with the aid of the microscope.

The study of physiology, begun by Galen in Classical times, made some headway with William Harvey's discovery of the circulation of the blood in 1578 and seventeenth-century studies of digestion and reproduction, but remained confused by vitalist theories of *life until the nineteenth century. Harvey's discovery was commemorated in Abraham Cowley's "Ode upon Dr. Harvey" (1663), while "The Development of the Embryo" was celebrated poetically in Sir Richard Blackmore's "The Creation" (1712), but the intense interest in physiological discoveries generated by their potential relevance to *medicine was frustrated by their obvious limitations. The interested readers of P. M. Roget's then-comprehensive study of *Animal and Vegetable Physiology* (1834) included Alfred, Lord Tennyson, but it offered scant inspiration to the substance of "Locksley Hall" (1842).

Taxonomic endeavours, amplified by discoveries in *palaeontology, permitted the development of theories of biological *evolution at the end of the eighteenth century, but their development was also handicapped by the lack of any supportive biochemistry. The theorisation of biology progressed in a fashion markedly different from that of physics and chemistry because the science generated no mathematically expressible laws, and very few candidate laws of any kind. A "biogenetic law" formulated by Karl von Baer in *Entwicklungsgeschichte der Thiere*

(Developmental History of Animals) (1828), stating that the forms through which embryos pass correspond to taxonomic phases of complexity, seemed to Ernst Haeckel to gain further significance when those phases were linked to stages in evolutionary history, but it was always rather impressionistic. It is echoed and speculatively elaborated in Edgar Rice Burroughs' *The Land that Time Forgot* (1918; book, 1924). The principles of comparative anatomy used by Georges Cuvier and his successors to deduce the whole forms of skeletons from fossil fragments were not quite as impressionistic, but had to be regarded as tentative and far from certain.

The literary response to the advancement of biological research in the nineteenth century was mostly concerned with medical speculations and responses to the controversy regarding theories of evolution. Its most obvious general feature was the development of the "yuck factor" in the use of the biological imagination to generate new *monsters, and in attitudes to the kinds of physiological investigation that were lumped together in the popular imagination under the heading of "vivisection". Traditional anatomists had been content to work with dead specimens, but attempts to link organic structure with function required the intimate investigation of living ones, calling forth protests in such works of fiction as Wilkie Collins' *Heart and Science* (1883). Scientists were by no means immune to this kind of horror themselves, as demonstrated by Sir Ronald Ross' gruesome account of "The Vivisector Vivisected" (written ca. 1890; published 1937), but images of vivisection became a key element of such exercises in antiscience fiction as S. Fowler Wright's "Brain" (1935).

The corollaries of this almost instinctive revulsion to seeming offences against *Nature were explored in J. B. S. *Haldane's comments on "biological inventions" in *Daedalus* (1923), which correctly anticipated the tenor of twentieth-century reactions to advancements in *biotechnology. Haldane's foresight was rapidly confirmed by such pulp horror stories as David H. Keller's "Stenographer's Hands" (1928) and "The Feminine Metamorphosis" (1929). Speculative fiction based on biological hypotheses of every kind has suffered more intensely than any other subgenre from the *Frankenstein complex, which took its name from a pioneering exercise in the investigation of the nature of life.

Whether biological innovations are depicted in fiction as technical inventions or mere discoveries, they tend to excite the same reflexive disgust. As the science of biology has progressed, therefore, *horror fiction has steadily increased the capital it draws from the biological imagination. The narrative energy of reflexive revulsion is readily exploited in such biological *contes philosophiques* as Nathaniel Hawthorne's "Rappaccini's Daughter" (1844), H. G. *Wells' *The Island of Dr. Moreau* (1896), and Edward Knoblock's *The Ant Heap* (1929). Even hypothetical discoveries answering desperate common desires—including keys to *longevity—are routinely treated with considerable suspicion. Social unease associated with *sex ensures that the yuck factor is extrapolated in a uniquely tortuous manner in the context of reproductive biology, as observed in Edward Heron-Allen's ironically self-censored but determinedly scabrous *The Cheetah Girl* (1922; initially by-lined Christopher Blayre).

The delicate nature of biological speculation ensured that it was considerably muted in pulp science fiction, to the extent that when James *Blish considered "The Biological Story" in a pioneering series of articles on "The Science in Science Fiction" (1951–1952) he lamented that he could only find one significant example—Norman L. Knight's "Crisis in Utopia" (1940)—that was not a horror story. The fact that British *scientific romance owed so much to the exemplary role of H. G. *Wells—who was educated in biology and enthusiastic to extrapolate contemporary biological ideas in a highly adventurous manner—ensured that European speculative fiction made more use of biological fantasias in a slightly more open-minded fashion. Heron-Allen was also a biologist by vocation, so many of the "strange papers" attributed to his pseudonym develop biological hypotheses. John Lionel Tayler, sometime lecturer in biology at University of London Extension College, wrote the far-reaching biological fantasia *The Last of My Race* (1924), while Wells' one-time collaborator Julian *Huxley produced "The Tissue-Culture King" (1926) in addition to such exercises in speculative non-fiction as "Philosophic Ants" in *Essays of a Biologist* (1923). It was Julian Huxley's brother Aldous who produced the ultimate literary extrapolation of the yuck factor in *Brave New World* (1932). Wells' influence extended beyond Britain; other significant pioneers of biological science fiction included the French Wellsian André Couvreur, in a series featuring the exploits of Professor Tornada (1909–1939), and the Russian Mikhail Bulgakov, in "Rokovy'e yaitsa" (1925; trans. as "The Fatal Eggs") and *Sobachy'e serdtse* (1925; trans. as *The Heart of a Dog*).

Biological science fiction—at least in its teratological varieties—received a considerable boost when it was demonstrated in the 1920s that radiation could produce genetic *mutations, instituting a subgenre of mutational romance. Its most important twentieth-century development was, however, the sophistication of stories of alien life by the input of the hypothetical science of *exobiology. After World War II, James Blish was in the vanguard of a new generation of science fiction writers willing to take a more balanced view of the prospects of biology—a project assisted by the heroic status conferred on James Watson and Francis Crick when they determined the structure of DNA from Rosalind Franklin's x-ray photographs and ushered in a new era in *genetics. Active ideological opposition to the yuck factor became evident in works such as Theodore Sturgeon's "It Wasn't Syzygy" (1952), "The Sex Opposite" (1952), and "The Wages of Synergy" (1953)—all of which employ exotic biological relationships as metaphors for human social relationships. A similar analogical method was employed by Alice Sheldon in "Your Haploid Heart" (1969) and "A Momentary Taste of Being" (1975)—both of which were by-lined James Tiptree Jr.—and "The Screwfly Solution" (1977), by-lined Raccoona Sheldon.

It is inevitable that literary responses to biological ideas should make much of metaphors of these unsettling kinds, given the nature of literary enterprise and the melodramatic potential of such concepts as "biological warfare". Literary images of biologists have always been more sinister than those of other kinds of *scientists; physicists might be better able to blow up the world, but only a biologist could institute a grotesque symbiosis between his wife and a fungus, as in Rosel George Brown's "Fruiting Body" (1962). This tendency became particularly marked during the explosion of biological science fiction that occurred in the 1970s when the possibilities of *genetic engineering—especially the idea of *cloning—became a major stimulus to the speculative imagination. Sympathetic fictional depictions of biologists became more common in that era, but the stigmata of Dr. Moreau, Dr. Jekyll, and Victor Frankenstein could not be erased, even in such even-handed accounts as the one featured in Greg Egan's *Teranesia* (1999).

BIOTECHNOLOGY

Biotechnology is usually defined as the use of living organisms in technological processes, although that definition has sometimes been restricted to the use of microorganisms. The narrower definition excludes agriculture and animal husbandry from the classification, and reduces biotechnology's early history to the production of alcohol by managed fermentation. On the other hand, the definition can be expanded to take in the technological manipulation of biological products; those kinds of technology have a much more elaborate history, cooking and clothing becoming the "primal biotechnologies".

Whichever definition is used, biotechnology became far more significant than ever before in the last quarter of the twentieth century, in connection with *food science and *medical technologies. Princess Vera Zaronovitch's *Mizora* (1880–1881) is an early example of biotechnological science fiction, featuring an all-female society whose members reproduce by means of artificial parthenogenesis and apply similar technological methods to other kinds of production.

A new kind of biotechnology seemed imminent when Alexis Carrel followed up experiments in skin grafting carried out in the 1890s with more elaborate attempts to grow and maintain tissues *in vitro*. His tissue cultures were not very successful, mainly because specialised cells could not divide indefinitely in nutrient solutions, but the basic idea seemed sufficiently promising to inspire Clement Fézandie's "The Secret of Artificial Reproduction" (1921), J. B. S. *Haldane's *Daedalus* (1923), and Julian *Huxley's "The Tissue-Culture King" (1926). Following Aldous Huxley's satirical extrapolation of biotechnological possibilities in *Brave New World* (1932), however, their image was badly tarnished. Even such farces as Eddin Clark's "Double! Double!" (1938), in which a technology for producing whole animals from single cells goes awry, retain a horrific edge, although *ecological parables such as Julian Chain's "Prometheus" (1951)—in which industrial civilisation is swept away by spinoff from research into plant hormones—were sometimes prepared to employ biotechnological plot levers.

The evolution of biotechnological speculation was closely allied with the notion of *genetic engineering, and was long restricted by the difficulty of imagining how the genetic material might be directly manipulated; it was not until the structure of DNA had been clarified that would-be speculators obtained a clearer view of what that kind of biotechnological manipulation might involve. Until then, such stories as S. P. Meek's "The Murgatroyd Experiment" (1929)—in which humans are equipped with chlorophyll-laden blood in order to alleviate their need for food—were devoid of any real argumentative basis. The ideas Haldane attempted to popularise in *Daedalus* received scant attention for the next half century; his sister, Naomi Mitchison, politely waited until he was dead before extrapolating them in a dourly cautionary fashion in *Solution Three* (1975) and *Not by Bread Alone* (1983).

By the 1970s several science fiction writers, most notably Samuel R. *Delany and John Varley, had begun to take it for granted that biotechnologies would have a significant impact on near-future societies; such scenarios as those detailed in Delany's *Triton* (1976) and Varley's *The Ophiuchi Hotline*

(1977), feature multiple applications. Their lead was followed by other writers, including Joan Slonczewski, in the novels *A Door into Ocean* (1986), *Daughter of Elysium* (1993), and *The Children Star* (1998); Brian Stableford, in stories collected in *Sexual Chemistry* (1998) and *Designer Genes* (2004) and the series of novels launched with *Inherit the Earth* (1998); and Alison Sinclair, in the novels *Blueheart* (1996), *Cavalcade* (1998), and *Throne Price* (2000, with Linda Williams).

Individual works of note featuring multiple applications of future biotechnology include Rebecca Ore's *The Illegal Rebirth of Billy the Kid* (1991), Ian McDonald's *Hearts, Hands and Voices* (1992; aka *The Broken Land*), Paul Di Filippo and Bruce Sterling's "The Scab's Progress"—whose biotechnological jargon was equipped with explanatory hyperlinks in the online version published on 29 December 2000—and Margaret Atwood's *Oryx and Crake* (2003). Thomas A. Easton's Organic Future series, comprising *Sparrowhawk* (1990), *Greenhouse* (1991), *Woodsman* (1992), *Tower of the Gods* (1993), and *Seeds of Destiny* (1994), offers an elaborate fictional account of a future in which biotechnology has taken over almost all the functions of organic technology.

Forms of biotechnology that did not involve genetic engineering or *cyborgisation became rare in the late twentieth century, although surgical modifications and various kinds of organic augmentation formed a substantial fringe to both subgenres. As with other literary uses of *biological ideas, constructive speculative accounts of new biotechnologies and their application have been heavily influenced by the *Frankenstein complex and its amplification by the yuck factor. The vast majority of novels elaborating biotechnological premises are alarmist *technothrillers, melodramatic *horror stories, and dark anticipations of biotechnological *weapons. The formularisation of such works—usually requiring that threats be overcome—inevitably encourages the construction of biotechnological "fixes" whose implications are intrinsically positive, but such fixes are often seen as improvisations temporarily holding back an inexorable tide of disaster.

BLACK HOLE

A term used in 1967 by John Wheeler to describe an aggregation of matter compressed to the point at which its surface gravity is so powerful that nothing—including light—can escape from it. The basic idea was much older; the possibility that there might be dark stars incapable of emitting light was suggested by John Michell in 1783. Karl Schwarzchild developed the notion in the context of Albert

*Einstein's general theory of *relativity in 1916; he calculated the curvature of space-time around a spherical mass required to create an "event horizon" surrounding a "singularity" cut off from the rest of the universe—a cosmos in its own right. The hypothesis was applied to processes of stellar collapse by Subrahmanyan Chandrasekhar in 1930, but the idea was ridiculed by Sir Arthur Eddington and more or less forgotten until it was revived in the 1960s, as an extrapolation of a burgeoning fascination with neutron stars. It was in that context that Wheeler's term caught on, taking a remarkably firm grip on the popular imagination and swiftly becoming a versatile metaphor in common parlance.

Although a black hole is, by definition, invisible, one resulting from stellar collapse may become evident by virtue of its effect on a nearby visible star, whose matter is stripped away to form an "accretion disk" of hot matter spiraling into the black hole. Several candidate objects were identified by astronomers in the 1970s. Stephen Hawking linked the notion of black holes to the *Big Bang theory by proposing that the cosmic explosion began with a singularity and calculating that vast quantities of tiny black holes must have resulted from the early expansion. He also modified the notion that nothing could escape from a black hole by considering quantum effects that convert the energy of its gravitational field into pairs of particles manifest outside the event horizon, only one of which is subsequently absorbed; by virtue of this "Hawking radiation" small black holes may gradually lose energy and "evaporate".

The idea of black holes had been vaguely anticipated in such constructs as the Hole in Space in Frank K. Kelly's "Starship Invincible" (1935), the hole created by the matter-annihilating giant positron in Nathan Schachner's "Negative Space" (1938), and the Pit generated by a collapsing star in Harry Walton's "Below—Absolute!" (1938). Fred Saberhagen's "The Face of the Deep" (1966) described the concept in detail ahead of the term's coinage. There were several ready-made science-fictional slots into which such a notion could fit when it was popularised, and black holes rapidly became commonplace. Many early stories elected to focus on the relativistic time-dilatation affecting objects falling towards event horizons; notable examples include Poul Anderson's "Kyrie" (1968), Jerry Pournelle's "He Fell into a Dark Hole" (1972), Brian Aldiss' "The Dark Soul of the Night" (1976), and Frederik Pohl's *Gateway* (1977). Such accounts of ominous cosmic encounters often found abundant dramatic fuel in analogies drawn between physics and psychology, as in Robert Silverberg's "To the Dark Star" (1968), Barry N. Malzberg's *Galaxies* (1975), and Connie Willis'

"Schwarzschild Radius" (1987). The heroes of Greg Egan's "The Planck Dive" (1998) protest against an attempt to impose unscientific meanings upon their endeavour.

Popularisations of the notion often yielded to a temptation to rhapsodic overstatement; John Taylor's *Black Holes: The End of the Universe?* (1973) proposed that "the black hole requires a complete rethinking of our attitudes to life". The intrinsic appeal of the notion was further demonstrated by the rapidity with which the Disney Corporation made the film *The Black Hole* (1979), although it pays scant attention to the scientific niceties of the concept. Artificially generated black holes soon put in an appearance; a malfunction at a nuclear power plant creates one in Michael McCollum's "Scoop" (1979), and an experiment in nuclear fusion produces a microstar that collapses into one in Martin Caidin's *Star Bright* (1980).

The fact that anything falling into a black hole was bound to be torn apart in the process placed an apparent limitation on the narrative utility of the device, but it was conveniently sidestepped by speculators avid to get inside, who seized on the possibility that rapidly rotating black holes might expose "naked singularities". As exit doors from the universe, black holes recommended themselves as a plausible means of dodging the relativistic limitations on cosmic travel—a notion used to shore up such existing facilitating devices as "star gates" and space-time "vortices", as in George R. R. Martin's "The Second Kind of Loneliness" (1972), Joe Haldeman's *The Forever War* (1974), and Ian Wallace's *Heller's Leap* (1979). Such hypotheses led to the further elaboration of the basic idea into that of a "wormhole": a metaspatial tunnel connecting a black hole with a complementary "white hole", which could operate as a faster-than-light transport mechanism or a means of interuniversal travel. The popularisation of the notion was assisted by John Gribbin's *White Holes: Cosmic Gushers in the Universe* (1977) and Adrian Berry's *The Iron Sun: Crossing the Universe Through Black Holes* (1977).

Wormholes became the most fashionable mode of interstellar travel in the last decades of the twentieth century, notably deployed in such novels as Paul Preuss' *The Gates of Heaven* (1980), Robert J. Sawyer's *Starplex* (1996), and Iain M. Banks' *The Algebraist* (2004). They also function as doorways through time, as in Preuss' *Re-Entry* (1981) and Stephen *Baxter's *Timelike Infinity* (1992) and "The Gravity Mine" (2000). In Roger McBride Allen's *The Ring of Charon* (1991) the Earth is kidnapped through a wormhole. In Arthur C. *Clarke and Stephen Baxter's *The Light of Other Days* (2000), a technology for manufacturing wormholes generates abundant spinoff, although its primary application is to allow the past to be viewed and recorded. Quantum wormholes feature as a means of local "teleportation" in Chris Moriarty's *Spin State* (2003). In the meantime, black holes continued to function as potential hazards in space travel, as in Mildred Downey Broxon's "Singularity" (1978), John Varley's "The Black Hole Passes" (1978), and Stephen Baxter's "Pilot" (1993).

Interest in cosmic black holes was further enhanced by the problem of dark *matter, some of whose suggestive manifestations could be explained by the hypothesis that many galaxies—including ours—had huge back holes at their centres. This notion soon became a standard element of science-fictional representations, spectacularly deployed in such works as Gregory *Benford's *Tides of Light* (1989); life inside black holes is also featured in Wil McCarthy's *Flies from Amber* (1995), while M. John Harrison's *Light* (2002) features a vast black hole bounded by a fecund shore.

Black holes also offered a potential solution to the enigma posed by the existence of "quasars"—a term derived by contraction of "quasi-stellar radio sources" to describe the discovery in the 1960s of intense radio sources of very small dimension, incapable of resolution by an optical telescope. When similar sources were found that did not emit radio waves, the collective term was changed to quasi-stellar object, but the contraction had stuck by then. The red-shifts of quasars turned out to be extremely high, implying they must radiate thousands of times more energy than a galaxy like the Milky Way—a phenomenon potentially accountable in terms of accretion of matter around an enormous black hole.

The idea that tiny black holes, as envisaged by Hawking, might still be around in some profusion was attractive to science fiction writers in search of manageable plot levers; such objects soon became commonplace in science fiction, having been trailed by Larry Niven in "The Hole Man" (1973) and adapted for use in a space drive in Arthur C. Clarke's *Imperial Earth* (1975). They were dubbed "kernels" in Charles Sheffield's *The McAndrew Chronicles* (1983). Black holes small enough to cause trouble on and below the Earth's surface once released from magnetic imprisonment are featured in such *technothrillers as Gregory Benford's *Artifact* (1985) and David *Brin's *Earth* (1990). Manipulable black holes are used as ultimate weapons in David Langford's *The Space Eater* (1982).

In Gregory Benford's "As Big as the Ritz" (1986), an idealistic plutocrat establishes a Utopian Brotherworld on the Hoop, an artificial habitat sustained by the energy output of matter falling into a black hole; Benford's speculations about black holes and their uses bore further fruit in "The Worm in the Well" (1995; aka "Early Bird") and *Eater* (2000), which features a sentient black hole. Indeed, no ambitious cosmic epic of the late twentieth-century was complete without at least one black hole; they are on particularly conspicuous display in Paul McAuley's *Eternal Light* (1991). The eponymous material featured in Wil McCarthy's *The Collapsium* (2000), manufactured from black holes, facilitates matter transmission.

BLISH, JAMES (BENJAMIN) (1921–1975)

U.S. writer. Blish studied microbiology at Rutgers University, obtaining his B.Sc. in 1942, and worked as an army medical technician during World War II. He did postgraduate work in zoology at Columbia University before abandoning his academic career in favour of writing, although he also worked as the editor of a trade newspaper from 1947 to 1951 and in public relations from 1951 to 1958.

From 1950 to 1962, Blish developed a series of stories whose future *history was derived by extrapolation of the central thesis of Oswald Spengler's *Der Undertang des Abendlandes* (1918–1922; trans. as *The Decline of the West*). Earth's cities are driven by economic recession to become gargantuan spaceships powered by antigravity devices called "spindizzies", wandering the galaxy as "Okies" in search of work as the West's decline becomes terminal and the "Earthmanist" culture goes through its own rise and decline. The stories assembled into *Earthman, Come Home* (1955) and *They Shall Have Stars* (1956; aka *Year 2018!*) were further augmented by the novels *The Triumph of Time* (1958; aka *A Clash of Cymbals*)—in which the decadence of Earthmanist culture is interrupted by an apocalyptic cosmic disaster—and *A Life for the Stars* (1962); all four volumes were combined in *Cities in Flight* (1970).

Alongside this series Blish wrote a number of stories pioneering the development of sophisticated *biological science fiction, including "Beanstalk" (1952; aka "Giants in the Earth"; exp. as *Titan's Daughter*, 1961) and the "pantropy" series, which developed the thesis that human *colonisation of alien worlds might only be practicable with the aid of drastic adaptations acquired by *genetic engineering. The pantropy stories, including the classic conceptual breakthrough story "Surface Tension" (1952), were assembled into the mosaic novel *The Seedling Stars* (1957).

Blish was consistently interested in the problem of developing rational foundations for psychologically plausible ideas, hypothesising a biological basis for traditional monsters in "There Shall Be No Darkness" (1950) and proposing a mechanism for extrasensory perception in "Let the Finder Beware" (1949; exp. as *Jack of Eagles* 1952; aka *ESP-er*). He became increasingly concerned with broader *philosophical issues, treating the paradox of prophecy with unusual seriousness in "Beep" (1954; exp. as *The Quincunx of Time*, 1973) and venturing into the field of speculative *theology in *A Case of Conscience* (1953; exp. 1959), in which a Jesuit confronted with a seemingly sinless alien world must reconcile its existence with his faith. In further pursuit of these interests, Blish became a prolific and exacting critic of the burgeoning science fiction genre, writing as William Atheling Jr.; his work in this vein is collected in *The Issue at Hand* (1964), *More Issues at Hand* (1970), and *The Tale that Wags the God* (1987, ed. Cy Chauvin).

Blish diversified out of science fiction in the historical novel *Doctor Mirabilis* (1964; rev. 1971), a biographical study of Roger *Bacon that focussed on the intellectual tension between Bacon's religious faith and anticipations of empirical scientific method. Blish coupled this novel with *A Case of Conscience* as elements in a trilogy collectively entitled After Such Knowledge, whose third component was the apocalyptic fantasy *Black Easter and the Day After Judgment* (2 vols., 1964–1971; combined 1980; aka *The Devil's Day*). The most notable of his later works were *A Torrent of Faces* (1967, with Norman L. Knight), which deals with social and political adaptations to the population problem, and the far-futuristic fantasy *Midsummer Century* (1972), in which the future evolution of life on Earth is complicated by competition with artificial intelligences.

Blish was a useful addition to John W. *Campbell Jr.'s stable of *hard science fiction writers, not merely because he helped to broaden the scope of hard science fiction to take in biological science, but because he was so keenly interested in fitting all kinds of science-fictional ideas into the largest possible philosophical framework. His perennial appreciation of the need to sell his work, initially in the action-adventure–orientated arena of the pulp magazines, never prevented him from undertaking literary experiments, although it certainly limited his opportunities to display their results. It was unfortunate that he never achieved financial stability in his writing career until he achieved an altogether unexpected celebrity writing prose versions of *Star Trek* scripts. Had the marketplace been more hospitable before he fell ill with the cancer that ultimately killed him, he would have undoubtedly pushed the envelope of genre science fiction even further than he contrived to do.

BOTANY

The major branch of *biology devoted to the study of plants. The practical significance of such knowledge in primitive society is so great that ethnobotanies tend to be much more elaborate than ethnozoologies and other traditional stocks of knowledge. By the same token, the account of plants contained in the *Historia Plantorum* of Theophrastos of Eresos—*Aristotle's appointed successor at the Lyceum—is much more elaborate than his predecessor's account of animals. In contrast to Aristotle's arrangement of animals into groups, the tentative taxonomic classification used therein bears no resemblance to modern botanical taxonomy. Pliny the Elder's *Naturalis Historia* (77 A.D.)—which similarly reflects the economic and *medicinal importance of plants, and the relative ease with which they can be studied—is similar; its division of plants into aromatic, alimentary, medicinal, and vinous categories, originated by Dioscorides, now seems entirely arbitrary.

Although it was a great advantage to botanists, the sedentary and passive nature of plants ensured that botany would always be less glamorous than *zoology. The speculative imagination has always sought imaginative compensation for this natural deficit by inventing fictitious ambulatory plants, man-eating plants, and plants whose flowers metamorphose into animals, all of which feature in Pliny. By the same token, the popularisation of botany tends to devote far more attention to predatory, parasitic, and poisonous plants than their actual prevalence seems to warrant.

The selective breeding of new crop plants is ancient, but it made relatively little impact on folklore, the historical record or the literary imagination. The use of plants in medicine is much more widely documented in fact and fiction alike, although it belonged to the realm of *occult science rather than that of empirical science until recent times; the medical textbooks associated with the New Learning in Tudor England—notably William Bullein's *Bulwarke of Defence againste Sicknes, Sorues, etc.* (1562) and John Gerard's *Herball* (1597) are shot through with mysticism. The cultivation of new crop plants, whose scale and scope was dramatically transformed in the sixteenth and seventeenth centuries following the discovery of the New World, was more important in generating popular interest in botanical science, especially when crop translocation became an important aspect of the process of *colonisation. The role played

in colonial adventures by *psychotropic plants was almost as important as that of food plants; tobacco and the potato are still linked in the historical imagination as key features of the discovery of the Americas.

A new appreciation of the patterns of plant relatedness was generated when attention was deflected away from leaves, stems, and roots towards flowers and fruit—a shift correlated with the improvement of drawing techniques in the Renaissance. Hieronymus Tragus (Jerome Bock) published an herbal in 1551 that reflected this change of emphasis; Andreas Caesalpinus' *De Plantis Libri* (1583) concentrated on the number of seeds and seed receptacles contained within each flower, thus laying the groundwork for the comprehensive taxonomy attempted by Carolus Linnaeus (Carl von Linné) in the 1730s. Caesalpinus and his successors were assisted by the foundation of public botanical gardens, which originated in Italy in the 1540s and spread into northern Europe in the 1570s, reaching Sweden in 1657 and England in 1680.

The new classification system involved the extension of analogies of animal reproduction into studies of plants, facilitated by the development of the *microscope. Nehemiah Grew's *The Anatomy of Plants* (1670) offered detailed accounts of the germination of various kinds of seeds. The attribution of *sex to plants had previously been very vague, although Robert Burton's *Anatomy of Melancholy* (1621) has a brief section on "vegetal love". Burton's citations include a fifteenth-century poem by the Italian humanist Jovianus Pontanus detailing the love affair of two date palms whose passion overcomes the difficulty of their geographical separation. Pontanus also wrote a better known poem about orange trees, *De Hortis Hesperidium*. It was not until the seventeenth century that microscopists such as Sebastian Vaillant were able to explain plant reproduction fully enough to allow Linnaeus to convert his unfolding artificial classification into a natural classification based on reproduction mechanisms, laying significant groundwork for theories of *evolution.

Linnaeus' decision to base his classification of plants on their *sex organs was not uncontroversial, although the sexuality of insect-pollinated flowering plants—involving the production of forms, colours, perfumes, and nectars designed to attract their go-betweens—had long been a significant component of their literary representation, readily lending itself to symbolism, euphemism, and occasional frank eroticism. Thomas Stretser's *The Natural History of the Frutex Vulvaria, or Flowering Shrub* and *Arbor Vitae; or, The Natural History of the Tree of Life, In Prose and Verse* (both 1732, initially by-lined Philogynes Clitorides) employ botanical metaphors as euphemistic coverage for the representation of human genitalia. The literary employment of flowers had always made much of their erotic symbolism and consequent cultural significance, and the Linnaean system wrought a subtle sophistication of such imagery.

Linnaean classification provided a framework for the description of collections of exotic plants amassed by world-travelling amateurs, and the collection of new specimens became an important element of many voyages of exploration. Joseph Banks, who traveled with James Cook's first expedition, refined Linnaeus' taxonomy and increased the number of known species by a quarter. Banks became president of the Royal Society and played a leading role in defining the missions of various naval expeditions; it was he who commissioned William Bligh to collect breadfruit from Tahiti, with a view to making it a significant staple crop in the Caribbean colonies, and made sure that the *Providence* completed the mission in 1793 after the *Bounty*'s crew mutinied in 1791. After taking charge of the Royal Gardens at Kew in 1798, Banks compiled a collection of plants from all over the world in order to equip the first Australian colonists with medicines and foodstuffs.

Banks was the dedicatee of James Perry's "Mimosa; or, The Sensitive Plant" (1779), which continued Stretser's euphemistic tradition, but his endeavours provided more substantial inspiration in prompting the production of Erasmus *Darwin's epic account of *The Botanic Garden* (1791), whose Linnaean observations of "The Loves of the Plants" were considered sufficiently radical to inspire a parody in the *Anti-Jacobin* and attracted such responses in kind as Elizabeth Moody's "To Mr. Darwin, on Reading His Loves of the Plants" (1798). Others inspired by Banks' example included Sir William Jones, whose *Design of a Treatise on the Plants of India* (1790) followed his translation of Kalidasa's fifth-century epic *Sacontalá* (1789); Jones made careful note of the elaborate floral/erotic symbolism of the latter work—not without embarrassment—and adapted Hindu mythology in a similar fashion in his own *Hymn to Camdeo* (1784). Jones' version of *Sacontalá* was influential in *Romantic literary circles, helping to inspire Robert Southey's *The Curse of Kehama* (1810) and the more picturesque Orientalism of Thomas Moore's *Lalla Rookh* (1817).

Banks' development of Kew was the scientific tip of a hobbyist iceberg; "gardening" in its broad sense became a widespread activity in eighteenth-century England as herb gardens and kitchen gardens were supplemented by flower gardens and a whole aesthetic movement devoted to "landscape gardening". The interrelationships of art, literature, and gardening are wide ranging and complicated, and

the influence of botanical science is decidedly peripheral, but the economic importance of aesthetic cultivation—remarkably dramatised in seventeenth-century Dutch "tulipomania", as reflected in such literary works as Alexandre Dumas' *La tulipe noire* (1850; trans. as *The Black Tulip*)—ensured that the science of horticulture would exert a powerful attraction on amateurs, eventually providing a key arena for the development of *genetics as well as the discovery of such biotechnologies as grafting.

The interrelationship of botanical science and colonial endeavour determined the origins and development of botany in the Americas. John Barton established a Botanic Garden in Philadelphia in 1728 and became the royal botanist—Banks' American equivalent—in 1765. After the revolution, Thomas Jefferson, George Washington, and John Quincy Adams established public botanic gardens, recognising the naturalisation and cultivation of useful plants as a primary economic necessity. Constantine Rafinesque, the author of the *New Flora and Botany of North America* (1836–1938) published a volume of poetry, *The World; or, Instability* (1836). Such endeavours helped to form the distinctive attitude to *Nature developed in Sarah Hoare's *Poems on Conchology and Botany* (1831) and the works of Henry David Thoreau and Ralph Waldo Emerson.

The enormous variety of plants revealed as a result of disciplined searches became an imaginative inspiration in itself. The bizarrerie of many specimens is celebrated in a remarkable chapter in Joris-Karl Huysmans' extended hymn to perversity *À rebours* (1884; trans. as *Against the Grain* and *Against Nature*), and the metaphorical imagery of flowers became a key element of the Symbolist Movement that Huysmans helped to launch, extravagantly developed by such writers as Rémy de Gourmont and Jean Lorrain. The illustrator Isidore Grandville had provided further inspiration for such adventures in *Les fleurs animées* (1847), in which beautiful women are elaborately costumed with flowers. Imaginary plants—including the mandrake, whose anthropomorphic root screams when detached, and the Upas Tree, which poisons the ground for miles around—were frequently drafted to serve as symbols, although the most significant of all symbolic trees remained the one that grew in Eden.

The Edenic tree was sometimes divided into two, on the assumption that the reference in *Genesis* 2:9 to "the tree of life" and "the tree of knowledge of good and evil" is to separate individuals; when the tree of knowledge had acquired new symbolic meaning in the context of the Age of Enlightenment, Tiphaigne de la Roche's allegorical *Giphantie* (1760; trans. as *Gyphantia*) introduced a third. However many they may have been, the corollary notion of Edenic "forbidden fruit" did sterling service in nineteenth-century literature; its representations in Victorian England—especially Christina Rossetti's "Goblin Market" (1862)—are particularly pointed. So all-pervasive is the Eden myth that horticultural symbolism found its influence virtually inescapable, even in such conscientiously secularised examples as Anton Chekhov's "Chernyi monakh" (1894; trans. as "The Black Monk") and *Vishnyovyy Sad* (1904; trans. as *The Cherry Orchard*).

The speculative botany of eighteenth- and nine-teenth-century popular literature made abundant use of traditional motifs. Plants to yield miraculous cures flourished as never before, as did plants to provide exotic poisons. Ambulatory plants, like the tree-men of Nazar in Ludwig Holberg's *Nicolaii Klimii Iter Subterraneum* (1741; trans. as *A Journey to the World Underground*) became incessantly restless. Carnivorous specimens, such as Phil Robinson's "The Man-Eating Tree" (1881) and Frank Aubrey's *The Devil-Tree of El Dorado* (1897), grew increasingly ambitious. The use of such motifs—especially the last—soon became sufficiently commonplace to warrant satirical treatment, as in H. G. Wells' "The Flowering of the Strange Orchid" (1894). Innovation was, however, rare; even the flying tree described in Edward Page Mitchell's "The Balloon Tree" (1883) is a straightforward extrapolation of the locomotion motif.

The development of palaeobotany in the nineteenth century facilitated the integration of the Linnaean classification into evolutionary theory, assisting the realisation that angiosperms (flowering plants) had been a late arrival on the evolutionary scene, largely displacing the gymnosperms (plants with "naked seeds") whose tree species had established vast forests during an earlier phase of life's conquest of the land. The first phases of that invasion were credited to algae. Fungi, which had long been considered to be part of the subject matter of botany, were difficult to accommodate within the sequence, and were eventually given a category of their own in the broad categorisation of the subsections of biology. While they remained part of the subject matter of botany, fungi occupied a special place in the subject's speculative literature by virtue of their association with decay, toxicity, and *psychotropic effects; elaborately sinister fungal ecosystems are featured in John Uri Lloyd's *Etidorhpa* (1895), William Hope Hodgson's "The Voice in the Night" (1905), and Philip M. Fisher's "Fungus Isle" (1923).

The twentieth-century literary development of already-familiar motifs found various means to increase their melodramatic component. The vegetable villains in Lyle Wilson Holden's "The Devil Plant" (1923),

Edmond Hamilton's "The Plant Revolt" (1930), and John Wyndham's "The Day of the Triffids" (1951) are straightforwardly violent, while those in James H. Schmitz's "The Pork Chop Tree" (1965) and "Compulsion" (1970) and Helen Cresswell's *The Bongleweed* (1973) are more subtly dangerous. The "man-eating" plant in D. L. James' "Beyond the Sun" (1939) and the psychotropic dahlias that "take over" the world in Mark Clifton's "The Conqueror" (1952) are, however, essentially beneficent. The economic roles traditionally played by plants had far less melodramatic potential, but lent themselves to occasional extreme extrapolation in accounts of new food plants, such as John Gloag's *Manna* (1940) and Aubrey Menen's *The Fig Tree* (1959); new plant-based textiles, such as Isaac *Asimov's *The Currents of Space* (1952); and panaceas, such as John Rackham's *The Flower of Doradil* (1970).

Earthly animate plants were largely relegated to such farces as Alfred Toombs' comedy *Good as Gold* (1955) in the twentieth century, but accounts of alien "plant-men" became common in such pulp stories as Edgar Rice Burroughs' *The Gods of Mars* (1913; book, 1918), Raymond Z. Gallun's "Moon Plague" (1934), and Murray Leinster's "Proxima Centauri" (1935). The notion of ambulatory plants was given more serious consideration in Clifford Simak's "Green Thumb" (1954), although the clever plants featured in Leinster's "The Plants" (1946) have to employ animals as motile instruments. The plants grown from Laurence Manning's "Seeds from Space" (1935) contend that, while vegetable life is widespread in the universe, animal life is scarce and humans are the only known example of animal intelligence.

The sentient plant in Stanley G. Weinbaum's "The Lotus Eaters" (1935) is philosophical about its destiny to provide food to stupid herbivores, but intelligent plant life is dominant on Mars in John Keir Cross' *The Angry Planet* (1945). Similarly ambitious vegetable intelligences are featured in Clifford Simak's *All Flesh Is Grass* (1965) and John Rackham's *The Treasure of Tau Ceti* (1969) and *The Anything Tree* (1970). More thoughtful exercises in vegetable existentialism include Ursula K. Le Guin's "Vaster Than Empires and More Slow" (1971) and Ronald Cain's "Weed Killers" (1973). The singing plants featured in L. Sprague de Camp's "Property of Venus" (1955) and J. G. Ballard's "Prime Belladonna" (1956) are, however, no smarter than the average songbird.

The sexual connotations of botanic science were given more leeway as the twentieth century progressed. Orchids—named for their alleged resemblance to an item of human reproductive apparatus—were frequently featured in this context, as in John Jason Trent's *Phalaenopsis gloriosa* (1906) and Edward Heron-Allen's *Passiflora vindicta Wrammsbothame* (1934, by-lined Christopher Blayre). Other species are employed in similarly suggestive ways in Evelyn E. Smith's "The Venus Trap" (1956), Rosel George Brown's "From an Unseen Censor" (1958), and Hugh Zachary's *Gwen, in Green* (1974). Large-scale ecosystems whose description stresses exotic methods of sexual reproduction include those featured in John Boyd's *The Pollinators of Eden* (1969) and *Barnard's Planet* (1975) and the bloomenveldt in Norman Spinrad's *Child of Fortune* (1985). Edenic symbolism inevitably figures in a great many sexual allegories, most conspicuously in David Lindsay's *The Violet Apple* (written ca. 1925; published 1975).

Botanists rarely recommend themselves for use as heroes in fiction, being less amenable than archaeologists to Indiana Jones–style makeovers, but Frank Belknap Long's *John Carstairs, Space Detective* (1949) is described as a "botanical detective". An ethnobotanist plays a heroic role in Howard V. Hendrix's "Singing the Mountain to the Stars" (1991; exp. as *The Vertical Fruit of the Horizontal Tree*, 1994), while the cyborgised heroine of Kage Baker's "Noble Mold" (1997; incorporated into *In the Garden of Iden*, 1998) is a botanist recruited by the mysterious Company to recover endangered plant species by means of time travel.

The twentieth-century development of *ecology inevitably proved to have the most significant influence on the use of botanical motifs in speculative fiction. Botanical *ecocatastrophes come in two main varieties, the more elementary featuring the failure of vital crops, as in John Christopher's *The Death of Grass* (1956), while the other features vegetable plagues like the one in Ward Moore's *Greener Than You Think* (1947). Descriptions of alien flora grew much more ambitious as ecological thinking advanced, with notable examples featured in Doris Piserchia's *Earthchild* (1977) and Ian McDonald's *Chaga* (1995; aka *Evolution's Shore*) and *Kirinya* (1998). The special role in maintaining the balance of the ecosphere attributed by early ecologists to rain forests—much elaborated in the wake of James *Lovelock's Gaia hypothesis—is reflected in a wide range of fiction dealing in a mystical spirit with forests. Stories imaginatively remaking humankind's ecological and spiritual relationships with trees include Jack Vance's *Son of the Tree* (1951; book, 1964) and *The Houses of Iszm* (1954; book, 1964) and Julian Chain's "Cosmophyte" (1952). Edward Rager's "Crying Willow" (1973) describes the rise of LEAF (the League to Eliminate the Abuse of Flora). A sentient tree is employed as a not-entirely-objective

observer of human affairs in Don Sakers' "The Leaves of October" (1983) and "All Fall Down" (1987).

Botany remains a central science in speculative fiction, the continued role of plants as primary producers seemingly assured by the dearth of accounts of artificial photosynthesis. The method devised in E. C. Large's *Sugar in the Air* (1937) goes sadly to waste, and such technologies attracted surprisingly little attention thereafter, although they are central to the background of the future history set out in Brian Stableford's emortality series.

BOVA, BEN(JAMIN WILLIAM) (1932–)

U.S. writer. He obtained a B.S. from Temple University, Philadelphia, in 1954, adding an M.A. from State University of New York, Albany, in 1983. He worked as a technical editor, documentary screenwriter, and science writer before succeeding John W. *Campbell Jr. as editor of *Analog* from 1971 to 1978, after which he served as fiction editor for the popular science magazine *Omni* from 1978 to 1982, becoming a freelance writer thereafter. One of his colleagues at the Avco Research Laboratory in the 1960s, Myron R. Lewis, collaborated on two of his early science fiction stories, "The Dueling Machine" (1963; aka "The Perfect Warrior"; book, 1969) and "Men of Good Will" (1964).

Bova's first book was the children's science fiction novel *The Star Conquerors* (1959), but he devoted more attention to the popularisation of science for young readers than to fiction during the 1960s. He produced *The Milky Way Galaxy: Man's Exploration of the Stars* (1961), *Giants of the Animal World* (1962), *Reptiles Since the World Began* (1964), and *The Uses of Space* (1965) in parallel with scientific articles in various science fiction magazines and the occasional science fiction story before returning to "young adult" science fiction of a more sophisticated kind. *The Weathermakers* (1967), whose short version had appeared in *Analog* a year before, features an altruistic scientist battling against short-sighted politicians and obsessive military men to secure technological progress in weather control. Much of Bova's subsequent work in the field of *hard science fiction followed a similar pattern, representing the central narrative of the history of science as a ceaseless heroic struggle against the inhibiting effects of short-term thinking and the monopolistic inclinations of militarists.

In the late 1960s and early 1970s, when his writings became more prolific, Bova continued to produce such young adult science fiction novels as *Out of the Sun* (1968), *Escape!* (1970), the trilogy comprising *Exiled from Earth* (1971), *Flight of Exiles* (1972), and *End of Exile* (1975), *When the Sky Burned* (1973; rev. as *Test of Fire*), and *The Winds of Altair* (1973) in parallel with children's nonfiction books whose range grew steadily more adventurous. The latter included *In Quest of Quasars* (1970), *The Amazing Laser* (1971; reprinted in *Out of the Sun*, 1984), *Starflight and Other Improbabilities* (1973), and the couplet *Man Changes the Weather* (1973) and *The Weather Changes Man* (1974). Once he had taken over the editorial chair at *Analog*, however, Bova began to produce similar works for adults, including the non-fiction books *The Fourth State of Matter: Plasma Dynamics and Tomorrow's Technology* (1971) and *The New Astronomies* (1972), and the mosaic novel *As on a Darkling Plain* (1972), based on a map of space exploration unfolded in "The Towers of Titan" (1962), "The Sirius Mission" (1969), and "The Jupiter Mission" (1970).

Bova's career as a writer changed direction in the mid-1970s, for reasons hinted at in four 1975 publications; two were children's nonfiction books, *Through Eyes of Wonder: Science Fiction and Science* and *Science—Who Needs It?*; one an adult nonfiction book, *Notes to a Science Fiction Writer*; and one a curious *roman à clef* satirically depicting the spoliation of a planned TV science fiction series by the intransigent stupidity of its producers, *The Starcrossed*. His shorter publications in that year included "The Shining Ones", which had been commissioned as a text for "reluctant readers" but then turned down by a panel of "experts" because it featured a hero suffering from a terminal disease.

Having pondered the socioeconomic situation of contemporary science fiction and its various connections with contemporary science, Bova published two novels in 1976 that were deliberately cast as thrillers for marketing outside the genre. *The Multiple Man* is a relatively straightforward political thriller whose plot involves cloning, but *Millennium: A Novel About People and Politics in the Year 1999* was an explicit bid for best-sellerdom, attempting to embed the myth of the Space Age in the matrix of a soap-operatic near-future history, a further segment of which was issued as the prequel novel *Kinsman* (1979). The intermediate novel, *Colony* (1978), also extended the enterprise, although it was not directly linked to the others.

When this attempt to reach a wider audience failed, Bova reverted to fiction much closer to the core of hard science fiction in the series comprising *Voyagers* (1981), *Voyagers II: The Alien Within* (1986), and *Voyagers III: Star Brothers* (1990), a sophisticated space opera in which politicians attempt to inhibit and conceal a first contact with aliens, prompting the protagonist to take exotic unilateral action in the interests of introducing humankind to a new phase in history. A similar theme, set against a more exaggerated background, is treated with slightly less reverence in the Space Age fantasy comprising *Privateers* (1985) and *Empire Builders* (1993).

Bova carried forward his satirical interests in *Cyberbooks* (1989), a witty exploration of possibilities inherent in the electronic reproduction of text, but he retreated temporarily from his didactic ambitions in a series of fantasy novels and two far-futuristic science fiction novels, *To Save the Sun* (1992) and *To Fear the Light* (1994), written in collaboration with A. J. Austin. He returned to near-future hard science fiction, committed to a more modest version of the Space Age, in *Mars* (1992), which became the first item in a loosely knit series he called the Grand Tour. The series includes the couplet *Moonrise* (1996) and *Moonwar* (1998), *Return to Mars* (1999), *Venus* (2001), *Jupiter* (2001), and *Saturn* (2003) and does indeed constitute a grand tour of the solar system revealed by contemporary space probes. One of its offshoots and the Asteroid War series launched in *The Precipice* (2001) was continued in *The Rock Rats* (2002).

In parallel with the early phases of the Grand Tour series, Bova dipped into alternative history in *Triumph* (1993) and continued to produce such techno-thrillers as *Death Dream* (1994) and *Brothers* (1995), the first featuring virtual reality and the second a breakthrough in medical biotechnology. He then settled into the kind of role expected of American science fiction writers, providing fictional propaganda for the continuation of the space program in the form of celebratory novels of frontiersmanship. Although his cynicism regarding politicians had always been widespread within that subgenre, his anxieties regarding the potential role of the military were less commonplace. The greatest virtue of his work remained the intelligence with which he researched his backgrounds and extrapolated his hypotheses; although he abandoned the popularisation of science in the late 1980s, after publishing *Welcome to Moonbase* (1987), *The Beauty of Light* (1988), and *Interactions: A Journey Through the Mind of A Particle Physicist and the Matter of This World* (1988; with Sheldon Glashow), he maintained his interest in contemporary scientific developments and his attention was always scrupulous.

BRIN, (GLEN) DAVID (1950–)

U.S. writer. Brin obtained a B.S. in astronomy from the California Institute of Technology in 1973 and then spent two years on the technical staff of the Hughes Aircraft Research Laboratory at Newport

Beach before receiving an M.S. in electrical engineering from the University of California, San Diego. He went on to obtain a Ph.D. in space science from UCSD in 1981. His scientific publications are distributed across a wide spectrum of topics, including papers on space station design, the theory of polarised light, the nature of comets, and the astronomical and philosophical questions implicit in the Search for Extra-Terrestrial Intelligence (*SETI).

While working for his doctorate, Brin completed his first science fiction novel, *Sundiver* (1980). He went on to teach physics and writing at San Diego State University between 1982 and 1985, during which time he was also a postdoctoral fellow at the California Space Institute. He then became a full-time writer, although he spent some time as a "visiting artist" at the University of London's Westfield College, served as a "visiting disputant" at the Center for Evolution and the Origin of Life in 1988–1990, and was a research affiliate at the Jet Propulsion Laboratory in 1992–1993.

Sundiver introduced a backcloth in which humankind has managed to augment the *intelligence and communicative ability of dolphins and chimpanzees, thus "uplifting" them to membership in a common moral community. Contact with alien species has, however, informed humans that their own seemingly spontaneous evolution of sapience is a dramatic exception to the normal pattern; all other known sapient species have been artificially uplifted by "patrons" who consider that favour a debt to be repaid by long periods of servitude. Humankind is thus considered to be a "wolfling" species, unready for participation in galactic civilisation. A novella set against the same background, "The Tides of Kithrup" (1981), was expanded into the second novel in the Uplift series, *Startide Rising* (1983).

The *Practice Effect* (1984) is a comic portal fantasy about a quasi-Mediaeval parallel world in which practice really does make artifacts perfect, and lack of usage results in a loss of virtue; like many a Campbellian hero before him, the zievatron-displaced physicist precipitated into this strange milieu finds the problem of introducing enlightenment into the Dark Age rather vexing, but eventually proves equal to the task. The mosaic *The Postman* (1985)—whose 1997 film version is a travesty of the text—describes how a man who masquerades as a postman to win the favour of townspeople in a post-holocaust America gradually becomes what he pretends to be in order to establish a platform for the rebuilding of democratic society. *Heart of the Comet* (1986), written by Brin in collaboration with his fellow Californian hard science fiction writer Gregory *Benford, attempted to take advantage of the long-anticipated reappearance of Halley's comet. Brin then

returned to the Uplift series in *The Uplift War* (1987), which foregrounds uplifted chimpanzees rather than the dolphins featured in its predecessor—the book is dedicated to Jane Goodall, Sarah Hrdy, and Diane Fossey, whose work with various primate species provided the basis from which the author's depiction of uplifted chimpanzees and the alien Garthlings is extrapolated.

Earth (1990), set fifty years in the future, is a definitive *ecocatastrophe novel—one of the first to foreground climate change—employing a mosaic narrative technique similar to the one that John Brunner had used for the same purpose in *Stand on Zanzibar* (1968), although Brin anchored his commentary embellishments to a robust central plot thread in which a scientific experiment with a tiny black hole goes disastrously awry. *Glory Season* (1993) is a bold exercise in social design, featuring a pastoral society run by *feminists, whose strict limitation of advanced technologies has been facilitated by the social marginalisation of males. The novel proved controversial, but Brin had always been eager to court controversy, developing a contentious speaking style and freely indulging his love of polemic in such articles as "Zero Sum Elections and the Electoral College" (1992) and "The Threat of Aristocracy" (1994) in *Liberty* and an interview in *Wired* entitled "Privacy Is History—Get Over It" (1996), all of which provided fuel for his nonfiction book *The Transparent Society: Will Technology Force Us to Choose Between Freedom and Privacy?* (1998).

Brin's next addition to the Uplift series was a trilogy comprising *Brightness Reef* (1995), *Infinity's Shore* (1996), and *Heaven's Reach* (1998), in which various alien species eking out a fugitive existence on a world that had supposedly been left to "lie fallow" by its former leaseholders are drawn back into the convoluted network of multigalactic society. *Kiln People* (2002, aka *Kil'n People*), which describes a near-future society in which people can delegate their aspects of their lives to temporary "golem" copies with various ability levels, has as much in common with *The Practice Effect* as his hard science fiction novels, but is extrapolated with the same relentless efficiency and eagerly confronts the various social and philosophical problems thrown up as corollaries of that extrapolation.

BRODERICK, DAMIEN (FRANCIS) (1944–)

Australian writer and scholar. Broderick obtained a B.A. in English from Monash University in Clayton, Victoria. His Ph.D. thesis, presented to Deakin

University, Victoria, in 1990, was on the work of Samuel R. *Delany; the perspectives developed therein led him to become one of the first writers to apply *postmodernist perspectives to science fiction in a more general fashion in *The Architecture of Babel: Discourses of Literature and Science* (1994) and *Reading by Starlight: Postmodern Science Fiction* (1995).

Broderick's early science fiction, including *The Sea's Furthest End* (short version, 1964; exp. book, 1993) and *Sorceror's World* (1970; rev. as *The Black Grail*, 1986) exhibited a strong interest in the far future that was more robustly rationalised in the *Omega Point fantasy *The Judas Mandala* (1982). He subsequently compiled a definitive showcase far-futuristic anthology that mixed fiction and nonfiction, *Earth Is But a Star: Excursions Through Science Fiction to the Far Futures* (2001). The chimerical melding of science fiction and magic characteristic of far-futuristic fantasy is also featured in *The Dreaming Dragons* (1980; rev. as *The Dreaming*, 2001) and the comedy *Striped Holes* (1988). Broderick eventually lumped all of these novels together—adding a naturalistic novel about science fiction fandom, *Transmitters* (1984), and a far-futuristic transfiguration of *Hamlet*, *The White Abacus* (1997)—within a collective he called the Faustus Hexagram.

Most of Broderick's other novels were written in collaboration with Rory Barnes. *Valencies* (1983)

"premembers" a future in which the entire universe of 4004 A.D. is colonised by humans, four billion to a world, their lives perfectly regulated by an Imperium employing its own predictive "mimetic hypercycles". *Zones* (1997) is a thriller about phone calls from the future. *Stuck in Fast Forward* (1999) features a bubble in space-time that becomes an unreliable time machine. *The Book of Revelation* (1999) is a millennial black comedy.

In the speculative nonfiction books *The Spike: Accelerating into the Unimaginable Future* (1997; rev. as *The Spike: How Our Lives Are Being Transformed by Rapidly Advancing Technology*, 2001) and *The Last Mortal Generation: How Science Will Alter Our Lives in the 21st Century* (1999), Broderick developed a notion very similar to Vernor Vinge's notion of a technological *singularity. Some of the ideas in the books are fictionally extrapolated in *Transcension* (2002) and *Godplayers* (2005); the latter novel's manifold of alternative histories is complicated by the conflict of the eponymous superhumans, who are obsessed with control of "Xon matter". These works established Broderick as one of the leading figures in the attempt to imagine the kinds of *posthuman evolution that might be associated with a technological singularity, and how such an evolution might foreshadow the ultimate destiny of humankind and life in general.

C

CAMPBELL, JOHN W[OOD] Jr. (1910–1971)

U.S. editor and writer who studied physics at the Massachusetts Institute of Technology from 1928 to 1931 before obtaining his B.S. at Duke University in 1933. He began publishing science fiction while still at college, with a story about a mathematically innovative supercomputer, "When the Atoms Failed" (1930). A larger device of a similar sort operates a mechanical invasion fleet in the sequel "The Metal Horde" (1930), Campbell's first venture into the hectic action-adventure space fiction that he was to develop more extravagantly than any of his contemporaries during the first phase of his career. The use of a galactic stage for action-adventure fiction had been pioneered only two years earlier by E. E. Smith and Edmond Hamilton; along with Jack Williamson, Campbell was one of the first writers to follow their lead. He conserved the fervent romanticism that characterised the works of the other three authors but injected massive doses of theoretical physics into the mix in *The Black Star Passes* (1930; book, 1953), *Islands of Space* (1931; book, 1956), and *Invaders from the Infinite* (1932; book, 1961). The series demonstrated the new subgenre's tendency to extreme melodramatic inflation, expanding out of the solar system with explosive verve.

Campbell moderated the narrative scale of "Beyond the End of Space" (1933) to more manageable dimensions, but the temptations of extravagance were irresistible and he returned to a vast stage in *The Mightiest Machine* (1934; book, 1947). His insistence on interrupting the spectacular action of his plots with extensive expository lumps prevented its sequels seeing print until they were belatedly collected as *The Incredible Planet* (1949), so he toned his work down again. His most notable subsequent work consisted of relatively brief but far-reaching *contes philosophiques* of a kind pioneered in "The Voice of the Void" (1930), in which force beings attack the ultimate descendants of humankind ten billion years in the future, when the Sun is about to go nova. "The Last Evolution" (1932) sketches out a future history in which a decadent human species threatened by a war for survival is replaced by intelligent machines designed to fight that war, which are superseded in their turn by "Beings of Force".

A similar evolutionary pattern was explored in two far-futuristic fantasies by-lined Don A. Stuart, "Twilight" (1934) and "Night" (1935), in which a Utopian lifestyle secured by mechanical production leads humankind to degeneracy and extinction. Subsequent Stuart stories elaborated various alternative scenarios for humankind's future evolution, but the only one seemingly indicative of a viable exit from the impasse of mechanical dependence was "Forgetfulness" (1937), in which the necessity for technology is sidelined by the development of *parapsychological powers. Most of Campbell's work in this vein was assembled in the omnibus *A New Dawn: The Complete Don A. Stuart Stories* (2003). Campbell's own by-line was replaced by the Stuart pseudonym because, after an interval of working as a salesman and in the research department of two technology companies, he had started work as assistant editor to F. Orlin Tremaine on *Astounding Stories*, and the magazine's owners did not like their employees to write for their own publications. The Stuart name vanished too, not long after Campbell succeeded Tremaine as editor and was held to a contract he had signed that forbade him to write science fiction for anyone.

Seemingly undismayed by this restriction, Campbell set about encouraging other writers to develop his ideas and to grapple with the problems he had encountered—including the practical problem of combining scientific exposition with exuberant narrative as well as the philosophical corollaries of human dependence on technology. He changed his magazine's title to *Astounding Science Fiction*, subsequently moving it through a series of phases reflective of his own aborted career; its early exploitation of space opera gradually gave way to increasingly sophisticated *contes philosophiques* written by a stable of writers whose initial key members included Robert A. *Heinlein, Isaac *Asimov, Clifford D. *Simak, L. Sprague *de Camp, Hal *Clement, *A. E. van Vogt, Lester del Rey, and the husband-and-wife team of Henry Kuttner and C. L. Moore. The first ten years of Campbell's editorship, when he successfully steered the magazine through the economic difficulties caused by the United States' involvement in World War II, were often described subsequently as science fiction's "Golden Age", when many new ideas were wide open to ingenious and adventurous exploration.

Campbell's Golden Age came to an end when *Astounding* veered into highly controversial territory during a 1950s boom in tales of *parapsychological superhumanity. Campbell's increasingly unreliable judgment—first compromised when he lent his support to Dianetics, a new kind of psychotherapy invented by one of the more colourful members of his stable, L. Ron Hubbard—led him to give publicity to a series of exotic devices in the 1950s and 1960s, including the Hieronymus Machine for detecting psychic force and an eccentric perpetual motion machine called the Dean Drive. He was not the first determinedly unorthodox thinker to follow a path into the further reaches of absurdity, but his waywardness reflected awkwardly on the *hard science fiction whose principal champion he had become, and whose production he continued to influence heavily by feeding the story ideas he could not develop himself to his favourite writers. His covert exercise of certain eccentric editorial preferences, one of which favoured a determined human chauvinism, also narrowed the scope of the fiction he published.

Campbell's faith in his own powers of prophecy was partly based in the early success of his fervent advocacy of the practicality of atomic power. He was also an enthusiastic advocate of the development of rockets as a means of space travel, and the progress of space science in the real world continually topped up his faith in his own judgment. His principal contribution to the development of modern futuristic fiction was, however, his insistence that it should be as respectful as possible of the boundaries of scientific possibility, to the extent that such scrupulousness was compatible with the demands of melodrama. He understood the importance of facilitating devices like faster-than-light travel and time machines, but insisted that they ought to be shored up by appropriate apologetic jargon, and that the premises used to establish them should be extrapolated carefully as well as boldly. He applied the same philosophy to *Astounding*'s short-lived fantasy companion *Unknown*, allowing its writers to employ all kinds of exotic premises but demanding that they employ rigorous logic in their extrapolation, thus producing a highly distinctive and conspicuously modern brand of "rationalistic fantasy".

Although he was only in charge of one science fiction magazine among many, whose heyday endured for little more than a single war-afflicted decade, Campbell contrived to establish his prospectus as an ideal at which all science fiction should aim, whose careless betrayal ought to be a source of shame. He insisted that conscientious science fiction ought to employ the future and other worlds as arenas for serious speculation rather than mere costume drama, and should apply an analogue of the scientific method to the business of constructing and testing its experimental visions. He eventually succeeded in emblazoning this manifesto on the figurehead of his magazine when he renamed it *Analog* in the late 1950s.

It is arguable that *Analog* was never the best advertisement for its own cause, being irredeemably tainted by Campbell's overinvestment in unorthodoxy and his constricted ideological agenda, but without such insistent advertisement the cause would have received far weaker and even more sporadic support than it did. Twentieth-century reflections of and responses to scientific progress, in Europe as well as the United States, would be fewer in number, vaguer in kind, and considerably less interesting had Campbell not committed himself so fully to his ambition. His fervent determination to import an intellectual sophistication into pulp science fiction made him a uniquely influential figurehead, who exerted more influence on the development of modern speculative fiction than any other individual, including H. G. Wells.

CARTOGRAPHY

The art and science of mapping. Map making, which presumably originated in association with the invention of *writing as an adjunct to hunting and trade, was one of the earliest technological practices to involve intellectual abstraction and graphic representation. The oldest indubitable specimens date back to the third millennium B.C., although some of the lines inscribed in neolithic cave art and bone fragments might have served a cartographic purpose. The first attempts to illustrate the *geography of the whole world appear to have been made around 1000 B.C., but the vast majority of maps remained utilitarian guides to navigation on land and sea.

Roman maps were more sternly utilitarian than those produced earlier by the Greeks, being adapted to the requirements of military campaigns and road building; one famous example was inscribed on the inner walls of a colonnade commissioned by the Roman admiral Vipsanius Agrippa in the first century B.C. The most outstanding cartographer of the Classical era was Ptolemy, whose attempts to describe the world extended beyond geography into *cosmology. His underestimation of the size of the *Earth's surface became accommodated within Renaissance learning along with his *Aristotelian model of the solar system, leading Christopher Columbus drastically to underestimate the distance he would have to sail in a westward direction to reach the Indies.

The heritage of Graeco-Roman cartography was largely lost during the Dark Ages, when social horizons suffered a drastic shrinkage, although maps of coastlines were employed as aids to marine navigation. Larger scale maps—"mappemondes"—evolved towards figurative representations of the Christian worldview, generally aggregating the bulk of the world's landmass into a single continuum with Jerusalem or Rome at the centre, often reformulating the synoptic landmass to form the image of a face or a fruit. The Renaissance expansion of trade, however, involved a rapid increase in the sophistication of portolans—pilot books indicating sailing courses, ports, coastal hazards, anchorages, and so forth.

The further ships went abroad, the greater their dependence became on maps and associated navigational aids, which created demands for better astronomical charts and better timepieces, greatly encouraging the observations and measurements on which the scientific revolution was based. Outside Europe, Oriental map making kept pace with early European developments in terms of accuracy of measurement, but it could not match the expansion of perspective associated with the great navigations of the fifteenth and sixteenth centuries.

All large-scale maps suffer from the problem of representing a curved surface on a flat one; the most popular solution originated when Gerardus Mercator published a map of Europe employing the projection named after him in 1554. The technology of manufacturing globes, pasting two-dimensional strips on to a spherical surface, also made rapid progress in the sixteenth century. The first modern world atlas was produced in 1570 by Abraham Ortelius.

From the seventeenth century onwards, mapping expeditions were sent out by all the major European powers, their collective endeavours laying the foundations for an eighteenth-century reformation that swept away the last vestiges of Mediaeval illustration and symbolic representation, substituting stern lines governed by precise scientific measurements. Such maps became increasingly detailed and accurate throughout the nineteenth and twentieth centuries, the work of surface-bound surveyors eventually being supplemented by aerial photographs, and ultimately including photographs taken by artificial satellites. Astronomers began constructing sketch maps of other planets as soon as they had *telescopes, to supplement maps of the near side of the Moon based on observations of the naked eye, but such designs remained intrinsically treacherous—maps of *Mars were particularly misleading—until the advent of space probes facilitated a rapid sophistication of such volumes as Patrick Moore's *Philip's Atlas of the Universe* (1994; rev. 1997).

In parallel with the latter phases of this history, the role of maps in prose fiction became increasingly important. A narrative is itself something that has to be navigated by writer and reader alike, and the business of constructing or following a story line has something in common with undertaking a journey—a correlation celebrated in such *contes philosophiques* as Jorge Luis Borges' "La Muerte y La Brujula" (1964; trans. as "Death and the Compass"). Narrative traction is routinely provided by the establishment of "landmarks" whose apparent direction and distance allow readers to orientate themselves. When plots involve actual journeys, as they very often do, maps are routinely provided, not merely for the internal use of characters but as external appendices for use by readers. It is only natural that one of the most common and enduring literary clichés is the treasure map. The fictional construction of hypothetical islands, nations, and cities often involves the construction of maps to be included in published versions, and this practice expanded naturally to the mapping of entire imaginary worlds. Map-based plotting became fundamental to the new kind of active fiction pioneered in the 1960s in such role-playing games as *Dungeons and Dragons*.

Cartographic impulses routinely transcend matters of narrative and geographical plausibility; the allegorical landscapes described by Dante's *Divina Commedia* (ca. 1307–1321), Phineas Fletcher's *The Purple Island; or, The Isle of Man* (1633), John Bunyan's *The Pilgrim's Progress* (1678), and Robert Ellis Dudgeon's *Colymbia* (1873) require and invite cartographical representation just as much as the imaginary plans of Thomas More's *Utopia* (1516) and Tommaso Campanella's *La Cittá del Sole* (written 1602; published 1623; trans. as *The City of the Sun*), the mariners' sketches of Robert Louis Stevenson's *Treasure Island* (1883) and its many imitations, the routes from known territories into the heart of the Dark Continent plotted in H. Rider Haggard's *King Solomon's Mines* (1886) and its many imitations, and the otherworldly maps that lend a further dimension of *hardness to such science fiction novels as Jules Verne's *Autour de la lune* (1870; trans. as *Around the Moon*), and Arthur C. Clarke's *Sands of Mars* (1951). The construction of maps of imaginary places—one of several classes of items aggregated as "cartifacts" by the curator Jan Smits—is practiced as an artform by such visual artists as Calyxa and Gregor Turk, and the production of "real" treasure maps is now a substantial industry.

Significant fictional accounts of cartographers at work include Jules Verne's *Aventures de trois russes et trois anglais dans l'Afrique australe* (1872; trans. as *Measuring a Meridian*) and Robert Whitaker's *The Mapmaker's Wife* (2004). Russell Hoban's *The Lion of Jachin-Boaz and Boaz-Jachin* (1973) offers a more impressionistic account of cartographical artistry and its psychological correlates. Notable science-fictional maps include the hi-tech treasure map featured in Charles Sheffield's transfiguration of Stevenson's *Treasure Island, Godspeed* (1993). Futuristic depictions of cartographers at work include Frederik Pohl's account of hyperspatial mapping in "The Mapmakers" (1955). Harlan Ellison's "Incognita, Inc." (2001) is a mildly surrealised cartographic fantasy. The atlas of *cyberspace available at www.cybergeography.org is one of several cartographic guides to the Internet.

Although the prolific use of stereotyped maps by modern writers of immersive fantasy—including many science-fictional variants—has attracted some derision, they are very useful to readers of such texts, and their function extends far beyond the mere matter of allowing the reader to follow the course of the story line through its various settings (although a dotted line is often included for this purpose). As well as displaying the setting and measuring the characters' movements, such maps characterise the worlds within the stories in a more fundamental and impressionistic

fashion, often conveyed by means of pseudo-Mediaeval embellishments or improvisations credited to their fictitious makers.

CATASTROPHISM

One of "two antagonist doctrines of geology" identified by William Whewell's *History of the Inductive Sciences* (1837), its antithesis being uniformitarianism. Whewell sought to distinguish theories of the Earth's history that imagined it to have been shaped primarily by sudden catastrophic events—floods, earthquakes, and volcanic eruptions—from those that imagined it to have been slowly sculpted by erosion and sedimentation. The former school embraced the ideas of such writers as Lazzaro Moro and Gerges Cuvier, whereas the latter thesis was developed by James Hutton and Charles Lyell. Given the abundant scope and apparent necessity for compromise, the dispute would not have assumed serious proportions had it not formed a key element of the *ideological conflict between *creationists, whose reliance on the Biblical deluge placed them squarely in the former camp, and *evolutionists, whose ideas required more gradual changes to have taken place over vast reaches of time.

Catastrophism inevitably has greater appeal to storytellers than uniformitarianism; the reliance of fiction on dramatic events strongly favours fire, flood, and trembling ground over processes on the margins of perception, although some scope is preserved for the latter in elegiac poetry, and in rhapsodic prose passages employed as narrative decor in works whose narrative energy comes from elsewhere. For this reason, fictional elaborations of the Earth's history have always been heavily biased towards catastrophic events and catastrophist explanations, and fiction writers have always reacted enthusiastically to new discoveries such as the evidence of an asteroid strike that might have completed the destruction of the *dinosaurs. Pseudoscientific accounts of Earth's history, like those contained in Ignatus Donnelly's *Ragnarok: The Age of Fire and Gravel* (1883) and Immanuel Velikovsky's *Worlds in Collision* (1950), exhibit a similar prejudice in favour of catastrophism; this helps to explain their popular appeal.

The major subgenres of the *disaster story made considerable leaps forward while the nineteenth-century dispute identified by Whewell was raging, and their popularity continued to increase throughout the twentieth century while the scientific debate colonised other fields. The same contrasting tendencies in explanation are evident in *cosmology, where catastrophist explanations—including the Comte du Buffon's suggestion that the planets were formed as a result of a collision between the sun and a comet, Big Bang theory, and theses awarding supernovas a key role in cosmic evolution—have been opposed by suppositions based on a uniformitarian "cosmological principle", such as the one that led Fred *Hoyle and his associates to formulate a "steady-state" cosmology. In the academic realm of *history, a castastrophist emphasis on the importance of wars and *disasters is opposed by uniformitarian theories of social development.

Historical fiction, inevitably, prefers to deal with what the proverbial Chinese curse calls "interesting times", but the preference for catastrophist explanation is also obvious in different styles of historical explanation. This is one of the reasons for the relative invisibility in historical writings of the subtler causal effects of *technology. The case made out in L. Sprague de Camp's *Lest Darkness Fall* (1939), which favours subtle *technological determinism over violent conflict as a causal agent, is a rare exception in any field; even those within the field of technological determinism prefer to speak in terms of revolution rather than evolution.

The legacy of nineteenth-century disputes between catastrophists and uniformitarians, and the significance they assumed in a theological context, is abundantly echoed in a catastrophist lexicon that has a particular appeal in tabloid *reportage and pulp fiction but is by no means restricted thereto. Legal jargon still refers to unpredictable catastrophic events as "acts of God", and such terms as deluge, Armageddon, judgment day, holocaust, and apocalypse retain a significant *rhetorical force within the vocabulary of common parlance. Uniformitarian rhetoric has a religiosity of its own, although it tends to imply a very different kind of God, whose primary characteristic is patience rather than wrath, as in such formulas as Henry Wadsworth Longfellow's "the mills of God grind slowly, but they grind exceeding small", translated from Friedrich von Logau's *Sinngedichte* (1653).

Catastrophist theory continues to thrive in the attempt to explain a series of "mass extinction events", of which there appear to have been five since the diversification of animal life that followed the end of the Cambrian period 570,000,000 years ago; a sixth is currently in progress. The most famous is the one that put an end to the *dinosaurs 65 million years ago, but it was the least devastating of the set. The mass extinction currently in progress is the result of human activity, but it may prove to be analogous to one of its predecessors; Paul Wignall's discovery of the three phases of the Permian/Triassic extinction—the most rapid of which was occasioned by a massive release of methane held in oceanic clathrates—was immediately linked to growing anxieties regarding the *greenhouse effect, feeding into the disaster stories linked to that phenomenon.

CHAOS

The antithesis of order. In creation *myths chaos often features as a primal situation from which the world is drawn by constructive godly action, and into which it might decay if not actively maintained. This perspective in echoed in the scientific worldview by the notion of *entropy contained within the second law of thermodynamics. There is a certain paradoxicality about the notion, in that total disorder bears a suspicious resemblance to perfect uniformity.

The chaos of creation myths is echoed in philosophical investigations of the question of how order can come into being, and maintain itself, in the absence of godly intervention—an issue considered in scientific terms in such works as *Order Out of Chaos: Man's New Dialogue with Nature* (1984) by Ilya Prigogine and Isabelle Stengers and *The Collapse of Chaos* (1994) by Jack Cohen and Ian Stewart. These works reflected a sudden fashionability generated by a new meaning attached to the term in *mathematical parlance, whose significance was popularised by James Gleick's *Chaos: Making a New Science* (1987). This fashionability was greatly enhanced by the significance within chaos mathematics of the "Mandelbrot set" whose "fractal" graphical extrapolation was an important aspect of early computer *art, generated by such packages as *James Gleick's Chaos: The Software* (1990) and illustrated in several books by Clifford A. *Pickover, whose *Chaos in Wonderland* (1994) makes extravagant use of illustrative fiction to support its popularising efforts. Anne Harris' *The Nature of Smoke* (1996) also makes ingenious fictional use of the Mandelbrot set.

The significance of the mathematical concept of chaos is associated with the observation that the behavior of complex systems governed by simple laws is sometimes extremely difficult to predict, because small variations in initial conditions can be magnified by idiosyncratic causal sequences to produce very different outcomes. The best-known dramatisation of the phenomenon is the "butterfly effect", commonly dramatised by the allegation that a butterfly flapping its wings on one continent might cause a hurricane in another should the causal sequence it initiates happen to magnify the effect at every stage. The popularity of the term might also owe something to Ray Bradbury's *conte philosophique* "A Sound of Thunder" (1954), which makes a similar point by suggesting that the accidental obliteration of a butterfly in remote prehistory might set off a causal chain that alters the political complexion of human society.

The notion of chaos is important in modern scientific thinking because it emphasises the weakness of the link between understanding physical laws and *predicting actual events. The imaginative device of Pierre Laplace's "daemon"—which suggests that if the present position and velocity of every particle were known, the universe's entire future and past might be extrapolated therefrom—is not entirely defeated by the application of chaos theory, but chaos theory highlights the extreme impracticability of making any such calculation, and the uselessness of approximation.

Literary creativity is often represented as a matter of drawing order out of chaos; the unlikelihood of the process being mimicked by chance is often metaphorically represented in terms of randomly typing monkeys reproducing the works of William Shakespeare. John Dewey's pragmaticist theory of *aesthetics suggests that aesthetic experience is born of the dual perception of harmony emerging out of disharmony, and then dissolving again, in an eternal alternation of union and separation. In this view, order and chaos are tendencies in eternal conflict—a notion that is extensively mirrored in literary work.

Order and Chaos are frequently substituted for Good and Evil in the conceptual frameworks of twentieth-century commodified fantasy, most explicitly by Michael Moorcock. Although order is sometimes conceived as innately good and chaos as innately bad, the usual presumption is that the ideal outcome to the conflict is not the annihilation of one or other of the contending forces, but the maintenance of some kind of cosmic balance. By the same token, order and chaos are both routinely cast as undesirable extremes in *dystopian fiction, the prevalence of excessive rigidity being accountable in terms of convenience of representation rather than political bias. Literary attempts to depict a state of chaos inevitably threaten to become chaotic themselves, and hence unreadable—Clark Ashton Smith's description of "The Dimension of Chance" (1932) is a rare example of an attempt to describe a reality unbound by physical laws—but literary manifestos recommending that writers should draw raw materials from the well of chaos are commonplace; Alfred Jarry's *pataphysics is the most explicit.

The capacity of chaotic systems to produce occasional unlikely results is inherently attractive to storytellers, and it is not surprising that the hypothetical butterfly and monkeys armed with typewriters have become celebrities of a sort, whose citation in modern literature is widespread. Science-fictional versions include Raymond F. Jones' "Fifty Million Monkeys" (1943) and Michael F. Flynn's "On the Wings of a Butterfly" (1989). The underlying thesis is sometimes used to support skepticism in literary representations of scientific enterprise; Michael Crichton's *Jurassic Park* (1990) invokes chaos theory as a counter to scientific *hubris*, construing it as a version of Murphy's *law. G. David Nordley's "A Calendar of Chaos" (1991), by contrast, features a Chaos Institute: a "retreat" for theoretical mathematicians concerned with the long-term behavior of hypersensitive systems. Michael Kallenberger's "White Chaos" (1991) draws an analogy with the *acoustic phenomenon of white noise. The idea that chaos mathematics might one day be tamable as a method of prediction is extrapolated, in spite of its paradoxicality, in such stories as Jeffrey A. Carver's melodrama *Neptune Crossing* (1994) and Connie Willis' comedy *Bellwether* (1996).

Late twentieth-century cosmological theory sometimes reformulates the traditional mythical problem of how order arose from chaos in wondering how the early universe became "lumpy", producing the disorder of material particles, which then aggregated into stars and galaxies. Theories of literary creativity have occasionally worked a similar switch, as in the celebration of *alienation by Bertolt Brecht, but the consensus in science and literature alike holds that the appropriate balance between order and chaos is closer to 99/1 than to 50/50; a little spontaneity can go a long way, even unaided by the butterfly effect.

CHEMISTRY

Science that deals with the composition and transactions of material substances. Its evolution was confused before and during the Renaissance by the mystical tendencies of *alchemy, which inhibited the replacement of the Classical theory of the four *elements by a more reasonable taxonomy—whose gradual achievement in the context of John Dalton's renewal of *atomic theory in *A New System of Chemical Philosophy* (1808) eventually culminated in the production of Dmitri Mendeleev's periodic table of the elements in 1869. The explanation of the pattern revealed by the periodic table connected chemistry to the underlying science of *physics.

Significant foundations for the transformation of alchemy into chemistry were laid in the twelfth and thirteenth centuries when a Mediaeval "Industrial Revolution" prompted an increase in mining that gave rise to considerable interest in metallurgy. The investigations thus prompted—summarised in Rodolphus Agricola's *De re metallica* (1556)— revealed the woeful inadequacy of the alchemical theory of metals. The process was supplemented by investigations connected with the gradual development of the most significant early chemical technology: the manufacture of dyes for use in the textile industry. The increase of the range of exploitable substances and the transitions that could be contrived therewith were summarised by Robert Boyle in *The Scyptical Chymist* (1661).

The first attempt to produce a general theory of chemistry to succeed *Paracelsus' revised version of alchemy was little better than its predecessor, being based on the ill-fated notion of phlogiston advanced by Georg Ernst Stahl in 1697. Phlogiston was a substance allegedly contained in all substances, in proportion to their readiness to be transformed by heat, and liberated therefrom by combustion. The aesthetic appeal of phlogiston theory maintained its popularity for a while in the face of such inconvenient facts as the gain in weight sustained by heated metals until Joseph Priestley's *Experiments and Observations on Air* (1777) assisted Antoine Lavoisier to invert the phlogiston theorists' account of combustion as a kind of dissociation. "Dephlogisticated air" was then reconceived as an element that combined with others in combustion: oxygen.

The rapid progress of experimental chemistry following the abandonment of phlogiston theory and the discovery of the atmospheric gases, assisted by Dalton's refinement of atomic theory, paved the way for a heroic era of chemistry. Its leading figures included Priestley's fellow "Jacobin scientist" Humphry Davy, a friend of the Romantic poets whose adventures in electrochemistry allowed him to discover several new elements, paving the way for Michael Faraday's revision of the theory of *electricity as well as helping to inspire Mary *Shelley's *Frankenstein* (1818).

This process of evolution was further boosted in the nineteenth century by the rapid progress of organic chemistry. It had long been assumed that the substances making up living bodies were governed by some kind of vital principle or *life force that rendered them unsynthesisable by vulgar means, but this assumption broke down in 1828 when urea was synthesised from ammonium cyanate. Justus von Liebig's *Die Organische Chemie in Anwendung auf Agrikultur und Physiologie* (1840; trans. as *Organic Chemistry in Its Application to Agriculture*) founded agricultural chemistry, prompting a boom in artificial fertilisation, while the same author's *Tierchemie* (1842; trans. as *Animal Chemistry; or, Organic Chemistry in Its Relations to Physiology and Pathology*) began the clarification of the metabolic processes of biochemistry.

The chemistry of carbon was rationalised with the aid of Edward Frankland's theory of valency, developed in the 1850s. One of the most popular legends of modern science describes Friedrich Kekulé's inspirational rationalisation of the chemical composition of benzene in terms of a ring structure, thanks to a dream he had in 1866. The new discipline was given added practical value by the development of the first aniline dye in 1856 and such *medical discoveries as the antiseptic effect of phenol (1867) and the analgesic effect of acetylsalicylic acid (1876). Jacobus Van't Hoff's *La Chimie en Espace* (1875; trans. as *Chemistry in Space*) founded stereochemistry, stressing the importance of the asymmetry of the carbon atom and the consequent existence of isomers.

Because the heroic age of chemistry coincided with the rapid evolution of the novel, while the succeeding development of organic chemistry implied a radical revision of human perceptions of the order of *Nature, the chemist provided the principal nineteenth-century archetype of literary images of *scientists at work. The chemist's laboratory similarly provided a definitive setting for scientific work; the test tube—where disparate substances were mixed, shaken, and heated in order to undergo some manifestly transformative reaction—became the iconic locus of the scientific experiment. Newly discovered elements and newly synthesised compounds became key facilitating devices of scientific romance, including such fabulous items as Charles Gaines' hydro-pyrogen in "The Sickle of Fire" (1896), H. G. Wells' cavorite in *The First Men in the Moon* (1901), and Frederic Carrel's sardinium in *2010* (1914).

The use of hypothetical chemical substances as quasi-magical devices continued long into the twentieth century, readily passing from scientific romance to pulp science fiction, which featured such innovations as Charles C. Winn's light-gathering lucium in "The Infinite Vision" (1924) and Richard Rush Murray's "Radicalite" (1933)—a sort of "metallic ammonia" whose usefulness was further enhanced by the extrapolation of its derivative "Stellarite" (1933). New discoveries, such as the discovery that many elements had distinct isotopes, were rapidly co-opted into this sort of role. The technological exploitation of allotropes of iron transforms the world in Cyril G. Wates' "A Modern Prometheus" (1930), while Nathan Schachner's "The Isotope Men" (1936) features isotopic split personalities.

The commercial exploitation of chemistry went through the same phases as the science itself, early ventures in industrial chemistry being greatly complicated by the advent of organic chemistry. The DuPont Corporation, founded in 1802 to manufacture gunpowder—supplemented by dynamite in 1880—underwent a dramatic expansion and diversification in the early twentieth century into dyes, plastics, and paints. It drew rich dividends from its careful sponsorship of research in "pure science" when polymer chemistry was pioneered within the company in the 1930s; Wallace Carothers' discovery of nylon became a key example of fundamental research as a fountainhead of technological innovation, leading to DuPont's eventual patenting of Dacron, Lycra, Kevlar, and Teflon. In the meantime, though, the image of the social utility of industrial chemistry and its research programs was badly dented by the role played in World War I by chemical *weapons, especially the poison gases that became the principal bugbear of future *war novels produced after 1918.

The industrialisation of organic chemistry, and its corollary effects on the tenor and tone of published research, is ironically reflected in such absurdist exercises in speculative nonfiction as Isaac Asimov's "The Endochronic Properties of Resublimated Thiotimoline" (1948), which offers a straightfaced account of an organic molecule that dissolves in advance of water being added, complete with fanciful references. The article became the first of a series as Asimov and others discovered further properties and potential applications of the remarkable substance. Industrial chemistry also prompted one of very few effective cinematic representations of science in relation to society, in the Ealing comedy *The Man in the White Suit* (1951).

The Italian industrial chemist Primo Levi would probably have spent his entire life working quietly in that capacity had not World War II interrupted his career, but his experiences in Auschwitz turned him into one of the twentieth century's most significant literary voices, his books attaining worldwide fame as the most minutely considered and carefully analytical accounts of the Holocaust. Levi always contended that the narrative voice he adopted was defined and determined by the fact that he was a chemist—a supposition he attempted to demonstrate in the reflective essays contained in *Il Sistema Periodico* (1974; trans. as *The Periodic Table*, 1984), in which his memories are decanted into fabular exercises in nonfiction, each inspired by the personal connotations of a particular chemical element. The collection is unique, although its method is an interesting extrapolation of Zolaesque *naturalism and Proustian introspective researches in the workings of memory. Its influence is evident in Michael Swanwick's Periodic Table of Science Fiction series, initially posted online at *Sci-Fiction* in 2002.

When anxieties regarding chemical warfare went into decline, it was only to be replaced by anxieties about *pollution of the environment by the byproducts of industrial chemistry. The role played by industrial organic chemistry in *food science also gave rise to anxieties about "additives". These factors combined to ensure that the heroic era of nineteenth-century chemistry gave way to a twentieth-century

era of chemical villainy, widely reflected in literature and reportage. Although the science still produced occasional heroes, they were usually based in academe rather than industry; the most notable was Linus Pauling, who became a leading figure in U.S. chemistry in the 1930s and produced one of its definitive textbooks, *The Nature of the Chemical Bond and the Structure of Molecules and Crystals* (1939).

The triumphant explication of chemistry's physical basis had reduced its perceived status considerably by comparison with physics, and the archetypal chemist was swiftly replaced by the archetypal physicist—incarnate in Albert *Einstein—as the very model of a modern scientist. The test tube did not lose its iconic status entirely, retaining sufficient authority to claim a component of the phrase "test tube babies" when *in vitro* fertilisation was first anticipated as a technical possibility, but its image was tarnished with a certain contempt. Within the education system, chemistry became irrevocably associated with bad smells and awkward stains, although the gift of a "chemistry set" remained a significant aspect of informal education for the greater part of the century. Chemical formulas—especially those describing important reactions—continued to claim a minority share of the mystique attributed to the calculative equations of physics.

One chemical notion that recommended itself for extensive literary use by means of its metaphorical potential was catalysis, in which a reaction is assisted by an agent that is continually regenerated; its deployments in speculative fiction include Malcolm Jameson's "Catalyst Poison" (1939), Poul Anderson's "Catalysts" (1956), Jesse Miller's "Catalyst Run" (1974), and Charles L. Harness' *The Catalyst* (1980). The use of colour-changing indicators, after the fashion of the pH-sensitive litmus test, retained a certain casual flamboyance abundantly displayed in the visual media; the development of a pregnancy test that worked in that fashion provided an abundance of dramatic moments in TV soap operas, while flushes of colour indicative of the presence of invisible blood helped chemical analysis secure a key role in TV dramatisations of *forensic science.

The term gained a new metaphorical significance in the context of its quasi-euphemistic use to refer to mutual sexual attraction, which proved very useful in fiction. The underlying metaphor was pioneered by J. W. Goethe in *Die Wahlverwandschaften* (1809; trans. as *Elective Affinities*)—the phrase was derived from a term coined by the Swedish chemist Torbern Bergman—but more explicit talk of "sexual chemistry" became increasingly common in the twentieth century; Greta Garbo offered a memorable reductionist account of erotic attraction in the movie *Ninotchka*

(1939), and the pattern is reinvested with literal implications in such works of speculative fiction as Brian Stableford's *Sexual Chemistry: Sardonic Tales of the Genetic Revolution* (1991) and James Patrick Kelly's "Chemistry" (1993).

CINEMA

A technology that takes advantage of the optical phenomenon of the persistence of vision to produce an illusion of continuous movement from a rapidly progressive series of still images preserved as a reel of photographic negatives. The development of cinema was preceded by a series of precursors, including Étienne Gaspard Robert's *Fantasmagorie*, magic lanterns, and zoetropes, all of which were echoed in literature, providing key metaphors to such works as Jean Lorrain's "Lanterne Magique" (1891; trans. as "Magic Lantern"). The frequent association of artificially reproduced moving images with apparitions is reflected in Thomas Amat's decision to call his pioneering moving-picture projector a "Phantoscope". Complex movements unanalysable by the unaided eye were first "atomized" by a series of still photographs in the late 1870s, the first use of the method being to study the motion of a galloping horse. The technique—standardised by E. J. Marey as "chronophotography"—was quickly adapted to study the aerodynamics of flight.

The advent of cinema in the 1890s was a highly significant advancement in recording technology, although it did not have as much impact in the scientific arena as the development of still photography, which had wrought a revolution in *astronomy. Early literary responses included Rudyard Kipling's "Mrs. Bathurst" (1904), which credits the cinema with a kind of *hypnotic effect. Until the late 1920s, cinematography was limited in the accurate representation of mundane life by the lack of an integrated soundtrack, but its cultivation of illusion was greatly facilitated by the opportunity to contrive an apparently seamless transition between sequences filmed at different times using strategically modified sets.

The most significant of the early filmmakers, George Méliès—who had previously worked as a stage magician—made conspicuous use of all the tricks at his disposal in representing impossible events. In 1896, he produced a film (the English version was titled *The Bewitched Inn*) whose flying candlesticks and disappearing bed were recapitulated in the more substantial *The Inn Where No Man Rests* (1902). He made several fairy-tale adaptations, including the hand-coloured *Kingdom of the Fairies* (1903) and *Cinderella, or the Glass Slipper* (1912),

four versions of *Faust* (1898–1904), and several films featuring such miracle-workers as the Devil and the enchanter Alcofrisbas (played by Méliès himself). He also made dream fantasies, including *The Astronomer's Dream* (1898), and early interplanetary fantasies, one of which—*Journey to the Moon* (1903)—was to provide one of the best-known movie sequences of the twentieth century.

Many other pioneers followed Méliès' lead, though none as prolifically. Another frequently replicated image was produced by Thomas *Edison's cinematographer Edwin S. Porter in *Fun in a Butcher Shop* (1901), which depicts a fully automated production line turning dogs into sausages, in support of a popular urban legend; Porter subsequently soothed public indignation by making *Dog Factory* (1904), in which sausages are transmuted into live dogs by a similar automated process. When the scientific photographer F. Martin Duncan combined cinema technology with the microscope in the pioneering documentary *The Unseen World* (1902), it was immediately parodied by the burlesque *The Unclean World, also known as The Suburban-Bunkum Microbe-Guyoscope*.

The use of cutting to make objects appear and disappear from scenes according to the director's whim was the most obvious cinematic manifestation of *impossibility, but almost every element of developing cinematographic technique was a similar violation of ordinary sensory expectation. Elmer Rice's scathing satire on the fictional worlds within movie texts, *A Voyage to Purilia* (1930), treats cutting, zooming, and fading out as manifest absurdities, and violations of temporal sequence such as flashbacks as items of bizarrerie—but cinema audiences had already learned to "read" all those devices, and to see nothing strange about them at all, accepting them as mere conventions of representation. Such devices were hardly noticed in the latter part of the century. Cinematographers also gave regular employment to a whole range of "special effects" that were not so readily accommodated within common sense, especially tricks with *time—speeding it up, slowing it down, and throwing it into reverse—and exotic biological transformations, illustrated by a flood of hair-restoring movies, surgical fantasies, and *Jekyll and Hyde* adaptations.

Whether or not it warranted the name "Purilia"—which Rice derived from "puerile", not from "pure"—the strange parallel world to which movies provided a window was soon established as a magical kingdom, irrespective of its explicit use of the supernatural, whose very essence was the casting of the kind of spell traditionally known as "glamour". It was the habitation of a new species of "stars" and "goddesses"—the vastness of whose close-up-exaggerated personalities easily survived the demise of the dumb show by which they signified emotion in pre-talkie days. The archaically rigid censorship of which Rice complained generated a new visual language of implication and irony, whose key product—labelled by the sensational novelist-turned-screenwriter Elinor Glyn in 1927—was *It*, also known as "sex appeal". Cinematography was by no means the first technology to facilitate "magic tricks" but none had ever been so intrinsically magical in the whole range of its manifestations. Although its enduring and overweening preference for *occult science and *pseudoscience over the authentic variety was partly a response to the attitudes of its mass audience, it was also intrinsic to the nature of the medium and the spectrum of opportunities offered thereby.

The employment of cinema as a means of documentary reportage was always secondary to its role as a medium of entertainment, and the high cost of making films ensured that many documentary endeavours were guided by the entertainment agenda. The scientific applications of cinema technology were primarily concerned with the *biological sciences, because the moving picture facilitated the depiction of active, living organisms. Cinematic adaptations of time-lapse photography became an important means of adapting slow processes like plant growth to sensory perception. The only significant overlap between this kind of endeavour and mainstream cinema was, however, the subgenre of "wildlife documentaries", which was long cursed by the embellishment of ludicrous anthropomorphising voice-overs.

The development of stop-motion animation greatly facilitated the cinematic depiction of imaginary creatures; it was rapidly used to dramatise *dinosaurs and became the foundation of a whole genre of *monster movies, epitomised by the Willis J. O'Brien–animated *The Lost World* (1925) and *King Kong* (1933). Although monster movies and other emergent movie subgenres such as the mad *scientist story and the superhero story drew on the vocabularies of science fiction and pseudoscience in the construction of narrative apologies, even sound-equipped cinema inevitably found authentic scientific explanations very difficult to accommodate, and a tradition was rapidly established whereby filmmakers adopted a frankly derisive attitude to the kind of fidelity idealised in the notion of *hard science fiction; the natural tendency was to regard illusion as an end rather than a means.

For this reason, the history of "science fiction films" followed a very different course from the evolution of science fiction in text form, entirely governed by the evolution of new means of contrivance that facilitated the incorporation of science fiction imagery without the least trace of extrapolative seriousness. The procedural principle that produced so many biological monsters was extrapolated to technologies, most notably in accounts of destructive rays such as those featured in the serial "The Flaming Disk" (1920) and the Russian *Luc Smerti* (Death Ray) (1925). The development of superhuman characters—anticipated by Fritz Lang's Dr. Mabuse in *Dr. Mabuse, der Spieler* (1922) and *Das Testament des Dr. Mabuse* (1933) before the invasion of cinema by comic book superheroes such as *Flash Gordon* (1936) and such analogues thereof as Philip Wylie's Superman-prototype *The Gladiator* (1939)—was also a natural extrapolation of cinematic trickery.

Early attempts to adapt futuristic fiction for the screen were few in number. Fritz Lang's *Metropolis* (1926) helped popularise the idea of the *robot, although the supportive imagery it provided was essentially magical and provided a cardinal example of Isaac *Asimov's Frankenstein complex. Lang's *Die Frau im Mond* (1929) attempted to advertise the imminence of the *Space Age, but its representations dissolved into absurdity. Alexander Korda's stilted version of H. G. Wells' *Things to Come* (1936) was the only significant attempt to accommodate the themes of British scientific romance to the medium, the earlier *The Island of Lost Souls* (1932, based on *The Island of Dr. Moreau*) and *The Invisible Man* (1933) having reduced Wells' stories to conventional thrillers, while a 1933 U.S. adaptation of S. Fowler Wright's *Deluge* was primarily notable for its model-based representation of a tidal wave swamping New York.

The devastation of Europe by World War II allowed the American philosophy of movie production to become totally dominant in its wake; Western science fiction motifs were almost exclusively reserved thereafter to exotic crime thrillers, horror movies, and space operas modeled on comic strips. Ultra-cheap "shockers" designed to assist teenage seductions in drive-in movie theatres played a major role in reducing the scabrous public image of science fiction to abysmal levels. Attempts to break this mould—including *Destination Moon* (1950), *Riders to the Stars* (1954), and *Forbidden Planet* (1956)—were rare and only partly successful.

By virtue of this pattern of development, scientific understanding remained offstage in the cinematic medium throughout the twentieth century. Although scientists were frequently featured as characters, and laboratories as settings, the standard role such characters played was that of instigator of catastrophe, whether by virtue of malice, madness, or foolishness; laboratories became, in consequence, quintessential sources of malignance and horror. James Whale's

Frankenstein (1931) supplemented Lang's *Metropolis* in securing the cinematic stereotypes of the scientist and his laboratory, echoed in *Island of Lost Souls* and *The Invisible Man*, and in other revisitations of silent classics such as *Mad Love* (1935) and *The Invisible Ray* (1936).

This stereotype was echoed in countless postwar images, including *Forbidden Planet*'s Dr. Morbeus, the horribly transmogrified protagonist of *The Fly* (1958), and Dr. Genessier in *Les Yeux Sans Visage* (1959; trans. as *Eyes Without a Face*). The amiably quirky variants of this image featured in such comedies as *The Man in the White Suit* (1951) and *The Absent-Minded Professor* (1961) sustained the pattern rather than challenging it. The Einstein-clone scientist in *The Day the Earth Stood Still* (1951) was displayed only to be contemptuously humbled, and there is also a conspicuous ineffectuality about heroic scientists, whose attempts to combat the tide of mutational and extraterrestrial disaster in such films as *Them!* (1954), *It Came from Beneath the Sea* (1955), and *The Monolith Monsters* (1957) are mere holding actions.

The motive for these representations was purely melodramatic—filmmakers had no ideological interest in stigmatising science or demonising the public image of scientists and their workplaces—but the net result of their endeavours probably included a marked diminution in respect for and trust in the activities of scientists. Some scientists chose to construe these cinematic representations as jokes, whereas others preferred to fulminate against the rational implausibility of cinematic clichés, misconstruing their absurdity as the result of accidental error rather than as an inevitable result of the technology's hospitality to illusions of impossibility.

Such sophistication as cinematic science fiction underwent in the 1960s was partly due to the injection of satirical black comedy, as in *Doctor Strangelove, or How I Learned to Stop Worrying and Love the Bomb* (1964) and *Planet of the Apes* (1968), and partly to an element of nostalgia, as in *First Men in the Moon* (1964) and *Jules Verne's Rocket to the Moon* (1967), but it was primarily a matter of the occasional use of special effects in a more stylistically polished fashion. Such films as *Fahrenheit 451* (1966), *Barbarella* (1966), and *Fantastic Voyage* (1966) had little to recommend them apart from their glossy effects, but Stanley Kubrick took the trend to a spectacular extreme in *2001—A Space Odyssey* (1968), whose Arthur Clarke–inspired space technology was slotted into a plot whose main lever was a mad computer and whose climax was a psychedelic trip into deliberate obscurantism. Kubrick's *2001* prepared the way economically for the visual spectaculars that would dominate science fiction cinema in the last decades of the twentieth century.

The narrative tradition in which the majority of these lavishly funded films would take their place was firmly established. The computer-assisted special effects that became commonplace when they were spectacularly advertised by George Lucas' *Star Wars* (1977) were immediately applied to the production of many other comic-strip space operas; monster movies such as *Alien* (1979), the 1982 version of *The Thing*, *The Terminator* (1984), and *Independence Day* (1996); and superhero stories such as *Superman—The Movie* (1978), the 1980 version of *Flash Gordon*, and *Robocop* (1987). *Close Encounters of the Third Kind* (1977) and *ET—The Extraterrestrial* (1982) took their inspiration from contemporary myths, not from scientific speculation, while the time-travel fantasies that followed in the wake of *Back to the Future* (1985) played gleefully with loops and paradoxes.

Because serious science fiction texts are so difficult to film, very few have ever been successfully adapted, and the rare partial successes—including Ralph Nelson's adaptation of Daniel Keyes' "Flowers for Algernon" as *Charly* (1968) and Jack Gold's 1974 film of Algis Budrys' *Who*—were all at the soft end of the spectrum. The most commercially successful adaptation of a science fiction text, Ridley Scott's *Blade Runner* (1982, based on Philip K. *Dick's *Do Androids Dream of Electric Sheep?*), was a drastically simplified version, and the subsequent Dick adaptations that followed in its wake were shoehorned into well-established cinematic formulas. The aspect of Dick's worldview that appealed most to filmmakers was its questioning of the stability of the experienced world, which chimed with the medium's ability to construct powerful illusions—a fusion illustrated by such metaphysical fantasies as David Cronenberg's *Videodrome* (1982) and taken to it furthest extreme in *The Matrix* (1999) and its sequels. The movie eventually based on Isaac Asimov's *I, Robot* (2004)—earlier, more faithful treatments having been aborted—deliberately inverted the book's explicit purpose, making it a cardinal example of the paranoid technophobia that Asimov had attempted to oppose.

Science-fictional extrapolations of cinema technology, in the days before the advent of the idea of *virtual reality, began by extrapolating the development of talkies to accommodate the other senses, especially in the development of "feelies", as anticipated in Aldous Huxley's *Brave New World* (1932) and John D. MacDonald's "Spectator Sport" (1950), and 3-D movies, as anticipated in George O. Smith's "Problem in Solid" (1947). As science fiction writers realised what Hollywood was doing to popular perceptions of science fiction, their extrapolations veered into the realm of satirical black comedy. The future of Hollywood is treated scathingly in such works as Henry Kuttner's "The Ego Machine" (1952), Bruce Elliott's "The Battle of the S....s" (1952), and Robert Bloch's *Sneak Preview* (1959; exp. book, 1971), although grudging acceptance of the inevitable introduced a greater subtlety and grudging affection into such continuations of the tradition as Michael Bishop's "Storming the Bijou, Mon Amour" (1979), Terry Bisson's *Voyage to the Red Planet* (1990), Connie Willis' *Remake* (1995), and Bruce McAllister's "Hero, the Movie: What's Left When You've Already Saved the World" (2005).

The relentless advance of special effects gave rise to the suggestion that filmmakers would soon be able to dispense with cameras altogether and work entirely with digitally synthesised imagery, thus transforming the medium into something else entirely. An intermediate phase in this development is described in Grey Rollins' "The Ghost in the Machine" (1993), but few contemporary writers of futuristic fiction in text form see any point in dwelling elaborately on a matter of inevitable extinction, over which few of them would shed a tear if it happened tomorrow.

CIVILISATION

A term whose literal meaning is the emergence and evolution of cities, although it is frequently applied approvingly to the kinds of cultural evolution facilitated by city life, especially their moral and aesthetic components.

Cities are manifestations of technological advance, their evolution mapped out in the development of building materials and techniques, the solution of such large-scale *engineering problems as water supply and waste disposal, the logistics of food distribution, and the evolution of manufacturing enterprises. These imperatives have provided the principal motive force for the advancement of applied science, and theoretical science may therefore be viewed as a by-product of civilisation. The first foundations of theoretical science were laid in Athens, the first city-state to escape the limitations of local agricultural supply by cultivating an economy based on trade; the second phase of its sophistication, in the seventeenth century, was correlated with a rapid expansion of cities, whose physical containment within strong defensive walls was being replaced by their political containment within nation-states.

Hypothetical cities, made or remade with the aid of new technology and inspired by intellectual progress, have played a central role in speculative fiction, from classical *Utopian fictions such as Francesco

da Cherso's *La Città Felice* (1553), Tommaso Campanella's *La Città del Sole* (written 1602; trans. as *City of the Sun*), and J. V. Andreae's *Christianopolis* (1619), through such euchronian visions as Louis-Sébastien Mercier's *L'an deux mille quatre cent quarante* (1771; trans. as *Memoirs of the Year 2500*), Edward Maitland's *By and By* (1873), and Edward Bellamy's *Looking Backward, 2000–1887* (1888) to such images of hypermetropolitan development as Pierre Véron's "En 1900" (1878), Ignatius Donnelly's *Caesar's Column* (1890), and H. G. Wells' "A Story of the Days to Come" (1897). Such imaginative projections reflect the sociohistorical process by which the same factors that made cities into centres of wealth, leisure, and architectural magnificence also made them into magnets for reckless but necessary migration and accumulators of industrial and organic wastes. The development of sophisticated sewage systems was too slow to prevent a nauseous reaction to city filth, resonantly echoed in much nineteenth-century literature. William Cobbett's description of London as a Great Wen struck a plangent chord, whose most extreme response was Richard Jefferies' *After London; or, Wild England* (1885).

Cities had been seen as the primary arenas of both cultural *progress and cultural *decadence since Classical times, and the revision of both ideas in the eighteenth and nineteenth centuries had much to do with the dramatic contrasts provided by the elaborate and exaggerated cross sections of larger societies contained within cities. The great European cities of the nineteenth century became the crucibles in which popular literature developed, providing compact audiences through which literacy gradually spread from top to bottom. One result of this was that cities became "characters" in their own right, explicitly so in such panoramic surveys as Eugène Sue's *Les mystères de Paris* (1842–1843; trans. as *The Mysteries of Paris*) and G. W. M. Reynolds' imitative *The Mysteries of London* (1844–1845).

The literary developments spearheaded by Sue and other popular celebrants of the idea of the city-as-organism were partly the product of the advent of artificial *light, initially with the equipment of city streets with gas lamps—with which London's Pall Mall was first fitted out in 1807. Liberation from the tyranny of night and day paved the way for a dramatic extension of economic and leisure activities—not to mention efficient policing—ushering civilisation into a new phase of enlightenment, but also bringing the nastier aspects of city life into the glare. In James Thomson's narrative poem, gaslight is impotent to redeem *The City of Dreadful Night* (1874), only serving to illuminate its horrors.

The application of science to municipal architecture and engineering, and the corollary role played by cities as hosts of scientific research and technological expertise, was given elaborate literary consideration in such nineteenth-century novels as Jules Verne's *Les cinq cents millions de la bégum* (1879, based on a first draft by Paschal Grousset; trans. as *The Begum's Fortune*), which carefully contrasts the political organisation of the cities of Frankville and Stahlstadt. In Verne's novel Frankville is triumphant, but it was the imagery of Stahlstadt that was more widely echoed in futuristic projections of city life. Mrs. Oliphant's afterlife fantasy "The Land of Darkness" (1887) depicts a sector of Hell as a City of Science: an Infernal factory complex ruled by mad Master. By contrast, the central exhibit at the Columbian Exhibition in Chicago in 1893 was the White City, designed by a host of architects, engineers, and artists to embody rather than merely to model the future of civilisation; its classically styled white buildings were topped by a series of gilded domes. The Pan-American Exposition in Buffalo in 1901 attempted to go one better with a Rainbow City organised around a central Electrical Tower, but its symbolic significance was direly compromised when the U.S. president, William McKinley, was assassinated in its Temple of Music.

The evolution of cities was always coupled with nostalgia for a mythical Arcadian past, when the various kinds of artifice represented by civilisation were allegedly unnecessary because *Nature provided everything necessary to human happiness. Such nostalgia increased rather than diminished as time went by, although the image of an Arcadian Golden Age was gradually replaced in Britain by the idea of an agricultural paradise whose relics still maintained a lingering presence in "the countryside". In America, whose geographical horizons were much vaster, the equivalent contrast was part of a more complex spectrum whose key axis, as far as literary images were concerned, was that between the city and the "small town" surrounded by broad tracts of cultivated land and wilderness. While inhabitants of the countryside and small towns fixed avidly ambitious eyes on cities, inhabitants of cities maintained an artificial affection for towns and villages—but the fact that the cities provided the core audience for literary endeavour ensured that the latter attitude would have the louder literary voice. Traditional agricultural practices and methods of transportation, especially the horse, are routinely rose tinted in twentieth-century literary mythology, as in such genres as the Western and such subgenres as horse-riding stories aimed at teenage girls.

It was partly due to this imbalance of envious viewpoints that the city was displaced from the core of Utopian imagery to become the focal point of its twentieth-century *dystopian opposition, routinely appearing in hypothetical examples either as a slum-ridden gargantuan sprawl where filth, crime, sickness, and vice flourish in appalling profusion—the rich and powerful having exiled themselves to luxuriously equipped baronial fortresses—or as an oppressive exercise in enforced orderliness, whose ruthless suppression of any and all deviance is ruthlessly dehumanising. The future of civilisation in scientific romance and science fiction is dominated by images of increasing *automation, pioneered in H. G. Wells' "A Story of the Days to Come" (1897), E. M. Forster's reactionary "The Machine Stops" (1912), Otfrid von Hanstein's enthusiastic *Elektropolis* (1928; trans. as "Electropolis"), and John W. Campbell Jr.'s deeply ambivalent "Night" (1934). The imagery of the future city reached an apogee of sorts at the 1939 New York World's Fair, whose central Perisphere contained a huge model of the futuristic "Democracity", and for which General Motors built a spectacular Futurama exhibit.

The city of the future was carried to various extremes of "perfection" in such images of "ultimate cities" as Isaac Asimov's Trantor, Arthur C. Clarke's Diaspar in *Against the Fall of Night* (1948; rev. 1956 as *The City and the Stars*) and its analogue in "The Lion of Comarre" (1949), the infinite city of J. G. Ballard's "Build-Up" (1957; aka "The Concentration City"), the solicitous cities of Bellwether in Robert Sheckley's "Street of Dreams, Feet of Clay" (1968) and Reflex in Ray Banks' "The City That Loves You" (1969), the culminating image of Thomas F. Monteleone's *The Time-Swept City* (1977), and the animate cities of Greg Bear's *Strength of Stones* (1981). There is, of course, a countertradition of defiant pastoralism, evident not merely in *disaster stories in which mortally wounded cities must be abandoned, but in images of deserted supercities such as those featured in John Campbell's "Forgetfulness" (1937), Clifford Simak's ironically titled *City* (1944–1952; book, 1952), and Ballard's "The Ultimate City" (1976).

The sharp tension between the attractions and repulsions of city life—clearly evident in the real world in the growth of intermediate suburban environments and the emergence of commuting as a way of life—is often evident in speculative fiction in an absolute division of the urban and the rural. In such imagery defensive city walls often reappear as encapsulating domes, as in Jack Williamson's "Gateway to Paradise" (1941; book, 1955, titled *Dome Around America*), Rena Vale's "The Shining City" (1952; exp. as "Beyond the Sealed World", 1965), and Daniel F. Galouye's "City of Force" (1959). Such re-enclosed spaces are often described in agoraphobia-inducing terms, reflected in such accounts of subterranean civilisation as Gabriel Tarde's *Fragment d'histoire future* (1896; trans. as *Underground Man*) and Fritz Leiber's "The Creature from Cleveland Depths" (1962; aka "The Lone Wolf"), and neatly summarised in Isaac Asimov's characterisation of *The Caves of Steel* (1954).

In the extreme case of James Blish's Cities in Flight series (1950–1962), domed cities literally tear themselves away from the Earthly soil in order to become rootless galactic wanderers. The vertical extension of Manhattan island provided a key model for both real and imaginary cities; hypothetical extrapolations of the skyscraper generated such images of urban isolation as Philip K. Dick's conapts, the Urbmons (urban monads) of Robert Silverberg's *The World Inside* (1971), and the "arcologies" featured in Larry Niven and Jerry Pournelle's *Oath of Fealty* (1981) and Elizabeth Hand's *Aestival Tide* (1992).

All of this imagery is abundantly represented in futuristic *art, which is understandably rich in cityscapes, and has lent considerable impetus to the notion of agglomerations of supremely tall buildings that scrape crystal domes for want of solid sky. Fritz Lang's *Metropolis* (1926) presented an influential image of a skyscraper city embellished with aerial walkways and airborne commuter traffic, while Frank R. Paul's cityscapes, featured on the covers and internal illustrations of the early science fiction pulps, largely defined what William Gibson was eventually to label "the Gernsback continuum". Gibson cited that assembly of images in order to highlight the fact that it never came to pass, but the imagery of the city as an extreme of technological enterprise has not yet developed any rival consensus, thus maintaining an impression that the realisation of Paul's megalopolis has merely been postponed.

The notion that the city has its own developmental imperatives beyond the control of planners retains its dominance of futuristic imagery—by contrast with the nostalgically exotic imagery of Italo Calvino's *Le città invisibli* (1979; trans. as *Invisible Cities*)—but is opposed by the multiple imagery of C. J. Cherryh's *Sunfall* (1981), the weird cities of Storm Constantine's *Calenture* (1994), and such depictions of custom-designed cities as Nightingale in Catherine Asaro's "Aurora in Four Voices" (1998).

CLARKE, SIR ARTHUR C[HARLES] (1917–)

British writer and populariser of science. He became an enthusiastic science fiction fan in his youth, contributing articles, stories, and reviews to various amateur publications while he was at school and while working thereafter as a civil servant. He did not like his job, and was glad when World War II allowed him to join the RAF, which put him to work on the development of radar. He extrapolated his expertise in various publications, including "Extraterrestrial Relays" (1945), an article that proposed the establishment of communications satellites in geosynchronous orbit.

After the war Clarke studied physics and mathematics at King's College, London, obtaining his B.Sc. in 1948. He also became a leading member of the British Interplanetary Society and an ardent propagandist for *space travel. It was during this period that he began publishing science fiction professionally, his first novel being *Against the Fall of Night* (1948; exp. as *The City and the Stars*, 1956) but he achieved greater success as a nonfiction writer when he followed *Interplanetary Flight* (1950) with the best-selling *The Exploration of Space* (1951), a landmark work in the development of the mythology of the *Space Age—whose most eloquent advocate he then became. He took advantage of the economic rewards the latter book provided to abandon the chilly climate of Britain for Sri Lanka, where he made his permanent home.

Clarke's propagandist efforts were so successful that when the *Apollo* program got under way he was hailed as a prophet, and retrospectively credited—on the basis of his 1945 paper—with the "invention" of the communications satellite. He was, however, scrupulous enough to call attention to the fact that he had envisaged such entities as manned space stations whose large crews would have to be perennially changing defective valves rather than tiny entities filled with reliable transistors. Much of his early fiction, including the novels *Prelude to Space* (1951; rev. 1954), *Earthlight* (1951; exp. 1955), *The Sands of Mars* (1951), *Islands in the Sky* (1952), and *A Fall of Moondust* (1961), and the short stories collected in *Expedition to Earth* (1953), *Reach for Tomorrow* (1956), *The Other Side of the Sky* (1958), and *Tales of Ten Worlds* (1962) consisted of calculatedly propagandistic dramatisations of his nonfictional speculations; his contribution to Reginald Bretnor's then-definitive account of *Modern Science Fiction* (1953) proudly declared science fiction to be "Preparation for the Age of Space".

The principal diversion from the main thrust of Clarke's *oeuvre* was *Childhood's End* (1953), which followed the example of *Against the Fall of Night* in developing a Stapledonian visionary element, coincidentally producing an image of humankind's evolutionary future reminiscent of Pierre Teilhard de Chardin's *Omega Point. A meditative short story in a similar vein, "Sentinel of Eternity" (1951; aka

"The Sentinel"), eventually became the basis of Stanley Kubrick's film *2001—A Space Odyssey* (1968; novelisation, 1968) while "The Star" describes the discovery by space travellers of worlds devastated by the explosion of the Star of Bethlehem. Oddly enough, Clarke's most popular short story was "The Nine Billion Names of God" (1953), in which Buddhist monks use a computer to complete the task set by God for humankind, resulting in the abrupt annihilation of the universe. Two other novels of this period—*The Deep Range* (1954) and *Dolphin Island* (1963)—reflected his interest in the sea as an unexplored wilderness akin to space, also dramatised in such nonfiction books as *The Coast of Coral* (1956) and *The Challenge of the Sea* (1960); his enthusiasm for diving was the key factor in his selection of Sri Lanka as a refuge, and he chronicled his exploits in such books as *The Reefs of Taprobane: Underwater Adventures Around Ceylon* (1957) and *Indian Ocean Adventure* (1961).

Clarke continued to popularise the possible rewards of space travel in *The Exploration of the Moon* (1954), *The Making of a Moon: The Story of the Earth Satellite Program* (1957), *The Challenge of the Spaceship* (1959), *Profiles of the Future: An Enquiry into the Limits of the Possible* (1962), *Voices from the Sky: Previews of the Coming Space Age* (1965), and *The Promise of Space* (1968). He wrote *First on the Moon* (1970) in collaboration with the *Apollo* astronauts, but the success of *2001—A Space Odyssey* had a more decisive impact on his public image and his economic opportunities. He returned to science fiction writing in earnest, with a sequence of best-selling hard science fiction novels. In *Rendezvous with Rama* (1973), human astronauts are fortunate enough to be able to investigate a huge alien artifact passing through the solar system en route to elsewhere. *Imperial Earth* (1975; restored text, 1976) is a sophisticated Space Age fantasy describing the future development of the solar system. *The Fountains of Paradise* (1979) describes the building of a "space elevator" that greatly facilitates commerce between the Earth's surface and orbital strata. Further elaborations of his new Space Age prospectus continued to occur to him, developed in the sequels *2010: Odyssey Two* (1982), *2061: Odyssey Three* (1988), and *3001: The Final Odyssey* (1997). *The Songs of Distant Earth* (1986) greatly elaborated a 1958 short story employing the lost colony device.

After *The Lost Worlds of 2001* (1972), which appeared in the same year as *Report on Planet Three and Other Speculations*, and a collaboration with space artist Chesley Bonestell, *Beyond Jupiter: The World of Tomorrow*, Clarke's nonfiction took a back seat to his fiction. When his health deteriorated in the 1980s, Clarke maintained the flow of his fiction by working with collaborators. Having extrapolated one of Clarke's ideas into *Cradle* (1988), Gentry Lee was entrusted with writing *Rama II* (1989), *The Garden of Rama* (1991), and *Rama Revealed* (1993), but Clarke elected to work with more experienced partners on other projects. The *technothrillers *Richter 10* (1996) and *The Trigger* (1999) were developed by Mike McQuay and Michael Kube-McDowell, respectively, while *The Light of Other Days* (2000) was the first of a sequence of novels extrapolated by Stephen *Baxter, a much more congenial collaborator; it was followed by the Time's Odyssey diptych comprising *Time's Eye* (2004) and *Sunstorm* (2005), in which the Earth is threatened with destruction by two catastrophic solar storms, and human attempts to build adequate defences are confused by the presence of enigmatic aliens. Clarke also contrived to produce a number of less burdensome solo works, including *Astounding Days* (1989), a memoir of his early infatuation with science fiction; *The Ghost from the Grand Banks* (1990), about the raising of the *Titanic*; and the asteroid-strike thriller *The Hammer of God* (1993).

Much given to sweeping statements, Clarke's fondness for aphorism led him to generate a series of oft-quoted "laws". The first one states that "When a distinguished scientist says that something is possible, he is almost certainly right. When he states that something is impossible, he is very probably wrong". Although intended as a comment on the pontificatory proclivities of eminent scientists, a corollary conclusion of this law is the thoroughly unscientific proposition that almost everything is possible. This view is slightly moderated by Clarke's second law—"The only way to discover the limits of the possible is to venture a little way past them into the impossible"—but is ringingly endorsed by the most popular law of them all, Clarke's third law: "Any sufficiently advanced technology is indistinguishable from magic". Unfortunately, the third law does not specify the viewpoint from which the difference is indistinguishable, thus leading many quoters to assume that science and magic are indistinguishable *in principle*, which is flatly contradictory to the truth and not what Clarke intended to imply.

Clarke's contribution to the development of modern science fiction was crucial; he is often cited as part of a key triumvirate along with Robert A. *Heinlein and Isaac *Asimov, but he was a better exemplar of the scrupulous and consistent practice of hard science fiction than either of those others, and his version of the Space Age encapsulated values more generously humanitarian—or at least less fundamentally misanthropic—than theirs. He is not often featured as a character in works of science fiction, but his name is frequently honored in such constructions as Allen Steele's *Clarke County, Space* and the spaceship *Arthur C. Clarke* in Thomas Wylde's "To the Eastern Gates" (1991).

CLEMENT, HAL

Pseudonym of U.S. science teacher and writer Harry Clement Stubbs (1922–2003). He obtained a B.S. in astronomy from Harvard in 1943, an M.Ed. from Boston University in 1947, and subsequently an M.S. from Simmons College, Boston, in 1963. In the latter years of World War II he served in the Eighth Air Force as a bomber pilot, and was in the Air Force Reserve from 1953 to 1976. From 1949 to 1987 he was a science teacher at Milton Academy in Massachusetts, and he did a great deal of work under his real name as a science journalist and populariser of science for children. His pseudonym's first manifestation was on a story published in John W. Campbell Jr.'s *Astounding Science Fiction* while he was in college, "Proof" (1942).

"Proof" features an *alien life-form whose physical makeup is very different from that of planet-bound material beings, and whose "first contact" with the Earth is both peripheral and fleeting. Although he was never able to become a prolific member of Campbell's stable because of his other commitments, Clement quickly established a unique position therein, defined by the exotic template of this ground-breaking story. He went on to design many more exotic aliens, carefully and cleverly adapted to various physical environments, thus becoming the leading literary exponent of *exobiology. His work in this vein was the most consistently conscientious attempt anyone ever made to live up to Campbell's prospectus for science fiction, and Hal Clement became the paradigm example of ultra-hard science fiction.

The short fiction Clement wrote for *Astounding* during and immediately after the war puts a heavy emphasis on problem solving, whether the problems arise because their protagonists are confronted with aliens (who are often humans seen from a different viewpoint) or because their protagonists find themselves in exotic physical predicaments. "Technical Error" (1943) and "Cold Front" (1946) are classic examples of humans being confounded by taken-for-granted assumptions that turn out to be incorrect in alien contexts. "Uncommon Sense" (1945) is a celebration of "lateral thinking" on the part of its hero, interplanetary explorer Laird Cunningham, whose further adventures were extrapolated into a short

series in "The Logical Life" (1974), "Stuck with It" (1976), and "Status Symbol" (1987).

Clement's first novel, *Needle* (1949; book, 1950), is an account of an alien policeman's pursuit of a fugitive on Earth, made difficult by the fact that both parties belong to a parasitic species descended from virus ancestors, and thus dependent on host bodies for nutrition and locomotion. The story must have been intended as a children's book, but was presumably deemed too challenging for its target audience; it appeared in *Astounding* as a serial before its book publication as an adult novel. The tense Robinsonade *Close to Critical* (1958; book, 1964), in which the castaways on the high-gravity world of Tenebra are children, evidently suffered a similar fate—an unfortunate one, given the author's strong commitment to science education. He was only able to publish two children's books in the course of his career—the calculatedly unchallenging *The Ranger Boys in Space* (1956) and the historical novel *Left of Africa* (1976)—and the latter was issued by a small press rather than a commercial publisher.

Iceworld (1951; book, 1953) offers an ingenious account of Earth as seen through exotic alien eyes, from which perspective it seems unreasonably cold, but Clement's talents were better displayed when he developed a detailed image of the giant planet Mesklin in *Mission of Gravity* (1953; book, 1954), a Robinsonade featuring an adult castaway. Mesklin spins so rapidly on its axis that the exacting gravitational attraction at its poles is considerably countered by centrifugal force at the equator—a gradient that causes the human protagonist's heroic alien rescuer problems directly contrary to his own. Clement revisited the milieu in *Star Light* (1971), in which Mesklinites explore the even more peculiar giant world of Dhrawn.

Cycle of Fire (1957) offers a similarly detailed account of the dual ecosphere of Abyormen, a planet in a binary star system whose surface suffers extremes of hot and cold. *Ocean on Top* (1967; book, 1973) is a further exercise in a similar vein, this time featuring humans biologically engineered for life in a liquid environment. *Through the Eye of a Needle* (1978) is a sequel to *Needle*, carrying forward its explanations of the alien biology of the Hunter and his kin. *The Nitrogen Fix* (1980) includes a further exercise in adaptive biology, concerning the inhabitants of a future Earth irredeemably altered by pollution, as well as alien visitors who feel more at home in the new atmosphere. *Still River* (1987) adopts a more brutal approach in its uncompromising account of humans exploring a dangerous alien environment. *Half Life* (1999) is a further exploratory drama in the same vein.

Clement's use of alien viewpoints is as interesting as his deployment of exobiological ecospheres, by virtue of his strong commitment to the idea that all intelligences are bound to approach the business of solving practical and theoretical problems in the same way—using the scientific method—if they are to be successful, and that they are bound to share certain aspects of the same existential situation as humans no matter how peculiar their biology may be. Although his work subsumes all other narrative considerations to the bold extrapolation and scrupulous exposition of scientific ideas, that mission was coupled with another, much subtler one, which provided it with underpinnings equally at odds with the bulk of popular pulp fiction. With the partial exception of two early stories, Clement steadfastly refused to employ villains as a means of generating dramatic tension. When radically different species meet in his stories, they often misunderstand one another and cause one another difficulties, but they are very rarely actively malevolent, and frequently go to extraordinary lengths of ingenuity and bravery in order to lend one another assistance.

Clement acknowledged that this strategy lessened the appeal of his work to readers who expected conventional conflict, but argued that the universe beyond the Earth's fragile ecosphere was sufficiently hostile and challenging without requiring the slightest further assistance from human or alien malignity. "I think it's a more interesting story", he said, in an oral discussion reprinted in *The New York Review of Science Fiction* in 1992, "when the expedition gets down to its last chocolate bar, not figuring out who gets the chocolate bar, but what they do to find out how to identify the local equivalent of a cocoa tree". Few readers ever agreed with him, but in a better world than ours he would surely have been right.

CLONE

A group of organisms comprising the asexually produced offspring of a single individual. The term was coined to describe genetically identical plants produced by taking cuttings, but is now more frequently used in connection with technologies that reproduce animals or their tissues, or with the duplication of lengths of DNA in genomic analysis. Asexual reproduction is the usual mode among many species of bacteria and protozoa, and in some plants and invertebrates, but is exceptional in more complex creatures, whose evolution has usually taken fuller advantage of the utility of *sex as a means of producing new gene combinations.

Fictional accounts of human cloning have a long history, originating in the tacit use of the notion in accounts of exaggerated psychological harmony between identical twins—members of a clone derived by the spontaneous splitting of an early embryo—such as Alexandre Dumas' account of *The Corsican Brothers* (1844), and in the creation of all-female societies like those featured in Princess Vera Zaronovitch's *Mizora* (1890) and Charlotte Perkins Gilman's *Herland* (1915; book, 1979). The idea was more explicitly popularised in the 1920s in connection with tissue culture experiments; speculations by J. B. S. Haldane and Julian Huxley led Aldous Huxley to feature cloning by embryo splitting in *Brave New World* (1932). Interest was renewed again in the 1950s when scientists at the Institute of Cancer Research in Philadelphia attempted to develop a nuclear transfer technique for cloning frogs; Poul Anderson's "UN-Man" (1953) employs a hypothetical technology of "exogenesis" for *eugenic cloning, while Theodore Sturgeon's "When You Care, When You Love" (1962) suggests that dedifferentiated cancer cells might be used as substitute egg cells in cloning processes.

The popularisation of the term by Gordon Rattray Taylor's *The Biological Time-Bomb* (1968)—which explicitly raised the question of "whether the members of human clones may feel particularly united, and be able to co-operate better, even if they are not in actual supersensory communication with one another"—prompted a flood of stories extrapolating this notion, the most notable of which include Ursula K. Le Guin's "Nine Lives" (1969), Richard Cowper's satirical *Clone* (1972), David Shear's *Cloning* (1972), Pamela Sargent's *Cloned Lives* (1976), Kate Wilhelm's *Where Late the Sweet Birds Sang* (1976), and Fay Weldon's *The Cloning of Joanna May* (1989). A further popularising boost to the idea of human cloning was provided by David H. Rorvik's journalistic hoax *In His Image: The Cloning of a Man* (1978).

The popularity of variations on the theme of *The Corsican Brothers* reflects the range of potential dramatic opportunities rather than any firm belief in the supernatural abilities of twins; the observation that most pairs of identical twins are enthusiastic to differentiate themselves from one another and have no difficulty in so doing is less plot friendly. Stories celebrating the limits of genetic determinism are rare; the exceptions include Ira Levin's *The Boys from Brazil* (1976), in which multiple clones of Adolf Hitler develop their own distinctive personalities in spite of crude attempts to reproduce the kind of environmental influences that helped formulate Hitler's own personality, and Richard Wilson's "The In-Betweens" (1957; aka

"The Ubiquitous You") in which six clones have contrasting personalities.

Verge Foray's "Duplex" (1968) develops a scenario in which conjoined twins are normal and dissociated twins are problematic exceptions, thus providing an ingenious investigation of the philosophy of identity that is echoed in many more orthodox accounts of clonal existentialism, including Gene Wolfe's *The Fifth Head of Cerberus* (1972) and Mildred Ames' *Anna to the Infinite Power* (1981). The inherent narcissism of self-cloning is ironically investigated in such cautionary wish-fulfillment fantasies as Kir Bulychev's "Another's Memory" (trans. 1986), while the hazards of cloning charismatic individuals are explored in such stories as Garfield Reeves-Stevens' *Children of the Shroud* (1990), in which Jesus is cloned thirty times over from the stains on the Turin shroud.

Elaborate accounts of hypothetical societies in which cloning is a routinely employed alternative to more familiar reproductive modes include Naomi Mitchison's *Solution Three* (1975), John Varley's *The Ophiuchi Hotline* (1977), C. J. Cherryh's *Cyteen* (1988), and Anna Wilson's *Hatching Stones* (1991). Copying people by "fax" produces routine "immorbidity" in Wil McCarthy's Queendom of Sol series, the cloning aspect coming to the fore in "The Policeman's Daughter" (2005). The potential utility of clones in facilitating experimental design—reflected in the real world in the production of cloned mice for use in medical research—is reflected in such imaginary experiments as the one begun in Thomas Sullivan's *Diapason* (1979).

The plausibility of the notion that people might go to any lengths in the admittedly futile attempt to "reproduce" lost loved ones—as featured in "When You Care, When You Love" and Jeremy Leven's *Creator* (1980)—has some observational support, although it has so far only been applied to pets. Clones also offer useful potential to writers of crime stories, by generating confusion related to the identification of corpses as well as expanding the range of possible motives for murder; such possibilities are exploited in Ben Bova's *The Multiple Man* (1976), John Varley's "The Phantom of Kansas" (1976), Michael Weaver's *Mercedes Nights* (1987), Michael F. Flynn's "The Adventure of the Laughing Clone" (1988), and Wolfgang Jeschke's *Midas* (trans. 1990).

Another possible application of cloning technology that has excited a good deal of journalistic and literary interest is the notion of "resurrecting" extinct species whose DNA is preserved in fossils. Mammoth carcasses preserved in the Arctic permafrost seem the most likely sources of usable DNA, which might be implanted in host egg cells provided by elephants—as described in Stephen Baxter's Mammoth trilogy

(1999–2001)—but the notion of cloning dinosaur DNA recovered from biting insects preserved in amber in denucleated frog egg cells, as featured in Michael Crichton's *Jurassic Park* (1994), makes up in melodramatic flair what it lacks in plausibility.

The advent of *in vitro* fertilisation and its widespread medical use in the 1980s made it relatively easy to create clones by dividing the resultant embryos—scientists at George Washington University created human clones by embryo splitting in 1993—but it remained more difficult to create a clone from the differentiated cell of a mature mammal; the nuclear transfer technique developed in 1997 by scientists at the Roslin Institute was a significant technical breakthrough. Subsequent debates about the future development of cloning technologies often drew a distinction between "reproductive cloning" (creating new individuals) and "therapeutic cloning" (the production of new tissues for use in medical treatments, usually using stem cells).

The premature death of the Roslin Institute's cloned sheep Dolly cast a shadow over the prospects of nuclear transfer technology, but Cumulina—a mouse cloned by nuclear transfer at the University of Hawaii Medical School in 1997—lived out a full span before dying in 2000, the year in which the first pigs, goats, and cattle were cloned by nuclear transfer. Research into therapeutic cloning underwent a spectacular renaissance in the same period, giving rise to intense bioethical debates because of the need to produce embryos in order to obtain a supply of "totipotent" stem cells. (Stem cells harvested from developed organisms are more limited in their ability to differentiate into specialised tissues.)

Accounts of cloning gone wrong are commonplace in horror-science fiction, in such dark farces as Russell M. Griffin's *The Blind Men and the Elephant* (1982) and the film *Multiplicity* (1996). The notion of therapeutic cloning has given rise to new nightmare scenarios like the one described in Michael Marshall Smith's *Spares* (1996), in which populations of hideously deformed, artificially produced twins live wretched captive lives while they wait for their organs to be harvested. Extrapolations of similar ideas include L. Timmel Duchamp's "How Josiah Taylor Lost His Soul" (2000), Nancy Farmer's *The House of the Scorpion* (2002), and Kazuo Ishiguro's *Never Let Me Go* (2005). The legal wrangles surrounding cloning technologies gave rise to such futuristic thrillers of illicit cloning as Kathleen Ann Goonan's *The Bones of Time* (1996). The possibility had become sufficiently familiar by the end of the century to warrant surreal celebration in the *recherché* Carrollian fantasy *Alice au pays des clones* (1999) by gynaecologist Claude Sureau.

COLONISATION

A term usually employed in a geographical and political context, in which a colony is a company of individuals transplanted from their mother country to a new land, where they set about reproducing their society of origin. It is also used in a biological context with reference to the spread of natural species, especially populations of bacteria developed from a single displaced cell. The latter meaning represents colonisation as a natural process impelled by a biological imperative, and this implication is often transferred to political programs by way of justification, especially when the extension of colonies by one political group involves the invasion and conquest of territory already occupied by another.

The cultural geography of the modern world has been largely determined by colonial movements, including the initial diaspora by which humans emerged from Africa to spread throughout the world and several subsequent westward migrations: from the Middle East to Western Europe (the Celts and others), from the Far East to Eastern Europe (the Tatars and others), and from Western Europe to the Americas. Modern colonialism is primarily associated with this final phase, which began in earnest in the sixteenth century. The subsequent discovery of Australia began a further phase in the eighteenth century, followed by various invasions of Africa in the nineteenth century. Such was the seeming inexorability of this endeavour that Thomas Gray's poem "Luna Habilitatis" (1737) imagined English colonialism extending to the lunar continents long before the idea became commonplace in science fiction.

Literacy and colonial activity have long been historically linked, partly because colonial endeavours necessitate long-distance communication, and the evolution of modern European literatures from the Renaissance to the twentieth century took place in a context of colonial expansion. Insofar as a literary work takes account of the future, even in the narrow sense of equipping characters with plausible ambitions, colonial projects have always loomed large within it. The conventional closure of the majority of novels was always secured by marriage and/or personal enrichment, but the third factor that frequently supplemented or complicated these narrative rewards is emigration—or, in an American historical context, heading west.

American science fiction developed alongside the genre that provided the United States with its "creation mythology": the western. It had the same ideological roots, and it is not surprising that its own guiding myth—the myth of the *Space Age—was a futuristic transformation of the western's image of history, which extrapolated an imperative process of colonisation from the last available terrestrial frontier to the "final frontier" of space, regarding the entire universe as territory ripe for conquest and civilisation. In speculative fiction and nonfiction, this project was routinely represented as a matter of destiny—neatly repackaged by James *Blish as "pantropy"—whose refusal or inhibition would be tantamount to a betrayal of human nature and the nature of life itself. In that context, the perceived generic centrality of Isaac *Asimov's Foundation trilogy—which imagines a galaxy filled to capacity with worlds inhabited by human beings—is perfectly understandable.

The discoveries of *astronomy from the mid-nineteenth century onwards provided a stream of evidence suggesting that colonisation of the other worlds of the solar system would be impossible, but astronomers like Percival Lowell were prone to interpret observations in the light of preconceptions that imprinted the surface of *Mars with illusory canals; it is not surprising that speculative fiction proved markedly resistant to contradiction, or that the reluctant acceptance of the inhospitablility of the other planets only served to increase interest in the colonisation of the worlds of other stars and calculated blindness to the extreme difficulties of interstellar travel.

The fact that the British Empire was already in decline before American science fiction got off the ground helps to explain the differences between scientific romance and science fiction. Although the Space Age was anticipated in some early scientific romances, such as Andrew Blair's *Annals of the Twenty-Ninth Century* (1874), the most innovative work in the genre explicitly modelled on British colonialism was H. G. Wells *The War of the Worlds* (1898), which the author envisaged as an inversion of the British colonialist invasion of Tasmania—except that bacteria side with the defenders in this case, whereas it was the diseases imported by colonists that devastated native populations in the real world. Subsequent writers of scientific romance were uninterested in the conquest of space; J. B. S. Haldane's "The Last Judgement" (1927) and Olaf Stapledon's *Last and First Men* (1930) imagine extraterrestrial colonisation as a last resort, motivated by extreme duress, and emigration from the solar system as an extremely distant project.

The situation of American science fiction was, of course, complicated by the fact that the independent nation's colonisation of the West had only become its definitive project once the English colonies founded in the east had successfully rebelled against their motherland. This crucial historical break was to be reenacted repeatedly in science fiction's futuristic narrative spaces, sometimes in very light disguise.

Notable examples include "Birth of a New Republic" (1930) by Miles J. Breuer and Jack Williamson, Isaac Asimov's "The Martian Way" (1952), Robert A. Heinlein's *The Moon Is a Harsh Mistress* (1966), and Poul Anderson's *Tales of the Flying Mountains* (1970). Similar events seen from a British perspective, in such novels as Arthur C. Clarke's *The Songs of Distant Earth* (1958; exp. 1986) and Paul J. McAuley's *Of the Fall* (1989; aka *Secret Harmonies*), tend to be far more ambiguous in their ideological outlook.

The notion that many of the first would-be colonists of America were religious sects and eccentric communards—a motif given mythical status in the story of the *Mayflower*'s Pilgrim Fathers—also lent itself readily to science-fictional transfiguration, and genre science fiction is remarkably rich in accounts of ideologically specialised colonial societies, whose satirical representation is often wryly sympathetic. Notable examples include Eric Frank Russell's "...And Then There Were None" (1951), Frederik Pohl and C. M. Kornbluth's *Search the Sky* (1954), Evelyn E. Smith's *The Perfect Planet* (1962), and H. Beam Piper and John J. McGuire's *A Planet for Texans* (1958). The "lost colony" formula became one of the significant clichés of science fiction in the 1950s, and continued to thrive for several decades thereafter. The notion that Earth might be a forsaken colony, as broached in B. and G. C. Wallis's "The Mother World" (1933), was elaborately developed in Ursula K. le Guin's Hainish series, which demonstrates the formula's potential for use in such serious sociological thought experiments as *The Left Hand of Darkness* (1969).

Skeptical accounts of the politics of Western colonisation began to appear in the U.S. science fiction pulps at an early stage—notable examples include Edmond Hamilton's "Conquest of Two Worlds" (1932) and Robert Heinlein's "Logic of Empire" (1941)—and became increasingly numerous and strident as time went by, under the influence of American foreign policy as applied in Korea and Vietnam. The murky politics of colonialist diplomacy were viewed with increasingly jaundiced eyes in such stories as Poul Anderson's "The Helping Hand" (1950), R. M. McKenna's "The Fishdollar Affair" (1958), and Keith Laumer's long-running Retief series (launched 1960). Problems of competitive colonisation are widely featured in 1950s science fiction; Clifford D. Simak's "No Life of Their Own" (1959) is a notable example.

Avram Davidson's "Now Let Us Sleep" (1957), Robert Silverberg's *Invaders from Earth* (1958), H. Beam Piper's *Little Fuzzy* (1962), and Ursula K. Le Guin's *The Word for World Is Forest* (1972) are among the more exaggeratedly polemical accounts of colonisation as spoliation. The increasing appeal of such stories is linked to a parallel growth in nostalgia for the mythical Golden Age fatally disrupted by *civilisation; accounts of Space Age colonisation are often infected by *ecological mysticism and Edenic imagery, as in Ray Bradbury's "The Million-Year Picnic" (1946) and Mark Clifton's *Eight Keys to Eden* (1960). Ironic reflections on the fundamental notion include William W. Stuart's "Inside John Barth" (1960), in which a human body is colonised by intelligent and ambitious microbes.

The idea that there might still be frontiers on Earth that warrant colonial endeavour was largely sidelined in American science fiction while the Space Age beckoned, although accounts of colonising the oceans always maintained a more conspicuous presence than accounts of civilisation extending beneath the Earth's surface or the building of cities in the *air, the primitive example of Robert Ellis Dudgeon's *Columbia* (1873) being carried forward in such works as Norman L. Knight's "Crisis in Utopia" (1940), Frederik Pohl and Jack Williamson's *Undersea Quest* (1954) and its sequels, Kenneth Bulmer's *City Under the Sea* (1957), Dean R. McLaughlin's "The Man on the Bottom" (1958; exp. as *Dome World*, 1962), Gordon R. Dickson's *The Space Swimmers* (1963; book, 1967), Keith Roberts "The Deeps" (1966), David Andreissen's *Star Seed* (1982), and Maureen F. McHugh's *Half the Day Is Night* (1994).

The space probes of the 1970s hammered the final nails into the coffin of traditional images of planetary colonisation, but the prospectus was repaired with the aid of the notion of building self-enclosed colonies in *artificial satellites, as advocated by Konstantin *Tsiolkovsky and repopularised by Gerard K. O'Neill's *The High Frontier* (1977). Another facilitating device used to bridge the widening gap in the Space Age timetable was that of *terraforming, defiantly applied to such colonisation projects as those featured in Kim Stanley Robinson's Mars series and Pamela Sargent's *Venus series, and flamboyantly mythologised in Ian McDonald's *Desolation Road* (1988). The processes of adaptation described in such works often attack the problem from both directions, involving strategic modifications of would-be colonists by *cyborgisation or *genetic engineering.

Although early accounts of the potential adaptive costs of space colonisation had been produced even before Blish's Pantropy series, in descriptions of the Thresholders contained in C. L. Moore's "Promised Land" and "Heir Apparent" (both 1950; by-lined Laurence O'Donnell), the 1970s saw a dramatic increase in such stories of literal *alienation, elaborate examples of which include Daniel Hatch's series about the colonisation of Asgard, launched with

"Den of Foxes" (1990), Alison Sinclair's *Blueheart* (1996), and Allen Steele's Coyote series, collected in the mosaics *Coyote: A Novel of Interstellar Exploration* (2002) and *Coyote Rising* (2004). Even in late twentieth-century and early twenty-first-century stories of Earth-clone colonisation, in which radical physical adaptations are not required, other kinds of problems tend to be extrapolated to extremes, as in McAuley's *Of the Fall* and Nancy Kress' *Crossfire* (2003) and *Crucible* (2004). The logic of the situation had made it clear by then that extending colonisation to the final frontier is almost certain to be a *posthuman project rather than a human one, if it should ever happen.

COMET

An astronomical phenomenon involving the relatively brief appearance of an object that moves relative to the stellar background and often extends a "tail". In ancient times comets—then considered as atmospheric phenomena—were routinely construed as omens of disaster, a reputation that assisted them in exercising a considerable fascination on the literary imagination. "Comet fear" is a detectable historical phenomenon in writings from 1200 onwards.

A large comet observed by Tycho Brahe in 1578, six years after his famous "new star", provided a second important demonstration of the fact that the heavens were not unchanging when measurements of its parallax demonstrated that it was further away than the Moon. This discovery did not diminish comet fear, and may have had the opposite effect; a pamphlet published a year after the comet of 1618 by Gotthard Arthusius—a professor of history and mathematics at the University of Main in Germany—construed it as an omen of the imminent end of the world. Accurate calculations of cometary orbits were made by several *astronomers in the seventeenth century, by far the most famous being Edmond Halley's determination of the 76-year period of the comet named after him, which allowed a prediction of its eventual return, whose eventual fulfillment was a significant testament to the competence of astronomical measurement and calculation.

The first telescopic discovery of a comet, by Maria Mitchell in 1835, paved the way for many more, revealing that such objects were not nearly as rare as had previously been imagined, and comets became objects of increasingly intense interest thereafter. The idea that the Earth might be struck by one, developed in jocular fashion in Oliver Wendell Holmes' poem "The Comet" (ca. 1833), increased

markedly in plausibility. One of its most enthusiastic popularisers was Camille *Flammarion, who also employed Halley's comet as a hypothetical narrator in his historical panorama "Histoire d'une comète" (1872) and assembled a fictitious international scientific conference to discuss a cometary threat in the first part of *La fin du monde* (1893; trans. as *Omega: The Last Days of the World*). Comets wreak disaster on the world in Edgar Allan Poe's "The Conversation of Eiros and Charmion" (1839) and Vladimir Odoevsky's *4338-J God: Peterburgskie Pis'ma* (1846), but such threats often loom only to be averted, as in William Minto's *The Crack of Doom* (1886) and George Griffith's "The Great Crellin Comet" (1897; exp. as *The World Peril of 1910*).

Other nineteenth-century literary comets included one that crashes into the Sun in Robert Duncan Milne's "Into the Sun" (1882) and the life-bearing examples of Humphry Davy's *Consolations in Travel* (1830). An exotic comet brought a message to a visitor from a world of Arcturus in Edward Spencer's "The Tale of a Comet" (1870). Comets featured in similarly meditative flights of fancy in such poems as Charles Harpur's "To the Comet of 1843" (1853), Gerald Manley Hopkins' allegorical "I Am Like a Slip of Comet" (1864), W. W. Strickland's "A Comet" (1893), and Thomas Hardy's "The Comet at Valbury or Yell'ham" (1898).

The comet in H. G. Wells' *In the Days of the Comet* (1906) is an arbitrary transformative device of rare benignity; most early twentieth-century accounts continued the disaster tradition, as in Jack Bechdolt's *The Torch* (1920; book, 1948), Geoffrey Helwecke's "Ten Million Miles Sunward" (1928), Dennis Wheatley's *Sixty Days to Live* (1939), and Lewis Sowden's *Tomorrow's Comet* (1949 as "Star of Doom"; book, 1951), although the role was increasingly taken over by giant *meteorites and stray *asteroids once such objects could be readily distinguished. Robert S. Richardson's *Getting Acquainted with Comets* (1967) includes a drama-documentary impact story. In Immanuel Velikovsky's notorious exercise in pseudoscientific catastrophism *Worlds in Collision* (1950), a "comet" expelled by Jupiter allegedly passed very close to Earth twice, reversing its direction of spin and altering its orbit before becoming the planet Venus.

The fragile construction of comets was popularised by Fred Whipple in the 1940s. Whipple proposed that they are conglomerates of ice and dust whose approaches to the Sun are associated with considerable evaporation—greatly expanding their heads and generating their long tails. His proposal was eventually confirmed by space probes; the Deep Impact probe impacted with Tempel 1 on 4 July 2005 revealing that its matter is very loosely aggregated and shot through with holes. Even so, large examples continued to figure in disaster-threat stories such as Robert S. Richardson's "The Red Euphoric Branch" (1967; by-lined Philip Latham); one shatters the Moon in Jack McDevitt's *Moonfall* (1998), while yet others strike the Earth in Michael McCollum's *Thunderstrike!* (1998) and Samuel C. Florman's *The Aftermath: A Novel of Survival* (2003). The familiarisation of their nature inhibited the production of fanciful stories, although Frederik Pohl's "Some Joys Under the Star" (1973) and Ian Watson's "The Descent" (1999) feature exotic examples, and they play a key role in Fred *Hoyle and Chandra Wickramasinghe's version of the *panspermia hypothesis, as dramatised in Robert R. Chase's "From Mars and Venus" (2000).

The projection of cometary orbits suggests that most of them originate from a "halo" of thinly distributed matter far beyond Pluto, which may contain far more mass than is combined in the planets. The main body of this halo was named the Oort Cloud, while an inner aggregation was dubbed the Kuiper Belt. The cometary halo was featured in Frederik Pohl and Jack Williamson's *The Reefs of Space* (1964) and played a cameo role in Arthur C. Clarke's *Imperial Earth* (1975) before Williamson developed the setting far more elaborately in *Lifeburst* (1984) and Pohl did likewise in *Mining the Oort* (1992). Robert L. Forward's *Camelot 30K* (1993) is an account of comets in their "natural habitat", and one such is colonised in Poul Anderson's *The Stars Are Also Fire* (1994). The Kuiper Belt is home to life in Stephen Baxter's "Sunpeople" (1997). The hypothesis that a dark star periodically triggers showers of comets from the Oort Cloud is explored in Poul Anderson's "Pride" (1986). The Kuiper Belt substitutes for the asteroid belt as a wild frontier in J. R. Dunn's "The Names of All the Spirits" (2002) and Matthew Jarpe's "City of Reason" (2005), while the Oort cloud becomes an arena of exotic romance in Mary Rosenblum's "Gypsy Tail Wind" (2005).

A comet is diverted to serve as a station for studying the sun in Hal Clement's "Sun Spot" (1960); a similar diversion is intended to cause a collision with the Moon in John Gribbin and Marcus Chown's *Double Planet* (1984; exp. 1988). The notion that long-distance space travellers might be able to "hitch" rides on comets is dramatised in Gregory Benford's "West Wind, Falling" (1971; with Gordon Eklund) and *The Heart of the Comet* (1986; with David Brin). The latter celebrated the long-anticipated return of Halley's comet, which had been anticipated for some years in such works as Philip Latham's "The Blindness" (1946) and John Calvin Batchelor's

The Further Adventures of Halley's Comet (1980); another novel produced to mark the event was Fred Hoyle's *Comet Halley* (1985).

COMPUTER

An automatic calculating machine that performs operations in response to a program. The earliest attempts to build such a machine involved devices whose programming systems were based on the punched cards governing patterns in powered looms. Charles Babbage contrived some simple devices of this kind but his attempt to develop a powerful "analytical engine" in the 1830s, in association with Ada Lovelace (the daughter of Lord Byron), was frustrated by the inadequacy of contemporary machine tools. Mechanical calculating machines always labored under the handicap of the decimal system, and it was not until the 1930s that the idea of developing calculators in which binary digits were represented by on/off switches paved the way for a new generation of machines using electromechanical relays. Konrad Zuse built an early binary calculating machine in 1936 and IBM began developing such machines in the early 1940s, while rival systems using thermionic valves were secretly developed for military purposes.

Although a few vaguely described "mechanical brains" gifting automata with *artificial intelligence were featured in nineteenth-century fiction, it was not until the early days of pulp science fiction that machines and mathematical processes bearing any resemblance to a modern computation system were described. The earliest examples included S. P. Meek's "Futility" (1929), an early account of predictive analysis, and the mathematically innovative device featured in John W. Campbell Jr.'s "When the Atoms Failed" (1930). Miles J. Breuer's "Mechanocracy" (1932) looked forward to the day when a mechanical brain would be entrusted with the task of World Government.

In 1936 Alan Turing conceived the "Turing machine"—a mathematically defined hypothetical construct invented to illustrate the theory of mechanical computation—and laid the methodical foundations for work carried out at Bletchley Park during World War II that involved the construction of a primitive computer, Colossus, dedicated to the task of cracking the Enigma code employed by the Germans. The U.S. Army and Navy mounted similar projects of their own, and the first electronic computer to be unveiled to the public in 1945 was ENIAC, built for the Army at the Moore School of Electrical Engineering at the University of Pennsylvania. John von Neumann adapted the ENIAC design to enable its use of electronically stored programs; by the time the resulting

EDVAC machine was constructed at Moore in 1949, a similar one had been constructed in Britain.

The first commercial installation of a UNIVAC computer was at the U.S. Census Bureau in 1951; its British equivalent, LEO, was employed by the food company Lyons & Co. IBM's 701 followed in 1952, rapidly achieving market domination before being superseded by later models in the series. Another early entrant into the commercial market was the Burroughs Atlas. These early mainframe computers filled large rooms and required constant maintenance to counter the problem of overheating vacuum tubes. Data was usually stored on and input from punch cards, although they were gradually replaced by magnetic tape systems, which were then displaced in turn by disk drives, initially marketed by IBM in 1957.

The advent of ENIAC awoke science fiction writers, rather abruptly, to the potential of computers, and it was the image of the massive ENIAC and its clones that dominated their notion of what computers were and might become. John D. MacDonald's "The Mechanical Answer" (1948) provided an early example of an ENIAC-inspired device built for military purposes. The use of names like Colossus and Atlas greatly encouraged the notion of the computer as a giant with the potential to become a tyrant. Accounts of human rebellion against machine intelligences were already commonplace, and the advent of actual computers was widely seen as an endorsement of such fears. Isaac *Asimov, already actively engaged in combating the *Frankenstein complex, was one of the few to question that rising tide of anxiety in such stories as "The Evitable Conflict" (1950). Fredric Brown's brief "Answer" (1954)—in which a new computer, asked whether there is a God, replies: "Yes, *now* there is a God"—encapsulated the prevailing mood of the era. The defence mounted against popular paranoia by such propaganda pieces as *They'd Rather Be Right* (1957; aka *The Forever Machine*) by Mark Clifton and Frank Riley revealed their desperation in their polemical excess.

Images of potential computer oppression rarely limited themselves to the modest extrapolative strategies of Walter M. Miller's "Izzard and the Membrane" (1951), in which a computer scientist and his creation fall into Soviet hands, and Poul Anderson's "Sam Hall" (1953), which suggested ways in which such instruments might serve the political ends of human despotism. They moved instead to extremes of totalitarian political domination and reckless hubris. Anderson moved swiftly on to imagine future society directly governed by the giant Technon in *The Long Way Home* (1955), and the fearful aspects of that possibility were profusely expressed in such varied alarmist fantasies as Francis G. Rayer's

Tomorrow Sometimes Comes (1951), E. C. Tubb's *Enterprise 2115* (1954; aka *The Mechanical Monarch*), Winston Brebner's *Doubting Thomas* (1956), Philip K. Dick's *Vulcan's Hammer* (1956; exp. book, 1960), Dino Buzzati's *Il Grande Ritratto* (1960; trans. as *Larger than Life*), Milton Lesser's *Spacemen, Go Home* (1962), Frank Herbert's *Destination: Void* (1966), D. F. Jones's *Colossus* (1966), Philip E. High's *The Mad Metropolis* (1966; aka *Double Illusion*), Harlan Ellison's "I Have No Mouth, and I Must Scream" (1967), Mack Reynolds' *Computer War* (1967) and *The Computer Conspiracy* (1968), Martin Caidin's *The God Machine* (1968), Paul W. Fairman's *I, the Machine* (1968), Lawrence Durrell's *The Revolt of Aphrodite* (in 2 vols. as *Tunc* and *Nunquam*, 1968–1970; combined ed., 1974), Christopher Hodder-Williams' *A Fistful of Digits* (1968) and *98.4* (1969), and Douglas R. Mason's *From Carthage Then I Came* (1968; aka *Eight Against Utopia*) and *Matrix* (1970).

In response to this torrent of anxiety, Asimov's most famous answer to "Answer", in "The Last Question" (1956), was not to deny the computer's potential to become a God, but to insist instead that it would be a good God—a reply that did not soothe many anxieties. Satires such as Arthur T. Hadley's *The Joy Wagon* (1958); in which a computer runs for the U.S. presidency, Olof Johanneson's *The Tale of the Big Computer* (trans. 1966), which updated the argument of Samuel Butler's "Book of the Machines" in *Erewhon* (1872); and Robert Silverberg's computer diary "Going Down Smooth" (1968) embodied the same sense of threat in their delicate dark edges.

The pattern of future computer development imagined by the science fiction of the 1950s and 1960s was relatively unaffected by the replacement of electronic valves with transistors, but it was abruptly subverted by a crucial new development that allowed large numbers of transistors to be etched into the layers of a "silicon chip"—the microprocessor, which was launched into the marketplace by Intel's 4004 in 1971. *Apollo*'s onboard computers, used in the 1969 Moon landing—made out of nickel-iron cores woven together with plastic wires and encased in plastic—suddenly seemed extremely crude. When the 4004 chip was superseded by the 8008 and the 8080 (launched in 1974), it became obvious that future computers would get smaller rather than bigger; the calculating power of an Atlas would soon be available on a desktop and all kinds of machines would soon be invested with managerial computers of varying sophistication. Personal computers were initially marketed as self-assembly kits, like the Altair 8800 launched in 1975, but the development of the CP/M operating system and the launch of the Apple II in

1977 ushered in a new era, secured when IBM launched its first PC—using Microsoft's MS/DOS operating system—in 1981. Apple introduced the Macintosh, equipped with a graphical user interface, in 1984.

Although it was rapidly observed that the only science fiction story of the 1940s that had imagined anything remotely resembling a personal computer was Will F. Jenkins' "A Logic Named Joe" (1946, by-lined Murray Leinster in most reprints), a few such machines had featured alongside the giants of the 1950s; Asimov's "Someday" (1956) imagined a desktop computer used to generate stories for children, while "The Fun They Had" (1957) employed a similar device in formal education. "Drafting Dan", which produces technical drawings in response to commands from a keyboard, had a cameo role in Robert A. Heinlein's *The Door into Summer* (1956). One could, however, find more ambitious imagery in the advertising sections of the contemporary magazines; *Galaxy* carried ads in 1956 for the Geniac "electric brain" construction kit, which allegedly composed music, computed and played games. Had more science fiction writers invested in the product, fewer might have been taken completely by surprise by the rapid advances of the early 1970s, when their imagery lagged conspicuously behind such melodramatic futurological studies as Ted Nelson's *Computer Lib/ Dream Machines* (1974) and Christopher Evans' *The Mighty Micro* (1979).

Although the imminence of the PC revolution was celebrated in the May 1973 issue of *Analog* by Stephen A. Kallis Jr.'s article on "Minicomputers", the magazine's fiction was slow to respond. Even Asimov was still couching such propaganda pieces as "The Life and Times of MULTIVAC" (1975) in "traditional" terms in middecade, and oppressive giant computers continued to feature in such works as Mick Farren's *The Quest of the DNA Cowboys* (1976), although that novel's grotesque exaggeration of their already-marked tendency towards insanity reflected the fact that the whole idea had got somewhat out of hand. The fictional exploration of the new spectrum of futurological possibilities was, however, competently begun in John Brunner's *The Shockwave Rider* (1975), whose anticipation of a vast profusion of networked computers immediately embraced the possible development of computer viruses and worms, and imagined the havoc such entities might wreak.

The geometrical increase in processing power soon gave birth to "Moore's law", which observed that the power of computing technology was doubling every eighteen months—a relationship that held good throughout the closing stages of the twentieth century, by which time the possibility that it would continue to hold good had given rise to the notion that the exponential ascent of the curve would bring about a technological *singularity. Images of a computer-rich future became so commonplace by 1980 that the notion hardly needed foregrounding by such titles as A. E. van Vogt's *Computerworld* (1983), and there seemed to be little need for science-fictional extrapolations of such notions as computer *art when even the simplest PCs could run programs producing fractal images by means of *chaos mathematics.

Science fiction writers tended to overleap the modest kinds of application on which futurological texts focused and move rapidly to extremes. The implication of intimacy contained in the notion of personal computers was extrapolated into the hypothetical science of "psychosynergistics" in Poul Anderson's "Joelle" (1977) whose preliminary exploration of the possibilities of building better interfaces between the human mind and computers pointed the way to the next spectacular explosion of science-fictional imagery: the development of the notion of *cyberspace and the advent of the cyberpunk movement. The great success of cyberpunk fiction ensured that hypothetical developments of computer technology that did not involve cyberspace would be relatively unobtrusive, although such examples as David Langford's "Blit" (1988) and its sequels—which feature computer images that wreak havoc on the human brain—are by no means uninteresting. By the turn of the century, such near-future speculations as Vernor Vinge's "Fair Times at Fairmont High" (2001), which describes the casual takeup of new technological opportunities by adolescents, and Richard Lovett's "Tiny Berries" (2003), which examines the problem of e-mail "spam", seemed astonishing in their modest restraint.

The cyberpunk science fiction of the 1980s and 1990s made much of the evolution of individual artificial intelligence in relatively small computers, but it also maintained its commitment to the notion that the worldwide network of small computers would merely be the matrix in which such intelligences would pursue their quests for totalitarian political control and effective godhood; the supercomputer refused to surrender the imaginative high ground entirely to the forces of anarchy, but simply amended its basic anatomy to suit the new imaginative environment. Further alternative anatomies appeared in such supercomputers as the one featured in Sean McMullen's Calculor series, initially launched by *Voices in the Light* (1994) but revised for the version contained in *Souls in the Great Machine* (1999), *The Miocene Arrow* (2000), and *Eyes of the Calculor* (2001).

Retrospective attempts to put the history of computers in perspective include a number of historical fantasies reexamining their evolution. Alternative histories wondering how the Babbage engine might have transformed the world if it had been practicable include Michael Flynn's *In the Country of the Blind* (1987; book, 1990) and William Gibson and Bruce Sterling's *The Difference Engine* (1990). Charles Sheffield's "Georgia on My Mind" (1993) looks back to the building of DEUCE (Digital Electronic Universal Computing Engine) in 1958 and hypothesises a quest for Babbage's lost analytical engine. Ada Lovelace's role is given greater prominence in John Meaney's "The Whisper of Discs" (2002). Lou Anders' anthology *Life Without a Net* (2003) imagines alternative worlds without the Internet—an idea that had already become challenging, less than twenty years after the advent of the phenomenon had seemed almost miraculous.

CONTE PHILOSOPHIQUE

A term employed by Voltaire to describe a series of fictions in which he used various fictional forms—the dialogue, the fantastic voyage, and especially the exotic tale of wonder, as popularised by Antoine Galland's *Les milles et une nuits* (1704–1717)—in the satirical extrapolation of various philosophical issues of his day. Although he devised the term by analogy with the *conte populaire* (folktale), the works to which he attached the label were very various in length; what he meant to emphasise was that the works had to be read as fabulations, their artificiality plainly manifest.

"Le Monde comme il va, vision de Babouc" (1746; trans. as "The World as It Is"') describes an educational excursion under the tutelage of the angel Ituriel, and many of Voltaire's subsequent *contes philosophiques* were similarly fantastic. Some, however, were much closer in substance and spirit to modern speculative fiction. "Zadig, ou la Destinée" (1748) tracks the misfortunes of a master of logical deduction whose brilliance is unappreciated by various interrogators—a significant precursor of detective fiction as well as a comment on the popular reception of scientific discoveries. "Micromégas" (1752) is a fierce assault on religious vanity whose apparatus—involving giant visitors from Sirius and Saturn—established it as a foundation stone of speculative fiction. *Candide, ou l'Optimisme* (1759; trans. as *Candide*) is a scathing juxtaposition of the Leibnizian insistence that ours is the best of all possible worlds—here credited to Dr. Pangloss—with a cynical analysis of the world as it is. "Les Oreilles du Comte de Chesterfield, et Le Chapelain Goudman" (1775) subjects an anatomist's views on the immortal soul to a painstaking thought experiment.

The term was borrowed by Camille Flammarion as a description of science-based speculative fiction—as in his collection *Contes philosophiques* (1911)—but it did not catch on as a generic description. Speculative fiction made its most significant early advances in a period when the principal model of fiction was the novel, cast in a mimetic rather than a diegetic *narrative mode, and in which self-consciously artificial *contes*/tales were being gradually displaced by *récits*/stories that replaced "telling" with "showing" to the extent permitted by their restricted word lengths. Because the themes of speculative fiction tend to be broad and abstruse, however, they are often better fitted to the format of the *conte philosophique* than to the mimetic short story, whose primary artistic triumph was the development of a "slice of life" format dependent on the reader's ability to invoke and skillfully deploy stocks of knowledge used in the interpretation of everyday experience.

The frequent use of *conte philosophique* methods by modern science fiction is one of the features that makes it seem "crude" to critics who consider the mimetic mode intrinsically superior. However, any serious attempt to investigate and display "the world as it is" (as revealed by the enhanced perceptions of science rather than the everyday traffic of mundane experience) is obliged to go beyond the limitations of mimetic presentation into the realms of diegetic *narrative. For this reason, the *conte philosophique* continues to survive and thrive in modern speculative fiction, assisting it in the exploration of the ways in which conceivable innovations might transform future society and in the use of nonhuman viewpoints—*aliens, *artificial intelligences, and so on—to illustrate and illuminate philosophical questions.

The main sequence of classic science fiction short stories—key examples include John W. Campbell's "Twilight" (1934), Isaac Asimov's "Nightfall" (1939) and his robot stories, Clifford Simak's "City" series (launched 1942), Daniel Keyes' "Flowers for Algernon" (1959), and Bob Shaw's "Light of Other Days" (1966)—exhibits a clear pattern of increasingly ingenious adaptation of their philosophical substance to a more conventionally mimetic mode of presentation. Kingsley Amis' characterisation of such works as "idea-as-hero stories" stresses their *conte philosophique* functionality, recognising that ideas can no longer function as "heroes" when they are consigned to the background of a text in order that its "human interest" may take precedence. The adaptation of Voltairean *contes philosphiques* to mimetic modes of narration by science fiction writers of the second half of the twentieth century was a compromise with reader preference rather than literary fashion, but the even balance between ideas and characters contrived by the most sophisticated *contes philosophiques* of that period helped to maintain the tradition of *hard science fiction against conspicuous and powerful softening tendencies.

Writers from outside the commercial genre have often felt freer than writers within it to indulge in the production of blatant *contes philosophiques*. American writers eager to avoid the stigmata of science fiction have mostly avoided similar imagery, but several high-profile European fabulators have taken a strong interest in the intellectual produce of science, including Primo Levi, whose relevant work from the 1960s is sampled in translation in *The Sixth Day and Other Stories* (1990); Italo Calvino, in the collections translated as *Cosmicomics* (1968) and *t zero* (1969); Josef Nesvadba, in *Vampire Ltd* (1964) and *In the Footsteps of the Abominable Snowman* (1970; aka *The Lost Face*); and Stanislaw Lem, in such collections as *The Cyberiad* (1974) and *Mortal Engines* (1977).

COSMOLOGY

The description of the universe as a whole, incorporating its present formation, origin, and evolution. Cosmological speculation originated as an important form of *myth, and its gradual metamorphosis into a science based on the integration of *astronomical observation and theoretical *physics is a central thread of the *history of science. The process began with the Greek philosophers who removed personalised deities from accounts of the condensation of the cosmos from primordial *chaos. The *Pythagoreans' notion of a cosmic sphere organised around a central *fire (whose light was reflected by the sun) was refined by later writers; *Plato and *Aristotle made crucial contributions to the emergence of the geocentric model of the cosmos detailed in Ptolemy's *Almagest* (ca. 130 A.D.). Aristarchos of Samos proposed a heliocentric model in the third century B.C., but it was dismissed, largely because the notion of an Earth moving through space and rotating on its axis seemed counterintuitive.

The Classical theorists' conviction that the fundamental motion of heavenly bodies must be circular was integrated into the fundamental physical geometry of the cosmos by the supposition that the various heavenly bodies were contained within concentric crystal spheres. Aristotle and Ptolemy accounted for anomalies in the movement of the planets in terms of subsidiary "epicycles" whose complexity was steadily increased by more accurate astronomical measurement. Cosmological speculation was reanimated in Renaissance Europe within the context of Christian theology. The geocentric model had been accepted into orthodox dogma—Dante Alighieri's *Paradiso* (ca. 1320) includes a detailed account of an ascent through the nine Aristotelian "heavens" to the empyrean (the realm of fire) beyond the fixed stars—but discussion of the possible *plurality of worlds opened new scope for argument.

In the early sixteenth century Nicolaus Copernicus' *De Revolutionibus Orbium Coelestrum* (On the Revolution of the Celestial Spheres) (written 1530; published 1543) revived the heliocentric model in the hope of overcoming the calculative inadequacies of the Ptolemaic system. Copernicus emphasised that his model was intended purely to improve calculations of planetary positions, but it was only slightly better than the Ptolemaic system, because it still assumed that the planetary orbits were circular. Even so, it gained popularity among astronomers; the Roman Church placed *De Revolutionibus* on the index of forbidden books in 1616 in the hope of stemming this support, but that action only heated up the dispute, which reached its climax in the trial following the publication of *Galileo's famous *Dialogue* of 1632. John *Kepler's elucidation of the laws of planetary motion in 1619 secured the calculative triumph that Copernicus had been unable to achieve, and Isaac *Newton completed the synthesis of Copernicus' model with Nicholas of Cusa's notion of an infinite number of solar systems distributed in infinite space.

Such literary works as George Buchanan's *De Sphaera* (1586) and Sir John Davies' "The Cosmic Dance" (ca. 1603) maintained allegiance to the Aristotelian cosmos but John Donne's *An Anatomy of the World* (ca. 1612) and Giambattista Marino's *L'Adone* (1622) are uneasily conscious of its obsolescence. Charles Sorel's *Vraie histoire comique de Francion* (1623–1626) is scrupulously even-handed, the first of its two satirical cosmic journeys mocking an Aristotelian universe while the second makes fun of the new cosmology. Sorel's nonfictional *La science universelle* (1635–1644), on the other hand, favoured a compromise position adopted by Tycho Brahe, in which the Sun orbits a stationary Earth but the planets orbit the Sun—a thesis also adopted in Athanasius Kircher's *Itinerarium Exstaticum* (1656). Juan Enríquez de Zúñiga's *Amor con vista* (1625) is proudly reactionary, representing the heavenly bodies within the Aristotelian spheres as the abodes of allegorical Classical gods. Henry More's didactic poem *Democritus Platonisans* (1646; trans. as *The Infinity of Worlds*) declared in favour of both the Copernican system and *atomism. Christian Huygens' posthumously published *Kosmotheoros* (1698; trans. as *The Celestial World Discover'd*) attempted a comprehensive literary summary of the new cosmology, as did Sir Richard Blackmore's *The Creation* (1712).

The distribution of the planets in the plane of the ecliptic caused heliocentric theorists such as Giordano Bruno to speculate that they might be floating on a sea of *ether—a notion taken up by René Descartes, who imagined the ether in motion, like a vortex with the Sun at its centre, and smaller vortices around each planet. He extrapolated this notion into a hypothetical account of the solar system's formation, which he integrated into his comprehensive *Principia Philosophiae* (1644). This eventually became the new orthodoxy that replaced the Aristotelian system in the European university curriculum. Literary responses to it included Gabriel Daniel's polemical rejection of Cartesian cosmology in *Voyage du monde de Decartes* (1690; trans. as *A Voyage to the World of Cartesius*), although Daniel directed his principal wrath against Cyrano de Bergerac, whose Cartesian *Fragment de Physique* had been appended to the second part of his account of *L'autre monde* in *Nouvelles oeuvres* (1662). Cartesian cosmology also exercised a considerable influence on the visionary adventures of Emanuel *Swedenborg.

The most significant of several attempts to modify Cartesian cosmology in the light of Isaac *Newton's *Principia* (1687) was made by Immanuel Kant in *Allegemeine Naturgeschichte und Theorie des Himmels* (1755; trans. as *Universal Natural History and Theory of the Heavens*), which included the contention that the Milky Way is one lenticular aggregation of stars among many "island universes" and offered a hypothetical account of the origin of the solar system by nebular condensation. The latter hypothesis was further elaborated by Pierre Laplace, in opposition to the Comte du Buffon's suggestion that the planets had formed as a result of a collision between the Sun and a comet.

Kant's notion of island universes obtained some empirical support in the early eighteenth century from William Herschel's studies of nebulae (which were in the process of being mapped by Charles Messier, in order to exclude them from the searches he was making for new comets). Herschel's observations of the Milky Way led him to conclude that some three hundred million *stars—most of them invisible—were arranged in a lens-shaped "sidereal system" measuring some 8,000 light-years by 1500. The first measurements of stellar parallax, published in 1838–1840, fitted neatly enough into the vastness of this imagined scale. The imaginative impact of these measurements was considerable; Edward Young's *Night Thoughts* (1742–1745) observed that "At once it quite engulfs all human thought; / 'Tis comprehension's absolute defeat" before relieving the shock with a sense of pride in being able to conceive of such things: "How glorious, then, appears the mind of man, / When in it all the stars, and planets, roll!"

Speculative accounts of the origin and evolution of the sidereal system initially replicated theories of the solar system on a larger scale, with much speculation about a "central Sun" and generalised theories of nebular condensation. The notion of the mortality of stars and star systems exercised a powerful grip on the first writers who attempted to embed the emerging cosmological narrative within literary frameworks, most notably Edgar Allan *Poe and Camille *Flammarion. Cosmological visions became a small but significant subgenre of speculative fiction as the nineteenth century drew to a close, significant examples being contained in Edgar Fawcett's *The Ghost of Guy Thyrle* (1895), H. G. Wells' "Under the Knife" (1896), and William Hope Hodgson's *The House on the Borderland* (1908).

Herschel's estimate of the size of the sidereal system was increased by his successors; Jacobus Kapteyn estimated in 1920 that its dimensions were $55,000 \times 11,000$ light-years. By that time, numerous nebular star clusters had been identified, and the proof that these lay outside the Milky Way emerged when the study of Cepheid variables provided a means of estimating their distance, demonstrating that the Magellanic Clouds and the Andromeda Nebula were other *galaxies. The exploitation of the Doppler effect in the calculation of the distance of nearer Cepheids allowed an initial calibration of the scale they provided, and an unexpected by-product of this enquiry was the observation that all but a few galactic Doppler shifts were towards the red end of the spectrum—implying that the universe is expanding—thus giving birth to the *Big Bang theory and its chief rival, the "steady-state" or "continuous creation" model.

The model of the universe produced by Albert *Einstein in consequence of his general theory of *relativity had already generated some controversy as to its stability. To conserve the cosmological principle that the universe ought to look the same from every viewpoint in space-time, Einstein had introduced a cosmological constant to oppose the effect of *gravity and maintain the model against the threat of collapse. William de Sitter had proposed alternative relativistic models that did not need any such constant, having a tendency to expand rather than collapse. De Sitter's model could not account for an expansion as rapid as that discovered empirically in the 1920s, but it did continue to supply cosmologists skeptical about the Big Bang with hope that alternative theories might still be viable.

These discoveries were difficult to accommodate within conventional narrative formats. Attempts to deal with the new cosmos as a whole within a literary text inevitably stretched their limits, as in Nathan Schachner's "Infra-Universe" (1937) and

Olaf Stapledon's *Star Maker* (1937). The action-adventure formats of pulp science fiction usually consigned cosmological speculations to background explanations, although that did not inhibit attempts to cash in on their grandeur. A few pioneers of interstellar space opera ventured outside the galaxy, but rarely went further than Andromeda. In narrative terms, a collapsing universe was more convenient than an expanding one, as illustrated by J. Lewis Burtt's "When the Universe Shrank" (1933), and science fiction writers were never shy about inventing new cosmologies in the context of *macrocosmic romance.

The expansion of the universe was rarely foregrounded as a topic, although Edmond Hamilton's "The Accursed Galaxy" (1935) suggested that all of the other galaxies might be fleeing in horror from ours because it is afflicted with the terrible disease of life. Clare Winger Harris attempted to extrapolate the nebular formation hypothesis in "The Menace of Mars" (1928), but the fanciful account of the solar system's origin contained in A. E. van Vogt's "The Seesaw" (1941) is more effective in dramatic terms. By contrast, the intellectually impeccable *contes philosophiques* contained within George Gamow's *Mr. Tompkins in Wonderland* (1939) have little in the way of story value, and the later fabulations that Italo Calvino called "cosmicomics" rely on their conspicuous *avant-gardism* in mounting their claim to literary worth. The difficulties of accommodating cosmological speculations within a story are carefully explained in Milton A. Rothman's metafictional "The Eternal Genesis" (1979).

Writers of *speculative nonfiction found it far easier to deal with the substance of cosmology, and such accounts began to take on literary attributes that other popularisations of science were usually content to leave to works of fiction. The history of cosmology offered in Svante Arrhenius' *Life of the Universe* (trans. 1909) does not extend as far as the inspiring discoveries of the 1920s, but works produced after the discovery of cosmic expansion were even more prone to bursts of rhapsodic lyricism—although some writers preferred to cultivate a triumphal laconism in dealing with momentous ideas in an ostentatiously casual manner. Such works extend from James Jeans' *The Universe Around Us* (1929) and Sir Arthur Eddington's *The Expanding Universe* (1940) to Steven Weinberg's *The First Three Minutes* (1977) and Stephen Hawking's *A Brief History of Time* (1988).

It was not only science fiction writers who found alternative cosmologies easier to deal with imaginatively; it became a fertile field for twentieth-century *pseudoscience. Inverted models conceiving of the Earth as a hollow sphere surrounding the Sun, Moon, and "phantom universe" of stars—as imagined in Cyrus Teed's "cellular hypothesis", the German *holtweltlehre* and "Koreshanity"—were dramatised in Marlo Field's *Astro Bubbles* (1928) and Laurence Manning's "World of the Mist" (1935), and recur in such fabulations as Barrington J. Bayley's "Me and My Antronoscope" (1973) and David Lake's *The Ring of Truth* (1982). Hanns Hörbiger's *welteislehre* (world ice theory), popularised in 1913 by Philipp Fauth's *Hörbiger's Galzial-Kosomogonie*, became fashionable in Germany during the Nazi era and was echoed in Otto Will Gail's *Der Stein vom Mond* (1926; trans. as *The Stone from the Moon*); Piers Anthony's *Rings of Ice* (1974) is a rare dramatisation in English of a similar thesis. Harold W. G. Allen, whose pseudoscientific cosmology is detailed in *Cosmic Perspective* (1998), *The Eternal Universe* (1999), and *The New Cosmology* (2001), attempted to popularise it further in his own science fiction novels, including *The Face on Mars* (1997) and *Lunar Encounter* (2000).

The romance of alternative cosmological speculation also appealed to more orthodox speculators, including those working with the kinds of models built by Einstein and de Sitter. J. B. S. Haldane's "A New Theory of the Past" (1945) and Martin Johnson's *Time, Knowledge and the Nebulae* (1947) attempted to popularise the theories of E. A. Milne, then president of the British Royal Astronomical Society, which included a new theory of primal matter formation and an idiosyncratic explanation of the galactic red-shifts. A BBC radio debate in 1959 gave rise to an Oxford University Press collection of *Rival Theories of Cosmology* (1960), in which the Big Bang and steady-state theories were supplemented by R. A. Lyttelton's suggestion that the universal expansion might be caused by a slight imbalance of charge between the electron and the proton. Reginald O. Kapp's *Towards a Unified Cosmology* (1959) offered a version of the steady-state theory in which matter *and* space are continuously created, although space is also obliterated within concentrations of matter; Kapp also proposed that all matter has a half-life of 400 million years—with the result that the Earth is slowly shrinking—and devised a new theory of gravity. William R. Bonnor's *The Mystery of the Expanding Universe* (1964) rejected both steady-state and Big Bang theories in favour of a cyclic theory in which the universe continually expands from and collapses into a cloud of hot nucleons.

Other exotic cosmologies with which science fiction writers have toyed include the idiosyncratic models deployed in Ian Watson's *The Jonah Kit* (1975), Philip José Farmer's *The Unreasoning Mask* (1981), and Barrington J. Bayley's *The Pillars of Eternity* (1982) and *The Zen Gun* (1983). A "Creator's Eye" view of applied cosmology is adopted in Don Sakers'

"Cycles" (1985). Ted Chiang's "Tower of Babel" (1990) describes a hierarchically organised recursive universe on a carefully limited scale. Adam Roberts' *Polystom* (2003) is set in a solar system in which air is omnipresent and planets are close enough to one another to facilitate travel by airship or biplane. Orthodox cosmology is rarely foregrounded in the same fashion, although its background situation is often far more than mere decor, as in Paul J. McAuley's *Eternal Light* (1991) and Greg Egan's *Schild's Ladder* (2001).

Scientific attempts to determine the size and nature of the universe were forced to become increasingly ingenious as astronomical observations continued to produce puzzling new data. One form of reasoning developed in the 1950s argued that the universe had to have certain characteristics in order to accommodate chemistry and biology; Robert Dicke argued that the existence of life implied certain limits to the conceivable size of the universe, while Fred Hoyle argued that the existence of organic carbon implied that a certain kind of fusion reaction must take place within stars. The observation that because life exists, the universe must be configured in such a way to contain it, gave rise to the weak and strong "anthropic principles" identified in 1974 by Brandon Carter. The weak principle is content to observe that if any one of the fundamental constants of physics had been slightly different, life could not have evolved, and that the values of the physical constants can therefore be deduced to a high level of accuracy from the mere fact that carbon-based life exists. The strong principle argues that there must be some kind of special significance in the observation and that it cannot be mere coincidence.

Acceptance of the strong anthropic principle does not necessarily imply an intelligent and purposive creator; one alternative explanation is that the observable universe may be the product of a process of natural selection, whereby universes reproduce themselves in such a way that those giving rise to stars of the kind likely to play host to life generate more offspring than those that do not. A version of this idea is extrapolated in Ian Stewart's "The Ape That Ate the Universe" (1993), in which the ultimate products of multiversal evolution are predatory cosmoses.

The idea that the observable universe is part of a much greater manifold had already been popularised by the Everett-Wheeler interpretation of quantum mechanical *uncertainty, which had lent support to the science-fictional notion of *alternative histories, but its cosmological extrapolation by such inflation theorists as Andrei Linde was quite distinct—at least until some science fiction writers began to confuse and conflate the two in such works as Stephen *Baxter's

Manifold series. The opposing view was, however, responsible for some remarkable conversions. Cosmologists who were driven by the implications of the strong anthropic principle to embrace some version of *creationist "intelligent design" included Fred Hoyle and Frank Tipler, while the most strident of all twentieth-century philosophical propagandists for atheism, Antony Flew, confessed in the early years of the twenty-first century that it had persuaded him to moderate his views. Interpretation of the anthropic principle became a key element of *Omega Point fiction, assisting it to become the primary form of cosmological science fiction in the latter part of the twentieth century.

Einstein's cosmological constant obtained a new lease on life in the final years of the twentieth century, when attempts to use ultrabright type Ia supernovas to estimate the distance of galaxies with the largest observable red-shifts, spearheaded by Saul Perlmutter, produced an unexpected result. Perlmutter had intended to calculate the rate at which the expansion of the universe is being slowed by gravity, but his results suggested that the universe's rate of expansion had actually increased since the Big Bang. This lent ammunition to dissenting theorists who believed that the galactic red-shifts might not be due to the Doppler effect, although the most popular explanations were offered by inflation theorists, who imagined the first phase of the Big Bang as a much more complex process than mere explosion.

John M. Ford's poem "Cosmology: A User's Manual" (1990) offers a whimsical commentary on the proliferation of arcane terminology within the science, allotting one couplet to each term. Inflation theory—an early literary echo of which is detailed in John Updike's philosophical novel *Roger's Version* (1987)—paved the way for science fiction writers to bring modern cosmological theory into the laboratory for experimental investigation in Gregory Benford's *Cosm* (1998). The corollary notion of variable laws of nature is developed on a more parochial scale in Bob Shaw's trilogy begun with *The Ragged Astronauts* (1986), which takes place in a region of space where *pi* equals three.

CREATIONISM

A philosophical doctrine holding that the world came into being through the action of a Creator. Although the fundamental thesis can be maintained in association with any scientific account, such collaboration became difficult in a Christian context when calculations of the timing of Creation based on Biblical chronology—most famously James Ussher's determination in the 1650s that creation took place in 4004 B.C.—established a timescale that became increasingly incompatible with the timescales suggested by such sciences as *cosmology and *geology. In spite of this incompatibility, Christian creationism retained its authority in respect of the origin of *life—although Georges Cuvier's *Ossements fossiles* (Fossil Bones) (1812) substituted a whole series of creations for the one described in *Genesis*—until the advent of theories of *evolution, which instituted a nineteenth-century contest in which the advent of Charles *Darwin's theory of natural election in 1859 seemed to both sides to be a pivotal moment.

Creationism became a common label in the twentieth century in connection with religious "fundamentalism". An early instance of fundamentalist rhetoric can be found in Alexander Ross's *The New Planet No Planet* (1646), which argues against John Wilkins' *Discovery of a New World* (1638)—and the *plurality of worlds in general—by stating that the Bible, the ultimate authority on all matters, speaks only of one creation, one humankind, and one Garden of Eden. Defences mounted against the implications of Darwinism in Victorian England were, however, more inclined to compromise. They ranged from the argument dramatised in Charles Kingsley's *The Water-Babies* (1863), to the effect that natural selection is merely God's creative method, to Philip Gosse's proposal, originally broached in *Omphalos* (1857), that, just as God had equipped Adam with a navel, he had created the world bearing the relics of a fictitious past. The Omphalos argument is deftly recast as the Re-Entrant Principle in R. A. Lafferty's "Inventions Bright and New" (1986).

Intellectual opposition to Darwinism in the United States initially rallied around a neo-Larmarckian position, but a more defiant and uncompromising Old Testament fundamentalism—championed in the early 1920s by populist Democratic politician William Jennings Bryan—had far more appeal to a great many laymen. Bryan's crusade culminated in a courtroom battle fought in Dayton, Tennessee, in 1925 against Clarence Darrow to determine the fate of John Scopes, who had confessed to teaching Darwinism in a local school in order to allow the American Civil Liberties Union (ACLU) to test a recently introduced legal ban. In the wake of the much-publicised trial, the statute was upheld and several other states passed similar bans, which were not overturned until the 1960s.

Although attacks on science by fundamentalists had become less frequent in the meantime, the removal of the statutes prompted a resurgence, calling for equal weight to be given in education to the theory of evolution and the oppositional stance, presented as

an alternative theory, initially called "Creation science" but subsequently retitled the "theory of intelligent design"—a position that combined William Paley's arguments in favour of natural *theology with more recent rhetoric drawn from the complexity of biochemical systems and the cosmological anthropic principle.

While some creationists gradually remodeled themselves as scientific theorists, some Darwinists took on the appearance of evangelical preachers; the spirit of a celebrated debate between "Darwin's bulldog", Thomas Henry Huxley, and Archbishop "Soapy Sam" Wilberforce was replicated more than a century later in a long series of journalistic confrontations between the most rhetorically fervent twentieth-century champion of Darwinism, Richard Dawkins, and a host of critics complaining about his alleged dogmatism. Ben Bova's editorial in the August 1973 issue of *Analog* complaining about the California Board of Education's decision to recognise creationism as a hypothesis of "equal validity" with Darwinism attracted a blizzard of counterargument, sampled in the letter column of the December issue.

The first climax of the early twentieth-century conflict is mirrored in Jerome Lawrence and Robert E. Lee's theatrical dramatisation of the Scopes trial, *Inherit the Wind* (1955; film, 1960), and parodied in L. Sprague de Camp's *The Great Fetish* (1978). An interesting *alternative history version of the trial, Stephen Kraus' "Frame of Reference" (1988), has Bryan prosecuting Albert *Einstein in Louisville, Kentucky, for teaching relativity, and Darrow achieving a compromise by proposing that if God were moving at near-light speed, six days might elapse while a billion years went by on Earth.

Creationism is usually treated in satirical fashion in twentieth-century fiction. Notable examples include Isaac Asimov's dialogue "Darwinian Pool Room" (1950); Jerry Oltion's "In the Creation Science Laboratory" (1987), in which God wonders why the numbers of the righteous are in decline on Earth and finds the answer by applying the theory of natural selection; and F. M. Busby's "Eden Regained" (1991), in which a breakthrough in Creation Science leads to a Manned Past Probe to investigate the crucifixion, the Flood, and the primal garden. Robert Gardner's *Mandrill* (1975) was an early exception, and some specialist religious presses in the United States set out to redress the balance when they began to produce children's fiction and sensationalist thrillers in some profusion in the 1980s.

Futuristic speculators disturbed by the dispute included Alexis Gilliland, whose *Long Shot for Rosinante* (1981) imagines evolutionists being driven into extraterrestrial exile and the operations of terrorist

Contra-Darwin hit squads. In Joseph Green and Patrice Milton's "With Conscience of the New" (1989), members of the Church of The Children of God's Plan set out to slaughter a herd of mastodons in order to protect their version of the truth. Earnest fictional representations of the debate are included in John Gribbin's *Father to the Man* (1989) and Stephen Utley's "Babel" (2004), while Robert J. Sawyer's *Calculating God* (2000) attempts an even-handed examination of the intelligent design thesis. Greg Beatty's "Parakeets and PBJs" (2004) is an attempted explanation of the persistence of the "creationism meme". Marcos Donnelly's *Letters from the Flesh* (2004) is a meditative account of the issues, ingeniously embodied in a series of parables.

CRIMINOLOGY

A branch of social science embracing elements of *sociology, *psychology, and *economics, devoted to the scientific study of crime. The term first became current in the 1880s, derived from an Italian version used by Rafaele Garofalo. The science is intimately associated with technologies facilitating the detection and prosecution of crime, considered herein under the heading of *forensic science. Its spectrum of concern extends into the politics of punishment, whose philosophies are sometimes aggregated under the rubric of penology, as pioneered by Cesare Beccaria's *Dei Delitti e delle Penne* (1764) and subsequently summarised in H. M. Boles' *The Science of Penology* (1902).

Crime is a legalistic concept that corresponds roughly with the religious idea of sin; the attempt by early social scientists to find a term that was not so deeply impregnated by value judgments resulted in its frequent reclassification as "deviance", but that term inevitably inherited similar evaluative overtones. The tension between different interpretations of the causes of deviance, in terms of the contrasted vocabularies of morality and causality, continue to vex contemporary arguments about the purpose and effectiveness of social responses to crime, in terms of punishment, deterrence, and rehabilitation. There is a similar tension between different scientific models of criminological explanation, neatly summed up in an old joke: "The difference between psychology and sociology is that, when a man beats up and robs his neighbour, psychology blames the man and sociology blames the neighbour". The enigma is equally difficult to resolve in a *theological context; the hypothesis of original sin has always been controversial within the Christian tradition, and the philosophical discipline of theodicy has long wrestled with the conundrum of how and why evil exists in a universe created by an omnipotent and good God.

In a literary context, the question of how some people come to do bad things, and how other people ought to respond, is more than a central topic of interest. Because writing is a process of "secondary creation" the author occupies a problematic position akin to that of the God of theodicy, solely responsible for the innate and inescapable moral order of the text. The author is not only the actual designer of all the deviant acts within the text but the administrator of "poetic justice" who must decide whether, and how, some characters are to be rewarded for their virtue while others are to be punished—or not—for their crimes. The vast and rich genre of "crime fiction" is, therefore, far more than a mere reflection of the development of criminological ideas. The originator of the phrase "poetic justice"—the Shakespearean critic Thomas Rymer—proposed that it was an author's moral duty to ensure that all fictional criminals receive their just desserts while all virtuous characters achieve happy endings (thus condemning all tragedy and much satire as morally defective) and there is a very obvious pattern of reader demand endorsing that opinion.

It is arguable that one of the key psychological functions of modern fiction, especially of popular fiction, is to provide insistently repetitive accounts of the appropriate punishment of crime, by way of offering some compensation for the fact that the justice systems of the actual world are so woefully ineffectual. This supplemented rather than replaced the traditional function of exemplary popular fictions as agents of moral terrorism, invoked by parents and priests alike in the attempt to persuade their charges to be good—a tradition that called forth a backlash in the form of picaresque fiction, which reached a peak in eighteenth-century glamorisations of highwaymen, pirates, and bandits, many of whose names became legendary as a result.

Actual legal systems in the Western world have made a gradual transition, within the fundamental context of Roman law, towards a more pragmatic attitude to and treatment of offenders. This trend was greatly assisted by the development of the scientific outlook and by the emergence of particular criminological theories, but its reflection in literature has been decidedly ambivalent; whereas actual legal systems have made significant attempts to set aside the sense of outrage that victims of crime and horrified onlookers routinely feel in favour of more objective considerations, much literary work has reacted against that policy, seeking instead to produce, flatter, and exploit exactly such a sense of outrage, and to give it free rein in the depiction of unusually horrible crimes and exceedingly dramatic compensatory moves. Even the most superficial comparison of the "world of fiction" formulated by twentieth-century books and visual media with the actual world reveals a very marked discrepancy between the frequency and nature of the criminal acts committed there, and in the regularity and nature of the retribution meted out in consequence.

Several early scientific studies of crime focused on the phenomenon of "juvenile delinquency"—a term coined in the 1840s and subjected to analysis in Mary Carpenter's *Juvenile Delinquency* (1853)—and the *psychopathology of crime, as investigated in such texts as J. C. Bucknill's *Criminal Lunacy* (1856). Psychological analyses of crime as madness and the sociological notion of "deviance", were, however, undermined by the fact that all known societies seemed to play host to criminality and the suspicion that the perfectly law-abiding citizen was a fabulous rarity.

The intrinsic irony of this observation is manifest in Karl *Marx's consideration of crime as a kind of service industry, "producing" the criminal law, police forces, and tragic literature and operating as a crucial balancing factor in protecting bourgeois life from stagnation, in the first volume of *Theorien über den Mehrwert* (written ca. 1863; published 1905). Marx cites Bernard Mandeville's crucial contribution to *economic theory in *The Fable of the Bees* in arguing that, from the point of view of encouraging the circulation of goods and money, crime can be seen as socially useful. Subsequent economists were routinely forced to concede that embarking upon a criminal "career" can qualify—at least in some circumstances—as a perfectly rational economic decision. Thomas Byrnes published his pioneering study of *Professional Criminals of America* in 1886.

The notion of crime as deviance entered a new phase of "criminal *anthropology" when Cesare Lombroso's *L'Uomo delinquente* (1876) attempted to identify the criminal "type" in terms of measurable criteria. Initially carried forward by Lombroso's compatriots Enrico Ferri and Rafaele Garofalo, this version of criminology was exported via such texts as Havelock Ellis' *The Criminal* (1890). Such attempts slotted comfortably into the context of race theory, using the methods of physiognomy and craniometry to demonstrate the essential inferiority of the criminal class. New fashions in explanation eventually redirected attention to other kinds of measurements—first to measurements of *intelligence and later to *genetic analysis—but the quest to find a physical basis for deviance never entirely let up. Fiction thrived on such notions, sustained by the need to construct and characterise "villains" in order to serve the ends of melodrama, although the requirements of ingenious plotting often required the production of deceptive villains whose appearance was the exact opposite to the criminal type, and whose intelligence was sufficiently acute to pose worthy opposition to that of a detective genius. In fiction, "criminal types" are abundant, but are often relegated to minor roles as hirelings and servitors of politely masked masterminds.

Socioeconomic explanations of crime in terms of poverty and poor education became a significant force in calls for political reform in the late eighteenth and early nineteenth centuries, extravagantly represented in the works of such philosophical novelists as Jean Jacques *Rousseau and William Godwin, and in the *Utopian fiction of the period. Novels attempting to investigate the causes and attempted remedies of crime with the aid of social scientific theories are very numerous, the most notable including Godwin's *Caleb Williams* (1794), Edward Bulwer-Lytton's *Paul Clifford* (1930) and *Eugene Aram* (1832), Charles Dickens' *The Chimes* (1844), Elizabeth Gaskell's *Mary Barton* (1848), Victor Hugo's *Les Misérables* (1862), and Fyodor Dostoyevsky's *Prestupleniye i nakazaniye* (1866; trans. as *Crime and Punishment*).

Within the literary arena socioeconomic hypotheses regarding the causes of crime gradually lost ground to psychological ones, more for reasons of literary convenience than scientific plausibility. The trend was inevitably exaggerated as the novel became steadily more introspective under the linked influence of Henry James and his psychologist brother William. The melodramatic potential of psychological arguments, and their capacity to overtake and reinvent traditional notions of good and evil, is extravagantly displayed in such literary accounts of "split personality" as Edgar Allan Poe's "William Wilson" (1839) and Robert Louis Stevenson's *Strange Case of Dr. Jekyll and Mr. Hyde* (1886) and in the analyses of literary works undertaken by such psychoanalysts as Sigmund *Freud and Carl *Jung. Psychology's increasing interest in and dependence on the sexual impulse is clearly reflected in crime fiction's increasing interest in and dependence on "sex crimes". Once Poe and Stevenson had prepared the way for psychological theory to produce new kinds of *monsters, many traditional types of monstrousness—including vampirism and lycanthropy—were co-opted by the burgeoning field of abnormal sexual psychology mapped out in Richard von Krafft-Ebing's *Psychopathia Sexualis* (1886). Many of Krafft-Ebing's paradigmatic examples of sexual psychopathology, including sadism and masochism, took their names and symptoms from literary sources.

The growth of a more pragmatic attitude to criminology in the twentieth century, reflected in such texts as Clarence Darrow's *Crime: Its Causes and Treatment* (1922), was echoed in a literary context by the growth of anxieties regarding the possible social effects of crime fiction. The accusation that crime fiction glorified crime and might itself be a cause of crime was strenuously rebutted by writers and publishers—although it resulted in the suppression of violence in crime comic books by the Comic Book Code in the 1950s—but many writers became anxious about the stigmatisation of villains. In much nineteenth-century fiction it had been taken for granted that anyone foreign was a suitable candidate for casting as a villain, but growing suspicions about the tacit promotion of xenophobia and racism gradually eroded that policy, while parallel anxieties questioned the association of villainy with particular social classes and modes of employment.

The slack generated by this anxiety was taken up by the widespread appropriation into fiction of two key criminological terms: "sociopath" and "psychopath". Characters of these types—whose evil tendencies are conveniently innate, whether imparted by nature or nurture—were villains by definition, and late twentieth-century crime fiction made extravagant use of the opportunities they presented. Particularly prolific use was made of psychopathic "serial killers" whose crimes were perfectly fitted to the necessities of plot development. The important archetype provided by Robert Bloch's *Psycho* (1959; film, 1960), loosely based on the case of Ed Gein, pioneered two significant subgenres. A "true crime" genre updating such eighteenth-century legendary constructions as Dick Turpin and Jack Sheppard in the distinctively modern mould of "Jack the Ripper" became highly significant as a form of narrative nonfiction, while the subgenre of fiction that attributed iconic status to such characters—Thomas Harris' psychiatrically trained cannibal genius, Hannibal Lecter, is a cardinal example—generated numerous best-sellers.

As the characterisation of fictitious criminals became increasingly elaborate in psychological and sociological terms, their adversaries in police forces were forced to become better educated in the relevant sciences. Writers of crime fiction were similarly required to intensify their research, as Colin Wilson did in composing his recherché crime novels *Ritual in the Dark* (1960), *Necessary Doubt* (1964), and *The Killer* (1970), which are derived from the same substance as his nonfiction works *Encyclopedia of Murder* (1961, with Patricia Pitman), *A Criminal History of Mankind* (1984), and *The Killers Among Us* (2 vols., 1996–1997).

Speculative fiction never had any shortage of criminal villains, but from Jules *Verne's Captain Nemo onwards they were distinguished more by the hi-tech apparatus with which they committed their crimes, or the exotic quality of the logical puzzles they set their adversaries, than by any application of scientific theory to their motivation. Penological theory is more prominently featured in science-fictional *contes philosophiques* than any other aspect of criminology; notable thought experiments include Robert A. Heinlein's "Coventry" (1940), Henry Kuttner and C. L. Moore's "Private Eye" (1949; by-lined Lewis Padgett), Damon Knight's "The Analogues" (1952), Robert Sheckley's "Watchbird" (1953), Alfred Bester's *The Demolished Man* (1953), William Tenn's "Time in Advance" (1956), Robert Silverberg's "To See the Invisible Man" (1963), John J. McGuire's "Take the Reason Prisoner" (1963), and Lucius Shepard's "Jailwise" (2003). Futures in which applied criminology has succeeded in eradicating crime are rare, except for perfectly ordered *dystopias desperately in need of mischievous relief.

Science fiction writers have been more creative in the matter of inventing new crimes for their agents to combat than in hypothesising new criminological theories. The subgenre of time police series gave rise to a new criminal class of would-be history-changers, called "degraders" in E. B. Cole's stories of the Philosophical Corps (launched 1951), who use advanced technology to set themselves up as gods on barbarian worlds for purpose of pillage. The sophistication of *biotechnology and the opening of the arena of *cyberspace both opened opportunities for the evolution of new crimes, but accounts of their execution and investigation rarely break new criminological ground; such works as K. W. Jeter's *Dr. Adder* (1984) and Kim Newman's *The Night Mayor* (1989) are primarily exceptional in terms of their grotesquerie.

CRYOGENICS

The science and technology of low temperatures. Because temperature is a reflection of the energy of atomic motion, the lowest conceivable temperature is that at which all motion ceases: "absolute zero" ($-273°$ Celsius, or $0°$ Kelvin). To a cryophysicist "low" means within a few degrees of $0°$ K, but cryobiologists are interested in the broader range of temperatures at which biological activity is suppressed, opening up the possibility of *suspended animation; the refrigeration temperature of liquid nitrogen, $81°$ K, is usually adequate for cryobiological purposes.

The phenomenon of most interest to cryophysicists is electrical superconductivity, which has numerous potential technological applications, although development was long inhibited by the difficulty of obtaining and maintaining such refrigerants as liquid helium. Although the notion of absolute zero once exerted a certain fascination on the speculative imagination—examples of its use include Harold M. Colter's "Absolute Zero" (1929) and Erle Stanley Gardner's "The Human Zero" (1931)—literary interest in cryophysics has always been limited, and was not significantly increased by the discovery of "high-temperature superconductivity" in 1986. Cryobiology is a different matter.

The preservative effects of low temperatures were known before the seventeenth century—Francis *Bacon's death was linked by rumor to a cryobiological experiment—so the notion of freezing-induced suspended animation was a ready recourse for subsequent tales of accidental time-displacement; Leonard Kip's "Hannibal's Man" (1873), W. Clark Russell's *The Frozen Pirate* (1887), Robert Duncan Milne's "Ten Thousand Years in Ice" and "The World's Last Cataclysm" (both 1889), and Louis Boussenard's *Dix mille ans dans un bloc de glace* (1889; trans. as *10,000 Years in a Block of Ice*) spearheaded a tradition that extended into the twentieth century in such stories as Edgar Rice Burroughs' "The Resurrection of Jimber Jaw" (1937) and Gerald Kersh's "Frozen Beauty" (1941, initially by-lined Waldo Kellar). The application of cryopreservative techniques to living tissues was, however, hindered by the problem of cell damage inflicted by ice crystals during freezing and unfreezing. The cells of freeze-resistant plants and animals are protected from such damage by "natural antifreezes"—mostly glycol derivatives and sugars—which allow supercooled tissue to vitrify.

Artificial cryopreservation made considerable progress in the last quarter of the twentieth century in connection with the freezing of egg cells and early embryos; by then, animal embryos treated with a crypoprotective solution could be preserved in liquid nitrogen for many years. Determining the practical limits of such preservation is likely to be a hazardous business whose experimental tests will inevitably last for centuries, but the narrative utility of the notion is considerable. The most significant extrapolation of the idea is that of "cryonics"—a term coined by Karl Werner for the use of cryogenetic techniques in preserving the human body, which entered common parlance after 1964, when R. C. W. Ettinger's treatise *The Prospect of Immortality*—self-published two years earlier and publicised in the science fiction magazine *Galaxy*—was reprinted in a mass-market edition. Ettinger advocated the freezing of recently dead bodies or severed heads in liquid nitrogen in order that still-viable brains might be preserved until medical technology is sufficiently advanced to reverse the various kinds of damage leading to "heart death".

The idea that the frozen dead might be reanimated by advanced technology had been broached in pulp science fiction by Neil R. Jones' "The Jameson Satellite" (1931), but was used sparingly thereafter. The notion of using suspended animation as a means of preserving a human body until it could be repaired by advanced medical technology was featured in Poul Anderson's "Time Heals" (1949), but was not initially coupled with the idea of cryonic preservation. In Leo Szilard's "The Mark Gable Foundation" (1961) freezing oneself to visit the future becomes a fad, but James White's *Second Ending* (1961; book, 1962)—whose protagonist's awakening is drastically belated—moved closer to Ettinger's prospectus. Ettinger not only inspired a sudden glut of such narratives but also the establishment of such corporations as Alcor and TransTime, which attempted to put his ideas into practice.

The first dead man "frozen down" in the hope of future revivification was Dr. James Bedford in 1967. The case immediately involved Alcor in a legal conflict with the California Department of Health Services (DHS), which refused to issue permits for the disposition of human remains to the company. The legal wrangle—which lasted until 1990, when the Los Angeles County Superior Court ordered the DHS to issue the forms—helped to add an extra dimension of melodrama to technothrillers featuring near-future cryonics such as Ernest Tidyman's *Absolute Zero* (1971) and Gregory Benford's *Chiller* (1993; by-lined Sterling Blake).

The potential social and political issues arising from cryonic projects were extrapolated in numerous literary works. In Clifford D. Simak's *Why Call Them Back from Heaven* (1967), trusts managing the financial assets of the frozen become significant power-blocs. In Norman Spinrad's *Bug Jack Barron* (1969), access to cryonic vaults—advertised as a ticket to immortality—becomes the ultimate bribe, and its denial the ultimate blackmail. Larry Niven's "The Defenseless Dead" (1973) points out that while the living have all the votes the "corpsicles" of the dead might become an exploitable resource. Tanith Lee's "The Thaw" (1979) examines the predicament of a distant descendant called on to welcome an "awakener". In Greg Bear's *Heads* (1990) the possibility arises that the memories of frozen heads—and hence their secrets—might be recoverable without their being defrosted. The problems of long-term storage space for corpsicles require their removal to Pluto in Charles Sheffield's *Tomorrow and Tomorrow* (1997). The fascination with cryonics was by no means limited to the United States; Nikolai Amosov's *Zapiski iz budushchego* (1967; trans. as *Notes from the Future*) and Anders Bodelsen's *Frysepunktet* (1969; trans. as

Freezing Point and *Freezing Down*) made significant contributions to the dialogue.

The notion that cryobiological storage of astronauts and extraterrestrial colonists might help to overcome the challenging time spans of interstellar *space travel—trailed in Walter M. Miller's "Cold Awakening" (1952)—was quickly co-opted into the myth of the *Space Age following Ettinger's popularisation; the considerable imagistic boost it received by virtue of its employment in Stanley Kubrick's *2001— A Space Odyssey* (1968) led to the motif becoming a common feature of cinematic science fiction, used in such works as John Carpenter's *Dark Star* (1974) and the *Alien* series (1979–1992). E. C. Tubb's "Dumarest" series (launched 1967) envisaged interstellar travel reproducing the class system of international flights, with "high" travellers enjoying the benefit of time-dilating drugs while "low" travellers must endure more hazardous cryonic procedures. This usage encouraged speculations about possible psychological effects of cryobiological preservation, as in Philip K. Dick's "Frozen Journey" (1980; aka "I Hope I Shall Arrive Soon") and James White's *The Dream Millennium* (1974).

Many stories in which people try to "cheat" death by committing themselves to cryonic storage are formulated as *contes cruels* in which fate finds suitably ironic ways to thwart them. The common assumption that one would be able to wake up rich by virtue of the effects of compound interest on their investments is casually overturned in Frederik Pohl's *The Age of the Pussyfoot* (1969) and M. Shayne Bell's "Balance Due" (2000). In Terry Carr's "Ozymandias" (1972) people who employ cryobiological methods to avoid a war fall victim to professional "tomb-robbers", like the mummified pharaohs of ancient Egypt. The angst-ridden protagonist of Brian Stableford's "...And He Not Busy Being Born" (1987; incorporated into *The Omega Expedition*, 2002) successfully delivers himself into a world of immortals, but fails to escape his own destiny. Ian Watson's "Ahead!" (1995) satirically examines awkward corollaries of being frozen down without a body.

One of Ettinger's earliest converts was Alan Harrington, who embedded advertisements for cryonics in his manifesto for longevity research, *The Immortalist* (1969), and the science fiction novel *Paradise 1* (1977). Another convert was K. Eric Drexler, who used the speculation that *nanotechnology might provide a means of repair and of providing protection against risks incurred during the thawing process as one of the key advertisements for his own hypothetical technology in *Engines of Creation* (1987). The latter supplementation increased the plausibility of cryonics to the point at which it became a standard feature of near-future scenarios in most science fiction published after 1990.

CRYPTOGRAPHY

The art and science of transfiguring information by means of codes or ciphers, usually for the purposes of concealment. Encryption is the process of converting information from a readily comprehensible format into an incomprehensible format, from which it can only be decrypted with the aid of a "key". Cryptography is closely related, especially in fiction, to steganography: the art and science of hiding messages by physical means. The most familiar forms of steganography, at least in fiction, involve invisible ink and microdots.

The two basic forms of cipher are transposition ciphers, which rearrange the order of the letters forming the message, and substitution ciphers, which replace letters or groups of letters with other letters or symbols. "Code" is a broader term that embraces the manipulation of meaning as well as symbols, although the most famous example—the Morse code used in telegraphy—is a simple substitution cipher. Substitution ciphers are usually soluble by frequency analysis. The desire to transmit information confidentially, for political or economic purposes, is ancient; an early technological aid was the scytale, a cylindrical rod used in ancient Sparta to produce a transposition cipher; the recipient deciphered the message by winding it around a rod of similar diameter. Early Christians in fear of persecution used such simple symbolic codes as fish symbols to signify Christ's name, and there are apparent references in the Bible to numerological codes, most famously "the number of the beast" (666) in *Revelation*.

As diplomatic relations became more complex and more duplicitous, the art of cryptography undoubtedly made considerable advances, but its history inevitably remains clouded in secrecy. It is impossible to be certain now whether or not the "Enochian alphabet" that John *Dee ostensibly used to communicate with angels might actually have been a code that he used to transmit secret messages. This uncertainty has led many people to look for codes and ciphers in places where they might not exist—a practice dramatically enhanced by the mind-set of *occult science, which is much preoccupied with hidden correspondences.

A tendency to treat the experienced world as a kind of vast cryptogram can be traced from the followers of *Pythagoras to the Renaissance, and the advancement of science—unraveling or unveiling the mathematical "mysteries of nature"—can easily be seen as an aspect of that tendency. Isaac *Newton spent a good deal of time attempting to identify and decipher codes hidden in the Bible—a practice that continued to bear "results" in the twentieth century. Ignatius Donnelly's *The Great Cryptogram* (1888) identifies ciphers hidden in William Shakespeare's plays that allegedly indicate their authorship by Francis *Bacon: an attempt to forge a correspondence between supreme exemplars of art and science that is very much in the spirit of occult science.

The first published discussion of cryptography is in the works of Roger *Bacon—where Dee undoubtedly read it—and is presumably reflective of the practices of contemporary *alchemists, although it may well have played a major role in prompting subsequent alchemists to use codes and ciphers. The use of codes in diplomatic communications led to the emergence in the sixteenth century of professional codecrackers, Giovanni Soro fulfilling such a function in Venice after 1506. By this time simple substitution ciphers had been superseded by complex variants that were more resistant to frequency analysis. Mary Queen of Scots was executed in 1587 on the evidence of coded messages allegedly deciphered by Sir Francis Walsingham's secretary. Despite the cloak of secrecy surrounding their history, guidebooks to the construction of ciphers began to appear in the seventeenth century; John Wilkins' *Mercury; or The Secret and Swift Messenger* (1641) provides an interesting parallel to his general survey of speculative technology *Mathematicall Magick* (1648).

Classic literary ciphers—notable nineteenth-century examples can be found in Edgar Allan Poe's "The Gold Bug" (1843), Jules Verne's *Voyage au centre de la terre* (1863; trans. as *Journey to the Centre of the Earth*) and *La jangada* (1881; trans. in 2 vols. as *Eight Hundred Leagues on the Amazon* and *The Cryptogram*), and Arthur Conan Doyle's "The Adventure of the Dancing Men" (1903)—are often offered to the reader as challenging puzzles to be solved, the last-named within the context of a detective story. Raymond McDonald and Raymond Alfred Leger's *The Mad Scientist* (1908) included a cipher without a solution, offering a cash prize to the first reader who solved it.

Such exercises were soon extracted from fiction to become a significant form of puzzle devised for leisure purposes. Modern guidebooks to the construction and solution of ciphers, such as Clifford A. Pickover's *Cryptorunes: Codes and Secret Writing* (2000), are usually accommodated within this context. In the meantime, they remained a highly convenient plot lever, exploited in much the same fashion as treasure maps in such works as Fergus Hume's "Professor Brankel's Secret" (1889) and Roland Pertwee's *MW.XX.3* (1929; aka *Hell's Loose* and *The Million Pound Cipher*).

In twentieth-century fiction, cryptography and steganography became staple elements of spy fiction, pioneered by William le Queux in such works as *Spies of the Kaiser* (1909) and *Cipher Six: A Mystery* (1919). Writers in the genre gradually developed an extraordinarily elaborate lexicon of methods of communicating information covertly. This accumulating wisdom was ingeniously exploited by such writers as Edward D. Hoch—whose Jeffery Rand heads a department of Concealed Communications in the series launched by *The Spy Who Didn't Exist* (1967)—Robert Ludlum, as in *The Bourne Identity* (1980), and Payne Harrison, as in *Black Cipher* (1994).

The extent to which such fiction reflects an actual cryptographic and steganographic "arms race" is open to conjecture, but the eventual lifting of the veil of secrecy shed belated light on the most spectacular success of actual codebreakers during World War II. Scientists working at Bletchley Park built the dedicated computer Colossus to decipher the German Enigma code, whose electrically powered rotating discs changed positions after each transmitted letter, thus making its substitution code indecipherable to anyone who could not duplicate the shift-pattern. The U.S. forces allegedly used a more straightforward method of concealment by exploiting the arcane Navaho language—a system whose particular vulnerability is graphically dramatised in the film *Windtalkers* (2002). Other movies illustrating the rapid sophistication of codes and their fictional representation include *The Secret Agent* (1936, based on Somerset Maugham's *Ashenden*, 1928), *Sebastian* (1976), and *Enigma* (2001).

The development of computers forced cryptograms to become considerably more elaborate, and the need to keep information held on computers safe from prying eyes put further pressure on cryptographic craftsmanship. A U.S. Data Encryption Standard (DES)—or Data Encryption Algorithm (DEA)—was introduced in 1976, requiring the use of 56-bit keys—a level of complexity that soon began to seem inadequate as the speed of processors continued to increase, considerably reducing the time needed to crack such codes.

A new vogue for books embodying codes that the reader is required to solve was launched by Kit Williams' *Masquerade* (1979), which deliberately recapitulated the story arc of "The Gold Bug" by concealing instructions for the location of a golden hare and launching a public treasure hunt. The book's success was, however, modest by comparison with other cryptographically informed best-sellers such as Michael Drosnin's "nonfictional" *The Bible Code* (1997), Arturo Perez-Reverte's *The Dumas Club* (1997), Neal Stephenson's *Cryptonomicon* (1999), and Dan

Brown's *The Da Vinci Code* (2003). Subtler uses of cryptographic plot devices include the mock-academic volume of commentaries of H. P. Lovecraft's fictitious book *The Necronomicon* edited by George Hay, which is supposedly based on a new decoding of Dee's Enochian alphabet.

CRYSTALLOGRAPHY

The branch of mineralogy devoted to the study of crystals. The Greek word *krystallos* referred primarily to ice—and hence to the quality of intense cold—and only secondarily to common quartz, which was initially conceived of as a kind of ice. The word "crystal" retained echoes of its original meaning, if only metaphorically, when it was reapplied to other minerals with similar properties to quartz. Such similarities were initially superficial, including clearness and rarity—thus leading to the categorisation of gemstones as crystals—but scientific crystallography rests on the geometric regularity of crystals.

This pattern of development led to some confusion, most obviously with respect to glass, which was once considered to be crystalline because of its transparency, although it has no geometrical regularity (by virtue of being a supercooled liquid). The eye, or its lens, was also once considered crystalline—a likeness that still survives in metaphor although the application of crystallographic science to organic substances is relevant to the structure of particular molecules rather than complex tissue structures.

Exotic properties were attributed to various kinds of crystals—especially gemstones—within systems of primitive medicine, magic, and *occult science, generating various kinds of "crystal healing", a quasi-astrological set of "birthstones" that is still commonly applied to jewelry and a set of symbolic colours employed in heraldry. The names borne by some gemstones were derived from such patterns—"amethyst" from a word meaning intoxication, because amethyst goblets were supposed to protect against the intoxicating qualities of liquids drunk from them, and "sapphire" from a word meaning moral purity, because sapphires were supposed to ward off lechers.

As usual, these occult connections had considerably more appeal to litterateurs than the development of scientific crystallography, although the significant roles played by gems in supernatural fiction and symbolist literature are outweighed and outshone by their role as economic objects of desire in such crime stories as M. P. Shiel's *The Rajah's Sapphire* (1896) and Fergus Hume's *The Mother of Emeralds* (1901) and such dramatisations of status envy as Henry James' "Paste" (1899) and F. Scott Fitzgerald's

"The Diamond as Big as the Ritz" (1922). Diamonds, in particular, represent a portable form of wealth whose double utility as an item of adornment is comparable to that of gold, over which it has the advantages of lightness, hardness, and scintillation.

Although the origin of gemstones remained mysterious, their mystique was secure—James Thomson's "The Seasons" (1726–1730; rev. 1744) represents gems as strange artifacts of the Sun's light: "The unfruitful rock itself, impregned by thee, / In dark retirement forms the lucid stone"—and their charisma was not significantly eroded by scientific accounts of mineral formation. Notable literary gems possessed of crystal charisma include William Makepeace Thackeray's *The Great Hoggarty Diamond* (1841), Wilkie Collins' *The Moonstone* (1868), and the Blue Water in P. C. Wren's *Beau Geste* (1924).

The foundations of scientific crystallography lay in the observation—recorded by Pliny the Elder, among others—of the geometrical regularity of crystals, but it was not until 1669 that Nicholas Steno observed that the angles of each particular kind of crystal were always the same, even though the technological skills of lapidarists had long become accommodated to the fact that gemstones could only be cut and shaped in a manner respectful of their fundamental geometry. Carolus Linnaeus' classifications of plants and animals inspired Romé Delisle, in *Essaie de Crystallographie* (1772), and his successor, René Just Haüy, to attempt something similar in mineralogy, using angular forms as criteria for the classification of crystals. The steady advancement of the chemical analysis of compounds enabled continual refinement of their work in the nineteenth century.

The popularisation of these scientific advances took what advantage it could from the inherent interest of gemstones, although the results could be peculiar; John Ruskin's *The Ethics of the Dust: Ten Lectures to Little Housewives on the Elements of Crystallisation* (1865) is a bizarre work. Crystal growing became a significant element of basic amateur chemistry. It is a challenging task because the crystals produced by familiar chemical compounds as they precipitate out of solution tend to be fragile, and the production of large crystals from smaller seeds is a delicate business. The growth of exotic dendritic forms from seed crystals dropped into solutions of sodium silicate, forming "crystal gardens", also became an esoteric hobby.

The raw aesthetic appeal of crystallisation as a phenomenon increased the literary range of crystals; its power as an imaginative stimulus is evident in such texts as George Sand's *Laura: Voyage dans le cristal* (1865; trans. as *Journey Within the Crystal*), in which the protagonist's discovery of a geode—an unprepossessing lump of rock that, when split, reveals a crystal-filled interior—sparks an imaginary polar voyage to a crystal world within the Earth. Inspiring crystal-lined caverns of more limited scope are featured in Robert Hunt's *Panthea* (1849) and Robert Ross's *The Child of Ocean* (1889).

In the meantime, the study of crystals became an important branch of stereochemistry; in the twentieth century, x-ray crystallography—analysing the manner in which x-rays are scattered by molecular crystals—became a key instrument of chemical analysis, crucial to such projects as the determination of the structure of DNA. The optical properties of crystals were extrapolated in numerous accounts of hypothetical crystals with extraordinary properties, including Fitz-James O'Brien's "The Diamond Lens" (1858), Norman H. Croell's "To the End of Space" (1909), and A. Hyatt Verrill's "Into the Green Prism" (1929). The capacity of crystals to grow and proliferate inspired numerous accounts of crystalline life, including J. H. Rosny aîné's "Les xipéhuz" (1887; trans. as "The Shapes" and "The Xipehuz"), John Taine's *White Lily* (1930; aka *The Crystal Horde*), Sidney D. Berlow's "The Crystal Empire" (1932), Dow Elstar and Robert S. McCready's "Stardust Gods" (1937), and Terry Dowling's "The Lagan Fishers" (2001).

Crystalline architecture became typical of "futuristic" scenarios in the nineteenth century; the idea of a "crystal palace", whose literary origins go back to folktales, was actualised in London to house the monuments to technological progress making up the Great Exhibition. Similar edifices featured in such Utopian fictions as Nikolai Chernyshevsky's *Chto Delat'* (1863; trans. as *What Is to Be Done?*) before becoming a staple of science fiction illustration in the pulp magazines. A Crystal Palace Mountain is featured in Mark Clifton's *Eight Keys to Eden* (1960). Notable twentieth-century examples include the synthetic diamond EigenDome in Catherine Asaro's "Aurora in Four Voices" (1998).

Because diamond is a crystalline form of carbon—also manifest in such dull forms as charcoal and graphite as well as being the basis of organic chemistry—it figures in many tales of quasi-alchemical transformation that double as moralistic fabulations, including C. J. Cutcliffe Hyne's *The Recipe for Diamonds* (1893) and Jacques Futrelle's *The Diamond Master* (1909). Such stories foreshadowed the development of actual techniques for manufacturing "industrial diamonds", although the establishment of such corporations as Lifegem, which offer to convert the carbonised corpses of beloved pets and cremated relatives into gemstones, was unanticipated. The possibility that extraterrestrial physical processes might produce extraordinary diamonds is treated with

appropriate irony in Malcolm Jameson's "Mill of the Gods" (1939) and Gregory Benford's "As Big as the Ritz" (1986).

Crystals sometimes function in speculative fiction as ordinary power sources, as in Lilith Lorraine's "In the 28th Century" (1930), but they are more frequently envisaged as sources of extraordinary power; they are often invested with magical properties of exactly the same kinds as the gemstones of occult and supernatural fiction, especially those enabling or enhancing *parapsychological psi-powers. Jewels routinely serve as psychically active talismans in hybrid science-fantasy stories that disguise fantasy tropes with science-fictional jargon, as in numerous works by Andre Norton. The strategy is capable of considerable sophistication, as in Ian Irvine's Well of Echoes series launched with *Geomancer* (2001), in which the forbidden art of geomancy is revived in order to combat crystalline alien "clankers".

The speculative framework of science fiction is conducive to the calculated exaggeration of such psychic effects, as in such stories as Theodore Sturgeon's *The Dreaming Jewels* (1950), John T. Phillifent's "Hierarchies" (1971), Christopher Hodder-Williams' *The Think Tank That Leaked* (1979), Cynthia Felice's *The Sunbound* (1981), and Robert Charles Wilson's *Memory Wire* (1988). On the other hand, it is equally hospitable to more subtle effects, such as those manifest in such works as Eric Brown "Star Crystals and Karmel" (1989) and "The Death of Cassandra Quebec" (1990), Vernor Vinge's "Gemstone" (1983), Bob Buckley's "World of Crystal, Sky of Fire" (1985), Roger Zelazny's "Permafrost" (1986), and Sheri S. Tepper's *After Long Silence* (1987; aka *The Enigma Score*).

Stories that credit hypothetical gemstones with musical as well as psychical properties include Thomas S. Gardner's "The World of Singing Crystals" (1936), Juanita Coulson's *The Singing Stones* (1968), and Anne McCaffrey's *The Crystal Singer* (1974–1975; book, 1982). The most elaborate attempts to exploit crystal charisma in twentieth-century science fiction are Cordwainer Smith's "On the Gem Planet" (1963), set on the world of Pontoppidan, which is extremely rich in gems but extremely poor in air and food, and J. G. Ballard's *The Crystal World* (1966), in which the substance of time begins to crystallise out in equatorial Africa, bringing about a striking metamorphosis of the rain forest.

CYBERNETICS

A term introduced into modern science by Norbert Wiener in 1947 and popularised in his best-selling *Cybernetics* (1948). Cybernetics describes the study of control and communication in organic and mechanical systems, especially with respect to generalised theories that cross the boundaries of the traditional disciplines of biology, psychology, and engineering. It overlaps considerably with what Ludwig von Bertalanffy called "general systems theory". The development of *computers and their adaptation to control other kinds of machinery made such interdisciplinary thinking seem vitally necessary. By the end of the century, the first element of the term was routinely detached in order to be chimerically fused with other components in portmanteau words such as "cyberculture", "*cyberspace", and "cyberpunk".

The most important core notion of cybernetics is that of regulation by feedback mechanisms, particularly in application to the functioning of neural networks. The notion of developing digital computers whose circuitry would be analogous to the electrochemical "wiring" of the human brain—extensively developed by John von Neumann—renewed the significance of philosophical attempts to analyse the relationship between the mind and the brain as well as practical attempts to develop *artificial intelligence. Wiener attempted to equip his new science with a fundamental theory of information mathematically analogous to the description of "negative entropy" in physical systems.

Cybernetics quickly became a buzzword in contemporary science fiction; the concept was introduced to readers of *Astounding* in 1949 by an article by E. L. Locke and much was made of its talismanic quality in Charles Recour's "The Cybernetic Brain" (1949). It was dutifully invoked in the first two issues of *Galaxy* in 1950, in Isaac Asimov's "Darwinian Pool Room" and Fredric Brown's "Honeymoon in Hell". Raymond F. Jones' *The Cybernetic Brains* (1950; book, 1962) was another early work to co-opt the term. Hypothetical cybernetic laboratories figured prominently in Bernard Wolfe's "Self Portrait" (1951).

The outlook and central ideas of cybernetics were elaborated and repopularised in Gregory Bateson's *Steps to an Ecology of Mind* (1972), which insisted that living systems—especially those giving rise to intelligence—are dependent on the accommodation of discontinuities or "logical contradictions" incorporating a measure of spontaneity and unpredictability in their behavior, forming the bedrock of creativity. Ideas flowing from cybernetics into *ecology became the basis of James *Lovelock's Gaia hypothesis.

Fictional extrapolations of cybernetics have mostly been concerned with its application to the development of artificial intelligence and to potential fusions of organic and inorganic systems to form *cyborgs; in these particular aspects, its literary influence is widespread. Fictional treatment of more general issues is hindered by their abstract nature, but the ambition to adopt its jargon remained strong. Frank Herbert's *Destination: Void* (1966) was one of several texts to borrow inspiration from Wiener's *God & Golem, Inc.* (1964), while Loren MacGregor's *The Net* (1987) is one of the most elaborate projections of cybernetic theory.

CYBERSPACE

A term popularised by William *Gibson's *Neuromancer* (1984), describing the "virtual *space" in which *computer-held data are located and through which electronic communication takes place. Gibson's characters can project their mental selves from the "inner space" of their minds into cyberspace through entry points into the wiring of a worldwide computer network. Stored data is manifest therein as architectural aggregations, while computer viruses and other programs are also manifest as visible entities.

Similar virtual spaces had previously been explored in a number of texts, including Daniel F. Galouye's *Counterfeit World* (1964; aka *Simulacron-3*), Chris Boyce's *Catchworld* (1975), and Vernor Vinge's *True Names* (1981), but Gibson's label acquired a talismanic significance. A similar significance was acquired at a later date by "the matrix"—a term similarly used extensively in *Neuromancer*, although it had been used before in a similar context, as in Douglas R. Mason's *Matrix* (1970). Many other descriptive terms were applied to the same idea, including the "metamedium" of Paul Di Filippo's "Agents" (1987) and the "metaverse" of Neal Stephenson's *Snow Crash* (1993), but never spread far beyond their source texts.

Gibson's novel was published at a time when the National Science Foundation's academically orientated network CSNET (founded in 1980) had recently been connected to the U.S. Defense Department's ARPANET with the aid of a compatibilising "Internet Protocol", and before the establishment of the NSFNET in 1985 laid down the backbone of the Internet that became the host of all the sites forming the World Wide Web. *Neuromancer*'s timeliness enabled it to capture the imagination of the engineers and users developing such systems, who were already forming the nucleus of a new "cyberculture", while its countercultural values and slick picaresque story line made it the paradigm text of a "cyberpunk movement" named by Gardner R. Dozois and showcased in Bruce *Sterling's anthology *Mirrorshades* (1986).

Cyberspace became a new Western frontier, whose particular lawlessness would work to the advantage of nerds instead of gunslingers, and a new escapist medium, in which the obsolescent *Space Age myth of cosmic breakout could be replaced by a kind of transcendent breakthrough to a new freedom from the burdens of the flesh. It also became a world of opportunity for ambitious *artificial intelligences (AIs), especially those intent on acquiring godlike dominion; while still functioning as a cosmos for refugees from personal inner space, *Neuromancer*'s cyberspace eventually becomes the inner space of a much vaster mind. The forging of intimate relationships between AIs and humans in cyberspace became commonplace, in spite of obvious inequities of magnitude and power.

Gibson was content to call cyberspace a "consensual hallucination", but the notion acquired a greater authority, as a seeming *a priori* necessity, as computers became better able to produce visible models of three-dimensional space incorporating sophisticated *virtual realities. The alternative descriptive term "matrix" combined the implication of abstraction contained in its mathematical meaning and the implication of substance contained in its geological and physiological meanings, thus becoming more closely akin to the Aristotelian notion of space as a plenum, etheric rather than empty; many science-fictional images of cyberspace are more reminiscent of an ocean in which uploaded minds "swim" than a void they traverse like spaceships.

The replacement of the "cosmic breakout" motif with breakthroughs in which human characters forsake frail flesh in favour of a new and more exciting life as pioneers of cyberspace, extravagantly celebrated in both *True Names* and *Neuromancer*, was carried forward into a host of "uploading" stories, notable examples including Roger Zelazny's "24 Views of Mt. Fuji by Hokusai" (1985), Roger McBride Allen's *The Modular Man* (1992), and Greg Egan's *Permutation City* (1994), eventually becoming the Holy Grail of *posthuman fiction. Significant variations of cyberspace include the virtual spaces featured in W. T. Quick's *Dreams of Flesh and Sand* (1988) in which a "meat-matrix" computer interfaces artificially with the "perceptual space" of its component brain cells, and Geoff Ryman's *Air (or Have Not Have)* (2003), which features a communication system that puts the Internet into people's heads, thus importing cyberspace into their inner spaces. The overlapping of cyberspace and inner space had previously been explored in several stories in which computer viruses cross over to the world of the flesh, including Pat Cadigan's *Synners* (1991) and Molly Brown's *Virus* (1994).

As a manifest movement, cyberpunk did not last long—Sterling boasted that the term was "obsolete before it was coined"—but the label easily outlasted the active propagandising of its early enthusiasts by virtue of its marketing value and its adoption into the jargon of *postmodernist criticism. Attempts to relabel the movement, as when Norman Spinrad championed Tappan King's coinage of "the Neuromantics" in 1986, failed, in spite of the fact that many writers interested in the literary uses of cyberspace were unhappy with the "punk" element. Cyberpunk's central motifs were so closely pursued by actual developments in computer technology that they soon lost their capacity to inspire awe and became taken-for-granted aspects of consensus images of the near future. The crime fiction elements of the subgenre were subjected to further exaggeration in "post-cyberpunk" thrillers that relished their own ready-made decadence, Pat Cadigan's *Tea from an Empty Cup* (1998) and K. W. Jeter's *Noir* (1998) offering self-conscious examples.

CYBORG

A contraction of "*cybernetic organism", contrived to describe products of organic/inorganic chimerisation, particularly the augmentation of the human body with mechanical devices. Although the notion was not new, it was enthusiastically updated and popularised by David Rorvik's *As Man Becomes Machine* (1971), which proclaimed the dawn of a new era of "participant evolution". The popularisation of the term was continued by Martin Caidin's *Cyborg* (1972) and its dramatisation in the TV series *The Six Million Dollar Man* (1973–1978), although the latter version favoured the alternative term "bionic man". Donna J. Haraway's highly influential essay "A Manifesto for Cyborgs: Science, Technology and Socialist Feminism in the 1980s" (1985; reprinted as "A Cyborg Manifesto: Science, Technology, and Socialist-Feminism in the Late Twentieth Century") invested the notion with a new ironic significance.

Anticipations of cyborgisation arose naturally enough as sophistications of such crude devices as wooden legs and the kind of hand-substitute worn by J. M. Barrie's infamous Captain Hook in *Peter Pan* (1904). Perley Poore Sheehan and Robert H. Davis' play "Blood and Iron" (1917) imagined that sufficiently ingenious replacements might remake wounded soldiers in a more powerful mould. The cyborg embodies anxieties about *automation in Guy Endore's "Men of Iron" (1940). Francis Flagg's "The Machine-Man of Ardathia" (1927) imagined the future evolution of humankind as a phased process of cyborgisation. The alien cyborgs featured in Jack Williamson's "The Alien Intelligence" (1929) and "The Moon Era" (1932) were cast as villains to capitalise on the "unnaturalness" of the motif, but the Zoromes in Neil R. Jones' "The Jameson Satellite" (1931) and its many sequels are benevolent.

Jones' Zoromes provided an instance of the most common form of science-fictional cyborg imagery: an organic brain in a mechanical body, as previously featured in Edmond Hamilton's "The Comet Doom" (1928) and various fantasies of *evolution that saw the future of humankind as one of increasing intellect but deteriorating physical presence. A more sophisticated speculative extreme of medical cyborgisation is featured in E. V. Odle's scientific romance *The Clockwork Man* (1923), which imagines a man of the future whose body and mind alike are regulated by a clockwork mechanism built into his head. Significant cyborgs from midcentury speculative fiction include the Director in Raymond F. Jones' *Renaissance* (1944) and the cyborg astronauts of Cordwainer Smith's "Scanners Live in Vain" (1950).

H. I. Barrett's "The Mechanical Heart" (1931) offered a more realistic depiction of medical cyborgisation, and as prosthetic limbs improved and augmentary devices such as pacemakers, Teflon joints, and arterial stents became commonplace in the later decades of the twentieth century, such speculative images drew further ahead of the pattern of actual progress. Bernard Wolfe's *Limbo* (1952), a scathing satire construing the term "disarmament" as a *double entendre*, made much of the proposition that people might begin to trade healthy limbs and organs for mechanical substitutes as soon as the latter became more adept or more powerful.

Although many items of personal technology, including keys and wristwatches, seemed perfectly adequate as items of luggage, the possibility of a more intimate integration of such devices as radio-telephones offered a number of advantages, some of which were elaborately trailed in spy fiction, in accounts of ingenious covert communication. Contemplation of such possibilities suggested to many writers that the early twenty-first century might be an era of elaborate elective cyborgisation.

The imagery of elective cyborgisation is readily divisible into accounts of "functional cyborgs", whose bodies are modified to perform specific tasks, and "adaptive cyborgs", whose bodies are modified to enable them to operate in alien environments. By the time the term was popularised, however, such technologies had already begun to be contrasted with purely organic strategies of functional design and environmental adaptation, by means of *genetic engineering. The idea soon developed of a contest between rival schools of adaptation, neatly encapsulated by the contrasted elements of Bruce *Sterling's Shaper/ Mechanist series (1982–1985).

The functional cyborgs most commonly featured in twentieth-century science fiction are those modified for the purposes of space travel and warfare. Notable examples of cyborg spaceships include James Blish's "Solar Plexus" (1941), Henry Kuttner's "Camouflage" (1945), Thomas N. Scortia's "Sea Change" (1956), Anne McCaffrey's "The Ship Who Sang" (1961), George Zebrowski's "Starcrossed" (1973), Zach Hughes' *Tiger in the Stars* (1976), and William Barton's "Heart of Glass" (2000), while a distinctive kind of cyborg astronaut is featured in Vonda McIntyre's *Superluminal* (1983). Notable examples of adaptive cyborgs working on alien worlds or in space itself are featured in Walter M. Miller's "Crucifixus Etiam" (1953), Arthur C. Clarke's "A Meeting with Medusa" (1971), Frederik Pohl's *Man Plus* (1976), Barrington J. Bayley's *The Garments of Caean* (1976), and Paul J. McAuley's "Transcendence" (1988). Early postwar examples of cyborg warriors, designed with varying degrees of subtlety include Jack Vance's "I-C-a-BEM" (1961), Poul Anderson's "Kings Who Die" (1962), James H. Schimtz's "The Machmen" (1964), and Keith Laumer's Bolo series, launched by *A Plague of Demons* (1965); almost all future *war novels published thereafter tended to employ soldiers subject to some degree of cyborgisation.

As the end of the twentieth century approached, the rapid advancement of *computer technology and the development of the cyberpunk sensibility greatly encouraged the use of cyborgs whose brains are augmented or adapted to work in intimate collaboration with various kinds of machinery; notable examples are featured in Gwyneth Jones' *Escape Plans* (1986), Walter John Williams' *Hardwired* (1986), J. R. Dunn's *This Side of Judgment* (1995), and Don DeBrandt's *Steeldriver* (1998).

The cyborg motif lends itself to use in existentialist *contes philosophiques* of a more intimate and inclusive kind than those featuring *robots or *aliens. Notable examples addressing the problem of identity include C. L. Moore's "No Woman Born" (1944), Walter M. Miller's "I, Dreamer" (1953), Algis Budrys' *Who?* (1958), Damon Knight's "Masks" (1973), and D. G. Compton's *The Continuous Katherine Mortenhoe* (1974; aka *The Unsleeping Eye*). William C. Anderson's comedy *Adam M-1* (1964) focuses on problems of cyborg sexuality; Joan Vinge's "Tin Soldier" (1974) and George R. R. Martin's "The Glass Flower" (1986) take a more refined view of similar issues. The Japanese movies *Tetsuo: The Iron Man* (1989) and *Tetsuo II: Body Hammer* (1992), and the animes *Ghost in the Shell* (1996) and *Ghost in the Shell 2: Innocence* (2004), offer surreal takes on cyborg imagery. The movie version of *Who?* (1974) and the American *Robocop* (1987) drew their narrative strength from the same source, although the latter's sequels were content to continue the cyborg superhero tradition popularised by Caidin.

The notion of progressive cyborgisation is used as a paradigm of *alienation in David R. Bunch's tales of *Moderan* (1959–1970; book, 1971), and cyborg imagery is used as an iconography of menace in Philip K. Dick's *The Three Stigmata of Palmer Eldritch* (1964), a strategy recapitulated in E. C. Tubb's employment of the Cyclan as adversaries in his Dumarest series (launched 1967), and in such *TV representations as the Daleks of *Doctor Who* and *Star Trek*'s Borg. Marge Piercy's *He, She, and It* (1991; aka *Body of Glass*) features the cyborg Yod, explicitly likened to the legendary golem. The strength of Rorvik's argument is reflected in the rapid manner in which much of this imagery was robbed of its power to impress by familiarity; by the beginning of the twenty-first century, all kinds of cyborgisation had become standard elements of the representation of the near future.

D

DARWIN, CHARLES (ROBERT) (1809–1882)

English biologist who explained the evolution of life on Earth by means of the theory of natural selection, which is frequently referred to as "Darwinism". One of his grandfathers was Erasmus *Darwin, who was also the grandfather of Francis Galton, the pioneer of *eugenics; the other was the famous potter Josiah Wedgwood. Darwin studied medicine at Edinburgh University but the subject disgusted him, although he developed something of a fascination with marine animals, to which study he returned late in life while sheltering from controversy. He also undertook preparatory studies for Holy Orders at Cambridge, but then applied for the post of naturalist on *HMS Beagle*'s 1831 survey expedition to South America, under the command of Captain Robert Fitzroy.

The observations Darwin made in the course of the *Beagle* expedition, including *geological arguments in support of Charles Lyell's uniformitarian theories and comments on the bird and reptile populations of the Galapagos Islands, were reported in *Journal of Researches into the Geology and Natural History of the Various Countries Visited by HMS Beagle* (1839; exp. 1845) and three further books. Although he had been skeptical about the common origin of Earthly species before the voyage, the obvious relatedness of variant species he had encountered in the Galapagos Islands convinced him of it. The stress that previous evolutionists had put on adaptation suggested the elements of the theory of natural selection to him in 1837, but his real breakthrough came in 1838 when he read Robert Malthus' *Essay on Population* and realised the relevance of the natural overproduction of offspring.

Darwin produced a written "sketch" of the theory of natural selection in 1842, which he expanded into an essay in 1844; he showed it to his friend John Dalton Hooker but did not publish it. He devoted himself thereafter to studies in the taxonomy of living and fossil barnacles. He expanded the essay in 1856 but still retained it for private circulation among a company that included Lyell and Thomas Henry Huxley. His procrastination might have extended indefinitely had he not received a paper by the naturalist Alfred Russel Wallace, whose observations in the Malay archipelago had guided him to the same thesis. A joint paper was read at the Linnaean Society in that year; Darwin's book *On the Origin of Species by Means of Natural Selection, or the Preservation of Favoured Races in the Struggle for Life* followed in 1859.

Like *Galileo before him, Darwin became the focal point of a fierce conflict between science and religious faith. Copernican cosmology had only threatened the Church's adoption of *Aristotle, but evolutionary theory threatened the central assumption of divine creation and the fabric of Holy Writ. French evolutionists—who included the Baron de Montesquieu, Pierre Maupertuis, and Denis Diderot as well as the Chevalier de Lamarck—had seemed less of a threat to religious faith because they had no explanatory mechanism save for a magical and mysterious impulse to improvement that was vaguely in keeping with religious thought. Darwin, by contrast, had an explanatory mechanism that seemed to many observers to be the absolute opposite of Christian values: a "struggle for life" in which only the "favoured" were "preserved". (The more familiar formulations, "the struggle for existence" and "the survival of the fittest", were supplied and popularised by his supporters, who included Herbert Spencer.)

The dramatic appeal of the new theory was understandably immense, both in terms of its intrinsic structure and its elevation as a banner in what seemed to many to be the ultimate conflict between science and religion. Although the contemporary debate was simplified by many—most famously Benjamin Disraeli—into a matter of whether humans were or were not "descended from monkeys", the literary influence of the central thesis was immense and very widespread.

Darwin's own notion of "Darwinism" was less harsh than that of his fiercest advocates. He conceived of natural selection as a subtler process than a bloody battle for survival, appreciating that such factors as choice of a mate and parental care of offspring must be important factors—to the extent that many species had developed elaborate strategies of these kinds, none more so than the one whose emergence and uniqueness he attempted to explain in *The Descent of Man and Selection in Relation to Sex* (1871). He followed the latter volume with an analysis of *The Expression of the Emotions in Man and Animals* (1872), an important contribution to evolutionary *psychology. The ideas in these two books were, however, sidelined in the war of ideas, and were neglected for the next hundred years, until the introduction into neo-Darwinian theory of such notions as "kin selection" paved the way for the development of *sociobiology. Darwin's subsequent books were scrupulous and calculatedly uncontentious studies of various groups of plants, although the idea of adaptation by natural selection remained a key explanatory instrument therein.

A rich narrative legend formed around Darwin while he was alive and persisted after his death, the preservation of many letters allowing his biographers to produce minute analyses of the road of intellectual trials that defined his heroism. It was falsely rumored that Karl *Marx had wanted to dedicate *Das Kapital* to him, but that Darwin refused because he did not wish to be associated with attacks on religion. Darwin did, however, maintain a careful distance while such champions of his thesis as Thomas Henry Huxley took issue with such opponents as Bishop Samuel Wilberforce, unhorsing their opponents skillfully and stylishly in a manner copied and further refined by such twentieth-century acolytes as Richard Dawkins.

Psychoanalysts and physicians competed to explain the severe illness Darwin suffered throughout his later life, invoking the Oedipus complex or Chagas' disease (a trypanosome infection discovered in 1909, which he might conceivably have contracted during the *Beagle* expedition). His home after 1842, Down House—where two of his ten children died, one in tragic circumstances—became a secular shrine. Three of his sons became eminent scientists, most famously Sir George Howard Darwin (1845–1912), an astronomer who published a monumental study of tides.

Darwin is not often featured as a character in literary works, although he provided the model for the scientist hero of Mrs. Gaskell's *Wives and Daughters* (1864–1866) and had previously thought himself the model for Professor Long in Edward Bulwer-Lytton's *What Will He Do with It?* (1858). He is one of the famous people engaged in conversation by God and His angels in Charles Wood's *Heavenly Discourse* (1927), is one of the heroes of science resurrected in Manly Wade Wellman's *Giants from Eternity* (1939; book, 1959), and is reverently invoked in Ray Bradbury's poem "Darwin in the Fields" (1970).

DARWIN, ERASMUS (1731–1802)

English physician and radical freethinker, grandfather of Charles *Darwin. He was educated at Cambridge and Edinburgh Universities. His successful practice at Lichfield became the focal point of the "Lunar Society", a group of scientists and technologists who met to exchange ideas and speculations. Its central members included James Watt, the steam engine pioneer, and his business partner Matthew Boulton; the chemist Joseph Priestley; the potter Josiah Wedgwood, who was to become Charles Darwin's other grandfather; Samuel Galton, who was to become the other grandfather of Francis Galton, the pioneer of *eugenic theory; Richard Lovell Edgeworth, the father of the novelist Maria Edgeworth; and Thomas Day, the author of the didactic children's book *The History of Sandford and Merton* (1783). Erasmus Darwin and the Lunar Society were also visited by such luminaries as Jean-Jacques *Rousseau and Samuel Johnson.

Erasmus Darwin's contributions to science were mostly in the field of *botany and *evolutionary philosophy. He followed his first account of *The System of Vegetables* (1783) with a long poem celebrating *The Loves of the Plants* (1789), which derived its theme and organisation from the fact that the system classifying plants originated by Carolus Linnaeus is based on the characteristics of their sexual organs. It attracted little attention until an expanded version was integrated into the much more popular *The Botanic Garden* (1794–1795), a poetic tribute to the work done at the Royal Gardens in Kew by Joseph Banks, which also included tributes to other contemporary scientific developments, including experiments with *electricity carried out by Benjamin Franklin. In this context, *The Loves of the Plants* seemed bizarre to some readers and indecent to others; it was parodied in the *Anti-Jacobin*—a Tory periodical that took an exceedingly dim view of the "Jacobin science" practised by such potential revolutionaries as Franklin and Priestley—by "The Loves of the Triangles" (1798), composed by George Canning and his fellow editors.

Darwin followed *The Loves of the Plants* with *The Economy of Vegetation* (1792), heavily influenced by the scientific aspects of contemporary French philosophy, particularly the ideas of Linnaeus' self-appointed rival, the Comte du Buffon. *Zoonomia; or, The Laws of Organic Life* (1794–1796) is more orthodox in manner, but more enterprising and unusual in its substance. *Zoonomia* helped pave the way for Charles Darwin's theory of evolution but it exerted little influence in its own day; the elder Darwin made more impact with his ideas on educational reform, as summarised in *A Plan for the Conduct of Female Education in Boarding Schools* (1797), and his championship of gardening, as summarised in *Phytologia; or, The Philosophy of Agriculture and Gardening* (1800).

The ultimate product of the epic project begun in *The Botanic Garden* was the posthumously published *The Temple of Nature; or, The Origin of Society* (1803), one of whose footnotes may have been the topic of discussion between Lord Byron and Percy Shelley that planted the seed of *Frankenstein* in Mary *Shelley's mind. Darwin's evolutionism was reiterated there, with a greater stress on the competitive element in Nature but with a relentless optimism based on his faith in the idea of *progress.

Darwin's literary influence was muted during his lifetime, in spite of the popularity of *The Botanic Garden*, but the German Romantics took him seriously, and reflected his influence back into English *Romanticism via Samuel Taylor Coleridge. The American George Tucker included an explicit response to *Zoonomia*'s evolutionist ideas in *A Voyage to the Moon* (1827, by-lined Joseph Atterley). Darwin's ideas also influenced the account of the evolution of science contained in Robert *Browning's *Paracelsus* (1835) and the discussion of the conflict between the scientific worldview and religious belief in Alfred, Lord Tennyson's *In Memoriam* (written 1833–1850). His own reputation as a poet did not wear well, and excerpts from *The Loves of the Plants* were prominently featured in D. B. Wyndham-Lewis and Charles Lee's showcase anthology of bad verse, *The Stuffed Owl* (1930); his importance as a scientist and freethinker, on the other hand, became increasingly evident in retrospect. Charles Sheffield employed him as a scientific detective in *Erasmus Magister* (1982; exp. 2002 as *The Amazing Mr. Darwin*).

DEATH

The cessation of *life. Foreknowledge of death is, according to existentialist philosophy, the fundamental curse of human experience: a prospect so horrifying that the human imagination has always struggled to deny or defy it, primarily by constructing mythical afterlives celebrated in funerary rites. Literary afterlife fantasies are common; the example of Dante Alighieri's fourteenth-century *Divina Commedia* gave rise, somewhat perversely, to an amazing profusion of "infernal comedies" designed to take the sting out of the idea of Hell, and the notion of cosmic *palingenesis gave rise to a significant subgenre of nineteenth-century scientific romance. Another significant subgenre of fantastic literature is posthumous fantasy, in which the dead continue to exist in the primary world rather than moving on to some further realm. Fantasies of extreme Earthly *longevity are also commonplace in myth and literature, but are rarely imbued with optimism.

The extent to which the *angst* associated with foreknowledge of death spoils the experience of life is obviously limited, but a gloomy tradition in philosophy extending from the Greek cynics to Arthur Schopenhauer asserts that only the capacity for self-delusion stands between humankind and despair. Literature supporting Sophocles' judgment that "the best thing of all is not to be born, and after that to die young" is relatively sparse, although it is echoed in a good deal of Victorian fiction anxious about the corrupting effects of adult consciousness, in which virtuous child characters are allowed by their benevolent creators to perish unspoiled.

Until the advent of organic *chemistry in the nineteenth century, the phenomenon of death was almost invariably seen as the loss of some kind of vital spark, equated with the soul in the case of humans. Its usual medical definition was the cessation of breathing and the beat of the heart, although the unreliability of such methods of perception as holding a mirror to the lips and feeling for a pulse generated considerable anxieties regarding the possibility of premature burial. Such anxieties shaped modern mortuary practices and inspired numerous horror stories, including Edgar Allan Poe's archetypal "The Premature

Burial" (1844). When vitalism declined as a theory, the problem of defining and detecting death became more awkward, and the advent of medical technologies designed to maintain the action of the heart and lungs artificially resulted in a new definition of "brain death", referring to a permanent loss of *neurological function.

Although the psychological anticipation of death plays a considerable role in life and literature alike, the principal material concern in both arenas has always been dominated by issues of inheritance. Death in politics, civil law, and fiction is primarily a means of passing on entitlements. Although the fundamental topics of literature are sex and death, their conventional manifestation is generally in terms of marriage and inheritance. The advances in medical technology and social hygiene that drastically altered the demographics of death in nineteenth- and twentieth-century Western societies brought about a dramatic change in the pattern of "expectations" of enrichment, and hence in the kinds of closure typical of fiction. Such twentieth-century advances in technology as *cryogenic preservation had little obvious impact on the phenomenon of death but had an immediate effect on the legal issues surrounding definitions of death and the propriety of wills and testaments, as reflected in such futuristic legal dramas as L. Timmel Duchamp's "Living Trust" (1998).

The symbolic personification of Death—usually, but not invariably, as a male figure—is a common stratagem of fantasy literature and art. He appears in works as early as Euripides' *Alcestis* (438 B.C.) and is very prominent in Renaissance work; he is the High Father's messenger in the sixteenth-century allegory *Everyman*. The image of the hooded Grim Reaper carrying his scythe, extensively featured in Mediaeval designs of life as a *danse macabre*, was cheapened by overuse and the gradual accumulation of parodies. Although some twentieth-century representations—notably Ingmar Bergman's *The Seventh Seal* (1957)—are earnest, the vast majority relegate the figure to scarecrow status. Even in humorous fiction, however—as in one of the main sequences of Terry Pratchett's Discworld series—the hooded Reaper retains considerable allegorical and philosophical potential.

Alternative depictions of personalised Death include the angel of death, often called Azrael, and urbane elderly gentlemen. Personable young men, like John Death in T. F. Powys's *Unclay* (1931), and female manifestations, such as Mara in George MacDonald's *Lilith* (1895), are rarer, but idiosyncratic guises are routinely improvised in melancholy fantasies and horror stories, including Pedro de Alarcón's *El amigo de la muerte* (1852; trans. as *The Strange Friend of Tito Gil*), Alberto Casella's oft-filmed play *La Morte in Vacanza* (1924; trans. as *Death Takes a Holiday*), Stephen Vincent Benét's "Johnny Pye and the Fool-Killer" (1937), L. E. Watkin's *On Borrowed Time* (1937; film, 1939), Nik Cohn's *King Death* (1975), and Dan Simmons' "The Great Lover" (1993).

The flamboyance and forcefulness of this literary apparatus easily override naturalistic representations of death, and the progress of science in accounting for death is principally reflected in the stock devices of modern hospital melodrama, which exploit the difficulties surrounding the decision to "switch off" mechanisms of artificial life support and the question of whether the deceased person's viable organs may be "harvested" for use in transplant surgery. Science-fictional extrapolations of such issues include Brad Ferguson's "Last Rights" (1988).

Experimental investigation of death was necessarily inhibited by ethical and practical factors. The decline of vitalism was, however, associated with significant attempts made by scientists to detect the departure of the soul from dying bodies; experimentalists frequently alleged that the moment of death corresponded with a measurable loss in weight. The actual history of such researches is briefly mapped out by Len Fisher's *Weighing the Soul: The Evolution of Scientific Beliefs* (2004), while literary extrapolations of the notion include Théophile Gautier's *Spirite* (1865), Charles B. Stilson's "Liberty or Death!" (1917; aka "The Soul Trap"), André Maurois' *Le peseur d'âmes* (1931; trans. as *The Weigher of Souls*), and Romain Gary's satire *Charge d'âme* (1973; trans. as *The Gasp*). The notion that such research is inherently sinister encouraged the production of such horror stories as George Manville Fenn's *The Man with a Shadow* (1888), in which a surgeon's experimental research into the phenomenon of death drives him mad.

Speculative fictions evaluating hypothetical technologies of longevity are commonplace, and are obliged to characterise death, if only tacitly, either as an enemy to be defeated or as a fate less undesirable than it may seem. Brian Stableford's "Mortimer Gray's History of Death" (1995; exp. 2000 as *The Fountains of Youth*) describes the career of a scholar writing a definitive history of death from an immortal viewpoint. Greg Egan's "Border Guards" (1999) also meditates on the changes wrought in the significance of death by new technologies of longevity. James Morrow's *The Eternal Footman* (1999) makes "death anxiety" manifest as an incarnate plague. The second strategy often makes much of the infinite tedium of extended life, although attempts to imagine societies in which death is or comes to be seen as a desirable goal in the absence of longevity go further; notable examples include James de Mille's *A Strange Manuscript Found in a Copper Cylinder* (1888), James Elroy Flecker's *The Last Generation* (1908), S. Fowler Wright's *The Adventure of Wyndham Smith* (1938), Gore Vidal's *Messiah* (1954), C. C. MacApp's "And All the Earth a Grave" (1963), Ian Watson's *Deathhunter* (1986), and Jack Dann's "A Quiet Revolution for Death" (1978).

Speculative accounts of technological resurrection tend to be dourer than the most pessimistic accounts of artificial longevity, heavily influenced by legendary accounts of zombies; notable examples include Raymond Z. Gallun's "Masson's Secret" (1939), William Tenn's "Down Among the Dead Men" (1954), Kevin J. Anderson's *Resurrection, Inc.* (1988), and Ian McDonald's *Necroville* (1994; aka *Terminal Café*). Even hypothetical futures in which resurrection becomes so easy that "recreational death" becomes a leisure pursuit—as in Michael Swanwick's "Moon Dogs" (2000)—are subject to an unusually intense yuck factor. Aliens bringing the gift of technological resurrection, like those in Eric Brown's Kéthani series—including "The Angels of Life and Death" (2001), "The Kéthani Inheritance" (2001), and "The Wisdom of the Dead" (2003)—are treated with greater suspicion than those merely bringing an elixir of life.

Much fiction dealing with the phenomenon of death is not so much concerned with the fact as the manner of passing. The advancement of medical technology has increased opportunities for easing the pain that is so frequently associated with dying, and most apparatus of that kind—including morphine—can also be used to hasten death. Legal issues surrounding the administration of "euthanasia" have caused controversy for centuries; its literary reflections have often considered the possibility of compulsory euthanasia for the elderly, as in the play *The Old Law* (1656) attributed to Philip Massinger, Thomas Middleton, and William Rowley, Anthony Trollope's novel *The Fixed Period* (1882), Nigel Kneale's teleplay "Wine of India" (1970), and Terry Bisson's "Greetings" (2003). Other novels dealing with the theme include William F. Nolan and George Clayton Johnson's *Logan's Run* (1967) and Sumner Locke Elliott's *Going* (1975). Notable examples of texts suggesting that compulsion would not be necessary if euthanasia technology were properly marketed include David Bunch's "Holdholtzer's Box" (1971) and Joseph Green's "Gentle into that Good Night" (1981).

The force of the existentialist argument regarding the *angst* generated by foreknowledge of death is reflected in the fact that modern medical technology that allows hearts to be stopped temporarily during surgical operations has given rise to a new mythology of "near-death experiences". Patients who have "died" on the operating table often report dreams of moving towards a light, with their progress being encouraged or impeded in various ways. Such imagery is in tune with the imaginative context provided by twentieth-century posthumous fantasies and afterlife fantasies; science-fictional extrapolations of the notion include Connie Willis' *Passage* (2001).

The reluctance of people trying to organise their worldviews within a scientific framework simply to dispose of the notion of the immortal soul has been an important stimulus to science-fictional invention; the more ingenious attempts to retain or find a substitute for it include Clifford D. Simak's *Time and Again* (1951), Bob Shaw's *The Palace of Eternity* (1969), Rudy Rucker's *White Light* (1980), Richard Cowper's "The Tithonian Factor" (1983), and Robert J. Sawyer's *The Terminal Experiment* (1995). Even speculative fictions that discard the notion of human souls sometimes credit them to *aliens, as in Poul Anderson's "The Martyr" (1960), George R. R. Martin's "A Song for Lya" (1974), and Nicholas Yermakov's *The Last Communion* (1981). A corollary reluctance to dispose entirely of the notion of an afterlife produced such accounts of artificial afterlives as Philip José Farmer's Riverworld series before the notion of uploading minds into *cyberspace added a new dimension of plausibility to the notion. In Patrick O'Leary's *The Impossible Bird* (2002), aliens establish an artificial afterlife for humans but find its beneficiaries perversely ungrateful.

The notion of existential *angst* is capable of cosmological extension to the argument that all human endeavours must be ultimately futile because the universe itself is ultimately doomed to the extinction of entropic heat-death or collapse. The subgenre of *Omega Point fantasy offers equal hospitality to gloomy reflections of this hyper-angst, attempts to combat it with a variety of mythical and speculative weapons, and accounts of the fashion in which the legacy of the present universe might be passed on to its heirs.

DECADENCE

A notion corollary to the hypothesis that cultures or civilisations have a natural life cycle akin to that of human individuals; a culture's decadence is a phase corresponding to an individual's senescence, and is held to manifest analogous symptoms. Images of cultural decadence usually involve jaded and morally anaesthetised aristocrats following sybaritic lifestyles whose futility is determined as much by the imminent doom of their culture as by their own inevitable deaths. The idea was first given quasi-scientific form by the Baron de Montesquieu in *Considérations sur les causes de la grandeur des Romains et de leur décadence* (Thoughts on the Causes of the Grandiosity of the Romans and their Decadence) (1734), but it was not new. The idea that the glories of imperial Rome had given way to the Dark Ages because its rulers had embraced debauchery rather than cultivating ambition was commonplace even while the process was in train; the Romans who complained of it had a conspicuous historical precedent of their own in the fate of the Greek empire built by Alexander the Great.

Montesquieu's thesis was adopted by Edward Gibbon into his account of *The Decline and Fall of the Roman Empire* (1776–1788), thus becoming an important influence on subsequent English literature, but it was more influential in post-Napoleonic France, where the notion that the decadent phase of a culture must be abundantly illustrated by its *art and literature was applied to the literary produce of contemporary France in Théophile Gautier's preface to the third edition of Charles Baudelaire's *Les Fleurs du Mal* (1857; exp. 1861 and 1869). Gautier's description of "Decadent style" and identification of the typical Decadent subject matter (derived from desperate attempts to combat *ennui* and *spleen*) assisted Baudelaire to become a model for future writers hoping to embody as well as depict the decadence of nineteenth-century European civilisation, prompting the proliferation of Decadent Movements in various nations from the mid-1880s to the end of the century. Joris-Karl Huysmans' sarcastic comedy *À rebours* (1884; trans. as *Against the Grain* or *Against Nature*) provided a definitive description of Decadent taste and sensibility.

The notion of cultural decadence was confused with the idea of "degeneration" in versions of *anthropological racial theory carrying forward J. F. Blumenbach's conviction that the coloured races had been produced by the deterioration of a Caucasian root stock. Count Gobineau's *Essai sur l'inégalité des races humaines* (1853–1855) rejected the idea of a single root race but attributed the decadence of great civilisations to the influence of "hybridism" caused by racial miscegenation—an idea widely reflected in subsequent literature. The advent of *eugenics extended the notion of degeneration into evolutionary biology, as in Ray Lankester's *Degeneration: A Chapter in Darwinism* (1880), further amplifying anxiety regarding the threat it posed to nineteenth-century Europe.

Max Nordau's *Entartung* (1893; trans. as *Degeneration*) applied an elaboration of Gobineau's hypothesis to the criticism of Decadent art and literature, including Pre-Raphaelitism, Wagnerism, Tolstoyism, Ibsenism, and Nietzscheanism, all of which Nordau construed as morbid symptoms of cultural twilight. Fashionable ideas relating to the *psychopathology of genius were accommodated in the allegation that "higher degenerates" often have some "exceptional mental gift" developed at the cost of atrophied faculties. Gobineau's theories, as reformulated and repopularised by Nordau, eventually assumed a central role in Nazi pseudoscience, where they were used to justify the extermination of inferior races and "hybrids", and stern opposition to the creeping menaces of decadence and degeneration.

The idea of decadence became a significant antithesis to the idea of *progress. Many writers who did not see nineteenth-century Europe as a decadent society saw the future in terms of inevitable decline rather than continuing technological and social advancement. Images of future decadence were sometimes offset by the assumption that their supersession by a newly emergent culture was equally inevitable, but the demands of melodrama inevitably encouraged greater concentration on the former aspect of the process; notable nineteenth-century images of future civilisation in irreparable decline include Louis Hippolyte Mettais' *An 5865* (1865), Alfred Franklin's *Ruines de Paris en 4875* (1875), Richard Jefferies' *After London* (1885), John Ames Mitchell's *The Last American* (1889), and Jules Verne's posthumously published "L'eternel Adam" (1910; trans. as "The Eternal Adam").

Montesquieu's notion of decadence made some inroads into nineteenth-century science, including evolutionist theory—where it was applied to certain fossil groups whose entire careers, culminating in extinction, were inscribed in rock strata—and economics, in Brooks Adams' *Law of Civilization and Decay* (1895). Its principal extension was, however, in two key works by twentieth-century philosophers of history, Oswald Spengler's *Der Undertang des Abendlandes* (1918–1922; trans. as *The Decline of the West*) and Arnold Toynbee's *A Study of History* (1934–1954), both of which offered panoramic surveys of a whole series of cultural life cycles. Spengler's influence on twentieth-century literature was particularly profound, affecting fiction set in the past, present, and future. Toynbee's account of the United States as the latest in a long list of civilisations whose day had come and gone (whose deterministic aspects he subsequently recanted) had a greater influence on American views of the decadence of Europe than on domestic anxieties about America's own future, but added to Spengler's influence in promoting the idea of a general "Western decadence" in cultures further to the east; by the end of the century many Europeans were equally enthusiastic to envision the United States as a hubristic, decadent culture in denial, as is suggested in such analyses as the essays translated in Umberto Eco's *Travels in Hyperreality* (1986).

Isaac *Asimov's futuristic replay of the decline and fall of the Roman empire on a galactic stage may have been more a matter of narrative convenience than theoretical conviction, but it is framed in explicitly Spenglerian terms. James *Blish's Cities in Flight series made very elaborate use of its Spenglerian schema. Charles Harness used Toynbeean theory in *Flight into Yesterday* (1949; aka *The Paradox Men*) to license an ambience of jaded Romanticism. A similar ambience was carried forward into such accounts of decadent future cities as Edward Bryant's *Cinnabar* (1976), Terry Carr's *Cirque* (1977), and S. P. Somtow's *I Wake from the Dream of a Drowned Star City* (1992).

The reiteration of Asimov's galactic schema in Poul *Anderson's Dominic Flandry series was more earnest in its contemplation of the advent of a "Long Night", and few science-fictional images of galactic civilisation were untouched by a conviction of the inevitability of decadence; even Iain M. Banks' defiantly formulated Culture was depicted in decadent mode in *Look to Windward* (2000). Dean McLaughlin's meditative archaeological fantasy "For Those Who Follow After" (1951) features a message left by a self-consciously decadent culture, forewarning others—no matter what their point of origin might be—of the inevitability of their fate.

Gautier's theory of Decadent style and substance was imported wholesale into the imagery of far-futuristic fantasy, and there extrapolated to its furthest extreme, in Clark Ashton Smith's 1930s tales of Zothique. The idea that the life cycles of the solar system and the entire universe have their own built-in decadent phase, consequent on the slow extinction of the Sun in the first instance and the ravages of entropy in the second, is frequently incorporated into such fantasies in a histrionically elegiac spirit. Jack Vance's tales of the Dying Earth, Michael Moorcock's accounts of the ultimate *ennui* of the Dancers at the End of Time, and such individual works as Elizabeth Counihan's "The Star Called Wormwood" (2004) continued Smith's Earthbound tradition, while the subgenre of *Omega Point fiction explored further extremes.

When the decline of *Space Age mythology pushed conventional images of space colonisation into a more distant *posthuman future, the new subgenre of far-futuristic space opera immediately adopted conventional decadent imagery in such works as Raymond Harris' *Shadows of the White Sun* (1988), which features a network of orbital constructs inhabited by a decadent social elite, the Hypaethra. Meanwhile, such stories as Jim Grimsley's "The 120

Hours of Sodom" (2005) added to a long literary tradition of reminders that it is not actually necessary to wait for the far future in order to enjoy an ostentatiously decadent lifestyle.

Although the term is rarely applied in such a context, the notion of decadence is tacitly mirrored in Thomas Kuhn's theory of scientific *paradigms, which credits theoretical frameworks with a kind of natural life cycle not unlike those superimposed on cultures by Montesquieu and Spengler. In Kuhn's account, paradigms enjoy an imperial heyday before being eaten away by accumulating anomalies, their sustenance increasingly dependent on the repair work of "secondary elaborations" carried out by change-resistant "aristocrats" of the scientific community—until their final collapse is ensured by the emergence of younger and more vigorous rivals. It remains to be seen how close the theory of decadence might be to the terminus of its own usefulness.

DE CAMP, L[YON] SPRAGUE (1907–2000)

U.S. writer who studied aeronautical engineering at the California Institute of Technology before obtaining his master's degree from the Stevens Institute of Technology. He began writing science fiction while working for a company organising patent applications, his early work including a satirical *evolutionary fantasy, in which future humankind has been superceded by intelligent apes, written in collaboration with P. Schuyler Miller. It was eventually published as *Genus Homo* (1941; book, 1950); by that time, de Camp had already become a key contributor to John W. *Campbell Jr.'s *Astounding* stable.

De Camp's fiction was conspicuously lighthearted, dealing in uninhibited adventures when not wholeheartedly comic. He seemed far more at home in *Astounding*'s fantasy companion *Unknown*, although his *Astounding* novella "The Stolen Dormouse" (1941) injected a welcome irreverence into the former magazine's imagery of the future, and his work for *Unknown* was informed by a sharp and highly distinctive sense of logical discrimination, even in the absurdist vein of "Divide and Rule" (1939), in which an alien conquest of Earth has magnificently silly results.

De Camp did not consider time travel plausible enough to rank as Campbellian science fiction, but that did not stop him from pointing out the language problems that time travellers would undoubtedly experience in "The Isolinguals" (1937), which he followed up with an article on "Language for Time-Travelers" (1938). Nor did it prevent him from setting out an earnest argument for *technological determinism in *Lest Darkness Fall* (1939; book, 1941; rev. 1949), whose timeslipped hero attempts to prevent the Dark Ages following the fall of the western Roman Empire's last remnant. His interest in *historical causality and the hiatus in scientific progress that followed the decline of the Roman Empire gave rise to two conscientiously researched, two-part articles in *Astounding* on "The Science of Whithering" (1940) and "The Sea-King's Armoured Division" (1941).

De Camp's intense interest in ancient technology was further developed in *The Ancient Engineers* (1963), such historical novels as *An Elephant for Aristotle* (1958), *The Bronze God of Rhodes* (1960), *The Dragon of the Ishtar Gate* (1961), and *The Arrows of Hercules* (1965) and the nostalgic science fiction novel *The Glory That Was* (1952; book, 1960). His interest in the process of invention and its role in social change was similarly developed in a book cowritten with A. K. Berle on *Inventions and Their Management* (1937; rev. 1951; rev. as *Inventions, Patents and Their Management*, 1959) and such solo works as *The Evolution of Naval Weapons* (1947) and *The Heroic Age of American Invention* (1961; rev. 1993 as *The Heroes of American Invention*).

The bulk of de Camp's science fiction consists of satirical comedies. One early series of short stories, begun with "The Command" (1938), featured the exploits of Johnny Black, a bear with artificially enhanced *intelligence. He eventually discovered a much more flexible future-historical backcloth in the Viagens Interplanetarias series, in which interstellar exploration is dominated by Brazil. Its early short stories were collected in *The Continent Makers and Other Tales of the Viagens* (1953) and *Sprague de Camp's New Anthology of Science Fiction* (1953), but its subsequent inclusions were almost all novels. With the exception of *Rogue Queen* (1951), which describes a humanoid hive society, *The Stones of Nomuru* (1988), and *The Venom Trees of Sunga* (1992), the novels in the series detail the eccentric history, geography, and *xenology of the planet Krishna, detailed in *The Queen of Zamba* (1949; 1954 book as *Cosmic Manhunt*; aka *A Planet Called Krishna*), *The Hand of Zei* (1950; some subsequent editions in 2 vols.), *The Virgin of Zesh* (1953; first collected in *The Virgin and the Wheels*, 1990), *The Tower of Zanid*, (1958), *The Hostage of Zir* (1977), *The Prisoner of Zhamanak* (1982), *The Bones of Zora* (1983), and *The Swords of Zinjaban* (1991).

The last two titles were cocredited to de Camp's wife Catherine Crook de Camp, whose collaborations with him were more numerous than the by-lines of his books acknowledge. De Camp's other significant works of science fiction include the black comedy "Judgment Day" (1955), *The Great Fetish* (1978),

which parodies *Creationist resistance to evolutionary theory—he had earlier written a nonfictional account of *The Great Monkey Trial* (1968)—and the mosaic *Rivers of Time* (1993), which collects a series of stories extrapolated from "A Gun for Dinosaur" (1956). Much of his fiction is pure fantasy, but no other writer of magical fantasy—at least until the advent of Terry Pratchett—ever made such conspicuous or conscientious use of the scientific outlook and the scientific method as de Camp, and his work in that genre is by no means irrelevant to the literary reflection of science.

In collaboration with fellow historian Fletcher Pratt, de Camp wrote a series of comedies in which the discovery of the mathematical foundations of magic allow access to a series of literary and mythical milieux, where the protagonists' scientifically trained, twentieth-century intellect becomes engaged in contests of wit with various gods, demons, magicians, and monsters. The early items, two of which were combined in *The Incomplete Enchanter* (1940; book, 1941) with the third being expanded for book publication as *The Castle of Iron* (1941; book, 1950), appeared in *Unknown*; two later ones were combined in *Wall of Serpents* (1960). *The Land of Unreason* (1941; book, 1942), also written with Pratt, is similar in spirit, as are some of de Camp's solo fantasies for *Unknown*. The latter include a parody of fairy-tale conventions, *The Undesired Princess* (1942; book, 1990, with a sequel by David Drake, "The Enchanted Bunny") and *Solomon's Stone* (1942; book, 1957), which features an astral plane inhabited by the dream projections of Earthly men.

In addition to these kinds of work, de Camp was also a leading populariser and writer of the "sword and sorcery" fantasy pioneered by Robert E. Howard (with whom he wrote numerous posthumous "collaborations"). His rigorously skeptical nonfictional investigation of the raw materials of modern fantasy fiction in such books as *Lands Beyond* (1952, with Willy Ley), *Lost Continents: The Atlantis Theme in History, Science and Literature* (1954), *Spirits, Stars, and Spells: The Profits and Perils of Magic* (1967, with Catherine Crook de Camp), *The Ragged Edge of Science* (1980), and *The Fringe of the Unknown* (1983) served to reemphasise his judgment that such fiction ought to be treated as pure entertainment, undertaken in a spirit of mildly mischievous fun. His biographies of H. P. Lovecraft and Robert E. Howard might, however, be reckoned a trifle uncharitable in charging both writers with taking their work and themselves far too seriously. In his own work, he demonstrated more convincingly than any other modern writer that the scrupulous application of scientific reasoning to all manner of premises was a game whose rewards could include hilarity as well as exhilaration, and the delights of absurdity as well as the joy of sanity.

The 1996 edition of *Lest Darkness Fall* was supplemented by a sequel by David A. Drake, "To Bring the Light". De Camp is featured as a character, along with his sometime coworkers Isaac Asimov and Robert A. Heinlein, in "Green Fire" (2000) by Eileen Gunn, Andy Duncan, Pat Murphy, and Michael Swanwick. He is also featured in one of the stories in a tribute anthology of fantasies edited by Harry Turtledove, *The Enchanter Completed* (2005).

DEE, JOHN (1527–1609)

English mathematician and astronomer who acquired a posthumous reputation as a magician. He was educated at St. John's College Cambridge, where he showed great promise in mathematics and began to make astronomical observations with the aid of a quadrant and cross-staff. He became a fellow of St. John's and a foundation fellow of Trinity College in 1546. In 1548, he went to study at the University of Louvain, where he became a close friend of the *cartographer Gerardus Mercator. He lectured on mathematics at the University of Paris before he returned to England in 1551, bringing back numerous navigational instruments, He first entered the service of the Earl of Pembroke, then obtained the patronage of the Duke of Northumberland, but his career nearly came to an end when his Protestant father, Roland Dee, was arrested after Queen Mary came to the throne in 1553.

Roland Dee was released but never recovered his assets; his fellow mathematician and astronomer Leonard Digges suffered a similar fate, hastening his premature death. Dee took responsibility for Digges' son Thomas, with whom he continued the elder Digges' work on the development of the *telescope, under the inspiration of Roger *Bacon (whose work Dee translated into English). Dee's release after his own arrest in 1555 has occasioned speculation that he became an informer, but he was in sufficient favour when Elizabeth succeeded Mary in 1558 to be entrusted with casting a horoscope to determine the most favourable day for her coronation. His liberty was more likely due to the fact that he had become an adviser on navigational matters to the Muscovy Company formed by Sebastian Cabot, assisting with the search for the northeast passage and instructing crews in geometry and astronomy; he held that position for 32 years, and undoubtedly made his expertise available to other navigators operating with the blessing of the crown, including Elizabethan privateers. His only work on navigation to have survived was printed in 1577—with a note asserting that it was being issued "24 years after its first publication"—but its earlier versions and parallel texts must have been circulated on a strict "need to know" basis.

Dee presented Mary with plans for a national library in 1556 and set out to build its nucleus on his own initiative; his collection was eventually superceded by the one assembled by Archbishop Matthew Parker, but was probably the largest in the kingdom for a while. Despite the respect in which Elizabeth held him, he never received any substantial financial support from the crown, and lived with his mother in Mortlake. He wrote prolifically, but relatively few of his works were printed and most slipped into obscurity, the most conspicuous exceptions being an introduction to a new edition of Euclid and his ambitious exercise in *occult science, *Monas Hieroglyphica* (1564). In 1568, Dee presented Queen Elizabeth with a copy of his *Propaideumata Aphoristica* and volunteered to give her lessons in mathematics to help her understand it; it contained a comprehensive survey of contemporary physics, mathematics, and astronomy—the latter heavily impregnated with astrological theory—and showed an interest in magic typical of its period, but was less inclined to occult syncretism than its predecessor.

Dee and Thomas Digges made disciplined observations of the "new star" of 1572, their calculations of its movement supplying valuable data to Tycho Brahe. They were already Copernicans, and the new star seemed to both of them to be proof of the heliocentric theory. In the late 1570s, Digges became a full-time military engineer, taking command of ordnance in the Netherlands until his death in 1595. In the meantime, Dee settled down with his third wife, Jane Fromands, who bore him eight children; his mother gave him the Mortlake house in order that he might do so. In March 1582, Dee found a far less suitable collaborator that Digges when he met Edward Kelley, a counterfeiter and confidence trickster who claimed that he could communicate with angels via a polished lump of obsidian stone that he alleged to be the Philosopher's Stone. Initially skeptical, Dee was seemingly persuaded that Kelley was genuine, and they embarked on a long collaboration, recording their intercourse with the angels in a code they called the Enochian alphabet.

From 1583 to 1589, Dee and Kelley travelled extensively in central Europe, mostly in Poland and Bohemia. When Dee returned to London—leaving Kelley in Prague, where he died in 1593—he found that most of his library had been stolen or confiscated; much of it ended up in the British Museum, along with the magic stone and documents relating to the Enochian code. Retrospective interpretations of the true significance of these materials differ sharply, but those who suppose Dee to have been a spy take the view that his journey to the heart of the Holy Roman Empire was a matter of gathering intelligence and that his arcane alphabet was a means of transmitting coded messages. Dee's attempts to obtain a position on his return were frustrated, but in 1596 he was appointed warden of the Collegiate Chapter (Christ's College) in Manchester. When Manchester was hit by the plague in 1605 his wife and several of their children died, and Dee returned to London.

It was not until fifty years after Dee's death that his reputation as a great magician took off, by courtesy of Meric Casaubon's highly fanciful *A true and faithful Relation of what passed between Dr. John Dee and some Spirits; tending, had it succeeded, to a general Alteration of most States and Kingdoms in the World* (1659). This was the source of the more widely read accounts of Dee contained in John Aubrey's *Brief Lives* (written ca. 1692; published 1813) and Charles Mackay's chapter on "The Alchymists" in *Memoirs of Extraordinary Popular Delusions* (1841; reprinted in *Extraordinary Popular Delusions and the Madness of Crowds*). Dee was widely credited thereafter with all manner of other clandestine magical endeavours, which threw his mathematical and scientific endeavours into the historical shade. The preservation of his magical apparatus in the British Museum, while his navigational endeavours and work on the telescope went largely unrecorded, ensured that he became a central figure in the retrospectively constructed neo-Hermetic tradition, a key inspiration for such lifestyle fantasists as Aleister Crowley, such literary fantasists as H. P. Lovecraft, and such historians of the occult as Frances Yates.

Dee's posthumous reputation guaranteed him a literary afterlife more extensive and more colourful than any other scientist of his era, although the inevitable price he paid for that peculiar celebrity was that his magical follies were magnified to a far greater extent than any of his primitive telescopes can ever have contrived. Notable examples of his literary employment as a magician include W. Harrison Ainsworth's *Guy Fawkes* (1841), Gustav Meyrink's *Der Engel vom Westlichen Fenster* (1927; trans. as *The Angel of the West Window*), Peter Ackroyd's *The House of Doctor Dee* (1993), and Liz Williams' *The Poison Master* (2003).

DELANY, SAMUEL R[AY] (1942–)

U.S. writer. His early novels were vivid futuristic fantasies in which scientific notions play a peripheral role, but his strong interest in contemporary literary theory—especially its intricate connections with *linguistics and cultural theory—increasingly informed his work. He published his first novel, the colourful science-fantasy *The Jewels of Aptor* (1962), while he was a student at the City College of New York, shortly after marrying his fellow student and poet Marilyn Hacker. He followed it with the three volumes constituting *The Fall of the Towers* (1963–1965), which deployed imagery typical of the action-adventure science fiction of the period in a far more polished fashion, and within a plot of highly unusual complexity and depth. His memoir of this era, *The Motion of Light in Water: Sex and Science Fiction Writing in the East Village* (1988; rev. 1990), explains the unusual experiential context from which these works emerged.

Delany continued to work as a full-time writer for a further decade. He followed the novella *The Ballad of Beta-2* (1965) with *Empire Star* (1966), a far-futuristic space opera that now seems far ahead of its time in every respect but its brevity, anticipating the *posthuman space operas of the 1990s. Its explanatory background includes a hierarchical classification of "simplex", "complex", and "multiplex" cultures incorporating distinct kinds of thought processes and worldviews; it attempts to anticipate future social evolution, taking aboard the assumption that further technological advancement would inevitably be correlated with new ways of thinking and new ways of creating artwork. Similar ideas were more elaborately reflected in *Babel-17* (1966), which includes an account of attempts to decipher an alien language whose structure involves similar advances in patterns of thought and creativity.

Broader philosophical issues of identity and sexuality are included in the casual sweep of the metafictional post-holocaust fantasy *The Einstein Intersection* (1967), which makes prolific use of syncretic mythological imagery. *Nova* (1968) is an elaborate Promethean fantasy cast in the form of a space opera, which continues the exploration of the social meanings and uses of myth in a more focused fashion, concentrating on the key elements of Romance. Delany and Hacker edited a conspicuously avant-gardist series of original anthologies, *Quark* (4 vols., 1970–1971), while Delany was working on the countercultural epic *Dhalgren* (1975), which he originally intended to publish in six volumes; it brought the decadent imagery of his work and his ongoing meditation on the social role of the artist much closer to home in its depiction of a contemporary city divorced from the history and geography of the United States, whose "dropped out" inhabitants formulate an anarchistic social order. His most ambitious science fiction novel, the "ambiguous heterotopia" *Triton* (1976;

aka *Trouble on Triton*), presents a bold analysis of future social possibilities that sets out to explore and extend the tacit assumptions built into the notion of *Utopia.

Delany began another similarly elaborate futuristic fantasy, but only published the first of two intended volumes, *Stars in My Pocket Like Grains of Sand* (1984), and virtually abandoned the genre thereafter as a writer, though not as an academic. He had obtained a post as Butler Professor of English at the State University of Buffalo, New York, in 1975 and held other short-term appointments thereafter, but in 1988 he settled as Professor of Comparative Literature at the University of Massachusetts, Amherst. Much of his subsequent work, including some of his fiction was issued by university presses and other small presses, and his forays into the mass market became increasingly abstruse—including his experiments with such formats as the graphic novel and such genres as pornography.

The early development of Delany's interest in the linguistics of science fiction had been mapped out in the essays collected in *The Jewel-Hinged Jaw* (1977) and *Starboard Wine* (1984) and a minutely methodical dissection of Thomas M. Disch's short story "Angouleme", set out in *The American Shore* (1978). From the mid-1980s onwards, his explorations made more elaborate use of semiotics and poststructuralist literary theory, but he continued to make concerted attempts to make his theses and arguments accessible to a nonacademic audience. In the essays and other materials collected in *Silent Interviews* (1994), *Longer Views* (1996), and *Shorter Views* (1999), he works hard to express his ideas in terms accessible to general readers as well as academics, and to students of creative writing who might want to put them into practice.

He moved from science fiction into the burgeoning commercial genre of fantasy in a series of books set in an imaginary prehistoric empire, comprising *Tales of Nevèrÿon* (1979), *Nevèrÿona* (1983), *Flight from Nevèrÿon* (1985), and *The Bridge of Lost Desire* (1987, rev. as *Return to Nevèrÿon*, 1989), in which issues of cultural and sexual identity are carefully explored in an arena that is both carefully simplified and scrupulously analogous to the modern world. Nevèrÿon is, to some extent, a transfiguration of New York, the Bridge of Lost Desire being a fantasised version of the Brooklyn Bridge, and its decadence is explicitly linked in the third book to the threat posed to New York's homosexual subculture by the AIDS epidemic. The books were equipped with a mélange of appendices, mostly signed by Delany's alter ego K. Leslie Steiner, which offered commentaries on their mythical, linguistic, and philosophical elements.

Although Delany's work always appeared to lie at the opposite pole of the science fiction spectrum from *hard science fiction, with his ostensibly commercial fiction eventually moving out of science fiction entirely into fantasy, he was always one of the most intellectually demanding writers in the genre, whose use of human sciences and literary theory was invariably as conscientious as it was intricate. No one else ever investigated the hidden workings of science fiction stories, in terms of the way they used language to generate "special effects", with such penetrating insight or such assiduity. His later work remains rather esoteric, but may well be crucial to a full understanding of the mechanics and artistry of constructing "fantastic" and "futuristic" narratives.

DICK, PHILIP K[INDRED] (1928–1982)

U.S. writer raised in California, who found social life and conventional employment difficult by virtue of various phobias. He became addicted to amphetamines prescribed for the relief of stress-induced asthma, which may have intensified his difficulties rather than relieving them. Although he worked briefly in a record store—he was passionately fond of classical music—his relative inability to deal with customers encouraged him to attempt to develop a career as a writer. Although he could not find a publisher for his naturalistic novels, he began to sell science fiction stories, and eventually devoted himself wholeheartedly to the genre.

Dick's work is located at the soft end of the science fiction spectrum, developing stock motifs with little or no regard to their rational plausibility, but he took such work to an unprecedented extreme by subjecting the notion of "rational plausibility" to scathing skeptical analysis. He constructed numerous *contes philosophiques* that mounted a variety of challenges to the notion that sensory information is trustworthy, developing various versions of the possibility that the world of phenomenal appearances might be concealing a very different reality.

Although his work was initially out of tune with the general run of contemporary science fiction, and tended to suffer from his amphetamine-fuelled method of production, whose hectic rushes of inspiration rarely lasted long enough to equip his novels with satisfactory denouements, the raw power and plaintive poignancy of Dick's best work attracted a considerable following. He became a figure of cardinal critical interest when *postmodernist critics discovered that work to be a perfect illustration of their theses—an opinion untroubled by the increasing influence exerted on his fiction by the actual paranoid delusions he began to suffer when his addiction got out of hand, and which lingered long after he had been forced to kick his amphetamine habit.

Such stories as "Beyond Lies the Wub" (1952) and "Roog" (1953) neatly encapsulated the wryly whimsical paranoia that became characteristic of Dick's early work, much of which focuses on the difficulty of distinguishing real individuals from *ersatz* imitations. These include such tales of mechanical *androids as "Second Variety" (1953) and "Imposter" (1953), such accounts of deceptive aliens as "The Father-Thing" (1954) and "Minority Report" (1956), and such tales of political chicanery as "The Variable Man" (1953) and *The World Jones Made* (1956). The hallucinatory fantasy *Eye in the Sky* (1957), in which a group of tourists caught in a freak accident experiences a series of distorted worlds, each based in the beliefs of one of their number, is markedly more intense, as are the extended delusional fantasies *Time Out of Joint* (1959) and *The Man in the High Castle* (1961).

Dick's analyses of the android condition increasingly likened it to schizophrenia, to whose paranoid variety he suspected himself of falling victim. *We Can Build You* (written 1962; published 1972), *Martian Time-Slip* (1964), *The Simulacra* (1964), *Dr. Bloodmoney* (1965), *The Three Stigmata of Palmer Eldritch* (1965), and *Now Wait for Last Year* (1966) all develop variants of this notion, which was refined to its philosophical extremes in *Do Androids Dream of Electric Sheep?* (1968) and *Ubik* (1969). Having no further to go in this direction, Dick then devoted himself to metaphysical fantasies of a more far-reaching kind, following the quirky analyses of the nature of godhood contained in *Galactic Pot-Healer* (1969) and *A Maze of Death* (1970) with the extraordinarily intense hallucinatory fantasies *Flow My Tears, the Policeman Said* (1974) and *A Scanner Darkly* (1977).

The writing of *A Scanner Darkly* was interrupted in February–March 1974 by a series of "visions" that obsessed Dick for the remainder of his life, which he struggled to represent and interpret in *Radio Free Albemuth* (written 1976; published 1985), and its revision as *VALIS* (1981), which formed the first part of a thematic trilogy completed by *The Divine Invasion* (1981) and *The Transmigration of Timothy Archer* (1982). The experience made his subsequent work relentlessly esoteric, but that only made his cult following more enthusiastic.

Dick's use of science fiction imagery without the least trace of any explanatory underpinning or extrapolative logic was completely contrary to the ideals of hard science fiction, but it reflected a significant trend within the evolution of the genre, which became greatly exaggerated as the commercial core of the genre moved out of text into the visual media. His work proved easily adaptable to the cinema once it was stripped of most of its subtlety and complexity. *Blade Runner* (1982) was a pale shadow of *Do Androids Dream of Electric Sheep?* but still seemed sophisticated by the standards of cinematic science fiction. *Total Recall* (1990) was a travesty of "We Can Remember It for You Wholesale" (1966), and *Screamers* (1996) did scant justice to the horrific quality of "Second Variety", although *Minority Report* (2002) captured the quality of its original more accurately. It is significant that such movies found more in Dick's work to develop within their own formal conventions than is extractable from most textual science fiction.

Dick's fearful but sympathetic representations of *psychopathology and alternative states of consciousness manifest an experiential authority rarely found in *psychotropic fantasy, and the distinctive quality of his *angst*-ridden *alienation made him an important contributor to modern existentialist fantasy. He did not belong to the extensive tradition of technophobic antiscience fiction; his work shows a consistent fascination with innovative gadgetry and its life-enhancing uses, although he was deeply suspicious of the vanity of the assumption that the human mind and the human sensorium are capable of deciphering the mystery of the world; his trust in science was, in effect, far greater than his trust in the intuitive methods of *occult science.

Dick is carefully referenced in Michael Swanwick's "The Transmigration of Philip K" (1985) and David Bischoff's *Philip K. Dick High* (2000). He is the key character in Michael Bishop's *The Secret Ascension; or, Philip K. Dick Is Dead, Alas* (1987), although his appearances are fleeting and deceptive. He also features in Paul J. MacAuley's alternative history "The Two Dicks" (2001)—the other being Richard Nixon.

DINOSAUR

A member of a group of extinct reptiles—which includes many giant specimens—whose gradual revelation has been the aspect of *palaeontology that has gripped the popular imagination more intently than any other. The term was coined in 1841 by Richard Owen to describe a new order of reptiles, whose first specimens had been identified in the 1820s and which was detailed in Geoffrey St. Hilaire's *Recherches sur de Grands Sauriens* (1831). In 1887, Harry Groves Seeley divided dinosaurs into two orders, the lizard-like *Saurischia* and the bird-like *Ornithischia*. Pterosaurs, icthyosaurs, and plesiosaurs—all of which had been discovered in the decade immediately preceding the discovery of the first dinosaur—are usually accommodated to the category in popular representations. The dinosaurs originated in the late Triassic period, some two hundred million years ago, and lived through the succeeding Jurassic and Cretaceous periods, before disappearing some sixty-five million years ago.

Dinosaurs became the most charismatic of all extinct creatures, and the unfolding narrative of their diversity became a considerable inspiration to the literary imagination. The spectacular size and forms of the most famous specimens—including the stegosaurus, the brontosaurus, the diplodocus, and the triceratops—prompted popular parlance to develop the notion that giant dinosaurs had "ruled the Earth" for 150 million years; the naming of *Tyrannosaurus rex*, which became the greatest saurian celebrity of all, added a curious official endorsement to this analogy of majesty. The popular excitement generated by dinosaurs is evident in the fact that the discovery of the first American specimens in 1855 quickly gave rise to a fervent competition between the rival "dinosaur hunters", Edwin Drinker Cope and his one-time associate Othniel Charles Marsh, a professor of palaeontology at Yale. Their feud is dramatised in Sharon N. Farber's alternative history story "The Last Thunder Horse West of the Mississippi" (1988).

The apparent abruptness of the dinosaurs' ultimate demise attracted a variety of *catastrophist explanations—including I. S. Shklovskii's suggestion that they might have been killed by ultraviolet radiation after the destruction of the ozone layer by charged particles from a supernova—before a 1980 paper in *Science* by Luis and Walter Alvarez, F. Asaro, and H. V. Michel argued that the presence of iridium in the boundary layer marking the end of the Cretaceous was evidence for the impact of an *asteroid about 10 kilometers in diameter, which might have prompted the volcanic eruptions associated with the Deccan Traps in India and blasted enough dust into the atmosphere to precipitate a worldwide *ecocatastrophe. A half-submerged crater some 180 kilometers in diameter, found at Chicxulub on the coast of the Yucatan peninsula in Mexico, was widely hailed as the "smoking gun" proving the Alvarez hypothesis (although it might be more appropriately compared to an exit wound).

The gradual realisation that the long evolutionary history of the dinosaurs had been one of continual change, associated with the gradual breakup of the supercontinent Pangaea and the development of flowering plants, supplemented catastrophist accounts of their tribulations with uniformitarian accounts of a long war of attrition between lumbering exothermic

reptiles and sprightly endothermic mammals, but that narrative too was subverted when Robert T. Bakker argued that many dinosaurs were, in fact, endothermic—a thesis popularised by Adrian J. Desmond's *The Hot-Blooded Dinosaurs* (1977). Bakker followed up his own account of *The Dinosaur Heresies* (1986; rev. 2001) with the documentary fiction *Raptor Red* (1996); his argument lent support to the notion that the group had not been wiped out at all, the bird-like *Ornithischia* being the ancestors of modern birds.

The principal problem afflicting the fictional representation of dinosaurs is that of bridging the temporal gap that separates them from human observers. Stories that adopt dinosaur viewpoints, such as Harley S. Aldinger's "The Way of a Dinosaur" (1928), Duane N. Carroll's "When Reptiles Ruled" (1935), and Fredric Brown's "Starvation" (1942), have limited appeal, and stories that feature extraterrestrial visitors to the Mesozoic Earth, such as Philip Barshovsky's "One Prehistoric Night" (1935), are similarly esoteric. Early fiction featuring dinosaurs usually cast them as exotic survivors lurking in remote enclaves, as in Jules Verne's *Voyage au centre de la terre* (1864; trans. as *Journey to the Centre of the Earth*), Robert Duncan Milne's "The Iguanodon's Egg" and "The Hatching of the Iguanodon" (both 1882), E. Douglas Fawcett's *Swallowed by an Earthquake* (1894), Wardon Allan Curtis' "The Monster of Lake La Mettrie" (1899), Charles Derennes' *Le peuple du pôle* (1907), and Arthur Conan Doyle's *The Lost World* (1912).

Although the Verne and Doyle classics became significant models for imitation in boys' books and pulp adventure fiction, including numerous fantasies by Edgar Rice Burroughs, this tradition grew thinner as the twentieth century progressed, eventually receiving nostalgic treatment in Greg Bear's sequel to *The Lost World, Dinosaur Summer* (1998). Such survivals were, however, extensively featured in the "fringe science" of cryptozoology, marine species akin to dinosaurs being routinely cited as hypothetical explanations of mythical lake creatures like the Loch Ness monster, but the possibility that dinosaur numbers might one day increase again is rarely entertained; Terence Roberts' *Report on the Status Quo* (1955) treats the notion satirically. An enclave of Cretaceous dinosaurs in the Palaeolithic era is featured in Piers Anthony's *Orn* (1971).

When twentieth-century science fiction pressed the facilitating device of *time travel into use, the age of the dinosaurs became one of the standard destinations of time machines. The prospect of hunting dinosaurs exerted a particular fascination, reflected in Eden Phillpotts' "The Archdeacon and the Deinosaurs" (1901), Ray Bradbury's "A Sound of

Thunder" (1952), L. Sprague de Camp's "A Gun for Dinosaur" (1956) and its sequels, Brian W. Aldiss' "Poor Little Warrior!" (1958), and several novels by the French writer Henri Vernes, including *Les chasseurs de dinosaures* (1965; trans. as *The Dinosaur Hunters*). The imagery of the hunting party continued to crop up in such stories as David Drake's *Time Safari* (1982; rev as *Tyrannosaur*, 1994).

Other notable expeditions to the era are described in Pauline Ashwell's "The Wings of a Bat" (1966) and "Boneheads" (1996)—both by-lined Paul Ash— Steven Utley's "Getting Away" (1976), Harry Turtledove's "Hatching Season" (1985), Tim Sullivan's "Dinosaur on a Bicycle" (1987), Joseph H. Delaney's "Survival Course" (1989), Robert J. Sawyer's *End of an Era* (1994), Stephen Dedman's "Target of Opportunity" (1998), and Michael Swanwick's *Bones of the Earth* (2002). In Charles L. Harness's time travel fantasy "A Boost in Time" (2000), an asteroid diverter is used in an attempt to save the dinosaurs from extinction. John *Taine's *Before the Dawn* (1934) is painstakingly restrained in employing a technology that can merely see through time, while Robert Chilson's *The Shores of Kansas* (1976) features parapsychological exploration.

*Cinema, with its ready-made accommodation of impossibility, saw no need for such facilitating devices as time travel; the anachronistic representation of prehistoric men living alongside dinosaurs became so commonplace as to rate as a cliché, and one of the most glaring of all "scientific errors" in cinematic science fiction. D. W. Griffith's blithely absurd *Man's Genesis* (1912) was remade by Hal Roach as *One Million B.C.* (1940; aka *Man and His Mate* and *The Cave Dwellers*) and as a straightforward drama by Britain's Hammer films as *One Million Years B.C.* (1966), although the juxtaposition reverted to joke status thereafter, in such parodies as *A Nymphoid Barbarian in Dinosaur Hell* (1991) and a sequence of TV commercials for Volvic mineral water (2004–2005).

The notion of dinosaur "survivals" acquired a spectacular new variant when the possibility of "resurrecting" dinosaurs by *cloning their DNA was raised by L. Sprague de Camp in "Employment" (1939). An article by Charles Pellegrino prompted Michael Crichton to write *Jurassic Park* (1990), which was filmed by Steven Spielberg in 1993; other dramatisations of the notion include Gregory Benford's "Shakers of the Earth" (1992). Tiny dinosaurs had previously "synthesised" from bone fragments in Brian W. Aldiss' "The Tell-Tale Heart Machine" (1968). Other images of present-day dinosaurs include Allen Steele's "Trembling Earth" (1990).

The notion that dinosaur evolution might have continued had it not been for their catastrophic destruction, so that they rather than their mammal rivals became ancestral to an intelligent species, is elaborately explored in numerous exobiological fantasies and alternative prehistory stories, including Norman L. Knight's "Saurian Valedictory" (1939), Anne McCaffrey's *Dinosaur Planet* (1978), Damien Broderick's *The Dreaming Dragons* (1980), David F. Bischoff and Thomas F. Monteleone's series begun with *Day of the Dragonstar* (1983), Harry Harrison's series begun with *West of Eden* (1984), Ward Hawkins' *Red Star Burning* (1985), Barry B. Longyear's *The Homecoming* (1989), Robert J. *Sawyer's Quintaglio trilogy (1992–1994), James Kelly's "Think Like a Dinosaur" (1995), Ken MacLeod's *Cosmonaut Keep* (2000), Stephen Baxter's "The Hunters of Pangaea" (2002), and Kathleen Ann Goonan's "Dinosaur Songs" (2004).

The notion of alternative dinosaurs, including intelligent species, was extensively developed in Dougal Dixon's illustrated book *The New Dinosaurs: An Alternative Evolution* (1988). It achieved best-seller status in a similar format in James Gurney's *Dinotopia: A Land Apart from Time* (1993), in which dinosaur intelligence does not require any modification of the familiar forms. *Dinotopia*'s abundant spinoff included Gurney's own sequel *Dinotopia: The World Beneath* (1995), Alan Dean Foster's *Dinotopia Lost* (1996), and a TV miniseries (2002). In combination with a spinoff from *Jurassic Park*, such material constituted a significant fad, satirised in Ian McDowell's "Bernie" (1994) and in Richard Chwedyk's account of the marketing of cute miniaturised "saurs" in "The Measure of All Things" (2001) and its sequels.

DISASTER

A large-scale, life-threatening event. The innate appeal of *catastrophist explanations in science and the melodramatic imperative of popular fiction combined to generate a significant subgenre of disaster scenarios based on speculative premises. The first instinct of journalists engaged in scientific *reportage is to look for "disaster potential", thus helping to maintain the prevalence of the *Frankenstein complex in public attitudes to science. History provides abundant demonstration of the vulnerability of the human race to natural disasters, including plagues and various kinds of *meteorological catastrophes and *ecocatastrophes.

The myths of Europe and the Middle East frequently contain accounts of large-scale disaster, including several versions of the Deluge and the Fimbulwinter of Norse mythology. The notion that the world's predetermined end will be signaled by or manifest as a large-scale disaster is similarly incorporated into religion, with particularly strident resonance in Christianity; the incorporation into the Bible of the surreally melodramatic *Revelation of St. John the Divine* encouraged the repeated resurgence within Christendom of Millenarian cults avid for signs of disaster, and such prospects have always been treated with considerable ambivalence.

The notion that contemporary civilisation might be so badly affected by some such affliction that the legacy of thousands of years of technological and social progress might be lost increased in proportion to the progress actually made. The potential dangers were multiplied and magnified by the advancement of science; the discoveries of *geology revealed the extent to which the Earth's surface had been modified by vulcanism, earthquakes, and Ice Ages, while astronomical discoveries suggested that the planet might be struck by a *comet or an *asteroid, and that the Sun might some day go *nova. The popularisation of the notion that nineteenth-century Europe was in the throes of its cultural *decadence lent further emphasis to such anxieties.

Although Mary Shelley's *The Last Man* (1826) was part of a minor glut whose other components were poems, including Thomas Campbell's "The Last Man" (1823) and Thomas Hood's parodic "The Last Man" (1826), the great majority of nineteenth-century disaster novels featured limited and local events; several stories threatened worldwide disasters only to avert them, as in William Minto's *The Crack of Doom* (1886) and the first part of Camille Flammarion's *La fin du monde* (1894; trans. as *Omega; the Last Days of the World*).

The advent of scientific romance helped to overcome literary inhibitions regarding the representation of large-scale natural disaster. H. G. Wells' "The Star" (1897) and M. P. Shiel's *The Purple Cloud* (1901) provided high-profile precedents that were echoed in J. D. Beresford's "A Negligible Experiment" (ca. 1916) and Arthur Conan Doyle's *The Poison Belt* (1913). Grant Allen's "The Thames Valley Catastrophe" (1897) and Fred M. White's "The Four White Days" (1903) featured more localised phenomena. Accounts of man-made catastrophe made their debut with tales of suffocating smog, including W. D. Hay's *The Doom of the Great City* (1880) and Robert Barr's "The Doom of London" (1892). Such stories inevitably called to mind Biblical accounts of the Deluge, whose moral dimension was frequently reproduced in comments on their implications regarding the attitudes and mysterious ways of the deity. Disaster stories became a significant device for assaulting human hubris, as in such *contes philosophiques* as Valery Bryusov's *Respublika yuzhnavo kresta* (1905; trans. as "The Republic of the Southern Cross").

The notion that a civilisation-shattering disaster might have its upside took early root in British scientific romance in the wake of Richard Jefferies' *After London; or, Wild England* (1885). The notion that hubristic European civilisation deserved destruction became commonplace in the years of disenchantment following the end of World War I—a sentiment expressed in S. Fowler Wright's *Deluge* (1920), J. J. Connington's *Nordenholt's Million* (1923), Victor Bayley's *The Machine Stops* (1936, by-lined Wayland Smith), and Storm Jameson's *The World Ends* (1937, by-lined William Lamb) as well as countless future war stories, and postdisaster Romanticism flourished in such works as John Collier's *Tom's a-Cold* (1933).

This ambivalent tradition was extended in such satires as R. C. Sheriff's *The Hopkins Manuscript* (1939), such *contes philosophiques* as Gerald Heard's "The Great Fog" (1944), and such moral tales as H. de Vere Stacpoole's *The Story of My Village* (1947) and John Beresford's *A Common Enemy* (1941), eventually being carried forward by a glut of thrillers produced in the wake of John Wyndham's best-seller *The Day of the Triffids* (1951), including Wyndham's *The Kraken Wakes* (1953), John Boland's *White August* (1955), John Christopher's *The Death of Grass* (1956), and *The World in Winter* (1962) and various works by John Lymington and Charles Eric Maine. British "cosy catastrophe" stories entered a more clinical and cynical phase thereafter in such works as the early novels of J. G. *Ballard, Brian W. Aldiss' *Greybeard* (1964), Keith Roberts' *The Furies* (1966), and Richard Cowper's *The Twilight of Briareus* (1974), but still retained a crucial ambivalence, sustained into the twenty-first century in such works as Adam Roberts' *The Snow* (2004).

The American pulp magazines began to exploit the melodramatic potential of disaster fiction before the advent of specialist science fiction pulps, following such native precedents as Simon Newcomb's "The End of the World" (1903). Disaster stories remained standard fare in general fiction pulps long after more specialised motifs had been hived off into the genre magazine, including such blatantly science-fictional versions as Victor Rousseau's "World's End" (1933), Philip Wylie and Edwin Balmer's *When Worlds Collide* (1933) and *After Worlds Collide* (1934), and John Hawkins' "Ark of Fire" (1937).

Many such works—notably Jack London's *The Scarlet Plague* (1912; book, 1915)—represented the destruction of civilisation as a terrible tragedy, but some writers began to take considerable delight in imagining the apparatus of civilisation swept away. The heroes of such stories, liberated from the shackles of complex social organisation, became free to roam and tame the wilderness, recapitulating the exploits of

America's Western pioneers. Key examples of this kind of story include Garrett P. Serviss's *The Second Deluge* (1911), George Allan England's trilogy begun with *Darkness and Dawn* (1912), and Victor Rousseau's "Draft of Eternity" (1918; in book form as *Draught of Eternity*, by-lined H. M. Egbert). Romanticism of this stripe was combined with reactions against technological civilisation in such works as David H. Keller's "The Metal Doom" (1932).

This kind of romanticism never disappeared entirely from American fiction, but a sharper awareness gradually developed of the magnitude of the loss that might be suffered, and of the vulnerability of an intricately linked technological infrastructure to sudden breakdown. A marked ambivalence is reflected in such satires as Ward Moore's *Greener Than You Think* (1947) and Kurt Vonnegut's *Cat's Cradle* (1963). More earnest works, such as George R. Stewart's *Earth Abides* (1949), laid the groundwork for sophisticated disaster stories to become something of a literary fad in the 1970s. Thomas N. Scortia and Frank M. Robinson's best-selling exemplar *The Glass Inferno* (1974) demonstrated the cinematic potential of the subgenre when it was filmed as *The Towering Inferno* (1974).

The Towering Inferno was followed by a plethora of meticulous cinematic accounts of the effects of huge fires, violent storms, endangered aircraft, floods, volcanoes, earthquakes, and so forth, interwoven with accounts of ingenious attempts to mount holding actions against them. The popularity of such fictions assisted the proliferation of the *technothriller subgenre. The traditional lexicon of disasters was augmented in this period by tsunamis, as in Crawford Kilian's *Icequake* (1979) and *Tsunami* (1983) and oil spills, as in Kevin J. Anderson and Doug Beason's *Ill Wind* (1995). Beyond the borders of the United States, fears of more drastic inundation were manifest in such novels as Sakyo Komatsu's *Nippon Shinbotsu* (1973; trans. as *Japan Sinks*). Images of cosmic disaster grew more drastic in such novels as Fred and Geoffrey Hoyle's *The Inferno* (1973).

The disaster movie fad was extravagantly satirised in David Langford and John Grant *Earthdoom!* (1987), which paid particular attention to the manner in which further science-fictional motifs had drafted in to supply extra measures of drama in accounts of plagues and asteroid strikes. A more earnest version of a compound "ultimate disaster scenario" is featured in Greg Bear's *The Forge of God* (1987). Similar motifs supplemented the imagery of *atom bomb devastation in the development of the standardised backcloth of the ultraviolent perverted Romanticism of survivalist fiction. The most remarkable development of disaster fiction as the end of the century approached, however, was the proliferation of religious fantasies looking forward to the fulfillment of the prophecies of *Revelation*, as exemplified by Tim LaHaye and Jerry B. Jenkins' best-selling Left Behind series (1995–2003).

Assisted by this resurgence of religious propaganda, disaster fiction reached a new level of intensity as the year 2000 approached, much of it labeled "millennial fiction". Although the term "Millennium" had originally signified the thousand years for which Christ would reign following his (supposedly imminent) return, the passage of time had refocused attention on calendrical Millennia. A legend became widespread in Renaissance Europe that the approach of the year 1000 had been marked by civil unrest and other symptoms of chiliastic panic, and the approach of the year 2000 gave rise to anticipations of similar distress, which might perhaps arise as a result of self-fulfilling *prophecies. Such anticipations were effective in actuality as well as in fiction, giving rise to "Y2K" anxieties about the inability of computer software in which dates were plotted in two-digit form to cope with the "reversion" to 00. Fictional anticipations of more various adverse reactions included Russell Griffin's *Century's End* (1981) and John Kessel's *Good News from Outer Space* (1989).

The hard science fiction imagery of cosmic disaster was exaggerated in the 1990s in parallel with the imagery of religious apocalyptic fantasy, in such novels as Charles R. Pellegrino and George Zebrowski's *The Killing Star* (1995), although the most extreme exemplars were postponed to more-or-less distant futures in Greg Egan's *Diaspora* (1997), Wolf Read's "Spindown" (1998), and Stephen *Baxter and Arthur C. Clarke's Time's Odyssey diptych (2004–2005). The movie genre had grown stale by then, although new special effects allowed its increasing desperation to be displayed to spectacular effect in such movies as *The Day After Tomorrow* (2004).

DYSON, FREEMAN (JOHN) (1923–)

English-born physicist who became a U.S. citizen in 1957, associated with the Institute for Advanced Study at Princeton since 1953. His scientific endeavours included contributions to quantum theory but he became better known for his cosmological calculations regarding the possible fate of the universe, as elaborated in "Time Without End: Physics and Biology in an Open Universe" (1979), and his speculations regarding the eventual fate of humankind and its analogues within that context, which made him a key contributor to the development of *Omega Point theory. Corollary speculations about the future evolution of technology and his enthusiasm for the *SETI project led him to popularise the notion of a "Dyson sphere": a vast artifact surrounding a sun and harvesting all its radiant imagery.

Dyson initially discovered the idea that advanced civilisations might surround their primaries with "light traps" in Olaf *Stapledon's *Star Maker* (1937), but made it his own when he introduced the proposition into a brief paper on the possibility of locating extraterrestrial civilisations published in *Science* in 1960. He argued that the strategy of scanning G-type suns for radio broadcasts might be the seriously flawed, because authentically advanced civilisations might be associated with stars rendered invisible by the construction of such artifacts. In developing this notion he took up a suggestion by the Russian astronomer Nikolai Kardaschev that civilisations in the universe might be classifiable into three types. Type 1 civilisations would eventually control the resources of an entire planet, type 2 civilisations the resources of a star, and type 3 civilisations the resources of a galaxy. Although a type 1 civilisation—which humans might achieve within a few hundred years—would have to grow by a factor of several billion times to develop into a type 2 civilisation, Dyson calculated that a society with one percent economic growth could make the transition in twenty-five hundred years.

Although stars exploited by type 2 civilisations would be permanently eclipsed, they would not be astronomically undetectable; the second law of thermodynamics requires a civilisation exploiting the energy output of a star to radiate away a fraction of that energy as waste heat, so a type 2 civilisation would appear to Earthly astronomers as a powerful source of infrared radiation, probably in a band of wavelengths distributed around a mean of ten microns. Dyson's suggestion that SETI astronomers should attempt to pick up radio broadcasts from such infrared sources did not, however, produce any immediate evidence of the existence of type 2 civilisations. The fictional deployment of Dyson spheres often places them in the distant narrative background, as in Fritz Leiber's *The Wanderer* (1964) and Linda Nagata's *Deception Well* (1997), while accounts of discoveries made by space travellers often involve smaller structures such as Larry Niven's *Ringworld* (1970).

This tentativeness is partly due to the narrative inconvenience of artifacts of that scale, but also reflects a technical difficulty widely publicised in the wake of Edgar Rice Burroughs' hollow Earth stories: Gravity cannot anchor anything to the inner surface of a sphere. Although gravity could be simulated by rotation, the g-force inside a rotating sphere would vary from the poles to the equator, where the atmosphere would tend to collect. For this reason, the basic notion is carefully modified in various ways in hard science fiction stories featuring Dyson spheres and similar objects, such as Frederik Pohl and Jack Williamson's Cuckoo series (1975–1983), Bob Shaw's Orbitsville series (1975–1990), Tony Rothman's *The World Is Round* (1978), Somtow Sucharitkul's Inquestor series (1982–1985), Timothy Zahn's *Spinneret* (1985), James White's *Federation World* (1988), Stephen Baxter's *The Time Ships* (1995), David Brin's *Heaven's Reach* (1998), and Peter F. Hamilton's *Pandora's Star* (2004).

Speculative engineers have made similar suggestions for the modification of Dyson's basic design; Dan Alderson proposed that a double sphere, consisting of two shells with an atmosphere enclosed between them, might be much more convenient than a single sphere. Alternatively, a disk shaped like a gramophone record—with the sun in the central hole—extending as far as the orbit of Mars or Jupiter might be more useful. The possibility of enclosing a sun or an artificial "starlet" with a whole series of connected concentric spheres is broached in Colin Kapp's Cageworld series (1982–1983) and Brian Stableford's Asgard trilogy (1979–1990). Pat Gunkel recommended that the first step in the evolution of an appropriate megastructure might be the construction of an ever-extending "topopolis" shaped like a hollow strand of macaroni, carefully looped around the sun, which might be gradually built up into a complex space-enclosing sphere. Dyson is the model for a key character in Gregory Benford's *Eater* (2000).

DYSTOPIA

A term used—and perhaps coined—by John Stuart Mill in 1868 as an antonym of *Utopia, tacitly construing the latter term as "eutopia" (good place), rather than "outopia" (no place), as Thomas More originally intended. Dystopian speculation describes hypothetical societies that are considerably worse than our own, tending towards the worst imaginable, although that extreme is hardly ever attained.

Although very many societies described in *satires are dystopian, the term is usually applied to relatively earnest images of futures in which political totalitarianism, economic ruthlessness, and/or the impetus of *technological determinism have had unfortunate consequences. Émile Souvestre's *Le monde tel qu'il sera* (1846; trans. as *The World as It Shall Be*) established the pattern in France, where it was further developed by Paschal Grousset and Jules Verne in the description of Stahlstadt in *Les cinq cents millions de la bégum* (1879: trans. as *The Begum's Fortune*). H. C. Marriott Watson's *Erchomenon* (1879), Walter

Besant's *The Inner House* (1888), and Ignatius Donnelly's *Caesar's Column* (1890) provided significant precedents in England and the United States.

Notable anti-Capitalist dystopias include Jack London's "The Iron Heel" (1907) and Claude Farrère's *Les condamnés à mort* (1920; trans. as *Useless Hands*), while notable anti-Socialist dystopias include Conde B. Pallen's *Crucible Island* (1919), John Kendall's *Unborn Tomorrow* (1933), and Ayn Rand's *Anthem* (1938). Anti-Fascist dystopias include Joseph O'Neill's *Land Under England* (1935), Sinclair Lewis' *It Can't Happen Here* (1935), and Murray Constantine's *Swastika Night* (1937). Extreme examples on both sides of the political spectrum often refer to a literal and metaphorical *automation of society, as in Owen Gregory's *Meccania* (1918) and J. D. Beresford and Esmé Wynne-Tyson's *The Riddle of the Tower* (1944); the latter also employs the imagery of the ant hive, which is widely invoked as a paradigm of dystopian organisation.

Notions of *decadence associated with excessive dependence on technology—exemplified by E. M. Forster's "The Machine Stops" (1909), Laurence Manning and Fletcher Pratt's "City of the Living Dead" (1930), and John W. Campbell Jr.'s "Twilight" (1934)—became increasingly important in dystopian fiction as anxieties regarding technological development gradually overtook and partially eclipsed twentieth-century political disputes. Bertrand *Russell's judgment, in *Icarus, or the Future of Science* (1924), that scientific progress was bound to make the world a worse place to live in, because it would allow society's power groups to oppress others more effectively, was echoed in many other works.

Egevny Zamyatin's *We* (1920; trans. 1924) provided an early exemplar of this kind of dystopia extrapolated to its logical extreme, in which political leaders employ all kinds of social and mechanical technology to secure absolute authority. The scrupulously modest development of the same thesis in George Orwell's *Nineteen Eighty-Four* (1949) made that novel a leading contributor of imagery to popular and political rhetoric. Aldous *Huxley's black comedy *Brave New World* (1932) argued on similar lines that technology would corrode the most valuable aspects of human life even in the hands of the most benevolent leaders. S. Fowler Wright's *The New Gods Lead* (1932) offered a similarly scathing indictment of the values of technocracy and the perversity of the "Utopia of comforts".

Although such suspicion contrasted strongly with Hugo *Gernsback's optimistic celebration of a coming "Age of Power Freedom", it became widespread in early pulp science fiction, starkly manifest in the antitechnological parables of David H. Keller. John

*Campbell encouraged the contributors to his *Astounding Science Fiction* to respond to this creeping anxiety with accounts of technically ingenious heroic rebellion against science-suppressing and science-monopolising dystopias, including Robert A. Heinlein's "If This Goes On..." (1940) and *Sixth Column* (1941; book, 1949), Fritz Leiber's *Gather, Darkness!* (1943; book, 1950), and Raymond F. Jones' *Renaissance* (1944; book, 1951). In the science fiction magazines of the 1950s, this formula became more refined and increasingly stylised, producing a glut of dystopian novels in which various organisations dominate society with the aid of technologically sophisticated means of persuasion, shaping it to their special interests.

The archetype of this subspecies is *The Space Merchants* (1953) by Frederik Pohl and C. M. Kornbluth, in which the power of advertising is fully mobilised; other notable examples include Damon Knight's *Hell's Pavement* (1955; aka *Analogue Men*) and James Gunn's mosaic *The Joy Makers* (1955; book, 1961). In the most impressive item of dystopian science fiction produced in the course of this flood, Ray Bradbury's *Fahrenheit 451* (1953), the state becomes the enemy of refined thought and emotion, elevating book burning to the status of a profession—but the focal point of heroic resistance in Bradbury's account is the preservation of literary appreciation rather than scientific thought.

Although the depth of its anguish was anticipated in a more conspicuously sarcastic fashion in Aldous Huxley's *Ape and Essence* (1948), Orwell's *Nineteen Eighty-Four* became the model for much subsequent fiction in which the future is imagined—as Orwell's O'Brien imagined it—as a metaphorical boot stamping on a human face forever, simply because it can. The adjective "Orwellian" was adapted to describe such works as Gerald Heard's *Doppelgangers* (1947), Bernard Wolfe's *Limbo* (1952), Evelyn Waugh's *Love Among the Ruins* (1953), David Karp's *One* (1953), L. P. Hartley's *Facial Justice* (1960), Anthony Burgess' *A Clockwork Orange* (1962), Michael Frayn's *A Very Private Life* (1968), and Ira Levin's *This Perfect Day* (1970), which seemed too surreal to qualify as straightforward political fantasies, although such hard-edged novels as Arthur Koestler's *The Age of Longing* (1951), Adrian Mitchell's *The Bodyguard* (1970), and Arthur Herzog's *Make Us Happy* (1978) kept Orwell's preoccupation with the advent of a quintessentially modern totalitarianism in much clearer focus.

As the Cold War's long winter settled in, the depiction of scientists and technologists as compliant civil servants—obediently following political instructions while comfortably alienated from the ultimate products of their labor—became a staple item of dystopian imagery, further reflected in a great deal of thriller fiction. It was especially prominent in the spy story subgenre, for which the Cold War provided an ideal context. The nuclear alarmism of the 1950s and early 1960s had not yet begun to wear thin when dystopian tendencies in futuristic fiction were further reinvigorated by a new wave of anxieties regarding the probable effects of the *population explosion and its attendant environmental *pollution, as expressed in such novels as Harry Harrison's *Make Room! Make Room!* (1966), John Brunner's *Stand on Zanzibar* (1968) and *The Sheep Look Up* (1972), Robert Silverberg's *The World Inside* (1971), Andrew J. Offutt's *The Castle Keeps* (1972), and Philip Wylie's *The End of the Dream* (1972).

The hysterical tone of such works, laid atop the existing stratum of Cold War disenchantment, was reflected in such dystopian *sociological analyses of the contemporary situation as Alvin Toffler's *Future Shock* (1970), which proposed that the sheer pace of technological change and its social effects threatened to make everyday life unendurable even in the absence of an *ecocatastrophic collapse—a prospect featured in such downbeat anticipations as Thomas M. Disch's *334* (1972). The advent of *computers in the 1970s added to such anxieties—inevitably, given

the tenor of previous science fiction stories about ruthlessly despotic giant computers.

The increasing urgency of feminism in the same decade gave rise to its own flood of dystopian imagery, in images of oppressive masculinity run wild such as those contained in Suzy McKee Charnas' *Walk to the End of the World* (1974) and Margaret Atwood's *The Handmaid's Tale* (1985). By the end of the twentieth century, the sum of all of these fears had ensured that the dominant question of near-futuristic fiction was not whether it might settle into an undesirable political configuration, stabilised by the oppressive use of new technologies, but whether *civilisation could survive at all as the reserves of fossil fuels sustaining the global economy began to dwindle rapidly, leaving an overcrowded world drowning in its own wastes subject to the slow or sudden onset of a Hobbesian war of all against all. As the twenty-first century began, almost all fictional images of the near future were permeated with dystopian imagery; even the traditional optimism of *futurology found it increasingly difficult to mount any kind of defense against the seeming inevitability of the fact that the world was bound to get a lot worse before it could possibly begin to get better.

E

EARTH

One of the four Classical *elements, whose establishment by Aristotelian cosmology as the bedrock of creation led to the term's eventual use as the name of the planet on whose surface humankind evolved. The notion of earth as an element retreated to the realm of metaphor as science advanced, but the term retained a crucial defiant ambiguity that identified the world as a whole with the soil in which its land-based plants—its "primary producers"—are rooted. Such phrases as "Mother Earth" continue to retain their mythic resonance.

Archimedes and Eratosthenes established that the Earth's surface was curved into a sphere in 200 B.C. or thereabouts, but the opinion that it was a flat disk—popularised by the Bible-based flat-earth *geography of Cosmas' *Topographia Christiana*—still retained some support in the Renaissance. Classical arguments regarding the shape of the Earth are dramatised in Charles L. Harness' "Summer Solstice" (1984), which features an argument between Eratosthenes and Ptolemy. The planet is depicted as a sphere in most diagrammatic representations of the geocentric *cosmology—it is thus represented in the thirteenth-century French poem *Ymage du Monde* and in Dante Alighieri's fourteenth-century *Divina Commedia*, which locates the mountain of Purgatory at the antipodes—but the opposite opinion retained some support until the sophistication of *cartography in the service of navigation established the roundness of the world beyond reasonable doubt.

Opinions also varied in the Renaissance as to what lay beneath the Earth's surface. The interior of the Earth had been the location of the Classical Underworld, and it became the site of the circles of Hell in Dante's *Inferno*. The notion of a hollow interior continued to echo long thereafter. Athanasius Kircher's *Mundus subterraneus* (1665) envisaged an intricate system of cavities and a channel of water connecting the poles—an image reflected in numerous works of fiction, including the anonymous *A Voyage to the World in the Centre of the Earth* (1755) and *Le passage du pôle arctique au pôle antarctique* (1780), Robert-Martin Lesuire's *L'aventurier français* (1782), Giacomo Casanova's *Icosameron* (1788), Jacques Collin de Plancy's *Voyage au centre de la terre* (1821), and Jules Verne's *Voyage au centre de la terre* (1863; trans. as *Journey to the Centre of the Earth*).

Kircher's model was complicated by Edmond Halley's attempt in "A Theory of Magnetic Variations" (1692) to explain variations in *magnetic north by means of the hypothesis that the Earth's interior was made up of a system of concentric spheres. Reproduced by Cotton Mather in *The Christian Philosopher* (1721), Halley's model became the ancestor of John Cleve Symmes' theory of the hollow Earth, popularised in his *Circular Number 1* (1818) and satirised in the pseudonymous *Symzonia* (1820, by-lined Adam Seaborn). Symmes called on Humphry Davy and Alexander von Humboldt to mount an expedition into the Earth to prove the thesis, but if they ever heard the call they declined. Humboldt's

Kosmos (1848) preferred a near-contemporary model proposed by the Scottish natural philosopher John Leslie, which represented Earth as a hollow sphere filled with a kind of "imponderable matter" whose pressure inflated it like a balloon, containing two radiant bodies—Pluto and Proserpine—that rotated like a binary star system. The Swiss mathematician Leonhard Euler proposed a similar model with a singular "internal sun".

Euler's model was reminiscent of the image of the world's interior contained in Ludwig Holberg's *Nicolaii Klimii Iter Subterraneum* (1741; trans. as *A Journey to the World Underground by Nicholas Klimius*)—in which the central sun has its own family of planets—and variants of it continued to recur in imaginative fiction, most famously in Edgar Rice Burroughs' representation of Pellucidar, although American writers tended to confuse the citation, often attributing the Leslie/Euler model to Symmes. This was because Symmes' propagandising had attracted the attention of a number of writers interested in the thesis—common to Kircher, Halley, and Symmes—that there was an opening at the pole giving access to the Earth's interior. Edgar Allan *Poe's *Narrative of Arthur Gordon Pym* (1838) is the best-known work employing the idea; notable variants include George Sand's *Laura: voyage dans le cristal* (1865; trans. as *Journey Within the Crystal*), Clara Holmes' "Nordhung Nordjansen" (1898), George Griffith's "From Pole to Pole" (1904), and Vladimir Obruchev's *Plutoniya* (1924; trans. as *Plutonia*).

The Leslie/Euler model of the Earth's interior continued to attract such twentieth-century adherents as Karl Neupert, Marshall B. Gardner, and Raymond Bernard, while Burroughs' influence ensured that hollow Earth stories remained popular in the pulp magazines—A. Hyatt Verrill's "The Inner World" (1935) is a notable example—in spite of his failure to realise that gravitational attraction would pull towards the central sun rather than the inner surface. Rudy Rucker's *steampunk novel *The Hollow Earth* (1990), which features Poe as a character, brought the idea ingeniously up to date. In the meantime, geological and seismological investigations suggested that the Earth's crust sat atop a fluid mantle and a hot, dense iron core. Although it was a good deal less useful for writers of Utopian or action-adventure fiction, this model still permitted accounts of future retreats from the surface as it became inhabitable because of the cooling of the Sun; notable examples include Gabriel Tarde's *Fragment d'histoire future* (1896; trans. as *Underground Man*), John and Ruth Vassos' *Ultimo* (1930), and R. F. Starzl's "If the Sun Died" (1931). Notable accounts of burrowing expeditions into the kind of Earth imagined by modern geology include G. N. Howard's "Depth" (1946), Paul A. Carter's "The Last Objective" (1946), Harry Harrison's "Rock Diver" (1951), Paul Preuss' *Core* (1993), and Nelson Bond's "Proof of the Pudding" (1999).

Flat Earths are much rarer in fiction than hollow ones, save for calculatedly perverse texts like S. Fowler Wright's *Beyond the Rim* (1932) and Richard A. Lupoff's *Circumpolar* (1984), but a stubborn minority of independent thinkers maintained a Flat Earth Society throughout the twentieth century, descended from the nineteenth-century Zetetic Society whose views were outlined in Samuel Birley Rowbotham's *Zetetic Astronomy* (1849). The Universal Zetetic Society was renamed by Samuel Shenton in 1956 and passed into the care of Charles K. Johnson in 1971; its Internet home page bears the proud legend "Deprogramming the Masses since 1547". Other unorthodox models—including the depiction of the Earth as the inner surface of a hollow sphere, as in Alfred William Lawson's *Lawsonomy* (1935–1939)—have excited even less literary interest, although the quasi-Aristotelian notion that the planet is surrounded by a solid transparent shell lingered in such exotic romances as Charles W. Diffin's "Land of the Lost" (1933–1934) and William Lemkin's "Beyond the Stratosphere" (1936).

A planet is too large, and its lifetime too long, to be comfortably accommodated within fiction as a topic in its own right, although that has not prevented the production of such panoramic overviews of Earth as those contained in Camille Flammarion's *Lumen* (1866–1869) and David Brin's *Earth* (1990). The development of global economic and *ecological worldviews greatly assisted such holistic thinking, encouraging the growth of such notions as Pierre Teilhard de Chardin's noösphere, evolving towards its *Omega Point, and James *Lovelock's Gaia hypothesis. It is sometimes argued that a significant perceptual threshold was crossed when photography was able to frame the entire Earth for the first time, in pictures taken from space; reproductions of such images of a cloud-strewn "blue planet" became very widespread in the late twentieth century.

The sheer size of the Earth also inhibits speculative accounts of attempts to modify its gross structure technologically, although attempts to straighten its wobbly rotation are featured in John Jacob Astor's *A Journey in Other Worlds* (1894) and William Wallace Cook's "Tales of Twenty Hundred" (1911–1912), and its tilt is further increased in Nathan Schachner's "Earthspin" (1937). Successful attempts to move it from its orbit are much more common, as featured in Homer Eon Flint's "The Planeteer" (1918), Neil Bell's *The Seventh Bowl* (1930; by-lined

Miles), and Edmond Hamilton's "Thundering Worlds" (1934), but later versions of the notion usually involve extraterrestrial agencies, as in Fritz Leiber's "A Pail of Air" (1951), Frederik Pohl and C. M. Kornbluth's *Wolfbane* (1957), and Roger McBride Allen's *The Ring of Charon* (1990).

Accounts of the ultimate fate of the Earth are usually dressed in ostentatious mourning, as displayed in George C. Wallis' "The Last Days of Earth" (1901) and Edmond Hamilton's "Requiem" (1962), although the latter's depiction of the event as a cynically marketed tourist attraction is rerun as slapstick comedy in Douglas Adams' "The Restaurant at the End of the Universe" (1980). Frank Belknap Long's "The Blue Earthman" (1935) depicts a far-future Earth tide-locked to the Sun and spiraling ever closer, while Brian W. Aldiss' *Hothouse* (1962) offers a conspicuously *decadent image of a far-future Earth tide-locked to the Moon and bound to it by giant cobwebs. However, science fiction writers often look back at the Earth from a distant *Space Age perspective in which Earth is merely one insignificant inhabited world among a multitude.

The Space Age perspective is taken to extremes in accounts of galactic empires in which the name has become legendary and the planet itself has been lost, as in Isaac Asimov's Foundation series and E. C. Tubb's Dumarest series. Such treatments are unaffected by the fact that science fiction writers often refer to planet Earth as "Terra"—or, if they are better Latinists, as "Tellus". Asimov's model of the galactic empire, which became the conventional framework of late twentieth-century science fiction, represents the galaxy as a cornucopia of Earth-clones, thus reproducing the imagery of early debates regarding the possible *plurality of worlds, save for the fact that the Earths in question have been populated by *colonisation rather than creation. James Blish's "Earthman, Come Home" (1953) encapsulates this worldview in its concluding line: "Earth isn't a place. It's an idea".

ECOCATASTROPHE

A term popularised by Paul Ehrlich, who used it in 1969 as the title of a futurological narrative summarising the anxieties about the threat of *population explosion and its corollary problems of resource management and environmental *pollution, as previously expressed in *The Population Bomb* (1968). Alvin Toffler's *Ecospasm* (1975) offered an alternative term, while Mark Budz's *Clade* (2003) and *Crache* (2004) refer to an "ecocaust". It was gradually realised that numerous cultures of the past must have suffered ecocatastrophic destruction, usually due to the deforestation of habitable enclaves such as the islands of Polynesia and the desert-trapped region in the southern United States, where the Anasazi ruins remain. Political "environmentalism" based on the notion that industrial civilisation might prove to be self-destructive, and thus fearful of the possibility of ecocatastrophe, first became evident in embryo in the nineteenth century, in such texts as Henry David Thoreau's *Walden* (1854) and George Perkins Marsh's *Man and Nature* (1864).

Robert Malthus' *Essay on Population* (1803) anticipates an enduring situation of strife and stress rather than a catastrophic reversal of progress, but catastrophist future imagery gradually became more evident in such texts as W. D. Hay's *The Doom of the Great City* (1880) and Richard Jefferies' *After London; or, Wild England* (1885). When the evolution of *ecology provided a firmer scientific framework for such anxieties, a clearer view was obtained of possible causal sequences that might precipitate ecocatastrophe. J. D. Beresford's "The Man Who Hated Flies" (1929) is an early "ecological parable" about the inventor of a perfect insecticide, whose annihilation of insect populations disrupts processes of pollination, thus precipitating massive crop failures and threatening the extinction of humankind. John Russell Fearn's "The Man Who Stopped the Dust" (1934; exp. as *Annihilation*, 1950) is a similar account of man-made ecocatastrophe. The future history mapped out in Laurence Manning's *The Man Who Awoke* (1933; book, 1975) includes an ecologically hyperconscious society in recovery from the self-destructive profligacy of the "Age of Waste".

The potential exhaustion of soil's crop-bearing capacities was dramatised in the United States by the emergence of the Midwestern Dust Bowl—popularised by such books as Stuart Chase's *Rich Land, Poor Land* (1936)—and received considerable literary attention in the works of such writers as John Steinbeck. These anxieties were extrapolated in pulp science fiction by such stories as Nathan Schachner's "Sterile Planet" (1937) and Willard E. Hawkins' "The Dwindling Sphere" (1940). British futuristic fantasies foregrounding the problem include A. G. Street's *Already Walks Tomorrow* (1938) and Edward Hyams' *The Astrologer* (1950). The vulnerability of humankind's agricultural base was satirically dramatised in Ward Moore's *Greener Than You Think* (1947), in which a single species of grass displaces all other plant life, while John Christopher's *The Death of Grass* (1956) provides an earnest description of an ecocatastrophe precipitated by a grain blight that destroys the world's staple crops.

Anxieties of this kind increased dramatically when Malthusian arguments resurfaced in the mid-1950s and the self-appointed Population Council became a significant disseminator of propaganda regarding the dangerous rapidity of world population growth. The scope of the arguments was rapidly broadened to take in the exhaustibility of other resources than food—especially oil—and the hazards of environmental pollution. Garrett Hardin, editor of *Population, Evolution, and Birth Control: A Collage of Controversial Ideas* (1964), sketched out a new discipline of "ecological economics" in a classic essay, "The Tragedy of the Commons" (1968), arguing that the fundamental logic of capitalism, as exemplified by the workings of Adam Smith's "invisible hand", was bound to lead to ecological devastation in the absence of powerful moral restraint.

After the publication of Rachel Carson's *Silent Spring* (1962), which argued that the use of such pesticides as DDT threatened ecocatastrophe because nonbiodegradable organic compounds accumulated in the tissues of higher animals, the environmental protection movement made considerable progress in the United States. Its concerns were stridently expressed in such texts as Richard Lillard's *Eden in Jeopardy: Man's Prodigal Meddling with His Environment* (1966) and *The Environmental Handbook* (1970), edited by Garett de Bell. Richard Nixon created an Environmental Protection Agency in 1970, although its political battles against proponents of economic growth were hard fought and largely unsuccessful.

The possibility of ecocatastrophe became a significant topic of political discourse, reflected in such texts as J. Clarence Davis' *The Politics of Pollution* (1970) and James Ridgeway's *The Politics of Ecology* (1971). Green Parties were founded in many European countries, linked to such pressure groups as Friends of the Earth (founded 1969) and Greenpeace (launched 1971). These developments were reflected in speculative fiction in such images of worldwide ecocatastrophe as James Blish's "We All Die Naked" (1969), John Brunner's *The Sheep Look Up* (1972), Philip Wylie's *The End of the Dream* (1972), and William Jon Watkins and Gene Snyder's *Ecodeath* (1972). The British TV series *Doomwatch* (1970–1972), originated by Kit Pedler and Gerry Davis, helped to export such anxieties to a wider audience. Accounts of ecocatastrophes precipitated by the inexorably spreading effects of singular causes became commonplace; notable examples include Zach Hughes' *Tide* (1974) and Chelsea Quinn Yarbro's *False Dawn* (1978). A sense of inevitability also haunts such accounts of attempted response as Cary Neeper's *A Place Beyond Man* (1975).

Discussion of the scientific bases of ecocatastrophic alarmism became increasingly heated as opposition to environmentalism took form and environmentalists responded, usually by hardening their views. Barry Commoner objected to Paul Ehrlich's "neo-Malthusianism" and Garrett Hardin's "ecological Hobbesianism" in *The Closing Circle: Man, Nature and Technology* (1971), but his own arguments about the "debt to nature" incurred by the "mythology" of wealth creation also tended to the apocalyptic. The argument was further amplified by such works as Angus Martin's *The Last Generation: The End of Survival?* (1975) and Jonathan Schell's *The Fate of the Earth* (1982). The latter added the *greenhouse effect and the depletion of the Earth's ozone layer to the ecocatastrophic mix—a supplementation reflected in Trevor Hoyle's *The Last Gasp* (1983), Paul Theroux's *O-Zone* (1986), Whitley Strieber and James Kunetka's *Nature's End* (1986), George Turner's *The Sea and Summer* (1987), David Brin's *Earth* (1990), and Michael Tobias' *Fatal Exposure* (1991).

Ecocastastrophic incidents in the actual world, though limited in scope, began to attract widespread attention. The oil spill generated by the *Torrey Canyon* in 1967 generated more surprise than alarm, but the *Exxon Valdez* disaster in 1989 was widely seen as symptomatic of a deep-seated malaise—a sensibility that gave rise to such disaster stories as Kevin J. Anderson and Doug Beason's *Ill Wind* (1995). The subgenre of post-holocaust fantasies, long dominated by the *atom bomb, increasingly took aboard post-ecocatastrophe scenarios such as the one described in Ian R. MacLeod's *The Great Wheel* (1998), while technothrillers began to make more of the notion of ecological sabotage and "ecoterrorism", as featured in such stories as Paul Di Filippo's "Up the Lazy River" (1993), Rebecca Ore's *Gaia's Toys* (1995), Thomas A. Easton's *Firefight* (2003), and Catherine Wells' "Point of Origin" (2005). Charles R. Pellegrino's apocalyptic fantasy *Dust* (1998) describes an unfolding ecocatastrophe precipitated by the mass extinction of insects.

Feverish alarmism was only one facet of the literary response to the perception of impending ecocrisis, but relatively few fiction writers echoed the more optimistic note of such anticatastrophist works as Murray Bookchin's *Towards an Ecological Society* (1980) or Fritjof Capra and Catherine Spretnak's *Green Politics: The Global Promise* (1984), reflected in such fictional images of future environmentalism as Alex Irvine's "Elegy for a Greenwiper" (2001). The imperatives of melodrama combined well with a general disenchantment with political short-termism, reinforced by the disintegration of the myth of the *Space Age and its corollary exit strategy of cosmic breakout. As the twenty-first century began, the vast majority of science-fictional images of the future took it for granted that the ecocatastrophe was not only under way but already irreversible, and that the backlash against environmentalism in the U.S. political arena was a manifestation of psychological denial—although Michael Crichton's *State of Fear* (2004) raised the banner of a defiant rearguard action, representing environmentalists as members of a global conspiracy intent on disrupting economic progress.

ECOLOGY

A term coined by Ernst Haeckel in 1866, referring to the study of organisms in relation to the physical components of the environment and the other organisms with which they share it. It was rarely used until the end of the century, when botanists began to consider the physical distribution of plants in the context of Darwinian evolutionary theory. The Ecological Society of America was founded in 1915, bringing botanists and zoologists together with soil scientists, agriculturalists, and other interested parties. Charles Elton's *Animal Ecology* (1927) was a landmark work, stressing the significance of "food chains" extending from "primary producers" that fix solar energy through a series of strata comprising herbivores, predators, and parasites, according to a pattern often called "the Eltonian pyramid" because the biomass of each layer is less than the one underlying it.

Ecological perspectives are vital to such hypothetical sciences as *exobiology and such notions as *terraforming as well as to alarmist fears relating to *population growth and *pollution, so they make up a powerful and broad framework in modern speculative thought. An acute awareness of human dependence on the natural environment developed long before the emergence of scientific ecology as an inevitable corollary of agricultural endeavour. Early *anthropologists observed that the primary purpose of practical magic and religious ritual in preliterate agrarian societies was to attempt to ensure bountiful harvests and success in hunting. Like other sciences descendant from religious and magical practices, the discipline is still fringed by pseudoscientific notions that may be grouped under the heading of "ecological mysticism", which tend to exaggerate the "balance" and "harmony" of *Nature. It was often suggested in the nineteenth century that the agricultural and technological aspects of the Industrial Revolution had resulted in a significant *alienation of modern humankind from Nature, a notion extravagantly displayed in W. H. Hudson's *A Crystal Age* (1887) and *Green Mansions* (1902). The latter text—a *Rousseauesque response to Joseph Conrad's *Heart of Darkness* (1902)—proposes that the horrific core of human

nature derives from the fact that all extant cultures, no matter how "primitive" or "advanced" they may be, have forsaken an intimate bond with the nurturing aspects of Mother *Earth.

Physical environments are considerably modified by the side effects of the food chains to which they are host; on the largest scale of all—the ecosphere—the atmospheric oxygen on which all respiration depends is a product of photosynthesis by plants and algae. Food chains are the context in which *Darwinian natural selection occurs, so *evolution is a prolific producer of organisms that enhance their reproductive fortunes by exploiting the feeding habits of other organisms; many plants produce nectar that recruits insects to serve as pollen disseminators, and seeds with edible packaging for distribution by the animals they feed. Such "symbiotic" patterns of mutual dependency further augment the complexity and intricacy of ecosystems.

Symbiosis—along with predation and parasitism, which lend themselves very well to social analogy and the creation of *monsters—is one of the ecological relationships of most obvious interest to the literary imagination, ingeniously extrapolated in numerous ecological puzzle stories, including Walt and Leigh Richmond's "Cows Can't Eat Grass" (1967). The manner in which native ecosystems could be disrupted by invaders was demonstrated by many actual cases of reckless importation, especially into Pacific islands and Australia—a theme extrapolated in such science fiction stories as Robert Abernathy's "Pyramid" (1954). Other *contes philosophiques* founded in ecological notions include Herbert L. Cooper's "A Nice Little Niche" (1955) and Robert Chilson's "Excelsior!" (1970) and "Ecological Niche" (1970).

A new kind of ecological mysticism was pioneered by C. S. Lewis's religious fantasy *Out of the Silent Planet* (1938), in which the harmony of the Martian ecosphere is ensured by active involvement of a spiritual overseer. Pierre Teilhard de Chardin had already worked out an evolutionary schema in which the destiny of the ecosphere was to fall increasingly under the sway of a superimposed "noösphere" until a harmonious integration was achieved at an *Omega Point, but the notion had to await posthumous publication in 1955. Secularised versions of similar notions were gradually integrated into the *exobiological descriptions of pulp science fiction during the 1930s, acquiring new levels of sophistication in the work of Clifford D. *Simak, whose celebrations of the pastoral first became mystically infused in the series begun with "City" (1944). Simak followed Lewis and Teilhard into the transfiguration of religious imagery in *Time and Again* (1951), where alien "symbiotes" provide stand-ins for souls and the raw material of potential noöspheres.

Godlike intelligences manifest within sentient ecospheres were also featured in such science fiction stories as Murray Leinster's "The Lonely Planet" (1949) and A. E. van Vogt's "Process" (1950), which spearheaded a remarkable resurgence of ecological mysticism in science fiction of the late 1950s and 1960s, when would-be *colonists were frequently humiliated by the belated discovery of sophisticated ecosystems blessed with quasi-supernatural harmony. Notable examples include Richard McKenna's "The Night of Hoggy Darn" (1958; revised as "Hunter Come Home", 1963), Robert F. Young's "To Fell a Tree" (1959), Mark Clifton's *Eight Keys to Eden* (1960), and Kris Neville's "The Forest of Zil" (1967). Images of symbiosis—imported into genre science fiction by such stories as Eric Frank Russell's "Symbiotica" (1943) and Will F. Jenkins' "Symbiosis" (1947)—took on extensive quasi-supernatural connotations, often sternly opposed to metaphors of vampirism and possession. Fictions of this kind included explicit ideological replies to earlier works—notably Ted White's *By Furies Possessed* (1970), which attacks the tacit xenophobia of Robert A. Heinlein's *The Puppet Masters* (1951). Symbiosis became a central element of ecological mysticism in such works as Sydney van Scyoc's Daughters of the Sunstone trilogy (1982–1984). The more ambivalent view of human/alien commensalism adopted in Octavia Butler's *Clay's Ark* (1984) and the first part of Dan Simmons' *Hyperion* (1989) undercut this modern sensibility while continuing to trade on it.

The remystification of ecological relationships is reflected in two of the best-selling science fiction novels of the 1960s, both of which took the form of messianic fantasies focusing on the reverent ritualisation of water relations: Robert A. Heinlein's *Stranger in a Strange Land* (1961) and Frank Herbert's *Dune* (1965). Piers Anthony's *Omnivore* (1968) and its sequels transformed the fundamental pattern of ecological relationships into a mystical trinity, while Herbert's *The Green Brain* (1966) described an active revolt of intelligent nature against the ecological heresies of humankind. The notion of fully integrated ecosystems—often extending to ecospheric dimensions—became very popular, as reflected in such stories as Stanislaw Lem's *Edem* (1959; trans. as *Eden*), James H. Schmitz's "Balanced Ecology" (1965), Arkady and Boris Strugatsky's *Ulitka na sklone* (1966–1968; trans. as *The Snail on the Slope*), Ursula K. Le Guin's "Vaster Than Empires and More Slow" (1971), Neal Barrett's *Highwood* (1972), Gordon R. Dickson's "Twig" (1974), Doris Piserchia's *Earthchild* (1977), and M. A. Foster's *Waves* (1980).

A similar upsurge of ecological mysticism occurred within the environmentalist movement, most conspicuously represented by the Findhorn Foundation, inaugurated in 1962 and named for a bay on the East Coast of Scotland where its first experimental Utopian community was based. The Findhorn community was tolerant of a wide range of ideologies, provided that they included the assumption of an "intelligent nature" in which God is incarnate and everpresent. The theoretical framework of ecology began to broaden to signify a worldview rather than a mere branch of science. Gregory Bateson's "Steps Towards an Ecology of Mind" (1972) proposed that the essential "holism" of the ecological perspective was appropriate to the study of mental as well as biological phenomena. Arne Naess' "The Shallow and the Deep: Long Range Ecology Movement" (1973) proposed a wide-ranging pursuit of "ecocentric wisdom", whose ambitions were resummarised in *Ecology, Community, and Lifestyle: Outline of an Ecosophy* (1989).

The idea that life on Earth could be viewed in terms of "intelligent nature", first advanced as a scientific proposition by Vladimir Vernadsky in *The Biosphere* (1926; trans. 1986), made a spectacular comeback in James *Lovelock's *Gaia: A New Look at Life on Earth* (1973). Although not mystical in itself, the language in which the Gaia hypothesis was couched lent tremendous encouragement to those who desired to construe it as if it were, so Lovelock's tentative assertion that the ecosphere could, in some respects, be usefully viewed *as if* it were a single organism was routinely extrapolated into a literal personification. The notion was rapidly fed back into science fiction in such works as John Varley's Titan trilogy (1979–1984), whose sentient superorganism is named Gaea. The more explicit versions of ecological mysticism contained in genre science fiction had no qualms about extrapolating their lyricism in the direction of spiritual transcendence; notable examples include Ursula Le Guin's *The Word for World Is Forest* (1972), Sally Miller Gearhart's *The Wanderground* (1979), Hilbert Schenck's *At the Eye of the Ocean* (1980), Somtow Sucharitkul's *Starship and Haiku* (1984), Octavia Butler's *The Parable of the Sower* (1993), and Cynthia Joyce Clay's *Zollocco: A Novel of Another Universe* (2000). The perspectives of Lovelock and Teilhard de Chardin were fused in a prospectus for a hyper-Gaian "Galaxia" set out in Isaac Asimov's *Foundation's Edge* (1982).

Ecological mysticism was trivialised at a vulgar level by a tendency to use the talismanic prefix "eco-" promiscuously, and by the development of such advertising phrases as "ecologically friendly". These developments occurred in parallel with a renaissance of pastoral nostalgia in many areas of popular fiction, whose meditative plaints became increasingly eloquent in science fiction in such heartfelt stories as Richard Cowper's trilogy begun with *The Road to Corlay* (1978), John Crowley's *Engine Summer* (1979), Kate Wilhelm's *Juniper Time* (1979), Norman Spinrad's *Songs from the Stars* (1980), Russell Hoban's *Riddley Walker* (1980), and Ursula Le Guin's *Always Coming Home* (1986) and extended into extraterrestrial settings in such works as Judith Moffett's *Pennterra* (1987) and Jack McConnell's "Into Greenwood" (2001).

The case for an actual technological retreat was forcefully made in Ernest Callenbach's Millenarian tract *Ecotopia: The Notebooks of William Weston* (1975; rev. as *Ecotopia: A Novel About Ecology, People and Politics in 1999*, 1978), which describes the secession from the United States of the western seaboard states, where a new low-tech society is established, based on the principles of "alternative technology" laid out in such texts as Ernst Schumacher's *Small Is Beautiful* (1973). Callenbach's neologism, reiterated in the nonfictional *The Ecotopian Encyclopedia for the 80s: A Survival Guide for the Age of Inflation* (1980) and the prequel novel *Ecotopia Emerging* (1981), gave rise to a broader movement, whose aims are summarised and dramatised in Kim Stanley Robinson's science fiction anthology *Future Primitive: The New Ecotopias* (1994).

The notion that an ideal society must be ecologically sustainable was integrated into more general Utopian philosophy in such stories as Louis J. Halle's *Sedge* (1963), Alexei Panshin's "How Can We Sink When We Can Fly?" (1971), Christopher Swan and Chet Roaman's *YV88: An Eco-Fiction of Tomorrow* (1977), D. J. L. Naruda's "Green City" (1982–1984), and Frederik Pohl's "Rem the Rememberer" (1984), but such societies are often envisaged as domed enclaves surrounded by blighted landscapes, as in Marie C. Farca's *Earth* (1972). The philosophy of "small is beautiful" is rather claustrophobically echoed in Robert Nichols' *Daily Lives in Nghsi-Altai* (1977–1978) and Mary Alice White's *Land of the Possible* (1979). Most ecotopias tend to be socialist or anarchist in their political organisation, in spite of Garrett Hardin's argument in "The Tragedy of the Commons" (1968) that *ecocatastrophe is inevitable in the absence of stern stewardship; Mary Rosenblum's "Jumpers" (2004) offers a rare glimpse of a privatised ecosphere. L. E. Modesitt's Ecolitan series, launched by *The Ecologic Envoy* (1986), adapted ecological politics to the requirements of action-adventure science fiction.

Warwick Fox's *Towards a Transpersonal Ecology* (1990)—a prospectus for "utopian ecologism"—and Freya Mathews' *The Ecological Self* (1991) continued the broadening process begun by Bateson. The transplantation of ecological concepts to other fields was continued by the development of a school of literary "ecocriticism". Ursula Le Guin's whimsical essay on "The Carrier Bag Theory of Fiction" (1986), which draws a basic distinction between "techno-heroic" tales of hunters and uncombative novelistic accounts of gatherers, was reprinted in more earnest surroundings in *The Ecocriticism Reader: Landmarks in Literary Ecology* (1996), edited by Cheryll Glotfelty and Harold Fromm. The latter volume became the doctrinal basis of an Association for the Study of Literature and the Environment founded in 1992. The British tradition of ecocriticism, founded by Jonathan Bate's *Romantic Ecology: Wordsworth and the Environmental Tradition* (1991), locates the origins of ecological concern in English literature in *Romanticism and discovers a coherent tradition extending therefrom in Arcadian literary responses to the industrial revolution.

ECONOMICS

A term derived from a Greek word signifying the art of household management, extended by analogy to pertain to "macroeconomic" studies of the management of the industry and finances of nations, while retaining a "microeconomic" dimension whose central focus in societies that use money is on the determination of prices. Economics is sometimes called "the dismal science", in spite of the capacity of economic issues to arouse powerful individual and political passions and the fact that economic issues play a central role in *Utopian fiction from Thomas More's *Utopia* (1516) on. According to St. Paul's first epistle to Timothy, "the love of money is the root of all evil"—although Jesus had been happy to use it as a metaphor in the parable of the talents—and it therefore became the central subject matter of much literature. Although conventional strategies of story closure often rank economic rewards second to romantic ones, there is near-universal agreement to the proposition that they work best in combination.

Money was one of the earliest and most significant of all technological innovations, facilitating the avoidance of problems of equivalence involved in barter by establishing an external scale in which exchange values are manifest as prices, and payments are made in the form of coins or promissory notes. The use of pieces of metal as tokens of exchange probably originated in the third millennium B.C., but the officially certified standardisation of coinage first became widespread in the seventh century B.C., early coins often being made of the gold/silver mixture called "electrum". Coins designed for counting rather than weighing immediately became vulnerable to "clipping"—the consequent preferential use of lighter coins being reflected in Gresham's law, "bad money drives out good"—and gave rise to the dubious art of forgery. Paper money, first introduced in China in the eighth century and widely adopted in Europe in the late eighteenth century, played a discreet but significant role in facilitating the industrial revolution.

Money is a unique technology, in that it involves the deliberate incarnation of an idea, sustained by social convention; although coins may have a substantial "objective" value by virtue of the metal they contain, bank notes have virtually none, and yet their perceived value makes them far more useful and desirable than objects whose value is crudely utilitarian. Money is essential to the economic organisation of all but the simplest societies; the development of accounting systems to keep track of it was a major force in the development of *writing. On the other hand, its confusing effect on traditional conventions of personal obligation is frequently reflected in religious suspicion, which has been particularly relevant to the charging of interest on loans.

The foundations of modern economic theory were laid down in the eighteenth century by the French "Physiocrats" and their English equivalents. The latter included Bernard de Mandeville, who formulated his ideas in the ironic poem *The Grumbling Hive; or, Knaves Turn'd Honest* (1705), which became the headpiece of *The Fable of the Bees; or Private Vices, Publick Benefits* (1714; second part, 1729); the literary form seemed appropriate because of the seeming ethical paradoxicality of the basic thesis that the net result of individuals independently seeking to maximise their own advantage in trade is the collective enrichment of their whole society. Mandeville's fable inspired a reply in the Baron de Montesquieu's fable of the troglodytes in *Lettres persanes* (1721), and Mandeville was represented unsympathetically as Lysicles in George Berkeley's dialogue *Alciphron; or, The Minute Philosopher* (1732). His argument is also echoed in John Gay's *The Beggar's Opera* (1728) in the philosophy of the roguish Peachum.

The condemnation of Mandeville's ideas as blasphemous in Simon Tyssot de Patot's *Voyages et aventures de Jacques Massé* (ca. 1715) was intended ironically, but Claude Helvetius' *De l'esprit* (1758; trans. as *Essays on the Mind*)—which argued that self-interest is the mainspring of mental and moral activity—actually was condemned by the Paris *parlement* and burned by the hangman. Even so, that notion became the foundation stone of economic theory, taken up by Adam Smith in his landmark analysis of *The Wealth of Nations* (1776), where its effects were likened to that of an "invisible hand". National governments had previously taken it for granted that national prosperity depended on the margin by which exports exceeded imports, and had thus imposed heavy excise duties on imports; Smith's argument that free trade would work to the benefit of the whole community of nations implied that all market regulation ought to be abandoned; this proposition became one of the most powerful transformative ideas of the modern era, although it remained an item of fervent political controversy into the twenty-first century.

The principal difficulty with the production of public benefits (that is, general economic growth) by the invisible hand of the market was that it seemed to be a temporary process, because competition was always forcing the price of goods down towards the cost of their production (the "law of diminishing returns"). David Ricardo refined Smith's arguments in *Principles of Political Economy and Taxation* (1817), partly by means of integrating into his economic model the ideas of Robert Malthus regarding the impossibility of sustaining economic growth purely by *population growth and the exploitation of new resources. One of the earliest and most sustained exercises in the popularisation of science employing both nonfictional and fictional instruments was undertaken by Harriet Martineau in order to demonstrate the principles of the new science, in such works as *Illustrations of Political Economy* (1832) and *Illustrations of Taxation* (1834).

Ricardo's analysis, further refined by John Stuart Mill's *Principles of Political Economy* (1848) became the lynchpin of governmental economic policy in Britain, while Smith's version remained more influential in the United States, whose population and natural resources had much greater scope for expansion and exploitation. The difficulties encountered by the "mature" economies of Europe exploded in a series of political upheavals in the year that Mill published his *Principles*, assisting the emergence of an alternative economic model proposed by Karl *Marx. From then on, economic theory became a political and philosophical battleground on which countless intellectual and actual armies carried forward increasingly bitter and bloody conflicts.

The extension of this battleground into the field of literature was most obvious in the field of Utopian satire, where moral and political arguments frequently overshadowed arguments derived from economic theory. David Stirrat's *A Treatise on Political Economy...in the form of a romaunt* (1824) is an exceptional didactic vision of the future of socioeconomic classes, but the discourses of Utopian fiction were more elaborately influenced by economic theory in the late nineteenth century, in such works as Cyrus Elder's

Dream of a Free-Trade Paradise (1872), Theodore Hertzka's *Freiland* (1890; trans. as *Freeland*), Adeline Knapp's *One Thousand Dollars a Day: Studies in Practical Economics* (1894), King Gillette's *The Human Drift* (1894), and Lebbeus Rogers' *The Kite Trust: A Romance of Wealth* (1900). Numerous American works in this vein showed the influence of Henry George's *Progress and Poverty* (1879), which concentrated on the role of land ownership and management rather than the entrepreneurial production of goods, advocating the nationalisation of all land and the replacement of all other forms of taxation by rents charged to its various users.

The commercial success of George's book helped pave the way for Edward Bellamy's *Looking Backward, 2000–1887* (1888) to become a huge best-seller. George's single tax system is adopted—but subsequently modified—by citizens of the free asteroid Henrygeorgia in the anonymous *Man Abroad* (1886), and is imposed temporarily by reformers in Thomas McGrady's *Beyond the Black Ocean* (1901) and James B. Alexander's *The Lunarian Professor* (1909). Anna Bowman's *The Republic of the Future* (1887) is an anti-Georgian tract. In Ingersoll Lockwood's *1900; or, The Last President* (1896) George becomes postmaster general when William Jennings Bryan wins the 1896 presidential election, and the country goes to rack and ruin in consequence. Georgian socialist analyses were not overtaken in the United States by Marxist ones until the mid-twentieth century, having exercised a strong influence on the distinctive American socialist tradition carried forward by Eugene Debs. Economic arguments deployed by socialist writers of British scientific romance, such as the one set out by M. P. Shiel in *The Lord of the Sea* (1901), were as likely to be derived from George as from Marx and Engels.

In terms of economic theory rather than political implication, what Smith, Ricardo, and Marx had in common was arguably more significant than their differences, in that all three accepted the labour theory of value—the notion that the price of an item was ultimately dependent on its cost of production, and hence on the labour invested in its manufacture. The growing awareness that prices were more heavily dependent on the subjective evaluations of buyers than the objective costs of sellers encouraged skeptical reflections on the amazing vagaries of subjective value, as illustrated by such notorious historical episodes as Holland's "tulipomania" and the scandal of the "South Sea Bubble", the later being satirised in Samuel Brunt's *A Voyage to Cacklogallinia* (1727). The replacement of the objective theory of value by a subjective one led to the development at the end of the nineteenth century of "marginal utility theory",

but the attempt to refine "supply-side" economics with theories of demand proved very difficult because of the essential mercuriality of demand, which was subject to such strange phenomena as "fashion".

As the twentieth century progressed, the economies of developed countries became increasingly focused on "luxury goods" that were enormously sensitive to the vagaries of demand, and hence to the pressures of advertisement, whose representations in speculative fiction—including Villiers de l'Isle Adam's "L'affichage céleste" (1873; trans. as "Celestial Advertising"), Skelton Kuppord's *A Fortune from the Sky* (1903), and George Allan England's "A Message from the Moon: The Story of a Great Coup" (1907)—became increasingly antipathetic. Such responses to the alleged crudity of advertising techniques were, however, a trifle disingenuous; fiction became increasingly significant as a celebrant of the idea and trappings of luxury, not only generating and amplifying an exacting status envy but peddling the notion that such rewards were within reach of anyone prepared to make the most of golden opportunity and native ability. The best-selling American writer of the 1890s was the dime novelist Horatio Alger, whose "rags to riches" stories equated poetic justice with material acquisition and founded one of the most prolific traditions of twentieth-century popular fiction.

Adam Smith's championship of the virtue of free trade was undermined towards the end of the nineteenth century by increasing anxieties about the tendency of competing corporations to fuse into monopolies or to form cartels. This tendency became an important focus of preventive regulations, and stimulated such fearful anticipations as Jack London's *The Iron Heel* (1907), J. C. Haig's *In the Grip of the Trusts* (1909), and George Allan England's *The Air Trust* (1915). The problems involved in regulating money supply by metallic standards also came under scrutiny in such works as Edgar Allan Poe's "Von Kempelen and His Discovery" (1849), Henry Richardson Chamberlain's *6000 Tons of Gold* (1894), and Garrett P. Serviss' *The Moon Metal* (1900). The notion of wrecking the world financial system by destroying its base was presented in an enthusiastic light by such socialist writers as Jules Lermina in *To Ho le tueur d'or* (1905; trans. as *To-Ho the Gold-Slayer*) and England in *The Golden Blight* (1912). Frank O'Rourke's satire *Instant Gold* (1964) updated the notion.

The tradition of Utopias based in economic theory continued in the mid-twentieth century in such works as Robert Ardrey's *World's Beginning* (1944), Henry Hazlitt's *The Great Idea* (1951; aka *Time Will Run Back*), and Ayn Rand's fervently propagandistic *Atlas Shrugged* (1957). Notable twentieth-century satires on economic theory included Upton Sinclair's *The Millennium* (1914; book, 1924), in which the economic phases of social development are rapidly reenacted by a small company of survivors in the wake of a disaster, and Archibald Marshall's *Upsidonia* (1915), which describes a society in which fundamental self-interest is overwhelmed by the pressure of social disdain.

Economic theory had little impact on early pulp science fiction, although an exotic exchange system is featured in Stanton A. Coblentz's *The Blue Barbarians* (1931). It was imported into John W. *Campbell's *Astounding Science Fiction* by Robert A. *Heinlein, extrapolating notions he had developed during his brief involvement with Upton Sinclair's EPIC ("End Poverty in California") campaign. In "The Roads Must Roll" (1940) a transport strike is called in the name of "Functionalism"—the proposition that the greatest economic rewards should go to the workers whose jobs are most vital to a society's infrastructure. "Let There Be Light..." (1940, by Lyle Monroe) discusses the economic logic of the suppression of innovation by power groups heavily invested in existing technologies. "Logic of Empire" (1941) includes similar discussions of the economics of slavery. "The Man Who Sold the Moon" (1950) describes the financing of a pioneering Moon voyage—an issue taken up by numerous subsequent Space Age fantasies, including Alexis Gilliland's "The Man Who Funded the Moon" (1989). Heinlein's economic theorising was comprehensively updated in *The Moon Is a Harsh Mistress* (1966), which helped to popularise the acronym TANSTAAFL ("There Ain't No Such Thing as a Free Lunch"); the precedents he set were enthusiastically followed up by numerous exponents of libertarian science fiction.

Notable science-fictional *contes philosophiques* exploring the consequences of economic theory include Henry Kuttner's "The Iron Standard" (1943; initially by-lined Lewis Padgett), in which human castaways disrupt the economy of an alien culture, and Poul Anderson's "The Helping Hand" (1950), which offers a scathing analysis of the economics of "foreign aid". The economics of *colonisation, which had provided a major bone of contention in British political economy throughout the nineteenth century, were extrapolated on a galactic stage by Anderson's Polesotechnic League series, including the novelettes collected as *Trader to the Stars* (1964), which feature Nicholas van Rijn, the ingenious manager of the Solar Spice and Liquors Company. The principal provider of economics-based science fiction to Campbell's magazine in the 1960s was Mack Reynolds, whose parents were socialist activists and whose ideas were strongly influenced by Eugene Debs; his work ranged

from low-key *contes philosophiques* such as "Subversive" (1962) to flamboyant accounts of economic subversion on a planetary scale such as "Ultima Thule" (1961; exp. as *Planetary Agent X,* 1965). "Adaptation" (1961; exp. as *The Rival Rigelians* 1967) describes an experiment in which spacefarers divide a planet's nations between themselves in order to compare the relative efficacy power of free enterprise and Marxist planning as forces of social evolution. Reynolds went on to write a substantial series of Utopian novels updating the ideas of Edward Bellamy, beginning with *Looking Backward, from the Year 2000* (1973) and *Equality in the Year 2000* (1977).

This work was produced against the background of a slow revolution in political economy brought about by recognition of the power and responsibility of governments to exercise a certain amount of control over demand, as analysed by John Maynard Keynes. The application of sophisticated mathematical analysis to the rapidly growing stock of historical and contemporary economic data—which came in quantified form, thanks to the ubiquity of money as an exchange mechanism—resulted in a dramatic complication of economic analyses, engendering a massive proliferation of "economic indicators". Increasing precision of analysis could not compensate, however, for the fundamental mercurialness of demand, which continued to limit the explanatory power of economic analyses. The practical application of economic theory was also undermined by the fact that any predictions issued by economists immediately affected the behavior of the people involved in the marketplace, altering the situation whose analysis had produced the prediction: a classic instance of the paradox of prophecy whose effects became increasingly obvious. This inability to anticipate the future of economic systems worked to the disadvantage of the public image of economists, who came to be seen as inept dogmatists continually outflanked by the unexpected, but it had considerable dramatic value for writers constructing plots, especially *contes cruels* celebrating the irony of fate.

The seeming perversities of economic theory were satirically extrapolated in science fiction by Frederik Pohl in such stories as "The Midas Plague" (1954), in which the efficiency of mechanical production results in citizens being afflicted with ever-more-burdensome consumption quotas to maintain economic growth, and "The Tunnel Under the World" (1955), which extrapolated the newly fashionable practice of market research to a new extreme. Pohl imported such concerns into two of the novels he wrote in collaboration with C. M. Kornbluth: *The Space Merchants* (1953), in which the economy of the United States is driven to extremes of conspicuous consumption and the advertising industry has become the principal instrument of government; and *Gladiator-at-Law* (1955), in which the stock market reigns supreme, strategically manipulated by monopolistic corporations run by the ultimate decadent capitalists.

The necessity of stoking up demand to maintain economic growth was further extrapolated in Robert Sheckley's "Cost of Living" (1952) and Louis Charbonneau's *The Sentinel Stars* (1963), in which the inheritance of wealth is replaced by the inheritance of ever-escalating family debt, and Damon Knight's *Hell's Pavement* (1955, aka *Analogue Men*). Knight's "A for Anything" (1957; exp. as *The People Maker*) explored the socioeconomic consequences of the instant disruption of the monetary exchange mechanism by the invention of a matter-duplicator, and makes an interesting contrast with other stories on an identical theme, including George O. Smith's "Pandora's Millions" (1945) and Ralph Williams' "Business as Usual, During Alterations" (1958).

The potential economic consequences of alien contact are explored in a number of stories by Clifford D. Simak, including *The Visitors* (1980). In D. C. Poyer's *Stepfather Bank* (1987), the dictatorial rule of a World Bank is secured by its ability to lure dissenters into debt. Almost all science fiction stories of this kind have a sarcastic edge, considerably sharpened in such satires as Christopher Anvil's "Compound Interest" (1967), Lee Killough's "Caveat Emptor" (1970), Joseph H. Delaney's "My Brother's Keeper" (1982), and Hayford Peirce's series featuring an "ethical stockbroker", which includes "The Boxie Rebellion" (1979; incorporated into *Jonathan White, Stockbroker in Orbit*, 2001). Economists using futurological scenarios to dramatise their ideas, as in the anonymous *Report from Iron Mountain on the Possibility and Desirability of Peace* (Dial Press, 1967) and Paul Erdman's *The Crash of '79* (1977), were readily infected by the tendency to sarcasm. The economic problems of Third World development became an increasingly important concern of global economists in the last quarter of the twentieth century, reflected in such literary works as Bruce Sterling's "Green Days in Brunei" (1985) and *Islands in the Net* (1988). The vulnerability of money held in *cyberspace to fraudulent manipulation also became a considerable concern, reflected in such speculative fictions as L. E. Modesitt Jr.'s "The Great American Economy" (1973).

EDISON, THOMAS ALVA (1847–1931)

U.S. technologist who became a legend in his lifetime and the archetype of the ingenious inventor; his remarkable life story became a key narrative in the popular understanding of technological evolution. Edison had almost no formal schooling, although he was tutored by his mother, a former schoolteacher. He set up a small laboratory in the cellar of his home when he was ten, becoming fascinated by electrical phenomena and gadgetry; when he "went into business" at the age of twelve, selling supplies to rail passengers, he moved his laboratory to a baggage car. He trained himself in telegraphy and spent the Civil War years as a peripatetic telegrapher before briefly obtaining a position with Western Union in 1868. Shortly afterwards he read Michael Faraday's *Experimental Researches in Electricity* (1839), which inspired him to intensify his own endeavours and to quit Western Union in order to work for himself.

Edison soon registered his first patent, for an electrical vote recorder. The device was a technical success but a commercial failure—an experience he accepted as a crucial lesson. After moving to New York in 1869, he was living in a Wall Street basement when the Western Union's telegraphic price indicator in the Gold Exchange broke down. After repairing it, he was installed as its supervisor, and the company commissioned him to improve the stock-ticker that had recently come into use. The Edison Universal Stock Printer, together with other modifications of contemporary telegraph machines, made him a fortune, providing him with the capital to set up as a manufacturer of telegraph machines in Newark, New Jersey. Western Union remained his leading client as he applied his knowledge to the refinement of a wide range of emergent electrical technologies, but he also hawked his wares to its rivals. In 1876, he moved his laboratory to Menlo Park, where he established a "scientific village" for his employees' families. Menlo Park became famous as the operating arena of the United States' primary genius.

Edison maintained a relentless pace, applying for patents at a greater rate than one a day. He missed out on patenting the telephone, but quickly improved Alexander Graham Bell's model with a carbon transmitter. He achieved two significant breakthroughs in quick succession when he patented the phonograph in 1877 and the electric light bulb in 1879, the latter securing the fortunes of the Edison Electric Light Company he had established with venture capital from J. P. Morgan and the Vanderbilts. His accidental discovery in 1883 of the current flowing between a hot and cold electrode—which he named the Edison Effect—found no immediate application, but eventually gave rise to the electron tube and the electronics industry. He increased the size of his operation when he moved it from Menlo Park to West Orange, whose Edison Laboratory eventually became a national monument; its products included the mimeograph, the alkaline storage battery, the fluoroscope, and the dictating machine, and he made highly significant improvements to motion picture cameras and projectors.

Even in the period of his greatest success, Edison's commitment to direct current rather than the alternating current developed by his one-time employee Nikola Tesla cost him dearly; he gradually lost control of his principal marketing instrument, the Edison General Electric Company—which subsequently forsook his name—and the millions he subsequently poured into the attempted exploitation of his movie technology completed the loss of his fortune. He continued to work hard, however, heading the Naval Consulting Board during World War I and establishing the Naval Research Laboratory in 1920.

Edison's celebrity stamped itself firmly on the early development of American science fiction in the dime novels medium, whose heroic gunslingers and detectives were supplemented by a flock of young inventors, one of whom was called Tom Edison Jr. and all of whom were cast in the same mould. John Clute coined the term "Edisonade" (by analogy with Robinsonade) to describe an entire subgenre of stories sprung from this fountainhead, in which heroic inventors devise technological fixes to save their communities from disaster—the ultimate celebration of individual improvisation under the spur of necessity.

Edison had a cameo role in Pearl Benjamin's "The End of New York" (1881), but he played much more important parts in the Comte de Villiers de l'Isle Adam's *L'Ève Future* (1886; trans. as *Tomorrow's Eve*) and Garrett P. Serviss' *Edison's Conquest of Mars* (1898; book, 1947), a newspaper-serial sequel to H. G. Wells' *The War of the Worlds*. He was credited as a source of ideas in George Parson Lathrop's futuristic fantasy "In the Deep of Time" (1897). He is featured in Manly Wade Wellman's *Giants from Eternity* (1939; book, 1959) and Kurt Vonnegut's "Tom Edison's Shaggy Dog" (1953), in which he tries out an intelligence analyser on his dog. He runs for president against William Jennings Bryan in Geoffrey A. Landis' alternative history story "The Eyes of America" (2003).

EGAN, GREG (1961–)

Australian writer and computer programmer. He became one of the outstanding *hard science fiction writers of the 1990s, publishing a series of unprecedentedly adventurous and philosophically sophisticated short stories and novels combining ideas drawn from physics, cosmology, and biology with uncompromising theoretical exactitude. "Beyond the

Whistle Test" (1989), describing the application of computers to the analysis of the brain's responses to music, is relatively tentative, but "Learning to Be Me" (1990) is a more robust exploration of possibilities of neurological manipulation that were further extrapolated in "Transition Dreams" (1993) before being taken to a remarkable extreme in "Reasons to be Cheerful" (1997). In "Fidelity" (1991) a *nanotechnological lock secures neural pathways so that love really can last forever. "In Numbers" (1991) features an exotic kind of space sickness.

Egan's first novel, *Quarantine* (1992), extrapolated the *uncertainty principle to a new extreme. When human astronomical observation begins to influence the nature of the universe by collapsing its inherent uncertainties, Earth is isolated in order to protect it. *Permutation City* (1994) found abundant new potential in the idea of achieving immortality by uploading personalities into *cyberspace; in one of its subplots a population of insectile cellular automata evolve to independence of thought and the acquisition of armed might. In the meantime, biochemical genetics provided a basis for "Cocoon" (1994), in which a bioartifact designed to protect embryos from AIDS has more controversial potential applications, including the prevention of homosexuality, and "Mitochondrial Eve" (1995), in which feminists and masculinists are driven to violent conflict by evolutionary extrapolations.

The *political fantasy *Distress* (1995), set on a quasi-Utopian floating island, has a principal plot organised around the impending announcement of a crucial advance in theoretical *physics, while one of its subplots features the Voluntary Autists—an organisation of sufferers from Asperger's syndrome whose resistance to the threat of compulsory corrective surgery leads them to challenge the notion that a "normal" ability to read other people's emotional states is anything more than a comforting delusion. The biological fantasy *Teranesia* (1999) is more restrained in its use of ideas than its predecessors, but the *cosmological extravaganza *Diaspora* (1997) more than made up for it. The sudden destruction of life on Earth by radiation from a gamma-ray burster forces a number of space habitats largely staffed by uploaded personas to set off on a series of exploratory expeditions, which eventually take them far into a hierarchical *macrocosm. *Schild's Ladder* (2002) tracks the creation and evolution of a "novo-vacuum" that begins to expand into a new cosmos in the wake of its own *Big Bang.

The sequence of *contes philosophiques* assembled in the collections *Axiomatic* (1995) and *Luminous* (1998) continued in his subsequent work. "The Planck Dive" (1998) features a suicidal journey into a *black hole.

"Oceanic" (1998) describes the conflict between the Deep Church and heretic Transitionals. "Border Guards" (1999) features virtual "quantum soccer" in the context of a meditation on the changes wrought in the significance of death by new technologies of longevity. In "Oracle" (2000) alternative-historical stand-ins for Alan Turing and C. S. Lewis confront one another in a 1950s TV debate about whether machines can think. In "Singleton" (2002) an artificial intelligence is painstakingly educated by its creator, who is troubled by the conviction that all of his choices are taken both ways in the many worlds of quantum uncertainty and is intent on shielding the artificial intelligence's host computer from quantum entanglements, so that all its decisions will be absolute.

EINSTEIN, ALBERT (1879–1955)

German theoretical physicist whose reputation became a counterpart of sorts to that of Thomas *Edison, in that he similarly became a legend in his lifetime and an archetype of the popular imagination, in his case of "pure" rather than "applied" science. As with Edison, his remarkable life story became a key narrative in the popular understanding of the evolution of science.

Einstein's schooling in Munich was rigidly disciplined, but he was not considered an outstanding pupil. Initially, he preferred music—he became an accomplished violinist—to science, and he failed to complete his diploma. His father and uncle owned an electrical factory and engineering works, but it did not flourish and his family moved to Milan. Einstein resumed his education in Switzerland, eventually studying physics at the Polytechnic Academy in Zurich before getting a job as an examiner in the Patent Office in Bern in 1900. He completed a thesis on "A New Determination of Molecular Dimensions" to qualify for his Ph.D., publishing it in the *Annalen der Physik* in 1905; in a remarkable burst of theoretical creativity, he published four further papers in the same journal before the year's end.

The first of these papers suggested an explanation of the phenomenon of Brownian motion—the random movements of microscopic particles suspended in a liquid medium—in terms of molecular kinetics. The second postulated that light is composed of individual quanta, using this hypothesis to explain the enigmatic photoelectric effect; it was this paper that was to win him the Nobel Prize in 1921. The third proposed the special theory of *relativity, based on the assumption that the speed of light is constant for all observers, whose subjective measurement of space and time varies according to their relative velocities.

The fourth added a footnote to this theory, which deduced the equivalence of mass and energy and culminated in the famous equation $E = mc^2$. The illimitable consequences of this flood of inspiration were all the more remarkable in light of the fact that his consequent attempts to supplement them came to very little once he had expanded the special theory of relativity into the general theory in 1916. Like Edison's eventual commercial failure, this decline from a spectacular zenith became part and parcel of his legend.

Einstein's work did not win universal acceptance immediately, but it captured the allegiance of many other theoretical physicists in advance of the first major demonstration of one of the general theory's consequences, when light rays passing close to the Sun were shown to suffer deflection by gravity during the solar eclipse of 1919. That vindication secured Einstein's international reputation as a genius, but he was then living in Berlin; his conversations with Alexander Moszkowski—the author of the Utopian satire *The Isles of Wisdom*—in *Einstein, Einblicke in seine Gedankenwelt* (1920) reveal the extent of his anxieties about that situation. The rising tide of German anti-Jewish feeling led to his being castigated during the 1920s as a champion of allegedly obscurantist "Zionist" or "Bolshevik" theory that flew in the face of commonsense. This persecution served to increase the dimensions of his heroism further; he travelled widely during this period, using his platform to preach pacifism as well as the new physics, eventually renouncing his citizenship and leaving Germany for good when the Nazis came to power in 1933.

Having accepted a position at the Institute for Advanced Study at Princeton, Einstein remained there for the rest of his life, conspicuously burdened by stoical sadness in the face of historical events and struggling heroically but unavailingly to produce a theory that would settle the conflict of apparent contradictions between relativity and quantum mechanics. In many minds, including his own, his failure to produce that "grand unifying theory" mirrored the political failure of Cold War politics; although he died in his sleep, rumor persisted in reporting that he was scribbling equations desperately until the end. The last item of writing he left incomplete was actually a speech in celebration of Israel's Independence Day.

Although he wrote a crucial letter to President Roosevelt on the feasibility of developing an *atom bomb, Einstein played no active part in the Manhattan Project, and learned about the destruction of Hiroshima in the same manner as the most ordinary of citizens. Public opinion, however, insisted on reckoning him among the fathers of the bomb. In Frederik Pohl's sarcastic fantasy "Target One"

(1955) he is assassinated on those grounds—but his killers do not return, as they intended, to a future without the bomb.

Einstein's imagistic influence was at least as great as Edison's, and his physical appearance—somewhat reminiscent of a frail but infinitely serious and deeply melancholy teddy bear—made him a far more sympathetic character in an age dominated by *photographic representations. Andy Warhol produced a portrait of him in 1980 and he was *Time Magazine*'s man of the century in 1999. The many anecdotes in which he features, and his most widely quoted aphoristic remarks, emphasise his modesty as much as his wisdom. The nature of his achievement, however, was much less amenable to literary imitation, becoming a byword for abstruseness and incomprehensibility—Arthur Eddington, asked in 1919 whether it was true that only three people in the world understood the theory of general relativity, allegedly replied "Who's the third?" In consequence, Einstein's fictional clones remained ineluctably mysterious, beyond the pale of common humanity. Representations of him in such historical fictions as Terry Johnson's play *Insignificance* (1982; film, 1985) invariably combine reverence with puzzlement, and a suspicion that his heartfelt commitment to pacifism and social justice was merely one more symptom of his unworldliness. Fictional simulacra such as Professor Barnhardt in *The Day the Earth Stood Still* (1951) and Dr. Know in Steven Spielberg's *AI* (2001) do not contradict this impression.

Although Einstein produced some autobiographical writings, including *My Philosophy* (1934) and *Out of My Later Years* (1950)—not to be confused with Gerhard Roth's novel *Die Autobiographie des Albert Einstein* (1972; trans. as *The Autobiography of Albert Einstein*), whose protagonist is delusional—they concentrate almost entirely on his scientific work, explicitly setting out to avoid the "merely personal". Anthony Storr's characterisation of "schizoid creativity" in *The Dynamics of Creation* (1972) includes a supplementary chapter devoted to him and Isaac Newton, as exemplars of highly intelligent men who expressed their schizoid tendencies in building "New Models of the Universe". Subsequent psychological analysts might be more likely to interpret the same "symptoms" in terms of Asperger's syndrome, with much the same effect.

Einstein plays an orthodox heroic role in Richard A. Lupoff's *Countersolar!* (1987)—in which his chief antagonist is Eva Peron. In Stephen Kraus' "Frame of Reference" (1988) it is he, not John Scopes, who is prosecuted in the Deep South for scientific heresy by William Jennings Bryan in the 1920s, and defended by Clarence Darrow. In George Alec Effinger's story of a time machine invented in a Naziless Germany in 1938, "Everything But Honor" (1989), he appears alongside Werner Heisenberg and Erwin Schrödinger. Alan Lightman's *Einstein's Dreams* (1993) is a philosophical rhapsody in which the great man dreams of alternate worlds in which time is experienced differently. Einstein is cloned in Robert Silverberg's "The Millennium Express" (2000). He features as the protagonist of Zoran Zivkovic's "The Violinist" (2002), and is insistently present in spirit in Michael Swanwick's "The Dark Lady of the Equations" (2003), which illustrates Einsteinium in the author's Periodic Table of Science Fiction. In Deborah Layne's Western transfiguration "The Legend of Jake Einstein" (2004) the eponymous gunslinger is involved in a shootout with Ned Bohr. Kevin McLaurty's *The Einstein Code* (2004) takes the form of a fictitious diary recording Einstein's responses to the evolution of speculative fiction (including a meeting with Isaac Asimov).

Einstein is the subject of Philip Glass' opera *Einstein on the Beach* (1976), Ed Metzger's one-man stage show *Albert Einstein: The Practical Bohemian* (1978), and Yahoo Serious' film *Young Einstein* (1988), and he also features in Steve Martin's play *Picasso at the Lapin Agile* (1996). No other scientist has enjoyed such a rich and varied existence in the worlds of modern legend and fiction.

ELECTRICITY

The phenomena aggregated under the heading of electricity are now known to be those arising from the *atomic property of charge, and have been theoretically fused with those of *magnetism, but those that were known before the nineteenth century seemed peculiar and deeply enigmatic. The adjective "electric"—used by William Gilbert, in *De Magnete* (1600)—was first applied to attractive forces generated by friction; the term "electricity" itself may have been used for the first time by Sir Thomas Browne in 1646.

Gilbert attributed the attractive power of a friction-charged object to the removal of a fluid "humor", which left a kind of aura around it. Such electrostatic phenomena were frequently studied by experimenters, but it was not until 1729 that Stephen Gray discovered electrical conductivity. Shortly thereafter Charles Dufay—Louis XV's gardener—pointed out that Gilbert's attractive force had a repulsive counterpart. Benjamin Franklin signified the opposed forces as + and – and proposed that they were always in balance; his experimental attachment of a key to a kite, which he flew in a thunderstorm to attract and conduct lightning—thus demonstrating that it was an electric phenomenon—became one of the best-known legends of science. A suggestion by Franklin led Joseph Priestley—who published a *History of Electricity* in 1767—to determine that electrical attraction was similar to gravitational attraction in that its force was subject to an inverse square law.

The notion that the fundamental property of *life might be electrical was enthusiastically extrapolated by James Graham, who concluded that electric shocks were of immense medical value. From 1775 onwards he offered a variety of electric and magnetic therapies at a series of Temples of Health and Hymen in Bath, Bristol, and London. The notion that life is "vital electricity" was encouraged by Luigi Galvani's discovery—made in 1780 and published in 1792—that electrical stimulation could cause a frog's muscle to contract; the study of electric currents became known as "galvanism" thereafter. Alessandro Volta applied Galvani's observations of the effects of contact between metals and moist surfaces to the development of the voltaic pile, the first electrical battery. In the early nineteenth century the English electrical experimenter Andrew Crosse became convinced that he had generated invertebrate life-forms by electrical stimulation, but Humphry Davy obtained much better results with his pioneering endeavours in electrochemistry.

In 1820, Hans Christian Oersted published his observations of the effect of electrical currents on compass needles; within five years André-Marie Ampère had produced an early formulation of the mathematical laws governing the interaction of currents and magnetic fields. The phenomenon of conductivity, and the "resistance" variously manifest by different substances, was mathematically analysed by Georg Simon Ohm. The various threads of this work were gathered together and further extended by Michael Faraday, who listed eleven fundamental propositions regarding electrical phenomena in 1834. His discovery of electromagnetic induction and development of the concept of "lines of force" making up an electrical field paved the way for electric motors, but the first important technological application of electrical theory was the development of telegraphy by Samuel Morse in 1830s; the commercially viable system he demonstrated in 1838 launched a new industry. The relationship between electrical currents and heat was investigated by James Prescott Joule, who published his findings in 1841.

The fusion of electrical and magnetic theory begun by Faraday was completed by James Clerk Maxwell in a definitive set of equations published in 1864, which also incorporated the connection, first made by Gustav Kirchhoff, between electromagnetism and

light. Faraday had suggested in 1833 that electricity might be particulate rather than fluid, and Maxwell also referred to "molecules" of electricity, even though his equations described *etheric waves. J. J. Thomson's experiments with primitive cathode-ray tubes in the mid-1890s proved that electricity did indeed consist of individual components that were soon named "electrons", whose discovery prompted new models of the atom. By this time, the revolution in electrical technology begun by Morse was accelerating rapidly, spearheaded by Thomas *Edison's pioneering endeavours in the industrialisation of invention.

The early impact of these developments on the literary imagination was mostly focused on the notion of vital electricity, their most striking reflection being Mary Shelley's account of the "modern Prometheus", *Frankenstein* (1818). Shelley's exemplar helped to ensure that the idea was mainly used throughout the nineteenth century to shore up horrific motifs, most graphically in such *fin-de-siècle* stories as J. Maclaren Cobban's *Master of His Fate* (1890) and Arthur Conan Doyle's "The Los Amigos Fiasco" (1892). A redemption of sorts began, however, when William Crookes' experiments with "cathode rays" in the 1870s were explicitly linked by him and others to the burgeoning field of "psychic research", later renamed *parapsychology, thus helping to stimulate the *occult revival. Marie Corelli's best-selling *A Romance of Two Worlds* (1887) celebrated the enlivening power of occult electricity, redefining God as a "circle of electric force", while Alfred Smythe's *The New Faust* (1896) explained all psychic phenomena as manifestation of an Electric Principle permeating the universe. In William Hope Hodgson's *The Night Land* (1912), the last hopes of humankind are invested in the invigorating "Earth-Current".

Such narrative moves reflected the fact that electricity was widely seen by nonscientists as a kind of magical force, and Maxwell's equations as arcane formulas. An important conceptual boundary had been crossed that placed the explanation of electromagnetic phenomena outside the range of common comprehensibility. Rather than life acquiring an appearance of explicability by virtue of its reconceptualisation as vital electricity, electricity took on something of the essential mysteriousness of life, remaining in the realm of the occult because many people simply could not conceptualise it clearly. The accelerating flood of technological applications demonstrated the competence of scientific understanding of electricity, but did not make that understanding any easier for the untrained mind to grasp.

Speculative extrapolation of the idea that electricity might become an important power source for machinery made exceedingly rapid headway after 1870, when the advanced capabilities of Jules Verne's *Nautilus* were casually explained as applications of electricity. The Utopian society of Edward Bulwer-Lytton's *The Coming Race* (1871) is powered by the ubiquitous electric force of *vril*, and Robert Dudgeon Ellis' *Colymbia* (1873) is also comprehensively electrified, drawing its power from the Earth's magnetic field. Albert Bleunard's *La Babylone électrique* (1888; trans. as *Babylon Electrified*) provided a striking symbolic depiction of the raising of an all-electric city, Liberty, from the ruins of Babylon, while Herbert D. Ward's "The Lost City" (1891) imagined an all-electric U.S. city of Russell, but few literary images bothered with such limited scales of representation. The majority of projections of electrical technology leapt directly to images of whole societies—or the entire world—completely transformed by electricity, as displayed in such Utopian romances as John O. Greene's *The Ke Whonkus People* (1890), Kenneth Folingby's *Meda* (1891), Robert Grimshaw's *Fifty Years Hence* (1892), Byron Brooks' *Earth Revisited* (1893), A. Garland Mears' *Mercia* (1895), Alexander Craig's *Ionia* (1898), Arthur Bird's *Looking Forward* (1899), Albert Adams Merill's *The Great Awakening* (1899), and Herman Hine Brismade's *Utopia Achieved* (1912).

L. Frank Baum declared in a didactic "electrical fairy-tale" that electricity was *The Master Key* (1901) to the future—a notion dramatised in similar fashion in John Trowbridge's *The Electrical Boy* (1891). Harry W. Hillman's *Looking Forward: The Phenomenal Progress of Electricity in 1912* (1906)—in which the author's employer, George Westinghouse (Thomas Edison's principal rival in the marketplace) appears as a character—is an early example of fiction used as advertising. By this time, electrical machinery was very widely distributed in popular fiction, being the chief stock-in-trade of tales of *invention. Electricity became an ubiquitous facilitating device, applicable to almost any hypothetical purpose—as, indeed, it seemed to be in actuality. The twentieth century saw Baum's and Hillman's hopes abundantly justified, particularly with the development of new "electronic" technologies employing "vacuum tubes" as electronic valves.

The Edison's company's British adviser, John Ambrose Fleming, developed a diode vacuum tube in 1904, which could filter current generated by *radio waves so that the output current only flowed in one direction. In 1907, Lee DeForest inserted a third electrode between the anode and cathode to produce a triode, which added the property of amplification to that of rectification, eventually leading to the development of radio broadcasting. The addition of further electrodes enabled vacuum tubes to acquire and refine further properties, including oscillation, frequency modification, and switching, which led to the eventual development of *TV receivers and cameras. Tubes filled with various gases also proved useful, especially those filled with neon adapted for lighting purposes. While these developments were taking place, the scope of electronics was dramatically widened by the development of semiconductors and the consequent rapid advancement of "solid-state" devices, which permitted a gradual replacement of vacuum tubes by transistors, greatly facilitating the development and manufacture of *computers.

To laypersons, electronic technology represented the perfection of electricity's arcana, its abstruse equations further supplemented by circuit diagrams whose straight lines and graphic symbolism belied the complexity of their significance. The peculiar properties of the vacuum tube—exemplified by its ability to produce eerie glows—and its amazing ubiquity secured it an iconic role in the visual representation of laboratories and *scientists at work, supplementing the chemical symbolism of the test tube. The descriptions of hypothetical machines in early twentieth-century speculative fiction routinely refer to glowing tubes, employing them as key emblems of power and ingenuity, and such imagery was readily transferred to the *cinema. Within little more than a generation, electricity had passed from the outer limits of the literary imagination to such wide fictional distribution that it had become exceedingly difficult to imagine a world without it, although its abrupt stoppage was featured in numerous *disaster stories. Christopher Anvil's "Not in the Literature" (1963) is a very rare attempt to imagine an alternative twentieth century whose technology is based entirely on chemistry, and in which electricity's belated discoverer is brusquely brushed off as a crackpot believer in magic.

ELEMENT

One of a set of fundamental components out of which all experienced substances are made. Early Greek philosophers proposed that there must be a single essential principle of matter, to which all forms of physical existence might ultimately be reduced, but they disagreed as to its nature. Thales suggested *water, Anaximenes *air, Heraclitus *fire, and Xenophanes *earth, while Anaximander proposed that there must be an invisible "fabric", the *apeiron* (unlimited), out of which these apparent elements must be made. Empedocles popularised the compromise view that the experienced world is made up of four elements, while the fabric of the heavens is a distinct *ether. In the Aristotelian cosmology the four elements are arranged hierarchically, in spite of their interaction and admixture, with earth as the foundation and the native spheres of water, air, and fire stacked sequentially upon it; Aristotelian *physics is based on the notion that each element has a tendency to return to its "natural location".

The theory of the four elements remained a conventional instrument of analysis until the Renaissance, when its use within *alchemy was subjected to new elaborations of mystical significance, which found parallels in other disciplines according to the invariable tendency of *occult science. The four elements were already mirrored in the four humours of Classical medical theory, and echoed in *astrology, where the twelve signs of the zodiac were divided into four affinity groups. *Paracelsus helped to revitalise the notion that each element had an associated "elemental spirit"—a notion extravagantly developed in German *Romantic literature, most famously in Friedrich de la Motte Fouqué's *Undine* (1812). The same symbolism was elaborately developed in England, notably in Erasmus *Darwin's *The Temple of Nature* (1803) and—in syncretic amalgam with other folkloristic analogies—the poetry of Percy Shelley. In France, the four "great elementals" were credited with a creative role in Tiphaigne de la Roche's allegorical *Giphantie* (1760; trans. as *Gyphantia*).

The notion of a single underlying principle resurfaced in alchemical speculation, reflected in such literary representations as the "primitive element" for which the anti-hero of Honoré de Balzac's *Le recherche de l'absolu* (1834: trans. as *The Quest for the Absolute*) searches in vain. The notion is also broached in Edward Bulwer-Lytton's occult romance *A Strange Story* (1862) and is fused with a hypothetical *electrical fluid in the *vril* featured in *The Coming Race* (1871). The development of modern chemistry produced a version of this notion in which all atoms are regarded as complications of the fundamental hydrogen atom, to which they might be reduced—a hypothesis that forms the basis of the apocalyptic technology featured in Fred T. Jane's *The Violet Flame* (1899). Another universal substance transmutable into any other is featured in William Cane and John Fairbairn's *The Confectioners* (1906).

The development of *chemistry out of alchemy involved a dramatic proliferation of the number of substances perceived as elements, although the old scheme lingered into the eighteenth century. Following precedents set in the revised atomic theory of Robert Boyle, the term was redefined by Antoine Lavoisier in *Traité élémentaire de chimie* (1789) as a substance that could not be decomposed into further substances. Lavoisier and Joseph Priestley had already demonstrated that neither water nor air was

an element in this sense; earth plainly did not qualify, and the same experimenters had also come up with a new theory of combustion to account for fire. As more substances were shown to be compounds, more new elements were discovered, assisted by new methods of isolation like Humphry Davy's electrochemistry. The process of identification made rapid progress in the early nineteenth century, and the new chemical elements were swiftly subjected to the taxonomic organisation of Dmitri Mendeleev's periodic table in 1869.

The periodic table of the elements became a stimulus to further discovery as researchers raced to fill in its various gaps and complete the pattern in to which the first ninety-two elements fell—relatively tidily, save for the anomaly of the "rare earths", which formed a sidebranch. Before this work had been completed, however, *atomic theory had moved into a new phase, having demonstrated that the chemical elements were not the ultimate constituents of matter at all. Early twentieth-century expectation that there might be only a few "elementary particles" making up the chemical elements were dashed in their turn when the number of subatomic particles observed in cyclotrons and predicted by hypothetical organising schemes began to grow profusely in the second half of the twentieth century. Theoretical physicists then took the search for relative simplicity to the even-more-fundamental level of quark theory.

In spite of their scientific supersession, the four Classical elements retained a powerful influence on literary imagery. The exemplars provided by Romantic literature, in which metaphorical representation of natural phenomena in terms of the four elements had not only taken aboard but further extended the mystical elaborations of the Paracelsians, assisted the Classical elements to become significant flag-bearers of Keatsian poetic resistance to the supposed imaginative corrosions of nineteenth-century science. The persistence of such phrases as "in one's element" and "the elements" (with reference to the weather), assisted by the extent to which biology and meteorology lagged behind the physical sciences, helped to maintain their metaphorical currency, and the twentieth-century resurgence of "alternative *medicine" gave new currency to similar pseudoscientific formulations, notably the "five elements" of Chinese medicine (earth, water, fire, wood, and metal). The genre fantasy produced on an increasingly prolific scale after 1976 also provided new imaginative space for the development and further elaboration of occult schemes based on the Classical elements.

Early writers of generic speculative fiction often used the discovery of fabulously powerful new elements as a plot lever, but post-Mendeleevian chemistry was already too sophisticated to allow such devices to carry much conviction, except as facilitating devices. In nineteenth-century scientific romance new metals and gases were usually used in the cause of *aeronautics, providing the means to construct or lift airships or spaceships, as in Harry Collingwood's *The Log of the "Flying Fish"* (1887), E. Douglas Fawcett's *Hartmann the Anarchist* (1893), and W. Cairns Johnston's *Beyond the Ether* (1898). Garrett P. Serviss' artemisium in *The Moon Metal* (1900) replaces gold as a currency standard. Stephen Chalmers' Saturnium in "Star-Dust" (1912) facilitates communication with the dead. Such casual miracles became a staple of crude action-adventure science fiction but were treated with much greater circumspection in science fiction that took its inspiration from actual chemistry.

Although the early science fiction pulps produced a rich crop of new elements, the harvest grew much thinner in the 1940s. The element aptly called X in E. E. Smith's *The Skylark of Space* (1928; book, 1946) opened up the galactic playground of space opera with a casual flourish, but Smith opted for a more elaborate jargon in later series as the well of plausible inspiration gradually ran dry. Other notable examples from the pulps include Gawain Edwards' undual in *The Earth-Tube* (1929), Ralph Linn's Carsonium in "Element 87" (1930), Donald Wandrei's rhillium in "The Blinding Shadows" (1934), and Nathan Schachner's transuranic element 93, evanium, in "The Ultimate Metal" (1935). The further reaches of the transuranic spectrum offered a brief respite from the general decline in such stories as Milton K. Smith's "The Mystery of Element 117" (1949), but most such inventions, including element 167 in A. E. van Vogt's *The House That Stood Still* (1950), were restricted to cameo appearances. The new inert gas agnoton, featured in Anthony Boucher's "Transfer Point" (1950), is relegated to a story within the story.

In the meantime, the speculative quest for a further underlying simplicity continued in such stories as Donald Wandrei's "Finality Unlimited" (1936) and "Infinity Zero" (1936)—which replace the Classical elements with five "ultimates" (time, space, matter, life, and intelligence) capable of independent variation—and Willard E. Hawkins' "The Dwindling Sphere" (1940), in which the single fundamental form of matter is "plastocene". Daniel F. Galouye's *Lords of the Psychon* (1963) carried that quest to its idealist extreme in suggesting that the ultimate component of reality is an aspect of id rather than matter. The discovery that many elements exist in several distinct isotopic states because of the variation of the number of neutrons contained in their nuclei permitted the invocation of new isotopes in place of new elements, but physical chemistry had already progressed to the point at which the properties of hypothetical isotopes could be calculated in advance, thus reducing their potential as fictitious miracle workers. In hard science fiction, at least, fictionally interesting discoveries of new elements became rare and somewhat treacherous; the dangerous "new element" jupiterium in Stephen L. Suffitt's "The Element" (1979) eventually turns out to be an isotope of silver, although its discoverer does succeed, belatedly in having his name attached to halberstamium.

ENGINEERING

The art of contrivance, involving the application of the scientific method to the design and construction of artifacts. Although the notion of engineering overlaps that of *invention, it usually involves more improvisation than innovation, solving practical problems by adapting general designs to suit particular circumstances—the term comes from the same Latin root as the word "ingenious"—so the engineer has become the archetype of the technological pragmatist who gets jobs done efficiently, elegantly, and economically (and usually anonymously). The term was first commonly used in connection with the design and construction of engines of *war: earthworks, forts, catapults, siege towers, improvised bridges, and so on.

Prodigious feats of early military engineering include the construction of a pontoon bridge across the Hellespont on the orders of the Persian king Xerxes in the fifth century B.C. and the construction of the Great Wall of China, begun in the third century B.C. Nonmilitary projects of similar scope were undertaken in the pursuit of monarchical grandiosity, especially in ancient Egypt. The first engineer whose name was committed to legend was the builder of the step pyramid at Saqqarah, Imhotep, but his was a rare privilege; most of the engineers of the seven wonders of the ancient world remain uncredited. Early theoretical investigations of the principles of engineering were carried out by Archimedes. Alexandria, established by the Classical world's greatest military genius, became and remained a key centre of improvisation, while the Athenian philosophers were more inclined to abstract cerebration. The pragmatically inclined and imperialistically ambitious Romans also made considerable advances in engineering while paying little or no heed to abstract matters. The first textbook of engineering was Roman: Vitruvius' *De architectura* (first century A.D.).

The history of warfare is easily representable as a long contest between offensive and defensive engineers, especially in the conduct of siege warfare, and the success of empire-builders was invariably founded on the superiority of their military engineers. Such is the politics of celebrity, however, that the lack of credit given to engineers in legend extended seamlessly to history and reportage, which invariably focus on the direct appliance of violence or the issuing of strategic commands. Among the host of Renaissance military engineers, only *Leonardo da Vinci achieved lasting fame, by virtue of the exceptional skill and fanciful tendencies of his technical drawing rather than any concrete achievements. Scientists who embarked on careers as military engineers, such as John *Dee's protégé Thomas Digges, tended to slip out of sight in the history of science, aided in their elusiveness by the fact that their discoveries were generally maintained as military secrets, at least for a while.

The first school of engineering, the École Nationale des Ponts et Chaussées, was founded in France in 1747. The École Polytechnique founded in 1794 was designed to train military officers in mathematics, science, and engineering. From its inception in 1775 the U.S. Army had a chief engineer responsible for fortifications; the Engineering Corps established in 1779 was reformed in 1794 as the Corps of Artillerists and Engineers, and in 1815 Sylvanus Thayer introduced an engineering school into the U.S. Military Academy at West Point. Civil engineering developed in the eighteenth and nineteenth centuries as an offshoot of military engineering. The U.S. Army Corps of Topographic Engineers, who mapped the West for military purposes, was co-opted by Congress to design and construct canals and railroads, while the skills of European military engineers diffused into the context of "public works": the building of roads, bridges, water supply systems, waste disposal systems, and so on. The first British civil engineer to use the title was John Smeaton, the designer of the Eddystone Lighthouse. The British Institution of Civil Engineers received its royal charter in 1828, its first president being Thomas Telford, builder of the Menai Bridge.

The term "civil engineer" was supplemented in the early nineteenth century by that of "mechanical engineer", primarily as a result of the endeavours of James Watt and Matthew Boulton in designing and building steam engines. The adaptation of steam engines to multiple functions in the textile industry, and the parallel development of the machine tool industry, brought the profession of engineering into its first heyday in the mid-nineteenth century, when Isambard Kingdom Brunel became the archetype of the engineer, much as Thomas Edison was later to become the archetype of the inventor and Albert Einstein the archetype of the theoretical scientist. Although Brunel's literary presence is far more elusive than that of his counterparts, Queen Victoria's diary, as envisaged in Stephen Baxter's "The Modern

Cyrano" (1999), suggests that he might have placed an object in orbit, and he is the builder of a problematic Thames tunnel in Paul J. McAuley's steampunk fantasy "Dr. Pretorius and the Lost Temple" (2002).

The heroic age of engineering was defined and detailed by Samuel Smiles' *Lives of the Engineers* (1861–1862; rev. eds., 1874 and 1904), a project that carried forward the argument of Smiles' best-selling *Self-Help* (1859), which had offered exemplary lives of various great men in association with the admonition "Do thou likewise". It was given more poetic expression, from the viewpoint of a machine-user rather than a machine-maker—by Rudyard Kipling in "M'Andrew's Hymn" (in *The Seven Seas*, 1896), which attempts to embody the worldview of a steamship's "engineer"—and helped to cement the cliché of the rough but ever-ready Scottish engine-minder. Engineers were famed for their versatility in the heroic era, but the profession was to undergo a long process of subdivision and specialisation thereafter, giving rise to such categories as electrical engineering, chemical engineering, and electronic engineering.

Like legend, history, and reportage, literature has always tended to short-change the engineer. Although the achievements of the heroic age of engineering are abundantly featured in naturalistic fiction and its potential achievements are extravagantly displayed in speculative fiction, the credit is invariably given to the characters who have the big ideas and drop the bombs rather than the people who actually build things. The objects manufactured by engineers routinely carry more charisma than their improvisers, as is evident in the description of such constructs as Jules Verne's *L'île à hélice* (1895; trans. as *Floating Island* and *Propellor Island*) and Curt Siodmak's *F.P.1 Antwortet Nicht* (1930; trans. as *F.P.1 Does Not Reply*), but there are some notable exceptions. The Brunelesque hero of Paschal Grousset's *De New York à Brest en sept heures* (1888, by-lined André Laurie; trans. as *New York to Brest in Seven Hours*) is equally hard-headed as an engineer and as a businessman. Bernard Kellermann's *Der Tunnel* (1913; trans. as *The Tunnel*), gives due credit to its hero's prowess as an engineer as well as to his invention of the supersteel Allanite.

John Lawrence Hodgson's *The Time-Journey of Dr. Barton: An Engineering and Sociological Forecast Based on Present Possibilities* (1929) is an ambitious futuristic projection by a civil engineer. The hero of John Knittel's *Amadeus* (1939; trans. as *Power for Sale*) does not actually succeed in building a dam across the straits of Gibraltar in order to increase the land surface of the Mediterranean countries (more water evaporates from the sea than flows into it from rivers), but gets full credit for effort and imagination.

The spirit of these Western European examples was amplified dramatically in Soviet science fiction by such writers as Alexei Tolstoi and Aleksandr Kazantsev, who preferred engineers to theoretical scientists on ideological grounds.

In early American science fiction inventors and theoreticians were awarded heroic status far more frequently than engineers, but John W. *Campbell Jr. strove to redress the imbalance in the pages of *Astounding Science Fiction*, where celebratory accounts of ingenious improvisation became part of the magazine's staple diet. Arthur J. Burks' "Hell Ship" (1938) transferred the cliché of the Scottish engineer into space opera, where it did long and noble service before it was taken up by *Star Trek*. It is significant, however, that this quasi-propagandist spirit was most evident in the work of those writers in Campbell's stable who gained the reputation of being competent journeymen rather than literary stars. The most conspicuous examples in the 1940s were George O. Smith, whose Venus Equilateral series (launched 1942) became archetypal of engineering science fiction, and Raymond F. Jones, in such stories as "The Toymaker" (1946), "The Model Shop" (1947), and "Tools of the Trade" (1950). Smith's "Rat Race" (1947) is an ironic extrapolation of the classic engineering problem of building a better mousetrap.

The adjustable spanner, or "monkey wrench", became an iconic symbol of engineering expertise in *Astounding*'s illustrations, often juxtaposed with more refined devices such as the slide rule, but it only played a significant part in the fiction when pressed into service as a makeshift weapon. On the other hand, the magazine's use of science fiction to develop interesting hypothetical exercises in engineering spilled out into the academy; John E. Arnold's article in the May 1953 issue described a creative engineering course at the Massachusetts Institute of Technology, including a project in which students designed a machine for a hypothetical alien race inhabiting a cold world with a methane atmosphere. Successful anticipations in the magazine's pages included the central image of Robert A. Heinlein's "Waldo" (1942): mechanical arms controlled with the aid of television monitors.

Other notable works of science fiction championing the talents of engineers include James Blish's "Bridge" (1952), Thomas N. Scortia's *What Mad Oracle?* (1961), and *Artery of Fire* (1972), which draw on the author's experiences in the aerospace industry, and Colin Kapp's series collected in *The Unorthodox Engineers* (1979). Philip K. Dick's "The Variable Man" (1953) offers only the vaguest account of how its repairman hero obtains results, but pays tribute to a growing mystique attached to talented handymen. Hypothetical engineering projects of heroic dimensions featured prominently in science fiction because of the crucial roles envisaged for them in the early phases of the *Space Age, not merely in the construction of spaceships but in the building and operation of space stations and other kinds *artificial satellites, and in the maintenance of *colonies in difficult physical circumstances. By the time *Astounding* became *Analog*, tales of engineering in space had acquired a fine gloss of realism, as displayed in stories by regular contributors Donald Kingsbury, as in "Shipwright" (1978), and John Berryman, as in "The Big Dish" (1986). Michael F. Flynn's series begun with *Firestar* (1996) pays close attention to the engineering problems involved in the space program it describes. Steven Popkes' "Stovelighter" (1987) is one of many stories extending this kind of exercise from near-contemporary space hardware towards the design of starships.

There was a further and more grandiose dimension to the representation of engineering in Campbellian science fiction, pioneered by such stories as Clifford D. Simak's *Cosmic Engineers* (1939), whose eponymous entities are mechanical beings working "at the rim of exploding universe" to avert its collision with another universe in five-dimensional "interspace". Carried forward by such stories as Harry Stine's "Galactic Gadgeteers" (1951), the tradition of cosmic engineering stories eventually expanded into a whole subgenre of stories featuring vast and enigmatic alien artifacts, unceremoniously dubbed "big dumb objects" in the 1992 edition of John Clute and Peter Nicholls' *Encyclopedia of Science Fiction*.

Early archetypes of this subgenre include Larry *Niven's *Ringworld* (1970), Arthur C. *Clarke's *Rendezvous with Rama* (1973), and Bob Shaw's *Orbitsville* (1975), and it was extensively developed thereafter in such extravagant sequences as Stephen *Baxter's Xeelee series and Charles *Sheffield's Heritage Universe series, drawing considerable inspiration from the ideas of Freeman *Dyson regarding projects that might be undertaken by type 2 civilisations. Similar structures constructed by future humans or *posthumans include the skyweb in Jack Williamson's *Lifeburst* (1984) and the Met in Tony Daniel's *Metaplanetary* (2001). Unsurprisingly, however, the engineers responsible for all of these projects are usually conspicuous only by their absence from the stories in which their achievements are featured.

ENTOMOLOGY

The branch of *zoology devoted to the study of insects. Although spiders and other arachnids are not insects, and thus not part of the scientific subject matter of entomology, they are routinely aggregated with insects in the "ethnoentomology" of the popular imagination and its literary extensions, and the meaning of the term will therefore be stretched for the purpose of this discussion to include them.

Although it is no more significant as a scientific discipline than any other sector of the study of the diversity of living organisms, entomology has had a grossly disproportionate influence on literary imagery, especially in the recent production of *monsters by their extreme magnification. The notion that insects could simply be scaled up to giant size is one of the most common "errors" of modern melodramatic fiction—ignoring the mechanical limitations of load bearing and problems of oxygen supply and nourishment associated with the fact that doubling the linear dimensions of an organism increases its body mass to a much greater extent than the dimensions of its limbs and internal transport systems—but the impulse producing such images has nothing to do with rational extrapolation, being far more concerned with matters of *psychology and *aesthetics.

It is not entirely clear why so many insects and creatures lumped with them in the vulgar category of "creepy-crawlies" are commonly held to be archetypes of ugliness, or why they should occasion phobic anxieties that extend far beyond the troublesome effects of their bites and stings, but that is very obviously the case. The quasi-instinctive horror with which many people regard creatures such as centipedes and spiders may have as much to do with the way they move as the way they look, but that does not assist the process of explanation. It is easy enough to understand why some elaborately coloured insects—especially butterflies—are considered beautiful rather than ugly, but night-flying moths and brightly coloured dragonflies are often regarded with distinct ambivalence in this respect. It is also easy to understand why the phenomenon of insect metamorphosis—which turns ugly caterpillars into beautiful butterflies, and many other larvae into even-less-prepossessing imagoes, following a sojourn in a chrysalis—excited particular interest in myth-makers and litterateurs, by virtue of its innate marvelousness as well as its abundant metaphorical scope.

The tendency of moths to be attracted by flames is another entomological phenomenon that recommends itself for metaphorical usage, and its association with death allowed the Egyptian scarab to take on a very elaborate symbolism. The most striking item of this kind is the organisation of social insects into hives: communities organised around a single fertile female, analogically dubbed the queen, supported by various castes of sterile females—including workers and soldiers—and male drones. Once the pattern was fully explicated, the hive provided a model of sexual reproduction strikingly different from that of human society (posing an awkward problem to theorists of natural selection, the explanation of its evolutionary logic being the cardinal triumph of *sociobiology). It also provided an apparent model of either the ultimate in totalitarianism or the ultimate in altruistic cooperation, according to political taste.

The origins of entomology in the classical zoology of Aristotle already reflected a keen awareness of insects as pests as well as the marvels of metamorphosis. The damaging effects of swarms of locusts are evident in literature descended from oral tradition; the afflictions visited on the Egyptians in *Exodus* 8–10 include swarms of biting flies and locusts. On the other hand, bees were appreciated for making honey, as well as becoming emblems of cooperative industry, along with ants. Silkworms became a prized component of early textile technology. These contrasted aspects of the science are sometimes reflected in their representation; the Elizabethan physician Thomas Moffet cast his account of *Silkwormes and their flies* (1599) as a Georgic poem. Moffet had already composed a pioneering textbook of entomology in Latin, but it was not published until 1634; it was translated into English as *The Theatre of Insects*. The image of the insect world as a "theatre" viewed by humans proved persistent and versatile, cropping up continually in satire, children's literature, and such unlikely locations as Théophile Gautier's *Mademoiselle de Maupin* (1835–1836). The anonymous *The Ants: A Rhapsody* (1767) is an early literary account of hive organisation, crediting "emmets" with an elaborate language.

The need to protect translocated crops from local pests made entomological investigations significant in the context of *colonisation, evidenced by such works as Thaddeus William Harris' *Treatise on Some of the Insects of New England Which are Injurious to Vegetation* (1842). The founder of American entomology, Thomas Say—whose *American Entomology* was issued in 1824–1828—was a member of Robert Owen's New Harmony community. The U.S. Entomological Commission, established in 1877 under the directorship of Charles V. Riley, was primarily interested in pest control. Leland O. Howard, the chief entomologist for the United States Department of Agriculture, was the first person to experiment with biological pest control when he imported parasites from England in the hope of limiting New England's gypsy moth population in 1905.

One of the deepest roots of literary accounts of giant insects and spiders extends back into nineteenth-century fairy tales, and particularly to the tradition of fairy painting established in that era, which made much of the notion that fairies were very tiny and possessed of insectile wings. This led to humanlike creatures being frequently depicted in illustration alongside similarly scaled insects. The imagery was not menacing at first—the partly anthropomorphised insects in William Roscoe's illustrated poem "The Butterfly's Ball and the Grasshopper's Feast" (1807) are charming—but it took on a more sinister edge in the paintings of Richard Dadd and John Anster Fitzgerald and such literary works as Sara Coleridge's *Phantasmion* (1837), whose eponymous hero is menaced by a giant stag-beetle. Like *archaeology and *palaeontology, entomology became a distinctly unglamorous profession in the nineteenth century, but its extension as an amateur hobby gave it greater scope. Its metaphorical resonances and certain items of its standard apparatus recommended it for literary use in such stories as H. G. Wells' "A Moth—Genus Novo" (1895), L. P. Hartley's "The Killing Bottle" (1927), and A. S. Byatt's "Morpho Eugenia" (1992).

The innately dramatic quality of insect reproduction excited a considerable sense of wonder in such nineteenth-century entomologists as Jean-Henri Fabre, who became a highly significant populariser of the subject in his *Souvenirs entomologiques* (10 vols., 1879–1907). Among those influenced by his work were the key Symbolist writers Rémy de Gourmont, who made abundant use of insect examples in his *Physique de l'amour* (1903; trans. by Ezra Pound as *The Natural Philosophy of Love*), and Maurice Maeterlinck, who rhapsodised on the subject in *La vie des abeilles* (1901; trans. as *The Life of the Bee*) and a 1926 sequel based on Eugène Marais' then-unpublished *Die siel van die Mier* (1937; trans. as *The Soul of the White Ant*). The subject retained a particular fascination in French literature, carried into the late twentieth century in the work of Bernard Werber, including the best-selling *Les fourmis* (1991; trans. as *Empire of the Ants*), *Jour des fourmis* (1992), and *La révolution des fourmis* (1995). The practice of drawing fabular symbolic links between insect and human behaviour reached an exotic apogee in Karel and Josef Čapek's play *Ze zivota hmyzu* (1921: trans. as "*And so ad infinitum...*" and *The Insect Play*).

Fabre and Maeterlinck laid the foundations for the quasi-mystical consideration of a hive of social insects as a kind of collective organism possessed of a "hive mind". The notion was accommodated within scientific discourse in such works as Auguste-Henri Forel's study of "insect psychology" *Le monde social des fourmis* (5 vols., 1923) and William Morton Wheeler's *Social Life Among the Insects* (1923), subsequently exercising a powerful influence on the literary

imagination. The hive became one of the most popular analogues developed in speculative *exobiology, and giant ants became common monsters of the science-fictional imagination. Notable expressions of this fascination include A. Lincoln Green's "The Captivity of the Professor" (1901), H. G. Wells' *The First Men in the Moon* (1901) and "The Empire of the Ants" (1905), F. Hernamann-Johnson's *The Polyphemes* (1906), Ralph Milne Farley's *The Radio Man* (1924; book, 1948), F. A. Ridley's *The Green Machine* (1926), Stanton A. Coblentz's *After 12,000 Years* (1929; book, 1950), Norman L. Knight's "Island of the Golden Swarm" (1938), Ben Hecht's "The Adventures of Professor Emmett" (1939), Bob Olsen's "The Ant with the Human Soul" (1932), William K. Sonnemann's "The Council of Drones" (1936), Alfred Gordon Bennett's *The Demigods* (1939), Will F. Jenkins' "Doomsday Deferred" (1949), Fredric Brown's "Come and Go Mad" (1949), Francis Rufus Bellaamy's *Atta* (1954), the film *Them!* (1954), Keith Roberts' *The Furies* (1966), Lindsay Gutteridge's *Killer Pine* (1973), Joseph L. Green's *The Horde* (1976), and Edward Bryant's "giANTS" (1979).

Newspaper reportage reflected anxieties about hive power in stories of "killer bees" that became popular in the early 1970s, reflected in such novels as Arthur Herzog's *The Swarm* (1974)—anticipated in Will H. Gray's "The Bees from Borneo" (1931). H. G. Wells' "Empire of the Ants" pioneered the notion that insect hives might be serious contenders to end human domination of Earth—a theme continued in Charles de Richter's *La menace invisible* (1927; trans. as *The Fall of the Eiffel Tower*) and Francis Flagg's "The Master Ants" (1928). In Homer Eon Flint's "The Emancipatrix" (1921) humans are enslaved by bees—a motif more elaborately developed in David H. Keller's *The Human Termites* (1929; book, 1978) and Frank Belknap Long's "The Last Men" (1934) and "Green Glory" (1935). Frank Herbert's *The Green Brain* (1966) imagines a multispecific hive evolving to restore the world's *ecological balance after its disruption by humans.

Literary images of hivelike human societies usually find the idea utterly horrific, and it is often invoked in *dystopian fiction. It is, however, proposed as a probable pattern for human's evolutionary future in Elizabeth Bisland's "The Coming Subjugation of Man" (1889), Edward Knoblock's *The Ant Heap* (1929), J. Harvey Haggard's "Human Ants" (1935), J. D. Beresford and Esmé Wynne-Tyson's *The Riddle of the Tower* (1944), Edward Hyams' *Morrow's Ants* (1975), and the series begun with Stephen Baxter's *Coalescent* (2003). L. Sprague de Camp's *Rogue Queen* (1951) describes a human-prompted rebellion in an extraterrestrial humanoid hive. More ambivalent treatments of the notion include T. J. Bass's *Half Past Human* (1971), Frank Herbert's *Hellstrom's Hive* (1973), John Boyd's *The Girl with the Jade Green Eyes* (1978), and Robert Silverberg's *The Queen of Springtime* (1989), but the eventual verdict of such works usually remains negative.

The idea of a collective mind is abstracted from hivelike reproductive systems in numerous imaginative accounts, which routinely find it more acceptable in decontextualised form. Group-minds are employed as images of enviable social harmony in Olaf Stapledon's *Last and First Men* (1930) and *Star Maker* (1937), Theodore Sturgeon's *More Than Human* (1953) and *The Cosmic Rape* (1958), and Arthur C. Clarke's *Childhood's End* (1953), although loss of individuality is often seen as a price too high to pay, as in Brian W. Aldiss' *Enemies of the System* (1978) and Mikhail Emtsev and Eremei Parnov's *World-Soul* (trans. 1978).

Alien hives are often matched against humans in what seems to be a fundamental Darwinian struggle for existence, as in Roscoe B. Fleming's "The Menace of the Little" (1931), Robert A. Heinlein's *Starship Troopers* (1959), Joe Haldeman's *The Forever War* (1974), and Orson Scott Card's *Ender's Game* (1977; exp. 1985), but the alien hives in Barrington J. Bayley's "The Bees of Knowledge" (1975) and Keith Laumer's *Star Colony* (1981) are granted more respect, and Card followed up *Ender's Game* with *Speaker for the Dead* (1986), in which the guilt-stricken genocidal hero searches for a new home for the last surviving alien queen. More detailed sympathetic accounts of alien hive societies are featured in C. J. Cherryh's *Serpent's Reach* (1982) and Linda Steele's *Ibis* (1985).

Romances of miniaturisation like Edwin Pallander's *Adventures of a Micro-Man* (1902) also deployed confrontations of similarly scaled humans and insects before pulp fiction began to make more prolific use of giant insects and spiders, in such stories as Murray Leinster's far-futuristic fantasies "The Mad Planet" (1920) and "The Red Dust" (1921), T. S. Stribling's "The Web of the Sun" (1922), and Russell Hays' "The Beetle Experiment" (1929). More inventive accounts of hypothetical arachnids include Charles Loring Jackson's "An Undiscovered Isle in the Far Sea'" (1926) and H. Warner Munn's "The City of Spiders" (1926).

Giant spiders lent themselves particularly well to cinematic representation in such movies as *Tarantula* (1955), *The Incredible Shrinking Man* (1957), and *Arachnophobia* (1990), which assisted them in acquiring a quasi-archetypal status as figures of menace, pressed into service as the very essence of horror in Stephen King's *It* (1986; film, 1990). In the meantime,

Franz Kafka represented the ultimate in human *alienation as transmogrification into a giant cockroach in *Die Vervandlung* (1915; trans. as *Metamorphosis*)—a notion recapitulated on a more popular level in George Langelaan's "La mouche" (1957; trans. as "The Fly"; films, 1958 and 1986).

Insect palaeontology did lend some support to the notion of giant insects, revealing the legacy of a Carboniferous heyday associated with the first development of flight, whose monstrous stars included giant dragonfly-like *Palaeoptera* and the burly ancestors of modern cockroaches and beetles. Such imaginative stimulation was, however, superfluous to the trend. The parallel revelation of the crucial role played by some biting insects in spreading disease—advertised by Ronald Ross' clarification of the manner in which mosquitoes spread malaria—also added little to the dread in which they were already held. On the other hand, further elucidation of the manner in which some insects parasitise other species, including mammals, by laying eggs inside them whose larvae become endoparasites, did lend itself to extrapolation into graphic images of exploitation, reflected in urban legends as well as science fiction stories featuring horrid *aliens, such as A. E. van Vogt's "Discord in Scarlet" (1939), Robert A. Heinlein's *The Puppet Masters* (1951), Philip José Farmer's *The Lovers* (1952; book 1961), the film series launched by *Alien* (1979), and Octavia Butler's "Bloodchild" (1984). An article by Ian Watson on the rational plausibility of such science-fictional images of such "necrogenes" sparked a combative correspondence in the pages of the journal *Foundation* in 1987–1988.

Awareness of the rational flaws in the notion of giant insects and spiders slowed the production of such images in more conscientious science fiction during the second half of the twentieth century. Hard science fiction stories based in entomology include W. Macfarlane's "Biological Peacefare" (1973) and Bruce Sterling's "Luciferase" (2004), while such works as Ian Watson's *The Flies of Memory* (1988; exp. book, 1990) and Scott Baker's *Webs* (1989) took on a surreal edge. The advent of *genetic engineering prompted some writers to look more realistically at the prospect of building bigger and better insects, as in Brian Stableford's "The Invertebrate Man" (1990) and Rebecca Ore's *Gaia's Toys* (1995). The possibility of using real or artificial insects as metaphorical "bugs" for surveillance purposes is explored in such stories as Stanley Schmidt's *Argonaut* (2002). In the title story of Darryl Murphy's *Wasps at the Speed of Sound* (2005), insects leave Earth just as humans are beginning to learn to communicate with them, thus emphasising the gulf of misunderstanding that has always affected the relationship, and the sense of injury that insects would probably feel if they knew what most humans thought of them.

The use of insects as food, although not uncommon, has a built-in yuck factor that encourages its literary use as a stomach-turning exercise—a service it also performs in many reality TV shows—and occasionally gives rise to speculative fiction of a blackly comic stripe, as in Edward Bryant's "The Human Side of the Village Monster" (1971), which features the creation of an edible cockroach.

ENTROPY

A term employed by the German physicist Rudolf Clausius in 1850 as a measure of the distribution of energy within a system; entropy increases as energy differentials—and hence the potential for energy transmission—decrease. The notion had been foreshadowed in Sadi Carnot's theoretical analysis of steam engines in *Réflexions sur la puissance motrice du feu* (1824). The invention of the term drew a swift response from William Thomson—later Lord Kelvin—in "On a Universal Tendency in Nature to the Dissipation of Mechanical Energy" (1852), which included the conclusion that the Earth must one day become uninhabitable because of the effects of entropy. The second law of thermodynamics—which states that entropy within a closed system always increases, until it reaches terminal equilibrium—seemed to Kelvin and others to encapsulate a kind of cosmic pessimism, testifying to the inevitable ultimate extinction of everything: the "heat death of the universe".

Kelvin followed up his first article on entropy with "On the Age of the Sun's Heat" (1862) in the popular periodical *Macmillan's Magazine*, which included the first of a series of calculations he made regarding the date when the sun's waning heat—which he assumed, falsely, to be produced by the energy of gravitational collapse—would no longer be adequate to sustain life on Earth. These calculations exercised a considerable influence on the literary imagination, echoed in such poems as James Clerk Maxwell's "A Paradoxical Ode" (1878), before providing the ideative underpinnings of a school of far-futuristic fantasy whose products included Camille Flammarion's *La fin du monde* (1893–1894; trans. as *Omega: The Last Days of the World*), H. G. Wells' *The Time Machine* (1895), and William Hope Hodgson's *The House on the Borderland* (1908). Kelvin also estimated the age of the Earth by the same method, coming up with a figure very much shorter than those favoured by geologists and lending considerable support to *Creationists.

Entropy is sometimes represented as a measure of "disorder", while "order" is construed as structural complexity, but the entropic "heat death" that promises to reduce the entire universe to a condition of uniform inactivity can also be conceived as a state of perfect order. The *evolution of complexity within *Earth's ecosphere is dependent on the inflow of energy from the Sun, so it is not a closed system, but the organising tendency of life is sometimes conceived as "negative entropy" or "negentropy", and the manner in which complex constructs emerge from systems whose built-in tendency is always to uniformity has become a considerable source of fascination to philosophically inclined scientists, especially in connection with the new understanding of the word "*chaos".

Although entropy is arguably the least dramatic of all scientific concepts, the notion that everything in the universe is caught up in an eternal and irresistible process of decay, against which background all constructive endeavour must ultimately prove futile, is imaginatively powerful. The distance of the prospect has not prevented philosophers, physicists, and litterateurs from expressing anxieties about the seeming indignity of universal entropic "heat death" and from producing such imaginative countermeasures as *Omega Point theory, which is partly based on J. D. Bernal's contention in *The World, the Flesh and the Devil* (1929) that humankind's ultimate descendants might well be able to cheat the heat death.

J. F. Sullivan's "The Dwindling Hour" (1893) is an early image of "reversed entropy", which imagines an "accelerating universe"; Christopher Anvil's "Untropy" (1965) is a more sophisticated version of the notion. Nathan Schachner's "Entropy" (1936), in which the heat death is accomplished, but becomes the prelude to a new creative process, is more typical of such exercises. In Jack Williamson's "Released Entropy" (1937) a plan to thwart the heat death goes awry. The hero of James Kahn's *Timefall* (1987) similarly attempts to prevent the world from "running down" by importing energy from parallel universes. Notable descriptions of an entropic universal anticlimax include David Langford's "Waiting for the Iron Age" (1991) and Stephen Baxter's "The Gravity Mine" (2000).

In more recent times the notion of entropy has been a prolific generator of "mood pieces" forging a quasi-justificatory link between universal entropy and personal feelings of *ennui* and despair. J. G. Ballard's "The Voices of Time" (1962), in which a cosmic signal intercepted by *SETI is found to be counting down to the end of time, and Pamela Zoline's "The Heat Death of the Universe" (1967), which subjects the dispiriting aspects of housework to a perverse glorification, became archetypal items of British "new wave" science fiction; their conscientious existential *decadence echoes in further stories, such as M. John

Harrison's "Running Down" (1975). The motif was frequently cited and elaborated in the work of the new wave's editorial guide, Michael Moorcock, and Colin Greenland titled his survey of the movement *The Entropy Exhibition* (1983). Although the temper of U.S. science fiction was markedly different, the notion was developed in a similar fashion in such genre stories as Robert Silverberg's "In Entropy's Jaws" (1971) as well as such literary fantasies as Thomas Pynchon's *Gravity's Rainbow* (1973).

ETHER

A Greek term—often rendered as "aether"—originally invented to describe the clear space above the clouds. It was widely conceived as the breathing medium of the gods, and was therefore sometimes used to refer to the substance of the soul, before being adapted by *Aristotle to serve as the substance of the heavens, enabling his philosophy to avoid the seemingly abhorrent notion of the "void" (empty *space).

The notion of void was not abhorrent to everyone—indeed, it was logically required by *atomic theory—and it seemed less troubling to some Mediaeval and Renaissance philosophers than it had to Aristotle. It seemed even less distressing in the context of the much vaster heliocentric model of the cosmos, which replaced the Aristotelian *cosmology of "crystal spheres" in the seventeenth century. Although Isaac *Newton conceived of his frame of absolute space as fundamentally empty, a plenum seemed necessary to many of his rivals in order avoid the problem of "action at a distance" posed by the theory of *gravity. René Descartes invoked an etheric "ocean" to explain the aggregation of the planets in the plane of the ecliptic; the notion of "etheric vortices" became a key element of his cosmology and others derived from it.

In the nineteenth century the term was borrowed by chemists for application to a volatile organic compound often used as an anaesthetic and occasionally as a stimulant. Its *psychotropic effects were far more excessive than the mere banishment of tiredness, as chronicled by one of its victims, Jean Lorrain, in a sequence of hallucinatory stories collectively known as *Contes d'un buveur d'éther* (1893–1895; trans. in *Nightmares of an Ether-Drinker*, 2002). The term was also revitalised by physicists to denote the hypothetical medium in which waves of light were propagated—a notion that gained considerably in popularity when James Clerk Maxwell fused the theories of *electricity, *magnetism, and *light, proposing that the "luminiferous ether" was a necessary hypothesis to account for the propagation of electromagnetic radiation in waves.

The reenshrinement of the luminiferous ether within physical theory was widely reflected in nineteenth-century accounts of *space travel, and it also provided an important theoretical foundation stone for the nineteenth-century occult revival. One of its most enthusiastic scientific popularisers, Oliver Lodge—who published "The Ether and Its Functions" in *Nature* in 1883—was also one of the most ardent scientific recruits to spiritualism and *parapsychology. It was one of the hypotheses attacked—along with the *atom—by such *positivist philosophers of science as Ernst Mach, who wanted to rid science of what he considered to be metaphysical embellishments, and therefore became a significant bone of contention by the end of the century. Although it was effectively killed off by *relativity theory—which reinterpreted the failure of the 1887 Michelson-Morley experiment's attempt to measure the Earth's velocity in the ether as conclusive proof of the ether's nonexistence—it continued to exercise an influence over the popular imagination, and is featured in numerous items of twentieth-century speculative fiction.

Hy Gage's "The Lord of the Ether" (1913) features an "ether annihilator" exploited by Universal Ether Controlling Corporation. Ether's manipulation is also the key to miraculous devices in Edmond Hamilton's *Outside the Universe* (1929), in which it is the raw material of continuous creation. Malcolm Jameson's "A Question of Salvage" (1939) features etheric storms in space. Twentieth-century occult fiction, which is obsessed with the notion of etheric "vibrations", continued to make much of the notion, and it made a comeback of sorts in theoretical physics in the 1960s when Peter Higgs and Phillip Anderson postulated a fundamental "Higgs Field" filling the universe and acting as a superconductor.

The classical ether is featured in such calculatedly anachronistic *steampunk stories as Richard A. Lupoff's *Into the Aether* (1974), and the notion is ingeniously varied in the elaborate exercise in cosmological and historical reconstruction contained in Ian MacLeod's *The Light Ages* (2003) and *The House of Storms* (2005), whose "aether" is a magical substance that precipitates an early industrial revolution.

ETHICS

The field of philosophy related to matters of moral responsibility. The history of the field has been dominated by attempts to detach ethics from *theology, and thus from the thesis that good and bad are solely determined by divine commandment. While some philosophers have attempted to substitute an alternative set of moral absolutes based in logic or intuition, others have attempted to build up pragmatic systems in which acts are evaluated according to the consequences that flow from them, often calculated on the basis of the utilitarian principle that the aim of moral action is "the greatest good of the greatest number". Such attempts have been fervently resisted by *religious believers; the consequent notion that secularised philosophy—including science—is innately evil is neatly encapsulated in the myth of *Faust, and is investigated in much of its abundant literary spinoff.

The evolution of pragmatic ethics was closely associated with the evolution of modern science; the two processes tended to move in step, notwithstanding the insistence of philosophers of science that statements of value and statements of fact belong to different orders, and can never be deduced from one another. Although the *positivist philosophy of science was extreme in this insistence, positivism as a social movement was heavily committed to the development of a new ethical regime. Such disciplines as *politics and *criminology are sometimes classified as "moral sciences", and their associated literary genres—*Utopian fiction and crime fiction—tend to be more directly and more combatively engaged with ethical questions than other kinds of fiction.

Wherever scientific and technological issues bear on the treatment of human beings—as they do very obviously in *medicine—ethical principles come into play, often resulting in the evolution of specialised subcategories of ethical philosophy. The development and application of formal and informal ethical systems is an important part of the subject matter of the human sciences, and questions of whether the psychological and sociological study of ethical decisions and institutions can or ought to be objective are inevitably controversial.

The idea that the development of ethical sensibilities ought to be an important part of the educational curriculum was taken for granted when education was monopolised by religion, and was preserved in that context into the nineteenth and twentieth centuries—as the evolution of such literary genres as the English school story readily testifies—but the customary placement of ethics within religious education ensured that ethical education was gradually marginalised or abandoned as twentieth-century education in Europe and America was gradually secularised. This ensured that the education system would remain a key battleground in *ideological disputes by means of which religious believers attempted to reclaim lost ground, as in the long war fought on behalf of *Creationism against the implication of *evolution theory.

The eighteenth-century philosophy of *progress supplemented the moral satisfaction of scientists by proclaiming that technology is a force for social good, and that scientific knowledge is a good in itself. The subsequent weakening of faith in the idea that technological progress inevitably promoted moral progress, and the growth of the suspicion that the former might be antithetical to the latter, generated new anxieties about the moral responsibility of scientists and technologists. If new knowledge could have a deleterious effect on society, by virtue of its technological applications, then it seemed that some science, at least, might be judged innately bad by utilitarian criteria—an argument elaborately developed by Bertrand *Russell in such essays as *Icarus* (1923). The notion of "scientific sin" gained further ground after the invention and use of the *atom bomb, generating such fervent literary reflections as Kurt Vonnegut's *Cat's Cradle* (1963).

Military applications of physics and chemistry generated increasingly heated moral debate throughout both World Wars, the Cold War, and such subsequent conflicts as the Vietnam War, prompting the New York Academy of Sciences to sponsor a conference on "The Social Responsibility of Scientists" in 1972. It was, however, the biological sciences that generated the deepest anxieties and the most fervent arguments, markedly intensified by the development of *biotechnology, which soon generated its own associated discipline of "bioethics" to supplement the long-standing category of medical ethics.

The best-known formulation of medical ethics is the so-called Hippocratic Oath—which was not originated by the followers of Hippocrates, although Hippocrates is credited with the fundamental tenet that a doctor's first duty is to make sure that the actions he takes will do no harm. The central principle of modern medical ethics is the principle of informed consent. Although controversies relating to the ethics of "vivisection" date back to the early nineteenth century, the applications of science in twentieth-century medicine have brought the ethical problems corollary to the *experimental testing of new treatments into much sharper focus. Scientific and technological advances have also complicated such issues as defining the commencement of independent life—important in determining the ethics of treating embryos—and the diagnosis of *death. The routinisation of the experimental testing of new treatments also complicated questions relating to the use of animals in research. All of these issues are extensively discussed in reportage and abundantly reflected in naturalistic literature.

The rapid advancement of molecular *genetics in the last quarter of the twentieth century introduced a new acuity to ethical questions connected with the human reproductive process, requiring the establishment of legal principles specifically geared to deal with the exploitation of new technological opportunities. These included *in vitro* fertilisation, the *cloning of early embryos, and the possibility of selecting embryos on the basis of their genetic makeup for various purposes, including their utility as organ donors for older siblings suffering from genetic deficiency disorders. The possibilities of strategic selection opened up by new reproductive technologies inevitably sharpened anxieties and apprehensions regarding social programs of *eugenics. The use of similar technologies in the genetic modification of animals complicated debates as to the nature and extent of moral consideration owed by humans to animals.

The range of bioethical debate was broadened in the 1980s to take in issues of intellectual property in gene sequences. Although patent law excluded the patenting of natural products, entrepreneurial geneticists began to argue that knowledge of gene sequences should not be excluded by that principle and that practical applications of such knowledge should be treated as inventions. When the advent of rapid sequencing machines prompted Craig Venter to set up the Celera Genomics Corporation, with the intention of obtaining patents for as many individual gene sequences as possible, the ethics of patenting genes with potential medical applications came into sharp focus.

Almost all medical dramas in naturalistic and speculative fiction involve some consideration of medical ethics, and some examples go much further in using medical problems as exemplars for more general ethical theses. Thus, James White's Sector General series (launched 1957) is science fiction's most explicit and most elaborate propaganda in the cause of pacifism—an ethical position that often receives scant consideration in a genre whose most popular subgenre is military science fiction and some of whose other subgenres are wholeheartedly committed to the pornography of violence. Notable individual works focusing on the manner in which scientific and technological progress impacts on medical ethics include Sinclair Lewis' *Arrowsmith* (1925), Alan E. Nourse's "Martyr" (1957), John Rowan Wilson's *The Double Blind* (1960), George R. R. Martin's "The Needle Men" (1981), Timothy Zahn's "The Final Report on the Lifeline Experiment" (1983), Rob Chilson and William F. Wu's "Be Ashamed to Die" (1986), Elizabeth Moon's "A Delicate Adjustment" (1987), Nancy Kress' "The Mountain to Mohammed" (1992), Michael Flynn's "Melodies of the Heart" (1994), Erin Leonard's "The Lab Assistant" (1994), Ben Bova's *Brothers* (1995), and Edd Vick's "The Compass" (2005).

More general questions relating to the ethics of scientific research are addressed in many stories dealing with the development of new *weapons or with discoveries and *inventions that turn out to have unexpected military potential. Notable individual examples include Edward Hyams' *Not in Our Stars* (1949) and Fredric Brown's "The Weapon" (1951). Alison Lurie's *Imaginary Friends* (1967) is a literary account of the entanglement of scientific and ethical issues in research in human science, based on the enquiry reported in Leon Festinger, Henry W. Riecken, and Stanley Schachter's *When Prophecy Fails* (1956).

Several subgenres of speculative fiction are particularly hospitable to *contes philosophiques* bearing on ethical questions—especially those dealing with hypothetical entities whose relationship to the human moral community is ambiguous or problematic, including *robots, *androids and other *artificial intelligences, and animals with enhanced *intelligence. Stories describing human relationships with *aliens provide a uniquely useful laboratory for the consideration of ethical questions, and are often used for that purpose. Stories of first contact sometimes suggest that it would be useful if an anticipatory set of moral principles were in place before any such event occurs, although many such works anticipate difficulties that might arise in their application. Human characters who attempt to establish ethical exemplars for aliens, whether or not they operate under the aegis of *religion, almost invariably come unstuck, as in such works as Katherine MacLean's "Unhuman Sacrifice" (1958) and Thomas N. Scortia's "Broken Image" (1966).

The ethics of human expansion into space have already attracted some academic and political consideration, and fictional accounts of galactic *colonisation often equip would-be settlers of other worlds with ethical principles regarding their treatment of indigenous populations. The idea of *terraforming other worlds for human use had called forth some particularly fierce reactions (Ernest Yanarella had suggested that it might be more appropriately rendered "terrorforming"). The most common suggestion for adoption by interstellar explorers is the observance of an ethic of noninterference—explicitly invoked in such series as the one assembled in Harry Turtledove's *Noninterference* (1988)—but such principles are more honoured in the breach than the observance. Lloyd Biggle's Cultural Survey series (launched 1961) describes a sequence of more-or-less ingenious circumventions of the principle that newly contacted cultures should not be disrupted by the introduction of new technologies. Spacefarers who deliberately set out to interfere with other cultures almost invariably do so in the name of progress, as in Mack Reynolds' United Planets series launched with "Ultima Thule" (1961). The relevant ethical questions are insistently posed in Dean R. McLaughlin's "The Brotherhood of Keepers" (1960).

Futuristic fiction envisaging the reversal of the trend marginalising ethical education is relatively rare, although such stories as John T. Phillifent's "Ethical Quotient" (1962) and Charles G. Oberndorf's *Testing* (1993) tackle it head-on. The hope that educational methods might become more effective in delivering such enlightenment, however, is very rarely expressed in twentieth-century fiction, reflecting a general cynicism regarding the very idea of social improvement. The modern consensus holds that many, if not all, ethical questions are "essentially contentious" and cannot ever be settled by rational argument, although that does not prevent attempts to do so, as in Robert J. Sawyer's courtroom drama *Illegal Alien*. The possibility of discovering "scientific ethics", which once seemed conceivable in the context of Utilitarian philosophy, has cropped up occasionally in twentieth-century science fiction stories; Murray Leinster's "The Ethical Equations" (1945) and "Adapter" (1946) look forward to "a logically valid association of ethics with probability" based on the dubious assertion that "favourable coincidences" tend to reward good deeds in actuality as well as fiction.

ETHNOLOGY

The term originally used to describe the study of different societies in terms of their customs, folkways, and beliefs. In the twentieth century the discipline was more usually called "cultural anthropology", but the older term has been retained here in order to avoid confusion with physical *anthropology. Its prefix still retains widespread currency within and without the scientific context, notably in connection with the notions of ethnobotany, ethnozoology, ethnogeography, ethnometeorology, and so on, those being the terms conventionally applied to the idiosyncratic stocks of knowledge and theory possessed by particular tribal societies regarding the subject matter of various areas of empirical concern.

The generalised study of tribal cultures originated in the fascination provoked by tales brought back by explorers and colonists of natives encountered in distant lands. Such notions underwent a significant ideological transformation when accounts of Tahiti as a kind of Earthly paradise were combined with the philosophical ideas of Jean-Jacques *Rousseau to provoke animated eighteenth-century debates about the pros and cons of technological *progress, and to

tempt analogies between the supposed "innocence" of the savage mind and the supposed "innocence" of childhood. Literary reflections of the debates include Denis Diderot's earnest dialogue *Supplément au voyage de Bougainville* (1772; trans. as "Supplement to Bougainville's Voyage") and Benjamin Disraeli's satirical *Adventures of Captain Popanilla* (1828), in which a blissful Pacific Arcadia is exposed to the principles of Benthamite Utilitarianism. E. B. Tylor's pioneering general survey of *Primitive Culture: Researches into the Development of Mythology, Philosophy, Religion, Language, Art, and Custom* (1871) represented itself as a study of "the savage as a representative of the childhood of the human race".

The Ethnological Society of Paris was founded in 1839, followed by American and British counterparts in 1842 and 1843. The first taxonomical distinctions imported to the discipline in order to assist in the classification of tribal cultures and the clarification of the idea of "primitive society" were those developed by race theorists and social evolutionists, so ethnology seemed to be a subsidiary discipline, and most of its separate societies were absorbed into broader anthropological societies. When the American Anthropological Association, founded in 1902, took over the discipline's most important scholarly journal, the *American Anthropologist*—which had been launched in 1888—the fusion was virtually complete, although it was at that point in time that race theories and the notion that all human societies followed the same evolutionary trajectory began to seem dubious.

Ethnological notions of race and primitivism were very widely reflected in nineteenth-century popular literature, in the depiction of the tribal societies of the Americas, Africa, Australia, and Oceania. In spite of the fact that far more violence was inflicted by "civilised" people on tribal populations, far more effectively, than was ever visited in the other direction, the notion that "primitive" people were intrinsically "savage" was promulgated by a rapidly expanding genre of adventure fiction, many of its ethnologically enterprising inclusions taking the form of "lost race" stories. Much of this fiction was marketed as juvenile fiction, especially in Britain, and it became routine for British "boys' books" to glory in the violence and oppression associated with the expansion of the Empire. The landmarks of this literary tradition included R. M. Ballantyne's *The Coral Island* (1858), Henry Rider Haggard's *King Solomon's Mines* (1885) and *She* (1887), and John Buchan's *Prester John* (1910), but there was an enormous volume of undistinguished popular fiction in a similar vein. The darker note sounded in more jaundiced works, most notably Joseph Conrad's *Heart of*

Darkness (1902), was no more complimentary to the quality of the "savage mind".

Ethnologists began to break away from the confining assumptions of evolutionist anthropology when the attempt to distribute tribal societies on a single linear scale according to the "level" of their technology proved difficult. Such simple measurements could not take account of the complexities of actual situations, and were also transient, because newly contacted cultures invariably adopted new technologies demonstrated by their "discoverers" with great alacrity. Ethnologists became preoccupied instead with drawing comparisons and contrasts between the religion and folklore of various tribal societies, which seemed more enduring, attempting to construct a more elaborate developmental scale based on the evolution of ideas. Ethnological attempts to theorise *myth became particularly significant in a literary context, partly because of the light they shed on the history and sociology of literature and partly because of the new inspiration they lent to writers.

A key figure in this phase of ethnology's evolution, especially with respect to its literary influence, was James Frazer, the last of the "armchair anthropologists" who devoted themselves to the collation and organisation of miscellaneous data submitted by travellers, with the aid of all manner of antiquarian sources. Frazer's massive *The Golden Bough* (2 vols., 1890; exp. in 3 vols. 1900; further exp. in 12 vols., 1911–1915) was an attempt to produce a general ethnological theory based on Auguste Comte's "law" stating that the explanation of phenomena invariably passes through three stages (religion, metaphysics, and science). Frazer argued that all cultures must pass through similar phases of evolution, although his three stages of "explanation" were magic, religion, and science. He assembled an enormous quantity of empirical data supposedly proving this thesis, but his indefatigable reinterpretation of his data in the light of his theory established *The Golden Bough* as one of the classics of *scholarly fantasy. Precisely because of that, however, it exercised an enormous influence on literary men in search of a philosophical framework for their endeavours, including such pioneers of Modernism as T. S. Eliot, Ezra Pound, and D. H. Lawrence, as well as countless historical novelists and fantasists.

Frazer was a great inspiration to subsequent scholarly fantasists; Margaret Murray reinterpreted the history of European witch-hunting as an assault on the relics of Frazerian cults; Robert Graves linked it to goddess worship in *The White Goddess* (1948); and Jessie Weston greatly expanded the analogical use Frazer made of the allegory contained in Chrétien de Troyes' *Conte du graal* to provide the ideological foundations of modern grail fantasy. Assisted by these elaborations, *The Golden Bough* became a key "taproot text" of modern genre fantasy, although its pretensions were soon shed, and its conclusions soon rejected, by academic ethnologists.

As new data was gathered and the political context shifted there was an increasingly powerful backlash against the implicit racism of nineteenth-century anthropology and the sloppiness of evolutionist theorising, which transformed the study of tribal cultures in the twentieth century. Frans Boas brought a more determinedly objective eye to the collation and interpretation of ethnographic data, as well as a profound hatred of its use in the justification of political oppression; his account of *The Mind of Primitive Man* (1911) rejected the idea of innate savagery, stressing the commonality of human nature underlying all cultures. Bronislaw Malinowski pioneered the investigative method of "participant observation", which required anthropologists to try to get "inside" other cultures rather than regarding them from afar as alien entities. Alfred Kroeber viewed all cultures as open and dynamic entities rather than closed and static ones, and attempted to surpass the limitations of previous theories of cultural evolution by introducing the notion of a "superorganic" level on which cultural phenomena interact in complicated ways. Ruth Benedict argued that the infinite variability of culture must, in the end, defy crude scientific generalisation, requiring more subtle comparisons and a kind of understanding much more akin to the literary understanding she brought to her poetry.

The latter half of the century saw a resurgence of generalisation in the work of such ethnologists as Claude Levi-Strauss, but lingering suspicion of the reckless tendencies of Frazerian thought ensured that it as a very different kind of generalisation, often based in ideas borrowed from *linguistic science regarding the fundamental structures of thought and its organisation. The interaction between the views of these twentieth-century writers and the litterateurs that reflected their work was far more complex than that between Frazer and his literary extrapolators—a point very clearly demonstrated by the career of Alfred Kroeber's daughter, Ursula K. *Le Guin.

Ethnologists and litterateurs soon became keenly aware of the fact that the subject matter of the science was vanishing, not because of the disappearance of *terra incognita* from the terrestrial map but because all the tribal cultures that had survived violent annihilation in previous centuries were being transformed out of all recognition by contact with remoter neighbors. Ethnological observation itself became a significant agent of change—an ironic version of the *uncertainty principle. Images of contemporary tribal societies in twentieth-century fiction had little alternative but to represent them not merely as endangered but doomed. When such exemplars were offered as superior alternatives to the folkways of civilised and technologically advanced neighbors, the relevant narratives inevitably became impregnated with tragedy, often infused with *ecological mysticism. Notable examples include Jacquetta Hawkes' *Providence Island* (1959) and Aldous Huxley's *Island* (1962). A similar sensibility affects accounts of small-scale societies improvised by castaways in such works as Rose Macaulay's *Orphan Island* (1924), W. L. George's *Children of the Morning* (1926), and William Golding's *Lord of the Flies* (1954).

The notion of deliberately setting up small-scale societies and making rigorous attempts to maintain their separate culture had a considerable tradition in Utopian politics, and the continued presence in the United States of separatist cultures like the Amish encouraged the resurgence of such ideals in the 1960s and 1970s, as the notion of "countercultural" communes took aboard environmentalist anxieties and revised their ideologies in an "ecotopian" vein. Separatist ideals also enjoyed a new popularity in the field of sexual politics, especially in the context of *feminism. These changes in the dominant culture had a profound effect on the way in which ethnological data were viewed, not only at a popular level but also in the academy; they became infused with a peculiar kind of reverence that often extended into *occult sensibilities, providing ethnological data with a special significance in the development of new "holistic" philosophies. There was much talk in the last decades of the century of a reconstitution of tribal culture in parts of the urban wilderness, aided by new communication technologies, exaggerated in such literary extrapolations as Cory Doctorow's *Eastern Standard Tribe* (2004).

The use of the future as a narrative space for hypothetical models of tribal society was pioneered by Richard Jefferies's *After London; or, Wild England* (1885), and the depiction of "post-civilisation" societies based on ethnological data became increasingly common in the twentieth century; notable examples include Cicely Hamilton's *Theodore Savage* (1922), John Collier's *Tom's a-Cold* (1933), J. Leslie Mitchell's *Gay Hunter* (1934), Angela Carter's *Heroes and Villains* (1969), Marge Piercy's *Woman on the Edge of Time* (1976), Russell Hoban's *Riddley Walker* (1980), the series of novels by Paul O. Williams begun with *The Breaking of Northwall* (1981), and Ursula K. Le Guin's extraordinarily elaborate *Always Coming Home* (1985). The reversal of the ethnological perspective is satirically employed in such works as Grant Allen's *The British Barbarians* (1895), Chad

Oliver's *Shadows in the Sun* (1954), and Horace Miner's "Body Ritual Among the Nacirema" (*American Anthropologist,* 1956). Some consciousness of this relativity is often incorporated into stories that feature ethnologists as protagonists, such as G. C. Edmondson's *Chapayeca* (1971; aka *Blue Face*).

A separate category of such stories emerged in the context of science fiction with the depiction of future tribal societies in extraterrestrial settings. The evolution of ethnologically informed depictions of future human tribal societies was closely paralleled by, and overlapped to some degree, the evolution of ethnologically-based *alien societies—a sociological discipline that relates to ethnology much as exobiology relates to biology, and eventually acquired the label *xenology. Because the actual colonisers of alien worlds have to be technologically advanced and in contact—however distantly—with a much vaster society, images of extraterrestrial tribal societies are mostly accommodated within their own subgenre of "lost colony" stories, in which the initial colonisation has been followed by a loss of contact with the galactic culture and a consequent decline in technological and historical resources.

Because of the difficulties inherent in accommodating hypothetical tribal societies in Earthly contexts, the lost colony story has become the chief literary instrument employed in the elaborate construction of such fictional societies. It is the chief instrument employed by Ursula K. Le Guin, the most sophisticated writer of ethnological and xenological science fiction, in her extensive Hainish series and similarly inclined works such as "The Wild Girls" (2002). Mike Resnick's *Kirinyaga* (1998) is similarly sophisticated in its representation of a reconstituted tribal culture desperately attempting to lose itself in an extraterrestrial setting. Jack Vance's planetary romances offer an elaborate array of makeshift societies improvised by castaways, refugees, and outcasts, including those distributed across *Big Planet*—further explored in *Showboat World* (1975)—the floating culture of *The Blue World* (1966), and the patchworks featured in the Planet of Adventure quartet (1968–1970), the Durdane trilogy (1973–1974), and the Alastor Cluster series (1973–1978).

The fact that science-fictional lost colonies generally have to be rediscovered in order to be described—the rediscoverers usually taking the place of ethnological observers—exaggerates the practical and *ethical problems involved in such observation considerably. The ethic of noninterference often applied to alien societies seems far less relevant to human societies whose cultural heritage has been lost, and many lost colony stories treat the restoration of technological progress as an urgent imperative, sometimes requiring active and ingenious cultural subversion, as in Ross Rocklynne's "The Infidels" (1945).

EUGENICS

The application of *evolutionary theory to the improvement of the human species. The term was coined and the notion popularised by Charles *Darwin's cousin Francis Galton, in *Inquiries into Human Faculty* (1883). He had earlier suggested in *Hereditary Genius* (1869) that gifted individuals might be produced by "judicious marriages". Earlier versions of the notion include the plural marriage program of John Humphry Noyes' Oneida community in the 1850s. Galton's initial recommendation that excellence might be cultivated by selective breeding (positive eugenics) was logically coupled with the notion that the propagation of undesirable characteristics might be prevented by persuading afflicted individuals not to have children, or refusing them that right (negative eugenics).

Galton pioneered the application of statistical methods to the study of human attributes in *Natural Inheritance* (1889). He recommended the study of twins in gauging the heredity of intellectual characteristics, forging a significant link between such studies—especially when devoted to the attempted measurement of *intelligence—and the idea of eugenic selection. He endowed a research fellowship in eugenics at University College, London, in 1904, which was converted into a chair in 1907; its first occupant was the mathematician Karl Pearson, whose development of "biometrics" was guided by his fervent advocacy of eugenics. Support for eugenic policies was boosted by fears of "degeneration" popularised by Ray Lankester's *Degeneration: A Chapter in Darwinism* (1880) and Max Nordau's *Entartung* (1893; trans. as *Degeneration*), which deepened the pessimism of fashionable theories of *decadence. Pearson's ideas and methods were imported into America by Charles Benedict Davenport, who worked in the Eugenics Record Office founded in 1910.

Eugenics provoked a spirited literary response, its advocates producing *Utopian propaganda while its detractors dramatised their moral outrage. Early fictional accounts of eugenic policies in operation included Edward Payson Jackson's *The Demigod* (1886; published anonymously), William Little's *A Visit to Topos* (1897), Ellison Harding's *The Demetrian* (1907; aka *The Woman Who Vowed*), Trygaeus' *The United States of the World* (1916), H. M. Vaughan's *Meleager* (1916), Jacques Binet-Sanglé's *Le haras humain* (The Human Stud-Farm) (1918), William Margrie's *The Story of a Great Experiment:*

How England Produced the First Superman (1927), Jacob Leon Pritcher's *A Love Starved World* (1937), and Robert A. Heinlein's *Beyond This Horizon* (1942, by-lined Anson MacDonald; book, 1948). "Eugenic eutopias" became so commonplace that the phrase is extensively used as a capsule description in Lyman Sargent's bibliography, although the threat of eugenic deselection became a favourite dramatic device of *dystopian fiction, exemplified in such horror stories as S. Fowler Wright's "P. N. 40—and Love" (1930; aka "P. N. 40"), whose setting is a future Eugenic Era, and such vitriolic comedies as Aldous Huxley's *Brave New World* (1932).

Other satirical accounts in which eugenic programmes go perversely awry include Alfred Clark's *In a State of Nature* (1899), Netta Syrett's *Drender's Daughter* (1911), Rose Macaulay's *What Not* (1918), William McDougall's "The Island of Eugenia: The Phantasy of a Foolish Philosopher" (1921), and Charlotte Haldane's *Man's World* (1927). Aelfrida Tillyard's *Concrete* (1930) also belongs to this tradition, although its depiction of a Ministry of Reason headed by a character named Big Brother, who operates with the aid of a propagandist Ministry of Aesthetics, presumably did not seem so amusing to George Orwell. Attempts to conduct balanced thought experiments were relatively rare, but Grant Allen's "The Child of the Phalanstery" (1884) is carefully ambivalent and Muriel Jaeger's *Retreat from Armageddon* (1936) summarises arguments on both sides.

The more extreme propositions of eugenic policy—including compulsory sterilisation—were opposed by the English Eugenics Society that Galton founded shortly before his death in 1907, but were regarded more far sympathetically in the United States, where a sterilisation program instituted in Indiana in 1907 was copied in fifteen other states in the following decade, and a further fourteen by 1931. The American Eugenics Society, founded in 1926, embraced notions of racial supremacy echoed by the National Socialist party in Germany. When the Nazis gained power they instituted programs of negative eugenics that eventually extended into mass murder, although legislation elsewhere in the world was usually restricted to the sterilisation of individuals suffering from various forms of alleged mental incompetence.

A rare *conte philosophique* studying eugenic possibilities in a conscientiously neutral manner is C. L. Moore's "Greater Than Gods" (1939), whose protagonist foresees two possible futures based on different potential applications of a technology allowing the sex of children to be selected. After World War II, eugenic social policies fell into such extreme disrepute because of their association with the Holocaust that such calculated neutrality became almost impossible.

The notion that all scientists, or at least all biologists, were overt or covert eugenicists, who would employ any political influence they were granted to promote programs of negative eugenics, became a common slander of antiscientific fiction, stridently exemplified in C. S. Lewis's *That Hideous Strength* (1945). This anxiety made relatively little impact in genre science fiction, where some diplomatically muted support for eugenic theory was still manifest. C. M. Kornbluth's striking black comedy "The Marching Morons" (1951) envisaged a future in which members of the intelligentsia have prudently exercised birth control, while the *lumpenproletariat* have continued to multiply, with spectacular counter-eugenic results.

Although Kornbluth's *conte philosophique* remained highly controversial, the challenge it posed was continually readdressed in late twentieth-century science fiction, especially in the pages of John W. Campbell Jr.'s magazine. Donald Kingsbury's article on "The Right to Breed" in the April 1955 issue of *Astounding* also proved controversial, prompting further editorial comment and a voluminous correspondence. Kingsbury's defence of eugenics was frequently echoed in *Astounding/Analog*'s fiction, occasionally very stridently, as in Piers Anthony's "The Alien Rulers" (1968; exp. 1974 as *Triple Detente*). Conventional opposition to eugenic schemes was maintained within the genre in such dystopian melodramas as Frank Belknap Long's *It Was the Day of the Robot* (1963) and such dark *contes philosophiques* as Theodore Sturgeon's "Necessary and Sufficient" (1971). Ideological alarmism in regard to eugenic politics was substantially revitalised after the 1970s by the rapid progress of molecular *genetics and the advent of new *biotechnologies, and further amplified by the institution and completion of the Human Genome Project. Fictional reflections of this revitalisation include Greg Egan's "Cocoon" (1994), the film *Gattaca* (1997), and a *Star Trek* novel series on *The Eugenics Wars* (launched 2001).

EVOLUTION

A term defined in Samuel Johnson's dictionary as the act of unrolling; it was first used in a scientific context to describe embryonic development. That meaning was displaced when the term was adopted by Étienne Geoffroy-Saint-Hilaire in 1831 to describe the process by which new species arise. By that time, the mutability of species had been an issue of controversy for a century, the struggle for its acceptance as a possibility providing the most conspicuous historical example of Francis *Bacon's proposition that the path to knowledge is obscured by "idols" that inhibit the exercise of clear sight. The notion that God had created all Earthly life-forms independently had long prevented clear perception of the fact that all life on Earth was related by descent, in spite of the gradual accumulation of overwhelming evidence.

The development of natural classifications in *botany and *zoology had reemphasised the obvious relatedness of many species, but such works as John Ray's *General History of Plants* (1686–1704) attempted to account for these phenomena in terms of accidental variations on fundamental divine designs. The eighteenth-century endeavours of Carolus Linnaeus called attention to the complexity and subtlety of degrees of similarity, and to the manner in which variant species were adapted to different environments, but Linnaeus did not represent his organisation of species into genera, families, classes, and orders as a "tree", after the modern fashion, preferring an aggregation of circles of various sizes, supposedly representative of the pattern of divine determinism.

The notion that species were not fixed was briefly advanced by the Baron de Montesquieu in 1721, reflecting on the recent discovery of a "winged monkey" (the colugo, *Galaeopithecus*), and given more detailed consideration by Pierre-Louis de Maupertuis, who suggested in 1751 that there might be a mechanism of variation involving "elementary particles" transmitted in sperm. The encyclopaedist Denis Diderot supported the notion, but the leading naturalists of the day remained hostile to the proposition. The fact that one of the most obvious patterns of resemblance among animals was that linking humankind to the great apes—as pointed out by such proto-*anthropologists as Edward Tyson and Lord Monboddo—was a considerable disincentive to the supposition that resemblance implied relationship, and the battle against evolutionist ideas often focused on the objection that they made cousins of humans and apes.

The Comte du Buffon took issue with Linnaeus on many points, but was forced to recant the allegedly heretical ideas he put forward in his *Natural History* (1749), even though he was diplomatic in his treatment of the relationships between living organisms, using the conventional language of the "infinite chain of being" and opposing René Descartes' proposition that living bodies could be treated as mechanical systems. He too interpreted the variation of living organisms as the elaboration of a creative design expressed via "internal moulds". Buffon's ideas were, however, combined with those of Diderot for more adventurous literary exploration by Nicolas Restif de la Bretonne, whose *La découverte Australe par un homme volant* (1781) includes a detailed allegory of evolutionary development.

Like Linnaeus, Buffon represented species and subspecies diagrammatically as circles distributed in a field, although he further emphasised the relationships between them by drawing connective lines. Buffon distinguished six "Epochs of Nature", accommodating various kinds of fossil organisms discovered in the eighteenth century. His successor Georges Cuvier was content to account for vanished vertebrate species by means of a theory of multiple creations in *Ossements fossiles* (1812), even though he recognised the obvious kinship of various sets of extinct and extant mammalian species. It was left to Jean-Baptiste de *Lamarck, who made the first systematic study of fossil invertebrates, to make the mutability of species the foundation stone of his intellectual system, and to represent his classification as the tracing of lines of historical descent extending across vast reaches of past time.

The key notion Lamarck used to explain mutability was adaptation, which he assumed to be the result of a dynamic impulse innate in all living things, expressed as a *sentiment intérieur* driving species to explore new habitats and means of sustenance, and to innovate in order to exploit them more effectively. The definitive version of his theory was set out in *Philosophie zoologique* (1809), but by the time it appeared evolutionist ideas had spread beyond France, surfacing in England in Erasmus *Darwin's *Zoonomia* (1794–1796), which similarly envisaged change occurring in response to impulses determined by "lust, hunger and danger".

Lamarck's ideas were applauded by Charles Lyell in the second volume of his *Principles of Geology* (1832), and the argument was carried forward by Robert Chambers' highly controversial *Vestiges of the Natural History of Creation* (1844) and Herbert Spencer's essay on "The Development Hypothesis" (1852). The term "evolution" had not yet come into common usage at that point; its arrival at much the same time as Charles *Darwin's *Origin of Species* (1859) helps to explain the common confusion still implicit in references to "the theory of evolution", which conflate the theory that the relatedness of species is explicable in terms of hereditary descent with the theory that the pattern of descent can be explained in terms of natural selection.

Early fictional treatments of evolutionist ideas often focused on the relatedness of humans and apes, as in Thomas Love Peacock's depiction of Sir Oran Haut-Ton in *Melincourt* (1817) and James Fenimore Cooper's establishment of another simian species at the top of the hierarchy of creation in *The Monikins* (1835). A. G. Gray Jr.'s "The Blue Beetle" (1856) considered the broader implications of the thesis. Alfred Lord Tennyson's *In Memoriam* (1850) conceded the strength of Chambers' arguments, which were published midway through its

composition, while Benjamin Disraeli reacted against them in *Tancred* (1847). There is a remarkable dream sequence in Charles Kingsley's *Alton Locke* (1850), in which the hero experiences the entire evolutionary history of life on Earth, imagined in Lamarckian terms.

Darwin's theory of evolution by natural selection did away with the necessity for any kind of innate "adaptive drive" but left open the question of whether acquired characteristics could be inherited. Herbert Spencer's *Principles of Biology* (1864–1867) admitted the possibility, and Darwin never explicitly rejected it. While Darwinism still remained unsupported by any *genetic mechanism of particulate inheritance, Lamarck's supposition of a fundamental "life force" imbued with some kind of progressive impetus retained its plausibility; it was carefully reformulated in Henri Bergson's *L'Évolution créatrice* (1907; trans. as *Creative Evolution*) as the notion of *élan vital*. The poetic dimension of Bergson's work was a key factor in his being awarded the Nobel Prize for Literature in 1928, and it exercised a considerable influence over French writers of evolutionist fiction. Some British writers of scientific romance, including J. D. Beresford and Olaf Stapledon, were also influenced by Bergson, but the notion that there was a crucial opposition between "Darwinism" and "Lamarckism" provoked a noticeable divergence of attitudes between the speculative fiction produced in different nations in the latter part of the nineteenth century, according to their various patterns of theoretical allegiance.

In France, the evolutionist ideas that Camille *Flammarion adopted in such hypothetical exercises in *exobiology as *Lumen* (1866–1969; book, 1872) owed more to the tradition that extended from Buffon and Lamarck, with literary support from Restif de la Bretonne, Louis-Sébastien Mercier, and the English Creationist Humphry Davy, than it did to Darwin. J.-H. Rosny aîné's many *anthropological fantasies, and such excursions into the representation of *alien life as "Les xipéhuz" (1887; trans. as "The Shapes") and *Les navigateurs de l'infini* (1925) similarly echoed Lamarckian and Bergsonian ideas. Jules Verne's anthropological fantasy *Le village aerien* (1901; trans. as *The Village in the Treetops*) is similarly wary of Darwinian ideas.

In England, Darwin's ideas made an immediate impact on Alfred, Lord Tennyson, whose reference in *In Memoriam* to "nature red in tooth and claw" seemed to have foreshadowed them; "Locksley Hall, Sixty Years After" (1886) is one of the most explicit and most plaintive Victorian literary reactions to Darwinism. Charles Kingsley's response was more rapid, expressed in fabular form in *The Water-Babies* (1863). Samuel Butler reflected his initial enthusiasm for the theory in a remarkable account of mechanical evolution, "The Book of the Machines", which he included in the Utopian satire *Erewhon; or, Over the Range* (1872), although he subsequently became disenchanted with it and became a significant champion of neo-Lamarckism in *Life and Habit; An Essay After a Completer View of Evolution* (1878), *Evolution, Old and New* (1879), and *Luck, or Cunning as a Main Means of Organic Modification?* (1887).

On the Origin of Species had a more general effect on many other contemporary writers, including George Eliot, Matthew Arnold, and George Meredith, although it was the following generation, introduced to the theory in adolescence, whose worldview was thrown into more profound turmoil by the controversy. Thomas Hardy absorbed it into his anxiously bleak notion of a purposeless and unguided *Nature whose God is a mere onlooker, while Winwood Reade tackled it head-on in the rhapsodic final section of *The Martyrdom of Man* (1872) and a novelistic account of the tribulations of a Darwinian convert, *The Outcast* (1875). The latter was followed by two novels by older writers that highlighted duels of wit between Darwinists and clergymen, with social exclusion as the forfeit: Eliza Lynn Linton's *Under Which Lord?* (1879) and Mrs. Humphry Ward's *Robert Elsmere* (1888). Linton and Ward were considerably less sympathetic to the new creed than Reade, but their works showed a clear awareness of the way the tide was running.

Henry Curwen's *Zit and Xoe* (1887) is a frothy satirisation of Darwinism, but Matilde Blind's book-length poem "The Ascent of Man" (1889) and J. Compton Ricketts' parable *The Quickening of Caliban* (1893) offered more earnest and somewhat gloomier reflections. May Kendall's poem "The Conquering Machine" (1887) saw evolution working inexorably towards "the Automatic Soul", and a note of regret was sounded even in such celebrations of Darwinism as Grant Allen's "The Lower Slopes" (1894), whose author could not entirely approve of a human ancestry in which "the strongest continued to thrive, / While the weakliest went to the wall".

For the first generation born into the Darwinian Era, Darwinism was already an intellectual foundation stone; H. G. *Wells, who attended Thomas Henry Huxley's lectures at the London School on Normal Science, was so profoundly affected by them that they became the central thesis of his early speculative fiction. Darwinist ideas were fundamental to the development of the entire genre of British *scientific romance, many of whose writers were freethinking sons of clergymen taking arms against obsolete faith, and the intellectual upheaval the idea had caused continued to echo in British historical novels

such as John Fowles' *The French Lieutenant's Woman* (1969).

In the United States, Darwinian evolutionism found powerful opponents in the nation's leading naturalist, Jean-Louis Agassiz, and its leading geologist, James Dwight Dana. Agassiz never relented in his opposition, although his son Alexander, a marine biologist, eventually conceded defeat. Dana was gradually convinced by the evidence, but when he finally admitted that evolution had occurred he still resisted the Darwinian theory of natural selection—as did many of his compatriots, including the palaeontologists Edward Cope and Alpheus Hyatt, the embryologist John Ryder, and the entomologist Alpheus Packard Jr. Packard coined the term "neo-Lamarckism" to describe the rival school of thought. Darwin's first American champion was the botanist Asa Gray, who arranged for publication of the *Origin of Species* in 1860, but when the neo-Lamarckian controversy reached its height in the early 1890s the fight against it was led by the zoologist August Weismann. Weismann became one of the key proponents of Mendelian *genetics following its rediscovery in 1900, immediately realising that it was exactly what Darwinism required to repel the threat of neo-Lamarckism.

Darwinian ideas were pilloried in J. L. Collins' parodic *Queen Krinaleen's Plague* (1874, by-lined Jonquil), which describes the theory of "Gibbon Darwin", but Leonard Kip's "The Secret of Apollonius Septrio" (1878) offered a bold Darwinist account of the future evolution of humankind. Austin Bierbower's *From Monkey to Man* (1894) attempted to reconfigure Genesis as an allegory of evolution. Edgar Fawcett's *The Ghost of Guy Thyrle* (1895) endorsed evolution, but the primary emphasis was on the fact of evolution rather than the mechanism. The persistence of neo-Lamarckian theories in American fiction is graphically illustrated by Edgar Rice Burroughs' *The Land That Time Forgot* (1918; book, 1924), which equips its lost land with an idiosyncratic evolutionary scheme echoing Ernst Haeckel's "law" of embryological development ("ontogeny recapitulates phylogeny").

The idea of evolution continued to distress some religious believers in America, who reacted by formulating *Creationism with which to fight evolutionism on the educational front. In the meantime, new controversies arose in connection with the application of evolutionist ideas to human history and politics in *Social Darwinist theories and *eugenic programs. Such ideas were offensive to many of those desirous of working towards the ideals of liberty, equality, and fraternity, to whom the Lamarckian thesis of a progressive and adaptive *sentiment intérieur* seemed markedly preferable. For this reason, neo-Lamarckism was sustained after the elucidation of the mechanism of genetic inheritance on *ideological grounds, most conspicuously—and problematically, for its American adherents—in post-Revolutionary Russia.

Subsequent objections to Darwinism, including objections to the theory's implicit uniformitarianism on the grounds that rates of evolutionary change manifest in palaeontological evidence vary considerably and objections based on examples of altruistic behavior that supposedly ran counter to the logic of natural selection, similarly raised their loudest clamor in the United States. The most significant literary defence of neo-Lamarckism is, however, George Bernard Shaw's play *Back to Methuselah* (1921), whose printed version has a long introductory essay sardonically explaining his renunciation of Darwinism on Socialist grounds. Gerald Heard's evolutionary allegory *Wishing Well* (1952; aka *Gabriel and the Creatures*), which attempts to "soften" the perceived harshness of the Darwinian perspective with neo-Lamarckian ideas, was also written by an Englishman, but one who had long been resident in the United States.

The ideological context of American speculative fiction influenced fictional treatments of the process of *mutation by which evolutionary variations arose. Pulp science fiction writers became fascinated by images of rapid evolutionary acceleration, as featured in Edmond Hamilton's "Evolution Island" (1927) and "The Man Who Evolved" (1931), John Taine's *The Greatest Adventure* (1929) and *Seeds of Life* (1931; book, 1951), R. R. Winterbotham's "Specialization" (1937), and Ray Bradbury's "The Creatures That Time Forgot" (1946; aka "Frost and Fire"). The operation of natural selection—or, indeed, of any actual mechanism of evolution—was virtually lost to sight in genre science fiction, even in the work of John W. Campbell Jr.'s stable, where mutational romances producing *supermen at a stroke were a conspicuous blot on the escutcheon of *hard science fiction. A corollary preoccupation with the notion of ultimate evolutionary destiny—often seen in terms of the kind of transcendence of the flesh featured in *Back to Methuselah*—was easily blended into genre science fiction's gathering fascination with *Omega Point fantasies.

British scientific romance became similarly fascinated with the notion of evolutionary destiny. John Lionel Tayler's *The Last of My Race* (1924) provided a blueprint of sorts for Olaf *Stapledon's magisterial *Last and First Men* (1930), and British writers played a significant role in developing such imagery in the science fiction pulps. Eric Frank Russell's "Metamorphosite" (1946) provided a figurative representation of humankind's ultimate descendants as radiant entities of pure energy, echoed in such stories as John Brunner's "Thou Good and Faithful" (1953, by-lined John Loxmith) and Daniel F. Galouye's "Country Estate" (1955). Arthur C. *Clarke's *Childhood's End* (1953) echoed Pierre Teilhard de Chardin's account of the evolution of an Earthly noösphere towards a climactic *Omega Point in offering a more elaborate account of that kind of evolutionary schemes, but images of a material evolutionary destiny continued to recur in genre science fiction, taken to elaborate extremes in such works as Robert Silverberg's *Son of Man* (1971) and Eric Brown's "Ascent of Man" (2001).

Accounts of *exobiological evolution made frequent and ingenious use of the logic of Darwinism, especially in the design of puzzle stories, but also played host to elaborate evolutionary schemes such as those described in Theodore Sturgeon's "The Golden Helix" (1954) and James Blish's *A Case of Conscience* (1958); the extensive penetration of exobiological science fiction by *ecological mysticism was partly rooted in American ambivalence towards Darwinist ideas. Science-fictional explorations of the past were more hospitable to earnest evolutionary speculation than its images of the future, and Darwinian theory is much more conspicuous in anthropological and palaeontological science fiction than futuristic science fiction; a notable example by an evolutionist is *The Dechronization of Sam Magruder* (1996), a novella left behind for posthumous publication by George Gaylord Simpson, author of a classic study of *Tempo and Mode in Evolution* (1944). It does, however, feature in some satirical examinations of the present, as in Alan E. Nourse's "Family Resemblance" (1953), which explains the case for believing than humans are descended from pigs rather than apes.

As the twentieth century progressed, the implications of Darwinism and its conflict with various kinds of ideological opposition came to seem less relevant to the future of human evolution—and perhaps all Earthly life. The realisation emerged that humans, having insulated themselves from the effects of natural selection by culture and technology, might take control of their own future evolution—and that of other species—by means of artificial selection or *genetic engineering. One result of this development was that late twentieth-century evolutionary fantasies retaining the theory of natural selection as a central mechanism tended to be set in futures from which the human factor had been removed, as in Dougal Dixon's exercise in *speculative nonfiction *After Man: A Zoology of the Future* (1981) and Kurt Vonnegut's satirical Jeremiad *Galapagos* (1985). Other works in a similar vein feature *alternative worlds in which evolution was sidetracked. Notable examples include Guy Dent's *Emperor of the If* (1926), Harry Harrison's *West of Eden* (1984), and Robert Charles Wilson's *Darwinia* (1998).

Although neo-Lamarckian explanations of life on Earth suffered a near-terminal decline in the latter half of the twentieth century—in spite of renewed attempts to recomplicate Darwinism such as Rupert Sheldrake's *The Science of Life: The Hypothesis of Formative Causation* (1981)—they continued to exert sufficient fascination to inspire science fiction writers to design hypothetical exobiological genetic systems capable of evolution by other means than simple natural selection. Notable examples include Barrington J. Bayley's "Mutation Planet" (1973), Brian Stableford's "The Engineer and the Executioner" (1975; rev. 1991) and *Dark Ararat* (2002); Paul Cook's Sheldrake-based *Duende Meadow* (1985); and Greg Bear's *Legacy* (1995). Fantasies of accelerated evolution maintained their situation at the heart of the subgenre, sometimes assisted by ideological considerations, as in the evolutionist fantasies of the British socialist writer Ian Watson, which include *The Martian Inca* (1977), *Alien Embassy* (1977), *Miracle Visitors* (1978), *God's World* (1979), and *The Gardens of Delight* (1980). Such extravagant and sometimes phantasmagoric fantasies tend to be more enterprising and colourful than conscientious extrapolations of Darwinian theory such as Elisabeth Malartre's "Evolution Never Sleeps" (1999).

EXOBIOLOGY

A term coined by Joshua Lederberg—in competition with the alternative label of xenobiology—to describe the disciplined construction of hypothetical alternatives to Earthly biochemistry. Although Lederberg was solely concerned with fundamental biochemistries, based on the assumption that the basic requirements for *life's existence were long-chain molecules and a suitable suspension medium, writers of speculative fiction had long been engaged in broader speculations whose principal emphases were on alternative patterns of *evolution, *ecological considerations, and the potential forms of *alien intelligence.

The origins of exobiological speculation can be identified in Plutarch's dialogue "On the Face that Appears in the Disc of the Moon" (ca. 100 A.D.), in whose concluding section the narrator argues that lunar life must be adapted to local conditions, and might well consider the Earth's surface "a damp, dark Hell". The thread of the argument was taken up in an identical context in John *Kepler's *Somnium* (1634), whose

conclusion points out that life on the Moon would have to be adapted to a very long cycle of day and night, and suggested some appropriate biological modifications. This set a precedent for such hypothetical exercises as Charles Defontenay's *Star* (1854), Camille *Flammarion's *Lumen* (1866–1869; book, 1872), H. G. *Wells' *The War of the Worlds* (1898), and George Griffith's *A Honeymoon in Space* (1901). Wells' representation of the *Martian ecosphere as a generator of predatory *monsters was particularly influential, founding a rich tradition of exobiological melodramas and horror stories, few of which were supported by competent exobiological arguments.

Wells had taken some inspiration from attempts to describe the Martian ecosphere made by Percival Lowell on the basis of *astronomical observations, and Lowell's ideas were a key source for exobiological speculative fiction during the early twentieth century, integrated into Edgar Rice Burroughs' accounts of "Barsoom" and many subsequent pulp science fiction stories. Exobiological speculations were, however, often confined to terrestrial enclaves and images of *panspermic invasions of Earth in scientific romance and early science fiction, notable examples including J. H. Rosny aîné's *L'étonnant voyage de Hareton Ironcastle* (1922; rev. trans. as *Ironcastle*, 1976), Arthur Conan Doyle's "The Horror of the Heights" (1913), A. Merritt's *The Metal Monster* (1920; book, 1946), and Jack Williamson's "The Alien Intelligence" (1929).

Science-fictional adventures in exobiology became more sophisticated in the 1930s as the myth of the *Space Age evolved. Primitive ecological sensibilities were integrated with a desire to produce more elaborate imagery in such works as Clark Ashton Smith's "The Amazing Planet" (1931), C. L. Moore's "The Bright Illusion" (1934), and numerous stories by Stanley G. Weinbaum, including "A Martian Odyssey" (1934), "The Lotus Eaters" (1935), "Flight on Titan" (1935), and "The Mad Moon" (1935). D. L. James' "Philosophers of Stone" (1938) imagined a mineral "ecosphere" on the surface of a protoplasmic planet, while Douglas Drew's "The Carbon Eater" (1940) equips silicon-based life-forms with dramatically implausible food requirements. The primary emphasis of all of these early flights of fancy was on bizarrerie rather than ecological coherence.

John W. *Campbell Jr.'s Penton and Blake series (1936–1938) attempted to build on Weinbaum's precedents, constructing peculiar life-forms with eccentric but plausible biochemical requirements—including the borax-eating Callistan "dog" Pipeline—and he insisted that writers working under his editorial aegis should put more thought into the exobiological issues inherent in "world-building"—especially their interrelationships with planetological and sociological factors. He helped the members of his stable to realise that such intellectual labour devoted to exobiological construction could work to their advantage by generating puzzles to be solved, thus supplying useful plot ideas and convenient story arcs. A notable nonfiction book on the subject by the British astronomer royal, Harold Spencer Jones' *Life on Other Worlds* (1940), lent some assistance to his cause.

This kind of opportunity was tentatively taken up by Clifford D. *Simak, in a loosely knit series including "Tools" (1942), and Eric Frank Russell, in a series including "Symbiotica" (1943), before Hal *Clement made extravagant exobiological speculation the foundation stone of his literary method, beginning with such stories as "Proof" (1942), "Uncommon Sense" (1945), and "Cold Front" (1946). From then on, conscientious exobiological extrapolation was a central thread of *hard science fiction, practiced with particular ingenuity by Poul *Anderson, in such stories as "The Big Rain" (1954), "Call Me Joe" (1957), "The Longest Voyage" (1960), and "Elementary Mistake" (1967, by-lined Winston P. Sanders). Anderson and Isaac *Asimov both became enthusiastic popularisers of alternative biochemistry. Exobiological puzzle stories did not remain confined to Campbell's *Astounding*, also becoming one of the significant subgenres featured in *Galaxy*, in such stories as F. L. Wallace's "Student Body" (1953) and Clifford D. Simak's "Drop Dead" (1956) and "The World That Couldn't Be" (1958).

Although narrative convenience ensured that exobiological science fiction was dominated by alternative ecospheres adapted to Earth-clone worlds, hard science fiction played host to many more radical alternatives, often involving the substitution of silicon for carbon as a structural molecule and the substitution of such molecules as ammonia and methane for liquid water as a low-temperature suspension medium. The surfaces of worlds following eccentric orbits within binary star systems and the vast atmospheres of gas giant planets became favourite locales, the former notably featured in Clement's *Cycle of Fire* (1957), Brian Aldiss's Helliconia trilogy (1982–1985), and Poul Anderson's "Hunter's Moon" (1983), and the latter in Arthur C. Clarke's "A Meeting with Medusa" (1971), Gregory Benford and Gordon Eklund's "The Anvil of Jove" (1976), and Jack Cohen and Ian Stewart's *Wheelers* (2000).

As exobiological science fiction continued to grow in sophistication, science fiction writers began to collaborate in the exploration of carefully designed worlds, in such exercises as *The Petrified Planet* (1952; ed. Fletcher Pratt), *Medea* (1985; ed. Harlan Ellison), and *Murasaki* (1992; ed. Robert Silverberg). The hypothetical world of Epona was designed for educational purposes by members of an organisation called Contact as one of a series of Cultures of the Imagination (COTI); its complex ecosphere was described in *Analog* in Wolf Read's article "Epona" (1996), with an accompanying story by G. David Nordley, "Fugue on a Sunken Continent". Read's stories "The Flowers That Bloom in the Spring" (1997) and "Duel for a Dracowolf" (1998) were also derived from COTI settings.

Individual efforts in exobiology continually tested new imaginative limits in such endeavours as Robert *Forward's Rocheworld series (launched 1982–1983) and *Camelot 30K* (1993) and Larry Niven's *The Integral Trees* (1984) and *The Smoke Ring* (1987). Images of Earth-clone worlds also became significantly more elaborate and ingenious as the twentieth century progressed; the range is vast, but notable examples include Harry Harrison's *Deathworld* (1960), Avram Davidson's *The Enemy of My Enemy* (1966), Juanita Coulson's *Crisis on Cheiron* (1967), Alan Dean Foster's *Midworld* (1975), Thomas Erickson's "Cocoon" (1982), Robert Reed's *The Leeshore* (1987) and "River of the Queen" (2003), Joan Slonczewski's *A Door into Ocean* (1987) and *The Children Star* (1998), Zach Hughes' *Life Force* (1988), G. David Nordley's "Poles Apart" (1992) and "The Forest Between the Worlds" (2000), Daniel Hatch's "In Forests Afloat Upon the Sea" (1995) and "Seed of Destiny" (2002), Alison Sinclair's *Blueheart* (1996), Robert Charles Wilson's *Bios* (1999), Ian Watson's "A Speaker for the Wooden Sea" (2002), Caitlin R. Kiernan's "Riding the White Bull" (2003), and Neal Asher's *The Line of Polity* (2003). Specialists in exobiological ecology feature in numerous texts of this kind, sometimes as explorers, as in Stephen Tall's *The Stardust Voyages* (1975) and *The Ramsgate Paradox* (1976), and sometimes as consultant troubleshooters, as in George R. R. Martin's mosaic *Tuf Voyaging* (1986) and Julia Ecklar's Noah's Ark series launched with "Blood Relation" (1992).

EXPERIMENT

A key element of the scientific method, which requires hypotheses to be subject to empirical enquiry. Laboratory experiments and field experiments were often seen as exercises intended to confirm scientific hypotheses, but Karl Popper's *philosophy of science insisted that their role is more appropriately viewed as a series of rigorous attempts to test hypotheses by establishing circumstances in which the hypotheses would be found wanting if they were false. The notion of experiments as crucial tests by which hypotheses might stand or fall is traceable back to *Galileo, but it was not fully refined or clarified until Popper's account of *Logik der Forschung* (1934; trans. as *The Logic of Scientific Discovery*).

This special scientific meaning of the term has always been confused with another meaning applied in common parlance, in which an experiment is simply a previously untried enterprise, undertaken in order to see what might happen. In this meaning, experimentation is a means of searching for new revelations rather than confirming or testing propositions. This kind of open-ended and exploratory experimentation has also been highly significant in the history of science, and a great many experiments of this kind are still carried out in laboratories; indeed, the significance of experiments as tests is often only realised retrospectively, as in the case of the Michelson-Morley experiment of 1887, which set out to determine the Earth's velocity in the *ether and ended up being elevated as proof of the ether's nonexistence, its apparent failure thus being transmuted into glorious success. In this latter sense, the term is used abundantly in a literary context, where "literary experiments" usually involve trying new formats to see whether they "work". Social experiments are generally of the same kind, although the fact that they are usually launched with the support of a theoretical prediction of success means that their almost-invariable failure does become a testing process of sorts.

The essence of experimentation is control. Ideally, the effect of a single variable is isolated, so that any change in a contrived situation can be attributed with complete confidence to the factor under hypothetical consideration. When such isolation is not practical—as it rarely is when working with living organisms, especially in "field experiments"—the separation of the effects of a set of variables is attempted by the statistical analysis of variance. The generalisation of experiments also requires that the contrived situation be essentially similar to all other situations to which the conclusion is to be extrapolated. As with the isolation of variables, this second criterion is easily met in physics and chemistry, but is harder to meet in biology, where idiosyncratic differences between individuals may be considerable, and very much harder in human science, where individual differences may be of paramount importance.

Experiments in biology—including medical science—are far more vulnerable than experiments in physical science to the "experimenter effect", which tends to prejudice observers in favour of the outcome they expect. In human science—again including medical science—a further complication of the same effect tends to prejudice experimental subjects in the same direction. For this reason, reliable experiments in medical science need to be "double-blinded", so that neither the immediate observers nor the subjects know which subjects belong to the experimental group and which are receiving a placebo. Experiments that cannot be subjected to this protection—which include almost all experiments in psychology and sociology, as well as medical experiments in which convincing placebos cannot be administered (such as attempted evaluations of surgical treatments)—are subject to a high degree of unreliability. It is for this reason that medicine and the human sciences remain cluttered with all manner of pseudoscientific hypotheses in spite of the best efforts of their practitioners to sort out the sound from the unsound.

These complications of experimental method are, for the most part, invisible to the *reportage of science, which tends to deal entirely in alleged revelations and their apparent consequences. For this reason, exercises in the *popularisation of science tend to expend a great deal of effort "debunking" notions that have been widely reported as scientifically proven on the basis of inadequate or corrupt evidence. Even within the field of formal *scientific publication problems arise because it does not seem worthwhile to publish negative results, even though negative results are, in the Popperian view, the ones that really matter. "Failed" experiments are frequently forgotten—which may lead to their futile repetition—and particular instances of "anomaly" may be discarded from repetitive runs, thus exaggerating the statistical quality of "successful" experiments.

Literary representations of science are often highly sensitive to the role played by experimentation in science, although they frequently overlook the niceties and frustrations of experimental practice. The success or failure of an experiment is a ready-made crisis point easily adaptable to a literary or cinematic climax, and is often used in that way, although melodramatists have a natural prejudice towards large-scale experiments whose failure is likely to produce devastating explosions (which are, for exactly that reason, of a type rarely carried out in actuality).

The usefulness of experimentation is also limited by the time required to produce effects, and by the size of the entities under consideration. Changes that occur within minutes or hours are ideal for experimental investigation, while those that happen in milliseconds or require years are not. Objects that fit readily into test tubes and whose changes can be tracked by the naked eye are similarly ideal, while the submicroscopic and the vast are not. Theoretical physicists interested in the very rapid transactions of very tiny entities have made heroic progress in overcoming these difficulties by means of exceedingly sensitive measuring devices, but scientists dealing with large, slow entities—especially living ones—have no such opportunity available to them. The fact that so much science is beyond the scope of easy experimentation, and that some is beyond the scope of any experimentation, has opened considerable scope within those areas for "thought-experiments"—a translation of *gedankenexperiment*, the term employed by Werner Heisenberg to describe the imaginative endeavour by which he arrived at the *uncertainty principle.

A thought-experiment is an imaginative construction that allows a scientist to extrapolate the consequences of a hypothesis in a situation whose contrivance is purely mental. There is a sense in which all actual experimental tests have to begin as thought-experiments in order to establish what would count as failure or success; but in circumstances where no real experiment is practicable, a thought-experiment may have considerable value in itself in generating surprising consequences, as when Albert *Einstein conducted the thought-experiment of "riding on a ray of light" in order to come up with the theory of *relativity. Charles *Darwin's theory of *evolution had to be worked out largely by means of thought-experiments comparing what might have happened in the generation of species in the wild with the processes of selective breeding employed in the differentiation of various kinds of domestic pigeons and dogs.

Some thought-experiments make use of entirely imaginary entities, like the daemon that Pierre Laplace imagined as having perfect knowledge of the position and velocity of every particle in the universe, or the daemon James Clerk Maxwell described in his *Theory of Heat* (1871), which manned a door between two halves of an air-filled vessel, only opening it to let fast-moving particles pass from compartment A to B and slow-moving ones from B to A, thus operating in contradiction to the second law of thermodynamics. The challenge posed to theory by Maxwell's daemon came to be seen as a significant enigma, finally "solved" by Leon Brouillon's observation in 1951 that providing enough illumination to allow the molecules to be seen and judged would increase the entropy of the system faster than the daemon could decrease it. Einstein's attempt to figure out the implications of a universe in which the speed of light was always constant, even when measured from standpoints travelling very rapidly in relation to one another, was even more provocative.

Some simple thought-experiments are conceived purely for illustrative purposes—many examples given in textbooks of physics are thought-experiments whose perfection could only be approximated in actuality, such as exemplary calculations in mechanics involving frictionless pulleys—while others are conceived in order to produce complex anticipations, like

the mathematical models run on computers. Many philosophical thought-experiments exploring the logical consequences of hypotheses in the philosophy of mind or the potential applications of moral principles are routinely cast in fictional form, and the literary subgenre of *contes philosophiques* can be seen as a series of thought-experiments of various kinds. Science-fictional thought-experiments range across a wide field of questions, and although their "results" are always subject to the prejudicial effects of dramatic imperatives they have the potential to be useful as well as entertaining.

Notable fictional examples of hypothetical experiments—of very various kinds—include David H. Keller's "A Biological Experiment" (1928), James Blish's "Bridge" (1952), Sidney Bliss' *Cry Hunger* (1955), Kate Wilhelm's *The Clewiston Test* (1976), Frank Herbert's *The Dosadi Experiment* (1977), Maya Kaathryn Bohnhoff's "Hand-Me-Down Town" (1989), and Robert Sawyer's *The Terminal Experiment* (1995).

EXTRAPOLATION

The process by which further possibilities are drawn out of a set of premises. It is fundamental to sophisticated mathematical and scientific reasoning, and also to sophisticated prose fiction, the extrapolation of theorems and theories being closely akin to the extrapolation of plots. The most satisfactory extrapolatory exercises in mathematics and science end with a triumphant flourish, sometimes explicitly signified by the phrase *Quod Erat Demonstrandum*, in much the same way that the most satisfactory stories achieve a sense of closure with some final summary comment, sometimes called a "punchline". The *aesthetics of science and literature are heavily dependent on the elegance of patterns of extrapolation and the rewarding quality of their conclusions.

Although mathematical extrapolation is a matter of strict logic, its artistry involves the exercise of the imagination to discover conclusions that are not obvious, and sometimes very surprising; conversely, although literary extrapolation is a much freer process, routinely tempted into farcical or suspenseful unlikelihood and unashamed fabulation, it is most powerful when it conveys a sense of inexorable inevitability. The "hardness" of *hard science fiction is contained in the artistry of its extrapolation as well as the rational *plausibility of its premises, although it is generally less rigorous in this regard than the hard core of detective fiction, as represented by such subgenres as the locked room mystery, which is far less hospitable to the intrusion of *deus ex machina* devices.

A sense of crushing inevitability is easier to cultivate in naturalistic fiction dealing with familiar *psychological types and everyday sequences of cause-and-effect than it is in speculative fiction, where the artistry of extrapolation is more likely to be revealed in boldness and originality.

The significance of extrapolation in speculative fiction is most obviously manifest in the production of expansive story series that continue to draw out further consequences of a hypothesis. Notable examples include Isaac *Asimov's Foundation series (launched 1942), Frank Herbert's Dune series (launched 1963), and Frederik *Pohl's Heechee series (launched 1971). One that is particularly elegant and compact is Bob Shaw's series of stories about "slow glass" collected in *Other Days, Other Eyes* (1972), in which an invention whose first plausible application seems trivial is shown by careful degrees to have the potential to bring about very dramatic changes in social organisation. All series in speculative fiction have—or ought to have—this kind of expansive potential, which may be contrasted with the "segmental" series typical of crime fiction, in which crime-fighters merely engage with a potentially infinite series of cases, while the milieu in which they operate hardly changes at all. The commitment of science fiction to a dynamic view of the world in which extrapolation is a duty as well as a necessity is reflected in the choice of *Extrapolation* as a title for the field's first academic journal, launched in 1959 by Thomas D. Clareson.

F

FAUST

A legendary character apparently named after a scholar based at the University of Heidelberg in the early sixteenth century. After the actual Faust's death, the rumour was spread that he had traded his soul to the Devil in exchange for "earthly knowledge"; his career thus became a parable in which science is represented as essentially satanic by virtue of its concentration on the empirical at the expense of the spiritual. The printed version of the legend appeared in 1587, in a pamphlet signed by Johann Spies, usually known as the *Faustbuch*.

Spies' pamphlet was widely reprinted and its story extensively copied, becoming one of the most successful of modern legends. It was translated into English as *Faustus: The History of the Damnable Life and Deserved Death of Dr. John Faustus* (1592) by "P. R., Gent." The original was rapidly followed by the *Wagnerbuch* (1593; trans. 1594 as *The Second Report of Dr. John Faustus; Containing His Appearances and the Deeds of Wagner*), which added further attestation to the story and tracked the adventures of Faust's servant. The story was immediately appropriated by Christopher Marlowe in *The Tragical History of Dr. Faustus* (written ca. 1592; published 1604), which became a highly significant literary exemplar.

Stories in which humans make formal pacts with the Devil were not new in the late sixteenth century; the earliest recorded is a medieval cautionary tale about a bishop named Theophilus, and the notion had undergone a dramatic repopularisation during the previous three centuries, when it had been adapted as an important instrument of the politics of persecution. The slander was used by Philippe le Bel of France to destroy the Knights Templar—a theatrical extravagance that became the seed of numerous twentieth-century secret histories. The stratagem was copied into other high-profile sorcery trials before becoming a standard instrument of the persecution of alleged witches, who were assumed to have made such pacts and forced by torture to confess to having done so. Faustian pacts, being contracted by males of relatively high social status, in exchange for knowledge rather than vulgar magical powers, were a cut above witch pacts, but the two were sufficiently confused to make Faust into a wizard rather than a scientist in many representations, somewhat undermining the original implication of the story.

The most famous literary transfiguration of Faust's story after Marlowe's was J. W. Goethe's (1808–1832), which shows a great deal more sympathy for the protagonist. Most of the works spun off from Goethe's version—including operas by Hector Berlioz (1845–1846), Franz Liszt (1854–1857), and Charles Gounod (1859) and a film by F. W. Murnau—pay more attention to the character of the demonic Mephistopheles than to Faust's quest for knowledge, and concentrate on the first part of the story, although Arrigo Boito's opera *Mefistofele* (1868) covers both parts. Philip James Bailey's verse drama *Festus* (1839) similarly blended Christian ideas with Hegelian idealism, and included an educative cosmic tour—a motif also co-opted into Gustave Flaubert's quasi-Faustian versions of *Le tentation de Saint Antoine*—as a prelude to Festus' final redemption.

Following the decline of Romanticism and its Gothic extensions, stories of diabolical pacts were mostly shifted into the realm of comedy, but a few still retained some relevance as parables of the scientific quest, including Austin Fryers' *The Devil and the Inventor* (1900). Many twentieth-century versions that reinfused the theme with allegorical seriousness—including Thomas Mann's *Doctor Faustus* (1947; trans. 1948), Jorge de Sena's *O Fisico Prodigioso* (1977; trans. as *The Wondrous Physician*), and Robert Nye's *Faust* (1980)—have other concerns than the reflection of the evolution and triumph of the scientific method, but Michael Swanwick's *Jack Faust* (1997) made a concerted attempt to revert to the spirit of Spies' parable, developing an alternative history based on the hypothesis that an early sixteenth-century scientist might indeed have tapped into a source of information that acquainted him with accurate and wide-ranging scientific knowledge.

The most earnest twentieth-century redeployment of the Faust myth was in Oswald Spengler's *Der Undertang des Abendlandes* (1918–1922; trans. as *The Decline of the West*), which characterised the modern culture whose life cycle was allegedly coming to an end as one possessed of a "Faustian soul"—by contrast with the Apollinian soul of Classical culture and the Magian soul of Arabic culture. Whereas the essence of Classical culture had been symbolised by the nude male of Greek statuary and that of Arabic culture by the dome, the essence of Western culture was the infinite *space that Faust had desired to grasp and master. Spengler's implication was that the attempt had failed, although Isaac *Newton and Albert *Einstein might both have disagreed, and the response of such Spenglerian science fiction writers as James *Blish was that the next culture in the sequence might yet succeed in the kind of grasp and mastery implicit in the myth of the *Space Age and the symbol of the spaceship.

Like the Romantics before them, genre science fiction writers mostly sided with Faust against the claims of Mephistopheles, convinced that the quest for knowledge was a sacred one no matter how much fonder a jealous God might be of blind faith. Characters in Hollywood monster movies were rarely able to do likewise, often signing off with a resigned admission that "there are things man was not meant to know", but such craven thinking was quite alien to the ethos of genre science fiction; even such straightforward transfigurations of the legend as Fred Saberhagen's "Some Events in the Templar Radiant" (1979) put a very different spin on it. The Faustian soul of twenty-first-century science, as mirrored in twenty-first-century science fiction, has not yet consented to decay, let alone to accept its allotted place in the afterlife.

FERMI PARADOX, THE

An enigma articulated by the nuclear physicist Enrico Fermi in the course of conversation, usually paraphrased as "If we are not alone, where are they?" The point Fermi was making is that if the evolution of intelligent *alien life on the planets of other stars is a matter of routine, there ought to be some discernible evidence of its existence. The problem began to seem increasingly acute as *SETI projects produced no results, and had become a hot topic of debate among astronomers and cosmologists by the 1970s.

The basic argument, elaborated since Fermi's initial proposition by further input, suggests that technologically sophisticated species only slightly more advanced than ours ought to be able to construct self-replicating space probes—often called "Von Neumann machines" because John Von Neumann published a paper in 1966 exploring the possibility—capable of exploring the ten-billion-year-old galaxy in a few hundred million years, as well as transmitting signals that should be detectable by radio telescopes. Species more advanced than that ought to be able to change their local environments in such astronomically detectable ways as the construction of *Dyson spheres. The fact that there is no credible evidence of the existence of such species calls into question the implications of the cosmological principle of mediocrity, which holds that Earth and its ecosphere are unlikely to be unique or very exceptional.

Gerrit L. Verschuur's "We Are Alone!" (*Astronomy*, 1975) and Michael H. Hart's "Atmospheric Evolution and an Analysis of the Drake Equation" (1981) summarise the ideas of a school of thought contending that the lack of evidence must be taken at face value. Other exobiologists, however, prefer the proposition put forward in Isaac Asimov's article "Our Lonely Planet"—which introduced the notion to science fiction readers in the November 1958 issue of *Astounding*—and echoed in John A. Ball's "The Zoo Hypothesis" (1973), which suggests that Earth may be a sort of "nature reserve" carefully protected from alien interference. Michael D. Papagiannis' "Are We Alone, or Could They Be in the Asteroid Belt?" (1978) concurred with this view.

Explicit science-fictional "solutions" to the Fermi paradox had been offered before it acquired that name, in such stories as A. E. van Vogt's "Asylum" (1942). Solutions involving some kind of strategic isolation are, however, melodramatically disadvantaged by comparison with solutions involving predatory species that descend like locusts on any solar system showing signs of life. Theses of the latter sort became increasingly fashionable in the last quarter of the twentieth century, although they continued to exist in parallel with more ingenious variants of their counterpart.

Notable examples of science fiction stories explicitly offering solutions to the Fermi paradox include David Brin's "Just a Hint" (1981), "The Crystal Spheres" (1984), and "Lungfish" (1986), Gregory *Benford's *Across the Sea of Suns* (1984), Charles Pellegrino's *Flying to Valhalla* (1993), Joe Haldeman's *The Coming* (2000), Alastair Reynolds' *Revelation Space* (2000), Paul J. McAuley's "Interstitial" (2000), Stephen Baxter's "The Children's Crusade" (2000), "Refugium" (2002), and "Touching Centauri" (2002), Robert Reed's "Lying to Dogs" (2002), and Jack McDevitt's *Omega* (2003). Ian MacLeod's "New Light on the Drake Equation" (2001) extrapolated the enigma into a poignant commentary on the demise of twentieth-century science fiction's mythical future. Stephen Webb's *Where Is Everybody? Fifty Solutions to the Fermi Paradox and the Problem of Extraterrestrial Life* (2002) summarised contemporary thinking on the issue.

An argument suggesting that if time travel were not impossible, time travellers from the future would already be here is sometimes described as "the Fermi paradox of time travel", as in Mat Coward's "The Second Question" (2001).

FIRE

One of the four Classical elements, favoured as the primal substance by Heraclitus. It is the odd one out of the four, being more readily seen as an agent that provokes changes of state in the three obvious states of *matter—from solid (earth) to liquid (water) and liquid to gas (air) through melting and evaporation, as well as the more complex transitions of combustion.

The Classical element of fire was associated with lightning—the probable source of the first fires domesticated by early humans—so the Aristotelian cosmology makes the "natural realm" of fire (the empyrean) the topmost of the four sublunar spheres. Although Aristotle located the heavens in a further sphere, it was often confused with the realm of fire, especially by writers who confused fire with *light and those who considered lightning bolts to be hurled down by angry gods. The representation of the *Sun as a kind of celestial fire was a further complication of the mythical scheme.

The domestication of fire, which probably began around 300,000 B.C., although the technology of *starting* fires did not emerge until much later—ca. 35,000 B.C.—was the key to the development of early technology, especially to cooking—the first foundation of all culture, according to the "culinary triangle" of Claude Lévi-Strauss' structuralist *anthropology. It may have been the domestication of fire that exerted the selective pressure causing human beings to become much less hairy than their primate relatives. Anthropological fantasies of prehistory routinely make the discovery of fire a key phase in human evolution, as in Jack London's *Before Adam* (1906) and Vardis Fisher's *The Golden Rooms* (1944), while such works as J. H. Rosny aîné's *La guerre du feu* (1909; trans. as *Quest for Fire*) put a heavy emphasis on its continued centrality.

Early *religion routinely reflected the key role of fire in the formation of culture in the forms of burnt offerings to the gods and the establishment of sacred flames; the latter are particularly prominent in the Vedic rituals associated with the god Agni and those of the Persian religion of Zarathustra. The foundations of Abrahamic religion mapped out in the Old Testament focus on the substitution of an animal sacrifice for a human one. Early persecutors of Jews and Christians within the Roman Empire sometimes used burning as a means of execution. Mediaeval Christians revived burning at the stake as a punishment for its own heretics and revitalised pagan psychological terrorism in a heavy emphasis on the supposed fires of Hell. Trials by ordeal frequently used fire as a test of fortitude.

Fire permitted the expansion of the human species into the colder regions of the planet, and the progressive development of an intricately interwoven sequence of technological discoveries. Cooking encouraged the development of ovens and bowls, and hence led to brickmaking, ceramics, and glassmaking. The evolution of ceramics encouraged the further development of ovens into kilns, which required the refinement of wood into charcoal, whose high temperatures facilitated the earliest developments of metallurgy and the evolution of the crucible. The use of fire as a *weapon—exploited in "Greek fire" long before the crucial discovery of gunpowder—eventually licenced the calculation of military might in terms of its "firepower".

Agriculture became feasible because ovens allowed the transformation of wheat into bread, while the heat-assisted fermentation of barley into beer produced the yeast that leavened bread and helped it become the staff of life. The crucible gave way to the forge as management of increasingly higher temperatures turned the Bronze Age into the Iron Age, and charcoal had to be augmented by fuels such as coal and oil. This elaborate network of fire-based technologies was precariously balanced for millennia because technologies for making fire were so restricted and so difficult to employ in cold or damp environments; this gave a particular significance to the advances in chemistry that facilitated the discovery of phosphorus, and hence the manufacture of matches.

The crucial importance of fire to the preliterate burgeoning of human culture is reflected in the myth of Prometheus, whose name means "forethought", the Titan who stole the fire of the gods and gave it to mankind—for which crime he was punished by being chained to a rock and having an eagle sent to devour his continually regenerated liver on a daily basis. When the myth was given literary form in a trilogy by Aeschylus, of which only one part survives—*Prometheus Bound* (ca. 468 B.C.)—the unrepentant Prometheus made it clear that his "theft of fire" had involved teaching men the rudiments of mathematics, science, and all the major branches of technology, as well as the art of divination. The imagery of this myth is frequently recapitulated in modern accounts of scientific and technological progress—most notably, perhaps, in Percy Shelley's defiant account of *Prometheus Unbound* (1820), in which the *meteorological analogies the poet had learned from his tutor Adam Walker inform his association of Promethean fire with the lightning of human rationality, which is about to spark a new era of creativity. Shelley's poem invokes Orpheus and Daedalus as well as Prometheus, drawing an explicit analogy between their endeavours and those of the chemist Humphry Davy and the astronomer William Herschel.

The preservation of the Classical element of fire within the pseudotheoretical frameworks of *occult science is particularly significant in the context of *alchemy, where it plays a crucial role in the kinds of transformations that were supposed to lead to the manufacture of gold. Salamanders are more extensively featured in mysticism and fiction than any of their rival elemental spirits, and other mythical creatures associated with fire—especially the phoenix—are similarly well represented. The alchemist's crucible, like Vulcan's forge, is often used as an emblem of creative transformation—a metaphor that received a new inspirational boost with the development of the steam engine powered by a furnace, and yet another when the source of the Sun's heat was discovered to be a new kind of fire, produced by nuclear fusion.

No satisfactory chemical explanation of fire emerged until the late eighteenth century, when Antoine Lavoisier explained combustion as rapid oxidation. Even thereafter it retained much of its mystery. A better understanding of the phenomenon facilitated a new wave of technological developments in all its traditional applications—cooking, ceramics, glassmaking, metalworking, and so on—and hastened the design and application of new kinds of fire-powered machines, including steam engines and internal combustion engines and such military hardware as flame-throwers and incendiary bombs, but fire—if only in the modest forms of candle flames and censers—also retained a key role in religious ceremony and ritual. Religions invented for use in fiction often exaggerate the role of fire in ritual and worship.

Although scientific confirmation had to wait until the late nineteenth-century sophistication of organic chemistry, Lavoisier's discovery that combustion was oxidation lent support to the mythical and metaphorical supposition that *life is a kind of fire. Although this was largely transformed in the nineteenth-century imagination into the notion of "vital *electricity", the notion of life-donating fire survived in such works of fiction as H. Rider Haggard's *She* (1887) and extended into the twentieth century in Arthur Leo Zagat's "The Living Flame" (1934) and Frank Belknap Long's "Flame of Life" (1939). It is, however, the emotional component of mental life that tends to be represented metaphorically in fiery terms, as the burning heat of passion, while the rational component of cerebration is typically considered to be cool at its finest, cold when allegedly excessive.

The mythical association of fire with life makes much—with good reason—of the generosity of the Sun's heat, and pre-twentieth-century fictions that imagined the Sun to be inhabited often represented its indigenes as creatures of flame. The discovery that solar heat was produced by nuclear fusion did not obliterate this imagery entirely; the notion of living beings that take the form of flames extended long into the twentieth century in such works as Henry J. Kostkos' "We of the Sun" (1936), Olaf Stapledon's *The Flames* (1947), and Edmond Hamilton's "Sunfire!" (1962). Fire also plays a key symbolic role in such celebrations of the exotic as Clark Ashton Smith's "City of the Singing Flame" (1931) and Samuel R. Delany's *Captives of the Flame* (1963) and in such titles as Ray Bradbury's *Fahrenheit 451* (1953)—the alleged temperature at which books catch fire, at which literacy, and all it stands for, is therefore consumed.

FLAMMARION, (NICHOLAS) CAMILLE (1842–1925)

French astronomer and leading exponent of the popularisation of science. He became fascinated with astronomy in childhood after observing the solar eclipses of 1847 and 1851, and became a keen amateur stargazer while apprenticed to an engraver in his teens. He began to write voluminously, producing an unpublished *Voyage extatique au régions lunaires; correspondance d'un philosophe adolescent* and a *Cosmologie universelle* that eventually saw print as *Le monde avant la création de l'homme* (1885). The latter won him an introduction to Urbain Le Verrier, the director of the Paris Observatoire, who put him to work in the Bureau de Calculs.

While he was working for Le Verrier, Flammarion wrote *La pluralité des mondes habités* (1862), a pioneering work of speculative *exobiology whose success launched his literary career. After two credulous works that contributed to the nascent boom in spiritualism and its associated *parapsychological research, he produced a scrupulously researched study of *Les mondes imaginaires et les mondes réels* (1864; exp. 1892), which compared fictional representations of other planets with calculations of conditions on their surfaces based on astronomical data, thus presenting an early historical analysis of speculative fiction in its scientific context. He began writing abundantly for periodicals, often using fictional formats to dramatise the information he presented. He constructed a telescope of his own but returned to the Observatoire in 1867 to take part in a project identifying and mapping binary stars. He also undertook parallel researches in *meteorology by means of balloon flights.

Three of Flammarion's fictionalised essays were collected in *Récits de l'infini* (1872; trans. as *Stories of Infinity*). The first uses Halley's *comet as a viewpoint for a series of snapshots of life on Earth. The most substantial is *Lumen* (1866–1869; separate ed. 1887; exp. 1906), in which the spirit of a dead man, now free to roam the universe, relates his observations in a series of dialogues with a living friend. The first three dialogues are preoccupied with the time-distorting effects of travelling close to and faster than the velocity of light, which cause the narrator to wax lyrical on the theme of the *relativity of time and space, and with the possibilities of cosmic *palingenesis. The fourth dialogue—expanded and divided into two in later editions—was written after Flammarion had read and translated Sir Humphry Davy's *Consolations in Travel* (1830), and attempts to offer descriptions of extraterrestrial life adapted to a wide range of physical conditions.

The idea of cosmic palingenesis was further developed in *Stella* (1877), a *bildungsroman* tracking the education of a female scientist, and the patchwork *Uranie* (1889; trans. as *Urania*), which includes an elaborate account of a reincarnation on *Mars. In the meantime, Flammarion's career as a populariser of science scored its greatest success when a publishing company, in which his brother Edward had become a partner, issued his paradigmatic guidebook for amateur astronomers, *Astronomie populaire* (1880; trans. as *Popular Astronomy*); he published updated editions at regular intervals during his lifetime, and the work was subsequently updated by others throughout the twentieth century.

An admirer of the *Astronomie populaire* made Flammarion the present of an estate at Juvisy-sur-Orge, south of Paris, where he constructed a new telescope, which similarly remained in use throughout the twentieth century. In 1892, he published a then-definitive study of observations made there in *La planète Mars et ses conditions d'habitabilité*, incorporating the "canali" publicised in the 1870s by Giovanni Schiaparelli. Percival Lowell was among the many visitors to this establishment, which included leading spiritualists—including Arthur Conan Doyle—as well as astronomers.

Flammarion's later endeavours were increasingly concentrated on parapsychological research, but he continued his enthusiastic popularisation of science in books and periodicals. He made much of the melodramatic potential of the possibility that the Earth might be devastated by a comet strike—a notion extravagantly explored in a long account of a fictitious conference held under the shadow of such a threat. This was translated for publication in the U.S. magazine *Cosmopolitan* before being supplemented with a long fictionalised essay describing the future history of the world as it might be if humankind were to survive until the extinction of the *Sun (according to Lord Kelvin's timetable) in *La fin du monde* (1894; trans. as *Omega: The Last Days of the World*). His other speculative fiction was collected in *Contes philosophiques* (1911) and—in company with various essays—*Rêves étoilés* (1914; abridged trans. as *Dreams of an Astronomer*).

Flammarion's scientific and literary reputations were compromised by the duality of his allegiance, his commitment to spiritualism, and his work as a populariser—by the time he died, his entry in the *Petit Larousse* had been reduced to the succinct description "séduisant vulgarisateur"—but he was a remarkably inventive writer who explored many different methods of popularising and celebrating scientific discovery and laid important groundwork for the development of *scientific romance and for historians of science fiction.

FLYING SAUCER

A term popularised in the late 1940s, adopting a comparison made in Kenneth Arnold's report of a mysterious group of flying objects near Mount Rainier, Washington State, in June 1947. It captured the popular imagination so thoroughly that it remained in use in media reportage long after the substitution of "unidentified flying object" (UFO) by people keen to maintain an appearance of objectivity in their recording and investigation of such sightings. Such reports were by no means new—many newspaper clippings relating to strange objects in the sky had been collated by Charles *Fort—but the Arnold sighting touched a raw nerve, and sparked the development of a significant modern *myth. The term was rapidly co-opted into fiction, its use in Bernard Newman's thriller *The Flying Saucer* (1948) being a prominent early example; a film with the same title was released in 1950.

A rapid side effect of the publicity given to the Arnold sighting was the reporting—allegedly on the basis of an Air Force press release—of the discovery of "the wreckage of a flying saucer" near Roswell, New Mexico, a few weeks later. Largely unheeded at the time, this incident acquired a central importance in UFO mythology in the 1990s, when rumour insisted that the wreckage had been transported to a secret research facility at an Air Force base in Nevada known as Area 51. The allegation soon followed that several corpses had been found, as featured in a notorious "alien autopsy" video of 1995. The fictional spin-off of the Roswell incident was very considerable in the 1990s, because it gave rise to so many melodramatic possibilities, which were lavishly exploited in such TV series as *The X-Files* (1993–2002) and *Roswell* (1999–2002). The Air Force's statement that the debris was a damaged weather balloon was widely construed as one more "cover-up".

Another rapid reaction to Arnold's report was that of Ray Palmer, editor of the pulp science fiction magazine *Amazing Stories*, who had published numerous works in the previous two years by Richard S. Shaver, beginning with "I Remember Lemuria" (1945). Shaver's stories insisted that misfortunate events on the world's surface were mostly caused by the radiation of "telaug" (telepathic augmentor) machines operated by underground-dwelling "deros" (detrimental robots) descended from servants left behind in the distant past when rival races of immortal giants abandoned the Earth. This had proved enough of a circulation booster to prompt Palmer to promote the "Shaver Mystery" as a revelation, and he had begun picking up other items of Fortean reportage to offer as evidence in its favour. Coincidentally, the issue of *Amazing* dated June 1947 was a special Shaver Mystery issue. The October issue—the first to go to press after the Arnold sightings—carried an enthusiastic editorial hailing the sighting as "proof" of Shaver's claims, listing the names and partial addresses of many other people who claimed to have seen the nine "ships", and asking for reports of further

sightings of "flying discs". Palmer claimed in subsequent editorials that he had received tens of thousand of responses to this contention.

Palmer used the "flying saucer" label for the first time in his November editorial, which fervently insisted on their reality. The magazine's back cover often illustrated Fortean items under the general heading "Impossible but True", sometimes adding a Shaverian twist in the captions, and the January 1948 issue's back cover referred to a "spaceship seen over Idaho" in 1910, described in the text as a "gigantic, glowing, golden disk"—although the picture, presumably drawn beforehand, showed a conventional aircar. The editorial for that issue exhorted readers: "Don't forget the flying saucers! Keep your eyes peeled on the skies". Shaver contributed a "non-fiction" item on the "Medieval Illicit", which claimed that Mars and Venus were inhabited by sadistic imperialists deeply resentful of Earth's surface civilisations.

Arnold's sightings were given pride of place on the cover of the first issue of *Fate*, a new magazine devoted to occult and Fortean subjects launched by Palmer—initially using the pseudonym Robert N. Webster—in 1948. The headline article was Arnold's "The Truth About Flying Saucers" and the cover showed a flying disk looming over a civilian aircraft. Palmer then launched a new science fiction magazine, *Other Worlds*, in 1949, whose first issue had a cover story by Shaver; Palmer abandoned his pseudonym in its second issue, having quit *Amazing Stories*, and continued to run his new magazines in close association, eventually retitling the latter *Flying Saucers from Other Worlds*.

The craze triggered by the 1947 sightings prompted the U.S. Air Force—moved by anxieties regarding national security—to investigate UFO sightings. Projects Sign and Grudge (both 1948) were supplemented by the longer running Project Bluebook (1952–1969), but an independent study by physicist Edward U. Condon concluded that further study was unwarranted and it was abandoned—which only served to encourage the theory that there was an "official cover-up". The alleged findings of the military enquiries were fused with amateur investigations in Donald Keyhoe's *The Flying Saucers Are Real* (1950) and *Flying Saucers from Outer Space* (1953), the latter presented in a drama-documentary format. Project Bluebook head Edward J. Ruppelt's *Report on Unidentified Flying Objects* (1956) was used as an incentive giveaway in ads for the Science Fiction Book Club.

The notion that flying saucers must be alien spacecraft was soon translated into autobiographical fantasy in such works as George Adamski's *Flying Saucers Have Landed* (1953, with Desmond Leslie) and *Inside the Space Ships* (1955). Adamski's account was soon supplemented by Gavin Gibbons' *They Rode in Spaceships* (1957), which tells the stories of Truman Bethurum and Daniel Fry. Such witnesses usually gave different accounts of the nature and motives of the saucer-men, but conserved enough of a core consensus to provide the foundations of an imagery whose eventual iconic core was the depiction of large-eyed grey midgets.

Donald H. Menzel's *Flying Saucers* (1953), which set out the history of such apparitions and offered hypothetical explanations, as well as comments on the jitters generated by the Cold War, headed a long tradition of sceptical works plaintively pleading the cause of rationality. Such efforts were futile; the myth was to become increasingly elaborate and to command increasingly bizarre behaviour for a further half century. The Committee for the Scientific Investigation of Claims of the Paranormal (CSICOP), publishers of *The Skeptical Inquirer*, fought a long rearguard action against the development of the mythology. One of the organisation's cofounders, Philip J. Klass, began addressing the topic in the late 1960s and began producing a *Skeptics UFO Newsletter* in 1994, but the reasons for its growth had nothing to do with rationality, and it could not be undermined by rational argument.

Ray Palmer's enthusiasm for the Shaver Mystery and flying saucers caused something of a schism in the science fiction community. The majority of editors and readers maintained a scrupulous scepticism in respect of flying saucers, reflected in the fact that the first issue of *Galaxy* in 1950 featured a specially commissioned article by Willy Ley, "Flying Saucers: Friend, Foe or Fantasy?"—which came swiftly and smoothly to the last-named conclusion. Objectivity rapidly turned to mocking disdain, although that made no difference to the genre's public image. The connection between science fiction and flying saucers forged in the consciousness of the American public from the outset was greatly encouraged by science fiction movies—especially *The Day the Earth Stood Still* (1951), which provided an iconic image of a flying saucer landing on the White House lawn. Science fiction writers soon began to exploit the imagery for their own purposes. Robert A. Heinlein's *The Puppet Masters* (1951) was one of many works to credit the saucers to its hypothetical aliens. Raymond F. Jones' *Son of the Stars* (1952) was one of many science fiction stories featuring a crashed saucer, and Sam Merwin's "Centaurus" (1953) one of several stories associating saucers with atomic bomb tests. Movies such as *Invaders from Mars* (1953) and TV series such as *The Invaders* (1967) were, however, far better placed to exploit the central icon of the myth,

whose form is probably traceable back to the ships used by the Mongol villains in the early Buck Rogers comic strips of 1929–1930.

A rich elaboration of cover-up theories began with Gray Barker's *They Knew Too Much About Flying Saucers* (1956), which launched the mythology of sinister "men in black" who would visit people who advertised their encounters too loudly. A far more influential elaboration was, however, the idea of "alien abduction", popularised by John Fuller's *The Interrupted Journey* (1966), which added a further string to the bow of *hypnotic regression. Large numbers of patients under hypnosis soon began to remember being abducted by aliens instead of (or as well as) past incarnations and memories of childhood sexual abuse, the "memories" in question carrying the same degree of psychological conviction as other revelatory experiences. The flying saucer craze had already attracted psychological interest, expressed in such texts as Carl *Jung's *Ein moderner Mythus: Von Dingen, die am Himmel gesehen werden* (1958; trans. as *Flying Saucers: A Modern Myth of Things Seen in the Sky*), but abduction accounts increased this kind of interest considerably.

The phenomenon also attracted sociological interest; *When Prophecy Fails* (1956) by Leon Festinger, Henry W. Riecken, and Stanley Schachter described the infiltration of a tiny "cult" whose chief protagonist, Marian Keech, had co-opted flying saucers into a quasi-spiritualist credo carried forward from Guy and Edna Ballard's "I AM" (Ascended Master) cult founded in 1930. Similar groups made increasingly elaborate use of UFO imagery in their credos and UFO groups as a recruitment route, notable examples including the Unarius movement founded by Ernest and Ruth Norman in 1954, the Aetherius Society founded in 1955 by George King, and the Raelian Movement founded in 1973 by Claude Vorihon (alias Rael).

The kinds of "truth" invented by such organisations tend to be much stranger than explicitly fictional deployments of flying saucers, but the mythical status of the relevant ideas is clearly evident in the fact that "flying saucer fiction" is the most conspicuous of several modern subgenres in which fantasy thrives on its representation as *reportage. Such work is not speculative but intensely dogmatic, and its adherents tend to be extremely scornful of speculative fiction that borrows its motifs for artistic reasons, such as Theodore Sturgeon's "Saucer of Loneliness" (1953) and "Hurricane Trio" (1955), J. G. Ballard's "The Encounter" (1963; aka "The Venus Hunters"), Josephine Saxton's *Vector for Seven* (1970), Ian Watson's *Miracle Visitors* (1978), and William Barton's "Off on a Starship" (2003), let alone such irreverent purposes as are manifest in Bernard Deitchman's "Man with a Past" (1977), Howard Waldrop's "Flying Saucer Rock 'n' Roll" (1985), Lawrence Watt-Evans' "A Flying Saucer with Minnesota Plates" (1991), and Arlan Andrews Sr.'s "The Roswell Accident" (1994).

Even such straight-faced fictional appropriations as Eando Binder's *Menace of the Saucers* (1969), David Bischoff's *Abduction: The UFO Conspiracy* (1990), and Mat Coward's "We All Saw It" (2000) tend to be seen as mocking trivialisations by UFO believers. Pastiches of UFO reportage like David Langford's *An Account of a Meeting with Denizens of Another World, 1871* (1979) arouse particular hostility, especially when they are co-opted into the mythology as if they really were sincere reports. In consequence, science-fictional representations of "UFO watchers" are often cruel and very rarely charitable, although the one in Robert Reed's *Beyond the Veil of Stars* (1994) is granted more respect than most. Fictional treatment of alleged abductees and UFO cultists is merciless, usually in a blackly comic vein; notable examples include Warren Miller's *Looking for the General* (1964), Shepherd Mead's *The Carefully Considered Rape of the World* (1966), George O. Smith's "The Night Before" (1966), Rory Barnes and Damien Broderick's *The Book of Revelation* (1999), Rudy Rucker's *Saucer Wisdom* (1999), and John Barnes' *Gaudeamus* (2004). Thomas M. Disch's comments on Whitley Strieber's alleged abduction experiences are masterpieces of acidic sarcasm.

Motifs originated within flying saucer literature, such as the tripartite classification of "close encounters"—exploited in spectacular fashion in Steven Spielberg's *Close Encounters of the Third Kind* (1976) —and Barker's "men in black", are routinely appropriated by the visual media, whose systematic traffic with the *impossible renders the implausibility of such notions redundant. The seemingly credulous employment of such ideas in comic books and the cinema is far less offensive to enthusiasts than any kind of intellectual investigation in fiction or nonfiction, whose prior assumption of scepticism is (rightly) seen as a threat to carefully maintained *Baconian idols. Echoes of the Roswell incident in the visual media are more likely to cement belief than challenge it, but the opposite is probably true of such textual treatments as Robert Reed's "Nodaway" (1999), Jamie Barras' "The Woman Who Saved the World" (1999), and Mat Coward's "Time Spent in Reconnaissance" (2002), even though they are not debunking exercises in the cheerfully disdainful spirit of Connie Willis' memoir *Roswell, Vegas, and Area 51: Travels with Courtney* (2002).

FOOD SCIENCE

A significant area of applied *biology; it is a subdivision of *biotechnology in the wider definitions of that term. The technological manipulation of food and its supply was the principal motor of human evolution in prehistoric times, expressed in cooking, agriculture, and animal husbandry, and it remained a key factor in subsequent technological revolutions.

The new technologies that laid the foundations for the Renaissance included windmills and watermills, whose primary function was to make flour for bread, and the Industrial Revolution of the eighteenth and nineteenth centuries brought about dramatic increases in agricultural productivity that were further enhanced by the advent of tractors and combine harvesters. In the meantime, primitive food technologies—especially the use of spices to render bad meat palatable—played a major role in stimulating trade and navigation. The expansion of *geographical knowledge and *colonisation were both motivated by the demands of food technology, and the discovery of new food crops was a major factor in determining dramatic shifts in *population such as those seen in Ireland as potatoes were introduced and then blighted. The term "food science" only came into common usage in the twentieth century, however, when major food producers began to devote considerable budgets to disciplined goal-orientated research.

The theoretical aspect of food science is the study of nutrition, pioneered in the 1880s by Wilbur Olin Atwater, who placed experimental subjects in respiration chambers in order to measure the energy values of fats, proteins, and carbohydrates. The dietary recommendations he published—designed to maximise calorie intake at minimum cost—seem absurd today, not so much because he had no knowledge of vitamins as because the modern priorities in developed nations have been reversed, the emphasis being on weight control rather than weight gain.

The same reversal of priority has been the central factor in determining sweeping changes in fictional representations of food. In pre–twentieth-century fiction, bread is a key symbol of life while most other foodstuffs are emblems of luxury; meat is a continual bone of contention between the upper and lower classes, reflected in the abundant literature of hunting and the relatively meagre literature of poaching. In the late twentieth century, by contrast, food becomes a significant bugbear in a great deal of contemporary fiction; in the modern Underworld, the descendants of Tantalus—especially the female ones—are given perfectly free access to their rations, their torment being calculated in corpulence and cellulite.

This inversion was largely unanticipated in early Utopian fiction, which routinely saw improvements in food supply as a fundamental key to the good life, but anxieties began to creep into late nineteenth-century speculative fiction. Synthetic food is the key to liberation from labour in Maurice Spronck's *An 330 de la République* (1894), as it had been in John Macnie's *The Diothas* (1883; by-lined Ingmar Thiussen), but in the later work it leads to obesity and listlessness rather than Utopia. A similar product has equally unfortunate results in Daniel Halévy's *Histoire de quatre ans, 1997–2001* (1903), while William Caine and John Fairbairn's satire *The Confectioners* (1906) satirises new food technology in a wholesale manner.

Other writers were content to object to the idea of synthetic food—and technologically processed food in general—on the grounds of taste. In one of the most extravagant of all benign *disaster stories, Henri Allorge's *Le grand cataclysme* (1922), the hero and heroine—having been raised on synthetic food—are as delighted to rediscover joys of meat and fruit as any true Frenchman and Frenchwoman would be. Robert Barr's "Within an Ace of the End of the World" (1900)—in which so much nitrogen is removed from the air by the Great Food Corporation Ltd. that the world becomes drunk on oxygen—is a rare example of idea-based "food science fiction". J. B. S. *Haldane's *Daedalus* (1923) looked forward enthusiastically to the day when the world's food problems would be solved at a stroke—a sentiment echoed in other *futurological projects such as J. P. Lockhart-Mummery's *After Us; or, The World As It Might Be* (1936)—but his sister, Naomi Mitchison, took leave to differ in *Not by Bread Alone* (1983).

On the other hand, some satirically inclined writers wondered whether new synthetic foods might be so much more efficient than natural ones as to provide a ticket to superhumanity. Notable examples include Alfred Jarry's *Le surmâle* (1901; trans. as *The Supermale*) and H. G. Wells' *The Food of the Gods, and How It Came to Earth* (1904). The ready-made analogy between such foods and familiar mythical devices, such as the Classical ambrosia and the Biblical manna that fed the Children of Israel in the desert, encouraged the endowment of such improving foods to take on a moral dimension, as in John Gloag's *Manna* (1940) and Peter Phillips' "Manna" (1949). In Aubrey Menen's *The Fig Tree* (1959), biotechnologically originated giant fruits turn out to have aphrodisiac side effects.

Concerns about the adulteration of processed food were a significant early manifestation of the *Frankenstein complex. The U.S. Federal Food and Drugs Act of 1906 was a belated response to public agitation, and the Food and Drug Administration (FDA) set up in 1927 to administer it eventually became one of the most fearsome bureaucratic institutions in the United States. The first major concern of the disciplined investigation launched by the 1906 Act was food preservation, whose traditional methods—including the salting of meat, the pickling of vegetables, and the dehydration of grains—had been technologically augmented in the early nineteenth century by bottling and canning.

Nicholas Appert published a guide to food bottling in 1810, although he was unable to explain why heating the food in advance delayed its decomposition. Peter Durand patented the idea of using cans instead of bottles, tin-plated steel containers being pioneered in the United States by William Underwood in 1819. The solder initially used to seal cans was eliminated by a new closure technique in the first decade of the twentieth century, by which time Pasteur's germ theory of disease had explained that heating food in sealed containers prevented its decomposition by killing bacteria (which became known as pasteurisation in consequence). Microbiological theory also provided the foundations for a better understanding of the fermentation processes involved in pickling and the manner in which salts and acids operated in other kinds of preserves.

Refrigeration was introduced as a preservative technology in the late nineteenth century but was greatly improved by the flash-freezing methods pioneered by Clarence Birdseye in the 1920s and was combined with dehydration with the development of vacuum-assisted freeze-drying techniques in the 1930s. Chemical methods of preservation were continually augmented as organic chemistry progressed and the preservative effects of such compounds as benzoates, propionates, and glycols were explored. Irradiation was first developed as a food preservation technology in the 1960s, although it did not become widespread until the 1980s. Food storage technology also made further improvements with the development of plastic containers and clingfilm wrap. As with so many other life-transforming technologies, this sequence of development was almost invisible in history and literature, save for suspicious cautionary tales in the tradition launched by mid-nineteenth-century urban legends of street urchins who made a living supplying restaurants with stray cats, and the related tale of the "demon barber" Sweeney Todd—told in Thomas Peckett Prest's *The String of Pearls* (1846)— who assisted his neighbour Mrs. Lovett to produce "the best pork pies in London".

Another significant range of additives pioneered in the nineteenth century were dyes, whose reckless use in the wake of the advent of organic chemistry increased the necessity of the U.S. regulatory system established in 1906. Anxiety regarding the safety of additive dyes limited their use in the latter part of the century, some countries banning them entirely. Other additives are used to alter the texture of foods, particularly fats and "fat substitutes" derived by the hydrogenation of natural oils. This range of technologies eventually brought about a revolution in preliminary food processing that facilitated the growth of "fast food" restaurants in the latter half of the twentieth century. Foods preprocessed for rapid domestic preparation became increasingly sophisticated and popular in the same period, following the initial marketing of "TV dinners" in the mid-1950s.

Technological alterations of the composition of foodstuffs advanced in step with the development of new devices employed in cooking. The transformation of kitchens was a major evolutionary feature of twentieth-century domestic technology, greatly assisted by the applications of *electricity. The electric toaster, introduced in 1909, was followed by a continual stream of gadgets, including increasingly sophisticated food mixers and devices for making tea and coffee, climaxing in the 1970s with the introduction of microwave ovens, sandwich machines, deep fryers, grilling machines, and juicers.

The latter developments were extensively reflected in twentieth-century naturalistic fiction, albeit indirectly; precisely because they are matters of everyday routine, food acquisition and food preparation are inherently undramatic. When food is foregrounded as a fictional topic, the actual foodstuffs tend to be conspicuously exotic, as in the description of Trimalchio's feast in Petronius' *Satyricon* (ca. 60 A.D.), or symbolic, as in such works as Isak Dinesen's "Babette's Feast" (1950; film, 1987) and T. F. Powys' "Come and Dine" (written ca. 1930; published 1967). From the viewpoint of writers of action-adventure fiction, the obligation to supply characters with food often becomes a nuisance, discharged in blatantly tokenistic fashion. Diana Wynne Jones' *Tough Guide to Fantasyland* (1996) comments sarcastically on the ever-presence of anonymous "stew" in the Secondary Worlds of commodified fantasy. There is, inevitably, greater scope for the literary imagination in starvation than satiation, as evidenced by Knut Hamsun's *Sult* (1890; trans. as *Hunger*).

For similar reasons, speculative fiction paid little attention to developments in food science as they occurred, although the instant preparation of preprocessed food is a common background item in pulp science fiction, routinely extrapolated to the extreme of imagining all nutriment being taken in the form of pills. This notion, blithely neglectful of the aesthetic component of eating, was not so much a symptom of entrenched utilitarian attitudes as an appreciation of an opportunity to do away with the burdensome aspects of the authorial obligation to provide meals for fictional instruments.

Serendipitous discoveries of convenient food sources, like the Heechee food factory in Frederik Pohl's *Beyond the Blue Event Horizon* (1980), are commonplace in science fiction. Bland synthetic foods are usually consigned to fictional interstices, except in rare cases where an additive produced plot potential, as in Rudy Rucker's *Spacetime Donuts* (1981). Foodstuffs designed to have the opposite effect—spices—are usually considered primarily in an economic context, as in H. H. Holmes' "Secret of the House" (1953), or in a quasi-magical one, as in Frank Herbert's *Dune* (1965). On the other hand, the inherent difficulty of describing taste sensations in mere words ensures that depictions of exciting new gustatory sensations are rare; John Brunner's "The Taste of the Dish and the Savour of the Day" (1977) is a notable example.

The negative glamour of food science is neatly illustrated by the fact that the pioneer of space opera, E. E. Smith, who turned the galaxy into a science-fictional playground, was seeking escape from his day job as a food chemist, specialising in doughnut mixes, and never used his own scientific expertise as a basis for fictional speculation. Cyberpunk fiction, which did for *cyberspace what Smith had done for interstellar space, was bathetically satirised by Marc Laidlaw in "Nutrimancer" (1987). Poul *Anderson's ingenious Nicholas van Rijn is explicitly represented as a dealer in spices and intoxicants and an accomplished trencherman, but there is relatively little food science in the stories in which he stars.

The continued automation of farming was given some focused consideration in twentieth-century speculative fiction in such stories as Otfrid von Hanstein's *Die Farm der Verschollenen* (1924; trans. as "The Hidden Colony"), Fritz Leiber's satirical "Bread Overhead" (1958), and Anne McCaffrey's "Daughter" (1971), but the hypothetical food-production technology that attracted most attention in science fiction was hydroponics—growing plants in a liquid substrate instead of soil—because of its possible applications in *space travel. Serious extrapolations of the notion include Hal Clement's "Raindrop" (1965), in which an orbital water world is used as a testing ground with a view to developing elaborate food farms. The vital importance of food technology to the prospects of extraterrestrial *colonisation is emphasised by Grey Rollins' "The Sweet Smell of Success" (1990). Anxieties about the future of food production in the overexploited and overfertilised soils of Earth often give rise to darker images of future food technology, as in Rob Chilson and William F. Wu's "The Ungood Earth" (1985).

There has always been a rich vein of horror fiction in which humans serve as food for predatory or parasitic species, most luridly exaggerated in vampire fiction. The advent of *aliens in speculative fiction provided an abundant new scope for people-eating monsters, but very little attention was give to matters of alien food science, save for the jocular evocation of alien cookery books in such stories as Damon Knight's "To Serve Man" (1950) and Ray Nelson's "Food" (1965).

The rapid growth of the U.S. "dieting industry" and the corollary fashionability of "eating disorders" in the latter half of the twentieth century inevitably called forth a good deal of satirical writing; speculative examples include several stories by Kit Reed, ranging from "The Food Farm" (1967) to "The Last Big Sin" (2002), and Robert Silverberg's "Chip Runner" (1989). The perverse holy grail of a "nutrition-free" food is sarcastically featured in Gay McDonald's "The Unfood" (1982), while anti-obesity pills are featured in Elizabeth Moon's "Sweet Dreams, Sweet Nothings" (1986). The newfound ambiguity of the notion of "sweetness", reflected in the actual development of artificial sweeteners and consequent economic guerrilla warfare by the embattled sugar industry, is extrapolated in such stories as W. R. Thompson's "Health Food" (1987). In Ian Stewart's "The Treacle Well" (1983), a technology for turning unextractable oil into sugar goes awry.

The last substantial flare-up of the Frankenstein complex in the twentieth century was a widespread moral panic regarding "Frankenstein foods" produced by genetic modification. Science-fictional reflections of the panic were mostly unsympathetic to its hysteria; notable sarcastic representations include Brian Stableford's "The Last Supper" (2000), Nancy Kress' "And No Such Things Grow Here" (2001), and Mike Resnick's "Old Macdonald Had a Farm" (2001).

FORCE

A term applied in human affairs to various kinds of physical and psychological coercion. In its specialised scientific meaning it is the fundamental agent of causation, a cornerstone of theoretical *physics. The scientific notion remained nebulous, confused by Aristotelian notions of elements seeking their natural station, until *Galileo came up with a clearer conception. Isaac *Newton's second law of motion defined it as mass times acceleration. Newton's theory of gravity introduced the notion of a "field of force" relating the force of gravitational attraction to the inverse square of the distance between two bodies of mass. These uncompromising definitions allowed a clear separation of the ideas of force, momentum, and energy in physical theory, although the meanings of force and energy remained confused in common parlance.

The discovery that the inverse square law also applied to magnetic attraction facilitated the fusion of *magnetism and *electricity into a second fundamental force. Karl von Reichenbach attempted to reach a further level of generalisation in the nineteenth century by hypothesising the existence of a basic "odic" force whose various expressions would explain the phenomena of electricity, magnetism, heat, light, chemical energy, life, and mind. The twentieth-century development of *atomic theory supplemented gravity and electromagnetic force with two forces governing the subatomic universe: the weak nuclear interaction force, intermediate in strength between gravity (the least powerful) and electromagnetic force, and the strong nuclear interaction force, the most powerful of all. The attempt to accommodate these four forces within a single mathematical system by establishing fundamental symmetries between them became a key goal of twentieth-century physics, but the unification remained tantalisingly out of reach.

While organic *chemistry remained mysterious, it seemed reasonable to many natural historians to account for the phenomenon of *life in terms of a fundamental "life force" or "vital energy", and this usage was largely responsible for the continued confusion of the two terms. This way of thinking persisted into the late nineteenth century in such notions as Henri Bergson's *élan vital*. The idea of vital force was increasingly confused with the notion of "mental energy" as psychological theories began to be framed in the language of impulse and compulsion; Sigmund *Freud's model of the mind—especially its conception of the id and the idea of repression—is permeated by analogies of energy and force.

Pseudoscientific accounts of the "power" of the mind, especially when expressed in such paranormal abilities as telepathic broadcasting and psychokinetic impulsion, greatly encouraged the notion of the human mind as a forcible instrument in the nineteenth and twentieth centuries. As with many commonsensical ideas overtaken by complex theories, the notions of vital and mental force persisted in common parlance and fictional representations, sustained by their metaphorical usefulness. Science-fictional references to living entities of "pure force" or "pure energy"— a common hypothetical endpoint of *evolution— refer to vital force and mental energy rather than physical force.

Physical forces have also been prone to this kind of metaphorical extrapolation; the notion of a "force field" has given rise to numerous analogical constructs in pseudoscience and speculative fiction. Attempts to explain *parapsychological phenomena in terms of mysterious "force fields" or "energy fields" are commonplace, such hypothetical fields often being linked to mental phenomena in such a way as to provide an apologetic licence for telepathy, the survival of the personality after death, and so on.

In science fiction "force fields" are frequently employed as virtual armour, resistant to penetration by matter, and sometimes by radiation. Science-fictional imagery often imagines such force fields as domes enclosing cities, like the ones in James Blish's "The Box" (1949) and his Cities in Flight series (launched 1950), and occasionally as cocoons enclosing spaceships, as in Arthur Leo Zagat's "The Lanson Screen" (1936). Charles L. Harness modified the notion in *Flight into Yesterday* (1949) to permit the penetration of slow-moving objects, thus forcing his future warriors and assassins to employ swords rather than guns in personal conflict—a useful melodramatic asset borrowed by several other writers. Poul Anderson's *Shield* (1963) is an attempt to analyse the logical implications of a personal force field of this kind. The "gluon field" in Damien Broderick's *The Dreaming Dragons* (1980) is a further variant.

Physicists have occasionally been tempted to hypothesise a fifth fundamental force. One such hypothesis, involving a secondary kind of gravity—which might have given a new respectability to the science-fictional notion of *antigravity—became briefly fashionable in the 1980s. Speculative fiction occasionally features the discovery and technological exploitation of some such hypothetical force, such as the "viticity" of L. Ron Hubbard's *The End Is Not Yet* (1947) and the "Alderson force" of Jerry Pournelle's "He Fell into a Dark Hole" (1972). The most widely popularised popular use of the term in recent science fiction, in the *Star Wars* film series (launched 1976), refers to a frankly supernatural prime mover.

FORENSIC SCIENCE

Science applied to the settlement of legal proceedings, often presented in court by "expert witnesses". Although such applications routinely invoke various kinds of *criminological theory, their principal focus is on technologies of identification and detection. Forensic science is, in consequence, a cornerstone of generic detective fiction, its importance paradigmatically emphasised by the first meeting of Dr. Watson and Sherlock Holmes in Arthur Conan Doyle's *A Study in Scarlet* (1887), which found the archetypal detective busy experimenting with a new method of typing blood. Watson soon discovered that Holmes was also the world's foremost expert in the analysis of tobacco ash.

Because the narrative utility of crime is so tremendous, in terms of generating drama and providing neat story arcs, the fictional utility of forensic science is similarly significant. In the first novel ever to feature a police detective in a central role, Paul Féval's *Jean Diable* (1862; trans. as *John Devil*), the hero is credited with having discovered a systematic process for collating evidence in such a way as to identify offenders objectively—and the villain thus sets out to lay an elaborate false trail with the specific intention of beating that system. A contest of wits was thus joined that was to provide an entire genre with rich dramatic sustenance.

The historical origins of forensic science were closely connected with the development of *photography; the first "rogues' galleries" were complied by police forces in the 1850s. The pioneering private detective Allan Pinkerton established a large collection of such photographs, and the New York Police Department's collection provided the core of Thomas Byrnes' study of the *Professional Criminals of America* (1886). The systematisation of photographic identification was pioneered by Alphonse Bertillon, who established a Bureau of Judicial Identification in Paris in 1881. His method employed a calibrated camera in a specific position, under consistent lighting, photographing both full face and profile, and supplementing the images with textual data recording anthropometric measurements and anatomical anomalies. The variant in widespread use today produces distinctive images—"mug shots"—abundantly used in reportage and fiction.

Francis Galton, who used composites of such photographs in an attempt to produce an empirical image of the "criminal type" in 1878, also pioneered the use of fingerprints in identification. His *Finger Prints* (1892) initiated a system of analysis further refined by Sir Edward Henry, London's acting police commissioner; the Metropolitan Police began taking fingerprints of suspects in 1894 and created the Criminal Record Office to store and collate the data. A similar method had previously been used in India in 1858, after the Indian Mutiny, at the instigation of Sir William Herschel. The Galton/Henry system was internationalised in 1914 in the wake of an International Police Conference.

The literary impact of fingerprint technology, in an era when detective fiction was becoming enormously popular, was immediate and widespread. Mark Twain read Galton's book while writing *Pudd'nhead Wilson* (1894) and promptly incorporated it into the text. The inevitable literary contest to come up with hypothetical technologies by which fingerprints could be plausibly faked inspired such works as Conan Doyle's "The Norwood Builder" (1903), Arthur Train's "Mortmain" (1906), R. Austin Freeman's *The Red Thumb Mark* (1907), and Maurice Renard's *Les mains d'Orlac* (1920; trans. as *The Hands of Orlac*).

The adaptation of a sphygmometer—a device for measuring blood pressure—for possible forensic use as a "lie detector" was first accomplished by Cesare Lombroso, the pioneer of "criminal anthropology", in 1895. The device was introduced to the United States by Hugo Munsterberg, who was invited to Harvard by William James in 1892. Munsterberg devised the technique of interrogation used to "calibrate" lie detectors that was used throughout the twentieth century in association with more sophisticated instruments such as the polygraph. The reliability and legal admissibility of such evidence was soon called into question, and its literary role remained similarly ambiguous, but the polygraph continued to play a peripheral role in the U.S. legal process and detective fiction throughout the twentieth century. Attempts to employ *hypnotism for the purpose of assisting witnesses to recover memories inaccessible to consciousness was pioneered in the same period but its results proved equally dubious. The quest to develop a useful "truth serum" by means of *psychotropic drugs that reduce inhibition, such as sodium pentothal, was more extensively used in spy fiction than detective fiction; the extent of its employment in the real world is difficult to estimate by virtue of being largely confined to a similar context.

Forensic science gradually but inexorably increased its role in the detection and prosecution of criminals during the twentieth century, but took a considerable leap forward when developments in molecular *genetics facilitated the development of technologies of "DNA fingerprinting", based on a technique pioneered in 1984 by Alec Jeffreys. Once this technique became standard police procedure in the late 1980s, it brought about a dramatic transformation of detective fiction; the involvement of scientists in the careful processing of evidence had already led to the devolution of a subgenre of detective fiction whose primary emphasis was on expert medical examiners rather than on "legmen", and that trend was abruptly accelerated. The dominance of amateur and private detectives over professional policemen had been waning for some time, but the increasing importance of police laboratories secured a conclusive victory for official procedures, which was secured by the evolution of closely knit teams of detectives involving medical examiners, groups of specialist scientists, interrogators, and armed officers.

The subgenre of postmortem-based detective fiction had been pioneered in the TV series as *Quincy, M.E.* (1976–1983) before being raised to a much higher level of sophistication by such writers as Patricia Cornwell, whose series of novels featuring Kay Scarpetta was launched with *Postmortem* (1990), and Kathy Reichs, author of the series launched by *Déjà Dead* (1997). A much broader range of scientific inquisitions was developed in the TV medium—which is intrinsically more accommodating to teams of characters—in such series as *Silent Witness* (launched 1996) and, most significantly, the Las Vegas–set *CSI: Crime Scene Investigation* (launched 2000), which soon spawned clones set in Miami and New York.

The subsequent development of sequencing machines that allowed very tiny traces of DNA to be analysed increased the recoverability of such evidence dramatically. DNA not only became the principal means of linking perpetrators to current crime scenes but a means of delving back into the evidence preserved from previously insoluble cases, giving rise to a new subgenre of detective fiction, whose most popular manifestations are the TV series *Waking the Dead* (launched 2000) and *Cold Case* (launched 2003).

The increasing importance in courtrooms of biological evidence was paralleled by an increasing importance of forensic psychology, initially because of the increasing use of psychological analyses to determine whether accused persons were mentally fit to stand trial or fully accountable for their actions. Such retrospective analyses were increasingly used in an anticipatory fashion in "psychological profiling", in which analysis of crimes was interpreted as evidence of the personality and circumstances of their likely perpetrator, thus assisting in the identification of suspects. Fictional extrapolations of the notion penetrated deeply into the subgenre of serial killer fiction, applied by such writers as Thomas Harris, in *Red Dragon* (1981), and James Patterson, in the series begun with *Along Came a Spider* (1992). It also had an impact in the TV medium, in series such as *Cracker* (1997–1999) and *Law and Order: Criminal Intent* (launched 2001). In concentrating so heavily on an artificial empathic link between the detective and the villain such fiction was occasionally extrapolated in a quasi-supernatural fashion, as in the TV series *Millennium* (1996–1998), thus forging a new link between orthodox detective fiction and fiction featuring "psychic" or "occult" detectives.

The use of forensic science in speculative fiction was far less extensive than in naturalistic detective fiction, although the subject's appeal to pulp science fiction fans is reflected in the fact that correspondence courses in "Scientific Crime Detection" were advertised in *Astounding* in 1937. The most explicitly scientific of all the heroes of series detective fiction, Craig Kennedy—who began his career in *Cosmopolitan* when it was still a pulp—was briefly co-opted into science fiction by Hugo *Gernsback, who hired his creator, Arthur B. Reeve, as "editorial commissioner" on *Scientific Detective Monthly* in 1930, but the magazine published only ten issues. The term itself was rarely used within the genre, although a "forensic sociologist" is featured in Henry Kuttner and C. L. Moore's "Private Eye" (1949; by-lined Lewis Padgett). As generic science fiction became more sophisticated in the postwar period, however, medical examiners were occasionally confronted with science-fictional enigmas, as in H. L. Gold's "The Old Die Rich" (1953), and futuristic police forces were routinely armed with ingenious forensic technologies, as in Rick Raphael's "Once a Cop" (1964).

A subgenre of "forensic science fiction" was pioneered in the wake of Jefferson's breakthrough by Paul *Levinson, in a series begun with "The Copyright Notice Case" (1996). Peter F. Hamilton's futuristic detective series featuring Greg Mandel also moved in that direction; "The Suspect Genome" (2000) features a further sophistication of DNA analysis. Although it seems highly likely to see further development, the subgenre is handicapped by the problem that afflicts all fantastic detective fiction—the ease with which *deus ex machina* devices can be improvised to bring story arcs to a conclusion. The artistry of detective fiction is heavily dependent on ruling out such arbitrary devices, so that once the impossible is eliminated, what remains—however unlikely it may seem—really must be the truth; as soon as the bounds of possibility become elastic, the aesthetics of that process are imperiled. It is the insistent naturalism of their fictional setting as well as the essential virtue of their endeavours that have permitted the heroes of such TV series as the *CSI* clones to become unprecedentedly charismatic exemplars of the heroic *scientist.

FORT, CHARLES (HOY) (1874–1932)

U.S. journalist who compiled four collections of "damned data": reports, culled from all manner of periodicals, of odd and supposedly impossible occurrences. Carefully setting aside the customary assumption that such items were evidence of the inherent unreliability of witnesses and the desperation of newspaper editors to fill space (especially evident in the August "silly season"), Fort interested himself in the classification of these data and wryly tongue-in-cheek analyses of the possible implications of the most consistent patterns. He took up a position that was both radically sceptical—refusing to accept any of the pronouncements of the "scientific priesthood"—and hypothetically adventurous.

The Book of the Damned (1919) dealt with odd *meteorological phenomena and other things reported to have fallen from the sky, including frogs and fishes as well as pebbles and *meteorites. *New Lands* (1923) continued in the same vein, widening the scope of its anomalous astronomical observations to take in the stars, and its atmospheric considerations to take in curious optical and acoustic phenomena, extending to what would later be seen as stereotypical reports of UFOs. All of these data, Fort contended, supported the view that there were more things in the local heavens than conventional science allowed.

Lo! (1931), reprinted in the science fiction pulp *Astounding* in 1934, took up the theme of strange showers yet again, but chose to interpret them in terms of a hypothetical "transportory force" that Fort chose to call teleportation. Accounts of blood flowing from religious statues and animals displaced from their customary habitats were accommodated within the same frame—the latter supplemented by a digression into cryptozoology—as were mysterious human appearances and disappearances and spontaneous combustions.

Wild Talents (1932) had a greater effect on the development of genre science fiction than *Lo!*, because it broadened its scope to take in a greater range of "working witchcraft"—that is, the supposed psi powers that fascinated the experimentalist J. B. Rhine and John W. *Campbell Jr.—and also took more interest in modern theoretical *physics as a potential source of explanatory hypotheses. Fort was, however, far more interested in the kinds of mysterious coincidences that Arthur Koestler subsequently elaborated into the pseudoscientific study of "synchronicity", mysterious cattle mutilations, unaccountable murders, stigmatic wounds, and the like. The author wondered at one point whether conventional psychic researchers might be right to think that ghosts exist, but immediately concluded that if it is so, then *we* must be the "ghosts" of spirits that have gone before.

In addition to these volumes, Fort published a little fiction, including the *microcosmic romance "A Radical Corpuscle" (1906)—but none of it belongs to the subgenre of "Fortean fiction" based on the extrapolation of his damned data. Notable examples of Fortean fiction from the science fiction pulps include Frank Belknap Long's "Skyrock" (1935), John Russell Fearn's "Subconscious" (1936), R. DeWitt Miller's "The Shapes" (1936), several items by Eric Frank Russell, most notably *Sinister Barrier* (1939), and H. Beam Piper's "He Walked Around the Horses" (1948) and "Police Operation" (1948). The tradition extended into several items in Edward D. Hoch's

Simon Ark series (1950s–1980s), Jerry Sohl's *The Transcendent Man* (1953), John Brunner's "A Better Mousetrap" (1963), Wilson Tucker's *Ice and Iron* (1974; rev. 1975), Gene deWeese and Robert Coulson's *Charles Fort Never Mentioned Wombats* (1977) and Caitlín Kiernan's collection *To Charles Fort, with Love* (2005). Fortean science fiction writer Damon Knight wrote the biography *Charles Fort: Prophet of the Unexplained* (1970).

Acknowledged Fortean fiction was always much thinner on the ground than calculated Fortean *reportage, which soon became a minor industry. A Fortean Society was formed in 1931, its stated aims including "To remove the halo from the head of Science" and "To destroy scientists' faith in their own works and thus force a general return to the truly scientific principle of 'temporary acceptance'". Its one-time secretary Tiffany Thayer described it as "the Red Cross of the human mind". The original *Fortean Society Magazine* was transformed into *Doubt*. The International Fortean Organization subsequently published *INFO Journal* while the U.K. branch published the slightly more lighthearted *Fortean Times*, which made a triumphant debut in the mass market in the 1990s, prompting the production of a *Fortean TV* show presented by one-time science fiction writer Lionel Fanthorpe, launched in 1997.

In the meantime, Fortean reportage became a key stock-in-trade of supermarket tabloids such as the *Weekly World News* and British equivalents such as the *Sunday Sport*. Classic examples of neo-Fortean reportage include Charles Berlitz's accounts of *The Bermuda Triangle* (1974) and *The Philadelphia Experiment* (1979, with William I. Moore; film 1984). The flying saucer craze that took off from Fortean foundations would have provoked Fort's severe disapproval as its supporters became increasingly dogmatic. Jeremy and Sarah Tolbert's *The Fortean Bureau*, an online magazine founded in 2002, published thirty-one issues before being closed to further submissions in 2005.

FORWARD, ROBERT L[ULL] (1932–2002)

U.S. physicist, populariser of science and science fiction writer, who obtained a Ph.D. in gravitational physics from the University of Maryland and spent the greater part of his career (1956–1987) at the Hughes Research Laboratories in California, obtaining numerous patents as well as publishing some seventy technical papers. He subsequently established his own space science company, Forward Unlimited, and became a partner in Tethers Unlimited.

The hardness of Forward's science fiction is comparable with that of Hal *Clement, but his active involvement in theoretical *physics and space science research allowed him to forge much closer links between his nonfictional and fictional speculations, as illustrated by his book *Indistinguishable from Magic* (1995), in which a series of popularising essays is each supplemented by an illustrative short story. The topics of the essays include antimatter, antigravity, *black holes, and *time machines as well as several on such space technologies as "beanstalks" (space elevators) and starships. The last-named subject is a particular fascination of Forward's; one essay maps out plausible technologies by means of which vessels might be constructed in the near future capable of reaching other stars at sub–light speeds, while another discusses the possibility of breaching the relativistic light-barrier.

Most of Forward's novels are much closer in spirit to Hal Clement's world-building exercises, developing elaborate exercises in *exobiology within extremely exotic physical circumstances. *Dragon's Egg* (1980) and its sequel *Starquake!* (1985) describe the long-term evolution of an ecosphere on the surface of a neutron star and the interaction of its sentient species with humankind. *Rocheworld* (1982; exp. book as *The Flight of the Dragonfly* 1985; further exp. under the original title 1990) describes the ecosphere of a double planet linked by a cosmic bridge; two sequels, *Return to Rocheworld* (1993) and *Rescued from Paradise* (1995), were written with his daughter Julie Forward Fuller and a further two, *Marooned on Eden* (1993) and *Ocean Under the Ice* (1994), with his wife Martha Dodson Forward.

The essential esotericism of these works inevitably restricted their market, and Forward appeared to be deliberately lowering his sights in an account of accelerated *terraforming (with the aid of a convenient *deus ex machina*), *Martian Rainbow* (1991). The story's libertarian rhetoric was further extrapolated in *Timemaster* (1992), but the latter novel's main emphasis is on the theoretical physics underlying the technologies of faster-than-light space travel and time travel developed within it. Forward had evidently decided that he would follow his own interests with appropriate scrupulousness rather than attempt to appeal to a broader audience.

Camelot 30K (1993) investigates the hypothetical biology of tiny aliens inhabiting an "iceball" in the Kuiper Belt, their ecosphere being a mere thirty degrees above absolute zero. *Saturn Rukh* (1997) describes an expedition to "mine" the Saturnian atmosphere and the expeditionaries' interaction with native life-forms—including one that swallows their "balloon" during a descent. Forward never became sufficiently famous to warrant extensive citation within the science fiction field, but he is featured as a character in Isaac Asimov's brief "Probability Zero" story "Left to Right" (1987).

FOURTH DIMENSION, THE

An addendum to the three dimensions by means of which *space is normally conceived. *Time is often considered as a fourth dimension, that representation being greatly encouraged by the artifice of co-ordinate *geometry, in which time is routinely represented as a linear axis. The popularisation of the idea that time could be represented as a fourth dimension was, however, historically confused with the popularisation of the idea that there might be a fourth spatial dimension even if time were left out of consideration. The leading populariser of the fourth dimension in the late nineteenth century, C. H. *Hinton, helped to inspire constructors of two-dimensional "flatlands" as well as providing the jargon that H. G. *Wells used to "explain" the functioning of The Time Machine (1895).

The nineteenth-century development of the idea was further confused by the combination of geometrical speculations with residues of *occult science, in the hope that a fourth spatial dimension might provide a "scientific" explanation for such phenomena as ghosts—another notion that Hinton found very interesting. The most ambitious theorist of this kind was Johann Zollner, whose Transcendental Physics (1865) provided considerable inspiration to spiritualists, theosophists, and other speculators anxious to preserve a relationship between the worlds of the living and the dead. Zollner's intellectual descendants included G. I. Gurdjieff and P. D. Ouspensky; the latter writer's key texts—originally published in Russian—were translated into English as Tertium Organum (1920) and A New Model of the Universe (1931). In the latter work's cosmology time "moves" in a spiral and there are six spatial dimensions; Ouspensky's version of the temporal dimension was dramatised in Kinemadrama (1915; trans. as Strange Life of Ivan Osokin). Hinton's studiously cautious but nevertheless adventurous approach was replicated in J. W. Dunne's An Experiment with Time (1927) and The Serial Universe (1934).

Most nineteenth-century literary references to higher dimensions are derived from occult appropriations of the notion, including the references made by Fyodor Dostoyevsky in Brat'ya Karamazovy (1879–1880; trans. as The Brothers Karamazov). Oscar Wilde's "The Canterville Ghost" (1887) pokes fun at such notions but Joseph Conrad and Ford Madox Ford used them more earnestly in their depiction of

the "dimensionists" of The Inheritors (1901). George W. Pawlowski's Voyage au pays de la 4ème dimension (1912) is an elaborate hybrid work. George Griffith's "The Conversion of the Professor" (1899), John Buchan's "Space" (1911), Algernon Blackwood's "A Victim of Higher Space" (1914) and "The Pikestaffe Case" (1924), Richard Hughes' "The Vanishing Man" (1926), and Charles Williams' Many Dimensions (1931) extrapolated this *pseudoscientific tradition.

The use of a hypothetical fourth dimension by occult scientists and pseudoscientists resulted in the idea acquiring a disreputable taint in the eyes of rationalists that it never entirely lost, even when the general theory of *relativity remodelled the space of theoretical *physics as a four-dimensional space-time and opened the door to speculation that a fourth spatial dimension—in effect, a fifth dimension— might explain electromagnetic attraction in the same way that Albert *Einstein had explained gravity, thus producing a unified "theory of everything".

When the notion of the fourth dimension was adopted into pulp science fiction, the occult projections of the idea were usually minimised, as in Ray Cummings' Into the Fourth Dimension (1926; book, 1943), Bob Olsen's series begun with "The Four-Dimensional Roller-Press" (1927), Miles J. Breuer's "The Appendix and the Spectacles" (1928), "The Captured Cross-Section" (1929), and "The Book of Worlds" (1929), and Murray Leinster's "The Fifth-Dimensional Catapult" (1931) and its sequels. The fourth dimension quickly became familiar in science fiction as the direction in which all *parallel worlds must lie, and it became a significant facilitating device by virtue of its association with that idea; interdimensional fishing expeditions were featured in such stories as Alan E. Nourse's "Tiger by the Tail" (1951) and Clifford D. Simak's "Dusty Zebra" (1954).

The possibility that human perception might be expanded, by evolution or education, to take in the fourth and other spatial dimensions was broached in E. V. Odle's scientific romance The Clockwork Man (1923) and Henry Kuttner and C. L. Moore's science fiction story "Mimsy Were the Borogoves" (1943, as by Lewis Padgett). The didactic fables in George *Gamow's Mr. Tompkins in Wonderland (1939) include significant attempts to make four-dimensional space-time imaginatively accessible. Other notable attempts to describe higher dimensions in literary terms include Norman Kagan's "The Mathenauts" (1964) and numerous works by Rudy *Rucker, including White Light (1980), some of the short stories in The 57th Franz Kafka (1983), The Sex Sphere (1983), and Spaceland: A Novel of the Fourth Dimension (2002). Ian Watson's "Hyperzoo" (1987) features four-dimensional creatures devised as artworks.

The notion of a fourth dimension came to seem rather modest and trivial, however, in the wake of suggestions by theoretical physicists that the universe might only be explicable in terms of a much larger number than four. Various versions of string theory expanded the likely number to nine, eleven, or even more.

FRANKENSTEIN

The surname of the antihero of Mary Shelley's *Frankenstein; or, The Modern Prometheus* (1818). The novel was one of the most influential ever published, its apparatus quickly acquiring legendary status. Early dramatic versions included the anonymous *Frankenstein; or, The Demon of Switzerland* (1823) and *Le Monstre et le Magicien* (1826) by Antoine Béraud, Charles Nodier, and Jean-Toussaint Merle. H. M. Milner adapted the latter into English as *The Man and the Monster; or, The Fate of Frankenstein* (1828). Jane Webb's derivative *The Mummy! A Tale of the Twenty-Second Century* (1827) was similarly earnest, but subsequent imitations displayed a conspicuous decline from *contes philosophiques* to crude horror fiction, illustrated by *Professor Stueckenholtz* (1880, by-lined J. A. A.), Patrice Latour's "Dr. Faber's Last Experiment" (1917), H. P. Lovecraft's "Herbert West—Reanimator" (1922), and J. C. Snaith's *Thus Far* (1922).

In the early twentieth century the name was often mistakenly applied to the monster that Frankenstein had assembled rather than the scientist himself, especially when the former character was equipped with an iconic visual image by James Whale's 1931 film version, which featured the actor subsequently known as Boris Karloff. Most modern references are to the film and its sequels rather than the novel, although such belated literary sequels as Howard Waldrop and Stephen Utley's "Black as the Pit, from Pole to Pole" (1977) and Michael Bishop's *Brittle Innings* (1994) and such variants as Brian W. Aldiss' *Frankenstein Unbound* (1973) and Fred Saberhagen's *The Frankenstein Papers* (1986), are more scrupulous. The stories in Byron Preiss' anthology *The Ultimate Frankenstein* (1991) are mostly movie inspired. The story has been frequently adapted into other media, including ballets choreographed by Wayne Eagling (1984), Matthew Wright (1988), and Lees G. Harris and Stephen K. Stone (2002) and operas by Libby Larsen (1990), James Wierzbicki and Ben Ohrmart (1999), and Ty Morse and Justin Perkinson (2003).

The name was eventually adapted for use as an adjective in popular *reportage, in such phrases as "Frankenstein foods" (that is, *genetically modified food products). It was freely bandied about in such titles as H. A. Highstone's "Frankenstein—Unlimited" (1936) and Edward D. Hoch's *The Frankenstein Factory* (1975). It was also appropriated by Isaac *Asimov in his description of the "Frankenstein Complex": a reflexively technophobic attitude of mind that he felt bound to oppose strenuously. In the preface to *The Rest of the Robots* (1964), Asimov claimed that all the stories in his robot series—earlier ones had been collected in *I, Robot* (1950)—were intended to challenge the careless assumption that any new technology was bound to run amok and threaten the destruction of its creators. Biophysicist Joe Allred's guest editorial in the May 1974 issue of *Analog* made similar complaints about the "Frankenstein phobia" manifest in TV talk shows, and the tendency was further satirised in Gray Greenwood's account of the routinisation of a "Frankenstein Process" in *Jigsaw Men* (2004).

Asimov had borrowed the title of *I, Robot* from Eando Binder's short story "I, Robot" (1939), in which a robot wrongly suspected of murdering its maker discovers why people are so very willing to think the worst of him when he reads Mary Shelley's novel and realises that it has become a template for modern attitudes to machinery. Like Binder, Asimov wanted to employ science fiction strategically to challenge and counter the assumption that technological invention is a hubristic usurpation of divine prerogatives that can only lead to disaster. It was for that reason that he equipped his robots with the "three laws of robotics", thus gifting them a seemingly simple system of ethics that would guarantee their benevolence.

The convenience of the normalising story arc associated with "intrusive fantasy", in which the world is briefly disturbed by an innovation that is eventually erased, thus restoring the *status quo*—a formula adapted to science fiction by such nineteenth-century writers as C. J. Cutcliffe Hyne—was sufficient to ensure that the fundamental pattern of Mary Shelley's novel was repeated incessantly. That kind of story arc had been adopted into pulp science fiction in spite of its tacit implication that all invention is bad, and was extravagantly developed there—a situation assisted by the fact that some prominent early writers of pulp science fiction, most notably David H. Keller, were obvious victims of the complex. In consequence, writers of *hard science fiction committed to the idea and ideals of technological progress had a hard fight on their hands from the very beginning.

In spite of the heroic efforts of Asimovian apologists, who were eventually forced onto the back foot as hard science fiction became a minority practice even within the genre, the Frankenstein complex increased its hold on the popular imagination in the latter part of the twentieth century, greatly encouraged by the advent of the *atom bomb, fears regarding the development of *artificial intelligence by *computers, and anxieties regarding new *biotechnologies. The fact that the 2004 film allegedly based on Asimov's I, Robot (unlike the unused Harlan Ellison script published in 1987 as "I Robot—The Movie") inverts his intention, becoming a stereotypical representation of the Frankenstein complex, testifies to the extent to which *cinema depends on normalising story arcs to generate dramatic tension and a sense of closure satisfactory to its audience.

The Frankenstein complex reigns supreme in thriller fiction, whose formula requires normalising endings, and hard science fiction writers venturing into that marketplace never had any chance of competing with such extreme victims of the complex as Michael Crichton. Hard science fiction writers continued to mount ideological opposition to the syndrome within the genre, but by the end of the twentieth century their effort had come to resemble a desperate and futile rearguard action.

FREUD, SIGMUND (1856–1939)

Austrian physician whose specialisation in the treatment of mental illness led him to develop a comprehensive theory of the mind and a distinctive technique of psychoanalysis. His *psychological model and its associated method of psychiatric treatment were always controversial, but their influence was enormous—colouring a great many literary texts—and they remain one of the landmarks of modern thought.

After completing his education at the University of Vienna, Freud worked as a medical student at the Brücke Institute. His early researches in physiology came to an end in 1882 when he went to the General Hospital of Vienna in order to obtain a qualification for private practice that would secure him the income he needed to marry; soon thereafter, he joined the staff of Theodor Meynert's psychiatric clinic, where he was introduced to a hallucinatory disorder whose study prompted some of the hypotheses he was later to build into his theory and published research on neurophysiological studies of the medulla oblongata and the physiological effects of cocaine. In 1885, he visited Jean Charcot, the neurologist who ran the Saltpêtrière hospital in Paris, and discussed potential uses of *hypnosis in treating mental illness.

Following his marriage in 1886, Freud worked with Josef Breuer in Vienna; the two published a paper in 1893 that became the preface to a collection of case studies, Fragen der Hysterie (1895; trans. as Studies in Hysteria). Freud soon abandoned hypnosis

as an investigative method in favour of the technique of "free association", and found a new collaborator in Wilhelm Fliess, with whom he formed the view that the basis of human psychology, in which all neurosis was rooted, was sexuality. He began work on the book that was eventually to appear as Die Traumdeutung (1900; trans. as The Interpretation of Dreams), and began to psychoanalyse himself in 1897, becoming his own paradigm example of the syndrome he called the Oedipus complex. The central thesis of his interpretative schema was that dreams were expressions of hedonistic wish fulfillment, which have to be disguised because the conscious mind is not prepared to acknowledge the desires thus represented, which have therefore been repressed into "the unconscious". Although the notion that the mind had an unconscious component was already a familiar notion—Eduard von Hartmann had already published Die Philosophie des Unbewussten (1869; trans. as The Philosophy of the Unconscious)—it was Freud's idiosyncratic conception of its contents and raison d'être that was to dominate twentieth-century thought.

In 1902, Freud set up a Psychoanalytical Society, inviting four friends—including Alfred Adler—to meet at his home once a week. By 1908, it had twenty-two members, including Carl *Jung. Discussions within the group formed the background to Freud's works subsequent to Zur Psychopathologie des Alltagslebens (1901; trans. as The Psychopathology of Everyday Life), including Der Witz und seine Beziehung zum Unbewussten (1905; trans. as Jokes and Their Relation with the Unconscious) and Drei Abhandlungen zur Sexualtheorie (1905; trans. as Three Essays on the Theory of Sexuality), all of which proved controversial, by virtue of their assertions about childhood sexuality. The Society suffered a series of fierce disputes that ultimately led to schisms as Adler, Wilhelm Stekel, and Jung broke away one by one to form rival schools of psychoanalysis.

In the meantime, Freud's theorising became increasingly ambitious, widening into *anthropological theory in Totem und Tabu (1913; trans. as Totem and Taboo) and *metaphysical philosophy in Jenseits des Lustprinzip (1920; trans. as Beyond the Pleasure Principle) and Die Zukunft einer Illusion (1927; trans. as The Failure of an Illusion), but he continued to refine his theory of the mind, publishing Vorlesungen zur Enführung in die Psychoanalyse (1917; trans. as A General Introduction to Psychoanalysis) and a definitive version of his model of the conscious self or "ego" as a dynamic compromise between the libidinous appetites of the "id" and the disciplined conscientious demands of the "superego" in Das Ich und das Es (1923; trans. as The Ego and the Id). He remained in Vienna until the Nazis arrived in 1938, when he relocated to London, but he was suffering from cancer and died soon afterwards.

The scientific status of Freud's theories was hotly debated from their inception, many scientists rejecting the introspective method and criticising its evidential basis in case studies whose interpretation was quite independent of the patients' actual experience of their condition. Freud was not averse to increasing the range of his evidence by analysing artists *via* the study of their works; his literary subjects included E. T. A. Hoffmann, whose Gothic tale "Der Sandmann" (1815; trans. as "The Sandman") became the developmental basis for a theory of "the uncanny" that became a key element in several later theoretical accounts of supernatural fiction. Hoffmann's *Die Elixiere des Teufels* (1813–1816) also provided fuel for an extensive analysis of the notion of doubles.

Sceptics considered Freud's own theory to be nothing more than a highly imaginative narrative, essentially fantastic and horrific. It was, however, an object of intense interest for artists, and Freud's theories formed an important part of the ideative background of modernist literature. Some modernists reacted fervently against it—Virginia Woolf wrote a scathing critique of "Freudian Fiction" (1920) couched as a review of J. D. Beresford's *An Imperfect Mother*, and D. H. Lawrence penned two critical essays—"Psychoanalysis and the Unconscious" (1921) and "Fantasia of the Unconscious" (1922)—attempting to defend the unconscious against Freud's alleged slanders, but many found it a fertile source of imagery and, more importantly, a useful means of organising symbolic imagery into meaningful and suggestive patterns.

One of the reasons that the Symbolist Movement petered out after 1900 was that symbolism had lost much of its mystery and had become rather obvious; when the further distortions of surrealism were not overtly guided by Freudian ideas, they very often absorbed Freudian methods of free association into their compository processes. The novel, as an art-form, had dedicated itself to the analysis of human psychology, and whether individual novelists loved or loathed the new schools of therapeutic psychoanalysis, they could not ignore them. Psychiatrists employing other methods of treatment, especially those rooted in *neurological research, found it easier to dismiss their rival out of hand than litterateurs whose own methods were introspective and whose own products were "case studies" of a sort. For this reason, the influence of Freudian thought on twentieth-century culture has been enormous, in spite of the dearth of belief in his theory.

Works that qualify as explicit Freudian fantasies and works actively promoting Freudian theory include David H. Keller's *The Eternal Conflict* (1939),

Guy Endore's *Methinks the Lady* (1945), several titles by D. M. Thomas—most notably *The White Hotel* (1981)—and several by Robertson Davies. W. H. Auden commemorated his passing in "In Memory of Sigmund Freud" (1940). He is featured in Irving Stone's *The Passions of the Mind* (1971), Nicholas Meyer's *The Seven Per Cent Solution* (1974)—in which he is consulted by Sherlock Holmes, as he also is in Keith Oatley's *The Case of Emily V* (1993)—Anthony Burgess' *The End of the World News* (1982), Kathleen Daniels' *Minna's Story: The Secret Love of Dr. Sigmund Freud* (1992) and—along with Carl Jung—Keith Korman's *Secret Dreams* (1995). Freud's early collaborator Josef Breuer takes centre stage in Irving D. Yalom's *When Nietzsche Wept: A Novel of Obsession* (1992), whose author went on to publish two collections of "tales of psychotherapy" and the novel *Lying on the Couch* (1996).

Literary accounts of liberation from repression that clearly have Freud in mind include various novels by Thorne Smith and Vincent McHugh's libidinous comedy *I Am Thinking of My Darling* (1943). Donald Barthelme's *The Dead Father* (1975) is a parody of Freudian fiction. Psychoanalytic fantasies involving further elaborations of Freudian theory include Judith Rossner's *August* (1983) and Daniel Menaker's *The Treatment* (1998). Speculative fiction based on Freudian ideas includes Frank Belknap Long's "Dark Vision" (1930), Alfred Bester's "The Devil's Invention" (1950; aka "Oddy and Id"), Franklin Abel's "Freudian Slip" (1952), and Philip José Farmer's "Mother" (1953; collected with similar endeavours in *Strange Relations*, 1960). Barry Malzberg's *The Remaking of Sigmund Freud* (1985) is an elaborate meditation on Freudian ideas featuring Freud as a character.

In spite of Freud's endeavours, there is still no general agreement as to what actual dreams mean, if they mean anything at all, but literary representations of dreams have to be loaded with meaning, or there is no purpose in reporting them. Once Freud's theory had been popularised, no literary dream could be designed or consumed without its possible sexual meanings being taken into account, even if much older theories of dreams as precognitive revelations were invoked. The fact that many artists attempt to mine dreams for inspiration and to adapt them into their work—a strategy painstakingly described by Roderick Townley in *Night Errands* (1998) and illustrated by his novels *The Great Good Thing* (2001) and *Into the Labyrinth* (2002)—only served to complicate the issue further.

By the time the twentieth century ended, it had almost become a ritual necessity for mentally aberrant characters in fiction—especially murderers—to issue derisive dismissals of Freudian interpretations of their behaviour well in advance of any actual confrontation with them, but the fact that they and their authors feel compelled to do so speaks volumes.

FUTURE

The range of unelapsed *time. Psychological attitudes to the future tend to differentiate between the near future and the far future, and the differentiation is clearly evident in fictional representations. Fred Polak's analysis of *The Image of the Future* (1973) distinguishes two categories of futuristic thought and imagery, which he calls "the future of prophecy" and "the future of destiny". The former category is primarily concerned with the unfolding consequences of present actions, decisions, and projects; the latter attempts to deal with matters of ultimate inevitability. J. D. Bernal had earlier drawn a similar distinction between "the future of desire and the future of fate". Exercises in *futurology, pseudoscientific prophecy and most *science fiction stories belong to the former category, while eschatological fantasies, images of far-futuristic *decadence and *Omega Point fantasies belong to the latter.

Within scientific discourse, the future is primarily an arena in which the *predictions generated by scientific hypotheses are put to the test, but the philosophy of science makes a crucial distinction between a contingent statement—that if a particular set of conditions is fulfilled then a particular event will follow—and an unconditional prophecy that is routinely blurred when the word "prediction" is used in common parlance, where it is usually taken to be synonymous with prophecy. Popular attitudes to futuristic fiction are inevitably polluted by this confusion.

The future is, essentially, an object of assumption rather than experience. Everything humans know—and, in consequence, what humans *are*—is a product of the past, but everything humans *do* is orientated towards ends situated in the future, organised by a combination of desire and hope on the one hand, fear and dread on the other. The fact that the only future certainty is death, and the overwhelming probability that at least some of our desires and hopes will fail to bear fruit before we reach that end, adds to the burden of that knowledge in formulating the *angst* that *existentialists define as the fundamental mood of human existence.

The instruments that humans use in attempting to steer a course into the future must, by necessity, include some sense of purpose and some kind of method; science is one provider of the second—self-defined as the only reliable one, its supporters being scornfully dismissive of intuition, superstition, and divine revelation—but is much weaker in calculating ends than means. Literature, by contrast, shares with *theology an intense fascination with ends that tends to be somewhat neglectful of means.

Because it is utterly impractical, if not logically impossible, to gather knowledge sufficiently complete and accurate to perfect our expectations and calculations of means, human ability to shape the future is extremely limited, even when people are not working at cross-purposes. This is so horrible a prospect that it is hardly surprising that one of the principal occupations of the human mind has always been a desperate quest for means of gaining supernatural insight into the future: the rewards of *prophecy. On the other hand, it is the unpredictability of the future that make conscious life possible; if the future *were* fully knowable, in a practical sense, there would be no necessity for anticipatory consciousness, because there would no longer be any choices to be made, all conceivable ends being either inevitable or unattainable. Because science is primarily a matter of calculating the inevitable, it stands in an odd relationship to human consciousness, whose avidity to know the inevitable is predicated on the impossibility of its ascertainment. The odd relationship in which science stands to literature, particularly to literature dedicated to the exploration and description of consciousness, is a corollary of this observation, as is the odd situation of the future within artistic—primarily literary—representation.

Anatole France's philosophical novel *Sur la pierre blanche* (1905; trans. as *The White Stone*), considering the representation of the future in human consciousness and art, observes that it is usually employed as a blank canvas whose users paint it with their hopes and fears. He acknowledges that it might be possible for artists and writers to explore the future in a more objective spirit, but in 1905 he could think of only one person—H. G. *Wells—who had tried. Ironically, Wells had just stopped doing it, having abandoned *scientific romance in favour of the *futurological mode of thought, but other writers readily took up where he had left off; throughout the twentieth century there was always a substantial, albeit tiny, minority of speculative writers who tried hard to wriggle free of the straitjacket of their hopes and fears in order to investigate a fuller range of rationally plausible possibilities. Literary images of the future, whose collation and comparison were considerably assisted by the development of imaginary technologies of *time travel, moved decisively into a new phase as they took up France's exploratory challenge with great enthusiasm.

Because the near future is imminent, some notion of its likely shape is a factor in all present plans; it is the reservoir of human ambition and is haunted by all manner of anxieties. Images of the near future are, in consequence, replete with reflections of contemporary hopes and fears. The demands of melodrama ensure that fears predominate in speculative fiction, leaving hopes to attain a more even balance in speculative nonfiction. Images of more distant futures, on the other hand, may be regarded with greater objectivity, and tend to take on a more clinical tone even when they are calculatedly melodramatic.

The sector of futuristic narrative space of most interest to humans is the timespan over which their own lives are likely to extend, although many people extend that interest by a further margin in worrying about the inheritance of their children. The certainty of *death creates further interest in hypothetical future narrative spaces that lie outside the pattern of history: afterlives shaped by religious faith, which often become ideatively entwined with images of more distant "post-historical" world futures. Images of the far future in scientific speculation and science fiction show a strong tendency to retain the kind of *theological overtones manifest in Omega Point hypotheses.

Futuristic imagery of both kinds is heavily dependent on scientific perspectives. Images of the far future could not be meaningfully elaborated until there was an appreciation of the true time scale of Earthly history and the forces involved in its long-term evolution, while images of the near future could not become interesting until it was generally realised that a human lifetime might bear witness to technological changes of considerable scope. Futuristic fiction was confined by the tradition of religious prophecy until an awareness of the effects of technological change developed. The anonymous *The Reign of King George VI 1900–1925* (1763) imagines a future England in which a king can still lead his cavalry into battle, but one in which canals have transformed internal trade and communications.

The exponential growth of futuristic fiction from the late eighteenth century to the early twenty first reflects a growth in the awareness that habits and strategies designed in the *past to cope with the *present might not be adequate to deal with the imminent future. Many people, even in the twenty-first century, probably have yet to cultivate a sound psychological appreciation of the scope of the changes that routinely overtake the world in the space of a contemporary lifetime; the difficulty of so doing was identified as a crucial personal and social problem is Alvin Toffler's *Future Shock* (1970). This factor further augments the natural tendency of fears to outweigh hopes in fictional representations; the near future is implicitly threatening because even the life-enhancing innovations it produces tend to *alienate people from the past experience on which their present consciousness is based.

The dimensions of the personal future change markedly over time, according to the proportion of an individual's anticipated lifetime that has yet to elapse. Adolescents have a natural interest in the future, because their entire adult life is yet to come, but the interest that old people have in the future often takes the form of clinging as hard as possible to the *status quo*—which involves opposing, resisting, denying, defying, and resenting change with all their imaginative might. Such resistance is futile, but that is little disincentive; it becomes increasingly difficult, as a person nears death, to strike any other attitude, although a substantial minority of people do seem to manage it. Life, and science, go on regardless, but this is their context and their curse; attitudes to speculative fiction are various in the young and old alike, but it is not surprising that the core audience for speculative fiction, speculative nonfiction, and the popularisation of science is a relatively young one.

Although there were significant precedents already in place, such as a "history of the future" published by the Portuguese Jesuit Antonio Vieria in the late seventeenth century, the calculated use of the future as a significant narrative space underwent its most significant development in France, as a consequence of the advent of the philosophy of *progress. Louis Sébastien Mercier's *L'an deux mille quatre cent quarante* (1771; trans. as *Memoirs of the Year 2500*) moved *Utopian speculation into a new euchronian mode, while Jean-Baptiste Cousin de Grainville's *Le dernier homme* (1805; trans. as *The Last Man*) attempted to accommodate the philosophy of progress within theologically based apocalyptic fantasy.

Félix Bodin's *Le roman de l'avenir* (1834) included an essay on the practical problems of writing novels set in the future alongside an exemplar that attempted to replace Mercier's static description of a future society with a more exciting story that would better advertise the potential rewards of progress. Émile Souvestre's *dystopian satire *Le monde tel qu'il sera* (1846; trans. as *The World As It Shall Be*) completed this initial set of variants by throwing down a challenge to the philosophy of progress, depicting a hypothetical future in which mechanical progress and the application of nineteenth-century economic theory have devastated moral and aesthetic ideals.

Almost all subsequent futuristic fiction followed one or other of these four fundamental precedents, with the traditions based on the third and fourth exemplars proving far more popular than the first and second. The translation of Cousin's *Last Man* prompted a minor English boom in "last man" fantasies—including one by Mary Shelley, whose archetypal account of

*Frankenstein set "the modern Prometheus" in the context of Gothic *horror fiction—and even Mercier seemed ominous to English readers made apprehensive by the Revolution it was widely credited with assisting. The tone of English futuristic fiction was, on average, darker than that of French futuristic fiction for two generations thereafter; even in postrevolutionary France, however, the fervour and optimism of the philosophy of progress died away; Jules *Verne, who wanted to write ambitious futuristic fiction, was dissuaded by his publisher, and had to confine his technological speculations to the hidden interstices of the present.

Futuristic fiction in Britain took a spectacular leap forward in the 1870s, when George T. Chesney's alarmist drama-documentary *The Battle of Dorking* (1871) was rapidly supplemented by Edward Bulwer-Lytton's account of *The Coming Race* (1871). Samuel Butler's *Erewhon* (1872) and early translations of novels by Jules Verne were not futuristic in their settings but they included significant futuristic projections that set them at the head of a new tradition of speculative stories exploring the probable effects of new technology on society—most particularly the business of *war. Chesney's propaganda piece did not feature any futuristic *weapons, but the subgenre whose founding he prompted soon became replete with them, thanks to striking contributions by George Griffith, H. G. Wells, and others.

Mercier's Utopia had been the best-selling book in France in the late eighteenth century, and the best-selling book in the United States in the late nineteenth century was also a mildly technophilic euchronian tract: Edward Bellamy's *Looking Backward, 2000–1887* (1888). Bellamy's book became an equally prolific stimulus to variant and opposing images, laying the foundations of a debate that was still the core of the American futuristic agenda when the fervently optimistic Hugo Gernsback wrote *Ralph 124C 41+: A Romance of the Year 2660* (1911–1912; book, 1925) and extrapolated it into the realm of pulp science fiction, setting out to "blaze a trail, not only in literature, but in progress as well".

Gernsback's prospectus for progressive science fiction faltered almost immediately, partly because it was immediately undermined by anxious dread in the work of such sceptical writers as David H. Keller but also—and more significantly—because pulp science fiction was hijacked by a particular set of hopes that reduced its open-endedness dramatically, much as the arguments set out in *The Discovery of the Future* and the trend analysis of *Anticipations* had sidetracked H. G. Wells. In the case of pulp science fiction the emergent consensus was the myth of the Space Age, which retained its swiftly won centrality

when John W. *Campbell Jr. took over *Astounding Science Fiction* in the late 1930s and began to ask for more carefully considered as well as more wide-ranging appraisals of future possibility. Many of Campbell's authors, and most of his readers, preferred the apparent freedom of the relatively distant but highly stereotyped future realms of space opera—whose uninhibited adventure stories gave futuristic fiction a reckless melodramatic edge of which Félix Bodin never dreamed—to varied and imaginatively disciplined accounts of nearer futures.

Insofar as Campbellian futuristic fiction consented to remain earthbound, it did retain a commitment to the philosophy of progress, even after 1945, when images of the near future were darkened by the shadow of the *atom bomb. Literary responses to this new situation were various, but many of them reflected a suspicion or conviction that the hopes of the past had been betrayed, and that the anxieties of the past had been innocently oblivious. A kind of flagrant perversity entered into many images of the future, very obvious in those produced outside genre science fiction—notable examples include Aldous Huxley's *Ape and Essence* (1948), George Orwell's *Nineteen Eighty-Four* (1949), Bernard Wolfe's *Limbo* (1952), and Evelyn Waugh's *Love Among the Ruins* (1953)—but also evident within it, in such examples as Fritz Leiber's "Coming Attraction" (1950), Wyman Guin's "Beyond Bedlam" (1951), Ray Bradbury's *Fahrenheit 451* (1953), and Frederik Pohl and C. M. Kornbluth's *The Space Merchants* (1953).

Although such works as these were set firmly within the tradition of dystopian satire that extended back to Souvestre, they reflected a sudden magnification of the fear that any and all individual ambitions might be overtaken by insane institutions whose ultimate support was the threat of doomsday. The baroque mode of such imaginative exercises was gradually transfigured by an acute awareness of the *ecocatastrophic threats posed by overpopulation and pollution, but the temper of their futuristic speculation remained fundamentally unchanged, and was significantly opposed only by the increasingly desperate extension of Space Age mythology. Within genre science fiction the myth of the Space Age provided a means of concluding dystopian fantasies with the escapist image of a "cosmic breakout", but futuristic fiction produced outside the genre found no such ready release, and became bleak in consequence. Even within the genre the proliferation of soft science fiction at the expense of hard science fiction deepened the tragic tone of its alarmist fantasies. Future *histories mapped out in near-future science fiction grew grimmer by degrees, except when they were interrupted by some sudden accession of *superhumanity or *posthumanity.

Literary images of the future produced in the late twentieth century contrasted sharply with the use of futuristic imagery in marketing, associated with the proliferation and increasing sophistication of domestic technology and a dramatic increase in *automobile ownership. In the world of advertising, the future of the home was seen in terms of hi-tech comfort and convenience—but the home came to seem a protective haven in a threatening world, connected by communicative threads to a network of friends and allies but increasingly beleaguered by hostile forces whose own technological impetus was accelerating.

Domestic and personal machinery was only one aspect of the cutting edge of technological progress, and new developments co-opted into it—such as personal *computers—had much grander applications in the wider world whose future potential was routinely seen in ominous terms. The general response to the possibilities inherent in *biotechnology was even more negative, exhibiting a considerable determination to keep all its applications save for medical ones out of the domestic arena. Even writers committed to the ideals of progress tended to see the near future in terms of rapidly multiplying and rapidly intensifying problems, and heroic contention in terms of the kinds of holding actions to which older people had always been committed.

The popularity of futuristic fiction continued to increase throughout the late twentieth century, but the balance between the two kinds of futuristic imagery shifted considerably in that period. The escapist component of the imagery of Space Age mythology maintained its popularity with the adolescent core audience to the extent that such imagery began to make a considerable impact in the visual media, but the more distant imaginative vistas of space opera became dominant in the visual media in spite of the economic problems of convincing representation. Near-future imagery in the visual media remained predominantly alarmist, much of it more akin to supernatural *horror fiction than to hard science fiction. In the print medium, the bookstore shelf space that futuristic fiction had colonised in the 1960s and 1970s was largely taken over by generic fantasy set in mythical pasts and parallel presents, and much of what remained of near-future narrative spaces was co-opted by *technothriller formulas whose normalising endings were a tacit general endorsement of the Frankenstein complex. By the time the twenty-first century began, the summary literary image of the future foreseeable by scientific and technological extrapolation—exclusive of quasi-miraculous parapsychological transformations—was one of near-total devastation.

The development of far-futuristic imagery followed a very different path—expectably, given its markedly different concerns and functions. Scientifically inspired images of the far future had emerged in the nineteenth century as estimates of the age of the *Earth grew dramatically in the wake of James Hutton's *Theory of the Earth* (1795) and Charles Lyell's *Principles of Geology* (1830). The notion of a universe that was infinite in both time and space had been around for some time, but in the absence of a graspable conceptual yardstick, it had produced no significant far-futuristic imagery. Edgar Allan Poe's *Eureka: An Essay on the Material and Spiritual Universe* (1848) was the first literary work to feature images of the future fates of the Earth, the Sun, and the entire sidereal system. Early extrapolations of Lord Kelvin's estimates of the likely duration of the Sun were incorporated into sober apocalyptic fantasy by Camille *Flammarion and into fantasies of future *evolution by H. G. Wells' "The Man of the Year Million" (1893) and *The Time Machine* (1895). William Hope Hodgson, having followed Poe's precedent in *The House on the Borderland* (1908), set a new one in *The Night Land* (1912), developing the exotic and allegorical potential of far-futuristic imagery in an earthbound setting.

The calculated bizarrerie of *The Night Land* placed it at the head of a twentieth-century subgenre of far-futuristic fantasies in which the kinds of magic featured in traditional accounts of the mythical past are revitalised and recomplicated, sometimes "rationalised" as relics of powerful technologies that are no longer understood but primarily employed to signify strangeness. The overwhelming sense of futility associated with many far-futuristic fantasies is as much an extrapolation of existentialist *angst* as of theories of *decadence. Far-futuristic imagery soon found new extremes to explore in the pulp magazines, in such extravagant fantasies as Donald Wandrei's "The Red Brain" (1927) and Clark Ashton Smith's tales of the magically blighted "last continent" of Zothique (launched 1932).

When Kelvin's low estimate of the Earth's future duration, based on the hypothesis that the Sun's heat was produced by gravitational collapse, was replaced by much higher ones based on a more accurate notion of the life cycles of *stars, new scope was opened up for accounts of future human evolution and for the development of Omega Point fantasies. A hybrid form of far-futuristic fantasy emerged in the science fiction pulps, combining the flagrant impossibilities indulged by Clark Ashton Smith with the supposed possibilities described by John W. Campbell Jr., in such stories as "The Voice in the Void" (1930), in varying proportions; notable examples of such hybridisation include Frank Belknap Long's "The Last Men" (1934), Raymond Z.

Gallun's "Seeds of the Dusk" (1938), several works by C. L. Moore, including *Earth's Last Citadel* (1943, with Henry Kuttner; book, 1964), and Arthur C. Clarke's *Against the Fall of Night* (1948; exp. as *The City and the Stars*). The last named ingeniously accommodated such imagery to the myth of the Space Age, whose galactic extension had threatened to render it redundant.

Far-futuristic fantasy became more prevalent in British science fiction than it was in the United States, partly due to the particular influence of Olaf *Stapledon but mainly due to the fact that British writers were far more likely to see their post-imperial society in decadent terms than their American counterparts. Brian W. *Aldiss produced far-futuristic fantasies in some profusion, including *The Canopy of Time* (1959; restored text as *Galaxies Like Grains of Sand*, 1979), "Old Hundredth" (1960), *Hothouse* (1962), "A Kind of Artistry" (1962), and "The Worm that Flies" (1968), while other notable examples of British far-futuristic fantasy included John Brunner's "Earth Is but a Star" (1958; book, 1959, as *The 100th Millennium*; exp. as *Catch a Falling Star* 1968), Michael Moorcock's *The Twilight Man* (1966; aka *The Shores of Death*) and the Dancers at the End of Time series (launched 1972), Michael G. Coney's *The Celestial Steam Locomotive* (1983) and *Gods of the Greataway* (1984), and Paul J. MacAuley's Confluence trilogy (1997–1999).

In the United States, the colourful postwar precedent set by Jack Vance's tales of the Dying Earth (launched 1950) were followed by Samuel R. Delany's *The Jewels of Aptor* (1962), Robert Silverberg's *Son of Man* (1971), James Blish's *Midsummer Century* (1972), Doris Piserchia's *A Billion Days of Earth* (1976) and *Earth in Twilight* (1981), and Crawford Kilian's *Eyas* (1982). Elegiac imagery reached a new extreme of affective delicacy in John Crowley's *Engine Summer* (1979), while the fusion of magical and science-fictional imagery was sophisticated by such works as Gene Wolfe's four-volume *Book of the New Sun* (1980–1983) and Robert Reed's mosaic *Sister Alice* (1993–2000; book, 2003).

The redevelopment of far-futuristic fantasy on a cosmic scale, in terms of Omega Point hypotheses, was hastened by the development of computer technology and further boosted by the advent of the idea of *nanotechnology. A gradual reduction in the plausibility of Space Age mythology resulted in the displacement of space opera, which was already a subspecies of far-futuristic fantasy, into futures that were even more distant, at least in conceptual terms—which is to say, futures that were essentially posthuman rather than human.

FUTUROLOGY

A term coined in the 1940s, when it was associated with a call for social scientists to develop more sophisticated methods of trend analysis in order to issue more accurate *predictions. Its early popularisers included Aldous *Huxley, who tried to practice what he preached in *Brave New World Revisited* (1958). The idea was, however, much older; the origins of futurological ambition can be retrospectively traced to Robert Malthus' *Essay on the Principle of Population* (1798), which argued that the tendency for population to grow exponentially while food supplies could only increase arithmetically would ensure the future preservation of the "Malthusian checks"—war, famine, and disease—in the absence of a degree of "moral restraint".

The term was subsequently co-opted as a general description of futuristic exercises in *speculative nonfiction. Academic courses generally preferred the label Future Studies, although many self-marketing "economic gurus" working in the area towards the end of the twentieth century preferred to term themselves futurists; they established an Association of Professional Futurists in the early twenty-first century. The methodology of futurology had made little progress in the meantime, although the Rand Corporation developed a "Delphic Technique" in the late 1960s based on the thesis—advocated by psychologist Christopher Evans—that a broad pool of opinions is likely to produce a consensus reflecting the eventual actuality. Nicholas Rescher's *Predicting the Future: Introduction to the Theory of Forecasting* (1997), Thomas Lombardo's *Doorways to the Future: Methods, Theories and Themes* (2001), and Wendell Bell's *Foundations of Futures Studies* (2003) survey current methods.

Nonfictional attempts to analyse the probable consequences of existing social trends continued throughout the nineteenth century as social statisticians gathered more data. All such projections involved a speculative element similar to that implicit in futuristic fiction, but the essence of futurological philosophy was the attempted minimisation of that uncertainty. Reportage of futurological findings sometimes employed fictional formats, but usually took care to emphasise that they were different from the general run of futuristic fictions, as in Robert Grimshaw's *Fifty Years Hence, or What May Be in 1943: A Prophecy Supposed to Be Based on Scientific Deductions by an Improved Graphical Method* (1892).

At the end of the nineteenth century, writers of speculative nonfiction, such as Henry Adams and H. G. Wells, became markedly more ambitious in their futuristic extrapolations and often more confident of their methods of anticipation. After publishing the series of newspaper articles collected as *Anticipations* (1901), Wells delivered a lecture published as *The Discovery of the Future* (1902), in which he claimed that certain aspects of the future were predictable with a reasonable degree of accuracy, and that reliable futurological calculations (although he did not use the term) were therefore possible. From then on, speculative nonfiction made much more use of ambitious projections of future history, often failing to specify whether the images they offered were supposed to be contingent or prophetic.

When the futurological ambitions of J. B. S. *Haldane's *Daedalus; or, Science and the Future* (1923) invited strident contradiction in Bertrand *Russell's *Icarus; or, the Future of Science* (1923), its publisher launched a series of similar pamphlets that eventually ran to more than a hundred volumes before petering out in 1930. Many of them were written by eminent natural and social scientists, some of whom certainly had prophetic ambitions, although others were content to regard what they were doing as an exercise in *satire. Most of the anticipations put forward in the series were scrupulously modest, but a few—especially J. D. *Bernal's *The World, the Flesh and the Devil* (1929)—were spectacularly far ranging. Exercises on a larger scale were similarly varied in their scope, the great majority confining themselves to the next fifty or a hundred years; such exceptions as Charles Galton Darwin's *The Next Million Years* (1952) and Kenneth Heuer's *The Next Fifty Billion Years* (1957) rarely lived up to their promises.

Futurology in the narrow sense of trend projection is most evident in the field of *economics, where short-range projections are vital to economic planning. The use of such techniques in the anticipation of *population growth and the analysis of its likely consequences became highly controversial in the 1960s, and their use in anticipating global climate change became similarly controversial in the 1990s. All three of these areas of application illustrate the difficulties that arise when the summary effect of a whole series of trends has to be combined, especially if their reliability varies considerably. All trends eventually break down, especially those whose dynamic is accelerative rather than linear; either they lose impetus—sometimes abruptly—or they enter a transfigurative phase akin to that envisaged by futurological projections of a technological *singularity. Attempts to analyse the methodology of this kind of futurology include Theodore Modis' *Predictions* (1992).

In the broader meaning of the term, futurological speculations appeared in increasing profusion as the century progressed. Those narrowly focused on technological projections—such as A. M. Low's *The

Future (1925) and *It's Bound to Happen* (1950; aka *What's the World Coming To?*), the Earl of Birkenhead's *The World in 2030* (1930), and C. C. Furnas' *The Next Hundred Years: The Unfinished Business of Science* (1936)—generally maintained a conspicuously more optimistic tone than futuristic fiction by virtue of concentrating on the opportunities afforded by new gadgets. The calculatedly awestruck tone of such exercises became typical of such popular periodicals as *Modern Wonder* (1937–1941) and such TV shows as *Tomorrow's World* (1965–2003).

While futuristic fiction grew steadily darker in tone in the latter part of the century, many futurologists remained defiantly optimistic, and that defiance was conserved to the end of the century and beyond in such texts as Michio Kaku's *Visions* (1997) and Bruce Sterling's *Tomorrow Now: Envisioning the Next Fifty Years* (2003). In the meantime, futurological works inspired by different kinds of technological advance were conspicuously different in tone, those prompted by advances in computer technology being mostly enthusiastic while biological exercises in futurology tended to be alarmist. Christopher Evans' *The Mighty Micro* (1979) contrasts sharply with Gordon Rattray-Taylor's *The Biological Time-Bomb* (1968) and Vance Packard's *The People Shapers* (1978).

This attitudinal division was complicated when anticipations of the future of computers began to grapple with the possibility that *artificial intelligence might soon outstrip human intelligence, so such texts as Hans Moravec's *Mind Children: The Future of Robot and Human Intelligence* (1988), Kevin Warwick's *The March of the Machines* (1997), and Ray Kurzweil's *The Age of Spiritual Machines* (1999) exhibit a noticeable trend towards greater ambivalence. The future of alarmism became a topic in itself in Alvin Toffler's *Future Shock* (1970), although the author took an optimistic view of our ability to cope with the phenomenon in question and progressed to more conventional defiant optimism in *The Third Wave* (1980).

Other significant exercises in near-futuristic futurology include Victor Cohn's *1999: Our Hopeful Future* (1956), Harrison Scott Brown, James Bonner, and John Weir's *The Next Hundred Years* (1957), George Soule's *The Shape of Tomorrow* (1958), Desmond King-Hele's *The End of the Twentieth Century* (1970), Herman Kahn's *Things to Come* (1972; with B. Bruce-Briggs) and *The Next Two Hundred Years* (1976), John Naisbitt's *Megatrends* (1982) and its sequels, Marvin Cetron's *Encounters with the Future* (1983), Norman Macrae's *The 2020 Report* (1984), Brian Stableford and David Langford's *The Third Millennium* (1985), Warren Wagar's *A Short History of the Future* (1989), Jonathan Weiner's *The Next One*

Hundred Years (1990), Richard Carlson and Bruce Goldman's *2020 Visions* (1990), Bill Gates' *The Road Ahead* (1995), Charles Handy's *The Age of Unreason* (1995), Jim Taylor, Watts Wacker, and Howard B. Means' *The Five-Hundred-Year Delta* (1997), Michael R. Dertouzos' *What Will Be* (1997), Ervin Laszlo's *Macroshift* (2001), and Martin Rees' *Our Final Century?* (2003). General surveys of futurology include *The Futurists* (1972), edited by Alvin Toffler, and Henry Winthrop's *Foreseeing the Future* (1978).

Exercises in far-futuristic futurology may seem hopelessly doomed by the *chaotic factors involved in multiple-trend extrapolation, but Wells claimed in *The Discovery of the Future* that certain kinds of far-futuristic prediction were possessed of far greater inevitability than short-term ones. The example of the Sun's demise proved slightly treacherous when Lord Kelvin's timetable for its extinction proved to be based on mistaken premises—and the kind of far-futuristic futurology that underlies *Omega Point fantasies always remains vulnerable to theoretical shifts in *cosmology—but the range of long-term futurological possibilities does indeed grow narrower as it grows vaguer.

G

GALAXY

A Greek-derived term whose original was often rendered in translation as "Milky Way" when applied to a strip of faint stars displayed in the night sky. When that aggregation was shown to be one among many, "galaxy" became the generic term for such clusters. The liquid analogy is often extended into references to a "sea of stars", and has been deliberately built into patterns of titles in series of novels by Gregory *Benford and David *Brin.

The suggestion that the Milky Way was actually a system of stars, analogous to the solar system, orbiting a central axis was broached by Thomas Wright in his *Original Theory or New Hypothesis of the Universe* (1750). It was rapidly taken up by Immanuel Kant, who extended the hypothesis to suggest that the Milky Way might be only one such system among a series of "island universes", whose existence was evident to Earthly observers only as faint nebulas. This hypothesis—eloquently elaborated in Edgar Allan *Poe's *Eureka* (1848)—received increasing support from astronomical observations throughout the nineteenth century, following William Herschel's initial attempt to classify nebulas into different types in 1811–1814, and was conclusively established by the 1920s.

Attempts to measure the spectroscopic Doppler shifts of other galaxies became feasible when dry photographic plates and longer exposure times made the techniques more exact. In 1912, the American astronomer Vesto M. Slipher, working with a new spectrograph at Percival Lowell's observatory in Flagstaff, Arizona, was able to establish that the Andromeda nebula M31 or NGC224 had a blue-shift, implying that it was approaching our solar system at 300 kilometres per second. By 1917, he had measured the Doppler shifts of fourteen more nebulas, of which thirteen were red-shifts. The red-shifts suggested that the galaxies were receding at an average velocity of 640 kilometres per second, far higher than the velocities attained by stars as they rotated around the galactic centre. By 1922, Slipher and his associates had measured forty nebular Doppler shifts, of which thirty-six were red-shifts.

Slipher's work was continued by Milton Humason and Edwin Hubble, who attempted to use the Andromeda nebula to calculate the relationship between red-shifts and distance, using Harlow Shapley's discovery of the link between the luminosity and periodicity of Cepheid variable stars. Estimating the luminosity of the Cepheid variables in Andromeda proved difficult, however, because of the effect of intergalactic dust on their perceived brightness. Hubble's initial estimates were modified several times before the present figure of 700 kiloparsecs was settled; estimates of the "Hubble constant" determining the general relationship between red-shift and distance remained controversial in the meantime, and is still subject to considerable uncertainty. In spite of these difficulties, Hubble's law—which states that the farther away a galaxy is, the greater its red-shift is—seemed to be firmly established, giving rise to the *Big Bang theory.

The only other galaxies apart from Andromeda that are visible to the naked eye are the two Magellanic

Clouds, but many more were discovered as more powerful optical instruments came into use, climaxing with the revelations of the Hubble Space Telescope in the 1990s, to which some fifty million galaxies were potentially visible. The distinctive shape of elliptical galaxies, involving trailing spiral arms projecting from a central hub, became a significant icon, lavishly reproduced in space *art. The mental image of a universe whose "units" are galaxies—each one containing hundreds of billions of stars—is central to modern *cosmology, and hence to an accurate appreciation of the relative magnitude of the human microcosm.

A galaxy is too vast a phenomenon to be easily accommodated within fiction; although space opera soon expanded to take in intergalactic conflict in such stories as J. Schlossel's "Extra-Galactic Invaders" (1931), the further order of magnitude made no perceptible difference to the scale of the action. Stories with galactic protagonists, such as Laurence Manning's "The Living Galaxy" (1934) and Barrington J. Bayley's "Combat's End" (1954), grope unavailingly for untapped grandeur.

As a distant prospect or generic concept, galaxies lend themselves to poetic or visionary representation, as in such imagistic phrases as Brian W. Aldiss' *Galaxies Like Grains of Sand* (1960). The word was a natural adoptee as the title of a science fiction magazine, just as it was a natural adoptee as the name of a bar of milk chocolate. In general, though, fictional galaxies—like actual ones—are a prospect of purely symbolic value. This does not prevent abundant use of the term's adjectival derivative as a signifier of ambition in such titles as Jack Williamson's "The Galactic Circle" (1935), E. E. Smith's *Galactic Patrol* (1937–1938; book, 1951), Harry Stine's "Galactic Gadgeteers" (1951), George Duncan's "Galactic Quest" (1953), and E. C. Tubb's "Galactic Destiny" (1959).

The inherently dramatic discovery in the 1960s that the cloud-shrouded centre of the galaxy appeared to be exploding was quickly reflected in science fiction in such stories as Larry Niven's "At the Core" (1966) and Stanley Schmidt's *The Sins of the Fathers* (1973), and the subsequent attribution of this appearance to the presence of a massive *black hole encouraged further melodramatic representations. The presence within the galaxy of starless rifts lends itself to stories of a different sort, notable examples being James Blish's "Bindlestiff" (1950) and James Tiptree Jr.'s mosaic *The Starry Rift* (1986).

The notion of the galactic rim also acquired a particular conceptual resonance as an ultimate frontier, most elaborately developed in the long series extrapolated from A. Bertram Chandler's "To Run the Rim" (1959), but the lack of much else in the way of structural organisation inhibited further extrapolations of this kind. Globular clusters such as the ones featured in Isaac Asimov's "Nightfall" (1941) and Poul Anderson's "Starfog" (1967) occasionally warrant strategic deployment in *contes philosophiques,* but other large-scale features such as the galactic maelstrom featured in Anderson's *Virgin Planet* (1960; exp. book, 1970) tend to be invented for use as facilitating devices.

GALILEO

The name by which Galileo Galilei (1564–1642) is usually known. He was the first person to make extensive and disciplined observations of the sky with the aid of a *telescope. He also made important studies of bodies in motion that laid the groundwork for Isaac *Newton's clarification of the laws of motion.

Galileo was born in Pisa, where two of the most famous anecdotes concerning his observations are set. One relates how his observations of a swinging lamp in the cathedral in 1581 inspired his discovery of the regularity of the oscillation of the pendulum, and the potential for its use in clocks; the other—almost certainly apocryphal—relates how he dropped two objects of different weights from the Leaning Tower, to demonstrate that they hit the ground at the same time. He withdrew from the University of Pisa in 1585 for lack of funds and rejoined his family in Florence, lecturing at the local academy. In 1586, he published an account of a hydrostatic balance, whose invention won him a wide reputation, and he was able to return to the University of Pisa as a lecturer in 1589, after publishing a treatise on the notion of the centre of gravity. Further financial difficulties led to his seeking a new post at the University of Padua in 1592, where he brought his work on bodies in motion to fruition.

Galileo was convinced that the heliocentric theory of the solar system was true before he began his astronomical observations, but kept his opinion to himself, with the exception of letters to such like-minded individuals as John *Kepler. The early observations he reported in *Sidereus Nuncius* [The Starry Messenger] (1610)—including sunspots, the phases of Venus, the rings of Saturn, and the fact that the Milky Way was composed of stars—were essentially uncontroversial. He left Padua to become "first philosopher" to the Grand Duke of Tuscany in 1610, and visited Rome in 1611 to show off his telescope; the welcome he received there encouraged him to propose publicly that the movement of sunspots proved that Copernicus was correct. A letter written in 1615 to the Grand Duchess, which argued that "experimental truth" is a better beginning in the quest for knowledge than scriptural truth and must be the final arbiter, sparked an ideological dispute with the orthodox academicians, which was soon complicated by political wrangles involving Galileo's patron, in which the Inquisition became involved.

The theologian Cardinal Bellarmine responded to this dispute by placing Copernicus on the index of forbidden books in 1616, warning Galileo that he must desist from his assertions. Galileo complied, devoting himself to private research at his house near Florence for the next seven years. He was provoked to reassert his views by a pamphlet on *comets by Orazio Grasi that made mock of his opinions. The recently elected pope, Urban VIII, was an old friend, to whom Galileo carefully dedicated his reply. In 1624 he went to Rome to ask for the ban on Copernican theory to be lifted; the pope declined, but gave him permission to write a comparison of the Ptolemaic and Copernican systems, provided that he came to the conclusion that human intellect is incompetent to decide between them, the responsibility for Creation being God's alone.

Galileo's response to this invitation, *Dialogo sopra i due massimi sistemi del mondo, tolemaico et copernicano* [Dialogue Concerning the Two Principal World Systems, the Ptolemaic and the Copernican] (1632), generated further controversy. While sticking to the letter of his promise, Galileo had taken advantage of irony and the careful characterisation of the participants in the dialogue to make a strong case in favour of Copernicanism. He was eventually forced to recant, although legend stubbornly insists that his public pronouncement was supplemented by a covertly muttered "*Eppur si muove*" [But it—i.e., the Earth—does move].

Galileo escaped imprisonment, but submitted to house arrest; this allowed him to complete a further dialogue in 1634 summarising and completing his work in mechanics. He went blind in the year of its publication, 1638, but he continued to correspond with other scientists, suggesting the application of the pendulum in clocks that Christian Huygens eventually put into practice in 1656. His persecution probably had at least as much to do with politics as religious doctrine, but it ensured his unparalleled reputation as a heroic champion of science against superstition. The range of his work, his ability to make complex deductions from primitive astronomical observations, the rhetorical flair of his first dialogue, his deployment of the notion of *force in the second, and his conception of experiment as *cimento* [ordeal]—that is, as a means of putting hypothetical propositions to the proof—fully entitle him to that status.

Galileo was subject to his own *Baconian idols; his aesthetic conviction that the planetary orbits had to be circular prevented him from acknowledging Kepler's laws, and he shied away from a theory of gravity because he could not abide the idea of action at a distance, but he played a greater part than any of his contemporaries in smashing the conceptual barrier dividing the Earth from the Heavens, setting their various phenomena firmly within a single conceptual framework.

The literary influence of Galileo's work was quick to take effect and has been long lasting. John Donne must have read *Sidereus Nuncius* in the year of its publication, because it is mentioned in his satire on the Jesuits, *Ignatius His Conclave* (1611), and it is echoed in several later poems. Galileo appears as a character in Giambattista Marino's cosmological epic *L'Adone* (1622), which praises his work with the telescope. John Milton visited Galileo in 1638/1639 and mentions him in *Paradise Lost* (1667)—in which Satan flies through infinite space "amongst innumerable stars". His name gave rise to an inevitable pun—the "Galilean gospel"—which recurred many times over in seventeenth-century literature, applied approvingly as well as pejoratively.

Galileo's status as a hero of science gave his name an iconic status that lasted into the twentieth century, celebrated in such fervently polemical works as Bertolt Brecht's *Leben des Galilei* (1938; published 1955; trans. as *The Life of Galileo in Seven Plays*) and Barrie Stavis' *Lamp at Midnight* (1947; TV version, 1966) and such revisionist accounts as Dava Sobel's *Galileo's Daughter* (1999) and Eric Flint and Andrew Dennis' *1634: The Galileo Affair* (2004). Fred Saberhagen's *Brother Assassin* (1969; aka *Brother Berserker*) engages a character modelled on Galileo in productive dialogue with a version of St. Francis of Assisi. Galileo also appears, although he is not named, in Zoran Zivkovic's *Time-Gifts* (trans. 1998).

GAME

A rule-bound pastime, usually of a competitive nature. A looser meaning applies it to the substance of all forms of play. Sporting contests of physical prowess, sometimes involving a ball, form one major subdivision of the category; gambling games, often involving dice or cards, constitute another. Both kinds of games may have originated in religious rituals; the former began a transition into a form of mass entertainment in Roman times, when gladiatorial contests and chariot races were staged for the edification of the masses. Puzzles and impostures of various kinds qualify as games under a loose definition, although they are usually excluded by narrower ones. The outcome of many games is entirely determined by the exercise of physical or intellectual skill, but gambling games routinely introduce an element of chance, which requires calculative skills to be exercised in situations of relative uncertainty.

Although they are usually defined in terms of leisure and recreation rather than work and vocational endeavour, games often reflect activities carried out in deadly earnest, especially warfare—for which they may provide useful training in tactics and strategy—and trials of courage. Johann Huizinga's *Homo Ludens* (1939) suggests that play is the very essence of human nature, pointing out that the most earnest human rituals, associated with religion and the law, routinely retain elements of symbolic pretence and elaborate rules closely akin to those characteristic of games. Politics is often considered as a game, of which war is merely an aspect. Science too may be considered a game, or at least as a quintessential series of puzzles.

The mathematical analysis of games and their associated competitive strategies provided the foundations of *probability theory and "game theory". The latter field, concerned with situations in which players' tactical choices have to be made in ignorance of the choices that other players will make, the outcome being dependent on the sum of the individual choices, casts valuable light on the psychology and politics of decision-making. The forms evolved by gambling games under the pressure of historical selection mirror various facets of "psychological probability", revealing disjunctions between subjective assessments of risk and objective calculations of probability. Games acquired a new significance in the development of *computer science, games of skill such as chess providing a series of crucial tests for programmers, while a new class of games specifically designed for computer play, of which the most significant early example was James L. Conway's *Life*, provided important new insights into the ways in which the application of sets of simple rules can produce surprisingly various and complex patterns of organisation.

The construction of literary works has aspects that strongly resemble games, most notably the design of plots as "puzzles" to be solved or "obstacle courses" to be negotiated by the characters and the reader. Although the most obvious examples of game-like fiction are provided by detective fiction, all plots tend to involve an element of mystery that presents itself to the reader, if not to the characters, as a puzzle to be solved. By the same token, all stories are representable as obstacle courses, even when the obstacles involved are purely psychological—as, according to Joseph Campbell's analysis of hero *myths, all obstacles to heroism really are.

The similarities and differences between challenging games of skill and viable plots were reflected in plots designed to mirror chess games, including Lewis Carroll's *Through the Looking-Glass* (1871) and John Brunner's *Squares of the City* (1965), and board games designed to mirror literary formulas, such as *Cluedo*, before becoming obvious in computer games based on literary imagery—most notably those based on the subgenre of quest fantasy whose archetype is J. R. R. Tolkien's *The Lord of the Rings* (1954–1955)—and films based on computer games. The advent of role-playing games such as *Dungeons and Dragons* (launched 1974; advanced version, 1978) confused the boundary between games and fiction considerably; anticipated developments in *virtual reality may complete a more intimate synthesis.

There is a significant sociological dimension to literature dealing with games by virtue of the fact that a game may symbolise a set of values definitive of a culture or a subculture. "National games" are readily available for allegorical use in commentaries on the moral condition of a society. The most abundant literature of this kind deals with American baseball, key examples being Robert Coover's *The Universal Baseball Association Inc., J. Henry Waugh, Prop.* (1968), W. P. Kinsella's *Shoeless Joe* (1982), Michael Bishop's *Brittle Innings* (1994), Nancy Willard's *Things Invisible to See* (1984), and Michael Chabon's *Summerland* (2002). Herman Hesse's *Der Glasperlenspiel* (1943; trans. as *Magister Ludi*; aka *The Glass Bead Game*) applies a similar logic to Utopian construction. In Pierre Boulle's *Jeux d'esprit* (1971; trans. as *Desperate Games*) a technocratic government brings about a eutopian society, but must devise hazardous games to relieve the general ennui.

Because of these cultural resonances, the futuristic extensions of sports fantasy in speculative fiction often carry considerable weight as *contes philosophiques*. As in the broader genre, the most abundant subspecies of science-fictional sports fantasies deals with baseball, as in Nelson S. Bond's "The Einstein Inshoot" (1938), Milton Kaletsky's "The Wizard of Baseball" (1940), Rod Serling's "The Mighty Casey" (1960), Allen Kim Lang's *Wild and Outside* (1966), several stories by George Alec Effinger, including "Naked to the Invisible Eye" (1973), John Kessel's "The Franchise" (1993), Ben Bova and Rick Wilber's "The Babe, the Iron Horse and Mr. McGillicuddy" (1997), and Louise Marley's "Diamond Girls" (2005).

American football is featured in Clifford Simak's "Rule 18" (1938), several stories by Jack C. Haldeman II, including "The Thrill of Victory" and "The Agony of Defeat" (both 1978), and W. R. Thompson's

"Touchdown, Touchdown, Rah Rah Rah!" (1995). The "gladiatorial" aspects of boxing recommend it for use in stories that feature individual effort rather than team spirit, as in William Campbell Gault's "Title Fight" (1956), Richard Matheson's "Steel" (1956), Brian Stableford's *The Mind-Riders* (1976), and Mike Resnick's "Mwalimi in the Squared Circle" (1993). Golf serves a similar function in James E. Gunn's "Open Warfare" (1954). Milton Lesser's *Stadium Beyond the Stars* (1960) features an interstellar Olympic Games. The possible applications of biotechnology to the enhancement of sorting performance are reflected in such stories as Howard V. Hendrix's "The Farm System" (1988) and Ian McDonald's "Winning" (1990).

The advent and rapid sophistication of computer games stimulated an abrupt flood of related fiction, much of which remained unpublished because one particular story idea occurred to a vast number of aspirant writers, becoming an instant cliché—the story's characters are revealed in the "surprise ending" to be pieces or icons in a game's *cyberspace. In simple variants of the theme, human characters become involved with communication with the "characters" in a computer game, as in Terry Pratchett's *Only You Can Save Mankind* (1992), or actually become trapped in such a game, as in Ian Watson's "Jewels in an Angel's Wing" (1988) and Gillian Rubinstein's *Space Demons* (1996). The latter stratagem belongs to a broader set of fictions; Watson's *Queenmagic Kingmagic* (1986) takes its characters through a whole sequence of "game-spaces," including such absurd universes as one based on Snakes and Ladders.

Speculative fictions more broadly concerned with the tactics of game-playing and their social echoes include Henry Kuttner and C. L. Moore's *The Fairy Chessmen* (1946; book, 1951; aka *Chessboard Planet*; all by-lined Lewis Padgett), Katherine MacLean and Charles V. de Vet's "Second Game" (1958; exp. book versions, 1962—as *Cosmic Checkmate*—and 1981), William Harrison's "Rollerball Murder" (1973), Barry N. Malzberg's *Tactics of Conquest* (1974), Gary K. Wolf's *Killerbowl* (1975), Barrington J. Bayley's *The Grand Wheel* (1977), Orson Scott Card's "Ender's Game" (1977; exp. book, 1985), William Gibson and Michael J. Swanwick's "Dogfight" (1985), and Iain M. Banks' *The Player of Games* (1988).

Various phases in the evolution of virtual reality gaming are reflected in Fred Saberhagen's *Octagon* (1981), S. C. Sykes' "The Cyphertone" (1981), Vernon Vinge's *True Names* (1981), Maureen F. McHugh's "A Coney Island of the Mind" (1993), and Melissa Scott's *Burning Bright* (1993). Robert Chilson's *Rounded with Sleep* (1990) describes the ultimate in computerised role-playing games. Games invented for use in fiction are occasionally adapted for actual play, but the more ambitious examples, such as J. K. Rowling's Quidditch and the virtual "quantum soccer" featured in Greg Egan's "Border Guards" (1999), are inevitably difficult to transfer into contemporary practice.

GENETIC ENGINEERING

A term coined in the late 1940s to describe the purposive manipulation of *genetic material. It was initially supposed that this would involve the surgical cutting and stitching of chromosomes so as to remove, rearrange, and augment sets of genes, and techniques of mechanical fragmentation were employed in early experimental techniques, although the discovery and use of restriction enzymes resulted in a rapid sophistication of techniques in the last quarter of the twentieth century. It became such an important aspect of *biotechnology in that period that the two terms became almost synonymous. The term was independently coined by the science fiction writer Jack Williamson in *Dragon's Island* (1951), although it did not make its way into common parlance for some time thereafter.

The notion of direct manipulation of genetic material had first been broached in response to the pioneering work by T. H. Morgan and his collaborators, which established that genes are located on chromosomes. Martin Swayne's *The Blue Germ* (1918) featured the calculated adaptation of bacteria by manipulation of their chromosomal material. The first of Clement Fézandie's series of didactic fantasies featuring "Doctor Hackensaw"—launched in Hugo *Gernsback's *Science and Invention* in 1921—made more elaborate use of the notion, as did J. B. S. *Haldane's essay *Daedalus; or, Science and the Future* (1923). Ambitious projects of biological engineering—tacitly, if not explicitly, involving genetic manipulations—were subsequently featured in numerous scientific romances, including Olaf Stapledon's *Last and First Men* (1930) and Aldous Huxley's *Brave New World* (1932), but quasi-allergic reactions against the idea of biological manipulation of the kind manifest in Huxley's novel had an inhibitory effect on the further use of the notion in both scientific romance and science fiction.

Stanley G. Weinbaum's "Proteus Island" (1936) employed a more sophisticated technology than its Wellsian model, while Norman L. Knight's "Crisis in Utopia" (1940) imagined a future shaped by multitudinous applications of "tectogenesis". A. E. van Vogt employed "gene transformation" to create the *superhuman *Slan* (1940; book, 1946). The most adventurous use of genetic engineering in pulp science fiction was in Robert Heinlein's *Beyond This Horizon* (1942, by-lined Anson MacDonald; book, 1948) which offered a moderately sympathetic description of a society that uses *eugenics and genetic engineering to ensure the physical and mental fitness of its population. Inhibition eased slightly in the 1950s, when James Blish's "Beanstalk" (1952) imagined a biotechnology based in the artificial multiplication of chromosomes and Katherine MacLean "The Diploids" (1953) employed a similar jargon; MacLean's "Syndrome Johnny" (1951; by-lined Charles Dye), on the other hand, imagined a material reconstruction of bodily tissues carried out by an artificial virus. The genetic engineering of animals excited less reaction than the engineering of humans, but stories like Walter M. Miller's "Conditionally Human" (1952), which dealt with "uplifted" *intelligence, tended to be fervently moralistic. The artificial creatures in Wyman Guin's "Volpla" (1956) are passed off as aliens for reasons of diplomacy.

The distinction between somatic genetic engineering (whose consequences are not heritable) and germ-plasm engineering, was not often made in early speculative fiction dealing with the theme, although it is fundamental to Cordwainer Smith's accounts of the genetically engineered Underpeople, being a key plot element in "The Ballad of Lost C'Mell" (1962). Debates regarding the *ethics of genetic engineering frequently confused the two types, although the evolving possibility of "gene therapy"—curing inherited conditions by means of somatic transformations—gradually made it clearer. The relative dearth of extra-medical applications in human beings, save for the kinds of adaptation to alien environments imagined in Blish's Pantropy series, continued to inhibit the use of the theme in speculative fiction, although the possibility of adapting humans for an amphibious existence, pioneered by Alexander Belyaev in *Tchelovek-Amfibia* (1929; trans. as *The Amphibian*) and Norman L. Knight's "Crisis in Utopia", was further explored by Kobo Abe's *Dai-Yon Kampyoki* (1959; trans. as *Inter Ice Age 4*) before Knight and James Blish revisited it in *A Torrent of Faces* (1967).

Interest in genetic engineering increased markedly in the 1960s and 1970s, although many stories of the period restricted their attention to the possibility of *cloning. The notion of tailoring viruses was extrapolated in Herbert Pembroke's "Situation Unbearable" (1964). The engineering component of the term was construed in an unusually rigorous manner in Hal Clement's "The Mechanic" (1966), in which diseased zeowhales are repaired.

The alarmist tone of such strident exercises in *reportage as Gordon Rattray-Taylor's *The Biological Time-Bomb* (1968)—a classic example of the

*Frankenstein complex at work—was reproduced in such thrillers as the pilot episode of the British TV series *Doomwatch* (1970; novelised as *Mutant-59*, 1972) by Kit Pedler and Gerry Davis. Kenneth F. Keyes and Jacques Fresco's *Looking Forward* (1969) offered a rare image of a eutopia based on the extensive application of genetic engineering; Frank Herbert's *The Eyes of Heisenberg* (1967), in which genetic engineering is used to produce "Optimen", is considerably more ambivalent about the prospect. Further images of aquatic humankinds were featured in Samuel R. Delany's "Driftglass" (1967) and Melissa Leach Dowd's "Mermaid" (1976), while the descendants of cetaceans engineered their return to the sea in Terry Mellen's "Whale Song" (1974).

Actual technologies of genetic engineering took a significant step forward in 1973 when recombinant bacteria were first produced by plasmid "transplantation". Such advances provoked a further exercise in journalistic hysteria in Vance Packard's *The People Shapers* (1978), which prompted a further crop of disaster stories, including G. C. Edmondson and C. M. Kotlan's trilogy, *The Cunningham Equations* (1986), *The Black Magician* (1986), and *Maximum Effort* (1987). Greg Bear's *Blood Music* (1985) and Paul Preuss' *Human Error* (1985) offered more realistic depictions of genetic engineers involved in tailoring viruses, and took a more objective attitude to the far-reaching consequences emerging from their work.

The first transgenic plant (tobacco) and the first transgenic animal (a mouse) followed in the wake of many recombinant bacteria and other single-celled organisms in 1983. Transgenic hybrids such as the "geep" (a goat/sheep chimera) were also produced in the early 1980s. The production of "knockout mice" modelling human deficiency diseases soon became standardised; the cancer-prone "Harvard oncomouse" was the first to be patented. As usual, the literary reflection of these developments initially tended to select for ominous potential, in such works as John Crowley's *Beasts* (1976) and Stephen Gallagher's *Chimera* (1982; TV version, 1985). Although more positive possibilities were explored in stories of medical applications, even stories of this type were often developed as Frankensteinian technothrillers, after the fashion of Bruce T. Holmes' *Anvil of the Heart* (1983). The potential uses of somatic engineering for cosmetic purposes—a logical extrapolation of the present day fashionability of cosmetic surgery—were usually treated sarcastically when they were foregrounded, as in Brian Stableford's "Cinderella's Sisters" (1989) and "Skin Deep" (1991).

In Leo Frankowski's *Copernick's Rebellion* (1987), two genetic engineers precipitate a "symbiotic Revolution", but Charles L. Harness' "The Cajamarca

Project" (1985) and Robert Reed's *Black Milk* (1989) were more tentative in their deployments of the technology. Accounts of functional adaptation began to grow progressively bolder as such accounts of modification for life in space as Linda Nagata's "In the Tide" (1989) laid groundwork for the further extremes of William Barton's "Heart of Glass" (2000), and Helen Collins' *Mutagenesis* (1993) took Blish's Pantropy hypothesis into strange new territory.

Attempts to produce transgenic plants carrying extra genes coding for antibodies against human diseases got under way in 1990, opening up the possibility of developing a "pharming industry" using genetically modified organisms (GMOs) to produce useful pharmaceuticals. In 1995, a transgenic sheep (Tracy) whose mammary glands produced milk containing AAT (alpha-1-antitrypsin) was born at the Roslin Institute, followed in 1996 by the first sheep cloned by nuclear transfer (Dolly) and in 1997 by the first transgenic sheep to be cloned (Polly). Newspaper and TV *reportage made a worldwide celebrity of Dolly, but parallel reportage routinely featured items reflecting public anxiety about the creation of GMOs, much of it precipitated by the aggressive marketing tactics of Monsanto, a company that produced an expanding range of GM crop plants.

Much anxiety focused on the possibility of transplanted genes "jumping" from modified crop plants to wild relatives by means of cross-pollination, and on the increasing use in plant genetic engineering of gene-carrying vectors such as the bacterium *Agrobacterium multifaciens* and tobacco mosaic virus (TMV). Other proposals that were reported in sensationalist terms included the use of genetic modification to produce animals (pigs) with organs more suitable for transplantation into humans, in order to counter shortages in transplantable human hearts and kidneys; experimental pigs whose blood contained human haemoglobin for potential use in transfusion were produced in the late 1990s.

The rapidity with which these developments occurred sharpened the urgency of alarmist fictional responses. The near-simultaneous arrival of so many individual applications forced science fiction writers to integrate a wide assortment of genetic engineering technologies along with other biotechnologies into conventional images of the near future from the late 1980s onwards, and the idea that future humans—or *posthumans—one or two generations hence would inevitably be products of genetic engineering passed from the outer fringes of the science-fictional imagination to the core in little more than a decade. In Hayford Peirce's *Phylum Monsters* (1989), fashionable "lifestyling" prompts a boom in promiscuous theriomorphy. Janet Kagan's *Mirabile* (1991) is set on a colony whose livestock has been engineered so that every organism may give birth to offspring of other species, with the consequence no one ever knows what might pop out next. Pick-and-mix transgenics are featured in a similar cavalier spirit in several of the stories in Paul Di Filippo's thematic collection *Ribofunk* (1998) and James Morrow's "The Cat's Pajamas" (2001).

The notion of movements politically dedicated to the transformation of humankind by means of genetic engineering, such as Bruce *Sterling's Shapers, the Edenists of Peter Hamilton's *The Reality Dysfunction* (1996), and the Forged in Justina Robson's *Natural History* (2003), became commonplace as the twentieth century gave way to the twenty-first—as did the idea of their opposition by *cyborgisation-minded rivals like Sterling's Shapers and/or diehard conservatives like Hamilton's Adamists. Mark Budz' *Clade* (2003) and *Crache* (2004)—which look forward to an "ecocaust" precipitated by the substitution of GM plants for natural ones as the primary producers of Earth's ecosphere, with humans being forced to modify themselves to survive in idiosyncratic "ecotectures" whose populations are genetically isolated from one another—laid the groundwork for a different kind of posthuman adaptive radiation, further emphasising the perceived likelihood that some such radiation would soon begin.

GENETICS

The branch of *biology concerned with fundamental processes of heredity. The genetics of plants and animals are considerably complicated by the phenomenon of *sex. Practical endeavours tacitly based on genetics existed long before the science acquired a substantial empirical basis; attempts to control the inheritance of plant and animal characteristics by selective breeding were central to early agricultural endeavour and the domestication of animal species. The followers of *Pythagoras proposed that heredity in animals must be determined by the mingling of "seminal fluids", and *Aristotle hypothesised that such fluids might be a kind of "purified" blood—a suggestion that had a powerful effect on the language of heredity, reflected in numerous terms and phrases (bloodline, blood relative, royal blood, and the like). The notion that male animals contributed "seed" that merely grew in "fertile ground" provided by female wombs led to a common overestimation of the importance of the male contribution to the characteristics of offspring.

It was not until the mid-seventeenth century that William Harvey's observations of early mammal embryos confirmed that they originated from egg cells and identified the ovary as the originating organ of egg cells fertilised by male sperm. The manner in which the characteristics of two parents were combined still remained mysterious, but Pierre de Maupertuis proposed in 1745 that the "seminal fluids" of every species must contain "an innumerable multitude of parts appropriate to form by their assemblage animals of the same kind", whose chance combinations produced offspring mingling the characteristics of two parents, with occasional variations.

The implications of this thesis remained vague, and little further progress was made until the late 1860s, when Johann Mendel (who was known as Father Gregor in his monastery) reported the statistical data he had collected relating to the ways that various hereditary traits were transmitted in plants. Mendel demonstrated that the contributions of the two parents remained distinct, although the expression of traits in cases where the parents communicated different causal factors depended on which of the two factors was "dominant".

The significance of Mendel's discovery with regard to Charles *Darwin's theory of evolution by natural selection went unnoticed until the early years of the twentieth century, when William Bateson published *Mendel's Principles of Heredity* (1902). The synthesis of Mendelian genetics with the notion of *mutation explained why the variations required by Darwin's theory were not lost by blending. The statistical principle on which population genetics is based, the Hardy-Weinberg "law", was published in 1908.

Literary notions of inheritance prior to 1900 were as vague as scientific ones, reflecting the same half-formed ideas in the same analogical language. A notion of hereditary fatality, built into such proverbs as "What's bred in the bone will not out of the flesh" and supernaturalised in the mythology of family curses, was useful to writers in search of ironic means of narrative closure, and was often used in that manner. Explicit fantasies of heredity, such as Oliver Wendell Holmes' *Elsie Venner* (1861) often drew on the melodramatic potential of a theory of prenatal influence that eventually turned out to be utterly mistaken. Stories in which family traits surface insistently and inappropriately were more closely in tune with actuality, but such titles as Mary Angela Dickens' *A Valiant Ignorance* (1894) summarised the state of the science with deadly accuracy.

The elucidation of the biochemical basis of genetics was begun when W. S. Sutton postulated in 1903 that the Mendelian units of heredity—the genes—were located on the chromosomes in the nuclei of cells. T. H. Morgan's studies of mutation in the fruit fly *Drosophila melanogaster* eventually convinced him

that Sutton was right, and he began mapping the positions of genes on *Drosophila* chromosomes—work summarised in *The Mechanism of Mendelian Inheritance* (1915, coauthored with A. H. Sturtevant, C. B. Bridges, and H. J. Muller). The journal *Genetics* was founded in 1916, and the synthesis of Darwinism and genetics was eventually completed by R. A. Fisher's *The Genetical Theory of Natural Selection* (1930) and Theodosius Dobzhansky's account of *Genetics and the Origin of Species* (1937). In the meantime, Morgan's collaborator H. J. Muller went on to induce mutations in *Drosophila* by means of x-rays, facilitating the process of location—a move that proved a dramatic stimulus to the literary imagination, giving rise of a subgenre of "mutational romances" and introducing a lurid element into many evolutionary fantasies.

In the 1930s, George Beadle and Edward L. Tatum demonstrated that many genes functioned by controlling the synthesis of enzymes. Max Delbrück's began studying bacteriophages as systems of genetic replication in 1937. By the mid-1940s, microscopic observations of the behaviour of chromosomes in the cell nucleus during cell division had provided further data about the mechanical processes involved in genetic replication and reassortment. In 1953, James D. Watson and Francis H. Crick produced a model of the structure of the molecule of heredity, deoxyribonucleic acid (DNA), which explained its self-replication and its production of ribonucleic acid (RNA) molecules that transmitted its gene templates to the body of the cell and built the enzymes. The Watson-Crick model implied that the genetic code had to be contained in the sequence of the four bases (adenine, thymine, cytosine, and guanine) that were arranged in complementary pairs within the two threads of a double helix. Cracking the code took a further decade, at which point it was revealed that each group of three bases corresponded to one of the twenty-two amino acids of which proteins are composed, save for those that signalled the beginning and end of coding sequences specifying chains of amino acids.

The explanation of the manner in which DNA serves as a genetic code was widely advertised in popular *reportage as the ultimate penetration of "the secret of life". Watson's account of how the discovery was made, *The Double Helix* (1968), caused a storm of controversy by virtue of its unashamed celebration of the casual arrogance of the two scientists and their use of X-ray crystallography data appropriated on their behalf by Maurice Wilkins from Rosalind Franklin—who missed out on the Nobel prize the other three received because she had died of cancer, a casualty of her vocation. This story became a central myth of the modern *history of science, and its publicisation had a considerable effect on literary representations of the way *scientists thought and worked.

The complex process by which genes produce proteins—involving the initial production of complementary strands of "messenger RNA", which migrate from the nucleus to the mitochondria, where they produce the transfer RNA templates on which amino acids are physically gathered into chains—was gradually elucidated in the 1950s. The first chromosomal "maps" were produced in the late 1960s, using a stain that bound to guanine; the resultant banding patterns of the different human chromosome were clarified in 1971, allowing the positions of individual genes to be plotted. By 1987, the locations of 403 genetic "markers" were known, providing the initial blueprint for the human genome project and the general science of genomics, which resolved such "physical maps" into sets of base sequences. The fine detail of these discoveries was exploited in such hard science fiction stories as Charles Sheffield's "Dancing with Myself" (1989).

The rapid progress of biochemical genetics following the elucidation of the genetic code had a profound effect on the pattern of late twentieth-century research in *medicine. The genetic origins of numerous hereditary conditions were identified, and links were discovered between defective genes and many kinds of disorders—especially cancers—caused by somatic mutations in cells that possessed only one functional copy of the damaged gene. Genes apparently did nothing but produce proteins—the "building materials" of organic substance—and the processes by which those materials were arranged according to particular "architectural designs" as embryos and bodies grew remained stubbornly mysterious, but scientists and laypeople alike fell into the habit of speaking of genes "for" particular physical attributes, and increasingly began to speak of hypothetical genes "for" behavioural characteristics. Speculative fiction began to throw up such candidates as Roy Hutchins' "The Nostalgia Gene" (1954), while journalists and fiction writers became equally interested in the possibility of finding genes for homosexuality, as featured in Geoff Ryman's "Birth Days" (2003).

This mode of representation had a powerful effect on the reportage of science, where the discovery of any statistical correlation between some item of human behaviour and the possession of a particular gene tended to be represented as a matter of causation. The speculative discipline of *sociobiology, which had been established in order to reconcile apparent instances of altruistic behaviour in various animal species with the logic of natural selection,

became strongly committed to the assumption that the ultimate basis of all behaviour, no matter how complex it might be or how peculiar it might seem, must be genetic. Opposition to this way of thinking usually concentrated on its human implications—seeking to defend such notions as the freedom of the will and the moral responsibility of the individual—and thus tended to appear "unscientific", although the casual assumption that all physical and behavioural phenomena in living organisms are determined by genes is a drastic overstatement in purely scientific terms. Literary reflections of genetic science, however—even within hard science fiction—tend to echo the polarisation of the popular debate, coming down either for or against strong genetic determinism.

Late twentieth-century progress in genetics had a dramatic effect on speculative fiction, opening speculation about possible *biotechnological applications of *genetic engineering and the development of such innovative techniques of reproduction as *cloning. In the field of *exobiology, the clarification of biochemical genetics allowed writers to design alternative genetic systems for extraterrestrial ecospheres, often with a view to equipping them with exotic patterns of evolution. Earth-clone worlds were often equipped with simple variants of DNA—justified by the logic of convergent evolution or by the theory of *panspermia—such as the one featured in David Lake's *The Right Hand of Dextra* (1977), which builds proteins from dextro-rotatory amino acids rather than the laevo-rotatory isomers preferred by Earthly DNA. Such exobiological extrapolations often increase the ease with which genes can be naturally "traded"; Octavia Butler's Xenogenesis trilogy launched by *Dawn* (1987) is an elaborate account of the "salvaging" of the human species by aliens interested in the economic value of its genetic heritage, and the means by which that potential is exploited. An inconvenient disruption of the human genetic code in an extraterrestrial environment is featured in Poul Anderson's "Mustn't Touch" (1964).

Most animal genomes consist of trillions of base pairs, about five percent of which belong to "expressible" gene sequences (exons) serving as instructions for the manufacture of proteins; the remaining ninety-five percent is distributed in intergenic regions and nonexpressed sequences within genes (introns). Most of the nonexpressed DNA appears to be functionless "junk", but writers of speculative fiction were quick to discover possible functions for it; it became a significant reservoir of facilitating devices employed in explaining such long-standing motifs as sudden accessions of *superhumanity and theriomorphic transformations. Its more ingenious deployments include Charles Sheffield's "The Double Spiral Staircase"

(1990) and Rudy Rucker and Bruce Sterling's "Junk DNA" (2002).

Techniques of genetic analysis were initially constrained by the difficulty of recovering adequate amounts of DNA for processing—a problem solved in 1977 when Fred Sanger devised a technique of "DNA sequencing" that was dramatically speeded up by the invention of automated PCR (polymerase chain reaction) sequencers. PCR machines allowed Craig Venter to set up the Celera Genomics Corporation in 1988, with the intention of mass-producing genomic data, selling access to its databases to interested parties, and obtaining patents for as many individual gene sequences as possible. The Human Genome Project was thus forced into a race to place its result in the public domain, publishing a "working draft" in 2000 and a definitive version in 2003. Venter's intervention ensured a dramatic heightening of an unfolding controversy regarding the patenting of genetic discoveries, which added a new aspect to the field of *bioethics. The chief reflection of this evolution in contemporary fiction was, however, the rapid sophistication of the *forensic science used as a basis in detective fiction, which similarly benefited from the introduction of PCR machines.

The sophistication of genetics was reflected in the manner in which "seed banks" established to preserve botanical specimens were gradually transformed in the imagination into "gene banks"—a notion that broadened further when the development of *cryogenics made it possible to freeze animal embryos. Such notions were inevitably associated with the mythical imagery of Noah's Ark, which had been generalised in imaginative fiction to refer to various fictitious devices invoked to preserve genetic capital against large-scale disasters or to export the raw material of Earth's ecosphere to other worlds. The sophistication is reflected in such Ark fantasies as Christopher Hodder-Williams' *The Chromosome Game* (1984). The notion that natural gene banks may have preserved the DNA of lost species for future reconstruction underlines numerous accounts of resurrected *dinosaurs and mammoths; the notion that living species might be regarded as a bank from whose resources extinct species might be "reverse engineered" is extrapolated in Michael Swanwick's "A Great Day for Brontosaurs" (2002).

Ideative spinoff from the development of genetic theory included the notion of "memes": mental constructs accidentally or deliberately designed for extensive replication and stubborn resistance to modification, thus equipping themselves for selection and proliferation in the struggle for intellectual influence. The term was popularised by Richard Dawkins, and picked up for use in numerous speculative fictions; the

notion is taken to uncomfortable extremes in the series begun with John Barnes' *Orbital Resonance* (1991).

GEOGRAPHY

The description of the *Earth's surface and its human habitations. The subject was first defined in such Classical texts as Strabo's *Geographia* (first century B.C.), which included accounts of the contours of countries, their natural resources, their commerce, and their politics. Their distribution was determined by Eratosthenes' determination in the third century B.C. of the sphericity of the Earth; he did so by comparing the lengths of shadows cast at noon at Alexandria and Syene (the modern Aswan), calculating the Earth's diameter as 250,000 stadia (24,662 miles). Eratosthenes imagined the habitable part of the globe as a single landmass, approximately rectangular in shape, with several inland seas and various associated islands, occupying about a third of the total surface area of the globe.

The sphericity of the Earth was known to Ptolemy, whose *Geography* (second century A.D.) was an early attempt to produce a definitive textbook, but Ptolemy significantly underestimated its diameter. The sixth-century *Topographia Christiana*, however—credited to an Alexandrian named Cosmas—deduced from Scriptural references to "the face of the Earth" that it must be flat. Mediaeval Christians were thus uncertain as to whether to represent the Earth as a central sphere nested within an Aristotelian hierarchy of spheres or as a flat plane contained within the innermost sphere.

Among scholars who preferred the former model, the idea that the southern hemisphere was a vast ocean persisted into the fourteenth century, when Dante Alighieri imagined such an oceanic hemisphere punctuated by the antipodean mountain of Purgatory. Ptolemy's miscalculation of the Earth's diameter persuaded Christopher Columbus that by sailing west he could reach the Indies without extending his journey too far—although most contemporary scholars knew better, thus making it difficult for him to attract patronage. His serendipitous discovery in 1492 of another continent where he expected the Indies to be began a sequence of new geographical revelations that gradually revealed the true distribution of the continental landmasses.

Geography was primarily important as an aid to navigation, and was thus expressed largely through the practical endeavours of *cartography for much of its history. It began to mature as a scientific subject when more sophisticated correlations were established between physical features of the Earth's surface and the variety of its human populations, establishing its pivotal position between the physical sciences of *geology and *meteorology and the human sciences. Its elaboration began with the collation of travellers' tales, which are notorious for exaggeration and fanciful embellishment, so it inherited a rich legacy of myth and legend that was preserved in literature long after it was expelled from the science because of the immense utility of exotic settings.

Marco Polo's *Travels*—recorded in a Genoese prison in 1298—became the most popular "true romance" of the early fourteenth century, but was deftly surpassed by the fictitious account of the travels of "Sir John Mandeville", which was preserved in four times as many manuscript copies, aided by its accounts of the imaginary kingdom of Prester John and its equipment of other distant realms with all manner of fabulous creatures. The legacy of such endeavours was long lasting, and such accounts of imaginary geography crop up in many different kinds of work. William Bullein's *A Dialogue Bothe Pleasaunte and Pietifull, Wherin Is a Goodly Regiment Against the Fever Pestilence, with a Consolation and Comfort Against Death* (1564), which masquerades as a treatise in *medicine, includes accounts of Mandragata, where headless men have eyes in their breasts, Selenetide, where human women lay eggs, and an Antipodean ideal state, all narrated by a traveller named Mendax.

Formal exploration for reasons of trade and *colonisation increased dramatically in the fifteenth century, assisted by sails that allowed ships to tack against the wind. Once Columbus had "discovered" the New World, such activities increased by an order of magnitude as the exploitation of the new continent began and companies were formed to mount searches for new passages to the Indies via the northeast and the northwest, in the hope of avoiding long transequatorial journeys to difficult passages around the southern tips of Africa and South America. Navigation became an important practical science, its lore sufficiently valuable to be kept secret by such sixteenth-century practitioners as John *Dee. Travel literature became a significant popular genre; Richard Hakluyt's *Principal Voyages, Traffiques and Discoveries of the English Nation* (1598–1600) mingled legend, history, and experience and was further extended after the explorer's death by Samuel Purchas. The first guidebooks to England and Europe were also produced in the sixteenth century, by such travellers as Andrew Boorde and Thomas Coryate.

The relationship between the expansion of geographical knowledge brought about by determined exploration and its literary reflection was always slightly perverse because the gradual decrease in *terra incognita* brought about by the former was a considerable inconvenience to certain aspects of the latter. Imaginary settings require to be hidden within geographical lacunae, so the slow shrinkage of those lacunae was a tax upon imaginative literature. Thomas More's *Utopia* (1516; exp. 1551) was written while the supply was still abundant, but the subsequent development of the genre to which it gave its name was faced with a steadily dwindling resource. Lands recorded by ancient geographers on the basis of rumour were delivered into a curious situation in the sixteenth century, with explorers uncertain whether, or where, to search for them. Plato's Atlantis was presumed to be out of reach beneath the ocean's surface, but El Dorado became the target of numerous American expeditions before it became a byword for illusion in such sarcastic fantasies as Voltaire's *Candide* (1759). Such "lost lands", whose omission from actual maps could never prove that they had never existed, became particularly interesting to litterateurs as mysteries as well as potential settings. The loss of various legendary lands was compensated, for a while, by the hope of discovering further new ones to add to the Americas—a hope fulfilled when the Comte du Buffon's speculations regarding a *Terra australis incognita* were proved correct, although Australia was not as vast as he had hoped.

The employment of *magnetic compasses in navigation, and the enigmas associated with magnetic north, greatly assisted the evolution of a particular sense of mystery surrounding the world's poles, which gave birth to a significant subgenre of geographical fantasy. Notable polar romances included Margaret Cavendish's *The Blazing World* (1666), Simon Tyssot de Patot's *Les voyages et aventures de Jacques Massé* (1710) and *La vie, les aventures et le voyage de Groenland du Réverend Père Cordelier Pierre de Mésange* (1720), Samuel Taylor Coleridge's "The Rime of the Ancient Mariner" (1800), Edgar Allan Poe's *Narrative of Arthur Gordon Pym* (1838), George Sand's *Laura: voyage dans le cristal* (1863; trans. as *Journey Within the Crystal*), and M. P. Shiel's *The Purple Cloud* (1901). When the poles were finally reached in the early years of the twentieth century, the subgenre became an endangered species, but it continued to play host to such calculatedly unorthodox works as S. Fowler Wright's *Beyond the Rim* (1932) and Duncan Lunan's "In the Arctic, Out of Time" (1989). Antarctica still retains a certain mystery by virtue of its emptiness, reflected in such earnest speculative fictions as Valerie J. Freireich's "Ice Atlantis" (1993) and Kim Stanley Robinson's *Antarctica* (1997).

Exploratory expeditions were increasingly financed by national governments in the context of imperial ambitions; the men who undertook them became national heroes and accounts of their voyages became huge best-sellers; notable examples include Louis-Antoine Bougainville's expedition of 1766–1769, James Cook's expeditions of 1768–1771 and 1776–1780, and Alexander von Humboldt's expeditions of 1799–1804. These voyages discovered the new austral continent anticipated by the Comte du Buffon and revealed the extravagant population of islands making up Oceania, extinguishing the hope of finding any further colonisable landmasses while producing much more elaborate accounts of those that still seemed wide open to exploitation. Humboldt's *Kosmos* (1845–1858) was one of the first attempts to collate the discoveries made by these voyagers into a coherent world picture, but the linkage of geography with other sciences had made rapid headway in the eighteenth century in the work of the Baron de Montesquieu. Various German philosophers—including G. W. F. Hegel and Immanuel Kant—had begun to speculate about the effects of different physical environments on the historical development of different nations. This work was dramatically extrapolated in Henry Thomas Buckle's misleadingly titled *History of Civilization in England* (1857–1861).

The botanist Joseph Banks accompanied Cook's first expedition and became an enthusiastic sponsor of such missions, on both scientific and political grounds, once he was president of the Royal Society from 1778, commissioning voyages undertaken by William Bligh, James Ross, John Franklin, William Parry, and Mungo Park. These exploits were a considerable stimulus to the literary imagination, assisting such exemplars as Daniel Defoe's *Life and Adventures of Robinson Crusoe* (1719) to found an entire genre of "adventure fiction" that was soon established as a key component of nineteenth-century popular fiction; its scientific component was further extrapolated by Jules Verne's *voyages extraordinaires* and the long-running *Journal des Voyages*, whose foundation Verne inspired. They also exercised a considerable influence on the development of *Romanticism, as well as lending new support to *Utopian romances and satires.

The penetration of the interior of Africa—from which no other expeditionary had previously returned —by Mungo Park in 1794 seemed particularly epoch-making. Park did not survive his own second attempt but his sensational memoir of the first, *Travels to the Interior Parts of Africa* (1799), was highly influential; the works it helped inspire included Robert Southey's Oriental romance *Thalaba* (1801). Southey's *Madoc* (1805) drew in similar fashion upon Benjamin Franklin's 1784 account of the tribes of the Susquehannna Valley, where Southey and Samuel Taylor Coleridge had once dreamed of establishing a Utopian community dedicated to the ideals of Pantisocracy.

While European powers sponsored naval voyages, the newly independent United States of America sent out Lewis and Clark's expedition in 1804 to explore the recently purchased "Louisiana", which was then a boundless territory extending westwards into the unknown. The collections amassed by the far more elaborate Wilkes expedition of 1838–1842 eventually formed the basis of a national museum at the Smithsonian Institution. Early American literature was deeply affected by these endeavours, which echo resonantly in the work of James Fenimore Cooper. The *National Geographic Magazine*, founded in 1888, became a spectacularly successful popular periodical.

The priority of marine explorers was to identify safe and rapid routes between significant points on shore, so the oceans themselves were seen primarily as obstacles. Even so, scientific oceanography made rapid progress in the late eighteenth century, encouraged by such heroic endeavours as those of the marine biologist Alexander Agassiz, who covered nearly 200,000 miles in various vessels. The literary representation of the oceans also tended to view them as challenging obstacles, even when they were viewed as a source of sustenance. Classical literature had drawn a sharp distinction between the docile Mediterranean and the ocean wilderness beyond the Pillars of Hercules, and when the global map was first completed, very different characterisations were produced of the Atlantic and the Pacific. In much the same way that legendary lands lingered in the literary imagination, so legendary waters like the Sargasso Sea retained a belated presence in such works as Julius Chambers' "*In Sargasso*"; *Missing* (1896), Thomas A. Janvier's *In the Sargasso Sea* (1898), William Hope Hodgson's "From the Tideless Sea" (1906) and its sequel, and Ward Muir's "Sargasso" (1908).

Further interest was added to geographical science by the speculation that the continents and oceans had not always been in their present conformation—speculation aided by such legends as the history of Atlantis, which gained new status in the eighteenth and nineteenth centuries in scholarly fantasies and literary fantasies alike. The hypothetical continent of Lemuria was invented by zoologists attempting to understand similarities between the ecosystems of Madagascar and India in the days when the theory of continental drift was considered to be a scholarly fantasy, and was promptly integrated into the newly designed syncretic mythology of Theosophy, along with the sub-Arctic realm of Hyperborea, popularised by Pliny the Elder.

Some later scholarly fantasists moved Lemuria from the Indian Ocean to the Pacific, a new variant being popularised in James Churchward's *The Lost Continent of Mu* (1926). Other lost continents of scholarly fantasy included John Newbrough's Pan and Lewis Spence's Antillia, but literary fantasists preferred the drowned land of Lyonesse or Ys, whose poetic and legendary credentials were much more extensive. Other lands reported in travellers' tales that maintained a fugitive legendary presence until the early twentieth century included the Biblical Ophir and the South American Cibola (the "seven cities" from which the Aztecs had allegedly sprung), but literary treatments of all these notions became increasingly nostalgic as geographical science extinguished their plausibility.

By the mid-twentieth century, even the tiniest imaginary enclaves were difficult to accommodate on the thoroughly mapped globe; the last few survivors took on the quasi-illusory quality exemplified by James Hilton's Shangri-la in *Lost Horizon* (1933). By then, the sophisticated understanding of actual places provided by the science was beginning to have a considerable, though not very obvious, effect on naturalistic fiction. Some sort of "ethnogeographical understanding" had always been tacitly present in literary endeavours focusing on the relationships between characters and their settings, and this kind of understanding was refined by degrees throughout the nineteenth century. William Sharp's *Literary Geography* (1907) attempted to analyse several important nineteenth-century novelists in terms of the manner in which particular authors responded to their native regions, and then reproduced their responses in the settings of their work.

Sharp's many successors—including Margaret Crosland, author of *A Traveller's Guide to Literary Europe* (1965), and Dorothy Eagle and Hilary Carnell, compilers of *The Oxford Literary Guide to the British Isles* (1977)—mostly presented their works as guidebooks, directing tourists to places of particular significance in the lives and works of famous authors, but the underlying thesis has a significant theoretical component; Sharp set out to investigate the manner in which real landscapes are translated into fictional ones, by a process of careful selection and metaphorical illumination. He also took note of the reverse process, by which perception of actual landscapes can be affected by their literary representations; he explored the relationship between the "Scott-Land" of Sir Walter and the actual Scotland, the construction of "Dickensian" England and the rebranding of part of Yorkshire as "Brontë Country"—whose surrounding landscape was informed and perceptually transformed by the representations of it in *Jane Eyre, Wuthering Heights,* and *The Tenant of Wildfell Hall.* (It is the literary geography of England, not the actual landscape, that makes it seem forever quaint in American eyes—an illusion to which the actual landscape soon began to pander, merchandising its own quaintness in the names and the stocks-in-trade of shops, parks, and public houses.)

Literary geography inherits a good deal from mythical geography, and preserves that inheritance, but it also continues the process of transformation—as reflected in the literary loading of such fundamental terms as the directions of the compass. East, defined by the dawn, is the direction of hope in literary geography, while west, defined by the sunset, is the direction of fatality—although the special circumstances of the United States make "going West" a bold move and "back East" a place of origin, while north and south are disconnected from the compass in becoming the politically defined poles of the Civil War. West and south are, in fact, so overloaded with meaning in America that they have spawned such subcategories as Midwest and Deep South as well as descriptive phrases like Wild West and Southern Gothic; the spirit of America's West is also carried over into the much grander version of "the West" that came to distinguish the primary political products of the Industrial Revolution from "the East" and the "Third World". England, by contrast, is socially organised along a different axis, the North being industrialised, provincial, and poor, while the South consists of prosperous rural shires encircling the even-more-prosperous and civilised capital. Throughout Europe the East is usually "mysterious", the Orient having a particular resonance in the literature of France, many of whose famous writers undertook eastbound pilgrimages in search of imaginative inspiration.

By virtue of these kinds of transformations, geography exists in a relationship with the settings of fiction similar to that in which psychology exists with characters. Just as literature might be held to add a further dimension to psychology that the scientific method cannot quite capture, so it adds a further dimension to geography, in terms of a "sense of place" and a notion of how landscape can inform and transform personality. The fact that the most elementary form of story is the journey, and that plots can often be represented as maps, is more significant than it may seem at first glance, as is the analogy that likens literary experience in general to a journey, carefully elaborated in such texts as John Myers Myers' *Silverlock* (1949) and Alberto Manguel and Gianni Guadalupi's *The Dictionary of Imaginary Places* (1980), the latter taking the form of a pastiche tourist guide.

The rich tradition of fiction referring nostalgically to imaginary geographies of the past is complemented by a very different kind of fiction looking forward to possible geographical modifications of the future. The notion of creating new islands dates back to the nineteenth century in such works as Jules Verne's *L'île à hélice* (1895; trans. as *Propellor Island*), and Verne considered the possibility of more extravagant exploits in "continental *engineering" in *L'invasion de la mer* (1905; trans. as *The Invasion of the Sea*). Albert Robida considered the possibility of gradually building a series of natural and artificial islands into a new continent in *Le vingtième siècle* (1882; trans. as *The Twentieth Century*), and a similar notion is extrapolated in Brian Stableford's *The Fountains of Youth* (2000). *Alternative histories also provide scope for geographical variation, as in Harry Turtledove's "Down in the Bottomlands" (1993), in which the straits of Gibraltar are blocked off and the Mediterranean is much smaller.

GEOLOGY

The study of the composition and structure of the *Earth. Its major components are mineralogy—the study of the substances making up rocks—and stratigraphy, the study of the various layers in the Earth's crust. The history of mineralogy is closely interlinked with the history of chemistry; the utility and commercial value of various kinds of deposits—primarily coal, metal ores, and gemstones—ensured the importance of chemical science within the economic context of mining.

The gradual elucidation, analysis, and explanation of the stratification of rocks brought about a drastic transformation in understanding of the age of the Earth and the changes it had undergone. The *palaeontological excavation of the fossils contained in various strata formed the empirical bedrock of *evolutionary theory. Occasional geological disturbances such as earthquakes and volcanic eruptions are significant threats to human enterprise, thus exerting a powerful effect on the imagination; they give rise to further components of geological science—seismology and vulcanology—and provide the evidential background to *catastrophist theories of geological change.

The elucidation of the geological timescale took its first important stride in 1669 when Nicolaus Steno proposed that geological strata must have been formed successively as horizontal layers by some kind of deposition, and subsequently distorted by various upheavals. His contemporaries and successors found it difficult to figure out how and when this had happened, but the thesis did not seem to pose an immediate or serious threat to Biblical chronology,

and could be construed as support for the notion of the Deluge as a key formulating force. In the mid-eighteenth century, Johann Gottlieb Lehmann and Giovanni Arduino proposed categorisations of rocks, recognising that two kinds of superficial layers were laid atop the "primary" or crystalline base; their primitive scheme was further refined by Abraham Gottlob Werner in the late eighteenth century.

Although the Deluge and similar events remained the central hypothesis in most accounts of geological formation, the uniformitarian theory put forward in James Hutton's *Theory of the Earth* (1795)—which proposed that the Earth was constantly being re-formed by a systematic cycle of erosion, deposition, consolidation, and elevation with "no vestige of a beginning, no prospect of an end"—represented a new train of thought. The uniformitarian thesis was carried forward by John Playfair and William Smith and further elaborated by Charles Lyell's *Principles of Geology* in 1830. It was possible by then to organise the various kinds of strata found in widely different locations into a single temporal scale, although the calibration of the geological timescale remained speculative until the development of radiometrics, which measured the decay of radioactive nucleotides since the deposition of the rocks containing them.

The ideological disturbance associated with the uniformitarian revolution in geology is reflected in numerous texts of the period, extravagantly elaborated in texts mounting a rearguard defence of *creationism against evolutionism, such as Humphry Davy's *Consolations in Travel* (1830) and Robert Hunt's *Panthea* (1849). Contemporary geological knowledge was set out in considerable detail in Jules Verne's *Voyage au centre de la terre* (1863; trans. as *Journey to the Centre of the Earth*). Apart from fossils, cave systems such as the one described by Verne were the static geological phenomenon that attracted most literary interest, assisted by the perennial fascination of stalactites and stalagmites. Strata have a certain aesthetic appeal in themselves, however, carefully extrapolated in Edward Bryant's "Strata" (1981) and employed satirically in Terry Pratchett's *Strata* (1981).

The demands of melodrama ensured that far greater literary interest has been shown in the dynamic phenomena of volcanoes and earthquakes. Their use as climactic *disasters took very little influence from the actual findings of vulcanology and seismology, which failed to produce any scientific means of reliable anticipation—a deficit speculatively remedied in William E. Cochrane's "Earthquake" (1973) and Grey Rollins' "Once in a Blue Moon" (1993). Such events were traditionally regarded as archetypal "acts of God", delivering judgement upon the likes of

Sodom and Gomorrah, and they are frequently employed in that fashion in fiction. The catastrophic earthquakes in Lisbon in 1755 and San Francisco in 1906 did, however, intensify demands for further scientific research as well as prompting numerous literary representations. The principal theoretical advance resulted from the belated acceptance of Alfred Wegener's theory of continental drift—following studies of magnetisation of the sea floor by Fred J. Vine and Drummond H. Matthews in 1963—when both sets of phenomena were linked to stresses generated by the relative movement of tectonic plates.

Among the various kinds of geological phases mapped out by the stratigraphic record, the one that has attracted most literary attention is the phenomenon of "Ice Ages". Ice Ages—usually speeded up for dramatic effect—have played a prominent role in fiction, in such stories as Marius' "The Sixth Glacier" (1929), Warner van Lorne's "Winter on the Planet" (1937), Sterling Noel's *We Who Survived* (1960), R. W. Mackelworth's *Tiltangle* (1970), John Gribbin and Douglas Orgill's *The Sixth Winter* (1979), James Gunn's "The North Wind" (1981), William R. Fortschen's *Ice Prophet* (1983) and its sequels, and Kim Stanley Robinson's "Glacier" (1988).

The theory that the Earth's crust suffers major "slips" relative to its axis of rotation, shunting whole continents around the globe, was broached in Charles H. Hapgood's *Earth's Shifting Crust* (1958) and adopted by several other scholarly fantasies in the last decades of the twentieth century. Earlier geological scholarly fantasies included various accounts of a hollow Earth and Eduard Suess' late nineteenth-century theory of a "collapsing Earth", which explained mountains as wrinkles formed by the planet's gradual shrinkage; James Dana's "permanence theory" was an American variant, but the notion provoked no significant literary extrapolation.

GEOMETRY

A branch of *mathematics concerned with relationships in *space, defined in terms of points, lines, angles, planes, surfaces, and solids. The original application of the term was to measurements on the Earth's surface—a practical art developed by the Egyptians that was theorised when Thales imported it into the Greek world, its foundations clarified by Euclid's *Elements* (fourth century B.C.). Euclid used deductive logic to construct a series of theorems—further augmented by such writers as Apollonius and Archimedes—based on five axioms that seemed intuitively indubitable (although the fifth axiom, which relates to parallel lines, seemed less indubitable than the rest).

Significant augmentations of geometric technique followed the reintroduction of Euclid's work to Europe in the Renaissance, the most important being René Descartes' development of an "analytical geometry" that permitted the graphical representation of algebraic relationships. Euclidean geometry continued to be considered a definitive description of spatial properties even though notions of "absolute space" were repeatedly challenged by idealistic notions of space as an artefact of perception. Immanuel Kant's proposal that space was a necessary *a priori* construct deflected attention away from the possibility that actual space might be significantly different from perceived space—or, at least, from the possibility of ever finding out if that were the case.

When mathematicians began developing "non-Euclidean" geometries based on the variance of Euclid's fifth postulate in the early nineteenth century, suspicion was aroused that real space might be non-Euclidean. Carl Friedrich Gauss and Nikolai Ivanovich Lobatchevsky both made measurements of actual triangular relationships in the hope of finding a discrepancy in the sum of their angles that would offer evidence of a curvature in actual space. The formulation of an abstract philosophy of geometry by David Hilbert, which refused to make assumptions about the properties of real space, did not long precede the development of the general theory of relativity by Albert *Einstein, which extrapolated Hermann Minkowski's notion of a non-Euclidean "space-time continuum".

Coordinate geometry began to produce literary spinoff when the representation of *time as an axis encouraged its mathematical consideration as a *fourth dimension equivalent to distance in any of the three spatial dimensions, thus assisting the notion of *time travel. The relevant apologetic jargon was not developed, however, until the mathematical consideration of hypothetical two-dimensional and four-dimensional objects and spaces began to make extensive use of fiction as an imaginative aid, as in Edwin Abbott's description of *Flatland* (1884, as by "A Square"). Abbott's hope was that if readers could be persuaded to identify with the predicament of a two-dimensional being attempting to imagine the third dimension, they would then find it easier to appreciate the limitations of their own perception. He used satirical humour as a means to make his account of Flatland more interesting and engaging, and to reflect the essential oddness of the idea.

Abbott's contemporaries included C. H. *Hinton, who made more elaborate attempts to popularise similar ideas in "A Plane World" (1886) and *An Episode of Flatland* (1907), and Alfred Taylor Schofield, whose *Another World; or, The Fourth Dimension*

(1888) tackled the problem more directly. Claude Bragdon's *A Primer of Higher Space: The Fourth Dimension* (1913) is a hectic combination of mathematics and occultism, concluding with "Man the Square: A Higher Space Parable". This kind of speculative fiction became more than an intellectual game once the refinement of relativity theory required physicists to think in terms of a four-dimensional space-time—a problem sharpened considerably when theoretical *physicists in search of a unifying theory began to hypothesise further spatial dimensions. The latter search renewed interest in the work of Abbott and Hinton, elevating them to heroic status in the eyes of such *popularisers as Rudy *Rucker and Michio Kaku.

Another aspect of geometry that attracted considerable literary interest in the twentieth century included topology: the study of the effects of deformation of geometrical figures. Mirror-imaging, as featured in H. G. Wells' "The Plattner Story" (1896), became empirically significant in organic chemistry, where most compounds could exist in two mirror-imaged isomeric forms, although Earthly life makes use of only one (laevo-rotatory) set. Arthur C. Clarke's "The Reversed Man" (1950) and David J. Lake's *The Right Hand of Dextra* (1977) extrapolate corollaries of this observation. The topological oddity that attracted most attention was, however, the Moebius strip: a loop of paper with a single twist, which thus acquires a single surface.

Moebius strips and their complex variants—including the three-dimensional version known as a Klein bottle—provided the bases for such fantasies as Nelson S. Bond's "The Geometrics of Johnny Day" (1941), Martin Gardner's "No-Sided Professor" (1946) and "The Island of Five Colors" (1952), A. J. Deutsch's "A Subway Named Mobius" (1950), Theodore Sturgeon's "What Dead Men Tell" (1949), Arthur C. Clarke's "Wall of Darkness" (1949), Bruce Elliott's "The Last Magician" (1951), Mark Clifton's "Star, Bright" (1952), Homer C. Nearing's "The Hermeneutical Doughnut" (1954), and Rosel George Brown's "Flower Arrangement" (1959). Robert A. Heinlein's "And He Built a Crooked House" (1941) features an architectural venture based on the geometry of the tesseract—the four-dimensional equivalent of a cube, also featured in H. H. Hollis' "Sword Game" (1968).

Such fantasies became increasingly elaborate as the precedents accumulated, according to a familiar pattern. In this case, however, the complication involved acute challenges to the reader's imagination, which was forced to grapple with increasingly awkward problems of conceptualisation, tending towards surrealism in Christopher Priest's *Inverted World* (1974),

which features a city whose inhabitants perceive the curvature of space as a hyperbola.

A. J. Dewdney's *The Planiverse* (1984) is a relatively straightforward account of an elaborate Abbotteque flatland, but Ian Stewart's *Flatterland: Like Flatland, Only More So* (2001)—in which A Square's descendant Victoria Line undertakes an educational voyage through the multiverse—is much more ambitious in its conceptual demands. Kim Stanley Robinson's "The Blind Geometer" (1987) finds that his lack of sight enables him to escape the limitations of Euclidean perception and explore the geometries of *n*-dimensional manifolds, but is inevitably distanced from the reader—although a reader's ability to convert a long and intricately folded line of symbols into a kind of virtual experience is a process of imaginative transformation that might seem similarly miraculous were it not so commonplace.

GERNSBACK, HUGO (1884–1967)

Luxembourg-born entrepreneur who emigrated to the United States in 1904. He set up in business as an importer of technical equipment from Germany, and quickly developed one of his mail-order catalogues into the magazine *Modern Electrics*, whose feature articles celebrated the social transformations that were soon to be precipitated by his wares. He wrote the *Utopian futuristic novel *Ralph 124C41+: A Romance of the Year 2660* (1911–1912; book, 1925) for serialisation in the magazine. He became particularly entranced by the possibilities of *radio, selling an early two-way communication system as the Telimco Wireless.

Modern Electrics was replaced by *The Electrical Experimenter*, for which Gernsback wrote a series of stories transforming the notorious teller of tall tales "Baron Munchausen" into an inventor. *The Electrical Experimenter* metamorphosed in its turn into *Science and Invention*, in which "scientifiction" by various writers became a regular feature. Gernsback launched *Amazing Stories* as a companion in 1926, thus founding the pulp *science fiction genre. He soon supplemented it with a quarterly companion. Although his primary purpose was didactic and inspirational, Gernsback recognised that if he were to make it attractive to readers, he would have to infuse scientifiction with the narrative zest of contemporary popular fiction. He began this quest by reprinting the exemplary works of Jules Verne and H. G. Wells, and by attempting to recruit the popular pulp fantasists A. Merritt and Edgar Rice Burroughs, but his inability to match the word rates of the mass-market magazines and a marked reluctance to let go of any money at all soon forced his executive editors to rely for their ordinary stock-in-trade on work submitted by enthusiastic amateurs who were carried away by the ideas contained in science fiction but paid little attention to matters of literary polish or narrative drive.

Practicing what he preached, Gernsback also invested heavily—but rather prematurely—in radio broadcasting. His radio station's losses bankrupted his company in 1929. *Amazing* and its companion were sold off with other assets, but Gernsback wanted to stay in publishing and started two rival magazines, *Science Wonder Stories* and *Air Wonder Stories*, labelling their contents "science fiction" rather than "scientifiction," although they were clones of *Amazing* in every other respect. They were soon combined as *Wonder Stories*, and competition within the nascent genre intensified as other pulp publishers—who were already embarked on a reckless expansionist phase that was rapidly multiplying the number and variety of genres—appropriated the science fiction label. The market was soon supersaturated, and Gernsback moved on in the late 1930s, concentrating his efforts thereafter on his most profitable magazine, *Sexology*—whose value as an exercise in the *popularisation of human science was probably not the principal reason for its success.

Sam Moskowitz persuaded Gernsback to return to the science fiction marketplace in 1953, but his new magazine, *Science Fiction Plus*, lost money prodigiously and was quickly killed off. Gernsback restricted his speculative endeavours thereafter to an annual *futurological pamphlet entitled *Forecast*, which he distributed privately as a Christmas gift. Some of his successors in the field he had fathered felt that the crudity of the fiction he published had imposed a handicap on the genre label from which it never recovered, but he was not responsible for the extrapolation of pulp action-adventure fiction into the extraterrestrial arena of "space opera", which seems to have been the major factor in securing the genre's early cult following, so it is doubtful that the genre would have fared any better had it been introduced into the marketplace by another route.

Gernsback's enthusiasm for technologically facilitated social transformation was all the more remarkable for being surprisingly rare in a nation that was to become the key venue of that social transformation; his example emphasises the extent to which it was forced by zealous immigrant converts to the American Dream, going directly against the grain of the nation's literary culture. Although his own ventures failed, his brand of cultural brutality eventually came to dominate American radio, TV, and the cinema—with the exception that his interest in science, invention, and science education was disdainfully discarded along with other matters supposedly unworthy of the attention of marketing men.

GIBSON, WILLIAM (FORD), (1948–)

U.S. writer who moved to Canada in 1968 to avoid the draft. He completed his education there at the University of British Columbia, Vancouver, graduating with a B.A. in English in 1977. He had little knowledge of or interest in science, but he was very interested in the "counterculture" formulated in opposition to the dominant trends in American political culture, and in the potential impact of new communications technology on its associated subcultures. He not only recognised the possibility but relished the thought that the rapid development of information networks facilitated by computer technology would become a kind of frontier on which outlaws and nonconformists would flourish, carrying forward a subversive crusade against the would-be monopolists of the military-industrial complex and its political puppets.

Gibson began chronicling life on this new frontier in "Johnny Mnemonic" (1981) and other stories eventually collected in *Burning Chrome* (1986), some of which were written in collaboration with other writers who shared his interests, including Bruce *Sterling and Michael Swanwick. His first novel, *Neuromancer* (1984), became the archetypal example of what soon came to be called "cyberpunk" fiction. The central character of the novel is an outlaw whose ability to "jack into" computers gives him the freedom to roam the wide-open virtual plains of *cyberspace, armed and dangerous in ways that were infeasible in real space. In actual space—most of which has decayed into a post-Industrial wasteland—he is permanently on the run, and there would be no scope for him to live a rewarding life even if he were able to settle, but in cyberspace he is a potential hero, and he feels a sense of belonging that the actual world can no longer offer.

Although its literary style was polished and its artfully designed narrative forceful, *Neuromancer* became a modern literary classic primarily by virtue of its status as a handbook of cybercultural aspirations. There really were hordes of dedicated nonconformists who were not only employable but in demand because of their skill in making computers do things that were beyond the capabilities of more orthodox thinkers—especially older ones trapped by the heritage of obsolete education and experience—and they all wanted to think of themselves as cyberpunks. In reality, of course, they mostly went native, using the economic rewards of their endeavour to escape the threat of abandonment in the urban wasteland—but that did not prevent them from fantasising, at least for a while. Gibson became a folk hero, and a guru, to an emergent generation of "hackers", in spite of the fact that he had no computer skills of his own, and had composed *Neuromancer* on a manual typewriter.

Neuromancer's sequels, *Count Zero* (1985) and *Mona Lisa Overdrive* (1988), carried forward Gibson's futuristic transfiguration of the kind of hard-boiled crime fiction whose cinematic reflection had become known as film noir. The film version of *Johnny Mnemonic* did not work, in spite of his involvement in the screenplay, because there was far too much internal experience in the original and its effect had been so dependent on its literary quality. No attempt was made to film *Neuromancer*, in spite of its status as a key text, but the basic concepts Gibson had helped to popularise were developed within a cinematic framework in such films as *The Matrix* (1999), which borrowed his alternative term for cyberspace. His subsequent novels moved even closer to the field of contemporary crime fiction, employing relatively modest hypothetical technologies but concentrating intently on the potential social changes they might facilitate. *Virtual Light* (1993), *Idoru* (1996), *All Tomorrow's Parties* (1999), and *Pattern Recognition* (2003) thus became the most sophisticated and least formulaic examples of contemporary *technothriller fiction.

With the cyberpunk movement's chief propagandist, Bruce Sterling, Gibson wrote the steampunk novel *The Difference Engine* (1990), set in an alternative history in which Victorian England has undergone a sweeping technological revolution thanks to the development of Charles Babbage's mechanical computer. The novel testifies, even more clearly than the noirish cynicism of his futuristic thrillers, to the deep scepticism with which Gibson regarded the progressive potential of such technology—a scepticism that had to be forgiven by the worshipful pioneers of cyberculture, but was welcomed and admired by the older celebrants of *postmodernism, who were almost as appreciative of his uneasy ambivalence as they were of his preoccupation with the rapidly increasing artificiality of experience.

GRAVITY

A term derived from the Latin *gravis*, which signified solemnity before it was adapted to describe the quality of having weight, associated with the Classical elements of earth and water—as contrasted with air and fire, which were allegedly possessed of the contrary quality of levity. It was adapted by *Galileo and Isaac *Newton to refer to a fundamental *force operative between all entities possessed of mass; Newton's law of gravity related its effect to the inverse square of the distance between two mutually attractive masses. The application of that law to objects at the Earth's surface and to the movement of planets in the heavens was a vital unification of explanation. When Newton's universal theory was eventually superseded, gravity again played a key role in Albert Einstein's general theory of *relativity, which reconceived it in *geometrical terms as a curvature of space-time.

Gravity had a particular significance in *cosmology because it imported a tendency to eventual collapse into cosmological models, as dramatised in such cosmic visions as Edgar Allan *Poe's *Eureka* (1848). This tendency caused some anxiety to Einstein, who had based his own theory on the cosmological principle that the universe ought to appear the same from every viewpoint in space-time, so he introduced a "cosmological constant" into his own model to counter the threat of gravitational collapse, but he was always unhappy with its arbitrariness and eventually rejected it as a mistake. Following the discovery in the 1920s that the universe was actually expanding, the question still remained open as to whether gravity would ultimately reverse the *Big Bang's impetus and institute a collapse—a central issue in *Omega Point fiction.

The difficulties involved in accommodating gravity within a "unified field theory" along with the other fundamental forces stimulated a twentieth-century search for a fundamental gravitational particle, the graviton, and associated phenomena of gravitational radiation. In the meantime, the extreme gravitational phenomena associated with *black holes became a popular item of fascination. The most significant roles played by gravity in speculative fiction, however, have always been connected with the possibility of *space travel. The law of gravity defines the thrust required to take a projectile out of the Earth's "gravity well", so it functions first and foremost as a retardant to be overcome, often licencing the invention of a facilitating device of "antigravity". Once a spaceship is free from Earth's gravity, however, the absence of the force becomes a considerable problem for space travellers, similarly compensated by the facilitating device of "artificial gravity".

The effects of the lesser gravity of the *Moon on visitors is noted in many early lunar voyages and almost all modern speculative fiction set there. The nullification of gravity's effect on bodies in free fall, as featured in Casanova's *Icosameron* (1788), and the effects of weightlessness on space travellers, as described by Jules *Verne in *Autour de la lune* (1870;

trans. as *Around the Moon*), became elements of the staple imagery of modern space fiction. The lesser gravity of *Mars is given partial credit for John Carter's heroic prowess in Edgar Rice Burroughs' interplanetary fantasies and is mentioned in many similar works, and designing adaptations to various levels of gravity became one of the key features of hard science-fictional "world building" in the wake of Milton A. Rothman's "Heavy Planet" (1939; by-lined Lee Gregor) and Hal *Clement's *Mission of Gravity* (1953).

Various versions of gravity nullification or reversal are used to propel spaceships in J. L. Riddell's *Orrin Lindsay's Plan of Aerial Navigation* (1847), Chrysostom Trueman's *The History of a Voyage to the Moon* (1864), Percy Greg's *Across the Zodiac* (1880), and Robert Cromie's *A Plunge into Space* (1890), although none of these examples actually uses the term "antigravity". Edwin Pallander's *Across the Zodiac* (1896) uses a gyroscope to nullify gravity. In Kurd Lasswitz's *Auf Zwei Planeten* (1897; trans. as *Two Planets*) the Martians use diabar, a substance "transparent" to gravity, for interplanetary travel and other technological purposes. The gravity-shielding Cavorite that H. G. Wells employed in *The First Men in the Moon* (1901) continued this tradition. Ludwig Anton's *Brücken über den Weltenraum* (1922; trans. as *Interplanetary Bridges*) similarly features the antigravitic mineral varium. Joseph Gray Kitchell's *The Earl of Hell* (1924) features the alloy nilgrav. Gravity nullification also featured in John Mastin's *The Stolen Planet* (1906), E. D. Ward's *Sir Pulteney* (1910), and John Ames Mitchell's *Drowsy* (1917) before variations of it were presented in such genre science fiction stories as Arthur J. Burks' "Hell Ship" (1938), James E. Gunn's "The Gravity Business" (1955), Arthur Sellings' *The Quy Effect* (1966), Lee Correy's *Star Driver* (1980), and Charles Sheffield's "The Double Spiral Staircase" (1990).

A world in which gravity operates—very inconveniently—in reverse is satirically described in J. G. Montefiore's "Gubmuh" (1874), and the metaphorical associations of the term and its correlates were further exploited in such nineteenth-century fictions as Fitz-James O'Brien's "How I Overcame My Gravity" (1864), Frank Stockton's "A Tale of Negative Gravity" (1884), and R. D. Blackmore's *Tommy Upmore* (1884). The last named made much of wordplay opposing "gravity" to "levity", and its self-consciously buoyant manner was carried forward with greater subtlety and wit into numerous twentieth-century accounts of levitation as Ronald Fraser's *The Flying Draper* (1924), Neil Bell's "The Facts About Benjamin Crede" (1935), Michael Harrison's *Higher Things* (1945), James H. Schmitz's *The Witches of Karres* (1949; exp. book, 1966), Brian Aldiss' "Pogsmith" (1955), R. A. Lafferty's "Snuffles" (1960), Timothy Zahn's *A Coming of Age* (1985), and John Shirley's *Three-Ring Psychus* (1980). In the late nineteenth and twentieth centuries, personal gravity defiance—"levitation"—became a common example of *impossibility, and a standard illusion of stage magicians, thus giving it a key role in many accounts of *parapsychological superhumanity, and generating problems of plausibility that are elaborately extrapolated in Isaac Asimov's "Belief" (1953).

Jules Verne's claim in a newspaper interview that the space gun he had featured in *De la terre à la lune* (1865; trans. as *From the Earth to the Moon*) was a rationally plausible way of overcoming the Earth's gravity, whereas Wells' Cavorite was not, gave rise to a good deal of subsequent debate. Arthur C. Clarke argued cogently in "What Goes Up" (1955) that the reverse was actually the case, because the space gun would kill its passengers while antigravity was the kind of apparent impossibility that might—with the aid of post-Einsteinian physics and sufficient technological ingenuity—be realised. Raymond F. Jones awarded antigravity the crucial role in his combative *conte philosophique* "Noise Level" (1952), which argued fervently that the principal bar to technological progress is the conviction that certain things cannot be done.

James Blish's Cities in Flight series (1950–1962) equipped its facilitating antigravity device with an aptly casual nickname, the spindizzy. The notion was based on the work of P. M. S. Blackett, who contended that a combination of gravity and rotation could produce magnetism, and that a combination of rotation and magnetism might therefore produce either gravity or antigravity. George O. Smith's "Meddler's Moon" (1947) hypothesises a similar relationship between magnetism and gravity, and Poul Anderson used a Blackettesque notion of "gyrogravity" to support both faster-than-light travel and *matter transmission in his "We Have Fed Our Sea" (1958; book version as *The Enemy Stars*). Blackett's thesis fell into neglect thereafter, although some of the gyroscopic phenomena that gave rise to it were subsequently popularised by the engineer Eric Laithwaite, notably in various lectures given at the Royal Institution in 1973–1975. *Physical Review Letters* published Hisdeo Hayasaka and Sakae Takeuchi's paper on "Anomalous Weight Reduction on a Gyroscope's Right Rotations about the Vertical Axis on the Earth" in 1989.

Science fiction stories employing the theory of gravity respectfully and ingeniously include Ross Rocklynne's *At the Centre of Gravity* (1936), Katherine MacLean's "Incommunicado" (1950)—which features a "slingshot" effect to accelerate a spaceship that was subsequently employed in reality—Ben Bova's "The Man Who Hated Gravity" (1989), and Stephen Baxter's *Raft* (1991). The problems of returning to Earth after long sojourns in low-g or zero-g environments are featured in such stories as Ross Rocklynne's "Touch of the Moon" (1968) and Fritz Leiber's *A Specter Is Haunting Texas* (1968). In order to avoid the undesirable physical consequences of such sojourns—including muscle wastage and the loss of skeletal calcium—spaceships and *artificial satellites often compensate for the lack of gravity by substituting "centrifugal force"—the tangential momentum that is subjected to restraint by the centripetal force of gravity—induced by spinning the habitat.

C. L. Moore's "Promised Land" (1950; by-lined Laurence O'Donnell) looked forward to a day when future space colonists might be born and bred in centrifuges, breathing alien atmospheres, in order to prepare them for the worlds to which they must go. Conversely, a "floater" born and raised in zero-gee is the protagonist of Syne Mitchell's *Murphy's Gambit* (2000). Centrifuges are used to train astronauts to withstand the increased g-forces of liftoff, but substituting that kind of force for gravity in relatively small living spaces is problematic because the effects of the force would not be uniform; the feet of someone standing on the inner surface of a spinning spaceship would be accelerated more rapidly than the head, with potentially dizzying effects. This inconvenience tends to be ignored when the notion is used as a fictional facilitating device.

Other varieties of "artificial gravity" are rarely supplied with any kind of supportive logic, although Poul Anderson used gyrogravity in that way too, initially in a lighthearted spirit, in "A Bicycle Built for Brew" (1959; book version as *The Makeshift Rocket*). In this story and subsequent ones an artificial gravity field makes interplanetary travel much easier by retaining an atmosphere about a ship, and allows *asteroids to be more easily colonised. Hypothetical environments in which gravity is perceived in exotic ways include the forest crown of Frederic S. Durbin's "The Place of Roots" (2001), where gravity is "the quiet wind", and the vertical surfaces on which precarious cultures live in Ian Watson's "The People of the Precipice" (1985) and Adam Roberts' *On* (2001).

GREENHOUSE EFFECT, THE

The term now given to a phenomenon first described in 1827 by the French mathematician Baron Fourier, by which some atmospheric gases absorb and retransmit the energy of solar radiation at different wavelengths, resulting in the heating of the atmosphere. The effect helps to even out the differences between day and night temperatures. Fourier's term, initially translated as "hothouse effect", is something of a misnomer, because energy conservation in greenhouses is mostly due to the inhibition of convection.

In 1860, John Tyndall determined that the greenhouse effect was produced by carbon dioxide, water vapour, and methane. Svante Arrhenius calculated in the 1890s that doubling the amount of carbon dioxide in the atmosphere would increase the Earth's surface temperatures by 5°C by virtue of the greenhouse effect, but the notion that carbon dioxide liberated by human industrial activity might alter the climate was not broached until 1938, by G. S. Callendar; it received little attention until it was revived by the American oceanographer Roger Revelle in 1957, after which it was soon added to other anxieties related to industrial *pollution. Although most alarmist attention tends to focus on greenhouse gases directly emitted from power stations, the destruction of "carbon sinks" by deforestation—especially in such areas as the Amazon basin—has a greater net significance, and probably allowed human beings to begin influencing global temperatures as soon as agricultural developments began, perhaps prolonging the current interglacial period.

Because the levels of carbon dioxide and water vapour in the atmosphere are largely determined by the photosynthetic activity and transpiration of plants, the regulation of the greenhouse effect is one of the chief homoeostatic systems featured in James *Lovelock's Gaia hypothesis. Several mass extinction events detected by *palaeontologists were eventually linked to catastrophic disruptions of this homoeostatic mechanism; the possibility of an imminent *ecocatastrophic disruption as a result of human activity thus became a key component of late twentieth-century *disaster fiction.

Fantasies of global warming were rare before the 1960s, and such exceptions as Travis Hoke's "Utopia by Thermometer" (1932) did not see it in catastrophic terms. When it was first built into ecocatastrophe scenarios, it generally played third fiddle to alarms generated by chemical pollution and the *population problem, but a shift in emphasis began in the late 1970s when such stories as Arthur Herzog's *Heat* (1977), Sam Nicholson's "Starships in Whose Future?" (1978), and Hal Clement's *The Nitrogen Fix* (1980) began to appear. It remained fugitive in the early 1980s, although new Deluges were featured in such stories as Gardner Dozois' "The Peacemaker" (1983) and George Turner's *The Sea and Summer* (1987; aka *Drowning Towers*) and a more extreme ecocatastrophe in Trevor Hoyle's *The Last Gasp* (1983). Anxiety increased markedly in the last years of the decade; Whitley Strieber and James Kunetka looked forward to *Nature's End* (1986). Fragments of a comet cause the greenhouse effect to go into overdrive in Frederik Pohl and Jack Williamson's *Land's End* (1988), but Fred Pearce's alarmist essay *Turning Up the Heat* (1989) argued that no such additional factor might be necessary. Science fiction stories dramatising this argument in various ways included John Gribbin's "The Carbon Papers" (1990), David Brin's *Earth* (1990), Laura J. Mixon's "Glass Houses" (1991), Jeff Hecht's "The Greenhouse Papers" (1991), Michael Tobias's *Fatal Exposure* (1991), and Patricia Anthony's *Cold Allies* (1993).

Increasing political concern resulted in a 1992 Earth Summit, which issued a resolution calling for world carbon dioxide emissions to be stabilised at 1990 levels by the year 2000. This was replaced by the Berlin Mandate of 1995, which committed industrial nations to the continued reduction of such emissions after 2000, although the situation was complicated by a U.S. proposal that the developed nations ought to be able to buy the emissions quotas of less favoured nations. The United States refused to ratify the renewal of the mandate called for by the Kyoto protocol of 1997, although the protocol came into force in the other signatory nations in 2004. This sequence of events generated an increasingly contentious debate in which scientists tracking global warming and modelling its likely future increase found themselves locked in ideological conflict with U.S. governments determined not to take any action that would slow economic growth.

By the end of the twentieth century, the greenhouse effect had become a factor in almost all science-fictional images of the near future—an accommodation recognised by the fact that the special June 2001 issue of *Whole Earth* devoted to the problem was edited by Bruce Sterling. Notable alarmist texts from the period included Norman Spinrad's *Greenhouse Summer* (1999), Steven Gould's *Blind Waves* (2000), William Sanders' "When This World Is All on Fire" (2001), Kim Stanley Robinson's *Forty Signs of Rain* (2004) and *Fifty Degrees Below* (2005), and Robert Reed's "Poet Snow" (2005). On the other hand, Michael Crichton's anti-environmentalist polemic *State of Fear* (2005) asserted that global warming caused by the greenhouse effect was negligible, and that anxieties about it were the result of an evil conspiracy.

The most extreme climate change scenarios developed in the early twenty-first century suggested that the sudden release of methane held in clathrates deposited in suboceanic carbon sinks and Arctic permafrosts might trigger a rapidly accelerating "Venus scenario" that could render the Earth uninhabitable in a matter of decades rather than centuries, as dramatised in Alain Castelbord's "Nyos 2030" (2004). By 2005, the widespread melting of northern permafrosts and the dwindling of the polar ice cap had increased the plausibility of this scenario considerably. In the meantime, proposals for strategic action to combat the greenhouse effect were not limited to the reduction of carbon dioxide emissions; other suggestions included the mass planting of fast-growing trees, the addition of iron to regions of the sea in which that element seems to be the principal limiting factor of marine algae growth, and increasing the reflectivity of the Earth's surface, either by enhancing the effects of atmospheric clouds and dust or painting the roofs of buildings white.

H

HALDANE, J[OHN] B[URTON] S[ANDERSON] (1892–1964)

British biologist and populariser of science. He was the son of a Scottish physician and physiologist educated at Eton and New College, Oxford, who was converted to socialism while serving with the Black Watch in World War I. He returned to New College thereafter until 1922; he then spent ten years at Cambridge before settling at University College, London, where he taught genetics until 1950, when he went to India.

In the 1920s, Haldane produced a sequence of notable essays in *speculative nonfiction, beginning with the anticipations of future *biotechnology contained in *Daedalus; or, Science and the Future* (1923). The essay looks forward optimistically to a day when biologists have created a new species of alga to solve the world's food problem, and in which "ectogenetic" children born from artificial wombs can be strategically modified. It observes, however, that there is always extreme resistance against "biological inventions", because they are invariably perceived, at first, as blasphemous perversions.

The published version of *Daedalus* became the first of the long-running series of *futurological "Today & Tomorrow" pamphlets when it provoked a reply in kind from Bertrand *Russell. It also prompted Julian Huxley to produce "The Tissue-Culture King" (1926), whose substance was greatly elaborated and its satirical slant heavily re-emphasised in *Brave New World* (1932), written by Julian's brother Aldous *Huxley. Haldane's other contribution to the Today & Tomorrow series was the similarly contentious *Callinicus: A Defence of Chemical Warfare* (1925), in which he analysed the role that poison gases were likely to play in the next war with a determinedly objective eye.

In the title piece of *Possible Worlds and Other Essays* (1927), Haldane extrapolated an idea broached in Julian Huxley's "Philosophic Ants" (1923), considering the likely worldviews of various animal species employing specialised sensory apparatus to scan and navigate particular physical environments. The last item in the collection, "The Last Judgment", is a far-ranging future history, which is markedly different from previous *Omega Point fictions in using an estimate of the Sun's probable lifespan very different from the one proposed in the nineteenth century by Lord Kelvin. After considering various cosmic accidents that might put an end to life on Earth before the Sun expires, it wonders what might become of humankind over billions of years, imagining our ultimate descendant species—a hivelike superorganism—adapting itself for relocation to *Venus, and then to *Jupiter, before contemplating the possibility of extending the human story to trillions of years by moving to the worlds of other stars. "The Last Judgment" was the principal inspiration of Olaf *Stapledon's *Last and First Men*, although Stapledon's Last Men baulked at the final hurdle. Other significant essays from this phase of Haldane's career included "On Being the Right Size" (1928), which argued cogently that size is an important determinant of the physiological systems a body can possess,

225

explaining—among other things—why such favourite images of fantastic fiction as giant insects are rationally implausible.

The Inequality of Man and Other Essays (1932) included three items relevant to the evolving tradition of British scientific romance. "Possibilities of Human Evolution" discusses speculations by H. G. Wells—with whom he was later to collaborate, along with Julian Huxley, on *Reshaping Man's Heritage* (1944)—George Bernard Shaw, and Olaf Stapledon. "Man's Destiny" suggests that once the human lifespan has been extended to thousands of years and the worlds of other stars have been colonised, "There is no theoretical limit to man's material progress but the subjection to complete conscious control of every atom and every quantum of radiation in the universe ... [and] no limit at all to his intellectual and spiritual progress". "Some Consequences of Materialism" suggests that a universe infinite in time must reproduce the same individuals over and over again—a curious kind of immortality. *Science and Life* (1934) included "If", an article on *alternative history.

Haldane's work in this vein was possessed of considerable rhetorical flair and gave rise to several oft-quoted aphorisms, one of which commented on the hypothetical Creator's remarkable fondness for beetles while another—sometimes known as "Haldane's law"—alleged that "the universe is not only queerer than we suppose, but queerer than we *can* suppose". One such throwaway line provided the ideative basis of the notion of "kin selection", on which the speculative science of *sociobiology was built. Haldane's political fervour, expressed in the science column he wrote for *The Daily Worker* after joining the Communist Party in 1937, initially led him to propose that T. D. Lysenko might be a great biologist, although he subsequently changed his mind and quit the party for good in 1950.

In *The Causes of Evolution* (1932), a significant summary of the synthesis between Charles *Darwin's theory of natural selection and Mendelian *genetics, Haldane laid the foundation for a good deal of subsequent work on population genetics. His classic paper on "The Cost of Natural Selection" (1957) calculated the number of individuals in a population that had to die in order for a new favourable mutation to become widely established within a population, thus introducing the concept of "genetic load".

Haldane ventured into speculative fiction on several occasions, although the only item of fiction in *Possible Worlds* is far less adventurous than the essays. The children's fantasies collected in *My Friend Mr. Leakey* (1937) are much livelier, although they make no attempt at rational plausibility. He abandoned his only attempt to write a full-length scientific romance, although the existing text was published posthumously as *The Man with Two Brains* (1976). The narrative "explains" William Blake's prophetic books in terms of visions of a distant planet. While dying of cancer in 1964, Haldane wrote a comic poem that includes the couplet: "I wish I had the voice of Homer / To sing of rectal carcinoma".

Haldane's wife Charlotte (née Franken) was a successful writer, mostly in the field of biography; her Utopian novel *Man's World* (1926) draws heavily on his ideas. His sister, Naomi Mitchison, was even more effective and far more prolific; in addition to numerous *anthropological and *ethnological fantasies, she wrote three science fiction novels, *Memoirs of a Spacewoman* (1962), *Solution Three* (1975), and *Not by Bread Alone* (1983), all of which extrapolate ideas from *Daedalus*. She might have written the second and third much earlier, but diplomatically waited until he was dead before publishing them, because they dissent strongly from his own optimism in regard to the envisioned technologies. Haldane's influence on other British writers of scientific romance was less direct but often considerable. Muriel Jaeger's *Retreat from Armageddon* (1936) offers one of the most balanced responses to *Daedalus*. Haldane is reflected with various degrees of disapproval in various literary characters, including Shearwater in Aldous Huxley's *Antic Hay* (1923), Codling in Ronald Fraser's *The Flying Draper* (1924), and Weston in C. S. Lewis' *Out of the Silent Planet* (1938). E. C. Large's *Sugar in the Air* (1937) is a careful satirical study of a key biological invention that receives a frustratingly chilly welcome; its anti-capitalist stance echoes the propagandistic Marxism that became very prominent in Haldane's work as a response to the rise of fascism in Europe.

HARD SCIENCE FICTION

J. R. Pierce's article "Science and Literature" (*Science,* 20 April 1951) complained that very few contemporary science fiction stories actually contained any scientific ideas. Pierce blamed this deficit on John W. Campbell Jr.'s editorial policy in *Astounding Science Fiction* of publishing fiction whose primary concern was the effects of potential discoveries on human individuals and society—which, he claimed, "has served as an excuse for a progressive deterioration of the hard scientific and technological core in much of science fiction".

This passage was quoted by *Astounding*'s regular book reviewer P. Schuyler Miller, who echoed Pierce's use of the word "hard" in a 1952 review of Wilson Tucker's *The City in the Sea*, calling it Tucker's first "hard-shell" science fiction book, and again in a 1957 review of three books, in recognition of the fact that it had become necessary to draw a distinction between "real" science fiction based in the careful extrapolation of rationally plausible premises and fiction that was content to use the imagistic vocabulary of science fiction without any regard at all for scientific plausibility. Significantly, the "fashionably soft" example under consideration, Murray Leinster's *Exploration Team*, had originated in *Astounding*'s pages, in accordance with the editorial policy identified by Pierce, while Hal *Clement's *Cycle of Fire*—hailed by Miller as paradigmatic hard science fiction—had gone straight into paperback, presumably having been rejected by Campbell.

Outside the pages of *Astounding*, no pulp editor since Hugo *Gernsback's departure from the field had been in the least concerned about matters of rational plausibility; all of them preferred to publish colourful action-adventure fiction that used science fiction motifs merely as literary décor. By 1957, the pulps were dead and a new generation of "digest" magazines had sprung up to replace them, but the situation had not altered significantly. Several of the new editors had determined to raise the *literary* quality of the material they published, but in many—though by no means all—instances this involved the development of an antiscientific (or at least antiscientistic) viewpoint for satirical or alarmist purposes. Significantly, the first labelled science fiction book to enjoy a *succès d'estime* in the wider literary world was Ray Bradbury's *The Martian Chronicles* (1950), a key example of fiction that used science fiction motifs without the least regard for scientific plausibility, developing them as symbols and metaphors.

Following Miller's use of the term, other reviewers and critics began to draw a similar distinction between "hard" and "soft" science fiction, recognising from the very beginning that hard science fiction was in decline because the softer varieties were far more reader friendly. Some subsequent users of the term took it to mean science fiction based in the "hard" (physical) sciences rather than the "soft" (human) sciences, while others took it to be a contraction of "hard-core", referring to the science fiction that lay at the heart, rather than the periphery, of the commercial genre. Hal Clement was generally retained as the archetypal example of a hard science fiction writer, while such writers as Robert A. *Heinlein and Poul *Anderson were seen as other key practitioners. The terminology was not unproblematic; Isaac *Asimov, though widely seen as a key hard science fiction writer, guiltily admitted that the bulk of his work was "social science fiction" of an intrinsically fanciful nature. Campbell's hospitality to *parapsychological

themes obliterated his entitlement to be considered as a champion of scientific plausibility in many eyes. The tendency of stories that once seemed rationally plausible to be exposed by the passage of time and the growth of new knowledge as flagrant impossibilities also confused the issue.

The word "hard" also had political connotations, being associated with the right wing of the U.S. political spectrum, while "soft" was associated with the left ("liberals" were routinely accused of being "woolly"). The political opinions expressed, sometimes fervently, by Campbell, Heinlein, and Anderson—and, in a slightly later period, by Larry *Niven—mapped onto this spectrum easily enough, and it also appeared that many prominent soft science fiction writers had conspicuously liberal leanings, although the situation was confused by the ambiguous situations of writers like Asimov and the left-leaning Frederik *Pohl. The association between hard science fiction and right-wing politics was, however, more firmly sealed by the intimate connection of hard science fiction to the myth of the *Space Age, which had built-in political imperatives associated with the key notions of conquest and *colonisation; this identification linked the "hardness" of science fiction to uncompromising and violent forms of libertarian entrepreneurialism.

However the hardness of hard science fiction was construed, subsequent fashionable innovations—such as British and American "new wave" science fiction, feminist science fiction, and the emergence of fantasy as a commodified genre—combined with the migration of science fiction from a small enclave of specialist magazines to mass market paperbacks and TV to bring about a dramatic emphasis of the softening trend identified by Pierce and Miller. Some users of the term—most notably David Hartwell, in *Age of Wonders: Exploring the World of Science Fiction* (1984) and his showcase anthologies *The Ascent of Wonder: The Evolution of Hard SF* (1994) and *The Hard SF Renaissance* (2002)—began to attribute "hardness" to any story containing a measurable amount of quasi-scientific exposition, and any that set out to support the cause of science against the "New Age" revival of superstition. It was taken for granted by the time Hartwell mounted his defence that hard science fiction, however loosely it might be defined, was a fugitive and endangered species in the literary marketplace.

From the viewpoint of this book, it remains not only desirable but necessary to separate out a category of science fiction stories that make a concerted attempt to maintain rational plausibility, because such stories stand in a unique relationship to the content and advancement of science. Soft science fiction also reflects and responds to changing scientific ideas, as some naturalistic fiction does, but it does so in a very different manner. Hard science fiction aspires to serve as a medium of thought experiments, significant not merely as a means of popularising scientific ideas but also—and primarily—as a means of their philosophical investigation. Hard science fiction is not the kind of science fiction that can appeal to literary critics in search of the same rewards that they find in naturalistic fiction, nor is it the kind of science fiction that can appeal to a mass audience, but it is the most intellectually interesting and imaginatively challenging kind of speculative fiction.

HEINLEIN, ROBERT A[NSON] (1907–1988)

U.S. writer who dabbled in politics after being forced out of the navy on health grounds, becoming involved with Upton Sinclair's EPIC (End Poverty in California) movement. He wrote a *Utopian novel, *For Us the Living* (written 1939; published 2004), heavily impregnated with ideas formed during that campaign, which did not find a publisher at the time and which he subsequently preferred to leave unpublished. He ventured instead into pulp *science fiction—a genre he enjoyed reading, although he despised its medium—in order to pay off a mortgage taken out to fund his unsuccessful candidacy for political office.

When John W. *Campbell Jr. recruited him to the burgeoning *Astounding* stable, Heinlein poured out work in profusion, publishing five stories in 1940 that became definitive of Campbellian ambitions. "If This Goes On—" transfigured memories of a Bible Belt upbringing into a cautionary account of a future America tyrannised by a Prophet Incarnate. "Requiem" is a sentimental celebration of *Space Age mythology. "The Roads Must Roll" follows the course of a futuristic labour dispute. "Blowups Happen" describes the social and psychological tensions generated in and around a *nuclear power plant. "Coventry" describes a reservation to which dissidents from a formal social contract are banished, where they stubbornly preserve the social problems that the surrounding society has solved.

In order to enrich the background of his stories, Heinlein fitted them into a loosely knit *future history, which prompted Campbell to propose that he should reserve his own name for stories set within it, publishing other works pseudonymously. Its idiosyncratic account of the Space Age was extended in "Logic of Empire" (1941), the couplet "Universe" and "Common Sense" (1941; combined in *Orphans of the Sky*, 1963), and *Methuselah's Children* (1941; book, 1958) but the project was abruptly abandoned

when the United States became embroiled in World War II and Heinlein was recalled to military service. Campbell had persuaded Heinlein to rewrite one of his unpublished political fantasies as *Sixth Column* (1941, by-lined Anson MacDonald; book, 1949; aka *The Day After Tomorrow*) and to return to his own Utopian ambitions in *Beyond This Horizon* (1942, as MacDonald; book, 1948) but that line of work was also cut short. Heinlein's career as a pulp writer was over; when he returned to science fiction writing after the war's end, he approached the business of building a writing career very differently, treating the specialist magazines as a market of last resort.

In the late 1940s and early 1950s, Heinlein tried hard to market work in the cinema and TV media, although his successes there were short lived. He also sold stories set in the nearer reaches of his future history to such "slick" magazines as *The Saturday Evening Post*, and began to write science fiction for children, because that was then the easiest way to market science fiction in a respectable (that is, hardcover) book form. He directed his new novels for adults—including the paranoid thriller *The Puppet Masters* (1951) and two transfigurations of classic works of popular fiction, *Double Star* (1956) and *The Door into Summer* (1957)—towards the few commercial hardcover publishers prepared to dabble in science fiction. He maintained a presence in the magazines, however, because he could sell serial rights to his novels there to earn extra money. He also allowed newly emergent specialist small presses to produce hardcover editions of his pulp stories, thus remaining central to the labelled genre even while he was trying to distance himself from it.

As genre science fiction migrated from the magazines into the general book market and more hardcover publishers started science fiction lines, Heinlein's career strategy came to seem less and less relevant to the prevailing circumstances. After producing twelve children's books for Scribner's on a yearly basis from 1947–1958, he allowed himself to test the limits of his editor's tolerance to destruction when he offered them the outspokenly militaristic *Starship Troopers* (1959), which was quickly taken up for publication as an adult book. He wrote one more children's novel, *Podkayne of Mars* (1963), expressly to test the limits of that market even further, but in order to get it published he bowed to editorial pressure and relented in his determination to kill off its heroine. He was less inclined to compromise elsewhere, however, and his career took off when the unusually long and unrepentantly polemical *Stranger in a Strange Land* (1961) became one of the genre's first best-sellers.

Stranger in a Strange Land is an account of a new messiah and his mentor, who serve as mouthpieces for

Heinlein's increasingly insistent political views and for a peculiar kind of *ecological mysticism. It was followed by an early experiment in generic fantasy, *Glory Road* (1963), and then by the uncompromising survivalist fantasy *Farnham's Freehold* (1964). His futuristic replay of the American Revolution, *The Moon Is a Harsh Mistress* (1966), which popularised the slogan TANSTAAFL (There Ain't No Such Thing as a Free Lunch) and featured an early quasi-adolescent *artificial intelligence, was widely celebrated as a return to form, but it proved to be his last aesthetically satisfying book. His work became increasingly self-indulgent thereafter.

When Heinlein took up the threads of his old future history again, in *Time Enough for Love* (1973), *The Cat Who Walked Through Walls* (1985), and *To Sail Beyond the Sunset* (1987), the whole enterprise seemed far crankier and far more dated than its early inclusions had in 1940–1941. Two of his other novels of the period, *I Will Fear No Evil* (1970) and *The Number of the Beast* (1980), were very weak, although they were stoutly defended by a company of loyal fans—many of whom had discovered science fiction as teenagers through his Scribner's novels—who felt that he could do no wrong. *Friday* (1982) and *Job—A Comedy of Justice* (1984) shone by comparison, but were essentially undistinguished. He was, however, forgiven his aged indiscretions by those who remembered what he had accomplished at the dawn of his career.

Heinlein's early contribution to pulp science fiction was groundbreaking, and set crucial precedents for other Campbellian writers to follow, but it did not do so by extrapolating scientific premises; what it did instead was to take new technological innovations for granted, wasting little time on accounts of how they might work, focusing on the social and psychological corollaries of their integration into the pattern of everyday life. His anticipations of future technological development were usually sound—although the space technology and nuclear technology he employed had already been standardised in pulp science fiction, he was unusually conscientious in making calculations, and he was able to imagine innovative applications of *biotechnology in *Beyond This Horizon*—but he rarely deployed his inventions within conventional story arcs, always attempting further steps into the political fallout of *technological determinism. His view of the future was always framed by practical political issues, tackled in a spirit of radical pragmatism. He encouraged other science fiction writers to develop a more sophisticated rhetorical style, and to employ it in the ritual celebration of the myth of the Space Age with an unashamed verve, but he also demonstrated more flagrantly than any other

writer that highly effective science fiction could be written without making any attempt at scientific discourse. The fact that he was fully capable of engaging in such discourse, had he so wished, only served to emphasise that there was no necessity to do so.

Heinlein's influence in genre science fiction is very persuasive, and his works—especially his children's novels—have often been imitated with a rare frankness, by such writers as Alexei Panshin, David Palmer, David Gerrold, and Jerry Pournelle. Explicit homage is paid to him in such stories as Jeffrey D. Kooistra's "The Return of the Golden Age" (1993) and in "Green Fire" (2000) by Eileen Gunn, Andy Duncan, Pat Murphy, and Michael Swanwick, in which he, Isaac Asimov, and L. Sprague de Camp become an anomalous presence in a classic *Fortean fantasy.

HINTON, C[HARLES] H[OWARD] (1853–1907)

English mathematician and writer. He was the son of a surgeon, James Hinton, who founded a cult that preached free love and polygamy—principles that Charles appears to have followed, in a discreet manner, until he was sacked from his post as a schoolmaster in 1885 and forced to flee England after being briefly imprisoned for bigamy.

Hinton's *Scientific Romances* (1886) helped popularise that term as a generic description, although it includes only two items of highly idiosyncratic fiction alongside essays in *speculative nonfiction developing the notion of the *fourth dimension. "A Plane World" is a fantasy in the *geometrical tradition of Edwin Abbott's *Flatland*, while "The Persian King" is a religious allegory developing a mathematical model of Christian redemption. The two novellas in *Stella and An Unfinished Communication* (1895) are slightly more orthodox, the first featuring an ingeniously theorised technology of *invisibility and the second employing the notion of time as a quasi-spatial dimension to develop an innovative notion of the afterlife. They were reprinted, along with more speculative essays, in *Scientific Romances: Second Series* (1902).

In the United States Hinton was briefly employed at Princeton University, where he invented the baseball pitching machine, but ended up working at the Patent Office after 1902. His efforts to spread the gospel of the fourth dimension prompted many articles in American popular magazines and a 1909 contest sponsored by *Scientific American* for the best short essay explaining the notion. His most sustained exercise in mathematical fiction was *An Episode of Flatland* (1907), whose two-dimensional beings live on the rim of a circular world, but his greatest influence was indirect, in the contribution his essays made to the explanation of the working of H. G. Wells' *The Time Machine*. Wells may also have taken some inspiration for *The Invisible Man* from *Stella*.

Hinton's work was rediscovered and publicised by the ingenious mathematical fantasist Rudy *Rucker, who gave an elaborate account of it in *The Fourth Dimension* (1984), along with details of Hinton's colourful life. Michio Kaku also paid tribute to Hinton's pioneering efforts in *Hyperspace* (1994).

HISTORY OF SCIENCE, THE

A subcategory of the broader discipline of *history, which has several peculiar features. It is subject to some of the internal differences, including the conflict between interpretations that give the primary credit for developmental change to the genius of great men and interpretations that stress independent causal factors that bring forth the great men when their hour has come, but there is a much greater tendency in the history of science to regard the accumulation of knowledge as a process in its own right.

Although it also makes sense to speak of *progress in political and social terms, it seems far more obvious that science makes progress, in the sense that as theories improve, the practical knowledge derived from them inevitably becomes more elaborate and more effective. This assertion is not undeniable—*relativists consider theoretical progress to be an illusion—but it does seem that twentieth-century science is more competent than the science of earlier eras, whether it is judged by the capability of the technologies it produces or the elaboration of its theoretical insights.

Explanations in the history of science can make considerable use of the kind of imaginative identification regarded as the basis of historical method by such theorists as R. C. Collingwood; we may try to understand how Isaac *Newton came up with the theory of *gravity or Albert *Einstein devised the theory of *relativity by trying to duplicate their trains of thought and trying to understand why it seemed reasonable for them to follow the tracks they did. In the history of science, however, such explanations usually contain an extra feature that is absent from similarly formulated accounts of why Julius Caesar crossed the Rubicon or why Charles I declared war on his own parliament: an element of revelation, provable by empirical investigation. The objectivity of this feature of scientific discovery gives the history of science an independent dynamic, making it more easily representable as a history of ideas, developing according to an unfolding logic of their own, than histories of power struggles and social reforms;

indeed, it is possible to represent the latter kinds of history as consequences of the history of science and technology, as theories of *technological determinism endeavour to do.

For this reason, histories of science—whose production began with William Whewell's *History of the Inductive Sciences* (1837; rev. 1846; further rev. 1857)—tend to find historical discontinuity puzzling and problematic. Explaining discoveries rarely seems problematic, because they follow logically from consultation of the appropriate evidence; the principal challenge to the historian of science is to explain the lack of discovery in periods when the evidence was not properly consulted. It was for this reason that Francis *Bacon produced his theory of "idols", seeking to explain the past nonprogress of science by means of a series of obstructive factors.

Whewell's history, being reluctant to blame dogmatic Christianity for the thousand-year gap in the history of science that seemed to him to yawn like an abyss between the direct inheritors of Greek philosophy and the scientific revolutionaries of the Renaissance, blamed the conceptual improprieties of Aristotelian physics and the general unwillingness of Athenian philosophers to get their hands dirty by trying to ascertain whether what they claimed was actually true. As a believer in natural *theology, Whewell was reluctant to construe the history of science as a struggle against oppressive religion, although such nineteenth-century histories of science as John William Draper's *History of the Conflict Between Religion and Science* (1874) moved in that direction. It was in this view of history that the trial of *Galileo became the fulcrum of the scientific revolution. Whewell's history ignored evolutionary theory, contentedly omitting the ideas of the Chevalier de Lamarck, Erasmus Darwin, and Robert Chambers and seemingly having no inkling whatsoever—even in the third edition of 1857—of what was about to materialise in Charles Darwin's account of *The Origin of Species*. The immediate response to that publication fitted in very well with the Draperian kind of history of science that saw its tribulations as a result of foolish religious persecution, and the lingering legacy of *Creationism still lends considerable support to that view.

It was an attempt to explain the phenomenon of discontinuity that caused Thomas Kuhn to come up with the notion of scientific *paradigms, which repositioned the Baconian idols inhibiting the continuity of scientific progress within the scientific community rather than seeing them as external forces of oppression. This view was very influential in academic circles—though considerably more so in the human sciences than the natural sciences—but it had far less impact on literary representations of the history of science, where the melodramatic quality of the war between science and superstition is far more appealing. Antiscience fiction tends to see the overall situation in similar terms, although it prefers to regard science itself—or certain aspects thereof—as a form of superstition against which intellectual crusades require to be launched.

When the history of science is represented by historians or litterateurs as a chronicle of the heroic endeavours of Great Men, the contexts in which these individuals function are very different from the political arenas and literal battlefields on which the Great Men of social history contend. The Great Men of science are typically seen as solitary workers without companions or followers, who either relish that condition or bear it stoically. The publication of their results is often met with incomprehension or hostility, but they usually bear that stoically too, content to let the world catch them up in its own time. They rarely make fortunes—if they do, they tend to deem them irrelevant—and rarely seek power over their fellow men, because they are possessed of a finer kind of power. That, in essence, is what it means, in legendary terms—and perhaps in fact—to be a *scientist.

There is relatively little *alternative history fiction that deals with the history of science, although there is a good deal that deals with anachronistic technological innovations. L. Sprague de Camp followed his long article in *Astounding Science Fiction* on theories of history with a similar two-part article in the September and October 1941 issues, "The Sea-King's Armored Division", asking why Greek science petered out after Heron of Alexandria, and what might have happened if it had continued to evolve. Few of de Camp's contemporaries took up the theme, and when such hypotheses did come into consideration, it was mostly in the calculatedly irreverent context of *steampunk fiction. It is similarly rare for historical fiction to focus on the processes of scientific theorisation and discovery, although the greatest English historical novel, George Eliot's *Middlemarch* (1871–1872), takes care to include such processes in its panorama. Such works as Neal Stephenson's *Quicksilver* (2003) and Gary Shockley's "Of Imaginary Airships and Minuscule Matter" (2004) stand out even in the early twenty-first century as works of considerable originality, although—as with the missing thousand years in the history of science—the real wonder is surely that they had so few conspicuous predecessors.

HISTORY

The description and explanation of *past events in human society, based on documentary evidence. The field of "oral history" consists of written records of orally formulated recollections. The earliest written "histories"—those compiled in the fifth century B.C. by Herodotus and others—inevitably contain a good deal of *mythical and legendary material, which was repeated by subsequent historians for whom Herodotus was a documentary source. History can never be entirely purged of this kind of "legendary pollution", and its fictional intrusions are often reproduced prolifically, precisely because they were designed to have a powerful rhetorical effect. The essential uncertainty of history is further confused by the fact that written documents can be deceptive, just as oral traditions can be accurate.

"Scientific" historians regard their work as an attempt to sort out the truth from the fiction, often recruiting *archaeological evidence to serve as a check on documentary sources, but some historians have seen their mission as a matter of drawing lessons—particularly moral lessons—from the past. The genre of historical fiction is similarly divided in its priorities, but its nature imposed a further level of complication, neatly illustrated by chapter IX of Robert Graves' *I, Claudius* (1934), in which the narrator is caught up in an argument between the historians Pollio and Livy. Pollio argues that history should be "a true record of what happened", forsaking all poetic and oratorical devices, whereas Livy argues that a history should have an "epic theme" so that it might better serve as an inspirational guide to its readers. Claudius, asked to arbitrate between the two, sides with Pollio, thus implying that his own narrative is of Pollio's sort—whereas it is, of course, actually Graves' composition and very definitely of Livy's sort. Most history and all historical fiction has, in fact, been written in accordance with Livy's prospectus, although many writers in both categories have pretended to be followers of Pollio for rhetorical purposes.

Philosophers of history from the Baron de Montesquieu to R. C. Collingwood have pointed out that historical explanation is significantly different from explanation in natural science. While natural scientists frame explanations by setting particular events in the context of general laws, historians seek their explanations in terms of idiosyncratic motives that can only be grasped by the historian "putting himself in the shoes" of the actor. This is a narrative process in itself, so history of this sort is much more closely akin to fiction than most other kinds of nonfiction, and the historical novel is potentially more useful as a quasi-scientific instrument than most other kinds of fiction. Speculative historical fiction involving *time travel may be even more useful in this respect than straightforward historical fiction, in that it introduces a privileged observer with a historian's interests and sceptical eye. It does not mater how arbitrary the timeslip might be that delivers the observer in question; what matters is the scrupulousness of his observations upon arrival. Timeslip romances written by academic historians, such as G. G. Coulton's *Friar's Lantern* (1906), may be a little more useful than those written by conscientious amateurs, such as J. Storer Clouston's *The Man in Steel* (1939), but those with additional complications born of narrative ambitions, such as Henry James' *The Sense of the Past* (1917), may be more useful still. (James did not manage to complete *The Sense of the Past*, but an ending was improvised when the story was adapted for the stage in 1929 by J. L. Balderston and J. C. Squire, as *Berkeley Square*.)

If potential misrepresentation is a problem in historical fiction, it is no more problematic than it is in history itself. Given the powerful reasons that routinely lead people to misrepresent their motives—in order to make their behaviour seem more rational and more moral than it usually is—the assistance lent to any act of identification by documentary evidence is inevitably treacherous. There is a sense in which *all* history is fantasy when it attempts to venture beyond mere matters of recorded happenstance. Because history inevitably intrudes upon the present, supplying justifications for decisions made and actions taken, the people to whom historians are responsible often have powerful reasons for wanting it to be slanted in a particular direction; writers of history and historical fiction may well be subject to equally powerful forces. The extremes to which William Shakespeare went when he set out to blacken the reputation of Richard III were born of political rather than literary dishonesty, and no Elizabethan historian would have dared to set the record straight.

The everyday reasons that all social actors have for misrepresenting their motives are greatly exaggerated in certain circumstances. Many actors involved in socially significant affairs have good reasons for wanting to keep their actions secret, and sometimes to engage in active dissimulation in the production of deceptive documents—economic historians relying on accounts made up for tax purposes often have reason to suspect that they may not be an entirely accurate record of business transacted—and this adds considerably to the mass of historical disinformation. There is, in fact, no other intellectual discipline so heavily burdened with disinformation (that is, calculated lies) as well as misinformation (honest mistakes).

This situation is further compounded by the fact that history is a very convenient medium for scholarly fantasy, because hypotheses relating to the causality of past events can rarely be tested to destruction. Not only can known events be reinterpreted, but historians are often able to indulge in wholesale invention, as in Geoffrey of Monmouth's *History of the Kings of Britain* (ca. 1135), which invented the myth of King Arthur. Such endeavours maintained the prolific production of wholly fictitious legends into the twentieth century, and the flow showed no sign of abating as the twenty-first century began. The imaginary components of scholarly fantasies invariably seize the popular imagination far more assertively than the mundane seeds of fact from which the foliage of fantasy sprouts, as demonstrated by *A General History of the Pyrates* (1724) by "Captain Johnson" (Daniel Defoe), which invented some of the pirates who became the most famous of the breed and embellished the careers of several others, and Jules Michelet's *La Sorcière* (1862; trans. as *Satanism and Witchcraft*), which invented the pagan witch cult on which many modern lifestyle fantasies are based.

Attempts by scientific historians to sift the truth of what happened from the misinformation and disinformation that surrounds it are further confused by the fact that the data they reject—"damned data" in Charles *Fort's terminology—are rarely simply forgotten. Such data often survive as legend even though it is universally accepted that they refer to events that never actually happened. The mythical past still thrives, to a remarkable degree, alongside the historical past, and intricately entwined with it. This offers considerable opportunities to writers of historical fiction, even if they are reluctant to stray into the realms of historical fantasy.

The notion that there were "secret histories" running alongside the fraction of recorded history saved by scientific historians supports various kinds of fictional enterprise, and is particularly hospitable to "conspiracy theories" in the broadest sense: the notion that scientific history is itself a patchwork of deceptive documents. Such fiction is equally amenable to the elaborate quasi-academic concoctions of such works as Umberto Eco's *Il Pendolo di Foucault* (1988; trans. as *Foucault's Pendulum*) and such melodramatic thrillers as Dan Brown's *The Da Vinci Code* (2003). Ironically, the most "scientific" of all kinds of historical fiction is not scrupulous naturalistic fiction but the subgenre of *alternative history, which is forced to engage with theories of historical causation in order to extrapolate patterns of events that might have happened if some crucial event had worked out differently.

Collingwood, in making his case for the idiographic nature of historical explanation, insists that generalisations of the kind typical of natural science have no place in its methodology—although his own thesis is based on the not entirely reliable generalisation that people try to behave in accordance with rational self-interest, thus making it possible to work out why they did what they did, given what they knew and were trying to achieve. Many other theorists have, however, claimed to have discovered an underlying logic or pattern to historical development, and there has long been a running dispute between "great man" theorists who credit historical change to the innovative actions of exceptional individuals and theorists who believe that great men are merely the product of their times and circumstances, enactors of some irresistible process of which they are unconscious. The greatest of all historical novels, Leo Tolstoy's *Voyna i mir* (1863–1869; trans. as *War and Peace*) represents itself as a scientific enquiry investigating this question, and comes down on the latter side, although it remains unclear whether Tolstoy was a genius who perceived this truth by his own efforts or merely an instrument of his era.

Historical fiction is very often idiographic in scale, but whenever it broadens its canvas significantly—whether laterally, as in Tolstoy's case, or temporally—it becomes dependent on generalisation of some kind. The most extensive panoramic views of human history, such as Eugène Sue's *Les mystères du peuple* (1849–1857; trans. in 21 vols. as *The Mysteries of the People*), Charles Godfrey Leland's *Flaxius* (1902), Johannes V. Jensen's *Den Lange Rejse* (1908–1922; trans. as *The Long Journey*), Katharine Burdekin's *The Rebel Passion* (1929), and Vardis Fisher's Children of God series (1943–1960), often extrapolate *anthropological theories or *theological theses, while the more modest accounts of historical change contained in the "family saga" subgenre deal far more frequently with matters of hereditary *psychology, but fiction's aesthetic dependence on patterns and holistic structures commits all authors of such works to *some* kind of theorisation.

The set of theories of history that proved to be most significant as a historical agent was that which represented historical change as a dialectical process, in which a series of theses generated antitheses, whose conflict created the motivation to bring about syntheses, which then became new theses generating new antitheses. In G. W. F. Hegel's version of the dialectic, the contending forces are ideas, and history is essentially a process of intellectual evolution, but in Karl *Marx's dialectical materialism, the contending forces are social classes, and history is essentially a matter of reforming and refining economic relations. Theories of this sort are not readily amenable to representation in historical fiction, although futuristic extrapolations of Marxist theory have given rise to a good deal of political fantasy.

Cyclic theories of history have not fared well in the context of historical science, where they are largely discredited, but they lend themselves much more readily to the literary exercise. The oft-quoted saw that "those who fail to learn from history are doomed to repeat it", even without the sarcastic addendum "first as tragedy, then as farce", is well adapted to the construction of story arcs leading to various kinds of closure. The early cyclic theories sketched out in Giambattista Vico's *Principii d'una scienza nuova* (1725) and the Comte de Volney's *Les ruines, ou Méditations sur les révolutions des empires* (1791) are reflected in numerous eighteenth- and nineteenth-century literary works, while Oswald Spengler's *Der Undertang des Abendlandes* (1918–1922; trans. as *The Decline of the West*) and Arnold Toynbee's *A Study of History* (12 vols.; 1934–1961) performed a similar function in the twentieth century, especially with reference to literary images of *decadence—although writers of fiction are very often willing to deal with eternal recurrences produced by arbitrary fate rather than any kind of underlying causative principle, as in such multistranded novels as Gerald Bullett's *Marden Fee* (1931), Nellie Kirkham's *Unrest of Their Time* (1938), and Alan Garner's *Red Shift* (1973).

Although the notion that theoretical analyses of history could provide a method of *futurological prediction was treated with considerable scepticism in the twentieth century, its logic flaws analysed in Karl Popper's *The Poverty of Historicism* (1957), futuristic fiction inevitably relies very heavily on the lessons of the past. Isaac Asimov's imaginary science of "psychohistory" suggested that the deficit might one day be made up, but it functions within his work as a facilitating device licencing the wholesale transfiguration of past events into future ones—a popular method of science-fictional story construction. Most theories of history—including theories of *technological determinism—resemble theories of biological *evolution in aspiring to provide competent accounts of the past while having no predictive power, because of their reliance on the input of random factors, but the construction of any futuristic scenario tacitly commits its designer to offer some sort of causative account of the manner in which the world of the present was transformed into the world of the story. Compilers of such accounts sometimes stress the unpredictability of the chain of connecting events, but if their purpose is alarmist or inspirational—as it very often is—they are more likely to argue that it *might* have been anticipated, if only people had been wiser.

Future histories have an obvious utility in futuristic fiction, in providing frameworks into which series of stories can be fitted; such frameworks are useful to readers, by providing backcloths that facilitate the understanding of particular stories, and are also useful

233

to writers, in that their extension and elaboration can generate story ideas and marketable series plans. The development of genre science fiction was considerably assisted by its adoption of the myth of the *Space Age as a future-historical framework, and many writers found it convenient to develop their own customised versions of it as venues for their particular endeavours. Even in the more loosely organised genre of British *scientific romance, the future history that Olaf Stapledon elaborated in *Last and First Men* (1930) not only provided an overt backcloth for *Last Men in London* (1932) but a tacit frame for several of his subsequent endeavours. Although the extensive future histories produced by writers of scientific romance prior to Stapledon's—including James B. Alexander's *The Lunarian Professor* (1909) and John Lionel Tayler's *The Last of My Race* (1924)—had not been elaborated in the same way, there is a sense in which all of them can be seen as variants of the scheme sketched out in H. G. Wells' "Man of the Year Million" (1893).

Pulp science fiction writers were given an unusually thorough introduction to theories of history by L. Sprague de Camp's two-part article on "The Science of Whithering" in the July and August 1940 issues of *Astounding*, which discussed Hegel, Marx, and Count Gobineau before going on to provide an elaborate subcategorisation of cyclic theorists. De Camp classified Spengler and Toynbee as "pessimistic mystics", contrasting them with "optimistic mystics" such as Pitirim Sorokin, "pessimistic materialists" such as Stanley Casson and Jose Ortega y Gasset, and "optimistic materialists" such as Vilfredo Pareto and Lewis Mumford. Robert A. *Heinlein published details of his future history in the May 41 issue of the magazine; its unmistakable echoes of Spengler and Toynbee may well derive from de Camp's account. The same issue carried the conclusion of de Camp's "The Stolen Dormouse", whose futuristic backcloth—the post-Imperial Feudalism of a future Corporate State—demonstrated that the scepticism shown in his article had not inhibited his willingness to indulge in pseudo-cyclic transfiguration.

A. E. van Vogt had already used Spenglerian theory to explain the patterns of human future history in "Black Destroyer" (1939)—which might well have prompted Campbell to commission de Camp's article—and he was to develop another cyclic model in "The Shadow Men" (1950; book as *The Universe Maker,* 1953). Jack Williamson extrapolated the Toynbeean thesis with some care in "Breakdown" (1942), and Charles L. Harness used it as background in *Flight into Yesterday* (1949; exp. 1953; aka *The Paradox Men*). C. M. Kornbluth's *conte philosophique* "The Only Thing We Learn"

(1949) applied a more cynical logic to the analysis of historical cycles.

The past-as-future history sketched out in Isaac *Asimov's Foundation series was eventually to prove the most influential of all such science-fictional devices, while the one developed from Spengler by James *Blish was the most ingeniously detailed. The modified Asimovian scheme employed in much of Poul Anderson's early work was similarly repetitive—his "Prophecy" (1949) cites both Spengler and Toynbee—but its underpinning by the *economic logic of evolving capitalism gave it a distinctive ideological complexion. Larry *Niven's future history of the exploration of Known Space makes similarly ingenious use of biological factors in accounting for the complex interactions of various species. Arnold Toynbee recanted his cyclic theory before he had completed the study that launched it, when such quasi-deterministic constructs fell out of fashion, but Toynbeean cyclicity continued to echo in such works as Walter M. Miller's *A Canticle for Leibowitz* (1960), Frederik Pohl and C. M. Kornbluth's "Critical Mass" (1961), Frank Herbert's *Dune* (1965), and Larry Niven's *A World out of Time* (1967), while the myth of the Space Age conscientiously echoed the myths of America's nineteenth-century past in its glorification of the "final frontier" and the tactics of its conquest and *colonisation. Like the mythical past of folklore, the mythical future of genre science fiction was very hospitable to cross-cultural and cross-temporal migrations, as exemplified by Poul Anderson's *The High Crusade* (1960), H. Beam Piper's *Space Viking* (1962), and Ben Bova's *Privateers* (1985).

The marked contrast of tone between American science fiction and British scientific romance is representable in terms of de Camp's subcategorisation of cyclic theorists; despite their extensive use of jargon drawn from Spengler and Toynbee, pulp science fiction writers were mostly "optimistic materialists", while their British counterparts tended towards pessimistic materialism. As citizens of a decadent empire in its terminal phase rather than the immediate inheritors of bold pioneers, many British writers of futuristic fiction imported elegiac and defeatist tones into such accounts of cyclic history as Edward Shanks's *People of the Ruins* (1920), Cicely Hamilton's *Theodore Savage* (1922; rev. as *Lest Ye Die*), and John Gloag's *Tomorrow's Yesterday* (1932). On the fringes of the genre, J. B. Priestley's various "Time Plays" dabbled unashamedly in pessimistic mysticism, while the qualified optimism of Olaf Stapledon's *Last and First Men* (1930) and H. G. Wells' *The Shape of Things to Come* (1933) took it for granted that hope for the future required long-term thinking; both books were roughly contemporary with Herbert

Butterfield's *The Whig Interpretation of History* (1931), which attacked historians who interpreted the past as a series of battles between progressive innovators and conservative forces of reaction—which the champions of progress always won in the end, aided by the forces of *technological determinism—on the grounds that the philosophy of progress was a mere illusion, conjured up by people in denial with regard to the inevitability of the Day of Judgement.

Toynbee's recantation was the prelude to an era in which grand theories of history fell into disrepute, although the decline of the consensual science-fictional future history forged in the 1940s was slow and grudging. The economic failure of the Soviet bloc prompted Francis Fukuyama's celebration of "The End of History" (1989), in the sense that dialectical materialism had no further phase to produce. (Many U.S. writers had, of course, always taken it for granted that liberal democracy was the evolutionary ideal and ultimate goal of all political systems.) Some philosophers of science—notably John Barrow—similarly began to contemplate an end to scientific progress as the limits of the discoverable were attained, although several technological discoverers were convinced that what had already been discovered was enough to produce a sociotechnological *singularity. It was perhaps inevitable, in such an intellectual climate, that so much imaginative fiction should turn away from the future towards the actual and mythical past, not only in the rapid proliferation of commodified fantasies with quasi-Mediaeval settings and alternative histories, but in the development of the *steampunk subgenre and the increasing sophistication of time travel stories dealing with past eras.

Time travel was extensively developed in the latter half of the twentieth century as a hypothetical method of historical research that might correct many inherited illusions, as in Isaac Asimov's "The Dead Past" (1955). Significant variants of the theme include Connie Willis' accounts of the endeavours of an Oxford History Department of the future, as featured in such works as "Fire Watch" (1982), *Doomsday Book* (1992), and *To Say Nothing of the Dog* (1998), Rebecca Ore's "Scarey Rose in Deep History" (1997), and Charles Sheffield's "Nuremburg Joys" (2000). As with many previous excursions into the past, stories of this kind that involved actual travel rather than mere chronoscopic viewing were routinely preoccupied with the necessity of conserving history from carelessly induced changes, but an interesting subgenre grew up of "historical rescue" stories in which time travellers snatch away historical characters on the point of elimination, leaving fake corpses behind to serve as evidence. John Varley's *Millennium* (1983) was only concerned with restocking a depopulated

future, but such stories as Nancy Kress's "And Wild for to Hold" (1991) and Paul Levinson's *The Plot to Save Socrates* (2005) went for high-profile targets whose experiences might be very valuable to historians.

Although science fiction writers continued to transfigure past events into future ones on a massive scale, they rarely invoked any kind of theory by way of apology, except to treat such theories satirically, as in Herbie Brennan's "Fourth Reich" (1974), Murray Yaco's "The Man Who Knew How to Make History" (1976), and James Van Pelt's "The Long Way Home" (2003). Paul J. McAuley's *Making History* (2000) revives the Great Man theory merely to dramatise the corollary thesis that behind every Great Man there is a manipulative woman.

A growing sense of the essential artificiality of history was greatly encouraged in the late twentieth century by an acute consciousness of the effect of the mass media on perceptions of history, as extrapolated in Kim Stanley Robinson's "Remaking History" (1989) and "A History of the Twentieth Century, with Illustrations" (1991). The same increasing consciousness of the artificiality of history prompted a boom in stories of secret history, which often became extraordinarily elaborate, as in Edward Whittemore's series *Sinai Tapestry* (1977), *Jerusalem Poker* (1978), *Nile Shadows* (1983), and *Jericho Mosaic* (1987). Accounts of the imaginary histories of all manner of secondary worlds were affected by the same trend, whose most noticeable by-products include Angélica Gorodischer's *Kalpa Imperial* (trans. 2003).

HORROR

An unpleasant sensation, usually classified as a compound of emotions such as fear, apprehension, and repulsion. It is distinct from terror because terror is normally a response to a direct personal threat, while horror is often a voyeuristic reaction to something happening to a third party. For this reason it may be defined as an *aesthetic response rather than an emotional one; it is seen as a key component of "the sublime" in Edmund Burke's aesthetic philosophy. Horror fiction is an anomalous genre, in that it is defined by the effect it is supposed to have on the reader rather than by its contents.

The relationship between science and horror is complex. On the one hand, science is a major factor in ordering our perception of the world and rendering it comprehensible, thus promoting a sense of well-being. On the other hand, it sometimes challenges other ideas—particularly religious ones—that serve a similar function and tends to undergo internal conceptual revolutions that call into question notions that previously produced a sense of well-being. Science also facilitates the development of socially disruptive technologies, which can give rise to a similar unease.

The revelation that the world of sensory experience, mundane time calculation, and social interaction is a network of appearances, behind which lie the arcane realities of cosmology, atomic physics, and geological time, gives modern theories in natural science an innate sublimity, in Burke's sense, which is linked to a subgenre of speculative "cosmic horror fiction". The literary reflection of this kind of horror, prominent in the works of H. P. Lovecraft and other members of his school, tends to be esoteric. Mass-market horror fiction makes much more use of a more visceral squeamishness, easily invoked by images of bodily violation, whether by virtue of violent attack or surgical intervention. That kind of "yuck factor" is—as J. B. S. *Haldane points out—also applicable to *biological inventions, insofar as they seem implicitly "unnatural", and is liberally exploited in fictional developments of what Isaac *Asimov called the *Frankenstein complex.

Another subgenre of horror fiction to which scientific theories are somewhat relevant is *psychological horror fiction; the literary exploitation of the "darkness" allegedly lurking in the hearts and souls of men is one of the principal motive forces of generic crime fiction as well as many exercises in existentialist fiction taking their thematic cue from Kurtz's final declamation in Joseph Conrad's *Heart of Darkness* (1902). Supernatural horror fiction is, by definition, outside the scope of science, but that very definition emphasises the subgenre's dependence on perceived breakdowns and violations of scientific determination. As Tzvetan Todorov pointed out in *Introduction à la littérature fantastique* (1970), there is particular dramatic tension to be obtained from stories that hesitate between psychological and supernatural interpretations of anomalous and disturbing events, effectively savouring a choice between different species of horror.

Genre science fiction includes a good deal of horror fiction, although *hard science fiction is intrinsically resistant to any suggestion that invention is innately horrific. The mass production of *monsters and the use of *aliens in menacing and disruptive roles also provoked a certain ideological resistance at the core of the genre. Although hard science fiction usually represents itself as a crusade on behalf of rational plausibility, it is also a crusade on behalf of the insistence that technological innovation really is socially beneficial and that a benign sense of wonder ought eventually to triumph over the paranoid aspects of the sublime and the yuck factor.

The narrative convenience and ready-made effectiveness of the standard horror fiction story formula —in which a nasty threat is intensified by degrees until it reaches a climax in which it is exorcised by a *deus ex machina*—ensures its continued survival and success in the media marketplace, and probably guarantees that it will always thrive to a greater extent than its ideological opposite. For this reason, enthusiasts for hard science fiction are apt to react to horror science fiction in exactly the same way that the heroes of horror science fiction react to their own antagonists, horrified by their hideously chimerical nature and direly threatening aspect. Champions of science frequently react to the very idea of the "supernatural" in much the same way, especially when it adopts *pseudoscientific disguise. The proposition that nothing should horrify us but horror itself is, however, just as untenable as the suggestion that there is nothing for us to fear but fear itself.

HOYLE, SIR FRED (1915–2001)

British astronomer, astrophysicist, and writer. He completed a turbulently unconventional education by graduating from Cambridge University, becoming a Fellow of St. John's College in 1939 but never bothering to submit a Ph.D. thesis. He worked on radar systems for the Admiralty during World War II, and it was while engaged on this research that he met Thomas Gold and Herman Bondi, with whom he formed an axis of opposition to what he disdainfully referred to as the *Big Bang theory of the cosmos. Their ideological opposition was formulated as the "steady state" or "continuous creation" theory, which maintained a cosmological principle of unchanging uniformity, in spite of evidence relating to galactic red-shifts, by proposing that new matter is spontaneously generated in intergalactic space, filling in gaps that would otherwise be left by universal expansion.

Hoyle, Gold, and Bondi clung hard to the steady state theory in spite of the absence of any plausible mechanism for the spontaneous generation of matter, and were reluctant to abandon it even when the discovery of the cosmic background radiation supplied the Big Bang theory with a key item of supportive evidence. In the 1960s, in collaboration with Jayant V. Narilkar, Hoyle modified his version of the steady state model to incorporate local phases of rapid expansion, anticipating the contribution of inflation theories to models of the Big Bang. Astronomical data provided by instruments such as the Hubble Space Telescope, however, continued to provide further evidence of universal evolution, making the cosmological principle on which the steady state theory had been based seem mistaken. Hoyle won more general support and acclaim with work done in the 1940s and 1950s—summarised in *Some Recent Researches in Solar Physics* (1949), *Star Formation* (1963), and *Nucleosynthesis in Massive Stars and Supernovae* (1965)—that explained the synthetic process by which heavier elements are manufactured in stars. This made a significant indirect contribution to the Big Bang theory, helping to explain the manner in which the primal elements were formed in the early universe.

Hoyle was a committed populariser of science, and took early advantage of the *radio medium—in accordance with the cultural improvement policy adopted by the BBC's first director-general, John Reith—to do work of that kind. Some of his early performances were reprinted in *The Nature of the Universe: A Series of Broadcast Lectures* (1950), which established the groundwork for such later texts as *A Decade of Decision* (1953), *Frontiers of Astronomy* (1955), *Man and Materialism* (1956), *Of Men and Galaxies* (1964), *Galaxies, Nuclei and Quasars* (1965), *Man in the Universe* (1966), *The New Face of Science* (1971), and *The Cosmogony of the Solar System* (1978). In 1958, Hoyle was appointed Plumian Professor of Astronomy and Experimental Philosophy at Cambridge, and in 1967 he founded the Institute of Theoretical Astronomy there. He was knighted in 1972 but resigned as director of the Institute and severed his ties with Cambridge in 1973 following disputes regarding the development of its research programme.

Hoyle's dogged pursuit of unorthodoxy continued in his insistent development of a sophisticated version of the *panspermia hypothesis, which held that life had originated in space and was initially brought to Earth by comets, whose debris continued to rain biological material—including agents of disease—upon the planet's surface. The idea was first exposed to public view in the science fiction novel *The Black Cloud* (1957), but Hoyle developed it much more elaborately in works of speculative nonfiction written in collaboration with Chandra Wickramasinghe, including *Lifecloud: The Origin of Life in the Universe* (1978), *Diseases from Space* (1979), *Evolution from Space* (1981), *The Intelligent Universe: A New View of Creation and Evolution* (1983), *Cosmic Life-Forces* (1988), and *Our Place in the Cosmos: The Unfinished Revolution* (1993). Although spectroscopic analysis of cosmic dust clouds produced increasing evidence of complex organic molecules, his peers remained sceptical, especially of the claim that epidemics are caused by temporary deluges of extraterrestrial viruses rather than interpersonal infection.

Hoyle's other science fiction novels include *Ossian's Ride* (1959), a relatively conventional thriller involving a scientific mystery, and *October the First Is too Late* (1966), in which the Earth's surface is disrupted by timeslips. *Element 79* (1967) collected his early short fiction. With John Elliot he developed two TV serials in which a radio broadcast from space provides instructions for building an advanced computer that turns out to have an agenda of its own, *A for Andromeda* (1961; novelisation 1962) and *The Andromeda Breakthrough* (1962; novelisation 1964). Most of his later fiction was written in collaboration with his son Geoffrey, much of it being aimed at children, extrapolating the popularising efforts of the Molecule Club, which mounted educational plays and displays in schools and theatres. The more adventurous items include the graphic *disaster story *The Inferno* (1973), in which the effects of an explosion in the galactic core devastate the Earth, and *The Incandescent Ones* (1977), whose android protagonist abandons a dystopian Earth for a transcendent existence on *Jupiter. His last solo novel, *Comet Halley* (1985), provided another vehicle for his ideas about the extraterrestrial origins of life.

The determined originality of Hoyle's thinking, the ingenuity with which he extrapolated his ideas, and the stubbornness with which he defended them against criticism are all typical of the habitual rebel against orthodoxy on whose efforts theoretical progress routinely depends. In two of his most sustained endeavours, he appeared to back the wrong horse, but the competition he provided was a useful stimulus in each case, and the precise extent of the historical credit due to him was still undecidable at the beginning of the twenty-first century. His literary endeavours were equally adventurous, their occasional awkwardness compensated by their determination to deal with scientific issues and their social significance in a forthright fashion.

HUXLEY, ALDOUS (1894–1963)

British writer. His brother Julian (1887–1975) was an accomplished biologist and populariser of science, and their relationship facilitated the exchange of ideas between two social circles that might otherwise have drawn apart more rapidly, in accordance with the process of diversification observed by C. P. *Snow. Huxley amalgamated the political ideas of the scientists he met in this fashion into a sketch of a future "Rational State" in his nostalgic conversation piece *Crome Yellow* (1920). One of them, J. B. S. *Haldane, was the model for the biologist Shearwater in *Antic Hay* (1923).

Following his brother's extrapolation of ideas from Haldane's *Daedalus* (1923) into the cautionary satire "The Tissue Culture King" (1926), Aldous Huxley incorporated ideas from the essay into a much more extensive account of the Rational State in the classic Utopian satire *Brave New World* (1932), whose scathing black comedy was taken very seriously by many of its readers. *Brave New World* is one of two futuristic fictions—the other being George Orwell's *Nineteen Eighty-Four*—that had a tremendous impact on British conceptions of the future and the threats contained therein, and many of its key images were adopted into common parlance and political rhetoric. Set in the year 632 A.F. (After Ford), it substitutes new institutions for the pillars of English society; the church is replaced by a "community singery", schools by "conditioning centres". The latter are attached to "hatcheries", where children are born ectogenetically in cloned batches, carefully fitted by embryological manipulation for life as alphas, betas, gammas, or deltas in a social hierarchy whose strata are biologically hypostasised.

The imagery of *Brave New World* is echoed in many subsequent *dystopian novels, most explicitly in L. P. Hartley's *Facial Justice* (1960), whose citizens are similarly classified into alphas, betas, and gammas and where envy of the ruling class is carefully discouraged by "betafication". Huxley's own subsequent ventures into speculative fiction included *After Many a Summer Dies the Swan* (1939: aka *After Many a Summer*), which features a lurid caricature of a *scientist, Dr. Obispo. Obispo's search for the secret of immortality in the guts of carp comes unstuck when it turns out that extension of the human lifespan merely allows the "neotenic ape" to attain full maturity. *Ape and Essence* (1948) is a full-blooded dystopia inspired by postwar alarmism, based on an unproduced film script.

Like many of his readers, Huxley began to take the warnings issued sarcastically in *Brave New World* very seriously, extrapolating them much more earnestly in the nonfictional *Brave New World Revisited* (1958). He had produced an earlier tract that was considerably less pessimistic, *Science, Liberty, and Peace* (1946), but his hopes for the future were increasingly distanced from the potentialities of science towards pseudoscientific mysticism. He began an empirical investigation of the liberating effects of *psychotropic drugs, whose results were reported in *The Doors of Perception* (1954) and *Heaven and Hell* (1956) before being incorporated into a blueprint for Utopia in *Island* (1962). The proposition that a new philosophy of life based in Eastern mysticism might save the world from the scientifically engendered horrors sketched out in *Brave New World Revisited* proved

unconvincing even within the narrative, however, and the hypothetical enclave of sanity seems to be doomed as the novel ends.

The Politics of Ecology: The Question of Survival (1963) was a significant contribution to the evolving debate about the necessity of paying more attention to *ecological matters, and *Literature and Science* (1963) was a carefully considered response to the debate started by C. P. Snow, but Huxley's death prevented him from carrying either train of thought any further. Although he now appears to be a central figure in the tradition of British antiscience fiction, there was always a determined scientific method in Huxley's approach to argument and exemplification; he could not have been nearly so effective in his satirisation had he not been able to extrapolate his ideas and arguments so skilfully. Unlike C. S. Lewis, whose equally vitriolic reaction against Haldane was visceral and based in religious faith, Huxley was primarily a rationalist, who never allowed aesthetic distaste to overrule the requirement to build a cogent argument.

HYPERSPACE

A term coined to describe the *space extended along a hypothetical extra dimension added to the three dimensions of conventional perception. It was introduced into science fiction by John W. *Campbell Jr. in *Islands of Space* (1931), in order to provide a jargon of apology permitting a spaceship to avoid the Einsteinian limitation on travelling faster than light. The notion that some such "higher space" might be the venue of the afterlife—which dated back to the works of C. H. *Hinton and nineteenth-century *occult theorists of the *fourth dimension—had previously been imported into pulp science fiction in Victor A. Endersby's "The Gimlet" (1930), but Campbell's application of the idea proved crucial. The possibility that shortcuts through interstellar space might be taken with the aid of some kind of topographical trickery was so useful in extending the scope of futuristic fiction to a galactic stage that it was taken up on a massive scale by other writers, although it was still sufficiently unfamiliar to be foregrounded as a novel idea in Nelson S. Bond's "The Scientific Pioneer Returns" (1940). The possibility of tapping hyperspatial energy is featured as a potentially apocalyptic one in Alfred Bester's "The Push of a Finger" (1942).

Hyperspace quickly became part of the standard vocabulary of science fiction, although a series of variants was developed alongside it. The most popular was "space warp" (another term used in *Islands in

Space), although many writers preferred "subspace", the term ultimately adopted in the *Star Trek* TV series for the realm into which the "warp field" projected around starships extends. Clifford D. Simak's *Cosmic Engineers* (1939) elaborated the notion into a multidimensional "inter-space" filled with existential shadows and phantoms of probability, while the starship in Eric Frank Russell's "Ultima Thule" (1951) is precipitated by a malfunctioning hyperdrive into the "unspace" into which Creation first expanded. Subsequent variants included the "N-space" of Robert A. Heinlein's *Starman Jones* (1953), the "tau-space" of Colin Kapp's "Lambda-1" (1962) and "The Imagination Trap" (1967), the "hypospace" of Michael Flynn's "Eifelheim" (1986), the "irrational space" of David Gerrold's *The Voyage of the Star Wolf* (1990), the "*nada*-continuum" of Eric Brown's *Engineman* (1994) and other stories, the "imaginary space" of Catherine Asaro's *Primary Inversion* (1995) and its sequels, and the "Q-Space" of Ian Watson's "One of Her Paths" (2001).

Science-fictional attempts to visualise what hyperspace might look like often depict it as a chaotic environment intrinsically confusing to the senses; notable examples include Frederik Pohl's "The Mapmakers" (1955), R. Lionel Fanthorpe's *Hyperspace* (1959), Clifford D. Simak's "All the Traps of Earth" (1960), Brian N. Ball's *Timepiece* (1968), and Elizabeth Lynn's *A Different Light* (1978). It is often portrayed as a challenging environment requiring physical or psychological modification of its travellers, as in Frank Herbert's *Dune* (1965), Michael Moorcock's *The Sundered Worlds* (1966), Vonda McIntyre's "Aztecs" (1977), David Brin's "The Warm Space" (1985), and Reginald Bretnor's accounts of Gilpin's Space, including a "A Taste of Blood" (1988). Science-fictional hyperspaces sometimes have exotic indigenous life-forms, like those featured in Christopher Grimm's "Someone to Watch Over Me" (1959). The notion of a hyperspace whose limiting velocity is slower than that pertaining to our cosmos is used as a gimmick in George R. R. Martin's "FTA" (1974) but given more elaborate consideration in John E. Stith's *Redshift Rendezvous* (1990). Timothy Zahn's *The Icarus Hunt* (1999) features an unusually elaborate account of a hyperspatial chase.

Hyperspace was adopted into theoretical physics when the development of modern *atomic theory encouraged widespread speculation as to the number of dimensions that must exist if the behaviour of the subatomic particles associated with the four fundamental *forces were to be accommodated within the same conceptual framework. It was repopularised as a scientific term by Michio Kaku's *Hyperspace* (1994).

HYPNOSIS

A term coined in the 1830s by James Braid to describe an induced "trance state" in which an individual seems unreceptive to environmental stimuli save for instructions issued by the hypnotist. Such instructions are obeyed automatically, even if they do not take effect until after the hypnotised individual is returned to ordinary consciousness. The latter phenomenon is usually termed "posthypnotic suggestion".

Although reports of similar trance states and their inducement go back to antiquity, the practice of induction was popularised in late eighteenth-century Europe by Anton *Mesmer, when he supposedly discovered that the magnets he had employed before 1780 were unnecessary to his treatments. Mesmer's technique was adapted in the early 1840s by a number of surgeons, most notably John Elliotson and James Esdaile, who claimed that it allowed operations to be carried out painlessly; it was the deriding of their claims as "mesmeric humbug" in the *Lancet* that prompted Braid to devise the new term. Braid conceded that no "magnetic fluid" was involved, claiming instead that the key to inducing the trance state was the intense concentration of the subject on a particular object; this gave rise to the popular image of hypnotists requiring patients to concentrate on spinning pocket watches or swinging pendulums.

In spite of Braid's defence, Elliotson was forced to resign his position at University College Hospital in 1838. He continued to contribute propagandistic articles to *The Zoist: A Journal of Cerebral Physiology and Mesmerism* (1843–1856), but hypnotism was largely relegated to the realms of *pseudoscience and the *occult revival in Britain. In France, however, mesmeric techniques continued in use until the 1880s, when they were taken up by Hippolyte Bernheim, the professor of medicine at Strasbourg. Bernheim was challenged by Jean-Martin Charcot, professor of neurology at the Sorbonne, who supplemented standard proofs of the irrelevance of magnets and fluids with a theory linking hypnotic suggestibility to "hysteria".

While Charcot's experiments using hypnosis to treat hysteria encouraged other psychologists, including Sigmund *Freud, to adopt it into their practices, Bernheim's position was supported by others, including Ambroise Liébault. They formed a "Nancy school", whose defiant contention that anyone could be hypnotised under the right conditions was imported into the Parisian courts by the advocate Jules Légois, who argued that people could be coerced into committing crimes by hypnosis—a suggestion that had a greater effect on contemporary crime fiction than jurisprudence. Notable fictions featuring hypnotically talented criminals include Violet Fane's *The Story of*

Helen Davenant (1889), Guy Boothby's Doctor Nikola series (1895–1901), George Griffith's *A Mayfair Magician* (1905), and Sax Rohmer's Fu Manchu series (launched 1913).

These controversies helped to make hypnotism into a fashionable talking point, reflected in many society novels of the period; it plays a particularly prominent role in Henry James' *The Bostonians* (1886). Writers of popular fiction exaggerated its supposed effects in various ways, following melodramatic precedents set by Edgar Allan Poe in "The Mesmeric Revelation" (1844) and "The Facts in the Case of M. Valdemar" (1845), Wilkie Collins' *The Woman in White* (1860), and Charles Dickens' *The Mystery of Edwin Drood* (1870). One that spawned a new legend was George du Maurier's development of the character of Svengali in *Trilby* (1894). Other pioneering tales of hypnotic domination included Francis Marion Crawford's *The Witch of Prague* (1891) and Mrs. H. D. Everett's *Nemo* (1900; by-lined Theo Douglas); the notion was eventually carried forward into pulp science fiction in such stories as Ross Rocklynne's "A Matter of Length" (1946).

Jean Lorrain's "L'égrégore" (1887; trans. as "The Egregore") invented a species of hypnotic life force predator; similar figures were featured in J. Maclaren Cobban's *Master of His Fate* (1890)—whose life force vampire is trained by Charcot at the Salpêtrière— Arthur Conan Doyle's *The Parasite* (1895), and George S. Viereck's *The House of the Vampire* (1907), while further antagonists whose hypnotic talents are essentially supernatural include those featured in H. Rider Haggard's *She* (1888), Richard Marsh's *The Beetle* (1897), and Bram Stoker's *Dracula* (1897). Stories of this type often contained a strong erotic element, further exploited in such works as Sax Rohmer's "The Black Mandarin" (1922) and Maurice Dekobra's *Flammes de velours* (1927; trans. as *Flames of Velvet; aka The Love Clinic*). The idea that hypnotised subjects might function as oracles became a commonplace of occult fiction, although it was rarely extrapolated as earnestly or as extensively as it was in William Ford Stanley's *The Case of The Fox, Being His Prophecies Under Hypnotism of the Period Ending AD 1950* (1903). The notion of hypnotically induced "past life regression" was advertised in such novels as Mrs. Campbell Praed's *Nyria* (1904) and H. Rider Haggard's *The Ancient Allan* (1920) and *Allan and the Ice Gods* (1927).

Hypnosis continued to be exploited by various twentieth-century neurologists and psychiatrists, including Pierre Janet in France, Morton Prince in the United States, and Ivan Pavlov in Russia. The notion of the quasi-somnambulistic "trance state" gradually faded into the background as most investigators and medical users of the technique concluded that the essence of the phenomenon was a form of hypersuggestibility. In the meantime, hypnosis was extensively developed as a form of stage performance involving the inducement of volunteers to carry out various amusing actions and making particular use of comical confusion generated by the delayed effects of post-hypnotic suggestion. This particular trick also proved useful in theatrical farce and humorous fiction; it played a role in such murder mysteries as Richard S. Prather's *Dagger of Flesh* (1956), although its propriety as a *deus ex machina* was always suspect. It was the association with stage performance rather than the lingering legacy of Mesmer's pseudoscientific theories that haunted therapeutic practitioners throughout the twentieth century, consigning them to the marginal wilderness of "alternative medicine" in spite of new successes in enhancing anaesthesia and treating psychosomatic conditions. Speculative fictions featuring constructive accounts of hypnotherapy such as John D. MacDonald's "Cosmetics" (1948) and Theodore Sturgeon's "The Other Man" (1956) occupied an uneasy situation on the genre's fringe.

The notion of hypersuggestibility was separately developed in the notion of "brainwashing", a term initially popularised in association with interrogation and indoctrination techniques practiced by the Chinese during the Korean war, and dramatised in that context by such novels as Richard Condon's *The Manchurian Candidate* (1959). The idea was not new, however, having featured in anxieties about the use of "subliminal advertising" by the mass media, as dramatised in Wallace West's "The Phantom Dictator" (1935). Other pulp science fiction stories exploring the implications of hypersuggestibility included Henry Kuttner and C. L. Moore's "Margin for Error" (1947). The idea of brainwashing was subsequently renewed with reference to the recruitment and ideative reinforcement methods of religious cults, especially when attempts by parents to recover children lost to such organisations began to involve professional "de-programmers" whose job it was to unravel and dismantle convictions planted and secured by the cults. Its scientific investigation is dramatised in James Kennaway's *The Mind Benders* (1963; film, 1963), and the notion is cleverly extrapolated in Paul J. McAuley's *Mind's Eye* (2005).

The image of hypnosis suffered a sharp deterioration in the last two decades of the century because of widespread attempts to exploit the supposition that hypnosis could assist the recovery of memories, although its success in curing amnesia was much greater in works of fiction, such as Mary Higgins Clark's "The Anastasia Syndrome" (1989), Joy Fielding's "Trance" (1977), and Elizabeth Adler's *The Secret of the Villa Mimosa* (1995), than it was in fact. Experimentation with hypnosis in the interrogation of witnesses to crimes soon revealed that the quality of the information thus recovered was highly suspect—again it worked much better in novels of "forensic hypnotism," such as Richard Kessler's *Trance* (1993), than it ever did in reality.

Hypnosis was used so prolifically in "recovering" memories of past lives—as featured in such sensationalist exercises in Fortean reportage as Morey Bernstein's *The Search for Bridey Murphy* (1956; film, 1956)—abduction by aliens in *flying saucers, and

sexual abuse by parents that it soon became necessary to identify and label the phenomenon of "false memory syndrome". (Freud had earlier used the term "screen memory" to describe false memories produced in the process of repressing true ones.) The theme of hypnotically recovered memories retained a significant presence in speculative fiction, however, in such stories as Paul Di Filippo's "Seeing Is Believing" (2003) and Lawrence Schoen's "Requiem" (2005). The Svengali myth continued to echo throughout the twentieth century, revamped in such works as Renée Guerin's *The Singing Teacher* (1995).

I

IDEOLOGY

A term introduced into English as a version of the French term "idéologie", which had been used in 1796 by the rationalist philosopher Antoine Destutt de Tracy—who thus came to be known as the primary example of an "idéologue"—in order to redefine the philosophy of mind as a "science of ideas" rather than an exercise in *metaphysics. It soon came to be used, like *mythology, to refer to an assembly of ideas rather than a general theoretical study, usually with reference to political ideologies held as doctrines, often with specific reference to revolutionary or socialist ideas. To describe a notion as "ideological" then became, in practice if not in theory, tantamount to calling it "false". This kind of usage was deliberately turned around by Karl *Marx and Friedrich Engels in *Die Deutsche Ideologie* (written 1845–1846; trans. as *The German Ideology*), who used the term in their condemnatory critique of conservative ideas and ideals.

Although Marx and Engels saw ideology as something distinct from science, and looked forward to an "end of ideology" when people became capable of seeing and thinking clearly about their *economic situations, subsequent Marxist analysis was perfectly prepared to condemn "bourgeois science" along with bourgeois economic theory as "ideological". Because Marx saw ideas as aspects of an intellectual superstructure constructed on an economic base, his use of the notion had a theoretical dimension, whereby an ideology is a product of economic self-interest, the fundamental thesis of Marxist ideological theory

being that every person's ideas are shaped, usually unconsciously, to sustain their economic interests as members of a particular socioeconomic class.

The Marxist theory of ideology was extensively elaborated by Karl Mannheim in *Idéologie et utopie* (1929; trans. as *Ideology and Utopia*), becoming a central element of the *sociology of knowledge and a key element of Marxist literary criticism, displayed in such exercises as Lucien Goldmann's analysis in *Le dieu caché* (1955; trans. as *The Hidden God*) of the ideas of Jean Racine as a product of the declining economic fortunes of the aristocratic subdivision known as the *noblesse de robe*. Because ideological analysis focuses on the underlying psychological reasons people have for holding beliefs and defending them against criticism, it routinely sets aside questions regarding the objective validity or otherwise of the beliefs in question. Ideological enquiries into scientific ideas and beliefs, therefore, disregard the empirical evidence relating to such ideas and beliefs in order to ask what other reasons their proponents and holders have for favouring them. Because the assumed processes are largely unconscious, ideological analyses tend to be untestable, but they sometimes appear to provide plausible explanatory accounts of puzzling phenomena.

When ideological analysis offers hypothetical explanations of cases in which people stubbornly refuse to accept what seems to other people to be overwhelming empirical evidence, or cases in which people leap to conclusions far beyond the warrant of the evidence they actually have, they provide potentially valuable explanations of the fact that the course of scientific progress has rarely run smoothly. On the other hand, when ideological analysis offers hypothetical accounts of the reasons that scientists might have to believe their findings, without reference to empirical evidence, it seems severely sceptical of the whole scientific enterprise. Opinions differ sharply as to the extent to which the accepted body of scientific knowledge might be "ideologically polluted", extreme *relativists being inclined to dismiss all supposedly objective knowledge as a set of ideological mirages.

Twentieth-century discussion of this issue often uses the jargon of "value freedom", reflecting a sharp philosophical distinction between statements of fact and statements of value. Science, in attempting to deal exclusively with matters of fact, aspires to be "value-free" in itself, no matter what values particular scientists might espouse as individuals or members of particular social groups; the extent to which scientists can set aside their values in the practice of their science is, however, controversial. The fact that scientists could hardly operate at all without a passionate ideological commitment to the search for the truth only serves to confuse the issue.

The attempt to produce a Marxist science distinct from Western science, allegedly purged of its bourgeois ideological components, was a significant feature of policy in Soviet Russia, whose consequences included T. D. Lysenko's championship of neo-*Lamarckian ideas against Darwinian orthodoxy. Carl C. Lindegren's *The Cold War in Biology* (1966) offers a minutely detailed account of the ideological conflict between American "Mendelists" and Soviet "Michurinists". A more brutal version of the same way of thinking led Nazi Germany to attempt to banish "Jewish science" along with its originators; Albert *Einstein's theory of *relativity attracted criticism in both Soviet Russia and Nazi Germany on the grounds of its supposed ideological origins.

Fictional accounts of ideological distortion in science often focus on matters of individual status rather than more general socioeconomic factors, self-interest being construed in the immediate contexts of career prospects and earning power rather than anything more general. Accounts of value distortion by more general cultural factors, such as Howard L. Myers' "Out, Wit!" (1972) and Christopher Anvil's "Ideological Defeat" (1972), are relatively rare in genre science fiction, and usually refer to non-economic factors. The most ingenious science-fictional analyses of hypothetical ideologies are found in Ursula K. *Le Guin's Hainish series, the ideological context of science coming into its sharpest focus in her meticulous account of how and why a scientist born and raised in an anarchist society, rather than his rivals in a technologically developed capitalist society, came up with the physical theory credited to him in *The Dispossessed* (1974).

The ideology of science fiction itself has, inevitably, come under close scrutiny from European observers sensitive to the political bias of its central *myths. American science fiction was scathingly criticised on Marxist ideological grounds by Stanislaw Lem in essays in *Fantastyka i Futurologia* (1970; partly trans. in *Microworlds*) and its alleged pessimism was analysed in Gérard Klein's "Discontent in American Science Fiction" (1977) by means of the assertion that the relevant writers were affiliated to a particular sector of the technical intelligentsia whose hopes for social advancement had been disappointed in the wake of World War II. A much more thorough analysis of this sort was carried out, at considerably longer range, in Darko Suvin's *Victorian Science Fiction in the UK: The Discourses of Knowledge and Power* (1983), which is extraordinarily scrupulous in gathering and setting out the relevant evidence. American analyses of the ideology of American science fiction can be just as scathing, as evidenced by H. Bruce Franklin's *War Stars: The Superweapon and the American Imagination* (1988) and Norman Spinrad's novel *The Iron Dream* (1972), in which an alternative Adolf Hitler sublimates his dreams of world conquest in writing action-adventure fiction, and slots quite comfortably into the Golden Age of pulp science fiction.

IMPOSSIBILITY

The range of things that cannot happen. Science is often seen as a process for defining the boundary separating possibility from impossibility—or, at least, the boundary beyond which an event would have to be considered "miraculous", "supernatural", or "paranormal". Proverbial wisdom continues to insist that "anything can happen" and that "nothing is impossible", and the scientific insistence that the opposite is the case occasionally arouses resentment in lay people.

From a religious perspective, the presumption of Godly omnipotence implies that the limits of possibility are perennially subject—if only theoretically—to miraculous disruption. In the literary arena of a world within a text, the author is intrinsically omnipotent, and no limits of possibility apply. Anything that a writer can state in words can happen within a story, although this fact is subtly obscured by *aesthetic philosophies such as that of Alexander Baumgarten, who held that the best art is, by definition, the most accurately representative and that "heterocosmic" creativity is intrinsically deplorable.

Even people who agree wholeheartedly with Baumgarten's judgement are, however, aware that it is purely advisory; fiction is perfectly free to deal with all manner of occurrences and actions that would be impossible in actuality—and it would be very surprising, if not frankly perverse, were it not to take full advantage of that licence. There are, therefore, whole genres of fiction—generally aggregated under the headings "fantasy" and "supernatural fiction"—that deal exclusively and definitively with the impossible, and whole fictional media, such as the *cinema, whose evolution has been driven and dominated by techniques for representing the impossible. *Science fiction is a special case, in that its dealings with impossibility are restrained by a real or pretended determination to feature ideas and events that, although presently impossible in the actual world, might be possible if circumstances were to change in the future according to a possible pattern of development (or had been different in the past, had some event worked out differently in a possible manner).

The *philosophy of science developed by Karl Popper is founded on the observation that although it is impossible to produce sufficient confirmatory evidence to prove that a general statement is true, it is relatively easy to produce proof that certain statements—especially universal generalisations—are false. In this perspective, the success of science is not measured inclusively but exclusively—by the extent of what it has ruled impossible. Its progress is measured by its improved definitions of the boundaries of possibility, and its power is exercised by its declarations of impossibility.

It was this forceful narrowing down of belief by science, and the consequent imperious banishment of certain cherished ideas and images, that made John Keats resentful of Isaac *Newton's "unweaving the rainbow"—although even the Romantics took delight in the corrosive effect when it was applied to conservative illusions they did not like. Other poets, including Mark Akenside, in "The Pleasures of the Imagination" (1744), and Edgar Allan Poe, in "Al Aaraaf" (1827), argued that science had donated more than it had taken away. Oscar Wilde's essay regretting "The Decay of Lying" (1891) pointed out that science had not actually taken away anything at all, given that litterateurs were still perfectly free to represent impossibility, and that the imagery of the impossible might be even more valuable when boldly employed in a spirit of calculated fabulation than it had been while its users still clutched at frail illusions of possibility like drowning men at straws.

All fiction—even the most doggedly naturalistic—is blithely disrespectful of the bounds of possibility. In the world of experience, as perceived through the lenses of science, million-to-one chances come off only once in a million times, but in fiction the probability of a million-to-one shot coming off, when the plot requires it, is one. In fiction, there is no chance; everything is a matter of determination. Even if a writer should choose to let chance direct his plot, by throwing dice or drawing cards to determine what happens next, that would be a matter of decision. Possibility in fiction is subject to authorial whim rather than causal necessity; that, in effect, is what fiction *is*. No matter how respectful a work of fiction seems to be of the ostensible bounds of possibility, "impossibility" cannot mean the same thing in works of fiction as it does in science. In mathematics, a *paradox is a conclusive proof of an assertion's falsity, or a deeply worrying puzzle; in fiction, a paradox may be an amusing rhetorical flourish.

This essential and irremediable difference between the universes of science and fiction has a considerable confusing effect on the relationship between the two, which becomes particularly acute with reference to explicit fictional treatments of scientific impossibility. New confusions began to emerge in the literary representation of scientific impossibility when notions of scientific impossibility began to diverge sharply from those of "common sense" at the beginning of the twentieth century, when such exotic *mathematical constructions as non-Euclidean *geometry and equations with ambiguous solutions began to be built into descriptive theories of *relativity and the subatomic world, and the distinction between rational and psychological *plausibility became sharper. The situation was further confused by the fact that the same historical period saw the advent of new media of fictional representation that were extremely hospitable to technically generated illusions, and hence to the representation of impossibilities whose particular plausibility was established by habitual consumption.

The concerted attempt by a handful of editors and writers to define a "hard core" of science fiction that differs intrinsically from fictions that deal deliberately and unrepentantly with impossibility has been largely unsuccessful. Most labelled science fiction, including most alleged *hard science fiction, is pure fantasy that elects to deploy scientific or pseudoscientific jargon in place of a frankly magical vocabulary. The immense difficulty of doing otherwise becomes more understandable, however, when one considers the extent of readers' prejudices in favour of the impossible. Tom Godwin's story "The Cold Equations" (1954) allegedly had to be rewritten several times before its author would accept the ending that John W. Campbell Jr. thought appropriate—which was that an innocent character would have to die, because it was impossible that she should be saved. The story in question generated a controversy that was still raging in the pages of *The New York Review of Science Fiction* more than forty years later, with readers and other writers queuing up to argue not merely that there *had* to be a way of saving the girl, but that it was the author's sacred duty to find or improvise it, and that to do otherwise was clear evidence of hideous misogyny, murderous fascism, or something unspecifiably worse. Responses in kind to Godwin's story, including Robert Sheckley's "The Cruel Equations" (1971), Don Sakers' "The Cold Solution" (1991), and James Patrick Kelly's "Think Like a Dinosaur" (1997), also added to the debate.

INTELLIGENCE

A term whose etymological composition implies "choosing between" or discrimination; it is nowadays used to refer to the faculty of understanding, conceived as an innate mental competence. The appropriation of the term into scientific *psychology was pioneered by Herbert Spencer and Francis Galton in the late nineteenth century, when the search soon began for an objective method of its measurement.

The measuring instruments systematised by such psychologists as James Cattell in the 1890s and Alfred Binet and Theodore Simon in the early 1900s focused on the solution of problems, tacitly equating intelligence with an ability to reason quickly and effectively. The tests that became standardised adopted a numerical scale with a mean IQ (intelligence quotient) set at one hundred, about which individual IQs were assumed to be normally distributed, the vast majority of the population falling in the 80–120 range. Intelligence was construed as an indication of potential rather than actual achievement, and its measurement in children was seen as an important indicator of what they might accomplish as adults. Unusual intelligence was seen as a necessary qualification for scientific genius, although its relevance to artistic genius was less obvious.

The attempted measurement of intelligence was closely associated with attempts to determine the extent to which it is determined by heredity factors, as opposed to environmental factors such as education—an issue hotly contested on various ideological grounds, especially insofar as it bore on questions of *eugenics, efficient parenting, the design of educational systems, and alleged differences in the mean IQ scores of different sexes and different races. Analysis of early IQ test results suggested that there is a degree of discorrelation between various "primary abilities"—numerical reasoning, verbal reasoning, and spatial perception—and these abilities were often

scored separately in the latter half of the twentieth century, although IQ scores continued to be issued as a single encapsulated figure.

Liam Hudson's *Contrary Imaginations* (1966) alleged that there is a marked discorrelation between IQ and "creativity", which had sometimes been assumed to be a simple derivative of it. It became a matter of common observation—and a source of considerable humour—that individuals with high IQs were often conspicuously inept in executing some simple tasks and negotiating many social routines that did not trouble people with lower IQs. This conformed to an established stereotype of the "absent-minded professor" who cannot cope with everyday life because his mind is constantly preoccupied with abstract matters. It also prompted observations of a discorrelation between IQ and "empathetic understanding" of other human beings—a faculty that Daniel Goleman called, by analogy, *Emotional Intelligence* (1995).

The literary reflection of this history often involved the use of IQ scores as indicators of hidden potentiality in child characters, whose treatment by adults changed markedly following the revelation of their high IQs. Speculative accounts of future societies or institutions whose organisation and policies are heavily dependent on psychometric testing, such as those featured in Victor Rousseau's *The Messiah of the Cylinder* (1917), J. A. Meyer's "Brick Wall" (1951), Kurt Vonnegut's *Player Piano* (1952), J. T. McIntosh's *World out of Mind* (1953), Edmund Cooper's "Tomorrow's Gift" (1958), and Michael Young's *The Rise of the Meritocracy 1870–2033* (1958), tend to be direly sceptical of their virtue.

Literary representations of IQ are inevitably more interested in extremes than mean performances, and in the higher extreme than the lower; indeed, the literary depiction of extremely low intelligence is an awkward technical problem, as illustrated by such examples as the first part of William Faulkner's *The Sound and the Fury* (1929) or the opening pages of Daniel Keyes' "Flowers for Algernon" (1959; exp. book, 1966). The contrary problem seems less acute, and there is a remarkably rich literature describing the trials and tribulations of the highly intelligent and elaborating the sense of grievance the allegedly intelligent often feel in response to the underestimation of their worth by others.

The difficulty writers have in constructing characters more intelligent than themselves is reflected in many works of speculative fiction that try to imagine what an individual with intelligence beyond the normal human range might think, feel, and want. Many works that foreground intelligence as a subject matter avoid the problem by describing the augmentation of low intelligence, as in accounts of animals technologically gifted with near-human intelligence; notable early examples include Edgar Fawcett's *Solarion* (1889) and F. C. Constable's *The Curse of Intellect* (1895), but the subgenre was significantly expanded as the twentieth century progressed in such works as L. Sprague de Camp's Johnny Black series (1938–1940), Olaf Stapledon's *Sirius* (1944), Miriam Allen deFord's "Oh, Rats!" (1961), and Kate Wilhelm's "The Planners" (1968). The reason for its proliferation had much to do with the pressure that developments in computer technology and the emergent possibilities of *artificial intelligence had on attempts to define intelligence more accurately; the connection is evident in such stories as M. C. Pease's "Devious Weapon" (1949).

The same strategy of examining the augmentation of low intelligence generated numerous accounts of highly intelligent children, notable early examples being J. D. Beresford's *The Hampdenshire Wonder* (1911) and Olaf Stapledon's *Odd John* (1934). Here too the second half of the twentieth century saw a rapid proliferation, in such works as Wilmar H. Shiras' "In Hiding" (1948; incorporated into *Children of the Atom*, 1953), Poul Anderson's "Genius" (1948), Mark Clifton's "Star, Bright" (1952), George O. Smith's *The Fourth "R"* (1959; aka *The Brain Machine*), and George Turner's *Brain Child* (1991). Poul Anderson's *Brain Wave* (1954) depicts a universal augmentation of Earthly intelligence, but uses characters with low starting points as its principal viewpoints.

Accounts of these kinds tend to become studies in isolation, the featured characters having little prospect of discovering or constructing a society adapted to their mental powers. Even in examples where gifted children eventually grow up, having found others of their kind in the meantime, as they do in *Odd John* and Stanley G. Weinbaum's *The New Adam* (1939), the resultant community usually provides scant protection against *alienation. The rare examples of works in which further increases in intelligence are gifted to intelligent adults also tend to feature isolated communities alienated from the social mainstream. Thomas M. Disch's *Camp Concentration* (1968) is set in an exotic prison, the superintelligent characters in Nancy Kress's *Beggars in Spain* (1993) and its sequels are forced into quasi-monastic retreat, and those in Frederik Pohl's *Starburst* (1982) are packed of to Alpha Centauri.

Such *contes philosophiques* as C. M. Kornbluth's "Gomez" (1954), Vonda N. McIntyre's "The Genius Freaks" (1973), and Ted Chiang's "Understand" (1991) offer neatly ironic encapsulations of the alienating effects of exceptional intelligence. The most

impressive of all science fiction stories of intelligence augmentation, "Flowers for Algernon", gains its remarkable poignancy from the tragic effect of its final pages, as the temporarily redeemed imbecile regresses to his former status, thus regaining the goodwill and companionship of his former "friends". Stories in which enhanced intelligence is reserved to such specialists as the operatives of the Mnemonic Bureau featured in Isaac Asimov's "Sucker Bait" (1954) often assume that such élites would be subject to a more spiteful kind of envy than that pertaining to the rich or famous.

In John Hersey's account of a society geared to fostering high intelligence contained in *The Child Buyer* (1961), the cultivation leads to dehumanisation, and the Utopia of the superintelligent featured in John T. Phillifent's *Genius Unlimited* (1972) is similarly problematic. In James E. Gunn's *The Dreamers* (1980), chemical learning enhances knowledge acquisition but suppresses imagination proportionately. Accounts of futures in which intelligence-boosting technologies become available—as in Lester del Rey's "The One-Eyed Man" (1945; by-lined Philip St. John), Walt and Leigh Richmond's *Phoenix Ship* (1969; exp. as *Phase Two*, 1979), John Boyd's *The IQ Merchant* (1972), Mack Reynolds' *Ability Quotient* (1975), and Kress' *Beggars in Spain*—it is anticipated that public demand would be avid, as demand already is in the developed countries for any means of giving children a head start over their rivals—a trend taken to a drastic extreme in David Brin's "Dr Pak's Preschool" (1989). Accounts of the attempted development of such technologies are easily able to anticipate nasty snags, as in G. C. Edmondson and C. M. Kotlan's *The Cunningham Equations* (1986) and its sequels.

Attempts to describe the augmentation of adult intelligence often mystify the process, offering accounts of transcendent metamorphosis into a superhuman condition beyond ordinary comprehension, as in A. E. van Vogt's *The World of Null-A* (1945; book, 1948) and "The Proxy Intelligence" (1968), Frank Herbert's *The Santaroga Barrier* (1968), and Ian Watson's *The Martian Inca* (1977). Accounts of superintelligent children overtaking and outstripping their parents often take on an edge of black comedy, as in "When the Bough Breaks" (1944; by-lined Lewis Padgett) by Henry Kuttner and C. L. Moore, and similar elements of black comedy sometimes infect accounts of rapid adult progress, as in Oscar Rossiter's *Tetrasomy 2* (1974). The chimerical combination of envy and frustration foregrounded by these stories is extrapolated with particular ingenuity in accounts of intellectually differentiated split personality such as Olaf Stapledon's *A Man Divided*

(1950) and Robert Charles Wilson's *The Divide* (1990).

Images of future human *evolution almost invariably take it for granted that the trend towards greater intelligence will continue; it is often seen as the essence of human evolution, although H. G. Wells did supplement his archetypal account of the big-brained "Man of the Year Million" (1893) with an essay wondering whether the higher faculties of the mind might be mere "Bye-Products of Evolution" (1895) conferring no selective advantage. Francis Donovan's "The Short Life" (1956) suggests that human intelligence might be a unique freak of nature, compensating for the lack of a much more useful advantage that all other world-dominating species possess. Evolutionary accounts that culminate in a transcendence of corporeal existence—as in Eando Binder's "Dawn to Dusk" (1934–1935) and "Spawn of Eternal Thought" (1936)—often describe the end products as creatures of "pure intelligence". *Exobiological speculators dramatically expanded the range of entities imagined to be capable of harbouring intelligence, including plants and micro-organisms as well as animals, and extending into further microcosms in such images as the intelligent molecules featured in John W. Campbell Jr.'s "Dead Knowledge" (1938; by-lined Don A. Stuart).

The prospect of animals evolving greater intelligence is sometimes represented in speculative fiction as an exceedingly ominous possibility. It is assumed by such works that the past human mistreatment of nonhuman beings might well lead to violent payback, as in J. T. McIntosh's *The Fittest* (1955; aka *Rule of the Pagbeasts*); even in the absence of an active revolt, the capacity of intelligent animals to outbreed slowly maturing humans is ominously pointed out in such black comedies as Cleve Cartmill's "Number Nine" (1950). In spite of such anxieties, there is a large body of speculative work that seems expressive of an earnest and passionate desire to discover, enhance, or create intelligence in other Earthly species, whose most obvious manifestation is the rich mixture of speculative fiction and nonfiction produced in the wake of John C. Lilly's *Man and Dolphin* (1961), which popularised the notion that dolphins might be far more intelligent than had previously been assumed.

Early spin-off from Lilly's work included Arthur C. Clarke's *Dolphin Island* (1963), William C. Anderson's *Penelope* (1963), Gordon R. Dickson's "Dolphin's Way" (1964), Joe Poyer's "Operation Malacca" (1966; exp. book, 1968), Roy Meyers' *Dolphin Boy* (1967; aka *Dolphin Rider*) and its sequels, Robert Merle's *Un animal doué de raison* (1967; trans. as *Day of the Dolphin*), Margaret St. Clair's *The Dolphins of Altair* (1967), and Robert Silverberg's "Ishmael

in Love" (1970). The notion that dolphins might be more interesting to alien communicators than humans, seriously developed in John Varley's *The Ophiuchi Hotline* (1977), became the ultimate joke in Douglas Adams' series of satirical farces, whose final completed volume was titled for the Earthly species' laconic farewell, *So Long, and Thanks for All the Fish* (1984). Stories of newly established human-dolphin communication continued to appear throughout the latter decades of the twentieth century in spite of the failure of actual attempts to make any headway; notable examples include John Boyd's "The Girl and the Dolphin" (1973) and Mark C. Jarvis' "Collaboration" (1982). In the same period, "swimming with dolphins" became a popular pastime to which mystical overtones and therapeutic effects were often attributed.

Cetaceans inevitably became favoured candidates for fictional intelligence augmentation, in such stories as Ian Watson's *The Jonah Kit* (1975) and Alexander Jablokov's *A Deeper Sea* (1989; exp. 1992), although the great apes maintained their traditional rivalry— foreshadowed in Robert A. Heinlein's "Jerry Is a Man" (1947)—in such works as Vernor Vinge's "Bookworm, Run!" (1966), Joseph H. Delaney's "Brainchild" (1982), Pat Murphy's "Rachel in Love" (1987), Mike Resnick's "Barnaby in Exile" (1994), Robert R. Chase's "Seven Times Never" (2001), and F. Paul Wilson's *Sims* (2003). Dogs also retained the place appropriate to man's best friend, following such classic precedents as Clifford Simak's *City* series (1944–1952), in Michael Sutch's "Nascent" (1975), and Orson Scott Card and Jay A. Parry's "In the Doghouse" (1978). David *Brin's Uplift series— which includes detailed accounts of the viewpoints of intelligent dolphins and chimpanzees—imagines a galactic civilisation in which artificial augmentation is the standard evolutionary route to intelligence, the prime movers of the system having long retreated into the realm of legend. In Brin's scheme, human beings are enormously proud of their exceptional achievement in having uplifted themselves, even though they have no idea how they did it—as, of course, they are in reality.

INVENTION

A noun originally used to refer to a general ability to devise new combinations of ideas or instruments, applied more often to artists than mechanicians. From the late Renaissance to the eighteenth century, however, its reference was increasingly narrowed to individual contrivances, especially to innovative machines, and to the act of producing them. It is possible to identify men who qualified as "inventors" from the late Renaissance onwards, and the word became commonplace in the seventeenth century, although it was not until the late nineteenth century that the image of the vocational inventor was brought to archetypal perfection by Thomas *Edison.

This heroic status was retrospectively extended to a handful of earlier inventors, beginning with Archimedes, the inventor of the screw pump, although the legendary cry that became the motto of scientific and technological inspiration, conventionally rendered "Eureka!" (it is more likely to have been "Heureka", signifying "I understand"), was allegedly occasioned by his discovery of the theoretical principle that bears his name. Historical fiction occasionally pays tribute to such ancient inventors, as in L. Sprague de Camp*'s *The Arrow of Hercules* (1965).

Most of the retrospectively recognised inventions that contributed to the technological revolution of the late Middle Ages—including the horse collar, the heavy plough, the windmill, and the water mill—are uncreditable, and the precise origins of many of the key inventions of the sixteenth and seventeenth centuries—including the *telescope and various items of clockwork—remain stubbornly vague. The development of patent law, pioneered in Venice in 1474 and adapted into English law as the 1623 Statute of Monopolies, sharpened such questions of entitlement considerably. By this time, practical scientists like Cornelius Drebbel—who was hired by James I of England as his "court inventor"—had begun to acquire considerable celebrity by their ingenious practical applications of the New Learning; Drebbel made a significant contribution to the development of compound *microscopes and thermostats, built three *submarines, and pioneered new methods for the manufacture of sulphuric acid and dyeing with cochineal.

The United States began issuing patents in 1790, and created its Patent Office in 1802. Although many modern inventions emerged from the work of considerable numbers of people working in collaboration or competition, the allocation of patents routinely focuses credit on a single individual, as with the attribution of credit for inventing the *telephone to Alexander Graham Bell. The gradual improvement and widespread application of the steam engine can be tracked with minute care by virtue of patent applications, creating a narrative that is as rich in heroic failures and near misses as it is in triumphs.

Literary reflections sometimes find more dramatic potential in frustrated hopes than ambitions fulfilled. William Golding's "Envoy Extraordinary" (1956; dramatic version 1957 as *The Brass Butterfly*) is an account of a Classical inventor ahead of his time who fails to attract patronage, while Gregory Feeley's

Arabian Wine (2004; exp. book, 2005) describes a similar seventeenth-century secret history. Several of Paul Féval's works, including *Jean Diable* (1862; trans. as *John Devil*), make regretful reference to the French steamboat pioneer Claude Jouffroy d'Abbans, who might have won the historical credit given to Robert Fulton had fate only been a little kinder, and the failed endeavours of Nicholas Tesla have acquired a retrospective fascination as Thomas *Edison's successes gradually surrendered to the contempt of familiarity, as reflected in such fictions as Lewis Shiner's "White City" (1990).

Contests to develop new gadgets were the subject of extensive reportage in the late nineteenth century, especially in the United States, where the demand for news of technical progress was sharpened by a widespread desire to invest in such projects. Such financial adventures are a significant background element of the literary reflection of invention; speculative writers sometimes speculated materially as well, as when Mark Twain lost most of his fortune investing in a new kind of printing press and Hugo *Gernsback was bankrupted by premature investments in *radio broadcasting.

Speculative fiction dealing with future invention inevitably runs into the paradox of prophecy; to describe a new invention in detail is, in effect, to make it. There is, however, a considerable margin of licence in the matter of detail, and writers have always been able to describe inventions in terms of what they are able to do rather than the mechanisms that permit them to do it. The first writer to make new inventions a focal point of his literary endeavours, Jules *Verne, became expert in marshalling such telling details as he could while glossing over those that were unspecifiable in his description of such devices as Captain Nemo's submarine, the Baltimore Gun Club's space shot, and Robur's airship. He made inevitable errors—his unpressurised diving suits would have been fatal to their users, as would the space gun—but he developed techniques of elliptical description that were borrowed and carried forward by a legion of successors.

The process of speculative invention is, by necessity, a matter of "reverse engineering", in which authors begin with notions of what their imaginary machine is to do, then devise the supportive apologetic jargon. The conscientious Verne was annoyed by the generous licence taken by his most famous successor, H. G. *Wells, in constructing supportive justifications for inventions whose real purpose was to supply facilitating devices—as with the dimensional jargon used to shore up *The Time Machine* and the gravity shields used to propel *The First Men in the Moon*—but it was Wells who planted the more significant signposts for twentieth-century writers. Vernian fiction that attempted to foreground the description of technically plausible inventions always took second place to Wellsian fiction, whose inventions were intended to open up new narrative spaces for exploration and development. The most conspicuous science-fictional exceptions to this general rule were the space *rocket and the *nuclear power plant, which were described in painstaking Vernian detail in science fiction stories before achieving actualisation.

These triumphs of science-fictional anticipation have to be set against the virtual absence from early twentieth-century science fiction of inventions that had a more profound effect on the century's historical development, such as the desktop *computer, the misestimation by science fiction writers of the breadth and depth of the social impact of such foreseeable inventions as *television, and the drastic misrepresentation of other plausible technologies, such as *robots. However, these failures of the imagination were not as profound in their effects as the collective results of the *Frankenstein complex in producing vast numbers of stories whose normalising story arcs require promising inventions to be obliterated before their possibilities can be sensibly investigated.

The vast science-fictional catalogue of imaginary machines is best sketched out under more specific category headings, such as *transportation—which similarly gives rise to such subcategories as *automobiles and *aeronautics—but there is a significant residual subcategory of stories that focus on the process of invention and the psychology of inventors. Many late nineteenth-century and early twentieth-century "Edisonades" are more satiric than heroic, portraying inventors as unworldly eccentrics whose inventions are mostly absurd in their impracticality, including the series partly collected in W. L. Alden's *Van Wagener's Ways* (1898), Henry A. Hering's accounts of Silas P. Cornu (1896–1899), Edgar Franklin's *Mr. Hawkins' Humorous Inventions* (1904), and Nelson Bond's Pat Pending series (1942–1957). The tradition was artfully continued by a long series of documentary fictions offered as light relief in *New Scientist*'s Daedalus column, some of which were collected in David E. H. Jones' *The Inventions of Daedalus, Inc* (1982), as well as such straightforwardly fictional examples as Christopher Anvil's accounts of the exploits of Doc Griswell in "The Gold of Galileo" (1980) and "Doc's Legacy" (1988).

More restrained depictions of the invention process often tend discreetly in the same direction. Walter Kateley's Kingston series (1928–1931), which feature an employee of the U.S. Patent Office, maintain a satirical irreverence that was further exaggerated in a sporadic series of *contes philosophiques* written for John W. *Campbell Jr. by "Leonard Lockhard"

(Charles L. Harness and Theodore L. Thomas, sometimes working individually). Lockhard's dialogues dramatising the perversities of patent law—sometimes advertised as "special features" rather than stories—extended from "Improbable Profession" (1952) into the 1990s, producing such spin-off en route as Raymond F. Jones' "Trade Secret" (1953). The highlights of Lockhard's series included "That Professional Look" (1954), which emphasises the terminological discretion requisite for a patent application for a synthetic baby, and "The Professional Approach" (1962), which features a tearproof paper with a fatal flaw. Harness extrapolated the spirit of the series in more elaborate works such as "The Venetian Court" (1981; exp. book, 1982), "H-TEC" (1981), and "The Picture by Dora Gray" (1986).

Accounts of the psychology of invention spanned a spectrum extending from the inspirational model dramatised in J. S. Fletcher's *Morrison's Machine* (1900)—which assumes that the line separating genius and madness is exceedingly thin—and the methodical model dramatised in Tom Godwin's "Mother of Invention" (1953), which states forthrightly that hard work is the father of technological brainchildren. Most such accounts agreed, however, that a talent for invention is a rarity that can be difficult to identify and develop—an argument wryly dramatised in Cleve Cartmill's "Some Day We'll Find You" (1942). On the other hand, Clifford D. Simak's "How-2" (1954) looks forward to a day when the business of invention can be automated.

Fictitious inventors are often disappointed and embittered by the ingratitude of the world they have laboured to enrich when they finally perfect their work, as in Arthur Conan Doyle's *The Doings of Raffles Haw* (1891) and John Taine's *Quayle's Invention* (1927). Individuals of this sort often turn to crime in response, making up a substantial minority of *technothriller villains and mad *scientists and formulating a central element of the rich mythology of comic book supervillainy. Many inventors need no such bad experiences to turn them in the direction of criminal enterprises, however, because the common assumption that scientific objectivity stifles the conscience serves to justify numerous accounts of criminally inspired invention. The melodramatic formula was a considerable boon to pulp science fiction, developed in advance of the emergence of specialist magazines in such stories as Murray Leinster's "A Thousand Degrees Below Zero" (1919), whose sequels included "The Darkness on Fifth Avenue" (1929), and "The Mole Pirate" (1934).

One of the advantages of science fiction's incarnation as a magazine genre was the medium's hospitality to story series, in which the development of inventions and their social impact could be tracked through a sequence of stages—a facility that John W. *Campbell Jr. attempted to exploit. Notable series extrapolating the gradually unfolding consequences of hypothetical inventions include those assembled in George O. Smith's *Venus Equilateral* (1947), Isaac Asimov's *I, Robot* (1950), and Bob Shaw's *Other Days, Other Eyes* (1972). The establishment of science fiction as a popular genre also permitted this kind of intellectual exercise to be generalised, as writers borrowed ideas from one another for alternative development. One of the significant aspects of Campbell's prospectus for genre science fiction was the recognition that technological progress is an aggregate of work carried out by large numbers of individuals applying the scientific method; science fiction can be regarded as a collective enterprise of much the same kind.

The twentieth century gave birth to a set of urban legends relating to the suppression of new inventions by vested interests financially dependent on the technologies they would replace—a myth endorsed by such science fiction stories as Robert A. Heinlein's "Let There Be Light!" (1940; by-lined Lyle Monroe) and Lee Correy's *Star Driver* (1980), although it is treated sceptically by such works as Randall Garrett's "Damned if You Don't" (1960). L. E. Modesitt Jr.'s "Power To...?" (1990) features an Office of Technology Evaluation—modelled on institutions that evaluate new medicines, such as the U.S. FDA and the British NICE—whose Byzantine bureaucratic processes render deliberate suppression quite unnecessary.

INVISIBILITY

The failure to excite a visual response. Strictly defined, it is effectively identical to perfect transparency, although it is sometimes secured in both reality and fiction by other means, including the kind of cryptic colouration adopted by many animals. Many supernatural beings are credited with the property, and facultative invisibility—often involving magical caps or cloaks—is a common motif in myth and legend. The psychological *plausibility of being or becoming invisible originates in the fact that people do not perceive their own viewpoint as a visible entity, and find it easy to imagine it coming adrift from its fleshy anchorage. It is equally easy to imagine other invisible viewpoints keeping watch on us.

In a mundane context, the possibility of invisible matter is demonstrated by air and other gases, although this was not always obvious; Lucretius' popularisation of Epicurean materialism, *De rerum natura*, begins with the defiant assertion that the atmosphere is material—that branches agitated by the wind are not shaking themselves but yielding to pressure—and deducing therefrom that all observable phenomena might and ought to be explained in terms of matter in motion, similarly agitated by forces whose agents are sometimes invisible. Conversely, the extent to which the transparency of solids and liquids falls short of true invisibility is readily demonstrated by the reflective and refractive properties of glass and water.

The psychological plausibility supporting the notion of invisibility sustained it as a standard motif of magical fantasy, so abundantly that early writers of speculative fiction immediately began searching for *pseudoscientific explanatory schemes that might add conviction to such fantasies. Literary accounts of invisibility often tend to acknowledge the rational implausibility of the notion by adopting a cautionary approach similar to that displayed in fantasies of *longevity, extravagantly extrapolated in such moralistic fantasies as James Dalton's *The Invisible Gentleman* (1833).

Early science-fictional accounts of people becoming invisible tend to be formulated according to the same cautionary principle; notable examples include Edward Page Mitchell's "The Crystal Man" (1881), H. G. Wells' *The Invisible Man* (1897), and Jack London's "The Shadow and the Flash" (1903). More positive accounts are, however, offered in C. H. Hinton's "Stella" (1895), Wells' "The New Accelerator" (1901), and Herbert C. McKay's "Spectral Adventurers" (1937). In London's story and "The New Accelerator", temporary invisibility is secured by moving at very high speed rather than by static transparency, a notion further extrapolated in Harry Bates' "A Matter of Speed" (1941).

Accounts of invisible others tend to follow a different narrative strategy, treating the phenomenon as a mystery to be solved, although the anxiety implicit in the idea of an invisible stalker comes to the fore in such works as Fitz-James O'Brien's "What Was It?" (1859), Guy de Maupassant's "Le Horla" (1887), Ambrose Bierce's "The Damned Thing" (1893), and George Allan England's "The Thing from Outside" (1923). Such anxiety is more readily set aside when the invisible other is a potential sexual partner, as in Charles de Kay's "Manmat'ha" (1876) and the frame-narrative of Hinton's "Stella".

The success of Wells' *The Invisible Man* prompted further accounts of invisible men who use their ability for nefarious purposes, including Fred MacIsaac's *The Vanishing Professor* (1926; book, 1927) and Philip Wylie's *The Murderer Invisible* (1931), but its early *cinematic adaptations—invisible agencies being a key application of cinematic special effects from the medium's inception—eventually gave rise to a rich *television tradition featuring heroes who dedicated their invisibility to the cause of fighting crime, after the fashion of several comic book superheroes.

Although the visual media have the tremendous, if slightly paradoxical, advantage of making invisibility visually manifest, print retains the prerogative of being able to establish subtle forms of invisibility that have more to do with the inattentive eyes of beholders than the actual transparency of objects, as in Christopher Priest's unfilmable *The Glamour* (1984). Other speculative accounts of invisibility via optical illusion include Donald A. Wollheim's "Mimic" (1947), Poul Anderson's "Peek! I See You" (1968), and Ron Goulart's Chameleon Corps series, launched by *The Sword Swallower* (1968). A particularly striking (and controversial) example is incidentally featured in Charles L. Harness' "The Rose" (1953).

Even if one sets aside the objection that rendering flesh transparent would not necessarily render it invisible, the notion of invisible humans runs into several practical problems. The most significant is that an invisible man would be blind, because light would pass straight through his retinas without exciting the optic nerves. John Sutherland's essay "Why Is Griffin Cold?" (1996), however, takes issue with Wells' assumption that his invisible man must go naked, on the grounds that he could manufacture invisible clothes with perfect ease. As with many themes blessed with innate psychological plausibility and daydream appeal, however, such issues rarely intrude upon a reader's enjoyment.

Daydreams of invisibility, which investigate and celebrate the amusing things one would be able to do if one were invisible, have a darker counterpart; being condemned to invisibility by the refusal of others to recognise one's existence is a very different matter. This kind of enforced invisibility is envisaged as a punishment in such stories of futuristic exile as Damon Knight's "The Country of the Kind" (1956) and Robert Silverberg's "To See the Invisible Man" (1963), and extrapolated psychotropically in Gardner R. Dozois' "The Visible Man" (1975). C. J. Cherryh's *Wave Without a Shore* (1981) makes more elaborate use of the notion of figurative invisibility.

A similar rhetoric is deployed in calculatedly ambiguous stories in which characters fading from inconsequentiality into invisibility cannot be entirely sure whether their situation is literal or psychological; notable examples include Charles Beaumont's "The Vanishing American" (1955), Harlan Ellison's "Are You Listening?" (1958), Sylvia Jacobs' "The End of Evan Essant" (1962), and Thomas Berger's *Being Invisible* (1988). Mark Rich's "Invisibility" (1993) uses a similar notion to add an extra gloss to a theme whose variations had been thoroughly explored by that date.

J

JUNG, CARL (GUSTAV) (1875–1961)

Swiss psychoanalyst who studied medicine at the universities of Basel and Zurich before practicing at the latter's Psychiatric Clinic and the Berghölzli Asylum from 1902; he used methods pioneered by Sigmund *Freud, with whom he entered into a close collaboration from 1907 to 1912, when his dissociation from the Freudian school was completed by the publication of *Wandflungen und Symbole der Libido* (1911–1912; trans. as *Psychology of the Unconscious*; rev. as *Symbols of Transformation*). He founded a new school of psychoanalysis in Zurich, beginning an analysis of psychological types whose most famous distinction was between the extrovert and introvert frames of mind.

In childhood Jung had experienced unusually vivid dreams and intense fantasies, so he began a long and intense introspective analysis of these phenomena, eventually concluding that they emanated from an aspect of the unconscious that was common to all human beings. He attempted to analyse the contents of this collective unconscious by means of a theory of "archetypes" that allegedly projected various kinds of "archetypal images" into conscious experience, often relayed therefrom into artistic and literary imagery.

This thesis had a tremendous cultural impact, especially on artists and writers who felt that it gave them an important key to understanding their own creative processes. The most important archetypes in Jungian theory include the "anima" (the male's conception of female nature) and its counterpart the "animus", the Mother, rebirth, the Spirit, and the Trickster. It is very easy to find such motifs replicated on a massive scale in literary works, and by no means difficult for critics to construe the creative motivation of writers in terms of the same creative apparatus. As with Freudian theory, however, it remains entirely possible that the whole theoretical edifice is a scholarly fantasy, closely akin to the imaginative constructs it is ambitious to explain.

Although most of his publications were technical works aimed at psychiatric practitioners, Jung wrote several popularisations addressed to a wider audience, including the essays translated in *Modern Man in Search of a Soul* (1933), which included a significant essay on "Psychology and Literature" first published in 1930. Jung drew a distinction between "psychological" and "visionary" literature—illustrating the difference as that between the two parts of J. W. Goethe's *Faust* (1808; 1832)—and was particularly interested in the latter, regarding its recurrent motifs as useful testimony to the power of archetypes and a useful guide to their taxonomy.

Jung was equally interested in religious heresy and occultism—especially the mystical elements of *alchemy—on the grounds that their various deviations from orthodoxy must offer similar testimony to archetypal attractions. *Myths provided him with his most elaborate evidence for the existence and nature of the archetypes, and his analyses thereof—collected in *Einführung in das Wesen in der Mythologie* (1941, with Károly Kerényi; trans. as *Essays on a Science of Mythology*)—had a considerable influence on some *anthropologists and *ethnologists, most notably

Joseph Campbell. Jung's psychotherapeutic techniques increasingly began to concentrate on helping patients afflicted by the failure of their religious faith—a problem from which his own father had suffered conspicuously—to discover their own idiosyncratic myth systems by a process of "individuation". Within this context, he became interested in the development of new and distinctly modern myths; his last book was *Ein moderner Mythus: Von Dingen, die am Himmel gesehen werden* (1958; trans. as *Flying Saucers: A Modern Myth of Things Seen in the Sky*).

Jung's literary influence has been very considerable, especially on writers of imaginative fiction such as Herman Hesse, Jorge Luis Borges, and Vladimir Nabokov. It gave rise to a school of Jungian literary criticism pioneered by Maud Boskin's *Archetypal Patterns on Poetry* (1924), whose most noted exponent was Northrop Frye. The school's extension into feminist criticism, in such texts as Bettina Knapp's *A Jungian Approach to Literature* (1984), was where it became highly influential. Jos van Meurs' *Jungian Literary Criticism 1920–1980* (1988) is a bibliography.

Jung's influence is widespread in genre fantasy, where it is sometimes featured as a quasi-scientific explanatory scheme, as in Robert Holdstock's series begun with *Mythago Wood* (1984). Although it was less noticeable in science fiction, it is manifest in the psychiatric science fiction of David H. Keller, most notably "The Abyss" (1947). The protagonist of Brian W. Aldiss' "When I Was Very Jung" (1968) dreams that he is Jung. Jungian ideas were frequently manifest in the work of feminist writers such as Josephine Saxton, Ursula Le Guin, and Margaret Atwood before they became fashionable in feminist literary criticism. Saxton's "The Consciousness Machine" (1968) and Le Guin's *The Word for World Is Forest* (1972; book, 1976) and "Social Dreaming of the Frin" (2002) are particularly notable examples. Other speculative fiction based on Jungian ideas includes Uncle River's *Prometheus: The Autobiography* (2003) and the stories in Kay Green's *Jung's People* (2004). Jung is featured as a character in Morris West's *The World Is Made of Glass* (1983) and Keith Korman's *Secret Dreams* (1995).

JUPITER

The fifth planet from the Sun, the largest in the solar system, and the paradigm example of a "gas giant." Its supposed significance in mystical *astrology gave rise to the adjective "jovial." Its four largest moons—Ganymede, Callisto, Io, and Europa—were discovered by *Galileo, but it was not until 1892 that E. E. Barnard discovered the fifth, Amaltheia. The number

increased dramatically in the twentieth century, especially when the space probes Pioneer 10 and 11 and Voyager 1 and 2 sent back data gathered at close range between 1973 and 1979; sixteen satellites had been named by 1980 and the number had grown to sixty-three by 2004. Subsequent passes were made by Ulysses in 1992 and Galileo in 1994, the latter launching an entry probe into the atmosphere.

Although the visible "surface" of Jupiter is fluid, it has stable striations and one spectacular enduring feature, first observed by S. H. Schwabe in 1831: the Great Red Spot. Initially thought to be a solid structure, closer observation proved it to be a vast cyclonic storm. The four large satellites were revealed by the Voyager probes to have markedly different surfaces, that of Io apparently being covered with sulphur and various salts, while Europa has a shell of water ice; both have rocky interiors containing large amounts of water, some of which might be liquid. Callisto's surface is mostly ice-covered rock, while Ganymede has more exposed rock.

Images of Jupiter produced before the end of the nineteenth century usually imagined it as a solid world not so very different from Earth, inhabited according to much the same pattern. It featured in numerous planetary tours, but attracted particular attention in Joel R. Peabody's *A World of Wonders* (1838) and J. B. Fayette's *The Experiences of Eon and Eona* (1886; published anonymously). In *The Narrative and Travels of Paul Aermont Among the Planets* (1873), its inhabitants are richly equipped with flying machines. In W. D. Lach-Szyrma's *Aleriel* (1886), it is a panthalassa with floating islands. In Harold A. Brydges' *A Fortnight in Heaven* (1886), it is America writ large. In John Jacob Astor's *A Journey in Other Worlds* (1894), it serves as a model of Earthly prehistory. It is a parallel Earth in the anonymous *To Jupiter via Hell* (1908) and a Utopia in Ella Scrymsour's *The Perfect World* (1922). Ganymede is equipped with domed cities in George Griffith's *A Honeymoon in Space* (1901).

Jupiter was an equally popular setting in early pulp science fiction. It is elaborately featured in George C. Wallis and B. Wallis' "The Star Shell" (1926–1927)—along with Europa, which exhibits extremes of temperature in Gawain Edwards' "A Rescue from Jupiter" (1930) and "The Return from Jupiter" (1931). It is a venue for conventional melodrama in Edmond Hamilton's "A Conquest of Two Worlds" (1932), J. Harvey Haggard's "Children of the Ray" (1934), and Edgar Rice Burroughs' "The Skeleton Men of Jupiter" (1943). Io plays host to more calculatedly exotic ecospheres in J. Harvey Haggard's "An Episode on Io" (1934), Stanley G. Weinbaum's "The Mad Moon" (1935), and Raymond Z. Gallun's "The Lotus Engine"

(1940). Frank Belknap Long's "Red Storm on Jupiter" (1936) imagines the Red Spot as a gelatinous landmass mined from Form Stations, while a vaporous Red Spot leaves Jupiter to precipitate an earthly catastrophe in Eando Binder's "Life Disinherited" (1937).

Even when a better appreciation developed of the extreme depth of the Jovian atmosphere—as reflected in Milton A. Rothman's "Heavy Planet" (1939; bylined Lee Gregor) and Clifford Simak's "Clerical Error" (1940)—accounts of Jupiter's *colonisation continued to appear. In Simak's "Desertion" (1944), humans discover a kind of paradise in its exotic exobiology and subject themselves to extreme biological metamorphoses in order to emigrate there. Isaac Asimov placed conventional aliens there in "Not Final!" (1941) and "Victory Unintentional" (1942). In the 1950s, images were still being produced of a solid world with an ecosphere shaped by the high pressure of an exotic atmosphere, as in Poul Anderson's "Call Me Joe" (1957).

Anderson updated his image of the Jovian surface in *Three Worlds to Conquer* (1964), which substitutes Ganymede as a world ripe for colonisation—a notion he had previously developed in *The Snows of Ganymede* (1955; book, 1958); other authors to do likewise included Robert A. Heinlein in *Farmer in the Sky* (1950) and Robert Silverberg in *Invaders from Earth* (1958), although James Blish gave the satellite a crucial role in the development of his argument that extraterrestrial colonisation would be impossible without heroic efforts of *genetic engineering, in "A Time to Survive" (1956; incorporated into *The Seedling Stars*). Blish had earlier offered an elaborate image of the hostile Jovian surface in "Bridge" (1952). By the end of the 1950s, however, science fiction writers had largely abandoned the hypothetical surface as a setting, accepting that the effectively bottomless atmosphere was where future action would have to be set.

Heroic descents into the Jovian atmosphere subsequently became a common motif, featured in Isaac Asimov's *Lucky Starr and the Moons of Jupiter* (1957; as by Paul French), the Strugatsky brothers' "Put'na Amal'teiu" (1960; trans. as "Destination: Amaltheia"), Arthur C. Clarke's "A Meeting with Medusa" (1971), Ben Bova's *As on a Darkling Plain* (1972), and Gregory Benford and Gordon Eklund's "The Anvil of Jove" (1976; incorporated into *If the Stars Are Gods*). The images of alien life offered by many of these stories usually employed models from earthly marine life, inflated to gargantuan proportions.

More elaborate Jovian ecospheres are featured in Paul Preuss' Clarke-inspired novels *The Medusa Encounter* (1990) and *The Diamond Moon* (1990), Ernest Hogan's *Cortez on Jupiter* (1990), Alexander Jablokov's *A Deeper Sea* (1993), Rick Cook and Peter L. Manly's "Symphony for Skyfall" (1994) and "Unfinished Symphony" (1995), and Jack Cohen and Ian Stewart's *Wheelers* (2000). The Jovian atmosphere becomes a venue for sailboat racing in Bud Sparhawk's "Primrose and Thorn" (1996), "Primrose Rescue" (1997), and "High Flight" (1998). The Red Spot continued to attract attention in such stories as Michael Kallenberger's "White Chaos" (1991). In G. David Nordley's "Out of the Quiet Years" (1994), Jupiter acquires a new magnetosphere.

The Jovian satellites continued to play host to accounts of careful colonisation while Jupiter's surface remained unscratchable. Ganymede remained the most frequent target, as in Gregory Benford's *Jupiter Project* (1975; rev. 1980), Charles Sheffield's *Cold as Ice* (1992) and *The Ganymede Club* (1996), and Charles L. Harness' "The Flag in Gorbachev Crater" (1997). Io is the primary arena in Kenneth W. Ledbetter's "Patera Crossing" (1985) and Michael Swanwick's "The Very Pulse of the Machine" (1998), while Europa comes to the fore in Bud Sparhawk's "The Ice Dragon's Song" (1998), Paul J. McAuley's "Sea Change, with Monsters" (1998), and Caitlin R. Kiernan's "Riding the White Bull" (2003), but complex movements and relationships between the entire satellite complex were frequently invoked, as in Jack McDevitt's "Melville on Iapetus" (1983) and "Promises to Keep" (1984).

The notion that Jupiter might be regarded as an unsuccessful star rather than a planet, and that its failure to ignite might be technologically remedied, is put forward in Arthur Clarke's *2010: Odyssey Two* (1982; film, 1984), Sakyo Komatsu's *Sayonara Jupiter* (1982; film, 1984), and Charles L. Harness's *Lunar Justice* (1991). The idea was earnestly explored in Martyn J. Fogg's *Analog* article "Stellifying Jupiter" (1989), and there are passing references to plans to achieve that goal in several other late twentieth-century science fiction stories, including Vernor Vinge's *Marooned in Real-Time* (1986).

K

KEPLER, JOHANNES (1571–1630)

German astronomer and astrologer. Kepler was born to a poor family in the "free city" of Weil der Stadt in the Holy Roman Empire, but obtained a good education thanks to a scholarship provided by the Duke of Würtemburg. At the University of Tübingen he was taught astronomy by Michael Mästlin, one of the very few Copernicans active as a teacher, and became a convert to the heliocentric theory.

After obtaining his M.A. in 1591, Kepler intended to become a Lutheran minister, but he did not finish his training in theology and became a mathematics teacher in Graz. In 1595, he became obsessed with the notion of accommodating the Copernican model of the solar system to a mathematical description that would relate the orbits of the planets to the five "Platonic solids"—the only such forms whose angles could be fitted to the surface of a sphere. He attempted to relate these five forms to the intervals between the six known planets in a book published in 1596, a copy of which he sent to Tycho Brahe, who was soon to be appointed Imperial Mathematician.

In 1600, Tycho invited Kepler to join the staff at his observatory at Benatek, near Prague, and Kepler succeeded him as Imperial Mathematician when he died in 1601. In that year he published *De Fundamentis Astrologiae Certioribus* [The Reliable Foundations of Astrology], which rejected the idea that the stars control or guide the lives of human beings, but asserted instead that the harmony of the universe ensured a reflective correspondence between the movements of the heavens and human lives, thus cementing the foundations of modern *astrological theory. His observation of a supernova in 1604, published in 1606, was offered as proof that the heavens were not changeless, while his analysis of the astronomical problems generated by the refraction of light in the Earth's atmosphere laid important groundwork in the science of optics.

Kepler's obsession with discovering some underlying logic to the planetary orbits finally bore unexpected fruit when he made the conceptual breakthrough that allowed him to realise that the orbits were not circular at all, but elliptical—a discovery he published, along with two laws of planetary motion, in *Astronomia Nova* in 1609. He was quick to acknowledge the accomplishments of *Galileo in a dissertation published in 1610, but Galileo would never concede that the planetary orbits were not circular, in spite of the fact that Kepler further elaborated his discovery with a third law of planetary motion in *Harmonies Mundi* [The Harmony of the Universe] (1619).

Although he had been reappointed as Imperial Mathematician when his first patron, Emperor Rudolph II, died in 1612—to be succeeded by his brother, Matthias—Kepler thought it prudent to leave Prague for Linz. Ferdinand of Austria, an enthusiastic persecutor of Protestants, was already making his presence felt within the Empire. In Linz, Kepler published his definitive account of the Copernican cosmology, *Epitome Astronomiae Copernicanae* (1618–1621). He had written another book in 1609, attempting to make his Copernican arguments more accessible and convincing by describing the astronomical observations of Earth that might be made by an observer on the Moon, but had not published it and had lost the manuscript in 1611, perhaps to theft. The narrative was represented as a dream, but the dreamer's trip to the Moon was facilitated by a "daimon" (a favourite term of the neo-Platonists, derived from the Greek word for knowledge), and this might have been misconstrued as "demon" by someone who read the manuscript. It is unclear whether this had anything to do with the fact that Kepler's mother was charged with witchcraft in 1620. At any rate, he defended her successfully, saving her from torture and execution; although he had rewritten his dream story by then, he never published it.

Kepler left Linz when he found a new patron, Albrecht von Wallenstein, but the turbulence of the times interrupted his work and he published nothing more after the *Tabulae Rudolphinae* (1627) he named in honour of his former patron. His dream story was belatedly published in 1634 as *Somnium*; it attracted little attention in the chaos of the Thirty Years' War (1618–1648) but it can be seen retrospectively as a remarkable work, not least because the concluding phase of the visionary voyage offers an account of the way in which lunar life might be adapted to the long day/night cycle. Kepler took up this theme from Plutarch's dialogue "On the Face that Appears in the Disc of the Moon" (ca. 100 A.D.), but he extrapolated Plutarch's *exobiological speculations considerably.

L

LAMARCK, JEAN-BAPTISTE DE MONET, CHEVALIER DE (1744–1829)

French biologist, who may have been the first person to use the French equivalent of the term "biology", in 1802. His father, a baron and infantry lieutenant, intended him for the priesthood, and he was sent to a Jesuit school at Amiens by way of preparation; when his father died, however, he enlisted in the infantry himself, serving from 1761 to 1768. Following his resignation from the army, he first studied medicine and then botany, obtaining a minor post at the Jardin du Roi (the royal botanical gardens). He published a three-volume work on French flora in 1778, which became the standard guide for an increasing number of hobbyists, and his weekly lectures at the Jardin became very popular—the hero of Charles-Augustin Sainte-Beuve's *Volupté* (1834) finds them a significant source of comfort in a city whose aspect and experience are generally distressing.

Lamarck was elected to the Académie des Sciences, and was engaged to tutor the Comte du Buffon's son on a two-year educational tour. He then took charge of the botanical entries for the *Encyclopédie méthodique*, the successor to Denis Diderot's pioneering enterprise, and became curator of the royal herbarium—a position in which he might have spent the remainder of his life had it not been for the revolution of 1789, which abolished it. He petitioned the National Assembly to establish a Museum of Natural History, which might become a paradigm of systematic organisation. When it was founded, however, he was passed over for the more prestigious supervisory appointments, presumably because he was an aristocrat and a former royal employee, and put in charge of invertebrate animals by way of subtle insult.

The *ci-devant* Chevalier devoted himself to the organisation and classification of the museum's collection of invertebrates with his customary assiduousness, making a concerted and ground-breaking attempt to place fossils and living species within a single taxonomic scheme. His philosophical ambitions were much wider, and he was ambitious to be a master of the entirety of natural history. He published attacks on the new theory of combustion developed by Antoine Lavoisier and a book on *Hydrogéologie* (1802), which attempted a compromise between *catastrophist and uniformitarian *geological theories.

In combination with his taxonomic enterprise, whose preliminary findings were published in 1801 as *Système des animaux sans vertèbres, ou table général des classes,* Lamarck's theoretical speculations impelled him strongly towards evolutionism, and to the notion of a progressive ladder extending from the simplest to the most complex animals, which all species were perennially engaged in climbing. He attempted to produce a physical theory of this innate tendency in *Recherches sur l'organisation des corps vivants* (1802), which was further elaborated in *Philosophie zoologique* (1809; trans. as *Philosophical Zoology*). The latter text stressed the role of adaptation to new environments in directing evolution, organisms being able to make such adaptations because organs and structures that are repeatedly exercised are improved while organs and structures that fall into disuse atrophy (his "first law"). He also asserted that these modifications are heritable (his "second law").

Lamarck's masterpiece was undoubtedly the culmination of his taxonomic studies in *Histoire naturelle des animaux sans vertèbres* (1815–1822), but he never gave up his attempts to make a significant contribution to scientific theory, devoting much of his later life—until he lost his sight—to studies in meteorology. Many of his post-revolutionary contemporaries regarded him as a crank left over from the *ancien regime*; the most celebrated anecdote to outlive him tells how he burst into tears when the Emperor Napoleon carelessly cast aside a presentation copy of one of his works without even glancing at it. His evolutionary philosophy gained ground steadily, however, and became a significant item of nineteenth-century scientific thought, perceived in France as an important precursor of Charles *Darwin's theory rather than a false doctrine rendered obsolete thereby. Its notion of an innately progressive "life force" was revitalised by Henri Bergson, and French notions of extraterrestrial life, as popularised by Camille *Flammarion, retained a Lamarckian emphasis on progressive impetus within a grandiose organisational scheme well into the twentieth century.

Apart from the notion that life on Earth had indeed evolved—which came to seem commonsensical—none of Lamarck's ingenious speculative hypotheses turned out to be correct, but his insistence on systematic organisation was a powerful influence on the development of biological thought, and his notion of what a museum ought to be is now taken for granted. In the grand narrative of the history of science, "Lamarckism" is commonly cited as a kind of heresy against which crusades need and ought to be directed, although its modern adherents—including Samuel Butler and George Bernard Shaw in Britain, T. D. Lysenko in Russia, and Jean-Louis Agassiz, Alpheus Packard Jr., and Luther Burbank in the United States—are often dismissed as more to be pitied than feared. Several science fiction writers have, however, attempted to design artificial or exobiological genetic systems that might be capable of transmitting acquired characteristics to future generations—most notably Greg Bear in *Legacy* (1995)—and *social Darwinists have never been able to set aside the inescapable fact that *cultural* evolution—including the evolution of science—is quintessentially Lamarckian.

LAW

A compulsory rule. The term is used in a social context to refer to the formal instructions that members of a community are supposed to follow, transgression of which is punishable, but in the context of natural philosophy it refers to inviolable principles governing the behaviour of material entities. The progress of science is frequently measured by its gradual elucidation of fundamental "laws of nature", the most important of which include Newton's three laws of motion and the laws of thermodynamics. Many such laws are named for their discoverers, thus retaining a record of heroic endeavours in science. The idea of a "natural law" is, however, somewhat confused by attempts by *Aristotle and many others to figure out what kind of moral laws human beings naturally tend (or are intended) to follow or institute.

The notion that laws of nature are dictates imposed by a Creator is readily transferred to the social sphere; the monotheistic tradition of Judaism, Christianity, and Islam has strongly favoured the notion that social and moral laws are also divinely determined, and hence absolute in spite of being so frequently broken. This has long been an important element of conflict in nations where law-making institutions have evolved in the direction of democracy, thus tacitly establishing statute law as a kind of social contract, continually subject to pragmatic readjustment. The introduction into legal systems of rights as well as duties is partly a response to the evolution of contract theory, but the concept of rights can be reformulated as "natural" or "divine" rights that pre-exist and limit any such contract.

In much the same way that the notion of natural law influenced the idea of social law as divine ordinance, so the notion of law as a negotiated settlement, in its turn, influenced the relativist idea that theoretical descriptions of the world are merely ways of seeing, with no absolute warrant. This fundamental attitudinal division is echoed in disputes as to whether scientific laws are prescriptive or merely descriptive, and whether the notion of "cause" is anything more than an observation of consistent coincidence.

Literature is inherently more interested in deviance than normality, because deviance is the source of drama. In fiction, therefore—to an even greater extent than in actual society—laws are routinely broken, and might even be judged to be elevated as topics merely in order to be broken. From the earliest days of Greek theatre and epic poetry to contemporary TV shows, the primary focus of literary activity has been disobedience of divine, religious, political, or moral laws, and the consequences of that disobedience. The simplest conventional story arc is one that requires a disturbed *status quo* to be recovered or repaired, and when such disturbances are not the result of human violation of written or unwritten laws, they are generally the result of natural *disasters ("acts of God") that devastate the pattern of everyday life.

Sophisticated literature conducts this kind of exercise thoughtfully and painstakingly, while popular fiction tends to formularise and melodramatise it.

Crime fiction—which might be more accurately described as "law-breaking fiction"—is one of the principal families of popular fiction, lending itself to the prolific production of segmental series in which heroic crimefighters face a potentially infinite series of lawbreakers. It gives rise to a series of commodified genres that includes detective fiction, spy fiction, thrillers, and Westerns. The other principal family of popular fiction—consisting of stories of self-improvement, whose endings are rewarding rather than normalising, distributed in such popular genres as romance and "family sagas"—is a fiction of violated rights rather than failed duties; its endings are rewarding precisely because they seem to be delivering entitlements that have been too long withheld. All kinds of fictional closure are, in a sense, impositions of law on disturbed narratives.

This quasi-adversarial relationship between literature and law poses problems for all fiction that attempts to deal with laws of nature in the scientific sense, because laws of nature are unbreakable in reality. Although fiction is perfectly able, and very often willing, to traffic in *impossibility, blatant deviations from naturalism are sometimes seen as foolish or depreciated in value. Sophisticated magical fantasy often excuses such deviations by using magic as a facilitating device to illuminate conventional deviations from existing moral principles, cautioning against the power of desire rather than indulging it. Speculative fiction, which attempts to avoid deviation from the principles of natural law while remaining imaginatively adventurous, often takes advantage of the same loophole, but runs into a problem in so doing. As Anatole France pointed out in *Sur la pierre blanche* (1905; trans. as *The White Stone*), serious speculative fiction ought to suspend judgement on the merit and durability of contemporary moral laws, in order to recognise the inevitability of their alternation, if not in the hope of making some contribution to their supersession. On the other hand, writers attempting to describe superior moral laws in successful operation—designers of Utopias—tend to separate themselves from the essence of the literary project, whose core is the depiction of deviance.

It is hardly surprising that some writers have come to see the tyranny of scientific law as something to be calculatedly violated in literature—and not in any subtle or apologetic fashion. It was for this reason that Alfred Jarry invented the hypothetical antiscience of *pataphysics while paving the way for the surrealist manifesto. Although there is no manifest connection, there is a similar spirit of rebellion in the manner in which a great deal of twentieth-century science fiction deals with calculated and unrepentant violations of scientific law such as faster-than-light *space travel, *time travel, *antigravity, and so on. The same spirit is evident among theoretical scientists, who often try to figure out ways to accommodate these same antagonistic ideas within their theoretical models. The speculative element of science, which serves a function analogous to that of *mutation in biological *evolution in generating new hypotheses for selective testing, can be seen as a form of deliberate deviance.

One "law" frequently cited in the parlance of scientists and engineers that has attracted intense but irreverent attention in science fiction, especially in the pages of *Astounding/Analog*, is the principle of perversity commonly known as Murphy's Law in the United States and Sod's Law in Britain, which states that "if something can go wrong, it will". Murphy's Law is a considerable inconvenience to practical men, but it is vital to conventional methods of narrative construction, because the development of dramatic tension depends on the plans formulated by characters to deal with the problems facing them going horribly awry before victory is finally snatched from the jaws of disaster. The part played by the careful application of Murphy's Law to the construction of science-fictional plots is, in principle, no different from the part it plays in the construction of naturalistic plots, but it poses a particular challenge to the ingenuity of science fiction writers, who must accommodate their schemes of error, complication, and ultimate redemption to schemes of scientific and technological plausibility.

When John W. Campbell Jr. made a passing reference to what he initially called "Finagle's Law" in *Astounding* in 1957, it called forth a flood of responses, which began appearing in the magazine's letters columns in February 1958. Numerous corollaries were suggested, including the "Bugger Factor" and the "Diddle Coefficient". The principle was explicitly acknowledged in such stories as Hugh B. Brous Jr.'s story "Murphy's Law" and Theodore L. Thomas' "The Law School" (both 1958). The feminist "Male-Versus-Female Laws", initially cited with ironic reference to a story by Katherine MacLean, soon made their appearance, as did the "Snafoo Series"—euphemistically misspelled to conceal the term's origin as an acronym—the Tohellwithit Factor, twenty axioms credited to the International Society of Philosophical Engineers, the Harvard Law of Animal Behaviour ("Animals will do what they damn well please"), and an elaborate network of "Stupidtheorems" (commencing with "The probability of predicting correctly in total ignorance is zero").

Arthur Bloch's *Murphy's Law, and Other Reasons Why Things Go Wrong* (1977) attempted to assemble a definitive collection of these terms, but the author had to publish several more volumes, including specific ones devoted to the medical and legal professions. The many happy returns of the principle to the pages of Campbell's magazine included a "spoof issue" of *Analog* (mid-December 1984) that featured A. Held, P. Yodzis, and E. Zechbruder's attempts to reconcile the work of two great lawgivers in "On the Einstein-Murphy Interaction", tacitly recognising that the ongoing quest in theoretical physics to fuse relativity theory with quantum mechanics would not really provide a Theory of Everything.

Coincidentally, the review column in the April 1958 issue of *Astounding* included an account of C. Northcote Parkinson's *Parkinson's Law* (1957)—a principle usually stated as "Work expands so as to fill the time available for its completion"—whose logic offered a convincing explanation of the fact that theoretically rational bureaucratic organisations always appear to be monumentally irrational in the way they actually work. The principle in question is akin to the seemingly perverse *economic theory of Bernard de Mandeville and Adam Smith, in which "private vices produce public benefits" and Garrett Hardin's account of "The Tragedy of the Commons". Although laws in natural science are much less prone to that kind of perversity, Werner Heisenberg's *uncertainty principle—especially as modelled in the thought experiment of Schrödinger's cat—seemed not dissimilar to many observers. The *Astounding* discussion was unleashed in the midst of the Cold War, whose fundamental logic of deterrence seemed perverse to some, while the subversively contradictory slogans featured in George Orwell's *Nineteen Eighty-Four* (1949) still seemed slightly shocking.

Science fiction writers produced numerous accounts of exotic legal systems, and were occasionally willing to hint at new laws of nature they could not specify in detail—although Charles Sheffield's "The Invariants of Nature" (1993) is unusually specific in detailing a new conservation law—but the most famous set of science-fictional laws is an interesting hybrid of the two. Isaac *Asimov's Three Laws of Robotics constitute a set of moral commandments, but one that permits no scope for disobedience. The story series generated with the aid of the laws that consisted largely of puzzle stories in which the anomalous behaviour of *robots had to be explained in terms of their conformity with these moral/natural laws. Writers considering similar hypothetical *artificial intelligences, including Jack Williamson in "With Folded Hands" (1947), proved equally adept at extrapolating seemingly simple and benign principles into perverse and dangerous behaviour-patterns—a kind of ingenuity that was subsequently to become

manifest in the actual scientific discipline of evolutionary psychology, spun off from *sociobiology.

Analog also played host to a series of stories by Randall Garrett, whose early examples were collected in *Too Many Magicians* (1967), featuring an *alternative world in which magic is bound by the laws deduced by the *ethnologist James Frazer, thus giving rise to a range of magical technologies. Although the fundamental conceit echoes the "mathematics of magic" pioneered in *Astounding*'s fantasy companion *Unknown* by L. Sprague *de Camp, Garrett developed it in a manner much more similar to Asimov's, his detective hero carefully analysing seemingly impossible events to show how they were produced as extrapolations of the Frazerian principles. David *Brin's *The Practice Effect* (1984) is a similar exercise in exotic world building based on a fantastic but proverbially sanctioned law.

The notion that the laws of nature might be variable is a difficult one to take aboard, because the assumption of their invariability is built into science at a fundamental level, but it is one that scientists have been forced to consider in a *cosmological context, not merely in the context of versions of inflation theory that hypothesise many universes but in attempts to explain apparent anomalies in the early evolution of the observable universe. Literary reflections of this notion include Vernor Vinge's *A Fire upon the Deep* (1992), in which the central regions of galaxies (the Unthinking Depths) have laws that prohibit thought, while the intermediate region inhabited by beings like us (the Slowness) eventually gives way by degrees to the Beyond, where the speed of light is unlimited and thought is extremely rapid; beyond the Beyond lies the Transcendent, whose Powers are godlike but ephemeral.

LE GUIN, URSULA K[ROEBER] (1929–)

U.S. writer, the daughter of the celebrated *ethnologist Alfred L. Kroeber. Her mother, Theodora Kroeber, was also a writer, whose books included an account of a displaced tribesman, *Ishi in Two Worlds* (1961). After obtaining her M.A. from Columbia in 1952, Le Guin worked in various colleges as an instructor in French and began raising a family of three children. She began publishing fiction in 1962, initially writing fantasies but soon beginning to develop a series of science fiction novels that underwent a spectacular maturation as it evolved.

The series in question is set within a community of Earthlike worlds known as the Ekumen, all of which—including Earth—originated as colonies of the planet Hain. Most, having been separated from the remainder for thousands of years, had developed their own highly idiosyncratic cultures before being recontacted and slowly reintegrated into a loose confederation. The first three novels in the series, *Rocannon's World* (1966), *Planet of Exile* (1966), and *City of Illusions* (1967), focused on the social and psychological problems associated with the evolution of telepathic "mindspeech", but most of the later works abandoned parapsychological motifs in order to concentrate on more rationally plausible exercises in hypothetical ethnology.

The Left Hand of Darkness (1969) moved the series to a new level of sophistication, offering a detailed and sympathetic critique of a society of human hermaphrodites. Two previous investigations of the notion, in Gabriel Foigny's *La Terre australe connue* (1676; trans. as *A New Discovery of Terra Incognita Australis* and *The Southern Land, Known*) and Theodore Sturgeon's *Venus Plus X* (1960), had given similarly earnest consideration to the question of whether the removal of sexual differentiation from society would facilitate social equality, but Le Guin's version set the relevant thought experiment much more firmly and deftly within the context of a novel whose characters' learning experiences change their lives profoundly.

"Vaster Than Empires and More Slow" (1971), the Hainish series' most significant sidestep into exotic *exobiology, displayed a fascination with forests echoed in *The Word for World Is Forest* (1972; book, 1976), a scathing condemnation of *colonialism and imperialism, which credits the native population of its imaginary world with unusual mental faculties based in the *Jungian theory of the collective unconscious. The first climactic high point of the series was *The Dispossessed: An Ambiguous Utopia* (1974), which carefully contrasts the quasi-Utopian anarchist society of an arid moon with the capitalist system of its technologically developed parent world, employing a theoretical physicist as a protagonist in order that the intellectual significance of his work can be set against the two contrasting social backgrounds, arguing that objective truth cannot be politically neutral.

Alongside these series stories, Le Guin wrote several other exceptional works. "Nine Lives" (1969) depicts a company of *clones whose emotional and existential links are devastated in the course of a disastrous expedition. "The Ones Who Walk Away from Omelas" (1973) is a *conte philosophique* dramatising a classic problem in ethical philosophy. "The New Atlantis" (1975) is a bleak fabular account of a devastating *ecocatastrophe. Her early short fiction, including some items in the Hainish series, were collected in *The Wind's Twelve Quarters* (1975) and *The Compass Rose* (1982). She also wrote several essays on

the nature and artistry of fantastic fiction, stressing the close kinship between conscientious science fiction and other kinds of fabulation. Her analytical investigations of the politics of the imagination and the techniques of imaginative writing established such collections as *The Language of the Night* (1979; rev. 1989) and *Dancing at the Edge of the World* (1989) as key guidebooks for writers in the field as well as critics.

Le Guin set the Hainish series aside for some time, but returned to it in a series of novellas collected in *Four Ways to Forgiveness* (1995), set in the problematic aftermath of a slave revolt in a double-planet culture. The stories investigate, from a series of carefully differentiated perspectives, the social and psychological difficulties involved in exercising political freedom once it has been notionally obtained. The central theme focuses on the necessity of setting aside the impulse to take revenge for past wrongs if cycles of violence are to be broken and an end to injustice secured. In *The Telling* (2001), an Ekumen observer visits a remote planet in order to compare and contrast the society of the Maoist Aka with that of fundamentalist Umists. Six of the eight stories in *The Birthday of the World and Other Stories* (2002) are also set in the Hainish universe, similarly establishing interesting *xenological test cases, and the longest of the collection's other inclusions, "Paradises Lost", is a similar study of a claustrophobic society evolved in the course of a generation starship's journey.

Le Guin's novels outside the Hainish sequence include a classic series of children's fantasies set in the secondary world of Earthsea, and numerous other works for children as well as secondary world fantasies for adults, some of which refrain from magical devices. One on the margins of science fiction is *The Lathe of Heaven* (1971), a metaphysical fantasy about dreams that have the power to alter reality, and the dangers of attempted wish fulfilment. Her other science fiction novels include the relatively brief *The Eye of the Heron* (1978; book, 1982), a political fantasy recalling the Biblical book of Exodus, in which an oppressed population on a colony world decide to seek its fortune in the wilderness, and *Always Coming Home* (1986), her most sustained and detailed exercise in imaginary ethnology. The latter borders on speculative nonfiction; it presents an extraordinarily elaborate description of the folkways, myths, and artwork of the post-technological society of the Kesh, the future inhabitants of northern California.

The mosaic *Changing Planes* (2003) collects a series of ethnological fabulations in a more whimsical and fabular vein, set within the frame of a multiverse whose elements—accessible via Earthly airports—are subject to the inquisitive investigations of the

Interplanary Agency. Its accounts of "The Royals of Hegn" and "The Flyers of Gy" (both 2000) describe societies significantly more exotic than those of the Ekumen. Many of the stories, including "The Island of the Immortals" (1999), re-examine standard science fiction motifs, while others, including the Jungian "The Social Dreaming of the Frin" (2002), develop Le Guin's own particular fascinations in new directions.

Le Guin's literary influence has probably been far greater in the field of genre fantasy, whose early commercial development she assisted considerably, than it has in genre science fiction. She felt compelled to rail against the swift domination of the fantasy genre by what she condemned as imitative and formularised "commodified fantasy", but she undoubtedly helped to inspire a great deal of work that was far more ambitious in its intent and methods. The standard she set in science fiction was so high that few other writers made any attempt to match it, but the subtitle of *The Dispossessed* was quickly complemented by Samuel R. Delany's description of *Triton* (1976) as "An Ambiguous Heterotopia", and explicit homage is paid to the Hainish series in Ian McDonald's "The Hidden Place" (2002), which replays the scenario of *The Left Hand of Darkness* in the context of an alternative Ekumen.

LEONARDO DA VINCI (1452–1519)

Florentine artist and engineer. The illegitimate son of a lawyer, Leonardo was apprenticed to the artist Andrea Verrocchio when Renaissance Florence was in its Medici heyday. He finished his training in 1472 and went into business for himself, developing his interests in mathematics and mechanics—including the mechanics of human anatomy and the flight of birds—alongside his painting. He began to record his ideas in notebooks, using mirror-writing to protect the textual contents from prying eyes. His studies of animal flight led him to speculate about the possibility of building machines to simulate the process, and when he despaired of the possibility of winged flight, he made drawings of "helicopters" seemingly inspired by the means adopted by certain airborne seeds. His mathematical interests were advanced when he illustrated Luca Pacioli's book on the "golden section", *Divina Proportione* (1509; trans. as *The Divine Proportion*), whose applications in artistic design he continued to explore.

In 1482, Leonardo left Florence for Milan, after successfully advertising his services to Ludovico Sforza in a famous letter, which stressed his talents as a military engineer and inventor. He attempted to exercise the latter ability during the next seventeen years, but his most abundant material achievements seem to have been minor contributions to the entertainment of the Milanese court, in the form of amusing automata. He may, however, have made contributions to the careful founding of cannon that were not so freely advertised. He drew sketches for ambitious schemes of irrigation and engines of war, as well as such devices as a screw-operated printing press, but none were ever constructed, and his most ambitious artistic scheme—the construction of a huge statue of Ludovico's ancestor Francesco Sforza, sitting upon a rearing horse—also came to nothing. His notebooks grew vastly—some 5,000 pages have survived—but their abundant anatomical representations and technological fantasies remained private, and mostly hidden. This phase of his life came to an end in 1499 when the French invaded Milan.

Leonardo fled the invasion and spent the rest of his life as a wanderer, serving numerous masters, including Cesare Borgia, who employed him as a military engineer during the campaign whose observation by Niccolo Machiavelli prompted that author's notoriously cynical study of the art of politics, *Il Principio* (written 1513, published 1532; trans. as *The Prince*). He went to Rome in 1513 when the son of Lorenzo de Medici became Pope Leo X, to work alongside Raphael and Michelangelo, but went to Amboise in 1516 when the king of France offered him a workplace free of any obligation; there he died a disappointed man—allegedly in the arms of the king, François I—having never fulfilled his ambitions.

Although Leonardo is seen in retrospect primarily as an idle dreamer, who filled his notebooks with designs for impossible machines, and did not value his genius for painting highly enough to put enough time and effort into it, he can also be identified as a great pioneer of empiricism. His fascination with accurate representation as a means to understanding was coupled with a keen appreciation of the delusory nature of what passed for knowledge among the alchemists and physicians of his era. When his notebooks were rediscovered in the late eighteenth century, it was the drawings they contained that claimed immediate attention, first as sketchwork by a great painter and only secondly as exploits in hypothetical design, while the accompanying text was relegated to a lower status, but the text is equally significant even though it had no opportunity to influence anyone before it was superseded. It included such interesting nuggets as a set of notes for a work of fiction describing a new Deluge; although little survived of the idea beyond the chapter titles, there was enough for Robert Payne to "edit" the prospectus into a complete text, published as *The Deluge* (1954).

Leonardo is featured in a good deal of historical fiction, including Theodore Mathieson's "Leonardo da Vinci, Detective" (1959), Peter Barnes' play *Leonardo's Last Supper* (1969), Rena De' Firenze's *Mystery of the Mona Lisa* (1996), R. M. Berry's *Leonardo's Horse* (1997), the film *Ever After* (1998), E. L. Konigsburg's *The Second Mrs. Gioconda* (1998), and Mario Puzo's *The Family* (2001), as well as such speculative works as Manly Wade Wellman's timeslip romance *Twice in Time* (1940; book, 1957), Poul Anderson's "The Light" (1957), Kit Reed's "Mister da V." (1967), Nathalie Charles-Henneberg's "Les non-humains" (1958, by-lined Charles Henneberg; trans. as "The Non-Humans"), Charles L. Harness' "The Tetrahedron" (1994), and episodes of the TV series *Star Trek* and *Doctor Who*. Notable *alternative histories in which his dreams bear more prolific fruit include Ted White's *The Jewels of Elsewhen* (1967), Garry Kilworth's "The Sculptor" (1992), Paul J. McAuley's *Pasquale's Angel* (1994), and Jack Dann's "Da Vinci Rising" (1995). Dann's earlier secret history, *The Memory Cathedral* (1995), concentrated on his work as a military engineer. His artworks are very frequently cited in fiction, especially his version of the Last Supper and the *Mona Lisa*; relevant speculative fictions include J. G. Ballard's "The Lost Leonardo" (1964), Bob Shaw's "The Gioconda Caper" (1976), and Dan Brown's *The Da Vinci Code* (2003).

LEVINSON, PAUL (1947–)

U.S. writer. He was born and raised in New York City, and attended City College there before dropping out to write folk-rock songs, of which he published more than a hundred; he recorded "Hung Up on Love" with the Other Voices in 1968 and the album *Twice upon a Rhyme* in 1972. He returned to New York University before obtaining an M.A. in media studies from the New School for Social Research, which had been founded in 1919 by John Dewey and others with a specifically futurist philosophy.

Levinson returned to the New School as a teacher after obtaining his Ph.D. from NYU in the philosophy and history of media and technology. He founded his own organisation, Connected Education Inc., in 1985, offering online courses linked to the NSSR's programs and those of several other universities. These include creative writing courses focused on science fiction as well as courses in social science focused on the social roles of science and technology. He was editor of *The Journal of Social and Evolutionary Systems* from 1990 to 2000.

Levinson began publishing fiction in 1991; the backbone of his work is a series of futuristic *forensic science mysteries launched with "The Chronology Protection Case" (1995) and other short stories before continuing in the novels *The Silk Code* (1999), *The Consciousness Plague* (2002), and *The Pixel Eye* (2003). "Loose Ends" (1997) considers the troubles afflicting the U.S. space program and the consequent fading of the myth of the Space Age. "The Orchard" (1998) features an eponymous artifact that provides previously elusive evidence of long-departed alien intelligence in an exobiological ecosphere.

Borrowed Tides (2001) describes the first manned interstellar mission, to Alpha Centauri, seen from the viewpoints of a philosopher of science and an ethnologist specialising in Native American mythology. *The Plot to Save Socrates* (2006) is an intricate time travel story in which characters from the nineteenth and twenty-first centuries are inveigled, along with the Athenian general and statesman Alcibiades, into a quest to prevent Socrates from committing suicide.

The main thread of Levinson's speculative nonfiction provides an elaborate account of the present and potential future impacts of information technology, begun in the essays collected in *Electronic Chronicles* (1992) and *Learning Cyberspace* (1995) and continued in *The Soft Edge: A Natural History and Future of the Information Revolution* (1997) and *Digital McLuhan: A Guide to the Information Millennium* (1999). The essays collected in *Realspace: The Fate of Physical Presence in the Digital Age, on and off Planet* (2003) continued the discussion.

LEY, WILLY (1906–1969)

German-born populariser of science who became a leading proponent of the myth of the *Space Age. His early life and career were confused by the troubled history of his native land; his father worked in the United States from 1910 to 1913 and then opened a delicatessen in London, but was interned during World War I and ruined by the postwar slump. He attended the University of Berlin and the University of Königsberg in 1924–1927 but left without graduating because of financial problems. Having popularised the ideas of the rocket pioneer Hermann Oberth in *Die Fahrt ins Weltall* [Journey into Space] (1926), he became a leading member of the Verein für Raumschiffart [Society for Space Travel] founded in 1927.

Die Mögelichkeit der Weltraumfahrt [The Possibility of Interplanetary Travel] (1928) helped inspire Fritz Lang's film *Die Frau im Mond* (1929; English version, *The Girl in the Moon*), although Ley was not directly involved in Oberth's failed attempt to build a working rocket for use in the film. He took an active part in subsequent successful experiments with liquid fuel rockets, but his attempts to build a career as a science writer were frustrated by Germany's economic collapse; when the Nazis took over supervision of the VFR in 1933, Ley resigned and left the country.

Having entered the United States on a visitor's visa, Ley was unable to obtain formal employment, but he supported himself as a freelance writer until he was allowed to apply for residential status in 1937. He published four science fiction stories in the pulp magazines, signed "Robert Willey", the most notable of which was "At the Perihelion" (1937), which attempted to bring a new technical realism to space fiction. The science fiction magazines became a regular market for his science articles after F. Orlin Tremaine's *Astounding Stories* published his propagandistic essay on "The Dawn of the Conquest of Space" (1937). In 1940, he joined the staff of the New York evening paper *PM*, but it folded when the United States entered World War II and he continued freelancing; his first book in English was a collection of articles on strange and mythical animals, *The Lungfish and the Unicorn* (1941; rev. 1948 as *The Lungfish, the Dodo and the Unicorn*)—a field he investigated further in *Dragons in Amber* (1951) and *Salamanders and Other Wonders* (1955), whose contents were combined and condensed in *Exotic Zoology* (1959).

The widespread publicity given in the war's final phases to the V-1 and V-2 rocket-bombs developed by Ley's former VFR colleagues at Peenemünde renewed interest in his articles on that subject, and helped his subsequent books on rocketry to become best-sellers. He also became famous as a radio and TV broadcaster. *Rockets: The Future of Travel Beyond the Stratosphere* (1944; rev. 1947 as *Rockets and Space Travel*; exp. 1951 as *Rockets, Missiles and Space Travel*), became a standard reference book, while *The Conquest of Space* (1949)—whose text he wrote to accompany paintings by Chesley Bonestell—helped prepare the imaginative ground for America's space program. His account of possible satellite-based weapons systems, "How We Could Wage Wars from Man-Made Stars" (1951), was the ultimate progenitor of Ronald Reagan's Strategic Defense Initiative. A further text illustrating Bonestell's paintings, *The Exploration of Mars* (1956; aka *Project Mars*), was written in collaboration with Wernher von Braun; he and Bonestell eventually added *Beyond the Solar System* (1964) to the set. *Satellites, Rockets and Outer Space* (1958) and *Missiles, Moonprobes and Megaparsecs* (1964) collected newspaper articles.

From 1947 onwards, Ley was a consultant to the U.S. Department of Commerce's Office of Technical Services, and eventually obtained an appointment as professor of science at Fairleigh Dickson University. From the early 1950s until his death, he contributed a monthly science column to the science fiction magazine *Galaxy*, which served as a model for Isaac *Asimov's column in *The Magazine of Fantasy & Science Fiction*; Ley also answered science queries from *Galaxy*'s readers. Some of his columns were reprinted in *Of Earth and the Sky* (1967) and *Another Look at Atlantis* (1969). Many were spun off from the books he published alongside them, including *Days of Creation* (1952), *Lands Beyond* (1952, with L. Sprague de Camp), *Engineers' Dreams* (1954), and *Watchers of the Skies: An Informal History of Astronomy from Babylon to the Space Age* (1963). *The Drifting Continents* (1969) was one of five books published in the final year of his life; he died three weeks before the first moon landing, for which he had written so much anticipatory propaganda.

LIFE

The quality that distinguishes animate organisms from inert matter; the subject matter of the modern science of *biology. In the absence of any means to analyse the differences between a living body and a dead one, early observers tended to see life in terms of some independent animating principle, such as the *pneuma* (divine breath) favoured by Zeno's Stoic school or the "vital spark" favoured by *Aristotle. It was not until the end of the eighteenth century that such views became challengeable in a scientific context, and the fundamental notion proved resilient in the face of criticism.

The vital element of animation was considered as a divine gift in a religious context, and the doctrine was initially secularised in terms of theories of "spontaneous generation". As the notion of independent creation came under increasing pressure, however, theories of spontaneous generation were also treated with growing scepticism. Theories of evolution proposed that all organisms might be descended from a single common ancestor, implying that the spontaneous generation of Earthly life need only have happened once, but the likelihood of it occurring even once seemed sufficiently remote to encourage such speculators as Svante Arrhenius to push its point of origin even further back with the theory of *panspermia. It was not until 1953 that an experiment conducted by Stanley L. Miller and Harold C. Urey—in which electrical discharges catalysed the formation of amino acids in a "hot organic soup" allegedly similar to the Earth's primordial oceans—was held up as proof that life might indeed have been spontaneously generated on Earth. However, the following fifty years failed to provide any hypothetical model, let alone any experimental evidence, of a sequence of chemical evolution extending all the way from simple organic molecules to a self-replicating molecular structure.

Attempts to conceptualise the mysterious spark of life moved in step with theories in physics, taking on new forms in the late eighteenth century, when the vital spark was increasingly seen as a kind of *force or energy, assisting the advent of such notions as Anton Mesmer's "animal magnetism". The associated concept of life as a kind of "vital electricity" was considerably boosted by Luigi Galvani's discovery that electrical stimulation could cause a frog's muscle to contract.

The most striking literary reflection of the electrical perspective was Mary Shelley's *Frankenstein* (1818). Numerous other nineteenth-century works extrapolated the analogy in different ways. Alvey A. Adee's "The Life-Magnet" (1870) describes the creation of simple life-forms and the reanimation of the dead by extracts of vital force. The transfer of an electrical life force facilitates an identity exchange in Edgar Fawcett's *Douglas Duane* (1887) and a rejuvenation in the same author's *A Romance of Two Brothers* (1891). Marie Corelli's *A Romance of Two Worlds* (1887) imagines the human body as a kind of "battery" that is sometimes in need of recharging, and is capable of being supercharged—a notion further extrapolated in Arthur Conan Doyle's "The Los Amigos Fiasco" (1892). The notion of life force also gave rise to tales of "psychic vampirism" such as J. Maclaren Cobban's *Master of His Fate* (1890).

As organic chemistry became more sophisticated, attention began to shift away from vital electricity towards the biochemical production of energy, but the metabolic pathways by which energy is stored and released, and the key roles of such molecules as ATP (adenosine tri-phosphate), were not fully elucidated until the 1960s. In the meantime, vitalism was defended by biologists such as Hans Driesch, who redeveloped the Aristotelian notion of "entelechy" (actualisation) as a replacement term for the increasingly unfashionable notion of vital electricity. The vitalist perspective was given a further overhaul by the evolutionist philosopher Henri Bergson, who popularised the term *élan vital*. Karl von Reichenbach's hypothetical "odic" force—applied to the creation of artificial life in Charles Edmonds Walk's "The Odyle" (1907)—also helped to sustain the vitalist perspective.

Vitalism maintained its grip on the popular imagination long into the twentieth century, cropping up continually in pulp science fiction, where the ultimate end of evolution was often envisaged as beings of "pure force" or "pure energy". The idea of innate biological energies retained its hold in many forms of "alternative medicine" into the twenty-first century, their status as alternatives generally deriving from an adherence to versions of vitalist theory instead of the chemical mechanisms envisaged by orthodox twentieth-century medicine, as expressed in drug therapies. Attempts to demystify biology by eliminating the notion of vital energy, such as Jacques Loeb's *The Mechanistic Conception of Life* (1912), often became stridently polemical in their attempts to smash the idol in question; Loeb became the model for Max Gottlieb in Sinclair Lewis's *Arrowsmith* (1925).

The eventual abandonment of the electrical version of vitalist theory as something applicable to Earthly life did not prevent speculative writers from trying to accommodate it to exobiological contexts. The notion that such a force might produce inorganic as well as organic life-forms was broached in such works as J. H. Rosny aîné's "La mort de la terre" (1910; trans. as "The Death of the Earth"). Discorporate electrical life is featured in such stories as Sewell Peaslee Wright's "Vampires of Space" (1932) and Fredric Brown's "The Waveries" (1945).

Earthly electricity is represented as an unintelligent remnant of a more versatile life-form in John Russell Fearn's "Metamorphosis" (1937), but retains its intellectual potential in Fritz Leiber's "The Man Who Made Friends with Electricity" (1962). The idea of vital electricity continued to thrive in metaphor, particularly in respect of the energy of thought—which is indeed electrical to the extent that neural transmission is an electrochemical phenomenon; talk of "brain waves" and "sparks of genius" is commonplace. Such analogies have a particular resonance in the context of speculative fiction and nonfiction, as reflected in the title of Catherine Asaro's periodical *Mindsparks*.

Alternative notions of an isolatable vital principle are featured in numerous twentieth-century speculative fictions, notably two stories called "The Wand of Creation", one (1929) by Stanton A. Coblentz and the other (1934) by Raymond Z. Gallun, P. Schuyler Miller's "Spawn" (1939), and Kit Reed's "The Quest" (1960; aka "Ordeal"). Exobiological fantasies played host to numerous accounts of life imbuing alternative states of matter, such as the vaporous life featured in Clare Winger Harris and Miles J. Breuer's "A Baby on Neptune" (1929), the fluid life-forms in Ralph Milne Farley's "Liquid Life" (1936) and Hal Clement's "Critical Factor" (1953), and the plasmatic life-forms of James Blish's *The Star Dwellers* (1961) and Mike Resnick's *The Soul Eater* (1981).

Inorganic solids continued to be a favourite medium of variation, as in the accounts of metallic life contained in Frigyes Karinthy's *Utazas Faremido* (1916; trans. as *Voyage to Faremido*), A. Merritt's *The Metal Monster* (1920; book, 1946), and Jack Williamson's "The Metal Man" (1928), and such accounts of crystalline life as J. H. Rosny aîné's "Les xipéhuz" (1887; trans. as "The Shapes" and "The Xipehuz"), John Taine's *White Lily* (1930; book 1952 as *The Crystal Horde*), Raymond Z. Gallun's "Mad Robot" (1936), and Thomas S. Gardner's "The World of Singing Crystals" (1936). In H. P. Lovecraft's "The Color out of Space" (1927), extraterrestrial life is manifest as a kind of stain. The most common variant of all, however, was the notion of silicon-based life, as featured in P. Schuyler Miller's "The Pool of Life" (1934), Nathan Schachner's "He from Procyon" (1934), Raymond Z. Gallun's "Blue Haze on Pluto" (1935), the stories assembled in Fletcher Pratt's anthology *The Petrified Planet* (1953), and Joan Vinge's "Mother and Child" (1975). The hectic confusion of such images abated somewhat as more attention began to be paid to the ecological contexts in which life-forms had to exist, although the notion of life adapted to the near-void of interstellar space continued to exert a particular fascination in such works as Raymond Z. Gallun's "The Revolt of the Star Men" (1932), Fred Hoyle's *The Black Cloud* (1957), and David Stringer's "High Eight" (1965).

The extension of the phenomenon of life to so many different media was justified by the notion that the essence of life is self-replication—a point explicitly made in Camille *Flammarion's *Lumen* (1866–1869), the first significant attempt to provide a panoramic view of the myriad forms that life might take in adapting to different physical circumstances. The principle is reflected in numerous accounts of exotic reproduction, both *sexual and asexual, and in such accounts of artificial life as S. P. Meek's "The Synthetic Entity" (1933). The effects of *radiation on *mutation, popularised in the 1920s, were a particular inspiration, reflected in such stories as A. Rowley Hilliard's "Death from the Stars" (1931) and "The Reign of the Star-Death" (1932) as well as conventional mutational romances. The use of *computers in modelling reproductive processes quickly gave rise to James L. Conway's "game" *Life*, which eventually gave rise to a wide range of simulation programs, featuring "cellular automata", some of which were "anthologised" in Rudy Rucker and John Walker's *Cellab Cellular Automata Laboratory* (1997).

The production of so many quasi-organic variants was counterbalanced by a reductionist attitude to "orthodox" organic life, which often came to be seen as an infinite series of variations on a single protoplasmic theme. The amoeba came to be seen as a kind of prototype of all multicellular organisms, and numerous images were produced of avid protoplasmic masses that reduced all organic material to their own undifferentiated state, including the aptly named movie *The Blob* (1958) and Theodore L. Thomas and Kate Wilhelm's *The Clone* (1965). Damon Knight's "Four-in-One" (1953) features a mass of this sort that obtains higher organic functions by absorbing other creatures. This kind of generalising, coupled with such ecological constructs as notions of the "ecosphere"—especially such collectivising models as James *Lovelock's Gaia hypothesis—encouraged the production of numerous images of vast life-forms covering or embodying whole planets. Notable examples include the entities featured in John T. Phillifent's "Flying Fish" (1964) and Robert Reed's *The Well of Stars* (2005).

LIGHT

The agent responsible for the sensation of sight. Because sight—whose study is the subject matter of *optics—is the most important of the five senses in human beings, light took on a special metaphorical significance. "Enlightenment" came to signify the process of obtaining a clearer and better understanding, especially as the result of a sudden "illumination" that allows someone to "see the light" where there was previously obscurity. Seeing is, as one aphorism has it, believing, and light metaphors are often used in the context of religious faith; the notion of Heaven as a realm of light is commonplace, as reflected in Dante's *Paradiso*.

*Pythagoras was credited with the suggestion that light might be a kind of radiation, but the Pythagoreans thought of it as something emitted by the eye rather than received by it, its rays functioning as "feelers". Epicurus suggested that radiation emitted by luminous objects was reflected by others before being intercepted by the eye, but the Pythagorean version retained its dominance after it was endorsed by Aristotle. Although the Greeks observed the phenomenon of refraction, the hypothetical account of it given by Ptolemy was devoid of any experimental measurements, and therefore very vague. When better accounts of the phenomenon became available in Renaissance Europe—especially when Isaac *Newton made the counterintuitive discovery in the seventeenth century that white light is a compound of various colours separable by refraction—the nature of light radiation became a central puzzle of physical theory.

The transmission of light was routinely assumed to be instantaneous until 1676, when Friedrich Römer correlated anomalies in the perception of eclipses of the moons of Jupiter with the season in which they were observed, allowing him to calculate that light takes approximately eleven minutes to cross the Earth's orbit. The implications of this discovery were not fully appreciated, however, until the true size of the universe was revealed by the first calculations of stellar parallax in the nineteenth century, when initial calculations rendered in parsecs (parallax seconds) were translated into light-years. Even then, it was not until it was proved that certain nebulas were actually other *galaxies that an appreciation grew that light took billions of years—far longer than the lifetime of a star—to traverse the observable universe.

The notion that light must consist of a series of particles, accepted by both René Descartes and Newton, was challenged by such writers as Robert Hooke and Christian Huygens, who thought that it must consist of vibrations in a medium. The early supporters of the former thesis were more prestigious, and it eclipsed its rival for more than a hundred years, but neither theory could give an entirely satisfactory account of the whole range of light's properties. The wave theory was revitalised by Thomas Young and Augustin Fresnel at the beginning of the nineteenth century, and soon established a new dominance by assisting the explanation of such phenomena as polarisation and diffraction, but James Clerk Maxwell's revitalisation of the *ether as the "luminiferous ether", required as a medium of electromagnetic radiation, ran into difficulties. The fact that light exhibited both vibratory and particulate properties became a key enigma of twentieth-century physics, confusing attempts to specify the properties of the photon.

The utility of light as a source or conveyor of knowledge was dramatically increased between the seventeenth and nineteenth centuries by the invention of such optical instruments as the *telescope and the *microscope, such enhanced beacons as lighthouses, and such techniques of fixing images as *photography. *Astronomy was transformed—and astronomers entranced—by the amazing quantity and quality of information deducible from the inspection of mere points of light in the night sky. Joseph von Fraunhofer's observation in 1814 that the solar spectrum is interrupted by dark lines caused by the absorption of particular wavelengths paved the way for Gustave Kirchhoff and Robert Bunsen to identify the elements present in the sun by spectroscopic analysis in 1859 and the first measurements of cosmic Doppler shifts by William Huggins in 1868, pioneering new dimensions of astronomical inquiry. The marvellous capacity of light as an agent of scientific enlightenment was celebrated by Camille *Flammarion when

he appointed it as the symbolic fount of wisdom in *Lumen* (1866–1869), and the awful tragedy of August Strindberg's *Fadren* (1887; trans. as *The Father*) is consummated when the protagonist's spectroscopic analyses of other worlds are construed as evidence of madness by his uncomprehending wife.

In the same period, technologies for producing artificial light made considerable progress, candles and oil lamps being supplemented by gas lamps and then by Thomas *Edison's electric light bulb. Improvements in artificial light made a considerable difference to the progress of science, not merely by facilitating reading in the hours of darkness but also by increasing and enhancing the zones of relative public safety secured by street lighting. It was the introduction of gaslight to the London streets in 1807 that cleared the way for the establishment of a Metropolitan Police Force and the proliferation of a protected nightlife that fostered education and discussion as well as entertainment. The changes were too subtle to attract a great deal of attention, but their significance was realised by Jules Verne, whose account of "Une fantaisie du Docteur Ox" (1872; trans. as "Dr. Ox" and *Dr. Ox's Experiment*) can be read as an allegory of the intoxicating effects of street lighting. Notable twentieth-century fictions featuring new lighting technologies are Donald Wandrei's "Murray's Light" (1935), Robert Heinlein's "Let There Be Light—" (1940; by-lined Lyle Monroe), and Lewis Shiner's "White City" (1990).

Light acquired a dramatic new significance in physics when the constancy of its velocity—from whatever standpoint it might be measured—became the foundation stone of *relativity theory, subsequently integrated by Albert *Einstein into the fundamental equation determining the equivalence of energy and matter, $E=mc^2$. However, the consequent impossibility of exceeding the velocity of light became an awkward stumbling block to writers of speculative fiction, because it put the worlds of other stars beyond practical reach. By the time pulp science fiction writers began to grope their way onto a galactic stage in the late 1920s, their facilitating devices had already been ruled inadmissible by the general theory of relativity published in 1916. That obstacle was not allowed to inhibit the development of the myth of the Space Age, but it forced a great deal of effort to be put into the construction of various kinds of apologetic jargon licensing faster-than-light travel.

The technological manipulation of light made further progress in the twentieth century, the most widely popularised breakthrough being the development of the laser—an acronymic term derived from the phrase "light amplification by the stimulated emission of radiation". In ordinary light sources the atoms emit electromagnetic energy independently, at many different wavelengths, but atoms can be simultaneously stimulated by radiation of a particular wavelength to duplicate that wavelength in their own emission, thus producing a beam of "coherent light", whose focused rays can drill through metals and crystals and carry out delicate surgical operations.

The possibility of light amplification had been recognised by Einstein in 1917, but it was not until 1954 that Charles H. Townes built the first "maser" (a microwave laser) and not until 1960 that the first laser using a visual wavelength—produced by a ruby rod—was assembled by T. H. Maiman. Similar models became the most popular educational exhibit since the x-ray machine. The similarities between laser beams and science-fictional "ray guns" produced a glut of laser *weapons in late twentieth-century science fiction, displayed in such stories as Frank Herbert's "Committee of the Whole" (1965), Ben Bova's *Out of the Sun* (1968), Martin Caidin's *The Mendelov Conspiracy* (1969), Cynthia Felice and Connie Willis' *Light Raid* (1989), and Geoffrey A. Landis' "In the Hole with the Boys with the Toys" (1993).

The symbolic uses of light in fiction did not always find it necessary to keep abreast of these scientific and technological improvements. The frequent metaphorical use of candles and torches as alleviators of darkness was supplemented rather than displaced by the imagery of lighthouses and electric light bulbs, although lighthouses had a firm advantage over candles in the matter of phallic symbolism—an edge exploited by James Joyce in *Ulysses* (1922) and Virginia Woolf in *To the Lighthouse* (1927) as well as less discreet examples such as Jeanette Winterson's *Lighthousekeeping* (2004). Such examples as these emphasise, however, that it is the absence, or threatened absence, of light rather than its presence that carries the greater melodramatic force. Sight may be a slightly dubious privilege in H. G. Wells "The Country of the Blind" (1904), but the most frequently quoted lines in modern poetry are probably Dylan Thomas' "Do not go gentle into that good night ... Rage, rage against the dying of the light" (1953).

Although true darkness renders purposeful action direly difficult, and is thus no better ally of plotting than literary description, it is for that reason a kind of ultimate fictional menace; the word "dark" and its derivatives probably outnumber their opposites by a considerable margin in the titles of works of fiction, and fear of the dark is an enormously significant motivating force in fiction. The dramatic device of reversing light and darkness—so that when the stage is lit the characters are assumed to be in darkness, and vice versa—in Peter Schaffer's play *Black Comedy* (1967) is a striking theatrical device, while Daniel F.

Galouye's *Dark Universe* (1961)—describing a society in which light is a legendary mystery—is something of a science-fictional tour de force. On the other hand, light can be represented as the threatening aspect of the paired opposites, as in Lawrence Watt-Evans' *Nightside City* (1989).

Speculative fictions that make considerable play with the metaphorical significance of light include Olaf Stapledon's *Darkness and Light* (1942), Somtow Sucharitkul's Inquestor series, launched with *Light on the Sound* (1982), Elizabeth A. Lynn's *A Different Light* (1978), and Jeffrey Ford's "A Man of Light" (2005).

LINGUISTICS

The scientific study of language, centred on the structural analysis of grammar. The grammar of Sanskrit compiled by Panini in the fourth century B.C. was the first great triumph of the discipline. The "art" of Greek grammar was first codified by Dionysius Thrax at the beginning of the first century B.C. and Latin grammar was similarly codified by Donatus and Priscian in the first century A.D. The first attempts to construct a generalised "universal grammar" were made in the thirteenth and fourteenth centuries, but little progress was made until late eighteenth- and nineteenth-century comparative studies began to explore and explain the relatedness of various languages, including the "Indo-European" group.

In 1822, Jakob Grimm postulated that there were certain typical patterns of *lautverschiebung* (soundshifts) governing the evolution of Germanic languages. Some of Grimm's fellows in the *Romantic Movement, notably Johann von Herder, emphasised links between the national language and national character (*volksgeist*) of German-speaking people, and linguistic theory—together with the folklore collected by Grimm and his brother Wilhelm—became a significant instrument in the campaign for the consolidation of Germany into a single nation. The Prussian statesman Wilhelm von Humboldt popularised the concept of a language as a dynamic project, continually actualising and extending the potential inherent in an underlying set of rules, anticipating the late nineteenth-century theories of Ferdinand de Saussure, the founder of "structuralism".

F. Max Müller proposed in the essays translated in *Lectures on the Science of Language* (1861) that the world's languages might have a common origin, and sought for evidence of a common root stock of *myths, in accordance with contemporary theories in *anthropology. This whole set of ideas is extensively reflected in literature, but its specifically linguistic aspects were rarely foregrounded; Bill Nye's "Personal Experiences in Monkey Language" (1894) and Charles Loring Jackson's "An Undiscovered 'Isle in the Far Sea'" (1926) were notable exceptions.

The idea of mechanical translation emerged during the rapid sophistication of communication technologies like wireless telegraphy and the *telephone, but early stories contemplating the possibility, such as Frank Stockton's "My Translatophone" (1900), could not take the notion seriously. The translation machines that became standard in pulp science fiction were mere facilitating devices, whose implausibility was parodied by Douglas Adams' Babel fish. In general, the plurality of languages was regarded by the vast majority of writers as a vexatious inconvenience to be got around with the minimum of inventive effort. Highlighting linguistic problems was, by definition, not reader friendly.

Saussure's structuralist theories were not widely communicated until the author was dead, his most influential book being the posthumous *Cours de linguistique générale* (1916; trans. as *Course in General Linguistics*), which drew a fundamental distinction between *langue* (the underlying regularities of linguistic formulation) and *parole* (the actualisation of language in speech), stressing the importance of differences in speech "performance" by various users of a language. This emphasis made the structuralist approach interesting to some academic literary critics, partly because it permitted them to cultivate an analytical expertise quite different from and independent of that of the "language users" they were studying. The dynamics of linguistic performance are, inevitably, explored in very many literary works, being a vital element in the style of such distinctive writers as P. G. Wodehouse and Damon Runyon, and the *raison d'être* of such exercises in dialect as R. Murray Gilchrist's Peakland tales, but the practical expertise reflected in such works had nothing to gain—and perhaps something to lose, in terms of spontaneity—by theoretical complication.

The structuralist approach was also influential in cultural anthropology, where it was further elaborated by Claude Lévi-Strauss, helping to sustain the intimate relationship between studies of language and mythology. This theoretical alliance had some influence on the writing of "mythopoeic fiction", especially by the Inklings group, whose linguist members—Owen Barfield, author of *Poetic Diction* (1928), and J. R. R. Tolkien—communicated something of their theoretical understanding to the other writers, including C. S. Lewis and Charles Williams. Tolkien's *Lord of the Rings* (1954–1955) was spun off from his fascination with the early evolution of the English language from its old Norse roots, and from the mock

epic he attempted to compose in order to embody that cultural evolution, a version of which eventually appeared as *The Silmarillion* (1977).

In America, where Native American languages were rapidly dying out, many without leaving any substantial record, linguistic theorists developed an acute sensitivity to the difficulties of translating Native American vocabularies into Indo-European languages. The ethnologist Franz Boas and his pupil Edward Sapir paved the way for Sapir's pupil Benjamin Whorf to develop the notion that language determines perception and thought to the extent that different languages contain incommensurable worldviews. In its most extreme form, this hypothesis implies that science ought to be seen as a product of Indo-European language rather than an objective account of the world, which cannot be used to pass judgements on worldviews based in other languages—a key foundation stone of twentieth-century *relativism and *postmodernist scepticism.

The Whorf-Sapir hypothesis lent considerable plausibility to the notion that language might be used as an instrument of political thought control, as extrapolated in such *dystopias as Ayn Rand's *Anthem* (1938) and George Orwell's *Nineteen Eighty-Four* (1949), or as a means of resistance to enforced conformity, as in Robert A. Heinlein's "Gulf" (1949). The notion continued to echo in subsequent Orwellian fiction, as in Benjamin Appel's *The Funhouse* (1959), Michael Frayn's *A Very Private Life* (1968), Robert Silverberg's *A Time of Changes* (1971), and Graham Dunstan Martin's *The Dream Wall* (1987). There is also a conspicuous Orwellian element in Russell Hoban's *Riddley Walker* (1980), a *tour de force* displaying a version of English produced in the wake of a devastating nuclear holocaust, which plays host to a great deal of ingenious wordplay.

The relevance of linguistic issues to writers of speculative fiction was discussed in the pages of *Astounding Science Fiction* by L. Sprague de Camp, in "Language for Time Travelers" (1938), having earlier been illustrated by his *conte philosophique* "The Isolinguals" (1937). Stories dealing with such issues remained few and far between, however; notable examples include Anthony Boucher's "Barrier" (1940), Poul Anderson's "Time Heals" (1949), C. M. Kornbluth's "That Share of Glory" (1952), Chad Oliver's *The Winds of Time* (1957), and Jack Vance's *The Languages of Pao* (1958), the last-named being an ingenious extrapolation of the Whorf-Sapir hypothesis.

Progress towards a general theory of language took a significant step forward when Noam Chomsky's *Syntactic Structures* (1957) attempted to identify a "generative grammar" common to all languages. Competition between Chomskian theory and its various rivals helped to make linguistic analysis and argument more fashionable in the United States, especially in academic literary criticism, where European structuralist ideas were imported and further elaborated on a massive scale in the last decades of the twentieth century. Spin-off from this new fashionability included a certain amount of academically sophisticated avant-gardist fiction, notably various works by Christine Brooke-Rose, including *The Dear Deceit* (1958), *Such* (1966), *Thru* (1975), and *Amalgamemnon* (1986).

The intensification of this debate spilled over into popular fiction in such sophisticated science fiction stories as Anthony Burgess' *A Clockwork Orange* (1962), Roger Zelazny's "A Rose for Ecclesiastes" (1963), Lawrence A. Perkins' "Delivered with Feeling" (1965), Samuel R. Delany's *Babel-17* (1966), David I. Masson's "A Two-Timer" (1966) and "Not So Certain" (1967), Robert Merle's *Un animal doué avec raison* (1967; trans. as *The Day of the Dolphin*), Christopher Anvil's "Babel II" (1967), Ian Watson's *The Embedding* (1973) and *The Jonah Kit* (1975), and Ursula Le Guin's "The Author of the Acacia Seeds and Other Extracts from *The Journal of the Association of Therolinguistics*" (1974).

Samuel R. *Delany became intensely interested in the issues touched on in these kinds of stories, which he developed at considerable length in his academic nonfiction and in his Nevèrÿon series of fantasy novels (1979–1989). Other writers who used related academic expertise in a science-fictional context included C. J. Cherryh, most notably in *Hunter of Worlds* (1977) and *Voyager in Light* (1984), and Suzette Haden Elgin, most notably in *Native Tongue* (1984), *The Judas Rose* (1987), and "We Have Always Spoken Panglish" (2004). Genre science fiction had always been a prolific source of neologisms, and its associated fan community began to take some pride in the profusion of its own arcane *argot*.

The linguistic sophistication of genre science fiction pioneered in the 1980s by Delany, Cherryh, and Elgin was further reflected by such works as M. A. Foster's *Waves* (1980), Octavia Butler's "Speech Sounds" (1983), Edward Llewellyn's *Word-Bringer* (1986), Shane Tourtellotte's "Finding a Voice" (1999), Ted Chiang's "Story of Your Life" (1998) and "Seventy-Two Letters" (2000), and Robert Thurston's "I.D.I.D." (2005). Iain M. Banks' *Feersum Endjinn* (1994) is narrated in a wordplay-loaded version of English akin to that developed in *Riddley Walker*. Sheila Finch began a series of stories featuring a Guild of Xenolinguistics in "Reading the Bones" (1998; incorporated into a similarly titled mosaic, 2003). In M. Shayne Bell's "Refugees from Nulongwe" (2001), the language of elephants is finally decoded,

but the independent state established in consequence proves short lived. In Ray Vukcevich's "The Wages of Syntax" (2002), a linguist thinks he has discovered the key to "spontaneous competence"—and hence to universal translation—but the translation machine's time proves to be still unripe.

LOGIC

The study of the principles and structure of sound reasoning, particularly the process of *extrapolative deduction. The term is sometimes extended to apply to the induction of rules from observations or to the kinds of practical reasoning implicit in moral calculation, but in its strictest sense it is a matter of analysing the "force of reason", whose compulsive power is based in the validity of argument rather than the truth of external reference. The academic consideration of logic founded by *Aristotle remained central to the curriculum throughout the Middle Ages, when it was included in the trivium with the related studies of grammar and *rhetoric.

The iconic form of logical construction is the syllogism, in which the juxtaposition of two propositions permits the deduction of a third—for instance, if all As are Bs and all Bs are Cs, then all As are Cs. Unfortunately, psychological *plausibility often attaches to false syllogisms, which duplicate the form but not the sense of the argument; thus, it is sometimes easy to persuade listeners that if all As are Bs and all Cs are Bs then As are highly likely to be Cs, and that kind of trickery is routinely applied by deceptive rhetoricians. The fallibility of incorrect premises can often be demonstrated by the process of *reductio ad absurdum*—the deduction therefrom of blatantly false consequences—but it is not always obvious exactly where the falseness lies, and some such absurd arguments become classic *paradoxes.

Scrupulous logicians are always willing to point out the errors into which everyday patterns of thought frequently fall, and are sometimes unable to comprehend why those corrected are so frequently ungrateful. It is, however, the case that the word "pedant" is usually used and perceived as an insult rather than a compliment. Many people perceive logic as a potential threat to their cherished beliefs and perceived competence, and thus as an enemy to be feared and loathed; this attitude is extensively reflected in literature, although it is rarely endorsed by writers. Voltaire's *conte philosophique* "Zadig, ou la Destinée" (1748; trans. as "Zadig, or Destiny") clarifies and laments the sad truth embodied in the proverbial statement that "nobody loves a smartass", and a similar bitterness is detectable in the tricks played with logic in Lawrence Sterne's *The Life and Opinions of Tristram Shandy* (1759–1767). In fiction, *reductio ad absurdum* is perceptible as a kind of aesthetic triumph as well as a demonstration of falsity, and this complicates the use and consideration of logic in literary criticism.

Aristotle's emphasis on the relationships between terms—as expressed in such axioms as "A is A" and "A is not B"—was replaced in late nineteenth-century analyses of logic by an emphasis on the relationships between propositions and an attempted sophistication of logic by the importation of mathematical terminology in George Boole's *An Investigation of the Laws of Thought* (1854). The early popularisers of Boole's algebraic "symbolic logic" included Charles Lutwidge Dodgson, *alias* Lewis Carroll, whose deployments of logic in his fiction—most notably in the Alice books (1865–1872)—took a thoroughly literary delight in perversity and paradox. The principles of mathematical logic were carried forward by Gottlob Frege, and by Bertrand Russell and Alfred North Whitehead's *Principia Mathematica* (1910–1913), into realms of abstract complication that seemed utterly incomprehensible to most laypeople, and thus more easily dismissible as quintessentially uninteresting. Although logic remained a fundamental part of the academic curriculum for most of the twentieth century, it was increasingly confined to the philosophy syllabus, and was eventually dropped as a compulsory requirement of many courses even there, because so many students found it impossible to master.

The fusion of logic and mathematics encouraged further attempts at synthesis, including the fusion of deductive and inductive logic in "logical positivism"—a project that also necessitated a logical reordering of semantics (the relationship between terms and their referents), as summarised in the title of A. J. Ayer's popularisation *Language, Truth and Logic* (1936). The failure of this project was an important step in the development of the twentieth-century *philosophy of science, shifting the emphasis towards the resistance of statements to falsification rather than the establishment of their absolute truth.

The dissonance between logic and common patterns of everyday thought has important consequences for literary endeavour. Although there is a sense in which all plots ought to "make sense", readers are, in general, very tolerant of plots that appear to make sense although they fall apart under scrupulous analysis. The aesthetics of literary surprise are heavily dependent on an author's ability to produce outcomes that are both unexpected and convincing, but the conservation of psychological plausibility is far more important in the contrivance of such effects

than sound logic. Some genres place heavier demands on writers than others—detective stories generally require more convincing argumentative performances—but the appearance of logical propriety is always more important than actual soundness.

This observation is particularly relevant to speculative fiction, where claims of rational extrapolation very often fail to stand up to scrupulous analysis, and where the use of calculated illogicality in a playful Carrollian fashion sustained such tributes to the aesthetics of logical perversity as the "Probability Zero" feature that ran in John W. *Campbell Jr.'s *Astounding Science Fiction* from 1942 to 1944 and was reintroduced into *Analog* in the 1990s. The whole point of such stories is to employ false logic and wordplay to generate impossible conclusions for humorous effect—a fascination explored in such science fiction stories as Eric Frank Russell's "Diabologic" (1955).

The late nineteenth-century fascination with non-Euclidean *geometry was echoed in considerations of "non-Aristotelian logic", but these proved less scientifically fertile. Even so, the train of thought was continued into the twentieth century in such texts as Alfred Korzybski's *Science and Sanity* (1933). Korzybski proposed that Indo-European languages might be purged of their built-in Aristotelian logic (which he considered unreasonably limited) by the development of a new General Semantics, whose mastery would enable human thought processes to take a significant leap forward. Korzybski's work had a significant influence on the evolution of pulp science fiction by virtue of the adoption of its jargon into A. E. van Vogt's *The World of Null-A* (1945; rev. 1948) and its sequels, and continued to echo in such images as the Institute of General Semantics in the film *Alphaville* (1965)—a narrative strategy that contrasts strongly with Ayn Rand's reverent use of Aristotelian axioms as headings for the various sections of *Atlas Shrugged* (1957), intended to provide the book's economic and political arguments with a gloss of indubitability. *Astounding* subsequently published several articles by Gotthard Gunther on "multi-valued logic", including "The Logical Parallax" (1953) and the three-part "Achilles and the Tortoise" (1954), arguing that the transcendence of Aristotelian "two-valued" logic might be useful in getting around the logical barriers to such favourite science-fictional devices as faster-than-light space travel. Colin Kapp's "Ambassador to Verdammt" (1967), which features an *alien species that employs an alien logic, sparked a considerable correspondence in *Astounding*'s letter column.

The treatment of logic as a topic in twentieth-century speculative fiction usually involves the construction of hypothetical beings whose logical thought processes are invulnerable to the dissonance that commonly afflicts human thought patterns. The dissonance in question is often falsely attributed in such examinations to the confusing effects of human emotion, as in the various *Star Trek* series' characterisations of Mr. Spock and the android Data, which demonstrated considerable authorial confusion as to what the words "logical" and "rational" actually signify. Such analyses spawned a number of literary clichés, including the notion that if one can trap an *artificial intelligence into self-contradiction, it will either cease functioning or blow up in frustration. A common variant has "logical" aliens confounded by confrontation with human "insanity", as in such stories as Robert Abernathy's "The Thousandth Year" (1954) and John Hunton's "What They're Up Against" (1956).

Anthony Boucher's theological fantasy "The Quest for St. Aquin" (1951) offers a calculatedly contentious account of what a perfectly logical *robot might deduce. Isaac Asimov's "That Thou Art Mindful of Him" (1974) is more conscientious in spelling out the steps of a robotic train of thought, but Douglas Adams' ultimate computer Deep Thought stubbornly refuses to elucidate the reasoning that generated its puzzling answer to the ultimate question of *Life, the Universe and Everything* (1982). In one of the most peculiar of all science fiction's *contes philosophiques*, logic becomes physically incarnate in Stephen Baxter's "The Logic Pool" (1994).

LONGEVITY

The span of life; the term is usually used to imply a protraction beyond the "natural" span. Given that awareness of inevitable *death is one of the least rewarding aspects of human self-consciousness—the consequent *angst* becoming the fundamental condition of human existence in the reckoning of existentialist philosophy—it is not surprising that the prospect of cheating death by acquiring unnatural longevity is one of the enduring fascinations of the human imagination, lavishly represented in myth, legend, folklore, and literature. Such evasions are often labelled "immortality" but the label is misleading, even in many of its applications to gods, let alone to human beings.

True immortality, in the sense of an absolute immunity to death, is usually seen in a religious context as the prerogative of some nonmaterial essence whose incarnation is a temporary affair, perhaps part of a potentially infinite series of incarnations. Within this perspective, flesh is often considered to be a direly inefficient vessel, and the notion of being trapped in it indefinitely is conceived as an implicitly horrific

prospect. In support of this judgement, myths and legends representing fleshly immortality routinely load the condition with some further penalty, such as the eternal restlessness that afflicted the legendary Wandering Jew or the continued aging that eventually withered the mythical Tithonus into an insect. The early literature of longevity carried this tradition forward; fictitious discoverers of such magical agents as the elixir of life and the fountain of youth invariably find their hopes frustrated somehow, no matter how much ingenuity the author requires to achieve that end.

The first response to the possibility that medical technology might find a means of extending the human life span was no different from the reflexive reaction to any other biological *invention, as illustrated by Jonathan Swift's depiction of the Tithonian Struldbruggs in *Gulliver's Travels* (1726) and the rich tradition of cautionary fantasies that extended unchecked through such works as William Godwin's *St. Leon* (1799), Charles Maturin's *Melmoth the Wanderer* (1820), W. Harrison Ainsworth's *Auriol* (1850), and W. Clark Russell's *The Death Ship* (1888).

Although objective consideration might suggest that the potential penalties of longevity—especially if they are conceived in terms of something as innocuous as boredom—are trivial by comparison with the inconveniences of dying, longevity continued to receive a surprisingly bad press in speculative fiction, in spite of the propagandistic efforts of philosophers such as Nikolai Fyodorov, whose essays arguing that technology would enable longevity and resurrection were collected shortly after his death in 1906. Elie Metchnikoff's *Études sur la nature humaine, essai de la philosophie optimiste* (1903; trans. as *The Nature of Man: Studies in Optimistic Philosophy*) argued that science is the only remedy for "disharmonies" in human nature, and must be given the opportunity to transform human nature. Metchnikoff applied this principle more specifically to the issue of achieving longevity in a treatise published in 1907, although his specific recommendations—he recommended sour milk as an antidote to senility—were mostly unhelpful.

William Harvey's discovery of the circulation of the blood in 1628 stimulated some speculation regarding the potential rejuvenating effects of blood transfusion, but early experiments were unsuccessful. The resumption of such investigations at the end of the eighteenth century—by Erasmus *Darwin, among others—were similarly frustrated, but when the idea resurfaced again in the late nineteenth century, it brought forth a considerable literary response. Georges Eekhoud's "Le coeur de Tony Wandel" (1884; trans. as "Tony Wandel's Heart") imagines a future in which the rich routinely obtain longevity by means of heart transplants, but represents it as an awful violation of the natural order of which no good could possibly come. Robert Duncan Milne's "A Man Who Grew Young Again" (1887) and M. E. Braddon's *Good Lady Ducayne* (1896) imagine transfusion as an innately repulsive kind of vampirism. J. Emile Hix's didactic Utopian novel *Can a Man Live Forever?* (1898) insists that blood substitution ought to be a perfectly acceptable method of cultivating longevity, but this was very much a minority view.

The balance of opinion regarding rejuvenation was not significantly affected when Karl Landsteiner's research into blood groups—which resulted in the publication in 1909 of the A/B/O categorisation—made successful blood transfusion and tissue-grafting possible, largely because actual blood transfusion proved to have no rejuvenating effects. Attention was largely switched to the possible revitalisation of the endocrine system in the 1920s, with Serge Voronoff suggesting that it might be achieved by the transplantation of animal testicles (euphemistically known as "monkey glands"); literary responses were divided into farces such as Bertram Gayton's *The Gland Stealers* (1922) and Thomas le Breton's *Mr. Teedles, the Gland Old Man* (1927) and horror stories such as Robert Hichens' *Dr. Artz* (1929).

Walter Besant's *The Inner House* (1888) employed a less gruesome longevity technology than transfusion or transplantation, but its author concluded that the social stagnation resulting from its use would be a thoroughly bad thing, even though the beauty of his young female protagonist is preserved. Marie Corelli's wish fulfilment fantasy *The Young Diana* (1915) took a much more positive view of an electrical method of rejuvenation employed to a similar purpose, but Gertrude Atherton's *Black Oxen* (1923)—which features rejuvenation by x-ray treatment of the endocrine glands—took a much dimmer view, as did Bertha Ruck's derivative account of *The Immortal Girl* (1925). Claude Farrère's *La maison des hommes vivants* (1911; trans. as *The House of the Secret*), Martin Swayne's *The Blue Germ* (1918), Harold Scarborough's *The Immortals* (1924), and Aldous Huxley's *After Many a Summer Dies the Swan* (1939) are all solidly set in cautionary tradition, endorsing the view that longevity would lead to existential, psychological, and social stagnation. When George Bernard Shaw expressed unqualified enthusiasm for universal longevity in the preface to *Back to Methuselah* (1921), Karel Čapek added a preface to his own play *The Makropoulos Secret* (1925) to argue that it would be an unmitigated curse even for a single individual.

On the other hand, George S. Viereck and Paul Eldridge's *My First Two Thousand Years* (1928) imagined that an immortal living in a world of mortals might find a great deal of self-satisfaction in his privileged situation, and Arthur Stanwood Pier's *God's Secret* (1935) followed Shaw in deeming the prospect of general longevity Utopian. One thing that this camp had in common with the other, however, was a recognition that the fervency of the human *desire* for longevity might have unfortunate consequences. Neil Bell's *The Seventh Bowl* (1930; initially by-lined Miles) and John Gloag's *Winter's Youth* (1934) do not oppose longevity *per se* but anticipate dangerous social upheavals ensuing from attempts by the rich and powerful to monopolise longevity technologies.

A similar division of opinion to that manifest in British scientific romance was evident in genre science fiction as it evolved from its pulp origins. Stories viewing the acquisition of longevity as the beginning of limitless opportunity included Neil R. Jones' "The Jameson Satellite" (1931), Laurence Manning's *The Man Who Awoke* (1933; book, 1975), Eando Binder's "Conquest of Life" (1937; incorporated with three sequels into *Anton York—Immortal*, 1965), Robert A. Heinlein's *Methuselah's Children* (1941; book, 1958), Roger P. Graham's *The Involuntary Immortals* (1949; book, 1959), J. T. McIntosh's "Live For Ever" (1954), James Blish's "At Death's End" (1954), and Clifford D. Simak's *Way Station* (1963). Stories representing it as a condition of dire stagnation included D. D. Sharp's "The Eternal Man" (1929), David H. Keller's "Life Everlasting" (1934; reprinted in *Life Everlasting and Other Tales*, 1947), John R. Pierce's "Invariant" (1944), Damon Knight's "World Without Children" (1951), Algis Budrys' "The End of Summer" (1954), Frederik Pohl's *Drunkard's Walk* (1960), and Brian Aldiss' "The Worm That Flies" (1968).

This kind of polarisation of opinion was not universal, but less polemical works tended to reflect it in their ambivalence. In Clifford D. Simak's "Spaceship in a Flask" (1941), a longevity treatment is concealed for fear of an economic collapse triggered by the obsolescence of life insurance, while Simak's "Second Childhood" (1951) considers possible undesirable side effects of rejuvenation. In Boyd Ellanby's "Category Phoenix" (1952), new longevity technologies are counterbalanced by new diseases. In Robert Silverberg's "To Be Continued" (1956), the deceleration of sexual maturation brought about by a longevity treatment makes reproduction problematic.

Damon Knight's "Dio" (1957) and Marta Randall's *Islands* (1976; rev. 1980) offered wry representations of the existential predicaments of common mortals in future societies in which longevity is almost universal. William E. Barrett's *The Fools of Time* (1963) and Chapman Pincher's *Not with a Bang*

(1965) offered equally wry accounts of social responses to the invention of longevity technology. J. L. Keith's "2131" (1935, but presumably written in 1931) describes a future society reshaped by a universal obsession with health and longevity. The prospect of immortality remains the ultimate temptation and lure in such stories as Jack Vance's *To Live Forever* (1956), James Gunn's *The Immortals* (1955–1960; book, 1962), John Wyndham's *The Trouble with Lichen* (1960), Kate Wilhelm's *The Nevermore Affair* (1966), and Norman Spinrad's *Bug Jack Barron* (1969), although that very fact threatens to undermine and spoil the reward.

The rapid advancement of twentieth-century medical science and hygiene brought about a dramatic transformation in the average human life span in developed countries, but it was initially due to a drastic reduction in infant mortality and the predations of common infectious diseases. Little improvement was seen in the Biblically-defined allotment of threescore years and ten until the 1970s, when the number of individuals reaching the ages of eighty, ninety, and then a hundred began to escalate dramatically. It was in this period that writers such as Alvin Silverstein, in *Conquest of Death* (1979), began to suggest that medical science might be on the brink of solving the problem of ageing and instituting an era of "emortality".

Silverstein defined emortality as a condition in which an organism is potentially capable of living indefinitely, while always remaining vulnerable to the possibility of violent death. Speculators who thought emortality a plausible medical goal soon began to suggest that people now alive might benefit from an "escalator effect" whereby each extra twenty years of life won by contemporary technology might win them the chance to benefit from the next suite of discoveries, and so on, all the way to the acquisition of authentic emortality. R. C. W. Ettinger's *The Prospect of Immortality* (1964) had already popularised the notion of winning access to future technologies of longevity by means of *cryogenic storage.

These propositions did not inhibit the production of such longevity-resistant works as Gardner Dozois' "Machines of Loving Grace" (1972), Thomas N. Scortia's "The Weariest River" (1973), Rene Barjavel's *Le grand secret* (1973; trans. as *The Immortals*), Michael Bishop's "A Few Last Words for the Late Immortals" (1979), Bruce McAllister's "Their Immortal Hearts" (1980), and Richard Cowper's "The Tithonian Factor" (1983), but did make writers work harder to invent new penalties that might spoil the experience. Bob Shaw's *One Million Tomorrows* (1970) couples longevity with impotence. Sharon

Webb's *Earthchild* (1982) and its sequels suggest loss of creativity as a cost. Kate Wilhelm's "April Fool's Day Forever" (1970) hypothesises the loss of a crucial bond with the collective unconscious, while her *Welcome, Chaos* (1983) makes its acquisition contingent on a gamble with sudden death.

Alongside such cautionary tales, however, there was a marked increase in the production of more earnest and even-handed considerations of the possibility of longevity. Notable examples included Raymond Z. Gallun's *The Eden Cycle* (1974), Octavia Butler's *Wild Seed* (1980), Pamela Sargent's *The Golden Space* (1982), and Poul Anderson's *The Boat of a Million Years* (1989). The notion that longevity would eventually give rise to unbearable ennui was carried to its ultimate extreme for satirical analysis in Michael Moorcock's *Dancers at the End of Time* sequence (1972–1976), and given more earnest treatment in such extended *contes philosophiques* as Robert Silverberg's "Born with the Dead" (1974) and *Sailing to Byzantium* (1985) and G. David Nordley's "Morning on Mars" (1992). One extensive exercise of this sort is a loosely knit series spun off by Brian Stableford from the future history sketched out in *The Third Millennium* (1985, with David Langford), begun in "... And He Not Busy Being Born" (1986) and extended in many other short stories and novels.

The most ambitious science-fictional *contes philosophiques* dealing with the subject of longevity became increasingly sophisticated as the twentieth century came to a close and the twenty-first began. Frederik Pohl's *Outnumbering the Dead* (1992) revisited the theme of a lone mortal in a world of immortals, who becomes an object of fascination by virtue of his mortality. Michael F. Flynn's "Melodies of the Heart" (1994) considers the ethics of the *genetic engineering of longevity. Joe Haldeman's "Four Short Novels" (2003) explores the social consequences of four variant kinds of longevity technology, while Robert Reed's alternative history "A Plague of Life" (2004) raises the question of how human evolution might have proceeded in the absence of inevitable death. The "immorbidity" resultant from copying people by "fax", as featured in Wil McCarthy's Queendom of Sol series, comes to the fore in "The Policeman's Daughter" (2005). By this time, the eventual fulfilment of Alvin Silverstein's hopes was taken for granted in a great many science-fictional visions of the future; although the cautionary tradition had not withered away, it had been drastically transformed by the assumption that the opportunity of longevity would become available, and would be taken up, no matter what its corollary problems might turn out to be.

LOVELOCK, JAMES (1919–)

British biologist. He obtained a Ph.D. from the London School of Hygiene and Tropical Medicine in 1948 and went on to do medical research at various U.S. universities, including Yale and Harvard. He also became an accomplished designer of scientific instruments, in which capacity he was hired by NASA in 1961 to help in the development of apparatus that space probes might use in the analysis of planetary atmospheres; when the Viking program began, this work became focused on the search for evidence of Martian life—a task that Lovelock came to consider superfluous, since the fact that the Martian atmosphere is chemically inert was proof enough in itself that there was no life there.

Lovelock applied the expertise gained during his NASA work to the development of a highly sensitive electron capture detector, which he used to measure the level of organic pollutants in the environment. His measurements of atmospheric levels of chlorofluorocarbons (CFCs) in the Antarctic in 1972 prompted a campaign to ban their use, although Lovelock was reluctant to believe that they might actually destroy the ozone layer until holes actually began to appear in it. In the meantime, his realisation that the existence of life was correlated with a chemically active atmosphere produced the "Gaia hypothesis", first publicly advanced in a brief paper written with Lynn Margulis, published in the journal *Atmospheric Environment* in 1972.

The fundamental proposition of the Gaia hypothesis is that the Earth's surface environment is not something fixed, to which evolving life simply had to adapt itself, but something transformable, which was so drastically altered by the early progress of life that the ecosphere eventually became the creator and maintainer of its own inorganic habitat. The fact that the Earth's atmosphere contains oxygen, and that water is liquid at the Earth's surface, are not fortunate accidents of fate, but the results of life's existence and activity, without which the dead Earth would have evolved towards a cold or hot extreme, following exemplars provided by Mars and Venus. Whenever the feedback mechanisms stabilising conditions at the Earth's surface are severely disrupted, surface conditions do indeed move towards one or other extreme until the biosphere recovers its grip. The uniformitarian geologist James Hutton had suggested in 1785 that the Earth might be regarded as a single vast organism, and the notion had been revived by Vladimir Vernadsky in the 1920s, but Lovelock was able to add much more detail to the idea in

Gaia: A New Look at Life on Earth (1979) and further elaborated it in *The Ages of Gaia: A Biography of Our Living Earth* (1988).

The Gaia hypothesis proved very controversial, not because of what it asserts—which is obviously true—but because of the way it was presented. The endowment of the ecosphere with the name of a mythical mother goddess seemed to many observers to be a step too far in the "personalisation" of the ecosphere, actively encouraging it to be discussed as if it were a purposive entity imbued with a kind of intelligence: the very essence of *ecological mysticism. The perceived problem was compounded by Lovelock's use of other fictional devices by way of illustration, such as the model of "Daisyworld" developed in 1983 and further elaborated in *The Ages of Gaia*, to clarify the fundamental principles of ecospheric evolution. The latter volume also includes a futuristic scenario sketched out in which an attempt by Dr. Intensli Eeger to palliate the *greenhouse effect by planting forests of fast-growing trees goes sadly awry.

The literary influence of the Gaia hypothesis was very widespread, at least in reviving the name Gaia (or its common variant Gaea) and equipping it with a new net of connotations to which reference is frequently made; it is invoked in this fashion in such works as Nancy Kress' *Brain Rose* (1990) and L. E. Modesitt, Jr.'s "Power To ...?" (1990), and became the logical appellation of such Earth-dominating intelligences as those featured in Robert Froese's *The Hour of Blue* (1990) and Poul Anderson's *Genesis* (2000).

Gaia is difficult to accommodate within stories as anything more than a background idea, although it does lend itself to the kind of exaggeration visited upon it by Isaac Asimov in *Forward the Foundation* (1993)—where it is deftly fused with the *Omega Point hypothesis, whose Teilhardian version is very much in tune with mystical versions of the Gaia hypothesis—but as a perspective from which life on Earth can be viewed, it informs the worldviews of many accounts of future Earth, including Amblin Entertainment's TV series *Earth-2* (1994–1995) and Chris Wills' *The Gaia Syndrome* (2000).

The notion that Mars and Venus might be far more Earthlike if they were home to life encouraged Lovelock to take an interest in the prospect of *terraforming Mars, for which he drew up a tentative plan in *The Greening of Mars* (1984, with Michael Allaby); this provided many subsequent science-fictional accounts of Martian colonisation with a guidebook of sorts.

M

MACROCOSM

One component of a contrasted pair of terms whose opposite is *microcosm. The terms were initially popularised in the context of neo-Platonism, which asserted that there was an essential affinity between the macrocosm (the universe) and the microcosm (the human body) representable by the slogan "as above, so below". This notion became popular again in the Renaissance, where it provided a justification of sorts for the mystification of *alchemy, *astrology, and other components of *occult science. Complementary accounts of the two were produced in considerable numbers, ranging from Bernard Sylvester's *De Mundi Universitate* (ca. 1150) to Robert Fludd's *Utriusque Cosmi Historia* (1617), reflected in such literary works as Thomas Browne's *Urne-Buriall* and *The Garden of Cyrus* (both 1658), in which the latter is the macrocosmic component. Emmanuel *Swedenborg retained the notion in his mystical writings, where he insistently refers to the universe as the "Great Man". The meanings of both terms became far more versatile in later eras; although "macrocosm" held its original meaning longer than its counterpart, it was dramatically expanded by twentieth-century speculations in *atomic theory and *cosmology.

Macrocosmic romances have generally been much rarer than microcosmic romances, although astrological imagery was occasionally animated to reproduce the narratives imposed upon it by the naming of the constellations; there is a notable visual example in the prologue to the film version of *The Man Who Could Work Miracles* (1936). Literary images of societies of giants, like that on the island of Brobdingnag in Jonathan Swift's *Gulliver's Travels* (1726), are macrocosms of a limited sort, and there is a small subgenre of speculative fictions whose protagonists must eke out a living in the interstices of a world built and governed by much larger beings; notable examples include A. Bertram Chandler's "Giant Killer" (1945), James Blish's "Sword of Xota" (1951; book 1953 as *The Warriors of Day*), William Tenn's "The Men in the Walls" (1963; exp. book 1968 as *Of Men and Monsters*), and Kenneth Bulmer's *Demons' World* (1964; aka *The Demons*). Such surreal fantasies of gigantism as Joe Orton's *Head to Toe* (1971) and Jane Gaskell's "Caves" (1984) can also be accommodated to the category. A similar inversion effect is contrived by science fiction stories in which the human body becomes a macrocosm for tiny inhabitants, as in Daniel F. Galouye's "Gulliver Planet" (1957), William W. Stuart's "Inside John Barth" (1960), and Joan Slonczewski's *Brain Plague* (2000).

The notion that solar systems might be atoms in a macrocosm was not as extensively developed in fiction as its opposite, but it was elaborated in R. A. Kennedy's *The Triuneverse* (1912; by-lined "author of Space and Time"), Ray Cummings' "Around the Universe" (1923), *Explorers into Infinity* (1927–1928; book, 1965) and *Beyond the Stars* (1928; book, 1963), G. Peyton Wertenbaker's "The Man from the Atom" (1923), Lloyd Arthur Eschbach's "The Light from Infinity" (1932), John W. Campbell Jr.'s "Atomic Power" (1934; by-lined Don A. Stuart), Donald Wandrei's "Colossus" (1934), Philip Dennis Chamberlin's "The

Tale of the Atom" (1935), Jack Williamson's "The Galactic Circle" (1935), John Russell Fearn's "Metamorphosis" (1937), and Stephen Barr's "The Back of Our Heads" (1958). It was used as a strategic humbling device in L. Ron Hubbard's "Beyond the Black Nebula" (1949; by-lined René Lafayette), in which it is discovered that our universe is located in the alimentary tract of a macrocosmic worm.

More ingenious extrapolations of the notion began to appear when the notion of the macrocosm was transfigured into a "multiverse" of *parallel worlds, initially containing all possible *alternative histories and eventually—in the cosmological versions associated with the notion of *black holes as universes-within-universes and the varieties of inflation theory that recast the observable universe as one of many "space-time bubbles" within a seething macrocosmic foam—all conceivable alternative universes. Notable fictional explorations of the macrocosm of modern cosmology include Greg Egan's *Diaspora* (1997) and Stephen Baxter's Manifold trilogy (1999–2002).

MAGNETISM

A property first observed in respect of iron ores, especially the oxide subsequently named magnetite, which exerted an attractive force on other iron objects. The property was familiar to the ancient Greeks, who named it—presumably because such ores were mined in the province of Magnesia, although Pliny the Elder attributed its discovery to a shepherd named Magnes—but they do not seem to have noticed that a magnetised iron rod, if allowed to swing freely, aligns itself in a north/south direction. Although such "lodestones" (that is, leading stones) were rumoured to have been in use in China as early as the eighth century, the first European historical references to them date from the thirteenth century; the first experimental investigation of the phenomenon of the "magnetic field" was reported by Petrus Peregrinus de Maricourt in 1269.

Magnetised compass needles became increasingly valuable in navigation as the scope of marine exploration increased, and they posed two significant puzzles in that context. A variation was observed between true north and magnetic north, which was being marked on navigational compasses by 1450, and it was eventually noted that the relationship was itself variable. It was also observed that compass needles dipped rather than remaining horizontal, and that the dip (or inclination) was also variable; instruments for measuring inclination were manufactured in the latter half of the sixteenth century, when attempts began in earnest to map the eccentricities of compass

behaviour in the hope that they might provide a means of calculating longitude. The earliest surviving account of compass variations in English is William Borough's *A Discours of the Variation* (1581), but the commercial and military value of navigational information probably kept others secret. The first definitive study of the phenomenon was William Gilbert's *De Magnete* (1600), which made much of the fact that the *Earth must have a magnetic field that causes compass needles to align.

The variation of magnetic north prompted Edmund Halley to propose that the Earth might have four magnetic poles, two situated on the axis of an outer shell and two on the axis of an inner shell whose rotation was dissimilar—a hypothesis that prompted much speculation about the planet's inner structure. In 1698, Halley was given command of HMS *Paramore* in order to chart compass variations in the Atlantic; he published his chart in 1701 and similar measurements were made by exploratory voyagers throughout the eighteenth and early nineteenth centuries, until it became possible to make accurate measurements of longitude by means of chronometers.

The mysteries of magnetism inevitably recommended it to *occult scientists such as Athanasius Kircher and Robert Fludd. The notion that magnetism might have curative effects applicable in *medicine might have been originated by *Paracelsus, who was convinced that the philosopher's stone must be a kind of magnet. More spectacular attempts were made to put the theory into practice by James Graham, who opened a famous Temple of Health and Hymen in late eighteenth-century London, and Anton *Mesmer, the pioneering theorist of "animal magnetism"—a notion that proved to have a much greater literary influence than the actual phenomenon, although the mysterious behaviour of lodestones had been widely cited as an enigma and compasses had played a key role in many a Robinsonade.

In 1785, Charles Coulomb discovered that magnetic fields are subject to the same inverse square law as gravitational fields. In 1802, Gian Dominico Romagnou found that electrical currents generate magnetic fields, but the discovery was overlooked until Hans Christian Oersted repeated it in 1820, paving the way for Michael Faraday's discovery of electromagnetic induction and the eventual integration of the two sets of phenomena in James Clerk Maxwell's theory of electromagnetism, summed up in his *Treatise on Electricity and Magnetism* (1873). In the meantime, new hypotheses attempting to account for the vagaries of the Earth's magnetism were produced by Jean-Baptiste Biot, Alexander von Humboldt, and Carl Friedrich Gauss, although none guessed that the planet's magnetic core might be liquid.

After many attempts, the north magnetic pole was finally reached in 1831 by James Clark Ross—a heroic endeavour that he supplemented in 1839 by setting out for the south magnetic pole. The expeditions leading up to these achievements were extensively celebrated in contemporary literature, including Eleanor Anne Proden's epic poem *The Arctic Explorers* (1818). While the property of magnetism remained mysterious, it seemed effectively magical, and to have obvious affinities with other kinds of supernatural attraction; Mesmer's was by no means its only extension into pseudoscience. Its aura of mystery remained sufficiently powerful even in the late nineteenth century to impel Jules Verne to solve the "problems" implicit in the open ending of Edgar Allan Poe's *Narrative of Arthur Gordon Pym* (1838) by invoking a magnetic sphinx in his sequel *Le sphinx des glaces* (1897; trans. as *The Sphinx of the Ice-Fields* and *An Antarctic Mystery*). Verne's sometime collaborator Pascal Grousset, who used the by-line André Laurie, used giant magnets to draw the Moon into the Earth's atmosphere in *Les exiles de la terre* (1887; trans. as *The Conquest of the Moon*).

The variability of the Earth's magnetic field was accommodated into disaster fiction in such stories as Victor A. Endersby's "When the Top Wobbled" (1936), but the extent of that variation was not fully appreciated until 1963 when it was observed that the magnetisation of rocks on the seabed, where tectonic plates were separating, followed a pattern of irregular inversions, which implied that the polarity of the field was reversed at intervals averaging about half a million years (and that the next such reversal is overdue). Various catastrophic results of such a reversal are extrapolated in such works as N. Lee Wood's *Faraday's Orphans* (1998) and Robert J. Sawyer's *Hybrids* (2003).

The Sun's magnetic field performs flips of this sort every eleven years, without any obvious consequence for humankind, but even a significant weakening of the Earth's field might prove catastrophic, because the field deflects dangerous solar radiation. Such a scenario is dramatised in the film *The Core* (2003), although it is barely mentioned in the book on which the movie is allegedly based (Paul Preuss' *Core*, 1993). Other disaster stories involving magnetism include Hugh Matheson's *The Third Force* (1960), in which magnetism is nullified, and various accounts of "electromagnetic pulses", such as Jerry Oltion's "Course Changes" (1993).

MARS

The fourth planet from the Sun, frequently called "the red planet". Its colouration facilitated its association by various ancient cultures with bloodshed; the Babylonians named it Nergal after their god of destruction, the Greeks Ares, and the Romans Mars, after their respective gods of war. Its satellites, discovered in 1877 by Asaph Hall, were named Phobos (fear) and Deimos (terror) by association. Mars retained its astrological connection with strife and masculinity into the twentieth century, at least in metaphor, in such symbolic narratives as John Gray's *Men Are from Mars, Women Are from Venus* (1992). Its movement against the stellar background seemed capricious because of its apparent changes in velocity and occasional retrograde motion—an enigma whose solution had to await John Kepler's modification of the Copernican model of the solar system.

Although some surface features of Mars were visible through early telescopes—the dark area known as Syrtis Major was recorded by Christian Huygens in 1659 and the polar caps were discerned by Giovanni Cassini in 1666—the first detailed maps were not produced until the 1860s, when a new generation of optical instruments came into use. One produced in 1877 by Giovanni Schiaparelli included the "canali" (channels) first described in 1876 by Pietro Secchi. The word was misconstrued by English speakers as "canals", inspiring Percival Lowell to establish an observatory in Flagstaff, Arizona, from which base he popularised the idea of Mars as the abode of a decadent civilisation struggling to survive in the red desert by means of vast irrigation projects. Lowell published a series of increasingly fanciful accounts of life on the Martian surface, including *Mars* (1896), *Mars and Its Canals* (1906), and *Mars as the Abode of Life* (1908). Much better maps were made in the 1920s by E. M. Antoniadi, casting severe doubt on the real existence of the *canali*, but the illusory canals retained their hold on the popular imagination until 1965, when Mariner 4 brought final confirmation of their non-existence.

By virtue of its relative proximity to the Earth—59 million kilometres distant at its closest approach—and the curious history of its astronomical observation, Mars has always held a special place in literary representations of other worlds, and in the science-fictional mythology of the Space Age. Early literary images were inevitably guided by classical and astrological associations. In Marie-Anne de Roumier's *Voyages de Mylord Céton dans les sept planètes* (1765–1766), Mars is the abode of the spirits of military men, but in Emmanuel Swedenborg's *Arcana Coelestia* (1749–1756), the spirits who live there are hailed as the best of all—a notion echoed in Camille Flammarion's palingenetic accounts of reincarnation on Mars, including those in *Lumen* (1872) and *Uranie* (1889; trans. as *Urania*), and Mortimer Collins' *Transmigration* (1874). Schiaparelli's map provided the bases for the images of Mars contained in W. S. Lach-Szyrma's *Aleriel* (1886) and Guy de Maupassant's "L'Homme de Mars" (1887; trans. as "Martian Mankind"), the mystical tradition continued in such spiritualist romances as Th. Flournoy's *From India to the Planet Mars* (1900) and Louis Pope Gratacap's *The Certainty of a Future Life on Mars* (1903).

Mars served as a site for conventional *Utopian romances, as in Percy Greg's *Across the Zodiac* (1880) and Alexander Bogdanov's *Krasnaia zvezda, utopiia* (1908; trans. as *Red Star*), but the Lowellian interpretation of Schiaparelli's map encouraged Utopian writers to incorporate more "local colour" into such works as Hugh MacColl's *Mr. Stranger's Sealed Packet* (1889), Robert Cromie's *A Plunge into Space* (1890), Gustavus W. Pope's *A Journey to Mars* (1894), and Kurd Lasswitz's remarkably elaborate *Auf Zwei Planeten* (1897; abridged trans. as *Two Planets*). H. G. Wells published a brief vision of decadent Martian life in "The Crystal Egg" (1897) before using a similar image of a dying world as the point of origin of the archetypal alien invaders in *The War of the Worlds* (1898). The novel planted the notion that Martians were malevolent *monsters so firmly in the popular imagination that it became a modern cliché; when Orson Welles' Mercury Theater dramatised it for radio in 1938, the mock-realistic mode of presentation precipitated a panic. The original was so successful as a newspaper serial that Garrett P. Serviss was hired to produce a continuation, *Edison's Conquest of Mars* (1898; book, 1947), in which Earthly scientists lead a military counterstrike that obliterates the last remnants of Martian civilisation. Mars was not always an abode of monsters thereafter, but the notion that its exhausted civilisation was on the brink of extinction dominated early twentieth-century imagery from George Griffith's *A Honeymoon in Space* (1901) onwards.

An unusually lush image of Martian decadence was offered in Edwin Lester Arnold's *Lt. Gullivar Jones—His Vacation* (1905; aka *Gulliver of Mars*), which borrowed a good deal of inspiration from Arnold's fellow writer of karmic romances, H. Rider Haggard. A similar spirit of reckless adventure was developed to an unprecedented extreme by Edgar Rice Burroughs in the Barsoom series launched by "Under the Moons of Mars" (1912; book 1917 as *A Princess of Mars*), which extended to eleven volumes over the next thirty years. Burroughs used Lowellian Mars as a venue for spectacularly uninhibited tales of derring-do in which sword-wielding heroes battle assorted villains and monsters, often from the decks of flying gondolas, to win the affections of beautiful princesses—a set of images so powerful that it continued to resonate plangently in pulp fiction and comic books throughout the twentieth century.

The early science fiction pulps were resonant with echoes of *The War of the Worlds* and *A Princess of Mars*; the first issue of Hugo *Gernsback's *Amazing Stories* reprinted Austin Hall's "The Man Who Saved the Earth" (1923), and he commissioned Burroughs to write a new Barsoom novel for the first issue of its companion magazine. Further attempts at invasion were featured in stories by various pioneers of space opera, including John W. Campbell Jr.'s "When the Atoms Failed" (1930), Edmond Hamilton's "Monsters of Mars" (1931), and Jack Williamson's "The Doom from Planet 4" (1931), while new layers of science-fictional complication were laid upon Burroughsian adventure stories in such stories as Clifford D. Simak's "The Voice in the Void" (1932) and C. L. Moore's "Shambleau" (1933). An ideological reaction against the stigmatisation of Martians was soon manifest in such accounts of meek Martian life as P. Schuyler Miller's "The Forgotten Man of Space" (1933) and Raymond Z. Gallun's "Old Faithful" (1934), while more elaborate exobiological constructions were featured in such stories as Laurence Manning's "The Wreck of the Asteroid" (1932–1933) and Stanley G. Weinbaum's "A Martian Odyssey" (1934).

In spite of the Wellsian precedent, British scientific romance made much less use of Mars than pulp science fiction; Wells never revisited it himself, although he invoked it whimsically in *Star-Begotten* (1937), and the assumptions implicit in *The War of the Worlds* were subject to a scathing ideological demolition in C. S. Lewis's religious fantasy *Out of the Silent Planet* (1938). The Orson Welles radio dramatisation represented a democratisation of the idea of Martians that encouraged genre science fiction writers to move on to fresher fields, and the problems afflicting the human *colonisation of Mars moved increasingly to the forefront of the pulp agenda. Clifford D. Simak's "The Hermit of Mars" (1939) and P. Schuyler Miller's "The Cave" (1944) foreshadowed a boom in the early 1950s comprised by such works as Arthur C. Clarke's *The Sands of Mars* (1951), C. M. Kornbluth and Judith Merril's *Outpost Mars* (1952; by-lined Cyril Judd; aka *Mars Child*), Walter M. Miller's "Crucifixus Etiam" (1953), and E. C. Tubb's *Alien Dust* (1955).

The decadence of Burroughsian imagery survived this shift, but was infected by a curious kind of nostalgia, which became increasingly evident in the work of Leigh Brackett as it evolved from "Martian Quest" (1940) through "Shadow Over Mars" (1944; book, 1951; aka *The Nemesis from Terra*) to "Queen of the Martian Catacombs" (1949; exp. book 1964 as *The Secret of Sinharat*) and "Sea-Kings of Mars" (1949; book 1953 as *The Sword of Rhiannon*). The ambience was further refined by Ray Bradbury, who completed Brackett's "Lorelei of the Red Mist" (1946) alongside "The Million Year Picnic" (1946) and went on to write "Mars Is Heaven" (1948), "... And the Moon Be Still as Bright" (1948), "The Naming of Names" (1949), and the other items making up the classic mosaic *The Martian Chronicles* (1950; aka *The Silver Locusts*). Bradbury's Martian civilisation is dead, but the planet's human colonists are haunted by its ghosts and are gradually captivated by its lingering legacy.

Similar nostalgic imagery continued to recur thereafter in such hybrid science-fantasies as Roger Zelazny's "A Rose for Ecclesiastes" (1963) and J. G. Ballard's "The Time-Tombs" (1963), and was increasingly manifest in accounts of colonisation such as Philip K. Dick's *Martian Time-Slip* (1964) and Algis Budrys' *The Amsirs and the Iron Thorn* (1967; aka *The Iron Thorn*). The Martian desert was an ideal setting for Robinsonades such as Rex Gordon's *No Man Friday* (1956; aka *First on Mars*), Theodore Sturgeon's "The Man Who Lost the Sea" (1959), and James Blish's *Welcome to Mars* (1967), and for the grim prison colonies in Frederik Pohl's "Mars by Moonlight" (1958; by-lined Paul Flehr) and D. G. Compton's *Farewell, Earth's Bliss* (1966), but it also served as the birthplace of a new messiah in Robert A. Heinlein's *Stranger in a Strange Land* (1961).

Mars was a key target of the U.S. space program from its inception, in accordance with a prospectus set out by Wernher von Braun in *The Mars Project* (1953); the Apollo program was considered by many to be a stepping-stone to the Mars mission rather than an end in itself. In 1962, NASA drew up plans for Early Manned Planetary-Interplanetary Roundtrip Expeditions (EMPIRE). In 1964, however, pictures sent back by Mariner 4 suggested that such propositions—along with contemporary science-fictional images of Mars—were far too optimistic. By the time the Viking landers of the early 1970s had confirmed that Mars was far more hostile than had earlier been hoped, NASA's 1969 proposal to make serious preparations for Mars missions had already been refused government backing.

The disappointment of finding an extremely inhospitable Mars instead of Burroughsian Barsoom or some manageable intermediate was grimly extrapolated in Ludek Pesek's *Die Erde ist nah* (1970; trans. as *The Earth Is Near*), while Ian Watson's *The Martian Inca* (1976) and John Varley's "In the Hall of the Martian Kings" (1977) conceded that the unpromising Martian terrain would require quasi-miraculous powers of recuperation if any echo of old science-fictional dreams were to emerge therefrom. A defiant reaction against despair was expressed in *Analog*'s special Mars issue of December 1974, whose

exemplary fictions included William Walling's "Nix Olympica" and Alex and Phyllis Eisenstein's "The Weather on Mars", but Viking's confirmation that Mars was dead was a considerable blow to the myth of the Space Age. It seemed that Mars henceforth could only feature in serious science fiction as a place where people might want to go simply because it was *there*, as in Stephen Baxter's alternative history of NASA, *Voyage* (1996). All was not quite lost, however; there still remained a possibility that the Martian environment might be redeemed from its extreme harshness and lifelessness by *terraforming.

James *Lovelock compensated for his earlier disappointment of NASA's hopes by investigating the possibility of redeeming Mars from its lifelessness in *The Greening of Mars* (1984, with Michael Allaby), which appeared amid a gathering flood of science fiction novels in which would-be colonists of Mars attempt to make up biotechnologically for nature's lack of provision. Notable examples included Frederik Pohl's *Man Plus* (1976), Lewis Shiner's *Frontera* (1984), Kim Stanley Robinson's "Green Mars" (1985)—whose themes were extrapolated into the definitive trilogy comprising *Red Mars* (1992), *Green Mars* (1994), and *Blue Mars* (1996)—Ian MacDonald's *Desolation Road* (1988), and Mick Farren's *Mars—The Red Planet* (1990). Robert L. Forward's *Martian Rainbow* (1991), Paul J. McAuley's *Red Dust* (1991), Philip C. Jennings' *The Fourth Intercometary* (1991), Jack Williamson's *Beachhead* (1992), Greg Bear's *Moving Mars* (1993), and Kevin J. Anderson's *Climbing Olympus* (1994).

The terraforming prospectus produced various backlashes and contradictions. Environmentalists protest against it in Daniel Hatch's "Intervention at Hellas" (1991). Terry Bisson's *Voyage to the Red Planet* (1990) proposes that missions to Martian are so pointless that only Hollywood would finance one—an idea recapitulated, with variations, in Alex Irvine's "Pictures from an Expedition" (2003) and Jason Stoddard's "Winning Mars" (2005). William K. Hartmann's *Mars Underground* (1997) suggests that burrowing beneath the surface might be a better option than terraforming it—a notion echoed in Alexander Jablokov's *River of Dust* (1996). On the other hand, A. A. Attanasio's *Solis* (1994) looks forward to a far-futuristic Mars whose terraforming has long been completed.

The idea of Martian life refused to die, although it was modified in NASA's discourse to the notion that there might have been life on Mars in the distant past. The detection of faint traces of methane by further probes suggested that the Martian atmosphere might not be absolutely inert, licensing such accounts of fugitive life as Gregory Benford's *The Martian Race*

(1999). One result obtained by the 1976 probes was a photograph of a rock formation that became known as "the face on Mars", which proved far more attractive to mystics and pseudoscientists than any mere whiff of methane. Richard Hoagland's *The Monuments of Mars: A City on the Edge of Forever* (1987) interpreted the formation and various neighbouring features as the ruins of a city, perhaps built by visitors from elsewhere. Photographs taken by the 1998 Mars Global Surveyor and the 2001 Mars Odyssey probes, which implied that the face was an artifact of poor resolution and idiosyncratic lighting, were inevitably dismissed by conspiracy theorists as a cover-up. The face was variously adapted into such works of fiction as Allen Steele's "Red Planet Blues" (1989; exp. 1992 as *Labyrinth of Night*, the film *Mission to Mars* (2000), and a 2002 episode of the animated TV series *Futurama*.

A determined realism was maintained through the turn of the century in such bleak accounts of the Martian surface as Bud Sparhawk's "Olympus Mons!" (1998), Allen Steele's "Zwarte Piet's Tale" (1998), Geoffrey A. Landis' *Mars Crossing* (2000), and "Falling onto Mars" (2002), Robert Reed's "The Children's Crusade" (2002), and most of the stories featured in Peter Crowther's *Mars Probes* (2002). Nostalgia continued to recur, however, in such deliberate homages as Harlan Ellison's "The Toad Prince, or Sex-Queen of the Martian Catacombs" (2000).

The Martian moons are too small to have attracted much attention as settings for science fiction stories, but Phobos is exotically embellished for deployment in Harl Vincent's "Lost City of Mars" (1934), Paul Capon's *Phobos, the Robot Planet* (1955), Tom Purdom's "Romance with Phobic Variations" (2001), and John M. Ford's "The Wheels of Dream" (1980), the last named describing the building of a Circum-Phobic Railway. It is not obvious why Deimos should not have been given similar treatment, but it seems to have fallen into relative neglect after featuring extravagantly in D. L. James' "Crystals of Madness" (1936).

MARX, KARL (1818–1883)

German social scientist. His father Heinrich, a Prussian political activist, was a champion of the Enlightenment and a great admirer of Immanuel Kant. Marx briefly attended the University of Bonn before enrolling at the University of Berlin to study philosophy, where he became engaged with the Young Hegelians, dedicated to carrying forward the ideas of G. W. F. Hegel into an era of rapid evolutionary change. His doctoral thesis, offering an analysis of Greek atomic theory based in the ideas of Hegel's Classical model, Heraclitus, was submitted to the University of Jena in 1841 because Marx's increasingly contentious political activities were attracting hostility in Berlin.

Under the influence of Ludwig Feuerbach, Marx became disenchanted with Hegel's interpretation of *history as the progress of the *geist* (spirit). He retained Hegel's notion of a dialectic dynamic in history—by which the contention of opposed ideas (thesis and antithesis) grows increasingly urgent until a settlement of their differences (synthesis) opens the way for the gradual development of a new opposition—but substituted socioeconomic classes engaged in political action for Hegel's abstract conflict of ideas. Marx explored the notion in the *Ökonomisch-philosophische Manuskripte aus dem Jahre 1844* (1959; trans. as *Economic and Philosophical Manuscripts of 1844*), but the bulk of his early publications consisted of brief polemical items of journalism.

Marx went to Paris after being expelled from Prussia, where he associated himself with various communist groups, but he was banished from France too and went to Brussels, where he entered into a long collaboration with another Young Hegelian convert to communism, Friedrich Engels. Engels' father owned a textile company, one of whose branches was in Manchester, and his first-hand knowledge of industrial conditions put meat on the bones of Marx's theoretical speculations. They published a critique of Hegelian idealism, but their more analytical examination of *Die Deutsche Ideologie* (written 1845–1846; trans. as *The German Ideology*)—which contained a detailed account of Marx's new theory of history—was not published. The ideas therein were not given a substantial public airing until Marx wrote a scathing response to Pierre-Joseph Proudhon's *Philosophie de la misère* (1846; trans. as *The Philosophy of Poverty*), sarcastically entitled *Misère de la philosophie* (1847; trans. as *The Poverty of Philosophy*). This set out a version of Marx's theory that saw history in terms of an uncompromising *technological determinism; it was, however, far outshone in terms of popular attention and acclaim by the truncated version incorporated into the manifesto that Marx and Engels were commissioned to write for the London-based Communist League, which benefited from fortunate timing in being completed early in 1848, just as a wave of revolutions began to sweep across Europe.

Marx returned to Germany to play his part in its unfolding revolution but was banished again in 1849, settling permanently in London. He continued to write polemical essays, living on a meagre income from journalism and handouts from Engels—who remained a mere clerk in the family firm until 1864, and was not well off himself—while labouring in the British Museum researching more substantial works.

Marx's first book on *economic theory was *Zur Kritik der politischen Ökonomie* (1859; trans. as *A Contribution to the Critique of Political Economy*), but this was merely a step on the way to his definitive study of *Das Kapital* (trans. as *Capital*), the first volume of whose first part appeared in 1867. Distracted by internal strife within the International Working Men's Association that had been founded in 1864 to spearhead the communist movement, and by the gradual deterioration of his health, Marx did not live to complete the second and third volumes. Versions edited by Engels from his notes were posthumously published in 1885 and 1894; the remaining two parts of the project were not even begun.

Capital set aside the technological determinism of *The Poverty of Philosophy* in order to concentrate on the evolutionary force of the opposition between social classes, particularly the opposition represented in the contemporary world by the bourgeoisie and the proletariat, whose increasing "immiseration" is chronicled at great length. Like Adam Smith and David Ricardo, Marx clung to an objective theory of value that interpreted value in terms of invested labour, but where Ricardo saw profit as a reward for entrepreneurial effort and a resource for further investment, Marx saw it as a penalty extorted from the workers to whom it belonged by moral right. The inevitable shrinkage of the margin of profit caused by competition, which Ricardo saw as an incentive to further entrepreneurial innovation, Marx saw as an incentive to further exploitation and immiseration, whose logical endpoint would be an irresistible insurrection.

This inversion of perspective provided a powerful antithesis to Ricardian orthodoxy, whose clash with its rival became the dominant theme of twentieth-century global politics. It expanded into a more general cultural critique via Marx's identification of art and literature as aspects of an ideological "superstructure" erected upon a society's economic base, in which the specific interests of the dominant economic class were represented and supported as "natural" and desirable. This facilitated the ingenious reinterpretation of the literature of the past and present in terms of its class affiliations, although it was less successful in its futuristic dimension, which anticipated the imminent emergence of a new "socialist realism" giving a clear cultural voice to the proletariat. The theory of *ideology, as elaborated by Karl Mannheim and others, became an important rhetorical instrument exposing supposedly hidden agendas everywhere—including science, which many Marxists came to regard as ideologically polluted, if not a product recently given over to the service of capitalist ends. Technology, which had once been the root determinant of social change in Marx's thesis, was converted in much twentieth-century Marxist thinking into an instrument of bourgeois oppression shaped by narrow economic interests—a preserver of privilege rather than an instrument of moral progress.

As with its general literary criticism, the theory of ideology worked better as a critique of American science fiction than as a generator of alternatives, although writers of Soviet science fiction certainly made a concerted effort to produce a kind of futuristic fiction that would not merely assume the future universalisation of the communist revolution but also help to promote it. Remarkably few images of what a future Marxist society might look like have been produced by writers sympathetic to the idea, although Marx's ideas are routinely cited in late nineteenth-century *Utopias such as Harold A. Brydges' *A Fortnight in Heaven* (1886). The explicit model in Anatole France's pioneering "Through the Horn or the Ivory Gate" in *Sur la pierre blanche* (1905; trans. as *The White Stone*) is curiously ambivalent. By the same token, writers anticipating a Marxist revolution with enthusiasm have often been reluctant to depict its actual course, mostly preferring—as Jack London did in *The Iron Heel* (1907)—to describe the vile oppressions that render it necessary and inevitable.

This situation is further complicated by widespread doubts as to whether the economic systems incarnated in post-1917 Russia, post-1949 China, and elsewhere are authentically communist. Marx's own writings are much stronger on criticism of existing economic structures than the design of potential replacements, and Lenin's task in building the actual economic institutions of postrevolutionary Russia involved a great deal of improvisation. Indeed, Leon Stover's *The Shaving of Karl Marx* (1982) slyly imagines Lenin taking English lessons from H. G. *Wells and basing the actual organisation of Soviet society on Wellsian scientific romance rather than Marxist theory. The bulk of what passes for Marxist literature, whether naturalistic or speculative, is content to echo Marx's vitriolic anticapitalist polemics without risking any constructive extrapolation of his economic theory, but much of it is highly effective in that vein. Many of his appearances in historical fiction are cameo roles, as in Tom Stoppard's trilogy of plays *The Coast of Utopia* (2002), or caricatures, as in the character of Old Major in George Orwell's *Animal Farm* (1945), but he takes centre stage in Grey Lynn's *The Return of Karl Marx* (1941), in which he is expelled from the English socialist movement for political deviation, Juan Goytisolo's novel *Saga de los Marx* (1993; trans. as *The Marx Family Saga*), and Howard Zinn's play *Marx in Soho: A Play on History* (1999).

MATHEMATICS

The analysis of quantitative relationships. The discipline is nowadays divided into arithmetic, algebra, and *geometry, the first exploring the calculative relationships between specified numbers, the second relationships including unspecified numbers, and the third the analysis of spatial relationships. Counting and calculation presumably evolved in prehistory in close association with agricultural endeavour, for the purposes of assessing wealth, negotiating trade, and determining the calendar by *astronomical means. The use of measurements in construction must also have provided a powerful incentive for the sophistication of arithmetic and geometry.

The gradual complication of *technology and the increasing importance of money required ever-greater facility and ingenuity in calculation as Classical culture developed, but the philosophical importance of mathematics was secured when the followers of *Pythagoras asserted that numerical relationships held the key to the interpretation and understanding of the universe, attributing a mystical significance to them whose echoes still linger. The abstract ruminations of the post-Pythagoreans and the practical calculations of the Egyptians and the Alexandrian school laid the foundations for what are now known as pure and applied mathematics. Although the former is fundamental to *philosophy and the scientific worldview it fostered, the latter can comfortably exist in a near-static culture, as it continued to do for more than a thousand years after the practically inclined Romans abandoned the more abstruse components of Greek philosophy. Roman numerals apparently served well enough for the utilitarian purposes of the Romans' expert surveyors, but pure mathematics required the "place-value" system of modern numerical notation and the development of a zero symbol to make further progress.

The arithmetical wonders that inspired Pythagoras quickly gave birth to the *occult methodology of numerology, which attributed special significance to various numbers and employed numerical resolutions of names in divination. The early literary extrapolation of numerology was widespread; one reference in the Biblical book of Revelation to the significant "number of the beast" (666) is echoed in much subsequent literary imagery, frequently cited in twentieth-century horror fiction. The supposed unluckiness of the number thirteen and the magical qualities of such numbers as five and seven also proved remarkably tenacious. Five is awarded special status in Thomas Browne's lyrical and mystical essay The Garden of Cyrus (1658), advertised as a celebration of "the Quincunciall", while seven exercised sufficient

authority over Isaac Newton—an enthusiastic numerologist in the context of his Biblical studies—to make him insist that there are seven colours in the visual spectrum, although orange and indigo are surely fringe effects rather than distinct colour bands.

The unsettling potential of arithmetic is touched upon in a legend to the effect that the Pythagorean who first discovered irrational numbers (numbers not expressible as fractional ratios between other numbers—pi and the square root of 2 are the most familiar examples) was put to death by his peers lest the secret get out. The eventual addition to the arithmetic canon of imaginary numbers, extrapolated from the square root of minus one, and transfinite numbers, extrapolated from the concept of infinity, amplified this sense of strangeness considerably and lent further encouragement to the notion of unusual mathematical concepts as quasi-magical arcana.

The development of mathematics was significantly extended in the Islamic world from the ninth century onwards, although it might have made much faster progress had Arab merchants adopted the Indian numerical system they first encountered in the sixth century. When Arabic numerals were imported into Europe at the end of the twelfth century, their facilitation of economic and theoretical calculations helped to provide the foundations of the European Renaissance. The earliest elaborations of mathematical lore produced in thirteenth-century Europe included the identification of the Fibonacci sequence by the thus-nicknamed Leonardo of Pisa in Liber Abaci (1202).

Algebra took its name from a treatise written by the Arabic mathematician al-Khwarizmi, although its popularisation in Europe had to await its elaboration in Gerolamo Cardano's Artis magnae sive de regulis algebraicis (1545). European mathematics made rapid progress in the seventeenth century in close association with the advancement of science. John Napier published his discovery of logarithms in 1614, a year before John *Kepler devised new methods of geometrical analysis that were further developed by Bonaventura Cavalieri in 1635. René *Descartes published his method of analytical geometry in 1637, assisting the conceptualisation of infinite *space and opening up the possibility of considering *time as a dimension. His work was carried forward by Pierre de Fermat, who also helped Blaise Pascal found *probability theory in 1654. Gottfried Leibniz and Isaac *Newton developed what is now known as calculus in the 1670s, fervently disputing the priority of their discoveries in the late 1680s.

In the eighteenth century, the evolution of mathematics became a determining feature of the Age of Enlightenment, symbolised in France by the work of encyclopaedist Jean Le Rond d'Alembert and the triumph of Joseph-Louis Lagrange's *Mécanique analytique* (1788), which provided a comprehensive analysis of the mathematical foundations of *mechanics. Pierre-Simon Laplace extended this work into the field of celestial mechanics in *Mécanique Céleste* (1799–1825), and developed several new analytical instruments, whose catalogue was further extended by Jean-Baptiste Fourier. Applied mathematics made a huge contribution to the development of human science, not merely in the assembly and correlation of social statistics—following precedents set by John Gaunt in the seventeenth century—but in such philosophical considerations as Jeremy Bentham's utilitarian calculations of the greatest good for the greatest number in *Introduction to the Principles of Morals and Legislation* (1789). These various threads of thought came together in Robert Malthus' *Essay on Population* (1798) and their combination continued to complicate mathematical schools of *economics.

The literary reflection of this pattern of progress and application was inhibited by fundamental differences of style and manner between mathematical and verbal descriptions and conclusions. Although the spaces of exotic geometry were eventually opened up to literary exploitation, the potential deployments of arithmetic and algebra remained far more limited. The occult aspects of numerology remained far more evident in eighteenth-century fiction than pure or applied mathematics. By the end of the century, mathematics seemed to lay people to be so far removed from the realms of common sense as to require a special kind of mind to engage with it. Such significant mathematical puzzles as "Fermat's last theorem" took on a quasi-iconic status as emblems of extreme difficulty, reflected in such stories as Jerry Oltion's "Fermat's Lost Theorem" (1994).

Early nineteenth-century crusades for popular education and attempts to popularise science paid as much attention to elementary numeracy as to fundamental literacy, but the deterrent effect of mathematical expressions was soon realised and such representations were largely reserved to the pages of academic publications. The aesthetic appreciation of mathematics became an esoteric achievement, although it did find occasional literary expression, as in George Boole's "Sonnet to the Number Three" (ca. 1850). The intrusions of mathematics into the fiction of such mathematicians as Charles Dodgson (Lewis Carroll) and C. H. *Hinton were often calculatedly surreal, founding a tradition of uninhibited bizarrerie carried forward into the twentieth century in such mathematicians' fantasies as David Eugene Smith's *Every Man a Millionaire: A Balloon Trip in the Mathematical Stratosphere of Social Relations* (1937), J. L.

Synge's *Kandelman's Krim* (1957), Philip J. Davis' *Thomas Gray, Philosopher Cat* (1988) and *Thomas Gray in Copenhagen* (1995), Clifford A. Pickover's *Chaos in Wonderland* (1995), and Eliot Fintushel's "Milo and Sylvia" (2000). Homer Nearing's *The Sinister Researches of C. P. Ransom* (1954), whose protagonist is head of the mathematics department of Uh-Uh University, is similar in spirit, as is Paul Di Filippo's "Math Takes a Holiday" (2001).

Heroic efforts were made in the twentieth century to make mathematics accessible and interesting to lay readers, one of the leading figures in the crusade being Eric Temple Bell—author of *The Queen of the Sciences* (1931), *The Handmaiden of the Sciences* (1937), and *Men of Mathematics* (1937)—who also wrote science fiction as John Taine. Lancelot Hogben's *Mathematics for the Million* (1937) sold very well, but its sales reflected the good intentions of its readers more than any triumph of educational achievement. The deterrent effect of mathematics continued to increase in the latter half of the century, to the point at which Stephen Hawking was advised before writing *A Brief History of Time* (1988) that every equation would halve his sales.

Martin Gardner made elaborate use of a strategy that attempted to popularise mathematics by means of puzzles, in his columns in *Scientific American* and *Isaac Asimov's Science Fiction Magazine*, although the principal effect of his endeavours was to help secure a cult following for mathematical puzzles. Although generally esoteric, the hobby in question proved capable of spawning a popular fad in the early twenty-first century Sudoku craze. Several notable showcase anthologies of mathematical fiction were produced in this cause, including Clifton Fadiman's *Fantasia Mathematica* (1958) and *The Mathematical Magpie* (1962) and Rudy Rucker's *Mathenauts* (1987); Gardner's contributions included *Science Fiction Puzzle Tales* (1981), *Puzzles from Other Worlds* (1984), and *The No-Sided Professor* (1987).

One simple arithmetical phenomenon that is widely featured in story form is the remarkable increase obtained by geometric series, featured in a traditional anecdote in which a wealthy potentate agrees to reward a petitioner by placing one grain of rice on the first of a chessboard's sixty-four squares, two on the second, four on the third, and so on, not realising that although 64 is not a huge number, 2^{63} most definitely is. Ingenious exactions of this kind feature in a number of *Faustian fantasies, including James Dalton's *The Gentleman in Black* (1831), whose hero unwisely commits himself to doubling the number of sins he commits every year in return for unlimited wealth, and Alexandre Dumas' *Le meneur de loups* (1857; trans. as *The Wolf-Leader*).

The power of compound interest to magnify sums of money over long periods of time is used as a plot lever in Eugène Sue's *Le Juif errant* (1845; trans. as *The Wandering Jew*), Edmond About's *L'homme à l'oreille cassée* (1861; trans. as *The Man with the Broken Ear*), and H. G. Wells' *When the Sleeper Wakes* (1899) and is extravagantly foregrounded in Harry Stephen Keeler's "John Jones' Dollar" (1915). The formula was reused in Charles Eric Maine's *The Man Who Owned the World* (1961), but the folly of neglecting the similarly geometrical erosions of inflation is pointed out in Frederik Pohl's *The Age of the Pussyfoot* (1968). Ideas are spread in a similar fashion in Edward Everett Hale's "Ten Times One Is Ten" (1871), which anticipates the theory of "chain letters" and "pyramid selling", as featured in numerous twentieth-century get-rich-quick schemes and such literary works as W. Laird Clowes' *The Great Peril, and How it Was Averted* (1893) and Katherine MacLean's "The Snowball Effect" (1952).

Early pulp science fiction provided a showcase for neo-Pythagorean celebrations of the cosmic significance of mathematics. New computer-generated equations alter reality in Nathan Schachner's "The Living Equation" (1934) and "The Orb of Probability" (1935), while the universe proves to be reducible to manipulable mathematical statements in John Russell Fearn's "Mathematica" and "Mathematica Plus" (both 1936). Although the fashionability of numerology as a divinatory means was far outstripped in the second half of the twentieth century by astrology and cartomancy, the mysticism of numbers remained more robust in literary imagery. Mathematical species of magic were sometimes dressed in apologetic disguise, as in L. Ron Hubbard's "The Dangerous Dimension" (1938), and sometimes featured explicitly, as in L. Sprague *de Camp and Fletcher Pratt's Harold Shea series (launched 1940). Both strategies were extensively echoed; John Rankine's "Six Cubed Plus One" (1966) and Stephen G. Spruill's *The Janus Equation* (1979) are examples of the former strategy, Geoffrey A. Landis' "Elemental" (1984) the latter. Jamil Nasir's *The Higher Space* (1996) offers a hybrid account of thaumatomathematics.

The extrapolation of similar modes of thinking to take aboard irrational, imaginary, and transfinite numbers is often treated in a whimsical Carrollian manner, as in such stories as James Blish's "FYI" (1953), J. W. Swanson's "Godel Numbers" (1969), Charles Mobbs' "Art Thou Mathematics" (1978), Rudy Rucker's *White Light* (1980), Ted Chiang's "Division by Zero" (1991), and John Barrow's play *Infinities* (2002), although Carl Sagan's *Contact* (1985) offers a more earnest account of pi as an encoded message and Stephen Baxter's "The Logic Pool" (1994) offers a reverent view of "metamathematics". Late twentieth-century advances in mathematical

theory that gave rise to similar literary spin-off included René Thom's "catastrophe theory", as set out in *Stabilité structurelle et morphogènese* (1972; trans. as *Structural Stability and Morphogenesis*) and *chaos theory.

The widespread use of statistical analysis in various kinds of social and economic research in the twentieth century encouraged the production of numerous works in which such research bears strange fruit. William Tenn's "Null-P" (1951) puts forward the ironic proposition that the perfectly average man would be the perfect democratic representative. Several statistical cycles peak simultaneously in Robert A. Heinlein's "The Year of the Jackpot" (1952). James Blish's "Statistician's Day" (1970) imagines statistics being converted from a form of measurement into a means of social design to which reality is then adjusted. The relentless search for statistical anomalies in *parapsychological research is mirrored in many psi stories, including Raymond F. Jones' "The Non-Statistical Man" (1956). Ominous breaches of the "law of averages" are also featured in such whimsical stories as Robert M. Coates' "The Law" (1974) and the opening scene of Tom Stoppard's *Rosencrantz and Guildenstern Are Dead* (1968).

Stories featuring mathematicians at work are understandably rare, given the nature of their labour, although there are numerous elliptical accounts of mathematical geniuses such as Robert A. Heinlein's "Misfit" (1939) and J. T. Lambery Jr.'s "Young Beaker" (1973). William Orr's "Euclid Alone" (1975) is a notable exception.

MATTER

The substantiality of physical entities, often cited—alongside *space and *time—as part of a fundamental triumvirate of concepts in natural philosophy. The nature of matter was hotly disputed in Classical philosophy between *atomist schools, whose members imagined it being constituted of tiny particles, and antiatomist schools, whose members thought it indivisible. This debate was complicated by contrasted opinions as to the nature of the "primordial substance", which were ultimately syncretised into Empedocles' theory of the four *elements. The fundamental assumption of Classical atomism, which was eventually transferred into post-Renaissance materialism, is that all phenomena can be explained in terms of "matter in motion".

The determined thrust of materialistic philosophy towards the exclusion of magical, spiritual, miraculous, and other metaphysical factors from explanations was a powerful driving force in the evolution of science. The term "materialism" was, however, significantly expanded into an *economic context, where its reference to a high regard for money and wealth, often at the expense of affection and compassion, tainted its implications. Modern philosophers of science tend, in consequence, to prefer the term "realism", whose extrascientific applications are less disreputable. Economic "materialists" are often credited with a high regard for mechanical technology, at the expense of living creatures, and with a blithe disregard for the kinds of boundaries identified with the *ethnological definition of dirt as "matter out of place"—a complex of ideas neatly encapsulated in the proverb "where there's muck, there's brass".

Materialism is routinely cast in an unflattering light in literary representations, and the economic extension of the term considerably increased the breadth and depth of that disfavour. Preoccupation with the world of matter at the expense of the spiritual realm, especially when the preoccupation extends to frank denial of the spiritual, is often represented in literary work as a cardinal sin, unaffected in its ignominy by the secularisation of terminology that prefers "emotional" to "spiritual". For reasons that are presumably connected with the abstract and emotion-driven nature of literary creativity, writers have a tendency to regard almost all matter as "dirty", even though some give evidence of a perverse affection for actual dirt.

As with space and time, an enduring philosophical controversy developed as to whether or not matter could be said to exist independently of its perception; idealists such as George Berkeley thought not—a position that cannot be refuted, as Samuel Johnson is said to have supposed, simply by kicking a stone. The controversy was further complicated by perspectives developed in theoretical *physics; in the 1870s, William Clifford suggested that matter might be no more than a distortion of the fabric of space, and similar views became increasingly plausible as models of the atom lost their solidity and retreated into realms of mathematical abstraction.

The three obvious fundamental states of matter are solid, liquid, and gas, which are roughly reflected in the Classical system of elements as earth, water, and air. Almost all substances can exist in all three states, changing from solid to liquid by melting, from liquid to gas by boiling, and from solid direct to gas by sublimation. The notion that there might be a fourth, equivalent to the Classical fire, was broached several times in the history of physics; Michael Faraday's speculation in 1819 that matter might have a "radiant" state was subsequently adopted by William Crookes, in connection with his discovery of "cathode

rays", before "plasma" was added to the list in the 1920s by Irving Langmuir.

The category of solids is subject to a fairly elaborate division into such naturally occurring subcategories as metals, stony substances, *crystals and the organic substance of living organisms, and such technological artefacts as glass and plastic, although the latter are actually supercooled liquids. Liquids are less obviously categorisable, although the immiscibility of oil and water is proverbial and such solvents as water and ethyl alcohol are markedly different in their capacity to absorb solids. In addition to solutions there are various other associational states, including colloids, vapours, and gels.

The transitions of matter are more interesting in literary terms than its stable states, and lend themselves well to the kinds of mystification imposed on them by *alchemical theory. A good deal of literary imagery has been devoted to the contemplation of such changes in state, especially those associated with *meteorological phenomena and the changing of the seasons. Speculative fiction similarly makes much of the imagery of solidification and liquefaction, especially with regard to living organisms. Such mythical motifs as the gorgon's stare that turns living entities to stone are frequently echoed—and often reversed—in fantastic fiction. Robert Sheckley's "The Petrified World" (1968; rev. as "Dreamworld") is a surreal fable whose viewpoint is native to a fluid world, for whom material constancy is the ultimate nightmare. John Updike's "The Dance of the Solids" (*Scientific American,* 1969) is a rare poetic celebration of the scientific view of matter.

Albert Einstein's equation establishing the equivalence of matter and energy, formulated in 1905, is frequently seen as an iconic summary of the triumph of scientific explanation. It paved the way for accounts of the primal formation of matter, and its subsequent transformation, that formed an important aspect of *Big Bang theory. The transformation of the matter into energy became a major theme of twentieth-century speculative fiction, embodied in accounts of *atom bombs and *nuclear power; examples notable for their focus on the nature of matter include Robert Cromie's *The Crack of Doom* (1895) and William Gerhardi's *Jazz and Jasper* (1928; aka *Eva's Apples*), both of which suggest—the latter explicitly—that matter is a "disease of space" best dissolved into pure energy. John Russell Fearn's "Dark Eternity" (1937) extrapolates the idealist notion of matter to an apocalyptic conclusion in a similar spirit. The extrapolation of Einsteinian relativity to take in matter as well as space and time was suggested by Gotthard Gunther's *Astounding* article "Achilles and the Tortoise" (1954), but seems to have had little influence on the magazine's fiction.

The gradual explication of the nature of matter and its cosmogonic formation spun off a number of scientific notions and puzzles. The revelation that matter consists of atoms in which negatively charged electrons orbit nuclei containing positively charged protons gave rise to the concept of antimatter, whose atoms would consist of "positrons" orbiting nuclei containing negatively charged anti-protons. The theoretical possibility was broached by P. A. M. Dirac in 1930, and a positron was observed in a cloud chamber in 1932 by Carl David Anderson, giving rise to a more extended search that resulted in many other fugitive antiparticles being observed in particle accelerators and as natural aspects of cosmic radiation.

If matter and antimatter were to be brought into contact, they would undergo an instantaneous mutual annihilation converting them both into energy, thus raising the possibility of employing such collisions as sources of power or destructive weapons—a notion quickly taken up in such pulp science fiction stories as Frank Belknap Long's "The Roaring Blot" (1936), which calls antimatter "Dirac ether". The notion that there might be "minus matter" in the universe that has not yet come into contact with matter was broached by John D. Clark's "Minus Planet" (1937), while Jack Williamson's "Collision Orbit" (1942; by-lined Will Stewart) introduced the term "contraterrene matter", abbreviated to Seetee in the subsequent series. The notion of using the energy of antimatter/matter annihilations to drive spaceships was subsequently employed by Arthur C. Clarke in *Imperial Earth* (1975) and Charles Pellegrino in *Flying to Valhalla* (1993). In Joe Haldeman's "Tricentennial" (1976), the Sun turns out have two "black dwarf" companions, one of which is made of antimatter.

Astronomical observation is restricted to radiant matter, and it always seemed likely to astronomers that there must be a significant amount of nonradiant "dark matter" in the universe. Most twentieth-century *cosmological theories presume that there must be a great deal of such matter, in order to account for the aggregation of stars into galaxies and for the rotation speeds of stars within galaxies seeming to be uniform rather than declining in proportion to their distance from the galactic centres. Inflationary models of the *Big Bang developed towards the end of the century suggested that there might be up to a hundred times as much dark matter in the universe as radiant matter, so the question of what forms that matter might take, and how it might be distributed, became central enigmas of cosmology. Although much of it, including matter held within *black holes, was accountable in terms of the same kind of matter—baryonic matter—that makes up radiant entities, it began to seem that there must be a much greater reservoir of at least one kind of exotic matter.

Various kinds of dark matter have been hypothesised in order to supply the missing mass, the most popular being "weakly interacting massive particles" (WIMPs). Shadow matter, first proposed in 1965—which can only interact with normal matter via the weak forces—is dramatised in Poul Anderson's "In the Shadow" (1967; by-lined Michael Karageorge) and John Cramer's *Twistor* (1989; rev. 1996); the notion of "mirror matter" is very similar. Cosmic strings—not to be confused with string theory—are extremely thin but massive entities, featured in such works as Rudy Rucker's "The Man Who Was a Cosmic String" (1987) and Bob Shaw's *The Fugitive Worlds* (1979). Other forms of exotic matter featured in science fiction include the Xon matter with which Damien Broderick's *Godplayers* (2005) are obsessed, but the general idea of dark matter has exerted more influence on literary imagery than specific attempts to identify it. It was given conspicuous exposure in Philip Pullman's trilogy assembled as *His Dark Materials* (1995–2000), and was metaphorically deployed in the title of a 2000 showcase anthology of speculative fiction by Afro-American writers edited by Sheree R. Thomas. The scientific enigma is, however, placed centre stage in Thomas R. McDonough's *The Missing Matter* (1992) and Charles Sheffield's "The Hidden Matter of McAndrew" (1992), and it becomes a matter of vital physiological interest to the protagonists of Robert Reed's "Melodies Played upon Cold, Dark Worlds" (2002).

MATTER TRANSMISSION

A means of transporting objects from one place to another without their passing tangibly through the intervening space. It is sometimes called teleportation, especially when represented as a parapsychological power of self-transportation.

The matter transmitter's utility as a facilitating device in literary work is obvious; it is, in effect, the ultimate short cut. Its imagined use is, however, limited by problems that can easily be extrapolated from the basic premise, as in Edward Page Mitchell's "The Man Without a Body" (1877) and Robert Duncan Milne's "Professor Vehr's Electrical Experiment" (1885). Early literary uses that ignore these potential problems included W. H. Stacpoole's "The Teleporon" (1886), Fred T. Jane's *To Venus in Five Seconds* (1897), and Garrett P. Serviss's *The Moon Metal* (1900).

The device had an obvious appeal to writers of pulp adventure fiction; Clement Fézandie's "The

Secret of Electrical Transmission" (1922) and Ralph Milne Farley's *The Radio Man* (1924; book, 1948) used it before the advent of specialist science fiction pulps, into which it was quickly appropriated by Edmond Hamilton's "The Moon Menace" (1927), Jack Williamson's "The Cosmic Express" (1930), George H. Scheer Jr.'s "Beam Transmission" (1934) and "Another Dimension" (1935), and J. George Frederick's "The Einstein Express" (1935). It was also employed outside the genre magazines in Norman Matson's *Doctor Fogg* (1929).

As genre science fiction grew more sophisticated the corollaries of the notion—especially the awkward ones—came increasingly to the fore in such stories as George O. Smith's "Special Delivery" (1945), Lester del Rey's "The Wind Between the Worlds" (1951), Alan E. Nourse's "The Universe Between" (1951), Damon Knight's "Ticket to Anywhere" (1952), Kenneth Bulmer's *Galactic Intrigue* (1953), Theodore Sturgeon's "Granny Won't Knit" (1954), Algis Budrys' *Rogue Moon* (1960; aka *The Death Machine*), and Clifford Simak's *Goblin Reservation* (1968). George Langelaan's "La mouche" (1957; trans. as "The Fly"), which featured one of the more ghoulish possibilities, was rapidly adapted for the cinema.

Concerted attempts to sophisticate the notion were made in Poul Anderson's *The Enemy Stars* (1959), Gordon R. Dickson's "Building on the Line" (1968), Harry Harrison's *One Step from Earth* (1970), Joe W. Haldeman's *Mindbridge* (1976), David Langford's *The Space Eater* (1982), and F. M. Busby's *The Singularity Project* (1993); Busby subsequently considered an intriguing variant in *Slow Freight* (1991). In the meantime, the motif was put to productive melodramatic use in Philip K. Dick's *The Unteleported Man* (1964; exp. 1982; aka *Lies, Inc*), Thomas M. Disch's *Echo Round His Bones* (1967), Roger Zelazny's *Today We Choose Faces* (1973), and Tak Hallus' "Stargate" (1974). It proved a considerable boon to TV space opera; the "transporter" with which *Star Trek*'s *Enterprise* was equipped presumably originated as a cost-cutting exercise, but its various malfunctions became a significant source of plot twists and its routine use generated the popular catchphrase "Beam me up, Scotty!"

A significant tradition developed in genre science fiction of *contes philosophiques* extrapolating of the possible social consequences of the development of such transportation devices. Notable examples include Arthur C. Clarke's "Travel by Wire" (1937), Lan Wright's "Transmat" (1960), Clifford Simak's *Way Station* (1963), George O. Smith's "Counter Foil" (1964), Poul Anderson's "Door to Anywhere" (1966), Gary K. Wolf's "The Bridge Builder" (1973) and *The Resurrectionist* (1979), and the novellas comprising *Three Trips in Time and Space* (1973) edited by Robert Silverberg: Larry Niven's "Flash Crowd", Jack Vance's "Rumfuddle", and John Brunner's "You'll Take the High Road". Brunner developed the idea further in *Web of Everywhere* (1974) and *The Infinitive of Go* (1980).

Bill Scotten's "A Matter of Condensation" (1987) carried this tradition forward in an Earthly context before John Barnes' *A Million Open Doors* (1992) extrapolated its implications onto a galactic stage. James Patrick Kelly's "Think Like a Dinosaur" (1995) employs a broader context in a *conte philosophique* of a different sort. Wil McCarthy's *The Collapsium* (2000) and its sequels employed another bold extrapolation in constructing its image of a twenty-sixth century Queendom of Sol linked by matter-transmitting "fax" machines. Several of these stories point out that transportation is not the only possible application of a "teleportation" device—a notion further explored in Bernard Deitchman's "All Which It Inherit" (1974), Joe Patrouch's "Your Privacy Is My Business" (1980), and Ray Brown's "Looking for the Celestial Master" (1982).

MECHANICS

In its broadest definition, the branch of *physics concerned with the transactions of material objects, usually divided into statics (including hydrostatics) and dynamics. The term is more often used to refer to the applications of science relevant to the construction of machines. Although early machinery was often ingenious, and five highly significant "primal machines"—the lever, the wedge, the wheel, the pulley, and the screw—were all improvised in prehistoric times, the productive application of general principles to *invention and *engineering was long inhibited by the lack of a useful concept of *force. It was not until that concept was integrated into the studies of motion made by Galileo and Isaac *Newton, and the mathematical analyses they produced, that science became properly applicable to the design of machinery.

The lack of a viable theory of mechanics had not inhibited such visionary sketchers of hypothetical machinery as *Leonardo da Vinci, but the possession of one made it easier to imagine how such dreams might be brought to fruition. The ability of artists and writers to imagine horseless carriages and flying machines was undoubtedly a significant inspiration to the actual development of *automobiles and *aeronautics, but the other side of the coin was that the one kind of machine ruled flatly impossible by mechanical theory—the perpetual motion machine—stubbornly lived on in the imagination as a kind of mechanical holy grail.

A machine is, in essence, something that facilitates labour, either by allowing the force of human or animal muscle power to be applied more efficiently to particular tasks, or by converting some other source of power—wind, water, or fire—to the same ends. The distinction is important, because the use of machines that direct human muscle power is usually seen as a skill, and hence as a triumph of endeavour, while machines that replace human muscle power can be seen as usurpers of privilege, giving rise to anxieties about potential redundancy. Such anxieties eventually came to dominate literary treatments of *technology, particularly of the trend towards *automation; ironically, anxiety itself has come to be conceived in mechanical terms, its excess allegedly leading to "nervous breakdown".

The language of mechanics is routinely transferred in a wholesale manner to *narrative theory, analysing stories as if they were machines for the manipulation of readers. Talk of "the mechanics of plotting" is commonplace, as are references to narrative flow and narrative hooks, to the levers, wheels, or threads of a plot, and to suspense and dramatic tension. The end of a story is conventionally described as a denouement, likening it to the untying of a knot. Although the essential subject matter of fiction is usually referred to as "conflict", the fact that it embraces sex as well as rivalry entitles it to more accurate description as "friction". The title of Henry James' "The Turn of the Screw" (1898) is derived from a metafictional prologue concerning the craftsmanship of the horror story rather than from the story itself.

The literary use of imaginary machines as facilitating devices—or as metaphors, as in Daniel Defoe's satire The Consolidator (1705), which features a "cogitator" to force rational thoughts into unwilling brains and a "devilscope" to detect and expose political chicanery—inevitably encourages the lay consideration of machines as "black boxes" whose workings are essentially mysterious. Although the working of primitive devices is obvious, the increasing complexity of such contrivances as clockwork—involving increasingly extravagant use of cogwheels, springs, and various escapement mechanisms to discipline time and generate chimes—conferred sufficient appearance of magicality to motivate as hardened a technophile as Jules Verne to represent it as something quasi-demonic in "Maître Zacharius" (1854; trans. as "Master Zacharius; or, the Watch's Soul"). The "mechanician" Coppelius—who builds automata—is extravagantly demonised in E. T. A. Hoffmann's "Der Sandmann" (1816; trans. as "The Sandman").

The mysterious qualities of mechanism were dramatically increased when machines began to make use of *electrical technology, and further increased when that technology began to include electronic devices. Machinery took on ominous qualities in the artwork of Giovanni Piranesi and a bizarre surreality in the contraptions designed by W. Heath Robinson. The excessive complication of Robinson's machines is echoed in numerous movies featuring inventors who have devised extraordinarily complicated devices to perform simple domestic tasks.

Science-fictional imagery tended to fall in with these patterns, and to emphasise them further in the depiction of such imaginary devices as gargantuan *computers and mysterious *alien artefacts. The demands of melodrama are not entirely sufficient to account for the attraction of such striking images of mechanical malevolence as Theodore Sturgeon's "Killdozer!" (1944), Fred Saberhagen's Berserkers (series launched 1964), or the whore-haunted fruit machine in Harlan Ellison's "Pretty Maggie Moneyeyes" (1967). The notion of a "doomsday machine" is often associated with variants of the *atom bomb, but extends beyond that in a more generalised commentary on the relationship between humans and machines, illustrated by such texts as James P. Hogan's The Genesis Machine (1978). In sum, the primary literary function of machines is to malfunction, and the science of mechanics is generally seen as a dark art dedicated to the substitution of cogwheels for cogitation.

MEDICINE

The treatment of injury and disease; the technological component of the science of *pathology. When *life was conceived in mystical terms, medicine was a form of magic, and the process by which the advancement of science transformed it into a species of applied *biology was slow and awkward. Various forms of quasi-magical "alternative medicine" survived and thrived alongside scientific medicine into the twenty-first century.

Although narrative theory is usually represented in terminology borrowed from *mechanics, the effects of literature on its readers are often seen as therapeutic, in terms of balms and tonics. Although it might be a step too far to classify fiction as a form of medicine, the kinship between the two probably extends beyond the merely metaphorical, and the history of medicine testifies very clearly to the fact that its practitioners have always relied more on the promptings of imaginative fiction than the scientific method.

Medical interventions can be roughly divided into surgical treatments and pharmacological treatments, both of which have prehistoric origins. Illness is frequently viewed by preliterate cultures as a form of demonic possession or curse, so folk medicine often involves rituals of exorcism and the use of protective magical talismans in addition to other forms of treatment. The first practitioners of medicine recognised by legend include the Egyptian vizier Imhotep, who lived at the beginning of the third millennium B.C. His approximate contemporaries in the Chinese imperial courts viewed medical treatment as a matter of balancing opposed forces of yin and yang in the context of five *elements by means of a subtle form of surgical treatment (acupuncture) and herbal treatments. Classical accounts of medicine begin with the legend of the god Asclepius, whose temples were ancestral to modern hospitals; the dogmas of his priests were, however, overhauled and overtaken in the sixth and fifth centuries B.C. by philosophers who developed a legendary figurehead of their own in Hippocrates.

The Hippocratics denied the divine and magical origins of diseases, considering them natural in origin, and hence best countered by the avoidance of artificial treatments—which, they believed, usually made matters worse. The emphasis of their practice was on the cultivation of healthy diets that stimulated the body's own natural resistance. The empirical researches pioneered by the Hippocratics were continued by Aristotle, but their emphasis on the power of natural healing was contested by a rival school in the first century B.C., popularised in Rome by Aulus Cornelius Celsus' De medicina (30 A.D.), which favoured active treatment. The controversy was supposedly resolved by Galen, who began practicing as a physician in 164 A.D. and pioneered empirical enquiries in anatomy and physiology, although human dissection was then illegal. The Christian church, however, reverted to a traditional view of the spiritual origin of disease, whose infliction as divine punishment could only be alleviated—miraculously—by prayer and divine grace.

Roman medicine was preserved in the Eastern empire and the Islamic world, whose leading legendary physician was Avicenna, before being reimported into western Europe during the Renaissance, when Galen was restored as a standard authority. The progress of Western medicine was, however, slow by comparison with the progress of physical science, and arguments from authority retained more power there. In spite of an abundance of empirical data, it was difficult to challenge the generalisations of authority. People who recovered from illness were always likely to credit their recovery to whatever medical treatment they had received, even though they might have recovered anyway; in the absence of massive field studies painstakingly reproducing *experimental design, it was impossible to tell exactly what difference a particular treatment made to the likelihood of recovery, or whether it had made matters worse.

The most obvious improvements in medical practice between the sixteenth and nineteenth centuries were in the field of surgery. Guy de Chauliac's fourteenth-century Chirugia magna became an important textbook and stimulus to further research, and the limitations of Galen's anatomy were far surpassed by Andreas Vesalius' De humani corporis fabrica (1543)—a work that had a profound effect on representative *art as well as the development of surgery, helping to cement an alliance between expert dissectors and the artists who depicted and drew upon their revelations. Ambroise Paré, whose writings were collected in 1561, was the most significant pioneer of "scientific surgery" based on new anatomical knowledge. The subsequent progress of anatomy and surgery was, however, inhibited by legal restrictions on dissection—a difficulty that was still abundantly reflected in urban legends and horror stories in the nineteenth century. The 1828 trial of William Burke and William Hare, who supplied bodies to the Edinburgh surgical school run by Robert Knox, generated considerable literary spin-off, including Robert Louis Stevenson's "The Body Snatcher" (1881) and James Bridie's play The Anatomist (1930), and French romans frénétiques of the same era made much on the fact that the bodies of criminals would pass from the guillotine to the dissecting table.

Meanwhile, the other major branch of medicine was caught in the toils of mystification. The "doctour of physick" in Geoffrey Chaucer's Canterbury tales (ca. 1387) relies on astrological diagnosis and couches his analyses in terms of an alchemical version of the theory of bodily humours (which saw health in terms of balancing occult principles, although it substituted an analogue of the four Classical elements for the Chinese distinction between yin and yang). This scheme proved remarkably persistent, the confusion between *alchemy and medicine being maintained and further enhanced throughout the fifteenth and sixteenth centuries. As the professionalisation of medicine in western Europe was consolidated, a conspicuous enmity developed between professional physicians and various practitioners of folk medicine, often characterised as "cunning men [or women]".

Competition between rival practitioners was further complicated when Galenist orthodoxy was challenged by a new school of "chemical medicine" pioneered by *Paracelsus. In Britain the Paracelsian Thomas Moffet had to fight his way into the Royal College of Physicians in the face of stern Galenist resistance to his disputatious dialogue De jure et praestantia chymicorum medicamentorum (1584; trans. as Of the Validity and Pre-eminence of Chemical Medicines), but eventually won a greater reputation as an *entomologist than he did as a doctor. William

Bullein's *Bulwarke of Defence Againste Sicknes, Sorues, etc* (1562) was divided into four parts: The first dealt with the Galenist use of herbal medicines based on theory of humours, the second with surgical methods, the third with pills, potions, and ointments formulated on vaguely Paracelsian lines, and the fourth with diet and fasting (including observations on sleep and mental disturbance).

The advancement of anatomy continued with William Harvey's discovery of the circulation of the blood in 1628, although a fuller appreciation of its significance had to await the eighteenth-century discovery of oxygen. In 1657, Harvey's friend Christopher Wren—the great architect—borrowed some equipment from him to carry out pioneering experiments in animal blood transfusion, but a French experimenter, Jean-Baptiste Denis, killed one of his patients and blood transfusions were outlawed thereafter until the end of the eighteenth century. In the meantime, competition in the medical marketplace was further complicated by commercial disputes between physicians (who prescribed medicines) and apothecaries (who supplied them). Sir Samuel Garth's "The Dispensary" (1699) is a satirical allegory dramatising the dispute in terms of a heroic descent into a monster-haunted "cave of disease".

One result of the combination of the physicians' price fixing and the increasing impact of new medical discoveries was the dramatic flourishing of "quacks"—unlicensed physicians who offered brand new treatments rather than the traditional ones favoured by cunning men and women (who had been harassed into secrecy, if not to the brink of extinction, by legal persecution, including charges of witchcraft). Quackery became the principal arena of the development of deliberate *pseudoscience, whose inventors mimicked the appearance of science by inventing pseudotheoretical jargon and deploying mysterious apparatus for the purposes of mystification and advertisement. A significant early dramatisation of quackery was Jean-Baptiste Molière's farce *Le médecin malgré lui* (1666; trans. as *The Doctor in Spite of Himself*). Edward Ravenscroft's *The Anatomist; or the Sham Doctor* (1697) is similar in spirit.

In Britain, the eighteenth century became the golden age of quackery, producing such legendary figures as "Crazy Sally" Mapp, the pioneer of techniques subsequently reinvented as osteopathy, and Gustavus Katterfelto, the inventor of styanography, palenchics, and the caprimantic arts. Henry Fielding's *The Mock Doctor* (1732) parodies the French quack Jean Misaubin, but the milieu of quackery is more extensively represented in the works of Tobias Smollett, who turned to writing after five years struggling to establish himself as a fashionable London physician;

Ferdinand Count Fathom (1753) is the most pertinent example. The popular joke about reading medical books inducing symptoms was first put about in this era, appearing in George A. Stevens' *The History of Tom Fool* (1760). The hijacking of the notion of medical progress by quacks lent a bitter irony to almost all eighteenth-century literature dealing with medical topics, including such ostensibly innocuous treatments of the theme as Edward Baynard's "Health: A Poem" (1740).

Quacks took abundant advantage of patent law, the first British "patent medicine"—Timothy Byfield's *Sal oleosum volatile*—receiving its grant in 1711. By the end of the century, more than a hundred medical patents had been granted, including those for trusses and various electric gadgets. The latter were dramatically popularised by James Graham, who took his inspiration from Benjamin Franklin's experiments with electricity; his Temples of Hymen and Health became very fashionable in Regency London, anticipating both the kinds of treatments made famous in France by Anton *Mesmer and their ostentatious mode of administration. Graham fared less well when he was forced to return to Edinburgh, although his *How to Live for Many Weeks or Months or Years Without Eating Anything Whatsoever* (1794) pioneered what is now called "Breatharianism". Quack nostrums played a key role in the early development of newspaper advertising, and continued to thrive as newspapers increased their audiences vastly in the nineteenth century. Physiognomy, phrenology, and homeopathy were among the greatest successes of quack medicine, their utility undoubtedly buoyed up by what would now be called the placebo effect, although their main virtue was their lack of toxicity.

The most significant eighteenth-century breakthrough in medical treatment was vaccination against smallpox, which was developed in India before being pioneered in England by Edward Jenner—although Jenner's initial submission to the Royal Society in 1798 was rejected because its president, Joseph Banks (for whom Jenner had formerly worked, dissecting specimens brought back by Banks from James Cook's first expedition) refused to sanction it. Jenner immediately set out to follow the standard quack strategy, mounting a publicity campaign advertising the virtues of vaccination, with the aid of testimonials from colonialists who had seen it in action. He commissioned a poem for use as propaganda in his cause—Robert Bloomfield's *Good Tidings; or, News from the Farm* (1804)—and obtained the support of the Romantic poets Robert Southey and Samuel Taylor Coleridge, although Southey's *A Tale of Paraguay* (1825) was a retrospective celebration of Jenner's heroic status rather than a contribution to its achievement. In the end, though, it was the potential military advantage conferred by vaccination that finally secured its success—a pattern repeated in both twentieth-century world wars, when the urgent necessity of keeping soldiers fit to fight prompted large-scale medical adventures that were field experiments in more than one sense. Subsequent inoculations against typhoid and tetanus were both made compulsory for soldiers fighting in World War I.

The relationship between literature and medicine was emphasised in this transitional era by a number of writers who represented their literary activity as self-medication. Laurence Sterne's *Tristram Shandy* (1760–1767) is described by its narrator as "a treatise writ against the Spleen". Such representations contributed to the development of the notion of "psychosomatic" disorders, and to the *psychopathological theories that linked literary genius so intimately with madness. Shandy's "spleen" eventually became the psychosomatic condition against which the entire works of Charles Baudelaire and the *Decadent Movement were raised in enmity; the movement's prose classic, Joris-Karl Huysmans' *À rebours* (1884; trans. as *Against the Grain* and *Against Nature*), is obsessed with medication, its climactic perversity being its hero's exultant discovery that it is possible to take nourishment by enema. A rather different alliance was wrought with the most popular nineteenth-century painkiller, laudanum—an alcoholic tincture of morphine whose hallucinogenic effects were explicitly exploited by such writers as Coleridge and Thomas de Quincey, and made a considerable contribution to the development of nineteenth-century imaginative fiction.

Nineteenth-century medical experimentation proceeded in fits and starts, undermined by its inherent hazardousness as well as its methodological problems. Humphry Davy's attempts to identify and counteract the gaseous "principle of contagion" that he considered to be the agent of disease involved testing his new chemical discoveries on himself in the hope of discovering curative effects; the inhalation of nitrous oxide made him laugh and intoxicated him—so he immediately sent some to Coleridge—but chlorine injured his lungs so badly that he never fully recovered, and he died a victim of his own curiosity. Progress remained unsteady, but it was gradually accelerated. The stethoscope, invented in 1813, revolutionised diagnosis as a kind of bodily seismology. The pulse-measuring sphygmograph followed in its wake. Johann Müller's *Handbuch der Physiologie des Menschen* (1833–1850) began to clarify the processes carried out by the various organs whose anatomical and histological description had been aided by the sophistication of the *microscope. The most crucial breakthrough was, however, Louis Pasteur's revivification of the germ theory of disease in the late 1850s.

The most celebrated of Pasteur's achievements as a physician—his treatment for rabies—was by no means conclusively proven to have an effect; its widespread adoption illustrated a key problem in medical research: the ethical difficulty of withholding a treatment that might be effective, given that its effect can only be accurately measured by a "double blinded" trial in which half the participants are given a placebo. His much simpler experiments proving the germ theory, on the other hand, cleared the way for a revolution in surgical practice that attacked the key problems of operational and post-operational infection. The disinfectant precautions pioneered by Ignatz Semmelweis in midcentury were supplemented by Joseph Lister's introduction of antisepsis in 1865. Further complemented by Joseph Simpson's development of chloroform as an anaesthetic in 1847, these advances dramatically enhanced the success rate of nineteenth-century surgery, and paved the way for the pioneering of hundreds of new procedures.

In the United States William Beaumont's *Experiments and Observations on the Gastric Juice and the Physiology of Digestion* (1831) was a highly significant text. The American Medical Association, founded in Philadelphia in 1847, stepped up the pressure on further research. Oliver Wendell Holmes, Semmelweis' U.S. counterpart as a champion of antiseptic surgery, was the first physician to build a considerable literary reputation; his poetry included such notable items as "The Stethoscope Song" (1849), although his prose fiction was restricted to studies in psychopathology. American quackery had still to reach its peaks of achievement, however, and those peaks proved to be higher than any scaled in Europe.

A new era in pseudoscientific quackery was pioneered by John Harvey Kellogg, the corn-flake pioneer, whose endeavours at the Battle Creek Sanitarium—including electrical baths like those pioneered by James Graham—are dramatised in T. Coraghessen Boyle's *The Road to Wellville* (1993; film, 1994). His relative, Wilfred Custer Kellogg, was a spiritualist whose channelling contributed to the development of the Urantia cult. The United States remained a significant host of "faith healing"; the notion of travelling salesmen mounting "medicine shows" to peddle "snake oil"—a term that entered common usage in the mid-1920s—became the twentieth-century archetype of deceptive quackery. Famous American twentieth-century quacks included Albert Adams, who advertised for patients to send their blood for diagnostic analysis in his "dynamizer" prior to treatment by "oscilloclast", and the realtor Gaylord Wilshire—after whom the Los Angeles

Boulevard is named—who marketed a curative magnetic belt. The fetishisation of health also reached a new peak in the United States, as advertised in Bernarr McFadden's physical culture magazines—which occasionally published science fiction. In the meantime, Joseph J. Kinyoun's bacteriological "laboratory of hygiene", founded in 1887 and given official backing by Congress in 1901, became the seed of the National Institutes of Health, which expanded rapidly after their creation in 1944 to become the world's leading sponsor of medical research.

The number of medical men who became more famous as writers than as doctors increased markedly at the end of the nineteenth century. Arthur Conan Doyle provided the most conspicuous example, although it was Sir Ronald Ross—who likewise served as a ship's doctor and nearly devoted himself to his burgeoning literary career instead of returning to India to solve the problem of the transmission of malaria in 1897—who inspired H. de Vere Stacpoole to follow in his footsteps. M. P. Shiel also studied medicine, although he did abandon it in favour of literature. Perhaps remarkably, the most obvious manifestation of their medical experience in the fiction produced by such writers tends to be in the formulation of horror stories—Ross' account of "The Vivisector Vivisected" (written ca. 1889; published 1932) is particularly horrific, while Shiel's account of *Dr. Krasinski's Secret* (1929) is a graphic study of a conscienceless medical researcher and Stacpoole's *The Story of My Village* (1947) wonders whether a universal plague of blindness might be regarded as a curative boon, given the cultural direction in which sighted humankind is headed. Oliver Wendell Holmes' successors in the United States were more constructively inclined; Robert Herrick's *The Web of Life* (1900) and *The Healer* (1911) were among the glossiest literary ads for the profession, while Silas Weir Mitchell's cautionary tales *The Autobiography of a Quack* (1900) and *The Case of George Dedlow* (1900) were painstakingly didactic.

The British doctors who took to writing "shockers" were carrying forward a rich tradition of European medical horror fiction, whose most influential root was Mary Shelley's *Frankenstein* (1818). The tradition gave birth to numerous urban legends as well as literary works; two nineteenth-century examples were dramatised by Villiers de l'Isle Adam in "Le secret de l'échafaud" (1883; trans. as "The Secret of the Scaffold") and "L'héroisme du docteur Hallidonhill" (1885; trans. as "The Heroism of Doctor Hallidonhill"). The strength of this tradition testifies to the fact that the successes of nineteenth-century medical science could not redeem the shady reputation of the medical profession. Frances Cobbe's *The Age of Science: A Newspaper of the Twentieth Century* (1877; by-lined "Merlin Nostradamus") offered a mock-horrific account of a future Britain run by Medical Houses of Commons and Lords, with the constant monitoring of health made compulsory—a theme echoed in James Granville Legge's *The Millennium* (1927).

George Eliot's sympathetic portrait of the medical researcher Tertius Lydgate in *Middlemarch* (1871–1872) was somewhat undermined by the devastation of his hopes and ambitions in consequence of a reckless marriage. George MacDonald's *Paul Faber, Surgeon* (1879) stood in dire need of a conversion to Christianity, in his creator's opinion—which was echoed by Georges Eekhoud, whose Dr. van Kipekap in "Le coeur de Tony Wandel" (1884; trans. as "Tony Wandel's Heart") is a harbinger of the Antichrist. The luckless antihero of Robert Louis Stevenson's *Strange Case of Dr. Jekyll and Mr. Hyde* (1886) could not help becoming a diabolical monster in spite of his best intentions. Grant Allen's *The Devil's Die* (1888) is one of many stories of medical experiments gone horribly awry; another, H. G. Wells' *The Island of Dr. Moreau* (1896), added a further archetype to the tradition, whose influence within scientific romance is reflected in such works as Neil Bell's *Death Rocks the Cradle* (1933; by-lined Paul Martens).

On the other hand, medical advances had a considerable impact on Utopian fiction, most obviously in such specialist works as Benjamin Ward Richardson's *Hygeia: A City of Health* (1876). The establishment of a medical science that could actually be proven to help people paved the way for money-grubbing physicians to seek more pragmatic conversions than the one forced upon MacDonald's Paul Faber; Clotilde Graves' *The Dop Doctor* (1910; by-lined Richard Dehan) spearheaded a subgenre of such tales whose subsequent examples included A. J. Cronin's *The Citadel* (1937). By far the most prolific twentieth-century subgenre of medical fiction was a subsection of genre romantic fiction in which doctors—especially surgeons—were recast as ideal objects of female desire; by the middle of the twentieth century, formularistic examples of the subgenre were dismissively labelled "nurse novels", but the subgenre was successfully transplanted into the milieu of TV soap operas, where it eventually recovered a measure of dramatic respectability in such shows as *Casualty* (launched 1986), *E.R.* (launched 1994), *Chicago Hope* (launched 1994), and *Grey's Anatomy* (launched 2005). Subgenres of speculative medical fiction also developed in the twentieth century around such themes as *longevity and aspects of *neurology.

As the twentieth century progressed, the horrific aspects of pathology were exploited in ever more gruesome melodramas, but they were increasingly counterbalanced by accounts of medical heroism and triumph. Speculative writers remained deeply sceptical of panaceas and other "miracle cures" such as those featured in H. G. Wells' *Tono-Bungay* (1909) and Robert Elson's *"Quack!" The Portrait of an Experimentalist* (1925), but they paid continual tribute to step-by-step advances facilitated by the application of increasing physiological and biochemical understanding to new forms of chemotherapy and immunisation. The continued balance of the war against disease was unfortunate for actual sufferers, but very useful to writers of fiction in search of dramatic tension. From a medical point of view the one substantial victory of World War I was the development of antibacterial sulfonamide drugs, forced by the need to combat syphilis rather than save battle casualties, while its heaviest losses were to the postwar epidemic of "Spanish flu". Alexander Fleming's discovery of penicillin in 1928 improved the effectiveness of antibacterial treatments, but proved ineffective against that literary star among diseases, tuberculosis, which had to await the advent of streptomycin in 1944.

The medical control of pain was improved markedly by the substitution of aspirin for opiates in less severe instances, and by the use of cocaine and diamorphine in the worst cases, but the latter intensified the problems of addiction associated with opium and laudanum, and took *psychotropic literature into a new and more sharply ambivalent phase. The development of treatments to compensate for endocrine dysfunctions, spearheaded by the discovery in 1921 of insulin as a means of treating diabetes, further augmented the list of celebrity drug therapies, although attempts to develop treatments based on sex hormones initially went awry; Serge Voronoff's attempts to restore male virility with animal testosterone (derived, in press parlance, from transplanted "monkey glands") were undermined by the tendency to transplant syphilis infections along with the relevant organs, although the idea seemed horrific enough in itself to such novelists as Robert Hichens, who dramatised it in *Dr. Artz* (1929).

The long-inherent conflict within the medical field was considerably reduced in the twentieth century as the medical profession's security was continually enhanced by the success of its treatments, but quackery did not go away, and the profession was subject to increasing internal stresses as the development and marketing of new medicines was subjected to the evolving priorities of "big business"—especially in the United States, which became the chief powerhouse of medical research. The growing tensions are carefully reflected and analysed in Sinclair Lewis' *Arrowsmith* (1925), whose qualification as the finest medical novel of its era was temporarily prejudiced by the fact that its hero prefers bacteriophages to

antibiotics as a potential method of treatment, although the ever-widening problem of resistant bacteria renewed interest in that line of research toward the end of the century. Several of the early recruits to pulp science fiction were doctors, all of whom were required to advertise their MDs in their by-lines in Hugo *Gernsback's magazines. David H. Keller and Miles J. Breuer were the most prolific, although neither made much use of their expertise, except that Keller's "The Feminine Metamorphosis" (1929) is the nastiest of all monkey gland stories.

The principal subgenre of medical science fiction is one that features peripatetic doctors travelling between worlds. The pattern was pioneered by L. Ron Hubbard's stubbornly unorthodox *Ole Doc Methuselah* (1947–1950, as by René Lafayette; book, 1970) but was more convincingly developed by Murray Leinster's "Med Service" series (1957–1966) and Alan E. Nourse's *Star Surgeon* (1960); James White's Sector General series (1957–1999) introduced the further sophistication of an interstellar hospital geared to cope with all manner of exotic *exobiologies. The heroes of such stories routinely find their task thankless, and frequently have to do good by stealth or in the teeth of fierce opposition, thus increasing the measure of their heroism. Theodore L. Thomas' "The Doctor" (1967) provided an exceptionally graphic archetype of this kind of character. Piers Anthony's "Prostho Plus" (1967) extended the extraterrestrial format to dentistry, but no writer of fiction had ever been able to take dentistry entirely seriously, so its development was inevitably comedic. Sharon Webb's *The Adventures of Terra Tarkington* (1985), featuring a starfaring nurse, also has a certain determined irreverence. A more earnest image of medical practice in space is Lee Correy's *Space Doctor* (1981).

Genre science fiction was, of course, hospitable to the continuation of the medical horror story tradition; its notable contributions included C. M. Kornbluth's "The Little Black Bag" (1950), Walter M. Miller's "Blood Bank" (1952), Cordwainer Smith's "A Planet Named Shayol" (1961), Sonya Dorman's "Splice of Life" (1966), Larry Niven's "The Organleggers" (1969), Laurence M. Janifer's "Amfortas" (1974), Arlie Todd's "Ultima Thule" (1979), K. W. Jeter's *Dr. Adder* (1984), Michael Blumlein's "Tissue Ablation and Variant Regeneration: A Case Report" (1984), and Richard Engling's *Body Mortgage* (1989). Tales of medical resurrection constitute a significant subcategory of such stories, exemplified by Raymond F. Jones' "Discontinuity" (1950), William Tenn's "Down Among the Dead Men" (1954), and Lisa Tuttle's "The Hollow Man" (1979).

Science-fictional accounts of panaceas, "wonder drugs", and other exotic cures balanced out the horror tradition to some extent, although the compensation they offered was often distorted by an inevitable tendency to seek ironic climactic twists. Relatively straightforward examples include Frank M. Robinson's "Untitled Story" (1951), Robert Moore Williams' "Medicine Show" (1953), Henry Slesar's "The Stuff" (1961), Jack Wodhams' "The Cure-All Merchant" (1967), Norman Spinrad's "Carcinoma Angels" (1967), Ian Wallace's *Dr. Orpheus* (1968), Rob Chilson and Lynette Meserole's "The White Box" (1985), and Roger MacBride Allen's "Side Effect" (1990). Those tending more in the direction of *contes cruels* include Christopher Anvil's "In the Light of Further Data" (1965), Larry Niven's "The Jigsaw Man" (1967), Sydney van Scyoc's "A Visit to Cleveland General" (1968), Eric Vinicoff's "Trauma" (1988), Stephen A. Kallis Jr.'s "Placebo Effect" (1992), and Greg Egan's "Cocoon" (1994).

Occasional science-fictional representations of future worlds run by doctors are by no means outrightly horrific, but do tend to the dystopian; notable examples include Ward Moore and Robert M. Bradford's *Caduceus Wild* (1959; book, 1978) and Alan E. Nourse's *A Man Obsessed* (1955; rev. as *The Mercy Men*, 1968) and *The Bladerunner* (1974). The science-fictional extensions of the medical subgenre of *technothrillers also tend to the horrific, as in such definitive works as Robin Cook's *Coma* (1977). The normalising thriller formula exercises a restraint on such stereotypical texts as Raymond Hawkey's *Side-Effect* (1979) and various texts by Stephen G. Spruill, including *Painkiller* (1990), and Sharon Webb, including *The Halflife* (1990), but such caution is shrugged off in the closely-related subgenre of medical *disaster stories, exemplified by Theodore S. Drachman's *Cry Plague!* (1953), Harry Harrison's *Plague from Space* (1965), Michael Crichton's *The Andromeda Strain* (1969), Chelsea Quinn Yarbro's *Time of the Fourth Horseman* (1976), Marshall Goldberg and Kenneth Kay's *Disposable People* (1980), Alan E. Nourse's *The Fourth Horseman* (1983), and Syne Mitchell's *The Changeling Plague* (2003).

Satirisation of the medical profession is less common in science fiction than melodramatisation, but the genre is a natural accommodation for such caricaturish representations as Andrew J. Offutt's "Population Implosion" (1967) and "For Value Received" (1972). Evelyn E. Smith's *The Perfect Planet* (1962) is a flamboyant satire of health fetishisation. Earnest accounts of exotic medical treatments are also rare, not so much because no such innovations could be anticipated but because two hundred years of quackery had sabotaged the seriousness of such efforts. Notable examples include the cancer-consuming crabworms in Elizabeth Moon's "Gut Feelings" (1988), the "soulminder" in

Timothy Zahn's "I Pray the Lord My Soul to Keep" (1989) and "The Hand That Rocks the Casket" (1989), and Neal Asher's "Strood" (2004).

The problems of financing and prioritising healthcare in an era when the advancement of medical science has vastly increased the range of potential interventions, and in which medical errors routinely result in litigation, came into increasingly sharp focus towards the end of the twentieth century, especially in the United States. Such trends are reflected in a great deal of naturalistic medical drama, and they are extrapolated in various ways by such science-fictional *contes philosophiques* as Nancy Kress' "The Mountain to Mohammed" (1992), H. D. Stratmann's "The Human Touch" (1998), Robert J. Sawyer's *Frameshift* (1997), and Brian Plante's "Dibs" (2004).

Late twentieth-century medical melodrama benefited tremendously from one particular technological innovation, which incorporated the ultimate in dramatic tension: the use of externally administered electrical shocks to stop and restart hearts that have lost their rhythmic beat. Such ready-made climactic moments are exploited on a prolific scale in TV soap operas (in which the success rate of the procedure is, understandably, much greater than it is in actuality). Although the irony is rarely pointed out, this is merely an extreme version of the electric shock treatments pioneered by the most daring of all the pseudoscientific quacks of the eighteenth century, James Graham.

Although quack treatments were far more likely to do more harm than good, the appearances they strove so mightily to cultivate did anticipate the techniques that authentic medical science would eventually cultivate. Nor was this success limited to charlatans; even the most Gothically gruesome of medical horror stories proved to be full of foresight in their anticipation of vivisections and organ transplants, and await the resurrection of the dead for their ultimate nightmares to be cosily domesticated. In the meantime, horror fiction continues to draw extravagantly upon the most benign medical applications of *biotechnology, especially those developments that have taken "transplantation" to a molecular level in *genetic engineering. The development of "pharming", in which generic modifications are employed to make animals and plants produce pharmaceutically useful by-products, have generated less anxiety than most such developments.

MERCURY

The nearest planet to the Sun, named after the Roman messenger-god who also lent his name to a chemical element; its astrological associations are summed up in the adjective "mercurial". Mercury's small size and proximity to its primary made its astronomical observation difficult, and defined its literary imagery. The Chevalier de Béthune's *Relation du monde de Mercure* (1750) imagines its winged inhabitants as unapologetic hedonists bathing in the Sun's bounty, unburdened by compulsory death but welcoming the occasional dissolution into the Eternal so that they might experience new incarnations. The Mercurian spirits of Emmanuel Swedenborg's *Arcana Coelestia* (1758) are uninterested in material things—even spurning the vulgarities of speech—and extremely knowledgeable, although this inclines them to conceit. In W. D. Lach-Szyrma's *Aleriel* (1886), the highly intelligent Mercurians live in the various layers of the planet's atmosphere, in "cars" that can easily mount expeditions into space.

In 1893, Giovanni Schiaparelli declared that Mercury's period of rotation matched its period of revolution, thus keeping the same face perpetually turned towards the Sun. Percival Lowell agreed with the judgement, which gave birth to numerous literary images of a world whose one side was extremely hot and the other extremely cold, with only a narrow "twilight zone" in between. Although this factor is ignored in the images of inhabited Mercury contained in Willis Brewer's *The Secret of Mankind* (1895) and William Wallace Cook's satire *Adrift in the Unknown* (1904–1905; 1925), it coloured most subsequent accounts of the kinds of life likely to be found there. This supposition persisted until 1965, when it was discovered that Mercury rotates on its axis every 58.6 years, by comparison with its orbital period of 88 days; the utter inhospitability of its surface and virtual absence of any atmosphere was confirmed soon afterwards by the Mariner 10 fly-past of 1974–1975.

Mercury is presently lifeless in Homer Eon Flint's "The Lord of Death" (1919), and its use as the setting of E. R. Eddison's *The Worm Ouroboros* (1922) is entirely arbitrary, but Schiaparelli's supposition governed the *exobiological imagery of a series of novels by Ray Cummings, including "The Fire People" (1922) and *Tama of the Light Country* (1930; book, 1965), the lives of whose winged Mercurians are determined by their relationship to the stationary Sun. It was taken into account by most subsequent pulp science fiction images, including Clark Ashton Smith's "The Immortals of Mercury" (1932), Frank Belknap Long's "Cones" (1936), Clifford D. Simak's "Masquerade" (1941; aka "Operation Mercury"), Isaac Asimov's "Runaround" (1942), and Leigh Brackett's "Shannach—The Last" (1952).

As genre science fiction became more sophisticated in the 1950s, such images became gradually more rigorous, and Mercury's extreme hostility lent a brutal edge to such stories as William Morrison's "The Weather on Mercury" (1953), Lester del Rey's *Battle on Mercury* (1956; by-lined Erik van Lhin), Asimov's *Lucky Starr and the Big Sun of Mercury* (1956; by-lined Paul French), Hugh Walters' *Mission to Mercury* (1965), Alan E. Nourse's "Brightside Crossing" (1956), Hal Clement's "Hot Planet" (1963), Larry Niven's "The Coldest Place" (1964), and C. C. MacApp's "The Mercurymen" (1965). There is a considerable continuity between the latter items in this list and those produced after the discovery of Mercury's rotation, including Eric Vinicoff and Marcia Martin's "Render unto Caesar" (1976), Poul Anderson's "Vulcan's Forge" (1983), and G. David Nordley's "Crossing Chao Meng Fu" (1997). Images of native Mercurian life became much rarer after 1950; the cave-dwelling Harmonia of Kurt Vonnegut's *The Sirens of Titan* (1959) are symbolic constructions.

Mercury provides a refuge for humankind as the Sun cools in such pulp fantasies as R. F. Starzl's "The Last Planet" (1934), Eando Binder's "Dawn to Dusk" (1934–1935), and Edmond Hamilton's "Intelligence Undying" (1936), but stories of that kind died out as it was belatedly realised that Lord Kelvin's estimate of the Sun's lifetime was badly mistaken. Mercury played a more sustained role in science fiction as a convenient base for the scientific study of the Sun, as in David Brin's *Sundiver* (1980), although it is occasionally mined for mineral wealth, as in Stephen Baxter's "Cilia-of-Gold" (1994). Although Mercury hardly seems suitable for *terraforming, the increasing interest in such projects produced such adventurous images as the one in Tom Purdom's "Romance in Extended Time" (2000), in which the planet is girdled by a huge "greenhouse". In Larry Niven and Brenda Cooper's "Kath and Quicksilver" (2005), Mercury is on the brink of being swallowed by the expanding Sun.

MESMER, (FRANZ) ANTON (1734–1815)

Austrian *medical practitioner. He was working in France in the 1770s when he began to claim—independently of the Scottish quack James Graham, who was then in the process of setting up his Temples of Hymen and Health to offer electrical and magnetic therapies—that *magnets are capable of marvellous therapeutic effects. Mesmer initially attributed this effect to the manipulation of an internal "magnetic fluid" by virtue of his own natural gift for "animal magnetism".

Rumours of Mesmer's activities caused a sensation, and the French government set up an investigative commission whose members included Antoine Lavoisier and Benjamin Franklin, who was then in Paris on a diplomatic mission. In 1784, the commission reported that it could find no evidence of the existence of such a fluid, and that Mesmer had achieved his alleged cures by exciting the power of the patients' imagination, but the publicity proved invaluable. Mesmer had prepared his response in advance; he had already announced his own conclusion that the magnets and the "mesmeric crises" they seemed to induce were actually superfluous, and he was in the process of developing a new therapeutic technique that subsequently became known as *hypnotism.

Mesmer's undiminished celebrity ensured that his ideas remained a significant influence on contemporary therapeutic practice, and they were more widely reflected in literature than any parallel medical fads. The importation of mesmerism into the United States in the 1830s was associated with a particular emphasis on the alleged ability of mesmerists to communicate with their patients by thought transference, effectively using them as oracles in much the same fashion as spiritualist mediums; the movement thus made a significant contribution to the ancestry of twentieth-century *parapsychology. The American mesmerist Phineas P. Quimby developed its fundamental theses into a kind of psychiatry by means of the "mind-cure" movement, while his one-time student Mary Baker Eddy reformulated and elaborated them as Christian Science. Andrew Taylor Still, the founder of modern osteopathy, and Daniel D. Palmer, the founder of chiropractics, both began their careers as mesmerists.

In accord with the general literary treatment of medical themes, mesmerists were often credited with sinister agendas, as in several stories by E. T. A. Hoffmann, Frédéric Soulié's Le magnetiseur (1834), Alexandre Dumas' La comtesse de Charny (1853–1855; trans. as The Countess de Charny and The Mesmerist's Victim), George MacDonald's David Elginbrod (1863), William Dean Howells' The Undiscovered Country (1880), and Ernest Oliphant's Mesmerist (1890). V. F. Odoevsky's "4338—i god" (1838–1840; trans. as "The Year 4338: Letters from Petersburg"), on the other hand, imagines that mesmeric theory will one day be the foundation of all medical practice. The idea that mesmeric trances might confer oracular powers or have other supernatural effects was employed as a facilitating device by Edgar Allan Poe in the visionary fantasy "The Mesmeric Revelation" (1844) and a mock-scientific report of "The Effects of Mesmerism on a Dying Man" (1845; aka "The Facts in the Case of M. Valdemar").

Twentieth-century fiction looking back on mesmerism usually views it as charlatanry—notable examples include Per Olov Enquist's Magnetisörens Femte Vinter (1964; trans. as The Magnetist's Fifth Winter), in which a mesmerist on the run captivates a small town, and Felice Picano's The Mesmerist (1977), in which a mesmerist practices dentistry in turn-of-the-century New York—but a scrupulous mesmerist is featured in Brooks Hansen's Perlman's Ordeal (1999). A mesmerist is murdered in Regency London in Amanda Quick's Don't Look Back (2002).

METAPHYSICS

A term used by *Aristotle to refer to the branch of *philosophy that attempts to determine the "true nature of things": that which supposedly underlies or contains the sensible substance making up the world of appearances. Analysis of the term as "beyond physics" suggests that its concerns are, by definition, outside the realm of science, but the relevant boundary has shifted considerably since the Classical era. Much of modern physics—especially its extensions in *cosmology—refers to ideas that were once quintessentially metaphysical. As the boundary has moved, the central concerns of metaphysics have changed, and the main force driving that mutation has been the expansion and evolution of scientific theory. All new discoveries in empirical science have implications for, and exercise powerful constraints on, the kinds of metaphysical framework that might underlie or contain them, and the fact that metaphysics deals with unprovable questions does not mean that its enquiries are beyond the scope of critical thought or unamenable to logical analysis. Metaphysics has, therefore, made progress in step with science, as a key component of the same intellectual process.

The speculative element of metaphysics is readily amenable to fictional representation and extrapolation. Almost all early speculative fiction, from *Plato's "Story of Er" to Voltaire's *contes philosophiques, extrapolates metaphysics rather than physics; although the balance shifted thereafter, there is still a considerable amount of metaphysical speculation even in the *hard science fiction whose definition claims to have forsworn it—as illustrated by the extrapolation of cosmology and *evolutionary theory into *Omega Point fantasy, theories of *hyperspace, and the imagery of *parallel worlds. The intense scrupulousness of serious metaphysical argument and analysis, on the other hand, does not lend itself to literary reflection or extrapolation. The most inventive sector of speculative metaphysics is that of *theology, whose alleged revelations have come into conflict with those of science as the boundaries of explanation have shifted, and the theological side of the conflict has always been more prolific, as well as more intense, in its literary produce.

The metaphysical debate that bears most directly upon the *philosophy of science is the conflict between realism and idealism, the former holding that such fundamental concepts as *space, *time, and *matter refer to objective entities, while the latter holds that such ideas are artefacts of perception. The philosophical extensions of this discussion included the assumption of controversial positions such as *positivism and *relativism, and exercised a powerful influence on the development of theories of *light and the *atom. Immanuel Kant's attempt to synthesise the two positions began with publications that compared and contrasted the fundamental metaphysics of Isaac *Newton's system of thought with that of Gottfried Leibniz, as popularised and revised by Christian Wolff, and also included an account of Emmanuel *Swedenborg's attempt to attain the same end by a very different route, which had similarly originated in scientific enquiries.

Kant's Critik der reinen Vernunft (1781; rev. 1787; trans. as The Critique of Pure Reason) remained a crucial account of the nature and placement of the boundary between physics and metaphysics. It contends that knowledge is a product obtained by the imposition of certain attributes of mind, determined a priori (in advance), on the data of sensory experience, facilitating their systematic arrangement a posteriori (subsequently) into science. The objects of knowledge thus become phenomena of perception rather than things "in themselves". Although the latter remain essentially mysterious, Kant was optimistic that the thinking mind could deduce a great deal about the nature of reality by careful a priori analysis of three different orders of "transcendental" information: intuitions of the form of time and space, categories and principles such as substance and causality, and ideas of self and the world.

Kant's influence on subsequent German philosophy was primarily a matter of the further development of a priori reasoning and the notion of the "transcendental subject", whose nature was construed by Johann Fichte and F. W. J. von Schelling as an absolute ego [self] before being reconstrued by G. W. F. Hegel as an aspect of a collective geist [spirit] and by Arthur Schopenhauer as a complex in which ideas of the world were confused by the wille [will]. The influence of this aspect of his philosophy on literature was muted by the difficulty as well as the abstraction of his ideas, but the ideas of Fichte, Schelling, Hegel, and Schopenhauer provided considerable nourishment to nineteenth-century literary endeavour, laying the ideological foundations of *Romanticism and all its descendant movements.

Another area of metaphysical debate that has considerable relevance to the evolution of science is the attempt to define the relationship between the mind and the body, whose crucial watershed was reached in René Descartes' definition of the mind as a metaphysical entity controlling the physical structures of the body. Although "Cartesian dualism" was soon discredited, the continuing argument, in both *psychology and "the philosophy of mind"—tended to be formulated as various schools of reaction against it, while "common sense" clung to it stubbornly as a major prop of psychological *plausibility. Descartes' influence on literature was as indirect as Kant's, but it was just as considerable. Henri Bergson's examination of the relationship between mind and body in Matière et mémoire (1896; trans. as Matter and Memory) was particularly influential in the literary arena; Marcel Proust's à la recherche du temps perdu (1913–1927) took considerable inspiration from it.

Such terms as "metaphysical poetry" and "metaphysical novel" are used very widely, the first term frequently being used as a synonym for "supernatural" or "mystical", thus embracing all exercises in *occult fiction and *parapsychology and all *religious fantasies. Most exercises in literary fabulation are also metaphysical in this broad sense. Many contes philosophiques are, however, narrowly definable as metaphysical fantasies, in the sense that they confront explicit metaphysical problems in a forthright fashion; there are numerous notable examples among the works of Jorge Luis Borges and Bertrand *Russell. Novel-length works of this sort are rarer, although René Daumal's posthumous Le mont analogue (1952; trans. as Mount Analogue) is a notable exception. Genre science fiction examples of metaphysical fabulation include K. Raymond's "The Great Thought" (1937)—which embodies a lecture delivered to a hypothetical American Metaphysical Society—Robert A. Heinlein's "Elsewhen" (1941), Fritz Leiber's "The Big Engine" (1962), C. J. Cherryh's Wave Without a Shore (1981), and Robert Thurston's "Slipshod, at the Edge of the Universe" (2001). R. A. Lafferty's works include several playful metaphysical meditations, the most notable of which are "Eurema's Dam" (1972) and "Inventions Bright and New" (1986).

METEORITE

A term referring to objects that appear to have fallen from the sky, equivalent to the now-obsolete "meteorolith". Such objects were immediately correlated with light trails in the sky (meteors), although many such "shooting stars" left no residue, and also seemed to some observers to be correlated with sounds, giving rise to such terms as "detonating fireball" and "bolide". The origins and nature of shooting stars remained controversial throughout the nineteenth century—the supposition that light trails were caused by actual objects and that meteorites had actually fallen from the sky was routinely criticised by sceptics who insisted on reckoning the former as optical illusions and the latter as odd terrestrial rocks—and the acoustic phenomena allegedly associated with them remained contentious into the twenty-first century. The ambiguity of their nature is cleverly exploited in Villiers de l'Isle Adam's "Une profession nouvelle" (1885; trans. as "A New Profession").

Shooting stars sometimes occur in thousandfold showers, which can be very impressive; the earliest record of such an event is from China in the seventh century B.C., but the reference in Revelation 6:13 to the stars falling upon the Earth may recall some such event. Virgil's *Georgics* (30 B.C.) asserts that meteor showers are omens preceding bad weather, and a character in William Shakespeare's *Richard II* testifies to their uncertain status in referring to meteors "[frightening] the fixed stars of heaven". Sixteenth-century travellers often took an interest in the phenomenon. Spanish soldiers who founded the city of Santiago del Estero in what is now Argentina in 1533 were told of a huge piece of metal that had fallen from the sky and sent an expedition to hunt for it in 1576. Their discovery that it was made of iron was widely reported, but it was forgotten amid political upheavals until its rediscovery in 1774.

A sample of the Santiago meteorite sent in 1788 to the Royal Society—whose interest had been awakened by the giant meteor of 18 August 1783—was compared with others brought from Siena, Benares, and Siberia, and then with one that fell at Woldnewton in Yorkshire in the late 1790s. Edward Howard's report, issued in 1802, confirmed their similarity and supported the hypothesis of their extraterrestrial origin. A rumour that the Santiago meteorite contained large silver deposits was rapidly proven false, but the notion of meteorites rich in precious stones or metals subsequently figured in such speculative fictions as M. P. Shiel's *The Lord of the Sea* (1900), Jules Verne's *La chasse au météore* (1908; trans. as *The Chase of the Golden Meteor*), and Théo Varlet's *Le roc d'or* (1927).

When it was observed in the early nineteenth century that meteor showers originate from particular regions of the sky, accumulated astronomical data were searched for recurrent events; the thirty-three/thirty-four year periodicity of the Leonid shower—regularly observed since 903 A.D.—was quickly established, permitting the successful prediction of its return in 1866–1867. The objects were shown to be following the same orbit as the *comet Tempel-Tuttle, establishing the hypothesis—soon confirmed by other such coincidences—that the showers were cometary debris.

Such showers are, however, caused by very tiny particles that evaporate in the atmosphere; it is presumed that most of the larger "meteoroids" whose remnants reach the surface as meteorites emanate from the *asteroid belt, sometimes consisting of debris ejected from Mars or the Moon in the remote past by asteroid strikes. "Meteor storms" occasionally featured in early space fiction as an astronautical hazard, as in Lowell Howard Morrow's "Through the Meteors" (1930), Frank K. Kelly's "Into the Meteorite Orbit" (1933), and John Berryman's "Special Flight" (1939).

Once their extraterrestrial origin was established, meteorites became objects of great scientific interest, offering clues to the origin of the solar system. They were classified into metallic siderites and stony aerolites and chondrites, the latter including carbonaceous material. Chondrites were co-opted into theories of *panspermia after fragments of a meteorite that fell near Orgueil in France in 1864 were examined by various scientists—including Marcellin Berthellot and Louis Pasteur—who confirmed that it contained organic material. Subsequent literary examples frequently turned out to bear the seeds or spores of extraterrestrial life; notable examples include Théo Varlet's *La grande panne* (1930), P. Schuyler Miller's "The Red Plague" (1930), and A. Rowley Hilliard's "Death from the Stars" (1931). The notion was extensively deployed in the science fiction pulps, where meteorites turned out to be alien spacecraft in such stories as Ed Earl Repp's "The Stellar Missile" (1929), Lloyd Arthur Eschbach's "The Gray Plague" (1930), and Eando Binder's "The Robot Aliens" (1935).

Other fictional meteorites served as interplanetary versions of the message-in-a-bottle motif, as in Charles Dixon's *Fifteen Hundred Miles an Hour* (1895), Henry James' "Mernos" (1929), James D. Perry's "Death Between the Planets" (1933), and Richard G. Kerlin's "The Alien Hah-Rah" (1935), or had quasi-miraculous effects such as those featured in John Taine's *The Iron Star* (1930), David M. Speaker's "The Message from Space" (1930), and Jack Williamson's "The Meteor Girl" (1931). Such motifs became less common as genre science fiction became more sophisticated and writers became more conscientious in estimating the probability of organisms or artefacts surviving the frictional heat generated by a descent through the atmosphere. William T. Powers' "Meteor" (1950) introduced the notion of irrational "meteor-strike anxiety" long before enterprising tradesmen began selling protective headgear in advance of the meteoric return to Earth of such *artificial satellites as Skylab.

The most significant shooting star of the twentieth century exploded at 7:17 a.m. on 30 June 1908 above the pine forests of the Podkamennaya Tunguska River valley in Siberia. The sound of the blast was heard a thousand kilometres away, but the remoteness of the region and the political turmoil of prerevolutionary Russia made it impractical to investigate the event until 1921, when Leonid Kulik—who hoped to find valuable deposits of *meteoric iron and nickel—attempted to find the object responsible. He reached the site in 1927 but found no crater, nor any substantial traces of magnetic metals, although the trees had been scorched and levelled for twenty kilometres around. I. S. Astapovich concluded that the exploding object must have been the nucleus of a *comet, consisting of fine dust held together by various ices, but the mystery soon attracted further hypotheses.

Lincoln La Paz suggested in 1941 that the Tunguska explosion might have been caused by a small piece of antimatter—a notion echoed in Jack Williamson's "Collision Orbit" (1942; by-lined Will Stewart), where the brightness of shooting stars is credited to the annihilation of "contraterrene matter". Aleksander Kazantsev—who was a science fiction writer as well as a scientist—proposed in 1945 that it might have been an atomic explosion in the drive unit of an alien spacecraft. Other venturesome hypotheses included the proposal that the damage might have been caused by the testing of an energy transmitter that the inventor Nikola Tesla had recently built at his Wardenclyffe research site on Long Island, whose potential as a weapon of destruction had been widely reported but never realised. Although Kulik's soil samples were found in the 1950s to contain tiny spheres of magnetic metal, suggesting that there had indeed been a meteorite that had exploded before impact, rival hypotheses continued to emerge. A. A. Jackson and Michael P. Ryan suggested in 1973 that the event might have been caused by a tiny *black hole.

Many of these suggestions attracted attention from writers of speculative nonfiction, but Kazantsev's—which had been anticipated in Ed Earl Repp's "The Second Missile" (1930)—seemed the most exciting; it is variously developed in D. R. Bensen's *And Having Writ* ... (1978), Ian Watson's *Chekhov's Journey* (1983), Rudy Rucker and Bruce Sterling's "Storming the Cosmos" (1985), Joseph Manzione's "Cold War" (1989), and Algis Budrys' *Hard Landing* (1993). John Baxter and Thomas Atkins popularised it in *The Fire Came By: The Riddle of the Great Siberian Explosion* (1976), which Baxter followed up with the novel *The Hermes Fall* (1978).

In 1961, Bartholomew Nagy and Douglas J. Hennessy claimed to have discovered fragments of once-living cells inside the Orgueil meteorite; although sceptics dismissed their findings as Earthly contamination, Nagy continued to search for similar evidence in other meteorites. NASA researchers reported in 1996 that microscopic structures in a meteorite found in Antarctica might be fossils of Martian bacterial life, reigniting interest in the panspermia hypothesis, as mirrored in such stories as Charles L. Harness' "The GUAC Bug" (1998) and Dan Brown's *Deception Point* (2001).

METEOROLOGY

The science of weather. The term derives from the title of Aristotle's *Meteorologica*, although that text had a wider reference, including *comets (which he assumed to be atmospheric phenomena), volcanoes, and earthquakes; very few of Aristotle's explanatory speculations turned out to be accurate. Bad weather is the principal agent of all *disaster stories, in myth and literature alike, routinely seen as the most significant threat that human societies face, and one of the two root causes of human misery. The related science of climatology, which relates to average conditions in seasonal cycles, has less inherent melodrama, although climate changes pose greater potential threats to long-term social welfare.

In mythical terms, weather is often seen as a product of the moods of the gods, storms being symptoms of divine wrath, gentle sunshine as a reflection of their contentment, and so on. This kind of thinking persisted in metaphor long after it had been labelled "the pathetic fallacy". It crops up routinely in *anthropological and *ethnological fiction as evidence of primitive superstition, but its most prolific literary reflection is its inversion in literary symbolism. Like literary dreams, literary weather is packed with symbolic meanings, reflecting the mood changes of the characters or the dramatic movements of the plot; a developing storm is a frequent element of a building climax. The use of weather in this fashion is graphically illustrated by the Biblical story of the Deluge and its consequent emblematic rainbow, from which fictional rainbows inherit their symbolic loading. Attempts to predict and control the weather are a significant aspect of divination, magic, and tribal religion; rain dances are another standard feature of stereotypical images of tribal society, and James Frazer's representation of "fertility rites" as the root-stock of all religion is widely featured in literary imagery. Literary symbolism also makes frequent use of technological devices used to judge wind direction.

The notorious capriciousness of weather made the development of a competent science of meteorology very difficult, but it was not until the development of *chaos theory that it became clear why meteorological prediction was so fraught with uncertainties, and would remain so no matter how well understood its causal mechanisms might be. Despite the difficulties of detailed prediction, the calendrical calculations used to anticipate seasonal changes, and hence to determine the patterns of agricultural endeavour, were the principal driving force in the development of the observational science of *astronomy and the associated analytical methods of *mathematics. There is a sense in which all science is derived from meteorological enquiry—which makes the lack of progress made in the narrowly defined science during the scientific revolution rather ironic. The importance of weather prediction sustained abundant divinatory activity into the twentieth century in spite of its manifest unreliability; astrological weather prediction was an important component of the demand for almanacs, which outnumbered all other printed books throughout the seventeenth and eighteenth centuries.

Climatic and meteorological conditions were often cited as causes of disease before the establishment of the germ theory, and a good deal of meteorological data was collected in the hope that it might be medically useful. The observations painstakingly recorded by John Lining of South Carolina in the 1740s provided the foundation for a far-ranging collaboration in the early nineteenth century between the U.S. Army Medical Department, the General Land Office, and various U.S. academic institutions. Such research was pursued with unusual enthusiasm in the United States because the climate and weather were perceived as alien, and strangely violent, by European colonists startled by Caribbean hurricanes and Midwestern tornadoes.

The origins of meteorological understanding were laid in the seventeenth century. Evangelista Torricelli invented the barometer in 1643, shortly before the reciprocal relationship of pressure and volume was established by Boyle's law. Barometers became key instruments of meteorological measurement, changes in atmospheric pressure being the primary indicator in scientific forecasting. The phenomenon of evaporation—the ascent of water vapour to form clouds—remained stubbornly mysterious for a further century, sufficiently so for the Academy of Sciences of Bordeaux to offer a prize for its solution in 1743. Attempted explanations remained confused by ideas of fusion and dissolution until James Dalton produced a theory of "independent vapour" in 1801, popularised by William Charles Wells' *An Essay on Dew* (1814). Although the reason for the conceptual linkage is unclear, several notable scientists interested in evolution and heredity also had a strong interest in meteorology. The Chevalier de Lamarck devoted the greater part of his later years to the study of the weather, Johann Mendel, *alias* Father Gregor, compiled a useful record of meteorological data alongside his experiments in plant breeding, and Francis Galton's *Meteorographica* (1863) provided a summary textbook of nineteenth-century advances.

The British *Romantic poets took a strong interest in the development of meteorological science, partly because Percy Shelley's tutor, Adam Walker, was intensely interested in meteorological phenomena, mingling his scientific sources with the ideas of the mystic Jacob Boehme. Walker's overestimation of the role of "atmospheric electricity" is reflected in Shelley's poems "Ode to the West Wind" (1819) and "The Cloud" (1820). British interest in meteorology was boosted by a month-long incident in 1783; between 23 June and 20 July the island was afflicted by a vast dust cloud (resulting from the eruption of the Icelandic volcano Skaptar Jokull) that obscured the Sun and generated considerable apocalyptic anxiety. Luke Howard—who was eleven at the time—was one of those whose attention was captured; he produced a classification of cloud types in 1802–1803—whose primary categories were cirrus, cumulus, and stratus—that is still in use in the twenty-first century. Howard's account of *The Climate of London* (1818–1820) helped formulate the perceptions of such artists as J. W. M. Turner and John Constable. The British Meteorological Society, founded in 1823, was the ancestor of the Meteorological Office founded in 1854. Another British poet who took an intense interest in meteorological science was Gerard Manley Hopkins, as exemplified in "That Nature Is a Heraclitean Fire and of the Comfort of the Resurrection" (written ca. 1880; published 1918), while reflections of the peculiarity of London's weather produced such fog fantasies as W. D. Hay's *The Doom of the Great City* (1880) and Robert Barr's "The Doom of London" (1892).

In the United States James Pollard Espy published a theory of hail in 1836, envisaging the atmosphere as an enormous heat engine, in which all disturbances were driven by updrafts; he generalised his theory in *The Philosophy of Storms* (1841). William Redfield disagreed, envisaging hurricanes as gigantic whirlwinds, while Robert Hare focused on the role of atmospheric electricity; all of them were partly right. The Smithsonian Institute launched a major meteorological project in 1848 under the direction of John Henry, and in 1870 Congress established a national weather service in the War Department, whose work was superseded by the U.S. Weather Bureau established by the Department of Agriculture in 1890. L. Frank Baum's *The Wonderful Wizard of Oz* (1900) includes one of the iconic American literary images of a storm, although George R. Stewart's *Storm* (1941) and Sebastian Junger's *The Perfect Storm* (1997; film, 2000) offer far more meteorological detail.

French weather is, in general, more benign than that of England, let alone the United States, and this is reflected in the relative delicacy of the weather symbolism of nineteenth-century French literature. The French always considered the British to be foolishly weather obsessed, and this obsession is reflected in literature as well as meteorological science; it became very noticeable in twentieth-century *disaster fiction, when English fiction of that sort developed a highly distinctive tradition of meteorological disaster stories, whose cardinal examples include Gerald Heard's "The Great Fog" (1944), a sequence of novels by J. G. Ballard begun with *The Wind from Nowhere* (1962), and Adam Roberts' *The Snow* (2004).

The possibility of developing weather-controlling *weapons also originated in British scientific romance, in such works as Fred M. White's *The White Battalions* (1900), recurring throughout that genre's history in such works as Francis Beeding's *The One Sane Man* (1934), W. Ashton Hamlyn's *Strange Weather!* (1941), and John Boland's *White August* (1955). Such weapons were imported into pulp science fiction in such works as Nathan Schachner's "Emissaries of Space" (1932) and subsequently cropped up in such technothrillers as Steve Frazee's *The Sky Block* (1953) and William E. Cochrane's "Weather War" (1976), but weather-controlling technologies were more frequently employed in American science fiction to tame the unruly native weather, as in Ed Earl Repp's "The Storm Buster" (1930), Malcolm Jameson's "Eviction by Isotherm" (1938), Isaac Asimov's "Rain, Rain, Go Away" (1959), Theodore L. Thomas' "The Weather Man" (1962) and "The Other Culture" (1969), Ben Bova's *The Weathermakers* (1967), and Hilbert Schenck's "Hurricane Claude" (1983).

A summary of contemporary meteorological knowledge was offered to readers of *Astounding Science Fiction* in Jack Williamson's two-part articles "Unpredictable" (February–March 1946), which included an account of the *greenhouse effect. It was quickly followed in the magazine's pages by Raymond F. Jones' "Forecast" in the June issue and Hal Clement's "Cold Front" in July, but meteorological science fiction made only sporadic appearances thereafter. Christopher Anvil's "The Gentle Earth" (1957), in which Earthly weather confounds invading aliens, was one of the more elaborate examples. Clement's venture into "exometeorological" hard science fiction was echoed in endeavours of other conscientious world builders, including Poul Anderson, Larry Niven, and Robert L. Forward, but most accounts of extraterrestrial bad weather are entirely arbitrary, generated by the same inversion of the pathetic fallacy that governs literary weather in naturalistic fiction, sometimes—as in Ray Bradbury's "Death-by-Rain" (1950) and

Cordwainer Smith's "On the Storm Planet" (1965)—exaggerated to new extremes.

In 1962–1963, however, *Analog* hosted Joseph Goodavage's "Crucial Experiment" series, in which the author compared "astrometeorological forecasts"—based on a method derived from Alfred J. Pearce's *Astrometeorology* (1889)—with actual weather, claiming a better hit rate than chance would permit, although he did not convince many sceptics. His failure emphasises that the difficulty of drawing good correlations from messy data cuts both ways; Leslie Gadallah's "The Butterfly Effect" (1991), in which a meteorologist finds a way to predict the weather but fails to convince anyone else of the virtue of the method, illustrates the problem.

While *atom bomb tests were being carried out in the early 1950s, they were frequently suspected of causing bad weather—as dramatised in Hilbert Schenck's "Tomorrow's Weather" (1953)—but no conclusive proof was produced. The link between industrial activity and "acid rain" was, however, easier to demonstrate. The claim that the global warming observed in the latter decades of the twentieth century was due to a *greenhouse effect induced by the burning of fossil fuels provoked another controversy of a similar sort. The anxieties thus provoked were reflected in numerous literary accounts of unprecedentedly bad weather and its painstaking investigation, including Tom Ligon's "Funnel Hawk" (1990), Bruce Sterling's *Heavy Weather* (1994), and John Barnes' *Mother of Storms* (1994).

MICROBIOLOGY

The subdivision of *biology concerned with single-celled organisms, which are sometimes called "microbes". Because such organisms are invisible to the naked eye, its origin had to await the development of the *microscope, and its progress has been dependent on the increasing power of such instruments.

Early microscopes revealed the existence of various kinds of protozoa, whose most celebrated stereotypes included the shape-changing amoeba and the ciliate *Paramecium*; single-celled plants, including various species of algae and fungi, were inherently less dramatic. More powerful microscopes revealed a range of even smaller entities, bacteria, whose role as agents of disease (germs) was quickly realised. Closer examination revealed that bacterial cells were prokaryotic (devoid of internal membranes), while protozoans and single-celled algae were eukaryots, with internal structures as complex as those in the cells of multicellular organisms. This classification became increasingly elaborate as finer discriminations became possible, and the development of electron microscopes in the twentieth century allowed a further range of even simpler entities—viruses—to be photographed.

The discovery and subsequent elucidation of the richness of microbiology was a considerable stimulus to the speculative imagination, opening the frontiers of further *microcosms contained within that of the human body. The inaccessibility of its contents to the naked eye was, however, a considerable narrative disadvantage, so much early speculative fiction dramatising the discoveries of microbiology uses facilitating devices to adjust the size differential, either by adopting a microcosmic viewpoint or by magnifying microbes. Notable examples of the former strategy include Patrick Dutton's "The Beautiful Bacillus" (1931). The latter strategy gave rise to a small subgenre of "giant microbe stories", including André Couvreur's *Une invasion de macrobes* (1909), Otis Adelbert Kline's "The Malignant Entity" (1926), and Arlton Eadie's "The Flowing Death" (1930); the amoeba provided a model for numerous aliens of considerable size, including those featured in Nictzin Dyalhis' "When the Green Star Waned" (1925).

The discoveries of microbiology were reflected most prolifically in accounts of new agents of disease, in such alarmist fantasies as Robert Potter's *The Germ Growers* (1892), A. Lincoln Green's *The End of an Epoch* (1901), J. J. Connington's *Nordenholt's Million* (1923), Clifton B. Kruse's "The Death Protozoan" (1934), and Thomas Painter and Alexander Laing's *The Motives of Nicholas Holtz* (1936; aka *The Glass Centipede*). They also encouraged the production of fantasies of artificial *life, such as Dudbroke's *The Prots* (1903), which tracks the evolution of artificially generated protoplasm from its microcosmic beginnings to the appearance of four-foot humanoids, and John Russell Fearn's "Dynasty of the Small" (1936), in which an artificial amoeba designed to feed on disease-causing protozoa escapes into the environment and precipitates an ecocatastrophe. Microorganisms were also recruited as speculative explanations in such works as Harriet Stark's *The Bacillus of Beauty* (1900).

Although these early fictions seemed highly fanciful, the notion of engineering microorganisms became increasingly plausible as the twentieth century progressed, and the *genetic engineering of bacteria eventually proved to be relatively easy because of the tendency of bacteria to hold genes in plasmid rings that could be absorbed from their environment. Viruses also became useful in genetic engineering as vectors carrying genes into eukaryot cells and attaching them to native genomes. Microbiology filled in significant gaps in theoretical accounts of the

*evolution of life on Earth—cyanobacteria play a crucial role in the scheme mapped out by James *Lovelock's Gaia hypothesis—and also supplied useful fuel to such supplementary accounts as the *panspermia hypotheses.

In all these contexts as well as accounts of microbial *pathology, the progress of microbiology gave rise to considerable literary spin-off, although its produce was generally consigned to the interstices of narratives whose main focus was on directly observable effects. Although particular microorganisms occasionally warrant star billing in titles, as in Kit Pedler and Gerry Davis' *Mutant 59: The Plastic Eater* (1972) and Joan Slonczewski's "Microbe" (1995), and microbiologists often feature as key characters in hypothetical scientific investigations, the substance of the science is innately peripheral to experience. In the absence of bizarre stretches of the imagination, microbes cannot feature as literary characters in their own right.

MICROCOSM

One element of a contrasted pair of terms, whose opposite is *macrocosm. In Classical and neo-Platonist thought, and hence in the Medieval mysticism that gave rise to *occult science, the microcosm is either the human body—although accounts of it often pay more attention to the "inner space" of the mind than to its physical anatomy—or the human world. In Christian philosophy the microcosm of Earthly creation is often contrasted with the divine macrocosm, as in Godefroy de Saint Victor's *Microcosmus* (twelfth century). The potential significance of the term became broader by degrees when the invention of the *microscope revealed a new organic microcosm beyond the threshold of visual perception and the development of modern *atomic theory opened imaginative access into the subatomic realm.

In a literary context the word is also used whenever a limited location or small institution is used as an allegory of something much greater, as in descriptions of *The Ship of Fools* (derived from Sebastian Brandt's *Narrenschiff*, 1494) or accounts of such symbolic dwellings as George Bernard Shaw's *Heartbreak House* (1919). The island of Lilliput in Jonathan Swift's *Gulliver's Travels* (1726) is also a literary microcosm of sorts, and there is a significant literary tradition of stories that allow humans access to an *entomological microcosm by means of various miniaturising devices.

Phineas Fletcher's *The Purple Island; or, The Isle of Man* (1633) is an early transfiguration of the mystical microcosm into an artefact of anatomical science, with organs represented as cities and the circulatory system a network of canals. Fitz-James O'Brien's "The Diamond Lens" (1858) and Charles Kingsley's *The Water-Babies* (1863) were significant surreal ventures into the microbiological microcosm; the more recherché items that followed in their wake included Morgan Robertson's "The Battle of the Monsters" (1899), Theodore Waters' "The Autobiography of a Malaria Germ" (1900), Mark Twain's "Three Thousand Years Among the Microbes" (written 1905; published 1966), Charles Fort's "A Radical Corpuscle" (1906), and Maurice Renard's *Un homme chez les microbes* (1928) before being imported into pulp science fiction in such works as Nathan Schachner's "Intra-Planetary" (1935; by-lined Chan Corbett) and Frank Belknap Long's "The Flame-Midget" (1936). The subgenre withered away in the latter part of the twentieth century, partly because it was replaced by a far more prolific subgenre of microcosmic romance developed from atomic theory, which made much of the early analogy drawn between atoms and solar systems.

The pulp subgenre of microcosmic romance was pioneered by Ray Cummings' "The Girl in the Golden Atom" (1919), which describes a world on the outside of an "atomic shell". Although the story's structure was modelled on H. G. Wells' *The Time Machine*, its content is much closer in spirit to the kind of planetary romance developed in the pulps by Edgar Rice Burroughs, and that remained the standard pattern of longer microcosmic romances in the science fiction pulps, as exemplified by S. P. Meek's "Submicroscopic" and "Awlo of Ulm" (both 1931) and Festus Pragnell's "The Green Man of Graypec" (1935; book 1936 as *The Green Man of Kilsona*). Shorter *contes philosophiques* included William Lemkin's "An Atomic Adventure" (1930), which presents the life story of a carbon atom, and Joseph W, Skidmore's Posi and Nega series (1932–1935), which features personalised subatomic particles.

The more ideatively adventurous contributions to the subgenre included Julian Kendig Jr.'s "Fourth Dimensional Space Penetrator" (1930), Edmond Hamilton's "The Cosmic Pantograph" (1935), Henry Hasse's "He Who Shrank" (1936), Nathan Schachner's "Infra-Universe" (1937), John Russell Fearn's "Worlds Within" (1937), and John W. Campbell Jr.'s "Dead Knowledge" (1938; by-lined Don A. Stuart). Significant use was made of the subsidiary notion that time might pass more rapidly in a microcosm than a macrocosm in G. Peyton Wertenbaker's "The Man from the Atom" (1926), R. F. Starzl's "Out of the Sub-Universe" (1928), Jack Williamson's "Pygmy Planet" (1932), and Theodore Sturgeon's "Microcosmic God" (1941).

As atomic models became more sophisticated, pulp microcosmic romance lost its slender imaginative warrant, but ventures into the exotic microcosms hypothesised by modern physics continued to feature in such didactic fictions as George Gamow's *Mr. Tompkins Explores the Atom* (1944) and such *contes philosophiques* as James Blish's "Nor Iron Bars" (1957) and a brief interlude in Rudy Rucker's *Space-time Donuts* (1981). The progress of twentieth-century physics opened up further microcosmic possibilities, especially in its dealings with the extreme compression of matter. Robert L. Forward's *Dragon's Egg* (1980) and Stephen Baxter's *Flux* (1993) describe microcosmic environments on the surfaces of neutron stars. The popularisation of the idea of *black holes offered even more exotic possibilities.

Pulp science fiction also made abundant use of miniaturising fantasies, in spite of their inherent logical difficulties—the notion is rationally implausible whether the mass of the miniaturised individual is supposed to be conserved and compacted or whether it is supposed to suffer a scalar reduction of some kind—and such fantasies proved very attractive to filmmakers interested in special effects; the melodramatic motifs of such pulp fantasies as Harry Bates' "A Matter of Size" (1934) and James Blish's "Surface Tension" (1952) were reproduced in the films *Dr. Cyclops* (1940) and *The Incredible Shrinking Man* (1957), which originated a tradition in the visual media. The stereotypical moves were reproduced in the TV series *Land of the Giants* (1968–1972) and sophisticated in such movies as *Fantastic Voyage* (1966), *The Incredible Shrinking Woman* (1981), *Innerspace* (1987), and *Honey, I Shrunk the Kids* (1989) and its sequels. Literary fantasies exhibiting a parallel evolution include Lindsay Gutteridge's *Cold War in a Country Garden* (1971) and Gordon Williams' *The Micronauts* (1977).

An opportunity to add a measure of rational plausibility to microcosmic fantasies emerged in connection with the idea of "telepresence", because the TV cameras relaying visual information are not subject to the perceptive limitations of human eyes. Microcosmic telepresence is achieved by means of *nanotechnological microbots in Pete D. Manison's "First Nanocontact" (1997), which refers back to much older models of the microcosm/macrocosm relationship in asking: "Are we God's nanites?"

MICROSCOPE

An optical instrument that produces greatly magnified images, allowing the perception of many entities invisible to the naked eye. Simple microscopes—or "magnifying glasses"—using a single lens were used in biological observations in the fifteenth century, improving in quality as techniques of lens grinding advanced to facilitate the production of clear, evenly curved convex lenses of considerable power. Compound microscopes, using two or more lenses arranged in such a way as to maximise their combined magnifying power with respect to a small but proximate visual field, were developed alongside *telescopes in the last decades of the sixteenth century, but their progress was much slower.

Robert Hooke's *Micrographia* (1665) included some early microscopic observations, and advances made in the study of the development of plant seeds made a vital contribution to *botanical taxonomy, but it was not until the highly skilled lens grinder Antoine van Leeuwenhoek published his observations in the early eighteenth century that compound microscopes demonstrated their worth in *microbiological observation. The chromatic aberration caused by the dispersal of light by convex lenses continued to inconvenience microscopists for a further century, until Joseph Lister published an account of the construction of achromatic microscope lenses in 1830. The theory of microscope construction was worked out in great detail by Ernst Abbe, but it was not until new "apochromatic" lenses eliminated chromatic aberration in the 1880s that microscopes were able to distinguish bacteria clearly and take full advantage of thin cross sections of various organic tissues.

*Photography could not revolutionise microscopy with the same rapidity that it revolutionised astronomy, because it was dealing with objects of far greater complexity than points of light. Producing good photographic images of objects on microscope slides proved awkward, but rapid progress was made after 1880. The advent of chemical staining increased the ability of microscopists to distinguish and analyse the internal structure of organic tissues, but it supplemented the problems caused by the mechanical distortion of specimens as they were made ready for examination. It was often difficult for microscopists to distinguish between natural attributes of the tissues under examination and artefacts resulting from the manner of their preparation: a kind of *uncertainty that occasionally resulted in new microscopic "discoveries" having to be undiscovered again when the relevant structures turned out to be artefacts of specimen preparation.

The literary uses of microscopy reflect these developmental problems; the facilitating device employed in the Chévalier de Béthune's *Relation du monde de Mercure* (1750) is a "philosophical microscope", and the same title might equally well be applied to such hypothetical instruments as Fitz-James O'Brien's "The Diamond Lens" (1858), constructed with the aid of the spirit of Leeuwenhoek, and to many other devices serving as actual or symbolic portals to various *microcosms, including those featured in Conde Hamlin's "A Criminal's Brain Cells" (1892), Richard Slee and Cornelia Atwood Pratt's *Dr. Berkeley's Discovery* (1899), Ray Cummings' "The Girl in the Golden Atom" (1919), Lloyd Arthur Eschbach's "A Voice from the Ether" (1931), and Stephen G. Hale's "The Laughing Death" (1931). Rudyard Kipling's "The Eye of Allah" (1926) imagines what Medieval schoolmen might have made of such an instrument had Roger *Bacon contrived one.

Early microscopists were often characterised as men obsessed with small matters and subject to delusions—Villiers de l'Isle Adam's self-deluding Tribulat Bonhomet, introduced in "Clair Lenoir" (1867; trans. in *The Vampire Soul*), is obsessively devoted to microscopic studies of "infusoria"—but the ability of the microscope to reveal the agents of disease turned the situation around. Although the iconic significance of the microscope never matched that of the telescope, it became a key symbol in the field of *medical research, occupying pride of place in every medical laboratory, and eventually acquired a similar status in the field of *forensic science. This iconic significance is most obvious in the visual media, but is evident in such earnest medical dramas as Sinclair Lewis' *Arrowsmith* (1925), and the microscope plays a key symbolic role in Brian Stableford's *The Empire of Fear* (1988).

The possibility of developing microscopes of much greater power than optical lenses permitted emerged in the 1920s when electrostatic and electromagnetic fields began to be used as "lenses" to focus electron beams. The first electron microscope was constructed in 1933, and such devices soon surpassed the resolution of the most powerful optical microscopes. The introduction in 1946 of a device that compensated for the inherent astigmatism of electromagnetic lenses increased the power of such instruments dramatically, allowing such entities as viruses to be photographed for the first time, and eventually producing images of individual organic molecules. Electron microscope images remained vulnerable to the problems of specimen preparation that had afflicted their optical counterparts, so the slicing and staining of specimens needed to be further refined, but the resultant images acquired a wondrous aesthetic quality of their own, elevating them to the first rank of works of scientific *art.

MONSTER

A term derived from the Latin *monstrum*, whose original reference was to a kind of divine omen taking the form of a grossly deformed example of a plant or animal, usually manifest in the latter case as an inviable embryo. Within this narrow definition the study of monsters became the quasi-scientific discipline of teratology, but the term broadened out in common parlance to refer to all manner of fabulous *zoological specimens, especially those derived by chimerical admixture, including the chimera itself, centaurs, gorgons, merfolk, and the minotaur, or those granted exceptional size, such as giant insects, worms, and snakes.

This broader meaning was further extended, by way of the commonly assumed equivalence of ugliness and wickedness, into the notion of monstrous conduct, and then to the notion that even handsome humans might become "inhuman monsters" by virtue of wickedness. In literary parlance, therefore, a great many entities used as narrative antagonists—particularly in horror fiction and heroic fantasies—are classifiable as monsters, and the notion of monstrousness is a significant component of the evolution of literary antagonists from Homer's *Odyssey* onwards. In demonising Richard III for propaganda purposes, William Shakespeare took care to make him a hunchback, and his characterisation of Caliban in *The Tempest* (ca. 1600) is only slightly more sceptical. Literary witches always came in two versions—the repulsive hagwife and the deceptive *femme fatale*, while giants and dwarfs got a terrible press in folklore and Medieval romances.

As *biological science made progress, the notion that narrowly defined monsters were omens of disaster fell into discredit, although it lingered for a long time in literary usage. The idea that newly discovered creatures with a hint of the fabulous about them could and should be construed as monsters proved more persistent. The early reputations won by great apes such as the orang-utan and Australian species such as the kangaroo were tainted by this mode of thinking, while fossil *dinosaurs were immediately labelled "prehistoric monsters". The notion that ugliness and wickedness were empirically linked also fell into discredit, although its use as literary metaphor was so deeply ingrained in habit that it required explicit challenge and bold opposition in such late Medieval moral tales as "Sir Gawain and the Loathly Damsel" and such reprocessed folktales as "Beauty and the Beast".

The relatively feeble impact of such moralising is evident in a great many subsequent literary works, some of which suggest that even if ugliness is unconnected with innate wickedness, the manner in which physical monstrosity is treated by its observers is highly likely to lead to monstrous behaviour—a thesis whose development is remarkably ambivalent in such texts as Mary Shelley's *Frankenstein* (1818) and

Victor Hugo's *Bug-Jargal* (1820), although Hugo tried to make amends in his groundbreaking attribution of a heroic role to Quasimodo in *Notre Dame de Paris* (1831) and his sympathetic depiction of a manufactured monster in *L'homme qui rit* (1869; trans. as *The Man Who Laughs*). The symbolic equation of beauty with goodness and ugliness with sin proved extremely difficult to shake off, however, and the difficulty was not helped in the least by the advent of the cinema, which provided a highly significant arena for the development of an elaborate catalogue of monstrous antagonists within a lurid subgenre of "monster movies", which co-opted and repackaged such traditional figures of supernatural menace as the vampire, the werewolf, the zombie, and the animated mummy.

The assumed equivalence of physical and moral monstrousness had a dramatic effect on the early development of the idea of the *alien, garishly exhibited in H. G. Wells' *The War of the Worlds* (1898), which instituted "monsters from Mars" as a central cliché of twentieth-century science fiction. The assumption was conscientiously opposed by such transfigurations of the Beauty and the Beast motif as Raymond Z. Gallun's "Old Faithful" (1934), but valiant dissent only served to illustrate the overwhelming force of the opposition, as *King Kong* (1933) did within the Hollywood tradition. Each new species of hypothetical beings introduced into twentieth-century speculative fiction tended to make its debut as a monster, whether it came prequalified for such a role—as *mutants did—or logically disqualified for it, as *supermen were. The fact that *robots were pressed into such a role prompted Isaac *Asimov to afford them a central role in his long crusade against the *Frankenstein complex.

Genre science fiction always ran the risk of being identified as a species of monster fiction—a risk greatly emphasised by the conventions of cover illustration developed in the late 1930s. The danger was recognised in 1939, when Martin Alger announced the establishment of a Society for the Prevention of Bug-Eyed Monsters on the Covers of Science Fiction Publications; in subsequent correspondence relating to the issue, "Bug-Eyed Monster" was frequently shortened to the acronym BEM, which soon became sufficiently commonplace to be accepted into Funk & Wagnall's dictionary in the 1950s. The term's reference was not restricted to insectile eyes, referring to any eyes that "bugged out"; Alger's ire was excited by the aliens featured on the covers of the first two issues (August and October 1936) of *Thrilling Wonder Stories*. The identification of science fiction and monster fiction became even easier when one of the genre's first best-sellers was John Wyndham's *The Day of the*

Triffids (1951), which succeeded in adding a new term to the lexicon of familiar monsters.

The result of these developments, in association with the parallel trend in the cinema, was that a considerable tension developed in twentieth-century speculative fiction between the desire to exploit the melodramatic potential of monstrousness and the desire to oppose the tacit assumptions of that kind of exploitation. This tension is clearly manifest in stories that "rationalise" the traditional monsters of horror fiction, including such science-fictionalised theriomorphic fantasies as John W. Campbell's "Who Goes There?" (1938; by-lined Don A. Stuart), Jack Williamson's *Darker than You Think* (1940; exp. book 1948) and James Blish's "There Shall Be No Darkness" (1950) and such accounts of quasi-vampiric parasitism as Eric Frank Russell's *Sinister Barrier* (1939; 1943; rev. 1948), A. E. van Vogt's "Asylum" (1942), Robert A. Heinlein's *The Puppet Masters* (1951), Richard Matheson's *I Am Legend* (1954), and Frank Crisp's *The Ape of London* (1959).

The essential perversity of common attitudes to monstrousness is summarised in the argument of Julian Huxley's "The Tissue-Culture King" (1926), which proposes that although the greatest fear attached to the idea of genetic engineering is that it might produce monsters, that is highly likely to be one of its first applications. Stories of carnival "freak shows" such as Todd Browning's film *Freaks* (1932), Charles G. Finney's *The Circus of Dr. Lao* (1935), and William Lindsay Gresham's *Nightmare Alley* (1946) often attempt or pretend to make the same point, as does Alexander Laing's murder mystery *The Cadaver of Gideon Wyck* (1934)—one of very few stories making use of scientific research in teratology—but the late twentieth-century upsurge in TV "documentaries" about human freaks of every sort suggests that such pleas and condemnations had had no lasting impact at all.

Monstrous antagonists became less fashionable in fiction as writers became steadily more anxious about promoting xenophobia, but the literary attractions of monstrousness remained irresistible even to the anxious. The sympathetic portrayal of "monsters" pioneered by Victor Hugo was extrapolated in numerous literary works portraying ugly and deformed individuals as victims rather than villains, and in such biographical accounts as that of the "Elephant Man", which fitted in neatly enough with the advent of sociological theories proposing that all villains might be better regarded as victims of deprivation and abuse. Within the various fields of imaginative fiction, however, it was as easy for this kind of rethinking to produce a fusion of seemingly incompatible ideas as to generate such parables of misfortunate

*alienation as H. P. Lovecraft's "The Outsider" (1926), Robert Silverberg's *Thorns* (1967) and *The Man in the Maze* (1968), and John Gardner's *Grendel* (1971). The fusion process was particularly evident in the cinema, where the ambiguous figure of King Kong was followed by a whole series of charismatic monsters—the most ambiguous being the Japanese *Gojiro* (1954; aka *Godzilla*)—and the ultimate human monster, Thomas Harris' Hannibal Lecter, won a spectacular liberation.

An explanation of sorts for this pattern of evolution was provided by the anthropologist Joseph Campbell in his analysis of the heroic "monomyth", which argues along *Jungian lines that all the monsters a hero meets as he passes along his road of trials are actually displaced fragments of his own personality, which must be symbolically slain in order to be subdued. The notion is abundantly reflected in literary images, even if one sets aside those directly inspired by it, such as the science-fictional transfiguration of *The Tempest* in the film *Forbidden Planet* (1956) and Ursula K. Le Guin's *A Wizard of Earthsea* (1968). In the most obsessively readapted of all literary versions of the motif, Robert Louis Stevenson's *Strange Case of Dr. Jekyll and Mr. Hyde* (1886), it is the displaced personality fragment that triumphs, as it does in many other *doppelgänger* stories. In versions tending to the contrary, the ritual victories won by heroes can only be temporary; the likes of Dracula and *Doctor Who*'s Daleks always come back again, and probably always will.

MOON, THE

The *Earth's satellite. As a heavenly body it seemed to early observers to be a good deal more mysterious than the *Sun, confusing the fundamental dualism of day and night by operating as an uncertain nocturnal lamp according to a complex cycle of its own. The lunar cycle formed the basis of some primitive calendrical systems and is built into the annual one, albeit approximately, as the month. Unlike the Sun, the Moon's face manifests visible features, which are sufficiently enigmatic to have invited a wide variety of mythical and folkloristic interpretations.

The Moon's relationship with tides was soon observed by coastal dwellers, and its approximate correlation with the human female menstrual cycle is reflected in the fact that the majority of deities associated with the Moon are female, including those providing such alternative names as Luna and Selene. All these features are extravagantly represented in *poetry, in which the Moon and its vagaries have been a perennial topic of interest. The Moon is also linked in myth and folklore to madness ("lunacy"), nonsense ("moonshine"), lycanthropy, unlikelihood ("once in a blue moon"), and unattainability ("crying for the moon"), and all these ideas were abundantly carried over into literary imagery. Classical mythology also suggested that the Moon might be the habitation of the souls of the dead—an idea carried forward by the neo-Pythagoreans—which became another recurrent literary image.

Such mythical and metaphorical associations continue to haunt fictional representations of the Moon even in the hardest science fiction, although the Moon also has a unique and particular significance in the evolution of speculative fiction. Early proto-scientific observations of the Moon were summarised in a dialogue by Plutarch, written about 100 A.D., usually known as "On the Face That Appears in the Disc of the Moon"; it concludes with a discussion of the possibility that there might be life on the Moon. The Moon was important in the early history of imaginative fiction as a key venue of Utopian satire; the necessity of improvising means of transport there was subject to a gradual refinement of rational plausibility whose effects were central to the evolution of scientific romance and science fiction.

Fictitious lunar voyages have a very elaborate history, the first recorded example, Antonius Diogenes' *Of the Wonderful Things Beyond Thule*, being known only through a brief secondary description in Photius' *Bibliotheca* (ca. 870). Two lunar journeys by the satirist Lucian survived, the more important being *Alethea Historia* (second century A.D.; trans. as *True History*), a parody of the fancies and exaggerations routinely encountered in travellers' tales. The satirical tradition was taken up again after the Renaissance when Lodovico Ariosto dispatched Astolpho to the Moon astride a hippogriff in *Orlando Furioso* (1516; exp. 1532), to find a repository of everything wasted on Earth: misspent time, broken vows, unanswered prayers, and so on. This too was added to the list of associations recalled and recycled by later writers.

The Moon replicates Earth in numerous satires, including the anonymous *Le supplément du Catholicon, ou nouvelles des régions de la lune* (1595) and *The Man in the Moone, Telling Strange Fortunes* (1609). *Galileo's telescopic observations had an immediate influence on such works as Ben Jonson's masque *News from the New World Discovered in the Moon* (1621), and farcical developments continued to dominate seventeenth century imagery; Nolant de Fatouville's comedy *Arlequin empereur dans la lune* (1684) was the basis of Aphra Behn's *The Emperor of the Moon* (1687) and Elkanah Settle's opera *The World in the Moon* (1697).

Earnest attempts to envision conditions on the Moon resumed with John *Kepler's *Somnium*

(1634), which took up its *exobiological theme from Plutarch, and John Wilkins' *The Discovery of a New World* (1638; exp. 1640), whose third edition was supplemented by an appendix giving serious consideration to the possibility of travelling there. The latter notion was extrapolated in David Russen's *Iter Lunare* (1703), although Russen's judgement that the best method might involve propulsion by a gargantuan spring must have seemed suspect even at the time. New notions spun off by the acceptance of the heliocentric theory were blithely mixed with exuberant satirical materials in Francis Godwin's *The Man in the Moone* (1638), which was quickly translated into French by Jean Baudouin and German by Hans Jakob von Grimmelshausen, and given far greater prominence in Savinien Cyrano de Bergerac's *L'autre monde* (1657).

The satirical tradition continued forcefully in such eighteenth-century works as Daniel Defoe's *The Consolidator* (1705), Samuel Brunt's *A Voyage to Cacklogallinia* (1727), Murtagh McDermot's *A Trip to the Moon* (1728), and William Thomson's *The Man in the Moon* (1783). Musical items included Joseph Haydn's comic opera *Il mondo della luna* (1777), with a libretto by Carlo Goldoni, and Maximilian Blaimhofr's *Die Luftschiffer oder der Strafplanet der Erde* (1786), in which the Moon becomes a penal colony. Thomas Gray's poem "Luna Habilitatis" (1737) imagines English *colonialism extended to the lunar continents. The attempts made by Kepler and Wilkins to found a realistic tradition bore far less fruit, although the supplementation of satirical fantasy with a spirit of pure adventure became very noticeable in such works as Ralph Morris' *The Life and Wonderful Adventures of John Daniel* (1751).

In the nineteenth century, the realist tradition was revived in such works as George Fowler's *A Flight to the Moon; or, The Vision of Randalthus* (1813) and J. L. Riddell's *Orrin Lindsay's Plan of Aerial Navigation* (1847). It was considered in a conspicuously tongue-in-cheek fashion in Edgar Allan Poe's "The Unparalleled Adventure of One Hans Pfaall" (1835; exp. 1840), but Poe was annoyed when a very similar account of lunar life was passed off as reportage in one of the most celebrated newspaper hoaxes of its era, written by Richard Adams Locke for the New York *Sun* in August 1835 and subsequently reprinted as a pamphlet. Locke's articles purported to be reprints from the *Edinburgh Journal of Science* publishing observations made by Sir John Herschel in South Africa.

John Herschel's father, William Herschel, had convinced himself that the Moon was habitable, and other astronomers exercising the eye of faith had discovered "evidence" of that habitation, much as

Percival Lowell was later to see canals on *Mars. Johann Schröter had reported surface formations of an artificial nature, while Francisco de Paula Gruithuisen had announced the discovery of an entire lunar city. Other observers, including William Beer and J. H. Mädler, deduced from contemporary observations that the Moon was devoid of air and water, and that the *maria* thought by *Galileo to be bodies of water were dry plains, but the notion of lunar life died hard, even among astronomers; W. H. Pickering convinced himself in 1924 that he had seen dark patches moving near the crater Eratosthenes, which might be swarms of migratory insects.

The realistic tradition of lunar voyages produced its first masterpiece in Jules Verne's *De la terre à la lune* (1865; trans. as *From the Earth to the Moon*) and its sequel, *Autour de la lune* (1870; trans. as *Around the Moon*). Verne was too scrupulous to let his travellers land when he had no plausible means of getting them back, but other armchair inventors were perfectly happy to equip their lunar travellers with versatile propulsion systems, no matter how implausible they might be, whether their intentions were didactic—as in W. S. Lach-Szyrma's *Aleriel* (1886)—or adventurous, as in André Laurie's *Les éxilés de la terre* (1889; trans. as *The Conquest of the Moon*). Images of the Moon as a world now dead, though still bearing relics of former habitation, proliferated in such accounts of cosmic tourism as Edgar Fawcett's *The Ghost of Guy Thyrle* (1895) and George Griffith's *A Honeymoon in Space* (1901). H. G. Wells, on the other hand, retained sufficient affiliation to the satirical tradition to imagine a Selenite society inside the Moon in *The First Men in the Moon* (1901). Wells' work was something of a watershed, helping to prompt an early twentieth-century flood of lunar fantasies, which made rapid headway in boys' books, American dime novels, and pulp magazines. Notable examples included Roy Rockwood's *Lost on the Moon* (1911), John Ames Mitchell's *Drowsy* (1917), Homer Eon Flint's "The Man in the Moon" (1919) and "Out of the Moon" (1923–1924), John Young Brown's *To the Moon and Back in Ninety Days* (1922), Bohun Lynch's *Menace from the Moon* (1925), Francis Grierson's *Heart of the Moon* (1928), and Otto Willi Gail's *Hans Hardt's Mondfahrt* (1930; trans. as *By Rocket to the Moon*).

In the meantime, a significant subgenre developed comprising fictions in which the Earth is credited with a second—necessarily exotic—moon. Verne's *Autour de la lune* featured a small second satellite postulated by Frédéric Petit in midcentury to explain discrepancies in the motion of the Moon. The second moon in Willem Bilderdijk's *Kort verhaal van eene aanmerklijke luchtreis en nieuwe planeetontdekking* (1813; trans. as *A Short Account of a Remarkable Aerial Voyage and a Discovery of a New Planet*) orbits within the Earth's atmosphere. Mary Platt Parmele's "Ariel" (1892) is invisible because it is always on the Earth's day side. Léon Groc's *La planète de cristal* (1944) is invisible by virtue of its transparency. Other exercises in a similar vein included Stacey Blake's *Beyond the Blue* (1914–1915; book, 1920). Paul Ernst's "The World Behind the Moon" (1931), J. M. Walsh's "Terror out of Space" (1934; by-lined H. Haverstock Hill) and Edmond Hamilton's "The Second Satellite" (1930). Raymond Z. Gallun's "N'Goc" (1935) and "Buried Moon" (1936) feature an ex-moon that fell to Earth in the distant past. Clyde W. Tombaugh and others searched for "small Earth satellites" at Lowell Observatory during the 1950s; he reported (mistakenly) in 1954 that he had found two. Kazimierz Kordylewski announced in 1961 that he had detected faint cloudlike objects at the L-5 point, but whether faintly luminous dust clouds can qualify as "moons" is highly dubious.

Many of the pulp science fiction writers who became the avid heirs of the adventure tradition of lunar romance were less particular than Wells, but Edgar Rice Burroughs similarly took the precaution of placing his lunar civilisation inside the Moon in *The Moon Maid* (1923–1925; book, 1926), and Jack Williamson sent his protagonist back in time to view the fecund ecosphere of "The Moon Era" (1932). Lunar voyages were relegated to a minor role, its place as a convenient habitation of alien life taken over by Mars—Lester del Rey's "The Wings of Night" (1942) offered a nostalgic elegy for lunar life—but the Moon retained its primary importance in speculative nonfiction. David Lasser's *The Conquest of Space* (1931) included a long "drama-documentary" sequence describing the first lunar voyage in the present tense, using the first person plural.

Lasser's successors as Space Age promoters often used similar devices; although Arthur C. Clarke's "We Can Rocket to the Moon—Now!" (1939) and *The Exploration of the Moon* (1954) are straightforward nonfiction, his novels *Prelude to Space* (1951) and *Earthlight* (1955) aimed for a kind of documentary realism. Wernher von Braun's *First Men to the Moon* (1958; exp. book, 1960) and Ludek Pesek's *Die Mondexpedition* (1966; trans. as *Log of a Moon Voyage*) are presented as drama-documentaries. Robert A. Heinlein supplemented his poignant propaganda piece "Requiem" (1940) with a quasi-documentary account of its central character's earlier fight to finance the first Moon-shot and sell the myth of space conquest to the world, in the title story of *The Man Who Sold the Moon* (1950), and tried to give his script for the George Pal film *Destination Moon* (1950) a documentary gloss. Charles Chilton's radio serial *Journey into Space* (1954) also made a feeble attempt to reproduce the techniques of verisimilitude employed by Orson Welles in his famous Mercury Theatre dramatisation of *The War of the Worlds*.

The notion that the Moon could be made habitable in spite of its airlessness and extreme aridity was valiantly maintained by the determined realism of images of lunar colonies produced by Heinlein, in the shorter stories in *The Man Who Sold the Moon* and *The Green Hills of Earth* (1951), by Clarke, in the two six-part story series "Venture to the Moon" (1956) and "The Other Side of the Sky" (1957), and by such individual works as Murray Leinster's *City on the Moon* (1957). John W. Campbell Jr.'s *The Moon Is Hell* (1950) and Charles Eric Maine's *High Vacuum* (1956) provided stirring accounts of lunar castaways whose triumphs of technological ingenuity recalled Douglas Frazar's ultimate nineteenth-century Robinsonade *Perseverance Island* (1885).

The last feeble flicker of the satirical tradition, Compton Mackenzie's *The Lunatic Republic* (1959), was produced in parallel with the first contrived lunar impact, by Luna 2, although the first soft landing was made by Luna 9 in 1966. Fiction featuring the first lunar voyage as a crucial cosmic breakout dwindled away somewhat in this period, but notable exceptions included Pierre Boulle's *Le jardin de Kanashima* (1964; trans. as *Garden on the Moon*) and William F. Temple's *Shoot at the Moon* (1966). Accounts of lunar colonies, on the other hand, grew bolder and more elaborate, as illustrated by Clarke's *A Fall of Moondust* (1961), Clifford D. Simak's *Trouble with Tycho* (1961), and Heinlein's *The Moon Is a Harsh Mistress* (1966).

There could be no more first lunar voyage stories after 1969, but accounts of lunar colonisation won an increase in plausibility that encouraged more serious attention to the design and organisation of such communities, as reflected in such works as Larry Niven's *The Patchwork Girl* (1980), Roger McBride Allen's *Farside Cannon* (1988), W. T. Quick's "High Hotel" (1989)—based on Ben Bova's design for a Moonbase, as described in a two-part *Analog* article in 1987— Michael Swanwick's *Griffin's Egg* (1990), Charles L. Harness' *Lunar Justice* (1991), John Varley's *Steel Beach* (1992), and John M. Ford's *Growing Up Weightless* (1993). Lunar colonies occasionally survived the devastation of Earth, if only briefly, as in Edmond Hamilton's "After a Judgment Day" (1963) and Ben Bova's *When the Sky Burned* (1973; exp. 1982 as *Test of Fire*), and occasionally went to war with Earth, as in Robert Reed's "Waging Good" (1995).

Although accounts of lunar life had virtually died out by 1969—John Christopher's "The Long Night" (1974) is a rare exception—the lifeless Moon remained a convenient place for spacefarers to find long-abandoned alien artefacts; Arthur Clarke's "Sentinel of Eternity" (1951; aka "The Sentinel") provided a significant exemplar that ultimately formed the seed of Stanley Kubrick's film *2001—A Space Odyssey* (1967); other notable examples include the enigmatic Death Machine featured in Algis Budrys' *Rogue Moon* (1960) and the space-suited skeleton in James P. Hogan's *Inherit the Stars* (1977). The Moon could still be subjected to spectacular fates, as it was in Bob Shaw's *The Ceres Solution* (1981) and John Gribbin and Marcus Chown's *Double Planet* (1988). The sequel to the latter work, *Reunion* (1991), offered a rare account of lunar *terraforming; Gregory Benford's "The Clear Blue Seas of Luna" (2002) is another. The Moon also retained its utility as a setting for dramas of difficult survival, as in Geoffrey A. Landis' "A Walk in the Sun" (1991), and for accounts of lunar mining, as in Kim Stanley Robinson's "The Lunatics" (1988). The traditional imagery still exerted its force, however, in such unashamed accounts of blatant lunacy as R. Garcia y Robertson's "Werewolves of Luna" (1994).

The fact that the notion of a Moon voyage, and all that it might imply for further exploits in space, came to occupy center stage in the mythology of the *Space Age was a significant factor in the decline of that mythology. Neil Armstrong's first words as he stepped onto the Moon in July 1969—which described that step as "a giant leap for mankind"—were the ultimate expression of the myth, and its knell of doom. Subsequent expressions of doubt as to whether the Moon landings actually took place, rather than being faked in a TV studio, reflected the disillusionment felt by many people when the mythic script was abruptly cut short.

MUSIC

The art and science of producing sound sequences that are pleasant, expressive, or meaningful. Song is music produced by voices; in the case of human voices it usually involves lyrics, thus creating a substantial overlap with *poetry. The technological creation of musical instruments—including drums, wind instruments, and stringed instruments—originated in prehistory, and the progress of such instruments is largely unchronicled; those few instrument makers who became famous—Antonio Stradivari is the most conspicuous example—tend to be engineers who developed previously existent designs to a new pitch of perfection rather than inventors. The science of music is better documented, the first significant applications of *mathematics to the analysis of harmony being attributed to *Pythagoras.

The affinities between *mathematics and music became a significant component of Pythagorean philosophy, and a vital seed of the kind of analogical thinking that came to underlie mysticism, echoing myths associated with the legendary father figure of Greek music, Orpheus. Pythagorean ideas of this sort were carried forward by *Plato in his analysis of the World-Soul. In particular, the Pythagoreans developed the notion that the organisation of the cosmos, as represented by the rotation of the heavenly bodies, must possess an innate harmony: the "music of the spheres". This notion is given a strikingly literal representation in the final passage of the *Republic*: the allegorical tour of the cosmos known as the Story of Er, in which each planet is equipped with its own singing Siren.

Similar imagery is reproduced in the corresponding allegorical conclusion of Cicero's *De republica* (55 B.C.), known in English as Scipio's Dream, and the notion became an important element of the mysticism of neo-Platonism, by which route it was integrated into early Christian philosophy. Saint Augustine produced a scholarly treatise, *De musica* (ca. 400), whose influence enabled music to be added to arithmetic, geometry, and astronomy as the fourth part of mathematics in the part of the Medieval academic curriculum dubbed the quadrivium ("fourfold path") by Boethius, whose *De institutione musica* (ca. 425; trans. as *Principles of Music*) became a standard textbook, remaining on the Oxford curriculum until the mid-nineteenth century.

The notion of the harmony of the spheres proved extremely resilient as a metaphor in subsequent literary expression, especially where the fields of music and literature overlap. The idea retained a stronger implication in *occult science, where it became a key expression of the fundamental holism that occult thought attempts to preserve against the diversifying tendencies of science. The importance of music and musicological theory within the Christian church secured a central role for church music in the elaboration of theory and musical technology. It was the mass that provided a context for the development of polyphonic chanting and its accompaniment by the organ. Modern musical notation was pioneered by Hucbald, author of *De institutione harmonica* (ca. 920; trans. as *The Principles of Harmony*) in the Abbey of Saint-Amand, and carried forward by Guido d'Arezzo's *Prologus in antiphonarium* (1020–1025).

The relationship between the church and musicological development—in both theory and practice—persisted until the eighteenth century in the work of such composers as J. S. Bach, although the secularisation of musical evolution took important steps forward in the late sixteenth century with the development of Florentine intermedi—the ancestors of the medium of Opera—and the first experiments in ballet. The "secularisation" of these new media was, however, largely a matter of making use of Classical mythology, in which such figures as Orpheus and Apollo, and the idea of the music of the spheres, played a major role—a role that Orpheus retained in numerous operas featuring his descent into the Underworld. As similar mythological material made its way back into Renaissance literature, its musical elements retained a powerful significance, celebrated in prose as well as poetry.

The late sixteenth century also saw significant theoretical attempts to rectify a flaw in the mathematical perfection of the Pythagorean scale—a slight discrepancy highlighted by the relationship between octaves and fifths—by the development of two new analytical systems, "just intonation" and "equal temperament". Their merits were fiercely disputed, the former being favoured by Gioseffo Zarlino and the later by Vincenzo Galilei (the father of *Galileo, who published a record of his own experiments in the mathematics of music). The idea of the music of the spheres is extensively featured in the work of Galileo's contemporary John *Kepler, whose third law of planetary motion was published in what was intended to be a final summation of his work, *Harmonies Mundi* [The Harmony of the Universe] (1619). Kepler's interest in mystical versions of musical theory was echoed by Isaac *Newton, but the notion faded into the metaphorical background of science thereafter, and its use in works of art became more flagrantly mystical, as in Wolfgang Amadeus Mozart's determinedly esoteric *Die Zauberflöte* (1791).

The mathematical analysis of music took another step forward with the work of Joseph Fourier, whose theorem describing the propagation of sound waves (published in 1807) facilitated the complete analysis of musical sounds. While composers and instrument makers made innovative use of advances in mathematics and technological methods, however, the literary aspects of music continued to be dominated by mythological, legendary, and mystical themes. Samuel Taylor Coleridge's "The Eolian Harp" (1817) celebrates the theoretical unification of sound and light as species of vibration and the potential of "natural music" as a source of enlightenment, but song lyrics and operatic librettos paid scant attention to the advancement of science. The imaginative aspects of speculative fiction occasionally proved attractive—Jacques Offenbach adapted Jules *Verne's *De la terre à la lune* as *Le voyage dans la lune* (1875), while Leoš Janáček produced an operatic version of Karel Čapek's *The Makropoulos Secret* (1925)—but Gustav Holst's *Planets* suite (1918) is based on the *astrological planets rather than their scientific equivalents. Hector Berlioz' *Euphonie, ou la ville musicale* (1844; rev. 1852) is a rare musical Utopia, whose city of Euphony is a celebration of the "expressive truth" of music, but what the work itself expresses is its author's bitterness consequent to the failure of his relationship with the pianist Camille Moke.

The mathematical foundations of music were shaken in the early twentieth century by the atonal music of Arnold Schoenberg, whose *Kammersymphonie no. 1* was composed in 1905, the year that Albert Einstein published the special theory of *relativity—a coincidence that seemed sufficiently significant to some observers for both men to be asked to comment on the apparent affinity. Schoenberg was fervently opposed by Paul Hindemith, who attempted to dramatise his defence of tonality in an opera based on the life of Kepler, *Die Harmonie der Welt* (1957). Herman Hesse's prose Utopia *Der Glasperlenspiel* (1943; trans. as *Magister Ludi* and *The Glass Bead Game*) describes a state founded on the harmonies of music and mathematics, which is similarly troubled by an insistent opposition.

The history of the increasingly complex relationships between music, mathematics, art, and technology were mapped out in an appropriately impressionistic fashion in Douglas R. Hofstader's "Metamusical Offering" *Gödel, Escher, Bach: An Eternal Golden Braid* (1979). The book takes its basic formal inspiration from J. S. Bach and presents its arguments as a series of variations on a theme; its meditations on such classical themes as the mind/body problem and such recently emergent ones as the possibilities of *artificial intelligence include a number of surreal dialogues, adding a literary dimension to its multiple facets.

Science fiction became a more significant resource for operatic and musical inspiration in the late twentieth century. Harry Martinson published a volume of songs, *Cicada* (1953), which was redeveloped as an epic poem about an interstellar voyage, *Aniara* (1956), which then formed the libretto for Karl-Birger Blomdahl's opera *Aniara* (1959). Vaclav Kašlík's *Krakatit* (1961) is based on a novel (1924) about an *atomic explosive by Karel Čapek. Tod Machover's *VALIS* (1987) is based on a novel (1981) by Philip K. *Dick. Paul Barker's *The Marriages Between Zones Three, Four and Five* (1987) and Philip Glass' *The Making of the Representative for Planet 8* (1988) are based on novels (1980; 1982) from a "space fiction" series by Doris Lessing. Glass also employed science-fictional motifs in his operas *Einstein on the Beach* (1976), *1000 Airplanes on the Roof* (1988), and *Christopher Columbus* (1992). Anthony Burgess wrote a musical stage version of his 1962 novel *A Clockwork Orange* in 1987.

The notion of "science-fictional music" developed in the 1940s, exemplified by various compositions by Harry Revel, three of which were released as 78 rpm records in that decade, the first being *Music Out of the Moon* (1947), arranged and conducted by Les Baxter. The ambience of "eeriness" they cultivated—largely achieved by the use of that quintessential science-fictional instrument, the theremin—was rapidly appropriated by the soundtracks used in science fiction *cinema. Revel's compositions reappeared in LP form in the 1950s, most notably on *Music from Out of Space* (1955), arranged and conducted by Stuart Phillips. Other items from that period included Larry Elgart's *Impressions of Outer Space* (1953), Walter Schuman's *Exploring the Unknown* (1955), Sid Bass' *From Another World* (1956), and the Jay Gordon Concert Orchestra's *Music from Another World* (1956). The launch of Sputnik in 1957 increased the flow of such items considerably, the highlights including Les Baxter's *Space Escapade* (1957), Russ Garcia's *Fantastica* (1958), Ron Goodwin's *Music in Orbit* (1958) and Jimmie Haskell's *Countdown* (1958).

This kind of "mood music" was recorded in considerable quantities in the early 1960s, when notable items included Frank Comstock's *Project Comstock* (1962), Attilio Mineo's *Man in Space with Sounds* (1962), and Dick Hyman and Mary Mayo's *Moon Gas* (1963), the last named anticipating the music Hyman was later to make with the aid of a Moog synthesiser. The pattern of development was, however, confused and to some extent usurped in the latter part of the decade by rock music. Such bands as Jefferson Airplane—which later metamorphosed into Jefferson Starship—discovered significant countercultural harmonies between science fiction and rock, and borrowed imagery freely.

Notable early examples of imagistic crossover included the Rolling Stones' "2000 Light Years from Home" (1967), Pink Floyd's "Insterstellar Overdrive" (1967), and David Bowie's "Space Oddity" (1969). Bowie's *The Rise and Fall of Ziggy Stardust and the Spiders from Mars* (1972) was the most successful science fiction–influenced "concept album", although it had been anticipated by Nirvana's *The Story of Simon Simopath* (1968), Van der Graaf Generator's *Aerosol Grey Machine* (1969), and Hawkwind's *In Search of Space* (1971). Michael Moorcock, a key influence on Hawkwind—who occasionally appeared on stage with them—briefly formed his own rock band, Deep Fix, with fellow *New Worlds* writers. The hybridising impulse spread to other new genres of music, being incorporated into the work of George Clinton's Funkadelic in *Cosmic Slop* (1973).

Jeff Wayne's adaptation of *The War of the Worlds* (1978) was one of the earliest "rock operas", and many of its successors in the subgenre incorporated science-fictional elements—although, like more traditional operas, they tended to favour imaginative extravagance unfettered by speculative discipline. Science fiction cinema's utter disregard for rational plausibility became a key element of the calculated tackiness of Richard O'Brien's *Rocky Horror Show* (1973) and such imitative shows as Bob Carlton's *Return to the Forbidden Planet* (1989) and Ben Elton's collaboration with Queen, *We Will Rock You* (2004). The adoption by science fiction of a cultural "punk" element into its early accounts of *cyberspace was reclaimed by Billy Idol's *Cyberpunk* (1993) but the impact of *computers on the making of music was much more considerable than any mere fad.

In 1956, the science fiction magazine *Galaxy* carried ads for the Geniac "electric brain"—an elementary desktop computer twenty years ahead of its time—which took care to emphasise that it could be used for composing music and playing games as well as computing (thus showing far more foresight than the vast majority of the stories of that era). Ten years later, under the heading "Music for Tomorrow", *Galaxy* advertised the Decca album *Music from Mathematics* (1968), consisting of music composed on computers and transducers by John R. Pierce and others. The rapid development thereafter of competent synthesisers brought about a democratising revolution in music composition, production, and recording whose potential was heralded when the German band Organisation metamorphosed into Kraftwerk in 1971; they went on to release the science-inspired album *Radioactivity* (1975) and the neo-technological *The Man Machine* (1978) and *Computer World* (1981).

The perceived countercultural links between rock music and science fiction may have been largely illusory, at least by comparison with the much more obvious links that exist between folk music and mythopoeic fantasy, but the idea proved resilient, especially with respect to that fraction of modern music that belongs more to "unpopular culture" than popular culture; the influence of H. P. Lovecraft on various kinds of esoteric modern music, especially Gothic rock music and German "dark wave" music, has been very considerable, although the speculative aspects of his writing have been far less influential than those co-opted by occultists. The reverse flow of influence has been much more considerable, and there is a great deal of late twentieth-century speculative fiction that is intensely interested in rock music and related modern genres.

Although Clark Ashton Smith's "The City of Singing Flame" (1931) is a notable adaptation of Platonic Sirens to the mythology of pulp science fiction, early twentieth-century speculative fiction usually considered music within the contexts of new technologies of recording and broadcasting. It encountered extreme difficulties of representation whenever it attempted to anticipate future developments in musical composition and performance, as in Frank B. Long's "Collector's Item" (1947) and J. B. Priestley's *Low Notes on a High Level* (1954). The most elaborate exploration of the relationship between music and science in genre science fiction was Charles L. Harness' "The Rose" (1953), which describes the production of a "Sciomniac equation" whose supposed ultimacy proves capable of further musical transfiguration. This proved to be a watershed work, its somewhat belated publication coinciding with the beginning of a deluge of science fiction stories featuring music and musicians.

Various musical notions are explored in Lloyd Biggle's thematic collection *The Metallic Muse* (1972), and Anne McCaffrey also made determined attempts to incorporate her musical training into her science fiction in such works as *The Ship Who Sang* (1961–1969; book, 1969) and *The Crystal Singer* (1974–1975; book, 1982). Thomas M. Disch's *On Wings of Song* (1979) and Orson Scott Card's *Songmaster* (1980) also attempt to explore the existential significance of music. Kim Stanley Robinson's "In Pierson's Orchestra" (1976; exp. as *The Memory of Whiteness*, 1985) attempts to envisage futuristic music technology. Sean McMullen's "The Colors of the Masters" (1988) features computerised synaesthetic translation of music into colour. Greg Egan's "Beyond the Whistle Test" (1989) considers the application of computers to the analysis of neurological responses to music. Paul Di Filippo's "Lennon Spex" (1992) attempts to actualise the world implicit in the song "Lucy in the Sky with Diamonds". The difficulties of representing dance in words are almost as acute as those of representing music, but that has not prevented writers of speculative fiction from trying; notable attempts include Spider and Jeanne Robinson's *Stardance* (1979), Nancy Kress' "Dancing on Air" (1993), and Catherine Asaro's *The Veiled Web* (1999).

Notable science fiction stories featuring musicians or music include Edgar Pangborn's "The Music Master of Babylon" (1954), James Blish's "A Work of Art" (1956), J. G. Ballard's "Prima Belladonna" (1956), Michael Moorcock's "A Dead Singer" (1974), Spider Robinson's "The Law of Conservation of Pain" (1974), Gregory Benford's "Doing Lennon" (1975), Carter Scholz's "The Ninth Symphony of Ludwig van Beethoven and Other Lost Songs" (1977), Barry Malzberg's *Chorale* (1978), Michael Swanwick's "The Feast of St. Janis" (1980), Thomas

F. Monteleone's "Sonata for Three Electrodes" (1980), Grant Carrington's *Time's Fool* (1981), Sharon Webb's *Earthchild* (1982), Howard Waldrop's "Flying Saucer Rock & Roll" (1982), "Ike at the Mike" (1982), and "Do Ya, Do Ya Wanna Dance" (1988), Timothy Zahn's "Music Hath Charms" (1985), Bradley Denton's *Wrack and Roll* (1986) and *Buddy Holly Is Alive and Well on Ganymede* (1986), Tom Purdom's "A Proper Place to Live" (1990) and "The Noise of Their Joye" (2000), Jack Womack's *Elvissey* (1993), Robert Silverberg's "Gianni" (1982), and Gwyneth Jones' series launched by *Bold as Love* (2001). Jack Vance's *Space Opera* (1965) extrapolates an obvious pun. Paul J. McAuley and Kim Newman's *In Dreams* (1992) is a thematic anthology. Attempts to envisage the future of rock music include Norman Spinrad's *Little Heroes* (1987), Lance Olsen's *Tonguing the Zeitgeist* (1994), and the Japanese anime movie released in English as *Perfect Blue* (1999). Works of speculative fiction issued with albums of illustrative music include Chris Williamson's *Lumière—A Science Fantasy Fable* (1982) and Ursula K. Le Guin's *Always Coming Home* (1986).

MUTATION

A term initially popularised in the context of theories of biological *evolution by Hugo de Vries' *Die Mutationstheorie* (1901–1903). De Vries used it to refer to gross physical deformities, usually generated by polyploidy, but Charles *Darwin had already dismissed the notion that such "sports" might play a significant role in evolution, and the word was quickly redefined to refer to the source of relatively trivial variations required by the nascent synthesis of Darwinism and Mendelian *genetics.

The revised version of the notion was eventually explicated in terms of minute variations of DNA base sequences within genes, but there was a long interval in which the biochemical nature of mutation remained unclear. During that interim the term retained de Vriesian implications in the popular imagination, especially in pulp science fiction, whose practitioners took immediate inspiration from Wilhelm Müller's discovery in 1927 that mutations could be induced in fruit flies by *radiation. The notion of radiation-induced mutation gave rise to an entire subgenre of mutational romances. "Mutation" and its derivative term "mutant" were widely employed as key items of apologetic jargon licensing the arbitrary production of monsters and *supermen by irradiation, as in Jack Williamson's "The Metal Man" (1928).

The most prolific pioneer of mutational romance was John Taine, whose works in that vein included

The Greatest Adventure (1929), *The Iron Star* (1930), and *Seeds of Life* (1931); Edmond Hamilton was also an enthusiastic practitioner, in such stories as "The Man Who Evolved" (1931), "Master of the Genes" (1935), and "He That Hath Wings" (1938). Other early examples included Stanton A. Coblentz's "A Circe of Science" (1930). The subgenre was given new impetus in 1945, when the *atom bomb made its debut on the historical stage. "Mutants" became a standard feature of stories set in the aftermath of a nuclear holocaust, while tales of wholesale transfiguration wrought by radiation sources became far more lushly extravagant; significant examples include Henry Kuttner's "I Am Eden" (1946) and "Atomic!" (1947) and Edmond Hamilton's *The Star of Life* (1947; book, 1959).

An indelicate balance was struck in many postwar mutational romances between "bad mutants", who were subject to moral as well as teratological disfiguration, and "good mutants", who might bear various physical stigmata—like the tendrils of A. E. van Vogt's slans in *Slan* (1940; book, 1946) or the bald heads of Henry Kuttner's "baldies" in *Mutant* (1945–1953; book, 1953)—but whose primary modification consisted of the acquisition of *parapsychological powers. Neutrality was rare, although Isaac Asimov's *Foundation and Empire* (1945; book, 1952) introduced the highly ambivalent character of the Mule, a random factor unforeseeable by psychohistorical calculations.

Whether they were stigmatised or not, "good mutants" were routinely subjected to xenophobic prejudice and unjust persecution, whether they emerged in the bosom of respectable suburban society, as in Wilmar H. Shiras' *Children of the Atom* (1948–1950; exp. book, 1953) and Theodore Sturgeon's *More than Human* (1953), or in post-holocaust scenarios like those featured in Poul Anderson and F. N. Waldrop's "Tomorrow's Children" (1947; exp. as *Twilight World*, 1961), John Wyndham's *The Chrysalids* (1955; aka *Re-Birth*), Walter M. Miller's *A Canticle for Leibowitz* (1955–1957; exp. book, 1960), Fritz Leiber's "Night of the Long Knives" (1960; aka "The Wolf Pair"), and Edgar Pangborn's *Davy* (1964). The eventual acceptance of such mutants into the moral community—or their eventual formation of a better moral community of their own—provided the climactic light at the end of many a story arc that had been turned into a dark tunnel by atom bomb-induced anxieties.

The representation of more extremely disfigured mutants as innocents remained relatively rare, but stories proudly defiant of the assumption that ugliness is synonymous with evil had been produced before the war—Robert A. Heinlein's "Universe" (1941) is a notable example, cleverly redeploying the casual cliché of the two-headed mutant—and they appeared in greater profusion thereafter. Technologies of directed mutation flourished briefly before being outmoded by *genetic engineering in such imagery as the "evolvotron" in Walter Miller's "Conditionally Human" (1952). In the meantime, the monster movie tradition of *cinema science fiction had developed its own fascination with human and animal mutants, which similarly went into overdrive in the 1950s, in such films as *Them!* (1954), *This Island Earth* (1955), *Tarantula* (1955), and *The Incredible Shrinking Man* (1957).

The paranoid component of postwar mutational romance was parodied in Norman Spinrad's *The Iron Dream* (1972), in which the mutant "dominators" are an analogue for Nazi attitudes to the Jews, but the tradition continued in such grim post-holocaust novels as M. John Harrison's *The Committed Men* (1971), Stuart Gordon's *One-Eye* (1973) and its sequels, Sterling Lanier's *Hiero's Journey* (1973), and Michael Swanwick's *In the Drift* (1984), while spin-off from the monster movie tradition was reimported into horror fiction by such works as James Herbert's *The Rats* (1974) and various novels by Guy N. Smith. Accounts of wholesale mutational metamorphosis retained their extravagance, seasoned with visionary exhilaration, in such texts as Samuel R. Delany's *The Einstein Intersection* (1967), Ian Watson's *The Gardens of Delight* (1980) and *Converts* (1984), A. A. Attanasio's *Radix* (1981), and Greg Bear's *Blood Music* (1985). By the end of the century, however, mutational romance had wilted under the burden of its clichés and had become rather passé, as reflected in such tongue-in-cheek examples as James Van Pelt's "The Last of the O-Forms" (2002).

MYTH

A term derived from the Greek word for "story", commonly used to refer to a narrative that was once believed but had been subsequently recognised as fiction. In a narrower definition employed by *ethnologists and folklorists, however, a myth is a sacred narrative concerning the interaction of the human and divine worlds. Legends and folktales can be subsumed under the general category of myths, but the narrower meaning separates it from the other terms, leaving "legend" to signify matters of imaginary history featuring heroic or charismatic individuals and "folklore" to describe fanciful stories set in the mythic past that were never afforded any significant reverence. The term retains a certain gravitas in literary usage, especially in such adjectival derivatives as "mythopoeic", which refers to the process of myth-making.

The word "mythology" is more often used to refer to a collection of myths, as exemplified by such Classical compendia as those of Hyginus, Appolodorus, and Ovid, than to a theoretical overview. Most collectors of myths had, however, some kind of taxonomic and explanatory purpose in mind. Edward Casaubon's ambition to produce a definitive *Key to All Mythologies* in George Eliot's *Middlemarch* (1871–1872) was overambitious; the efforts of his actual predecessors and successors in compiling syncretic "encyclopaedias" of mythology—the earliest post-Renaissance example seems to have been Giovanni Boccaccio's *De genealogia deorum gentilium* (1350–1374)—were defeated by the fact that the data piled up more rapidly than they could assimilate it.

The ethnologist and *linguist F. Max Müller conceived of myth as "a disease of language"; because he believed that all languages had a common root stock, he assumed that all myths must therefore have similar common roots, and made much of the notion that a wide range of myths were derivatives of a primal "solar myth". His method was parodied by Andrew Lang's "The Great Gladstone Myth" (1886), and Lang's own books on the subject—including *Myth, Ritual and Religion* (1887) and *Modern Mythology: The Book of Dreams and Ghosts* (1897)—paid much more attention to the variety of myth, as befitted an accomplished mythopoeic fantasist and popular anthologist of fairy tales. Müller's syncretic tendencies were, however, recapitulated in James Frazer's *The Golden Bough* (1890; rev. 1900; further rev. 1911–1915), and continued to recur in such twentieth-century theses as Joseph Campbell's contention in *The Hero with a Thousand Faces* (1949) that all hero myths are variants of a common "monomyth". Whether such theories can be considered anything more than *scholarly fantasies is open to argument, but they had a tremendous influence on literary imagery, not merely in terms of the depiction of actual and hypothetical societies but in terms of strategies of mythopoeic literary composition.

The Müllerian perspective was applied to literary analysis in such essays as Matthew Arnold's "The Study of Celtic Literature" (1866), and soon became a standard method of studying ancient literature. The practice of mining Greek drama, epic poetry, and other early literary works for presumed insights into the evolution of mythology was still commonplace by the end of the twentieth century, producing such notable scholarly fantasies as Jessie Weston's *From Ritual to Romance* (1920) and Robert Graves' *The White Goddess* (1948), both of which had a tremendous influence on further work in their respective areas. That work includes a great deal of fiction that deliberately re-creates the mythical patterns supposedly discovered by scholarly analysis, the most significant of which marks the alleged replacement of neolithic goddess worship by patriarchal religions in the wake of social changes designed to secure and protect patrilineal inheritance.

If there were a scientific "key to all mythologies", it would presumably investigate the complex relationships between three categories of shaping forces. The first would be universals of cultural experience such as the observation of natural cycles, the fundamentals of linguistic communication, and the various technological consequences of the domestication of *fire. The second would be the *aesthetic and *narratological factors influencing the construction of stories capable of providing psychologically satisfactory "explanations" of these universals of experience. The third would be the idiosyncratic influence of particular individuals who attained authoritarian status in various cultural groups. None of these kinds of factors is irrelevant to the history and progress of science, so there is a sense in which science cannot help resembling myth in its formulation and representation; it has spawned a supportive structure of heroic legends and anecdotal folktales in much the same fashion that myth systems spin off similar accoutrements.

Scientific narratives have replaced many key examples of myth on a global scale, especially with respect to the important subcategory of creation myths, which have been substituted in a macrocosmic context by the *Big Bang theory and in an Earthly context by biological accounts of *evolution. The rearguard action fought against the advancement of science by the Christian church can be seen as an attempt to defend its own creation myth against supersession; the last redoubt of that defence in respect of the origin of life often advertises itself as *creationism. Scientists and philosophers are tacitly forsworn to avoid conscious mythopoesis, but the incidental mythopoeic thrust of cosmological and evolutionary theories is unavoidable. This is evident in the work of many *popularisers of science, from Robert Hunt and Camille *Flammarion through James Jeans and Loren Eiseley to Fred *Hoyle and Richard Dawkins, as well as the characteristically inspirational tone of *hard science fiction. It is, in consequence, not surprising that theorists of *ideology—whose interest is in the psychological reasons people have for holding beliefs rather than the truth or otherwise of the beliefs in question—can construct plausible explanations of the progress of science that consider its revelations as mythical as well as, or rather than, objective.

The fact that some scientific narratives supply answers to questions that were once only answerable in entirely imaginary terms actively encourages sceptical *relativists to represent it as one more mythology in a potentially infinite catalogue. Philosophers of science, on the other hand, see the displacement in more fundamental terms, as a gradual and painful, but nevertheless comprehensive and final, demolition of *Baconian idols. The fact that every human culture invents myths to fill lacunae of explanation left by the absence of scientific knowledge is evidence of a powerful psychological craving, whose effect drives as well as hampers the scientific enterprise.

The relationship between myth and modern fiction is just as complex as that between myth and modern science. In oral cultures, where stories appear to exist independently of individual tellers, and gain their authority from the impression of being handed down from remote antiquity, all stories are set in the mythic past. The replacement of such stories by modern narratives attributed to particular authors, whose usual setting is the distant or immediate *historical past, was a gradual process fraught with difficulty and confusion. Like the evolution of science, it has generally been seen as a progressive transcendence of the primitive and the obsolete, and those relics of the mythic past that survived—with remarkable obstinacy—in modern literary activity are often stigmatised as implicitly naive or childish. Ethnological analyses of myths, legends, and folktales lent assistance to this attitude in the nineteenth century.

Science fiction is sometimes represented in casual parlance as a "modern mythology", although the more elaborate ethnological terminology would relegate it to the status of "modern folklore", while science itself would be the mythological component and the history of science its associated assembly of legends. Some writers of speculative fiction have regarded themselves as mythopoeic writers—H. G. Wells boasted that The Time Machine (1895) was "the new Delphic oracle"—and speculative fiction has given rise to significant legendary figures, including individuals like Mary Shelley's *Frankenstein, Robert Louis Stevenson's Dr. Jekyll, and George Orwell's Big Brother and more generalised figures like *robots, *supermen, and *mutants.

The early twentieth-century development of the future as a narrative space became heavily dependent on a mythical future similar in many respects to the mythical past of early narrative, centred on the myth of the *Space Age. The sheer multiplicity of modern science fiction, however, pushes it towards the folkloristic end of the spectrum and consistently undermines its own quasi-mythic core; its relationship with modern mythologies that draw heavily upon its imagery—*flying saucers providing the most conspicuous example—is highly ambiguous. The closest resemblance between late twentieth-century speculative fiction and Classical myth-making is not its reflection of new scientific accounts of creation, nor even its construction of Space Age future histories, but its reflection of emergent scientific ideas of destiny in accounts of the *Omega Point. There, if nowhere else, a certain reverence and sense of exaltation is conserved.

Whether it is entitled to be considered as modern mythology or not, however, modern speculative fiction has certainly taken an intense interest in the substance of ancient myths, and in their calculated transfiguration. The extent of that transfigurational activity is remarkable even if one only considers published material, but the material submitted to science fiction publishers that never reaches print includes an astonishing profusion of what Brian Aldiss dubbed "Shaggy God stories": stories whose climactic twists reveal them to be crude transfigurations of Biblical or Classical mythology. The fact that such ideas occur spontaneously to large numbers of aspirant writers offers further testimony to the force of the psychological impulse of confabulation and to the adaptive manner in which that force usually operates.

Transfigurations of ancient myths into superscientific science fiction can be curiously obsessive, as manifest in J. Lewis Burrt's six "Lemurian Documents" (1932) and "The Never-Dying Light" (1935), Nelson Bond's tetralogy comprising *Exiles of Time* (1940; 1949), "Sons of the Deluge" (1940), "Gods of the Jungle" (1942), and "That Worlds May Live" (1943), and Emil Petaja's series begun with *Saga of Lost Earths* (1966). Other notable transfigurations of a similar sort include Wallace G. West's "Dragon's Teeth" (1934), Lester del Rey's "When the World Tottered" (1950; book 1959 as *Day of the Giants*), and Ian Watson's couplet *Lucky's Harvest* (1993) and *The Fallen Moon* (1994). The transfigurative process is also applied to literary works that are themselves transfigurative; science fiction versions of Homer's *Odyssey* include Fletcher Pratt's "The Wanderer's Return" (1951), R. A. Lafferty's *Space Chantey* (1968), and David A. Drake's *Cross the Stars* (1984). The

notion that a better understanding of mythopoeic process might generate technological spin-off of various sorts is developed in such stories as Trevor Hoyle's Q series, launched with *Seeking the Mythical Future* (1977), and Jamil Nasir's *Tower of Dreams* (1999). None of this work can possibly qualify as rationally plausible extrapolation, but it does reflect and symbolise an acute awareness of the manner in which science's replacement of confabulatory myth has wrought a fundamental epistemological change while conserving psychological functionality.

The development of prose fiction and the particular narrative techniques of the novel included a concerted attempt to set aside the mythic past in which all the stories of the earlier, newly literature, culture had had to be set. The evolution of prose fiction was, in consequence, intimately involved with the development of the possibility, and an insistence on the value, of representing the world "as it is". From the late Renaissance onwards, the great strides made by science involved looking outwards, while those made by literature involved looking inwards, but the attitude of the seeing minds had as many similarities as differences.

Conscientious practitioners of modern science and conscientious writers of modern fiction have been equally determined to penetrate the sham of appearances in order to find a deeper truth than the kind that earlier myths had created and preserved. The fact that literary attempts to see the world "as it is" always tended to satirical irony, while scientific accounts preferred mathematical exactitude, is a contrast that not only overlay but sprang from a common determination. The sense in which myth could be set aside and superseded, however, was the trivial sense in which the term meant no more than obsolete belief. In the more profound sense that myth aimed for a coherent overview of humankind's relationship with the macrocosm, both science and fiction aspire to be better, brighter, and broader myths than those they replaced and remoulded.

N

NANOTECHNOLOGY

A term popularised by K. Eric Drexler's highly influential work of speculative nonfiction *Engines of Creation* (1987), often abbreviated to "nanotech" and readily giving rise to such derivatives as "nanoware" and "nanobots" (nanotechnological robots). *Engines of Creation* summarised a train of thought that Drexler had first set in motion in "Molecular Engineering: An Approach to the Development of General Capabilities for Molecular Manipulation" (1981), although similar ideas had previously been broached in Richard Feynman's essay "There's Plenty of Room at the Bottom" (1961, in H. D. Gilbert's *Miniaturization*). Nanotechnology is a drastic extrapolation of the notion of technological miniaturisation, proposing the development and use of extremely tiny machines capable of manipulating individual atoms and molecules, simulating and vastly extending the "natural molecular technologies" used by living cells to manufacture proteins, organs, and whole bodies.

In general, mechanical devices become more powerful as they increase in size, so the main thrust of technological development in respect of such epoch-making devices as mills and locomotives had tended towards giantism. A contrary trend towards miniaturisation had, however, been generated by the demand for portability. The first significant trend towards miniaturisation was that reducing clockwork to the dimensions of pocket watches, which necessitated a transfer of fine-working skills from jewellers to watchmakers—a generalisation of application that played a significant role in the development of other devices, such as movable print and *microscopes. Another trend towards miniaturisation prompted by the necessity of portability led from cannon through muskets to handguns, although the utility of portable guns was limited by the corresponding loss of killing power.

Similar trends became increasingly evident in the nineteenth century, with the development of such domestic apparatus as typewriters and vacuum cleaners and the replacement of public transport by private *automobiles—reflected in speculative fiction in the imagery of personal aircraft and helicopter backpacks. The possibilities of ultra-miniaturisation remained beyond the imaginative horizon until the development of the microchip and its deployment in personal *computers brought about a sudden and drastic change of attitude; the idea of nanotechnology appeared soon thereafter.

The progress of surgical techniques in the last decades of the twentieth century, involving the computerised direction of tiny probes with the aid of microscopic cameras in order to perform such operations as placing stents to widen clogged arteries, soon tested the limits of what could be achieved by direct manipulation, but Drexler proposed that the inherent limitations of human fingers and eyes could be overcome. He suggested that it ought to be possible to build self-directing "assemblers" in successive generations, using small machines to manufacture even smaller machines in series. He also suggested that problems of design could be solved with the aid of self-improving *artificial intelligence programs that would make ever-more-rapid progress as the machines they guided descended the space-time scale.

The economic potential of nanotechnology immediately excited interest; *Fortune* discussed it in "Where the Next Fortunes Will Be Made" in 1988 and *The Economist* considered it in "The Invisible Factory" in 1989. The notion was taken up with equal alacrity by science fiction writers, following a popularising article by Drexler and Chris Peterson in the mid-December 1987 issue of *Analog*. Gregory *Benford was one of the participants in *Nanocon 1: The First Northwest Conference on Nanotechnology* in Seattle in February 1989.

Science-fictional anticipations of nanotechnology had been relatively rare, although R. A. Lafferty's "McGruder's Marvels" (1968) is a significant exception that might have taken its inspiration from Feynman. Ian Watson was one of the first post-Drexlerian science fiction writers to declare that the nascent phase in history was "Nanoware Time" (1989), but many others joined enthusiastically in the business of further elaborating the notion, including Michael J. Flynn, in the stories combined in the mosaic *The Nanotech Chronicles* (1989–1991; book, 1991).

The obvious utility of nanotech in *medicine prompted many of the early fictitious depictions of nanotech at work. Pat Cadigan's *Mindplayers* (1987), W. T. Quick's "The Healing" (1988), Greg Bear's *Queen of Angels* (1990) and its sequel *Slant* (1997), and Mark O. Halverson's "Incident at the Angel of Boundless Compassion" (1993) speculate about its potential impact in that arena. Jeffrey Carver's *From a Changeling Star* (1989) foregrounded the potential of internal nanotechnology. Maya Kaathryn Bohnhoff's "If It Ain't Broke...". (1991) featured "large" nanomachines—"meganannies"—designed to fix tiny things and clean up miniature messes, while her "Sunshine, Genius and Rust" (1993) fused nanotech with *genetic engineering in "genano engineering".

The idea that Drexlerian assemblers or nanobots could be used to process extremely raw material into any object of desire prompted speculation about amorphous "utility mists" awaiting temporary metamorphosis into useful objects and melodramatic accounts of "grey goo catastrophes" precipitated by out-of-control nanotechnologies, as foreshadowed (in a different hue) in Greg Bear's *biotechnological fantasy *Blood Music* (1985). Later variants of the grey goo catastrophe scenario similarly gave rise to goos of many other colours, but blue was conventionally reserved for defensive measures intended to prevent such catastrophes.

Given that the hypothetical assemblers were to be designed and operated by artificial intelligences derived by natural selection, it seemed only natural to many writers that the nanotechnologies in question might develop goals and purposes of their own, which might well remain incomprehensible to human beings, as in such postdisaster scenarios as those mapped out in Katherine Ann Goonan's *Queen City Jazz* (1994) and its sequels and Alastair Reynolds' *Chasm City* (2001). Alien nanotechnology begins to dismantle the solar system in Roger McBride Allen's *The Ring of Charon* (1990), and threatens to do likewise in Kevin J. Anderson and Doug Beason's *Assemblers of Infinity* (1993). A leisure society is sustained by nanotech in Walter Jon Williams' *Aristoi* (1993).

Ian Watson's contention in a futurological seminar hosted by British Telecom that nanotechnology would deliver immortality prompted Ian McDonald to wonder whether it might also facilitate resurrection—an idea he developed in *Necroville* (1994; aka *Terminal Café*). Linda Nagata's work, from *The Bohr Maker* (1995) on, made extravagant use of nanotechnology, which reached a strange extreme in *Memory* (2003), set on a ring-shaped planet afflicted by mysterious nanotechnological fog controlled by insectile mechanical "kobolds". Wil McCarthy's *Murder in the Solid State* (1996) is an early nanotech murder mystery, while *Bloom* (1998) carried the development of an organic nanotechnology further forward. The notion of microcosmic telepresence was developed in such stories as Pete D. Manison's "First Nanocontact" (1997). The first decade of science-fictional speculation was summarised in Jack Dann and Gardner Dozois' theme anthology *Nanotech* (1998).

By the end of the twentieth century, the continued evolution of nanotechnology was taken for granted in most of the futuristic scenarios of hard science fiction, although opinions differed widely as to the expectable pace of that progress. The second part of Drexler's thesis, regarding the potential use of artificial intelligences derived by natural selection to incorporate themselves in progressively smaller forms, encouraged the notion that technological advancement would accelerate towards a technological *singularity, pioneered in such works as Neal Stephenson's *The Diamond Age* (1995).

The nanotech menace inevitably occupied its niche within *technothriller fiction, as in Michael Crichton's *Prey* (2002) and John Shirley's *Crawlers* (2003), but always threatened to smash through the normalising boundaries of that genre, as in such accounts of pestilential nanoware as Paul J. McAuley's *Fairyland* (1995). Joan Slonczewski's *Brain Plague* (2000), in which intelligent nanotechnological commensals must decide whether or not to rebel against their host, summarised the ambivalent situation reached at the end of the twentieth century.

In Tony Daniel's *Metaplanetary* (2001) and *Super-luminal* (2004), nanotech cables provide literal connective tissue for an elaborate future society, while Karl Schroeder's *Ventus* (2000) and *Permanence* (2002) look forward to a nanotechnological vitalisation of the entire human environment and Justina Robson's *Mappa Mundi* (2001) carries forward the potential medical applications of nanotech. On the other hand, Alastair Reynolds' *Century Rain* (2004) looks forward to a hyperdestructive "nanocaust" and Schroeder's *Lady of Mazes* (2005) inverts the situation in a different direction, with internal nanotech controlling human perception of the world.

NARRATIVE THEORY

The analysis of the techniques of storytelling. The discipline originated in *Aristotle's *Poetics*, which identified the three key elements of a plot as *harmatia* (a crucial fault), *anagnorisis* (a moment of revelation or recognition), and *peripeteia* (an abrupt reversal of fortune). The strategy of narrative construction had previously been touched upon in classical accounts of *rhetoric, and in an argument advanced by *Plato in the *Republic*, which suggested that an ideal society could have no place for poets and dramatists, because their work nourishes the emotions that rational human beings in quest of *ataraxia* (calm of mind) ought to subdue and suppress. Aristotle countered the latter allegation with the theory of catharsis, arguing that participation in public performances allowed the expressive discharge of pent-up emotions that might otherwise cause continuing disturbance, thus guaranteeing the social utility of both tragedy and comedy—a thesis that is difficult to support empirically.

Aristotle's notion of *harmatia* leading to *peripeteia* was further developed by Thomas Rymer in *Reflexions on Aristotle's Poetics* (1674), into the notion of "poetic justice". Rymer contended that the power authors have to determine the rewards and punishments distributed in their texts implies a responsibility to do so according to a moral code; thus, the tragic protagonist must suffer his reversal of fortune as a just consequence of his manifest fault. Rymer—who was primarily a historian, although he dabbled in dramatic criticism and wrote a play himself—criticised William Shakespeare for his occasional failure to ensure that evil characters are punished and good ones rewarded.

Shakespeare had, of course, been well aware of the fact that the audience's expectation that an author will exercise power in this way is subject to manipulation, and that the calculated disappointment of the expectation can be used to generate an acute sense of "the irony of fate", which can seem either tragic or comic, or partake of a chimerical alloy of the two. By the seventeenth century, it was well understood by accomplished dramatists that it is precisely because the world within a text is intrinsically subject to moral order that an authorial refusal to distribute rewards and punishments in accordance with a particular moral code is so highly effective. Shakespeare certainly understood—although some commentators still seem dubious—that it is not sadism that makes members of an audience so avid to see a villain bloodily done to death, but merely the inflationary effect of melodrama on moral currency.

In the nineteenth century, when prose fiction began to displace poetry as the dominant literary medium, writers began to focus more intently on the narrative aspects of their work; notable contributions to the development of narrative theory were then made in essays by Edgar Allan Poe and Edward Bulwer-Lytton, letters written by Gustave Flaubert, and Henry James' introductions to his collected works, reprinted in *The Art of the Novel* (1934). These were supplemented by such twentieth-century discussions as E. M. Forster's *Aspects of the Novel* (1927) and Erich Auerbach's *Mimesis* (1946). Robert Scholes and Robert Kellogg's *The Nature of Narrative* (1966) offered a significant summary in advance of the more elaborate theoretical account offered by Gérard Genette in *Figures I–III* (1967–1970; abridged trans. as *Narrative Discourse: An Essay in Method*). Further theorisation led to the widespread use of the term "narratology" in the 1980s, as in Mieke Bal's *De theorie de vertellen en verhalen* (1980; trans. as *Narratology: Introduction to the Theory of Narrative*), although that discipline tends to be narrowly focused on structural issues, avoiding the kind of argument developed by Rymer.

Aristotle's own analyses were structural in kind; he anatomised the artistic construction of stories in terms of three distinct phases (referred to in common parlance as the beginning, the middle, and the end) and the manner in which the holistic organisation of these phases conserves an overall "dramatic unity". Rhetoricians interested in the art of persuasion were more likely to use mechanical analogies, referring to such items as the dramatic tension generated by oppositional relationships between protagonists and antagonists, and making reference to such notions as narrative hooks, the cultivation of suspense, and the levers, wheels, or threads of plots. By contrast, the nineteenth-century theorists—especially Henry James, whose brother William was a pioneering psychologist—paid more attention to the way in which stories functioned as a kind of surrogate experience, making use of such notions as "point of view" and "stream of consciousness"; their analyses were much more sensitive to the kinds of argument employed by Rymer—and, for that matter, the dispute between Plato and Aristotle as to the emotional resonances of drama.

These two broad frames of reference continued to overlap in twentieth-century narrative theory, underlying the discussion of story content and language. Writers and compilers of manuals for writers took a particular interest in viewpoint—or "focalisation", in Genette's terminology—because this determines the "voice" in which a story is told; the development of the novel has largely replaced the traditional "omniscient narrator" or the oral folktale by viewpoints apparently located in the consciousness of particular characters; the methodology of this approach was extensively discussed in Percy Lubbock's *The Craft of Fiction* (1921) and more elaborately considered in Wayne C. Booth's *The Rhetoric of Fiction* (1961). This discussion gave rise to a crucial theoretical distinction between what Plato had called mimetic and diegetic modes of narration—or, in common parlance, between "showing" and "telling" the reader what happens in the story. The gradual replacement of the diegetic mode by the mimetic allows the author to become effectively "invisible" within a text, assisting readers to "identify" with the viewpoint character, thus entering into the story almost as if it were their own experience—a facility that only became possible when *writing was standardised as print.

The gradual displacement of the diegetic mode by the mimetic created problems with respect to filling in data relevant to the story but outside its actual timespan—particularly the elaboration of the various characters' "back stories"—but techniques developed whereby this kind of information could be intruded incidentally and unobtrusively. The emergence and evolution of the mimetic mode was also closely associated with the development of literary naturalism, because it is well adapted to the cultivation of an impression of actuality; for this reason novels were often contrasted in the nineteenth century with "romances" allegedly dealing with less probable events, and characterised by the heightened sense of the dramatic signified by the term "melodrama". Popular fiction tended to retain its romantic and melodramatic qualities, and was increasingly distinguished from "literary fiction" on that account.

Another significant argumentative thread in narrative theory draws a subtler distinction between "story" and "plot" (although Genette prefers "discourse" to plot). A story, in this limited definition, is a chronological sequence of events. In the simplest stories, the events are effectively independent of one another, although they usually share the same orientation towards some ultimate goal. Such sequences may, however, be "thickened" in various ways as various plot strands draw connections between the events, by means of various forms of complication, often changing the temporal order in which the events are narrated. The most significant kinds of complication involve conflict generated by characters' competing agendas, and elements of mystery that add new levels of potential meaning to the story's events and the characters' discoveries.

The concerns raised by Rymer broadened out in subsequent considerations of narrative theory to taxonomic studies of the various ways of achieving "closure" in the conclusion of a story. As prose fiction has evolved, the traditional nineteenth-century rewards of marriage and inheritance have been extravagantly supplemented, and to some extent displaced, by intellectual rewards of the kind that James Joyce called "epiphanies": moments of insight that constitute minor or major existential breakthroughs. Such endings can be combined, but may also be contrasted, with endings in which antagonists are conclusively defeated, the disruptive effects of their antagonism being healed or exorcised, thus contriving a kind of normalisation. Normalising story arcs proved particularly useful in extrapolating series, as in the various popular genres of crime fiction. Shorter stories often make use of a kind of closure extrapolated from the "punch lines" of jokes and anecdotes, although more sophisticated examples cast in the mimetic mode may develop "slices of life" whose descriptions of trivial events in a social microcosm become significant of much broader theses.

David Lodge argues in *Consciousness and the Novel* (2002) that the evolution of modern mimetic techniques—especially the "third person limited" viewpoint—has equipped fiction with better methods of describing and understanding the phenomenon of consciousness than *psychology has yet contrived, and the novel is routinely held up as a means of gaining a special insight into the way that people are motivated. Indeed, it can be argued that the inner lives of literate people—their actual "streams of consciousness"—are largely modelled upon and shaped by literary accounts of thought processes, and that even illiterate people often have a tendency to interpret their lives, and the lives of others, in narrative terms. The genre of biography—especially its autobiographical subsection—is much given to the construction of life *stories*, which attempt to superimpose a narrative structure on the events making up a life as well as offering rationalisations and moral justifications of problematic actions. *Reportage has a similar tendency, continually converting the world's events into "news stories" whose appeal to newspaper readers—their "newsworthiness"—has much to do with such narrative qualities as "human interest" and the irony of fate.

The evolution of narrative technique mirrors the general pattern of intellectual development in Western culture from the Renaissance onwards; if descriptions of the world are considered as narratives, there has been a movement away from the employment of an omniscient creator towards a seemingly-objective account in which events and their organising processes are directly shown to the observer, and a similar movement away from a simple sequential understanding of temporal processes towards a more complex integration of time, space, and instrumentality. The significant transformations in both science and literature can be seen as symptoms of a more general transition from "telling" to "showing" that took place as the perceived power of arguments from authority lost their persuasive precedence to arguments based on empirical experience and logical analysis. Seen from this point of view, the increasing importance of naturalistic fiction—including the emergence of a formal theory of literary *naturalism—appears less puzzling than it does if it is seen purely in terms of *aesthetic arguments.

All representations of science, including formal *scientific publication, have a narrative component. The evolutionary sequence that led from the Classical dialogue to the modern scientific paper is a striking example of a transition from a mode of presentation involving active tellers to one in which the data and its analysis are simply shown, as if from an entirely depersonalised viewpoint. The underlying anatomy of a scientific paper is similar to the dramatic anatomy dissected by Aristotle, leading inexorably from introduction to conclusion, and it has its own built-in rhetorical strategy. The scientific paper is definitively different from mimetic fiction in that it specifically excludes the surrogate human viewpoints that novels usually aim to cultivate, but it is by no means unconcerned with the kinds of complication and mystery that constitute the thickening of story into plot, and it has a distinct strategy of closure intent on delivering a particular intellectual epiphany.

Writers of speculative fiction are frequently accused of failing to deliver the same rewards as writers of conventional narrative, because they routinely pay less attention to the cultivation of character identification, and more attention to the diegetic establishment of data within their narrative schemes. This is necessary in all fiction that deals with exotic worlds-within-texts, because the "back story" of the entire world has to be filled in, along with that of the characters. This was not the reason why Alexander Baumgarten thought that "heterocosmic creativity"

was intrinsically inferior to mimetic realism in aesthetic terms, but it is a significant limitation of narrative technique, especially in its application to speculative fiction.

The more complex the speculative process is by which the world within a text has been generated, the more detailed its heterocosmic back story is likely to be. This means that serious speculative fiction remains so heavily committed to diegetic narrative modes that its twentieth-century examples often seem markedly different in tone and manner from contemporary naturalistic fiction. Heterocosmic creativity also makes it more difficult for writers to employ conventional methods of closure. Normalising story arcs are often unsatisfactory because the assumption that the *status quo* is a privileged situation that ought to be restored is much more secure in naturalistic fiction than it is in fiction that deals directly with the dynamics and irresistibility of social change, as serious speculative fiction is bound to do. Conventional rewards are equally unsatisfactory, in that they tend to reflect contemporary moral evaluations that serious speculative fiction is bound to call into question.

These differences are characterised in various ways by different observers, one of the more commonsensical versions bring Kingsley Amis' contention in *New Maps of Hell* (1960) that science fiction stories are mostly "idea-as-hero" stories, in which the reader's narrative focus is shifted from identification with characters to confrontation with enigmatic phenomena that demand explication, and whose extrapolation usually poses a challenge to the reader's conventional assumptions. Robert Scholes argues that the most interesting speculative fiction has to be regarded as a subspecies of "fabulation", a term he uses to describe narratives that retain the diegetic mode in order to deal with blatantly fantastic material for philosophical purposes, sacrificing the illusion of identification in favour of intellectual stimulation and provocation.

In Scholes' narrative taxonomy, serious science fiction becomes "speculative fabulation", contrasted with the various types of "dogmatic fabulation" associated with *myth, allegory, *occult fiction, and so on. Scientists occasionally dabble in fabulation in the course of constructing thought *experiments along the lines of James Clerk Maxwell's "demon" or Albert Einstein's twin paradox, while literary fabulators such as Italo Calvino employ scientific theses in such works as those collected in *Le Cosmicomiche* (1965; trans. as *Cosmicomics*) and *ti con zero* (1967; trans. as *t zero* and *Time and the Hunter*). The mass of speculative fiction extends across a spectrum connecting these extremes, but the middle of the spectrum is drastically curved by the gravitational attraction of the mimetic modes favoured by the much vaster mass of conventional prose fiction.

Speculative fiction has inevitably considered the possibility that mastery of narrative theory might enable the automation of narrative production, as envisaged in such stories as Clifford D. Simak's "So Bright the Vision" (1956), Fritz Leiber's *The Silver Eggheads* (1958; exp. 1962), Christopher Anvil's "The New Boccaccio" (1964), and Robert Escarpit's *Le littératron* (1964; trans. as *The Novel Computer*). The very few science fiction stories to deal directly with matters of narrative theory include Milton A. Rothman's "The Eternal Genesis" (1979), which explores the difficulties involved in accommodating cosmological speculations within a conventional narrative, and Hilbert Schenck's "The Geometry of Narrative" (1983), in which a seminar on that subject is presented as a modernised Platonic dialogue.

NATURALISM

A term initially applied to a philosophical position whose central assertion was that everything was explicable in terms of natural—as opposed to supernatural—agents; the notions of "natural philosophy" and "naturalistic fiction" are derivatives of this meaning. In the nineteenth century, however, the literary meanings of the term became more complicated. It was sometimes used to describe prosaic writing, by contrast with various kinds of ornate contrivance, and in the wake of Charles *Darwin's use of the term "natural selection", a new school of literary Naturalism emerged, which attempted to refine literary representation into a kind of scientific description.

The principal propagandist for the quasi-scientific kind of literary Naturalism was Émile Zola, who proposed in *Le roman experimental* (1880) that the novel might and ought to be employed as an instrument for the study of human nature, constructing and considering characters as products of the interaction of heredity and environment, after the fashion of the pioneering human scientists Hippolyte Taine and Claude Bernard. Zola's manifesto carried forward earlier literary arguments, put forward by such writers as Gustave Flaubert, to the effect that novelists should not pass moral judgements on their characters, limiting themselves to the neutral description of motivational processes, but it called for an increased intensity and theoretical sophistication as well as a greater objectivity of authorial attitude and method.

Zola's proposals, and his attempts to exemplify them in *Thérèse Raquin* (1867) and the novel series *Les Rougon-Maquart: Histoire naturelle et sociale d'une famille sous le Second Empire* (1871–1893), influenced several of his contemporaries, at least temporarily. They included Guy de Maupassant, Paul Bourget, Henrik Ibsen, and August Strindberg; the last named summarised his own Naturalist prospectus in the preface to *Fröken Julie* (1888; trans. as *Miss Julie*). Several American writers espoused Naturalist ideas and methods, some taking as much inspiration from the "medicated novels" of Oliver Wendell Holmes as from Zola; the most notable included Harold Frederic, whose account of *The Damnation of Theron Ware* (1896; aka *Illumination*) is a key exemplar, William Dean Howells, and Edgar Fawcett. Fawcett's attempts to reconcile the spirit of Naturalism with his strong desire to write speculative fiction led to his prefacing *The Ghost of Guy Thyrle* (1895) with a manifesto for "realistic romance" that anticipated later apologias for science fiction. Zola also ventured into speculative fiction, albeit tentatively, in the futuristic passages of *Fécondité* (1899; trans. as *Fruitfulness*), the first of an unfinished quartet of novels extrapolating a family saga to the year 1980.

Although the echoes of the explicit Naturalist movement faded away in the early years of the twentieth century, along with the echoes of such antithetical movements as Symbolism, its ambitions did not vanish entirely, becoming discreetly accommodated within the broader pastures of ordinary naturalism. The examination of intricately interwoven influences of heredity and environment on characters became part and parcel of the routine business of characterisation in all sophisticated narrative, thus contriving an interesting overlap, if not an intimate alliance, between modern fiction and the human sciences, especially *psychology. The philosophy of Naturalism also affected the development of speculative fiction, some of whose practitioners—notably Robert A. *Heinlein—took care to insist that *hard science fiction ought to be considered as a species of naturalistic fiction, essentially different in kind from the various subspecies of imaginative fiction that employ supernatural apparatus. The use of speculative fiction as a medium of thought *experiments, especially those exploring hypotheses in human science, can be seen as an extrapolation of Zola's method.

NATURE

A deceptively simple term derived from the past participle of a verb meaning "to be born", which is also reflected in such English words as native, nation, and innate. Its trivial meaning refers to the character or constitution defining the members of a set or a species, and is often encountered in common parlance in the context of the phrase "human nature". In a more grandiose sense—often signified by a capital letter—Nature signifies the essential makeup of the entire world, particularly the fundamental processes of its animation. The Latin root is notably featured in the title of Lucretius' summary of Epicurean philosophy, *De rerum natura*, variously translated as *On the Nature of Things* and *On the Nature of the Universe*, in which context it gives rise to the notions of "natural philosophy" and the elementary meaning of *naturalism.

Initially, the implicit antithesis of the idea of Nature was God, or the supernatural in general, and the notion gradually became personalised in much the same fashion. In the eighteenth century, personalised Nature was most frequently seen as a stern lawgiver, as in the first section of Alexander Pope's *Essay on Man* (1733), but after Jean-Jacques *Rousseau's championship of the natural state and the advent of the *Romantic Movement, its characterisation became more various. Rousseau and his fellow "men of feeling" went walking in the country in order to experience and respond to Nature, their responses being informed and enlightened by developments in scientific knowledge. Percy Shelley's tutor, Adam Walker, popularised this attitude in *A System of Familiar Philosophy* (1799), whose sentiments are echoed in such popularisations of science as Robert Hunt's *The Poetry of Science* (1984).

One passage derived by Hunt from Walker inspired the Scottish poet William Wilson to issue a brief manifesto for a new genre of "science-fiction" in 1851, but it proved premature—although Wilson's chosen exemplar, Richard Henry Horne's *The Poor Artist; or, Seven Eye-Sights and One Object* (1850) is a good illustration of the manner in which scientific knowledge can inform and transform the imagery of Nature. The thesis struck a particular chord in America, where Ralph Waldo Emerson's *Nature* (1836) analysed the concept in a similar fashion, echoed by Henry David Thoreau's *Walden* (1854) and J. P. Mowbray and Andrew Carpenter Wheeler's *A Journey to Nature* (1901). In the meantime, similar perspectives were enthusiastically extrapolated in Britain by the champions of "natural *theology", who saw Nature as a teacher engaged in demonstrations of God's ingenuity, subtlety, and majesty.

Alfred, Lord Tennyson's reference in *In Memoriam* (1850) to "Nature red in tooth and claw" became ominously famous in the wake of Charles *Darwin's theory of natural selection, but more benign depictions flourished alongside it. The deployment of maternal imagery became increasingly common, hinting at a new opposition between Mother Nature (or Mother *Earth) and God the Father. Nature and science had started out as members of a common category, yoked together in natural philosophy, but the last-cited characterisation licensed a new scheme in which maternal Nature could also be opposed to a depersonalised Science, and this kind of metaphorical analysis became increasingly common as the nineteenth century gave way to the twentieth.

Contrasts between Nature and Science were also drawn in a post-Romantic context by writers who became increasingly interested in pagan nature imagery, often embodied in the image of the god Pan, who became a prolific source of inspiration in poetry of the latter half of the century; a curious kind of Nature worship quite distinct from Christian natural theology developed in the work of such writers as Richard Jefferies, displayed in the nonfictional *The Dewy Morn* (1884) as well as his antitechnological tract *After London; or, Wild England* (1885), and in the anticipatory *ecological mysticism of W. H. Hudson.

The development of the human sciences, especially *anthropology and *ethnology, gave rise to another dialectical distinction, between Nature and Culture. Initially, practitioners of the new sciences, reacting against the notion of divinely gifted privilege, tended to see human nature as a product of heredity and the natural environment, but the emphasis began to change before the end of the nineteenth century. George Perkins Marsh, who started out as a hardline environmental determinist, reversed his position in *Man and Nature* (1864), concentrating instead on the human ability to transform, control, and disrupt the environment, thus lending impetus to a train of thought that led to the notion of Nature as a hapless victim of human agency rather than a dominating force—an image that fit in well with the increasingly fashionable feminising imagery, opposing Mother Nature to a *technology that was not merely impersonal but actively rapacious.

In twentieth-century common parlance, "natural" and "scientific" were far more often used as opposed terms than identical ones, as they might have been a century earlier. In contexts where "natural" implied "maternal", and hence "good", the contrasted use of "scientific" inevitably came to imply "impersonal", and hence "bad". In considerations of human nature, the opposition of Nature and Culture was frequently replaced by an opposition of nature and *nurture*, emphasising the maternal aspects of cultural determinism. The use of "natural" and "scientific" as opposites became particularly prominent in "alternative *medicine", whose practitioners reimported the pagan/maternal concept of Nature into the narrower context of human nature even more enthusiastically than the followers of Rousseau, using its resonance to support essentially supernatural views of the body and the contrasted states of health and illness.

"Nature" was also increasingly used as a synonym for the rural environment of "the countryside", again in implicit contrast to "technology"—an attitude that turned a blind eye to the fact that the modern countryside is a product of agricultural artifice.

The development of the maternal notion of Nature, especially in its neo-pagan variants, had an enormous impact on twentieth-century literary representations of cities, the countryside, and human nature, in both naturalistic and speculative fiction. In Europe there was a dramatic resurgence of Arcadian imagery, in tacit or explicit opposition to Utopian imagery tied to the ideals of material and political *progress. This pattern was less obvious in America, where the business of taming the Western wilderness still seemed to be a historical work-in-progress, but sharp contrasts developed there between literary representations of city life, small town life, and frontier life, which routinely glorified "Big Country" and homes on the range. The increasing hostility between the pagan/maternal view of Nature and the scientific worldview was brought dramatically into focus by responses to James *Lovelock's Gaia hypothesis, whose tacit attempt to synthesise the opposed perspectives resulted in much misunderstanding and annoyance.

In late twentieth-century common parlance, "natural" has gradually come to seem almost synonymous with "good", while such antonyms as "artificial" and "technological" and "chemical" have acquired an increasingly sinister gloss. This is a peculiar development, given that almost everything we unthinkingly call "natural" is a product of technical artifice, but it has a profound effect on the way in which contemporary literary *rhetoric employs the term.

NEPTUNE

The eighth planet from the Sun—although its orbit intersects with that of *Pluto periodically (as in the last two decades of the twentieth century), relegating it temporarily to ninth. Its existence was postulated in 1820 by Alexis Bouvard, in order to explain perturbations in the orbit of *Uranus; Friedrich Bessel launched a search for it in 1842 that was continued by John Couch Adams and Urbain Le Verrier, whose calculations of its likely position led to its discovery by Johann Galle in 1846. Within a month its largest satellite, Triton, had been observed; a second, Nereid, was discerned in 1949.

Neptune's discovery was swiftly acknowledged by Charles Rowcroft's The Triumphs of Woman (1848), which features a visitor from "Leverrier's Planet", but

it was rarely included in imaginary planetary tours because of its extreme distance. Information about its inhabitants is obtained by occult means in Marie Corelli's The Soul of Lilith (1982), a wandering planetoid collides with it in H. G. Wells' "The Star" (1897)—igniting a new star that threatens the Earth with destruction—and space battles rage around it in Robert W. Cole's The Struggle for Empire (1900), but it did not feature as a significant literary location until it appeared in Clare Winger Harris and Miles J. Breuer's "A Baby on Neptune" (1929) and became the home of the ultimate human race in Olaf Stapledon's Last and First Men (1930). It was also visited by human spacefarers in Edmond Hamilton's "The Universe Wreckers" (1930), Henrik Dahl Juve's "The Monsters of Neptune" (1930), and J. M. Walsh's "The Vanguard to Neptune" (1932), and was ignited into a star again in Donald Wandrei's "Raiders of the Universe" (1932). Stapledon's influence may have been responsible for the role attributed to Neptune in John W. Campbell's "Twilight" and "Night" (1934–1935; by-lined Don A. Stuart), where it is the final refuge of humankind's mechanical successors, but it retreated into obscurity again as pulp science fiction grew more sophisticated.

Twentieth-century spectroscopic analyses revealed that Neptune is a gas giant closely akin to its immediate neighbour, although it appears to have a significant source of internal heat. The only spacecraft to fly past the planet was Voyager 2 in 1989. It identified six more minor satellites—one of them, Proteus, being larger than Nereid but much more difficult to discern because of its closeness to its primary—and a tenuous ring system. Voyager 2 also observed a Great Dark Spot on the planet's apparent surface, but that had disappeared by the time the Hubble Space Telescope began to produce images of the planet in 1996, testifying to the unusual activity of the atmosphere. Triton also seemed unexpectedly varied and active, featuring geysers of liquid nitrogen and pink polar snow. As with other gas giants, Neptune attracted less literary attention in late twentieth-century science fiction than its major satellite; Triton is the *terraformed site of the "ambiguous heterotopia" featured in Samuel R. Delany's Triton (1976; aka Trouble on Triton), and Gordon Eklund's A Thunder on Neptune (1989) and Jeffrey A. Carver's Neptune Crossing (1994) are partly set there. The planet itself is featured as a hazard to be escaped in Gregory Feeley's "Neptune's Reach" (1986), but its atmosphere plays host to exotic mining enterprises in Alex Irvine's "Shepherded by Galatea" (2003). Mike Resnick's "The Elephants of Neptune" (2000) is a moral conte philosophique.

NEUROLOGY

The branch of physiology concerned with the study of the nervous system; it is of particular relevance to human science because it includes the study of the brain, and hence supplies scientific underpinning to philosophical discussions of the interface between *biology and *psychology, particularly in respect of attempts to understand *psychopathology.

The location of psychological functions within the brain got off to a shaky start in the *pseudoscience of phrenology, but more secure foundations were laid in Charles Bell's *Idea of a New Anatomy of the Brain* (1811), which clarified the brain's structure in terms of two "hemispheres" and three progressively accumulated "layers", in which the parts of the hindbrain common to all vertebrates are overlain by the structures of the cerebellum in mammals, supplemented in their turn by the cerebrum, with which nineteenth-century neurologists associated human brain's "higher functions". This hierarchical organisation of structures slotted neatly enough into philosophical models of the mind that had long represented it as an entity whose "higher" impulses are in constant competition with "baser" ones.

*Plato, René Descartes, Charles *Darwin, and Sigmund *Freud had all concurred in the view that the forces of human reason and free will are continually subverted by "animal" appetites and urges, expressed as potentially uncontrollable emotions that need to be suppressed, contained, or tamed if humans are to live sane and balanced lives. The idea that brain surgery or the administration of *psychotropic drugs might alter the relationship between these higher and lower impulses led to such literary reflections as Robert Louis Stevenson's *Strange Case of Dr. Jekyll and Mr. Hyde* (1886). Other early neurological fantasies hypothesised interventions in whatever mechanisms the brain might have to retain memories, and hence to organise the personality. Notable early examples of these kinds of neurological tampering are featured in Edward Bellamy's *Doctor Heidenhoff's Process* (1880), Walter Besant's "The Memory Cell" (1902), and Vincent Harper's *The Mortgage on the Brain* (1905). Twentieth-century extrapolations of similar hypotheses included Keith Laumer's "The Body Builders" (1966).

The scientific study of the human brain is severely restricted by ethical difficulties, although patients in mental hospitals were long regarded as fair game for experiments, even in the twentieth century, when experiments with direct electrical stimulation were carried out in the hope that they might help pave the way for new treatments of epilepsy and various surgical procedures—including prefrontal lobotomies—

were carried out in order to alleviate various kinds of mental distress. Such practices were a considerable inspiration to writers of *medical horror fiction.

Horror fiction also made abundant use of the melodramatic potential of the notion of brain transplantation. Potential corollaries of such surgical operations are amply displayed in such works as Emeric Hulme-Beaman's *The Experiment of Doctor Nevill* (1900), Edgar Rice Burroughs' *The Master Mind of Mars* (1927), Edmund Snell's *Kontrol* (1928), and Carl F. Keppler's "Mr. Pichegru's Discovery" (1929). The idea was swiftly taken up in the *cinema, in the silent movie *Go and Get It* (1920)— one of many such fantasies to implant a human brain in the body of a gorilla—and the Boris Karloff vehicle *The Man Who Lived Again* (1936). More sophisticated versions of the theme are featured in Lester del Rey's "Reincarnate" (1940) and C. L. Moore's "No Woman Born" (1944)—both of which explore the sensory effects of transplanting brains into robot bodies—John Boyd's *The Organ Bank Farm* (1970), and M. Lucie Chin's "The Best Is Yet to Be" (1978).

The notion of brains detached from bodies, with or without their enclosing heads, was equally inspiring to writers of horror fiction, notable examples including Aleksandr Belayev's *Golova Professora Doueillia* (1925; trans. as *Professor Dowell's Head*), Curt Siodmak's *Donovan's Brain* (1943; movie versions 1944, as *The Lady and the Monster*, 1953, and 1963, as *Vengeance*). Other movies on the same theme included *The Man Without a Body* (1957), *The Colossus of New York* (1958), *The Brain That Wouldn't Die* (1959), and *The Man with Two Brains* (1983). Detached brains are put to work in such pulp science fiction stories as Miles J. Breuer's "The Strength of the Weak" (1933), Eando Binder's *Enslaved Brains* (1934; book, 1965) and "Spawn of Eternal Thought" (1936), and Raymond F. Jones' *The Cybernetic Brains* (1950; book, 1962), but they attain extravagant achievements in Lloyd Arthur Eschbach's "The Time Conqueror" (1932; rev. as "The Tyrant of Time") and Frank Belknap Long's "The Vapor Death" (1934). Many pulp *supermen were equipped with huge brains, and sometimes ended up with very little supplementary tissue. Others were equipped with extra brains, as in A. E. van Vogt's *The Mixed Men* (1943–1945; book, 1952) and *The World of Null-A* (1945; book, 1948).

Against this lurid background, more ingenious extrapolations of neurology such as William Lemkin's "A Matter of Nerves" (1932) and Walter Anton Coole's "A Surgical Error" (1937)—both of which feature synaesthetic effects—and Raymond E. Banks' "The Happiness Effect" (1953) seemed distinctly undramatic. The situation was not assisted by the fact that research into the functioning of the brain made slow progress in the twentieth century, although James Papez located the origins of emotion within a network of subcortical brain structures, centred on the hippocampus, in the 1930s, and Paul MacLean subsequently extended this work to conceptualise the "limbic system" as the emotional centre of the brain.

The electroencephalograph (EEG), which made brain activity trackable in a nonintrusive fashion, was invented in 1929. Its use eventually revealed the existence of certain rhythmic patterns, named for letters of the Greek alphabet, whose possible significance was popularised by W. Gray Walter's *The Living Brain* (1953). The EEG became a common item of cinematic imagery, where it was often used to display the brain activity of dreaming subjects. Notable examples of the extrapolation of such notions include Arthur Leo Zagat's "Slaves of the Lamp" (1946), William T. Richards' semi-autobiographical *Brain Waves and Death* (1940; by-lined Willard Rich), Don Thompson's "The Telenizer" (1954), Diana and Meir Gillon's *The Unsleep* (1961), Jack Wodhams' "The Fuglemen of Recall" (1968) and "Androtomy and the Scion" (1969), D. G. Compton's *Synthajoy* (1969), and Ralph Blum's *The Simultaneous Man* (1970). The protagonist of Walker Percy's *Love in the Ruins* (1971) and *The Thanatos Syndrome* (1987) invents an advanced neurological reading device called a lapsometer.

The neurological discovery that had the greatest impact on the popular imagination was James Olds and Peter Milner's identification in 1954 of "pleasure centers": areas of the brains of rats whose direct electrical stimulation had a more powerful conditioning effect than that of any indirect reward. The image of "wireheads" hopelessly addicted to electrical self-stimulation became commonplace in science fiction of the 1960s and 1970s, in spite of the fact that experiments with human subjects could not demonstrate the kind of intense reaction observed in rats. One of the more imaginative extrapolations of the notion is featured in Kurt Vonnegut's "The Euphio Question" (1991), in which a signal incorporated into radio programmes stimulates the pleasure centres. A similar kind of addiction involving more elaborate effects is featured in Philip E. High's *Reality Forbidden* (1967).

The immense difficulty of regenerating neural links broken by spinal injury gradually emerged as one of the crucial medical challenges of the twentieth century, and research intensified considerably in the second half of the century. The frustrating nature of the problem is highlighted by such literary reflections as Charles Sheffield's *My Brother's Keeper* (1982), in which the basic problem is solved but gives rise to awkward side effects.

The development of more sophisticated imaging devices, which mapped metabolic activity in the brain as well as electrical activity, allowed further progress to be made in the late 1960s in identifying the different specialisms normally adopted by the right and left hemispheres, and different uses of specialist functions correlated with individual aptitudes and activities. The apparent potential for the two hemispheres of the brain to function independently, though not identically, is reflected in such science fiction stories as Verge Foray's "Duplex" (1968) and Robert Charles Wilson's *The Divide* (1990).

Attention was swiftly drawn in this context to differences between the usual patterns of neuronal usage in male and female brains—which seemed to be correlated with the effects of sex hormones, especially testosterone, on the embryonic development of the brain—but it was still unclear at the end of the twentieth century to what extent the differences might result from innate predisposition and to what extent they were the consequence of experiential learning.

Potential neurological applications of new technologies developed in the second half of the twentieth century always received enthusiastic publicity; Isaac Asimov's "Think!"—which details potential applications of lasers—was used in advertising by Coherent Radiation before its publication as a story in 1977. Asimov also addressed the possibility of chemical memory enhancement, in a more ironic spirit, in "Lest We Remember" (1982). Neurological augmentation became one of the key themes of *cyborg fiction, particularly in respect of such cyberpunk stories as Pat Cadigan's *Synners* (1991) and Melissa Scott's *Trouble and Her Friends* (1994). Neurophysiological intervention also seemed to be a significant corollary of the possibilities of *nanotechnology.

The notion of radical neurophysiological intervention underlies numerous sophisticated *contes philosophiques*, including Greg Egan's "Fidelity" (1991), "TAP" (1995), and "Reasons to Be Cheerful" (1997), Ted Chiang's "Understand" (1991), and Shane Tourtelotte's "Acts of Conscience" (2005). Similar philosophical issues are raised, albeit far more tentatively, in Ian McEwan's *Saturday* (2005), whose protagonist is a neuropsychologist.

NEWTON, SIR ISAAC (1642–1727)

English natural philosopher. He played a key role in the scientific revolution of the Age of Reason, his *Philosophiae Naturalis Principia Mathematica* [Mathematical Principles of Natural Philosophy] (1687) becoming one of the pivotal works in the history of science.

Newton's father died before he was born and his mother abandoned him upon her remarriage in 1644 to the care of his grandmother, instilling in him an extreme resentment that permanently coloured his character. When his mother was widowed again in 1653, she recruited him to help manage the property she had inherited, but his neglect of this commission was so blatant that he was swiftly packed off to school. He moved on to Trinity College Cambridge in 1661, having developed a legendary prowess in the construction of machines. Traditional Aristotelianism was still being taught at Cambridge, but Newton's discovery of the work of René Descartes showed him a new direction of rebellion. He also read Pierre Gassendi's new version of *atomic theory, Robert Boyle's work in *chemistry, and Henry More's neo-Platonist analyses of the *occult Hermetic tradition, all of which studies he attempted to carry forward.

Newton's first manifest achievement was an extrapolation of Descartes' algebraic *geometry, first circulated in a privately circulated manuscript in 1669; his discovery of what he subsequently called the method of fluxions (differential calculus in modern terminology) won him a select reputation, but he did not publish it. While the university was closed in 1665–1667 because of an epidemic of the plague, he carried out experiments with prisms and lenses, which were to provide the foundations of his *Opticks*, but he did not publish the resultant essay "On Colours" either.

Newton was elected to a fellowship at Trinity in 1667 and was recommended by Isaac Barrow—one of the few men acquainted with his work—to succeed him as Lucasian professor of mathematics in 1669. He continued to develop his theory of *optics in the context of an annual lecture course, and eventually presented a paper on the subject to the Royal Society in 1672. One of the Society's leading members, Robert Hooke—who considered himself an expert in the subject—wrote a condescending critique of the paper, which so enraged the psychologically fragile Newton that he became a virtual recluse until 1675, when he heard what he took to be a recantation by Hooke, and presented a second paper on refraction, which became the basis for the second volume of *Opticks*. He was, however, soon embroiled in a new dispute with Hooke, who accused him of stealing the ideas he had incorporated in a further paper on the underlying physics of light.

Newton controlled his anger for a while, but was tipped over the edge again when a group of Jesuits in Liège contended that his experiments were invalid. He suffered what would nowadays be called a "nervous breakdown" in 1678, whose effects were compounded by the death of his mother the following year; his correspondence with others ceased, although he continued to work in isolation on all the problems that intrigued him. It was not until Edmond Halley visited him in 1684 that Newton revealed that he had solved the problem of orbital dynamics and reluctantly promised to show him the proof. The paper Newton sent to Halley did not contain the three laws of motion or the law of universal gravitation, but all of them were subsequently incorporated into the expanded version that he published as the *Principia*.

On seeing the manuscript of the *Principia*, Hooke again charged Newton with plagiarism; Newton reacted by cutting almost all the references to Hooke from the book (the famous anecdote relating how the idea of gravity occurred to Newton when an apple fell on his head as a boy was invented as an element of his defensive strategy against Hooke's allegation). Newton decided not to publish *Opticks*, and swore that he would never accept the presidency of the Royal Society while Hooke was alive.

The international reputation won by the *Principia* made Newton by far the most prominent scientist in England, and he took advantage of his fame to make a political career for himself in London, eventually becoming Warden of the Royal Mint in 1696. The new friends he made in London, who included John Locke and Samuel Pepys, thought it likely that Newton would go mad in 1693, when his relationship with the young mathematician Nicholas Fatio de Duillier came to an end, but he recovered. His principal intellectual labours were devoted thereafter to studies of the text of the Bible based in ideas taken from *occult science, but he never published anything of that sort.

Newton accepted the Presidency of the Royal Society in 1703, when Hooke was safely buried, and was knighted in 1705. Again he became embroiled in fierce disputes, with the astronomer John Flamsteed and the philosopher Gottfried Leibniz, but he now had sufficient authority to support his wrath, and that may have protected him from the possibility of another breakdown. He finally prepared *Opticks* for publication in 1704, but he augmented the text twice, in the Latin edition of 1706 and a second English edition of 1717–1718, incorporating new material derived from his general physical theories. He imported similar new material into a second edition of the *Principia* in 1713. The final versions of his two key works completed the definitive edition of his model of the universe. Some of his less adventurous esoteric studies were posthumously published as *The Chronology of Ancient Kingdoms Amended* (1728) and *Observations upon the Prophecies of Daniel and the Apocalypse of St. John* (1733).

Newton became the primary symbol of the New Science among litterateurs. When he died, Allan Ramsay wrote an *Ode* in his memory and Alexander Pope wrote an epitaph for him: "Nature and Nature's laws lay hid in night; / God said, Let Newton be! and all was light!" William Wordsworth characterised him in "The Prelude" (1805) as "Newton with his prism and silent face, / The marble index of a mind for ever / Voyaging through strange seas of thought, alone", while James Thomson—who also wrote "A Poem Sacred to the Memory of Sir Isaac Newton" (1727)—described him in "The Seasons" (1726–1730; rev. 1744) as "Newton, pure intelligence, whom God / To mortals lent to trace his boundless works". Other tributes included Richard Glover's "A Poem on Newton", which was printed in Henry Pemberton's *A View of Sir Isaac Newton's Philosophy* (1728), but a more profound philosophical influence can been seen in such poems as Richard Blackmore's "The Creation" (1712), David Mallett's "The Excursion" (1728), Henry Baker's "The Universe" (1734), and Henry Brooke's "Universal Beauty" (1735).

For those hostile to the produce of the scientific revolution, Newton became the great antagonist. A famous illustration by William Blake shows him crouched in a craven pose, equipped with measuring dividers similar to those employed by the Creator (of whom Blake also disapproved). Blake bracketed Newton with Francis Bacon and John Locke as leading enemies of "vision", allegedly offering up the regular prayer "May God us Keep From Single vision and Newton sleep" and complaining in one of his notebooks that "The Atoms of Democritas / And Newton's particles of Light / Are sands upon the Red sea shore, / Where Israel's tents do shine so bright"). The artist Benjamin Haydon recalled Charles Lamb abusing him for putting Newton's head into a picture, and calling on John Keats to support his allegation that Newtonian analysis had destroyed the poetry of the rainbow—support that Keats was glad to lend. The Romantics were not all of one mind on the issue—Samuel Taylor Coleridge complimented Newton's "serener eye" in *Religious Musings*—but the antagonistic clamour proved to be more easily audible in the literary world.

Blake's argument was not new; before Newton had published either of his masterworks, Margaret Cavendish had written *Observations upon Experimental Philosophy* (1666) in response to Hooke's *Micrographia*, appending to it a "romantical" and "fantastical" Utopian romance, *The Description of a New World, Called the Blazing World*, which expresses the anxiety that the wonderful discoveries of the Enlightenment might obscure a broader vision based in occult philosophy. Voltaire, on the other hand, saw Newton as a welcome flood of common sense, cleansing philosophy's Augean stables of undesirable detritus; he popularised Newtonian ideas in *Éléments de la philosophie de Newton* (1738), after his lover, Émilie du Chatelet, had translated the *Principia* into French; he also imported them into his *contes philosophiques, especially *Micromégas* (1752). The contrast between these two viewpoints became acute in the early nineteenth century, and not merely in the context of *Romanticism. David Brewster's *Life of Sir Isaac Newton* (1831) popularised an anecdote about Newton's dog, Diamond, upsetting a candle in 1692 and destroying several years' work, threatening the delicate balance of his mind—a balance that came under increasing scrutiny as the science of *psychology evolved.

Newton seemed to some proto-psychologists to be a perfect illustration of the alleged link between genius and madness, and the retrospective analysis of his personality provided fertile ground for speculative psychoanalysts. The notion that his scientific analyses were a product of abnormal psychology gained ground in the twentieth century, when Newton was initially diagnosed as "schizoid" and later as a victim of Asperger's syndrome. Anthony Storr's *The Dynamics of Creation* (1972) holds up Newton and Albert *Einstein as paradigmatic examples of "schizoid creativity", although Newton's resentful and vituperative tendencies contrast strikingly with Einstein's placid pacifism. Frank Manuel's *A Portrait of Isaac Newton* (1968) attributed Newton's breakdowns to repressed homosexual feelings, calling attention to his relationship with Fatio de Duillier. Such speculations, combined with the belated revelation of the full extent of Newton's occult investigations, added a certain ambivalence to his heroic status.

Newton's appearances as a literary character include his alleged reincarnation in Jakub Jan Arbes' surreal "Newtonuv mozek" (ca. 1866; trans. as "Newton's Brain") and his anachronistic inclusion in the crew of a pioneering space rocket in Konstatin Tsiolkovsky's *Vne zemli* (written 1896–1920; trans. as "Outside the Earth"). Manly Wade Wellman recruited him to a similarly symbolic cause in *Giants from Eternity* (1939; book, 1959). In Randall Garrett's satirical alternative history "Gentlemen: Please Note" (1957), military and academic authorities prove so obdurate in their incomprehension of the practical applications of fluxions to ballistics that Newton gives up on science and becomes a clergyman. In J. Gregory Keyes' Age of Unreason series, launched by *Newton's Cannon* (1998), he is a rather ominous background presence, but in Neal Stephenson's Baroque Cycle, comprising *Quicksilver* (2003), *The Confusion* (2004), and *The System of the World*

(2004), he is the pivot on which the whole scheme turns. In Gregory *Benford's "Newton's Sleep" (1968, in Janet E. Morris' *Heroes in Hell*), Newton is one of three personal heroes encountered by the author's alter ego, the others being Ernest Hemingway and Che Guevara.

NIVEN, LARRY (I.E., LAURENCE) (VAN COTT) (1938–)

U.S. writer. He attended the California Institute of Technology in Pasadena from 1956 to 1958 before continuing his education at Washburn University, Topeka, Kansas, obtaining his B.A. in mathematics in 1962. He then spent a year doing graduate work at the University of California, Los Angeles. He was financially supported at this time by a trust fund established by his great-grandfather on his mother's side of the family; he recalled his father saying to him on his twenty-first birthday words to the effect of "Here's a million dollars, son—don't lose it", but he was enthusiastic to make his own way in life as a writer.

Niven began publishing science fiction in 1964, quickly establishing a reputation as a definitive writer of *hard science fiction. Although he wrote a certain amount of comic material and chimerical science-fantasy, his most important early venture was the development of an elaborate future history of expansion into "Known Space", involving surprising discoveries about the origin of the human species and its relationship to the exotic Pak Protectors, and crucial encounters with other intriguing alien races, including the paranoid Puppeteers and the feline Kzin. The early short stories in this series were first collected as *Neutron Star* (1968), the book being titled for the most notable of them, but a definitive collection was eventually assembled, along with an explanatory chronology, in *Tales of Known Space* (1975).

Some of Niven's other work from the first phase of his career subjected familiar ideas to further extrapolation and careful reanalysis, as in the re-examination of the notion of *alternative histories held in a multiverse of *parallel worlds in "All the Myriad Ways" (1968). "Inconstant Moon" (1972) is a fine *conte philosophique* in which the Moon suddenly increases dramatically in brightness, suggesting to scientifically aware Americans that the Sun might have gone nova and that dawn will bring devastation, although there is also a possibility that it might be the result of a brief solar flare whose destructive effects will be confined to the Earth's day side.

The early novels in the Known Space series were *World of Ptavvs* (1966), *Protector* (short version,

1967; book, 1973), *A Gift from Earth* (1968), and *Ringworld* (1970); the last named, featuring a massive alien artefact—a narrow slice from a *Dyson sphere—became his most successful early work and an emblem of his determination to maintain rigorous rational plausibility; objections to the viability of the artefact raised by readers were carefully compensated in *Ringworld Engineers* (1979), and further refinements were introduced in the subsequent sequels *The Ringworld Throne* (1996) and *Ringworld's Children* (2003).

Other works spun off from the early phases of the future history included a series of futuristic mysteries, three of which were reprinted in *The Long ARM of Gil Hamilton* (1976), while the fourth was issued separately as *The Patchwork Girl* (1980). The later phases of the future history provided a backcloth for a *tour de force* of *exobiological speculation detailing a planetless ecosphere distributed around a star, comprising *The Integral Trees* (1984) and *The Smoke Ring* (1987). Another sector of the scenario was opened up to other writers in a series of shared world anthologies detailing *The Man-Kzin Wars* (4 vols., 1988–1991).

The main sequence of Niven's light-hearted comedies is a series extrapolating the ingenious tradition of time *paradox stories; it includes the short stories collected in *A Hole in Space* (1974) and the novel *Rainbow Mars* (1999). *The Magic Goes Away* (1978), the final item in a brief heroic fantasy series, examines the predicament of a society whose magical world is undergoing a metaphysical metamorphosis into the world described by science. The protagonist of *A World out of Time* (1976), whose personality has been relocated in another man's body, returns to the solar system after a three-million-year excursion through space-time to find its society changed in various ominous ways, and embarks upon a quest for an unusual *longevity technology. *Destiny's Road* (1997) is a grim planetary romance in which the failure of one group of would-be colonists to adjust to the awkward reality of their situation is severely punished by their allegedly wiser counterparts.

Much of Niven's later work was written in collaboration; he formed an early partnership with Jerry Pournelle, whose libertarian political views he shared. Their earliest works in collaboration were the nostalgic but sophisticated space opera *The Mote in God's Eye* (1974) and the calculatedly irreverent Dantean fantasy *Inferno* (1976), in which a comatose science fiction writer's guide to Hell turns out to be Benito Mussolini. They followed the latter with a definitive account of the effects of an *asteroid strike, *Lucifer's Hammer* (1977). *Oath of Fealty* (1981) is a political fantasy set in an arcology—a vast building containing an entire city. *Footfall* (1985) is a story of alien invasion that the writers had originally intended to incorporate into *Lucifer's Hammer* but had been persuaded to leave out in order not to compromise its potential as a best-selling *disaster story. *The Gripping Hand* (1993; aka *The Moat Around Murcheson's Eye*) added a belated sequel to *The Mote in God's Eye*.

A third partner was added to the Niven-Pournelle partnership when Steven Barnes joined them to produce an elaborate account of difficult *colonisation transfiguring the legend of Beowulf, *The Legacy of Heorot* (1987) and *Beowulf's Children* (1995). Between the two elements of the couplet Michael F. Flynn joined Niven and Pournelle as a third participant in the tongue-in-cheek political fantasy *Fallen Angels* (1991), which describes an utterly horrid future in which the majority of people are steadfastly opposed to space travel, science, and science fiction, forcing science fiction fans to become the core of a subversive underground movement. Niven also collaborated with Barnes on a series about an ultimate theme park making extravagant use of *virtual reality technology, begun with *Dream Park* (1981), the disaster story *The Descent of Anansi* (1982), and the futuristic thrillers *Achilles' Choice* (1991) and *Saturn's Race* (2000).

The extent of Niven's collaborations is striking evidence of the extent to which seriously intended hard science fiction is a collective endeavour obliquely mirroring the collective endeavour of science; hypotheses introduced by one writer are routinely taken up for further extrapolation by others, often resulting in productive dialogues and synergistic effects. He was virtually unique in undertaking this kind of work solely as a vocation, his inheritance having given him the freedom to do anything he wished, or nothing at all, but his potential disregard for commercial considerations never led him into esotericism; he was always determined to write for a substantial, if somewhat select, audience. His work showed a certain loss of innovative energy over the years—as is far from uncommon, among scientists and writers alike—but the rigor of his method was never compromised, and he remained a key exemplar of his genre into the twenty-first century.

NOVA

A stellar explosion that produces a bright but temporary object in the night sky; the phenomenon was sometimes confused by early astronomers with *comets. The attentive observation of one such "new star" by Tycho Brahe, John *Dee, and others in 1572, followed by the observation of another by John *Kepler in 1604, offered significant evidence that the heavens were subject to change, greatly assisting the progress of new *cosmological theories.

Records of previous events of a similar kind had been made by ancient astronomers, including one that might have been the Biblical Star of Bethlehem. *Astrologers had considered them to be omens, and that seemed for a long time to be their principal literary utility, given the impossibility of any more active engagement with Earthly affairs—although J. S. Fletcher's "The New Sun" (1923) did try to contrive a (highly implausible) close encounter. The possibility that the *Sun might go nova had little potential in *disaster stories because the resultant destruction would be absolute, although provision for the event's aftermath to be briefly witnessed was made in Simon Newcomb's "The End of the World" (1903).

The prospect of surviving the Sun going nova—thus permitting its integration into melodramatic works of fiction—emerged with the popularisation of the myth of the *Space Age. Far-futuristic humankind must emigrate to avoid the Sun's fate in John W. Campbell Jr.'s "The Voice of the Void" (1930), while a few near future spacefarers are fortunate enough to survive the Sun's unanticipated explosion in Joseph W. Skidmore's "Dramatis Personae" (1931). Aliens come to the aid of humans who have used suspended animation to escape the worst effects of the Sun's explosion in E. V. Raymond's "Nova Solis" (1935).

The latter themes were combined in Arthur C. Clarke's "Rescue Party" (1946), in which humankind proves not to need alien assistance to cope with the Sun's extinction. Robert Sheckley's "Potential" (1953) is a story of survival similar in spirit to Clarke's, while the opening sentence of Theodore Sturgeon's "The Skills of Xanadu" (1956) casually records that the Sun has gone nova before progressing to the substance of the story. George O. Smith's *Fire in the Heavens* (1958) is a more orthodox disaster-threat story. Arthur Clarke made further use of the notion in "The Star" (1955), in which human spacefarers discover the worlds devastated by the explosion of the Star of Bethlehem, and "The Songs of Distant Earth" (1958; exp. book, 1986), in which human colonies survive among the stars after the Sun's explosion.

Artificially induced novas soon became the ultimate *weapon of flamboyant space opera. They were a favourite device of Edmond Hamilton, first introduced as a threat in "The Universe Wreckers" (1930) and subsequently deployed several times over, coming into sharp focus in "Starman Come Home" (1954; book 1959 as *The Sun Smasher*) and *Doomstar* (1966). Sun-smashing acts of war or revenge became a standard climactic flourish of such crude works as the pseudonymous Karl Zeigfreid's *Beyond the Galaxy* and *Chaos in Arcturus* (both 1953), and acquired an even more flamboyant gloss in Norman Spinrad's account of the ultimate booby-trap bomb in *The Solarians* (1966). Spinrad also deployed the motif in his ironic apocalyptic fantasy "The Big Flash" (1969).

The largest novas—including those observed by Tycho and Kepler—were renamed supernovas in 1934 to distinguish them from lesser events. Supernovas only occur a few times per century in a galaxy like the Milky Way (as opposed to twenty-five lesser novas per year), but Fred *Hoyle's investigation of the manner in which stars produce heavier elements by fusion revealed that they play a key role in galactic evolution by producing large quantities of heavy elements and scattering them over interstellar distances.

Hoyle's work suggested that all the elements in the solar system with atomic weights greater than iron had originated from a distant supernova, and that the solar system was a "second generation" phenomenon. The realisation that we and our world are largely made of supernova debris ("stardust") was a considerable inspiration to late twentieth-century literary imagery, plangently echoed in the chorus of Joni Mitchell's song "Woodstock" (1969) and the final words of Paul Newman's 1972 film version of Paul Zindel's play *The Effects of Gamma Rays on Man-in-the-Moon Marigolds* (1965), and adding a new dimension to such disaster-anticipation stories as Hoyle's *The Inferno* (1973; with Geoffrey Hoyle).

The further theorisation of supernovas established that they occur when the core of an aging star collapses into a neutron star or—in extreme cases—a *black hole. Both these concepts made considerable contributions to the imaginative vocabulary of speculative fiction, the former making a notable debut in Larry Niven's "Neutron Star" (1968). Evidence of the existence of neutron stars was provided by pulsars—astronomical objects that produce intermittent beams of radio waves—the first of which was discovered in 1967; a pulsar was identified at the heart of the supernova debris known as the Crab Nebula in 1969.

Other phenomena of a similar kind, discovered in 1973 by X-ray astronomers, were labelled bursters; they are thought to be explosions caused when accretion to the surface of a neutron star reaches a critical point, and are incorporated into such speculative fictions as Greg Egan's *Diaspora* (1997). A further discrimination of Type I and Type II supernovas prepared the way for observations of supernovas in distant galaxies by Saul Perlmutter and others using the Hubble Space Telescope, which proved—contrary to expectations—that the expansion of the universe appeared to have accelerated over time, posing a challenge to cosmological theorists.

Science fiction stories establishing circumstances that enable human observers to study distant supernovas—sometimes attempting rescue missions in the process—include Poul Anderson's "Supernova" (1966; aka "Day of Burning"), Stephen Tall's "The Bear with the Knot on His Tail" (1971), Michael McCollum's *Antares Dawn* (1986), Robert Silverberg's "The Iron Star" (1987), and Jeffrey Carver's *From a Changeling Star* (1989) and *Down the Steam of Stars* (1990). Sophisticated disaster stories involving actual or anticipated supernovas include Richard Cowper's *The Twilight of Briareus* (1974), Alice Sheldon's *Brightness Falls from the Air* (1985; by-lined James Tiptree Jr.), Doug Beason's "Ben Franklin's Laser" (1990), and Roger McBride Allen and Eric Kotani's *Supernova* (1991). In Edward Bryant's "Particle Theory" (1977), a galactic "plague" of supernovas brings intimations of mortality to an astronomer, but the definitive science-fictional exploration of the potential symbolic significance of the motif is Samuel R. Delany's *Nova* (1968).

NUCLEAR POWER

Energy derived from controlled nuclear fission reactions—or, potentially, from nuclear fusion reactions—usually used in the generation of *electricity. Although the phenomenon of *radioactivity had been familiar for some time, and Enrico Fermi had begun bombarding various elements with neutrons in the 1930s, the possibility of using a controlled nuclear chain reaction as a power source emerged from experiments conducted in 1938 by Otto Hahn and Fritz Strassman, along with the possibility of making *atom bombs.

The first controlled chain reaction was established in 1942 in a reactor established by Fermi at the University of Chicago. Subsequent experimental work on the fissibility of uranium-235 and plutonium-239 was conducted in the context of the Manhattan Project, but when the war was over the research was rapidly diversified, the building of nuclear power stations becoming a key target. The Atomic Energy Commission was set up in 1946 to promote and control the development of nuclear energy in the United States.

The idea of setting up a "breeder" reaction—in which a reaction started by U-235 would prompt U-238 to produce Pu-239 at a faster rate than the U-235 was consumed—prompted the building of an experimental reactor in Idaho, which first operated successfully in 1951. It proved easier to control reactions in which plutonium and other fission products were washed out with water; when such systems were pressurised—in pressurised water reactors (PWRs)—the heat generated by the system became adequate to generate electricity.

Commercial reactors made rapid progress in the early 1950s, assisted by the demand for plutonium from the weapons industry. The establishment of a gas-cooled reactor at Windscale in the United Kingdom (since renamed Sellafield) pioneered a new generation of reactors. When the demand for plutonium was reduced as a result of strategic arms treaties, however, the plutonium was effectively reduced to the status of problematic "waste" that needed "reprocessing" before it could be reused in other reactors—a change that transformed the economics of the industry. By the early 1960s, there were more than two hundred reactors of various types operating in the United States, but Western Europe still had fewer than fifty in 1970, and the economic transformation restricted their subsequent proliferation. The situation was further constrained when the prospect of catastrophic nuclear accidents was brought into sharp focus by meltdowns at Three Mile Island in 1979 and Chernobyl, Ukraine, in 1986. The nuclear power program received a new boost, however, when the contribution made by conventional coal- and oil-burning power stations to global warming via *greenhouse gas emissions became a political issue at the end of the twentieth century.

The theory of nuclear fusion advanced in step with that of nuclear fission after Hans Bethe proposed in 1939 that the energy of stars is derived from fusion reactions. The possibility of creating such a reaction was rapidly and successfully fed into nuclear weapons research, but the problem of stabilising and controlling such powerful reactions posed much greater technical difficulties than those involved in the development of fission reactors. Many enthusiasts for nuclear power thought of fission reactors as a mere stepping-stone to fusion reactors that would solve humankind's power-supply problems for good, but the problem of stabilising a fusion reaction for long-term maintenance proved extremely frustrating following the establishment of experimental fusion devices in the United States and the USSR in 1953 and at Harwell in the United Kingdom in 1954.

A new cycle of fusion research began in the 1970s when several new reactors based on the Soviet Tokamak model were built—including the Joint European Torus (JET)—but there was a marked contraction in funding in the 1980s in response to a further round of disappointing results. In 1989, B. Stanley Pons and Martin Fleischmann claimed to have produced fusion reactions in deuterium atoms at room temperature with the aid of a palladium electrode; a National Cold Fusion Institute was immediately founded in Utah, but attempts to duplicate the experiment elsewhere failed and interest in the possibility dwindled rapidly. By the end of the century, the possibility of fusion power had come to seem chimerical.

The notion of a stabilised atomic power source had been used in fiction long before the first nuclear chain reaction was produced, as soon as Albert Einstein published his famous equation $E=mc^2$. Atomic power was used as a means of spaceship propulsion in Garrett P. Serviss's *A Columbus of Space* (1909), and the notion became a staple of pulp science fiction. Hugo Gernsback wrote an editorial on "The Wonders of Atomic Power" in the May 1932 issue of *Wonder Stories*. John W. Campbell Jr.'s first published story, "When the Atoms Failed" (1930), assumed such a power source, and he developed the idea further in such stories as "Blindness" (1935; by-lined Don A. Stuart). As soon as he became editor of *Astounding Science Fiction* in 1937, Campbell wrote an article advertising the possibility of nuclear power, "Atomic Generator", and continued to respond to new research findings in "Isotope 235" (1939) and "Atomic Ringmaster" (1940), both of which were by-lined Arthur McCann.

Campbell frequently discussed the implications of these developments in his editorials, and actively encouraged his writers to consider the possibilities seriously, feeding them ideas that resulted in such works as Harl Vincent "Power Plant" (1939), Theodore Sturgeon's highly atypical "Artnan Process" (1941)—whose plot hinges on the problems of isotope separation—and Robert A. Heinlein's "Blowups Happen" (1940), about the psychological and social stresses generated by the establishment of an urban nuclear power plant. The latter theme was further expanded in Lester del Rey's *Nerves* (1942; exp. 1956), in which an accident in a nuclear power station threatens to turn into a major disaster. Clifford D. Simak's "Lobby" (1944) anticipates the political problems involved in the introduction of atomic power to the United States.

After 1945, atomic power plants were frequently employed in science fiction as sources of quasimagical *mutation, but in the shadow of Hiroshima they also came to seem even more problematic than they had before. The protagonist of Henry Kuttner and C. L. Moore's *Tomorrow and Tomorrow* (1947; book 1951, by-lined Lewis Padgett), employed at Uranium Pile Number One under the auspices of the Global Peace Corporation, is afflicted by futuristic dreams prompting him to start a chain reaction leading to a third world war, which might be prelude to Utopia or annihilation. Kelley Edwards' "Radiation" (1952) revisited the theme of *Nerves* in an ominous account of the aftermath of a "minor" accident in a nuclear power plant.

As nuclear power became a reality, the issues treated in "Blowups Happen" and *Nerves* passed into the field of naturalistic fiction, where their exploration was undertaken in such novels as Henri Queffélec's *Combat contre l'invisible* (1958; trans. as *Frontier of the Unknown*) and Daniel Keyes' *The Touch* (1968), and into such technothrillers as Christopher Hodder-Williams' *The Main Experiment* (1964) and Thomas N. Scortia and Frank M. Robinson's *The Prometheus Crisis* (1975). The use of speculative fiction to extrapolate the moral, political, and practical issues inherent in the use of nuclear power was, however, robustly continued in such stories as H. Beam Piper's "Day of the Moron" (1951), Poul Anderson's "The Disintegrating Sky" (1953) and "Progress" (1962), Boyd Ellanby's "Chain Reaction" (1956), and Wade Curtis' "Power to the People" (1972).

The meltdown at Chernobyl—dramatised by Frederik Pohl in the documentary novel *Chernobyl* (1987)—renewed interest in nuclear power stations as potential agents of disaster, and the fact that Three Mile Island happened on U.S. soil sharpened local interest even further. Anxieties regarding nuclear accidents and the contaminant effects of nuclear waste were explored in such works as John Clagett's *The Orange R* (1978), the film *The China Syndrome* (1979), Michael McCollum's "Scoop" (1979), and Michael Swanwick's *In the Drift* (1984). Opinions within the genre as to the wisdom of maintaining nuclear power programs became polarised as alarmist fiction became a significant battleground for anti-nuclear propaganda. Champions of nuclear power made its preservation or revivification a condition of recovery from global catastrophe in Larry Niven and Jerry Pournelle's *Lucifer's Hammer* (1977) and Poul Anderson's *Orion Shall Rise* (1983).

The possibility of a breakthrough in fusion research helped to maintain optimism among fictional propagandists for nuclear power, the anticipated moment being invested with transcendental implications in Herbert Jacob Bernstein's tongue-in-cheek "Phantasmaplasmagloria" (1968)—which was not billed as story on *Analog*'s contents page—and Kevin J. Anderson and Doug Beason's earnest "Reflections in a Magnetic Mirror" (1988). Abundant energy produced by nuclear fusion is the lynch-pin of the various Utopian futures sketched out in alternative images of the year 2000 designed by Mack Reynolds, beginning with *Looking Backward from the Year 2000* (1973)—a reliance which made the entire project seem sadly redundant when that year actually arrived. Fusion reactions figured in disaster stories too, as in Martin Caidin's *Star Bright* (1980). A "low-energy fusion" device was featured in Christopher Anvil's "The Gold of Galileo" (1980) some time before the flurry of excitement generated by cold fusion, but it went awry. Paul Levinson's cold fusion story "Late Lessons" (1999) was no more optimistic.

O

OCCULT SCIENCE

The term occult is derived from a Latin word meaning "hidden", but its significance was extrapolated to a more general suggestion of mystery, routinely applied to matters beyond common understanding, and hence to the supernatural. The term "occult science" is often used merely as an umbrella term embracing such disciplines as *alchemy and *astrology, but it also signifies a complex network of parallels and analogies between such disciplines, secured by their common descent from *Pythagorean and neo-Platonic philosophy. Such analogical connections formed the sinews of Mediaeval mysticism, and provided a fundamental core linking the philosophies of many writers who wanted to retain a holistic and intimate notion of the universe in the face of its infinite expansion and dispersion by *Newtonian science.

The most important neo-Platonic philosopher was Plotinus, whose *Enneads* were assembled by his disciple Porphyry. The fundamental holism of Plotinus' thought was embodied in the notion that the intelligibility of the world had to be attained by a threefold path—integrating the routes to understanding followed by the Musician, the Lover, and the Philosopher—and a key analogy likening and linking the *microcosm of the human soul to the *macrocosmic motions of the heavens. The fifth book of the third Ennead introduced the notion that every human being has an accompanying "daemon", which was invested by some later writers with a visible aspect and personal character; it made a spectacular return to literary fantasy in Philip Pullman's *His Dark Materials* (1995–2000).

Porphyry's chief successor, Iamblichus, attempted to reconcile all forms of religion within a single syncretic system, with the sole exception of Christianity—a response to the Christians' determined exclusivity that established a crucial rivalry whose effects were long lasting, permanently colouring Christian attitudes to neo-Platonist ideas and causing problems in the Renaissance for philosophers who wanted to recover the legacy of Neoplatonism along with other Classical learning. The satanic taint attached to such ideas was a major cause of the care with which they were dressed up and mystified by scholars, especially within the field of alchemy—to the extent that Mysticism became a significant topic in its own right, sprawling across the boundaries of church doctrine. The repopularisation of the Hermetic tradition, which prompted a considerable "occult revival" in nineteenth-century Europe, was assisted by a significant dissertation on Mysticism affixed by Barthelemy Saint-Hilaire to his prize-winning *Rapport* (1841).

The revivification and mystification of the Pythagorean and neo-Platonic traditions in Renaissance Europe continued the syncretising efforts of Iamblichus by incorporating another holistic and mystical tradition that similarly claimed descent from antiquity: the Jewish Kabbalah. This new synthesis eventually came to be called the Hermetic tradition, because of its alleged origins in the works of the legendary Hermes Trismegistus—to whom a passing reference had been made by St. Augustine in *De Civitate Dei*. Two significant documents relating to this supposed tradition began to circulate in manuscript in the fifteenth century, a copy of one of which—the *Corpus Hermeticum*—was acquired by Cosimo de Medici in 1460 and given to the neo-Platonist scholar Marsilio Ficino. Ficino's version of the *Corpus*, together with his commentary and extrapolations of its claims, was widely circulated; its admirers included the infamous Rodrigo Borgia, who became Pope Alexander VI, and Giordano Bruno, one of the most prominent advocates of the heliocentric theory of cosmology.

The idea of the Hermetic tradition was remarkably flexible, and its elasticity was seized upon by such determined innovators as *Paracelsus, who became the first of a new breed of inventive occultists bent on usurping ancient authority and claiming its nebulous weight for their own ideas. Paracelsian occultism played a significant background role in the ideological and actual conflicts associated with the Reformation, whose consequent wars of religion made sixteenth-century Europe exceedingly turbulent. The notion of hidden traditions of supernatural belief and activity also became confused with the witch-hunts pursued by peripatetic friars, cropping up insistently in such philosophical studies as Reginald Scot's *The Discoverie of Witchcraft* (1584), whose scathing scepticism was not reflected in the abundant Elizabethan and Jacobean literature it helped to inspire.

The *Corpus Hermeticum* was exposed as a fraud in 1614 by Isaac Casaubon, who traced many of its sources and identified some of its anachronisms, but Casaubon's scepticism had no more effect than Scot's. Time had, in any case, moved on; the very same year saw the emergence of a new and spectacularly successful mystical mythology cast in the Paracelsian mould, originated on Paracelsus' home ground. The new occult philosophy made its debut in a pamphlet generally known as the *Fama Fraternitus*, which offered a brief biography of a magician named Christian Rosenkreutz; it was followed by the *Confessio Frateritas* (1615), which described his magical initiation, and then by the allegorical *Chymische Hochzeit Christiani Rosenkreuz* (1616; trans. as *The Heretick Romance; or, the Chymical Wedding*). The third of these items was signed by Johann Valentin Andreae—who was later to publish the Utopian romance *Christianopolis* (1619)—and who may well have written all three.

The Rosicrucian pamphlets excited an enormous amount of attention as would-be members searched high and low for the mysterious Brotherhood of the Rosy Cross. One early enthusiast for Rosicrucianism was the English philosopher Robert Fludd, who published two apologias for the Brotherhood before setting out to write his own encyclopaedia of the *macrocosm and the *microcosm between 1617 and 1626. He engaged in fierce arguments with John *Kepler, who criticised his anthropocentric cosmology in *Harmonies mundi*. Fludd's account of the macrocosm fused the Aristotelian cosmology of the Church with neo-Platonic ideas and infusions from the Kabbalah, while his account of the human microcosm—which he never completed—was a grandiose synthesis of contemporary anatomy, mystical interpretations of the body's proportions, *astrological linkages between various organs and the signs of the zodiac, neo-Pythagorean theories of musical harmony, and so on. He went on to develop new theories of *medicine—harassed by critics who claimed that his treatments were useless—and analyses of "Mosaic philosophy" that laid the groundwork for Isaac *Newton's Biblical studies.

A similar spirit of encyclopaedic inclusivity is represented in the work of the unorthodox Jesuit and pioneering Egyptologist Athanasius Kircher, who published his first book—one of several treatises on *magnetism—in 1631, a year before witnessing the trial of *Galileo in Rome. Kircher was careful to maintain discretion in his own writings on astronomy and optics and, like Fludd, remained an obstinate geocentrist. He allowed himself greater extravagance in two significant imaginary voyages; *Itinerarium extaticum* (1656; aka *Iter exstaticum*) described an excursion through the Aristotelian heavens, while *Iter exstaticum II* (1657) described a journey within the Earth; the latter provided a prologue to his most successful work, *Mundus subterraneus* (1665–1678), an early account of *geology. He too diversified into Biblical studies in speculative accounts of the roles played by the Deluge and the Tower of Babel in the evolution of languages.

Fludd and Kircher were, in a way, truer "Renaissance men" than Kepler and Galileo, in that they were interested in the entire spectrum of human knowledge and in binding all of it together into a coherent whole. The only way that such a whole could be held together, however, was by means of essentially mystical connections, which allowed apparent contradictions between belief and evidence to be set aside in favour of some underlying harmony representable in exotic symbolism and geometrical patterns. In retrospect, it is easy to see that the Age of Reason was making rapid progress by sifting, testing, and selectively discarding ideas and propositions, and that the scientific refinement of truth was moving in the opposite direction to the occult quest to bind all kinds of ideas into a single philosophical system, but it was not so obvious at the time.

What the occult scientific quest for holistic connection lacked in rational plausibility, it made up in psychological *plausibility; its syncretic generosity had considerable *aesthetic attractions, which impressions of esotericism and secrecy could only magnify. The Newtonian revolution could not sweep away the mystical geocentrism of men like Fludd and Kircher, but it did sweep it under the carpet of orthodoxy, into an esoteric ecological niche to which it was very well adapted. Geocentrism was not, however, an essential component of mysticism, whose microcosmic and macrocosmic analogies could easily be reformulated in a heliocentric mould, as Emmanuel *Swedenborg set out to do. Charles Fourier's *Théories de l'unité universelle* (1822) attempted something similar, asserting that the macrocosmic force of gravity has a microcosmic analogue that provides the driving force of progress; like Swedenborg, Fourier attempted to describe life on the other worlds of the solar system, and also offered futurological descriptions of technological advancement. Like Swedenborg, he became a great inspiration to numerous disciples, who founded dozens of Fourierist communities—most of them in the United States—based on his model of the *phalange*, usually translated into English (as in a notable scientific romance by Grant Allen) as "phalanstery".

The Rosicrucian renewal of the Hermetic tradition had a powerful effect on literary fantasy; it is a Rosicrucian who provides the protagonist with the "philosophical microscope" used to observe Mercury in the Chevalier de Béthune's *Relation du monde de Mercure* (1750), and his kindred hover in the background of much subsequent French imaginative fiction, including the philosophical components of Honoré de Balzac's celebration of the *Comédie Humaine*. Edward Bulwer-Lytton's depiction of a Rosicrucian sage in *Zanoni* (1842) was a major inspiration to subsequent lifestyle fantasists as well as writers of occult fiction, and Robert Hunt's *Panthea, the Spirit of Nature* (1849) testifies to the enduring appeal of Rosicrucian mysticism, even to a man who became one of the foremost exponents of the *popularisation of empirical science. Bulwer-Lytton peppered the serial version of *A Strange Story*—published in Charles Dickens' *All the Year Round* in 1861–1862—with footnotes referring to contemporary science and the Bridgewater treatises on natural *theology as well as arcane sources, and he attempted a further synthesis of contemporary physics and occult science in his scientific romance *A Coming Race* (1871).

Some of those tempted by this kind of synthesising, like Robert Hunt, eventually plumped for pragmatic science, but others went to the opposite extreme in becoming ardent scholarly and lifestyle fantasists. The most flamboyant was "Éliphas Lévi", the pseudonym adopted by the failed littérateur Alphonse Louis Constant, whose *Dogme et rituel de la haute magie* (1854–1856; trans. as *The Doctrine and Ritual*

of Transcendental Magic*) and highly fanciful *Histoire de la magie* (1859; trans. as *The History of Magic*) became the principal sourcebooks of all subsequent handbooks of "high magic". They prompted the foundation of numerous "Rosicrucian lodges", whose example spread far and wide from Paris—where their most enthusiastic propagandists included Joséphin Péladan and Édouard Schuré, both of whom made elaborate use of fiction in popularising their ideas. The most celebrated English lodge of this stripe was the Order of the Golden Dawn, which attracted numerous literary men of some note, including W. B. Yeats, Arthur Machen, and Aleister Crowley.

The most successful new synthesis emergent from the nineteenth-century occult revival was Theosophy, founded by Madame Blavatsky, whose *The Secret Doctrine: The Synthesis of Science, Religion, and Philosophy* (1888) drew extensively on nineteenth-century *anthropology in compiling a highly imaginative account of the *evolution of humankind, which featured seven "root races" (two of which had yet to materialise) associated with various primordial continents, including Hyperborea, Lemuria, and Atlantis. Theosophical ideas spawned an entire subgenre of literary fantasy, overflowing abundantly into popular pulp fiction, where they made a significant mark on early "sword and sorcery" fiction by Robert E. Howard and his contemporaries. The most successful writer of "occult science fiction" was Marie Corelli, who was the best-selling writer in the English language during the *fin-de-siècle*, promoting her own idiosyncratic synthesis of ideas drawn from contemporary science—including *electricity and *radioactivity—with Christian mysticism in such works as *A Romance of Two Worlds* (1886), *Ardath* (1889), *The Soul of Lilith* (1892), and *The Secret Power* (1921).

Blavatsky and Corelli formed the tip of a huge conglomerate iceberg, whose components extended into the field of *parapsychology descendent from Spiritualism, and into the *fourth-dimensional mysticism of writers like C. H. *Hinton. The same syncretic impulse is manifest in all of the most popular exercises in *pseudoscience, including the works of such writers as Immanuel Velikovsky, Erich von Däniken, Lyall Watson, Robert Temple, and Graham Hancock. This is not surprising, given that the most obvious source of psychological plausibility is the impulse to search for hidden connections, and to make patterns out of them that will serve as guides to action and preparatory thought. The notion of a hidden "science" that might somehow "complete" the recognised one, by reconnecting it to and reamalgamating it with various kinds of religious and traditional notions, continues to thrive in such fields as alternative *medicine, whose various cults are proud to describe themselves as "holistic" in defiant opposition to the "reductionism" of empirical science.

The intimate association within occult science of scholarly, literary, and lifestyle fantasies extended throughout the twentieth century. Its syncretic enthusiasm did not balk at such tongue-in-cheek exercises as the works of Charles *Fort, and animated countless idiosyncratic clusters of ideas that seemed utterly bizarre and frankly crazy to uninvolved onlookers. The cultish adherents of such occult microsyntheses were perfectly prepared to borrow from science fiction as well as science in producing new occult philosophies and mythologies; the advent of *flying saucers in 1947 merely provided new grist to an inexorably grinding mill.

The literary treatment of *history made ample room available for secret histories integrated by all manner of occult connections, producing the first huge best-seller of the twenty-first century in Dan Brown's *The Da Vinci Code* (2003). Much past-set science fiction produced immediately before and after the end of the twentieth century displayed a conspicuous nostalgia for one or other Golden Age of occult science, and for the great synthesis that it might have wrought but never could; Mary Gentle's alternative history *1610: A Sundial in a Grave* (2004), whose hero is Robert Fludd, is a paradigmatic example.

OMEGA POINT

A term coined by the evolutionary philosopher Pierre Teilhard de Chardin to describe his notion of the divinely ordained terminus of the human historical narrative. The phrase refers back to Revelation 1:8—"I am Alpha and Omega, the beginning and the ending, saith the Lord". The key word had been used in a similar context before, notably in the English title of Camille Flammarion's *La fin du monde* (1894; trans. as *Omega: The Last Days of the World*), whose ultimate counterpart of Adam is named Omegar, deliberately recalling the equivalent figure in Jean-Baptiste Cousin de Grainville's *Le dernier homme* (1805; trans. as *The Last Man*), whose name is Omegarus. An entity of "pure thought" capable of assuming any material form is named Omega—signifying its evolutionary ultimacy—in William Gray Beyer's *Minions of the Moon* (1939; book, 1950).

Religious *myths pertaining to the ultimate *future are intrinsically less vulnerable to disproof and displacement by empirical science than creation myths, but are by no means immune to competition. In discovering the true age of the Earth and the universe *geologists and *astronomers also extended their probable future; James Hutton was careful to

point out that his uniformitarian thesis was not only devoid of any vestige of a beginning but also any prospect of an end. With respect to humankind, the account of its past evolution from a sequence of ancestral species suggested the possibility of a further evolution, as well as the possibility of ignominious extinction while other species continued to produce descendants. Cousin de Grainville was still able to reconcile the implications of eighteenth-century science with Biblical prophecy although it became increasingly difficult in the nineteenth century, when a series of new images of the ultimate future appeared, whose landmark texts included Edgar Allan Poe's *Eureka: An Essay on the Material and Spiritual Universe* (1848) and H. G. Wells' "The Man of the Year Million" (1893) and *The Time Machine* (1895).

Teilhard began to formulate his Omega Point thesis in the 1920s but was forbidden to publish by the Society of Jesus, of which he was a member. Its first version eventually appeared posthumously, in *Le phénomène humain* (1955; trans. as *The Phenomenon of Man*). Teilhard argued that the Earth's evolving ecosphere is supplemented by an equivalent intellectual entity, the noösphere, whose future evolution will involve its progressive integration into a coherent whole, until a climactic "concurrence of human monads" brings the divinely planned story of human evolution to its terminal. The notion is reminiscent of G. W. F. Hegel's notion of the progressive *weltgeist* (world spirit)—especially the revised versions described by George Bernard Shaw in the final act of *Back to Methuselah* (1921), by J. D. Bernal, in his speculative essay *The World, the Flesh and the Devil: An Enquiry into the Future of the Three Enemies of the Rational Soul* (1929), and by Olaf *Stapledon, in such works as *Death into Life* (1946).

The Omega Point of *The Phenomenon of Man* is a local phenomenon; Teilhard extrapolated the notion on to a universal stage in a 1945 lecture reprinted in *L'avenir de l'homme* (1959; trans. as *The Future of Man*), which suggested that the Earthly noösphere might detach itself from the planet in order to join a universal collective comprising all the intelligences in the universe. By the time this essay had been reprinted in book form, that notion too had been significantly echoed in speculative fiction, in the climax of Arthur C. *Clarke's *Childhood's End* (1953).

Teilhard's ideas were explicitly debated in Fred Saberhagen's *Brother Assassin* (1969; aka *Brother Berserker*), and his cosmic Omega Point was appropriated and modified by George Zebrowski, in *The Omega Point* (1972; reprinted with associated works in *The Omega Point Trilogy*, 1983), A. A. Attanasio, in the tetralogy begun with *Radix* (1981), and Damien Broderick in *The Judas Mandala* (1982; rev. 1990).

The vague promise of a Teilhardian Omega Point called the Sea of Perpetual Peace—a term that also recalls the imagery of William Hope Hodgson's *The House on the Borderland* (1908)—comes under threat in John Crowley's *Great Work of Time* (1989; book, 1991). Julian May's Galactic Milieu series, begun with *Jack the Bodiless* (1992), offered a further account of a Teilhardian World Mind and Galactic Mind before the notion of the Omega Point was taken up, and dramatically reconfigured, by the physicist Frank Tipler in *The Physics of Immortality: Modern Cosmology, God and the Resurrection of the Dead* (1994).

Tipler combined Teilhard's model with ideas drawn from Freeman *Dyson's "Time Without End: Physics and Biology in an Open Universe" (1979), which had taken their own inspiration from Jamal Islam's "Possible Ultimate Fate of the Universe" (1977; exp. as *The Ultimate Fate of the Universe*, 1983). Dyson's paper attempted to calculate the conditions in which life might endure and evolve forever, concluding with the seemingly paradoxical judgement that "the total energy required for indefinite survival is finite" because "subjective time is infinite". It also included the assertion that "an immortal civilisation should ultimately find ways to code its archives in an analog memory"—a notion that Tipler calls "the Eternal Life Postulate".

Tipler also took inspiration from the strong version of Brandon Carter's anthropic *cosmological principle, which he took as proof that there must be some special significance in humankind's existence. Building on the assumption that any space-travelling species ought to be able, ultimately, to engulf and take control of the entire universe, Tipler suggested that such a civilisation would undoubtedly want to deploy some of the resources of the universe to the purpose of recapitulating its entire history, contriving the resurrection of every entity that has ever existed within the *cyberspace of the Ultimate Computer, thus fulfilling the most ambitious dreams of *theology. Like Dyson, Tipler relied on the notion of "subjective time" to allow human beings to exist "forever" in spite of the fact that the universe must either culminate in an *entropic heat death or a *gravitational collapse. Whereas Dyson's "forever" had relied on an open universe, however, Tipler's was contingent upon the universe collapsing into a singularity—an Omega Point contrived by the ultimate product of universal evolution.

Fugitive aspects of the Tiplerian Omega Point had been sketchily prefigured in such science fiction stories as John W. Campbell Jr.'s "The Last Evolution" (1932), Isaac Asimov's "The Last Question" (1956), and James Blish's *The Triumph of Time* (1958; rev. as *A Clash of Cymbals*), but nothing so grandiose had been proposed before. Variants of Tipler's scheme of future evolution were rapidly appropriated into such science fiction stories as Robert Reed's *An Exaltation of Larks* (1995), Charles Sheffield's "At the Eschaton" (1995; exp. book 1997 as *Tomorrow and Tomorrow*), Frederik Pohl's Eschaton series begun with *The Other End of Time* (1996), J. R. Dunn's *Days of Cain* (1996), William Barton and Michael Capobianco's *White Light* (1998), Robert Charles Wilson's *Darwinia* (1998), Arthur C. Clarke and Stephen Baxter's *The Light of Other Days* (2000), various items in Sherwood Sith's theme anthology *Beyond the Last Star* (2002), and Ken Wharton's "Aloha" (2003). "Eschaton"—adapted from the theological discipline of eschatology—became a significant alternative term for the Omega Point, also employed in Charles Stross's *Singularity Sky* (2003; aka *Festival of Fools*) and *Iron Sunrise* (2005). Dunn's *Days of Cain* preferred Moiety, while James Patrick Kelly's "The Edge of Nowhere" (2005) substituted a "cognisphere" for Teihard's noösphere. Damien Broderick's *Godplayers* (2005) updated the Teilhardian Omega Point of *The Judas Mandala* to a Tiplerian version.

Some of these works depicted singular versions of the Omega Point, but others followed the example set by Poe's *Eureka* in favouring the notion of a beating "Heart Divine" that echoes the human heart as its pulses produce an infinite series of new universes, ceaselessly alternating Alphas and Omegas (or, in vulgar parlance, *Big Bangs and Big Crunches). Tipler's Omega Point—as befits a physicist's God—is uninterested in minor moral issues, but the science fiction writers redeploying Tipler's ideas, working in a morally ordered medium, had to be more concerned with matters of judgement. Although some novelists were content to concede, in the great tradition of theological pusillanimity, that mere humans could not hope to understand the mysterious ways of the Omega Point, others bravely attempted to provide accounts of its motivation, in the hope of justifying its ways to their contemporaries.

OPTICS

The science of vision, relating to the perception of *light. Aristotelian physics hypothesised visual rays passing through a medium extended between the eye and objects of vision, but assumed that such rays were emitted by the eye rather than received by it—a supposition that was a considerable hindrance to the future development of optical theory. Euclid's *Optica* included some observations regarding the phenomenon of reflection, and Ptolemy's *Optics* includes some measurements of refraction, but neither phenomenon was usefully analysed. The Islamic scientist Alhazen and Roger *Bacon improved on Classical understanding, as did *Galileo, but Isaac *Newton's experiments with prisms detailing the refractive division of white light into its constituent colours was a pivotal breakthrough, and his experiments with lenses clarified the processes by which real and virtual images were formed, facilitating a better understanding of the operation of the human eye.

The phenomena of optics were, inevitably, of considerable intrinsic interest to visual *artists, who may have begun using primitive image projectors based on the principle of the camera obscura (or "pinhole camera") to assist their draughtsmanship in the fifteenth century, recruiting the assistance of lenses not long afterwards. An elaborate argument supporting this contention was made by David Hockney's Secret Knowledge (2001), although his conclusions remained controversial.

The progress of optics before and after Newton was closely associated with the technology of lens grinding, and with the evolution of the technology of glass manufacture, from classical origins described by Pliny to the publication of the secrets of Venetian glass-making in Antonio Neri's De Arte Vitraria (1612). The field of optics was much elaborated after the end of the sixteenth century by virtue of the gradual evolution of a series of optical instruments, including *telescopes, *microscopes, and spectroscopes, and further enhanced by the development of *photography. Newton's account of colour was not universally accepted, a rival theory being produced a century later by the central figure of German *Romanticism, J. W. Goethe, but Goethe's account proved mistaken.

Although particular optical instruments were often featured in fiction, more general issues of optical theory had less potential for literary extrapolation. The mysteries of colour were recomplicated in W. H. Rhodes' "The Story of John Pollexfen" (1876) and the camera obscura was further extrapolated in Robert Duncan Milne's "The Aerial Cone Deflector" (1881), but the most prolific subspecies of optical speculative fiction to emerge in the nineteenth century was that dealing with hypothetical extensions of the faculty of sight, whether by virtue of freaks of nature—as in W. H. Rhodes' "The Telescopic Eye" (1876), H. G. Wells' "The Remarkable Case of Davidson's Eyes" (1895), and J. H. Rosny aîné's "Un autre monde" (1895; trans. as "Another World")—or by means of hypothetical optical instruments.

Both of these notions had significant precedents in supernatural fiction, in legends of "second sight" and magical devices—often imagined as "crystal balls"—permitting remote viewing, and the transition to

speculative fiction often carried forward similar literary motifs, as in such transitional works as Erckmann-Chatrian's "Les Lunettes de Hans Schnaps" (1859; trans. as "Hans Schnap's Spy-Glass"). Although Eugène Mouton's "L'historioscope" (1883; trans. as "The Historioscope") is carefully provided with a scientific rationale borrowed from Camille *Flammarion, and the observations made by means of the instrument are set within the context of academic *history, it retains a playful absurdity frequently seen in contemporary literary revisitations of supernatural motifs. William Wirt Howe's "A New Spectroscope" (1891) is also well aware of its supernatural associations. The symbolisation of augmented sight as a "third eye" also had a supernatural pedigree, which acquired a new lease of life in the nineteenth-century *occult revival, leading to the adoption of the "cycloptic eye" as a key symbol of imaginary enlightenment by the surrealists.

The production of these works coincided with a growing awareness of the fact that what the eye sees is a mental construct rather than a mere reflection of an assembly of external objects and that the process of its construction can be deluded, thus producing "optical illusions" such as mirages—whose most notorious examples, including the spectre of the Brocken and the Fata Morgana, had always excited literary interest. Technological devices like the zoetrope were produced to exploit the phenomenon of "the persistence of vision" in order to produce the illusion of movement from a series of still images, while exercises were developed to demonstrate the unapprehended gap in the visual field associated with the "blind spot" at which the optic nerve emerges into the retina. While the former effect was still being integrated into *cinema technology the perceptive effects of time dilatation were explored in such stories as H. G. Wells' The Time Machine (1895) and "The New Accelerator" (1901) and Jack London's "The Shadow and the Flash" (1903), and such works of *art as Giacomo Balla's Dynamism of a Dog on a Leash and Rhythms of a Bow (both 1912). It was, however, the cinema medium that eventually became the natural medium for optical illusions to be accommodated and extrapolated in fiction.

The discovery of x-rays in 1895 added a new item to speculative extensions of sight, the obvious flaws in its rational *plausibility being readily compensated by psychological plausibility and the innate attractiveness of the notion. Notable accounts of x-ray vision include Guy de Teramond's L'homme qui voit à travers les murailles (1914; trans. as The Mystery of Lucien Delorme), Noel Godber's Amazing Spectacles (1931), Edmond Hamilton's "The Man with X-Ray Eyes" (1933), and the film X—The Man with X-Ray Eyes

(1963). More restrained twentieth-century accounts of augmented vision include Maurice Renard's *L'homme truqué* (1921) and *Le maître de la lumière* (1933), Leslie F. Stone's "The Man with the Four-Dimensional Eyes" (1935), Eando Binder's "Strange Vision" (1937), A. E. van Vogt's "The Chronicler" (1946), G. McDonald Wallis' *The Light of Lilith* (1961), and Ray Nelson's "Eight o'Clock in the Morning" (1963; film 1988 as *They Live*). One actual sight-augmenting "technology"—the equipment of blind people with guide dogs—was extrapolated in numerous stories of artificially enhanced *intelligence, but such stories rarely paid attention to the optical aspects of the compensation; Daniel F. Galouye's "Seeing-Eye Dog" (1956) is an exception.

An ingeniously simple item of hypothetical optical technology, "slow glass"—through which light takes years to pass—was developed by Bob Shaw in "Light of Other Days" (1966) and other stories gathered into the mosaic *Other Days, Other Eyes* (1972). Science fiction writers also extrapolated the notion of "subliminal perception" that became fashionable in the 1960s with rumours that single frames inserted into cinematic projections or TV broadcasts could evoke subconscious responses even though they could not be consciously apprehended. Notable stories of this sort included J. G. Ballard's "The Subliminal Man" (1963) and Keith Roberts' "Sub-Lim" (1965). The domination of the theme of augmented vision within relevant speculative fiction became even more conspicuous, however, when such notions acquired new plausibility in the last decades of the century as the notion of employing various ingenious kinds of *neurological implants became more plausible.

Stories that benefited from this additional plausibility included Ursula K. Le Guin's "Field of Vision" (1973), Joseph L. Green and Patrice Milton's "To See the Stars That Blind" (1977), Sean McMullen's "Colors of the Soul" (2000), and Simon Ings' "The Convert" (2002), but the principal development was the extrapolation of technologies facilitating the optical experience of *cyberspace and the establishment of "telepresence" within actual environments and *virtual reality.

ORNITHOLOGY

The branch of *zoology devoted to the study of birds. Like *entomology it has a substantial hobbyist following, mainly because of the aesthetic appeal of the brightly coloured plumage that many birds exhibit and the fascination of their ability to fly. The observation of patterns of bird migration had a particular scientific significance in ancient times by assisting agricultural calculations; the arrival of a particular species in a locality was often employed as a signal when calendars were still primitive.

This utility undoubtedly assisted various bird species to acquire a reputation as omens, although the establishment of carrion crows and vultures as birds of ill omen had a more obvious cause. Various legendary birds were added to traditional bestiaries, including the giant roc, but the most important was the phoenix, which continually renewed its life by rising afresh from its own funeral pyre—a symbol of regeneration that guaranteed it frequent literary citation. Significant symbolism was also granted in the West to the dove, as manifest in its use by Noah in the aftermath of the flood, and the owl, as manifest in its association with Athene, the Classical goddess of wisdom. Eagles eventually became significant symbols of empire and ostriches acquired an entirely unwarranted reputation for burying their heads in sand to avoid unpleasant sights.

The symbolic potential of birds allowed them to be used in a significant series of allegorical literary works ranging from Aristophanes' fifth-century B.C. satire *The Birds* through such Medieval works as a twelfth-century dialogue between *The Owl and the Nightingale*, such Renaissance works as Geoffrey Chaucer's *Parlement of Fowles* (ca. 1380) and "The Nun's Priest's Tale" in *The Canterbury Tales* (ca. 1387), such post-Renaissance poems as John Webster's "Call for the Robin Redbreast and the Wren" (1612) and William Davenant's "The Lark now Leaves His Wat'ry Nest" (1650), such Romantic poems as Percy Shelley's "Ode to a Skylark" (1820) and John Keats' "Ode to a Nightingale" (1820), such post-Romantic poems as Alfred, Lord Tennyson's "The Eagle" (1891), such moral fables as Hans Christian Andersen's "The Ugly Duckling" (1845) and Maurice Maeterlinck's *L'oiseau bleu* (1909; trans. as *The Blue Bird*), and such calculated mockeries as Edward Lear's "The Owl and the Pussycat" (1846) and James Thurber's "There's an Owl in my Room" (1934), to earnest fabulations such as Richard Bach's *Jonathan Livingston Seagull* (1973).

The progress of ornithological science made hardly any impact on this tradition, and remained overshadowed by it even in literary works desirous of offering more naturalistic accounts of bird life. The postal service role played by owls in the literary phenomenon of the early twenty-first century—J. K. Rowling's Harry Potter series—testifies to the residual authority of the symbolic tradition.

The domestication of various bird species was important in the addition of protein to the human diet, in the form of eggs as well as meat, and acquired a new significance after the invention of *writing, when quills became significant instruments of inscription—a role they maintained until the invention of the steel nib in the late eighteenth century. Magical eggs and quill feathers feature abundantly in folklore, and hence in fairy tales, but literature took more inspiration from the fact that certain birds are capable of imitating human speech, as famously represented in Edgar Allan Poe's "The Raven" (1845). This equipped them for such purposes as forming courts to put humankind on trial, as they do in such literary fantasies as the second volume of Cyrano de Bergerac's *L'autre monde* (1662)—an idea recapitulated in such twentieth-century works as Geoffrey Dearmer's *They Chose to Be Birds* (1935) and James Blish's *Midsummer Century* (1972), and tacitly echoed in such stories of *Nature's rebellion as Frank Baker's *The Birds* (1936) and Daphne du Maurier's "The Birds" (1952; film, 1963). Satires featuring avian cultures, such as Samuel Brunt's *A Voyage to Cacklogallina* (1727) and Anatole France's *L'île des pingouins* (1908; trans. as *Penguin Island*), also draw upon this resource.

Comparative observations of variation in wild and domestic birds played a crucial role in supplying Charles *Darwin with the evidence he needed to support his theory of evolution by natural selection. *The Origin of Species* begins with a long discourse on the selective breeding of pigeons, whose mechanism is then analogised to the natural differentiation of the finches specialised for life on different Galapagos Islands. Birds also made a considerable exemplary contribution to the understanding of *sex, not in physiological terms but in terms of their frequent sexual differentiation; male birds often have elaborately coloured plumage, whose effect is often further enhanced by elaborate competitive displays of singing, occasionally augmented by "dancing" and nest decoration; various aspects of this art of display are taken to extremes by such species as peacocks, birds of paradise, and bowerbirds.

Speculative explanation of the *genetic economics of brilliant plumage and elaborate courtship behaviour became a key factor in the development of *sociobiology, but their analogical relevance to human behaviour was noted long before, elaborately depicted in metaphor and literature. Studies of birds also played a major role in the development of the behavioural science of ethology, particularly in revealing the role of *psychological "imprinting" in establishing bonds between chicks and their mothers. This too seemed to have some analogical relevance to human behaviour. Literary reflections of this kind of scientific research, and the potential for its confusion with human affairs, include Graham Billing's *Forbush and the Penguins* (1966; film 1971 as *Mr. Forbush and the Penguins*).

The most extensive literary use of birds is concerned with the mysterious mechanics of their flight, whose inspirational quality is extensively celebrated in poetry, as exemplified by Charles Baudelaire's "L'albatros" (1857; trans. as "The Albatross") and Gerard Manley Hopkins' "The Windhover" (1918). It gave rise to cautiously modified hopes of technical mimicry, from the myth of Daedalus and Icarus to *aeronautical designs of imaginary "ornithopters" and such literary extravaganzas as Robert Paltock's *The Life and Adventures of Peter Wilkins* (1751). Images of winged humans often symbolise transcendent freedom, as in Barry Pain's *Going Home* (1921), J. G. Ballard's "Storm Bird, Storm Dreamer" (1966) and *The Ultimate Dream Company* (1979), Vera Chapman's *Blaedudd the Birdman* (1978), and William Mayne's *Antar and the Eagles* (1989); by the same token, the clipping of wings—often done to restrict the movement of domesticated species—becomes a striking metaphor of female oppression in Inez Haynes Gillmore's feminist allegory *Angel Island* (1914).

Science-fictional images of birdlike aliens extend the various elements of this symbolism in a striking fashion, notable examples including Otis Adelbert Kline's "The Bird People" (1930), Francis Flagg's "The Land of the Bipos" (1930), Poul Anderson's *The People of the Wind* (1973) and "The Problem of Pain" (1973), R. Garcia y Robertson's "A Princess of Helium" (1999) and "Bird Herding" (2000), James Van Pelt's "A Flock of Birds" (2002), and Carol Emshwiller's series including "All of Us Can Almost ..." (2004).

In the twentieth century, several bird species became significant symbols of the dangers of extinction, largely because of publicity given to the recent fates of the dodo—ironically echoed in Howard Waldrop's "The Ugly Chickens" (1980)—and the once-common passenger pigeon. The discovery of relics of giant birds in New Zealand—as featured in such stories as H. G. Wells' "Aepyornis Island" (1894) and Gregory Feeley's "A Different Drumstick" (1988)—lent further impetus to this symbolism, and the particular fascination of giant flightless birds was further represented in Robert Reed's "In the Valley of the Thunder Quail" (2000).

P

PALAEONTOLOGY

A term coined at the beginning of the nineteenth century to describe the branch of *biology dealing with ancient life-forms, especially those preserved as fossils by the gradual petrifaction of the hard parts of their bodies. The fossil record played a highly significant role in the development of *geology, enabling rock strata in different places to be matched, and in the development of *evolutionary theory, particularly with respect to the prehistory of humankind mapped by physical *anthropology.

The existence of fossils was known in ancient times, and such writers as Xenophanes came close to an understanding of their nature, but their speculations were obscured in the Christian world by Biblical chronology. Resemblances between fossils and existing organisms were noted in the Middle Ages, but were interpreted either as the detritus of the process of divine creation or as evidence of divine whimsy. *Leonardo da Vinci was one of the first people to revive the hypothesis that fossils were the remains of long-dead life-forms, but it was not until the seventeenth century that Nicolaus Steno was able to integrate them into a general theory of rock formation. Robert Hooke brought early *microscopes to bear on the study of tiny fossil invertebrates, whose results were reported in his *Micrographia* (1665), and he pioneered the comparative anatomy of living and fossil plants; he campaigned for the establishment of a national museum to collect and organise such specimens.

The chalk cliffs of the British isles were prolific sources of fossils, and their collection became increasingly popular after the publication of a catalogue of John Tradescant's collection in 1656; a pioneering attempt at a comprehensive survey of British fossils compiled by Edward Lhuyd, *Lithophylacii britannici iconographia* (1699), included the first description of a trilobite, but his notion of their origin and nature was utterly mistaken. Scholars in Italy, Switzerland, Germany, and France published similar national catalogues in the early eighteenth century, stimulating the quest for a general theory of fossil formation and distribution. Such endeavours also prompted a famous hoax perpetrated in Germany in 1710, when a number of fake fossils were laid out for discovery by Johann Beringer, the Dean of the Faculty of Medicine at the University of Würtzburg, who reported the findings in *Lithographae Wirceburgensis* (1726) and then tried to buy back all the copies when he realised that he had been tricked.

As awareness of the vast number and various ages of extinct species increased, explanations in terms of a singular Deluge became increasingly implausible; fossils gradually moved to the foreground of geological controversies regarding the age of the Earth and the forces of change that had shaped it, as reflected in the Comte du Buffon's *Théorie de la Terre* (1749) and *Époques de la nature* (1778). Several spectacular discoveries in vertebrate palaeontology were made in the late eighteenth century, including the discovery near Whitby in 1758 of a "fossile allegator". The first complete megatherium (giant sloth) skeleton was found in 1789, and a further species, *Megalonyx*, was discovered in 1797 by Thomas Jefferson, but the fossil mammals that became central to the debate were relatives of elephants.

Many discoveries of mastodon bones, in Europe and America, had initially been construed as evidence of the existence of human giants (as advertised in Genesis 6:4) but their elephantine affiliations were recognised in the 1760s: Charles W. Peale founded the institution that became the Philadelphia Paleontological Museum to display the mastodon bones he had excavated in New Jersey. In 1772, Peter Simon Pallas published a description of the corpse of a woolly mammoth preserved in the Siberian ice, and Osip Shumakov excavated one in 1799, although it deteriorated considerably before it was transported to St. Petersburg. Georges Cuvier's first comparative study of extinct species of elephants appeared in 1799.

Cuvier integrated his work on fossil elephants with other mammalian studies in *Recherches sur les ossements fossiles* (1812), which laid the foundations of a method for extrapolating whole skeletons from partial remains by means of a generalised biomechanical "principle of correlation". Lord Byron cited Cuvier in the preface to *Cain: A Mystery* (1821), and his interest in fossil species is further reflected in the body of the poem and in both *Don Juan* (1823) and *Heaven and Earth: A Mystery* (1823). The latter works appeared in the same year as William Buckland's survey of *Reliquae Diluvianae*, which tried hard to sustain the notion that fossil animals were relics of the Biblical Deluge, but other users of Cuvier's method were inexorably driven to doubt this thesis. Étienne Geoffroy Saint-Hilaire's study of fossil crocodilians persuaded him to embrace evolutionism.

As more and more fossil discoveries were made in Britain—including an ichthyosaur discovered at Whitby in 1819 by Rev. George Young and a plesiosaur discovered at Lyme Regis in 1823 by Mary Anning—the dispute between Creationist geologists like Buckland and Sir Roderick Murchison and such sceptics as Charles Lyell and Richard Owen became increasingly heated. The devout Hugh Miller, who recorded his discoveries of fossil fish in Scotland in *The Old Red Sandstone* (1841), felt compelled to modify his *Creationist stance in *The Testimony of the Rocks* (1857) but did so by arguing that the six days of Creation could not have been literal days, but must instead refer to phases of the "Mosaic vision" by which the books of the Pentateuch had been revealed to their writer.

Although Charles *Darwin said little about fossil animals in the *Origin of Species*, the book's publication in 1859 had a considerable impact on palaeontology and its public perception, especially in view of the discovery of remains of "Neanderthal man" in 1857 and remains of "Cro-Magnon man" in 1868. The theory of evolution was still treated with careful reservation in the supposedly definitive *Handbuch der Paläontologie* (1876–1893) compiled by Karl von Zittel, however, and American palaeontologists were reluctant to take it aboard, at least in its Darwinist version.

Fossil collecting became a significant craze in America in the 1860s; its competitive element was dramatically increased in 1873 when Othniel C. Marsh, the professor of palaeontology at Yale, fell out with his early associate Edward D. Cope. They embarked on a long feud, striving to outdo one another in the excavation of a plethora of new fossil reptiles from the Jurassic and Cretaceous periods, and early birds and mammals from the Cretaceous and Eocene. Cope became a vociferous supporter of neo-Lamarckian evolution, providing an exemplary image of the palaeontologist as flamboyant "dinosaur hunter" whose image was to be prolifically reproduced in American fiction and the news media, giving palaeontologists a significant early edge over *archaeologists. The Marsh-Cope feud is dramatised in Sharon N. Farber's alternative history story "The Last Thunder Horse West of the Mississippi" (1988), and Mark W. Tiedemann's "The Disinterred" (2002) offers a further account of the way that nineteenth-century palaeontology might have gone.

Invertebrate palaeontology never seemed as exciting as vertebrate palaeontology, in spite of the minor celebrity won by ammonites, trilobites, and the dragonfly-like Palaeoptera of the Carboniferous era, but the fortunes of the investigative science improved markedly when Joseph Augustine Cushman and John J. Galloway found that foraminifera deposits were good indicators of oil deposits, thus creating new employment opportunities for its practitioners. Palaeobotany was similarly disadvantaged with respect to palaeozoology, although the narrative of the first invasion of the land and the subsequent replacement of the gymnosperm forests and giant ferns of the Carboniferous—whose substance is preserved as coal—by angiosperms and flowering plants added a significant dimension to the history of the Earth and to imaginative representations of that history.

The produce of palaeontological science nourished a significant subgenre of fiction in which explorers came across isolated enclaves where relics of past eras still survived. Jules Verne's *Voyage au centre de la terre* (1863; trans. as *Journey to the Centre of the Earth*) set an early example, followed by H. G. Wells' "Aepyornis Island" (1894), Jack London's "A Relic of the Pliocene" (1901), Robert W. Chambers' *In Search of the Unknown* (1904), Vladimir Obruchev's *Plutoniya* (1924; trans. as *Plutonia*), Arthur Conan Doyle's *The Lost World* (1912), and Alan Sullivan's *In the Beginning* (1927). Although the subgenre of prehistoric fantasy's focus on *anthropological issues restricted its use of vertebrate palaeontology to contemporary megafauna, this allowed considerable scope for dramatic incident, as in J. H. Rosny aîné's *Le félin géant* (1918; trans. as *The Giant Cat*). Palaeontology was rarely featured in any elaborate way as a scientific practise in early twentieth-century fiction, but one notable exception is Karel Čapek's *Vàlka s Moloky* (1936; trans. as *War with the Newts*), in which much attention is paid to the fossil record of the rediscovered species *Andrias Scheuchzeri*.

The imaginative re-creation of remote eras produced far more speculative nonfiction than fiction in the twentieth century, while geographical enclaves harbouring interesting survivals became increasingly difficult to accommodate plausibly in adventure fiction. Certain palaeontological discoveries, however, exerted such a powerful fascination on the popular imagination that they overrode questions of rational plausibility, securing the extraordinary posthumous celebrity of the *dinosaurs. Mammoths and mastodons achieved a lesser, but nevertheless significant, measure of fame, celebrated in such works as Stanton A. Coblentz's "The Reign of the Long Tusks" (1937), Clifford D. Simak's "Project Mastodon" (1955), L. Sprague de Camp's "The Mislaid Mastodon" (1993), and Stephen *Baxter's Mammoth trilogy (1999–2001). The last named was one of several works prompted by the discovery of the "Jarkov mammoth" (named after the family who discovered it) in 1997, which ignited the hope that enough DNA might be recoverable from the corpse to clone the species, using an elephant as a surrogate mother. John Varley's *Mammoth* (2005) is another. Various species re-created by cloning are exhibited in a circus in Howard Waldrop's "Winter Quarters" (2000).

Speculative fiction occasionally credits future palaeontologists with the potential to make unprecedentedly exciting discoveries, as in Jeff Hecht's "Extinction Theory" (1989) and Michael Swanwick's *Bones of the Earth* (2002), but a greater flexibility is conceded to "exopalaeontologists" operating on alien worlds or alternative Earths, as in Robert Reed's "The Dragons of Summer Gulch" (2004). Human and alien palaeontologists achieve a significant meeting in Robert J. Sawyer's *Calculating God* (2000), and a shady palaeontologist caters to the demands of alien tourists in M. Shayne Bell's "Homeless, with Aliens" (2000). Cuvier's principle of correlation is sometimes extrapolated to remarkable reconstructive extremes, as in Robert R. Olsen's "Palaeontology: An Experimental Science" (1974).

The most elaborate reconstruction of a past era in recent speculative fiction is the image of the palaeozoic contained in a long sequence of stories by Steven Utley, extending from "The Tall Grass" (1989) and "There and Then" (1993) to a connected series about a wormhole connection to the Silurian era, which includes "The Wind over the World" (1996), "Chain of Life" (2000), "Foodstuff" (2001), "Exile" (2003), and "Promised Land" (2005). An earlier image of the palaeozoic had been presented in Robert Silverberg's "Hawksbill Station" (1967; exp. book, 1968). The literary solidification of such imaginary landscapes sometimes deflects attention away from the fact that palaeontology is a highly speculative science, many of its images being the product of extrapolations even less reliable than Cuvier's principle of correlation, but its meditative and visionary aspects are celebrated in such stories as Bud Sparhawk's "Iridium Dreams" (1994) and Greg Beatty's "Midnight at the Ichnologists' Ball" (2003).

PALINGENESIS

A Greek term meaning "to be born again". It was often applied to the doctrine of continual rebirth, otherwise known as metempsychosis, associated in Greek thought with *Pythagoras. It was adapted into *biology to refer to the reproduction of unchanging characteristics from generation to generation. Another significant adaptation was made by Charles Bonnet in *Contemplation de la nature* (1764) and *Palingénésie philosophique* (1769); the latter formally introduced the notion of "cosmic palingenesis", proposing that the immortal soul might progress through a series of incarnations on different worlds, gradually ascending a scale of moral perfection. The idea that the worlds of the solar system might provide a framework for such opportunities had previously been broached by Christian Huygens' *Kosmotheoros* (1698).

The idea of cosmic palingenesis was tentatively deployed in Louis-Sébastien Mercier's "Nouvelles de la lune" in *Songes et Visions Philosophiques* (1768), and more extensively popularised by Johann Gottfried Herder, a pupil of Immanuel Kant's at Königsberg, who attempted to extrapolate Kant's *cosmological ideas in *Zerstreute Blätter* (1785). The notion had no scientific value, but it was a considerable inspiration to scientists and writers interested in getting to grips with the new cosmos revealed by astronomical observation, gifting the vast *plurality of worlds with an appropriate divine plan.

Mercier's precedent was flamboyantly followed up by his friend and fellow "Rousseau de ruisseau" [gutter *Rousseau] Nicholas Restif de la Bretonne, in *Les posthumes* (written 1788; published 1802), which includes an account of the extraterrestrial discoveries of Lord Multipliandre—an "everyman" figure who is considerably less anxious about the judgement of others than the dead friend featured in Mercier's story. Jacques Bernardin de Saint-Pierre, a one-time director of the Jardin des Plantes, elaborated a similar morally based scheme in *Harmonies de la Nature* (1815), describing many extraterrestrial humankinds.

Patterns of cosmic palingenesis took a significant step forward when Humphry Davy spent the final months of his life penning a series of philosophical dialogues published posthumously as *Consolations in Travel; or, The Last Days of a Philosopher* (1830). The first of these includes a remarkable cosmic vision, which imagines life as a series of incarnations—some of them in radically alien biospheres—in which the soul has the opportunity to ascend (or slip back down) a divinely established scale of moral perfection. Camille *Flammarion translated the book into French while he was midway through the sequence of dialogues making up *Lumen* (1866–1869), whose later sections are heavily influenced by it.

Although *Lumen* features a considerable array of exotic extraterrestrial species, all produced by evolutionary adaptation to their particular exobiological niches, Flammarion remained firmly committed to the idea of a spiritual evolution whose central mechanism is serial reincarnation. Alfred, Lord Tennyson's *De Profundis* (1880) also integrates evolutionist notions into a pantheist metaphysical system whose notion of serial reincarnation recalls Humphry Davy's. George du Maurier's *The Martian* (1897) also features a version of the thesis.

Flammarion's model of cosmic palingenesis, as reiterated in *Uranie* (1889; trans. as *Urania*), was integrated into a number of other late nineteenth-century spiritualist fantasies, including Mortimer Collins' *Transmigration* (1874) and Th. Flournoy's *From India to the Planet Mars* (1900), but lost fashionability thereafter. It was, however, retained by several of Flammarion's successors as pioneers of French science fiction, including J. H. Rosny aîné, Théo Varlet, and Gustave le Rouge. Most of these were led by this assumption to regard aliens as fellow participants in a great cosmic scheme rather than potential rivals of humankind; Rosny's *Les navigateurs de l'infini* (1925) finds nothing implausible or reprehensible in the idea of a love affair between a human and a six-eyed tripedal Martian.

The lingering effects of the religious conviction that God's creation of a plurality of worlds could not be futile was one of the factors that helped to sustain the idea that the other planets in the solar system must be habitable by humans long after the time when astronomical discoveries had rendered it untenable. It is also a significant factor in sharpening the discomfort of the *Fermi paradox. It is not surprising, therefore, that the idea of cosmic palingenesis is echoed in a number of American science fiction stories, where technological artifice sometimes makes up for nature's lack of provision—as in Clifford D. Simak's "Desertion" (1944), in which the human race reincarnates itself in alien bodies on Jupiter. Fainter echoes include Philip José Farmer's Riverworld series (1965–1983), Robert Sheckley's *Mindswap* (1966), and Rachel Pollack's *Alqua Dreams* (1987), the last named featuring an alien society whose members believe that they are dead and experiencing an afterlife. The notion was, however, spectacularly overtaken in the last decades of the century by the notion of reincarnation in *virtual worlds by courtesy of the "uploading" of human souls to *cyberspace.

PANSPERMIA

A term whose modern usage was popularised by Svante Arrhenius in a paper on "The Propagation of Life in Space" (1903), *Varldarnas utveckling* (1906; trans. as *Worlds in the Making*), and a *Scientific American* article on "Panspermy: The Transmission of Life from Star to Star" (1907). Arrhenius proposed that all life in the universe might have a common point of origin, uniquely favourable to spontaneous generation, and that planets and other life-bearing bodies are routinely seeded by space-travelling "spores".

The panspermia hypothesis was severely criticised in A. I. Oparin—in the 1924 book translated as *The Origin of Life*—whose model of the Earthly evolution of life became the orthodox narrative, but it exercised a considerable influence on the literary imagination, reflected in such works as Edward Heron-Allen's "The Cosmic Dust" (1921; by-lined Christopher Blayre), Eric North's "The Satyr" (1924; aka "Three Against the Stars"), P. Schuyler Miller's "The Arrenhius Horror" (1931), and Raymond Z. Gallun's "A Meteor Legacy" (1941). Brian W. Aldiss' *Hothouse* (1962) features a mechanism by which far-future Earthly life fires its spores into space. The panspermia hypothesis was frequently invoked in science fiction to facilitate explanation of the narrative convenience that introduced so many interplanetary travellers to beings recognisably akin to themselves.

The hypothesis was revitalised and lent new credence by Fred *Hoyle and Chandra Wickramasinghe in the 1970s. Hoyle's novel *The Black Cloud* (1957) had featured intelligent living creatures composed of comic dust—finely divided interstellar material whose spectroscopic analysis had shown that it contains a good deal of carbon and that its particles might be coated in water and ammonia ice—and he went on to develop this notion seriously, in collaboration with Wickramasinghe, in *Lifecloud: The Origin of Life in the Universe* (1978). The authors argued that the evolution of the basic biochemistry of life—involving the intimate systematic integration of such complex molecules as DNA, NAD, chlorophyll, and ATP—could not possibly have happened so rapidly in the relatively constricted and violent environment of a newly formed planetary surface; they contended that it is far more likely to have happened in a much vaster and less violent arena, over much longer periods of time, and that elementary life-forms are likely to have been transmitted to the Earth's surface—as to many other worlds—by cometary impacts.

In subsequent works, including *Diseases from Space* (1979), *Evolution from Space* (1981), and *The Intelligent Universe: A New View of Creation and Evolution* (1983), Hoyle and Wickramasinghe argued that new biological material was continually delivered to the Earth's surface throughout its history, its input providing a highly significant resource for the evolution of the biosphere, and being responsible even now for major epidemics of disease. This sophisticated version of the thesis was extrapolated in such science fiction stories as John Barnes' *Sin of Origin* (1988) and Robert R. Chase's "From Mars and Venus" (2000), and endorsed by such essays in speculative nonfiction as Christian de Duve's *Vital Dust: Life as a Cosmic Imperative* (1996), but it remained unorthodox. It will presumably continue to remain unorthodox, until relevant empirical evidence turns up, or a chemical model is produced that provides a coherent account of the emergence of self-replicating systems from a mere admixture of organic compounds.

PARACELSUS

The nickname of Theophrastus Bombast von Hohenheim (1493–1541), the most influential of all *occult scientists, whose real name became the source of the term "bombastic". He was important to the transition between *alchemy and *chemistry, and prompted a revolution in *medicine, at a time when physicians made elaborate use of alchemical theory in their work. His fondness for stating that "Reason is a Great Open Folly" placed him in direct opposition to the early champions of empirical investigation, but his reverence for the occult tradition did not extend to a determination to protect its authority against revision; indeed, he had an altogether atypical determination to subject the supposed wisdom of accepted authorities to a thoroughgoing overhaul. His father, a German-speaking schoolmaster who

taught chemistry in a mining community—with an understandable bias towards practical metallurgy—presumably set the context for his rebellion.

After leaving the school in Villach, Austria, where his father taught, the younger Bombast von Hohenheim moved from one great German university to another, affecting to despise them all and to find more inspiration in various traditions of folk wisdom. He claimed that he had graduated in medicine from the University of Vienna in 1510 and then studied at the University of Ferrara—because its teachers were critical of Galen and the Islamic school of medicine—allegedly receiving his doctorate in 1516 (there is no documentary evidence to support the latter claim). He had begun styling himself Paracelsus by the latter date; the Celsus that he was claiming to have transcended had been a Roman physician of the first century A.D.

Paracelsus apparently wandered through Europe for several more years, serving as an army surgeon in the perennial wars that were in the process of being heated up by the spreading Reformation. He also claimed to have visited Egypt and Asia Minor in search of alchemical wisdom. He had acquired a reputation by the time he returned to Villach in 1524, and was appointed town physician not long thereafter, as well as obtaining a lectureship at the University of Basel. He opened his lectures to the general public, wrote in his native tongue rather than Latin, and held a public burning of books by the authorities he refused to teach, but he denied charges that he was a "medical Luther".

Paracelsus' tenure at Basel did not last long; he had to leave and to resume a peripatetic way of life while he prepared his medical textbook, *Die grosse Wundartzney* (1536), for publication. It was in this period that he proposed the most famous of his new treatments, the mercury treatment for syphilis. It was still in use in the early twentieth century, as were many of his other metallurgical treatments. The most effective aspect of his treatment may have been his insistence on small doses, which prevented most of his medicaments from doing much harm, but if the rumour is true that he pioneered the dissolution of opium in alcohol—a technique subsequently used to mass-produce laudanum—he might have been very effective in treating pain. One way or another, though, he became a great success and a highly fashionable physician. He eventually obtained a position as physician to Duke Ernst of Bavaria, but died in Salzburg under what his followers insisted on regarding as suspicious circumstances. His posthumous reputation continued to grow, and the revolution in medicine he tried to bring about spread slowly throughout Europe, eventually becoming an orthodoxy to rival Galenism.

Whatever the shortcomings of Paracelsian medicine may have been, the fact that its pioneer successfully challenged accepted authority, and casually replaced it with a system of his own devising, was of very considerable importance as a demonstration of potential. Paracelsus was the great forefather of quack medicine, who inspired a thousand charlatans to do exactly as he had done, but he was also one of the fathers of modern chemistry, whose injection into alchemical lore of knowledge derived from recent technological refinements in metallurgy helped to create the room for chemistry to grow within its decaying corpse. He attempted to draw a good deal of new information into his system, adapting it to the Classical theory of four *elements by means of a revamped theory of quintessence.

Had Paracelsus nailed his flag to the mast of empiricism he would have acquired a better reputation as a pioneer of science, but he would probably have been a great deal less influential and far less famous. What he tried to do was to replace one system based in rather haphazard analogies by another based in a different set of analogies; perhaps his was slightly better designed to appeal to psychological *plausibility, but its real appeal was that it was new, in an era where novelty was in the process of replacing antiquity as a source of fascination and a guarantor of commitment. Even if his reputation as a physician was entirely based on the placebo effect, at least he helped to demonstrate the power of that effect and the manner of its psychological mobilisation.

The influence of Paracelsus' new system of analogies extended far beyond the fields of medicine and proto-chemistry; he repopularised the Germanic names for elemental spirits, adding sylph, kobold, and undine to the already fashionable salamander, and ensuring those terms a very prominent place in the symbolism of Romantic literature, not merely in his homeland but in France and Britain too. It was Paracelsus who paved the way for the mode of discourse employed in Erasmus Darwin's *Temple of Nature* (1803), in which Teutonic elemental spirits serve as metaphorical organisers for an attempted scientific description of the world, and thus became entitled to the central symbolic role in Robert Browning's verse drama *Paracelsus* (1835), which celebrates the emergence of science from scholastic superstition. Georg Pabst's 1943 film *Paracelsus*, however, represents him as a wholehearted occultist.

The inventiveness of Paracelsian thought, which evidently recommended it to many of his followers, also appealed to many litterateurs. One of his fanciful recipes explained in some detail how to manufacture a homunculus—an artificial human being. Anyone who actually tried it must have been disappointed, but the idea was understandably fascinating to imaginative writers who had their own allegorical reasons for producing such entities in a fictional medium; modern variants of his formula are imagined to be workable in such works as Fred T. Jane's *The Incubated Girl* (1896), John Hargrave's *The Artificial Man* (1931), and David H. Keller's *The Homunculus* (1949). Although he lived and died a Catholic, he really was a medical Martin Luther, whose particular beliefs were less important than the reformation he helped to kick-start.

PARADIGM

A term whose ordinary meaning refers to an exemplar, especially a model to be copied, such as a specimen conjugation or declension in grammar. It acquired a new meaning in the context of the *philosophy of science when it was used by Thomas S. Kuhn in *The Structure of Scientific Revolutions* (1962; exp. 1970) to refer to "universally recognised scientific achievements that for a time provide model problems and solutions to a community of practitioners". Kuhn proposed that the *history of science could be seen in terms of occasionally punctuated equilibrium, in which long periods of "normal science"—consisting of the investigation of phenomena within the context of a theoretical consensus—were periodically interrupted by revolutionary shifts in perspective.

Kuhn's argument sparked considerable controversy because he argued that data standing in apparent contradiction to a theoretical consensus—whether produced by observation or experiment—are not normally held to be fatal to it until the accumulation of such anomalies reaches a critical mass, at which point the whole theoretical edifice undergoes an abrupt reformulation, in such a manner as to eliminate the anomalous quality of most of the rogue data. This brought it into conflict with Karl Popper's view of the essence of scientific method as a selective process involving the continual testing and attempted falsification of individual hypotheses. In addition to this apparent challenge to orthodoxy, Kuhn suggested that if the process of paradigm shifts could be explained sociologically, in terms of the political dynamics of the scientific community, it might be necessary to "relinquish" the notion that paradigm changes bring scientific knowledge gradually closer to the truth. Although Kuhn subsequently recanted this judgement, it was taken up with alacrity by sociologists of science, whose foregrounding of *ideological issues inevitably inclined them to *relativism.

Kuhn's principal examples of large-scale paradigm shifts included the replacement of the geocentric cosmological model by its heliocentric rival, and the replacement of the luminiferous *ether with a theory of electromagnetism in which light needed no medium in which to form its waves. He also used the term to refer to theoretical systems of much smaller magnitude, held in common by relatively small groups of specialists, which were often replaced much more frequently. The latter meaning was frequently used in specific studies in the sociology of science, some such uses bringing it much closer to the original meaning of the term by referring specifically to analogical models, such as those constructed by early *atomic theorists, and hypothetical exemplars such as *black holes.

The interest in the sociology of the scientific community provoked by Kuhn's analysis is reflected in numerous late twentieth-century literary representations of scientists at work. In particular, it supplies a useful logic to images of heroic independent thinkers who experience difficulties in winning acceptance for their ideas from communities heavily invested in theories they have put under threat. Notable examples include Isaac Asimov's accounts of Hari Seldon in the later volumes of the Foundation series and Ursula K. Le Guin's description of Shevek in *The Dispossessed* (1974), but Kuhnian paradigm shifts are investigated with particular care and concern in Neal Stephenson's Baroque Cycle, comprising *Quicksilver* (2003), *The Confusion* (2004), and *The System of the World* (2004). James O. Farlow's "The Paradigmatic Dragon-Slayers" (1978) is a curious Kuhnian allegory.

Kuhn's notion of a paradigm bears some similarity to the notion of a "conceptual breakthrough" devised by Peter Nicholls in *The Encyclopedia of Science Fiction* (1979; rev. 1993) to describe a fundamental theme of science fiction. A conceptual breakthrough is, in essence, the effect of shattering one of Francis *Bacon's inhibitory idols, so that it ceases to constrain and distort thought, allowing new horizons of possibility suddenly to be glimpsed. The notion of conceptual breakthrough has considerable narrative value, because it offers a possibility of contriving story climaxes that are both dramatic and progressive. In narrative terms, however, the device works best when it produces a specific and easily appreciable reward: an inspirational shock like the one that allegedly made Archimedes leap out of his bath when he discovered the hydrostatic principle named after him.

Describing paradigm shifts and conceptual breakthroughs in historical fiction and such past-set speculative fictions as Liz Williams' "Tycho and the Stargazer" (2003) is relatively easy, but contriving them in futuristic fiction is problematic because of the *paradox of prophecy: to anticipate the conceptual breakthroughs of the future would be to make

them. Many science fiction stories employing such narrative payoffs to celebrate the power of scientific method are thus forced to place their characters in a state of artificial ignorance in order that readers may celebrate their breakthrough to an awareness we already possess. Notable examples of this stratagem include Isaac Asimov's "Nightfall" (1941), James Blish's "Surface Tension" (1952), and Philip C. Jennings' "Otherness" (1999). One of the reasons that *parapsychological themes are so attractive to science fiction writers is their facilitation of apparent climactic breakthroughs to *superhuman enlightenment, as featured in Charles L. Harness's "The Rose" (1953) and Theodore Sturgeon's *More than Human* (1953). More ambitious examples of futuristic conceptual breakthroughs include those featured in James White's *Tomorrow Is too Far* (1971) and John Gribbin's *Innervisions* (1993).

Another term that has associations with the notion of paradigm shifts and the conceptualisation of intellectual progress as a series of conceptual breakthroughs is "lateral thinking"—popularised by Edward de Bono's *The Use of Lateral Thinking* (1967)—whose occasional rendering as "thinking outside the box" recognises the constraining effects of accepted theoretical frameworks and procedural models. One of the explicit functions of didactic fabulations, thought experiments, and *contes philosophiques* is to encourage readers to take up new viewpoints in order to get a fresh perspective on familiar ideas. This is often advanced as one of the merits of science fiction, tacitly celebrated by such science fiction stories as Walt and Leigh Richmond's *The Probability Corner* (1977).

PARADOX

A false proof whose *logical flaw is not obvious, or a seductive self-contradiction. A distinction has to be drawn in either case between logical paradoxes and semantic paradoxes, the latter being a form of wordplay based in linguistic ambiguity.

The most venerable example of a paradox is Epimenides' paradox, in which his allegation that "all Cretans are liars" became problematic because he was himself a Cretan. The most famous example is one of four formulated by Zeno of Alea in the fourth century B.C. in opposition to the ideas of the Pythagoreans. It imagines Achilles giving a tortoise a head start in a race, arguing that Achilles must first cover the distance separating him from the point at which the tortoise started, by which time the tortoise will have moved on to a further point; by the time Achilles reaches that point, however, the tortoise will have moved on again—and so, *ad infinitum*, suggesting that Achilles can never overtake the tortoise. This paradox is soluble by the realisation that a calculation with an infinite number of terms may still have a finite sum, but some paradoxes resist such resolution, notably Bertrand *Russell's "set paradox"—an extrapolation of Epimenides' paradox that asks whether the set of all the sets that do not contain themselves contains itself or not. The set paradox extrapolates an anecdotal paradox about a village whose resident barber "shaves everyone who does not shave himself", thus rendering the question "who shaves the barber?" unanswerable.

As these examples demonstrate, there is a natural affinity between paradoxes and fictitious representations. Stories that serve to dramatise paradoxes gain narrative energy from their puzzling quality. Given that complications, puzzles, and mysteries are the essence of plotting in *narrative theory, paradoxes can be seen as uniquely clever examples of plot formation, and they are often used in that fashion, particularly in fiction based in *mathematics (arithmetical operations involving zero or infinity often produce seemingly paradoxical results). James Clerk Maxwell's "A Paradoxical Ode" (1878) offers a poetic celebration of the perversities of emergent analytical science. Fiction dealing with transgressions of the sequence of *time is also a ready means of producing paradoxes—a strategy whose propriety seemed to be endorsed by nature when theoretical *physics produced the "twin paradox" by means of a simple *thought experiment in *relativity theory.

The aesthetic delight that can be obtained by the production of paradoxes is readily illustrated by the frequent use of semantic paradoxes by such writers as Lewis Carroll, G. K. Chesterton, and Oscar Wilde, who collaborated in the establishment of paradoxicality as the soul of wit—a tradition extrapolated by such late twentieth-century writers as Tom Stoppard, whose play *Jumpers* (1973) includes an intensive revisitation of Zeno's paradox. John W. Campbell Jr. attempted to cash in on that delight by introducing the Probability Zero feature that ran in *Astounding Science Fiction* from 1942–1944, and was reintroduced to *Analog* by Stanley Schmidt in 1990. Its most conspicuous example is, however, the rich subgenre of stories in which time travel into the past obliterates the history that led to its possibility. The standard example involves murdering a grandparent or other ancestor, so that one could never have been born to carry out the deed.

Self-contradictory time paradoxes were adopted into comic fantasy in the nineteenth century, F. Anstey's *The Time Bargain* (1891, aka *Tourmalin's Time Cheques*) providing an entertainingly convoluted

example. They were rapidly taken aboard by the science fiction pulps, in such celebratory stories as Charles Cloukey's "Paradox", "Paradox +", and "Anachronism" (all 1930), Nathan Schachner's "Ancestral Voices" (1933), William Sell's "Other Tracks" (1938), Alfred Bester's "The Probable Man" (1941), Norman L. Knight's "Short-Circuited Probability" (1941), and Fredric Brown's "Paradox Lost" (1943). As science fiction became more sophisticated, the paradoxes created by time travel became increasingly convoluted, as in William Tenn's "Brooklyn Project" (1948), Alfred Bester's "The Men Who Murdered Mohammed" (1958), Ursula K. Le Guin's *The Lathe of Heaven* (1971), and Robert Sheckley's "Slaves of Time" (1974), and gave rise to such self-conscious fabulations as Andrew Weiner's "The Grandfather Problem" (1988).

In much the same way that there are self-fulfilling *prophecies as well as self-negating ones, there are also time paradoxes that pervert causal sequences into closed loops instead of severing them. Such causal loops, especially when they are ingeniously convoluted, also have an intrinsic aesthetic satisfaction, reflected in such science-fictional examples as Ross Rocklynne's "Time Wants a Skeleton" (1941), Robert A. Heinlein's "By His Bootstraps" (1941; by-lined Anson MacDonald), P. Schuyler Miller's "As Never Was" (1944), Charles L. Harness' "Time Trap" (1948), Murray Leinster's "The Gadget Had a Ghost" (1952), and Mack Reynolds' "Compounded Interest" (1956). In Heinlein's sarcastic existentialist fantasy "All You Zombies ..." (1959), the protagonist completes such a loop by becoming his own father and mother. The innately disturbing quality of paradoxes readily licenses the subgenre of time police stories.

If time travel stories were entirely confined to fiction, their paradoxical quality would be entirely a matter of aesthetics, but the notion is not difficult to accommodate within theoretical *physics at the so-called "quantum level", where *uncertainty is normal. Such thought experiments as the one relating to the fate of Schrödinger's cat have a paradoxical quality about them, challenging the axiomatic assumption of Aristotelian logic that the cat must either be alive or dead and cannot be both, neither, or any combination of the two mutually exclusive opposites.

Quantum mechanics is a prolific generator of seeming paradoxes, whose disturbing effect moved Albert *Einstein to declare that he could not believe that "God plays dice with the world"—a statement that has called forth all manner of witty corollaries and rejoinders. Ilya Prigogine referred to quantum mechanical paradoxes as "The Nightmares of the Classical Mind"—a phrase borrowed for use as a story title by Charles Sheffield in 1989. Analogues of the uncertainty principle on a larger scale often result from the "paradox of prophecy", which arises in situations where the fact that a *prediction is issued is sufficient to prevent its fulfilment, by prompting the hearer of the prediction to take precautionary action. The paradox of prophecy is a useful generator of narrative complication in stories dealing with such means of divination as *astrology, and *parapsychological precognition.

The ability to entertain—and be entertained by—paradoxes is often seen as a virtue, whose possession might serve to separate humans from less flexible thinkers. Fictitious *artificial intelligences such as *computers and *robots are often defeated by confrontation with paradoxes, and the motif extends into fantasy fiction in such stories as L. Sprague de Camp and Fletcher Pratt's Land of Unreason (1941; book, 1942), where the barber paradox is employed to confound a monster.

PARALLEL WORLD

A world neighbouring the world of experience, but displaced from it in such a fashion as to be imperceptible and inaccessible in normal circumstances. In the days when people routinely thought of the world as a plane, it seemed reasonable to think of parallel worlds above and below it, the former often being identified with the realm of the gods and the latter with the realm of the dead. In Greek mythology both realms were equipped with portals, Mount Olympus serving as a conduit between Earth and heaven while various caverns gave admittance to the Underworld. Both notions are reflected in cosmological ideas that persisted throughout the Middle Ages and into the Renaissance, although notions of divine reward and punishment often redistributed the dead between the two realms; they were preserved in various descendant schools of *occult science, in which the notion of "higher planes"—especially the "astral plane"—retains considerable imaginative authority.

The Underworld is associated with many western European folkloristic accounts of supernatural beings, cropping up in many of the tales that served as ancestors to modern fairy tales, but is confused with conceptualisations in which such beings live invisibly alongside human society, either as animistic "elemental spirits" or in variously veiled enclaves only partially or periodically accessible to humans. The latter version became the standard strategy of literary fairy tales, laying imaginative groundwork for the extrapolation of the notion that there might be an array of parallel universes laterally displaced from ours in a *fourth dimension. The latter notion was popularised at the end of the nineteenth century by such writers as C. H. *Hinton and dramatised in such stories as H. G. Wells' "The Plattner Story" (1896), William Hope Hodgson's The House on the Borderland (1908) and The Ghost Pirates (1909), and Gerald Grogan's A Drop in Infinity (1915). Such stories often retain echoes of the mythical thesis, placing the shades of the dead in a parallel world, while The House on the Borderland transplanted a notion commonly associated with dream fantasy, using the landscapes of a parallel world to map and symbolically display the psyche of its protagonist.

The idea of parallel worlds displaced in a fourth spatial dimension underwent a spectacular boom in twentieth-century fiction. It was established as a useful framework for the science-fictional accommodation of *alternative histories in the 1930s, encouraged by such exercises in speculative nonfiction as J. W. Dunne's attempts to explain supposedly prophetic dreams in An Experiment with Time (1927), which led him to construct an ambitious account of The Serial Universe (1934). It was accommodated into the pulp magazines before the advent of specialist science fiction pulps in such stories as A. Merritt's classic portal fantasy "The Moon Pool" (1918), Austin Hall and Homer Eon Flint's The Blind Spot (1921; book, 1951), and Philip M. Fisher's "Worlds Within Worlds" (1922), and was thus established as a standard generic motif, given a more scientific gloss in such versions as Murray Leinster's "The Fifth-Dimension Catapult" (1931) and "The Fifth-Dimension Tube" (1933).

The notion of Faerie as a parallel world made similar progress in twentieth-century fantasy fiction, generalised in J. R. R. Tolkien's notion of fantasy settings as "Secondary Worlds". Secondary Worlds are usually conceivable as parallel worlds even when the inclusion of connective portals does not make the relationship explicit. The narrative utility of fantasies featuring such portals is obvious, in that they allow characters to step from the experienced world into a Secondary one, arriving as naive and inquisitive strangers whose own learning process educates the reader; Farah Mendlesohn's "Towards a Taxonomy of Fantasy" (2003) identified portal fantasy as a major sector of modern fantastic fiction, intermediate in its narrative technique between immersive fantasy and intrusive fantasy. Although much science-fictional portal fantasy deals with shortcuts through space and trips through time rather than shifts into parallel worlds, the development of parallel worlds in genre science fiction made a very significant contribution to the broader genre of portal fantasy, evolving a new jargon of "dimensional doorways" and "gates" that helped to add psychological plausibility to their fantasy counterparts.

Science-fictional portals retain the same essential magicality as well as the same narrative function as portals to Faerie and its analogues, and such devices became—very appropriately—a key motif of the hybrid subgenre of science-fantasy. They facilitated genre crossovers with the same ease that they facilitated transfer between primary and secondary worlds, as illustrated by such archetypal hybrids as A. Merritt's *The Face in the Abyss* (1923–1930; rev. book, 1931), C. L. Moore's *The Dark World* (1946; book, 1965; by-lined Henry Kuttner) and Andre Norton's *Witch World* (1963), and the chimerical crossovers that became typical of *Astounding Science Fiction*'s fantasy Companion *Unknown*, whose key templates were established by L. Sprague *de Camp.

The occult tradition of parallel worlds fiction, which had latched on to the notion of the fourth dimension in the late nineteenth century, also gave rise to a hybrid subgenre, carried forward by such works as John Buchan's "Space" (1911) and Algernon Blackwood's "The Pikestaffe Case" (1924). This too was imported into the pulp magazines, most conspicuously by H. P. Lovecraft—whose deployment of the relevant jargon was echoed by his many disciples, including August Derleth, Frank Belknap Long, and Clark Ashton Smith. Some of these writers brought a new ingenuity into their developments of the idea, especially Smith, whose "City of the Singing Flame" (1931) introduced Merrittesque portal fantasy into the science fiction pulps, and whose "The Dimension of Chance" (1932) attempts to describe a parallel world with variant physical laws.

Early pulp science fiction writers initially mined the melodramatic potential of parallel worlds in a brutally straightforward fashion, in such accounts of monstrous invasion as Edmond Hamilton's "Locked Worlds" (1929) and Donald Wandrei's "The Monster from Nowhere" (1935) and such accounts of heroic expeditions as Clifford D. Simak's "Hellhounds of the Cosmos" (1932) and E. E. Smith's *Skylark of Valeron* (1934; book, 1949). Its uses became more sophisticated in the 1940s, in such stories as Harry Walton's "Housing Shortage" (1947), but it enjoyed a spectacular leap forward in the 1950s and 1960s in the context of what eventually came to be called the "multiverse": an infinitely extendable manifold of alternative histories.

The notion of the multiverse is implicit in such early pulp science fiction stories as Harl Vincent's "Wanderer of Infinity" (1933) and "The Plane Compass" (1935)—the latter refers to a "superuniverse"—and became more explicit in such time police stories as Fritz Leiber's *Destiny Times Three* (1945) and Sam Merwin's *House of Many Worlds* (1951) before Michael Moorcock pasted the new label on it, and

demonstrated its utility as a framing concept linking the very various worlds described within his texts into an inherently chimerical superstructure. Clifford D. Simak's *Ring Around the Sun* (1953) is an early celebration of the extrapolation of the idea of parallel worlds to embrace an infinite series of Earth clones—all empty of humankind in this version, and hence available for *colonisation. Simak went on to examine the possibilities of interparallel trade in "Dusty Zebra" (1954) and "The Big Front Yard" (1958).

Traditional notions of parallel existence continued to echo in science fiction—as the notion of invisible coexistence did in Gordon R. Dickson's "Perfectly Adjusted" (1955; exp. book 1961 as *Delusion World*) and transfigurations of dream fantasy in Christopher Priest's Dream Archipelago series (1976–1999)—but the more interesting developments of the notion involved its extension in new philosophical directions. These included the extensive exploration of parallel selves in such existential fantasies as Adolfo Bioy Casares' "La trame céleste" (1948; trans. as "The Celestial Plot"), Robert Donald Locke's "Next Door, Next World" (1961), Brian W. Aldiss' *Report on Probability A* (1968), Larry Niven's "All the Myriad Ways" (1969), and Graham Dunstan Martin's *Time-Slip* (1986). Other existential fantasies employing parallel worlds include Richard Cowper's *Breakthrough* (1967), Robert A. Heinlein's *The Number of the Beast* (1980), and Kevin J. Anderson's "The Bistro of Alternate Realities" (2004), and such tales of transuniversal tourism as Robert Silverberg's "Trips" (1974), Robert Reed's *Down the Bright Way* (1991), and Alexander Jablokov's "At the Cross-Time Jaunter's Ball" (1987) and "Many Mansions" (1988).

One significant narrative advantage of the use of parallel worlds is that it cuts out the necessity for elaborate modes of *transportation between fictional constructions. Faster-than-light travel is no less arbitrary a facilitating device than interdimensional portals, as is evident in the synthesis of the two kinds of portal in the "stargate", but the idea of a galactic community did retain an imaginative advantage by virtue of its resonance with the majesty of the night sky: the "higher" of the two original parallel worlds.

For much of the twentieth century, the idea of parallel worlds was regarded by scientists as an amusing corollary of mathematical fancy, but it became increasingly significant in theoretical *physics as *atomic theory and *quantum mechanics became increasingly complicated, eventually acquiring a certain respectability when it was co-opted in 1957 by Hugh Everett and John Wheeler as the "many worlds" interpretation of quantum mechanical *uncertainty. The number of dimensions theoretically required to account for the exotic behaviour of subatomic particles increased dramatically with the advent of string theory, and the notion of parallel universes became a key element of some versions of inflationary *cosmology.

Parallel worlds stories illuminated by ideas drawn from these developments in theoretical physics include Isaac Asimov's *The Gods Themselves* (1972), Bob Shaw's *A Wreath of Stars* (1976), Frederik Pohl's *The Coming of the Quantum Cats* (1986) and *The Singers of Time* (1991; with Jack Williamson), and Stephen Baxter's *Manifold* trilogy (1999–2002). This is, however, one instance in which fiction has conspicuously failed to keep imaginative pace with the theory. One of the originators of string theory, Michio Kaku, became an outspoken advocate of the notion that the real existence of parallel worlds is no mere *metaphysical hypothesis, but can be proven, providing a definitive summary of the issue in *Parallel Worlds* (2005). The inflationary version of the many worlds hypothesis was given an added twist by the proposition that there must be an ongoing process of "natural selection" favouring the proliferation of those universes that are most hospitable to the formation of new sub-universes, and that this intra-multiversal evolutionary process might be responsible for the implication of intelligent design inherent in the cosmological anthropic principle*. *Scientific American* devoted a special issue to such questions in May 2003. Liza Randall's *Warped Passages: Unraveling the Universe's Hidden Dimensions* (2005) calls individual universes "branes" (short for membranes) and the multiverse "the bulk".

PARAPSYCHOLOGY

A term coined by J. B. Rhine in *Extra-Sensory Perception* (1934) in an attempt to isolate a scientific sector within the wider field of "psychic research", which was widely perceived as tainted by its long association with spiritualism and the study of hauntings. The term became standard usage, usually used in association with the definition of its field of interest as "paranormal phenomena", its definitive status secured by Rhine's *Parapsychology: Frontier Science of the Mind* (1957). Sceptics, however, regard the whole field as *pseudoscientific.

The origins of parapsychological research lie in the support won by certain spiritualist mediums from such physicists as William Crookes and Oliver Lodge, who became convinced that the phenomena were real and susceptible to scientific analysis. The initial involvement of scientists owed much to the efforts of the celebrity medium D. D. Home between the late 1850s and the early 1880s. His performances were also witnessed by many of the leading literary figures of the day, impressing William Thackeray but annoying Charles Dickens and exciting a more powerful antipathy in Robert Browning, who pilloried Home in "Mr. Sludge, the Medium" (1864). Spiritualism was also attacked in Thomas Love Peacock's *Gryll Grange* (1860), although its concerns were treated far more reverently in much of the fiction that accompanied the *occult revival, as in Frances Trollope's *Black Sprits and White* (1877).

Crookes' controversial investigations of mediums, including Home and Florence Cook, carried out from 1869 onwards, caused a sensation when they were reported in the *Quarterly Journal of Science* (after the *Proceedings of the Royal Society* had declined the paper) in 1874. A criticism made of Crookes by W. B. Carpenter, to the effect that he was a specialist used to investigating phenomena that had no intrinsic interest in misleading him, and was therefore easy prey to calculated deception, has been routinely levelled at scientific investigators ever since. The stage magician Harry Houdini established himself as an investigator with the necessary expertise to penetrate such deceptions—a tradition carried forward into the twentieth century by such practitioners as James Randi and Ali Bongo. The investigation and exposure of fraudulent mediums was a significant component of the work of the pioneering detective agency set up by Allan Pinkerton, as reported in *The Spiritualists and the Detectives* (1877).

A Society for Psychic Research (SPR) was founded in 1882 by F. W. H. Myers and various associates, including the moral philosopher Henry Sidgwick and the physicist Sir William Barrett. One of the SPR's six committees was set up to investigate telepathy—a term Myers had coined—while the others were devoted to the study of mediums, *mesmerism, apparitions, Reichenbach's theory of the odic force and to the collation of existent data. The last named eventually gave rise to Myers' posthumously issued study of *Human Personality and Its Survival of Bodily Death* (1903), but its first product was Myers and Edward Gurney's *Phantasms of the Living* (1886). Myers' younger brother Arthur, a physician, became expert in *hypnotism and continental *psychology, assisting Myers to develop an occult theory of the "subliminal consciousness" and to introduce *Freudian ideas to England in a paper on "Hysteria and Genius" read to the SPR in 1897. Barrett's *On the Threshold of the Unseen* (1918) imagines a telepathic utopia where shared thoughts would inevitably produce social justice by making the rich party to the misery of the poor (and providing the poor with a new metaphorical opium).

Psychic research of this sort was taken seriously by many writers and scientists, although Samuel Clemens' application to join the society in 1884 attempted to cover its manifest embarrassment with the wit typical of his Mark Twain persona. William and Henry James were far more earnest, as was Thomas *Edison. Other members of the American SPR founded in 1884 were more inclined to scepticism than their British counterparts, but the societies merged in 1889.

Writers directly influenced by the SPR's researches included Rudyard Kipling, as in "Wireless" (1902), Algernon Blackwood and other writers of "occult detective stories", and such scientifically inclined writers of spiritualist fantasy as Camille *Flammarion and Arthur Conan Doyle. The institution of scientific inquiry stimulated literary attempts at more careful extrapolation of the implications of possessing such powers, including John Strange Winter's *A Seventh Child* (1894), Louis Tracy's *Karl Grier, The Strange Story of a Man with a Sixth Sense* (1906), Stephen McKenna's *The Sixth Sense* (1915), and—most impressively—Muriel Jaeger's *The Man with Sixth Senses* (1927). The French journalist Léon Groc was a significant early developer of parapsychological themes with a science-fictional sensibility, in such works as *Ville hantée* (1913) and *L'autobus évanoui* (1914); the latter is an early example of telepathy induced by *radiation. Unfortunately, attempts to find explanations for such phenomena as ghosts in terms of conventional physics—as in George Wycherley Kaye's "The Hydrogen People" (1910)— usually seemed blatantly absurd.

The replacement term emphasises the close involvement of the twentieth-century development of psychic research with the parallel advancement of psychology. Under this influence the primary focus of psychic research gradually shifted away from such external phenomena as ghosts, concentrating more intently on the occult powers of the human mind. Traditional ideas of "second sight" underwent a series of jargonistic transfigurations, renamed as a "sixth sense" and Latinised as "clairvoyance", before Rhine redefined it as "extra-sensory perception" (ESP) in the same monograph that defined parapsychology. Rhine, originally a plant physiologist, turned to such work in 1926, taking advantage of one of several endowments given to U.S. universities for such research. Harvard had previously played host to such research under the auspices of its professor of psychology, William McDougall; Rhine initially went to Duke University, where he carried out the bulk of his research, as McDougall's assistant.

Rhine, who founded a *Journal of Parapsychology* in 1937, attempted to support the reality of such paranormal phenomena as telepathy and precognition with experimental evidence gleaned in the laboratory. His research, conducted in allegedly controlled conditions—using an iconic set of symbols printed on sets of "Zener cards"—produced masses of quantified data. These data were then subjected to statistical analysis, comparing the number of "hits" obtained by his subjects with the number expectable by chance. His methods were imitated by others, including S. G. Soal and Frederick Bateman, whose account of *Modern Experiments in Telepathy* (1955) was issued by Yale University Press—a circumstance that occasioned a fierce attack by George R. Price in a long article on "Science and the Supernatural" in *Science* (26 August 1955). Soal had earlier made his crucial addition to the terminology of parapsychology by referring to the range of phenomena investigated by Rhine as "psi powers"; these included Rhine's initial set of extrasensory perceptions, plus psychokinesis or telekinesis (the ability to move objects by the power of thought), pyrolysis (the ability to start fires with the power of thought), and teleportation (the ability to move oneself by the power of thought, by a process of *matter transmission rather than *gravity-defying levitation).

The findings of such research were greeted with widespread scepticism—not unnaturally, given the *a priori* objections raised against such notions as "telepathy" and "precognition" by philosophers such as Antony Flew, in *A New Approach to Psychical Research* (1953)—and Price was one of many crusaders who undertook to slay the pseudoscientific dragon. Investigators commissioned to check up on the claims made by such experimenters as Rhine and Soal soon began to detect deceptions on the part of their star subjects. The Welsh Jones brothers, whose investigation was reported in Soal and H. T. Bowden's *The Mind Readers* (1960), were quickly exposed as cheats. The fact that telepathy, clairvoyance, and precognition are essentially *plausible impossibilities guaranteed, however, that the "evidence" would also be avidly seized by believers as the foundations of an authentic scientific discipline.

The "traditional" versions of ESP had been a staple feature of fantastic fiction throughout history, but the Rhinean reconfiguration was surprisingly slow to take effect, given the tremendous fashionability it eventually acquired in the years following the end of World War II. He was not as influential in literary circles during the 1930s as Charles *Fort, who frankly admitted that his reliance on newspaper *reportage rendered his findings dubious, except as incontrovertible evidence of enduring preoccupations of the human imagination. One notion implicit in Rhine's alleged findings that had considerable literary potential, however, was the suggestion that large numbers of people might have "latent" psi powers of which they were quite unaware, which might be further developed by proper training or by sudden traumatic access.

This idea became a considerable inspiration to accounts of future human *evolution, and the notion that the species destined to replace ours—commonly called *Homo superior*—would achieve that by virtue of cultivating psi powers became a standard feature of the literary image of the *superman. Pulp science fiction writers became increasingly entranced by this idea, with the active encouragement of the emergent field's tacit leader, John W. *Campbell Jr. His "Forgetfulness" (1937; by-lined Don A. Stuart) offered a significant account of a future human race that has outgrown its dependence on *technology because the mind can do everything that once required tools, reproducing in pulp science fiction the occult Utopianism of Edward Bulwer-Lytton's *The Coming Race* (1870).

The fact that Campbell had been a student at Duke when Rhine arrived there presumably assisted his subsequent acceptance of the reality of "psi powers" and his insistence on building them into the core assumptions of *hard science fiction. His advocacy helped to popularise the related term "psionics"—which included a seductive echo of "electronics"—and encouraged a boom in "psi stories" in science fiction magazines after the end of World War I. Jack Williamson's review of J. B. Rhine's *The Reach of the Mind* (1948)—which appeared shortly after his "... And Searching Mind" had finished serialisation, in the August 1948 issue of *Astounding*—provided a manifesto of sorts for the boom, arguing that "The paraphysical attributes of mankind are the final answer to the overgrown physical science of the humanoids" and citing Rhine's hope for a "nuclear psychology [that] might rescue mankind from the devastating aftermath of nuclear physics".

The consequent evolution of *Astounding*'s contents was mirrored by the transformation of the career of L. Ron Hubbard, the least earnest member of Campbell's stable, who had displayed an amiable cynicism in his early psi story "The Tramp" (1938), but spent the late 1940s developing a new form of psychoanalysis called Dianetics, which Campbell allowed him to advertise in a long article in the May 1950 issue of *Astounding*. Dianetics, which promised to endow its clients with a modest superhumanity by "clearing" them of the accumulated psychological blocks inhibiting their existential progress, was subsequently integrated into Scientology, a religion whose core doctrine embraced the notion of human evolution towards psionic godhood. A. E. van Vogt, the author of the classic psi-superman novel *Slan* (1940;

book, 1946), and several other science fiction writers became recruits to Hubbard's cause, temporarily abandoning their literary careers to live their dreams as lifestyle fantasists.

In post–World War II science fiction, psi powers became a standard aspect of fictitious *mutation, sometimes induced by fallout from *atom bombs or accidents in *nuclear power stations but often represented as an aspect of the human heritage that had previously been hidden away or subject to persecution. Science-fictional psychic researchers of the period often began their searches in lunatic asylums, and such titles as Wilmar H. Shiras' "In Hiding" (1948), James H. Schmitz's "The Witches of Karres" (1949; exp. book, 1966), Mark Clifton and Alex Apostolides' "Hide! Hide! Witch!" (1953), and George O. Smith's *Highways in Hiding* (1955; book, 1956) became commonplace.

Although much psi boom science fiction was content to dramatise the notions codified by Rhine, narrative pressure put a heavier emphasis on the emotional component of science-fictional telepathy, sometimes separating out a supernatural version of empathy practiced by "empaths". This emphasis became particularly evident in the work of Theodore Sturgeon, who analysed its potential *existential consequences in such works as "The Touch of Your Hand" (1953), *More than Human* (1953), *The Cosmic Rape* (1958), and "Need" (1961), and in such heavily sentimentalised psi stories as Zenna Henderson's accounts of "the People" in the series launched with "Ararat" (1952). The notion that supernatural empathy might be transmitted as well as received generated such accounts of parapsychological tranquillisation as Roger Dee's "Assignment's End" (1954).

The thesis favoured by Sturgeon and Henderson—that psi powers might provide a cure for existential *angst* and provide the basis for a better human morality—provided a useful kind of redemptive conclusion. It was not confined to sentimental fantasies, being readily adaptable to such melodramas as Alfred Bester's *The Demolished Man* (1953)—which relocates the plot of Feodor Dostoyevsky's *Crime and Punishment* in a society of "espers" in which secrets are extremely difficult to keep—and *The Stars My Destination* (1956; aka *Tiger! Tiger!*), which similarly transfigures the vengeance-driven plot of Alexandre Dumas' *The Count of Monte Cristo*. Other writers, however, explored the opposite possibility: that the acquisition of psi powers would give their users unprecedented power over their fellows, which would corrupt them absolutely. Previously developed in such works as Andrew Marvell's *Congratulate the Devil* (1939) and Norvell W. Page's "But Without Horns" (1940), the notion was given sharper expression in such postwar *contes philosophiques* as Jerome Bixby's "It's a Good Life" (1953) and Frederik Pohl's "Pythias" (1955), and more elaborate expansion in Jack Vance's "Telek" (1952), Frank M. Robinson's *The Power* (1956), Henry Slesar's "A God Named Smith" (1957), John Wyndham's *The Midwich Cuckoos* (1957), and Frank Herbert's "The Priests of Psi" (1959; exp. book as *The God Makers*, 1972).

The development of the Cold War added considerable impetus to the progress of spy fiction, and the utility of espers in espionage inevitably became a topic in 1950s science fiction, encouraged by rumours that the U.S. military was investigating the possibility. The straightforward introduction of telepathy made covert spying *so* easy, though, that considerable narrative ingenuity had to be applied to the problem of developing dramatic tension in, or adding new layers of complication to, such accounts of covert operations as Hal Clement's *Needle* (1950), Richard Matheson's "Witch War" (1951), J. T. McIntosh's "Spy" (1954), Eric Frank Russell's *Three to Conquer* (1956), and Randall Garrett and Laurence M. Janifer's "That Sweet Little Old Lady" (1959; book 1962 as *Brain Twister*, by-lined Mark Phillips). Beyond the limits of the genre, however, it became increasing easily to market crime and espionage thrillers that deployed ESP without being reckoned as supernatural fiction; notable examples include Angela Tonks' *Mind out of Time* (1958), Margery Allingham's *The Mind Readers* (1965), and L. P. Davies' *The Paper Dolls* (1966).

Telepathy was by far the most popular psi power in the boom years, although teleportation was foregrounded in Bester's *The Stars My Destination* and Gordon R. Dickson's *Time to Teleport* (1955; book, 1960) and precognition was useful in explorations of the paradox of prophecy. Dowsing (water divining) attracted some interest as a psi power in *Astounding*'s nonfiction sections, but did not lend itself to literary development. The fictional potential of psychokinesis was occasionally aided by the hypothesis that some such ability might be the only viable means of distant space travel, as in Clifford Simak's "The Fisherman" (1961; book as *Time Is the Simplest Thing*).

As the boom ended and parapsychological fiction had to strive harder for effect, telepathically gifted individuals began to make headway as psychotherapists in such stories as John Brunner's *The Whole Man* (1964) and Roger Zelazny's *The Dream Master* (1966), although the antithetical notion that the invasion of mental privacy by extrasensory images and thoughts would be tantamount to instant insanity—previously explored in such pulp science fiction stories as Frank Belknap Long's "Dark Vision"

(1939)—permitted more dramatic development, as in such stories as Joanna Russ' *And Chaos Died* (1970). The boom was inevitably followed by a period in which psi stories came to seem passé within genre science fiction, but when they were revisited in earnest they required some kind of sophistication; in the 1970s and 1980s, science fiction writers were required to be more careful as well as more adventurous in extrapolating the logical correlates of various parapsychological abilities, as reflected in such works as Lester del Rey's *Pstalemate* (1971), Robert Silverberg's *Dying Inside* (1972) and *The Stochastic Man* (1975), Stephen King's *Carrie* (1974), *The Dead Zone* (1979), and *Firestarter* (1980), Tom Reamy's *Blind Voices* (1978), Jack Dann's *The Man Who Melted* (1984), Leigh Kennedy's *The Journal of Nicholas the American* (1986), Orson Scott Card's "Eye for Eye" (1987), and Rachel Murphy's "Prescience" (1989).

Parapsychological research acquired a new fashionability in the 1970s by virtue of the media attention paid to Uri Geller, who popularised a particular form of psychokinesis that became known as "spoonbending" in honour of his favourite trick. The TV publicity brought forth a host of children who claimed to be able to work the same trick, and were sufficiently accomplished in the art of misdirection to fool the physicist John Taylor, who wrote them up in his book *Superminds* (1975). Other popularisers picked up by the same media bandwagon included Lyall Watson, author of *Supernature* (1971). Other ideas that attracted much media attention in the period included the "auras" revealed by "Kirlian photography", popularised in Kendall Johnson's *The Living Aura* (1976)—although Semyon Kirlian had begun producing such images in 1939.

The TV chatshow circuit offered Geller and Watson opportunities for self-publicity that had not been available to D. D. Home, and the following thirty years saw a steady growth in the population of "TV psychics", who spanned a wide spectrum from traditional spiritualist mediums and astrologers through "psychic detectives" and ghosthunters to celebrity parapsychologists. The exploitation of newspaper columns, premium phone lines, and the internet allowed practitioners of various forms of divination to become far more economically successful in the last quarter of the twentieth century than ever before. The phenomenon was satirically mirrored in such literary works as Barry N. Malzberg and Bill Pronzini's *Night Screams* (1979), and steadfastly opposed by sceptics, but such opposition was entirely ineffectual.

One of the principal effects of the dramatic *fin-de-siècle* increase of media parapsychology was, ironically, to make genre science fiction writers much warier of psi themes—much as they had always been wary of the SPR-style investigation of ghosts, which had always been considered an aspect of supernatural fiction, save for such lighthearted exceptions as Charles Eric Maine's "Scholarly Correspondence" (1974) and Michael F. Flynn's "Mammy Morgan Played the Organ, Her Daddy Beat the Drum" (1990). The increasingly fugitive subgenre of science fiction stories attempting to subject psi powers to more rigorous extrapolation and analysis did, however, continued to the end of the century in such stories as Connie Willis' "Jack" (1991), Steven Gould's *Jumper* (1992), Paul Ash's "The Man Who Stayed Behind" (1993), Jim Aikin's *The Wall at the Edge of the World* (1993), Pamela Sargent's "Common Mind" (2000), and Sean McMullen's "Colors of the Soul" (2000).

PAST

The range of elapsed *time, which remains mentally accessible via memory and culturally accessible to literate societies via *history. In preliterate societies the past is a construction of *myth, legend, and folklore, so early literature produced in connection with the advent of literacy inevitably offers elaborate accounts of the mythical past. Indeed, the techniques of artistry inherited by literate culture from oral culture—the meter and rhyme of poetry, the heroic and moralistic aspects of storytelling, and the ritual aspects of drama—must have been conceived and developed as efficient means of preserving, sustaining, decorating, and dignifying the mythical past. The association of literature and myth is deep rooted and very intimate.

The history of modern literature—particularly the recent history of prose fiction—is, to some extent, a narrative of the gradual replacement of the mythic past by the historical past in such genres as the novel. Although modern readers and critics are likely to think of the historical novel in contrast to the contemporary novel, it originally materialised in opposition to fiction dealing with the mythical past. It is hardly surprising that aspects of the mythical past still survive and thrive in the interstices of the historical past represented in fiction and nonfiction alike; nor is it surprising that the historical past continually generates mythical aspects of its own. Since the early nineteenth century, fiction that deals frankly and self-consciously with the mythical past has been distinguished from naturalistic fiction by means of such labels as Gothic fiction, supernatural fiction, fairy tales, and fantasy, but not all myths and legends are supernatural or fantastic, so the historical past cannot be isolated from its mythical roots and correlates merely by the exclusion of the supernatural and the

fanciful—nor is the exclusion of the supernatural as simple a matter as it may seem.

The evolution of folkloristic and literary representations from the near-universality of various mythical pasts to the privileged dominance of the historical past is sometimes viewed retrospectively as a process taking place in the world that folklore and literature supposedly mirrors. As cultures evolve history, therefore, they routinely come to see their residual mythic representations as images of a world now lost: a Golden Age replaced by an Age of Iron, or a magical Age of Miracles that has now given way to an era of toilsome mundanity. Fantastic fiction—especially modern fantastic fiction—is often hyperconscious of this kind of imagined dynamic, so literary images of the mythical past routinely represent it as a world in the process of what John Clute calls "thinning": a world whose enchantment is gradually and inexorably dwindling away.

This notion of the past is often transferred to an individual context, in the common idea that childhood is an existential phase possessed of its own innate magicality, which leaks away as individuals grow to adulthood and put aside childhood illusions. This way of thinking is so powerful, in fact, that it conditions the culture of childhood manufactured in the West, which deliberately conserves and fiercely protects various mythical notions for the alleged benefit of children—most conspicuously the myth of Santa Claus. A child's relationship with books is not merely one of the means that literate culture uses to protect and conserve a mythical element in childhood experience, but one of the items to be protected; the recognition that the act of reading can be, and often is, a kind of "enchantment" in itself is the basis of a significant thread of *aesthetic philosophy.

The notion of personal thinning is sustained by the mind's essential existential relationship with the past—which is, inevitably, dominated by the antithesis of *angst*, nostalgia. In the prologue to his anti-nostalgic novel *The Go-Between* (1953), L. P. Hartley contends that "The past is a foreign country: they do things differently there", but this is only true from the assumed objectivity of the novelistic stance. In experiential terms, it is the present that is the foreign country where "they do things differently"; the past is, by contrast, where we are able to feel "at home", even though we did not feel at home there while we were living through it. We can feel at home there because the past, from the viewpoint of the present, is a known quantity, already survived and contextualised.

The chief sources of *angst*—death and uncertainty—belong to the future; the worst that the personal past can contain is the kind of dire experience that generates post-traumatic stress, and no matter how bad that might be, there was always a time before it to which nostalgia can be attached. Even as minds deteriorate, losing connection with the immediate past under the assaults of such conditions as Alzheimer's disease, they tend to retain their nostalgic connection with the more distant past, which becomes their last refuge and comfort. In personal terms, as the original translator of Marcel Proust's *À la recherche du temps perdu* (1913–1927) had him observe, "The past not merely is not fugitive, it remains present".

The history of science, especially as viewed by literature, needs to be seen within this context if the widespread contemporary hostility to science—especially among literary men—is to be fully understood. Within the perspective that sees the mythical past as a world in the process of thinning, science is the chief agent of corrosion, the irresistible spirit of the Iron Age. The fact that some of its specific assertions insult and shatter specific items of the mythic past is an aspect of a much broader and far-reaching erosion, which is as antagonistic to nostalgia as it is to faith.

Because history is, by definition, based in documentation, it cannot help preserving and recognising—no matter how dismissive it may be of their claim to factual status—all the aspects of the mythical past that were ever committed to *writing. Other past-orientated sciences, however, especially when they deal with prehistoric eras, are bound to be less respectful. Proust's judgement is not only applicable to the personal past of memory and the cultural past of traditions and monuments, but to the physical past too, which leaves relics and traces everywhere, for the consultation of *geologists, *archaeologists, *palaeontologists, and *cosmologists. The early discoveries of such sciences were, inevitably, often construed in the context of ideas deeply infected by mythical images of the past, but the accumulating mass of those discoveries was more severely and more comprehensively corrosive of false belief than any re-examination of historical documents could ever be. As such sciences evolved, they generated a few myths of their own, especially in the field of physical *anthropology—which are abundantly represented in literary imagery—but their general thrust was always more brutally anti-mythic than the progress of history.

Although Hartley's judgement of the past is not in strict accordance with personal experience, it is perfectly accurate in its judgement of the literary treatment of the past, in naturalistic, speculative, and fantastic fiction alike—as is recognised in David Lowenthal's monumental survey of attitudes, *The Past Is a Foreign County* (1985). The literary past *is* a foreign country, to which readers must be carefully introduced, and in which they must be imaginatively

immersed. This is a difficult narrative project, and it is often skimped, so that the literary past routinely ends up seeming much more like the present than the historical, prehistoric, or mythical past under representation could possibly have done. Even so, it remains foreign by definition. The scientific past, as reconstructed by archaeology, palaeontology, geology, and cosmology, is also different in its detail—so different that it poses very considerable difficulties to writers intent on the imaginative immersion therein of the contemporary reader—but the whole basis of its construction is the notion that the underlying agents of its causality have always been the same.

The scientific past can only be extrapolated on the assumption that the laws of physics and the phenomena of chemistry have been constant; even such restricted sciences as geology and palaeontology moved inexorably from *catastrophist explanations towards uniformitarian ones. The fundamental assumption of science is that the world was never magical, and has always been as thin as it is at present. The scientific past, especially in the context of the more theoretically inclined sciences, is defined in such a way that it cannot be a foreign country. Small wonder, then, that the scientific past always feels far less comfortable in fiction than the mythic past, no matter how hard writers of speculative fiction might strive to make it seem hospitable.

The scientific past is bound by chronological order, in which events are organised in linear order and causality follows time's arrow. The personal past and the literary past are not so tightly confined. Memory discards and rearranges, and the mind is free to flit from memory to memory along eccentric paths of association, without regard for chronological connection or order. Literary texts can do the same, routinely ignoring tracts of uneventful time by consigning them to text breaks or synoptic summaries and performing "flashbacks" to fill in aspects of "back-story". Speculative literature can do more, by virtue of the various ways it has of playing more expansive tricks with time. Even the personal past is limited in its mutability to the scope of forgetfulness, confabulation, and self-delusion; the literary past is far more mutable than that in such subgenres as *alternative history, although the mutability is disciplined by the same logic of extrapolation that applies to the retrospective projection of the scientific past.

PATAPHYSICS

A term coined by the French writer Alfred Jarry, one of the pioneers of surrealism (who had been educated in science and was fascinated by the metaphysical philosophy of Henri Bergson). While physics deals with regular phenomena that can be organised within a framework of laws, pataphysics supposedly deals with exceptional phenomena that cannot be accommodated within such a framework: events that are, in essence, uncaused and inexplicable. The term is sometimes rendered as 'pataphysics, precisely because the prefatory apostrophe is redundant and meaningless.

Jarry was aware of the fact that certain scientific theses past and present required unaccounted intrusions. The Epicurean cosmology, as popularised by Lucretius in *De rerum natura*, imagined the ultimate origin of motion as *clinamen*, a tiny random swerve of an atom falling through space, occasioning its collision with other atoms, which initially set in train the whole sequence of cause and effect. Charles *Darwin's theory of evolution by natural selection similarly required some such source of spontaneous variation to provide the differences on which selection could operate, which could not be accounted for in the days before the causes and mechanisms of genetic mutation were understood. Jarry's notion of a "science" of such exceptions is, however, a deliberate contradiction in terms: an aesthetically pleasing *paradox.

Pataphysics was primarily a prospectus for artistic procedure; Jarry asserted that writers ought not to be content to provide their audiences with material that was comprehensible within conventional structures of belief and expectation, but should attempt to startle them out of their complacency by presenting them with the unexpected and the nonsensical, unconstrained by any limits of plausibility or possibility. He attempted to put this prospectus into practice in his classic absurdist play *Ubu roi* (1896), whose antihero—like the protagonist of *Gestes et opinions du docteur Faustroll* (1911; trans. as *Exploits and Opinions of Dr Faustroll, Pataphysician*)—was modelled on one of his science teachers.

The latter work was an explicit response to the advent of Wellsian speculative fiction; Jarry's typically perverse reaction to Wells' first novel had been a speculative essay, "Commentaire pour servir à la construction pratique de la machine à explorer le temps" (1900; trans. as "How to Construct a Time Machine"), which revised Wells' notion of time travel along Bergsonian lines, describing a hypothetical mechanism to isolate its user from the ceaseless pressure of "becoming", thus achieving eternal stasis. Jarry also dealt with Wellsian themes in *Le surmâle* (1901; trans. as *The Supermale*), a deceptively orthodox mock-scientific romance whose exceptionally endowed protagonist eventually proves to be not quite exceptional enough.

The pataphysical prospectus was echoed, and combined with other notions, in Andre Breton's surrealist

manifesto, which named Jarry among its primary exemplars. The more familiar term is derived by a similar linguistic extension. The spirit of pataphysics is also echoed in such mock-scientific generalisations as Murphy's *law. All forms of storytelling—including *reportage as well as fiction—are, of course, more interested in the exceptional than the usual, and often manifest a particular interest in the bizarre and inexplicable, even within a supposedly naturalistic framework. Even the kind of pseudoscientific literary *naturalism developed by Émile Zola was primarily interested in grotesque human specimens whose literary interest was defined by their deviance rather than their normality.

Admirers of Jarry's literary philosophy eventually established a Collège de Pataphysique in 1948, whose *"dignitaires"* included numerous significant *avant-gardist* writers, most notably Boris Vian and Raymond Queneau, the surrealist artist Max Ernst, and the filmmaker René Clair. It issued a series of *Cahiers* and *Dossiers*, followed by the *Subsidia Pataphysica* and the *Carnets trimestriels*, which built up a considerable retrospective tradition of pataphysical literature. Jules Verne was one of many writers drafted to exemplify the cause, although François Rabelais was appointed its founder. Queneau and others, including Georges Perec and Italo Calvino, went on to found the Ouvroir de Littérature Potentielle [Workshop of Potential Literature]—usually contracted as Oulipo—whose poetry is produced by various extraordinary and calculatedly nonsensical methods; its English language spin-off includes the Cybership of Fools based on the University of Melbourne's website. After a period of eclipse the Collège de Pataphysique was revitalised in 2000 by a new generation of enthusiasts—including Jean Baudrillard and Umberto Eco—and began publishing a new journal. Similar institutions sprang up in many other places in that auspicious year, including an Institute of Pataphysics in London.

PATHOLOGY

The branch of *biology pertaining to the physiology and causation of disease. Its history is intimately linked with that of *medicine, the technology of treatment, and literary works very often combine explorations of the nature of disease with accounts of its treatment. The notion that many diseases are caused by imperceptible physical agents (germs) transmissible by physical contact or atmospheric circulation was first broached in Classical times by Varro in the first century B.C. and repeated by Girolamo Fracastoro's *De Contagione* (1546), but it could not be backed up with evidence until the invention of the microscope opened the way to a science of *microbiology.

The crucial proof of the germ theory was offered by Louis Pasteur in "Nouvelles expériences relatives aux générations dites spontanées" (1860), and its significant early applications included the identification of the bacilli causing tuberculosis and cholera by Robert Koch in 1882–1883. Prior to this establishment, the afflictions of disease were very often considered in spiritual terms, as divine punishments or magical curses that could only be alleviated, if at all, by prayer or magical countermeasures. The identification and description of new diseases made progress during the early phases of the scientific revolution, however, even though their treatment did not. *Paracelsus' mercury treatment for syphilis was a toxic disaster, but the verse description of the disease in Fracastoro's *Syphilis sive morbus Gallicus* (1530) was a significant exercise in pathology as well as a pioneering work of epidemiology. The fact that its title contains an unjustified slur on the French reflects a common tendency to stigmatise whole nations or cultures by means of pathological or *psychopathological references. Arguments raged for centuries as to whether syphilis had been imported to Europe from America or *vice versa* (different strains probably existed on both continents, whose mutual transfer into populations with no natural immunity was disastrous), although there is little doubt that smallpox was exported from Europe on a massive scale by explorers, with devastating—and sometimes calculated—effects on distant native populations that had no resistance to it.

While early literary representations often mocked medical practitioners, they remained in awe of disease, particularly of destructive epidemics. The vulnerability of civilised society to the ravages of bubonic plague—to which the fourteenth-century Black Death was routinely, though dubiously, attributed—is a significant theme of early prose fiction, amply reflected in the frame narrative of Giovanni Boccaccio's *Decameron* (1349–1351). That awareness continued into the eighteenth century in such works as Daniel Defoe's *A Journal of the Plague Year* (1722) and became a significant feature of early speculative fiction, in such works as Mary Shelley's *The Last Man* (1826). Edgar Allan Poe's "The Masque of the Red Death" (1842) is a striking symbolic fantasy. The significance of ill health as a motivation to literary endeavour is emphasised by the number of writers who became "career invalids", including Laurence Sterne, Samuel Johnson, Elizabeth Barrett Browning, Algernon Swinburne, Marcel Proust, and Eugene Lee-Hamilton. The notion that the deliria associated with disease-induced fever

might offer similar inspirational rewards to the hallucinations induced by *psychotropic drugs became commonplace.

The attitudes and methods of nineteenth-century European imaginative fiction were deeply coloured by the vulnerability to venereal diseases of writers committed to a "Bohemian" lifestyle. Although syphilis was not solely responsible for the cynicism and fatalism of writers involved in the *Decadent movements, it was certainly a major contributor. J. K. Huysmans' definitive Decadent novel, *À rebours* (1884), includes a striking visionary sequence in which the disease is seen as the ultimate *femme fatale*, which helps to explain the constant association of female beauty with fatality in nineteenth-century Romantic and post-Romantic fiction. Huysmans went on to produce a novelisation of a legend of martyrdom by disease, *Sainte Lydwine de Schiedam* (1901), which is one of the most remarkable examples of the pornography of pathology.

Many writers in nineteenth-century France were also greatly fascinated by tuberculosis, whose association with pulchritude ran in the opposite direction; post-Romantic and Decadent literature is replete with eroticised accounts of the transfiguration of young women worn away by its ravages, including such novels as Alexandre Dumas fils' *La dame aux camélias* (1852; trans. as *The Lady of the Camellias*) and Marcel Schwob's *Le livre de Monelle* (1894) and such *contes cruels* as Maurice Level's "Nès yeux" (1904; trans. as "All Saints' Day" and "Blue Eyes").

The dual association of disease with artistic creativity and erotic fascination was preserved into the twentieth century by such writers as Thomas Mann, in *Der Tod in Venedig* (1911; trans. as *Death in Venice*) and—in a more ambitious existential extrapolation—*Der Zauberberg* (1924; trans. as *The Magic Mountain*). The notion that infatuation can be regarded as a kind of disease, preserved in the adjective "lovesick", was extrapolated into the post-Pasteur era by such works as Jane Emily Gerard's *The Extermination of Love: A Fragmentary Study in Erotics* (1901), whose protagonist believes that he has discovered *bacillus amoris*.

Pasteur's clarification of the nature of infectious diseases did not give rise in the short term to many new means of actively fighting diseases, although it did prompt a revolution in hygiene and disease avoidance—a trend hypothetically extrapolated to its ultimate extreme in such stories as Allen Kim Lang's "World in a Bottle" (1960) and various actual cases of twentieth-century children being raised in plastic "bubbles". There was also a time lag before the mechanisms for combating disease innate in living bodies began to be clarified, when Elie

Metchnikoff—working at the Pasteur Institute—pioneered the study of the immune system and discovered the operation of white blood corpuscles in 1898. Infectious diseases continued to serve in fiction as implacable menaces well into the twentieth century, when they continued to do equally sterling service as a convenient means of authorial murder.

Although the notion of disease as an agent of divine punishment declined in fashionability while prose fiction increased its popular appeal, literary disease remained a kind of curse visited by writers upon their characters as a means of generating dramatic tension or disposal. The strategic uses made of cholera in Eugène Sue's classic proto–soap opera *Le Juif errant* (1844–1845; trans. as *The Wandering Jew*) set a series of examples that many future writers of serial fiction took to heart. Striking down a key character by injury or disease became—and still remains—a standard device of melodrama, its potential impact summed up by the classic line in the 1863 stage adaptation of Mrs. Henry Wood's *East Lynne* (which does not appear in the 1861 novel): "Dead! Dead! And never called me Mother!"

So useful is life-threatening disease as a plot lever that the twentieth-century literary history of disease was largely a matter of keeping one step ahead of medical treatment, abandoning curable ailments in favour of incurable ones. Cancer became the favourite weapon of authorial murder, leukaemia replacing tuberculosis as the agent most commonly deployed against children. In the latter part of the century, such instruments were deployed with particular brutality, on an individual level, in the TV medium. They were routinely used to pick off selected individuals in soap operas and hospital dramas, and also featured in the emergence of a whole new genre of "freak show" documentaries chronicling exotic diseases.

In early twentieth-century speculative fiction, new diseases were routinely used as agents of mass destruction in *disaster stories. Their potential was enhanced within genre science fiction by the possibility of importing new diseases from outside the earth, in the context of the *panspermia hypothesis, as in such works as Théo Varlet's *La grande panne* (1930) and A. Rowley Hilliard's "Death from the Stars" (1931). The theme was further sophisticated in such late twentieth-century examples as Harry Harrison's *Plague from Space* (1966) and Michael Crichton's *The Andromeda Strain* (1969), by which time it was formally reintroduced into Fred Hoyle and Chandra Wickramasinghe's revitalised version of the panspermia hypothesis, in *Diseases from Space* (1979). Accounts of quarantine regulations intended to protect Earth from Space Age infections include Bernard

I. Kahn's "For the Public" (1946) and Randall Garrett's "What's Eating You?" (1957).

The notion that new diseases might be deliberately produced as weapons of war, introduced in an exotic fashion in Robert Potter's *The Germ Growers* (1892), also made considerable headway in the twentieth century, although those employed as threats in thriller fiction—as in Robert W. Service's *The Master of the Microbe* (1926), Thomas Painter and Alexander Laing's *The Motives of Nicholas Holtz* (1936; aka *The Glass Centipede*), and Alastair Maclean's *The Satan Bug* (1962; by-lined Ian Stuart) rarely ran riot. The advent of *genetic engineering in the latter part of the century brought a dramatic increase in anxiety regarding the actual possibilities of biological warfare, and hence in fictional representations of manufactured diseases. Notable examples of such anxious responses include Frank Herbert's *The White Plague* (1982), Terry Gilliam's film *Twelve Monkeys* (1995), and Mike Conner's alternative history novel *Archangel* (1995).

By far the most important disease of the twentieth century, in terms of its literary impact, was AIDS (Acquired Immune Deficiency Syndrome), which was first identified in 1981 in New York and California. The apparent selectivity of the disease, whose early victims in the West were often homosexual men who transmitted the disease through sexual intercourse and drug users who transmitted it by sharing needles, provided a complex network of associations whose potential melodramatic utility was exploited to the full, especially by homosexual writers. The agent responsible, which eventually became known as HIV (Human Immunodeficiency Virus), could not be directly attacked, but the complex development of disease meant that the secondary symptoms induced by its suppression of the immune system could be significantly retarded; the fact that HIV-positive patients varied extensively in the rapidity with which they developed "full-blown AIDS" added further flexibility to literary representations of the disease.

Further complications were added to the AIDS narrative when palliative treatments—involving drug cocktails including azidothymindine (AZT)—became widely available in the 1990s in the West, although restricted access in developing countries, especially in Africa, failed to slow down a global pandemic affecting tens of millions of people. Notable responses to AIDS in speculative fiction—where the scientific aspects of the epidemic received most attention—included Michael Blumlein's *The Movement of Mountains* (1987), F. M. Busby's *The Breeds of Man* (1988), Norman Spinrad's "Journals of the Plague Years" (1988), Michael Bishop's *Unicorn Mountain* (1988), Charles Sheffield's "Dancing with Myself"

(1989), Judith Moffett's "Tiny Tango" (1989), Nancy Kress' *Brain Rose* (1990), Paula May's "The Solomon Solution" (1990), and Charles G. Oberndorf's *Sheltered Lives* (1992).

One other newly defined disease that attracted a great deal of attention in naturalistic fiction as the century drew to a close was Alzheimer's disease, whose effects on old people became increasingly obvious as the effects of the agents that had killed the great majority of their predecessors were gradually reduced. Speculative fictions dealing with the possible future impact of the disease include Shane Tourtellotte's "The Return of Spring" (2001), Maureen McHugh's "Presence" (2002), and Alexander Glass' "Lucid" (2002).

Most accounts of hypothetical diseases in late twentieth-century speculative fiction belong to the rich tradition of medical horror fiction. The most elaborate practitioner of this kind of fiction is Octavia Butler, whose works in that vein include "Speech Sounds" (1983), *Clay's Ark* (1984), and "The Evening and the Morning and the Night" (1987). Notable examples by other writers include Gregory Frost's "In Media Vita" (1985) and Tanarive Due's "Patient Zero" (2000). There is, however, a substantial tradition of stories featuring diseases whose undeniably awkward symptoms are offset by various kinds of existential rewards, greatly exaggerating the psychotropic effects of mere fevers; notable examples include Walter M. Miller's "Dark Benediction" (1951), Thomas M. Disch's *Camp Concentration* (1968), Maya Kaathryn Bohnhoff's "Blythe Magic" (1990), and—in a more blackly ironic spirit—Greg Egan's "Silver Fire" (1995). Egan's "In Numbers" (1991) is also significant as an ingenious account of a kind of "space sickness". Diseases invented for satirical purposes include Thurston's disease in J. F. Bone's "Pandemic" (1962), which spares heavy smokers, and allergic pseudomononucleosis in Harry Harrison's "A Matter of Timing" (1965; by-lined Hank Dempsey).

The notion of infatuation as an actual disease was resurrected by D. G. Compton's *A Usual Lunacy* (1978), making more sense in an era when the Darwinian logic of disease transmission was better understood. David Brin's "The Giving Plague" (1988) makes ingenious use of that logic in an account of a disease that makes a rather different somatopsychic provision for its transmission to new hosts. These are by no means the only stories in which hypothetical pathology remains a tacit instrument of moral judgement; similarly frank deployments include Eric Vinicoff and Marcia Martin's "The Ultimate Arbiter" (1977)—the title refers to cancer—and Jerry Oltion's "The Uncommon Cold"

(2003). Despite all the sophistication of twentieth-century diseases, however, there is a sense in which none can ever duplicate the imaginative impact that the plague once had, as is tacitly recognised in such modern accounts of the Black Death as Sharon Farber's "A Surfeit of Melancholic Humours" (1984) and Connie Willis' *Doomsday Book* (1992).

Although the bacterial flagellum became a key item in arguments for "intelligent design" bandied about in the early twenty-first century, pathogens were still generally regarded as blots on the face of Creation whose extermination is devoutly to be desired. Even the most hardened conservationists hesitate to demand their preservation, although the November 1977 issue of *Analog* did feature a satirical article by Joe Patrouch calling for "Legal Rights for Germs", which drew forth a response from Dennis Latham Cox giving an account of "Universal Medical versus *Diplococcus pneumoniae*" (1978). There is, however, a certain strange aesthetic in the symptoms of exotic diseases, very amply reflected in the pages of *The Thackeray T. Lambshead Pocket Guide to Eccentric and Discredited Diseases* (2003) edited by Jeff VanderMeer and Mark Roberts, whose contributors were invited to invent the strangest diseases they could imagine, purely for the fun of it.

PHILOSOPHY

A term translatable from the Greek as a love of wisdom, or a passion for truth. Its field of reference is difficult to define or delimit, although it would certainly include careful analysis of that very difficulty. It has accumulated a range of subsidiary meanings, whereby reference to a personal philosophy can mean an attitude or a set of beliefs, and the adjective "philosophical" sometimes implies no more than a refusal to get excited.

The field of Classical philosophy, as mapped out by *Plato, *Aristotle, Epicurus, and other pioneering philosophers is broadly divisible into two principal categories: the investigation of what is in the world (natural philosophy), and the discussion of how people ought to behave. Before such questions can be answered, however, the philosopher needs to determine how answers might be sought, and upon what foundations they might safely be erected; that preliminary phase has not yet been exhausted, and to the extent that knowledge of the former kind has moved beyond such fundamental analysis it has been displaced into the new category of *science. Other significant subcategories or extensions of the principal categories that are separately covered in this volume are *logic, *metaphysics, and *aesthetics, while literary treatments of fundamental philosophical questions are also mentioned in the articles on *space, *time, and *matter.

The aspect of philosophy most relevant to science in its attempt to underpin the endeavours—which forms the substance of the subsequent article on the *philosophy of science—but various other fields retain connections and associations with the progress of science. Although science is independent of *ethics in the sense that one cannot deduce an ought from an is, it is nevertheless the case that no system of ethics can be of much practical use if it does not take into account the resources of the world and the limits of its manipulability; for this reason, new technologies frequently give rise to specific moral problems, and may give rise to new subcategories of ethical philosophy such as bioethics. Aesthetic judgements cannot be deduced from scientific statements either, but that is not to say that science does not have an aesthetic dimension. Scientific knowledge can, and perhaps must, be reckoned as a good in its own right whose acquisition is both morally and aesthetically desirable. Such issues are, inevitably, relevant to the representation of science in art and literature as well as to the artistic and literary components of science.

Philosophy has always had a considerable literary element, built in at its inception by Plato's choice of the dialogue as a means of investigating and clarifying philosophical questions—a method echoed by numerous successors, including *Galileo. Social philosophy, insofar as it required the construction of hypothetical societies, often made use of imaginary *geography, again following the Platonic precedent of Atlantis. Drama routinely retained a philosophical component in its dialogue, and embraced another standard philosophical genre—the meditation—in the development of the soliloquy. When dialogue was imported into prose fiction on a massive scale as its *narrative method evolved from the diegetic to the mimetic mode, its philosophical potential was often imported and exploited, remaining in the foreground in the work of Thomas Love Peacock and his imitators.

Prose fiction also accommodated the meditation, especially in its use of first-person narration, whose fictional exemplars often mimic the supposedly nonfictional genre of "spiritual autobiography". Most works of fiction cast as first-person narratives have a philosophical aspect, but some—including most texts classified as bildungsromans—are primarily philosophical in their intent. Some specifically examine the consequences of holding particular philosophical positions; notable examples include J. W. von Goethe's Die Leiden des jungen Werther (1774; trans. as The Sorrows of Young Werther), William Henry Smith's Thorndale; or, The Conflict of Opinions

(1857), J. H. Shorthouse's John Inglesant (1880), and Paul Bourget's Le Disciple (1889; trans. as The Disciple). The introspective method of René Descartes' Meditationes (1641) became the fountainhead of a rich French tradition of explicitly philosophical fiction that extended into the twentieth century in the existentialist explorations of Jean-Paul Sartre and Albert Camus.

There is a sense in which all serious literature is philosophical, immediately and intimately concerned with questions of what is and what ought to be and the tangled relationship between the two. It still makes sense, however, to separate out a distinct genre of *contes philosophiques, which adopt a distinctive interrogative attitude and aspire to exceptional analytical depth. They usually introduce hypothetical and comparative dimensions, setting what is within the context of what might be. Although *science fiction has been displaced into a literary category of its own, all serious speculative fiction is rooted within the tradition of the conte philosophique; this is equally obvious whether one considers the genre's primary parental text to be John Kepler's Somnium, Francis Bacon's New Atlantis, Voltaire's Micromégas, Mary Shelley's Frankenstein, Jules Verne's Voyage au centre de la terre, or H. G. Wells' The Time Machine, or whether one considers the acme of its twentieth-century achievement to be found within the work of Olaf Stapledon, Isaac Asimov, Arthur C. Clarke, Robert A. Heinlein, Philip K. Dick, Ursula K. Le Guin, or Greg Egan.

Literary characters identified as philosophers are generally distinguished by their unworldliness and impracticality, much as *scientists often are, but are rarely treated with such scant respect as Dr. Pangloss—a parodic follower of Gottfried Leibniz—in Voltaire's Candide (1759). Such caricatures are not uncommon, but examples of fictitious philosophers who are not based on real individuals, such as Georg Engel's Hann Klüth, der Philosoph (1905; trans. as The Philosopher and the Foundling), are understandably rare. Philosophers are difficult to characterise in the visual media, as exemplified by the highly stylised depiction of Don Joselito in the 1922 film version of Vicente Blasco-Ibanez' Sangre y arena (1909; trans. as Blood and Sand).

PHILOSOPHY OF SCIENCE

The component of *philosophy that attempts to prove and sustain empirical science's entitlement to be reckoned the most reliable product of human intellectual endeavour, and to differentiate it from the imitative and aberrant endeavours of *pseudoscience and *occult science.

The foundations of the philosophy of science, as a distinct enterprise, were laid in the sixteenth and seventeenth centuries, the result of a crucial and distinctive evolution of Western thought. In that period there was a gradual inversion of the priority afforded to two fundamental styles of argument: argument from authority and argument from experience. Thomas Aquinas had brought the legacy of Classical philosophy back into the bosom of Christendom, but he had done so by fusing the authority of the scriptures with the authority of ancient philosophy—primarily that of *Aristotle—into an ostensibly seamless whole. The settlement of any argument was largely dependent upon the prestige of the authority holding that argument, with the scriptures having the ultimate power of judgement. If the evidence of experience came into conflict with the power of authority in Medieval Christendom, then it had to be set aside as illusory, mistaken, or misunderstood.

By degrees, this assumed priority was overturned during the Renaissance. Significant numbers of individuals inverted the hierarchy of doubt, preferring the evidence of their own senses and the force of their own reason to authoritarian declaration. When disputes of this kind became famous, as in the case of the trial of *Galileo, the Church tended to win the battles, but science won the war: In the end, the majority of the intelligentsia came to favour the view that empirical evidence, not written authority, is the final arbiter of all claims to reliable knowledge. This inversion was the foundation of modern individualism as well as modern science, and was ultimately responsible for the global success of Western politics and culture.

Seventeenth century analyses of the scientific method, including the description issued by Francis *Bacon, represented the essence of empirical analysis as the "induction" of generalisations from the careful observation of the world, whose refinement would reveal underlying *laws of nature. The application of processes of logic and mathematics to particular circumstances controlled by these laws could then produce a fuller understanding, including predictions of their future development. The role of experimentation in setting up and refining circumstances for analysis was already appreciated, and the achievements of eighteenth century science were largely built on these philosophical foundations.

The literary reflection of this evolution of thought is rather clouded. Litterateurs are understandably inclined to respect the authority of the written word, and to attribute both literal and metaphorical sacredness to texts, so the most conspicuous literary response to the advancement of the modern philosophy of science was defensive and defiant. The fact that speculative fiction has frequently been seen as an unusual or frankly aberrant form of literary endeavour testifies to the extent to which the majority of litterateurs have regarded the development and progress of empirical argument with unease, suspicion, and distaste.

Once the brute force of argument from authority had been successfully resisted, opposition to the scientific notion of explanation in terms of material causes and effects was displaced into other philosophical fields. One redrawn line attempted to remove the human world from the scope of scientific explanation because the scientific notion of determinism seemed to be in conflict with the human experience of "free will". The most notable attempt to make that distinction came to be known as Cartesian dualism in response to the ideas of René Descartes, who proposed that although the human body is a mechanical system subject to physical laws, the human mind operates according to different principles, able to intrude upon the mechanical working of the body from without.

The mind/body problem, and its implications for the nature of the human sciences, remained a significant confusing factor in the philosophy of science despite such attempts to override the Cartesian model as Pierre Laplace's *Essai philosophique sur les probabilités* (1814), which asserted that if the present state of the universe were entirely knowable and fully describable, then its entire past and future history could be calculated. Laplace's hypothetical knower—usually called Laplace's daemon (or demon)—became a significant icon of the determinist position, widely cited in philosophy and literature. In general, the literary response to determinism was negative, often fervently so; litterateurs tend to regard literature as a particularly self-evident product of free will. Arthur Hugh Clough's "The New Sinai" (1849) is one of many literary objections to Laplace's argument.

The philosophy of science was identified as a significant area of discussion in the nineteenth century, when John Herschel's *A Preliminary Discourse on the Study of Natural Philosophy* (1831) helped pave the way for William Whewell's *The Philosophy of the Inductive Sciences* (1840) and Auguste Comte developed the philosophy of *positivism. Further additions to Whewell's prospectus included John Tyndall's *Essays on the Use and Limit of the Imagination in Science* (1870) and Karl Pearson's *The Grammar of Science* (1892).

Comte's crusade to dispose of the last few Baconian idols cluttering science with stubborn residues of religious and metaphysical thought reached its terminus in early twentieth century "logical positivism", which was retrospectively summarised in A. J. Ayer's *Language, Truth and Logic* (1936). Logical positivism proved unsatisfactory, partly because it proved impossible to purge sensory perception of an interpretative element that made observations dependent on theories rather than *vice versa*, and partly because of the "problem of induction", which could find no logical justification for the induction of a universal law from the observation of a finite series of coincidences. The exit from this apparent dead end was supplied by Karl Popper, by means of an inversion of perspective.

Popper cast aside the notion that generalisations could or should be passively induced from observation, preferring the representation of hypothesis formation as an active and adventurous process. This changed the primary role of *experimentation from the strategic increase of the range of observation to the testing of hypotheses. No matter how many confirmatory cases of a generalisation one accumulates, Popper observed, one can never be certain that the generalisation is universally true—but one single counter-example is sufficient to demonstrate that it is not. Knowledge, therefore, can only consist of generalisations that have not yet been falsified, and the most reliable knowledge is that which has resisted falsification most sternly, having been very severely tested. Statements that are unfalsifiable by empirical evidence—*metaphysical statements—cannot, in this view, be admitted as claimants to the status of knowledge.

In this perspective, theory is indeed prior to observation, and the point of observation and experiment is not to confirm theories but rigorously to attempt their refutation; science progresses not by the accumulation of truths but by the careful elimination of falsehoods. The process is akin to Darwinian selection: only the fittest propositions survive, while those that are tested and found wanting are comprehensively defeated in the struggle to command conviction. In this philosophy, scientific knowledge can never attain final perfection, but can only attempt to shed as much imperfection as is practical.

There is a sense in which the Popperian philosophy of science is psychologically unsettling and unsatisfying. It is fundamentally at odds with the mental predispositions that favour and maintain the ambitious holism of *occult science and the illusory certainties of religious faith. For this reason, the logic supporting Popper's case often proves less powerful, in terms of individual cognition, than a hunger for the kind of certainty that is forever unattainable. That hunger is very obvious in fiction, whose popular formulas thrive on a diet of certainty; the sense of closure that provides *narratives with their ultimate payoff may be intellectual, emotional or spiritual, but its Joycean description as an "epiphany" emphasises

the extent to which it mimics one of the key rewards of religious belief in providing a metempirical warranty.

The notion that the essence of science is falsification rather than confirmation remains problematic, particularly with reference to those sciences that are not based on universal and mathematically specifiable laws. These include disciplines that are devoted to the study of specialised sets of physical and chemical phenomena, such as geology and biology, as well as the human sciences. Despite their dearth of universal generalisations, however all these disciplines do seem to benefit considerably from the application of the scientific perspective and the disciplined organisation of their data. There are also useful generalisations, even in physics, that are statistical in nature rather than absolute; they cannot be falsified by single instances of exception, but only by analyses of considerable accumulations of data.

Another significant set of problems arising in connection with the Popperian model of science derives from the fact that the observations that are supposed to operate as objective tests are conditioned—even at the most elementary level of optical perception—by prior assumptions. This renders scientific theories vulnerable to the charge that they sometimes corrupt their own referees, and may therefore be *ideologically loaded. In view of the sociological factors relevant to the abandonment of *paradigms, and the psychological factors favouring the stubborn defence of faith against the corrosions of scepticism, the possibility of such loading is evidently a genuine hazard. Nevertheless, Popperians argue that their prospectus is all that science can amount to, and that its imperfections as a route to reliable knowledge are mere motes by comparison with the beams blinding the alternatives.

Continuing the trend initiated in the seventeenth century, literary reflections of the modern philosophy of science are mostly nebulous or frankly negative. The Popperian perspective is, however, significantly reflected—and was to some extent anticipated—in detective fiction, which routinely pays heed to Sherlock Holmes' oft-quoted maxim that when you have eliminated the impossible, whatever remains—however unlikely it may seem—must include the truth. The analysis of crimes in modern detective fiction routinely proceeds by the rigorous elimination of apparent suspects from consideration, until only one remains. Speculative fiction often proceeds in the same manner, especially in the subgenre of *hard science fiction, many of whose exponents are explicit champions of Popperian philosophy; those who have waxed lyrical on the subject include Paul *Levinson and David *Brin.

PHOTOGRAPHY

The technology of recording visual images by means of light-sensitive chemicals. The attractions of such a technology were demonstrated by the camera obscura, a dark room with a small hole in one wall, which enabled inverted images of objects outside the room to be projected on the opposite wall. The principle was discovered in the late Middle Ages; Renaissance descriptions include one in *Leonardo da Vinci's notebooks. Lenses were placed in such apertures in the sixteenth century, by Giovanni della Porta and others; variants of the *optical device were used by artists in the seventeenth century, and perhaps much earlier. Techniques of fixing such images were anticipated in a number of literary works produced in the eighteenth century, including Tiphaigne de la Roche's *Giphantie* (1760; trans. as *Gyphantia*).

The blackening of silver salts had been observed by the seventeenth century, although it was not immediately obvious that the effect was caused by light rather than heat; the first use of silver salts to capture a picture within a camera was in the 1820s, but it was not until 1839 that Louis Daguerre described a process of development and fixation. Daguerrotype images were mirror-reversed, but that was remedied by the calotype system of development and fixation pioneered by William Fox Talbot in 1840. The invention of the daguerrotype and calotype sparked a boom in commercially sponsored photochemical research, whose potential was popularised in Robert Hunt's *Popular Treatise on the Art of Photography* (1841). The new technology was applied to *astronomy by John William Draper in 1840, who also pioneered spectroscopic photography in 1844; his son Henry made the first photomicrographs in 1850 (at the age of thirteen), although further progress in that area was considerably slower. The adoption of photography into *forensic science was also very rapid, the first galleries of criminal photographs being assembled in the 1850s.

Wet plates introduced in 1851 by F. Scott Archer became the standard recording method because of the speed of their reaction to light. Development of wet plates had to be immediate, but news photography soon took off, in spite of the necessity of transporting portable darkrooms. The cumbersome nature of the technology did not prevent Matthew Brady from making a photographic record of the American Civil War, whose significance is earnestly commemorated in Kristine Kathryn Rusch's *The Gallery of His Dreams* (1991). Dry photographic plates capable of storage, and hence of mass production, were first marketed in 1873, along with developable papers for photographic printing. Plates sensitive to particular parts of the colour spectrum were first introduced in the mid-1880s but panchromatic plates did not become generally available until 1904. Early hobbyist photographers included Charles Lutwidge Dodgson, whose "Hiawatha's Photographing" (1887, in *Rhyme? and Reason?*) is an elaborate description and celebration of the technology.

The transition from glass plates to celluloid was pioneered by the Eastman-Kodak company in the late 1880s; the new technology opened the way for the development of *cinema photography. Handheld cameras with automatic shutters had first been developed in midcentury, but the Eastman-Kodak box camera, launched in 1888 and adapted for celluloid film rolls in 1891, backed up by a commercial processing and development service, gave a tremendous boost to the spread of amateur photography. The challenge that photography posed to painting was a significant factor in the development of nonrepresentative schools of art. Its impact on the illustration of nonfictional material, across the entire spectrum extending from scientific publication through popular journalism to portraiture and pornography, was immense. Photographic plates also played a key role in the extension of the electromagnetic spectrum when they facilitated the discovery of x-rays in 1895.

The possibility of expanding the capability of photographic apparatus became a significant theme of nineteenth-century speculative fiction; notable examples include W. H. Rhodes' "The Case of John Pollexfen" (1876), Robert Duncan Milne's "The Palaeoscopic Camera" (1881), Edward S. van Zile's "Chemical Clairvoyance" (1890), and Mary Platt Parmele's "Answered in the Negative" (1892). One of the most enthusiastic appropriations of the technology was its exploitation by spiritualists and the psychical researchers investigating them. It was in this context that the development of deceptive photography made very rapid progress, producing countless "spirit photographs" by means of double exposure.

The development of x-ray photography—immediately celebrated in such stories as George Griffith's "A Photography of the Invisible" (1896)—was a considerable stimulus to the hopes of psychic researchers as well as the speculative imagination, prompting such extravagant fancies as Charles Melville Shepherd's "The Confessions of a Scientist" (1898), Walter Herries Pollock's "The Phantasmatograph" (1899), Richard Marsh's "The Photographs" (1900), Frank Atkins' "The Magic Camera" (1904), and Victor Whitechurch's "Mitchinson's Developer" (1906). Such hopes remained largely unrealised, in spite of such innovations as Semyon Kirlian's photographic depictions of personal "auras" in 1939 and the claims made by Ted Serios in the 1960s regarding his ability to produce photographic images by the power of thought, but the theme continued to crop up in such works of fiction as Avram Davidson's "The Montavarde Camera" (1959).

Spirit photography enjoyed a new lease on life after 1918, while families grieved for the casualties of World War I; the desperate hopes buoyed up by deceptive photography in the period assisted such blatant and improbable impostures as the notorious "Cottingley fairies", whose authenticity was certified by Sir Arthur Conan Doyle. The advent of the cinema soon made it clear what effects could be obtained by "trick photography", and the dictum that "the camera cannot lie" was quickly exposed as a lie itself—although the exposure did not affect the utility of photographs as narrative devices. Throughout the twentieth century, "compromising" photographs remained the most significant instrument of fictional blackmail. Photographs also function routinely in fiction both as stimuli to investigation and as instruments of investigation.

The capacity of photographs to capture and preserve private moments—much enhanced by the advent of Polaroid cameras in 1947, and further increased by the development in the 1980s of digital cameras capable of downloading images directly into personal computers—ensured that the discovery of revealing photographs would remain a useful plot lever in all kinds of fiction throughout the twentieth century. The use of photography in the calculated invasion of privacy increased dramatically as the century progressed, eventually spawning hordes of *paparazzi* whose employment consisted of photographing people in whom the public were interested, reflecting the visual media's key role as brokers of celebrity and notoriety. On the other hand, striking evidence of the extent of the camera's unconsidered absorption into the fabric of everyday experience was offered in the early years of the twenty-first century by snapshots of war crimes casually taken—and then handed over for commercial development—by soldiers in Iraq.

The utility of photographs as narrative instruments was readily taken aboard by fantastic fiction in the "impossible photograph" motif, in which anachronistic photographs, such as those featured in Lance Sieveking's "The Prophetic Camera" (1923), or photographic images of impossible entities are used as sources of mystery or as climactic revelations. The visual media spawned a significant variant in the changing photograph, whose images fade or are reconfigured as history is changed by time travellers, as in the sequels to *Back to the Future* (1987–1990).

Although far less dramatic in textual fiction, such notions remain capable of significant development there, as in Lisa Goldstein's "Cassandra's Photographs" (1987). The photographic innovation most commonly anticipated in twentieth-century speculative fiction is three-dimensional photography (an anticipation only partly fulfilled by Dennis Gabor's development in 1947 of holography); notable examples include the "largoscope" in Robert Zacks' "Don't Shoot" (1955). A more fanciful extrapolation of the technology is featured in David Marusek's "The Wedding Album" (1999). Sophisticated versions of the impossible photograph motif include Clifford D. Simak's "The Marathon Photograph" (1974) and Daniel Grotta's "RAW" (2005).

The enormous significance of photography in astronomy—amply displayed by the photographic archive compiled by the Hubble Space Telescope—was increasingly supplemented in the late twentieth and early twenty-first centuries by photographs taken by space probes orbiting other worlds and occasionally by landers on the surface. The photographs taken during the *moon landings remain significant icons of achievement, although they have also become the basis for sceptical suspicions that the missions were fictitious.

PHYSICS

The science of *matter and motion, first defined by *Aristotle. Aristotelian physics—which sought explanations in terms of each *element seeking its "natural place", with an alacrity dependent on the degree of its displacement therefrom—was completely mistaken; the authority afforded to it became an awkward hindrance to the development of a proper understanding of the principles of motion and impulsive *force, the actual structure of matter, and its relationship with various forms of energy, including *light.

The clarification of laws of motion by *Galileo and Isaac *Newton, and the latter's theory of *gravity, were foundation stones of the scientific revolution, and the same investigators' work on *optics laid further groundwork for the future development of physics. As advances in *mechanics facilitated the acceleration of mechanical *technology, another further set of fundamental principles—the laws of thermodynamics and the principles of conservation—were added in the early nineteenth century as a result of the work of such theorists as Sadi Carnot and Hermann von Helmholtz.

Physics was subjected to a radical overhaul in the later part of the nineteenth century and the early years of the twentieth as the fusion of theories of *electricity and *magnetism paved the way for the development of modern *atomic theory, quantum theory, and *relativity theory. Thereafter, physics attempted to analyse phenomena in terms of the operation of mathematical laws formulated in terms of the relationships between a series of fundamental physical constants—including the gravitational constant, the speed of light, and Planck's constant (which relates the energy of a photon to its frequency)—reflecting and regulating the operation of the four fundamental forces determining the structure and dynamics of the universe.

This reconstruction, especially when it was further complicated by such embellishments as Heisenberg's *uncertainty principle, wrought a crucial alienation of theoretical physics from common sense, placing it beyond the comprehension of most laymen and conferring a special intellectual status on the individuals—notably Albert *Einstein—who had made key contributions to the reconstruction. Even Einstein struggled imaginatively with the implications of the fact that photons and other subatomic entitles appeared to have two sets of properties, one of which suggested that they ought to be conceived as waves, the other as particles; one of the consequences of this enigma was that relativity theory could not be entirely reconciled with quantum mechanics.

Einstein and Niels Bohr clashed over the "Copenhagen interpretation" of the enigma, which tacitly credited the apparent irreconcilability of the two conceptions to the limitations of the human imagination and suggested that physicists should simply ignore it, using whichever scheme was appropriate to a particular phenomenon. The dream of reconciling quantum mechanics and relativity within a "grand unifying theory" (GUT) or "theory of everything" (TOE) became the Holy Grail of twentieth-century theoretical physics, embodied in such specific quests as the search for the Higgs boson—an elementary particle whose discovery might lay the groundwork for a theory of "quantum gravity".

The search for the Higgs particle was an important motivating factor in the building of such items of experimental apparatus as the CERN supercollider, the ultimate emblem of twentieth-century "Big Science". When a planned American Superconducting Supercollider (SSC) was cancelled in 1993, it seemed to physicists, and some science fiction writers, to be a significant diminution of the United States' status as a superpower. The SSC is defiantly featured in such fictitious advertisements for Big Science as John Cramer's *Einstein's Bridge* (1997) and Michael A. Burstein's "Broken Symmetry" (1997), "Absent Friends" (1998), and "Reality Check"

(1999), although Kevin J. Anderson and Doug Beason's equally celebratory *Lethal Exposure* (1998) is more modestly set at the actual Fermi National Accelerator Laboratory (Fermilab) in Illinois.

The extrapolation of theoretical physics beyond the limits of popular comprehension was seen as a central problem by would-be popularisers of science, but attempts to rise to the challenge, such as Bertrand Russell's *The ABC of Relativity* (1925; rev. 1958) and Johnnie T. Dennis' *The Complete Idiot's Guide to Physics* (2003), failed to solve the problem. One of the most heroic such attempts was undertaken by George Gamow, who employed a series of fabular visionary accounts of alternative universes to dramatise fundamental issues of modern theoretical physics in *Mr Tompkins in Wonderland* (1939) and *Mr. Tompkins Explores the Atom* (1944). The two volumes—which had been combined in *Mr. Tompkins in Paperback* (1965)—were reverently updated by Russell Stannard in *The New World of Mr. Tompkins* (1999), although it was obvious by then that their appeal was essentially esoteric, and that only a few of their readers could grasp the points that the *contes philosophiques* were attempting to make.

Inevitably, genre science fiction writers struggled even harder to extrapolate such ideas in a responsible and comprehensible manner. Most pulp science fiction stories dealing directly with issues in theoretical physics were risible, although John W. Campbell Jr. tried harder than most in such stories as "Uncertainty" (1936; book as *The Ultimate Weapon* 1966). The stories that worked best in literary terms usually restricted their use of such ideas to mere allusion, as in J. George Frederick's "The Einstein Express" (1935), or restricted their field of view to such peripheral issues as the notorious differences of attitude between theoreticians and engineers, as brought into sharp focus by George O. Smith's "Trouble Times Two" (1945) and "Trouble" (1946).

The ostentatious esotericism of twentieth-century physics provided a context for the attachment of a new kind of charisma to the image and idea of Albert Einstein, which was transferred after his death to the remarkable figure of Stephen Hawking, a British theoretical physicist who fell ill in 1962 with motor neurone disease. Hawking's progressive physical deterioration confined him to a wheelchair and forced him to use a mechanical voice box—which became increasingly hard to operate—in order to speak. The resultant combination of intellectual brilliance and physical helplessness produced a uniquely striking iconic image of genius. When Hawking attempted to popularise his work—which dealt with the theory of *black holes and their relevance to models of the *Big Bang—in *A Brief History of Time* (1988), the book became a huge best-seller, its notorious incomprehensibility merely adding to its status.

Hawking appeared in episodes of the animated TV show *The Simpsons* and *Star Trek: The Next Generation*, and played cameo roles in such science fiction stories as Stephen Baxter's "Imaginary Time" (1993), Jack McDevitt's *Ancient Shores* (1996), and Zoran Zivkovic's *The Fourth Circle* (2004). Other "media physicists" who made bids for celebrity based on their combination of presumed genius and manifest eccentricity—including David Deutsch and Michio Kaku—could not begin to compete with Hawking's condition. Such fictitious geniuses as the hero of Charles Sheffield's *The McAndrew Chronicles* (1983; exp. as *The Compleat McAndrew*, 2000) also paled by comparison, although there is a sense in which theoretical physicists are relatively easy to characterise in science fiction. The reader does not expect to understand what they have accomplished, which can therefore be signified in elegantly elliptical fashion, as in such works as Ursula K. Le Guin's *The Dispossessed* (1974), Dean McLaughlin's "Ode to Joy" (1991), Jeffrey D. Kooistra's "Young Again" (1993), and Greg Egan's *Distress* (1995). Outside the genre, Friedrich Dürrenmatt's play *Die Physiker* (1962; trans. as "The Physicists", 1965) took the even easier option of making its central characters madmen.

As the twentieth century ended, the best hope for a unification of physical theory seemed to lie with some variant of string theory, a system initially developed in the 1960s as a means of modelling the strong nuclear interaction force, and generalised in the 1980s. String theory postulates that fundamental entities are more like lines than points, and that their one-dimensional forms twist and move through a complex multidimensional manifold. In the 1990s, string theory was hybridised with an earlier GUT candidate, twistor theory, which had been developed in the 1960s by Roger Penrose, advancing to become "superstring theory", as advertised by Michio Kaku's *Introduction to Superstrings and M-Theory* (1988) and dramatised in John Cramer's novel *Twistor* (1989; rev. 1996).

The problems of literary representation posed by theoretical physics were never solved, but the recruitment of such physicists as Cramer and Geoffrey A. Landis to the ranks of hard science fiction writers certainly allowed dramatic progress to be made beyond the follies of the pulp era. Russell McCormach's *Night Thoughts of a Classical Physicist* (1982) and Alan Lightman's ventures into poetry and parables, along with the novels *Einstein's Dreams* (1993) and *Good Benito* (1995), attempted to bring the imagery of twentieth-century physics into literary works of a more prestigious stripe.

Notable examples of hard science fiction stories envisaging theoretical advances in physics include Robert Chilson's "The Wild Blue Yonder" (1970), D. A. L. Hughes' "Rare Events" (1970), James P. Hogan's *The Genesis Machine* (1978), Landis' "Vacuum States" (1988), Charles Sheffield's "A Braver Thing" (1990), and Stephen Baxter's "Planck Zero" (1992). The tradition of George Gamow's popularising endeavours was ingeniously carried forward by Colin Bruce in *The Strange Case of Mrs. Hudson's Cat and Other Science Mysteries Solved by Sherlock Holmes* (1997). As the twenty-first century began, literary explorations of the world of physics found various ingenious means of sidestepping its most esoteric aspects. Carter Scholz's *Radiance* (2002) focuses on the rivalry between two physicists competing for funding to develop a death ray, and Ian Creasey's "Demonstration Day" (2003) offers an account of social interplay and horseplay at a physicists' conference, while theoretical ideas are cleverly mined for metaphorical resonance in such novels as J. Frederick Arment's *Backbeat—A Novel of Physics* (2004) and Alison McLeod's *The Wave Theory of Angels* (2005).

PICKOVER, CLIFFORD A. (1957–)

American populariser of science who obtained his Ph.D. from Yale's Department of Molecular Biophysics and Biochemistry and became a member of the research staff at IBM's T. J. Watson Research Center.

Pickover's early publications aimed at a popular audience were mostly devoted to fractal imagery and other aspects of *computer-assisted art; they included *Computers, Patterns, Chaos and Beauty* (1990), *Computers and the Imagination* (1991), *Mazes for the Mind: Computers and the Unexpected* (1992), *Visions of the Future: Art, Technology and Computing in the Twenty-First Century* (1992), and *Chaos in Wonderland: Visual Adventures in a Fractal World* (1994). His later works in the same vein included *The Loom of God: Mathematical Tapestries at the Edge of Time* (1997). After coediting *Frontiers in Scientific Visualization* (1993) with Stuart K. Tewkesbury he produced a book of his own on the computer-aided representation of data, *Visualizing Biological Information* (1995). His work began a dramatic diversification of concern and method with *Keys to Infinity* (1995), which attempted to take the reader on a "mental journey" through mathematical theory.

Keys to Infinity made abundant use of fictional techniques, attempting to educate its readers by means of the classical Socratic method, as illustrated by *Plato. *Black Holes: A Traveler's Guide* (1996) used a similar method, designating the reader as the captain of a spaceship probing interesting phenomena. A collection of "brain teaser" puzzles packaged as *The Alien IQ Test* (1997) was followed by a more extended study of *The Science of Aliens* (1998). Pickover's use of fictional devices became even more adventurous in *Time: A Traveler's Guide* (1998), in which a second-person narrative records discussions between a Chopin-obsessed museum curator, his assistant Zetamorph (an alien from Ganymede), and a female student.

Pickover followed a survey of *Strange Brains and Genius: The Secret Lives of Eccentric Scientists and Madmen* (1998) with *Surfing Through Hyperspace: Understanding Higher Universes in Six Easy Lessons* (1999), which alternates expository sections with a didactic science fiction narrative in which a second-person viewpoint investigates the nature and lifestyle of hyperbeings. His first orthodox science fiction novel, written in collaboration with Piers Anthony, was *Spider Legs* (1999), in which crustacean monsters from the deep terrorise a Newfoundland town. *Wonders of Numbers: Adventures in Math, Mind and Meaning* (2000) included conversations between Dr. Googol and his pupil Monica, as well as puzzles dramatising the issues raised. *Cryptorunes: Codes and Secret Writing* (2000) is an account of cryptographic techniques, while *The Girl Who Gave Birth to Rabbits: A True Medical Mystery* (2000) is an account of an eighteenth-century prodigy.

A new ambition became evident in *The Paradox of God and the Science of Omniscience* (2001), an analysis of the philosophical problems inherent in the idea of God and the interpretation of the scriptures. *The Stars of Heaven* (2001) attempted to cover both "the science and spirituality of the stars", alternating its expository argument with dialogues between futuristic humans and their alien peers. *Dreaming the Future: The Fantastic Story of Prediction* (2001) is a critical history of divination, which includes an analysis of the psychology supporting the demand for such information and some suggestions for practical experiments.

In 2002, Pickover produced a set of four science fiction novels aimed at teenagers, collectively entitled the Neoreality series. In *Liquid Earth* religious robots help humans cope with the dissolution of their reality. In *The Lobotomy Club* people perform brain surgery on themselves in order to reach a "higher reality". *Sushi Never Sleeps* features a fractal society whose inhabitants live at different size scales. In *Egg Drop Soup* an alien entity permits the characters to explore the multiverse. "Neoreality" is used to refer to a shift of mental perspective rather than an alternative world: to the kind of conceptual transformation that C. H. *Hinton's writings about the *fourth

dimension were supposed to bring about, giving access to a "religious reality" beyond space or time.

The Mathematics of Oz: Mental Gymnastics from Beyond the Edge (2002) is a further puzzle book, in which Dr. Oz tests human intelligence. *The Zen of Magic Squares, Circles and Stars* (2002) continued the author's exploration of the wonders of mathematics. *Calculus and Pizza: A Math Cookbook for the Hungry Mind* (2003) extended the discussion further, employing chef Luigi as a mouthpiece for the popularisation of calculus. Pickover then began to draw the threads of his various endeavours together in *A Passion for Mathematics: Numbers, Puzzles, Madness, Religion, and the Quest for Reality* (2005) and the even wider-ranging *Sex, Drugs, Einstein, and Elves: Sushi, Psychedelics, Parallel Universes, and the Quest for Transcendence* (2005). No other populariser of science had ever been as adventurous in the co-option of fictional formats, but very few had tried to deal with such a wide range of challenging ideas, and none at such a furious pace.

PLANET

A term derived from the Greek "wanderer" to designate heavenly bodies that moved against the background of the "fixed stars". Ancient astronomers identified five of those currently recognised—*Mercury, *Venus, *Mars, *Jupiter, and *Saturn—although references to "the seven planets" persisted until the demise of geometric models of the solar system because the *Sun and *Moon were also credited with planetary status. A fascination with the number ten moved the followers of *Pythagoras to hypothesise that there must be an invisible *antichthon* or "counter-Earth" beyond the Sun to make up that number along with the seven planets, the Earth, and the realm of the fixed stars.

In *astrological theory the planets were associated with different aspects of the human personality; the metaphorical remnants of the system survive in such adjectives as mercurial, venereal, martial, jovial, and saturnine. The aesthetically-based assumption that the planetary orbits must be circular was a considerable handicap to *cosmologists in search of an accurate model; John *Kepler's discovery that they were actually elliptical was a crucial breakthrough in understanding.

The definition of a planet within a heliocentric context became problematic when it was realised that in addition to large objects too faint to be obvious to the naked eye, like *Uranus and *Neptune, there were large numbers of smaller "minor planets" or *asteroids orbiting the Sun. Although *Pluto was added to the list by general consent, the subsequent discovery of the Kuiper Belt of asteroidal bodies between the orbit of Neptune and the cometary halo suggested that it might better be regarded as a sub-planetary mass. Planetary status was generally withheld from Quaoar (discovered in 2002) and Sedna (discovered in 2004), although they were not much smaller than Pluto. A larger object whose identification was publicised in 2005, officially designated 2003 UB313—but nicknamed Xena by its discoverers—initially seemed a better candidate for the status of the "tenth planet".

Many other additional planets were hypothesised in fiction and speculative nonfiction from the eighteenth century onwards. Most were set in a variety of remote locations, although Ludwig Holberg's *Nicolaii Klimii Iter Subterraneum* (1741; trans. as *A Journey to the World Underground by Nicholas Klimius*) imagines a planet circling an internal sun inside the hollow Earth. Planetary tours were featured in cosmological fiction before the replacement of the geocentric model by the heliocentric one, and continued to appear in some quantity thereafter. Theories of planetary origin were a key element in cosmogonic theses put forward by such philosophers as René Descartes and Immanuel Kant. Several nineteenth-century astronomers, including Camille Flammarion and Percival Lowell, attempted to produce generalised accounts of planetary evolution; Lowell summarised his in *The Evolution of Worlds* (1909).

As soon as it was realised that the *stars are bodies akin to the Sun, the possibility became apparent that they too might have planetary systems—a notion that helped to refine arguments regarding the *plurality of worlds. The notion remained hypothetical until astronomers were able to detect the gravitational effects of large planets on some neighbouring stars. The Hubble Space Telescope facilitated the discovery of a considerable number of extrasolar planets after 1996, all of them gas giants—a generic term apparently coined by James *Blish to describe planets surrounded by vast, thick atmospheres, like Jupiter and Saturn—in much tighter orbits than the gas giants in our own solar system.

The distribution of the planets within the solar system attracted continual attention from mathematicians intent on finding a logic to it. Kepler's attempts to rationalise it with the aid of solid geometry failed, but an arithmetical series named after the eighteenth-century mathematician Johannes Bode—although it was first observed by Johann Titius—seemed more successful for a long time. Bode's "law" observes that the ratios of the mean astronomical distances of the planets in the solar system follow the sequence 4 + (0, 3, 6, 12, 24, 48, and 96), except for the fact that there is no planet corresponding to 28. When Uranus was discovered in 1781, at a mean distance from the Sun very close to the 196 predicted by the sequence, the discovery was hailed as proof of the law. It obtained further credit in the nineteenth century when the first asteroids were discovered in orbits roughly corresponding to the gap in the sequence, encouraging the hypothesis that there must once have been a planet in between Mars and Jupiter, whose disintegration had generated an abundance of interplanetary debris.

Literary works featuring the disintegrated planet hypothesis were greatly encouraged by the inherent melodrama of hypotheses accounting for its destruction. Florence Carpenter Dieudonne's *Rondah; or, Thirty-Three Years in a Star* (1887) is an early work of this sort, but writers of pulp science fiction were more adventurous; notable examples include Harl Vincent's "Before the Asteroids" (1930), John Russell Fearn's "Before Earth Came" (1934), and Raymond Z. Gallun's "Godson of Almarlu" (1936). Stories of this kind enjoyed a new vogue of fashionability following the revelation of the *atom bomb, which immediately became a prime candidate for the destructive agent, as featured in Ray Bradbury's "Asleep in Armageddon" (1948) and James Blish's *The Frozen Year* (1957; aka *Fallen Star*).

The relative insignificance of Pluto's gravitational pull lent credence to the notion that it was not, after all, the planet for which Percival Lowell had searched, and that there must be a still-undiscovered tenth planet. This hypothetical body is called Cerberus in Raymond Z. Gallun's "The World Wrecker" (1934), Euthan in J. Harvey Haggard's "A Little Green Stone" (1936), Persephone in Jack Williamson's "The Blue Spot" (1937), and Mephisto in George O. Smith's *Nomad* (1945, by-lined Wesley Long; book, 1950). It also features in John W. Campbell's *The Planeteers* (1936–1938; book, 1966), Henry Kuttner's "We Guard the Black Planet" (1942), Philip K. Dick's *Solar Lottery* (1955; aka *World of Chance*), Edmund Cooper's *The Tenth Planet* (1973), and Larry Niven and Jerry Pournelle's *Lucifer's Hammer* (1977).

Urban Le Verrier, who predicted the existence of Neptune in order to explain perturbations of the orbits of the outer planets, also suggested that there might be a planet closer to the Sun than Mercury, in order to account for perturbations in that world's orbit. When an amateur astronomer claimed to have detected such an object in 1859 (he had actually seen a sunspot), Le Verrier named it Vulcan. Literary representations of Vulcan are included in Donald Horner's *By Aeroplane to the Sun* (1910), Leslie F. Stone's "The Hell Planet" (1932), Harl Vincent's "Vulcan's

Workshop" (1932), and John Russell Fearn's "Mathematica" (1936). A similar body is called Circe in Victor Rousseau's "Outlaws of the Sun" (1931) and Inferno in the same author's "Revolt on Inferno" (1931). The idea is echoed in Poul Anderson's "Vulcan's Forge" (1983).

The hypothetical planet that made the most appeal of all to writers of fiction was the Pythagorean counter-Earth, whose situation was ripe for satirical mirror-imaging of various kinds. Notable examples of its use include D. L. Stump's *From World to World* (1896) and *The Love of Meltha Laone* (1913), Edison Tesla Marshall's "Who Is Charles Avison?" (1916), Edgar Wallace's *Planetoid 127* (1929), Paul Capon's trilogy begun with *The Other Side of the Sun* (1950), and John Norman's Gor series (launched 1966).

The stability of the planetary orbits gives their motion a reliability that was one of the first significant proofs of the predictive power of science, and a significant stimulus to divinatory optimism. Disturbances of that regularity have, in consequence, a particular ominous or portentous significance. In George C. Wallis' "The Great Sacrifice" (1903), Martians move the outer planets to shield the inner system from a meteor swarm, then sacrifice their own world to save Earth. In Edmond Hamilton's "Thundering Worlds" (1934), the nine planets become literal wanderers, accelerating towards a new star when the Sun is destroyed. New planetary bodies entering the solar system from without, sometimes colliding with or passing disastrously close to Earth, are featured in numerous disaster stories, including Edwin Balmer and Philip Wylie's *When Worlds Collide* (1933). A similar *catastrophist scenario became the basis of Immanuel Velikovsky's *pseudoscientific explanation of the early crises of Mediterranean civilisation, *Worlds in Collision* (1950).

Another exercise in catastrophist pseudoscience, Zechariah Sitchin's *The 12th Planet* (1976), hypothesised a planet named Nibiru as the source of colonialists who arrived on Earth 450,000 years ago, and whose subsequent approaches at intervals of 3,600 years were associated with Earthly disasters. A similar hypothesis, involving a companion dark star and much longer intervals between catastrophes, was suggested in 1985 by Daniel P. Whitmore and John J. Matese; literary representations of the planets of the hypothetical companion star include Isaac Asimov's *Nemesis* (1989).

The category distinction between gas giants and smaller planets like Earth and Mars was initially drawn in the speculative context of *exobiology, on the grounds that floating ecosystems designed to inhabit the atmospheres of gas giants would form a complex class radically different from the class of surface-hugging ecosystems adapted to smaller worlds. Science-fictional world builders have also paid particular attention to the design of habitable planets within multiple star systems, and the adaptation of their ecospheres to the complexities of the stars' orbits. Charles Defontenay's *Star, ou Psi de Casseipoée* (1854; trans. as *Star*) is an early exercise of this kind; kindred ventures in *hard science fiction include Hal Clement's *Cycle of Fire* (1957), Brian W. Aldiss' Helliconia trilogy (1982–1985) and Harlan Ellison's shared world anthology *Medea* (1985).

The variety of extrasolar planets imagined by science fiction writers is vast, including many examples whose rational plausibility is highly dubious. Relatively common variants include starless planets, such as the ones featured in Neil R. Jones' "The Sunless World" (1934) and George R. R. Martin's *Dying of the Light* (1977); double planets, like the ones in Homer Eon Flint's "The Devolutionist" (1921), Robert L. Forward's *Rocheworld* (1982; rev. 1990), and Bob Shaw's *The Ragged Astronauts* (1986); and liquid worlds, like the ones featured in Neil R. Jones' "Into the Hydrosphere" (1933) and Bob Shaw's *Medusa's Children* (1977). In Jack Williamson's "Born of the Sun" (1934), planets are reconceived as eggs, which are eventually destined to hatch.

Local and long-distance planetary tours remained a fashionable format in genre science fiction, often extended over long series—as in the elaborate tour of extrasolar planets contained in E. C. Tubb's Dumarest series (1967–1997)—but sometimes collapsed in a minimalist cause, as in "Archaic Planets: Nine Excerpts from the *Encyclopedia Galactica*" (1998) by Michael Swanwick, with assistance from Sean Swanwick.

PLATO (CA. 428–347 B.C.)

The nickname (meaning "broad") of an Athenian philosopher whose family name was Aristocles; opinions vary as to whether the nickname's reference was to his shoulders or his forehead. Plato's political interests led him to support Socrates against the enemies who eventually condemned him to death for "corrupting" the city's youth, and his subsequent career was moved by outrage against this sentence. Socrates' trial is described in some detail, presumably fictionalised for effect, in the *Phaedo*, and many of Plato's other dialogues feature Socrates in the leading role, preserving and promulgating his ideas and displaying the "Socratic method" of education, in which a teacher constructs a persuasive argument to guide a pupil from truths already admitted to a further conclusion. After Socrates' execution, Plato travelled for some years before returning to Athens, in 387 B.C. or there-abouts, to found his pioneering school of philosophy, the Academy.

Plato's dialogues provided a key model for philosophical discourse and established the principle that knowledge ought to be obtained by intellectual effort rather than the acceptance on faith of authoritarian statements. His early works were primarily devoted to the quest for clear definitions of qualities such as courage, excellence, and soundness of mind, and often occupy themselves with the puzzling question of why men in pursuit of good so often do evil. In these works Socrates usually takes up a critical position, ruthlessly exposing flaws in the reason of others (while overlooking flaws of his own, in the judgement of later philosophers from *Aristotle onwards). In a second group of dialogues, the Platonic Socrates set out his own beliefs much more elaborately and explicitly; the shift in emphasis took place in the course of the *Republic*, which had commenced as a critique of the idea of justice.

The *Republic* became Plato's most famous work, partly because it sets out the theory that the ultimate components of reality are Forms or Ideas, which became the basis of his idiosyncratic *metaphysics. It also set several significant and highly influential precedents in the philosophical use of literary method. It includes a pioneering attempt to design an ideal society, which became the foundation stone of the *Utopian literary tradition, and two bold exercises in didactic fabulation: the allegory of the cave and the story of Er.

The allegory of the cave likens the imperfections of human perception to the plight of prisoners in a cave, chained with their backs to the mouth, so that they are aware of the reality of the world—its constituent Forms—only by means of a series of reflections cast upon the wall by firelight. The story of Er, which concludes the dialogue, is an afterlife fantasy and cosmic vision in which a dead soldier is borne away to the Meadow to be judged, before seeing the Spindle of Necessity, on which the cosmic whorl—a primitive version of the Aristotelian cosmology, owing much to the ideas credited to *Pythagoras—is spun, to the accompaniment of the Siren song that constitutes the *music of the spheres. The remaining dialogues of this second period expanded considerably on these metaphysical notions, before Plato added a third and final sequence to his works.

From a purely philosophical point of view, the most important of the final group of Plato's dialogues was the *Laws*, which contains the summation of his moral and political philosophy. The most relevant to the development of science and to Plato's subsequent literary influence, however, was the *Timaeus*, which sets out a more elaborate version of his cosmology, as well as his comments on physics and biology. The *Timaeus* attempts to combine the mathematical ideas of the Pythagoreans with the Empedoclean theory of the *elements by giving the *atoms of the four elements different geometrical forms and employing a *spatial void as the basic metaphysical substrate containing such atoms. Significantly, the *Timaeus* makes further use of the literary allegorising that made the *Republic* so distinctive, further elaborating its hypothetical construction of an ideal state by incarnating that state on the vanished island of Atlantis. The description of Atlantis was continued in the *Critias*, but that dialogue was never completed.

Plato's use of literary methods of exposition was often seen as an embarrassment by later philosophers, who marginalised that aspect of his work in order to focus on Plato as Socrates' alleged mouthpiece, applying reasoned argument to the exploration of fundamental concepts and their relationship to "the good". That representation of Plato can, however, be strongly contrasted with the Plato who became the father figure of neo-Platonism and many subsequent schools of mysticism and *occult science. Greek neo-Platonism, developed by Plotinus in the third century A.D. and carried forward by Porphyry and Iamblichus, turned out to be the final phase of European pagan philosophy, which was subsequently overtaken and overwhelmed in the Dark and Middle Ages by Christian scholasticism. The neo-Platonists treated Plato as an authority to be revered rather than an exponent of critical argument, and established versions of his post-Pythagorean cosmology and theory of Forms as central dogmas whose literary extrapolations were viewed as mystical representations offering key revelations to "initiates" capable of decoding them.

Less adventurous forms of Platonism were echoed in Christian thought, but they were always deemed unorthodox—in spite of Plato's considerable influence on St. Augustine—and never achieved the kind of accommodation that was granted to Aristotelian ideas. Neo-Platonist ideas were viewed with even greater hostility—unsurprisingly, in view of the neo-Platonists' specific exclusion of Christianity from their ambitious syncresis of religious ideas—and became inextricably entangled with other components of occult science, including the Jewish tradition of Kabbalistic thought and the so-called Hermetic tradition. Although some pioneers of science—most notably John *Kepler—were strongly influenced by Platonist ideas, those ideas lost much of their force when Kepler had to throw the Platonic solids out of his model of the solar system to make room for elliptical planetary orbits bound by very different mathematical laws.

Plato's influence on literature also has two partly contrasted elements. Although the Platonic dialogue died out as a form of scientific reportage not long after *Galileo's combative employment of it, the adaptation of dialogue as a significant mode of mimetic literary discourse transformed prose fiction. That transformation involved the gradual evolution of carefully told tales into stories whose narrative voice faded further and further into the background as their characters loomed ever larger and their dialogue became relentlessly naturalistic. On the other hand, Platonic allegory and the method of exemplification that established the archetypal republic of Atlantis—casually drowning it again in order to explain its contemporary non-existence—became key strategies of modern diegetic fabulation, as elaborately displayed in quasi-scientific *contes philosophiques* as in various kinds of occult fiction.

Platonic fiction is dominated by the extraordinarily prolific subgenre of Atlantean fantasy, but few such works include any significant measure of scientific speculation; notable exceptions include Jules Verne's *Deux milles lieues sous les mers* (1870; trans. as *Twenty Thousand Leagues Under the Sea*), C. J. Cutcliffe Hyne's *The Lost Continent* (1900), and Stanton A. Coblentz' *The Sunken World* (1928; book, 1948). The associated subgenre of speculative nonfiction, on the other hand, is host to a great deal of speculative *geography and *ethnology. Ignatius Donnelly's best-selling *scholarly fantasy *Atlantis, the Antediluvian World* (1882) provided substance adapted as a central element of Theosophical dogma by Madame Blavatsky in *The Secret Doctrine* (1888) as well as many other pseudoscientific tracts.

The ideal society described in the *Republic* is reproduced for revaluation in a number of Utopian romances, including Gabriel Daniel's *Voyage du monde de Descartes* (1690; trans. as *A Voyage to the World of Cartesius*), Alexandr Moszkowski's *Die Insent der Weisheit* (1922; trans. as *The Isles of Wisdom*), and David F. Bischoff and Ted White's *Forbidden World* (1978). P. Schuyler Miller's "Through the Vibrations" (1931) invokes a lost continuation of the *Timaeus*, but Plato is relegated to a minor role in Paul Levinson's *The Plot to Save Socrates* (2006).

PLAUSIBILITY

A term whose original meaning signified "worthy of applause", and which was subsequently adapted to refer to arguments and assertions that seem believable. Although it can be used to refer to statements that really are credible, the term routinely retains the suspicion that the credibility to which it refers is a mere gloss, perhaps intended deceptively. A "plausible argument" is often one that seems sound at first glance, but is rotten at the core. This ambiguity reflects an important distinction between rational plausibility, in which credibility is based in logical or scientific analysis, and psychological plausibility, in which credibility is a reflection of gullibility. A similar ambiguity inevitably afflicts the concept of *rhetoric—which is, in essence, the set of techniques by which plausibility is manufactured.

Science is necessarily suspicious of psychological plausibility. Literature, on the other hand, thrives on it. Narrative plausibility is routinely associated with events that defy the calculus of *probability, sometimes to the extent of being frankly but unrepentantly *impossible. The cultivation of narrative plausibility is often deliberately deceptive, as in the telling of "tall tales", in which the hearer's predisposition to trust the veracity of the teller is exploited in order to lead the audience along a seductive path to a climactic absurdity, worthy of laughter if not always of applause. The existence of an extremely rich and various fantastic literature not only demonstrates that entities and events impossible or highly unlikely in the world of experience can be forcefully endowed with literary plausibility but also illustrates the remarkable fact that such narrative devices often seem far more plausible than everyday entities and events: an awareness summarised in the dictum that "truth is stranger than fiction".

The history of actual beliefs testifies very clearly to the power of irrational plausibility, and the history of science can easily be seen as a series of hard-fought battles to cast down idols whose shabby feet of clay were stoutly and elegantly booted by psychological plausibility. When Francis *Bacon offered his account of the ideological origins of those idols, he did not foresee the problems that would arise as a result of their replacement. As science progressed from the seventeenth century to the twentieth, the progress of its understanding took it further and further into realms of implausibility whose capacity to defy "common sense" became starkly manifest with the advent of modern theoretical *physics. However powerful the representations of twentieth-century physics might be in mathematical and predictive terms, they are certainly not psychologically plausible. There is a challenging imaginative gulf between modern science and the human mind's faculty of comprehension, whose crossing many people are afraid even to attempt.

The principal reason for this increasingly awkward dissonance between rational and psychological plausibility is the adaptation of human senses to the necessities and vicissitudes of our immediate environment. The extension of the human sensorium by such optical instruments as *microscopes and *telescopes and such measuring devices as barometers, voltmeters, and Geiger counters is a marvel, but the farther such instruments take us into the realms of the ordinarily invisible and the ordinarily intangible, the more inadequate the assumptions built into our senses become, and the less capable our powers of imagination are to "visualise" what we know is actually there. The universe of modern science, in terms of its vastness, its age, and its fine structure, is an intellectual construct that beggars the imagination, whose effect on the mind is so profoundly unaccountable that the English language routinely refers to it by means of derivatives of the frankly nonsensical verb "to boggle".

The difficulties of imagining the world outside ourselves on the basis of the immediate objects of our perception pale into insignificance, however, when the "mind's eye" tries to look back on itself, following the introspective philosophical method of René Descartes. There are no objects of perception inside the mind except for thoughts, feelings, and sensation, whose role as instruments of perception catches them in an awkward trap when they are perceived in their turn. The Cartesian mind—a ghostly entity of mental substance that sits in the pineal body, pulling the levers that control the body-machine—is easily revealed by rigorous Socratic criticism to be a sham, but it really is how we *appear* to ourselves when we attempt to examine ourselves from within. Cartesian dualism is seductively and quintessentially *plausible*; not only is it easy for us to "picture" our minds as ghosts in fleshy machines, but it is difficult in the extreme to picture ourselves in any other way.

This way of imagining the mind has numerous corollaries blessed with elementary psychological plausibility. They include the notion that the ghost-mind might be able to exist—and seem not much different to itself—outside the body or after the body's death, and the notion that if another ghost-mind were to invade and take possession of the body, it might displace or enslave its native inhabitant.

Because the ghost-mind can create mental pictures and thoughts formulated in words, it seems plausible that the pictures might be "seen" by other ghost-minds, or the verbalised thoughts overheard by mental eavesdroppers—and because the ghost-mind can pull the levers of the body machine, it seems plausible that it might extend its reach to more distant levers.

Moreover, because the ghost-mind is aware of the limitations of its own self-control, the authority of reason being compromised and undermined by the impulses and urges produced by appetites and emotions, it seems plausible that the self is a battleground between opposed forces—which can just as easily be categorised as guardian angels and tempting demons as the *Freudian *superego* and *id*—on which all kinds of alien forces might intrude, as magic spells ranging from curses to love potions.

Then again, because the ghost-mind is gifted with memory, it seems to be a traveller in time, capable by mental effort of bringing back yesterday or projecting itself into tomorrow—wishing all the while that it might have done something other than it did, or that events yet to come will actually work out as planned rather than suffering any of the myriad possible disasters conjured up by fear.

The exterior universe revealed by scientific analysis is difficult to grasp, but there is much in it that can be convincingly described, even if it remains outside the scope of visualisation, by the language of mathematics. The rational arguments that reveal the idolatrous nature of the Cartesian ghost-self, on the other hand, can put no other image in its place; the vacuum they leave is unfillable by describable possibilities, however implausible.

By virtue of this void, the Cartesian attempt at rational self-confrontation remains unresolved, uneasy, and fundamentally anxious. This anxiety is clearly reflected in *all* the literary images built upon Cartesian plausibility: not merely the intrinsically monstrous notions of demonic possession and temptation, curses, and lycanthropy, but those which might otherwise seem quite hopeful and exciting, such as life-after-death and out-of-body experiences, telepathy and psychokinesis, time travel, and prophecy. The literature of the psychologically plausible is insistent and prolific, but by no means overblessed with self-confidence. This creates particular problems for speculative fiction, especially the *hard science fiction that attempts to come to terms with the imaginative substance of psychological plausibility's nemesis, rational plausibility.

Literary plausibility is not solely a matter of exploiting Cartesian and other delusions. The innate moral order of worlds within texts creates a powerful desire in readers to see poetic justice done, and this routinely lends poetic licence to improbable or impossible events and actions, whenever they are invoked in good causes. Worlds within texts tend to be inordinately generous, both in providing resources for heroic characters to employ and in granting them the ability to perform extraordinary feats under extreme duress—thus creating a palpable narrative attraction towards the superheroic that affects crime and thriller fiction as well as heroic fantasy.

Similar pressures assist in the conversion of literary love into an irresistible romantic force, readily likened to the pull of gravity, and in the detachment of literary luck from any vestige of restraint by the principles of probability. This too creates problems for speculative fiction, which inevitably experiences a contrary pull by virtue of its allegiance to the scientific worldview—but hard science fiction has never shown the least sign of ungenerosity to its heroes, or the least reluctance to play fast and loose with their luck. Love has been a conspicuously different matter, but that might have other causes than conscientious adherence to rational standards of plausibility.

There is a substantial sector of speculative fiction that is taken up by shadowboxing with the phantoms of psychological plausibility, much of whose produce is discussed under the heading of *parapsychology. The imaginable detachability of the Cartesian ghost from its fleshy envelope fuels a great deal of genre science fiction—including a good deal of cyberpunk fiction and much *Omega Point fantasy—that deals with the "uploading" of ghost-minds into some kind of *cyberspatial *virtual reality. Traditional notions of *possession and compulsion have been remodelled in terms of *alien invasion. The entire subgenres of *time travel stories and *alternative histories have roots in psychological plausibility that are cleverly extrapolated in science fiction's principal subgenre of tall tales, which deal in time *paradoxes. In its extrapolations of ideas in *neurology, on the other hand, science fiction can get to grips with some decisive shifts in the spectrum of plausibility that result from advances in our understanding of the mind/body problem and the manner in which the structure of the brain is related to thought and memory.

The dissonance between rational and psychological plausibility is also reflected, to slightly varying degrees, in various fields of "nonfiction", ranging from *reportage and *scholarly fantasy through pseudoscience, history, and conduct books to the popularisation of science and scientific publication. Ironically, it is easier to cultivate psychological plausibility in "nonfiction" than in fiction, because the assertion that a statement is true—especially if it is insistently repeated—is itself one of the principal rhetorical devices used in the manufacture of plausibility. The kinds of actual truth that really are stranger than fiction—which is to say, the abstruse realms of twentieth-century scientific theory—tend to be much stranger than the kinds of fake truth that deliberately set out to substitute psychological plausibility for rational plausibility. A work of fiction has the distinction of being an "honest lie", devoid of any delusion, and the farther-reaching honesty of the best fictional narratives is far more significant than their hypothetical status.

PLURALITY OF WORLDS, THE

A philosophical thesis whose original argument was that the world imagined by Aristotelian *cosmology—in which the Earth is surrounded by a supplementary network of heavenly bodies bounded by the sphere of the fixed stars—is not unique. The thesis became confused with, and eventually overtaken by, the notion that the heavenly bodies and fixed stars were themselves worlds akin to the Earth or the Sun, rather than mere points of light.

The case for the plurality of worlds was initially argued on *theological grounds, based on the contention that the assumption of a single world was an insult to God's creative capability. Nicholas of Cusa's *De Docta Ignorantia* (1440) proposed that the universe ought to be as infinite as God Himself, and filled with an infinite number of worlds of equal status. This philosophy of plenitude was further developed in a didactic poem, *Zodiacus Vitae* (ca. 1534) by "Marcellus Palingenius Stellatus" (Pier Angelo Manzoli), which suggested that the human race might be the only one to have experienced a Fall, while its multitudinous peer races remained perfect—an idea echoed in such modern theological fantasies as Marie Corelli's *A Romance of Two Worlds* (1886) and C. S. Lewis's *Out of the Silent Planet* (1938).

The notion of the plurality of worlds was not considered heretical at first, although it came to seem far more dangerous when Aristotelian orthodoxy was challenged by Copernican theorists. When an updated version was argued as a matter of empirical truth by Giordano Bruno in *La cena de le ceneri* (1584) and *De l'infinito universo e mondi* (1584), it contributed to his condemnation to death in 1600. The controversy surrounding *Galileo's discoveries with the *telescope was increased by the support his discovery of new heavenly bodies lent to the notion of a much greater plurality. John *Kepler and Christian Huygens added further empirical and theoretical observations favouring the ideas of plurality and plenitude.

The landmark texts of this theological dispute included Pierre Borel's *Discours nouveau prouvant la pluralité des Mondes* (1657), Pierre Gassendi's posthumous *Syntagma Philosophicum* (1658), and Bernard de Fontenelle's enormously popular *Entretiens sur la pluralité des mondes* (1686; trans. as *Conversations on the Plurality of Worlds*). The controversy could still excite a sense of urgency in the mid-nineteenth century, when the diehard negativity of William Whewell's *Of the Plurality of Worlds* (1853) was immediately countered by David Brewster's *More Worlds than One: The Creed of the Philosopher and the Hope of the Christian* (1854).

PLUTO

Most of the participants in the theological debate took it for granted that the inhabitants of other worlds must be human, because they too would be made in God's image, but the notion that they might differ in various ways crept into the debate by slow degrees, eventually giving rise to the idea of the *alien. Nicholas Hill's *Philosophia Epicurea, Democritiana, Theophrastica* (1601) argued that the size of created individuals must vary in proportion to the size of their worlds. The idea that there might be a more wide-ranging diversity of form was broached by Bruno and carried forward by Gassendi and—much more elaborately—Otto von Guericke's *Experimenta Nova (ut Vocantur) Magdeburgica de Vacuo Spatio* (1672).

The literary spin-off of the debate was more adventurous than its purely academic arguments. Charles Sorel's *Vraie histoire comique de Francion* (1623–1626) includes two satirical cosmic journeys, the first mocking an Aristotelian universe and the second mocking the plurality of worlds, employing the possibility of an alien invasion of Earth as a seemingly absurd corollary of the notion. John *Kepler's *Somnium* (1634) inverted Hill's assumption about the correlation of size and world size, and made other amendments to the habits of his lunar giants in order to adapt them to the long lunar day/night cycle. Cyrano de Bergerac's *Histoire des états et empires du soleil* (1662; trans. as *The States and Empires of the Sun*) used a good deal of calculatedly absurd imagery, but asserts robustly that the other planets in the solar system must indeed be inhabited, and probably not by humans. Christian Huygens' *Kosmotheoros* (1698), which set a pattern for many subsequent cosmic voyages, similarly favours the notion of a variety of planetary inhabitants.

Kosmotheoros also helped to popularise the notion that the inhabitants of the other worlds in the solar system might be arranged on a progressive scale of moral and cultural advancement—a proposition that soon gave birth to the corollary notion of interplanetary *palingenesis. Such schemes of moral assortment tended to be heavily influenced by the Classical naming scheme of the planets and its elaboration in *astrological theses associating each planet with a particular personality type. Marie-Anne de Roumier's *Voyages de mylord Céton dans les sept planètes* (1765) provides a cardinal example of this kind of symbolic schema, whose echoes extended throughout the nineteenth century in such works as W. D. Lach-Szyrma's *Aleriel* (1886) and George Griffith's *A Honeymoon in Space* (1900).

Immanuel Kant's *Allegemeine Naturgeschichte und Theorie des Himmels* (1755; trans. as *Universal Natural History and Theory of the Heavens*), which

included the contention that the Milky Way was merely one lenticular aggregation of stars among many "island universes", modernised Nicholas of Cusa's hypothesis as well as extrapolating it to a greater scale of magnitude. It was further extrapolated as the "cosmological principle of mediocrity": the axiomatic assumption that the universe is uniform, and that the Earth's situation within it is in no way privileged. Isaac *Newton's theory of gravity had provided a significant application of the assumption that the same laws of nature apply everywhere, to everything—a notion that seemed extraordinary to Aristotelians, who took it for granted that different rules applied in Earth and in the heavens.

The cosmological principle was employed by many subsequent cosmologists, including Albert *Einstein and Fred *Hoyle, in building models of the universe, but its application did not yield uniformly satisfactory results; Einstein's theory of relativity proved much more successful than Hoyle's theory of continuous creation. The supposition that the Sun is a star like many other *stars proved true, although astronomers discovered that stars are very various. The supposition that other stars—or Sun-like stars, at least—have their own elaborate systems of orbiting planets has yet to be fully tested, although new extrasolar planets have been discovered in considerable quantities by the Hubble Space Telescope. The once-common supposition that the planets in the solar system are all alike proved flatly false, although it is partly responsible for the fact that descriptions of *alien beings and the *exobiological conditions sustaining them always lagged behind the implications of current astronomical data. A version of the cosmological principle derived from the plurality thesis is still commonly applied to debates about the likely existence of alien life, giving rise to the *Fermi paradox.

The persistence of ideas retained from theological disputes regarding the plurality of worlds licenced such twentieth-century speculative ventures as the use of an alien ecosphere as a model of possibly diabolical creation in James Blish's *A Case of Conscience* (1953; exp. 1958). Other examples of its influence include the use of aliens to stand in for angels in Ray Bradbury's "In This Sign" (1951; aka "The Fire Balloons"), immortal souls in Clifford D. Simak's *Time and Again* (1951), and a creative demiurge in Philip José Farmer's "Father" (1955).

PLUTO

The ninth planet of the solar system. It is usually the farthest from the Sun, although its eccentric orbit sometimes brings it within the orbit of *Neptune. Pluto's existence was predicted by Percival Lowell, on the basis of calculations similar to those that led to the discovery of Neptune. Lowell launched the search that eventually bore fruit in 1930, when Clyde W. Tombaugh found it, using a telescope specially designed for the task; the planet's name and its associated symbol were chosen in order to incorporate Lowell's initials.

Pluto is a smaller world than Earth's *Moon, more akin to an *asteroid than the other planets; its tide-locked companion body, Charon—discovered in 1977—has a diameter more than half as large as Pluto's. Although no twentieth-century space probe flew past them, the Hubble Space Telescope produced clearer images of Pluto and Charon in the late 1990s. Pluto's surface appears to be covered in methane ice but is highly variegated, suggesting that its nitrogen/methane atmosphere is unexpectedly active.

In spite of its presumed inhospitability, Pluto figured more prominently in pulp science fiction than Neptune because its status as a newly discovered planet increased interest in it. Stanton A. Coblentz's *Into Plutonian Depths* (1931; book, 1950) was an early deployment; others include Kenneth Sterling's "The Brain-Eaters of Pluto" (1934), Leslie F. Stone's "The Rape of the Solar System" (1934), Stanley G. Weinbaum's "The Red Peri" (1935), Wallace West's "En Route to Pluto" (1936), Laurence Manning and Fletcher Pratt's "Expedition to Pluto" (1939), Ross Rocklynne's "The Last Outpost" (1945), and Murray Leinster's "Pipeline to Pluto" (1945). Clifford D. Simak's *Cosmic Engineers* (1939; book, 1950) begins in its vicinity.

Pluto was always an unlikely target for *colonisation, although it is turned into habitable paradise in George O. Smith's "Circle of Confusion" (1944; by-lined Wesley Long) and settled in Algis Budrys' *Man of Earth* (1958). It offered greater scope as a challenging destination, as in Wilson Tucker's *To the Tombaugh Station* (1960), or as a base for aliens investigating the solar system, as in Robert A. Heinlein's *Have Space Suit—Will Travel* (1958)—or both, as in Donald A. Wollheim's *Secret of the Ninth Planet* (1959). In Clifford Simak's "Construction Shack" (1973), Pluto turns out to be an artefact, while Rick Gauger's *Charon's Ark* (1987) imagines it drastically modified to serve as a *dinosaur reserve.

Although Pluto's status in defining the rim of the solar system was undermined by the discovery of the Kuiper Belt—which seems to contain several objects of similar size—and the *cometary halo, it retained a certain mystique to the end of the twentieth century. It is the setting of Kim Stanley Robinson's *Icehenge* (1984) and the starting point of the planetary

tour featured in the same author's *The Memory of Whiteness* (1985). Larry Niven's "Wait It Out" (1968), Robert Silverberg's "Sunrise on Pluto" (1985), and Stephen Baxter's "Gossamer" (1995) feature life-forms capable of existing there, while Gregory Benford's "Proserpine's Daughter" (1988, with Paul A. Carter; aka *Iceborn*) and *The Sunborn* (2005) credit it with a complex ecosphere.

In Roger McBride Allen's *The Ring of Charon* (1990), Pluto is the site of experiment that has unexpectedly far-reaching consequences, and it is briefly featured in Charles Sheffield's *Tomorrow and Tomorrow* (1997). Charon's lack of atmosphere makes it an even more inhospitable setting, but it is featured in Colin Greenland's *Take Back Plenty* (1990) and its sequels, and is linked to its primary by a curious bio-artefact in Larry Niven and Brenda Cooper's "The Trellis" (2003).

POE, EDGAR ALLAN (1809–1849)

U.S. writer best known as a poet and short story writer. In the latter capacity he pioneered several modern genres and subgenres, including the detective story, psychological horror fiction, and science fiction, making extensive experiments with narrative form. These extended to fiction imitative of contemporary scientific reportage, in "The Effects of Mesmerism on a Dying Man" (1845; aka "The Facts in the Case of M. Valdemar"), and an extraordinary book length "poem in prose" popularising and extrapolating contemporary discoveries in *astronomy in *Eureka: An Essay on the Material and Spiritual Universe* (1848).

Poe's unparalleled literary inventiveness received such a hostile reception in his homeland that one of his biographers, J. A. T. Lloyd, titled his life story *The Murder of Edgar Allan Poe* (1931), identifying Poe's literary executor, Rufus W. Griswold, as the chief assassin. It was Griswold who permanently saddled Poe's by-line with a middle name derived from the surname of his stepfather (which Poe incorporated only briefly while he was alive) and wrote the deceptive memoir that gave him a posthumous reputation as a drunkard of dubious sanity. In fact, Poe drank little—although alcohol did go straight to his head, perhaps because he was perpetually on the brink of starvation—and was perfectly sane, but it is conceivable that he instructed his executor to demonise him. It is difficult to imagine that the nakedly vicious obituary that appeared under Griswold's name could have been penned without prior sanction, and it may even have been written by Poe himself, as an ironic gesture. That would have been typical of Poe's traffic with what one of his fictionalised essays called "The Imp of the Perverse" (1850).

Poe was much more successful in France than in the United States. His leading French translator was Charles Baudelaire, who saw his own perceived plight—as an unjustly neglected poet and a harshly treated stepson—mirrored in Poe's unlucky life. Aided by Baudelairean style, Poe became a highly influential writer in Europe, and might be regarded as the true progenitor of the *Decadent Movement, whose central myth he developed in "The Fall of the House of Usher" (1839); he also modelled its stylistic affectations in "The Masque of the Red Death" (1842) and provided a guide to decadent life-style fantasy in "The Murders in the Rue Morgue" (1841).

Poe was the first writer seriously to tackle the problem of finding appropriate narrative forms for literary extrapolations of the scientific imagination, and he did so in a determinedly experimental spirit. In addition to the innovative formats cited above he toyed with visionary poetry in "Al Aaraaf" (1829), extraordinary voyages in "MS Found in a Bottle" (1833), *The Narrative of Arthur Gordon Pym of Nantucket* (1838), and "The Unparalleled Adventure of One Hans Pfaall" (1835; rev. 1840), mock-philosophical dialogue in "The Conversation of Eiros and Charmion" (1839) and "The Colloquy of Monos and Una" (1841), the tall tale in "The Man That Was Used Up" (1839), visionary fantasy in "Mesmeric Revelation" (1844) and "A Tale of the Ragged Mountains" (1844), and fake newspaper reportage in material reprinted in "The Balloon Hoax" (1844) and "Mellonta Tauta" (1849).

The experimental tentativeness of this material makes much of Poe's science fiction seem odd to modern readers, but no one else—not even H. G. *Wells—ever matched his innovative flair and daring. The imaginative reach of *Eureka* seemed merely bizarre at the time, and no one noticed that it contained the first correct solution of Olbers' paradox: the question of why the night sky is dark if the universe is illimitably vast and replete with stars. The analysis of the pretensions of empirical science contained in its early chapters—which dismisses the methods favoured by "Aries Tottle" (*Aristotle) and "Hog" (Francis *Bacon) in favour of intuitive inspiration—is sufficiently pompous and sarcastic to alienate lay readers and scientists alike, but it is best regarded as a typical example of defensive perversity. The middle section of the book is an earnest and perceptive description of astronomical discovery, whereas the final section is a poetic vision of the death and rebirth of whole cosmic systems (what would now be termed galaxies) whose transient light takes unimaginably long periods of time to reach the Earth. All *Omega Point fantasies and similarly grandiose visions of universal crisis owe their ultimate origin to *Eureka*.

Poe's literary influence was enormous, but is most evident in genres other than speculative fiction; he is much more frequently cited, acknowledged, and imitated in the fields of horror fiction and detective fiction. Stories in which he features as a character usually focus on his relevance to these other genres; examples include Manly Wade Wellman's "When It Was Moonlight" (1940), Robert Bloch's "The Man Who Collected Poe" (1951), Fritz Leiber's "Richmond, Late September" (1969), Anne Edwards' *Child of Night* (1975), Barbara Steward's *Evermore* (1978), Marc Olden's *Poe Must Die* (1978), Manny Meyers' *The Last Mystery of Edgar Allan Poe* (1978), N. L. Zaroulis' *The Poe Papers* (1978), Angela Carter's "The Cabinet of Edgar Allan Poe" (1982), Walter Jon Williams' "No Spot of Ground" (1989), Charles L. Harness' *Lurid Dreams* (1990), Stephen Marlowe's *The Lighthouse at the End of the World* (1995), Sophia Kingshill's play *The Murder of Edgar Allan Poe* (1997), Kim Newman's "Just Like Eddy" (1999), Harold Schechter's *Nevermore* (1999) and its sequels, Randall Silvis' *On Night's Shore* (2001), and Hugh Cook's "The Trial of Edgar Allan Poe" (2002). Rudy Rucker's *The Hollow Earth* (1990) and Fred Saberhagen and Roger Zelazny's *The Black Throne* (1990) are notable exceptions.

POETRY

A form of literary expression initially characterised by devices evolved to assist listening and memorisation. The skill involved in managing these devices and the authority of tradition maintained the prestige of poetry, relative to prose, until the early twentieth century, although the utility of print in facilitating "direct reading"—i.e., reading without translation into aural imagery—facilitated changes in poetic form as well as the evolution of the particular literary virtues of prose, as reflected in the development of "free verse".

Sir Philip Sidney's *Defence of Poesie* (written 1579–1580; published 1595; aka *An Apologie for Poetrie*) advertises poetry as a particular form of knowledge, linking it to post-Renaissance New Learning by proclaiming it "the Monarch of the Sciences" and praising the "planetlike music of poetry". Sidney felt that a defence was needed because of Puritan objections that poetry was a kind of existential frippery, ostentation devoid of utility. Percy Shelley's *Defence of Poetry* (written 1821; published 1840) was begun as a reply to a tongue-in-cheek article by Thomas Love Peacock arguing that the best minds of the future must devote themselves to the social sciences instead of poetry, but it is not anti-scientific. In the spirit of revolutionary *Romanticism it praises the moral and creative worth of poetry in terms of its liberating potential, hailing poets as "the unacknowledged legislators of the world".

The residuum of *Pythagorean thought in Renaissance science was powerful enough to maintain the notion of "the harmony of the spheres" through the Copernican revolution, at least as a highly significant metaphor, and it is not surprising that an affinity was established and maintained between cosmologists and poets. John Donne's lament in "An Anatomie of the World" (1611) that "And new Philosophy calls all in doubt, / The Element of fire is quite put out; / The sun is lost, and th'earth, and no man's wit / Can well direct him where to look for it" was not the horrified reaction it has come to seem. Giambattista Marino's L'Adone (1622) combines Classical imagery with that of the new science, the goddess Venus rubbing shoulders with *Galileo. A growing tension between the scientific and literary worldviews did, however, become more evident as time went by. John Milton's response to the new cosmology was ambivalent, and the best advice Raphael can give Adam in Book VIII of Paradise Lost (1667) is not to trouble himself with such matters while there are more important concerns at hand—a sentiment echoed by Alexander Pope's judgement that "the proper study of mankind is man" (1733).

John Dryden was happy to associate himself with the Royal Society, as was Abraham Cowley, and it is possible to identify an entire school of poets who responded enthusiastically to Isaac *Newton's revelations. The German poet Berthold Heinrich Brockes attempted a synthesis of science and theology in Irdiches Vergnügen in Gott (9 vols., 1721–1748), while his compatriot Friedrich Gottlieb Klopstock made modern science—particularly cosmology—the basis and subject matter of all his poetry, most significantly Messias (1748–1773). Although Mark Akenside's "Hymn to Science" (1739) construes the term in a wide sense, his "Pleasures of the Imagination" (1744) gives full credit to the imaginative impact of the Newtonian revolution. Akenside combined the careers of poet and physician, as Erasmus *Darwin was later to do. Darwin's *botanical verse fitted readily enough into an existent tradition, and it is possible to identify a similar, albeit much weaker, tradition in the early development of *entomology.

At its inception, the *Romantic Movement was very sympathetic to the scientific component of the Enlightenment, and that sympathy is widely reflected in its poetry; it is only in retrospect that Blakeian and Keatsian dissent seems to stand out as a plangent plaint against the advent of industrialisation and utilitarianism. Edgar Allan *Poe resolved the doubts expressed in his early "Sonnet—To Science" (1829), moving swiftly on to the visionary "Al Aaraaf" (1829) and the magisterial Eureka (1848), while his compatriot Oliver Wendell Holmes thought it perfectly appropriate to write "medicated" poetry. Several nineteenth-century scientists and popularisers of science dabbled in Romantic verse, including Humphry Davy, Robert *Hunt, and James Clerk Maxwell. Scientific American routinely published poetry in its pre–Civil War issues, although it increasingly advertised it as a "break" from scientific matters, and the tradition was preserved into the twentieth century—albeit rather fugitively—by some other journals, including Science. By the end of the nineteenth century, though, it seemed necessary to Ronald Ross that he make a choice between a literary career as the last of the Romantics and the scientific career that ultimately won him the Nobel Prize for medicine.

Among several significant developments in the nineteenth century that were relevant to this apparent change of situation, two stand out: the relentless evolution of prose fiction and the relentless evolution of *evolutionary theory. When Sidney and Shelley had penned their defences of poetry, they were really defending literature in general, but as the artistry of prose advanced, it came to seem that the "poetic" aspects of poetry might be seen as superfluous frippery after all. On the other hand, the Newtonian poets who had given expression to a new harmony of the spheres had still been able to retain their traditional respect for divine creation; they were able to argue, along with other champions of the *plurality of worlds, that the new cosmos was a higher achievement than the old. Evolutionary theory, especially the version of Charles *Darwin's theory of natural selection that was rapidly popularised, seemed to offer a worldview that was not nearly so flattering to imaginative—and hence to poetic—ambition. The shift in attitude and mood is clearly reflected in the differences between Alfred, Lord Tennyson's In Memoriam (1850) and "Locksley Hall, Sixty Years After" (1886) and the moodiness of Thomas Hardy's meditations on evolution. In an 1861 treatise on Education, the evolutionist Herbert Spencer fervently denied "the current opinion that science and poetry are opposed" as a delusion, insisting that "Science is itself poetic", but the temper of his protest was suggestive of a man swimming against a tide.

The new movements in poetry that developed at the end of the nineteenth century and the beginning of the twentieth did so partly in reaction against the prosaic qualities of prose and the emergent scientific worldview, but they were not necessarily unsympathetic to scientific inspiration. Although the method of symbolist poetry was somewhat at odds with scientific representation, it could accommodate such works as Giovanni Pascoli's "Emigranti nella Luna" (1905), which is an account of lunar emigration by modified *palingenesis. New notions of the relativity of time gave birth to a movement of their own in "simultaneous poetry". Henri-Martin Barzun founded a journal in 1912 to showcase such work, whose first issue included a poem about the unification of the world by wireless and aviation. Blaise Cendrars' "simultaneous book" *La prose du Transibérien et de la petite Jeanne de France* (1913)—a poem printed on two-meter-long sheets—transforms a railway journey into a world-embracing odyssey. Guillaume Apollinaire's *Zone* (1912) sought to collapse past and future into the texture of present experience, while *Ondes* (1913) celebrated the Eiffel Tower's contribution to time signalling. The poetry associated with futurism was equally enthusiastic about the same themes—but seemed equally eccentric in consequence.

Although a chasm seemed to have opened up between the two topics, I. A. Richards' *Science and Poetry* (1926) was still able to defend the past and present connections between the two and hope for further alliance in future. Working scientists were still embarking on poetic endeavours in that period—Julian Huxley's "Cosmic Evolution" and "Cosmic Death" (both written ca. 1925) are notable examples—and poetic champions of science such as Alfred Noyes were still to be found, but they were becoming increasingly rare. More significantly, self-appointed champions of poetry were beginning to turn against the poets of the past who had interested themselves in science.

D. B. Wyndham-Lewis and Charles Lee's definitive anthology of Bad Verse, *The Stuffed Owl* (1930), opens with those pillars of the Royal Society, Cowley and Dryden, employing them to bracket Margaret Cavendish—who was not allowed to join the Society because of her sex, but devoted much of her writing to reactions against its produce, especially that of Robert Hooke. Sir Richard Blackmore is abundantly represented, as is Erasmus Darwin. One of the few unknown poets selected for inclusion was T. Baker, singled out for being "inexhaustibly impressed by the powers of steam". Numerous passages from his epic poem *The Steam-Engine; or, The Power of Flame* (1857) were included, and the alleged risibility of the subject matter was further emphasised by the subsequent inclusion of John Close's extremely obscure celebration of "The Beelah Viaduct" (whose reference is to the then-famous Belah Viaduct).

Twentieth-century epic poetry found speculative scientific input useful in generating the scope and imaginative grandeur required by the form. Examples such as Harry Martinson's *Aniara* (1956), Buckminster Fuller's *Untitled Epic Poem on the History of Industrialization* (1962), and Frederick Turner's *The New World* (1985) and *Genesis* (1988) embraced such imagery wholeheartedly. Ben Schumacher's supposed cetacean epic—"translated by Robert Gerard" as "The Great Gray Dolphin" in the June 1978 issue of *Analog*—is not entirely serious, but not entirely mocking. On the whole, however, poetry dealing with speculative materials found itself subject to the same critical suspicions that Wyndham-Lewis and Lee had visited upon its predecessors—suspicions that seemed to be confirmed by the development of "science fiction poetry".

Although pulp magazines were generally too conscientiously lowbrow to make much room for poetry, Hugo Gernsback occasionally published verse in his specialist magazines, partly in order to emphasise their higher pretensions. Many of the fans attracted by the science fiction magazines were enthused by the notion of expressing its visionary quality in poetry, and such poetry became a prominent feature of science fiction fanzines. The most significant pioneer of work expressly labelled science fiction poetry was "Lilith Lorraine"—the pseudonym of Mary Maude Wright—who regarded it as an ideal medium for visionary speculation because it was free of the constraining shackles imposed on pulp fiction by marketing considerations. In 1940, she founded the small press Avalon, which published the first science fiction poetry magazine *Challenge*—although her first collection of science fiction poetry, *Wine of Wonder* (1952), appeared under another imprint. The tradition was continued in such volumes as Lilian Everts' *Journey to the Future* (1955) and Roscoe Fleming's *The Man Who Reached the Moon* (1958).

Much of the poetry published in the more downmarket science fiction pulps was pastiche, often in the vein of Nelson S. Bond's "The Ballad of Blaster Bill" (1941) and "The Ballad of Venus Nell" (1942), which followed precedents set by the frontier poet Robert W. Service. Similarly unprestigious models were also employed outside the genre, in such works as *The Space Child's Mother Goose* (1958) by Frederick Winsor and Marion Parry, whose "scientific nursery rhymes" included a robust account of "The Theory That Jack Built".

The science fiction magazines became hospitable to more earnest poetic endeavours in the 1960s. *Galaxy* published Sheri S. Eberhart's "Extraterrestrial Trilogue on Terran Self-Destruction" in 1961, but the most significant breakthrough was connected with the British "new wave", many of whose writers extended their experiments in that direction; the work they did was extensively sampled in Edward Lucie-Smith's anthology *Holding Your Eight Hands* (1969). Although new wave science fiction was generally suspicious of the myth of the *Space Age, it was in the same period that the actual space program began to provide significant inspiration to poets, reflected in such endeavours as E. G. Valens' *Cybernaut* (1968), John Fairfax's *Frontier of Going* (1969), Robert Van Dias' *Inside Outer Space* (1970), and Edwin Morgan's *From Glasgow to Saturn* (1974). Science fiction poetry even made it into the *New York Times* with "A Poem by Buckminster Fuller" (1971).

Scientific American and *Science* both attempted to revitalise their old poetry traditions in this period; John Updike's "The Dance of the Solids" (1969) appeared in the former, although it was the latter that stuck to its guns in continuing to feature poetry in every issue, providing a venue for such physicist-poets as Alan Lightman and helping to bring into being a new school of "hard science poetry" represented by such works as Diane Ackerman's *The Planets: A Cosmic Pastoral* (1976), Andrew Joron's "The Sonic Flowerfall of Primes" (1982) and "Antenna" (1989), and Michael Newman's "Cloned Poem" (1982).

Science fiction writers with a strong interest in poetry found far more publishing opportunities in the second half of the twentieth-century. Those who took early advantage of such opportunities included Ray Bradbury, John Brunner, Thomas M. Disch, Ursula K. Le Guin, Michael Bishop, and Joe W. Haldeman. A Science Fiction Poetry Association was founded by Suzette Haden Elgin in 1978, giving out an annual Rhysling Award (named after the "blind singer of the spaceways" who was given the task of rendering Robert A. Heinlein's poetry into imitation folk songs in "The Green Hills of Earth", 1947). Science fiction writers specialising in poetry—or at least devoting the bulk of their effort to that medium—became considerably more numerous and prolific thereafter. The most notable included Bruce Boston, author of the poetry collections *Nuclear Futures* (1987) and *Cybertexts* (1991), his sometime collaborator Robert Frazier, with whom he produced *Chronicles of the Mutant Rain Forest* (1992), Keith Daniels, and K. V. Bailey. David R. Bunch wrote a good deal of science fiction prose poetry, as well as such verses as "The Heartacher and the Warehouseman" (2000).

When Gardner R. Dozois took over the editorship of *Asimov's Science Fiction* in 1984, poetry became a more regular and prominent feature of the magazine, its regular contributors including several of the specialists cited above as well as writers also notable for their prose, such as Geoffrey A. Landis, Michael R. Collings, Tony Daniel, and John M. Ford, whose "Winter Solstice, Camelot Station" (1988) won a World Fantasy Award. *Analog* editor Stanley Schmidt briefly followed suit with Michael F. Flynn's "The Engineer Discourses upon His Love" (1989) but soon abandoned the experiment. The bulk of science fiction poetry remained confined to such small press magazines as *Kinesis* (1968–1970), *Speculative Poetry Review* (1977–1980), *Uranus* (1978–1984), *Umbral* (founded 1978)—sampled in Steve Rasnic Tem's *The Umbral Anthology of Science Fiction Poetry* (1982)—*Star*Line* (founded 1978), and *The Magazine of Speculative Poetry* (founded 1984), although there is a remarkable abundance of it to be found on the Internet. Steve Sneyd undertook the difficult task of compiling a history of poetry in science fiction fanzines and reprinting exemplary selections via Hilltop Press, and an "Ultimate Science Fiction Poetry Guide" is located at www.magicdragon.com.

Speculative fiction has offered numerous accounts of the future of poetry, frequently bewailing its inevitable mechanisation, as in Émile Souvestre's pioneering dystopian satire *Le monde tel qu'il sera* (1846; trans. as *The World as It Shall Be*). One item of prediction on which the vast majority of subsequent futurists were united was that poetry would perish one way or another. The few dissenters were confounded by the usual problem of trying to describe what the progressive poetry of the future might actually look or sound like. In Robert F. Young's "Emily and the Bards" (1956; aka "Emily and the Bards Sublime"), the android poets in a museum are discarded to make way for classic automobiles. When poets are featured as protagonists in science fiction novels, as in Edmund Cooper's *Five to Twelve* (1969), Damien Broderick's *The Judas Mandala* (1982), and Adam Roberts' *Jupiter Magnified* (2003), their verse is usually sampled with careful parsimony. They occasionally attempt to play the role defined for them by Percy Shelley, as in Robert Silverberg's "A Man of Talent" (1966).

Poetry composed by fictitious *computers is often quoted in science fiction to illustrate the limitations of its style, as in G. C. Edmondson's "One Plus One Equals Eleven" (1973), although John Wain's "Poem Feigned to Have Been Written by an Electronic Brain" (1956) is more respectful. On the other hand, poetry composed by—or at least with the aid of—actual computers tends to be quoted in a rather different spirit, more akin to such endeavours as the infamous Ern Malley hoax, by means of which two Australian journalists set out in 1944 to expose the absurd pretensions of the poetic *avant garde*. Thomas A. Easton's *Analog* article "Poetry with Rivets"

(1988) described a method of generating poetry by computer and left it to readers to judge the implications of the fact that twenty items had, at the time of writing, been accepted for publication by various editors.

POHL, FREDERIK (GEORGE JR.) (1919–)

U.S. writer and editor, whose entire career was dedicated to the science fiction genre, save for an interval of wartime service with the U.S. Air Force, a brief spell as an advertising copywriter, and a few exercises in literary hackwork. He also worked within the field as a literary agent from 1949 to 1953.

Before World War II, Pohl was a member of a New York–based group of science fiction fans known as the Futurians, and his early writing and editing was done in the context of the group's activities. Initially more inclined to editorial work, his early fiction—much of which was signed James MacCreigh—was undistinguished pulp fare. While he was employed as an editorial assistant on *If* and *Galaxy*, however, he began to produce an abundance of short fiction that extrapolated social trends in a satirical manner and supplied familiar ideas with new twists.

Pohl's early novels were all done in collaboration, mostly with his fellow Futurian Cyril Kornbluth. Three of his collaborations with Kornbluth were non–science fiction, but the four science fiction novels set important precedents within the genre. *The Space Merchants* (1953), which offers a garish image of a future United States of America politically and culturally dominated by the advertising industry, is a satirical extrapolation along the same lines as his short fiction, enlivened by a fast-moving action-adventure plot (so fast moving, in fact, that it features an unexplained murder, as the epilogue wryly admits). *Search the Sky* (1954) is an episodic Odyssean fantasy featuring a series of similarly distorted societies, each of which takes some contemporary ideology to an absurd extreme; the fact that one of the ideologies pilloried is feminism did not endear the book to later generations of readers. *Gladiator-at-Law* (1955) is similar in manner and tone, but more vividly dystopian, while the dystopian society described in *Wolfbane* (1957) is so odd that the book becomes a surreal thriller rather than the indictment of herd mentality it apparently set out to be.

The template from which these stories were stamped, in which heroic rebels struggle unavailingly to return some semblance of normality to an insane future society, was the standard format of the 1950s Earth-set science fiction novel. Although the

Pohl-Kornbluth versions of it were deliberately caricaturish—far more so than *Preferred Risk* (1955; by-lined Edson McCann), which Pohl cobbled together with Lester del Rey in order to win a *Galaxy* competition for which no adequate entries had been submitted—their garish quality gave them an edge that compensated for the triteness of their story arc. The short fiction that appeared under the Pohl-Kornbluth joint by-line—some of which consisted of story ideas brought to fruition by Pohl after Kornbluth's career was cut short by a heart attack in 1958—was more various, but similarly ebullient in its manner; it is collected in *The Wonder Effect* (1962) and *Critical Mass* (1977).

Pohl struggled to replicate the imaginative flair of his collaborative work in his early solo novels. *Slave Ship* (1957) and *Drunkard's Walk* (1960) followed the same narrative pattern, but in a slightly toilsome fashion that contrasted strongly with the buoyancy of his short fiction, whose high points included a farcical depiction of economic growth run wild in "The Midas Plague" (1954), a dramatic account of market research taken to its ultimate extreme in "The Tunnel Under the World" (1955), and an equally far-reaching extrapolation of consumerism in "The Man Who Ate the World" (1956). A series of collections extending from *Alternating Currents* (1956) through *The Case Against Tomorrow* (1957), *Tomorrow Times Seven* (1959), *The Man Who Ate the World* (1960), and *Turn Left at Thursday* (1961) to *The Abominable Earthman* (1963) cemented his early image as an essentially frivolous writer incapable of working effectively at novel length.

When he was left in sole charge of *Galaxy*, *If*, and their new companion magazine *Worlds of Tomorrow* in the 1960s, Pohl's own work began to seem even more casual than it had when he was assisting H. L. Gold. *A Plague of Pythons* (1965) and *The Age of the Pussyfoot* (1969) marked no significant advance on his earlier solo novels. He still seemed more comfortable working in collaboration, Jack Williamson having replaced Kornbluth as his preferred partner. They had produced a trilogy of juvenile novels about undersea colonisation, *Undersea Quest* (1954), *Undersea Fleet* (1956), and *Undersea City* (1958), and now went on to produce a trilogy of colourfully sophisticated space operas in *The Reefs of Space* (1964), *Starchild* (1965), and *Rogue Star* (1969). In 1969, however, Pohl quit his magazine posts in order to edit paperback book lines, initially for Ace and then for Bantam. The flow of his own work was temporarily stemmed, but when it resumed it swiftly underwent a considerable transformation.

Prior to 1970, Pohl had always seemed to sit contentedly at the soft end of the science fiction spectrum, primarily interested in speculative extrapolation as a means of producing absurd extremes, but he did not approve of science fiction's gradual displacement from bookstore shelves by commodified fantasy, and he remained firmly committed to the progressive ideology at the core of genre science fiction. The short fiction collected in *In the Problem Pit* (1976) continued a trend towards more intense extrapolation begun in the material collected in *Day Million* (1970); "The Merchants of Venus" (1971) eventually became the prelude to the far-reaching Heechee series, whose plotting demonstrated a new energy and cohesion and whose scope continued to broaden out long after the initial project had been completed, as further ideas and possibilities occurred to him. The series, which eventually comprised *Gateway* (1977), *Beyond the Blue Event Horizon* (1980), *Heechee Rendezvous* (1984), *The Annals of the Heechee* (1987), and the mosaics *The Gateway Trip* (1990) and *The Boy Who Would Live Forever* (2004), offered a bold account of the history, population, and prospects of the galaxy.

Alongside the early phases of the Heechee saga, *Man Plus* (1976) and *JEM: The Making of a Utopia* (1979) provided hardheaded accounts of extraterrestrial colonisation, stressing the difficulties and costs that any such prospect would involve, even if the galaxy did turn out to be full of terraformable planets. The theme was further extrapolated in *Stopping at Slowyear* (1991), *Mining the Oort* (1992), *The Voices of Heaven* (1994), and—in an ostentatiously light-hearted vein—*O Pioneer!* (1998).

Pohl also produced a series of near-future thrillers, all of them embellished with carefully controlled science-fictional motifs. Works of this sort included a sarcastic account of *The Cool War* (1981), an earnest mosaic future history of New York, *The Years of the City* (1984), and an ingenious account of subtly different parallel worlds, *The Coming of the Quantum Cats* (1986). *Black Star Rising* (1985), *Narabedla Ltd* (1988), and *The Day the Martians Came* (1988) stepped up the element of political satire contained in the earlier items in the sequence. The belated extrapolation of "The Midas Plague" into *Midas World* (1983) and the provision of a sequel to *The Space Merchants, The Merchants War* (1984) did not work as well, although they brought the earlier stories' concerns up to date. The recent exercises in a similar vein contained in *Pohlstars* (1984)—along with some fine *contes cruels*—were much sharper, and the documentary novel *Chernobyl* (1987) further illustrated the intensity of Pohl's concerns regarding the hazards likely to be thrown up in the near future by ominous trends.

Starburst (short version 1971 as "The Gold at the Starbow's End"; book, 1982) and *Homegoing* (1989)

featured considered confrontations with *alien intelligence. *The World at the End of Time* (1989) was a relatively tentative venture into the far future, which prepared the way for an ambitious series of *Omega Point fantasies comprising *The Other End of Time* (1996), *The Siege of Eternity* (1997), and *The Far Shore of Time* (1999). *Outnumbering the Dead* (1990) is a thoughtful *conte philosophique* cast as a Utopian satire. In parallel with these works Pohl continued his work in collaboration with Jack Williamson. *Farthest Star* (1975) and *Wall Around a Star* (1983) are action-adventures stories featuring a *Dyson sphere, *Land's End* (1988) is a topical disaster story, and *The Singers of Time* (1991) is an extravagant cosmological fantasy.

By the early years of the twenty-first century, when Pohl was in his eighties, he had established himself as a key exemplar in the genre, capable of poignant sentimentality and bleak tragedy as well as flamboyant satire, and expert in every shade of wit, from the blackest comedy to the blithest farce. He never departed from the prospectus of speculative fiction, always basing his projections—however ambitious they might be—in scientific ideas, and developing them within the context of the scientific worldview. Like Williamson—who was eleven years older—he retained a remarkable sharpness of mind and clarity of prose style.

POLITICS

The organisation of power within society in patterns of legal authority and systems of government. The birth of political philosophy was intimately bound up with the development of democracy in Athens, when the opportunity first arose for political institutions to be designed and chosen rather than merely imposed by brute force and varied according to tyrannical will. It was the perceived failure of the democratic process, in ordaining the death of Socrates, that moved *Plato to lay important foundations of political philosophy in the *Republic, Statesman,* and *Laws,* favouring the notion that, in order to promote the ultimate ends of social harmony and individual prosperity, the apparatus of the state must be rigorous and exacting. Aristotle's *Politics* is more liberally inclined, and also more empirically enriched than many of his works, containing much useful observation on the workings of the Greek city-states.

The history of Western political philosophy after Plato and *Aristotle was considerably affected by the growth of Roman power and its attempted universalisation of political authority, in which context republicans consistently lost out to imperialists on actual battlegrounds, although a moral victory of sorts was secured in the eyes of historians by the blatant viciousness and incipient madness of so many of Rome's emperors. The replacement of Rome's temporal empire with Christendom's spiritual one reduced the function of civil authorities, in St. Augustine's view, to keeping order in a sinful world awaiting its judgement, but the judgement did not arrive before secular power—assisted by a milder climate, better harvests, and increasing wealth and population—began to outstrip religious authority again in the Middle Ages. The consequent power struggle extended across the entire second millennium of the Christian calendar, the progress of science being conceivable as one of many political battles.

Political philosophy retained a basic bipolarity reflective and extrapolative of Plato's and Aristotle's positions, represented in modern parlance as a spectrum extending from authoritarian and totalitarian theories of restrictive government to libertarian and anarchist theories favouring a minimal state apparatus. The situation was long confused by the role of *religion, which was often employed as a justification for authoritarianism—as in the notion of the "divine right" of kings—but whose separability from the state permitted a situation in which a rigid moral authoritarianism specified by religion could exist, albeit awkwardly, in parallel with a libertarian legal and governmental apparatus. The notion of a secularised political system running in parallel with organised religion, first formulated by Marsilius of Padua's *Defensor Pacis* (1324), came to dominate European politics after the Renaissance, becoming increasingly attractive following the development of *economic theories suggesting that the wealth of nations could best be promoted by free trade and a *laissez faire* political economy. The continued entanglement of religious and political authority, however, served to ensure that references in common parlance to the "right" and "left" wings of the political spectrum are rarely as straightforward as they sometimes seem.

The principles of virtuous and dutiful Christian kingship elaborated in the thirteenth century by St. Thomas Aquinas in *De regimine* were counterbalanced not only by Marsilius' prospectus for a secular state but by the cynical analysis of Niccolo Machiavelli's *Il principe* (1513; trans. as *The Prince*), which suggested that the actual behaviour of powerful men, and the strategies that served to preserve their power, were essentially deceptive, and that the rhetoric of political theory only served to conceal the true motivation and apparatus of government. This suspicion was incorporated into much subsequent "political science", notably the account offered by Thomas Hobbes in *Leviathan* (1651), which conceived politics as a pragmatic matter of preserving and maintaining a perennially precarious order and stability. Hobbes secularised St. Augustine's opinion that the world is fundamentally sinful in an account of selfish and unscrupulous human nature, direly in need of authoritarian restraint.

The Machiavellian account of politics, as elaborated by Hobbes, was echoed and elaborated in Bernard Mandeville's economic analysis of the body politic as a "grumbling hive", whose resentful stir cannot (and should not) ever be permanently soothed. It also had a profound effect on the literary representation of politics, although the acceptance of the pragmatism of political methodology by writers also served as a sharp reminder of the desirability of diplomacy. Literary representations of politics such as those featured in William Shakespeare's plays began to develop and exploit a sophisticated admixture of superficial flattery, directed at the works' patrons and overseers, and subtly submerged cynicism.

Hobbes' method of political analysis was carried forward by John Locke, who adopted a more generous view of human nature and therefore favoured less exacting means of social control. Locke advanced a *tabula rasa* theory of the mind, in which individuals were the product of their society rather than having a predetermined nature, so he saw government and law as active moulding processes rather than mere shackles. This line of dissent was taken much further by Jean-Jacques *Rousseau, who proclaimed that human nature was fundamentally virtuous, that it was the shackles of bad social organisation and government that spoiled the lives and minds of civilised folk, and that just and proper government could only be secured by a fundamental social contract secured by informed consent.

Similar notions—repackaged and revised by polemicists such as Thomas Paine, the great proponent of *The Rights of Man* (1791)—formed the ideological basis for the political revolutions of the eighteenth century. They also paved the way for the development of *Utopian socialism in the nineteenth century, building on ideas proposed in such works as William Godwin's *Political Justice* (1793) and Pierre-Joseph Proudhon's *Système des contradictions économiques, ou philosophie de la misère* (1846). Utopian socialism was challenged in its turn by the "scientific socialism" of Karl *Marx.

All of these developments had been reflected in Utopian literature and in the literature of complaint, whose howls of protest against political injustice were incessant. It was in the late eighteenth and early nineteenth centuries that such literary work began to take on a more analytical and theoretical slant, attempting to take aboard the ideas of political economy and social science in both its constructive (Utopian) and destructive (*satirical) variants. The fact that destructive criticism is much easier—and more entertaining—than satisfactory construction ensured that most Utopian fictions retained a strong satirical element. The contests within political philosophy regarding the nature of the individuals whose social organisation had to be politically determined are clearly reflected in the history of literary Utopias and satires, the latter routinely taking a much darker view of human nature than the former.

Literary work was always a significant instrument of political propaganda, and the earliest professional writers—active in seventeenth-century Europe—usually made most of their money from political propaganda. Satire was a keen weapon in this context, as deployed by such eighteenth-century British writers as Daniel Defoe and Jonathan Swift, but the promulgators of political philosophies were inevitably more interested in earnest Utopias an euchronias. Charles Fourier's attempt to dramatise his *socialisme phalanstérien* in this way in *Le nouveau monde amoureux* (written 1817; published 1967) came to nothing at the time, leaving the novelistic development of his ideas to more carefully ambivalent works such as Grant Allen's "The Child of the Phalanstery" (1884) and Paul Adam's *Les coeurs nouveaux* (1896).

The nineteenth century saw the widespread development of a pragmatic liberalism orientated towards the amelioration of poverty, which was manifest in strikingly different ways in different parts of the industrialising world. In France, under the influence of such writers as Henri de Saint-Simon and his positivist disciple Auguste Comte, this project had an implicit technological dimension and was integrated into the philosophy of *progress. In England, it was closely associated with the utilitarian principle that the aim of government was to secure the greatest happiness of the greatest number, although it was confused there by the strength of an antagonistic philosophy of imperialism.

Theoretical analyses of utilitarian liberalism produced by Jeremy Bentham and James Mill—which were to be further elaborated by the latter's son, John Stuart Mill, author of *On Liberty* (1869)—were subjected to cautionary empirical checking by Alexis de Toqueville's *De la démocratie en Amérique* (1835–1840; trans. as *Democracy in America*), investigating the manner in which the post-Revolutionary United States was attempting to build a society on the basis of a fundamental Constitution, as modified by the series of amendments popularly known as the Bill of Rights. Within the strongly contrasted tyranny of Tsarist Russia, the liberal creed was linked to the development of ambitious revolutionary politics, as

dramatised in Nikolai Chernyshevsky's *Chto Delat'* (1863; trans. as *What Is to Be Done?*), whose title was copied by Lenin.

The development of Western national democracy from the late nineteenth century on was steered by variants of this kind of pragmatic philosophy, while Eastern Europe followed a markedly different path that eventually produced a nominally Marxist "state socialism". The latter's centralisation licenced the charge that it was actually the opposite of what it claimed to be, mirroring the totalitarian systems of government by brute force that were still commonplace throughout the as-yet-unindustrialised world. The opposition between pragmatic democracy and centralised socialism became the central bipolarity of twentieth-century political philosophy and administration, their manifestations still complicated and confused by religion. Their fates were ultimately to be judged by the yardstick of personal wealth, as secured for their populations (or not) by economic growth, but judgement was passed in the meantime in a continuous flood of vitriolic satires directed against caricaturish versions of either end of the spectrum.

The cynicism of political satire is usually twofold, in that it doubts both the readiness of the governed to remain governable and the readiness of those in government to act in anyone's interest but their own. On the latter point there tends to be a sharp contrast between political philosophers, whose primary interest is the design of better systems of law and government, and literary commentators, who routinely take the view that *no* political system is likely to work, however cleverly it is designed, if its institutions are badly manned. The cautionary empiricism reflected in the philosophical tradition by such writers as Machiavelli and de Tocqueville is much more evident in the literary tradition than the academic one; its preponderance became ever greater as literature forsook diegetic modes of representation for mimetic ones, which required much more specificity in the design of characters and their settings.

Constructive utopian design became increasingly difficult in nineteenth- and twentieth-century literature as long fiction came to be dominated by the novel, but satirical assaults became more effective as well as easier as narrative techniques for depicting the plight of individuals harassed by political machinery gained much greater authority to generate indignation and outrage. The rise of *dystopian satire from the late nineteenth century onwards, its inexorably increasing bitterness, and its acquisition of an unchallengeable literary dominance over the broadly defined Utopian tradition was inevitable and irresistible—although it is arguable that the sadder reflection of political cynicism is the similarly irresistible rise of speculative *war stories, which take it for granted that the ultimate settlement of political disputes is always likely to be violent. The British genre of *scientific romance and serious American proto–science fiction were dominated by these kinds of fiction, whose suppositions also coloured conventional futuristic and extraterrestrial action-adventure fiction.

Writers of speculative fiction often adopt a viewpoint that tacitly overturns the Saint-Simonian perspective, thinking of the progress of science and *technology not as a derivative aspect of political evolution, nor even as its determining cause, but as a principal goal that political organisation ought to facilitate. This opens an ideological gulf between speculative fiction and naturalistic fiction, which usually remains committed to the idea that the primary goal of government is to maximise or control individual freedom. This kind of thinking is particularly conspicuous in the context of the myth of the *Space Age, whose centrality in American science fiction encouraged the production of numerous stories accepting that all kinds of political chicanery might be licenced in the interests of making sure that the conquest of the final frontier might go forward as planned. Notable examples include Robert A. Heinlein's "Requiem" (1940) and "The Man Who Sold the Moon" (1950), Poul Anderson's "The Double-Dyed Villains" (1949), and Dean McLaughlin's *The Man Who Wanted Stars* (1965). Norman Spinrad's *The Iron Dream* (1972) suggests that if Adolf Hitler had become a pulp science fiction writer instead of a dictator, his sublimated dreams would have been readily accommodated within the mythology of the Space Age.

Many early pulp science fiction writers tacitly adopted the view that politics was supposed to foster progress, and that American democracy was virtuous primarily because it did. Miles J. Breuer's "The Gostak and the Doshes" (1930) dismissed the kind of political rhetoric that was then beginning to tear Europe apart as so much silly hot air, while "The Birth of a New Republic" (1930; with Jack Williamson) looked forward with nationalistic pride to the day when another new world—the Moon—would follow the example of the United States and declare its independence of the old world from which its colonists had come. Pulp fiction became increasingly politicised in the 1930s, however, as it took aboard more explicit and more anxious reactions to the rise of fascism in Europe. Notable science fiction stories in this vein included Wallace West's "The Phantom Dictator" (1935) and Nat Schachner's series begun with "Past, Present and Future" (1937). This tendency was markedly increased in the science fiction genre by the importation into John W. Campbell Jr.'s *Astounding Science Fiction* stable of the highly influential Robert Heinlein,

whose radical political pragmatism permeated all his futuristic fiction and struck a powerful chord in the attitude and policies of his editor and mentor, although his early political fantasy *For Us the Living* (written 1939; published 2004) remained unpublished in his lifetime.

Twentieth-century speculative fiction continued reacting to the threat of fascism long after its neutralisation. Stories of what might have happened had Hitler triumphed in World War II continued to dominate the subgenre of *alternative history. The substitution of Stalin as the leading bugbear of U.S. politics after 1945 caused some confusion among popular writers who had previously thought of him as an ally in the fight against Hitler, and the establishment of Joseph McCarthy's Un-American Activities Committee provoked some reaction in the science fiction community. John Campbell was prepared to publish James Blish's explicitly anti-McCarthyite "At Death's End" (1954; exp. in *They Shall Have Stars*, 1956) and also to provide a home for political fantasies by the socialist writer Mack Reynolds, although Robert Silverberg has alleged that Howard Browne terminated Roger P. Graham's career as a regular contributor to the Ziff-Davis pulps because of his expressed support for communism in "Frontiers Beyond the Sun" (1953; by-lined Mallory Storm). Postwar science fiction clung even harder to its anti-fascist ideals in its treatment of race relations, both directly and through the medium of accounts of anti-*alien prejudice. The most effective use of science fiction devices in a *conte philosophique* dealing with race relations is, however, Derrick Bell's extrageneric account of "The Space Traders" (1992).

Such commitments were not recognised by Soviet writers attempting to develop their own distinctive science fiction genre. The June 1949 issue of *Astounding* printed a translation of a review of an anthology of U.S. science fiction from *Literatunaya Gazyeta*, by Viktor Bolkhovitinov and Vassilij Zakhartchenko, which characterised it as a "world of nightmare fantasies" replete with "nauseating evil ravings". Soviet science fiction writer Ivan Yefremov set out to write an ideological reply to one of the stories in the anthology, Murray Leinster's "First Contact" (1945), which was translated into English by Moscow's Foreign Languages Publishing House in 1959 as "The Heart of the Serpent" (aka "Cor Serpentis").

The increasing dependence of genre science fiction of the 1940s and 1950s on the "galactic empire" framework as a reservoir of interesting alien worlds had the accidental side effect of making magazine science fiction seem politically backward-looking. The glorification of interstellar "empires" by writers like Isaac Asimov, A. E. van Vogt, and Edmond

Hamilton was motivated by the attempt to capture their Romantic glamour rather than by any kind of political affection, but it was very difficult to imagine how a galaxy-wide culture might actually be governed. John Campbell pointed out in one of his editorials, "Arithmetic and Empire" (1943), that even the meanest count would require a galactic government to have in excess of four hundred billion employees, and that elected representatives in any kind of galactic parliament would have to speak for trillions of constituents. The problem was dramatised by Murray Leinster in "Plague" (1944), which features a galactic society hopelessly bogged down by bureaucracy. The simplest solution—calculated anarchism—was never taken seriously by U.S. writers, although the Scottish writer Iain M. Banks found it much more congenial when he set out to write space operas such as *Consider Phlebas* (1987), set within and around the anarchistically inclined Culture.

By the time that Campbell's *Astounding* became *Analog* at the end of the 1950s, it had acquired a reputation for right-wing politics, in spite of Mack Reynolds' continued appearances in its pages. The particular brand of right-wing politics it favoured, however, was a type of libertarianism praised for its hospitality to technological entrepreneurialism, and hence to the cause of progress—a cause to which Mack Reynolds was just as committed as such determinedly anti-socialist *Analog* regulars as Poul *Anderson, Gordon R. Dickson, and Larry Niven. The elaboration of libertarian political theory in Robert Nozick's *Anarchy, State and Utopia* (1974) used arguments based in human rights to sustain its case for the maximisation of individual freedom by the careful minimisation of government into a "night-watchman state"—whose obligations are confined to robust defence and a streamlined criminal justice system—but the literary arm of libertarian thought, primarily represented by the "Objectivist" writings of Ayn Rand, including the futuristic *Atlas Shrugged* (1957), tended to place much more emphasis on both technological development and the sacredness of intellectual property.

Libertarian science fiction is even more inclined to insist that the maximisation of individual freedom must go hand in hand with the maintenance of the scientific innovation and technological inventiveness requisite to the advancement of such projects as extraterrestrial colonisation. The cause of libertarian science fiction, as carried forward by such writers as Vernor Vinge, James P. Hogan, Jerry Pournelle, David A. Drake, and libertarian political activist L. Neil Smith, remained intimately tied to advocacy of the space program and the removal of political checks on technological adventurism. The Libertarian SF

Society proved ready and willing in 1996 and 1998 to present its annual Prometheus Award to the stridently socialist Scottish writer Ken MacLeod, for *The Stone Canal* and *The Star Fraction*, partly in recognition of the fact that MacLeod's left-wing anarchism is explicitly tied to the ideals of the Space Age.

Reynolds' socialism was not the only "left wing" political philosophy to be aired in Campbell's *Astounding*. Eric Frank Russell's robust championship of the pacifism of Mahatma Gandhi, "And Then There Were None..." (1951; exp. in *The Great Explosion*) appeared there, along with several other stories scathingly opposed to the tradition of military science fiction founded in the same pages by Gordon R. Dickson's *Dorsai* (1959; book 1960 as *The Genetic General*). British science fiction's other polemical pacifist, James White, only appeared in *Astounding/Analog* once, but that probably had more to do with the closeness of White's relationship with his primary editor, John Carnell, than any hostility to his brand of *medical science fiction on Campbell's part. Campbell published Murray Leinster's Med Ship stories, which show a similarly principled allegiance to the Hippocratic principle of doing everything humanly possible to avoid causing harm. Campbell also published early work by Norman Spinrad, whose *Agent of Chaos* (1967) endeared him to student radicals by expressing an enthusiasm for rebellious anarchism, which was echoed by long-time Campbell stable member A. E. van Vogt in *The Anarchistic Colossus* (1977). Other significant leftwardly inclined works produced within the bounds of U.S. science fiction include Gordon Eklund's *All Times Possible* (1974), Alexis Gilliland's *The End of the Empire* (1983), John Shirley's *Eclipse* (1985), and Dennis Danvers' *The Fourth World* (2000) and *The Watch* (2002).

By the time that *Analog* had obtained its reputation as a right-wing stronghold, there was a widespread perception that British science fiction was, in general, more left wing than its U.S. counterpart, but this generalisation requires similar modification. British science fiction of the 1950s and 1960s had its own brand of conservative politics, clearly evident in the work of such writers as John Wyndham and Brian W. *Aldiss, but it tended to fall into a more nostalgic vein, far more suspicious of technological development and buccaneering frontiersmanship than U.S. science fiction. The conservative sector of British science fiction carried forward one aspect of the tradition of *scientific romance—which had no obvious affection for the myth of the Space Age—while its left wing, as represented by such writers as Ian Watson, Iain Banks, and Ken MacLeod, carried forward another aspect, rooted in the crusading socialism of such writers as

George Griffith and H. G. *Wells and such genre associates as J. B. S. *Haldane and J. D. Bernal.

The complications introduced into British scientific romance by the persistence of imperialistic ideas was also carried forward into British science fiction in works that sought to break the mould of Cold War opposition. David Wingrove's Chung Kuo series (1989–1996) bears on this issue tangentially, but Jon Courtenay Grimwood's *Pashazade* (2001) and its sequels and Ian McDonald's *River of Gods* (2004) tackle postcolonial situations directly. The parallel arguments in American science fiction tend to take the form of investigations of the politics of "development", as in John Barnes' *The Man Who Pulled Down the Sky* (1987), *Sin of Origin* (1988), and the Thousand Cultures series launched by *A Million Open Doors* (1992). U.S. science fiction has its own residual idiosyncratic preoccupation in the form of continuing echoes of the political divide that sparked the Civil War of 1861–1865, which continues to play a very substantial role in alternative history fiction, and in such futuristic political fantasies as Bruce Sterling's *Distraction* (1998) and Allen Steele's "Stealing Alabama" (2001).

Literary images of the democratic process became increasingly cynical in the late twentieth century as the impact of new media and marketing theory had a dramatic impact on the manner in which political campaigns were run and won. Such sarcastic fantasies as William Tenn's "Null-P" (1951) and "The Masculinist Revolt" (1965), John Schneider's *The Golden Kazoo* (1956), and Arthur Hadley's *The Joy Wagon* (1958) were succeeded by the more earnestly melodramatic representations of Norman Spinrad's *Bug Jack Barron* (1969) and *A World Between* (1979) as well as further satires such as Ward Moore's "Frank Merriwell in the White House" (1973), Frederik Pohl's "Servant of the People" (1983), Daniel Hatch's "Senator Space Cadet" (1993), and Philip Roth's *The Plot Against America* (2004).

The East/West divide was also subjected to scathing satire in such late twentieth-century works as Kim Newman and Eugene Byrne's *Back in the USSA* (1997) and Howard Waldrop's *A Better World's In Birth!* (2003). Such cynicism was, however, counterbalanced by the extension of the tradition of political *contes philosophiques* introduced into genre science fiction by Mack Reynolds, which continued to produce forthright commentaries on the fundamental issues of political philosophy into the twenty-first century in such short stories as Gregory Benford's "Brink" (2001) and Tom Purdom's "A Champion of Democracy" (2002) and more extended analyses in such novels as Neal Asher's series begun with *Gridlinked* (2001) and Kim Stanley Robinson's *Forty Signs of Rain* (2004).

One form of political organisation that received rather scant attention in science fiction after the early 1930s is technocracy, which faded from view in the wake of the meteoric career of Hugo Gernsback's propagandistic *Technocracy Review*. A case can be made, however, for the fact that explicit advocacy of technocracy is unnecessary in a genre that often takes *technological determinism for granted. If technology is the ultimate determinant of economic and political organisation, as Marxism and science fiction both assert, with slightly different political emphases— then every form of political organisation, from divinely sanctioned tyranny to dogmatic anarchy—is merely a variation of technocratic instrumentality.

POLLUTION

A term whose original meaning was to render impure or unclean—not in the commonplace sense of muddying, but within a moral and spiritual context, more akin to defilement or desecration. Its use in the context of "environmental pollution", with reference to the problems of waste disposal associated with the growth of cities and the rapid proliferation of industrial enterprise, always retained an echo of that implication. Problems of sanitation afflict all cities and frequently make themselves offensively manifest; attempts to restrict waste disposal by law—exemplified by laws to abate smoke production and restrict garbage disposal enacted by the English Parliament in 1273 and 1388—have always proved difficult to enforce, and many major *engineering projects were inspired by the necessity of waste disposal. London's sewer system was inspired by the "Great Stink" of the 1850s, which made long sections of the banks of the river Thames— including the one on which the Houses of Parliament stood—unendurable.

Early literary images of industrial pollution, including W. D. Hay's *The Doom of the Great City* (1880) and Robert Barr's "The Doom of London" (1892)—both featuring smog—tend to be formulated as tales of richly deserved punishment. Similar attitudes are manifest in the common nineteenth-century representation of London as the "Great Wen" (William Cobbett's phrase), whose decay into a mere scar is celebrated in such exercises in future pastoralism as Richard Jefferies' *After London; or, Wild England* (1885). Late nineteenth-century British Utopias routinely yearn for the kind of civic cleanliness displayed in *The Coming Era; or, Leeds Beatified* (1900; by-lined "A Disciple" [of H. G. Wells]).

In the early part of the twentieth century, pollution in Britain seemed to be on the decline as sewage systems improved and industrial emissions were subject to legal controls. U.S. industry, being more localised and easier to distance from living space, seemed even less problematic. Even so, some anxieties began to creep into the images of the future contained in pulp science fiction. Raymond Z. Gallun's "Magician of Green Valley" (1938) imagines lunar landscapes disfigured by the spoil-heaps of burgeoning industry. The pollutant side effects of modern warfare were starkly extrapolated in Robert A. W. Lowndes and John B. Michel's "The Inheritors" (1942) on the eve of the United States' involvement in World War II.

A sharp increase of such anxieties in the 1950s, due in part to nervousness about radioactive wastes produced by *nuclear power stations, was reflected in such stories as C. M. Kornbluth's black comedy "Shark Ship" (1958) before Rachel Carson's alarmist best-seller *Silent Spring* (1962) caused a sensation with its assault on the nonbiodegradable insecticide DDT. Pollution was rapidly absorbed thereafter into fantasies of impending *ecocatastrophe, where it was routinely linked to the problem of the *population explosion. It plays the major role in such *dystopias as George Bamber's *The Sea Is Boiling Hot* (1971), John Brunner's *The Sheep Look Up* (1972), Frank M. Robinson's "East Wind, West Wind" (1972), and Douglas R. Mason's *The Phaeton Condition* (1973), and such moralistic melodramas as Norman Spinrad's "The Lost Continent" (1970), Kurt Vonnegut's "The Big Space Fuck" (1972), Gordon R. Dickson's *The Pritcher Mass* (1972), Herbert W. Franke's "In den Slums" (1970; trans. as "Slum", 1973), Kit Pedler and Gerry Davis' *Brainrack* (1974), Wynne N. Whiteford's *Breathing Space Only* (1980), Trevor Hoyle's *The Last Gasp* (1983), and Paul Theroux's *O-Zone* (1986).

Other notably graphic science-fictional treatments of pollution include *The Clone* (1965) by Theodore L. Thomas and Kate Wilhelm—a horror story in which household and industrial pollutants combine and come to life—and Charles Platt's *Garbage World* (1967), in which extraterrestrial disposal generates new worlds of waste. More earnest and meditative treatments of the theme include Peter Tate's *The Thinking Seat* (1970), Hayden Howard's "The Biggest Oil Disaster" (1970), Gardner Dozois' "King's Harvest" (1972), Dean McLaughlin's "To Walk with Thunder" (1973), and Connie Willis' "Blued Moon" (1984).

POPULARISATION OF SCIENCE, THE

Although significant precedents were set in the seventeenth century by such works as Bernard de Fontenelle's *Entretiens sur la pluralité des mondes* (1686; trans. as *Conversations on the Plurality of Worlds*), the popularisation of science did not become manifest as a collective activity backed by an educational ideology until the eighteenth century. An early propagandist was Johann Christoph Gottsched, who set himself up as an "educator of the German nation", in the first half of the century, but it was not until the revolutionary decades of the 1770s and 1780s that they began to make rapid progress in the United States and Europe. A two-pronged crusade was then undertaken in the context of two general causes: the extension of literacy to the working classes and the education of women. In both cases, science was seen as a crucial element of the dispersal of Enlightenment and the advancement of democracy.

In 1799, the Royal Institution was founded in London to disseminate "practical knowledge"; Humphry Davy and Michael Faraday lectured there, and the latter's Christmas lectures for children became a custom that extended into the twenty-first century. To some extent, the Institution was a reaction against Joseph Banks' insistence on running the Royal Society as a kind of gentleman's club for wealthy amateurs. Most learned societies still operated along similar lines, but natural history societies and philosophical societies open to all comers soon began to spring up in large towns. A London Mechanics' Institution founded in 1824 was widely copied. Scientific education was seen as essentially democratic, because it was not dependent on knowing Latin and Greek. The most widely read British periodicals of the early nineteenth century—the *Quarterly Review*, the *Edinburgh Review,* and *Blackwood's*—all printed lengthy analyses of new scientific texts and summary surveys of contemporary knowledge in particular areas of science.

Several of the leading figures in the movement were women. Maria Edgeworth used her children's novels as vehicles for scientific education, most notably *Frank* (1801) and *Harry and Lucy* (1801; with Richard Levell Edgeworth). Jane Marcet's *Conversations on Chemistry, Intended More Especially for the Female Sex* (1806) went through sixteen editions in the next half century and sold 160,000 copies in the United States. Marcet used dialogues and exemplary fictions in *Conversations on Political Economy* (1816), *Conversations on Natural Philosophy* (1819), and *Conversations on Vegetable Philosophy* (1829), the first named including an account of "A Manchester Strike" ancestral to the "social problem novels" of Benjamin Disraeli and Mrs. Gaskell. Mary Somerville translated Pierre Laplace's *Mécanique Céleste* (1825) as *Mechanism of the Heavens* (1831) and her *On the Connexion of the Physical Sciences* (1834) was a significant expression of the notion that all the physical sciences could and would be united into a coherent whole, although its main emphasis was on the underlying unity of scientific method. Harriet Martineau published a significant series of fictional *Illustrations of Political Economy* (1832–1934) and became a leading light of Henry Brougham's Society for the Diffusion of Useful Knowledge, founded in 1826.

Popularisations of science aimed specifically at children included Thomas Day's didactic novel *Sandford and Merton* (1783), Samuel Parkes' *Chemical Catechism for the Use of Young People* (1806), Jeremiah Joyce's *Scientific Dialogues* (1807), Margaret Gatty's *Parables from Nature* (1855–1871), Charles Kingsley's *Glaucus; or, The Wonders of the Shore* (1855) and *Madam How and Lady Why* (1869), and John Ruskin's *The Ethics of the Dust: Ten Lectures to Little Housewives on the Elements of Crystallisation* (1865).

British scientists who lent themselves to the cause included Sir John Herschel, who became one of the most successful populotatiofs of astronomy; his *Treatise on Astronomy* (1833) and *Outlines of Astronomy* (1849) were very successful, helping to demonstrate that astronomy is the most readily popularised science, with a large amateur following. There was little evidence of any fundamental cultural division between scientists and litterateurs at that time. George Eliot made every attempt to promote science in the *Westminster Review* (founded 1852), which she helped to edit, and one of her early recruits in that line was her future partner in life G. H. Lewes, whose early contributions included "Goethe as a Man of Science". Lewes also contributed "Studies in Animal Life" to the early issues of William Thackeray's *Cornhill Magazine*, founded in 1860.

A new breed of specialist popularisers of science began to emerge in midcentury, a key pioneer being Robert Hunt, whose books included a lyrical account of *The Poetry of Science* (1848). Hunt worked on the Great Exhibition of 1851—whose official catalogue he produced—and many other exercises in the public communication of science; following the Exhibition, he began to set aside his early experiments in photochemistry, becoming increasingly involved in mining technology and the education of miners. Although Brougham's Society for the Diffusion of Useful Knowledge was satirised by Thomas Love Peacock in *Crotchet Castle* (1831) as "The Sixpenny Science Company", it thrived. *The Penny Magazine*, founded in 1832 as a disseminator of practical information, was similarly successful, although it eventually had to give more space to popular fiction in order to hold its audience in the face of expanding competition.

The Great Exhibition of 1851, housed in the Crystal Palace, was a huge success, not least in provoking a remarkable flood of celebrations, satires, and didactic

stories for children—including E. G. M.'s *The Crystal Palace* (1851), Robert Franklin's *Wanderings in the Crystal Palace* (1851), Samuel Warren's *The Lily and the Bee—An Apologue of the Crystal Palace* (1851), and C. T. W.'s *The Crystal Hive; or, The First of May* (1852)—and Henry Mayhew's comic novel *1851; or, The Adventures of Mr. and Mrs. Sandboys and Family, Who Came up to London to "Enjoy Themselves" and See the Great Exhibition* (1851; with illustrations by George Cruikshank). It was swiftly imitated in Paris, where every effort was made to improve upon it in later exhibitions such as the Universal Expositions of 1889—for which the Eiffel Tower was built—and 1900.

The more rapid spread of literacy in post-Revolutionary France and the unchecked growth of newspapers and popular magazines in the early nineteenth century had ensured that it was not necessary for crusaders like Brougham to make such heroic efforts there, but the popularisation of science was undertaken with similar vigour. The works of Jean-Sébastien Julia de Fontenelle, including a *Manuel de physique amusante* (1826), provided significant early exemplars before Camille *Flammarion took over Herschel's role as the primary populariser of nineteenth-century astronomy.

The exhibition tradition was also imported into the United States, where various cities competed with one another in hosting a series of spectacular "world's fairs", initiated by the 1876 Centennial Exposition in Philadelphia's Fairmount Park, whose focal point was the Machinery Hall, decked out with electric lights and elevators powered by a huge Corliss steam engine. The popularisation of astronomy also followed a course similar to its development in Britain and France; Ormsby MacKnight Mitchel's lecture tours became very successful in the 1840s and Simon Newcomb published a *Popular Astronomy* (1878), while Garrett P. Serviss' journalistic pieces gradually turned him into an expert. Lectures remained an important vehicle of popularisation in the United States; John Tyndall's New York lectures on physics in 1872 were followed by Thomas Henry Huxley's lectures on evolution in 1876, reprints of both series selling tens of thousands of copies.

Scientific American, founded as a weekly in 1845, took on a distinctive slant when it came under the control of patent attorney Orson D. Munn, who directed its focus toward technological innovation, introducing an element of practical ambition into American popular science whose context provided crucial scope for such inventive entrepreneurs as Thomas *Edison and Hugo *Gernsback. By contrast, the *Popular Science Monthly*, founded in 1872 by Edward L. Youmans, was far more intent on promoting theoretical ideas, especially those of Herbert Spencer.

This heroic age of scientific education could not last. The task became increasingly problematic in the latter part of the century as the specialist vocabularies of science and its mathematical underpinnings became more elaborate and difficult to grasp. The popularisation of science increasingly became a matter of "translation into layman's language"—a phrase that was the ancestor of the modern idea of "dumbing down". The two cultures of science and literature began to draw apart, and their relationship came to be seen as problematic before the end of the century, the opening of the rift detailed by Matthew Arnold in "Literature and Science" (1882).

The emerging pattern of distinction was dramatised by W. H. Mallock in *The New Republic: Culture, Faith and Philosophy in an English Country-House* (1877), a work intermediate between Peacock's *Crotchet Castle* and Aldous *Huxley's *Crome Yellow*. There is a very obvious distinction of narrative complexity between the popular articles that Thomas Henry Huxley wrote for *Macmillan's Magazine* and the *Nineteenth Century* in the 1880s and his formal scientific publications. By that time, scientific *publication had become formularised as well as formalised, having adopted a kind of pedantry that almost seemed to have the purpose of excluding the understanding of ordinary people. The revolution in theoretical physics that took place over the next thirty years completed the process of alienation. *Popular Science Monthly* was taken over in 1900 by James McKeen Cattell, the editor of *Science*, but Cattell sold it on in 1915, when it shed its educational ambitions and began catering to established hobbyists. Cattell founded *The Scientific Monthly* to move in the other direction, addressed to readers who had already received their scientific education in schools and universities.

As this esotericisation gathered pace, interest in the uses of fiction as a didactic instrument increased, largely because it seemed to popularisers that greater efforts would have to be made to make information accessible. Although Jules *Verne did not consider himself a populariser of science, the kind of fiction he produced seemed to some of its admirers to be a useful packaging device, whose particular strength in this regard was its ability to appeal to the young— thus cultivating sufficient interest in science to steel them for the increasingly difficult task of coming to grips with its challenges. Already, however, the impetus imparted by writers like Maria Edgeworth and Jane Marcet had been lost; an interest in science, and the potential for its mastery, was increasingly seen as a male prerogative.

The adaptation of Vernian romance as a didactic medium was not conspicuously successful; the more scientific exposition was pumped into the texts, the less appealing they became as conventional reading experiences. Such experiments as Luke Theophilus Courtenay's *Travels in the Interior* (1887)—which features an educative voyage through the human body—John Trowbridge's *The Electrical Boy* (1891) and Mark Wicks' *To Mars via the Moon* (1911) became paradigm examples of the kind of "science fiction" that was dubious in scientific terms and more or less devoid of narrative value. When Hugo Gernsback reinvented scientifiction, he knew that this was a problem in need of a solution, but he made little headway in that mission. Such nakedly didactic pulp science fiction stories as Daniel Dressler M.D.'s "The White Army" (1929)—the reference is to white blood corpuscles—and "The Brain Accelerator" (1929) made no appeal whatsoever to the readers the new genre was courting.

The Century of Progress Exhibition in Chicago in 1933–1934 made the most determined effort of all the U.S.'s World's Fairs to popularise science and technology, but emphasised in doing so the extent to which science and technology were becoming esoteric and controversial. The decision of the exhibition's planners to eliminate windows from its halls, replacing them with sheets of asbestos and plywood held in steel frames, did not work to its advantage, and its most extravagant exhibit—showing dinosaurs in a "natural" setting—proved provocative in an era when *Creationism was gathering impetus.

Similar difficulties afflicted straightforward exercises in scientific popularisation. *Scientific American* reverted to a monthly schedule in 1921, and the Munn family eventually sold it in 1947 to science journalist Gerard Piel and his associates. Its new editors altered its slant dramatically, featuring in-depth articles by scientists aimed at other professional scientists who were interested in reading outside their specialties. Assisted by the research legacy of World War II, that population had now swelled to a very considerable size, and the new version of the magazine was a great success. Its nearest British counterpart, the weekly *New Scientist*—founded in 1956—followed a similar policy, and also thrived. The demand for popular science was by no means extinct, but it had become specialised in a few relatively distinct areas, most of which are associated with particular groups of hobbyists, such as "ham *radio" enthusiasts and amateur astronomers. The only "popular science" magazine Hugo Gernsback thought it worthwhile to continue in the 1930s, when *Modern Electrics* and *Science and Invention* were dead and buried and *Technocracy Review* had been stillborn, was *Sexology*.

Popular science books could still achieve best-selling status on occasion in the mid-twentieth century, but sales of such texts as Lancelot Hogben's *Mathematics for the Million* (1937) and *Science for the Citizen* (1938) were probably sustained by a desire to seem interested, or pipe dreams of self-improvement, rather than by any kind of productive engagement with the texts. A more direct and gripping engagement was achieved, however, by a number of books whose appeal was directly to the *aesthetics of the sublime, which used the grandeur of modern *cosmology and the vast timespans of evolutionary biology and *geology to tap into a sense of wonder. One of the most successful writers in this vein was Sir James Jeans, author of *The Universe Around Us* (1929), *The Stars in Their Courses* (1931), and *The New Background of Science* (1933); it was probably not coincidental that Jeans was as interested in music as astronomy—he became director of the Royal Academy of Music in 1931 and wrote a definitive text on *Science and Music* (1937). The writer who initially took this kind of popularisation to its most lyrical extreme was the polymathic Loren Eiseley, author of *The Immense Journey* (1946), *The Firmament of Time* (1960), and *The Unexpected Universe* (1969).

Eiseley became the prototype of a new wave of generalist scientific popularisers whose tone was inspirational and whose manner was evangelical. Their work was often far ranging, identifying associational links between different areas of scientific data and various aspects of personal experience, but even when it was more detailed and tightly focused, its primary purpose was to spread the gospel of science. This kind of popularisation embraced and transformed the kinds of *speculative nonfiction produced by writers like J. B. S. *Haldane, thus dovetailing neatly with the interests and methods of writers of *hard science fiction. Some of its key exponents, including Isaac *Asimov and Arthur C. *Clarke, were also science fiction writers; others, like George Gamow, Fred *Hoyle, Carl Sagan, John Gribbin, Ian Stewart, and Jack Cohen, became dabblers in the genre, while even those who never bothered with it, like Freeman *Dyson, Stephen J. Gould, Richard Dawkins, and John Barrow, sometimes drew part of their own inspiration and some of their examples from fictional discourse. This kind of popularisation frequently extended its associational links far beyond the confines of science itself, inevitably finding an affinity with other kinds of preaching, producing such strange hybrids as Pierre Teilhard de Chardin's speculations regarding the *Omega Point and Fritjof Capra's *The Tao of Physics* (1975).

The educative mission of the popularisation of science was never forsaken, nor was it entirely relegated to publications aimed at young readers, but it never lost the edge of desperation that it had acquired in the 1880s. That desperation is particularly obvious in works that attempt to use popular works of fiction as hooks to catch the interest of readers, offering to explain the science "behind" the ideas displayed therein. The vogue for this kind of work was launched by Laurence Krauss's *The Physics of Star Trek* (1995), which was rapidly supplemented by the same author's *Beyond Star Trek Physics: Physics from Alien Invasions to the End of Time* (1997), Richard Hanley's *The Metaphysics of Star Trek* (1997; aka *Is Data Human?*), Robert Sekuler and Randolph Blake's *Star Trek on the Brain: Alien Minds, Human Minds* (1998), Susan and Robert Jenkins' *Life Signs: The Biology of Star Trek* (1998), and Athena Andreadis' *To Seek Out New Life: The Biology of Star Trek* (1998).

This method was extended to extremes in such texts as Mark C. Glassy's *The Biology of Science Fiction Cinema* (2001), although that assisted the realisation that there is no need for the texts under consideration to be science fictional at all. It is just as easy to plot scientifically interesting pathways from entirely fantastic texts, as in Terry Pratchett, Ian Stewart, and Jack Cohen's *The Science of Discworld* (1999) and its two sequels, John and Mary Gribbin's *The Science of His Dark Materials* (2003), Michael Hanlon's *The Science of The Hitchhiker's Guide to the Galaxy* (2005), and Henry Gee's *The Science of Middle-Earth* (2005). Indeed, the most useful model text for educational exercises of this kind had long since been demonstrated to be Lewis Carroll's Alice books, as employed in such works as Frank Debenham's *Navigation with Alice* (1961).

More serious examinations of the science in science fiction were routinely carried out in the nonfictional sections of *Analog* from the 1940s onwards, and similar concerns were occasionally exhibited in such small press publications as Catherine Asaro's *Mindsparks* (4 issues, 1993–1994), but items of that sort were, like the post-1947 *Scientific American*, preaching to the converted. Attempts to reach out to a more general audience were far more problematic, although the desire to *appear* interested in manifestly important scientific matters, and to have some elementary understanding thereof, remained sufficiently powerful to generate such famous largely unread best-sellers as Stephen Hawking's *A Brief History of Time* (1988). Hawking's success helped to revive the fortunes of scientific popularisation as a marketable genre, and to sharpen awareness of the acute problems involved in trying to translate modern science into "layman's language". The sheer magnitude of that challenge, however, was an incentive in itself. The most ardent of the late twentieth-century popularisers refused to be daunted by it, and set out to make more abundant and productive use of their ingenuity than had ever been made before.

The best results of this heroic determination provide striking examples of determined *rhetoric and applied *narrative theory, as well as re-emphasising the utility of speculative nonfiction and hard science fiction as potential instruments of scientific popularisation. The most extensive and adventurous use of fictional techniques in the cause of didactic popularisation was begun by Clifford A. *Pickover in the 1990s, and the same period saw similarly ambitious combinations in such works as Ian Stewart and Jack Cohen's *The Collapse of Chaos* (1994) and *Evolving the Alien: The Science of Extraterrestrial Life* (2002). Some hard science fiction writers began issuing nonfictional texts that were, in effect, companions to their fiction, including Damien Broderick's *The Spike* (1997; rev. 2001) and *The Last Mortal Generation* (1999), Stephen Baxter's *Deep Future* (2001) and *Omegatropic* (2001), and Wil McCarthy's *Hacking Matter: Levitating Chairs, Quantum Mirages, and the Infinite Weirdness of Programmable Atoms* (2003). Theoretical scientists like Michio Kaku increasingly drew in their popularisations on work previously done by such cross-generic writers as Rudy *Rucker, extending the ideative links they had forged. The Internet, appropriately enough, became a significant location for the development of these kinds of links, abundantly illustrated by the online publications of Sten Odenwald at such sites as www.astronomycafe.net.

POPULATION

The human inhabitants of a particular place. The scientific study of population—demography—is concerned with the age structure of populations and factors determining mortality in their various subdivisions. The first important work of demography was John Graunt's groundbreaking study in social statistics, *Natural and Political Observations upon the Bills of Mortality* (1662). The term is usually restricted to the human population, leaving animal studies to be classified under the looser heading of "population dynamics". The latter field became closely associated in the twentieth century with that of population genetics, which tracks changes in the biological constitution of populations. The notion of subjecting demography to political control was entangled with the politics of *eugenics some time in advance of the establishment of a coherent science of population genetics, and that confusion remained manifest in literary

treatments of the "principle of population" throughout the twentieth century.

The principle of population was introduced into human science by Robert Malthus, who published the first edition of his *Essay on the Principle of Population as it Affects the Future Improvement of Society* in 1798. The essay argued that *Utopian dreams of universal peace and plenty were impossible of achievement, because food supply tends to increase arithmetically while population tends to increase exponentially—with the result that human societies always require numerical restriction by war, famine, and plague: the "Malthusian checks".

In a second edition of his essay published in 1803, Malthus modified his thesis to take aboard criticisms made by William Godwin and others—which were to be repeated and further amplified in such works as William Hazlitt's *Reply to Malthus* (1807) and Godwin's *Of Population* (1820). In the revised version Malthus conceded that the voluntary restriction of population by the exercise of "moral restraint" might solve the problem—but he found it difficult at first to put his faith in any such effect, and many other writers who took up his argument were far more pessimistic than he eventually became.

Malthus' thesis was a significant influence on the development of theories of natural selection by Charles *Darwin and Alfred Russel Wallace, and it was used as the centrepiece of more wide-ranging *sociological theories in George Drysdale's *Elements of Social Science* (1854). Its impact on the nineteenth-century literary imagination was muted by comparison, but the challenge it posed to Utopian romancers and satirists could not be ignored. George Tucker cited Malthusian ideas in his satirical *A Voyage to the Moon* (1827; by-lined Joseph Atterley) and envisaged overpopulation as a major political problem of the future in the more earnest *A Century Hence* (written 1841; published 1977). The pseudonymous Nunsowe Green, in *A Thousand Years Hence* (1882), also centralised Malthusian ideas within his extrapolation, although Richard Whiteing's dream fantasy *All Moonshine* (1907) brought the entire human population of the world to stand on the Isle of Wight in order to assert defiantly that anxieties about overpopulation were nonsensical.

Anxieties derived from the principle of population increased, as they were bound to do, with the actual population of the world, subject to the same pattern of geometrical increase. The near-universal lack of faith in general moral restraint is starkly represented in numerous accounts of futures in which population control is carried out covertly, seen as a policy that could never win a democratic mandate in spite of its dire necessity. In T. S. Stribling's "Christ in Chicago"

(1926), the returned messiah is one of the victims of such a policy. The not-quite-unthinkable alternative was displayed in such dystopian fantasies as S. P. Meek's "The Murgatroyd Experiment" (1929), which imagines a world population of 31 billion in the year 2080, and Tiffany Thayer's *Doctor Arnoldi* (1934). Futuristic Malthusian fantasies were a continual presence in the pulp magazines, ranging in time and sophistication from Homer Eon Flint's "The Planeteer" (1918) to Fritz Leiber's "Let Freedom Ring" (1950; aka "The Wolf Pack").

In the second half of the twentieth century, anxieties were amplified in the notion of a global "population explosion". The Population Council, established by John D. Rockefeller III in 1952, became a significant disseminator of propaganda regarding the dangerous rapidity of world population growth; the March 1956 issue of *Scientific American* carried an alarmist article on "World Population" by Julian Huxley that assisted the Council's efforts. Science fiction writers had already begun to take an interest in the issue; *Marvel Science Stories* had featured a "symposium" in its November 1951 issue on the question of whether the world's population should be limited. The topic was squarely addressed in Isaac Asimov's *The Caves of Steel*, Damon Knight's "Natural State", and Kurt Vonnegut's "The Big Trip up Yonder" (all 1954); the last named pointed out that technologies of longevity would inevitably compound the problem.

The Population Council's continuing efforts over the next decade were reflected in such science fiction stories as Frederik Pohl's "The Census Takers" (1956), William Tenn's "A Man of Family" (1956), Robert Silverberg's *Master of Life and Death* (1957), Louis Charbonneau's *No Place on Earth* (1958), Robert Bloch's "This Crowded Earth" (1958), J. T. McIntosh's *The Million Cities* (1958), Jack Vance's "Ullward's Retreat" (1958), J. G. Ballard's "Billennium" (1961), and Lester del Rey's *The Eleventh Commandment* (1962). By then, the Council itself had become irrelevant, because its concerns had been taken up on a much wider front. The continuing amplification of its concerns was evident in such works as John Brunner's *The Dreaming Earth* (1963), Harry Harrison's *Make Room! Make Room!* (1966; very loosely adapted as the film *Soylent Green*, 1973), James Blish and Norman L. Knight's *A Torrent of Faces* (1967), D. F. Jones' *Implosion* (1967), Kurt Vonnegut's "Welcome to the Monkey House" (1968), Robert Sheckley's "The People Trap" (1968), and Brunner's *Stand on Zanzibar* (1968). The last named pointed out, *pace* Whiteing, that the Isle of Wight was no longer big enough to accommodate the human population, even in a huddle. Accounts of countermeasures involving variously organised mass homicide became commonplace; notable examples included D. G. Compton's *The Quality of Mercy* (1965), William F. Nolan and George Clayton Johnson's *Logan's Run* (1967), Jack Beeching's *The Dakota Project* (1969), and Robert Bloch's "Sales of a Deathman" (1968).

The widespread popularisation of the issue was continued by Paul Ehrlich's melodramatic account of *The Population Bomb* (1968) and a series of extrapolations based on mathematical models, *The Limits to Growth: A Report for the Club of Rome's Project on the Predicament of Mankind* (1972), by D. H. Meadows and others. A pressure group calling for Zero Population Growth was established in the United States; early attempts to popularise its aims included a futuristic film, *Z.P.G.* (1971; novelised by the screenwriter, Max Ehrlich, as *The Edict*) and an anthology of science fiction stories edited by Rob Sauer, *Voyages: Scenarios for a Ship Called Earth* (1971). Other overpopulation dystopias published in 1971 included T. J. Bass's *Half Past Human*, Gordon R. Dickson's *Sleepwalker's World*, and Robert Silverberg's *The World Inside*. Silverberg's "Going", also published that year, was a rare account of future moral restraint, undermined by dark irony; Philip José Farmer's "Seventy Years of Decpop" (1972) was similarly ironic. Other notable accounts of overpopulation and its Draconian amelioration from the 1970s included William Earls' "Traffic Problem" (1970), Leonard C. Lewin's *Triage* (1972), Michael Elder's *Nowhere on Earth* (1972), Michael G. Coney's *Friends Come in Boxes* (1973), John Hersey's *My Petition for More Space* (1974), Juanita Coulson's *Unto the Last Generation* (1975), and Chelsea Quinn Yarbro's *Time of the Fourth Horseman* (1976).

Specific anxieties regarding population peaked in the early 1970s, but they did not die away thereafter; they were already being combined with corollary fears regarding environmental *pollution, and gathered into a more wide-ranging prospectus for *ecocatastrophe. The principle of population continued to play a key role in visions of that catastrophe until the end of the twentieth century, even though it was increasingly displaced from centre stage by such competitors as the consequences of the *greenhouse effect. The persistence of a near-universal lack of confidence in moral restraint—even aided by modern methods of birth control, which Malthus had been unable to anticipate—encouraged the continued production of Draconian science-fictional "solutions" to the population problem, which became surreal in such works as Snoo Wilson's *Spaceache* (1984), Philip José Farmer's *Dayworld* (1985), and Margaret Peterson Haddix's *Among the Hidden* (1988).

In spite of this lack of confidence, it had become obvious by 1990 that birth rates in the developing countries had dropped sharply, to the point at which many Western nations were no longer reproducing a sufficient rate to maintain their populations in the absence of substantial immigration. When the assumption that the rest of the world would follow a similar pattern as global development continued was built into mathematical models, they began to suggest that world population might peak some time in the twenty-first century even in the absence of a global ecocatastrophe. By the first decade of the twenty-first century, popular demographic anxieties had been diverted away from a straightforward preoccupation with numbers, the increasing preponderance of the aged in many Western nations—and the consequent economic burden of providing them with pensions—becoming a key issue. On the other hand, the ecocatastrophic dangers posed by rapid population growth were increasingly illuminated by studies of animal population dynamics and historical studies of human population crises, as summarised in Claire and W. M. S. Russell's broad survey of *Population Crises and Population Cycles* (1999).

The difficulties that might be caused by a shift in the demographic structure of the population had earlier been extrapolated in such scientific romances as Neil Bell's *The Seventh Bowl* (1930; by-line Miles), S. Fowler Wright's "Justice" (1932), and John Gloag's *Winter's Youth* (1934)—all of which foresaw violent conflicts between the young and the old becoming inevitable if conventional patterns of dependency and inheritance were disturbed—and science fiction stories exploring the consequences of the medical preservation of increasing numbers of old people, such as Kit Reed's "Golden Acres" (1967) and "The Revenge of the Senior Citizens" (1986), Gordon Eklund's "Embryonic Dharma" (1976), and Ray Brown's "Like a Fine Wine" (1983). Other fictional exemplifications of the complication of anxieties regarding population trends included John Christopher's *A Dusk of Demons* (1994). Straightforward fantasies of apocalyptic overpopulation continued to be produced as the twentieth century gave way to the twenty-first, but the overfamiliarity of their predecessors ensured that they would require more ingenious narrative twists, such as the one in Michael Kandel's "Multum in Parvo" (2000).

POSITIVISM

A term whose primary significance in the history of science derives from the work of Auguste Comte, whose *Cours de philosophie positive* (1830–1842; trans. as *A Course of Positive Philosophy*) further developed previous uses of the term "positive" by Pierre-Simon Laplace and others to describe a particular philosophy of science. Comte advanced the thesis that human understanding had passed through three fundamental historical phases—the theological, the metaphysical, and the positive, or scientific—which progression constituted a gradual process of refinement by attrition. Comte proposed that explanations of events in terms of hidden gods had been depersonalised into explanations in terms of abstract metaphysical forces, and then pared down to what was empirically demonstrable in the hierarchy of the "six great sciences": mathematics, astronomy, physics, chemistry, physiology, and "social physics". Comte's own work was mostly concerned with the last named, which he divided into "social statics" and "social dynamics"—a terminology echoed in such works as Herbert Spencer's *Social Statics* (1851). Positivist philosophy was popularised in Britain by G. H. Lewes' *Comte's Philosophy of the Sciences* (1853) and Harriet Martineau's *The Philosophy of Comte* (1853).

Comte extrapolated his system of thought into the realm of practical politics in the ambitious *Système de politique positive* (1851–1854; trans. as *A System of Positive Politics*), in which he proposed that the obsolete worship of God should be replaced by the worship of humanity, and that political organisation should be redirected to serve the cause of scientific progress rather than the ideals of liberty, equality, and fraternity. Among other suggested reforms he proposed a new positivist calendar, consisting of thirteen four-week months plus a Universal Fête of the Dead, with Catholic saints' days replaced by a progression of models symbolising the evolution of thought. Thus, the first month of the year would be Moses, and its first day Prometheus, whereas the thirteenth month would be Bichat (named after the physician and pathologist Xavier Bichat), and its days would be named for Copernicus, Galileo, Isaac Newton, Antoine Lavoisier and so on.

Although such ideas seemed risible to many—one notable satire is W. H. Mallock's *The New Paul and Virginia, or Positivism on an Island* (1878)—Comtean churches sprang up in some profusion; literary representations of similar institutions include the church described in the final sequence of M. P. Shiel's *The Last Miracle* (1906) and Miles J. Breuer's Church of the Scientific God in "A Problem in Communication" (1930). Positivism became identified, in the thinking of many laymen and social philosophers, with the ultimate in what John Keats called "cold philosophy", intent on unweaving rainbows and all other phenomena by ruthlessly stripping them back to bare essentials.

Within the scientific community, positivism was manifest as a determination not to exceed the warrant provided by facts by including any speculative element in theory. Its most fervent adherent in physics, Ernst Mach, became a dedicated enemy of such imaginative constructs as the *atom, continually challenging the developers of modern atomic theory with the question: "Have you ever seen one?" Mach was equally ruthless in his treatment of such notions as the luminiferous *ether, where his assaults assisted in the discarding of that notion, helping to pave the way for the development of *relativity theory.

Comtean ideas permeated many areas of nineteenth-century science, including *anthropology. James Frazer's account of the intellectual development of tribal societies was a variation on Comte's law of the three stages. The philosophy was carried forward into the twentieth century by "logical positivism", whose ultimate failure to purge science of metaphysical residues turned the tide against the whole enterprise. The term fell into considerable disrepute thereafter; by the 1960s, it was commonly used as an item of abuse hurled at human scientists who were considered to be overly concerned with measurable phenomena and the establishment of simple causal connections, after the alleged fashion of behaviourist *psychologists.

Although litterateurs were always disinclined to favour positivist accounts in human science for the same reasons that Charles Dickens attacked "utilitarianism" in *Hard Times* (1854), there was a fugitive literary contribution to the positivist crusade, which tended to be all the more fervent by virtue of its authors' awareness of the fact that they were issuing a minority report. A cardinal example is Vincent Harper's *The Mortgage on the Brain* (1905), which overflows with assertive positivist rhetoric. Marie Corelli's *Boy* (1900) and Marguerite Tinayre's *L'ombre d'amour* (1910; trans. as *The Shadow of Love*) stand at the opposite end of the spectrum, the former mounting a virulent attack on the dispiriting effects of a positivist education and the latter extrapolating the philosophy into ruthless *eugenic policies.

POSTHUMAN

A term popularised in the 1980s, with reference to various conditions in which humans might have modified themselves so extensively by *cyborgisation and *genetic engineering as to liberate themselves from the traditionally recognised "human condition". A commonly encountered derivative is "posthumanism"—a term also used with regard to schools of philosophy subsequent to humanism—whose reference in this context is to a group of assertive creeds whose members want to hasten the evolutionary process. Some of them follow a Posthuman Manifesto extracted from Robert Pepperell's *The Posthuman Condition: Consciousness and the Brain* (1995).

Alternative terms for the assertive variety of posthumanism include transhumanism and extropianism. The term "transhumanism" was coined by Julian Huxley in 1957, but its modern use derives from F. M. Esfandiary's *Are You a Transhuman?* (1989; by-lined FM-2030), which dramatised the notion that the transitional phase in human history had already begun. This version of the term was further extrapolated by Max T. O'Connor, who became Max More in 1989—in which guise he founded the Extropy Institute ("extropy" being a newly minted antonym of *entropy). This pattern of complication was further confused when moral philosophers interested in animal rights began using "posthumanism" to refer to the cause of extending the notion of the moral community beyond its traditional limitation within the human species.

Although it overlaps with the notion of the *superman, the idea of posthuman evolution is distinguished by its emphasis on calculated technological modification and—more importantly—by its insistence that there is no single linear thread of human evolution potentially mapped out for the species. In stark contrast to such fantasies of future evolution as Olaf Stapledon's *Last and First Men* (1930), posthumanists see the future evolution of humankind in terms of a dramatic diversification of types, partly accountable in terms of adaptive radiation and partly in terms of aesthetic impulses. Posthuman modification is essentially idiosyncratic, prolific, and promiscuous, involving a rapid and rather haphazard emergence of new types. The origins of the thesis are traceable back to J. D. Bernal's *The World, the Flesh and the Devil: An Enquiry into the Future of the Three Enemies of the Rational Soul* (1929), whose consideration of the likely course of human self-guided evolution dismissed then-conventional linear sequences in favour of promiscuous metamorphoses, by which multifarious bodies might be equipped with new combinations of sense organs and limbs, eventually progressing to a seamless synthesis of the organic and inorganic in individual bodies and the development of systems for networking brains into collective and effectively immortal superorganisms.

Although posthumanism was identifiable as a manifest social movement by the end of the twentieth century, whose ancestry could be tracked to works of speculative nonfiction popularising the ideas of cyborgisation and genetic modification, its imagery has been largely developed in the medium of speculative fiction, particularly cyberpunk fiction. One of its key themes is the establishment of a much closer symbiosis between human and *computers, both in "meatspace" and *cyberspace. The first significant popularisers of the notion of posthuman evolution in science fiction included Bruce *Sterling, in the Shaper/Mechanist series (1982–1985), and Michael Swanwick, in *Vacuum Flowers* (1987). Other early fictional representations of posthumanist philosophy in action include the Cultists of Cybernetic Temple in David J. Skal's *Antibodies* (1988) and the Ousters in Dan Simmons' *Hyperion* (1989) and its sequels.

Numerous *fin-de-siècle* accounts of future history imagine an ideological conflict emerging between conservatives clinging to the original model of human form, and diversifying progressives, as in the contest between the Naderites and Geshels in Greg Bear's *Eon* (1985) and *Eternity* (1988). Gregory Benford's "Naturals" (2003) draws the crucial distinction more economically, while a far more complex series of philosophical struggles engages such groups as the Conjoiners, Ultras, Demarchists, Slashers, and Threshers featured in Alastair Reynolds' series launched with *Revelation Space* (2000) and *Redemption Ark* (2002). Notable attempts to describe mature posthuman societies can be found in Damien Broderick's *The White Abacus* (1997), Robert Reed's "Coelacanths" (2002) and *Sister Alice* (2003), Karl Schroeder's *Permanence* (2002), Justina Robson's *Natural History* (2003), and Charles Stross and Cory Doctorow's "Flowers from Alice" (2003).

Patterns of posthuman evolution became extremely fashionable when explosive diversification was established as a logical corollary of post-*singularity social evolution, as detailed in such works as Charles Stross' *Accelerando* series (2001–2004; book, 2005), but they are also featured in accounts of relatively sedate future evolution such as Brian Stableford's Emortality series (1998–2002). Posthumans look back unregretfully on their ancestry in Bruce Sterling's "AD 2380: *Homo sapiens* Declared Extinct" (2001), while Geoffrey A. Landis' "A History of the Human and Post-Human Species" (2000) and Stephen Baxter's "The Children of Time" (2005) offer compact Stapledonian accounts of their evolution and future history.

POSTMODERNISM

A term originated in the field of architecture, where it was used to refer to a new eclecticism that displaced the minimalist styling of "modernism". It was appropriated into literary theory in the late 1960s, again to describe that which seemed to have replaced "modernist" literature, including the metafictional meditations, *contes philosophiques,* and hallucinatory texts of such writers as Samuel Beckett, Jorge Luis Borges, and William Burroughs, all of which seemed to fit loosely under the same umbrella in regard to their self-referential explorations of the creative process. The notion expanded to embrace a much more ambitious scepticism regarding the possibility of depicting "reality" in a text.

Viewed in this light, postmodernism seemed to be a logical extrapolation of literary modernism, if the modernism were conceived as a movement concerned with questions about the extent to which the world is "knowable" within the limits of our instruments of discovery. Postmodernism takes such questions to a further level by challenging the basic assumption that the world is sufficiently definite and stable to be known, no matter what instruments might be brought to the task—in effect, by assuming that all culture (including science) is best understood as an ideologically guided system of convenient delusions.

Postmodernist criticism picked up the notion of "deconstruction" from Jacques Derrida's *De la grammatologie* (1967; trans. as *Of Grammatology*), which opposed "thematic criticism" on the grounds that the alleged "theme" of a text is a matter of the reader's perception rather than the text's content. The deconstructive method attempted to examine the process by which "themes" are negotiated between text and reader. Postmodernism was also "poststructuralist", in that its adherents borrowed logical and theoretical tools developed in *linguistic theory and linguistic philosophy in order to examine the ways in which words carry meaning.

The "postmodernity" of Jean-François Lyotard's *La condition postmoderne* (1979; trans. as *The Postmodern Condition*) is a related concept, although it does not relate straightforwardly to the field of postmodernist study. It refers instead to an alleged interruption of the unfolding Age of Enlightenment, involving a return to anxious uncertainty by virtue of increasing incredulity regarding the "metanarratives" of religion and twentieth-century science. Whereas modernism's consciousness of this uncertainty had been nostalgic for lost certainty, postmodernism's accepts its inevitability, indulging in ironic celebration of the impossibility of accurate representation and moral certainty. Jean Baudrillard's *Simulacres et simulation* (1981; trans. as *Simulacra and Simulation*) describes a world permeated by "inauthenticity", in which all cultural representations are "simulacra" devoid of original models, which constitute a "hyperreality". The last term was popularised in English by a collection of Umberto Eco's translated essays *Travels in Hyperreality* (1986).

Postmodernism is, of course, unabashed by the criticism that in ruling everything to be false, it undermines its own claim to be true; *paradoxicality is intrinsic to the exercise. Its adherents were, however, somewhat embarrassed when Alan Sokal, the professor of physics at New York University, succeeded in publishing a paper entitled "Transgressing the Boundaries: Toward a Transformative Hermeneutics of Quantum Gravity" in *Social Text* in May 1996, consisting of buzz words and fashionable phrases strung together without any intention of making sense—a hoax whose success was gleefully advertised the following month in *Lingua Franca*. The ensuing scandal resulted in a great deal of argument and reportage. Sokal followed it up with a book written in collaboration with Jean Bricmont, *Impostures intellectuelles* (1997; trans. as *Intellectual Impostures* and *Fashionable Nonsense*).

The postmodernist worldview does not simply embrace philosophical scepticism about the supposed certainty of scientific knowledge, but takes various aspects of modern science as clear evidence of an ultimate *uncertainty, especially the implausibilities of *quantum mechanics. Academic critics interested in science fiction would probably have embraced postmodernist methods in the late 1980s merely because they were fashionable, but they had no difficulty in finding attitudes reflective of their own within the genre, especially in the sceptical fantasies of Philip K. *Dick and the manner in which cyberpunk writers such as William *Gibson, Bruce *Sterling, and Pat Cadigan played with the evolving notion of *virtual reality. One of the cyberpunk movement's most important showcase anthologies, Larry McCaffery's *Storming the Reality Studio: A Casebook of Cyberpunk and Postmodern Fiction* (1991), juxtaposes work by Kathy Acker, Don DeLillo, Thomas Pynchon, and Joseph McElroy with that of genre science fiction writers.

The science fiction writer most conspicuously influenced by academic postmodernism was Samuel R. *Delany, whose later science fiction novels—especially *Dhalgren* (1975) and *Triton* (1976)—embody a similar consciousness of uncertainty and a similarly introspective fascination with the processes of literary and cultural creativity. The postmodern version of the term hyperreality is extrapolated in a science-fictional fashion in Haruki Murakami's novels, notably *Sekai no owari to hâdo-boirudo wandârando* (1985; trans. as *Hard-Boiled Wonderland and the End of the World*).

POWER

The capacity to produce effects. In terms of individual *psychology, power is manifest in the freedom of the will; in social terms it is the sphere of *politics. In terms of natural science, it is *force or energy applicable to particular tasks; in biology it is primarily represented by muscle power, while the central thread of the history of *technology is the exploitation and application of external power sources, beginning with the harnessing of *fire. Literary endeavour is sometimes represented as an exercise of power—Robert Browning declared that "poetry is power", while Percy Shelley claimed that poets are "the true legislators of mankind"—and the opinion is not entirely unwarranted.

The particular role of fire in the history of technology causes a common distinction to be drawn between "renewable" and "nonrenewable" power sources, although the distinction is technically one of degree rather than kind. Muscle power is renewable by nutrition and rest, whereas wind power is permanently—albeit capriciously—laid on by the weather, but the burning of fuel is a more avid process whose consumption is less easily repaired. The burning of wood requires the replacement of forests—a process so slow that geographically-limited societies can easily precipitate local ecocatastrophes by deforestation.

The industrial revolution of the eighteenth and nineteenth centuries was largely powered by the exploitation of coal, and its continuation in the twentieth and twenty-first centuries was heavily dependent on the exploitation of oil—but coal, oil, and "natural gas" are "fossil fuels" whose deposition and refinement takes millions of years, so they represent energy capital that, once spent, is effectively irrecoverable. The realisation in the late nineteenth century that the ultimate source of all Earthly energy was the Sun became a significant factor in images of the far *future that considered the plight of the world once the Sun's own fuel ran out.

The notion that the developed world is facing a near-future resource crisis as recoverable reserves of coal, oil, and gas are used up—long anticipated in such stories as Harold Donitz's "A Visitor from the Twentieth Century" (1928) and John M. Corbett's "The Black River" (1934)—was swiftly integrated into the *ecocatastrophe scenarios of the 1960s, in combination with the *population problem and increasing environmental *pollution. Opinions vary sharply as to the exact extent to which the impending crisis of fossil fuel production can be postponed, but its ultimate inevitability is beyond question. The extent to which *nuclear power can compensate for the gradual exhaustion of coal and oil also remains controversial, as does the extent to which the side effects of fossil fuel usage—particularly their contribution to the *greenhouse effect—are ecocatastrophic in themselves.

The generation of power is the subject of one of the most common examples of plausible *impossibility, represented in the history of technology by countless "perpetual motion machines"—whose design, description, and construction has long been a perverse form of *art, reflected in literature in such stories as John W. Campbell's "The Irrelevant" (1934; by-lined Karl van Campen) and Theodore Sturgeon's "Brownshoes" (1969). The stubbornness of the idea that power might be freely and abundantly available in nature if one could only master the trick of obtaining it is reflected in the manner in which newly described phenomena tend to be rapidly taken up by hopeful speculative fiction as potential sources of unlimited power.

*Electricity was often seen as a potential primary power source when it was conceived in terms of natural lightning, although the dull reality of its generation by the conversion of energy produced from other sources damped down the enthusiasm manifest in such texts as Mary Shelley's Frankenstein (1818) and Edward Bulwer-Lytton's The Coming Race (1871), forcing the substitution of similarly quasi-miraculous agents such as the "apergy" featured in Percy Greg's Across the Zodiac (1880).

In the twentieth century, attention shifted to various means of generating electricity; the necessity of developing "sustainable" energy sources inspired a good deal of speculative nonfiction, although the idea's inherent lack of dramatic potential limited its scope in fiction. Hydroelectric power has the advantage of requiring huge dams, but—like windmills—they tend to be a more effective presence in cinema and TV representations than they are in fiction, where their principal function is symbolically to burst, as in D. H. Lawrence's The Rainbow (1915). A notable exception is The Diamondking of Sahara (1935), written in English by a Finnish writer signing himself Wettenhovi-Aspa, which describes a series of transformative hydroelectric projects. The exploitation of solar power gave rise to more speculative fiction; notable examples include Murray Leinster's "The Power Planet" (1931) and Nathan Schachner's "Stratosphere Towers" (1934), both of which focus on problems of transmitting solar power from the points at which it can most conveniently be gathered, and Robert A. Heinlein's "Let There Be Light!" (1940).

The discoveries of x-rays in 1895 and natural radioactivity in 1896 provoked innumerable stories in which unlimited power could be casually generated by various newly discovered "rays", or at least transmitted wirelessly, as in Robert L. Hadfield and Frank E. Farncombe's Ruled by Radio (1930). The optimism thus generated is manifest in such bold fictional anticipations as E. E. Smith's The Skylark of Space (1928)—in which interstellar spaceships are powered by the release of "infra-atomic energy"—and John W. Campbell Jr.'s "Atomic Power" (1934; by-lined Don A. Stuart), which illustrates contemporary attitudes to the scientific elucidation of the phenomena of nuclear fission and fusion.

Such was the confidence of early twentieth-century speculators in the potential availability of unlimited power that their most thoughtful variations on the theme were earnest considerations of the moral responsibility that would devolve upon the scientist fortunate enough to make the breakthrough. Stories of this kind include Karel Čapek's The Absolute at Large (1922) and Krakatit (1924; trans. 1925), Neil Bell's The Lord of Life (1933), Sydney Fowler Wright's Power (1931), and Jack Williamson's "The Equalizer" (1947). When the expert engineer Thomas N. Scortia submitted a carefully worked out story about a new power supply system, "Artery of Fire" (1960; exp. 1972), to Astounding Science Fiction, John W. Campbell rejected it because he could not believe that a much better system, such as fusion power, would not be available by the date in which the story was set: 1973.

The persuasiveness of the idea of free power is demonstrated by the reception given by worshippers in the temple of hard science fiction, Astounding Science Fiction, to Raymond F. Jones's "Noise Level" (1952), which suggests that the only thing standing between science and the discovery of limitless power (here represented as antigravity technology) might be the belief of scientists in its impossibility. So convincing was its line of argument it prompted a rash of letters to the editor and supplementary articles criticising contemporary patent law for its mistrust of perpetual motion machines and its discrimination against discoveries of new fundamental principles in science.

This optimism waned dramatically during the 1960s when the intellectual climate changed. When the Organization of Petroleum-Exporting Countries (OPEC) demonstrated its ability to dictate energy policy to the Western world—a least for a while—in 1972–1973, it brought about a new awareness of the politics of energy supply, vividly reflected in such works as Poul Anderson's "Wildcat" (1958), Frederik Pohl's JEM: The Making of a Utopia (1979) and The Cool War (1981), Wolfgang Jeschke's Der Letzte Tag der Schöpfung (1981; trans. as The Last Day of Creation), and Rory Harper's Petrogypsies (1989).

Images of a future of unlimited power were by no means obliterated by the catastrophic anxieties of the 1960s and 1970s. The possibility of harnessing nuclear fusion was supplemented by ingenious schemes for extracting energy directly from the substrate of *space. Unlimited supplies of power are fundamental to the prospects for the development of technological civilisations set out by Nikolai Kardaschev and Freeman *Dyson, and to Frank Tipler's version of *Omega Point theory; the latter assumes that the ultimate energy source will arise from the spatial "shearing" of the collapsing universe. Stories featuring new energy sources tended to become more tongue-in-cheek, however—as illustrated by Charles L. Harness' "H-TEC" (1981) and L. E. Modesitt Jr.'s "Power To ...?" (1990).

PREDICTION

A foretelling of a future event. Its common usage overlaps that of "prophecy" almost to the point of synonymy, but it is important to distinguish contingent predictions of the form "if X happens, then Y will follow" from absolute assertions that something is bound to happen no matter what. There is a considerable difference between scientific predictions, which normally specify what will happen if certain carefully specified preconditions are met, from religious prophecies, which tend to presuppose—albeit somewhat hypocritically—that the pattern of future history is subject to divine predestination.

Prediction is intrinsic to the scientific method, because scientific theories are tested by their ability to issue correct predictions, especially in controlled circumstances formulated as *experiments. The twentieth-century *philosophy of science developed by Karl Popper places this process at the heart of the scientific enterprise, defining the progress of knowledge in terms of the rejection of theses whose predictions have been proven false.

Popper took some trouble to exclude from his conception of science certain theories in human science, including *Marxist theory, that seemed to him to be assuming that the future course of human history was broadly predictable—a position he called "historicism" in *The Poverty of Historicism* (1957). Popper produced several arguments proving that the future course of history is implicitly unpredictable, two of which are particularly noteworthy. One asserts that, to the extent that the future of human society is dependent upon scientific discovery, it cannot be predicted, because we cannot know now what we might—and might not—discover in the future. The other calls attention to "the Oedipus effect": the effect that the issuing of a prediction has on the likelihood of its fulfilment.

In discussing the Oedipus effect Popper concentrates on the phenomenon of "self-fulfilling prophecies", which enhance their own chances of coming true—as, for instance, when an influential figure in

the stock exchange predicts that the price of a certain share will fall, precipitating a wave of selling that causes the price to fall. Self-negating predictions are, however, more frequent and significant; people confronted with a prediction that they will suffer misfortune will usually take steps to ensure that the prediction cannot come true. The latter phenomenon is also known as "the *paradox of prophecy".

One of the key differences between natural and human science is that the objects of the former rarely react to attempts to observe them—although various exceptions may be aggregated under the heading of the *uncertainty principle—while the objects of the latter invariably do. Since the inception of human science, human beings have reacted to the conclusions of psychology and sociology in various ways, often attempting to defy or subvert them as well as to exploit them. It is arguable that the science of *economics is continually being thwarted by its subject matter, because every analysis that is produced of the way economic systems work leads people active within those systems to use the analysis to their own advantage, changing their behaviour sufficiently to alter the systems, which then require further analysis.

Futuristic fiction is often viewed as a series of attempts to "predict" the future, although its creators are often fervent in their insistence that they are doing no such thing. The science fiction writer John Brunner, following a precedent set by Ray Bradbury, used to reply to the charge by saying "I'm not trying to predict the future, I'm trying to prevent it". C. E. M. Joad had earlier ended his futurological essay "Is Civilization Doomed?" (1930) by saying that, although he had no idea whether or not civilisation was doomed, he considered it his moral duty to insist that it was, because people would not otherwise be persuaded to do what was necessary to save it. Although John W. Campbell was happy to proclaim that science fiction's successful anticipation of new technologies such as *atom bombs and space *rockets was firm evidence of its virtue and utility, he was always careful to point out that all science-fictional predictions are conditional, based on the *extrapolation of premises that might be invalidated at any moment by new discoveries or events.

Predictions vary considerably in terms of the probability that they might be upset by unforeseen contingencies. The success of the *astronomical predictions on which the calendar is based reflects the fact that there are relatively few likely occurrences that could upset a planetary orbit. Some would-be predictors assert that some aspects of future history are far less unpredictable than others, and may thus be accommodated within a scientific discipline of *futurology. One of the pioneers of futurology, H. G. *Wells, argued in *The Discovery of the Future* (1902) that certain aspects of human future history can be confidently anticipated because they are subject to inescapable constraints that leave free will no scope for operation. Wells had already represented *The Time Machine* (1895) as a "modern Delphic Oracle" on the grounds that the ultimate extinction of the Sun, and hence of the human species, was quite inevitable—an example not assisted by the subsequent discovery that the calculation of the Sun's likely lifetime on which Wells based his future chronology was completely mistaken. A similar line of thought is carried forward by *Omega Point hypotheses such as Frank Tipler's *The Physics of Immortality* (1994), although the sheer variety of such hypotheses casts doubt on their alleged inevitability.

Insofar as religious prophecies represent the supposed intentions of God, the implication is that no human agency can prevent their fulfilment; they are usually issued as promises guaranteeing that the moral inequities of the present will one day be corrected, usually by a rain of destruction from which only the righteous will be spared. On the other hand, such prophecies tend to have a built-in "escape clause", by which the wicked are promised that if they will mend their ways in the meantime, they may join the ranks of those who will be spared. Such escape clauses attempt to negotiate a solution to logical incompatibility between the ideas of free will and destiny—both of which are routinely supported by religious doctrine—by a strategy similar to that subsequently adopted by futurologists, arguing that free will can only operate within certain bounds.

The paradox of prophecy derives from the fact that religious prophecies must claim to be absolute if they are to be psychologically compelling, but can only serve as a useful instrument of influence if they leave individuals room to make choices. The contradictions that arise when specific dates included in prophecies actually arrive have always plagued religious cults expecting an imminent end to the world, but historians and sociologists of religion have had abundant opportunities to observe that believers rarely react to the failure of religious prophecies in the way that scientists are supposed to react to the failure of theoretical predictions. Ethnologists studying the manner in which divination works in tribal societies, as in E. E. Evans-Pritchard's classic study of *Oracles and Magic Among the Azande* (1937), routinely make the same observation: that the failure of an oracular prediction is never blamed on the incompetence of the oracular system, but is always attributed to some particular exceptional circumstance, a "secondary elaboration" of the system.

Leon Festinger, Henry W. Ricken, and Stanley Schachter's account of events following the expiration of prophecies uttered within an American cult, *When Prophecy Fails* (1956), argues that various psychological strategies are available to avoid the "cognitive dissonance" that might arise from the failure of a prophecy—and sociologists of science have pointed out that science is by no means immune to secondary elaboration in the interests of such avoidance. When Saturn's orbit was found to be at odds with the predictions of the theory of gravity, no one wanted to discard the theory; instead, a secondary elaboration was introduced, in the form of a previously unknown planet whose gravitational effects must be responsible for the perturbation. When that secondary elaboration turned out to be true, in the form of the planet Uranus, it still did not settle the anomaly—with the result that cosmologists hypothesised yet another unknown planet rather than sacrifice the theory. The psychological strategies with which people deal with the paradox of prophecy are of considerable literary interest, to the extent that Leon Festinger's study was dramatised in Alison Lurie's novel *Imaginary Friends* (1967).

The psychological hunger for information regarding the future remains insatiable in spite of the paradoxes inherent in such information. Almanacs blending accurate astronomical predictions with hopeful divinations outsold all other books for the first few centuries of the history of printing, and the 353 oracular quatrains issued in 1555 by the Frenchman who styled himself Nostradamus gave birth to an extraordinary industry; the catalogue was subsequently extended to 1,040 quatrains, each one supposedly referring—rather obscurely—to a year of future history. The flexibility of their meaning allowed serial rereadings of his works to be fitted to the unfolding historical record, with every manufactured hit increasing the seer's reputation. *Scholarly fantasies devoted to his work were produced in some profusion in the late twentieth century, and his literary manifestations, as in Manly Wade Wellman's "The Timeless Tomorrow" (1947), tend to be respectful.

Literary accounts of predictions fulfilled are inevitably multitudinous, given that the success or failure of a fictitious prediction is entirely at the discretion of the author. There is no point in manufacturing a literary prediction unless it is either going to come true or fail in an interesting fashion. Literary dreams are frequently used as oracular devices, with a prophetic accuracy many orders of magnitude greater than the oracular accuracy of actual dreams. Fictitious representations of the Oedipus effect are extremely easy to contrive, and to complicate in melodramatic fashion. The story of Oedipus, as dramatised by Sophocles and many others, is itself evidence of the manner in which authorial power can design elaborate patterns of cause and effect to embody "the irony of fate". In this respect, fiction is much closer in its methods to the aspirations of religious prophecy than the contingencies of the scientific method; in the world within a text, everything that happens really is determined by the will of a creator, and the characters' free will is entirely illusory.

Examples of fictitious prediction are very numerous, and mostly trivial. John Buchan's *The Gap in the Curtain* (1932) gathers together a series of exemplars that offer a particularly stark illustration of the extent of authorial privilege and the typical manner of its deployment. *Contes philosophiques* featuring variants of the Oedipus effect include S. P. Meek's "Futility" (1929)—an early account of the use of *computers as predictors—Anthony Boucher's "Pelagic Spark" (1943), and Brian Stableford's "The Oedipus Effect" (1991). It is tacitly featured in many *time paradox stories—time travel is used strategically to institute exactly such an effect in Robert Charles Wilson's *The Chronoliths* (2001)—and all sophisticated accounts of *parapsychological precognition.

PROBABILITY

A term referring to the relative likelihood of alternative outcomes of a situation. The mathematical calculation of probabilities was pioneered in the seventeenth century by Blaise Pascal and Pierre de Fermat, the former having taken an interest in the calculations of probabilities relevant to various gambling *games.

Even the simplest calculations of probability can be psychologically confusing. The observation that the probability of a tossed coin coming down heads or tails is 0.5 is perfectly straightforward, but it can easily give rise to false expectations. Probabilities cannot be arithmetically added in the way that ordinary numbers can, so the probability of two coin tosses including at least one head is not 1 (0.5 + 0.5) but 0.75 (1 − 0.5 × 0.5); although this example is reasonably obvious, the calculation of probabilities relevant to a six-sided die or a thirty-seven-slotted roulette wheel is more challenging, and routinely tempts gamblers to make "additive errors" in forming rough estimates. There is also an innate psychological tendency to draw connections between events, tempting the supposition that when a tossed coin has come down heads four times in a row, the likelihood ought to be greater than 0.5 that the next toss will come down tails. Such phenomena as these ensure that psychological estimates of probability are often at odds with the actual calculus of probability—a margin frequently exploited by common gambling games that tempt players into making bad bets. The first significant

academic analysis of these phenomena was John Cohen and Mark Hansel's *Risk and Gambling: The Study of Subjective Probability* (1957), although they had been known and exploited for centuries by predatory gamblers.

The tendency to seek patterns in sequences of events is connected to one of the commonest forms of fallacious argument, often described by the Latin phrase *post hoc ergo propter hoc*: the supposition that because one event happened after another, the earlier must have caused or influenced it. The tendency to see phantom connections of this kind gives rise to the phenomenon of superstition, whereby people repeat an action they performed before a successful endeavour in the hope of increasing the likelihood of a repeat success, and frequently continue to do so in the absence of any substantial reinforcement. The effect is exaggerated by the tendency for rewards obtained from risks successfully taken psychologically to outweigh disappointments accruing from unsuccessful ventures. This is especially obvious in cases when infrequent but substantial wins make more psychological impact than frequent but relatively trivial losses, no matter how far the total loss exceeds the total gain—the principle that allows fruit machines to obtain a "house percentage" that is often in the region of 50%.

The calculus of probability is sometimes referred to as "the laws of chance"—a term whose incipient *paradoxicality is reflected in the concept of "luck": the notion that success or failure in a risky venture depends on a mysterious supernatural agency that will decide which of the various possibilities will be fulfilled on this particular occasion. In combination with the tendency to superstition, this notion frequently leads to the supposition that certain objects and actions, or whole classes of objects and actions, are lucky or unlucky. It is very common for people whose risky ventures have failed to feel victimised by fate, even when the probability of success was mathematically slight. It is also common for people to believe that the probability of success in a venture is increased when "their luck is in" or when they are "on a roll", and decreased when the opposite is the case.

The mechanisms of psychological probability are a major aspect of game theory—a discipline that attempts both to observe how people actually make decisions whose outcomes are partly dependent on the decisions made by other people, and to calculate how people ought to make such decisions in terms of the calculus of probability. The most familiar exemplar is that of the "prisoner's dilemma", in which a person under interrogation can obtain a reward by giving nothing away, provided that others under interrogation do likewise, but can also obtain a benefit by testifying against the others, provided that he is the first to break the silence. The logic of the situation suggests that keeping silent is the optimum course, but the fear of being betrayed ensures that the psychological calculation usually tends towards betrayal—an item of knowledge exploited in large numbers of fictitious interrogations featured in crime fiction, and presumably in many actual ones.

In spite of such coincidental tendencies as this one, the workings of probability in fiction are very different from its workings in the actual world. The calculus of probability determining real events is quite meaningless in the world within a literary text, where all occurrences are entirely at the discretion of the author. In the actual world, luck is a phantom of the imagination, but the events within a fictional text really are subject to a "supernatural" whim that often works in accordance with the suppositions of psychological probability. As the writer Terry Pratchett is fond of observing, whenever the hero of a story says "it's a million-to-one shot, but it might just work", the actual probability of it working is one. Literary representation thrives on the improbable to a far greater extent than it thrives on the impossible; even the most determinedly naturalistic fiction makes little concession to the calculus of probability in arranging its plots, and readers hoping for the morally appropriate outcome to a story are prepared to find the most ludicrous improbabilities perfectly *plausible, provided that they produce an aesthetically satisfactory explication of the achievement of the outcome.

Although Pratchett's observation is a derisive one, the fact is that the million-to-one shot that comes off is far more effective in literary terms than any highly likely contingency, because it maximises dramatic tension and narrative suspense; literary closure is far more satisfying when it seems to be won against overwhelming odds than when it seems so nearly inevitable as to be expectable. In fiction, the mathematically probable is worthless as a narrative device, and is therefore highly improbable as a course of narrative development, while the mathematically improbable can be very valuable indeed, and is thus cultivated with relentless ingenuity. This radical disjunction between the world as it is in fact and the world as it is in fiction is the most important factor determining that no fictional world, however naturalistic it may be, can possibly stand up to rigorous logical analysis. This creates particular problems for speculative fiction, which deals with events that are supposedly amenable to probabilistic calculation, but which do not belong to the class of everyday events that could, in principle, be manufactured by "luck".

The most common evocation of the concept of probability in speculative fiction is metaphysical rather than mathematical, imagining that events whose outcomes can be estimated in probabilistic terms can be seen as the points of origin of *alternative histories diverging into a manifold of *parallel worlds. The phenomena of mathematical and psychological probability, and the disjunction between them, can be interesting in themselves, however. Such topics are addressed in such *contes philosophiques* as Raymond F. Jones' "Fifty Million Monkeys" (1943), E. L. Locke's "The Finan-seer" (1949), Connie Willis' "Blued Moon" (1984), Rudy Rucker and Marc Laidlaw's "Probability Pipeline" (1988), and Gardner R. Dozois' "The Hanging Curve" (2002), and more extensively explored in Brian Stableford's *Streaking* (2006). The difficulty of accommodating them in fiction is illustrated by Mark Haddon's *The Curious Incident of the Dog in the Night-Time* (2003), in which the autistic narrator can see with perfect clarity what the mathematically correct solution to a particular puzzle is, although the attractions of psychological probability lead the vast majority of normal individuals to a wrong answer. The discussion and explanation of the problem is, inevitably, consigned to an appendix lest it get in the way of the story's flow.

PROGRESS

A term whose literal meaning, "to step forward", was initially applied to physical journeys or processions. A particular connection with going forward into the *future was secured in the seventeenth century and popularised by John Bunyan's *The Pilgrim's Progress from This World to That Which Is to Come* (1678). A similar notion of purposive moral progress was secularised in the eighteenth century and used to construe *history as a process of problematic but continual improvement. Even before the advent of theories of evolution, Edward Young could write in *The Complaint; or, Night Thoughts* (1742–1745) that "Nature delights in progress; in advance/From worse to better".

In 1750, Anne-Robert Turgot characterised the Enlightenment as the latest phase in an unfolding history whose general trends included the increase of knowledge, increasing harmony within and between nations, the improvement of manners, and an irresistible march towards "higher perfection". Turgot's philosophy of progress, popularised in France by the Marquis de Condorcet and in Britain by William Godwin, took it for granted that moral and material progress went hand in hand, each supportive of the other—a notion that is intrinsic to the first futuristic *Utopia, Louis Sébastien Mercier's *L'an deux mille quatre cent quarante* (1771; trans. as *Memoirs of the Year 2500*).

The notion of the unity of material and moral progress was soon challenged by such sceptical analyses as Robert Malthus' essay on *population, which proposed that such evils as famine, war, and "vice" were resistant to improvement because they were necessary by-products of the tendency of human populations to increase faster than their food supplies. Utopian accounts of the future were soon supplemented by *dystopian accounts such as Émile Souvestre's *Le monde tel qu'il sera* (1846: trans. as *The World as It Shall Be*), which took the view that scientific and technological progress, as guided by *positivist philosophy and the *economics of self-interest, would bring about a drastic decline in the quality of life.

The term became one of the watchwords of the Industrial Revolution, which was seen by its champions as the embodiment of a technological progress that was inevitable, irresistible, and intrinsically good. Opponents of this kind of progress were labelled Luddites, after the weavers who smashed the mechanised looms that were putting them out of work in the name of Ned Lud. The literary reaction against the Industrial Revolution, on the grounds of the misery it spread and the blight it generated, varied in its attitude, sometimes rejecting "progress" altogether but more usually seeking to discriminate between material and moral progress, calling for the former to be restrained in the context of the latter.

It became increasingly common for the view to be expressed that material progress had outstripped moral progress, and that the consequences of the disjunction were appalling. This view was succinctly summarised by Bertrand *Russell's *Icarus; or, The Future of Science* (1923), written in reply to J. B. S. *Haldane's call for an end to resistance against "biological inventions" in *Daedalus; or, Science and the Future* (1923). This argument remained heated throughout the twentieth century, providing the context for the evolution of science fiction, which was initially formulated by Hugo *Gernsback as propaganda for technological progress but soon became a fierce ideological battleground.

Early histories of the idea of progress, including John B. Bury's *The Idea of Progress* (1932) and similarly titled books by Morris Ginsberg (1953), Charles van Doren (1967), and Sidney Pollard (1971), tended to begin in the eighteenth century with Turgot's definition, but Robert Nisbet's *History of the Idea of Progress* (1980) cites abundant evidence of the existence of similar notions in ancient Greece and Rome. Its development thereafter was, however, hindered by the tendency of political entities to undergo conspicuous cycles of prosperity and collapse—lending considerable credence to cyclic theories of history—and was further confused by religious concepts of singular revelation.

Religious opposition to the idea of progress continued to crop up in the twentieth century, most notably in Herbert Butterfield's account of *The Whig Interpretation of History* (1931), which objected on Christian grounds to the tendency of contemporary historians to represent history as a series of battles between stubborn reactionaries and progressive opponents (which the latter always won, thus bringing about the modern world). Butterfield did highlight the danger of the kind of retrospective reasoning that regards the past as a series of preliminary phases leading inexorably to the present rather than an accumulation of the unintended collective consequences of the sum of individual actions.

All historical and futuristic fiction takes up a position, overtly or tacitly, on the philosophy of progress, but the subset of fictions that engages with the notion most directly and analytically consists of episodic endeavours that attempt to tell the story of humankind *in toto*, moving across centuries or millennia of past time, and sometimes extending into the future. The narrative thread of Eugène Sue's *Les mystères du peuple* (1849–1852; trans. as *The Mysteries of the People*) is one of endless class struggle, as is that of Henri Barbusse's *Les enchaînements* (1925; trans. as *Chains*), but *anthropological theses provide the core narratives of Johannes V. Jensen's *Den Lange Rejse* (1908–1922; trans. as *The Long Journey*), several story series by F. Britten Austin, including *When Mankind Was Young* (1927), and Vardis Fisher's Testament of Man series (1943–1960).

Broadly speaking, writers of *hard science fiction remain key propagandists and apologists for technological progress, routinely arguing that its contribution to moral progress has been, is, and will continue to be positive rather than negative. Writers of antiscience fiction, on the other hand—including some, but by no means all, writers of "softer" science fiction—routinely justify their hostility on the grounds that technological development is deleterious to moral progress and the quality of human life. The ambivalence has long been reflected in *Faustian fantasies, and within fabulations in which the rewards and costs of progress are weighed against one another, such as Bruce Sterling's "Flowers of Edo" (1987). The persistence and complication of the conflict offer eloquent evidence of the fact that the trends towards social, political, and ideological harmony optimistically identified by Turgot have not continued smoothly.

PSEUDOSCIENCE

A set of assertions devoid of any rational support, which is presented in a jargon imitative of scientific terminology and supported by apparent empirical evidence, in the hope and expectation of gaining credence thereby. Alternative terms attempting to avoid its pejorative qualities include "fringe science" and "alternative science", while those intended to further increase the pejorative implications include "pathological science" and "junk science". As the latter coinages suggest, pseudoscience is regarded as a manifest and dangerous evil by many scientists.

Some modern pseudosciences preserve the names and ambitions of traditional divinatory practices such as astrology, numerology, and chiromancy (palmistry), and some others are similarly inclined, although the oracular *prediction of events is often de-emphasised and sometimes entirely displaced by the analysis of personality. Others belong to the field of *parapsychology, which similarly attempts to reclothe traditional magical ideas in quasi-scientific terminology, and to the field of unorthodox *cosmological speculation—including fanciful accounts of the *Earth's history and composition. David Starr Jordan, the first president of Stanford University, coined the alternative term "sciosophy" to describe "systematized ignorance" in *The Higher Foolishness* (1927), but it did not catch on. Pseudoscientists are often described as cranks—from the German *krank*, meaning "sick"—but this says more about the inability of sceptics to comprehend why people adopt such beliefs than about the epistemology of the beliefs.

A scientific backlash against the pretensions of pseudoscience became increasingly noticeable in the late nineteenth century; Augustus de Morgan's *A Budget of Paradoxes* (1872) is an early example of a wide-ranging "debunking" exercise. The natural resentment felt by scientists against pseudoscience—or, rather, against the frequent rhetorical successes of pseudoscience—tends to infect the tone of such debunking exercises with furious sarcasm and other forms of argumentative brutality. Such mannerisms delight fellow sceptics, but can seem reminiscent of religious enthusiasts denouncing heretics, thus giving rise to the kind of antipersecution rhetoric deployed by Charles *Fort and his admirers. The tradition founded by de Morgan required elaborate continuation in the twentieth century as *scholarly fantasies proliferated vastly—a Herculean task undertaken by Martin Gardner in a series of books begun with *In the Name of Science* (1952).

Pseudoscience inevitably flourished wherever the scientific method made least historical progress, and wherever there was an urgent but unfulfilled demand for effective technology; its most spectacular manifestations were in the field of *medicine from the sixteenth century onwards, when the orthodox pseudoscience of Galenian theorists was challenged by the followers of *Paracelsus, and then by a floodtide of quack theories, many of which reflected new fashions in other sciences. In the late eighteenth century, James Graham advertised the therapeutic value of *electricity, Antoine *Mesmer advanced a theory of animal *magnetism, and Johann Lavater pioneered physiognomy, which attempted to diagnose diseases and divine character by means of the features. Physiognomy's emphasis on the divinatory potential of the shapes of the forehead and skull was carried forward into the pseudoscience of craniology, pioneered by Franz Josef Gall's *Sur les fonctions du cerveau* (1825) and renamed phrenology by his followers, which attempted to identify differences in brain development from the shape of the skull.

Phrenology was popularised in Britain by George Combe, author of *The Constitution of Man* (1828) and founder of *The Phrenological Journal and Miscellany* (1823–1847), who once read George Eliot's "bumps" but failed to convince her of the method's merits. Most other litterateurs were similarly sceptical, but by no means uninterested; the pattern of thought underlying physiognomy and phrenology had a considerable influence on nineteenth-century literary discussion of character formation and motivation. Speculative fictions extrapolating its theses included John Trotter's *Travels in Phrenologasto* (1825; by-lined Don Jose Balscopo) and William Windsor's *Loma: A Citizen of Venus* (1897), in which applied phrenology enables a hypothetical society to obtain a *Utopian order and harmony.

The disjunction between the level of demand for curative treatments and the ability of nineteenth-century physicians to deliver them, coupled with such phenomena as the placebo effect, assisted medical quacks to thrive while there was no possibility of medical treatment based in an understanding of physiology and biochemistry, and it is not surprising that they continued to thrive alongside scientific medicine, given that many kinds of illnesses prevail for which no effective scientific treatment is yet available. One of the most effective nineteenth-century medical pseudosciences, renamed homeopathy by Samuel Hahnemann, probably owed its success to the fact that the elaborate pretence of treatment coupled with the actual avoidance of treatment minimised the possibility of doing patients further harm by medical intervention. The success of medical pseudosciences was greatly assisted by the psychological factors leading people to make mistaken estimates of *probability and causality—especially the application of the principle of *post hoc, ergo propter hoc*—and the similar factors responsible for psychological *plausibility also sustain whole schools of parapsychological pseudoscience.

Such medical pseudosciences as physiognomy and phrenology were based on hypotheses that are susceptible to scientific enquiry—Charles *Darwin produced a more effective analysis of *The Expression of the Emotions in Man and Animals* (1872)—but empirical studies of localisation of brain function had to await sophisticated instruments of *neurological measurement whose development did not begin until the late twentieth century. What qualified them as pseudoscientific was their founders' insistence on filling the empirical void with remarkably detailed confabulations whose supportive evidence was either nonexistent or purely anecdotal, and did not lend itself to any kind of experimental testing. Similar criticisms can be levelled against many schools of human science, especially in the field of *psychology, including *sociobiology-based "evolutionary psychology", and it is arguable that the entire project of "character analysis" or "personality analysis" is inherently pseudoscientific. Medical pseudoscience was only partly displaced by scientific medicine during the twentieth century; as with other kinds of divinatory pseudoscience, it underwent a dramatic resurgence in the last decades of the century in the proliferation of "alternative medicine", many of whose theses overlap or derive from theories of personality.

In spite of the fact that literary endeavour is so hospitable to improbability, implausibility, and frank *impossibility, the literary heritage is not conspicuously sympathetic to pseudoscientific schools of thought. Indeed, literary works often seem suspicious of pseudosciences precisely because they attempt to don scientific disguise. Litterateurs suspicious of or hostile to science frequently regard false science as doubly damnable. There is a certain irony in the fact that the literary genre most hospitable to pseudoscience is science fiction, whose dependence on and advocacy of real science inevitably renders it vulnerable to the impostures of false science, to the extent that John W. *Campbell Jr. spoiled his ambition to set science fiction on firm rational foundations by making *Astounding/Analog* so hospitable to the cranks to whom he was willing to lend his audience.

The treatment of various pseudosciences in early science fiction pulps usually adopted an intellectual position of "interested scepticism" similar to that of Charles Fort, but Ray Palmer's *Amazing Stories* began a much more enthusiastic advocacy of Richard S. Shaver's "Shaver Mystery", launched in its pages with "I Remember Lemuria!" (1945; reprinted in *I Remember Lemuria and The Return of Sathanas*). Palmer subsequently alleged that Shaver had spent time in Ypsilanti State Hospital suffering from paranoid schizophrenic delusions, but this did not prevent him from promoting those delusions, nor

from claiming early *flying saucer sightings as "proof" of their allegation that the world's political troubles were due to telepathic sabotage by evil *androids lurking in hidden caverns beneath the Earth's surface.

The appeal of these fantasies to readers obviously had much to do with the intellectual climate of the late 1940s—a connection strongly re-emphasised by John Campbell's decision to embark on a similar promotional endeavour on behalf of L. Ron Hubbard's "Dianetics", launched as a new kind of psychoanalysis before it became the basis of the religion of Scientology. John A. Winter's introduction to Hubbard's Dianetics in the May 1950 issue of *Astounding* claims that "in this present civilisation of ours, where our techniques of destruction dangerously exceed our abilities to survive, there have been many thinkers engaged in a frantic search for a method to control Man's race-homicidal, race-suicidal tendencies". The article itself introduces the human brain as "the optimum computing machine"—it is shot through with *computing analogies—and concludes with the proposition that the human future is a straightforward choice between the stars and the *atom bomb, which urgently requires the facilitation of good "mental hygiene".

Campbell went on to lend his support to other pseudoscientific notions, showing a particular fondness for exotic technological devices such as the psi-detecting Hieronymus Machine (publicised in the June 1956 *Astounding*). When the unorthodox cosmological theories of Immanuel Velikovsky became a *cause célèbre* in the 1960s—assisted by a set of articles in the September 1963 issue of *The American Behavioral Scientist* and the consequent book *The Velikovsky Affair* (1966)—Campbell opened the pages of *Analog* to the debate, expanding it to take in the fallout of Erich von Däniken's *Chariots of the Gods* (1968), although he sided with the sceptics. His successor as *Analog*'s editor, Ben Bova, published a special "Velikovsky issue" of the magazine in October 1974, in which Isaac Asimov briskly demolished Velikovsky's theory. The fiction Campbell published that reflected such interests tended to be far more lighthearted in its Fortean scepticism. A notable example is Walt and Leigh Richmond's *The Lost Millennium* (1967; aka *Siva!*), a response to the 1970s fad for "pyramidology" in which solar taps located in pyramids broadcast electrical power and manipulate history.

The perils of trafficking with pseudoscientific unorthodoxy are illustrated by John Gribbin and Stephen Plagemann's *The Jupiter Effect* (1974), a popular science book based on a letter published in *Science* in 1971, about correlations between cyclic sunspot activity and earthquakes, which broaches the possibility that both might be linked to the gravitational effects of alignments of the major planets. By way of dramatisation, Gribbin added a chapter to the book regarding the possible effects of the next sunspot maximum—a scenario that became increasingly apocalyptic in secondary reportage, much of which construed Gribbin's "predictions" (somewhat to his distress) as a kind of "scientific astrology". The exaggerated thesis inevitably made its way into *disaster stories, although it is treated with appropriate scepticism in Frederik Pohl's *Syzygy* (1982).

Many science fiction writers follow the example of scientists by going out of their way to treat pseudoscientific material scathingly—often cruelly so—because they resent being lumped together with *flying saucer enthusiasts and followers of such unorthodox theorists as Velikovsky, von Däniken, and Graham Hancock—whose *The Message of the Sphinx* (1996; with Robert Bauval) provided the initial impetus for several pseudoscientific fads of the late twentieth century. Even so, such notions continue to attract considerable attention among the genre's fans, especially in the context of media "sci-fi", which is much more hospitable to pseudoscientific theses than science fiction in print.

Some members of the science fiction community—notably John Sladek and Thomas M. Disch—are among the most vitriolic debunkers of pseudoscientific nonsense, but the very fierceness of their attacks tends to give their victims free publicity. Their efforts are not only counterbalanced by the pseudoscientific fantasies of writers publishing under the science fiction label, such as Piers Anthony, but those of writers who consider themselves to be a cut above it in marketing terms, such as Whitley Strieber. "Pseudoscience fiction" is, however, a fugitive subgenre in the field of acknowledged fiction, because packaging such imaginative endeavours as "fiction" is self-defeating; the whole point of pseudoscience is to command undeserved credibility, so its natural habitat is tabloid reportage and the equivalent sector of the book market. Even fictional parodies of popular pseudoscience such as Zach Hughes' *Seed of the Gods* (1974) tend to seem a trifle pointless.

PSYCHOLOGY

The scientific study of the human mind. The internal subdivision of the science reproduces the philosophical mind/body problem; it includes both introspective schools that make no attempt at *neurological anchorage and physiological schools that build on neurological discoveries but have great difficulty in accounting for the mental phenomena of self-consciousness. A conspicuous explanatory gap yawns between accounts of hormonal release and neuronal firing on the one hand and emotion, sensation, and thinking on the other.

Psychology is the most self-referential of all the sciences, and thus encounters the worst effects of methodological *uncertainty. It is also the science whose entanglements with literary endeavour are the most fundamental, the most intricate, and the most problematic. The elements of psychological experience are usually cited as thought and emotion, but fantasy—the faculty of forming images, in its narrowest definition—is also a fundamental psychological process as well as the fundamental literary process. The production of fiction, whether privately or for public consumption, is an exceedingly complicated psychological phenomenon, and the everyday production of psychological phenomena within the mind is subject to the pressures and demands of *narrative construction.

Although conscious fantasising is mostly subject to conscious control, as in processes of recall and daydreaming, it also has a significant spontaneous component, and sleep produces the remarkable phenomenon of dreaming: the spontaneous production of fantasies of a puzzling and sometimes disturbing nature. Literary fantasising is subject to a greater measure of conscious control—further emphasised by the facility of rewriting—but it too has a highly significant spontaneous component, often described as inspiration, which is intrinsic to the process of literary creativity. Writing fiction can be represented as an unusually elaborate and disciplined form of daydreaming, but simulating dreams in a literary context is much harder, as exemplified by the efforts of surrealist writers. Literary dreams cannot resemble real dreams, because the meaning of real dreams remains stubbornly elusive, while every literary dream has to carry a meaning of *some* sort in order to warrant its inclusion in the narrative.

The German *Romantic writer Jean Paul Richter—who signed his work Jean Paul—attempted to secularise and desupernaturalise the idea of poetic inspiration by means of reference to "the unconscious": an idea whose subsequent development was intimately shared by psychologists and litterateurs. Richter's theory was introduced to English readers and writers in 1821 by Thomas de Quincey, immediately influencing writers such as Elizabeth Barrett Browning, who published *An Essay on Mind, with Other Poems* in 1826, three years before James Mill published his pioneering text on *The Analysis of the Human Mind* (1829). The naturalist and physiologist William Benjamin Carpenter, who elaborated the term to "unconscious cerebration" in 1853, was personally acquainted with

Mrs. Gaskell, who reflected his ideas in the behaviour of the heroine of *North and South* (1855); Carpenter's *Comparative Physiology* (1855) was also one of George Eliot's sources, and the notion is similarly reflected in the behaviour of Maggie Tulliver in *The Mill on the Floss* (1860).

While George Eliot was writing *Daniel Deronda* (1876), her long-time partner G. H. Lewes was working on *The Physical Basis of Mind* (1877), and she applied his ideas to the characterisation of Gwendolen Harleth. (It is no coincidence that the characters so far cited are female, as the workings of the female mind were then supposed to be less rational and more amenable to explanation in terms of hidden motives than those of their male counterparts'.) Wilkie Collins used the notion of the unconscious in *The Moonstone* (1868), in which he cited the work of his friend John Elliotson, who had been professor of medicine at University College Hospital before being forced to resign in 1838 because of his interest in *hypnotism. Charles Dickens followed Collins' example in the unfinished *The Mystery of Edwin Drood* (1870).

Carpenter's thesis was further popularised when Francis Cobbe wrote two articles on "Unconscious Cerebration: A Psychological Study" and "Dreams as Illustrations of Unconscious Cerebration" for *Macmillan's Magazine* in 1870. The phrase crops up in numerous subsequent novels, including Henry James' *The Aspern Papers* (1888), which appeared two years before his brother William's *Principles of Psychology* (1890). Both James brothers became intensely interested in the description of the "stream of consciousness"—a term that William coined—and Henry's influence assisted it to become a key notion of modernist literature, whose simulation in print was attempted by Dorothy Richardson, James Joyce, Virginia Woolf, Hubert Selby Jr., and many others, although a notable pre-Jamesian example can be found in Édouard Dujardin's *Les lauriers sont coupés* (1887).

A significant prospectus for physiological psychology was set out in Herbert Spencer's *The Principles of Psychology* (1855), which conceded the unique difficulties posed by the subjectivity of consciousness, but also made much of such notions as reflex action and instinct and stressed the role of memory as the source of reason, emotion, and will. A pioneering laboratory for psychological experimentation was established by William Wundt in 1879. The potential contribution of studies in animal psychology to the understanding of human psychology was investigated by Lloyd Morgan's *Introduction to Comparative Psychology* (1894). The field of psychometric measurement also underwent rapid progress in the 1890s, with the development of early *intelligence tests.

The literary response to these developments was not nearly so rapid or so respectful—their utility in the matter of characterisation seeming far more limited—although it did include such speculative *contes philosophiques* as Kurd Lasswitz's "Psychotomie" (1893; trans. as "Psychotomy"), in which mental processes are gifted with an objectivity that is convenient from the point of view of a scientific observer, but not for the subject who experiences them. The mechanism of memory attracted considerable literary attention, most of it fascinated by the phenomenon of amnesia, which was to prove so useful a plot device that amnesiac fiction became a significant subgenre of mystery fiction. The more scientifically inclined treatments of memory in late nineteenth-century fiction include Edward Bellamy's *Dr. Heidenhoff's Process* (1880), Richard Slee and Cornelia Atwood Pratt's *Dr. Berkeley's Discovery* (1899), and Walter Besant's "The Memory Cell" (1900).

The further development of the concept of the unconscious in the context of *psychopathology—including the clinical uses of *hypnosis and the consequent evolution of Sigmund *Freud's psychoanalytic techniques—inevitably provided a tremendous stimulation to literary studies of deviant behaviour and motivation. Freud and Carl *Jung each provoked a considerable number of doctrinaire literary works, while Freud's other one-time disciple Alfred Adler also prompted such fictitious exemplars as Miles J. Breuer's "The Inferiority Complex" (1930). Such introspective approaches to psychology came to seem increasingly *pseudoscientific to physiological psychologists in the early twentieth century, however, and generated something of a *positivist backlash, dramatised in Vincent Harper's polemical novel *The Mortgage on the Brain* (1905). The backlash gave rise to behaviourism, a school of psychology committed to the restriction of its observations and conclusions to observable items of behaviour. Using concepts developed by I. P. Pavlov in Russia—especially the notion of the "conditioned reflex"—and placing a heavy emphasis on experimental methods, the behaviourist manifesto was published in the United States by John B. Watson in *Psychological Review* (1913; exp. as *Behaviorism*, 1925).

Behaviourist psychology instituted a long tradition of experiments in which the behaviour of rats was conditioned by delivering rewards or electric shocks in response to various stimuli in "Skinner boxes"—named after B. F. Skinner, the author of *Science and Human Behavior* (1953) and the Behaviourist Utopian romance *Walden Two* (1948). Stories in which human protagonists discover that they are actually experimental subjects in glorified Skinner boxes became commonplace in the latter half of the century—Frank M. Robinson's "The Maze" (1950) is a notable early example. The idea that a suitably elaborated behaviourist psychology might pave the way for psychologically sophisticated government only enjoyed a brief fashionability, eccentrically reflected in Gerald Heard's *Doppelgängers: An Episode of the Fourth, the Psychological Revolution* (1947) and half-heartedly extrapolated in Poul Anderson's "Question and Answer" (1954) and James E. Gunn's "Tsylana" (1956), although occasional behaviourist science fiction stories were produced thereafter, including Herbert Jacob Bernstein's "Stimulus-Response" (1969) and Tom Purdom's *The Barons of Behavior* (1972).

Rats were also extensively used as experimental subjects by German *gestalt* psychologists whose accounts of learning processes were rather different, leading Bertrand Russell to observe that experimental animals tended to replicate the national characteristics of their observers: whereas American rats ran around haphazardly until they received a positive or negative stimulus purely by chance, German rats would allegedly retire to a corner and devote themselves to serious cogitation before taking any action. Although such research produced some notions of some potential relevance to human behaviour—especially when it was extended to encompass neurological experiments like those leading to the identification of "pleasure centres" in the brain—it also generated a certain amount of repugnance, dramatised in such works as James Tiptree Jr.'s "The Psychologist Who Wouldn't Do Awful Things to Rats" (1976). Its competence in the explanation of animal behaviour was challenged by studies of animal behaviour in the wild, which resulted in the growth of a far more flexible school of "ethology"—a term first coined by John Stuart Mill but redefined by Darwinists interested in the interaction of instinct and learning. The terms produced and popularised by the school included Konrad Lorenz's notion of "imprinting", referring to a process by which young animals identified parental models for attachment and imitation.

In extreme cases, such as Jane Goodall's observations of chimpanzees from 1960 to 1990 and Diane Fossey's observations of gorillas between 1963 and 1985, ethological methods became closely akin to the *ethnological method of participant observation. Although such ethologists as Lorenz and Niko Tinbergen did a great deal of work on birds, the use of rats as models for understanding human behaviour was set firmly aside by ethologists in favour of much nearer biological relatives in such works as *Human Behaviour* (1961) and *Violence, Monkeys and Man* (1968) by Claire and W. M. S. Russell. The application of ethological explanatory schemes to the

analysis of human behaviour was popularised by Desmond Morris' *The Naked Ape* (1967) and *The Human Zoo* (1969).

The attention paid by all these schools of psychological thought to learning processes encouraged the development of a significant subsidiary science of child psychology, which stressed the differences between the thought processes of children and adults. Such work inevitably impacted on the characterisation of children in fiction, and on the composition of fiction for children; notable literary works foregrounding the supposed idiosyncrasies of child psychology include Ray Bradbury's "Zero Hour" (1947) and "The World the Children Made" (1950; aka "The Veldt"), Jerome Bixby's "It's a *Good* Life" (1953), and William Golding's *Lord of the Flies* (1954).

The progress of introspective schools of psychology in the twentieth century was increasingly dominated by practical concerns; to many interested observers, the point was not to explain minds but to change them. This was evident not merely in the field of psychiatry but also in the increasing interest taken in the effects of *psychotropic drugs inducing "altered states of consciousness" and in the commercially significant field of "self-help" manuals. People desirous of changing their psychology in the interests of success were encouraged by Émile Coué in the early years of the twentieth century to mobilise the power of "positive thinking"—a crusade carried forward by Norman Vincent Peale and many others, especially in the United States. A subsequent school of American psychology developed by such writers as Carl Rogers and Abraham Maslow offered guidance in the matter of "self-actualization". Similar theories were subsequently extrapolated into various kinds of training programs, including the "neuro-linguistic programming" developed in the mid-1970s by Richard Bandler and John Grinder. Speculative fiction extrapolating such notions includes Peter Phillips' "P-Plus" (1949).

These various kinds of motivational psychology routinely came under suspicion of being entirely pseudoscientific. Critics, such as Paul C. Vitz in *Psychology as Religion: The Cult of Self-Worship* (1990), complained that they were merely narcissistic cults, which replaced God with the self as an object of worship—a claim lent considerable credence by such examples as the integration of L. Ron Hubbard's psychoanalytical Dianetics into the religion of Scientology. Literary reflections of the cynical application of such principles of psychological management include Norman Spinrad's *The Mind Game* (1985).

In fiction, of course, the power of positive thinking is absolute, because its rewards are always at the discretion of the author, and matching literary rewards to the nature, extent, and virtue of a character's effort is one of the fundamental aspects of the moral order of fiction, intrinsic to narrative theory. Indeed, the ability of fiction to provide inspirational models of this kind for readers to emulate is often advanced as an important social utility, particularly in respect of formularistic popular fiction that has no truck with tragic or ironic variants and never fails to deliver an appropriate payoff. The literary novel, as a genre, largely consists of an extensive series of studies in more-or-less successful self-actualisation; even chronicles of abject failure are usually redeemed by Joycean "epiphanies" that allow characters to develop new insights as a result of their follies and humiliations.

As in the late nineteenth century, the most prolific twentieth-century literary derivative of physiological psychology consists of tales dealing with the hypothetical mechanisms of memory. Amnesiac fantasies broadened out in the wake of the Freudian notion of repression to develop a rich mythology of traumatic suppression, taken to elaborate extremes in H. P. Lovecraft's "The Shadow Out of Time" (1936). L. Ron Hubbard's development of the repression theory underlying Dianetics was anticipated by his pulp fantasy "Fear" (1940), in which an amnesiac is tortured by "demons" of guilt.

Writers of speculative fiction became increasingly interested in the possibility of transferring memories from one mind to another by chemical or electrical means; notable developments of the notion include Curt Siodmak's *Hauser's Memory* (1968), A. E. van Vogt's *Future Glitter* (1973; aka *Tyranopolis*), David Skal's *Scavengers* (1980), and James Gunn's *The Dreamers* (1980). Recording devices transcribing memories, dreams, or emotional experiences—often enabling them to be replayed or marketed—also became commonplace; notable examples include Charles Eric Maine's *The Man Who Couldn't Sleep* (1958), Lee Harding's "All My Yesterdays" (1963), D. G. Compton's *Synthajoy* (1972), Chelsea Quinn Yarbro's *Hyacinths* (1983), and James Morrow's *The Continent of Lies* (1984).

The development of speculative fiction gave rise to a host of speculative entities credited with consciousness—including *aliens, animals and humans with augmented *intelligence, and such *artificial intelligences as sentient *computers and *robots—whose psychological construction was intrinsic to their characterisation. Isaac *Asimov was moved to invent a hypothetical science of robopsychology for use in the stories collected in *I, Robot* (1940–1950; book, 1950), and robopsychologist Susan Calvin's various confrontations with the anomalies of robot behaviour—inevitably derived from nonobvious extrapolations

of the three laws of robotics—became a standard plot device within the series.

The evolution of speculative fiction also encouraged the development of the literary modelling of the psychological realm of "inner *space". The literary representation of dreams had always presented them as adventures in hypothetical worlds, and the notion of the mind as a kind of "theatre" on whose stage images might appear and thoughts could be voiced was also old. Fiction itself—easily representable as a series of excursions into psychologically generated spaces—provided a key exemplar of the notion of the mind as a venue where whole worlds might be created, elaborated, and annihilated. The notion of inner space acquired a particular fashionability in speculative fiction of the 1960s, when J. G. *Ballard produced a polemic calling for a redress of a generic balance that had previously been tipped in favour of outer space.

Science fiction writers had already extrapolated the notion of taking trips in other people's psychological spaces—notable examples included Peter Phillips' "Dreams Are Sacred" (1948), Roger P. Graham's "The Mental Assassins" (1950; by-lined Gregg Conrad), John Brunner's, "City of the Tiger" (1958), Daniel F. Galouye's "Descent into the Maelstrom" (1961), and Robert F. Young's "The Girl in His Mind" (1963)—but Ballard's call to arms helped bring about a marked sophistication. Fantasies of this kind had usually involved some kind of machine-assisted connection, and such stories were further assisted in becoming more elaborate and dramatic by the development of the notion of machine-generated *cyberspace, which gave private fantasies a much larger arena in which to operate in such works as Pat Cadigan's *Mindplayers* (1987), Kim Newman's *The Night Mayor* (1989), Jamil Nasir's *Quasar* (1995), and the film *The Cell* (2000).

PSYCHOPATHOLOGY

The branch of *pathology dealing with mental illness—the modern version of the traditional notion of madness. "Mental illness" and "madness" are both problematic concepts; Ambrose Bierce's commentary on the word "mad" in *The Devil's Dictionary* (1881–1906; book 1906, initially as *The Cynic's Word Book*) offers the prefatory definition "Affected with a high degree of intellectual independence", and goes on to observe that most accusations of madness are offered by "officials destitute of evidence that themselves are sane".

Madness was initially viewed as a divine affliction, as represented in Euripides' oft-quoted dictum that

"Whom the gods destroy they first make mad". The history of its relocation within a medical context in the seventeenth century is detailed, with a cynical resentment similar to Bierce's, in Michael Foucault's *Histoire de la folie* (1961; trans. as *Madness and Civilization: A History of Insanity in the Age of Reason*). The process had begun in England when the fifth book of William Bullein's *Bulwarke of Defence againste Sicknes, Sorues, etc.* (1562) attempted to deal with phobias and other disturbances of the mind. Subsequent academic studies of madness often had a polemical bent and sometimes a calculated perversity. Robert Burton's *The Anatomy of Melancholy* (1621; rev. repeatedly until 1676)—which poses as a methodical study of every aspect of its subject—is explicitly based on the proposition that "All the world is mad" and the tradition thus founded extended into the twentieth century in such works as Thomas Szasz' *The Myth of Mental Illness* (1961) and R. D. Laing's *The Politics of Experience* (1967).

Foucault suggests that the medicalisation of madness had much to do with the necessity of developing new scapegoat enclaves following the virtual disappearance of leprosy in the late Middle Ages, and that the insane asylum was the natural heir to the leper colony. Historical fiction dealing with the incarceration and attempted treatment of madmen from the seventeenth century to the twentieth routinely takes the same view, often casting the keepers of asylums as out-and-out villains whose sanity is far more vicious and inhumane than the insanity of their victims. Notable examples include Charles Reade's *Hard Cash* (1863), Amalie Skram's *Professor Hieronimus* (1899), and the highly fanciful account of the Marquis de Sade's imprisonment in Charenton in the film *Quills* (2000).

As with other aberrations from the norm, madness has been a perennial preoccupation of literature, from Classical representations of the madness of Orestes through such post-Renaissance representations as Ludovico Ariosto's *Orlando Furioso* (1516), William Shakespeare's *Hamlet* (1600) and *King Lear* (1606), and Miguel de Cervantes' *Don Quixote* (1605–1615), to modern representations of the sociopath and psychopath as the archetypal villains of modern *criminological fiction. The difficulty of determining the bounds and causes of the various conditions lumped under the label has added a useful component of ambiguity and ambivalence to literary consideration, enabling literary madness to take on various kinds of meaning that are usually absent from actual madness; literary madness, like literary dreams, always has method in it.

Notions of what counts as madness have shifted somewhat over time, not so much in terms of the assessment of what qualifies as mental aberration as in terms of the extent and manner of the tolerance extended within different social contexts. Thus, infatuation or "romantic love" has always been considered a kind of madness, but is now regarded as something to be suffered kindly rather than something to be deplored—and perhaps treated surgically, as it was in the case of Abelard and Heloïse. The Medieval sin of *accidie* was eventually reclassified as the disorder of "melancholia"—Burton's melancholy—and then as "depression" (or "clinical depression", to distinguish the supposed illness from ordinary sadness and natural grief).

Literary sympathy for the mad and cynicism regarding the definition of madness reflect the circumstance that writers and artists have often been considered mad by their neighbours and contemporaries; academic sympathy and cynicism reflect the circumstance that the same judgement is often made of philosophers. The notion that the scientific worldview is a kind of madness was advanced in Erasmus' *Encomium Moriae* (1509; trans. as *In Praise of Folly*), which refers to the "insane self-deception" of "bearded and gowned philosophers" whose measurements and computations give them the illusion that they know everything when they really know nothing—an image reproduced in such satires as Jonathan Swift's *Gulliver's Travels* (1726) but given more ambivalent treatment in such accounts of obsession as Honoré de Balzac's *La recherche de l'absolu* (1834; trans. as *The Quest of the Absolute*). The notion continued to echo in such twentieth-century examples of anti-science fiction as Stanislaw Lem's representations of natural and human science as ultimately hopeless delusional quests, including *Glos pana* (1968; trans. as *His Master's Voice*).

The common assertion that madness is closely akin to genius—first made by *Aristotle and subjected to sarcastic comment in William Shakespeare's grouping of "the lunatic, the lover and the poet" and John Dryden's observation that "Great wits are sure to madness near allied, /And thin partitions do their bounds divide" (1681)—is tantamount to an affirmation that some aberrations from the norm are socially and existentially desirable, more akin to a superior state of preternatural health than to illness. Artistic and scientific creativity are the most obvious candidates for this honour; it is by no means unknown for would-be artistic creators deliberately to go in search of mental derangement with the aid of *psychotropic drugs, and fairly common for them to accept the licence to behave badly that forgivable madness appears to grant. It is not surprising, therefore, that the general tendency of self-regarding litterateurs is to sympathise with the mad, unless and until their mania becomes homicidal; even then, fascination is often mingled, overtly or covertly, with admiration.

Pseudoscientific studies of the relationship between madness and genius became commonplace in the late nineteenth century, often conducted by early criminologists such as Cesare Lombroso, whose *L'uomo di genio in rapporto all psichiatria* (1889; trans. as *The Man of Genius*) nourished the craze. J. F. Nisbet's *The Insanity of Genius* (1891) judged all great men "neuropathic", offering (with supporting evidence) an exemplary list of "insane" writers that included Swift, Samuel Johnson, almost all of the *Romantics, and Edgar Allan Poe, although the case made out for Shakespeare is a trifle hesitant. Nisbet's list of neuropathic musicians is even comprehensive, while his register of mad scientists and philosophers begins with Socrates and takes in Nicolaus Copernicus, Galileo, John Kepler, Francis Bacon, René Descartes, Isaac Newton, Immanuel Kant, Carolus Linnaeus, Georges Cuvier, Auguste Comte, the Herschels, James Watt, Humphry Davy, Michael Faraday, and Charles Darwin. He observes in laconic conclusion that "there is every reason to believe that the habitual criminal owes his characteristics to the same set of causes".

The construction of a taxonomy of mental illness, on the basis of different sets of symptoms, did not begin in earnest until the nineteenth century, when "alienists" specialising in the treatment of mental illness were gradually redefined as "psychiatrists" in the context of the theoretical evolution of *psychology. There is, however, a significant anticipatory "psychiatric literature", whose landmark works include Samuel Johnson's *Rasselas* (1759), Laurence Sterne's *Tristram Shandy* (1760–1767), and James Hogg's *Confessions of a Justified Sinner* (1824). *Rasselas* includes retrospectively recognisable descriptions of schizophrenia and depression, and its accounts of the genesis of mental illness were so convincing that it was required reading at the John Hopkins Medical School until the early twentieth century.

The notion of madness is inherent in a particular formula of prose fiction, which takes the form of an autobiographical account of escalating encounters with exotic experience, which may be seen by the reader as a hallucinatory descent into delusion or as an account of supernatural persecution. The reader's hesitation between these rival explanations, whether or not it is eventually resolved by the narrative, is often held to produce a particular aesthetic sensation that is the basis of a good deal of *horror fiction. Poe—the most prolific nineteenth-century writer of psychiatric fiction—wrote several classic tales in this vein, including "William Wilson" (1840) and "The

Tell-Tale Heart" (1943). Sigmund *Freud gave it a label normally translated as "the uncanny", although Tzvetan Todorov preferred to restrict the French equivalent (*l'inconnu*) to stories in which the narrative is resolved as a madman's delusion, defining the subgenre of stories in which ambiguity is retained as *le fantastique*.

Notable early examples of the madman's narrative that have a speculative component include Poe's "The Unparalleled Adventure of One Hans Pfaall" (1835; rev. 1840), Jean Richepin's "La machine à métaphysique" (1877; trans. as "The Metaphysical Machine"), Guy de Maupassant's "Le Horla" (1887; trans. as "The Horla"), and Edgar Fawcett's *Douglas Duane* (1887) and "Solarion" (1889). Such narratives are routinely prefaced by a complaint in which the imaginary writer bewails the fact that people think that he is mad, and proceeds to offer his account, orally or in manuscript form, as a retrospective explanation and justification of extraordinary conduct. The adaptation of the formula into speculative fiction often turns its innate irony on its head; in science-fictional madmen's manuscripts, the general opinion is more often at fault than the narrator's mind, because the narrator is usually a visionary who knows, accepts, and welcomes the fact that the world is more wondrous, and more rapidly changing, than his contemporaries would prefer to believe. As George Bernard Shaw observed, *progress depends on unreasonable men, who are prepared to think innovatively in spite of the risk of being thought and called mad.

As the medical taxonomy of mental aberration evolved, it was rapidly transplanted into literary "case studies" of a sort pioneered by Oliver Wendell Holmes' "medicated novels": *Elsie Venner* (1861) employs an account of unusual ante-natal effects as a test case for the religious notion of predestination, although it can be seen retrospectively as an early study of schizophrenia; *The Guardian Angel* (1867) is a more conventional representation of what would now be called multiple personality syndrome; *A Mortal Antipathy* (1885) is an account of a neurotic phobia. Thomas Bailey Aldrich's *The Queen of Sheba* (1877) is similarly "medicated".

The English physician who first described alcoholism as a disease, William Gilbert, collected a more extensive and inventive series of hypothetical case studies in *Shirley Hall Asylum* (1863) and *Dr. Austin's Guests* (1866). Walter Besant, who dramatised Gilbert's account of alcoholism as a disease in *The Demoniac* (1890), also wrote one of the earliest novels construing multiple personality—which had a long literary history in *doppelgänger* stories—as a clinical disorder in *The Ivory Gate* (1892). Homicidal mania began to be treated in case study terms in such novels as Mary Angela Dickens' *Against the Tide* (1898). The various fetishisms explored in lovingly minute detail in Richard von Krafft-Ebing's *Psychopathia Sexualis* (1886) provided abundant fodder for the literary explorations of such *decadent writers as Jean Lorrain and Rémy de Gourmont, although their development in the English language was inhibited by Victorian moralism—a delay that caused something of a backlash in such rebellious explorations as Edward Heron-Allen's *The Cheetah Girl* (1923), Ronald Fraser's *The Flower Phantoms* (1926), and George Sylvester Viereck and Paul Eldridge's *The Invincible Adam* (1932).

The new taxonomy also encouraged the "discovery" of new or hitherto-unrecognised psychopathological phenomena. One of the most significant of these newly identified syndromes was neurasthenia (nervous exhaustion). The term was coined in 1881 by George M. Beard, who explained the seemingly recent prevalence of the condition by describing it as a response to the acceleration of the pace of everyday life brought about by new technologies such as railways and telegraphy. Not everyone agreed about neurasthenia's cause, but there was no doubting its fashionability. Identified as a disease to which artists were particularly prone, it became a key symptom of "degeneracy" in Max Nordau's *Entartung* (1893; trans. as *Degeneration*). The notion was more sympathetically popularised by Octave Mirbeau's *Les vingt-et-un jours d'un neurasthénique* (1901), whose protagonist observes life in an enclave of sufferers while taking a "rest cure", John Girdner's *Newyorkitis* (1901), Willy Hellpach's *Nervosität und Kultur* (1902), and an autobiographical account of *The Education of Henry Adams* (1907). The epidemic of madness described in Valery Brussof's remarkable account of "Respublika yuzhnavo kresta" (1905; trans. as "The Republic of the Southern Cross") is also conceived in terms similar to Beard's.

As the twentieth century progressed, the bifurcation of psychology into introspective and physiological schools was reflected in psychiatric theory and psychopathological fantasies by opposed schools of interpretation and treatment. While introspective interpreters sought explanations in terms of repression, problematic family relationships, and traumatic experiences, and cures by means of analytical interrogation and expert counselling, physiological interpreters sought explanations in terms of *neurological malfunctions, and cures by means of *psychotropic drugs, electrical shocks, and psychosurgery. The rivalry between these two traditions was often manifest as overt enmity, sometimes associated with polemical condemnation.

Most litterateurs, inevitably, tended to side with the introspective school in matters of analysis and treatment, although writers of speculative fiction generally found it more convenient to think in terms of physical causes, which were often exaggerated to bizarre extremes, as in the case of tumorous multiple personality described in Stanley Weinbaum's *The Dark Other* (written 1934; published 1950) or the epidemic madness induced by solar radiation in Philip Latham's "Disturbing Sun" (1959). Maya Kaathryn Bohnhoff's "A Tear in the Mind's Eye" (1993) is carefully sceptical of the tendency.

The apparent violence done to the mentality and personality of patients by large doses of major tranquillisers, electro-convulsive therapy, and prefrontal lobotomy excited particular revulsion and complaint in a great many fictional representations, including Tennessee Williams' *Suddenly, Last Summer* (1958; film, 1959), Ken Kesey's *One Flew over the Cuckoo's Nest* (1962), and Jeremy Leven's *Satan* (1982). That reaction encouraged literary support for R. D. Laing's "anti-psychiatry" movement, which recast schizophrenics as voyagers in inner space, embarked upon journeys of self-rediscovery necessitating the perceptual restructuring of time and thought. Doris Lessing's *Briefing for a Descent into Hell* (1971) is a notably elaborate dramatisation of Laing's map of a schizophrenic expedition, and J. G. Ballard described several similar excursions, including those in "The Overloaded Man" (1961) and "The Enormous Space" (1989).

The divergence of the two rival schools of psychopathology further confused the taxonomy of mental illnesses, in spite of the attempt made to clarify the relevant definitions in the American Psychiatric Association's *Diagnostic and Statistical Manual, Mental Disorders* (1954). Although some distinctions emerged, the general tendency was for rival practitioners to apply the same labels, but to offer different accounts of symptoms reflecting different theories of their causality.

The principal additions to the basic vocabulary of schizophrenia, paranoia, and various manias made by the introspective school were psychoanalytical "complexes" such as Freud's Oedipus complex and Alfred Adler's inferiority complex, while more empirically inclined practitioners played a key role in identifying and treating such childhood disorders as "attention deficit hyperactive disorder" (ADHD), dyslexia, and autism. Some terms were progressively redefined, including schizophrenia, one of whose early referents was redefined as multiple personality disorder, having been dramatically popularised by Corbett H. Thigpen and Hervey M. Cleckley's *The Three Faces of Eve* (1957; film, 1957). The "residue" of the description was increasingly fused with one of its alternatives as "paranoid schizophrenia". In the meantime, "manic depression" was recategorised as "bipolar disorder". Some aberrations previously thought of as mental illnesses were uncontroversially reclassified as neurological disorders, most notably epilepsy.

Many aberrations were reconceived in terms of spectra that extended from normal behaviour through mild eccentricity to neurosis *en route* to the psychotic extreme, and the relationship between creativity and madness was re-explored in terms of symptomatic intensity. Particular attention has been paid to the relationship between the mildly manic phase of bipolar disorder and artistic creativity, culminating in such analyses as Kay Redfield Jamison's *An Unquiet Mind* (1995).

Anthony Storr's *The Dynamics of Creation* (1972), which attempted to account for different kinds of creativity in terms of variant tendencies towards different subspecies of madness, categorised the cosmological creativity of Isaac Newton and Albert Einstein as "schizoid"—a judgement first made more than two decades earlier and gleefully repeated by L. Sprague de Camp's article on "The Care and Feeding of Mad Scientists" in the July 1951 issue of *Astounding Science Fiction*. Storr's reiteration helped to reopen discussion regarding the proximity of scientific genius to madness, although his diagnoses were challenged by Michael Fitzgerald, whose claim that Newton and Einstein were sufferers of the mild form of autism known as Asperger's syndrome became central to a much more general account, *The Genesis of Artistic Creativity: Asperger's Syndrome and the Arts* (2005).

The gradual alienation of literature from science had long been reflected in fictional portraits of "mad scientists" that characterised scientists almost entirely by means of psychopathological symptoms. Such portraits were sometimes aided by autobiographical accounts, such as John C. Lilly's blithely unrepentant *The Scientist* (1979). The twentieth-century evolution of science fiction only provided a slight amelioration of the literary trend, achieved primarily by the stratagem of developing a specific subcategory of mad scientists for use as villains—whose tacit assumption that scientists would have to be mad to be plausibly cast as villains is a compliment of sorts. The visual media, however, routinely featured characters who were essentially practitioners of "mad science" rather than dangerous lunatics who merely happened to be scientists; the cinematic *Frankenstein became an important archetype of the subspecies.

Clichéd media depictions of mad scientists were inevitably supplemented by similarly clichéd depictions of mad science fiction fans, who were generally represented in very unflattering terms (having, of course, no vestige of a claim to redeeming qualities of genius). Although Erasmus' notion of mad science

became increasingly difficulty to sustain as the technological spin-off of scientific genius transformed the world, the hypothesis that science fiction is an implicitly mad genre was much easier to argue, and fit in very well with the general contempt in which the genre was held by many scientists and literary men.

Ray Palmer's allegation that Richard S. Shaver's pulp *pseudoscience fiction series launched with "I Remember Lemuria!" (1945) had originated in paranoid schizophrenic delusions for which the author had been hospitalised—nourished, as actual delusional patterns reported by psychiatrists increasingly seemed to be, by such literary sources as H. G. Wells and H. P. Lovecraft—was echoed in an article by Robert Plank in *International Record of Medicine and General Practice Clinics* (July 1954), "The Reproduction of Psychosis in Science Fiction". Plank diagnosed various science fiction writers as schizoid personalities ("especially of the paranoid type") on the basis of their "schizomorph" stories.

Plank's ideas attracted sufficient attention to be further elaborated in an article in the Winter 1957 issue of *Partisan Review* entitled "Lighter than Air but Heavier than Hate", advertised on the cover as "Space Travel and Psychotic Fantasy". Here Plank made much more of the argument that the very idea of space travel was a flight from unacceptable reality, akin to a psychotic retreat. The notion had been anticipated in such science fiction stories as J. T. McIntosh's "Hallucination Orbit" (1952)—an account of the hypothetical disease of "solitosis"—and was to be more explicitly echoed in many others, including Barry N. Malzberg's *Beyond Apollo* (1972) and *Herovit's World* (1973), Robert F. Young's "Glimpses" (1983), Norman Spinrad's *The Void-Captain's Tale* (1983)—which elaborates the common corollary notion of spaceships as phallic symbols—and John Kessel's "Invaders" (1990). A similar notion was effectively dramatised soon after the publication of Plank's first article in a case study represented as nonfiction in Robert Lindner's *The Fifty-Minute Hour* (1955).

Lindner's account, individually titled "The Jet-Propelled Couch", describes his alleged treatment of a patient working in atomic weapons research who falls under the delusion that he is actually the hero of a popular science fiction series (the implication seems to be that it is Edgar Rice Burroughs' Martian series, although its description bears more resemblance to space operas by Edward E. Smith or Edmond Hamilton). Significantly, this is the one case in the book that so captivates the psychiatrist that he becomes party to the delusion himself. Equally significantly, it prompted a long controversy in the science fiction community as to whether the hypothetical—

and probably imaginary—patient might "actually" have been the diplomat Paul Linebarger, who wrote science fiction as Cordwainer Smith (almost all of which was published after 1955).

"The Jet-Propelled Couch" is tacitly echoed in numerous twentieth-century examples of the madman's narrative subgenre, which was increasingly displaced into the framework of the psychiatric case study—thus shifting the story's implicit viewpoint from a lay listener to a supposedly scientific arbiter and interpreter. As in nineteenth-century examples, examples cast as speculative fiction had a far greater tendency to favour the romance, if not the reality, of accounts given by patients over the psychiatrists' inevitable conviction that they must be delusional. Notable examples include Henry Kuttner and C. L. Moore's "The Cure" (1946; by-lined Lewis Padgett), Murray Leinster's "The Strange Case of John Kingman" (1948), Roger P. Graham's "The Yellow Pill" (1958; by-lined Rog Phillips), John Brunner's *Quicksand* (1967), Sonya Dorman's "Lunatic Assignment" (1968), Jack Wodhams' *Looking for Blücher* (1980), Andrew Weiner's "Klein's Machine" (1985), Gene Brewer's *K-Pax* (1995), and Patrick O'Leary's *Door Number Three* (1995). Psychiatrists were treated much more kindly in naturalistic fiction, where their assumptions about their patients were much more trustworthy—especially in mystery stories where they functioned as detectives, as in Henry Kuttner and C. L. Moore's four Michael Gray mysteries (1956–1958).

Whether or not science fiction's denigrators were right to stigmatise it as a mad genre, it is not at all surprising that it should have generated so many fantasies siding with the allegedly mad against the allegedly sane. Insanity becomes the norm and sanity an aberration in Fritz Leiber's "Sanity" (1944; aka "Crazy Wolf"). In Wyman Guin's "Beyond Bedlam" (1951), civil rights are extended to alternative personalities; by contrast, Trevor Hoyle's *Seeking the Mythical Future* (1977) features Psychological Concentration Camps. In Eric Frank Russell's *Dreadful Sanctuary* (1948), the entire Earth is a lunatic asylum populated by rejects from other worlds. In Edmund Cooper's *All Fools' Day* (1966), "normal people" commit mass suicide while artists, eccentrics, and psychotics inherit the Earth. Larry Niven's "Madness Has Its Place" (1990) explores the potential usefulness of paranoid schizophrenics. Maggy Thomas' *Broken Time* (2000) features a galactic Institute for the Criminally Insane.

Several twentieth-century science fiction writers took a particular interest in psychopathology and cleverly exploited the ambiguities of its delusional components. Alfred Bester's notable works in this vein include *The Demolished Man* (1953) and "Fondly Fahrenheit" (1954). Theodore Sturgeon's include "Baby Is Three" (1953), "Mr. Costello, Hero" (1953), "Who?" (1955), and "The Other Man" (1956). Philip K. Dick's *Clans of the Alphane Moon* (1964) features a full panoply of neuroses, while his representations of schizophrenia in *We Can Build You* (written 1962; published 1972) and *Martian Time-Slip* (1964) are unusually heartfelt. Christopher Hodder-Williams' *Coward's Paradise* (1974) makes graphic use of prefrontal lobotomy, while *The Prayer Machine* (1976) features schizophrenic delusions.

The elaborate accounts of nonhuman psychology developed in genre science fiction did not extend far into psychopathological fantasy, for the simple reason that the psychology of exotic beings is sufficiently "aberrant" in itself, although accounts of *computers driven "mad" by confrontation with *logical puzzles—especially *paradoxes—formed a significant subgenre of stories about *artificial intelligence. The last psychiatrist on Earth has to treat robots for want of human patients in Robert Bloch's "Dead-End Doctor" (1956), but accounts of human treatment by mechanical psychiatrists—as in Robert Sheckley's "Bad Medicine" (1956; by-lined Finn O'Donnevan)—were more commonplace.

The slow progress of neurological science inhibited the development of hypothetical psychiatric methods in science fiction, although the advent of *nanotechnology prompted such anticipations of technologically assisted sanity as Greg Bear's *Queen of Angels* (1990). Such a possibility is treated more sceptically in Greg Egan's *Distress* (1995), in which an organisation of "voluntary autists" is formed to defend sufferers from Asperger's syndrome against the threat of compulsory surgical "normalization" and in which the new mental illness of "acute clinical anxiety syndrome" is described. The fashionability acquired by autism as the twentieth century gave way to the twenty first is reflected in such works as Elizabeth Hand's "The Boy in the Tree" (1990; integrated into *Winterlong*), Michael F. Flynn's "Captive Dreams" (1992), and Elizabeth Moon's *The Speed of Dark* (2003). Charles Stross and Cory Doctorow's "Appeals Court" (2004) pays similarly timely attention to Asperger's syndrome.

PSYCHOTROPIC

An adjective signifying "mind changing", most commonly encountered in the term "psychotropic drug", which describes chemical compounds capable of inducing altered states of consciousness. Common descriptions of various psychotropic effects include intoxication, euphoria, ecstasy, hallucination, and narcosis, but the taxonomy is as confused as the experiences it attempts to classify. Almost every human culture known to *ethnologists—the Inuit were the principal exception until they were introduced to alcohol—has employed psychotropic substances on a routine basis, often in the context of religious beliefs allowing experiences of altered states of consciousness to be interpreted in terms of divine inspiration.

Human use of psychotropic drugs is very ancient; opium poppies appear to have been cultivated by the fifth millennium B.C., but the use of psychotropic compounds was probably commonplace before the advent of agriculture. Terence McKenna's *Food of the Gods: The Search for the Original Tree of Knowledge* (1992) hypothesises that mushrooms containing such hallucinogens as psilocybin and muscarine might have been the catalyst responsible for the initial development of human self-consciousness and the subsequent development of religion and art. It has been suggested that the differences between religions can be partly explained by their origins in different psychotropic experiences. Hallucinogens are usually associated with shamanistic cults, while the religions of the ancient Mediterranean generally focused their rituals—from the Dionysian rites of ancient Greece and the Egyptian festivals of Hathor to the Christian Eucharist—on alcoholic intoxication.

The history of Western civilisation has been associated with the development of a distinct ambivalence toward the social role of psychotropics, perhaps reflecting the relative ease with which alcohol can be obtained by technological manufacture. A significant boundary between the sacred and the profane might have been crossed when the domestication of fermentation technology made alcohol freely available for recreational use and intoxication was reduced to mere drunkenness. Traces of the early development of this ambivalence can be identified in Graeco-Roman myth and folklore relating to such figures as Dionysus, Bacchus, and the Sileni, and their literary development in such tragic dramas as Euripides' *The Bacchae* (404 B.C.).

Although Homer called upon his Muse merely to assist him in remembering the lines of the long poems that he had to recite, later writers divided Mnemosyne into a company of nine daughters, instituting a long tradition. The association of artistic creativity with *psychopathology—reflected in the oft-cited link between genius and madness—is based in the conviction that such creativity is an inherently psychotropic process, more akin to the sacred functions of intoxication than mere drunkenness. Given this inherent link between poetic expression and psychotropic experience,

it was only to be expected that literature's relationship with the philosophy of temperance first popularised by *Plato would be a troubled one—especially when "temperance" was redefined by many of the word's users to mean "abstinence".

The psychological rewards of psychotropic adventures appear to have been consistently adequate, at least for some users, to outweigh considerable costs in terms of toxic side effects. If the Eleusinian Mysteries associated with the Greek goddess of the harvest, Demeter, were associated with the deliberate ingestion of ergot, the risk and consequent damage must have been considerable, and the ingestion of various hallucinogenic drugs by North and South American tribespeople routinely involves dire discomfort before and after the desired effect takes place. This compensatory downside to psychotropic adventurism is by no means inconvenient in dramatic terms; literary representations of artistic creativity, like religious representations of revelation, frequently call attention to the costliness of such inspirational experiences—and muses are frequently represented as exacting, even vampiric, mistresses.

The history of psychotropic technology in Western society is largely a matter of viniculture and the brewing of beer. As in many parallel fields, however, psychotropic technology made significant advances in the Renaissance, including the techniques of distillation employed in manufacturing liqueurs and spirits—whose early development was connected with the practice of *alchemy. Tobacco, imported to Western Europe from the Americas in the sixteenth century, and caffeine, lavishly imported in the seventeenth century in tea, coffee, and chocolate, provided alcohol with two new and important rivals, and prompted the development of new technological apparatus for their processing and consumption. Coca was imported along with tobacco, but its psychotropic effects were more difficult to exploit because the active compound decayed when the leaves dried out. Caffeine, especially in the context of coffeehouse culture, probably had a considerable effect on literary culture, but it was nonobvious because the costs of caffeine-fuelled creativity were far less conspicuous than those of more powerful psychotropics—although the writer Honoré de Balzac is sometimes said to have been the only man ever to have died of work-related coffee poisoning.

The displacement of beer by industrially-distilled gin in eighteenth-century England was perceived as a significant social menace. The increasing importation of opium from the Far East and its large-scale processing as laudanum was regarded more kindly, because laudanum was the most effective painkiller available throughout the nineteenth century. Its potential role in literary inspiration was popularised by the British *Romantic poets, especially Samuel Taylor Coleridge, who credited *Kubla Khan* to it. Coleridge was first introduced to opium in the form of "bang" by the *botanist Joseph Banks, who supplied psychotropics drawn from distant parts of the world to various willing experimentalists. Thomas de Quincey's *Confessions of an English Opium-Eater* was serialised in the *London Magazine* in 1821—the same year that he introduced the English public to the German writer Jean Paul [Richter], who conceived of poetic inspiration in terms of the activation of "the unconscious".

Coleridge also obtained new means of psychotropic stimulation from the chemist Humphry Davy, whose discovery of nitrous oxide was swiftly followed by his discovery of the delights of its inhalation (as "laughing gas")—an experiment whose frequent repetition in kind was ancestral to a complex modern culture of hazardous inhalation variously known as "glue sniffing" and "solvent abuse". Scientific exploration of the effects of various psychotropic substances—with the willing assistance of literary men—was thus well advanced before the advent of organic chemistry. Its most widely publicised arena of enquiry was *Le Club des Hachichins*—as it was dubbed by Théophile Gautier—whose Parisian experimenters were supplied with materials by the physician Jacques-Joseph Moreau. Moreau published several early studies of psychopathology and was keenly interested in the relationship between genius and madness.

Moreau reprinted Théophile Gautier's account of his experiences under the influence of cannabis, first published in 1843, in his study of *Du haschich et de l'aliénation mentale* (1845; trans. as *Hashish and Mental Alienation*). Charles Baudelaire—whose own membership of the club was brief—also relied on Gautier's observations in his study of "Du vin et du hashish" (1851; incorporated into *Les paradises artificiels*, 1860; trans. as *Artificial Paradises*). Fictional descriptions of similar experimental ventures were included in many of the key documents of the Decadent movement, including J. K. Huysmans' *À rebours* (1884; trans. as *Against the Grain* and *Against Nature*), Jean Lorrain's *Monsieur de Phocas* (1901), and Claude Farrère's *Fumée d'opium* (1904; trans. as *Black Opium*). English fictional accounts of the effects of opium and cannabis, such as Fergus Hume's "Professor Brankel's Secret" (1889), George Griffith's "A Genius for a Year" (1896), and Victor Rousseau's "The Draught of Eternity" (1918; book 1924, bylined H. M. Egbert), seem distinctly underresearched by comparison.

The technological refinement of psychotropic effects made rapid headway in the late nineteenth century. Although morphine was first extracted from

opium in 1805, it did not begin to replace laudanum until Andrew Wood's development of the modern hypodermic syringe in 1853—which facilitated its recreational as well as its medicinal use. In 1874, C. Alder Wright discovered its acidic derivative diacetylmorphine, which was renamed heroin after 1898 when a German pharmaceutical company began its industrial manufacture and gave it a brand name. Cocaine was extracted from coca in 1880, and techniques for its purification were rapidly perfected when its potential as a local anaesthetic was discovered; Sigmund *Freud became one of its earliest medical advocates. Amphetamine was first synthesised in 1887, but its properties were not extensively investigated until the 1920s, when it became significant as a stimulant, being more powerful in that respect than caffeine and less toxic than other compounds previously used to procure similar effects.

The literary subgenre of hallucinatory fantasies—which extends from earnest visionary fantasies presented as quasi-religious revelations to hectically anarchic dream fantasies offered as the purest possible form of entertainment—took considerable inspiration from these advances. Real and imaginary psychotropic drugs were routinely used as facilitating devices in such works from the mid-nineteenth century on, as in J. Sheridan le Fanu's "Green Tea" (1869), Algernon Blackwood's "A Psychical Invasion" (1908), and Arthur Conan Doyle's "The Adventure of the Devil's Foot" (1910). Speculative writers also began to investigate hypothetical psychotropic effects, in such works as Robert Louis Stevenson's *Strange Case of Dr. Jekyll and Mr. Hyde* (1886). Such fantasies became commonplace in pulp science fiction and fantasy; notable examples include Clark Ashton Smith's "The Light from Beyond" (1933) and "The Plutonian Drug" (1934), J. Harvey Haggard's "Fruit of the Moon-Weed" (1935), Stanton A. Coblentz's "The Glowworm Flower" (1936), and George O. Smith's "The Hellflower" (1952; book, 1953).

The twentieth-century continuation of psychotropic research and experimentation was inhibited and confused by legal controls, whose most spectacular manifestation was the U.S. Volstead Act of 1919, prohibiting the sale of alcohol. The act had to be repealed in 1933, but its brief reign had a tremendous effect on American culture, facilitating the evolution of organised crime and its attendant corruption of the police and judiciary—developments vividly reflected in the evolution of American crime fiction, which was infected with a "hard-boiled" cynicism whose legacy proved extraordinarily powerful. Prohibition also generated a new subgenre of fantasy fiction celebrating the disinhibitory effects of alcohol, whose chief proponent was the humorist Thorne Smith. Smith's extravagant accounts of the beneficial effects that uptight Americans might derive from psychotropic "loosening up" were widely imitated, producing a number of speculative fictions featuring mass releases of inhibition, ranging from Vincent McHugh's light-heartedly satirical *I Am Thinking of My Darling* (1943) and Fletcher Pratt's amiable *Double Jeopardy* (1952) to David H. Keller's grimly paranoid "The Abyss" (1947).

The catastrophic experience of 1920s prohibition did not inhibit governments in the United States and elsewhere from imposing similarly stringent restrictions on other psychotropic substances, thus preserving organised crime and promoting "secondary deviance" on a massive scale as addicts of various drugs were driven to crime to fund their habits. Although a good deal of fiction was produced that fell into step with political policy in attempting to demonise psychotropic drugs, the more significant literary response took advantage of that demonisation in order to mount an ideological opposition, liberally seasoned with hard-boiled cynicism, in documents that became central to the development of a mid-twentieth-century "counterculture", ranging from relatively flirtatious works such as Aleister Crowley's *Diary of a Drug-Fiend* (1922) to extravagantly avant-gardist works such as William S. Burroughs' *The Naked Lunch* (1959). It was against this cultural background that progress in organic chemistry produced a host of new psychotropic products.

These new products included newly purified extracts from traditional sources, such as DMT (dimethyltryptamine), from the virola tree, but many were synthesised in the laboratory. MDMA (3.4 meth-ylene-dioxy-methylamphetamine), first produced in 1912, became popularly known as ecstasy. Whole families of psychotropic drugs were developed, including tranquillisers derived from chlorpromazine in the late 1950s and tricyclic antidepressants, launched in the same period but replaced in the late 1980s by a new generation of drugs whose most popular exemplar was Prozac. Tranquillisers prompted an ambivalent literary response, in such accounts of mass pacification as John Gloag's *Manna* (1940) and Mark Clifton's "The Conqueror" (1952). Far the most significant of the new drugs in terms of literary influence was LSD (lysergic acid diethylamide), first produced by Albert Hoffman in 1938 as a secondary derivative of the natural alkaloid ergotamine.

Hoffman discovered LSD's powerful hallucinogenic effect in 1943, and the process of its popularisation began almost immediately. It attracted considerable attention from the military, whose scientific advisers had become intensely interested in the possibility of developing a "truth serum" (in which

capacity the off-touted sodium pentothal had proved disappointing). More significantly, its potential as a generator of religious experience was loudly advertised by Timothy Leary, who began experimenting with it in 1961 after undertaking similar adventures with "magic mushrooms".

The attempted rehabilitation of psychotropic effects as a route to raw religious—or "transcendental"—experience was well under way by the time Leary got involved. A determined attempt at its popularisation had been made in 1954, when Aldous Huxley published *The Doors of Perception*. In *Heaven and Hell* (1956), Huxley went on to argue that there must be a psychophysiological basis for the "sense of wonder", and commented on certain common features of reported hallucinatory experiences; when the book was reviewed in *Astounding Science Fiction*, P. Schuyler Miller had no difficulty in finding the same features in fantasy fiction—and agreed with Huxley that the motifs might be losing their effect as it was blunted by overfamiliarity. A broadly sympathetic response to such propaganda was featured in Evan Hunter's "Malice in Wonderland" (1954), in which champions of "vicarious experience" (Vikes) are portrayed as heroic rebels against repressive addicts of dull reality; the sensitivity of the subject was reflected, however, in the choice of the by-line Hunt Collins for its book length expansion *Tomorrow's World* (1956), although it was reprinted in a later era under the author's more famous pseudonym, Ed McBain. Algis Budrys' account of "lobotomol" in "The Sound of Breaking Glass" (1959) is more typically anxious. The advent of LSD, however, changed the attitudinal climate dramatically.

LSD seemed a more attractive proposition than such alternatives as mescaline, and it was advertised far more cleverly by the trans-American bus trip undertaken in the early 1960s by Ken Kesey and his "merry pranksters"—colourfully detailed in Tom Wolfe's *The Electric Kool-Aid Acid Test* (1967)—while the substance was still legal. Leary's advocacy of the drug—especially his coinage of the slogan "Turn on, tune in, drop out"—helped place it at the core of a rapidly evolving counterculture, which produced a spectacular harvest of "psychedelic" literature and music. The most widely consumed products were rock music lyrics by such bands as Jefferson Airplane, the Grateful Dead, Pink Floyd, and the Moody Blues, which imported LSD into the heart of pop culture—an achievement recognised in the widespread (but false) rumour that the title of John Lennon's "Lucy in the Sky with Diamonds" (1967) was an encoded ad.

Direct fictional responses to the LSD fad included such stories as Thomas M. Disch's "Invaded by

Love" (1966)—in which pills that cause everyone to love one another destroy civilisation—William Tenn's "Did Your Coffee Taste Funny This Morning?" (1967; aka "The Lemon-Green Spaghetti-Loud Dynamite-Dribble Day"), Dean R. Koontz's "The Psychedelic Children" (1968), and Brian Aldiss' *Barefoot in the Head* (1969), and such films as *The Trip* (1967) and *Easy Rider* (1969). Heroin continued to feature in such speculative fictions as Ted Thomas' "The Swan Song of Dame Horse" (1971), but accounts of futuristic addiction were more often inclined to cut out the chemical middleman and feature direct neurological stimulation of the brain's "pleasure centres".

The ideological recoupling of hallucinogenic drugs with transcendental experience prompted a boom in speculative fiction featuring extravagant psychotropic effects, whose notable produce included John Brunner's *The Gaudy Shadows* (1960; exp. book, 1970) and *The Dreaming Earth* (1963), Stephen Bartholomew's "Last Resort" (1963), Philip K. *Dick's amphetamine-fuelled *The Three Stigmata of Palmer Eldritch* (1964), *Now Wait for Last Year* (1966), *Flow My Tears, the Policeman Said* (1974), and *A Scanner Darkly* (1977), Norman Spinrad's "Subjectivity" (1964), "The Weed of Time" (1970), and "No Direction Home" (1971), Christopher Anvil's "Is Everybody Happy?" (1968), John Rackham's *Ipomoea* (1969), Paddy Chayefsky's *Altered States* (1978; film, 1980), and James Morrow's *The Continent of Lies* (1984). The tone of such stories varied from wild enthusiasm to dark tragedy via ironic ambivalence, but all of them testified to a seemingly widespread discontent with the limitations of ordinary consciousness. As the fad began to lose its fashionability, however, the ironic component of such fiction became increasingly corrosive, darkly reflected in such works as Gwyneth Jones' *Kairos* (1988) and extrapolated into flippant sarcasm in such stories as Alexander Jablokov's "The Ring of Memory" (1989).

The neurological basis of psychotropic effects was gradually clarified in the last decades of the twentieth century following the discovery of endorphins (endogenous morphines) in 1975. The physiological roles of neurotransmitters—including epinephrine, dopamine, and serotonin—were determined, along with the psychotropic effects of their stimulation and inhibition. This resulted in a considerable sophistication of the explanatory jargon underpinning such stories as Lucy Sussex's *Deersnake* (1994), Gregory Frost's *The Pure Cold Light* (1993), and Leah Bobet's "Bliss" (2004), although their story arcs tended to follow familiar trajectories. The most significant development in late twentieth-century psychotropic fantasy was the emergence of new competition in the form of a whole new field of hallucinatory fantasy associated with the notion of *virtual reality. Accounts of virtual reality often used psychotropic drugs as facilitating devices, as in Jeff Noon's *Vurt* (1993), but the emphasis on the calculated and computerised production of synthetic experience diminished the elements of spontaneity and bizarrerie that had formerly seemed so vital to psychotropic transcendence, drastically altering the spectrum of its perceived potentialities and dangers.

PUBLICATION, SCIENTIFIC

The dissemination of information, as technologically transformed by the development of *writing and its mechanisation by printing. Both developments were vital to the evolution of science.

The publications now regarded as early classics of science used all the standard formats of philosophy, including the dialogue and narrative poetry, but became increasingly focused on the essay or treatise, whose *rhetoric was formulated to create an impression of extreme objectivity, in which reported facts and extrapolations drawn from them by logical or mathematical reasoning appeared to speak for themselves. The formalisation and formularisation of scientific publication was assisted by the regular reprinting of papers presented orally to various learned societies for appraisal and discussion. Anthologies of such presentations became prolific during the eighteenth century as the number of specialist societies increased and their meetings became more formal and formulaic. Their format helped to cement the image of science as a collective, collaborative, and highly methodical endeavour.

The notion of publishing a periodical comprising scientific papers, to be sold for profit rather than being distributed as a service to a society's members, originated in France. François Rozier launched *Observations sur la physique, sur l'histoire naturelle et sur les arts* in 1771; it survived the revolution and the Napoleonic wars, although its editors' insistence on mounting a stern opposition to Antoine Lavoisier's new chemistry reduced its significance considerably before it folded in 1823. Its regular and reliable schedule made it more appealing to members of the Académie des Sciences than the Académie's own *Mémoires*, which were routinely subject to two-year delays.

The British Royal Society and such specialist analogues as the Linnaean Society, the Geological Society, the Zoological Society, the Royal Astronomical Society, and the Royal Botanic Society—which all issued records of their proceedings, transactions, or annals— were subject to the same relaxed scheduling as their French equivalents in the late eighteenth century, and material awaiting publication piled up as the pace of progress accelerated. When the journalist William Nicholson founded the *Journal of Natural Philosophy, Chemistry and the Arts* in 1797 and Alexander Tilloch launched a rival *Philosophical Magazine* in 1798, a new era of independent scientific publication began in Britain. Responsibility for the printing of the latter periodical was taken over in 1800 by Richard Taylor, who printed most of the society periodicals; his firm, subsequently renamed Taylor & Francis, became the leading scientific publishing company in nineteenth-century London, assisted by the development of mechanised printing presses driven by steam engines.

The *Philosophical Magazine*, which initially accepted papers across a broad range of sciences, saw off such early rivals as *Annals of Natural Philosophy* (founded 1813), but as the volume of submissions grew and rival journals found success in specialisation, it began to specialise in physical science and to hive off companions such as the *Annals of Natural History* (founded 1838) and *The Chemical Gazette* (founded 1842). The pattern was replicated in the United States, where the *American Journal of Science and Arts* (launched 1818) soon dropped the last two words of its title and became increasingly specialised as rivals sprang up. By the mid-nineteenth century, generalisation was largely the prerogative of popular periodicals, although new journals like *Nature* (founded 1869) and *Science* (founded 1880) bid for a privileged centrality, with some success; the latter journal, initially funded by Thomas *Edison, ceased publication in 1894 but secured its fortunes following its revival when it was incorporated into the membership package of the American Association for the Advancement of Science in 1900.

As twentieth-century science became increasingly prolific and specialised, so did the journals in which it was published; as with other forms of publication, the process of diversification was interrupted by both world wars, but the period following the end of World War II saw a dramatic proliferation of new and more specialised journals, and the advent of such international journals as Elsevier's *Biophysica Acta* (launched 1947) and Taylor & Francis' *International Journal of Radiation Biology* (launched 1959). The structural formalisation of the scientific paper was by now complete, although the standardisation of bibliographies was complicated by rival formats. The establishment of summary abstracts permitted the growth of a secondary layer of journals whose function was to provide thematic indices of the primary journals. The singular judgement of journal editors was gradually replaced in this era by a system of "peer appraisal" in which papers submitted to journals would be judged by pairs or panels of experts in the relevant field.

The economics of scientific publication developed in an idiosyncratic fashion, quite distinct from the economics of other kinds of publishing. The anthologies produced by the learned societies and distributed to their members were not commercial products, and did not pay their contributors. The journals of the early nineteenth century were commercial products, and some of them did begin paying their contributors in the same way as other commercial periodicals, but many never did—partly because so many society members merely wanted to accelerate the process of getting their work into print. Those journals that did make payments soon began to lose out in economic competition with those that did not. The situation might have been reversed as the number of journals proliferated, but priority of publication became such an important aspect of academic status and advancement that a pattern developed by which authors willingly donated their publications to scientific journals, then went on—if there was any demand—to produce popularisations of their ideas for more generalised popular periodicals.

This pattern was strongly reemphasised in the twentieth century, when publication became the currency by means of which academic careers were structured, to the point where some journals began to charge their contributors fees in order to fund the process of peer appraisal, which was gradually transformed into a competitive marketplace. As academic publishers adopted the peer appraisal system, it became commonplace for the readers passing judgement on submissions to be paid considerably more than the author of the book was ever likely to receive in royalties. The struggle to obtain priority of publication increasingly favoured "prepublication" in the form of letters notifying readers of journals that a significant paper was in the works, and—whenever a discovery had news value in the context of newspaper *reportage—"publication by press release". The advent of electronic publication via the Internet posed a considerable threat to the journal system, which had come to seem oppressive to many working scientists.

The net result of this evolutionary process was the development of an economic dichotomy between scientific publication and literary publication that was as great as, if not greater than, the dichotomy that had developed between the rhetorical style of scientific papers and literary works. This significantly increased the difficulty of building bridges between the scientific and literary worlds, in spite of the commercial and stylistic hybridisation of "popular science". When the editor of *Nature* approached well-known science fiction writers with a view to running a series of speculative vignettes in its pages, a dispute immediately developed as to whether the writers would be paid for their work (as was their normal expectation) or not (as was the journal's habitual practice). The vignettes—for which a modest fee was eventually paid—were published between November 1999 and December 2000, but the economic problems that would have arisen in connection with a potential book version did not encourage their subsequent reprinting. This illustrates the fact that the cultural divide between science and literature has a material dimension as well as an attitudinal one, which exerts its own inhibitory effects on bridging exercises.

PYTHAGORAS

The legendary founder of a Greek school of philosophy, who was allegedly born in Samos, although he was said to have settled in Croton after fleeing his native isle, eventually dying near the end of the sixth century B.C. He appears in the historical record as the first of a significant series of inspirational teachers whose intellectual efforts helped lay the foundations of natural science, his key ideas being further developed and selectively refined by *Plato and *Aristotle. The Pythagoreans believed in metempsychosis (the transmigration of souls) and hence in the kinship of all living things—a notion that remained a pervasive influence on Western mystical thought and resurfaced within a cosmic context in the idea of *palingenesis.

The most important contribution to the development of science attributed to Pythagoras was the empirical discovery—presumably by the analysis of notes sounded by plucked strings of various lengths—that musical intervals are representable as *mathematical relationships. This became an iconic illustration of the general notion that mathematical analysis might provide a key to the comprehension of all the transactions of nature. The Pythagoreans pursued this quest in various ways, symbolising it by means of an emblem known as the "tetractys of the decad": a triangular arrangement of ten dots with four at the base, tapering through rows of three and two to a single dot at the apex.

The Pythagoreans laid the foundations of *geometry that were subsequently codified by Euclid, although they were probably not responsible for what became known as Pythagoras' theorem, which states that the square on the hypotenuse of a right-angled triangle is equal to the sum of the squares on the other two sides. They did important early work in arithmetic, although they were reputed to have been horrified by the discovery of "irrational numbers", which are not expressible as fractions. They developed a model of the universe whose fundamental harmonising principle they described as "the *music of the spheres"—a

notion echoed in many subsequent *cosmological models, from Plato to John *Kepler. Their insistence on seeking keys to understanding in mathematical relationships laid the foundations for scientific measurement and quantification, and also left a legacy of puzzles and enigmas whose attempted solution was an important driving force in the development of pure and applied mathematics.

Neo-Pythagoreans of the first century B.C., led by Apollonius of Tyana, tried to synthesise Pythagorean ideas with such later philosophical developments as Platonism and Stoicism. They were forced by the syncretic nature of their aim to emphasise the analogical correlations between different schools, which tended to mystify the elements of their own tradition. That strategy of mystification, and the resulting elaborations of such disciplines as *astrology and numerology, laid important groundwork for the holistic inclinations of the neo-Pythagoreans' direct intellectual descendants, the neo-Platonists, and for the subsequent evolution of *occult science; Pythagoras was awarded a central role in the mythology of the "Hermetic tradition".

Literary representations of Pythagoras are scarce, although he is featured in Willis Brewer's *The Secret of Mankind* (1895) and is present in spirit in numerous historical occult fantasies of the sort pioneered by Edouard Schuré. Generous literary homage has, however, been paid to his theories, whose colourful imagery recurs in countless literary fabulations and *contes philosophiques*, from Plato's story of Er to Paul Di Filippo and Rudy Rucker's "The Square Root of Pythagoras" (1999). His ideas were often derided by commentators—from Heraclitus, in the fifth century B.C., onwards—so his reputation acquired a conspicuous ambiguity, reflected in such tongue-in-cheek references as that of the Scottish writer Robert MacNish, who signed himself "A Modern Pythagorean" after setting a precedent in the irreverent comedy "A Metempsychosis" (1826).

The neo-Pythagorean Apollonius of Tyana, on the other hand, had the dubious distinction of being posthumously promoted as a miracle-working rival to the Christ of the gospels in a fictionalised biography written by Philostratus in the third century A.D. The reputation as a magician thus foisted upon him was imported into numerous striking literary representations, including one in Alexandre Dumas' *Isaac Laquedem* (1853). One particular anecdote from Philostratus, reproduced in Robert Burton's *Anatomy of Melancholy* (1621), became the basis for several nineteenth-century works, including John Keats' "Lamia" (1820)—the poem into which he incorporated his fervent indictment of "cold philosophy" on the grounds of its attempt to "unweave the rainbow".

R

RADIATION

The emission of energy. The most familiar forms of radiation are *light and radiant heat, the directly sensible aspects of solar radiation and Earthly *fire. The notion of radiation became much more complex in the context of nineteenth-century physics, when light and heat were integrated in a more elaborate electromagnetic spectrum by James Clerk Maxwell. That spectrum was elaborated in the ultraviolet direction to accommodate the *radio waves detected by Heinrich Hertz in 1887 and the x-rays discovered by Wilhelm Röntgen in 1895, while the infrared direction—which accommodated radiant heat—was further extended into "microwave radiation".

Röntgen's discovery had an immediate and powerful effect on the popular imagination, by virtue of the ability of x-ray *photography to display skeletal features concealed within flesh—which soon became the basis of a new kind of stage "magic". Early dramatisations of this facility included George Griffith's "A Photograph of the Invisible" (1896) and Clara Holmes' "A Tale of the X-Ray" (1898), but the imaginative impact extended far beyond that as speculative writers began to attribute all kind of miraculous powers to hitherto undiscovered "rays", further encouraged by Henri Becquerel's discovery in 1896 of the radioactivity of uranium. Marie Curie's discovery of radium in 1898 made her a heroine of feminism, often pictured holding up a glowing test tube, in a pose reproduced in many other illustrations of scientific enlightenment. The radium glow—technologically exploited in luminous watches—became a potent indicator of miraculous science at work in all manner of visual representations, including cinematic ones.

The radium glow seemed benign and gentle at first—when it was often confused with phosphorescence—so many of its early literary appropriations, including Edgar Mayhew Bacon's "Itself" (1907) and Richard Dehan's "Lady Clanbevan's Baby" (1915), attributed curative and creative powers to it. It infuses luminous alien Murani with astonishing powers—including interplanetary flight at light speed—in J. Henry Harris's *A Romance in Radium* (1906), and confers "x-ray vision" on the protagonist of Guy de Teramond's *L'homme qui voit à travers les murailles* (1914; trans. as *The Mystery of Lucien Delorme*). X-rays were credited with their own curative powers in such romances as Gertrude Atherton's *Black Oxen* (1923). The priorities of melodrama ensured, however, that rays would be swiftly adapted as *weapons in future *war fiction, which soon became replete with "death rays", disintegrator rays, and "heat rays" like those deployed by H. G. *Wells' Martians.

Pierre Curie distinguished alpha and beta radiation in 1900, while Pierre-Ulrich Villard added gamma radiation to the set in the same year. Alpha radiation was found to consist of helium ions, beta radiation of electrons—the elementary particles of *electricity—and gamma radiation of high-energy photons. Frederick Soddy's popularisation of radioactivity in *The Interpretation of Radium* (1909; the highly speculative last chapter was omitted from subsequent editions) inspired numerous scientific romances. It exerted a particularly strong influence on "John Taine" (the mathematician Eric Temple Bell), most obviously on *Green Fire* (written 1919; published 1928). The French writer Léon Groc developed a similar fascination; *L'autobus évanoui* (1914) features telepathy induced by radioactivity, *Le chasseur de chimères* (1925) is an early fictional treatment of nuclear disintegration, and "La révolte des pierres" (1930; book version as *Une invasion des Sélénites*) features radioactive mineral life on the Moon.

Such was the enthusiasm for new rays that much excitement was generated in 1903 by René Blondlot's announcement of the discovery of N-rays, which were allegedly emitted by x-ray tubes but were subject to prismatic refraction and polarisation. Blondlot's colleague at the University of Nancy, Augustin Charpentier, published supportive papers and three hundred more articles appeared in the next three years, although R. W. Wood of Johns Hopkins had visited Nancy in 1904 and had proved the rays illusory by secretly removing and replacing Blondlot's prism from the apparatus. This became an oft-quoted anecdote: a moral fable warning against the scientific hazards of "the eye of faith". Fictional N-rays were featured in Gustave Mertins' *A Watcher of the Skies* (1911)—in which they are the medium of thought—and E. Charles Vivian's *Star Dust* (1925).

The iconography of the skeletal x-ray photograph and the radium glow was further augmented by Johannes W. Geiger and Walther Müller's radiation counter, first devised in 1908, whose accelerated clicking became a key signal of invisible menace in science fiction movies. Rays of all kinds became key facilitating devices in pulp science fiction from its inception, although their already clichéd status was reflected in such blithely irreverent treatments as C. Sterling Gleason's account of "The Radiation of the Chinese Vegetable" (1929).

The seeming benignity of radiation soon proved deceptive, and awareness grew of the dangers of "radiation sickness". Workers in watch-making factories who licked their radium-impregnated paintbrushes to a fine point began to develop oral cancers in frightening profusion, and scientists working with radioactive compounds and x-rays—including both Curies and another feminist icon, Rosalind Franklin—became martyrs to their work. In 1927, Wilhelm Müller discovered that radiation caused *mutations in fruit flies—another development that had an immediate impact on the popular imagination, making radiation into a prolific source of *monsters, especially in mutational romances of the kind pioneered by John Taine.

New technological applications of electromagnetic radiation continued to appear throughout the twentieth century, but the only one to reproduce something of the imaginative impact of x-ray photography was radar, whose development began in the 1930s at the U.S. Naval Research Laboratory and became crucial as World War II approached. Britain, France, and Germany all had working systems in 1939, and raced to improve them year by year as the war progressed; the U.S. Navy rejoined the race with all due fervour in 1942. The science fiction writer Arthur C. Clarke played a leading role in radar research in Britain, while Isaac Asimov, Robert A. Heinlein, and L. Sprague de Camp were all employed in the U.S. Naval Research Establishment. The battle of rival radar technologies proved vital to the war in the air, playing a major role in determining the outcome of the conflict between the Royal Air Force and the Luftwaffe that became known as the Battle of Britain.

The advent of the *atom bomb in 1945 immediately stimulated anxieties about the biological effects of radiation produced by "radioactive fallout" from atomic explosions, as garishly featured in Roger P. Graham's pulp science fiction novel *So Shall Ye Reap!* (1947; by-lined Rog Phillips). These fears were supplemented by similar anxieties about radioactive isotopes contained in waste from *nuclear power stations, with the result that the word "radiation" became a significant bugbear of late twentieth-century common parlance. The infiltration of the term by reflexive horror is clearly reflected in crime thrillers where radiation is used as a means of murder, including Eden Phillpotts' *The Fall of the House of Heron* (1948) and Gerald Heard's *Murder by Reflection* (1942), although it is deployed with much greater extravagance in countless post-holocaust fantasies.

In the meantime, further applications continued to emerge; radiocarbon dating methods were developed in the mid-1950s. Radioactive tracers, first used in studies of plant metabolism in 1948, were widely employed in medicine in the mid-1950s, when radioactive isotopes became increasingly plentiful as by-products of nuclear reactors. Radiation was also used in the treatment of cancer and in the sterilisation of food and medical supplies. The development of lasers in the 1960s was hailed by many observers as a vindication of early romances featuring miraculous rays.

Radiant entities discovered by astronomers became increasing exotic as radio *astronomy and x-ray astronomy extended and complicated their observations; such phenomena as pulsars and quasars played a key role in the development of a growing fascination with the idea of *black holes, while the discovery of the cosmic background radiation provided important confirmatory evidence of the *Big Bang theory. The discovery of an x-ray "burster" in 1973 gave rapid birth to the idea of gamma-ray bursters emitting a lethal tide of radiation: the ultimate *disaster scenario, as employed in Greg Egan's *Diaspora* (1997).

The danger posed to astronauts by radiation was gradually integrated into earnest accounts of space travel, often in association with hypothetical protective technologies such as the one featured in Michael F. Flynn's "The Washer at the Ford" (1989). The dangers posed to the Earth by a potential alteration in the Earth's protective magnetic field and the disappearance of the atmospheric ozone layer were also added to the imaginative lexicon of the disaster story. By the end of the twentieth century, radiation had suffused throughout the entire spectrum of speculative fiction.

RADIO

The production and reception of signals transmitted through space as electromagnetic *radiation. The possibility was anticipated in Robert Duncan Milne's "The Great Electric Diaphragm" (1879) before being demonstrated by Heinrich Hertz in 1886. The phenomenon was developed technologically for the purpose of wireless telegraphy by Guglielmo Marconi, who moved to England and patented his system in 1896. He transmitted signals from his base on the Isle of Wight across the English Channel in 1899, having already sent the first paid radiotelegram in 1898 as a publicity stunt when he was visited by Lord Kelvin. His first transatlantic transmission in 1901 attracted even more public attention, quickly reflected in such literary works as Rudyard Kipling's "Wireless" (1902).

The progress of wireless telegraphy was hastened by the discovery and development of electronic vacuum tubes—John Ambrose Fleming's diode in 1904 and Lee DeForest's triode in 1907—and by the ability of radio to transmit speech as well as Morse code. Popular fiction began to make prolific use of the technology, especially in spy thrillers such as Eden Phillpotts and Arnold Bennett's *The Statue* (1908). Many ships were equipped with radio equipment by 1910, when the murderer Henry Crippen was undone by a radio transmission to the ship on which he had taken flight and radio distress signals alerted the world to the sinking of the *Titanic*.

Amateur radio enthusiasts proliferated rapidly enough to require regulation—to prevent their interfering with official broadcasts—by 1911. Lee DeForest was prosecuted for mail fraud in 1913 when he suggested that it would soon be possible to transmit speech across the Atlantic as a way of advertising stock in his company, but the American Telephone & Telegraph Company (AT&T) did indeed contrive a transatlantic speech transmission in 1915. In 1916, the Marconi Company recommended that transmitting stations be established in the United States for the broadcasting of speech and music.

The implementation of the latter proposal was delayed by U.S. involvement in World War I—during which amateur radio use was strictly banned—so members of the German Army were the first beneficiaries of entertainment broadcasts in 1917. The first public broadcasting station in the United States, KDKA, was established in Pittsburgh in 1920. Early advertisements for radio broadcasting included the movie serial *The Radio King* (1922), produced by Universal Studios in association with *Radio News*; the serial itself did not survive but a novelisation by George Bronson Howard and Robert Dillon did.

Hugo *Gernsback's WRNY broadcast live music and scientific lectures on a regular basis in 1928, but Gernsback went the way of many technological pioneers when he went bankrupt in 1929, just before the boom in broadcast radio took off. The U.S. President Herbert Hoover declared that it was inconceivable that such a powerful medium should be allowed to fall into the hands of advertisers, but within five years that is exactly what happened in the United States. Governments in Europe kept a much tighter rein on the technology—which was thus permitted to play a key role in Adolf Hitler's achievement and maintenance of political power in Germany. The United States had, however, to introduce a regulatory authority—which eventually grew into the Federal Communications Commission (FCC)—to arbitrate the fierce competition for waveband space.

Early extrapolations of radio in speculative fiction included Ralph Milne Farley's series begun with *The Radio Man* (1924; book, 1948), in which radio becomes a means of *matter transmission, and Norman Matson's *Doctor Fogg* (1929), in which an advanced radio receiver intercepts a message from space—thus anticipating the subgenre of *SETI fantasies. The development of radio and the evolution of genre science fiction were closely connected by virtue of Hugo Gernsback's involvement in both; his initial ventures into magazine publishing were extensions of mail order catalogues selling technical apparatus, especially radio hardware, to hobbyists. His science fiction pulps continued to advertise the potential of the technology loudly, at least until his bankruptcy.

Notable pulp science fiction stories foregrounding radio technology included Raymond Z. Gallun's "Old Faithful" (1934), Eric Frank Russell "The Great Radio Peril" (1937), Bertrand L. Shurtleff's "Silence Is—Deadly" (1942), George O. Smith's Venus Equilateral series (1942–1947), and Fredric Brown's

"The Waveries" (1945). In Henry Kuttner and C. L. Moore's "The Twonky" (1942; by-lined Lewis Padgett), an advanced radio set turns out to be a mechanical wolf in sheep's clothing. The rapid spread of radio provided an incidental boost to the *parapsychological notion of telepathy, which was frequently reconceived as "mental radio". The notion of human brains picking up actual radio signals was only rarely deployed, although Anthony Pelcher's "The Soulless Entity" (1931) features a neurological adaptation facilitating such reception.

Radio dramatisations of science fiction, beginning with the space operatic adventures of Buck Rogers in 1932, helped popularise the genre, and the panics sparked by Orson Welles' notorious Mercury Theater adaptation of *The War of the Worlds* in 1938 provided a spectacular demonstration of the power of science fiction imagery as well as the medium's authority. Advertising-dominated U.S. radio went in for melodramatic dramatisation on a massive scale, but the British Broadcasting Corporation (BBC), pretentiously run as a public service by its Calvinist director-general, John Reith, developed a very different tone and manner. In spite of these differences, radio dramas in the United Kingdom and the United States were equally subject to the restrictions and opportunities of the medium, whose absence of visual display was ingeniously compensated by acoustic special effects that soon established their own symbolic vocabulary.

In the United States, dramatisation was standardised, but the BBC featured an abundance of short stories and serial novels that were simply read aloud. Stories specifically written for radio broadcasting were, however, adapted to the medium in being brief and carefully measured, often making deft use of punch lines. Gernsback's scientific lectures were swiftly banished from U.S. radio, but the BBC became an important medium for popularisers of science such as James Jeans and Fred *Hoyle. Speculative fiction was, however, largely excluded from BBC broadcasting—save for occasional interjections by H. G. Wells and Olaf Stapledon—until Reith was persuaded to relax his narrow standards during World War II in order that morale could be maintained by "light entertainment".

When the war was over, a BBC "light programme" was permitted to continue broadcasting thereafter. Among many other experiments, it played host to a number of science fiction serials—including *The Other Side of the Sun* (1950) by Paul Capon, *Spaceways* (1952; book, 1953) by Charles Eric Maine, and *Journey into Space* (1953; book, 1954) by Charles Chilton—which greatly assisted the popularisation of the genre in Britain. The U.S. anthology series *Dimension X* (launched 1950; retitled *X Minus 1*

before its demise in 1958) provided a similar boost, especially to the magazine *Galaxy*, from which its writers borrowed many of the stories they adapted. By the mid-1950s, however, radio was in the process of being overtaken as a medium of broadcast mass entertainment by *television.

Although TV swiftly replaced radio as the most important form of home entertainment, the process was retarded by the relative portability of radio receivers—especially after the advent of transistor radios—and the fact that radio was more compatible with other activities, especially in the provision of a sonic "background". From the 1960s onwards, the most important venues of radio reception, in cultural terms, were the bedroom and *automobile, where its deployment exerted a highly significant pressure on the evolution of popular music.

Speculative fiction foregrounding radio technology became much sparser in this period, although the limitations of radio in interplanetary and interstellar communication—as dramatised in Floyd L. Wallace's "Delay in Transit" (1952)—became a significant thorn in the side of images of galactic *colonisation. Notable exceptions include John M. Iggulden's *Breakthrough* (1960), which describes a radio-facilitated dictatorship, Christopher Anvil's sarcastic "Two-Way Communication" (1966), which features a problematic "back-talker", and Christopher Hodder-Williams' *The Silent Voice* (1977), in which radio interference with human thought causes delusions.

By the end of the century, a hundred years after the technology's debut, writers of speculative fiction had to go to extraordinary extremes to make radio interesting as a futuristic topic. Examples of such extremes include Robert Reed's "Frank" (2000), in which a talk show host uses quantum interface machines to broadcast to a vast audience of alternative selves, Cory Doctorow's "Liberation Spectrum" (2003), in which a multinational company markets "cognitive radio", and Geoff Ryman's *Air (or Have Not Have)* (2003), which features a communication system that allows the Internet to be broadcast directly into people's heads.

RELATIVISM

A philosophical position based on the assertion that beliefs have no universal validity, being the arbitrary products of particular social groups at particular times.

*Ethical relativism seems to have been implicit in the arguments of Greek Sophist philosophers, but became unfashionable as Greek philosophy developed further. It was abhorrent to the moral absolutism of the religious systems that dominated Western philosophy thereafter, and its gradual resurgence after the Renaissance was slow and tentative. *Aesthetic relativism has always been much more acceptable, in spite of attempts by aesthetic philosophers to establish objective criteria of beauty and literary merit. The popular adage "one man's meat is another man's poison" is usually used in an aesthetic context, although it is occasionally cited in moral contexts, reflecting an overlap between the two fields. By contrast, relativism in matters of factual belief is relatively rare, at least with respect to "brute facts" that cannot be denied; scientific theories are sometimes regarded with greater suspicion.

The development of empirical science involved a separation of judgements of fact from judgements of value, on the grounds that only judgements of fact could be supported empirically, and thus be proved true. The erosion of the privilege of authority in dictating matters of fact inevitably cast doubt on authoritarian judgements of moral value, but the lack of any obvious means of ethical judgement other than authoritarian presupposition provided a tacit endorsement of ethical relativism and created awkward problems for secular moral philosophy. It was mainly for this reason that science was seen by many observers—including many litterateurs—as a manifest threat to the moral order of society.

Relativistic suspicions began to creep back into science with a growing awareness of the extent to which empirical observation was shaped and limited by the senses—an idea broached in Voltaire's *Micromégas* (1752), which features *alien beings with much more elaborate sensoria. A careful distinction between the phenomenal world of experience and the noumenal world of "things in themselves" was made by Immanuel Kant's *Critik der Reinen Vernunft* (1781; rev. 1787; trans. as *The Critique of Pure Reason*). Auguste Comte's *positivist philosophy of science responded to this dimension of uncertainty with a crusade to minimise the margin of error inherent in phenomenal observation, but its extrapolation ultimately proved the impossibility of its ultimate extinction, thus giving new hope to supporters of various kinds of alternative belief, including numerous subspecies of *occult science.

In the twentieth century, the adoption of a relativist standpoint became a methodological principle in the context of *ethnology, as a reaction against the tendency of early ethnologists to load the notion of "primitive" society with evaluative judgements. The necessity of withholding all judgements of that sort, in the interests of scientific neutrality, was insistently argued by such practitioners as Melvile J. Herskovits, in *Man and His Works* (1948). Ethnological data had

already been extensively cited in earlier attempts to sustain the view that there are no moral absolutes and that all ethical judgements are relative, most conspicuously in the calculatedly provocative works of the Marquis de Sade, whose production and reception illustrate the difficulty relativist philosophers encountered while making headway in the toils of Christendom. Sade had not been willing to argue that other societies' judgements of fact could be taken equally seriously, by comparison with the rewards of the Enlightenment, but ethnologists can only obtain an understanding of the complexity and coherency of a particular tribal society's ethnobotany, ethnoastronomy, ethnochemistry, and so on by setting aside their own concepts.

In the wake of the ethnological popularisation of cultural relativism and the development of the Marxist theory of *ideology, it became increasingly common for Kantian doubts regarding the limitations of human senses as a guide to objective reality to be used to sustain the view that alternative accounts of empirical reality are self-validating in exactly the same way as alternative moral systems, and that the presumed objectivity of Western science is a self-serving sham. Such a position tends to be a methodological presupposition of *postmodernist thought, and is frequently adopted by proponents of various kinds of *pseudoscience, especially practitioners of alternative *medicine. It is a view that lends itself to more elaborate and extensive development in speculative fiction than naturalistic fiction; the use of exotic hypothetical viewpoints—including those of *aliens and *artificial intelligences—to explore the implications of both moral and empirical relativism became a standard strategy of science-fictional *contes philosophiques*.

Extreme theoretical relativism attracts as little sympathy among writers of *hard science fiction—whose "hardness" is contained in its commitment to the objectivity of facts and the solid competence of theories in the physical sciences—as it does among dogmatic religious believers, but it is recognised there as a kind of metaphysical "nightmare scenario", whose force is illustrated by the perverse popularity of Arthur C. Clarke's relativist parable "The Nine Billion Names of God" (1953).

RELATIVITY

The noun derivative of the adjective "relative", which forms a contrasted pair with "absolute", referring to entities that can only be defined by comparison with other entities rather than in isolation. In *physics, the theory of relativity refers to the specific proposition that time and space are not independent of one another but different aspects of a "space-time continuum", and that their experience and measurement may vary according to the velocity of the observer.

The idea that space and time are relative terms was advanced and dramatised by Camille *Flammarion in *Lumen* (1866–1869), which points out that because the velocity of *light is constant and finite, fast-moving observers would be able to see distant events in slow or accelerated motion, while observers travelling faster than light would see events happening in reverse order. Flammarion's relativity is, however, a subjective illusion; Albert *Einstein adopted the contrary hypothesis that all observers would perceive the same constant velocity of light, and that observers whose standpoints were moving rapidly relative to one another would experience time and space differently, thus eliminating the incompatibilities identified by Flammarion. In this view, it would be impossible for any object, as perceived from another standpoint, to accelerate to or beyond the velocity of light. The special theory of relativity, developed by Einstein in 1905, dealt with the propagation of electromagnetic phenomena in space and time; the general theory propounded in 1916 expanded its scope to incorporate a new theory of *gravity.

Einstein's theory provided an explanation of the failure of an experiment carried out by Albert Michelson and Edward Morley in 1887 to determine the velocity of the Earth relative to the luminiferous *ether by measuring the velocity of light at opposite points of the Earth's orbit. They had found that the velocity seemed to be almost identical irrespective of the direction in which the Earth was moving. George Fitz-Gerald and Hendrik Lorentz pointed out that the result could be explained by the hypothesis that the Earth was "foreshortened" in the direction of its movement through the ether, to a degree that varied with its velocity. Einstein's theory proposed that exactly such a foreshortening—which became known as the Lorentz-Fitzgerald contraction—must become apparent in an object moving rapidly relative to the point of measurement, although it would not be evident to observers within the object, whose "frame of reference" would be different.

The stern challenge to psychological *plausibility posed by consequences of relativity theory became a key factor in the increasing distance that opened after 1905 between theoretical physics and common sense. Popularisers of science made several heroic attempts to make the consequences of the theory imaginatively graspable; a notable one cast in fabular form is featured in George Gamow's *Mr. Tompkins in Wonderland* (1939). Attempts to test the theory of relativity by observation and experiment became highly significant endeavours of twentieth-century science; Arthur

Eddington made a loudly publicised expedition to observe a solar eclipse in 1919, with the intention of discovering whether the light of distant stars was deflected as it passed close to the Sun, as predicted by the general theory. A hypothetical experimental test is featured in H. R. Wakefield's parodic story "Imagine a Man in a Box" (1931).

One consequence of the relativistic disassociation of frames of reference, often used to illustrate it, is the "twin *paradox", whereby a twin who leaves Earth in a spaceship that accelerates to a relative velocity close to that of light would prove, on his return, to have aged less than his Earthbound brother. The time dilatation effect is featured in numerous science fiction stories, including Miles J. Breuer's "The Fitzgerald Contraction" (1929) and "The Time Valve" (1930), Fredric Brown's "Placet Is a Crazy Place" (1946), L. Ron Hubbard's "To the Stars" (1950; book 1954 as *Return to Tomorrow*), James Blish's "Common Time" (1953), Poul Anderson's "Ghetto" (1954; incorporated into *Starfarers*, 1998) and *The Long Way Home* (1955; aka *No World of Their Own*), Robert Heinlein's *Time for the Stars* (1956)—which actually features a pair of time-dissociated twins—Charles L. Fontenay's *Twice upon a Time* (1958), Vladislav Krapivin's "Meeting My Brother" (trans. 1966), Joe Haldeman's *The Forever War* (1975) and "Tricentennial" (1978), Larry Niven's *A World out of Time* (1976), Tom Allen's "Not Absolute" (1978), George Turner's *Beloved Son* (1978), John Varley's "The Pusher" (1981), and Robert L. Forward's "Twin Paradox" (1983). Carol Hill's *Amanda, the Eleven Million Mile High Dancer* (1985) includes a more elaborate exploration of the theory's fabular potential.

If the time dilatation effect is taken to its logical extreme, it permits such a radical disjunction between the reference frame of a spaceship and that of its initial reference frame that a human lifetime aboard the ship might outlast the lifetime of the universe—a possibility displayed in such science fiction stories as Poul Anderson's *Tau Zero* (1970) and Frederik Pohl and Jack Williamson's *The Singers of Time* (1991). The radical implausibility of such extrapolations helps to sustain the use within science fiction of facilitating devices that defy relativity theory by permitting faster-than-light travel, simultaneously avoiding the conceptual problems generated by different frames of reference and the narrative problems caused by galactic distances.

The imaginative challenge posed by Einstein's relativity theory is further increased by variants of it. The Dutch astronomer Willem de Sitter published a paper on the general theory in 1917 that suggested that the curvature of space would cause the radiation spectra of distant objects to be red-shifted—though not to the extent actually observed when Edwin Hubble and his associates began tabulating galactic red-shifts. Variants of relativity theory were, however, invoked by such theorists as E. A. Milne to provide interpretations of galactic red-shifts that challenged the *Big Bang theory. The extra strain put on plausibility by unorthodox science-fictional extrapolations of the theory—such as the one featured in A. E. van Vogt's "Rogue Ship" (1950; aka "The Twisted Men")—tends to work against them, so they are rarely attempted. The relationship between the scientific notion of relativity and other notions, including those implicit in various notions of *relativism, is explored in Alan Lightman's account of *Einstein's Dreams* (1993).

RELIGION
A system of *metaphysical beliefs associated with reverential rites. Most religions involve belief in and worship of one or more gods, although Buddhism reveres human teachers whose accounts of universal metaphysics do not include a personalised creator. The religions of literate cultures usually focus on scriptures that contain definitive accounts of its doctrines, which are often held to have been divinely inspired. The adjectival form of the term is often used in the phrase "religious experience", referring to the alleged apprehension or intuition of metaphysical reality, which usually consists of brief intervals of revelation.

Although the religions of different cultures vary markedly—and usually constitute the most obvious manifestations of cultural difference—religion seems to be a universal feature of human society, implying that its basic features are deeply rooted in human psychology, although not so uniformly as to produce an effective unanimity of belief. Seemingly trivial differences in doctrine can, however, produce fierce enmities; religion is sometimes manifest as phobic intolerance of difference and dissent, even when its basic moral tenets include the instruction to be tolerant. This observation confuses attempts to account for the social and psychological functions of religious faith. On one hand, religion seems to promote a sense of community solidarity and peace of mind; on the other, it appears to make individuals holding variant beliefs seem dangerously alien, promoting a sense of threat severely injurious to peace of mind.

Religion is often conceived as antithetical to science, based on the fact that religious faith is founded in arguments from authority and scientific knowledge in arguments from experience, and the two are therefore in fundamental disagreement as to how intellectual disputes should be arbitrated. On the other hand, the two modes of thought have always coexisted, and Western science emerged from and within a culture whose primary organisation was religious. The perceived threat posed by science to Western religion was countered intellectually by attempts to construe it as "natural *theology", and attempts by scientists and religious men to find compromises or to construe the two disciplines as complementary rather than antithetical persisted throughout the twentieth century, alongside such manifest struggles as the one between *Creationism and evolutionism.

Attempts to study religion scientifically as a social phenomenon were initially confined to the consideration of tribal and ancient religions within the contexts of *ethnology and *anthropology. It was, however, impossible to avoid the implication that the generalisations contained in such summary works as Charles-François Dupuis' *L'origine de tous les Cultes ou Religion universelle* (1795) and Andrew Lang's *The Making of Religion* (1898) could not also be applied to Christianity and other major extant religions. Similarly, attempts to analyse the individual psychology of faith and revelation, such as Edwin Starbuck's *The Psychology of Religion* (1889) and William James' *The Varieties of Religious Experience* (1902), were methodologically committed to treating the central and most fundamental attribute of faith and revelation—the conviction of truth—as a phenomenon requiring explanation rather than something to be taken for granted.

Early anthropological studies of religion embraced the evolutionism that dominated the science, trying to account for changing patterns of belief in terms of movements from animism through polytheism to monotheism, associated with shifts in conceptions of causality. This was, in essence, an extrapolation and elaboration of Auguste Comte's "law of the three stages", which imagined human thought progressing from theological explanations through metaphysical explanations to *positivist (that is, scientific) explanations. James Frazer's version of the evolutionary sequence described the three phases as magic, religion, and science. One post-Frazerian analysis, popularised in Robert Graves' *The White Goddess* (1948), suggested that the worship of Mother Goddesses had been replaced by the worship of All-Fathers, assisted if not prompted by the discovery of paternity and the consequent shift in patterns of inheritance from matrilinearity to patrilinearity. Another construed the legend of Abraham—which is fundamental to Judaism, Christianity, and Islam—as an allegory of the abandonment of human sacrifice in favour of animal sacrifice as a key rite of divine palliation.

The twentieth-century decline in the fashionability of Comtean and evolutionist explanations was reflected in the growth of theories of religion of a markedly different stripe. For instance, Greg Retallack attempted to account for ancient differences in the conception of deities in terms of *ecology, correlating the various gods to which Greek temples were dedicated with the types of soil on which they were erected, and hence to the agricultural possibilities of the surrounding terrain. In broader terms, the argument held that agriculturalist tribes usually worship gods associated with their specific surroundings and productive activities, while nomadic tribes usually worship singular gods identified with the sky. In this thesis, the Abrahamic religion was originally produced by recently settled nomads, and their continued success in periods of rapid social evolution was due to their celebration of dynamic processes such as colonisation.

Early images of religion in fiction inevitably viewed them from a standpoint of religious faith, but all accounts of hypothetical religions inevitably raise questions similar to those addressed by sociologists and psychologists of religion, sharpened by the dissatisfactions writers usually feel with regard to the imperfections of their own religious culture. The construction of such images was greatly encouraged in Christendom by Martin Luther's calls for reform and the consequent evolution of Protestantism. Thomas More's *Utopia* (1516), the product of a man sufficiently devout to be appointed a saint, features an extensive discourse on the subject of "natural religion", whose extension remained central to the tradition of *Utopian satires and romances for the next two hundred years as Utopian writers struggled to design better religious cultures and organisations, and to explain why existing religious observance and its associated institutions seemed to have gone so badly awry.

Whether literary representations of imaginary religions were designed in order to mount vitriolic satirical attacks on real ones or to offer earnest visions of better ones, their authors had to view the phenomenon of religion in a quasi-scientific way while their endeavours remained overtly and proudly fictional. Thinkers and writers who could not set aside their own propensity for faith produced new cults rather than literary images. Some such cults withered on the vine, while others thrived. Numerous Utopian writers crossed this divide, or became confused as to which side of it they were on; the tendency extended to *occult scientists such as Emmanuel *Swedenborg, practitioners of quack *medicine such as James Graham (whose Temples of Health and Hygiene lost their fashionable appeal when he decided that they

were indeed the temples of the New Jerusalem), and even to pulp science fiction writers like L. Ron Hubbard.

Dramatic priorities ensured that the most striking and memorable images of fictional religion were the horrific and comic ones; earnest attempts to design happy and peaceful religious cultures provide a perfect illustration of the limitations of eutopian fiction, achieving the worst possible combination of implausibility and tedium. The appeal of melodrama has never been confined to the literary sphere; it has always played a significant role in the politics of persecution, which routinely represent the religious ideas of the groups to be attacked as Satanic, whether they were Christians in certain phases of the Roman Empire, Jews in the days of the Spanish Inquisition, Knights Templar in the sights of an avaricious French king, or alleged perpetrators of twentieth-century child abuse. The stigmatisation of tribal religion by means of the same accusatory libels—especially cannibalism and human sacrifice—was a central element of the ideological armoury of colonialism and imperialism as well as a staple of adventure fiction.

Fictional representations of horrid religions tend to be constrained by a diplomacy that pales their reflection of actual accusations. Only fantasies represented as "nonfiction" can be used—as they routinely are—to justify torture and murder on a massive scale, so fictional representations may be held more virtuous in spite of their accomplice role. On the other hand, fictional representations of comic religions tend to be gleefully undiplomatic, even though the savagery of their satirical assaults is often masked by conspicuous playfulness, and are usually steadfastly opposed to the excesses associated with fantasies of horrid religion, so the virtue of such works as Samuel Butler's *Erewhon* (1872), James Branch Cabell's *The Cream of the Jest* (1917), and Bertrand *Russell's "Zahatopolk" and "Faith and Mountains" (both 1954) is far more obvious. Theocracies are frequently employed in speculative fiction as paradigms of arbitrary despotism, starkly opposed to liberal cultures in such works as Neal Asher's Polity series begun with *Gridlinked* (2001) and Iain M. Banks' Culture series.

The depiction of religion in historical fiction was also affected by the politics of persecution, which became one of the most significant topics within the genre. Creatively confined as it is by the supposed facts of recorded *history, which leave a relatively narrow margin for elaborations of secret history, historical fiction inevitably derives much of its narrative energy from lamentation and fervent partisanship, and the history of religious persecution offered abundant scope for the cultivation of a heady cocktail of empathy and outrage—as it does, of course, in the scriptures. The subgenre of "Biblical epics" recycles doctrinal tales as novels, using new narrative techniques to enhance the effects of the originals, sometimes greatly elaborating incidents that obtained only passing mention in the Testaments.

Fiction dealing with the history of the Christian church routinely draws, in similar fashion, on documents compiled by churchmen in order to cash in on the same combination of empathy and outrage, such as the thirteenth-century *Golden Legend* compiled by Jacobus de Voragine and John Foxe's sixteenth-century "Book of Martyrs". Historical treatments of conflicts between religion and science are sometimes given a similar slant, as in many accounts of the near-martyrdom of *Galileo, and examples of historical speculative fiction tend the same way; Patricia Anthony's *God's Fires* (1997) suggests that the Spanish Inquisition would not have been a suitable institution to deal with visiting aliens and their contactees.

The nostalgic element of religious conviction, which supposes that faith must have been stronger in the *past—having been subjected to a thinning process similar to that corroding the mythic past— and therefore stands in constant need of "revival", is also extravagantly developed in historical fiction, extrapolated in timeslip stories such as SMC's *Brother Petroc's Return* (1937) and Upton Sinclair's *Our Lady* (1938), although the imaginative component of such endeavours inevitably generates a sceptical opposition, represented by such works as G. G. Coulton's *Friar's Lantern* (1906).

Early speculative fiction based in various forms of scientific theory made no conspicuous attempt to escape the literary tradition portraying hypothetical religions as horridly or comically absurd. Indeed, its fundamental assumption that the very idea of religion is absurd sometimes exaggerated these tendencies, although early writers of scientific romance like H. G. *Wells and M. P. *Shiel had a manifest regard for the Comtean notion of designing rituals that would duplicate the socially cohesive effects of religion while disposing of such inconvenient and unaesthetic notions as God. A similar respect for "sacred scepticism" continued to echo in such twentieth-century works as Pierre Boulle's *Histoires perfides* (1964; trans. as *The Marvelous Palace and Other Stories*), whose stories are narrated by a minister of the Religion of Doubt.

Because genre science fiction originated in the United States during a period whose moral climate was symbolised by Prohibition, it tended to follow a diplomatic policy similar to that of Jules *Verne (who did not want to offend his devout family by making his own atheism public), so the religious beliefs of *aliens were initially disregarded, although "fake" religions explicitly designed for purposes of covert social control—such as the Durna Rangue cult introduced in Neil R. Jones' "Escape from Phobos" (1933)—were a different matter. Even that restricted licence soon began to generate more challenging corollaries, however; Robert A. Heinlein conscientiously balanced the evil fake religion in "If This Goes On ..." (1940) against the well-intentioned fake religion in *Sixth Column* (1941; by-lined Anson MacDonald; book, 1949). It only required one small step thereafter for Cleve Cartmill's "With Flaming Swords" (1942) to reintroduce an element of sharp satire, and one more for Fritz Leiber's *Gather, Darkness!* (1943; book, 1950) to provide a virtuous fake Satanism as a remedy for an evil fake godliness.

Once genre science fiction's early diplomacy began to wane, it soon evaporated; after World War II religion became a significant topic within the genre, explored in numerous *contes philosophiques* that gained extra appeal from their "taboo-breaking" efforts. Walter M. Miller's *A Canticle for Leibowitz* (1955–1957; book, 1960) painstakingly mapped out the role played by a neo-Catholic Church in the rebuilding of society after a nuclear holocaust—and in paving the way for the next such holocaust. Many such stories engaged directly with matters of theology, but accounts of alien religious institutions became commonplace in the second half of the twentieth century; notable examples include Robert Silverberg's *Nightwings* (1969) and *Downward to the Earth* (1970), George R. R. Martin's "A Song for Lya" (1974), Gregory Benford and Gordon Eklund's *If the Stars Are Gods* (1974; fix-up, 1977), Rachel Pollack's *Alqua Dreams* (1987), and Dan Simmons' *Hyperion* (1989).

The problems of exporting existing religions within the context of a galactic diaspora were subject to analysis in numerous accounts of problems faced by interstellar missionaries, including Katherine MacLean's "Unhuman Sacrifice" (1958), Harry Harrison's "The Streets of Ashkelon" (1962), James White's "Sanctuary" (1988), and Maria Doria Russell's *The Sparrow* (1996). The narrative pattern is satirically reversed in D. G. Compton's *The Missionaries* (1972) and James Patrick Kelly's "The Glass Cloud" (1987). The proposition has been made several times that the human religious culture best adapted to coexist with alien ones is that of the Society of Friends, by virtue of its emphases on pacifism, sobriety, and tolerance, but accounts such as Joan Slonczewski's *Still Forms on Foxfield* (1980), Judith Moffett's *Pennterra* (1987), and Molly Gloss' *The Dazzle of Day* (1997) also take care to point out that such tendencies have often resulted in Quakers becoming refugees fearful of their own species. The galactic diaspora is supervised by a militant ecclesiastical organisation in Robert Silverberg's "We Are for the Dark" (1988).

The use of improvised religions in the instrumentality of future tyranny was further explored in such late twentieth-century genre science fiction stories as James E. Gunn's *This Fortress World* (1955), Zack Hughes' *The Stork Factor* (1975), Dean McLaughlin's "Dawn" (1981), Keith Roberts's *Kiteworld* (1985), K. W. Jeter's *The Glass Hammer* (1985), Stephen Leigh's *The Bones of God* (1986), Lawrence Watt-Evans' *Shining Steel* (1986), and Grey Rollins' "Ashes to Ashes" (1998). Such accounts were, however, supplemented by more ingeniously various accounts of religions improvised by human societies in the context of a galactic diaspora or in post-holocaust conditions; notable examples include Robert A. W. Lowndes' "A Matter of Faith" (1952; by-lined Michael Sherman; exp. book as *Believers' World*, 1961), John Brunner's *Rites of Ohe* (1963), Sylvie Louise Engdahl's *This Star Shall Abide* (1972; aka *Heritage of the Star*), Richard Cowper's "Piper at the Gates of Dawn" (1976; incorporated into the U.S. edition of *The Road to Corlay*, 1978) and its sequels, John Morressy's *The Mansions of Space* (1983), and Frank Herbert and Bill Ransom's trilogy comprising *The Jesus Incident* (1979), *The Lazarus Effect* (1983), and *The Ascension Factor* (1988).

Accounts of religions improvised in response to specific existential and ecological circumstances were also developed in respect of *artificial intelligences such as *robots and *androids, as in Robert F. Young's "Robot Son" (1959), Roger Zelazny's "For a Breath I Tarry" (1966), Gordon Eklund's "The Shrine of Sebastian" (1973), and Alastair Reynolds' "Angels of Ashes" (1999). Humans sometimes become objects of reverence in such stories, as they also do in Robert Silverberg's "The Pope of the Chimps" (1982), but are more often treated as obstacles to salvation. Some such accounts imagined complex collaborations in the improvisation of new religions; the one in Clifford D. Simak's *Project Pope* (1981) is a human-robot coproduction. The system-wide Syncretist Church of the Transcendental High in Glen M. Bever's "Snowball at Perihelion" (1975) is one of several attempts to design a church specifically adapted to a burgeoning *Space Age. Borders between science and religion are blurred in a more complex manner in Ray Brown's "Credos" and "Identity Crisis" (both 1983), in which future religious evolution produces a hectic multitude of new and recycled cults.

The potentially problematic future of existing religions became a significant topic in such stories as Riley Hughes' *The Hills Were Liars* (1955), Robert Silverberg's "Good News from the Vatican" (1971), Connie Willis' "Samaritan" (1978), Richard Bowker's

Forbidden Sanctuary (1982), Jack Dann's "Jumping the Road" (1992), and James Morrow's "Auspicious Eggs" (2000). The satirical tone adopted by many works of this sort obtained more extravagant expression in accounts of new cults arising in opposition to existing ones, as in L. M. Fallaw's *The Ugglians* (1956) and its sequel, Kurt Vonnegut's *The Sirens of Titan* (1959), *Cat's Cradle* (1963), and *Slapstick* (1976), Robert F. Young's "L'Arc de Jeanne" (1966), Kate Wilhelm's *Let the Fire Fall* (1969), Gerald Jonas' "The Shaker Revival" (1970), Greg Bear's *Heads* (1990)—whose Logologists are modelled on Hubbard's Scientologists—and Frederik Pohl's "Redemption in the Quantum Realm" (1994), in which the Holy Church of Quantum Redemption attempts to answer the enigma of why wave functions retain their *uncertainty if God is an observer.

Earnest extrapolations in a similar vein include Robert Silverberg's *To Open the Sky* (1967) and several works by John Barnes, notably *The Man Who Pulled Down the Sky* (1987) and *Sin of Origin* (1988). Barnes carried his interest in the politics of religion forward into the Thousand Cultures series comprising *A Million Open Doors* (1992), *An Earth Made of Glass* (1998), and *The Merchant of Souls* (2001). Ed Naha's *The Suicide Plague* (1982), which features the Church of the Ancient Astronauts, is one of several stories in which the people of hypothetical future eras see the myth of the Space Age for what is it is, but elect to dress it with religious reverence. Greg Egan's "Oceanic" (1998) describes the ideological conflict of the Deep Church and the Transitionals in a *posthuman context.

*Time travel was increasingly used in the twentieth century as a means of investigating the history of religion, hypothetical explorers frequently targeting the crucifixion as an item of investigation, as in Michael Moorcock's *Behold the Man!* (1966; exp. 1969), Brian Earnshaw's *Planet in the Eye of Time* (1968), Garry Kilworth's "Let's Go to Golgotha" (1975), and Barry N. Malzberg's *Cross of Fire* (1982). *Alternative history was similarly used to explore different ways in which Christendom might have developed, in such works as Keith Roberts's *Pavane* (1968), Kingsley Amis' *The Alteration* (1976), and Robert Charles Wilson's *Mysterium* (1994).

One of the side effects of the late twentieth-century boom in speculative fictions foregrounding religion was a backlash of futuristic religious fantasies, strikingly exemplified by Tim LaHaye and Jerry B. Jenkins' best-selling Left Behind series (1995–2003). The series was founded on the proposition that the authority of Biblical prophecy is absolute, but in expanding that thesis to generate additional empathy and outrage—after the fashion of pious Biblical epics—it could not help taking aboard various elements of futurological thought, which tended to confuse that assumption. The ultimate fictional religion is, of course, the Great New Fictional Religion (GNFR) featured in Fay Weldon's *Rules of Life* (1987), whose deity is Our Writer.

REPORTAGE

The recording of contemporary occurrences, especially as practised in the pages of European and American newspapers from the early eighteenth century onwards. There was always a marked division between respectable news media that gave priority to the workings of government, the exploits of royalty, the conduct of international relations, and major economic transactions and popular news media—such as the eighteenth-century "broadside"—whose stock-in-trade was the sensational reportage of crime, punishment, and "marvels".

The sociopolitical role of respectable newspapers was generally supposed to be that of informers of democratic society, as enshrined in the principle of the freedom of the press. As the economics of newspaper production evolved, however, the money obtained from their selling price declined in proportion to the money obtained from advertisers; the priorities of reportage shifted in parallel, becoming more closely reflective of the interests of their readers, and their informative role was increasingly compromised. Although the gap between respectable and popular news media never closed, it became gradually narrower as time went by.

This shift affected both the nature of events covered by reportage and the manner of the coverage, eventually producing a situation in which newspapers tend to be organised according to the geography and hierarchy of their audiences—the basic axes of differentiation being national/local and broadsheet/tabloid—regulating their attention accordingly. Reportage was increasingly permeated by the methods and priorities of narrative theory, producing "news stories", while the "news value" of events in the world became heavily dependent on such factors as human interest, local interest, and—above all—melodramatic potential. Long before the advent of weekly and daily newspapers, the "news" sections of almanacs had been dominated by personal advice and tales of "prodigies" of various kinds; the personal, the monstrous, and the allegedly miraculous continued to provide a steady flow of news value throughout the modern history of reportage.

By the beginning of the twentieth century, this process of evolution had created a situation in which the primary function of reportage was to provide an incentive for newspaper readers to expose themselves to advertising, and in which many of the events reported in newspapers only happened in order that they might be reported. The implicit ironies of this situation ensured that journalism would become the most cynical of all twentieth-century professions, reflected in such judgements as William Randolph Hearst's dictum that "news is what someone wants to stop you printing; all the rest is ads". The trend was noted by several nineteenth-century writers of futuristic fiction, but the only one who seems to have been fully alert to its import was Albert Robida, who has the heroine of *Le vingtième siècle* (1882; trans. as *The Twentieth Century*) try out several jobs, finding news reportage to be the most absurd, corrupt, and hazardous of them all.

The reportage of science was, inevitably, subjected to exactly the same pressures as the reportage of other social processes as this evolution occurred. The initial assumption that the reportage of scientific discoveries would reflect their importance was undermined from the beginning by the difficulty of estimating that importance, given that the crucial nature of particular findings is often realised only in retrospect. The assessment of events in the world of science according to their "news value", however, introduced more drastic distortions. The priorities of human interest and melodrama exerted a powerful influence on the choice of discoveries to be reported, the manner of their reporting, and an occasional willingness to invent such material—a propensity dramatically illustrated by the entirely false reportage by Richard Adams Locke of the discovery of lunar life by Sir John Herschel, published in the New York *Sun* in August 1835.

A respectable tradition of science journalism developed in the nineteenth century in connection with the *popularisation of science, to which articles in periodicals made a considerable early contribution. Robert Hunt's frequent contributions to the scientific column of the *Athenaeum* in the 1840s and 1850s provided paradigm examples for others to follow. Such columns were, however, more common in monthlies and weeklies than in daily newspapers, and when daily papers did carry such features, they usually restricted them to a weekly schedule. That remained standard practice throughout the twentieth century, contriving a literal marginalisation of science journalism within the world of reportage. In order to make the news pages rather than being retained in specialist columns, science stories had to contain news values of exactly the same kind as conventional news stories, in broadsheets as well as tabloids.

The scientific columns of twentieth-century newspapers tended to be written by "guest" contributors, or by specialists educated in science, but science stories in the news pages were more often written by staff reporters—and when specialist reporters moved from their dedicated columns into the news pages they tended to adapt their style and manner to suit the different environment. As the century progressed, the specialist columns were subject to pressure to increase their news value—a process which became strikingly evident in the evolution of science reportage on *television, where the TV equivalent of specialist columns, documentaries, were considerably transformed in the latter half of the twentieth century, according to the principles of "infotainment". The intensified competition generated by the advent and proliferation of satellite, cable, and digital channels accelerated this trend, even in channels supposedly specialising in didactic material.

One result of this pressure was the personalisation of science reportage, which began increasingly to concentrate on the "human interest" aspects of scientific discoveries, emphasising the life stories of scientists and their involvement in theoretical rivalries and conflicts, while deemphasising the objective content of their discoveries. This has the effect of construing scientific research as a species of heroic endeavour—which many scientists find flattering—but also of tacitly encouraging the *relativistic view that it is a conflict of ideologies in which success has at least as much to do with personality as empirical arbitration. It is, however, capable of considerable sophistication, as in Jeremy Bernstein's science articles for the *New Yorker* from 1960 onwards—whose method is explained in the first essay in his *Cranks, Quarks and the Cosmos* (1993)—and Alan Lightman's essays on the "human side of science" collected in *Time Travel and Papa Joe's Pipe* (1984) and *A Modern Day Yankee in a Connecticut Court* (1986). A further corollary of the pressure, much less amenable to sophistication, was the evolution of specialist science reporters into a population of "experts" whose utility was determined by their ability to find or manufacture news value in their reportage rather than their scientific acumen.

These institutional arrangements added to the difficulties imposed on reportage by the increasing esotericism of twentieth-century science. Even within specialist columns, popularisers of science had their work cut out trying to explain their subject matter to a lay audience; outside those columns, such efforts were likely to be futile, greatly encouraging reporters to attack that esotericism as an insult to the intelligence of laymen. Resentment of and hostility to the complexities of scientific explanation were readily transformed, in the context of newspaper reportage,

to resentment of and hostility to science itself. This hostility also infected newspaper coverage of science fiction, where it was more easily transfigured into naked contempt—but that did not prevent the intellectual descendants of Richard Adams Locke continuing to find a prodigious utility in science-fictional ideas that could be presented as "facts".

The consistent interest shown by newspaper reportage in the exotically melodramatic furnished Charles *Fort with an abundance of "damned data" for painstaking collection and collation, and the willingness of newspapers to print fanciful material played a leading role in the development of such *pseudosciences as cryptozoology, such occult practices as *astrology, and such modern *myths as *flying saucers. The tendency of such items to proliferate during the August "silly season" reflects both the annual slowdown in the production of political and business news during holiday seasons and the fact that it has usually been safer, in the context of modern libel laws, to invent highly fanciful news than false stories about actual people.

The mass production of "celebrity" in the latter part of the twentieth century eased the pressure on editors desperate to fill space—or, in the context of TV, time—by increasing the supply of actual individuals likely to be detected in the commission of exotic and melodramatic exploits (and to engage in such exploits in order that their reportage might sustain their celebrity) but never entirely filled the gap. The margin remained amply able to accommodate another class of mass-produced news items, supposedly scientific in nature, consisting of the reportage of statistics—whether independently produced or manufactured by means of survey techniques—and it also remained exceedingly hospitable to accounts of prodigies. Increasingly, as the twentieth century progressed, reporters looked to science and technology for the production—both actual and hypothetical—of such prodigies. This context coloured the public reception of a great many scientific discoveries and speculations, especially *biotechnological discoveries and speculations capable of generating a "yuck factor". It also created a situation in which scientific "experts" who provided specialist coverage in newspapers and on TV gradually became celebrities too, thus opening the potential for them to be of service in more than one role.

Given this pattern of evolution, there is nothing surprising in the regularity with which tabloids at the bottom end of the newspaper hierarchy routinely use stories whose contents are closely akin to *cinematic B-movies in their casual celebration of the prodigiously bizarre. The U.S. *Weekly World News* and the British *Sunday Sport* take manifest pride and joy in their improvisation of such notorious story head-lines as SPACE ALIEN BABY SURVIVES UFO CRASH and WORLD WAR 2 BOMBER FOUND ON MOON. Nor is it surprising to see controversies whipped up by reportage of genetic modification as "Frankenstein Foods".

This kind of exploitation cut both ways; there was an increasing tendency in the late twentieth century for scientists to take swift advantage of the potential news value of their discoveries. In 1960, Theodore Maiman announced his development of the first laser by press release after *Physical Review Letters* rejected his paper. In 1987, Paul Chur announced his discovery of "high-temperature superconductivity" to the press with the paper still pending. In 1989, B. Stanley Pons and Martin Fleischmann claimed to have discovered "cold fusion" in a press release, perhaps anticipating the difficulty they might have in getting a paper through a peer review. In 1998, Arpad Pusztai issued a press release claiming that genetically modified potatoes "caused toxicity to rats"—an allegation unsupported by the evidence set out in his 1999 paper. Whether this sequence of events reflects a gradual corruption of scientific standards remains controversial, although the practice of "publication by press release" was severely criticised in 2005 by Ben Goldacre in his *Bad Science* column in *The Guardian* (whose *raison d'être* is putting the boot into reckless claims made by advertisers and rival columnists).

The literary reflection of these processes is some-what confused by the prevalence of various myths regarding reporters, the most prevalent being that of the investigative reporter who pursues the news as defined by Hearst with dogged determination, in spite of all obstruction and opposition. Although this is somewhat at odds with the everyday reality of paraphrasing press releases, it thrives because of its narrative utility, and investigative reporters are sec-ond only to detectives in their potential as protago-nists in mysteries and thrillers. It is also supported by the fact that, while processors of press releases are largely invisible, the most conspicuous of all reporters are those engaged in the tedious game of pursuing celebrities with cameras and prurient questions.

Although investigative reporters, in their capacity as literary characters, do occasionally stray over the borders of crime fiction into neighbouring subgenres of science fiction, they are—quite appropriately—more commonly featured in pseudoscience fiction and horror science fiction than any kind of serious speculative fiction. They are particularly prominent in cryptozoological science fiction, stories featuring fly-ing saucers, and stories featuring sinister research installations where horrid investigations are being secretly carried out, although there are exceptions; Alastair Reynolds' "The Real Story" (2002) is a nota-ble example. Accounts of the manipulation of news coverage in the interests of promoting the Space Age often take advantage of the utility of ingenious tech-nology in the manufacture of publicity stunts; James E. Gunn's "The Cave of Night" (1955) is a notable example.

Modern writers of futuristic fiction occasionally follow in Robida's footsteps in satirising the domi-nant trend of the business of reportage, as in Gore Vidal's account of TV coverage of the crucifixion in *Live from Golgotha* (1992) and Mark Rich's account of the tabloid coverage of a first contact in "Foggery" (1996), but are also willing to take a serious interest in the future development of the news media, as in several stories by Norman Spinrad, most notably *A World Between* (1979) and *Greenhouse Summer* (1999), and David Marusek's "VTV" (2000).

RHETORIC

The art and science of persuasion, pioneered in Clas-sical times by the pre-Socratic philosophers who were subsequently labelled sophists. Rhetoric was subjec-ted to considerable criticism by *Plato, who thus gave "sophistry" a bad name; his characterisation of the rhetorician as a "speech-rigger" (*logodaedalus*) took it for granted that rhetoric is basically a form of cheat-ing: a means of cultivating psychological *plausibility at the expense of rational plausibility. *Aristotle dis-agreed; his *Rhetoric* insists on the essential neutrality of the art, and argued that the truth must have its own persuasive support if it is to prevail against falsehood. The scientific method can be regarded as a form of rhetoric—as a means of providing *proof*, without which statements have no justified claim of belief.

Aristotle's support assisted the enthusiastic adop-tion of rhetoric into the educational curriculum of the Roman Empire, where the art of oratory was highly esteemed. It was carried forward into the Mediaeval curriculum of Christian education as an instrument of doctrinal defence, eventually becoming the principal instrument of scholastic philosophers intent on re-conciling Aristotelian wisdom with the dogmas of Christianity. This proved Aristotle's point, by ensur-ing that when new empirical knowledge became avail-able, thanks to applications of the experimental method and the enhancement of observation by new optical devices, its supporters had to be very persua-sive indeed to establish their findings in a hostile intellectual climate. The publications of *Galileo, John *Kepler, Isaac *Newton, and many others are no mere statements of discovery but powerful examples of rhetoric, and such pioneers often had to be as innovative in their rhetorical methods as they were in their techniques of discovery.

Rhetorical theory divides the persuasive process into three basic components: ethos, pathos, and logos (a combination that helps to explain how Alexandre Dumas named two of the three musketeers but cannot account for Aramis). Ethos is an impression of trustworthiness cultivated by the orator or writer. Pathos involves the cultivation of a particular state of mind in the hearer or reader, by means of appeals to emotional or aesthetic sensibilities. Logos is the structure—that is, the *logic—of the argument itself.

Ethos is further divisible into personality and stance. Personality is more relevant to oral discourse, in which an impression of warmth, friendliness, charm, and status can be cultivated by tricks involving body language, eye contact, and tone of voice, with the aim of making the speaker seem knowledgeable, competent, and—above all—honest. Although *writing is intrinsically more impersonal, such matters as the vocabulary, tone, and apparent authority of the discourse remain significant, but the relative importance of stance—where the speaker or writer is "coming from", in terms of attitudes, beliefs, and principles—is considerably greater.

Pathos is as vital to oratory as personality; the ability to control the emotions of an audience—as evangelical preachers do when they attempt to mobilise guilt feelings in order to create a state of mortal terror before offering the hope of salvation—is invaluable in face-to-face situations. The ability to create excessive moral indignation is particularly useful to polemical orators—hence their frequent designation as "rabble-rousers". Writers have less scope in this respect, but manufacturers of popular fiction and newspaper *reportage are easily able to "push the buttons" that obtain a strong reader response to the predicaments of their characters. Such techniques are by no means absent from nonfiction writing that pretends to far greater dispassion. Aesthetic effects, on the other hand, are more suited to writing than oratory, its more subtle effects being reliant on the cultivation of complex ornamentation that is impractical in oral discourse.

Logos is the component of rhetoric that consists of the construction of logical and mathematical proofs, and the marshalling and analysis of empirical evidence; it becomes far more important in writing than in oratory, and writing is vitally necessary to the competent organisation of complex data. Various techniques of presentation are involved in such organisation, whose application has produced such formulas as that of the geometric theorem and the modern scientific paper. Various quasi-oratorical devices that are psychologically rather than rationally persuasive can, however, easily be built into such documents; the simplest are repetition, which exploits the crude psychological rule that what an audience is told three times over it tends to take aboard, and the "QED flourish", with which a logical chain of argument concludes by connecting its end to its beginning, as if closing a circle.

Although the logos component of an argument seems less hospitable to accidental and deliberate deception than ethos or pathos, there are several familiar strategies by which illusions may be constructed, including terminological obfuscation—"blinding with science"—and, more significantly, the ordering of information so as to take advantage of psychological vulnerability to *post hoc ergo propter hoc* reasoning: the innate tendency of the human mind to suppose that if two events or two statements occur in sequence, there is likely to be a causal connection between them.

A language has an inherent rhetoric built into its grammatical structure, but it remains pliable; the careful selection of words and organisation of words into sentences are the primary instruments of rhetoric. Language is naturally prone to such celebrations of its own accidental qualities as wordplay and rhyme, and its usage is routinely subject to such phenomena as wit and irony; the tendency of rhetorical strategies that rely heavily on the component of logos is to formulate special languages supposedly purged of such elements, whereas the tendency of strategies relying more heavily on ethos and pathos is to exaggerate them, but the situation is complicated by the double-edged nature of humour, which may be an asset in developing a personality but implies an unreliability of stance. Wit, especially when it plays with paradoxes, deliberately confuses meaning, thus creating a rhetorical uncertainty useful in satire, whose mockery of logos may be just as intense as its mockery of ethos and pathos.

The rhetoric of science is now standardised; all scientists are supposed to conform to the same model. Its basic strategy is to pretend to set aside matters of personality and emotion, so that its ethical component appears to be a stance of strict objectivity, and its pathetic component purely aesthetic, stressing values of neatness, economy, and elegance. This was not always so; throughout the seventeenth century and for much of the eighteenth—as chronicled in Donald Davie's *The Language of Science and the Language of Literature, 1700–1740* (1963)—many British writers on scientific subjects aspired to "literary style" just as much as writers of fiction or political commentary. Although *The Charters and Statutes of the Royal Society* (1720) specified that "Matters of

Fact should be barely stated, without any Preface, Apologies or Rhetorical Flourishes" it was not until the end of the eighteenth century that plainness of statement became widely seen as a virtue, and then not so much for its own sake, but rather in order that what was written might be more broadly accessible, for the benefit of those who had not the benefit of academic learning. George Gregory's *Economy of Nature* (1798) was by no means alone in proclaiming that it had been written as clearly and plainly as possible "for the sake of female readers".

When the rhetoric of science is used deceptively—whether by mistake or deceptive design—the result is *pseudoscience. Such impostures are supposed to be obvious to the educated eye, but the reality of the situation is more complicated. When a set of data is incomplete, as it very often is—in retrospect, we can see that very few sciences could claim to have recovered even a tiny fraction of the data relevant to a competent understanding of their phenomena before 1900, and we have no guarantee that the same will not appear to be true of 2000 when another century has elapsed—it can be very difficult to eliminate plausible conjectures that might eventually turn out to be utterly mistaken.

Although the rhetoric of science, as embodied in the structure and presentation of scientific papers, is supposed to be transparent, it is not above suspicion. The biologist Peter Medawar broadcast a talk on BBC radio in 1964 entitled "Is the Scientific Paper a Fraud?" in which he argued that the standardised structure is an artifice implying an "inductive" model of discovery—which he attributed to John Stuart Mill—whereby a general conclusion appears to emerge spontaneously out of an array of reported facts. Medawar argued, with reference to Karl Popper's *philosophy of science—that observations and experiments are invariably made with a hypothesis already in mind, and that the structure of the scientific paper tends to obscure rather than highlight this fact. Since 1965, scientific papers have edged in the direction pointed out by Medawar, routinely specifying in advance the hypotheses that the reported observations or *experiments were intended to support or refute—but that too is an artifice, which might not reflect the actual thought process of the scientist at all. Sometimes, scientists really do gather data or try "experiments" simply to see what emerges, only reporting their endeavours if something actually does emerge, and only then attempting to determine what has been demonstrated or proved. Rational plausibility is more often the product of afterthought than the rhetoric of science is prepared to allow.

The rhetoric of fiction is much more flexible in its strategy; although certain features are more common than others, modern litterateurs tend to strive for "originality" in the ethical and pathetic components of their work, routinely aiming to cultivate a distinct personality, stance, and aesthetic impression, although emotional manipulation is more likely to be regarded as a generalised skill. The logical component of literary work, while inevitably reduced in relative importance and often far from central to the concerns of individual works, remains significant; it is worth observing that works of fiction that set out to contrive "nonsense"—including Edward Lear's verses and the fiction of Lewis Carroll—have to be cleverly and coherently organised at the logical level, and that stories that fail ignominiously to "make sense" almost invariably do so by virtue of carelessness. It is also worth noting that works of art that seem devoid of any kind of "argument" in the strictly logical sense often retain a firm discipline in the organisation of their pathetic materials—thus, it becomes possible to speak of an "aesthetic logic" by which such impressions as beauty, sublimity, and elegance are constructed. In general, however, the logos of fiction is more often devoted to the cultivation of psychological plausibility than rational plausibility.

Speculative fiction is only a partial exception to this last generalisation; although advocates of *hard science fiction claim to adhere strictly to principles of rational plausibility, the pretence is compromised by the literary necessity of employing such facilitating devices as time travel, superluminal space travel, and galactic empires. Very little science fiction, even of the hardest stripe, makes any attempt to strike the same objective pose as scientific publication; for the most part, it is entirely content to employ the personality aspect of ethos and the emotional aspect of pathos. In this it bears a strong resemblance to scientific journalism, which similarly reilluminates the personal and emotional aspects of scientific endeavour and discovery.

Within this general pattern, there are certain differences and divergences worthy of note. The rhetoric of science is by no means uniform across the entire range of sciences, its epitome being represented by those areas of science subject to the greatest mathematical sophistication and those that are replete with observational detail. A "narrative science" like *cosmology, although underlain by the observational science of *astronomy and integrated with the theoretical science of *physics, is bound to develop a rhetoric bearing a more obvious resemblance to the rhetoric of narratives in general. Such narrative sciences—the most conspicuous example is *evolutionary biology—tend to lend themselves much more readily to literary adaptation and extrapolation than "purer" sciences, and are considerably more vulnerable to the intrusion of aesthetic devices useful in fiction, as illustrated by various debates between *catastrophists and uniformitarians. Similar intrusions and confusions occur as the data of scientific publication are extended through endeavours in *popularisation to become the subject of specialist and nonspecialist reportage.

Scientific publication attempts to escape the kinds of "literary dishonesty" that inevitably infect other kinds of nonfiction—especially biography and history—in which efforts to "make sense" of what happened are innately polluted by rationalisations and justifications. The success attained by such attempts is variable, and science inevitably retains a certain vulnerability to the kinds of argument it seeks to exclude. Although scientific conclusions are eventually reducible to the results that produce them, the fact that such results have to be obtained, collated, reported, and evaluated by human beings ensures that, in practice, matters of personality cannot be entirely excluded from the ethical element of scientific rhetoric; some people are deemed more trustworthy than others, and findings that gain prestigious support are more likely to be heeded than those that do not. In commanding belief, reputations matter—and so, too, do emotions. No matter how unemotional scientific reportage strives to be, certain statements will still evoke emotional responses in hearers and readers, and those emotional responses are likely to have a profound effect on the manner in which scientific ideas are communicated and received. Science cannot entirely escape the necessity of polemica argument; that is one reason why science is often vulnerable to, and sometimes benefits from, the polemics of fiction.

ROBOT

A term coined by Karel Čapek in his allegory *R.U.R.* (1921), where it describes the artificial labourers who represent the working class; he derived it from the Czech *robota*, meaning forced labour. The label was borrowed by other writers for application to mechanical humanoids capable of being mistaken for human beings, that association being firmly cemented by Fritz Lang's film *Metropolis* (1926). Its application to mechanical devices resulted in organic humanoids of the kind described in *R.U.R.* being more frequently labelled *androids. The term was subsequently applied in a looser sense to industrial machines substituting for human labourers on automated production lines, especially mechanical arms, and to machines capable of self-determined locomotion.

The notion of machines that mimic human or animal form was already old when Čapek's term was appropriated as a label. "Talking statues" are said to have been constructed in the third millennium B.C., and Heron of Alexandria apparently build various automata as toys in the first century A.D. Although the mechanical servant allegedly constructed in the thirteenth century by Albertus Magnus and the talking head allegedly made by Roger *Bacon are certainly mythical, clocks began to be equipped with elaborate automatic striking devices in the fourteenth century and Gianello dell Torre of Cremona built a mechanical figure of a girl playing the lute in the 1540s. A Japanese tradition of theatrical automata was launched in the seventeenth century. There was a considerable vogue in eighteenth-century Europe for the construction of ingenious mechanical automata; the most famous example was a duck designed by Jacques de Vaucanson. The Baron Wolfgang von Kempelen's chess-playing automaton, which became famous in the 1770s, was certainly a fake, although the machine was long gone by the time Edgar Allan Poe published a speculative essay explaining how the deception was achieved.

The literary response to the eighteenth-century vogue was not immediate, but the nineteenth century produced numerous notable fictional automata, including the Talking Turk in E. T. A. Hoffmann's "Automata" (1814), Olympia in the same author's "Der Sandmann" (1816; trans. as "The Sandman"), the hour-striking automaton in Herman Melville's "The Bell-Tower" (1855), and the mechanical musician in Edmund Gosse's *The Secret of Narcisse* (1892); Vaucanson was belatedly referenced in Fredric Perkins' "The Man-ufactory" (1877) and Jerome K. Jerome's "The Dancing Partner" (1893). The famous automata of the era included a "steam man" built by Zadoc P. Dederick of Newark, New Jersey, in 1868, which was featured in the "dime novel" that launched the American tradition of Vernian fiction, Edward S. Ellis' *The Steam Man of the Prairies* (1868; aka *The Huge Hunter*), its invention recredited to the teenage Johnny Brainerd.

"Der Sandmann" and *Metropolis* were elements of a significant subgenre of accounts of automated female beauty, whose early examples also included George Augustus Sala's "The Patent Wife" (1876), the Comte de Villiers de l'Isle Adam's *L'Ève future* (1886; trans. as *The Future Eve* and *Tomorrow's Eve*), and E. E. Kellett's "The New Frankenstein" (1900). Most feature as potential brides; the remainder are servants, as in Howard Fielding's "The Automated Bridget" (1889), Elizabeth Bellamy's "Ely's Automatic Housemaid" (1899), and the anonymous dramatic skit *Mechanical Jane* (1910). It was in the latter context that "male" automata of the kind featured in *R.U.R.* were more widely featured, in such works as Cyrus Cole's *The Auroraphone* (1890), in which the advanced inhabitants of Saturn are served by robotic "dummies", W. M. Stannard's "Mr. Corndropper's Hired Man" (1900), William Wallace Cook's *A Round Trip to the Year 2000* (1903; book, 1925)—which calls its mechanical labourers "mugwumps"—and Charles Hannan's *The Electric Man* (1910). Čapek's story was followed by other dystopian visions in which all work is done by humanoid and other machines, including Henri Allorge's *Le grand cataclysme* (1922), and other accounts of automata turned murderous, including Gaston Leroux's *La machine à assassiner* (1924; trans. as *The Machine to Kill*).

Čapek's term was popularised just in time to be imported into the science fiction pulps in prolific fashion. Early genre stories tended to be stridently alarmist—David H. Keller's "The Psychophonic Nurse" (1928) and "The Threat of the Robot" (1929) reacted violently against the notion that machines could be adequate replacements for human workers—and contrasted strongly with such British scientific romances as J. Storer Clouston's Wodehousian comedy *Button Brains* (1933), in which a robot is continually mistaken for its human model, with amiably farcical consequences; Max Blore's poem "The Robot", which appeared in *The London Aphrodite* in 1929, is also wryly humorous; the spirit of both items survived World War II in Wallace Geoffrey and Basil Mitchell's conspicuously British play *The Perfect Woman* (1948; film, 1949).

Keller's gloomy prognostications were further extrapolated by such works as Abner J. Gelula's "Automaton" (1931), which pioneered a peculiar tradition of stories in which sinister robots become enamoured of human females and are moved to murder by their unnatural lust, and Harl Vincent's "Rex" (1934), whose protagonist conceives megalomaniac ambitious. The use of robots as figures of menace was, however, overtly challenged in the mid-1930s. Eando Binder's "The Robot Aliens" (1935) and "I, Robot" (1939) featured benevolent robots subject to wholly unjustified attacks by humans conditioned to assume that robots must be evil. The latter story, whose robot protagonist realises why people react to him with unreasoning hatred when he reads Mary Shelley's *Frankenstein*, inspired Isaac *Asimov to become a fervent propagandist against the ravages of the "*Frankenstein complex".

Asimov set out to redeem robots from such prejudice in a long series of stories featuring robots whose ethical behaviour was programmed into them in the form of the Three Laws of Robotics: 1. A robot may not injure a human being, or through inaction allow a human being to come to harm. 2. A robot must obey the orders given it by human beings, except where such orders would conflict with the First Law. 3. A robot must protect its own existence as long as such protection does not conflict with the First or Second Law. The laws emerged from "Reason" (1941), but "Liar" (1941) was the first of many Asimov stories formulated as explications of seemingly odd robot behaviour in terms of their logic. The early stories in the series—culminating in "Evidence" (1946), in which a robot politician can only get elected by convincing voters that he is human, but does the job far better than the man he replaces—were collected in *I, Robot* (1950).

Similar sympathy for robots was displayed in many other stories. Ray Cummings' "The Robot Rebellion" (1934) features robots comfortably integrated into human society, although they play a minor role in a revolt, and "The Robot God" (1941) features a megalomaniac robot, but "Zeoh-X" (1939) and "X1-2-200" (1938) featured sympathetic robots, the latter suffering a conflict generated by innate psychological compulsions similar to the Asimovian laws. Other pre-Asimovian examples include Lester del Rey's love story "Helen O'Loy" (1938), Robert Moore Williams' "Robots Return" (1938), whose protagonists overcome the disappointment of discovering that their creators were made of frail flesh, and Joseph E. Kelleam's "Rust" (1939), which describes the tragic decline of mechanical life on Earth. F. Orlin Tremaine's "True Confession" (1940) and Ray Cummings' "Almost Human" (1941) feature altruistic acts of robotic self-sacrifice. A robot is granted a social status superior to its weaker model in Harry Bates' "Farewell to the Master" (1940), while another is a valued member of a starship crew in Eric Frank Russell's "Jay Score" (1941; incorporated into *Men, Martians and Machines*, 1956).

This rehabilitation process continued as robots became clownish comic figures in the stories assembled in Henry Kuttner's *Robots Have No Tails* (1943–1948; book 1952, by-lined Lewis Padgett). The robot servants who survive mankind in Clifford D. Simak's *City* series (1944–1952; book, 1952) are perfect gentlemen's gentlemen rather than mere slaves, and help to ensure that the emergent canine society is conspicuously more polite than the human society it replaces. A cautionary note was sounded by Anthony Boucher, whose "Q.U.R". and "Robinc" (both 1943 as by H. H. Holmes) championed "usuform robots" against anthropomorphous ones, on the grounds that they would be less offensive to human and divine dignity—an argument also put forward in Eando Binder's "Orestes Revolts" (1938).

The real "robots" of the 1930s and 1940s were still set firmly in the tradition of Vaucansonian automata, and were most commonly encountered at science fairs and exhibitions. The London Radio Exhibition of 1932 featured several, most spectacularly the chromium plated giant Alpha, while the New York World's Fair of 1939 featured Elektro, specially designed by the Westinghouse Electric Corporation. Elektro could perform twenty-six different movements in response to spoken commands. Significantly, urban legends had begun to circulate regarding a robot at the Chicago World's Fair which killed its creator, but this did not deter Mechanical Man Inc. from setting up a production line in 1939 to manufacture automatons for use as salespersons. The situation changed in the 1940s, however, when the rapid advancement of *computer science in World War II opened up the actual possibility of equipping such automata with "mechanical brains".

Asimov's endeavours had already helped to establish the robot as a key figure for use in *existentialist fantasies exploring the possibilities of *artificial intelligence. Such stories as Malcolm Jameson's "Pride" (1942)—in which a robot equipped with Asimovian behaviour controls solves his problems by self-lobotomisation—reproduced the pessimism of human existentialism in full force, but other accounts were more optimistic; the dancer resurrected in a robot body in C. L. Moore's feminist fantasy "No Woman Born" (1944) concludes that the robot condition is decidedly preferable to the human. This train of thought was, however, initially handicapped by the consistent use of viewpoints external to the robots' own consciousness. The reports of Asimov's robots were usually filtered through "robopsychologist" Susan Calvin, and Moore's roboticised dancer conveys her feelings in conversation with a male protagonist. Chan Davis' "Letter to Ellen" (1947) uses a standard distancing device, and the self-dissatisfied robot in Poul Anderson's "Quixote and the Windmill" (1950) is also restricted in its self-expression. After 1950, direct explorations of the quality of artificial intelligence became more common—but the enhancement of the idea of robot intelligence was not the only imaginative legacy left by World War II.

After 1945, when the *atom bomb renewed suspicion of technological progress, attitudes to robots in science fiction became noticeably more ambivalent; in 1947, Asimov published his first sinister robot story, "Little Lost Robot", and Jack Williamson published the sceptical "With Folded Hands", in which robot "humanoids" charged "to serve man, to obey, and to guard men from harm" take their mission to unwelcome extremes. Williamson modified this position in the sequel "... And Searching Mind" (1948; rev. as

The Humanoids, 1949) and steadfast robot apologists such as Asimov and Simak followed the example of John S. Browning's "Burning Bright" (1948) in taking up a defiantly defensive stance, but many generic robot stories of the 1950s involved confrontation and conflict.

Robots attempted homicide, sometimes unwittingly but often successfully, in Peter Phillips' "Lost Memory" (1952), Philip K. Dick's "Second Variety" (1953), Margaret St. Clair's "Short in the Chest" (1954; by-lined Idris Seabright)—whose philosophical robot is called a "huxley"—Algis Budrys' "First to Serve" (1954), Asimov's *The Naked Sun* (1956), and Cordwainer Smith's "Mark XI" (1957; aka "Mark Elf"). The mistaken identity motif took sinister turns in Asimov's "Satisfaction Guaranteed" (1951), Philip Dick's "Imposter" (1953), Walter M. Miller's "The Darfsteller" (1955), and Robert Bloch's "Comfort Me, My Robot" (1955).

Robots feature in courtroom dramas in Simak's "How-2" (1954), Asimov's "Galley Slave" (1957), and Lester del Rey's "Robots Should Be Seen" (1958). Human-robot boxing matches were featured in William Campbell Gault's "Title Fight" (1956), Richard Matheson's "Steel" (1956), and Robert Presslie's "The Champ" (1958). Robots became hard moralistic taskmasters in Robert Sheckley's "Watchbird" (1953) and Henry Kuttner and C. L. Moore's "Two-Handed Engine" (1955). Tom Godwin's "The Gulf Between" (1953) argued that the differences between human and robotic understanding would always render robotic obedience deficient, while two robots strive unavailingly to be more human in Richard Wilson's "If You Were the Only—" (1953). Asimov's *Caves of Steel* (1954) brought contemporary anxiety sharply into focus by attempting a close psychological study of its protagonist's antirobot prejudice.

More relaxed attitudes to robots became evident again as the 1950s progressed, wry humour coming to the fore in such stories as William Moy Russell's *The Barber of Aldebaran* (written 1954–1955; published 1995). Robert Bloch's "Dead-End Doctor" (1956) has to treat robots for lack of human customers; the same issue of *Galaxy* included Arthur Sellings' "The Category Inventors", in which the roles are reversed by humans flocking to robot psychiatrists. Other works in the same vein include Robert Sheckley's "Human Man's Burden" (1956), Harry Harrison's "War with the Robots" (1958)—and other items in his similarly titled 1962 collection—Fritz Leiber's *The Silver Eggheads* (1958; exp. book, 1961), and Poul Anderson's "The Critique of Impure Reason" (1962).

Sentimentality returned in full force in Simak's "All the Traps of Earth" (1960) and reached new extremes of sickliness in Ray Bradbury's "I Sing the Body Electric" (1969). Randall Garrett's *Unwise Child* (1962) is set firmly in the Asimovian tradition that sees robot-generated problems merely as puzzles to be solved. Robots acquire a new sense of purpose in Lester del Rey's "To Avenge Man" (1964), and strive to become more human themselves in A. Bertram Chandler's "The Soul Machine" (1969). Sylvia Jacobs' "Slave to Man" (1969) writes erotica. A darker irony was, however, preserved in such stories as Brian W. Aldiss' "Who Can Replace a Man?" (1958) and Robert Sheckley's "The Cruel Equations" (1971).

In the meantime, the first computer-controlled industrial robot arms appeared on production lines in 1960; in the same year, the Hughes Aircraft Corporation built Mobot, a mobile robot designed to work in areas too dangerous for humans. In 1968, the Stanford Research Institute's Shakey, connected to a computer by a cable, was equipped with television camera "eyes" and a "bump detector" to provide the elements of a sensorium; the development of computers using integrated circuits facilitated the establishment of the first specialist robotics company, Unimation Inc., in 1972.

It was against this background of rapid technological advancement coupled with postatomic suspicion that exercises in robot existentialism really took wing, gifted with a new imaginative intensity by Philip K. Dick's analyses of the "android condition" and Stanislaw Lem's robotic fables, whose English versions were collected in *The Cyberiad* (1974) and *Mortal Engines* (1977). Cardinal examples included Barrington J. Bayley's *The Soul of the Robot* (1974) and *The Rod of Light* (1985) and Asimov's final sequence of robot stories, extending from "That Thou Art Mindful of Him" (1974) and "The Bicentennial Man" (1976) to the novels that integrated his robot stories into the future history of his Foundation series, including *The Robots of Dawn* (1983) and *Robots and Empire* (1985). Other notable exercises in robot existentialism from the 1970s and 1980s included Sheila MacLeod's *Xanthe and the Robots* (1977), Walter S. Tevis' *Mockingbird* (1980), Tanith Lee's *The Silver Metal Lover* (1982), and John Sladek's *Roderick* (1980) and *Roderick at Random* (1983). In all of these stories robots share the burden of providing viewpoint characters, sometimes assuming it as a sole privilege.

Robots continued to play sinister roles, as in Roger Zelazny's account of a robot executioner in "Home Is the Hangman" (1975) and John Sladek's account of a robot "psychopath" whose "asimov circuits" have failed in *Tik-Tok* (1983), but the consciousness of such machines now demanded explanation in much the same way as violent tendencies in humans. Robert Reed's *The Hormone Jungle* (1987) features deeply enigmatic robots. The tenor of robotic satire changed dramatically in such works as Barry B. Longyear's *Naked Came the Robot* (1988), in which the ranks of the robot working class are infiltrated by subversives, and Alan Ayckbourn's play *Henceforward* (1988), which added a sharp new twist to the long theatrical tradition of mechanical domesticity. A new spirit of brotherhood was, however, celebrated in such works as James P. Hogan's *Code of the Lifemaker* (1983), in which human libertarians fight for the freedom of ex-colonial robots.

Hans Moravec's *Mind Children: The Future of Robot and Human Intelligence* (1988) provided works of this stripe with a firmer ideological basis, assisting further complications and confusions. Pat Murphy's *The City, Not Long After* (1989) features a robot builder called Machine. The posthuman citizens of the future are jewel-encrusted robots in Marc Laidlaw's "Kronos" (1989). In Jeffery Liss' "A Robot in Every Job" (1990), the advent of "omnibots" requires the establishment of new principles of social justice. Tony Daniel's "The Robot's Twilight Companion" (1996; incorporated into *Earthling*) is a surreal heroic fantasy about a robot's acquisition of self-consciousness. Robert Sheckley's "The Quijote Robot" (2001) continued the sophistication of his long series of robot farces, and Asimovian tropes are subjected to similarly satirical reconsideration in David Langford's "The Last Robot Story" (2002), Mike Resnick's "Robots Don't Cry" (2003), and Cory Doctorow's "i, robot" (2005). Tony Ballantyne's "Teaching the War Robot to Dance" (2002) is an ingenious post-WWII secret history.

In the meantime, while industrial robot slaves continued to proliferate and grow in sophistication, performing robots made a striking comeback, in a fashion very different from the demonstrations carried out at exhibitions and trade fairs earlier in the century. The impresario who started the new trend, Mark Pauline, called his first show in 1979 Machine Sex, but what the machines actually did was collide brutally, demolishing one another. A 1980s show entitled Useless Mechanical Activity paved the way for 1990s "circuses" that fully recaptured the spirit of the Roman arena, mounting elaborate spectacles of destruction that were swiftly co-opted by TV in the gladiatorial show *Robot Wars* (launched 1998). The fashionability of this new spectator "sport" was reflected in such fictional works as G. Harry Stine's Warbots series (1988–1992), the film *A.I.* (2001), and Alex Irvine's "Jimmy Guang's House of Gladmech" (2002). Its influence on future robot attitudes to their parent species remains to be judged.

ROCKET

A missile propelled—in accordance with Isaac *Newton's third law of motion—by its mechanical reaction against a jet of gas expelled from its hind end, usually in consequence of an explosive chemical reaction. Rockets were used as fireworks in China in the eleventh century, and were adapted as weapons of war in the thirteenth century. Europeans borrowed the idea, but rocket-propelled missiles were largely abandoned in favour of muskets and rifles. The protagonist of a fifteenth-century Chinese legend, Wan Hoo, attached rockets to a chair and blasted off into the unknown; a similar device—employing three sets of rockets intended to ignite in stages—was unsuccessfully tested as a means of *space travel by Cyrano de Bergerac's protagonist in the first part of L'autre monde (1657).

Rocket weapons became fashionable again when they were used against the British in India at the end of the eighteenth century. The possibility of using them as a means of transportation allegedly inspired Claude Ruggieri to send mice up in a rocket in 1806, returning them safely to Earth by parachute. The British subsequently used rocket missiles in the Napoleonic Wars and the American War of 1812; those used in an attack on Fort Henry in 1814 inspired the reference to "the rocket's red glare" in The Star-Spangled Banner—whose author, Francis Scott Key, witnessed the battle. They fell into disuse again, however, as field artillery improved.

In 1898, the Russian scientist Konstantin *Tsiolkovsky wrote an article on "The Probing of Space by Means of Jet Devices", which reached print in 1903; he attempted to popularise the notion in the didactic novel Vne zemli (1916; exp. book, 1920; trans. as Beyond the Planet Earth and Outside the Earth). The American engineer Robert Goddard, allegedly inspired by H. G. Wells' The War of the Worlds (1898), began experimenting with rockets in 1911, working towards the development of a liquid-fuel stage rocket—whose potential as means of interplanetary travel had been advertised in John Munro's A Trip to Venus (1897). Goddard launched his first liquid-fuel rocket in 1926.

Tsiolkovsky, Friedrich Zander, and Yuri Kondratyuk established a Soviet Society for Studies of Interplanetary Travel in 1924. Shortly thereafter, the German rocket pioneer Hermann Oberth, author of Die Rakete zu den Planetenräumen (1921) and other enthusiasts—including Otto Willi Gail, Max Valier, Willy *Ley, and Wernher von Braun—formed a similar society in Germany. In 1928, Oberth was offered the opportunity to build a rocket by a German film company, which hired him as technical adviser for Fritz Lang's film Die Frau im Mond (1929; aka The Girl in the Moon); it was supposed to be launched before the film's premiere as a publicity stunt, but the project collapsed. Gail and Valier—who became the first fatal casualty of rocket research in 1930—both used fiction to popularise their vocation, Gail in Der Schuss ins All (1925; trans. as The Shot into Infinity), and Valier in Auf kühner Fahrt sum Mars (1928; trans. as "A Daring Trip to Mars"). Ley and von Braun joined in later; Ley became a contributor to the U.S. science fiction pulps in the late 1930s, and von Braun's didactic novella First Men to the Moon (1960) was serialised in This Week before appearing in book form.

Interplanetary societies similar to the Soviet and German ones were soon established in Britain and the United States, forming similar links with potential popularisers and propagandists. David Lasser, a leading member of the American Rocket Society, was hired by Hugo *Gernsback to edit Science Wonder Stories and its companions, celebrating his appointment with an article in the December 1929 issue entitled "The Rocket Comes to the Front Page". Lasser included a fictional account of a trip to the Moon in his propagandist book on The Conquest of Space (1931). He also recruited the president of the society, G. Edwards Pendray, and fellow member Laurence Manning to write for the Wonder group (Pendray used the pseudonym Gawain Edwards). Manning described the first flights of a liquid-fuelled rocket in "The Voyage of the Asteroid" (1932) and "The Wreck of the Asteroid" (1932–1933). Another member of the society who became a pulp science fiction writer was Nathan Schachner.

The impetus provided by these propagandists was soon picked up by other pulp science fiction writers, who began to integrate space rockets into attempts to produce realistic images of future technological development. The British Interplanetary Society—founded by P. E. Cleator, author of Rockets Through Space (1936)—included Arthur C. Clarke, William F. Temple, and A. M. Low among its members, all of whom went on to use science fiction as propaganda for the *Space Age they assumed to be imminent. Clarke published an article entitled "We Can Rocket to the Moon—Now!" (1939) in Britain's first science fiction pulp magazine, Tales of Wonder.

Oberth and his assistants managed to launch a number of rockets in 1931, but the project was abandoned when Germany's economy crashed. Ley went to the United States when the Nazis took control but Wernher Von Braun joined a rocket development project instituted by the German Army, which acquired a large research centre on the Baltic island of Peenemünde in 1937. While Robert Goddard spent

World War II developing rockets to assist U.S. Navy aeroplanes in taking off from their carriers, Von Braun and his staff developed the V-1 and V-2 rocket bombs. When the war ended, Von Braun surrendered to the Americans and went to work for an American research program, whose funding increased dramatically as competition with Russian programs intensified, becoming hectic after the launch of the space satellite Sputnik in 1957.

Von Braun and his new colleagues developed the Jupiter rocket, which launched America's first space satellite in 1958, and then the Saturn rocket used in the Apollo program, which eventually carried the first men to the Moon in 1969. In the meantime, the use of science fiction as propaganda for interplanetary rocket travel moved up a gear. George Pal's supposedly realistic film *Destination Moon* (1950) was scripted by Robert A. Heinlein, although more convincing imagery was provided by such ultra-hard science fiction writers as Arthur Clarke, in *Prelude to Space* (1951), and Lee Correy, in *Rocket Men* (1955) and *The Contraband Rocket* (1956). The foremost pioneer of ultra-soft science fiction, Ray Bradbury, was equally fascinated by rockets and their symbolism, celebrating their potential in "King of the Grey Spaces" (1943; aka "R is for Rocket"), "I, Rocket" (1944), "Rocket Skin" (1946), "Rocket Summer" (1947), and "Outcast of the Stars" (1950; aka "The Rocket").

The rocket ship became the ultimate iconic symbol of 1950s science fiction, the moment of its blast-off encapsulating the ideals of the Space Age and providing a suitably melodramatic climax for "cosmic breakout" stories. Notable deployments of the motif include C. M. Kornbluth's *Takeoff* (1952) and Fredric Brown's *The Lights in the Sky Are Stars* (1953; aka *Project Jupiter*). The rocket's potential as a phallic symbol came to its peak in this period, when the orgasmic quality of blast-off was extensively exploited and celebrated.

The close association of rocket research with science fiction presumably influenced the remark made in 1956 by British Astronomer Royal Richard Woolley to the effect that all talk of space travel was "utter bilge", but Sputnik's debut the following year made him look silly. There is no other technological sequence of events in which fact and fiction entwined so intimately. The near-unanimous testimony of rocket scientists that their first inspiration came from science fiction seemed to be good evidence of the genre's potential to influence the shape of the future while it still remained plausible that rockets really did have the potential to launch a Space Age.

Although the funding for their research came from the military gutter, it seems entirely likely that the rocket scientists of the late 1930s and early 1940s really did have their eyes fixed on the stars, as represented in Pierre Boulle's *Le jardin de Kanashima* (1964; trans. as *Garden on the Moon*). The mythical significance of rockets was given a new twist in Thomas Pynchon's *Gravity's Rainbow* (1973), whose central character fantasises about becoming a Rocketman in much the same fashion as Ray Bradbury's aspirant heroes and the protagonist of Elton John's song "Rocket Man" (1972). Rocket pioneer Robert Goddard is the key character in Allen Steele's alternative history "Goddard's People" (1991), while he and Wernher Von Braun are featured as characters in Christopher McKitterick's alternate history "Paving the Road to Armageddon" (1995). The romance of amateur rocket research is celebrated in such fictions as Tom Ligon's "Amateurs" (1996) and the BBC TV series *Rocket Man* (launched 2005).

ROMANTICISM

A movement in the arts and philosophy whose reverberations had a profound effect on intellectual, social, and political life between the 1780s and the 1840s. It was originally conceived, in Germany, as the dialectical antithesis of Classicism. Its adherents developed an *aesthetic theory that put more emphasis on Edmund Burke's concept of the sublime, and extrapolated his championship of the exercise of the imagination, in opposition to the more conventional view favoured by Alexander Baumgarten, which emphasised the disciplined cultivation of beauty and the avoidance of "heterocosmic" creativity. It can also be seen as a vital component of the European cultural development of individualism.

The leading members of the German Romantic movement included "Novalis" (Friedrich von Hardenberg)—whose allegorical märchen in the posthumously published *Heinrich von Ofterdingen* (1802) symbolised the Romantic ideal as a blue flower—Ludwig Tieck, Johann Musäus, Friedrich de la Motte Fouqué, E. T. A. Hoffmann, and the Brothers Grimm. Johann Wolfgang von Goethe was initially hostile to the movement, declaring his steadfast allegiance to Classicism, but he was retrospectively conscripted to it, partly on account of his dabbling in allegorical märchen—which assisted Novalis to found a tradition of kunstmärchen [art fairytales]—but mainly because of a drastic change of emphasis between the two parts of his *Faust* (1808, 1832), which seemed to many critics to represent a conversion to Romantic ideals.

British Romanticism, foreshadowed by James Macpherson's invention of Ossian and by the "graveyard poetry" of Edward Young, was theorised by Nathan Drake, Walter Scott, Samuel Taylor Coleridge, William Wordsworth, and Thomas Carlyle, the last named being a highly significant translator of relevant German materials. William Blake, Robert Southey, Percy Shelley, Lord Byron, John Keats, Thomas de Quincey, and John Wilson (better known, in his capacity as presiding genius of *Blackwood's Magazine,* as "Christopher North") were among its most significant converts.

The French movement was foreshadowed by the endeavours of revolutionary literary philosophers, especially Jean-Jacques Rousseau and the Marquis de Sade, but it was expressly formulated and named by Charles Nodier, whose pioneering Romantic *cénacle* set an example that transformed the *salon* tradition of Parisian literary culture and laid the foundations of modern writers' workshops. His followers included Victor Hugo, Théophile Gautier, Alexandre Dumas, and the Parnassian poets; because the United States had no Romantic movement of its own to speak of, the French movement belatedly co-opted Edgar Allan *Poe in its twilight, his work combining with that of his translator, Charles Baudelaire, to lay the foundations of the *Decadent Movement.

Many contributors to the romantic movements were enthusiastic about the progress of science, and the movement's emphasis on individualism was inherently favourable to arguments based in empirical experience rather than ideas inherited from authority. Several associates of the German movement saw themselves as contributors to scientific evolution. The anti-Newtonian theory of colour that emerged from Goethe's work in *optics had little to recommend it, but his work in *botany, most significantly *Die Metamorphose der Pflanzen* (1790; trans. as *The Metamorphosis of Plants*; rev. as *Zur morphologie* 1817)—which sought to explain the formation of growing plants in terms of the progressive differentiation of elements extending from a central axis—was much more successful. Jakob Grimm made a considerable contribution to the development of *linguistics, and the interest in folklore he took over from Musäus laid useful groundwork for future *ethnological studies of *myth.

Percy Shelley's tutor, Adam Walker, instilled in him a strong interest in science, especially *meteorology. The ideological opposition that scientific progress mounted against traditional religious ideas made science seem quintessentially Romantic to Shelley, who was hailed as *A Newton Among Poets* (1930) by Carl Grabo in a minute study of the enthusiastic use of science in his poetry. Coleridge, who

had briefly been tutored by the anthropologist J. F. Blumenbach, was an enthusiastic participant in early meetings of the British Association for the Advancement of Science and a close friend of Humphry Davy, whom he met at a Pneumatic Institution in Clifton in 1799.

Davy was a wholehearted participant in the movement for a while, writing poetry alongside his researches—most notably "After Recovery from a Dangerous Illness" (ca. 1808), which expresses a broadly informed and enthusiastic belief in natural *theology, and "The Sons of Genius" (written 1805), a teenage paean to the scientific method. The account of Davy's early work published in *Researches, Chemical and Philosophical* (1800) was read by Mary Shelley and her husband shortly before she began work on *Frankenstein; or, The Modern Prometheus* (1818; rev. 1831), and helped to inform the ideative background of the novel. Robert Hunt, who became prolific in the *popularisation of science, was also a Romantic poet, his work in that vein being published in *The Mount's Bay* (1829), and a pioneering folklorist.

The input derived from Rousseau forged close links between French Romanticism and social philosophy, strongly reflected in the early development of images of the *future in French fiction. The development of science is a subsidiary theme in Victor Hugo's *La légende des siècles* (1840–1877), but it is a key component of his depiction of the evolution of the spirit of Liberty, and he extrapolated his scheme into the future in such terminal episodes as "Plein ciel". Nodier made a significant contribution to the development of philology, although his principal commitment was to the "Illuminist" tradition of *occult science, to whose "folklore" he produced a significant guide in *Infernaliana* (1822). The accounts of diabolism, hauntings, and vampires contained in that text provided invaluable fuel for subsequent French supernatural fiction, as well as inspiration to such lifestyle fantasists as "Éliphas Lévi".

Nodier was by no means the only Romantic to compound orthodox scientific interests with a keen interest in occult science. Adam Walker was an admirer of the mystic Jacob Boehme, and many of the Romantics became fascinated with the ideas of Emmanuel *Swedenborg. Robert Hunt's fictionalised account of his own intellectual odyssey, *Panthea* (1849), inverts the pattern of Swedenborg's progress from empirical science to mysticism, recording an early fascination with Rosicrucian *occultism derived from the works of Edward Bulwer-Lytton. Some of the more mystically-inclined Romantics were suspicious of science, on the grounds of its supposed destructive effects on the finest products of the imagination, but others—including Bulwer-Lytton—looked forward to a day when science might be triumphantly reabsorbed into a holistic occultism.

In Britain, William Blake and John Keats were the most outspoken adversaries of the scientific world-view. In Blake's *Europe* Los, the spirit of poetry, is at war with Urizen (Reason). Keats supported Charles Lamb's attack on Isaac *Newton at a dinner recalled by Benjamin Haydon, agreeing that optical science had robbed the rainbow of its poetry—a notion to which he gave poetic form in an attack on the disillusioning tendencies of "cold philosophy" in *Lamia* (1820). Wordsworth, who was also present at the dinner in question, was far more ambivalent about the argument, and made a conscientious attempt to be evenhanded in his elaborate discussion of the relationship between science and poetry in the prefaces to the 1800 and 1802 editions of *Lyrical Ballads*; the latter supposes that the Poet will be "at the side" of the Man of Science as future "material revolutions" are created, "carrying sensation into the midst of the objects of the Science itself".

Even those Romantics who were suspicious of theory, however, took inspiration from the contemporary explorers who were enabling advances in *geographical and cultural science. Keats asked Joseph Ritchie—who wrote Romantic poetry of his own—to take *Endymion* with him on an expedition to Timbuktu from which he never returned. When a new edition of Mungo Park's *Travels to the Interior Parts of Africa* (1799)—which had inspired Southey's *Thalaba* (1801)—appeared in 1818, Keats joined with Shelley and Leigh Hunt in a sonnet contest whose subject was the geography of the Nile. Byron's "The Island" (1822–1823) imagined the aftermath to the mutiny on the *Bounty* (the actual fate of the mutineers was not determined until much later) in Rousseauesque terms.

On the other hand, even the Romantics who were most interested in science took a considerable delight in the Gothic aspects of the imagination, and made abundant use of the imagery of the supernatural that Nodier called *Infernaliana*. In the light of that tendency, it is not entirely surprising that the Romantics' retreat from formal constraints in art and poetry came to be seen by a large section of their audience as a radical rebellion against the ideas, rewards, and supposed lessons of the Enlightenment, issuing a challenge to the supposed intellectual hegemony of science and reason as well as the orthodoxies of religion. It is not difficult to find examples of Romantic art, poetry, and prose that champion subjectivity against the supposed excesses of objectivity, and rhyme against the supposed excesses of reason, even though their use of the supernatural was initially undertaken in a spirit of conscientious fabulation.

The Romantic emphasis on subjectivity and the Gothic aspects of sublimity bore scientific fruit of its own in helping to formulate certain key ideas in *psychology, especially the role of "the unconscious". In retrospect—as provided, for instance, by Mario Praz' classic account of *La carne, la morte e il diavolo nella litteratura romantica* (1930; trans. as *The Romantic Agony*)—one can see Romanticism's dealings with the subject of *sex, especially its rich development of the motif of the *femme fatale*, as a significant precursor of Sigmund *Freud's account of the role of the libido in psychological development and the formation of neuroses. Even when Romanticism became decadent—in consequence of a long decline begun in 1848—and more unrepentantly antirationalistic, it retained significant links with psychological science, especially *psychotropic science, and with cyclic theories of *history.

Given the ambiguities of its interests and purposes, it is not surprising that the most outstanding examples of Romantic speculative fiction in both prose and verse seem so perversely tentative and ambivalent in their attitude to science. The eponymous antihero of *Frankenstein* fails conspicuously to live up to his subtitular billing as "The Modern Prometheus", and Mary Shelley's subsequent speculative novel, *The Last Man* (1826), is an expression of grief following the death of her husband. Critics continue to argue as to whether the imagery of Lord Byron's "Darkness" (1816) is supposed to refer to the past, the present, or the future.

Percy Shelley's attempts to express a scientific worldview in the language of myth and folklore in "Queen Mab" (1813) echo Erasmus *Darwin's attempts to do something similar in *The Temple of Nature* (1803), but the superiority of his poetic skills does not result in a more comfortable fusion. Other scientists with Romantic leanings, including Davy and Robert Hunt, attempted similar projects in prose, but their success was limited; even Poe, in the magisterial *Eureka* (1848), could not persuade his audience of the merits of that kind of extended poetry-in-prose as an ideal vehicle for the scientific imagination.

These precedents serve as reminders of the extent to which the lyrical element of twentieth-century speculative fiction—including *hard science fiction—is, in its essence, Romantic. The debt is frequently admitted, especially in *steampunk fiction, which might be regarded as the Romantic science fiction that the Romantics themselves neglected to produce. Alternative versions of Lord Byron and the Shelleys are featured in Walter Jon Williams' *Wall, Stone, Craft* (1993), while secret histories of the origins of Frankenstein are ingeniously shaped in Brian Aldiss'

Frankenstein Unbound (1973) and Philip C. Jennings' "Original Sin" (1994). Alex Irvine's Wordsworth-inspired "Intimations of Immortality" (2000) is a meditation on Romantic ideas and ideals.

ROUSSEAU, JEAN-JACQUES (1712–1778)

French philosopher. His education was informal and he worked as a clerk and music teacher before becoming ambitious to be a writer, publishing some early works on music and writing several dramatic works before making the acquaintance of the banker and royal counsellor Claude Dupin in 1744. He struck up a friendship with Denis Diderot and contributed to the score of an opera with words by Voltaire and music by Jean-Philippe Rameau before obtaining an appointment as Dupin's secretary from 1745 to 1752. Diderot encouraged him to enter a competition sponsored by the Dijon Academy for an essay on the subject of whether contemporary trends in science and art worked to the advantage of morals; his winning submission—arguing with considerable rhetorical fervour that they did not, merely serving to decorate and conceal the chains that bound people to effective slavery—made him famous, or at least notorious, as a political radical.

Rousseau wrote all the articles on music for Diderot and Jean d'Alembert's *Encyclopédie* and composed an opera in 1752 that was performed before the court of Louis XV, but he refused to accept a pension from the king and gave up his position with Dupin, in order to demonstrate the sincerity of the values he had expressed in his prize-wining essay. He entered a second competition of the same sort with a new *Discours sur l'origine et les fondements de l'inégalité parmi les hommes*; it did not win the prize, but its publication in 1755 added to his celebrity. The second *Discours* argues, with considerable fervour, that the "natural state" of humankind was one of equality, but that the prehistoric era in which that idea had been realised had given way—via the cultivation of wheat and the development of iron tools—to the corruptions of civilisation and perpetual warfare. The essay's combative tone, illustrative method, and nostalgia for a lost Golden Age recall the general manner, if not the sparse style, of *Plato's more extravagant dialogues.

In 1756, Rousseau left Paris, initially taking up residence in a country house owned by Louise d'Épinay, a friend of the Encyclopaedists; there he began the novel *Julie, ou La nouvelle Heloïse* (1761), which he finished at another house nearby after being forced to move by one of the quarrels that kept him perpetually on the move throughout his life—episodes he laboured long and hard to explain and justify in his *Confessions*. He broke with the Encyclopaedists following another such quarrel, but contrived to finish two more substantial books before moving on again. The first was his determinedly unorthodox tract on education, *Émile* (1762), which recommended withholding all books, except *Robinson Crusoe*, in order that children should learn self-sufficiency by direct interaction with their environment.

The political principles summarised at the end of *Émile* were elaborated in *Du contrat social* (1762; trans. as *The Social Contract*), which sought to establish all social relationships and obligations as tacit contracts between free individuals, requiring democratic government and religious tolerance. Both books were proscribed by the French government and Rousseau fled to Switzerland, but he was unable to find a permanent refuge; he went to England in 1766 at the invitation of the empiricist philosopher David Hume, but quarrelled with him the following year and returned to Paris, adopting a *nom de guerre* and moving continually, working all the while on his *Confessions*—from which he read frequently in public, with the aim of putting his perceived enemies to shame. The *Confessions* eventually appeared, posthumously, in 1782, along with *Les rêveries du promeneur solitaire*, a much calmer work about humankind's psychological relationship with *nature, written when his paranoia had eased somewhat.

During his lifetime, Rousseau was much better appreciated outside France than within; he was invited to write a constitution for the as-yet-nonexistent nation of Corsica and to advise Polish nationalists as to how their national constitution ought to be reformed. After his death, however, he was recognised as an important prophet of the Revolution of 1789—after which his remains were moved to the Panthéon—and an important precursor of French *Romanticism. His influence was extended through a cult of *sensibilité*, whose adherents advocated trust in natural instincts and active rebellion against the corrupting influences of civilisation. Cynical commentators suggested that he had not set a good example for such ideals, having sent all the children borne by his long-time mistress, Thérèse Levasseur, to foundling homes where they died, but such paradoxes only served to increase the fascination he exerted upon the literary imagination, which far outweighed the influence of any of his contemporaries. When he appeared as a character in such Romantically-inclined historical novels as Alexandre Dumas' *Joseph Balsamo* (1846–1848; trans. as *Memoirs of a Physician*), he was treated with great affection and reverence.

Rousseau's notion of humankind in a state of nature is an imaginative construct devised to serve a rhetorical purpose, so it is not surprising that it makes more appeal to the literary imagination than any reasoned account of what prehistoric human existence might actually have involved, but it had a considerable effect on early *ethnological observations. Louis Antoine Bougainville's *Description d'un voyage autour de monde* (1771–1772), which describes a voyage made in 1766–1768, includes accounts of the Patagonians and the allegedly Edenic islands of the South Seas that are heavily coloured by Rousseauesque preconceptions. Diderot's fictitious dialogue, *Supplément au voyage de Bougainville* (1772; trans. as "Supplement to Bougainville's Voyage"), further complicated the pattern of influence.

The idea of the social contract is similarly argumentative, although one need not suspect it of having been improvised merely to avoid orthodoxy at all costs (that being the first necessity of bidding to win a debating competition). Although the idea that Rousseau glorified the "noble savage" was foisted on him by others, his ideas became parent to a significant subgenre of nineteenth-century adventure fiction in which noble savages are discovered and respectfully depicted; Henry Rider Haggard's *King Solomon's Mines* (1885) is a cardinal example. Rousseau was not an advocate of technological retreat either, let alone a celebrant of *ecological mysticism, but that did not prevent his image of the natural state of human society guiding several nineteenth-century fantasies in which the obliteration of civilisation is represented as a desirable Romantic prospect, as in Richard Jefferies' *After London; or, Wild England* (1885). Although Jules Verne's own work was not conspicuously Rousseauesque, the Vernian fiction produced in profusion for such periodicals as the *Journal des Voyages* was replete with nostalgia for the supposed natural state of human tribal society.

The direct literary influence of the cult of sensibility was brief, although its extension into English literature is manifest in Henry Mackenzie's *The Man of Feeling* (1771) and Jane Austen's *Sense and Sensibility* (1811), but the literary cult of the noble savage gathered momentum over time, receiving a further boost in popularity when the notion became literally incarnate in the early years of the twentieth century, in the character of Edgar Rice Burroughs' Tarzan. Earlier images of the same archetype, such as the one contained in Ronald Ross's *The Child of Ocean* (1889), were eclipsed by Burroughs' version, which became one of the key hero myths of the twentieth century. Rousseauesque philosophy echoed plangently in the work of some of the core writers of British

*scientific romance, including S. Fowler Wright and J. Leslie Mitchell.

RUCKER, RUDY (I.E., RUDOLPH) (VON BITTER) (1946–)

U.S. scholar and writer who obtained a B.A. in *mathematics from Swarthmore College in Pennsylvania in 1967, then went to Rutgers University to obtain his M.A. in 1969 and his Ph.D. in 1973. From 1972 to 1978, he was an assistant professor at the State University of New York, Geneseo, and then spent two years at the University of Heidelberg and two more as an associate professor at Randolph Macon Woman's College in Lynchburg, Virginia, before becoming a full-time freelance writer in 1982.

In his professional capacity Rucker became particularly entranced with transfinite *mathematics and multidimensional *geometry, popularising the relevant ideas in *Geometry, Relativity and the Fourth Dimension* (1977), *Infinity and the Mind: The Science and Philosophy of the Infinite* (1982), and *The Fourth Dimension: Toward a Geometry of Higher Reality* (1984; aka *The Fourth Dimension: A Guided Tour of the Higher Universe*). The last named paid appropriate homage to the work of C. H. *Hinton—whose work he brought back into print in *Speculations on the Fourth Dimension: Selected Writings of Charles Howard Hinton* (1980)—and to Edwin Abbott's account of *Flatland* (1884).

Rucker's first venture into fiction was the hectic *Spacetime Donuts*, which failed to complete the serialisation in *Unearth* whose second part appeared in 1979—it eventually appeared in book form in 1981; it attempted to explore the future of information technology in a breezily irreverent manner somewhat reminiscent of another nineteenth-century mathematician-writer, Lewis Carroll, anticipating the concerns and rebellious ideology of cyberpunk fiction, but equipping them with a distinctive narrative style. His first novel to appear in print, *White Light* (1980), is an unusually vivid didactic exercise cast as an afterlife fantasy, in which life after death provides abundant opportunities to model and explore arcane mathematical concepts and problems. *The Sex Sphere* (1983) and *The Secret of Life* (1985) provided a prequel and a sequel, in which the Carrollian aspects of his style came even further to the fore—although the Reverend Dodgson would probably have been severely discomfited by their unrepentant interest in sex. He subsequently called attention to the autobiographical elements of the trilogy, whose transfigurative method he described as "transrealism".

A similarly cavalier literary style, and similar erotic content, were employed in many of the fabulations reprinted in the story collection *The 57th Franz Kafka* (1983), whose contents were subsequently reprinted—in company with poems and essays—in the significantly titled *Transreal!* (1991), and again in the elliptically labelled *Gnarl!* (2000). Rucker's Carrollian inclinations were also given free rein in the laid-back wish-fulfilment fantasy *Master of Space and Time* (1984). He adopted a more earnest manner in a trilogy of novels extrapolating the possibilities of *artificial intelligence more boldly than he had in *Spacetime Donuts,* comprising *Software* (1982), *Wetware* (1988), and *Realware* (2000).

The cyberpunk credentials of the Software trilogy are more obvious than those of *Spacetime Donuts*, although Rucker's irrepressible imaginative and narrative exuberance took the edge off the noirish tone usually considered *de rigeur* in such fiction. *The Hacker and the Ants* (1994; rev. as *The Hacker and the Ants, Release 2.0*, 2003) developed similar subject matter in a more broadly comic manner. Rucker also adopted a studiously earnest manner, well suited to the Romantic flamboyance and mock naivety of *steampunk fiction, for *The Hollow Earth* (1990), in which a party of explorers—including Edgar Allan *Poe—venture into the interior of the Earth, to find an inner-surface ecosphere lit by energy emitted by the accretion disk of a central *singularity (of the *black hole variety), where gravitational attraction in the direction of the core is perpetually problematic.

In parallel with the later novels in this sequence Rucker produced another popularisation of mathematical ideas, *Mind Tools: The Five Levels of Mathematical Reality* (1987), before broadening his range in *Artificial Life Lab* (1993) and his co-editorship with R. U. Sirius (Ken Goffman) and Queen Mu (Allison Kennedy) of *Mondo 2000*'s *User's Guide to the New Edge* (1992), whose subtitle lists its concerns as "Cyberpunk, Virtual Reality, Wetware, Designer Aphrodisiacs, Artificial Life, Techno-Erotic Paganism, and More". The magazine *Mondo 2000* had started out as *High Frontiers* before becoming *Reality Hackers*; it subsequently expired—as it had to do before the millennium—in 1998.

The later novels in the Software trilogy were punctuated by *Saucer Wisdom* (1999), a metafictional novel whose hypothetical narrator is abducted by aliens in order to receive enlightenment regarding the future of technology—particularly the development of a metamorphic "femtotechnology" that takes the concept of *nanotechnology to its logical extreme. *Spaceland: A Novel of the Fourth Dimension* (2002) further elaborates Rucker's fascination with dimensional fantasy, cementing his status as the modern writer best able to transform the imaginative acrobatics of complex mathematics into intoxicating literary exhilaration. *Frek and the Elixir* (2004) returns to the method and concerns of *Saucer Wisdom* in its account of a boy embarked on an exploratory quest in a phantasmagoric future whose *biotechnology has run amok.

Long after the bulk of post-cyberpunk fiction had shrunk into a rather stereotyped enclave of futuristic thriller fiction, Rucker's transrealist fiction retained an exploratory exuberance, a fascination with cutting-edge ideas, and an interest in various didactic formats that allowed his work to keep pace with that of Bruce *Sterling—the only other comparable writer in the world was Damien *Broderick—but Rucker's sophisticated understanding of mathematics gives his best work a unique surrealism that no one else can duplicate.

RUSSELL, BERTRAND (ARTHUR WILLIAM) (1872–1970)

British philosopher. He studied mathematics and philosophy at Trinity College, Cambridge, and subsequently held a variety of academic posts there and at other universities. He was a remarkably prolific writer who tried hard to make the arcana of philosophy accessible to lay readers in books ranging in breadth from his succinct summary of *The Problems of Philosophy* (1912) to his sweeping account of *The History of Western Philosophy* (1945).

Russell's early work in philosophy, reported in *The Principles of Mathematics* (1903) and *Principia Mathematica* (1910–1913 with A. N. Whitehead) attempted to synthesise *logic and *mathematics into a single coherent system. His subsequent work extended the range of his analysis of the foundations of knowledge into the *philosophy of science, reacting against logical *positivism while resisting the opposite tendencies of *linguistic philosophy; his own version of the realist philosophy of science was eventually summarised in *Human Knowledge: Its Scope and Limitations* (1948).

The attitudes to the progress of science and technology manifest in Russell's work shifted somewhat over time, but were always ambivalent. On the one hand, he tackled the confusions of theoretical physics in the context of his popularising endeavours, in *The ABC of Relativity* (1925). On the other hand, he continually manifested anxieties regarding the social consequences of the advancement of knowledge. While the memory of World War I was still fresh in his mind, he wrote a scathing reply to J. B. S. Haldane's essay *Daedalus; or, Science and the Future* (1923), wittily entitled *Icarus; or, The Future of Science* (1923), which argued succinctly that because the progress of technology gave people more power to indulge their passions—which seemed to be mostly destructive—it was a bad thing, and might easily bring about the destruction of civilisation. The dispute prompted the publisher to bring out an extended series of *futurological pamphlets with titles in a similar style, under the collective title *Today & Tomorrow*, which eventually ran to more than a hundred volumes.

Russell elaborated the argument of *Icarus* in a more detailed examination of *The Scientific Outlook* (1931), whose final chapter drew a distinction between "science considered as metaphysics" and "science considered as a technique for the transformation of ourselves and our environment". In the former guise, Russell considered that science had been intrinsically disappointing, leaving the power generated by science unconstrained, "only obtainable by something analogous to the worship of Satan, that is to say, by the renunciation of love". By the early 1950s, however—after winning the Nobel Prize for Literature in 1950—this *Faustian perception was somewhat ameliorated in the essays making up *The Impact of Science on Society* (1953), whose final chapter conscientiously listed the factors threatening the stability of a "scientific society", comprising practical problems of *ecology, and sociopolitical problems of ensuring equality of prosperity. The conclusion conceded that only "an infinitesimal minority" of people seemed ready, willing, or able to interest themselves in trying to solve these problems, but suggested that it might be too early to give up all hope.

Russell's Faustian interpretation of the condition of a scientific society was echoed in the allegorical title novella of his first collection of *contes philosophiques*, *Satan in the Suburbs and Other Stories* (1953), which also includes a speculative account of an unprecedently sensitive photographic device, "The Infra-redioscope", and three relatively modest satires of intellectual high society. The contents of *Nightmares of Eminent Persons and Other Stories* (1954) are more unrepentantly fantastic, the main sequences of vignettes including "The Mathematician's Nightmare: The Vision of Professor Squarepunt" and a vision of the author's worst fears about the future of technology fulfilled, "Dr. Southport Vulpes's Nightmare: The Victory of Mind over Matter". The remaining novellas, "Zahatopolk" and "Faith and Mountains", are blistering satires on religion that have no doubt at all that the scientific worldview is absolutely correct. The "Divertissements" section of the mixed collection *Fact and Fiction* (1961) added two more nightmares and a complementary sequence of dreams, although its only item of speculative fiction was the parable "Planetary Effulgence" (1959), in which a divided Martian society fails to learn a crucial lesson from the tragic history of Earth. The contents of the first two collections were reassembled, with the fictional items from the third, in *The Collected Stories of Bertrand Russell* (1972).

Russell, who defined a pedant as a person "who cares about whether what he is saying is true or not", was somewhat distressed by the attitude of mind that regards logic as an enemy to be feared and loathed, but had to acknowledge that dissenters from that view were a tiny and beleaguered minority. This accounts for the fervency of his desire to popularise philosophy and science, for the slightly injured tone that much of his philosophy adopted, and for the sarcastic wit with which his popular writing was invariably decorated. He remains an exceptionally clear and articulate exemplar of an attitude that was very widespread during the twentieth century, which was both fascinated by the advancement of science and fearful of it, deeply committed to the notion that knowledge is good in itself while despairing of the uses to which knowledge was mostly put. That kind of ambivalence saturated the major fraction of the twentieth-century literary response to science.

S

SAGAN, CARL (EDWARD) (1934–1996)

U.S. astronomer and populariser of science. He completed his education at the University of Chicago, obtaining degrees in physics before obtaining his Ph.D. in astronomy and astrophysics in 1960. He taught at Harvard before moving to Cornell University in 1968, where he was appointed professor of astronomy and space science in 1971; he was also the director of a Laboratory for Planetary Studies and was editor-in-chief of *Icarus*, the principal journal of planetary studies, for twelve years. The first of his three marriages, in 1957, was to Lynn Margulis, the biologist who collaborated with James *Lovelock on the development of the Gaia hypothesis, and he retained a strong interest in environmental issues, helping to popularise the dangers of the *greenhouse effect and the notion that the use of *atom bombs in warfare would precipitate a "nuclear winter".

After producing an English adaptation of a book by the Russian astronomer I. S. Shklovskii, published as *Intelligent Life in the Universe* (1966), Sagan went on to produce numerous essays and books of his own on the same subject, including *The Cosmic Connection: An Extraterrestrial Perspective* (1973), the anthology *Communication with Extraterrestrial Intelligence* (1973), and *Other Worlds* (1975). These works were significant in promoting the search for extraterrestrial intelligence (*SETI).

In symbolic pursuit of a first contact with *alien intelligence Sagan persuaded NASA to place a message plaque on the Pioneer 10 space probe, which was designed to fly past Jupiter in 1973 and then to exit the solar system. The gesture was so successful, in terms of NASA's public relations, that he was allowed to compile a much more complex advertisement for the human race, including photographs and music, encoded on a CD carried by both the Voyager probes launched in 1977—a project whose history is chronicled and selective logic explained in *Murmurs of Earth: The Voyager Interstellar Record* (1978). Although the probability that the artefact will ever be found is presumably negligible, the task of compiling a capsule account of the human species and its cultural achievements had to address the question of what kind of image that species might want and be able to project into an infinite posterity.

Sagan won a Pulitzer Prize for *The Dragons of Eden: A Speculative Essay on the Origin of Human Intelligence* (1977), which presented a narrative account of the evolution of the human brain, helping to popularise the notion of its hierarchical *neurological organisation. He reached an even larger audience with the TV series *Cosmos: A Personal Voyage* (1980), whose accompanying book was a huge best-seller. In the TV series he posed as a traveller on the bridge of a hypothetical starship, using dramatic special effects to represent recent discoveries of astronomy and space exploration. His commentary made some attempt to place the discoveries in a broader theoretical context but was primarily notable for its dramatic pleading for the virtue and aesthetic majesty of the scientific world-view. His final summation of his views on the subjects covered in the series was contained in *Pale Blue Dot: A Vision of the Human Future in Space* (1994).

The essays collected in *Broca's Brain* (1993) presented a similar mix of lyrical celebrations of the achievements of science and polemical assaults on its various opponents, including a painstaking demolition of Immanuel Velikovsky's *pseudoscientific cosmic catastrophism. He took the polemical aspect of this work further in *The Demon-Haunted World: Science as a Candle in the Dark* (1996), which illustrates its championship of the scientific method by exposing the false pretensions of various fashionable beliefs. His "baloney detection kit" remains available on the internet as a resource for assisting the penetration of pseudoscientific claims.

An unprecedentedly large advance was offered to Sagan for a science fiction novel that would anticipate the success of the SETI project, *Contact*; he accepted the commission, but had difficulty completing the project. The eventual appearance of the floridly portentous text in 1985 disappointed many readers, and its adaptation as a film in 1997 was similarly overblown. Some of Sagan's later books were written in collaboration with his third wife, Ann Druyan, including *Comet* (1985), about the return of Halley's *comet, *Shadows of Forgotten Ancestors: A Search for Who We Are* (1993), and the posthumous *Billions & Billions: Thoughts on Life and Death at the Brink of the Millennium* (1998). The effects of the cancer that eventually killed him made it difficult for this later work to recapture the imaginative drive and fervour of his earlier endeavours. During the late 1970s and early 1980s, however, Sagan was the most prominent face of the popularisation of science in the United States, embodying an alchemical combination of stern reverence for hard facts and boundless imaginative enthusiasm that was typical of the vocation in that era.

SATIRE

A term derived from the Latin *satura*, referring to a mixture of fruits or other foodstuffs, applied analogically to poetic medleys produced by such Roman poets as C. Lucilius (second century B.C.). The form was sophisticated by Horace, Persius, and Juvenal. Satires written in a mixture of verse and prose were called Menippean—after a Greek writer whose works were similarly mixed (although they were not satirical)—by their pioneer, M. Terentius Varro. The other principal Roman satirists in the Menippean tradition were Petronius and Seneca. The term subsequently broadened out to describe any literary composition whose purpose was to ridicule and censure some perceived vice or folly by exaggerating its incongruities, or to ridicule the pretensions of particular powerful individuals.

Satire enjoyed a significant resurgence in seventeenth-century England, in the poetry of such writers as Samuel Butler and John Dryden, and a rich tradition of English prose satire was established in the early eighteenth century by Daniel Defoe and Jonathan Swift. Elements of the satirical method of comic exaggeration had, however, previously been adopted into such genres of prose fiction as the traveller's tale; the caricaturish methods of satire readily lent themselves to the construction of hypothetical societies reached by means of fantastic voyages, so there was always a strong element of satire in fanciful accounts of *space travel and *Utopian fiction. The great majority of the texts that can be seen retrospectively as ancestral to *scientific romance and *science fiction have some satirical component, and satirical motives refined the narrative methods and devices of the Voltairean *conte philosophique*.

Although Voltaire used satire as a weapon against religious and philosophical dogmatism, it had already been used to assault the supposed delusions of scientists in the third part of Swift's *Travels into Several Remote Nations of the World in Four Parts ... by Lemuel Gulliver* (1726; aka *Gulliver's Travels*), which mocks the Academy of Projectors of the flying island of Laputa (a parody of the Royal Society) and regrets such technological transformations of human life as the uncomfortable immortality of the senile Struldbruggs of Luggnagg. The fourth part, in which the natural nobility of the equine Houyhnhnms is contrasted with the disgusting habits of the anthropomorphic Yahoos, established an important prototype for the use of *alien viewpoints in the sceptical examination of the human condition. *Gulliver's Travels* became one the most influential of all literary exemplars; the example of its breadth, fervour, and extremism combined with that of the savage irony of the nonfictional "A Modest Proposal for Preventing the Children of the Poor People from Being a Burthen to Their Parents" (1729) to establish archetypes of a uniquely vigorous species of "Swiftian satire".

Most subsequent "Gulliveriana" imitated Swift's softer targets—subsequent voyages to Lilliput and Brobdingnag far outnumber those to Laputa or the land of the Houyhnhnms, although *Mr. Oscar Preen in Japan and Laputa* (*Tinsley's Magazine* 1869–1870) and Wendell Phillips Garrison's *The New Gulliver* (1898) are exceptions—but the bolder writers who invented entirely new realms for Gulliver and his clones to explore often made use of scientific speculation in constructing their imaginary societies. Notable examples include Barry Pain's "The New Gulliver" (1913), Frigyes Karinthy's *Utazas Faremido* (1916; trans. as *Voyage to Faremido*) and *Capillaria* (1921), and the first and last stories in Adam Roberts'

Swiftly (2004). A contest of sorts between antiscientific Swiftian satirists and proscientific Voltairean satirists extended from the mid-eighteenth century to the twenty-first, both sides increasing their offensive weaponry as the battleground gradually became wider and its ideological landscape progressively more complex.

The fervent disputes of twentieth-century political satire were, in general, far more superficial than those of the Swift-Voltaire contest, but the progressive development of technology remained a key element of their background, because one of the charges most commonly issued against political parties and attitudes was that of being "behind the times", unready and unable to respond to new challenges. The failure of shortsighted statesmen to make adequate provision for future change is a constant preoccupation of political satirists, which became increasingly acute as the pace of social change accelerated. Twentieth-century examples of political satire became increasingly inclined to take such considerations aboard, as in Anatole France's *L'île des pingouins* (1908; trans. as *Penguin Island*), Rose Macaulay's *What Not* (1919), Hilaire Belloc's *But Soft—We Are Observed* (1928), Upton Sinclair's *Roman Holiday* (1931), Harold Nicolson's *Public Faces* (1932), and John Gloag's *Winter's Youth* (1934).

The customary rhetorical stance of satirists identified with the emergent British genre scientific romance—whose archetypal products included H. G. Wells' *The Wonderful Visit* (1895), Grant Allen's *The British Barbarians* (1895), Eimar O'Duffy's *The Spacious Adventures of the Man in the Street* (1928), and Eden Phillpotts' *Saurus* (1938)—was defiantly Voltairean, although Aldous Huxley's *Brave New World* (1932) introduced a powerful Swiftian exemplar to the genre. American science fiction preferred action-adventure formulas developed from Vernian romance, but the works of Edgar Rice Burroughs were by no means innocent of satire, and a much more obvious subspecies was soon imported to the pulps by Stanton A. Coblentz, in *The Sunken World* (1928; book, 1948), *The Blue Barbarians* (1931), and *In Caverns Below* (1935; book 1957 as *Hidden World*). Pulp science fiction's political satires were notable for their tendency to assume that political disputes are essentially meaningless within the greater context of insistent *technological determinism—a view given striking expression in Miles J. Breuer's "The Gostak and the Doshes" (1930).

The use of *aliens for satirical purposes was always considered fair game in pulp science fiction, but the example set by Voltaire's *Micromégas* (1752)—in which intellectually superior aliens demonstrate the folly of human vanity—seemed uncongenial to many genre stalwarts. John W. *Campbell Jr. preferred to invert the formula in the magazines he edited, featuring stupid aliens who had much to learn from humans, although writers such as Eric Frank Russell occasionally contrived to twist this pattern advantageously, in such stories as "The Waitabits" (1955), and also to make ingenious use of a galactic society background in which widely different human societies could be satirically compared, as in "... And Then There Were None" (1951). On the other hand, Campbell—encouraged by his brief association with Robert A. *Heinlein—presided over a marked change in genre science fiction's uses of political satire, developing a much keener appreciation of the ways in which political reorganisation might assist the cause of technological progress, especially in the context of the *Space Age: an awareness common to the satirically inclined works of writers from opposite ends of the political spectrum, such as H. Beam Piper and Mack Reynolds.

The demise of the action-orientated pulps and the rise of a new post–*atom bomb cynicism regarding *progress and *technology combined their effects to make 1950s science fiction particularly hospitable to satire—a licence indulged to the full by such writers as Frederik *Pohl, C. M. Kornbluth, Damon Knight, Fritz Leiber, and Robert Sheckley. All of these writers contrived to find fertile middle ground between the Voltairean and Swiftian traditions, mercilessly attacking misapplications of technology while retaining a fundamental respect for science, at least as a precious antidote to its poorer alternative, dogmatism. Writers outside the genre were less inclined to make such fine distinctions, a thoroughly Swiftian scepticism being retained by such writers as Bernard Wolfe, in *Limbo* (1952), and Kurt Vonnegut, in *Player Piano* (1952), *The Sirens of Titan* (1959), and *Cat's Cradle* (1963), although the Voltairean opposition was maintained in Doris Meek and Adrienne Jones' *The Golden Archer* (1956; by-lined Gregory Mason).

This difference in inclination was preserved into the 1960s, when several U.S. satirists using science fiction motifs—most notably Thomas M. Disch and John T. Sladek—allied themselves with British "new wave" science fiction before winning acceptance in their own country. The association of Disch and Sladek with the British movement had an invigorating effect because much of the movement's domestically produced satire was conspicuously polite—Brian W. Aldiss' *The Primal Urge* (1961) and *The Dark Light Years* (1964) are cardinal examples. The sharpness of Disch's sarcasm, as displayed in "White Fang Goes Dingo" (1965; exp. book as *Mankind under the Leash*, aka *The Puppies of Terra*) and *The Genocides* (1965), and the hectic quality of Sladek's wit, as displayed in

The Reproductive System (1968; aka *Mechasm*), provided useful exemplars, although the United States also produced such scrupulously polite satires as Hortense Calisher's *Journal from Ellipsia* (1965). The most significant extension of satire into cinematic science fiction, Stanley Kubrick's *Dr. Strangelove; or, How I Stopped Worrying and Learned to Love the Bomb* (1963), appeared in this period.

The principal evolution of satire in the 1970s and 1980s, both within and without the science fiction genre, was associated with the rapid growth of feminism, which provided a new challenge to assumptions about the scope, virtue, and significance of techno-fetishism and technologically determined social change, reflected in such works as Ira Levin's *The Stepford Wives* (1972), Joanna Russ's *The Female Man* (1975), James Tiptree Jr.'s "Houston, Houston, Do You Read?" (1977), Josephine Saxton's *The Travails of Jane Saint* (1980), and Candas Jane Dorsey's "(Learning About) Machine Sex" (1988).

Speculative fiction inevitably became a target for satirisation itself, especially the manifest imaginative excesses of pulp science fiction, which were further exaggerated in the visual media and comic books. Such satire inevitably began with "in-jokes" such as Fredric Brown's *What Mad Universe?* (1948; exp. book, 1949), Harry Harrison's *Bill the Galactic Hero* (1965), and George O. Smith's "Speculation" (1976), and a strong tradition of incestuous parody was maintained within the fan community by such writers as David Langford, who extended his wit to such demolitions of commercial work as *Earthdoom!* (1987; with "John Grant" [Paul Barnett]). A much greater scope for such work was, however, opened by the expansion of generic science fiction into other media, where a substantial satirical sector was eventually established by such productions as Douglas Adams' *Hitchhiker's Guide to the Galaxy* (radio version, 1978; novel series launched 1979; TV adaptation, 1981; film, 2005), Rob Grant and Doug Naylor's *Red Dwarf* (TV series launched 1988; tie-in novel series launched 1989), *Third Rock from the Sun* (TV series launched 1996), and the film *Galaxy Quest* (1999).

The riotous clamour produced by this kind of self-referential satire far outshone other kinds of satire using speculative tropes from 1980 onwards, although futuristic satires reflecting contemporary trends, such as John Kessel's *Good News from Outer Space* (1989) and Harvey Jacobs' *Beautiful Soup* (1993) continued to maintain an elegantly sophisticated edge to such fiction. The Voltairean tradition was forcefully maintained by such writers as James Morrow, especially in the trilogy begun with *Towing Jehovah* (1995), while such works as James Lovegrove's *Untied Kingdom*

(2003) and John Reed's *Snowball's Chance* (2003) kept the tradition of technologically sophisticated political satire alive into the twenty-first century.

Attitudes to the use of satire within speculative fiction tend to differ sharply in critical evaluations. Critics affiliated to the genre, who share *hard science fiction's commitment to the notion of technological progress as a good in itself, tend to regard satire as a marginal activity, whose primary merits are Voltairean; critics trained in the academy, on the other hand—who are far more likely to be sceptical about the connection between technological and social progress—usually conserve their loudest applause for Swiftian materials. Scientists are, however, occasionally willing and able to use satire as a weapon against their critics, as in Alan Sokal's parody of *postmodernist analysis.

SATURN

The sixth planet from the Sun, now known to be a gas giant somewhat smaller than Jupiter. It was the most distant planet known in the ancient world, and was named for a Roman god of agriculture who was subsequently equated with the Greek Cronus, the ruler of the Titans. Its most spectacular feature, the surrounding ring system, was observed by *Galileo and explained by Christian Huygens in 1656. Two bright rings were distinguished by G. D. Cassini in 1675; a third inner ring was discovered in 1850 and a fourth outer one in 1907, but the structure proved to be much more elaborate when viewed at close range by the space probes Pioneer 11, Voyager 1, and Voyager 2, which flew past the planet in 1979–1981. The visible surface of the planet seems less varied than that of Jupiter, which has always overshadowed it in speculative fiction by virtue of being bigger and closer.

Saturn has one large satellite, Titan—discovered by Huygens in 1656—and numerous smaller ones. Rhea, Iapetus, Dione, Tethys, Enceladus, Hyperion, and Mimas were identified by telescopic observation, and ten more were added as a result of data gathered by the Pioneer and Voyager probes. Titan was closely examined by the Cassini-Huygens probe launched in 1997, which sent out a subsidiary craft to make a landfall on its surface in 2004. Pictures taken during the descent were successfully relayed back to Earth; they appear to show evidence of both solid objects and expanses of liquid—perhaps methane—on the surface.

Saturn was visited *en passant* by Voltaire's Sirian visitor, *Micromégas* (1750), the Saturnian who accompanied him thereafter being intermediate in size and sensory equipment between the star-dwellers and humans. The planet's inhabitants play an intermediate role between humans and angels in Emmanuel *Swedenborg's cosmic scheme; in Marie Corelli's *A Romance of Two Worlds* (1886) and John Jacob Astor's *A Journey in Other Worlds* (1894), its spiritually superior inhabitants confirm the theological convictions of travellers from Earth. Humphry Davy's *Consolations in Travel* (1830) offers a significant image of radically alien Saturnian life, while retaining the notion that its inhabitants are far superior to humans, but the planet's biosphere is more orthodoxly primitive in other works. It is dominated by giant mushrooms and insects in W. D. Lach-Szyrma's *Aleriel* (1886), and by Sargassoesque seaweed in George Griffith's *A Honeymoon in Space* (1901). In Cyrus Cole's *The Auroraphone* (1890), the advanced Saturnians possess robotic "dummies".

Relatively few pulp science fiction writers used Saturn as a venue, although it is the home of gaseous humanoids in Stanton A. Coblentz's "The Men Without Shadows" (1933) and provides a refuge for dispossessed humankind in Henry J. Kostkos' "Earth Rehabilitators Consolidated" (1935). The more Earthlike Titan seemed a far more promising location even then, equipped with a lavish biosphere in such stories as Bob Olsen's "Captain Brink of the Space Marines" (1932), Edwin K. Sloat's "Loot of the Void" (1932), Harl Vincent's "Creatures of Vibration" (1932), and Stanley G. Weinbaum's "Flight on Titan" (1935). Other Saturnian satellites occasionally featured in similar extraterrestrial adventures, as Iapetus does in Harl Vincent's "Water-Bound World" (1932). The rings of Saturn provided raw material for a weapon in Clifton B. Kruse's "Menace from Saturn" (1935) but otherwise seemed to offer little in the way of melodramatic potential, although they came into their own in more modest accounts of the colonisation of the solar system such as Otto Binder's "The Ring Bonanza" (1947) and Isaac Asimov's "The Martian Way" (1952) and *Lucky Starr and the Rings of Saturn* (1958; as by Paul French). The latter belonged to a tradition of didactic juvenile science fiction that also included Philip Latham's *Missing Men of Saturn* (1953).

Titan's apparent potential as a site for a colony kept its relatively high profile in *Space Age science fiction, in such works as R. D. Nicholson's "Far from the Warming Sun" (1953), Alan E. Nourse's *Trouble on Titan* (1954), and Arthur C. Clarke's "Saturn Rising" (1962), and it maintained that role into the 1970s in such stories as Ben Bova's *As on a Darkling Plain* (1972) and Clarke's *Imperial Earth* (1976). It provides a key location in Kurt Vonnegut's *The Sirens of Titan* (1959), but is more interestingly employed as a source of alien life in Gregory Benford and Gordon Eklund's *If the Stars Are Gods* (1977). Although the post-Voyager image of Titan seemed far less hospitable to life, it provided a memorable backcloth for Stephen M. Baxter's *Titan* (1997) and Michael Swanwick's "Slow Life" (2002).

The tradition of observing Saturn from a distance, in order to have the full effect of the rings, was preserved in Diane Ackerman's poetry collection *The Planets: A Cosmic Pastoral* (1976), in which "Saturn" is the longest inclusion. An artificial world hidden among the Saturnian satellites is the setting of John Varley's *Titan* (1979) and its sequels, while the rings come into sharper focus in the same author's "Gotta Sing, Gotta Dance" (1976). The planet's minor satellites are foregrounded in such works as Poul Anderson's "The Saturn Game" (1981) and Grant D. Callin's "Saturn Alia" (1984; exp. as *Saturnalia*, 1986), both of which are centred on Iapetus. The rings are mined for ice in Joe Martino's "The Iceworm Special" (1981). Descents into the Saturnian atmosphere are not nearly as common as the Jovian equivalents, but are featured in Roger Zelazny's "Dreadsong" (1985), Michael A. McCollum's *The Clouds of Saturn* (1991), and Robert L. Forward's *Saturn Rukh* (1997).

SAWYER, ROBERT J[AMES] (1960–)

Canadian writer. He completed his education at Ryerson Polytechnic University, obtaining a B.A. in radio and television arts in 1982. He had already begun publishing science fiction stories and had edited a showcase anthology of stories by members of the Ontario Science Fiction Club, although his work did not begin to appear regularly in professional outlets until 1988. He worked briefly at Ryerson as an instructor-demonstrator in TV production but was able to write full time from then on.

Much of Sawyer's early work hybridised science fiction and crime fiction. *Golden Fleece* (short version, 1988; book, 1990; rev. 1999) fuses a transfiguration of the Greek myth of the questing Argonauts with a murder mystery. Mysteries of a more explicitly science-fictional variety serve as narrative frames in the loosely knit Quintaglio trilogy, comprising *Far-Seer* (1992), *Fossil Hunter* (1993), and *Foreigner* (1994), in which saurian aliens must figure out how to avoid extinction when their world comes under threat from meteoritic bombardment. The time travel fantasy *The End of an Era* (1994) includes an elaborate commentary on possible reasons why Earthly dinosaurs failed to avoid that fate, as well as a fanciful account of the actual reason for their extinction. His temporary fascination with dinosaurs was further reflected in the *conte cruel* "Just Like Old Times" (1993).

Sawyer's work became conspicuously more ambitious in the late 1990s. *The Terminal Experiment* (1995) has a murder mystery subplot, but foregrounds an enquiry into the roots of ethical philosophy, employing three artificial "clones" of its protagonist's personality as subjects in an elaborate thought experiment. *Starplex* (1996) is more relaxed, taking a trip around the galaxy by means of wormhole portals, but *Illegal Alien* (1997) returned to arguments regarding the fundamental principles of moral philosophy, here deployed in a courtroom drama. *Frameshift* (1997) is initially formulated as a conventional technothriller, but it develops a powerful flow of rhetoric regarding the ethical and pragmatic implications of the regulations controlling medical insurance schemes.

The SETI fantasy *Factoring Humanity* (1998) features an alien message whose decoding opens spectacular new evolutionary possibilities, as well as solving an awkward domestic problem for its female protagonist. The ambiguous disaster story *Flashforward* (1999) attempts to resophisticate the notion of a sudden access of superhumanity, which had been the favourite theme of Canada's most prominent resident science fiction writer, A. E. van Vogt.

Human and alien palaeontologists become involved in an ideological contest in *Calculating God* (2000), which sets up a series of cosmic coincidences in order to reexamine the arguments from nineteenth-century "natural theology" that contemporary Creationists were recycling as the "intelligent design" thesis. The Neanderthal Parallax series, comprising *Hominids* (2002), *Humans* (2003), and *Hybrids* (2003), begins in an alternative world where Neanderthal humans were never superseded, and the narrative proceeds to develop an ingeniously scrupulous comparison between the civilisations of the two different human species in parallel worlds.

Sawyer's literary method—displayed in the short fiction sampled in *Iterations* (2002) as well as his novels—is typical of *hard science fiction (much of his work first appeared in *Analog*) but he remained determinedly and combatively sceptical of ideological assumptions that U.S. writers seem to take for granted. This philosophy of procedure increased the pressure on his arguments to move in unfamiliar directions while maintaining great care in their development, helping to establish him as one of the leading figures in the genre as the twenty-first century began.

SCHOLARLY FANTASY

A work of the imagination passed off as scholarly nonfiction. The category includes, but is by no means restricted to, all kinds of *pseudoscience. Any work presented as nonfiction may legitimately be called a scholarly fantasy if it can be objectively demonstrated that the case made therein far exceeds the warrant of available evidence, especially if it employs fanciful "secondary elaboration" in an attempt to nullify countervailing evidence and logical contradiction.

There are, inevitably, accidental elements of scholarly fantasy in many early works of attempted scholarship that had little or no reliable data on which to base their conclusions, or that construed such evidence as was available in the light of entirely fanciful hypotheses. Almost all of *Pythagorean philosophy and many of the works of *Plato and *Aristotle now stand revealed as scholarly fantasies in spite of the enormous intelligence that went into them, as do substantial parts of Galen's *medicine, Herodotus' *history, Ptolemy's *geography, and Pliny the Elder's *botany and *zoology. The whole point of the scientific method is that such aggregates can be painstakingly sifted as new evidence become available, but arguments from authority tend to give equal weight to the true and false elements, while the holistic mode of thought typical of *occult science tends to preserve false elements by obfuscatory mystification.

The effect of these preservative factors was that falsehoods accidentally incorporated into ancient philosophical endeavours often became *Baconian idols inhibiting intellectual progress. Intellectual history testifies to the remarkable tenacity of certain falsehoods, especially those gifted with psychological *plausibility. Psychological plausibility inevitably functions as a prolific generator and supporter of scholarly fantasies.

The most notable deliberate scholarly fantasy in *Classical literature is probably Plato's invention of Atlantis—which demonstrates that notions improvised as exemplary fictions can easily be misread in such a way as to become deceptive. Other exercises in deliberate scholarly fantasy that had a very considerable deceptive effect include the story of King Arthur in Geoffrey of Monmouth's *Historia Regnum Britanniae* (ca. 1135; trans. as *History of the Kings of Britain*), Johann Valentin Andreae's Rosicrucian pamphlets (1615–1619), and the account of the history of witchcraft in Christendom contained in Jules Michelet's *La sorcière* (1862; trans. as *The Witch of the Middle Ages* and *Satanism and Witchcraft*).

All of these examples have been extraordinarily powerful in the inspiration of literary works—which serve to illustrate an important means by which scholarly fantasies continue to command allegiance. Successful scholarly fantasies routinely establish ideological feedback loops linking them to literary fantasies, and often also to lifestyle fantasies—in which people set out to live in accordance with the fantasies, as loyal heirs of imaginary traditions. Speculations circulate freely around these feedback loops; any innovation in one field routinely infects the others.

Whatever their followers may claim, and however sincere their practitioners might be, all treatises on *alchemy, *astrology, *flying saucers, *parapsychology, and other kinds of *occult science are scholarly fantasies in which accidental models have been imitated—sometimes deliberately—on a massive scale. In terms of the history of literature, however, such texts are of less significance than historical, *anthropological, and *ethnological studies that produce fanciful hypotheses to "explain" the history of magical, occult, and pseudoscientific beliefs in unduly credulous terms.

Scholarly fantasies are bound to emerge from the human sciences in some profusion, because the understanding at which those sciences aim involves trying to see things as other social actors see or have seen them. Such acts of imaginative identification are intrinsically difficult to test, and such evidence as the past leaves behind usually fits several different accounts of what the relevant actors might have thought they were doing. When interpretations of the past have to come to terms with the fantasies entertained by the people of the past, attempts to sort out what was actually believed, to what extent, and on what grounds become extremely difficult; such attempts not only risk infection by the fantasies of the objects of study, but by fantasies born of earlier attempts to understand them.

In consequence of this confusion, scholarly fantasies once thought extinct or obsolete often make spectacular comebacks, sometimes in transfigured forms. This is one reason why belief in magic and divination seems to be more widespread now than ever before—and why both accidental and deliberate scholarly fantasies are more widespread now than they have ever been before. Not all histories of magical and occult belief are scholarly fantasies, by any means, but they are uncommonly amenable to accidental and deliberate fantastic extrapolation. Scholarly fantasies also thrive in the field of medicine, where they support all forms of quackery and "alternative medicine", benefiting from the rewards of the placebo effect.

Literature inevitably makes avid use of scholarly fantasies whenever such borrowing is convenient or aesthetically appealing; even the most candid fabulation requires the cultivation of narrative plausibility.

Thus, modern Arthurian fantasy draws extensively on the revisionist scholarly fantasies of such writers as Jessie Weston, modern literary accounts of witches on the Micheletesque scholarly fantasies of Margaret Murray, and late twentieth-century fantasy featuring Mother goddesses draws on the post-Frazerian scholarly fantasies of Robert Graves. Literary poseurs are, however, less prone to the danger of falling prey to their own rhetoric than scholarly fantasists; many overt scholarly fantasists—like most lifestyle fantasists—appear to have been failed litterateurs, for whom nonfictional representation of their ideas, and belief therein, was a fallback position. Speculative fiction routinely extrapolates scholarly fantasies, often doing so in order to achieve a *reductio ad absurdum*, but the tolerance extended to different kinds of scholarly fantasy varies considerably.

Natural science is much less hospitable to scholarly fantasy than human science, and has been much more successful in fulfilling its historical mission to extirpate it. Even so, the use of speculation in constructing hypotheses for testing generates a great many potential scholarly fantasies, some of which are seductively easy to integrate into theoretical systems. Although such obvious examples as the phlogiston theory of combustion, the "Lamarckian" thesis of the inheritance of acquired characteristics, various theories of the hollow *Earth, and the "steady state" theory of cosmology have all been laid conclusively to rest, suspicions may still be entertained regarding extant theoretical exotica in physical and biological science alike, in which the extravagance of speculation far outweighs the actual material evidence; string theory and *sociobiology are potential candidates. One of the consequences of the advancement of twentieth-century science into exotic theoretical realms, however, is that very few of its modern constructions benefit from psychological plausibility in the same way that long-established scholarly fantasies do, so there is little likelihood of any abundant ideological feedback being produced in support of any scholarly fantasies that do still lurk on the fringes and in the interstices of twenty-first-century science.

SCIENCE

A term whose Latin equivalent, *scientia*, means "knowledge". It was used in a similarly broad fashion in English until the seventeenth century, often in complementary partnership with "conscience", which usually referred to a more intuitive or passionate sense of knowing. It was also used more narrowly to refer to an academic discipline or a body of skills, being virtually synonymous in the latter sense with one of the meanings of *art.

The principal items of the Medieval university curriculum—the quadrivium (logic, arithmetic, geometry, and astronomy) and the trivium (grammar, rhetoric, and music)—were sometimes lumped together as the "seven sciences", as in Stephen Hawes' allegorical *Passetyme of Pleasure; or, the Historie of Graunde Amoure and La Belle Pucel, Containing the Knowledge of the Seven Sciences and the Course of Man's Life in This Worlde* (written 1506; printed 1509), but as the "New Learning" made further progress in the sixteenth and seventeenth centuries, it became increasingly common to draw distinctions between "arts" and "sciences", resulting in a gradual restriction of the latter term to disciplines requiring theoretical understanding.

Andrew Maunsell's pioneering *Catalogue of English Printed Bookes* (1595) employed a tripartite fundamental division of the New Learning. The first (and much the largest) category was that of "Divinitie"; the second contained two subdivisions, "Arithmetick, Geometrie, Astronomie, Astrologie, Musick, The Art of Warre and Navigation" being lumped together as *Mathematicall*, while *Physick and Surgery* were combined in their own subcategory; the third section—which was never completed—lumped "Gramer, Logick, Rethorick, Lawe, Historie, Poetrie, Policie, etc." under the general heading *Humanity*. This taxonomic scheme is still echoed in modern university organisation, in the slightly blurred distinction between theology, theoretical and applied sciences, and "the humanities".

From the early eighteenth century onwards, the distinctive meaning of "science" became more sharply refined, referring to a body of observations subject to theoretical organisation; this became the word's modern meaning, displacing "natural philosophy" to become the key element in a parcel of terms that also included the modern meaning of "empirical" investigation and "experimental" proof. Mark Akenside's "Hymn to Science" (1739) retains a broader meaning of the term, but is aware in so doing that the meaning is old-fashioned and requires a certain exercise of poetic licence. It was not until the early nineteenth century, however, that such phrases as "the scientific method" and "scientific truth" entered common currency, and retrospective reference to a "scientific revolution" within the New Learning, led by such heroes as Francis *Bacon and Isaac *Newton, became commonplace. William Whewell's summaries of the *history and *philosophy of science in 1837–1840 cemented the modern notion of what science is—or what sciences are—within the English language.

The original synonymy of science and knowledge is retained in the *positivist view that only the contents of science constitute authentic knowledge of the world, all other claims being metaphysical, and hence bogus. Such a view is, however, controversial, often cited as evidence of the kind of arrogance that licenses use of the term "scientism". Attempts by the logical positivists and Ludwig Wittgenstein's *Tractatus Logico-Philosphicus* (1921) to rule all statements that are incapable of scientific justification devoid of meaning caused considerable resentment, and were soon overtaken by more generous and more flexible theories of meaning. The idea persisted that there is some kind of supplementary or "higher" truth of which scientific truth is only a component; the notion is very often given literary expression, assisted by a widespread belief among litterateurs that great literature is itself a component of that higher knowledge.

The most obvious literary reflection of the history of the term "science" is the emergence and proliferation of the genres of "*scientific romance" and "*science fiction", whose dominance by speculative futuristic fiction emphasises the notion of science as a dynamic force determining the evolution of human thought and—via its *technological spin-off—practical endeavour. It is this notion, rather than any mere acquaintance with sophisticated theory, that was responsible for the growth in the twentieth century of a "culture of science" distinguishable, in C. P. *Snow's sense, from the culture of literature and the arts. Even litterateurs who would not endorse the proposition that literature is a component of higher knowledge tend to be preoccupied with its heritage, thus tending to a nostalgic conservatism that is at odds with the transformative tendencies of science and technology. (Even those aspects of science that are "finished"—in the sense that the relevant laws are fully elucidated—are usually regarded by scientists as instruments of future practical endeavour rather than precious items of conservation.)

SCIENCE FICTION

A term first coined by the Scottish poet William Wilson in *A Little Earnest Book upon a Great Old Subject* (1851), in response to his reading of Robert Hunt's *The Poetry of Science* (1848). Wilson wanted to provide a manifesto for a kind of fiction that would dramatise discoveries in science, celebrating the insight thus gained, but the term was not taken up by anyone else, having no ready field of reference. An item published in the 1830 edition of the annual giftbook *The Keepsake*, "A Dialogue for the Year 2130", had, however, already proposed that the popular fiction of that era would consist of trashy "scientific novels", including such titles as *Love and Algebra* and *Geological Atoms; or, The Adventures of a Dustman*. A similar proposition was advanced, pessimistically, in Frances Cobbe's *The Age of Science: A Newspaper of the Twentieth Century* (1877; by-lined "Merlin Nostradamus"), in which the last surviving examples of fiction include the wittily titled *The Procession of the Equinox* and a romance in which love is interpreted and described in terms of glandular secretions.

When the existence of a popular genre of futuristic fiction based in scientific speculation did become sufficiently obvious to require a label in the 1890s, reviewers and critics initially preferred other terms, *scientific romance and "Vernian fiction" being the only ones to achieve widespread acceptance, the latter being primarily applied to juvenile fiction. Jules *Verne had not considered himself an author of children's books, but his publisher, Pierre Hetzel, was enthusiastic to serialise them in his "family magazine", where they might serve a didactic purpose, embedding information about contemporary scientific instruments and devices in exciting adventure stories such as *Voyage au centre de la terre*. The utility of this kind of didactically embellished fiction as an educative instrument was dubious, but the idea was attractive as a justificatory ploy; Vernian fiction became an important enclave of the "boys' book" market in Britain and a significant species of "dime novel" fiction in the United States. Such fiction tended, however, to borrow Vernian means of locomotion without bothering with the painstaking technological detail in which Verne revelled (much of which was ruthlessly expunged from translations of his works).

The notion that Vernian fiction had a unique educational value was enthusiastically taken up by Hugo *Gernsback, who made it a key element of his advertising of the fiction he called "scientifiction" in the early 1920s. "The Magazine of Scientifiction" was the original subtitle of pioneering specialist magazine *Amazing Stories*, launched by Gernsback in 1926, and that label might have stuck had he not been forced to sell the title in 1929. He probably substituted "science fiction" in the rivals he elected to found, *Science Wonder Stories* and *Air Wonder Stories*, to distance the new magazines from their model, but it seemed much more convenient to readers and writers alike. Once *Amazing* had changed its subtitle from "The Magazine of Scientifiction" to "The Magazine of Science Fiction"—in the November 1932 issue— the establishment of the new term was ensured.

Gernsback's promotion of "scientifiction" made much of the educational and inspirational value of the new genre, although the didactic component of the fiction specifically written for *Amazing* in the late 1920s—appearing alongside reprints of work by Jules *Verne and H. G. *Wells—tended to follow the narrative conventions typical of pulp fiction. *Amazing* was initially larger in size and printed on sturdier paper stock than the general run of pulp magazines, but its pretensions were not reflected in the quality of its prose. Indeed, science fiction rapidly demonstrated that it was innately vulnerable to an unfortunate potential for literary incompetence that went far beyond the capacity of naturalistic fiction. While the badness of naturalistic fiction was limited to incompetence in describing the experienced world, science fiction's creation of hypothetical futures and alien worlds could easily extend into hitherto-unexplored realms of ludicrous incongruity.

The pulp magazines were by no means devoid of futuristic fiction and extraterrestrial adventures before Gernsback founded *Amazing*; indeed, he was encouraged to try his experiments by the great popularity already won by Edgar Rice Burroughs' interplanetary romances, A. Merritt's exotic portal fantasies, and Ray Cummings' wild adventures in space, time, and the subatomic microcosm. He had persuaded Merritt and Cummings to write for him before launching *Amazing* and obtained a new Martian novel from Burroughs for the *Amazing Annual* that was swiftly transformed into *Amazing Stories Quarterly*, but he gave them little incentive to repeat the experience. If his insistence that they included more scientific discourse in their work had not been sufficient deterrent, his attitude to making payment for the work he published would have completed the disincentive.

When *Amazing* made its debut, Burroughsian interplanetary fiction and futuristic fiction were regularly featured in several of the general fiction pulps. *Weird Tales*, which had been founded in 1923, used a good deal of futuristic and interplanetary fiction alongside the supernatural fiction in which it was later to specialise. The principal difference between the "scientifiction" in *Amazing*'s early issues and the kinds of imaginative fiction that were appearing in other pulps was, ironically, that *Amazing*'s contents were predominantly antique, consisting largely of reprints from Wells and Verne. Although Gernsback's editorial posturing was very distinctive, relatively little of the new fiction he published embodied his ideals in any conspicuous fashion; the main effect of his demand for didactic content—where it was actually answered—was to inhibit narrative pace and render the construction of plots very awkward.

By the time former Gernsback employee T. O'Conor Sloane inherited sole control of *Amazing* in 1929 and David Lasser took charge of Gernsback's rival *Wonder* group, it had begun to seem that Gernsback's affirmations of educational value only served to exaggerate the fatuity of the worst examples of pulp science fiction. Sloane and Lasser both allowed the fiction they published to drift in the direction of the conventional pulp action-adventure fiction—a movement dramatically reemphasised when Harry Bates persuaded William Clayton to launch a new specialist magazine, *Astounding Stories of Super-Science*, under his editorship in 1930. Bates ignored Gernsback's didactic pretensions, regarding the "science fiction" label merely as a specification for conventional pulp melodrama of a particularly lurid stripe. Because he paid a higher word rate than his rivals, he immediately began to cream off the most ambitious of the fledgling genre's new recruits, but the "science" in the stories he published was, in essence, mere jargon shoring up the extravagance of plots that involved hectic adventures in space and time, and extraordinary crimes and invasions.

Gernsback and his managing editors tried hard to recruit practicing scientists to work in the new genre, and were enthusiastic to publish their degrees in their by-lines. Locating practicing scientists who were capable of writing fiction, and interested in doing so in the pulp medium, was not easy, but they did find several significant recruits. Two of them, Miles J. Breuer and David H. Keller—who made their debuts in 1927 and 1928, respectively—were M.D.s, although neither made much use of their particular expertise in their fiction. Breuer produced dimensional fantasies, such as "The Appendix and the Spectacles" (1928) and "The Capture Cross-Section" (1929), an expansive account of "Rays and Men" (1929), and a notable novel about a hi-tech society, "Paradise and Iron" (1930), but the last named was a cautionary tale somewhat at odds with Gernsback's own optimism. Although Keller set up a close working relationship with Gernsback that far outlasted their involvement with scientifiction, their views of the future of technology were flatly opposed; for Keller, all kinds of technological advance, no matter how seemingly benevolent, posed a terrible threat to human psychological and spiritual wellbeing. His first-published scientifiction story, "The Revolt of the Pedestrians" (1928), took a stridently alarmist view of the booming automobile culture, while "Stenographer's Hands" (1928) and "The Threat of the Robot" (1929) offered horrified responses to different aspects of industrialisation. His fiction provided an archetypal example of what Isaac Asimov would later call "the *Franken-stein complex".

Sloane continued Gernsback's recruitment policy when *Amazing* changed ownership in 1929. He was not permitted to reveal that "John Taine" was mathematician Eric Temple Bell, but the blurbs he attached to Taine's novels boasted about the author's membership of the National Academy of Sciences. Bell, who had been writing a novel during every summer vacation since 1921, had published several thrillers with speculative components, but had not been able to find an outlet for his more adventurous works. *White Lily* (1930; book 1952 as *The Crystal Horde*) and *Seeds of Life* (1931; book, 1951) were garish melodramas that may well have been written with the pulps in mind, although they made use of interesting speculative premises, but *The Time Stream* (written 1921; published 1932; book, 1946) was a more meditative piece, significantly more original and mature in its handling of ideas than most pulp fiction. Taine made little contribution to the pulps thereafter, however, and his example bore scant fruit. It turned out that by far the most influential of all Sloane's "discoveries" was another writer who had set out to produce a new kind of fiction some years earlier but had not so far found a market for it: the food scientist he was able to advertise, proudly, as E. E. Smith, Ph.D.

Smith had written *The Skylark of Space*—a Burroughsian adventure story that used the entire galaxy as a playground rather than a single other world—in 1920 (with some input from Lee Hawkins Garby, a female neighbour who had inserted "the love interest"). It finally began serialisation in an issue of *Amazing* bearing the same date (August 1928) as the issue of *Weird Tales* in which Edmond Hamilton's novella "Crashing Suns" began serialisation. The two stories, in which starships hurtle across the galaxy, getting involved in an assortment of interstellar conflicts, provided templates for a new subgenre, whose imaginative reach made a tremendous impact on science fiction's burgeoning fan base, and became a key element of the new genre. This new kind of pulp adventure fiction—which ultimately came to be known as "space opera" (by analogy with "horse opera" and "soap opera")—rarely had any serious speculative content, but in taking pulp fiction on to a galactic stage it added an important new frontier to the sketch-map of the future that would become the myth of the *Space Age.

Other practitioners attracted to the subgenre, most significantly Jack Williamson and John W. *Campbell Jr., did have sufficient commitment to Gernsbackian ideals to put considerable emphasis on the scientific hypotheses that provided the seeds of their plots—and Campbell was very fond of wedging speculative lectures on theoretical physics into the interstices of his fast-paced plots—but its enthusiastic adoption by Harry Bates' *Astounding Stories of Super-Science* had far more to do with the scope of its action. It was the advent of space opera rather than the careful speculations of David Lasser's fellow *rocket enthusiasts from the American Interplanetary Society that secured the U.S. genre's commitment to the myth of the Space Age, because it was space opera that provided that futuristic prospectus with its authentic mythic dimension: its promise that the Golden Age of infinite opportunity and godlike power could be plausibly relocated in the future instead of the past.

Clayton's magazine chain was one of those that collapsed when the expansion and diversification of the pulp magazines hit its limits in the Great Depression. *Astounding*'s title was bought in 1933 by Street & Smith, who abbreviated it to *Astounding Stories* and installed F. Orlin Tremaine as editor. *Amazing* reverted to a conventional pulp format in 1933, lost its quarterly companion shortly thereafter, and languished until it was sold to the Ziff-Davis chain in 1938; its new editor, Ray Palmer, immediately converted it into a conventional pulp fiction magazine slanted towards a juvenile audience. By then, Gernsback had already sold the ailing *Wonder Stories*, which was in the process of being repackaged for the same audience as *Thrilling Wonder Stories*. Gernsback's didactic ambitions were, however, reimported—albeit in a carefully modified form—into the Street & Smith version of *Astounding Stories*. Tremaine had begun to advertise for ingenious "thought variant" stories based on scientific speculations in 1934, and this process of ideative sophistication was accelerated when John Campbell took over editorial responsibility for the magazine in 1937.

Campbell leavened the fiction in *Astounding* with popular science articles, and made a show of insisting that the stories he published were rational extrapolations of scientific and technological possibility. He gradually built a stable of writers who were more or less in tune with his ambitions, whose key members included Clifford D. *Simak, Robert A. *Heinlein, Isaac *Asimov, and L. Sprague *de Camp. His ambition was assisted by the fact that science fiction—as it was now routinely abbreviated—or sf, had built up what would now be called a "cult following". The genre had never had mass appeal—its audience was much narrower than the audiences for pulp Western and crime fiction—but the people who liked it tended to like it a great deal, becoming obsessive followers of the genre and forming a community linked by the production and circulation of amateur magazines (fanzines). Gernsback had tried to cultivate this community by sponsoring a Science Fiction League, whose members included many future writers and editors—some of whom, like Donald A. Wollheim, were so obsessive that they volunteered to edit pulps for parsimonious publishers without the benefit of a salary or an editorial budget. Campbell had this relatively small but steadfastly loyal audience at his disposal, and their support was vital to his cause.

Having started out as a writer of space opera before transforming himself into a writer of *contes philosophiques*, Campbell was fully conscious of the utility of science fiction's limitless stage, but the work in that subgenre he published integrated it into the myth of the Space Age and facilitated the kind of sophistication to which it was subjected by Isaac Asimov. While the science fiction in *Astounding* retained and refined its speculative scientific core, however, the material in its rival pulps favoured exotic costume drama and Frankensteinian fables. There was some overflow as fiction designed for sale to Campbell had to be redirected elsewhere, but that was more than compensated by the increasingly heavy dependence of *Amazing Stories* and *Thrilling Wonder Stories*—and their new companions *Fantastic Adventures* and *Startling Stories*—on melodrama and monstrous menaces. These were the models imitated by new outlets, including *Planet Stories* and *Super Science Stories*, whose attempts to distinguish themselves from their rivals went even further in the same downmarket direction.

Campbell tried hard to distinguish *Astounding* from the other science fiction pulps, first by reverting to the "bedsheet" size of the original *Amazing* and then converting it into a "digest" magazine (the same size as *The Reader's Digest*). The latter switch enabled it to maintain a monthly schedule during World War II, when the pulps suffered so badly from paper shortages that the medium never recovered, fading away in the postwar decade, when "pulp fiction" became the prerogative of cheap paperback books and new digest magazines sprang up in droves to displace the pulps. The war did, however, kill off *Astounding*'s fantasy companion, *Unknown*, which Campbell had founded to pioneer a distinctively modern subspecies of magical fantasy, reshaped and enlivened by powerful injections of rationalistic scepticism.

From 1929 to 1945, the term "science fiction" was almost exclusively reserved to American magazines; the sole exception in text form being *The Pocket Book of Science Fiction* (1943) edited by Donald Wollheim. Once World War II was over, however, it began a rapid process of proliferation, not only into paperback books but also into such hardcover showcases as Groff Conklin's *The Best of Science Fiction* (1946). It had already been used with reference to comic books, and to radio shows and films spun off from comic books, but it now began to be used much more generally in all those media and on TV. It was also exported on a considerable scale to Britain and continental Europe, where labelled science fiction magazines and books began to appear in some profusion. The produce of the expanded genre consisted almost entirely of jargonised costume drama, but while the assumption remained in place that its core was still situated in the speculative fiction promoted by John Campbell, the "science" part of its label did not seem entirely redundant.

Britain had developed a small community of science fiction fans, assisted by the fact that pulp publishers often cleared redundant stock out of their warehouses by selling it for use as ballast in transatlantic ships; when such filler survived the crossings it was sold to Woolworth's department stores for resale as "Yank Mags". This unsteady supply had prompted a number of British writers, including John Russell Fearn and John Beynon Harris (later renamed John Wyndham), to launch careers as pulp science fiction writers, and had inspired the establishment of several British fanzines, and a British science fiction pulp, *Tales of Wonder* (launched 1937). Wartime paper shortages were even more acute in Britain than the United States, but they caused a boom in publications printed on bootleg paper, which frequently imitated the garish style of American pulp fiction, including pulp science fiction. As paper rationing eased in the late 1940s, there was an explosion of such imitative fiction, a substantial fraction of which carried the science fiction label. Unfortunately, the straitened economic conditions of its production ensured that such fiction plumbed depths of awfulness never previously attained, and never to be attained again.

The exporting of American science fiction into Britain and continental Europe was closely associated with the new economic hegemony of the paperback book, whose publishers had taken advantage of the artificial market situation of the war to occupy the middle ground between the pulps and hardcover books, taking up the slack left by the paper starvation of both sets of rivals. Although paperback publication had long been normal in nations like France, the new American models were much more colourful and used cheaper technologies of production, so they were widely imitated. Because U.S. paperbacks inherited the marketing policies associated with the generic differentiation of the pulps, science fiction soon became a familiar concept and label everywhere in the world.

While western European science fiction was formulated in the image of American science fiction, eastern European science fiction was formulated in conscious ideological opposition to it. The contrast eventually became particularly stark in West and East Germany, but the most abundant production of ideologically

competitive science fiction was in the USSR, where futuristic fiction had been employed in the 1920s as an instrument of political propaganda by such writers as Alexei Tolstoi, and as an educational aid by such writers as Alexander Belayev. After World War II the genre was enthusiastically promoted by the palaeontologist Ivan Yefremov, whose early works had been translated into English in *Meeting over Tuscarora* (1946; by-lined Efremov). The Foreign Languages Publishing House in Moscow reissued the material therein in *Stories* (1954), adding two novellas of a more ambitious stripe, and also issued a translation of Yefremov's Utopian novel *Andromeda* (1958; trans. 1959) before using his "Cor Sepentis" (1959)— explicitly framed as an ideological reply to Murray Leinster's "First Contact"—as the title story of the first in a series of showcase collections, *The Heart of the Serpent* (1961). The stories in these anthologies were advertised in accordance with a sternly Gernsbackian prospectus, which made much of their scientific bases and the scientific credentials of their writers; Western science fiction was criticised both tacitly and explicitly for its abandonment of scientific speculation in favour of enthusiastic expansions of the ideologies of imperialism colonialism and technofetishism.

Astounding lost its market leadership in the magazine arena as new digest magazines like *Galaxy* and *The Magazine of Fantasy & Science Fiction* (*F&SF*) broadened the horizons of the genre in the 1950s, but in the paperback arena editors anxious to mine the stored-up riches of the pulp genre found much richer pickings in the old *Astounding* than they did elsewhere. Aided by specialist small presses established by fans to put that heritage into hard covers, the paperback publishers made the cream of pulp science fiction available to a new audience in the 1950s and 1960s. The historical background—in which *atom bombs had created a Cold War whose most obvious technological front was the space race—assisted the appreciation of writers who had taken such notions seriously, and whose contributions to the myth of the Space Age could now be seen as definitive.

Genre science fiction remained magazine based until the mid-1960s, in that the magazines were the primary target of all fiction written with the science fiction label in mind, so the editorial policies of *Galaxy* and *F&SF* were important forces guiding new production until then. They were, however, increasingly subject to new patterns of demand associated with book publication. Although both magazines preferred "softer" kinds of science fiction to the Campbellian science fiction that was now relabelled *hard science fiction, their editors were uninterested in space opera—which had come to seem imaginatively naive as well as awkwardly crude in literary terms, and they preferred their Frankensteinian fables dressed in stylish wit. *Satire became very prominent in magazine science fiction of the 1950s, but much of it steered a clever course that aimed for Swiftian literary elegance without reproducing Swift's deep-seated antipathy to science and technology.

Campbell reacted to *Astounding*'s loss of market leadership by changing its title to *Analog* in the late 1950s, reasserting his insistence that science fiction ought to be analogous to science in providing a medium for serious thought experiment; he had recovered its position as the best-selling science fiction magazine from the faltering *Galaxy* by the time he died in 1972, but economic power had shifted by then to book publishers. The science fiction magazine market proved surprisingly resilient, allowing it to survive the extinction crisis that killed off other kinds of fiction magazines in the 1960s, but it was book publishers who set the genre's agenda thereafter. The most important corollary of this shift was that science fiction was transformed from a genre whose fundamental forms were the short story and the novella into one whose primary form was the novel. While the typical length of paperback fiction was sternly controlled there was still a substantial overlap between the long novellas favoured by the magazines and the short novels favoured by the new medium, but that era ended in the mid-1970s when editorial theory underwent a paradigm shift that encouraged much longer books.

The increasing dominance of the science fiction novel posed new challenges to writers, putting much more stress on techniques of "world building". The new regime greatly favoured stories set on Earth-clone scenarios and modestly transformed futures, whose backgrounds did not need much detailed explanation. It saw a dramatic proliferation of the softer subspecies of science fiction, with the successful emergence of writers like Brian *Aldiss, Philip K. *Dick, Ursula *Le Guin, and Robert *Silverberg. The genre broadened its reader base considerably, but the presumed analogy between science and science fiction was weakened to the point at which it came to seem quite unnecessary to readers whose primary interest was in exotica for exotica's sake. One result of this shift in supply and demand was the rehabilitation of such pulp subgenres as "sword and sorcery" fiction and the proliferation of similar subgenres of magical fantasy employing stereotyped and technologically stripped down secondary worlds; the paperback success of J. R. R. Tolkien's *The Lord of the Rings* in the mid-1960s prepared the way for the development of commodified genre fantasy, whose magic was sometimes equipped with a *pseudoscientific disguise by means of *parapsychological jargon.

A similar pattern of development was seen in children's science fiction, which was first distinguished as a significant hardcover subgenre in the early 1950s. Many of the more ambitious writers of Campbellian science fiction—including Heinlein, Asimov, Arthur C. *Clarke, and James *Blish—took full advantage of a brief interval when hard science fiction for children was promoted by U.S. publishers for its supposed educational value, but children's publishers soon realised that softer kinds of science fiction, devoid of theoretical explanations and mechanical devices—as pioneered in the United States by Andre Norton and Madeleine l'Engle—had far more sales potential, because hard science fiction content was a deterrent to the female readers who made up the bulk of the teenage audience.

The supposed educational value of hard science fiction, and its presumed ability to attract male readers who would not otherwise be interested in reading, helped maintain its fashionability in the children's market through the last quarter of the twentieth century—allowing hard science fiction specialists like Ben *Bova, Gregory *Benford, Charles *Sheffield, and Stephen *Baxter to continue to work in the sector—but soft science fiction and magical fantasy reaped much larger commercial rewards, and the phenomenal success of such children's fantasies as J. K. Rowling's Harry Potter series and Philip Pullman's His Dark Materials trilogy eventually turned the victory into a rout.

The dominance of genre science fiction by paperback publishers was itself threatened, not long after it had been achieved, by the increasing success of science fiction in the visual media. The *television series *Star Trek* (1966–1969) overcame the handicap of its restricted initial viewing figures when repeat showings demonstrated the strength of its cult following, and the tremendous success of George Lucas' film *Star Wars* (1976) as a merchandising instrument provided a further demonstration of the exceptional features of the science fiction marketplace. Once the field's economics were fully understood, their exploitation proceeded with all due vigour, and by the mid-1990s, the genre was dominated by its visual formats and by the textual spin-off therefrom. The necessity of appealing to mass audiences, the formularising demands of TV broadcasting, and the innate hostility of the visual media to cogitation, explanation, and intricate plotting combined to reemphasise the softening trends that had already set in within the genre, forcing hard science fiction farther out into the margins of the field—where it continued to survive, in spite of seeming an endangered species, by virtue of a narrower version of the cult following that sustained the entire genre.

The end result of this pattern of evolution was that the bulk of science fiction was gradually shorn of any meaningful relationship with science—but that the minority of texts that struggled to maintain some such relationship in defiance of market pressures continued to attract the support of a small but equally determined sector of the audience. The genre's public image, blighted from its inception by its pulp origins, occasionally showed slight signs of recovery—especially in the late 1960s, when it acquired some useful countercultural associations—but the increasing dominance of TV and movie science fiction extrapolating the concerns and methods of comic book illustration obliterated any chance it had of retaining any significant measure of respectability. Although certain aspects of the genre were integrated into popular culture, those aspects that retained any connection—however tenuous—with the culture of science were firmly condemned to the eccentric ranks of unpopular culture.

SCIENTIFIC ROMANCE

A term used in the plural by C. H. *Hinton as the title of an 1886 collection of speculative nonfiction, whose singular form was subsequently taken up by journalists and reviewers in the 1890s as a convenient label for the kind of fiction popularised by H. G. *Wells. Wells resisted it for some time, preferring the subtitle "Fantastic and Imaginative Romances" in the lists of his previous works printed in his books, but he eventually capitulated by sanctioning the release of an omnibus edition of *The Scientific Romances of H. G. Wells* (1933). By that time it had become standardised in Britain, actively embraced by such writers as Neil Bell and S. Fowler Wright, although it never became popular in the United States—which generated its own alternative term, *science fiction, in the 1920s.

"Scientific romance" remains useful as a label, as a means of highlighting the marked differences between the British and American traditions of speculative fiction that persisted until they were eroded by the importation of American science fiction into Britain in the wake of World War II; it is employed in that fashion in Brian Stableford's history *Scientific Romance in Britain, 1890–1950*. The term retained some currency after 1950, occasionally used as a subtitle—or even, as in Ronald Wright's *A Scientific Romance* (1997), as a title—by writers intent on making the point that the works thus advertised have more in common with the classics of the British tradition than those of American science fiction.

The most important writers associated with the first flourishing of Wellsian scientific romance were George Griffith, M. P. Shiel, C. J. Cutcliffe Hyne, Arthur Conan Doyle, J. D. Beresford, and William Hope Hodgson. Its most significant subgenre was future *war fiction, although the distinctive element introduced by Wells between 1895 and 1901 was the bold use of imaginative motifs in exploratory *contes philosophiques* that were unconfined by the subgeneric boundaries of war stories and Utopian fiction.

The foundation of the genre was associated economically with the rapid proliferation of new middle-brow periodicals following the launch of *The Strand Magazine* in 1891. For slightly more than a decade, the fierce competition between these periodicals encouraged their editors to experiment with various different genres, but by 1905 it had become obvious to the survivors that detective stories and other kinds of crime fiction were by far the most popular and manageable forms of magazine melodrama. Scientific romance went into a decline in the first few years of the twentieth century that was completed by World War I, when the hopes expressed in prewar futuristic fiction came to seem absurd.

Scientific romance made a slow comeback in the 1920s, but only made very occasional appearances in popular magazines; it was mainly restricted to books. A more substantial renewal of its popularity after 1930 was closely associated with political developments in Europe, which made a new world war seem likely; the general tenor of scientific romance between 1919 and 1939 ranged from strident alarmism to bitter pessimism. The new writers who carried forward the Wellsian tradition between the wars, in addition to Bell and Fowler Wright, included Olaf *Stapledon, John Gloag, J. Leslie Mitchell, Katharine Burdekin (who also used the pseudonym Murray Constantine), Muriel Jaeger, C. S. Lewis, and Gerald *Heard, although the most successful individual work written in the period was Aldous *Huxley's *Brave New World* (1932).

When World War II was over, the tradition of scientific romance showed brief signs of recovery, but it was soon swamped by imported American science fiction and British works imitative of that example. It produced one final classic in George Orwell's *Nineteen Eighty-Four* (1949), but became fugitive thereafter as writers who were interested in the future as a narrative space increasingly accepted the science fiction label and made themselves familiar with the American science fiction tradition. Even futuristic writers who refused to publish under the science fiction label in case it should injure their reputation or sales—most notably John Wyndham (who had previously been one of Britain's handful of pulp science fiction writers, as John Beynon Harris)—tended to take more inspiration from the American tradition than the British one, although some British science fiction retained a distinctive flavour consciously carried forward from such writers of scientific romance as Wells and Stapledon.

The most conspicuous difference between scientific romance and science fiction, while the two traditions remained separate, was the total absence from scientific romance of the myth of the *Space Age. Although scientific romances did feature expeditions into space, they never portrayed such expeditions as the initiation of an inexorable sequence of colonial expansion. Even such wide-ranging works as Stapledon's *Last and First Men* (1930) remained confined to the solar system, envisaging the colonisation of its other worlds as last resorts compelled by dire circumstance; such excursions to infinity as the same author's *Star Maker* (1937) were invariably presented as visionary rather than actual experiences. Scientific romance was also noticeably darker than science fiction, by virtue of the deeper scars left in Britain by World War I, and the consequent heightening of anxieties about the effect of bombing raids were a new war to begin—an anxiety that the United States, conveniently out of range of any enemy capable of sending forth aerial fleets of bombers, never had to take seriously.

Britain's empire was in terminal decline throughout the history of scientific romance, and the future always seemed to its practitioners be one of shrinking rather than expanding horizons, and of difficult survival rather than triumphant progress. In spite of these tendencies, writers of scientific romance did occasionally sound hopeful notes, but confined them almost entirely to some notion of human transfiguration that would supersede the seemingly insoluble problems of the contemporary human condition.

The advent of the *atom bomb exposed American futuristic fiction of the 1950s to anxieties similar to those faced by Britain after 1918—causing an increase in visions of transcendent superhumanity, among other effects. In the meantime, British futuristic fiction—led by the example of Arthur C. *Clarke—became much more ready to take aboard, and actively to promote, the myth of the Space Age. In spite of this convergence, however, a certain cultural difference was still distinguishable between American and British science fiction at the end of the twentieth century, which testified to the lingering legacy of scientific romance. Such writers as J. G. *Ballard remained steadfastly suspicious of the values and futuristic imagery typical of American science fiction, but the mythological devastation that Ballard foresaw did not herald a mass retreat on the part of British futuristic fiction to the values of scientific romance, whose echoes remained faint, fugitive, and rather forlorn. Eric Brown's "The Blue Portal" (2002), which is set in 1930s England, pays homage to the genre's accomplishments while regretting its limitations, in featuring two imaginary writers of scientific romance confronted by a dimensional gateway.

SCIENTIST

A practitioner of *science. The term is specifically associated with the modern meaning of "science", its coinage being suggested (by analogy with "artist") by William Whewell in 1833. The terms "natural philosopher" and "man of science" had been in use for some time, but "scientist" had a pithiness that ensured its proud and widespread adoption by practitioners. Images of scientists in art and literature, however, inherited many features previously attributed to alchemists and magicians. Early literary images of "scientists" were routinely mistrustful, suspecting that their interest in abstract matters might be a symptom of social maladjustment and occult interests that might easily be extrapolated into something more dangerous.

Images of natural philosophers and men of science, produced before Whewell's new term became widespread, had often stressed their eccentricities and their alienation from the interests and values of common men. The various specialist researchers of Margaret Cavendish's *Blazing World* (1666) are described as metaphorical chimeras, including bird-men, fish-men, and worm-men. The astronomers of Laputa in Jonathan Swift's *Gulliver's Travels* (1726) have twisted themselves out of shape by continually lifting one eye to the heavens while keeping the other fixed on the ground. The "mechanician" Coppelius in E. T. A. Hoffmann's "Der Sandmann" (1816; trans. as "The Sandman") is a frankly diabolical figure. Victor Frankenstein in Mary Shelley's novel (1818) threatens to fill the world with monsters. The protagonist of Honoré de Balzac's *La recherche de l'absolu* (1834; trans. as *The Quest of the Absolute*) sacrifices everything that sensible men hold dear to his obsession. Literary representations accepted Whewell's new term readily enough, but did not employ it to signify any break in this exotic tradition.

Although the image of the scientist evolved in parallel with a more specific and more materialistic definition of "science", the suspicion lingered in popular perception that there is something essentially strange, if not explicitly magical, about such people. The suspicion continued to haunt late nineteenth-century technologists as well as abstract theorists, in spite of Thomas *Edison's insistence that his kind of genius was "ninety-nine percent perspiration". Late nineteenth-century speculative fiction added further type specimens to the image of the antisocial and incipiently dangerous scientist, many of them contributed by the founding fathers of modern speculative fiction. Jules Verne offered a relatively generous account of the eccentric Professor Lidenbrock in *Voyage au centre de la terre* (1863; trans. as *Journey to the Centre of the Earth*) but went on to imagine more sinister figures in Captain Nemo, the antihero of *Vingt milles lieues sous les mers* (1870; trans. as *Twenty Thousand Leagues Under the Sea*), and *Robur le conquérant* (1886).

H. G. Wells similarly followed the kindly and heroic time traveller of *The Time Machine* (1895) with a sequence of less appealing figures, including the megalomaniac Moreau in *The Island of Dr. Moreau* (1896), the paranoid Griffin in *The Invisible Man* (1897), and the scatterbrained Cavor in *The First Men in the Moon* (1901). Robert Louis Stevenson's well-intentioned Dr. Jekyll turned out to be a mask for the demonic Mr. Hyde. Arthur Conan Doyle offered Professor Challenger as a heroic exaggeration of himself—he posed for the character in the fake photograph included in the first edition of *The Lost World* (1912)—but seemed to take particular pride in the great man's ready assumption that his scientific genius gave him a licence to disregard social conventions of politeness and discretion and behave like a boor.

A significant break in the tradition of socially isolated and alienated scientists might have occurred when the American public made a hero of Edison, and some of his literary imitations did represent the ingenuity of inventors as a natural expression of progressive American pragmatism, but the general impression remained that Edison was a very remarkable man, and such fictitious dime novel inventors as Johnny Brainerd (in Edward S. Ellis' *The Steam Man of the Prairies*, 1868), Frank Reade Jr., Tom Edison Jr., and Tom Swift remained essentially nerdy no matter what heroic feats they accomplished. The advent of generic science fiction made only modest inroads into this established pattern. Hugo Gernsback's *Ralph 124C41+* (1911–1912) was intended to be an appealing character in every respect, as youthful, vigorous, and brave as any hero of popular fiction, but he was a striking exception to the general pattern of pulp fiction.

Ralph 124C41+'s avatars were rare even in the specialist science fiction magazines, where grey-bearded eccentrics far outnumbered brilliant adventurers like Edward E. Smith's Richard Seaton. The heroes of the great majority of pulp science fiction stories were young men of no great intellectual attainment, who often became involved with scientists merely by virtue of falling in love with their lovely daughters. The narrative utility of naive viewpoint characters, who could legitimately ask for detailed explanations of a story's scientific background—and pursue its thornier points until they were able to grasp the gist—was keenly appreciated by writers and readers alike. Unworldly eccentrics abounded in both popular scientific romance and pulp science fiction—notable examples included W. L. Alden's Professor Van Wagener (some of whose exploits were collected in *Van Wegener's Ways*, 1898), Paul Bold's Jerome Mudgewood (in a similar series in *The Idler*, 1910), Clement Fézandie's Dr. Hackensaw (in the Gernsback pulps, 1921–1926), and Stanley G. Weinbaum's Professor van Manderpootz (in a pulp science fiction series, 1935–1936)—but they were much more useful as characters when their esoteric ideas could be filtered through a man-in-the-street's viewpoint *en route* to the reader.

Many scientists in pulp fiction turned to crime in order to supply the stories in which they appeared with an adequate component of melodrama, after the fashion of the cultish scientists in Neil R. Jones' Durna Rangue series. Very few of them ever followed the example of the villain of John W. Campbell Jr.'s "The Black Star Passes" (1930), who repented his delinquency in order to add his expertise to that of his pursuers in tackling much bigger problems. Some early twentieth-century scientists did stretch the envelope of conventional heroism in the direction of "superheroism"—Caesar Brent in Frederic Carrel's *2010* (1914) is a notable example—and S. P. Meek's Dr. Bird series (1930–1932) imported that notion into the pulps, but the subsequent evolution of superhero fiction soon settled into a standard pattern by which scientists who acquired superpowers were highly likely to become supervillains, while the secret identities of the superheroes who opposed them would very often be conspicuously ordinary.

Because "science" is an abstract concept, it was the scientist who provided a tangible public and literary image. That image was gradually refined by various iconic associations, most of which were standardised in twentieth-century fiction and reportage by virtue of lending themselves to illustrative representation. One such association was with scribbled equations, sometimes formalised as formulas inscribed on a blackboard but often jotted down on the backs of envelopes or other haphazard scraps of paper, reflecting the unexpectedness with which inspiration is widely supposed to strike. Another such association was with laboratory apparatus, often aggregated on benches in chaotic clusters, reflecting the cumulative effect of hasty experimental endeavour and its tendency to outstrip the imperatives of tidiness—although those imperatives were reflected in the scientist's emblematic costume (the lab coat) and his readiness to elevate significant items of apparatus (especially test tubes) above the general chaos, to symbolise the emergence of order and discovery therefrom. The movement from experimental enquiry to theoretical conclusion was routinely symbolised in fiction by the journey from laboratory to lecture hall, from the private struggle with raw data to confrontation with a company of peers—which, in accordance with the imperatives of dramatic tension, rarely received the hero with due enthusiasm, and often rejected his findings, quite unjustly, with manifest contempt.

Louis Macneice's "The Kingdom" (1944) summed up the conventional attitude to this kind of image in a paradigmatic poetic representation of a scientist as "A little dapper man but with shiny elbows / And short keen sight, he lived by measuring things / And died like a recurring decimal / Run off the page, refusing to be curtailed ..." Twentieth-century scientists who turned to writing fiction, however, tended to evaluate this attitude as an unfortunate misunderstanding, or at least a misappreciation, of the true social value of such individuals. The plant physiologist E. C. Large produced a very detailed account of Charles Pry's struggle to maintain the cause of progress against all kinds of odds in *Sugar in the Air* (1937). Sometimes, novelists who were not scientists themselves took a similar view, although Sinclair Lewis's painstaking portrait of a medical researcher in *Arrowsmith* (1925) offers a slightly ambivalent account of an ideological struggle very similar to Pry's.

This kind of imagery was further exaggerated when it moved from the printed page into the cinema medium. Although the way had been pointed by such literary works as Raymond MacDonald and Raymond Alfred Leger's *The Mad Scientist* (1908), it was in cinematic representations that the stereotypical eccentricity of scientists moved decisively in the direction of full-blown madness. Classic silent movie images of this kind include *The Cabinet of Dr. Caligari* (1919) and *Dr. Mabuse, der Spieler* (1922; English version as *Dr. Mabuse, the Gambler,* 1922). Mad scientists became much more expressive in the early talkies, where actors whose use of facial expression had been trained in the caricaturish fashion of silent films were able to mutter and screech as well—a mode of performance demonstrated by Colin Clive's portrayal of *Frankenstein* (1931) and further augmented by Ernest Thesiger's portrayal of Dr. Praetorius in the sequel, *The Bride of Frankenstein* (1935). Actors who played cinematic monsters, including Boris Karloff and Bela Lugosi, routinely extended their range by playing mad scientists, as Karloff did in *The Invisible Ray* (1936) and Lugosi in *Black Dragons* (1942).

Outside the realm of monster movies scientists fared only a little better; Alec Guinness' character in *The Man in the White Suit* (1951) provided the perfect cinematic exemplification of the unworldly eccentric, while Cary Grant's uptight and absent-minded scientist in *Monkey Business* (1952) benefited enormously from psychotropic loosening up. L. Sprague de Camp's article on "The Care and Feeding of Mad Scientists" in the July 1951 issue of *Astounding Science Fiction* suggested that it was the stereotypical image of the scientist that invited psychopathological classification as "schizoid", but was teasingly uncertain as to the extent to which actual scientists resembled the stereotype—and de Camp took obvious relish in the composition of "Judgment Day" (1955), in which a scientist mocked by his fellow men is only reluctant to destroy the world with an atomic chain reaction because he has no way of subjecting it to a slower torture. Late twentieth-century fictional images of scientists often embody the notion that the attempt to purge knowledge of value judgements encourages scientists to put their consciences to one side, so that they become voluntary sociopaths.

The image of the scientist was not helped by the role that technologists played in the two world wars in developing new *weapons, especially chemical and biological weapons. Those involved in World War I remained behind the scenes, but some of those involved in World War II achieved a legendary notoriety. The exploits of Josef Mengele in Auschwitz gave rise to a new archetype, as did those of the rocket scientist Wernher von Braun, whose recruitment to the U.S. space program never entirely redeemed the sinister aspects of his larger-than-life personality. Von Braun and his fellow rocket scientists did, however, provide a convincing paradigm of the heroic scientist whose eyes were fixed on the stars while his feet were planted in the mire.

By the time World War II ended, the myth of the *Space Age was so well developed in genre science fiction that a new generation of heroic scientists had emerged therein, whose heroism consisted in the fact that they were organising and taking a fully active part in the conquest of the next frontier. It was in extraterrestrial contexts that the heroic scientists of genre science fiction found their true vocation, and the opportunity to be fully integrated into the new societies that would form and grow beyond the limits of Earth's surface. When Isaac Asimov's Foundation series introduced social scientists to pulp science fiction, their primary function was to explain and justify the mythos of the Space Age.

Even Earthbound scientists were able to demonstrate their heroic credentials when extraterrestrial entities arrived on Earth, because they were the experts who might find a way to deal with such incursions. Even in the visual media, scientists could become out-and-out heroes when alien invasions threatened; Nigel Kneale's Dr. Quatermass became one of the archetypal characters of BBC TV. The television medium ultimately proved to be a useful arena for the development of series-based scientists who could function as puzzle solvers and crimefighters in continual confrontation with problematic dangers to the public, whether the dangers in question were exotic—like those faced by Dana Scully in *The X-Files* (1993–2002)—or mundane, like those faced by the *forensic scientists in the various *CSI* series (launched 2000).

In the context of confrontation with problematic dangers, as in others, however, the legacy of World War II generated considerable anxiety about the interaction between scientific and military priorities, and scientists whose primary interest was in learning more were frequently juxtaposed in fiction of the latter half of the twentieth century with military men whose first instinct was to destroy anything unfamiliar and take exclusive control of any knowledge or technology with weapon potential. Notable accounts of idealistic scientists victimised by or heroically resistant to attempts to hijack their work for military applications include Edward Hyams' *Not in Our Stars* (1949), C. M. Kornbluth's "The Altar at Midnight" (1952), David Duncan's *Dark Dominion* (1954), Algis Budrys' *Who?* (1958), Haakon Chevalier's *The Man Who Would Be God* (1959), and W. J. J. Gordon's "The Nobel Prize Winners" (1963). Edward Peattie's "The Conners" (1954) offered an anxious depiction of future scientists as objects of murderous hatred under perpetual army protection. Scientists ready and willing to cooperate with military schemes came to seem even more sinister than their predecessors, in such representations as the eponymous antihero of Stanley Kubrick's film *Dr. Strangelove* (1963), Felix Hoenikker in Kurt Vonnegut's *Cat's Cradle* (1963), and the various scientists featured in Thomas Pynchon's *Gravity's Rainbow* (1973).

The fact that so many late twentieth-century science fiction writers were trained in science to degree level, and that a considerable number worked as scientists, helped to make the characterisation of scientists within the genre more credible as well as more sympathetic. This imagery remained confused with caricaturish imagery, but did provide a balancing factor that exposed the more eccentric portraits as dramatic contrivances. Outside the genre, the relative dearth of scientifically educated novelists—and the frequent critical hostility directed against such rare examples as C. P. *Snow—resulted in a marked

dominance of dark-edged satirical representations such as those found in C. S. Lewis's description of the National Institute of Co-ordinated Experiments in NICE in *That Hideous Strength* (1945), Lawrence Durrell's *The Revolt of Aphrodite* (in 2 vols. as *Tunc* and *Nunquam,* 1968–1970; combined ed., 1974), Harvey Jacobs' "Accepting for Winkelmeyer" (1973), and Don deLillo's *Ratner's Star* (1976).

No matter how sympathetic writers were to scientists pressed into service as characters, representations of their work had to cope with the problem of equipping the ninety-nine percent of genius that consists of mere perspiration with a measure of dramatic interest. All literary images of scientists at work in the laboratory inevitably tended to concentrate on the rare high points of actual discovery, while consigning routine work to the narrative background as mere decor. Even in the respectful and celebratory varieties of science fiction, therefore, convincing images of scientists at work and laboratories in operation are relatively rare; notable attempts can be found in Raymond F. Jones' "Noise Level" (1952), Kate Wilhelm's *The Clewiston Test* (1976), Gregory Benford's *Timescape* (1980), Hilbert Schenck's *A Rose for Armageddon* (1982), Paul Preuss' *Broken Symmetries* (1983) and *Human Error* (1985), Stephen Baxter's *Timelike Infinity* (1992), and Alan Lightman's *Good Benito* (1995).

More profound narrative problems arise in the depiction of theorists engaged in calculation and cogitation without the aid of laboratory apparatus, and the task is rarely attempted; even Ursula K. Le Guin's representation of Dr. Shevek in *The Dispossessed* (1974) takes up his story some time after he has made his epoch-making discovery. Scientific theorists are most useful, in a dramatic sense, when they are engaged in fierce ideological and professional disputes with their rivals, as they are in Eleazer Lipsky's *The Scientists* (1959), Isaac Asimov's *The Gods Themselves* (1972), Wil McCarthy's *The Collapsium* (2000), and Carter Scholz's *Radiance* (2002).

In spite of all these difficulties in representation, science fiction remains the favoured leisure reading of many practicing scientists—a phenomenon sufficiently obvious by the 1950s to prompt Arthur S. Barron to pose the question "Why Do Scientists Read Science Fiction?" in the February 1957 issue of *The Bulletin of the Atomic Scientists.* Barron—employing conventional functionalist "uses and gratifications" theory—identified three flattering processes at work: the glamourisation of scientists' endeavours; the expression of protest against the use of scientists' work for "antihuman ends"; and the reaffirmation of the fundamental belief that that "human intellect, come to its final flowering in the scientist, will save mankind".

SETI

An acronym signifying the search for extraterrestrial intelligence. It was coined in association with Project Ozma, established in 1960 by Frank Drake at the National Radio Astronomy Observatory in Greenbank, Virginia, to scan G-type stars for radio signals that might be communications.

The possibility that radio telescopes might pick up signals from extraterrestrial civilisations had first been broached in the 1940s, and had been popularised within the science fiction field by an article in *Astounding*'s April 1947 issue by Lorne MacLaughlan. Pre-Ozma science fiction stories of radio contact included Robert Crane's *Hero's Walk* (1954), Arthur C. Clarke's "No Morning After" (1956), and J. G. Ballard's "The Voices of Time" (1960; rev. as "News from the Sun", 1982). Drake and other interested parties, including Carl *Sagan, thus had a head start in trying to figure out which frequency an alien species might employ for such broadcasts—R. N. Bracewell had proposed that the most likely wavelength for interstellar communication is the 21-cm "hydrogen line"—and how information might be encoded within a sequence of binary digits.

This speculative nonfiction laid the groundwork for a substantial subgenre of SETI fiction, which built on the inspiration of the "Drake equation": a device for estimating the number of advanced technical civilisations in the galaxy, which involves multiplying the number of stars in the galaxy by the proportion that have planetary systems, the average number of habitable planets in each system, the proportion of habitable planets in which life actually arises, the proportion of planetary ecospheres in which intelligence evolves, the proportion of intelligent species that develop communication technologies detectable by radio astronomy, and the fraction of a planetary lifetime for which such civilisations are likely to exist.

All these figures except the first are conjectural, and might have values very close to zero, but the application of the "cosmological principle"—which assumes axiomatically that our solar system must be relatively ordinary—tempted many speculators to insert figures much closer to one, yielding estimates on the order of tens of thousands, or even millions. Stephen H. Dole's *Habitable Planets for Man* (1964; popular version with Isaac Asimov as *Planets for Man*), based on the U.S. Air Force's RAND study, employs conservative estimates.

Had the figures initially estimated for the terms in the Drake equation been correct, Ozma might have been expected to produce results within a few years; its continued failure—reflected in the *Fermi paradox—suggested that at least one of the terms in the equation must be a great deal closer to zero than the cosmological principle had suggested. One optimist, Duncan Lunan, suggested in "Space Probe from Epsilon Boötis" (1974) that evidence might already exist of a SETI contact, buried in the archives of early radio astronomy, but failed to convince sceptics.

Science fiction writers, who had long been interested in the prospect of a first contact with *alien intelligence, were enthusiastic to imagine what the consequences might be of Project Ozma's success. In John Brunner's "Listen! The Stars!" (1962; exp. book *The Stardroppers*) the project is democratised, as "stardroppers" listen to signals from stars on walkman-like earphones. Notable post-Ozma representations of SETI contacts include Fred Hoyle and John Elliot's *A for Andromeda* (TV serial, 1961; book, 1962), Chloe Zerwick and Harrison Brown's *The Cassiopeia Affair* (1968), James E. Gunn's *The Listeners* (1968–1972; book, 1972), Perry A. Chapdelaine's "Initial Contact" (1969), Richard and Nancy Carrigan's *The Siren Stars* (1970), Scott W. Schumack's "Longevity" (1976), Ben Bova's *Voyagers* (1981), Jack McDevitt's "Cryptic" (1983), *The Hercules Text* (1986), and "Voice in the Dark" (1986), Thomas Wylde's "The Oncology of Hope" (1984), Frederick Fichman's *SETI* (1990), Mary Doria Russell's *The Sparrow* (1996), Robert J. Sawyer's *Factoring Humanity* (1998) and "Ineluctable" (2002), and Tobias S. Buckell's "The Fish Merchant" (2000).

The gravitas attached to the notion of first contact inevitably produced such cynical SETI fantasies as Stanislaw Lem's *Glos pana* (1968; trans. as *His Master's Voice*), in which the received message is profoundly unhelpful, and a story in Pierre Boulle's *Quai absurdum* (1970), in which it turns out to be an advertising slogan, but the more interesting late additions to the subgenre are those reflecting the gradual disillusion of the project's continued failure, including Lee Killough's "The Lying Ear" (1982), Francis Cartier's "The Frequency of the Signals" (1986), "The Day the Signals Started" (1991), and "The Day the Signals Stopped" (1993), Robin F. Rowland's "Wait Till Next Year" (1988), Francis Marion Soty's "Call to Glory" (1991), Ian R. MacLeod's "New Light on the Drake Equation" (2001), and Robert Reed's "Oracles" (2002) and "Lying to Dogs" (2002).

NASA withdrew its funding for SETI in 1993, but the project continued, generating a remarkable collaborative enterprise in the early twenty-first century, when its data processing was dispersed to hundreds of thousands of internet-connected PCs whose owners volunteered their use—a project explained and publicised in *Are We Alone in the Cosmos? The Search for Alien Contact* (2000) edited by Ben Bova and Byron Preiss.

SEX

A *biological phenomenon, whereby reproduction of an organic species requires the combination of two different kinds of cells produced by different organs, identified as "male" and "female". In angiosperm plants the different reproductive organs are usually held within a single structure—a flower—although some flowers only have one kind of organ, male and female flowers being borne by separate individuals. Even when both kinds of organs are held within the same flower, though, it is often the case that the pollen produced by the male stamens cannot fertilise the female ovule contained within the style of the same flower, requiring it to be carried to another by the wind or by an intermediary vector (often an insect). In animals it is relatively rare for individual organisms to be equipped with both male and female sex organs; as in plants, such hermaphrodite species are usually incapable of self-fertilisation.

The mobility of animals obviates the necessity for vectors, although sedentary aquatic species rely on the surrounding water to bear the produce of their male sperm to the female equivalents; the usual pattern of sexual reproduction in animals is for individuals of opposite sexes to come together at an appropriate moment and engage in some form of mechanical intercourse. The determination by natural selection of various patterns of sexual differentiation and mating behaviour among animals is a complex process whose results often seem puzzlingly exotic; identification of the logic of such patterns is the subject matter of *sociobiology.

Human sexual intercourse is subject to extraordinarily complex social regulation and surrounded by intricate patterns of taboos. The logic of this situation has much to do with the necessity of providing elaborate parental care for human offspring, which are neotenic (born at a relatively early developmental stage) and thus require careful protection and education for a period considerably longer than the entire lifespans of many other species. It is arguable that all human culture is an extrapolation of the biological and social necessities of sexual reproduction, and inevitable that the psychological by-products of the social institutions surrounding sexual intercourse and parental care should be one of the principal subjects of literature and the visual arts.

There is a sense in which complex multicellular organisms and their behaviour patterns are merely mechanisms by which egg cells reproduce themselves—usually summed up in the aphoristic observation that a chicken is only an egg's way of making more eggs. From this standpoint, the real purpose of everything that human beings are, do, think, and believe—including science and fiction—must be seen as a derivative, however remote or oblique, of the process of sexual reproduction. Within this perspective, both science and fiction may be regarded as by-products of the sexual impulse, which tends to be diverted into "displacement activities" in many animal species whenever its direct expression is frustrated or unprofitable. This thesis is often contained, overtly or covertly, in theories of literary creativity—George Bernard Shaw is reputed to have believed that every orgasm cost him three chapters—but is less frequently encountered in the philosophy of science, although it does figure in some pejorative explanations of science and technology as typical extensions of male psychology and behaviour.

Sexual differentiation in most animal species is obvious, and the significance of sexual intercourse in reproduction is easily observed in animal husbandry. *Anthropological opinions as to when various human societies became conscious of the connection between sexual intercourse and reproduction are, however, various. One thesis suggests that the evolving consciousness was responsible for a relatively recent prehistoric shift from matrilineal patterns of inheritance to patrilineal ones, reflected in drastic changes in *religious culture. At any rate, awareness of the connection still left much to be discovered in terms of the mechanisms of generation and heredity. It was not until the invention of the microscope that studies in embryology began to make progress and Antonius von Leeuwenhoek was able to observe "animalcules" (sperms) in semen. The hypotheses built on that observation—including the Comte du Buffon's theory of "organic molecules", which interpreted the newly observed microscopic entities as generative agents whose function was to activate "interior moulds"—were initially vague and often fanciful.

The initial attribution of sex to plants was made in Classical times—and celebrated in a handful of eccentric classics of *botanical literature in the fifteenth and sixteenth centuries—but it was not until Sebastian Vaillant's seventeenth-century microscopic observations that the fecundation of plants was explained in sufficient detail to permit Carolus Linnaeus to formulate a natural classification of plants based on their reproductive organs. The treatment of plant sexuality in literature provides a vivid reflection of the remarkable extent and power of the taboos surrounding the entire topic of sex, whose history in respectable literature has been screened by censorship and euphemism, while generating an antithetical "undergrowth" of fiction defiant of that censorship.

Litterateurs had, of course, begun to scrutinise the psychology and sociology of sex long before its biological basis was elucidated, in spite of the fact that such explorations excited controversy and censure, after the fashion of the works of François Rabelais. Attitudes to the literary uses of sex reflect a discomfiting awareness of the potential sexual uses of literature: the knowledge—expressed in the term "pornography"—that literary works featuring sexual intercourse, whatever their supposed or actual intention, have a technical utility of their own in the assistance of masturbation. The relationship between respectable literature and pornography reflects that between institutions of legitimate marriage and their own dubious counterpart, prostitution.

While scientific research gradually exposed and explained the mechanisms of animal—and therefore human—reproduction, and the variety of sexual regulation in different human cultures, the producers of respectable literature were mostly content to avert their attention, while producers of pornography avidly soaked up the new wisdom and attempted to integrate their own endeavours into it. The Marquis de Sade's eighteenth-century adventures in pornographic extremism are replete with discourses in primitive ethnology, physiology, and psychology, and manifest a keen interest in tabulation, classification, and experimentation. Scholarly extrapolations of the same objectives, from Richard Krafft-Ebing's *Psychopathia Sexualis* (1886) to Margaret Mead's account of *Coming of Age in Samoa* (1928) and Alfred Kinsey's reports on *Sexual Behavior in the Human Male* (1948) and *Sexual Behavior in the Human Female* (1953), were read with far greater avidity than most scientific treatises. There are some remarkable hybrid texts in this field—including Rémy de Gourmont's *Physique d'amour* (1903; trans. as *The Natural Philosophy of Love*), Sigmund Freud's *Die Traumdeutung* (1900; trans. as *The Interpretation of Dreams*), and Augustin Cabanes' *The Erotikon* (1933)—that are equally interesting as literary and scholarly works.

The differences between the treatment of sex in respectable literature and pornography are largely describable in terms of the complementary accounting schemes of love and lust. The involvement of science in the explanation of sexual phenomena often tended to reduce the former to the latter—in which matter its effects ran contrary to the involvement of Christian religion, which tended to pull them apart by exalting love beyond the physical while denigrating and suppressing lust. There is no historical evidence of any movement towards compromise in this ideological dispute; the twentieth century saw the extravagant proliferation of a literary genre of formularised "romantic fiction" whose *raison d'être* is to elaborate and celebrate a quasi-religious notion of love, in dialectic opposition to rapidly proliferating pornography elaborating and celebrating the biological and psychological imperatives and perversities of lust. The representation of love as a kind of supernatural force, as unaccountable as it is irresistible, is the most significant enclave of resistance to the general disenchantment of the world by scientific explanation.

Within the tradition of Utopian fiction the complexities and embarrassments of the social regulation of sex often seemed to be awkward barriers to the establishment of an ideal society. In many Utopias sexual relations are rudely stripped of their passionate component and sternly regulated, although it is hard to believe that such supposedly rational systems of sexual regulation as the astrological calculations employed in Tommaso Campanella's *La Città del Sole* (written 1602; trans. as *The City of the Sun*) could ever gain consensual support. In others, the regulatory systems are casually discarded so that the passionate component can be given free rein, as in Denis Vairasse's *L'histoire des Sevarambes* (1677–1679; trans. as *History of the Sevarites or Sevarambi*).

Gabriel de Foigny's *Les aventures de Jacques Sadeur* (1676) uses a hypothetical race of hermaphrodites to explore the question of whether the ideal of social equality can ever be fulfilled while sexual differentiation exists. Denis Diderot's *Les bijoux indiscrets* (1748) took an opposite tack, imagining a race whose sexual organs come in so many different shapes and sizes that mate choice is determined entirely by geometrical coincidence. Giovanni Casanova's *Icosameron* (1788) features another hermaphrodite species, whose individuals live in inseparable pairs. Other writers, following an example set by Thomas d'Urfey's play *A Common-Wealth of Women* (1686), wondered whether a society entirely composed of women—reproducing by means of parthenogenesis or by a contrivance such as the one attributed to the legendary Greek tribe of Amazons—might be happier and more prosperous than one confused by differentiation; most male writers contemplating such a notion, however, clung to the narcissistic assumption adopted by d'Urfey, that it would only require the appearance of one virile man to persuade an entire society of that sort to revert to "normality".

The inversion of typical social relations between men and women became a significant topic of satire in the eighteenth century—although the text of the play that apparently led the way, Pierre Marivaux's *La Nouvelle colonie, ou la Ligue des femmes* (1729), is lost—and remained a favourite speculative strategy thereafter. The principle of "free love" exemplified in James Henry Lawrence's *The Empire of the Nairs* (1811) and endorsed by Charles Fourier in *Le nouveau monde amoureux* (written ca. 1832; published 1967)—on the grounds that monogamy is implicitly antisocial—became a significant slogan of several euchronian social movements. Dystopian images exhibit exactly the same range of representation, the differences of evaluation being in the eyes of the beholders.

European social and literary attitudes to sex were complicated in the sixteenth century by the advent of syphilis, although the epidemiology of the disease is difficult to track because of the inadequacies of contemporary diagnostic techniques. At any rate, it was soon realised that it was an especially virulent and dangerous form of "venereal disease". The extent to which it inspired the ideological upheavals of Puritanism must remain conjectural, but its effect on literary culture is more obvious. The association of a considerable sector of literary culture with a sexually liberal lifestyle had been limited while literate men were mostly monks, but from the sixteenth century onwards, there was a noticeable correlation between literary activity and licentiousness that reached its apogee in the nineteenth century, although it was held at bay in England by the strictures of "Victorianism". In France, the transformation of the optimistically passionate *Romantic movement into the fatalistically passionate *Decadent movement—and the centrality to the imagery of both movements of the *femme fatale*—was at least partly attributable to the physical and psychopathological effects of syphilis.

The scientific advances of the nineteenth century made slow but significant headway in penetrating the physiological mysteries of sex and made a beginning on the biochemistry of the sex hormones. The logic of the whole phenomenon became a little clearer when Charles *Darwin developed the theory of evolution by natural selection and Johann Mendel clarified the elementary principles of genetic inheritance—after which it became evident that sex ensures the continual reassortment of genetic information, producing new combinations subject to the judgement of natural selection. In the same period, technological means and methods of intervention also made significant progress, in spite of being subjected to drastic repression; the proliferation of cosmetics was not uncontroversial, and the development of technologies of birth control excited such strong reactions that George Drysdale felt obliged to publish his innocuously titled *Elements of Social Science* (1854) anonymously lest its

discussion of such issues should cause irreparable distress to his family. Literary interests became deeply confused as the long-traditional inclination of litterateurs to oppose the corrosive effects of scientific explanation on the mythology of love was counterbalanced by a by-now traditional inclination to favour "Bohemian" sexual licence against Puritan denial.

Although actual scientific progress in this field was gradual, a significant boundary of awareness and attitude was passed in the final decades of the nineteenth century, which transformed the literary treatment of sex. The brief flourishing of literary *Naturalism combined with the popularisation of Richard Krafft-Ebing's work on sexual psychopathology by such works as Havelock Ellis' *Studies in the Psychology of Sex* (1897)—all the more significant because of Ellis' endeavours in literary criticism—and the sensation generated by Sigmund Freud's psychology to transform the manner in which sex was treated in the literary representations of modernism. The consequent rhetorical stance was never wholeheartedly scientific, or even pseudoscientific, but it did take aboard an awareness of new findings in physiology, biochemistry, and psychology and inevitable correlations between them. Once the boundary had been crossed, however, there was a very obvious pause, which brought a swift halt to any further development.

The boundary transgression was reflected in speculative fiction in a small number of exploratory works such as J. H. Rosny aîné's "Les xipéhuz" (1887; trans. as "The Shapes" and "The Xipehuz"), which equips its alien invaders with a third sex (a notion he was to revisit in *Les navigateurs de l'infini*, 1925), and Alfred Jarry's *Le surmâle* (1901; trans. as *The Supermale*), but such explorations made little progress. It was more obvious in the transformation of feminist fictions such as the pseudonymous *Mizora: A Prophecy* (1880–1881; book, 1890, by-lined Princess Vera Zaronovich), in which biotechnology sustains a society that has no further biological or social use for males. Feminist writers had taken a strong interest in the *popularisation of science in the early part of the nineteenth century, but it was obvious by 1880 that education was not as powerful an instrument of liberation and equality as writers like Jane Marcet and Harriet Martineau—working in a tradition that extended back to Margaret Cavendish—had hoped.

The feminist movement's cutting edge had switched to the active political campaigning of the suffragettes, but its supporters had a ready-made interest in Utopian speculation. Lillie Devereux Blake's "A Divided Republic" (1887), Mrs. George Corbett's *New Amazonia: A Foretaste of the Future* (1889), and Alice Jones and Ella Marchant's *Unveiling a Parallel*

(1893; by-lined "Two Women of the West") carried the cause forward in a bold manner, but subsequent images of a similar kind—including Charlotte Perkins Gilman's *Herland* (1915; book, 1979) and its sequel—tended to be markedly less adventurous in their use of scientific ideas and technological speculation. Anti-feminist fantasies such as Thomas A. Janvier's *The Women's Conquest of New York* (1894; published anonymously), J. Wilson's *When the Women Reign, 1930* (1908), and Arthur Charles Fox-Davies' *The Sex Triumphant* (1909) followed a similar trajectory.

Speculative fiction was subject to the same inhibitions as any other discussion of sexual science, which tended to be particularly severe when applied to "popular fiction", especially fiction slanted at a juvenile audience, as Vernian fiction was. There was an inevitable reaction against such restriction, exemplified by such works as Edward Heron-Allen's spectacular celebration of perversity *The Cheetah Girl* (privately published 1923) and Isidore Schneider's account of facultative transsexualism *Doctor Transit* (1925; by-lined I. S.), but they remained effectively invisible. Circumstances did permit the publication of occasional far-reaching thought experiments—notably Katharine Burdekin's *Proud Man* (1934; by-lined Murray Constantine), in which a hermaphrodite Genuine Person from the far future visits the present in order to observe the failures of contemporary sexual differentiation—but stifled far more. M. E. Mitchell's *Yet in My Flesh*—(1933) exercises such extreme terminological restraint that the purpose and procedure of the biological experiment at the heart of its plot remain clouded in obscurity (although the alert reader can infer that it involves a female equivalent of Serge Voronoff's attempts to rejuvenate male patients by means of transplanted animal testicles).

The Utopian tradition of thought experiments in state-controlled reproduction retained a certain respectability by virtue of its antiquity, and received a further boost from the fashionability of *eugenics, giving rise to a few relatively ingenious scientific romances, such as Charlotte Haldane's *Man's World* (1926) and S. Fowler Wright's "P. N. 40—and Love" (1930; aka "P. N. 40"). The most adventurous early twentieth-century attempt to construct a hypothetical society with a radically different sexual organisation was Frigyes Karinthy's Swiftian satire *Capillaria* (1922), but it is a conspicuously isolated example. It was, however, from the relatively respectable direction of eugenically inspired Utopian modelling that speculations regarding future developments in regulatory institutions and their potential technological support made their way into pulp science fiction, in such stories as David H. Keller's "A Biological Experiment" (1928) and "Unto Us a Child Is Born"

(1933), Francis Flagg's "An Adventure in Time" (1930), Leslie F. Stone's "The Conquest of Gola" (1931), Thomas S. Gardner's "The Last Woman" (1932), and Raymond F. Jones' *Renaissance* (1944).

The biochemistry of sex made rapid advances in the 1930s, when all the principal sex hormones were first isolated, their structures determined, and their synthesis (from cholesterol) begun. This research made little direct impact on speculative fiction, in spite of the fact that Hugo Gernsback's interest in scientific insights into sex was sufficient to ensure that when he abandoned science fiction publishing in the 1930s, he continued to publish *Sexology* (with continued assistance from David H. Keller). Gernsback belatedly incorporated various themes from that magazine into his novel *The Ultimate World* (written 1958–1959; published 1971), but diplomacy restrained their literary influence for decades. The analysis of insect pheromones—chemical sex attractants—also made significant advances in the 1930s, reigniting interest in the long folkloristic and literary tradition of tales of aphrodisiac "love potions", but literary reflections of the notion were similarly restrained; notable examples include William Moy Russell's *The Barber of Aldebaran* (written 1954–1955; published 1995) and Ernestine Gilbreth Carey's *Giddy Moment* (1958).

The intrinsic gaudiness of pulp science fiction did, however, open up scope for the continuation of other, more elaborately cloaked and costumed literary traditions—particularly the extrapolation of male fantasies of exotic female sexual magnetism. Stories such as Bob Olsen's "The Superperfect Bride" (1929), Don Mark Lemon's "The Scarlet Planet" (1931), and Jack Williamson's "The Lady of Light" (1932) demonstrated scope for development that was enthusiastically taken up by cover illustrators, who gradually developed some remarkable conventions of futuristic costuming. Notable recurrent features included colourful thigh-boots, diaphanous skirts, and metallic brassieres. Although the science fiction pulps were always slightly disadvantaged in the depiction of *femmes fatales* by comparison with *Weird Tales*—which hosted such experiments with *alien *femmes fatales* as C. L. Moore's "Shambleau" (1933)—the co-option of biological models eventually facilitated a distinctive kind of excess in such works as Philip José Farmer's *The Lovers* (1952; exp. book, 1961).

The spirit of carefully measured and rather coy "daring" contained in Philip José Farmer's early science fiction is detectable in many other works that seemed to be testing the water for an impending sea-change that was not quite ready to happen. Notable speculative works of this kind included Theodore Sturgeon's "The Deadly Ratio" (1948; aka "It Wasn't

477

Syzygy"), William Tenn's "Venus and the Seven Sexes" (1949), Philip Wylie's *The Disappearance* (1951), Margaret St. Clair's "Vulcan's Dolls" (1952; book, 1956 as *Agent of the Unknown*), Fritz Leiber's "Yesterday House" (1952), Sam Merwin Jr.'s *The White Widows* (1953; aka *The Sex War*), and Aubrey Menen's *The Fig Tree* (1959). All of these stories address issues connected with sex in a manner that suggests an aspiration to be far bolder, constrained by diplomatic necessity. Although the pulp medium was now dying off, its immediate replacements—digest magazines and paperback books—were equally committed, at first, to providing "family entertainment".

The cultural situation of speculative fiction in the first part of the twentieth century was confused by the fact that male and female readers exhibited obvious differences of literary taste, especially in respect of popular fiction. The readers of pulp fiction were predominantly male, female readers being more likely to favour "slick" magazines printed on better quality paper. This situation had come about because U.S. advertisers armed with pioneering techniques of market research had figured out that it made good commercial sense to direct the advertising of consumer goods at women rather than men, because they were more active in generating and responding to the social pressures that guided purchasing decisions. Advertising-supported periodicals—which needed better quality paper in order to carry glossy illustrations—therefore began to specialise in the fictional genres that female readers preferred (genteel social dramas, especially love stories, and nonviolent mysteries), leaving those preferred by male readers (Westerns and the action-orientated forms of crime fiction) to the sales-supported pulps.

Pulp science fiction was further inclined to pander to male readers because Hugo Gernsback knew that the hobbyist radio enthusiasts and other budding technologists to whom *his* advertising was directed were mostly male; even so, the Gernsback pulps published feminist Utopias such as Lilith Lorraine's "Into the 28th Century" (1928) and M. F. Rupert's "Via the Hewitt Ray" (1930), and promoted such writers as Clare Winger Harris and Leslie F. Stone. Although Stone, C. L. Moore, and Leigh Brackett had ambiguous by-lines, the fact that they were female was advertised rather than concealed by the editorial blurbs attached to their stories.

Pulp science fiction was always more hospitable to female writers than other kinds of pulp fiction, in spite of the claims of implicit hostility made by feminist critics in the 1970s. It is hardly surprising that the genre remained as exceedingly hospitable to male fantasies and misogynistic expressions as other pulp genres, but it is not surprising either that genre science

fiction eventually provided fertile ground for the gestation of more assertive feminist ideas and ideals. It is undoubtedly true that genre science fiction's treatment of sexual themes was conspicuously adolescent throughout the pulp era, and for the remainder of the 1950s, but the relative adulthood of speculative fiction produced outside the genre was mostly expressed in terms of a thoroughly respectable aversion of gaze.

Genre science fiction writers were often very conservative in their view of the future development of sexual relations in the context of the Space Age—Raymond F. Jones' "The Farthest Horizon" (1952), blurbed "There will be those who go up to the sea of space in ships—and there will be the women who wait for them, too. And there will be the inevitable fights to keep the men from going, waged by women who fear the waiting", and Randall Garrett's "The Queen Bee" (1958) provided cardinal examples—but such assumptions did not go unchallenged. Robert A. Heinlein's "Delilah and the Space Rigger" (1948) assumed that there would soon be laws against sexual discrimination in employment, Judith Merril's "Survival Ship" (1951) offered a very different account of the sexual imperatives of space travel, and Chan Davis' "It Walks in Beauty" (1958) satirised the stigmatisation of career women.

While the Utopian tradition remained dominated by eugenic concerns, the scientifically informed consideration of sexual matters in such fiction was painstakingly tentative throughout the first half of the twentieth century, but the situation changed rapidly and decisively in the second half, following another abrupt boundary shift. The new licence granted to the exploration of sexual themes in fiction after 1960 was widely referred to as a liberation, and the appropriateness of the term is reflected in the manner in which so many key works picked up themes that had been broached long before but whose exploration in the light of modern knowledge had been long inhibited. The timing of the abrupt shift was not unconnected with the twentieth century's most socially significant advancement in reproductive technology, the contraceptive pill, but it would be a drastic oversimplification to credit that invention with being its root cause.

The thread of Gabriel de Foigny's experiment in hypothetical equality was picked up in such works as Theodore Sturgeon's *Venus Plus X* (1960), Ursula K. Le Guin's *The Left Hand of Darkness* (1969), Storm Constantine's *The Enchantments of Flesh and Spirit* (1987) and its sequels, and James Alan Garner's *Commitment Hour* (1998), while the broader Utopian tradition was brought up to date by such carefully methodical works as Joanna Russ's *The Female Man* (1975) and Marge Piercy's *Woman on the Edge of*

Time (1976). The thread of Thomas d'Urfey's ruminations on gynecocracy was picked up—sometimes with and sometimes without the assistance of his narcissistic convictions—in such works as Mack Reynolds' *Amazon Planet* (1966–1967; book, 1975), Edmund Cooper's *Five to Twelve* (1969) and *Who Needs Men?* (1972; aka *Gender Genocide*), Sally Miller Gearhart's *The Wanderground* (1980), Pamela Sargent's *The Shore of Women* (1986), Joan Slonczewski's *A Door into Ocean* (1986) and its sequel *Daughter of Elysium* (1993), Nicola Griffith's *Ammonite* (1993), Catherine Asaro's *The Last Hawk* (1997), John Kessel's "The Juniper Tree" (2000) and "Stories for Men" (2002), and Tricia Sullivan's *Maul* (2003) and "Men Are Trouble" (2004). The pattern was satirically inverted in A. Bertram Chandler's *False Fatherland* (1968) and Lois McMaster Bujold's *Ethan of Athos* (1986). The thread of Denis Diderot's contemplation of the possibilities of multisexuality was picked up in such works as Ian MacLeod's "Grownups" (1992) and James Patrick Kelly's "Lovestory" (1998).

More recently emergent threads were also taken up. Edward Heron-Allen's exploration of polymorphous perversity was continued in J. G. Ballard's *Crash* (1973), Samuel R. Delany's *Triton* (1976), Pat Cadigan's "Fifty Ways to Improve Your Orgasm" (1992), and Maggie Flinn's "50 More Ways to Improve Your Orgasm" (1992), and L. Timmel Duchamp's "Things of the Flesh" (1994). The subgenre of pulp science fiction that used science-fictional ideas in the quest for the ultimate in sexual magnetism was extended in J. F. Bone's *The Lani People* (1962), Piers Anthony's *Chthon* (1967), Ian Watson's *Orgasmachine* (1976), and Elizabeth Hand's "In the Mouth of Athyr" (1992). Biologically exotic reproductive systems were detailed in such works as Marion Zimmer Bradley and Juanita Coulson's "Another Rib" (1963), James Tiptree Jr.'s "Your Haploid Heart" (1969) and "Love Is the Plan, the Plan Is Death" (1973), Robert Thurston's "Aliens" (1976) and "The Oonaa Woman" (1981; exp. book, 1985 as *Q Colony*), Octavia Butler's Xenogenesis trilogy (1987–1989), and Harry Turtledove's *A World of Difference* (1990). All of these themes were integrated into a proliferating subgenre of science-fictional pornography and reflected in burgeoning subgenres of gay and lesbian science fiction.

Twentieth-century scientific accounts of reproductive biology, as elaborately represented in Michael Blumlein's *X, Y* (1993), are most commonly extrapolated in accounts of the possibilities inherent in future sexual technology, especially as such technologies become more intimate—as graphically advertised in Donna Haraway's "Cyborg Manifesto" (1985). The rapid progress from simple accounts of new masturbatory technologies to images of *posthuman transfiguration is illustrated by such works as John Boyd's *Sex and the High Command* (1970), K. W. Jeter's *Dr. Adder* (written 1972; published 1984), Martha Soukup's "Master of the Game" (1987), Candas Jane Dorsey's "(Learning About) Machine Sex" (1988), James L. Cambias' "A Diagram of Rapture" (2000), Neal Barrett Jr.'s "Hard Times" (2003), and Vonda N. McIntyre's "Little Faces" (2005).

Sarah Lefanu's feminist study of speculative fiction *In the Chinks of the World Machine* (1988) draws a useful distinction between feminist fiction and "feminised fiction", the former analysing existing (male-designed) sexual-political power structures—and thus arguing, overtly or covertly, in favour of a female infiltration or usurpation of those structures—while the latter merely extol the virtues of an alternative and overtly feminine social organisation that would value empathy more highly than technical competence, patience more highly than assertive action, and intuition more highly than rationality. Feminists who consider "femininity" an oppressive male construction inevitably disapprove of feminised speculative fiction, but the speculative fiction produced in the late twentieth century by female writers—and by many male writers—was heavily biased in that direction, not merely in its descriptions of the balance of power in hypothetical future and extraterrestrial societies but in its broader considerations of the biology of reproduction. No matter what the term may imply by way of crude innuendo, this applies to *hard science fiction as well as its softer rivals.

SHEFFIELD, CHARLES (1935–2002)

British-born physicist and writer. He completed his education at King's College Cambridge, obtaining his B.A. and M.A. in mathematics and a Ph.D. in theoretical physics, before moving to the United States in the 1960s. He began writing science fiction at a relatively late stage in his career, but made up for lost time by becoming remarkably prolific. His early short fiction, collected in *Vectors* (1979), *Hidden Variables* (1981), and *The McAndrew Chronicles* (1983; exp. as *One Man's Universe*, 1993; further exp. as *The Compleat McAndrew*, 2000)—especially the last-named series—mostly consisted of archetypal *hard science fiction based in theoretical physics, often possessed of an uncompromising expository density even when his plots took the form of light comedies, as they often did.

Sheffield's early novels made conscientious attempts to be more reader friendly than the short fiction he published in such specialist magazines as

Analog, and employed a markedly different range of themes. *Sight of Proteus* (1978) features a highly implausible metamorphic biotechnology, but extrapolated its central premise conscientiously enough to supply ideative elaborations to two sequels, *Proteus Unbound* (1989) and *Proteus in the Underworld* (1995). *The Web Between the Worlds* (1979), which describes the building of a "skyhook", suffered an accident of timing when it appeared almost simultaneously with Arthur C. *Clarke's similarly themed *The Fountains of Paradise*. *My Brother's Keeper* (1982) is a neurological fantasy in which the hemispheres of two different brains are combined in the same skull, the problems of compatibility ameliorated by the fact that they originated from identical twins. The mosaic novel *Erasmus Magister* (1982; exp. as *The Amazing Dr. Darwin*, 2002) is an intriguing work of historical fiction in which Erasmus *Darwin serves as a peripatetic scientific detective.

The scope of Sheffield's long fiction became broader and bolder in *Between the Strokes of Night* (1985; rev. 2002), a far-reaching epic including a trip to the end of time. It laid significant groundwork for some of the author's more ambitious later endeavours, including the far-futuristic fantasy *Godspeed* (1993) and the *Omega Point fantasy *Tomorrow and Tomorrow* (1997). Sheffield ventured into sophisticated space opera in *The Nimrod Hunt* (1986; exp. as *The Mind Pool*, 1993)—to which he added a belated sequel in *Spheres of Heaven* (2001)—and post-holocaust fantasy in the mosaic *Trader's World* (1988) before undertaking an extensive world building exercise in the Heritage Universe series of exotic planetary romances, which initially comprised *Summertide* (1990), *Divergence* (1991), and *Transcendence* (1992); again he added more items to the series at a much later date in *Convergence* (1997) and *Resurgence* (2002).

Cold as Ice (1992) and its sequels, *The Ganymede Club* (1995) and *Dark as Day* (2002), are thrillers in which the development of the solar system becomes a necessity following the devastation of Earth. *Brother to Dragons* (1992) describes a similarly problematic future in which the dialectical relationship between the principal socioeconomic classes becomes awkwardly polarised. *Aftermath* (1998) and *Starfire* (1999) comprise an extravagant disaster story in which Alpha Centauri goes supernova and Earth is devastated by an electromagnetic pulse. Like many other hard science fiction writers Sheffield diversified into didactic juvenile fiction in a series consisting of *Higher Education* (1996; with Jerry Pournelle), *The Billion Dollar Boy* (1997), *Putting Up Roots* (1997), and *The Cyborg from Earth* (1998).

While producing these novels, Sheffield continued to write shorter *contes philosophiques* whose method

was not so flagrantly melodramatic, although they are equally ambitious in their own fashion; their frequent use of humour, sometimes in combination with flagrant sentimentality, gives their celebrations of lateral thinking a distinctive effervescent charm that contrasts with the staid quality of much hard science fiction. His later work in this vein was collected in *Dancing with Myself* (1993), *Georgia on My Mind and Other Places* (1995), *Space Suits* (2001), and *The Lady Vanishes and Other Oddities of Nature* (2002). Although his longer narratives always had a tendency to become garrulous, and to wander in pursuit of distractions, both qualities were aspects of his fascination with scientific ideas and their eccentric extrapolation; they need not be reckoned as faults by sympathetic readers.

SILVERBERG, ROBERT (1935–)

U.S. writer. He graduated from Columbia University, New York, in 1956 and immediately embarked upon a career as a full-time writer, having already prepared the way with a number of short story sales and the juvenile novel *Revolt on Alpha C* (1955). He established a "fiction factory" with his friend Harlan Ellison and the older writer Randall Garrett to supply the magazine market with stories produced on a prolific scale, using stereotyped formulas in whose deployment and variation he soon became an expert. His efficiency was legendary, and by the time the science fiction magazine market went into a decline after 1959, he had diversified into enough other markets to maintain the production of hackwork at a rate of approximately two million words a year for several more years.

This pattern of production required Silverberg to work with familiar motifs, continually making small modifications to their customary patterns of development, without any elaborate exposition or extrapolation. He became, in consequence, an archetypal writer of "soft" science fiction, which used conventional science-fictional ideas without paying much attention to their scientific underpinnings. His work in this vein was by no means unintelligent—indeed, the level of production he maintained required great ingenuity as well as extraordinary discipline—and the best work he did in this phase of his career was not without ambition. *Master of Life and Death* (1957), in which a bureaucrat struggles to implement policies to counter social problems generated by rapidly expanding *population, was topical and timely. *Invaders from Earth* (1958), in which the colonisation of a Jovian moon is orchestrated by venal organisations, builds up a fine pitch of political indignation. *Recalled to Life* (1958;

book, 1962) is a neatly developed thought experiment tracking society's transformation by a technology of resurrection. *Collision Course* (1959; book, 1961) is a morally earnest first contact story, which had the distinction of being rejected by John W. *Campbell Jr. because of its antichauvinistic ideology.

Following the publication of the existentialist *conte philosophique* "To See the Invisible Man" (1963), Silverberg abruptly changed direction in the development of his career. He abandoned his furious production schedule and began a methodical deployment of science fiction's vocabulary of ideas in modelling various situations of existential *alienation, and mapping potential routes to psychological fulfilment. He produced a series of highly effective images of spiritual isolation, including *Thorns* (1967), *Hawksbill Station* (1968; aka *The Anvil of Time*), *The Man in the Maze* (1969), *A Time of Changes* (1971), *The World Inside* (1971), *Dying Inside* (1972), *The Second Trip* (1972), *The Stochastic Man* (1975), and *Shadrach in the Furnace* (1976). He complemented these works with a parallel sequence in which similar existential situations are relieved by various kinds of metamorphic transcendence, including *To Open the Sky* (1967), *Nightwings* (1969), *Downward to the Earth* (1970), *Tower of Glass* (1970), and the allegorical far-futuristic romance *Son of Man* (1971).

These mature works were as lacking in fundamental science-fictional hardness as Silverberg's earlier fiction, but once their fundamental premises had been granted, they were both conscientious and elegant in their extrapolation, especially of the potential social consequences of the developments of new technological capabilities or the possession of particular parapsychological abilities. In the course of this phase of his career Silverberg became an accomplished literary stylist and an expert manager of narrative technique. His occasional new ventures into juvenile science fiction, including *The Gate of Worlds* (1967) and *Across a Billion Years* (1969), brought an exceptional sophistication to work of that sort, extrapolating the serious concern of the educational nonfiction he produced in considerable abundance in the 1960s. Although that work too began as mechanical hackwork, it eventually extended into useful collations of information and authentic scholarship, in such studies as *The Golden Dream: Seekers of El Dorado* (1967), *Men Against Time: Salvage Archaeology in the United States* (1967), *Mound Builders of Ancient America* (1968), and *The Challenge of Climate: Man and His Environment* (1969). By the time he wrote *Clocks for the Ages: How Scientists Date the Past* (1971), he had become a significant populariser of science—particularly of archaeology—but he stopped producing such work abruptly in 1972.

The shorter fiction assembled in such collections as *The Cube Root of Uncertainty* (1970), *The Reality Trip and Other Implausibilities* (1972), *Earth's Other Shadow* (1973), *Sundance and Other Science Fiction Stories* (1974), *Born with the Dead* (1974), and *The Feast of St Dionysus* (1975) included numerous highly polished *contes philosophiques*. After finishing *Shadrach in the Furnace*, however, Silverberg decided that he had done enough science fiction as well as enough nonfiction and that—given that he had made more than enough money to ensure that he never need work again—it was time to retire. He did, however, continue one other thread of his work; he had become one of the most prolific anthologists in the field, and continued to edit further volumes, including his annual series featuring original works, *New Dimensions* (1971–1981).

His retirement did not last long; he returned to the fray in the 1980s to exploit new commercial opportunities presented by the genre, abandoning the philosophical pretensions of his mid-period work in order to concentrate on the production of best-sellers capable of appealing to the widest possible audience. The planetary romance *Lord Valentine's Castle* (1980), which deftly duplicated the key features of the burgeoning genre of commodified fantasy, immediately hit the mark. Silverberg went on to produce numerous calculatedly unambitious novels in the same vein, although he could not keep his enduring preoccupations entirely at bay; the Majipoor series launched by *Lord Valentine's Castle* moved gradually into much deeper waters. The short fiction he produced in this period also had more polish than depth to begin with, but he could not help formulating many of his stories as *contes philosophiques*, so the work collected in *The Conglomeroid Cocktail Party* (1984) and *In Another Country and Other Short Novels* (2002), together with such separately issued novellas as *Sailing to Byzantium* (1985), *The Secret Sharer* (1988), and *In Another Country* (1990), also recovered much of the intellectual penetration of his mid-period work.

The colourful Odyssean fantasies Silverberg wrote in this period, including *The Face of the Waters* (1991), *Kingdoms of the Wall* (1992), and *The Longest Way Home* (2002), placed increasing emphasis on their quasi-allegorical aspects. He also began to produce much darker works such as the satirical apocalyptic fantasy *Hot Sky at Midnight* (1994), the extended parable of desperation *Starborne* (1996), and an ironically sophisticated revisitation of the theme of H. G. Wells' *The War of the Worlds*, *The Alien Years* (1998). The mosaic *Roma Mater* (2003) painstakingly developed an elaborate alternative history in which the Roman Empire is untroubled by monotheistic religions. Although he maintained his resolve never to revert to the fervent intensity of his middle period, therefore, Silverberg retained his status as an important writer of sophisticated and intellectually adventurous soft science fiction.

SIMAK, CLIFFORD D[ONALD] (1904–1988)

U.S. journalist and science fiction writer. He attended the University of Wisconsin, Madison, before going to work for the *Minneapolis Star* in 1924; he continued to work as a journalist—winning promotion to various editorial posts and eventually moving to the *Minneapolis Tribune*—until he retired in 1976. He published his first science fiction story in 1931; writing fiction was always a sideline, but he produced work steadily after John W. Campbell Jr. assumed editorial control of *Astounding Stories* in 1937.

Simak's early work for Campbell included the extravagant space opera *Cosmic Engineers* (1939: book, 1950), but he was more comfortable working on a limited scale. He produced a sequence of stories set on the various planets of the solar system, including "Hermit of Mars" (1939), "Clerical Error" (1940), and "Tools" (1942), but found his true métier in the more parochial stories assembled into the mosaic novel *City* (1944–1951; book, 1952). The series maps out a future history in which humankind abandons Earthly civilisation for a radically new way of life on Jupiter, leaving a considerable material inheritance to humanoid robots and dogs with artificially enhanced intelligence, which collaborate in the establishment of a gentle pastoral Utopia.

Simak was to return to the notion of evolutionary transcendence in such novels as *Time and Again* (1951; aka *First He Died*) and *A Choice of Gods* (1972), but it was his evident delight in rural life and its associated values that fuelled much of his subsequent work, which formed the core of a subgenre of "pastoral science fiction". *Ring Around the Sun* (1953) and *Way Station* (1963) take care to acknowledge that lifestyles of the kind Simak favoured are only fully sustainable within a much more elaborate technological context, but insist that the purpose of technological progress ought to be the liberation of humankind from the awkward restrictions of primitive agricultural economy, not the institution of an all-encompassing automation of existence. His robots are more perfect and loyal servants than Isaac *Asimov's, not because they are fitted with a more rigid innate morality but because they are free to develop a more elaborate etiquette and a more painstaking concern for the well-being of all organic creatures.

In their most idealised versions, Simak's green pastures are not only integrated into a complex Earthly civilisation but a limitless galactic and interdimensional network of civilisations glimpsed in such exploratory works as "The Big Front Yard" (1958) and *Time Is the Simplest Thing* (1961) and more fully developed in *Way Station*. He was always conscious that the sustainability of any such technological system would depend on the willingness of everyone in the world, universe, or multiverse to get along peacefully, ever ready to assist one another in a spirit of neighbourliness, and he was aware of the many unfortunate tendencies and active agencies that might spoil such a situation, but he remained convinced that it was not an impossible goal, even for human beings. This conviction underlies and continually becomes manifest in the short fiction collected in *Strangers in the Universe* (1956), *The Worlds of Clifford Simak* (1960; aka *Aliens for Neighbors*), and *All the Traps of Earth* (1962).

As he approached his eventual retirement, the quality of Simak's fiction became patchier. *All Flesh Is Grass* (1965) and *Why Call Them Back from Heaven?* (1966) are ambitious and coherent extrapolations of science-fictional premises, but a tendency to whimsy first exhibited in *They Walked like Men* (1962) gained fuller expression in the chimerical fantasies *The Werewolf Principle* (1967) and *The Goblin Reservation* (1968), which deliberately mixed science-fictional and folkloristic motifs without achieving a plausible synthesis. Although his abiding preoccupations continued to produce highly effective imagery on occasion, as in *A Choice of Gods, Cemetery World* (1973), *Shakespeare's Planet* (1976), *A Heritage of Stars* (1977), *The Visitors* (1980), and *Project Pope* (1981), his habit of making up his plots as he went along, often developing them in short snatches—because he rarely found opportunities to work on his fiction for long periods—left many of his novels with no strong sense of direction and little opportunity to reach satisfactory denouements. The later short fiction assembled in *The Marathon Photograph and Other Stories* (1986) was spared this problem, but the relative sparseness of its production testifies to the waning of his creativity as he moved through his seventies into his eighties.

Simak was an enterprising member of the Campbell stable for more than twenty-five years, and also became a regular contributor to *Galaxy* in the 1950s, during which time he raised questions about the purpose and potential scope of technological development whose importance has not diminished with the subsequent passage of time.

SINGULARITY

A term used in mathematics to describe critical points at which functions become indefinable, usually by tending to infinity. One such description, Roger Penrose's "singularity theorem", was applied to the collapse of matter into a *black hole, for which reason the space inside the black hole came to be known as a singularity—a usage echoed in such science fiction stories as Mildred Downey Broxon's "Singularity" (1978). In the 1980s, that meaning was supplemented and largely displaced by another, whose initial derivation was from a reference by John von Neumann to an "essential singularity" beyond which the future becomes unanticipatable. The popularisation of the new meaning was hastened by Vernor *Vinge's use of the phrase "technological singularity" in a 1983 article in *Omni* and the novel *Marooned in Real-Time* (1986). Damien *Broderick's *The Spike* (1997) offered an alternative term for the technological singularity, which could have avoided confusion with black hole singularities, but it arrived too late to have any chance of displacing its rival.

The proposition that humankind will attain a technological singularity in the near future assumes that the evolution of information technology, self-transforming *nanotechnologies, and various *biotechnologies will continue to accelerate, to a point at which they bring about an abrupt and dramatic breakthrough to *posthuman nature. It is the end towards which various "transhumanist" and "extropian" movements began to work in the 1990s, with the encouragement of such futurist philosophers as Hans Moravec. The literary depiction of the arrival of the technological singularity and the consequent transformation of individuals and society became a significant challenge to science fiction writers; it was first attempted by Marc Stiegler in "The Gentle Seduction" (1989), by way of supplementing his essay on "Hypermedia and the Singularity" in the January 1989 issue of *Analog*. W. T. Quick's *Singularities* (1990) pays homage to Vinge, but makes only peripheral use of the notion, as does Neal Stephenson's nanotechnology fantasy *The Diamond Age* (1995).

The most detailed response to the challenge was the sequence of stories collected in Charles Stross' *Accelerando* (2005), begun with "Lobsters" (2001), which sets out an elaborate future history that includes a series of technological singularities. In the eighth story, "Elector" (2004), the inner solar system—except for Earth—has been converted into a cloud of computronium by humankind's Vile Offspring; refugees from this domain flood the moons of Saturn, while the *Omega Point appears to be drawing ominously near. In the ninth and last story, "Survivor" (2004),

the refugees move on again, colonising the systems of brown dwarf stars by way of calculated anticlimax. The attempted stigmatisation of the term by unsympathetic critics as "the rapture of the nerds" was proudly appropriated by Stross and his sometime collaborator Cory Doctorow.

The notion that a technological singularity might provide the means for the revival and refurbishment of the myth of the *Space Age is incorporated into such post-singularity space operas as Karl Schroeder's *Ventus* (2000) and *Permanence* (2002), Wil McCarthy's Queendom of Sol series—comprising *The Collapsium* (2000), *The Wellstone* (2003), *Lost in Transmission* (2004), and *To Crush the Moon* (2005)—John C. Wright's trilogy comprising *The Golden Age* (2002), *The Phoenix Exultant* (2003), and *The Golden Transcendence* (2004), and Scott Westerfeld's *The Risen Empire* (2003). Alex Irvine's "Chichen Itza" (2002), Stross and Doctorow's "Jury Service" (2002) and "Appeals Court" (2004), and Geoff Ryman's *Air* (2004) offer more tightly focused accounts.

SNOW, C[HARLES] P[ERCY] (1905–1980)

British writer. He was educated at Christ's College, Cambridge, where he became a tutor after obtaining a Ph.D. in physics in 1930. During World War II, he was recruited by the government as a scientific adviser, and remained in the civil service thereafter until 1960. In 1964, he was elevated to the peerage as Baron Snow of Leicester and became undersecretary of state in the Ministry of Technology formed by Harold Wilson's recently elected Labour government.

Snow published a detective novel in 1932 and an anonymous scientific romance, *New Lives for Old*, in 1933. The latter describes the development of a technology of longevity, taking a conventionally dim view of the likely consequences of its use. After the political novel *The Search* (1934), however, he became considerably more ambitious in his literary endeavours, launching an extensive series tracking the evolution of British society from the early 1930s on with *Strangers and Brothers* (1940). Although the central character of the early novels in the sequence is a lawyer, his brother is a physicist, whose wartime travails are the central subject of the fifth novel, *The New Men* (1954).

In 1959, Snow gave the Rede lecture at Cambridge, which was reprinted as *The Two Cultures and the Scientific Revolution*. Its delivery and subsequent publication launched a storm of controversy that had not entirely died down by the end of the century. Snow suggested therein, regretfully, that a steadily widening gulf had opened up between "traditional" literary culture of the kind identified by Matthew Arnold's *Culture and Anarchy* (1869) and an emergent culture of science. He distinguished the two in a quasi-ethnological fashion, as distinct communities with their own characteristic bodies of knowledge, attitudes, and ambitions, and argued that it would be a good thing if the participants in each culture were to make more effort to familiarise themselves with the fundamental concepts and concerns of the other. His tentative suggestion that more literary men were guilty of wilful ignorance about science than *vice versa* called forth a scathing attack by the critic F. R. Leavis, who was insistent that there was and could be only one "culture"—in the sense of that which created a "cultured individual"—and that science could not possibly constitute a rival or substitute.

The fervent discussion that became known as "the Two Cultures debate" generated a good deal of interest in the possibility of bridging the gap, but relatively little success; Martin Green's reminiscences in *Science and the Shabby Curate of Poetry* (1964) illustrated the difficulties. The most profound effect was achieved in combination with that of Raymond Williams' analysis of the evolution of *Culture and Society, 1780–1950* (1958)—which presumably prompted Snow to adapt the word "culture" to his own purpose—and the volume with which Williams followed it, *The Long Revolution* (1961). The debate instituted by Snow undoubtedly assisted Williams in the foundation of a new academic discipline of "cultural studies", although the discipline developed within the context of the humanities and most syllabuses framed under the rubric made no attempt to accommodate the culture of science.

Snow reexamined and slightly modified his argument in a supplementary essay combined with the original in *The Two Cultures, and A Second Look* (1963), although the gulf of angry incomprehension that yawned between his position and Leavis' was, in a sense, the ultimate proof of his argument that the two cultures had drawn so far apart as to be fundamentally antipathetic. Snow's own attempts to ameliorate the situation outlined in *The Two Cultures* were initially accommodated within the later phases of the Strangers and Brothers series. *The Affair* (1964) picked up where *The New Men* had left off—two more titles had appeared in the interim—in dealing directly with the ethics of scientific discovery in a politicised context. He took the theme further forward in a nonfictional study of *Science and Government* (1961) and in the next novel in the sequence, *Corridors of Power* (1963). The last two novels in the series, however, *The Sleep of Reason* (1968) and *Last Things* (1970), reverted to more reader-friendly concerns, perhaps reflecting a growing awareness of the intractability of the problem.

Snow's later works included a popular history of twentieth-century physics, with particular emphasis on the development of *atom bombs, *The Physicists: A Generation That Changed the World* (1981), but his subsequent novels were crime stories. The torch was subsequently taken up by other writers, notably John Brockman—a literary agent specialising in popular science books—who set his own endeavours in the context of the debate in *The Third Culture: Beyond the Scientific Revolution* (1996). Edward O. Wilson also carried the debate forward in the hope of a possible reconciliation in *Consilience: The Unity of Knowledge* (1998).

SOCIAL DARWINISM

A hypothesis asserting that social evolution is determined by the same factors that determine the evolution of natural species, with the least efficient cultures being eliminated by natural selection while the most efficient survive and thrive. The notion, as commonly understood, is implicit in the social theory of Herbert Spencer, who coined the phrase "the survival of the fittest" to describe its mechanism, and several commentators have argued that it ought to be called "social Spencerianism". A very different kind of "social Darwinism" is contained in the account of *The Descent of Man* (1871) offered by Charles *Darwin. Instead of focusing on negative selection determined by the greater likelihood of certain individuals or groups perishing in open competition for resources, Darwin focused on the protective selection associated with parental and social care, and with the collaboration of groups in the management of their resources.

As with many theories in social science, social Darwinism is readily invoked in justification of certain kinds of political programs. The Spencerian theory of selection is mirrored in economic theories of *laissez faire* market competition and is easily applicable to the theorisation of *war as destructive competition between tribes or nations, as in Walter Bagehot's *Physics and Politics* (1873). Darwin's own account of the social implications of his theory, by contrast, could easily be invoked to justify economic protectionism and pacifism. The phrase has always been historically associated with the adoption of the Spencerian view by such American industrial theorists as Andrew Carnegie and William Graham Sumner as a justification the aggressive tactics of American capitalism. Sumner's frank anticipation of open warfare between social classes is reflected in Ignatius Donnelly's apocalyptic novel *Caesar's Column* (1890;

initially by-lined Edmund Boisgilbert) and Claude Farrère's similarly anti-Capitalist *Les condamnés à mort* (1926; trans. as *Useless Hands*).

Social Darwinist ideas were a major factor in the futuristic speculation of H. G. Wells, evident in such anticipations of the future evolution of society as *The Time Machine* (1895) and *When the Sleeper Wakes* (1899), such accounts of potential competitive threat as *The War of the Worlds* (1898) and "The Empire of the Ants" (1905), and such exercises in social design as *A Modern Utopia* (1905) and *Men like Gods* (1923). Wells' futurological projections routinely assume that the emergence of a better society presupposes the destruction of the present one, to be followed by a process of rigorous winnowing, as described in *The World Set Free* (1914) and *The Shape of Things to Come* (1933). When Wells finally despaired of the world's salvation, he invoked the logic of social Darwinism to condemn its failure in *Mind at the End of Its Tether* (1945). The most fervent ideological opposition to Wellsian social Darwinism is contained in C. S. Lewis' *Out of the Silent Planet* (1938).

Social Darwinist rhetoric is found in many other early scientific romances, including W. D. Hay's *Three Hundred Years Hence* (1881), Louis Tracy's *The Final War* (1896), and M. P. Shiel's *The Yellow Danger* (1898). The latter titles extrapolate the argument that there must ultimately be a war for possession of the Earth between different human races (although Shiel subsequently abandoned his Spencerian views in favour of a Nietzschean theory of progress). The thesis was employed as a justification of race hatred by Heinrich von Treitschke, whose work was a major source of theoretical inspiration for Adolf Hitler's *Mein Kampf* (1925–1926) and the political ideology of Nazism.

Racist social Darwinism was carried forward into post–World War I scientific romance by such works as P. Anderson Graham's *The Collapse of Homo Sapiens* (1923). It was, however, largely displaced thereafter by a significantly different kind of social Darwinism, which glorified the struggle for existence on *Rousseauesque grounds, as a healthy antidote to the corrupting influence of civilisation; this version was enthusiastically dramatised by S. Fowler Wright, in such novels as *Deluge* (1928) and *Dream, or the Simian Maid* (1931), and J. Leslie Mitchell, in such works as *Three Go Back* (1932) and *Gay Hunter* (1934).

Racist social Darwinism was extrapolated in numerous pulp science fiction stories, including J. Schlossel's "The Second Swarm" (1928) and Arthur J. Burks' "Earth the Marauder" (1930), but also called forth ideological opposition in such works as Walter Kateley's "Room for the Super Race" (1932) and Raymond Z. Gallun's "Old Faithful" (1934). Social Darwinist rhetoric was frequently invoked by John W. *Campbell Jr. in support of his own fervent human chauvinism, and his sympathy to such rhetoric secured it an enduring base within the pages of *Astounding* and *Analog*. It was sometimes taken to extremes in works extrapolated by other writers from Campbell's ideas, including L. Ron Hubbard's *Return to Tomorrow* (1954) and Lloyd Biggle Jr.'s *The World Menders* (1971). Such ideas were sometimes expressed in uncompromising terms in the work of Robert A. Heinlein, most starkly in *The Puppet Masters* (1951), *Starship Troopers* (1959), and the collection of aphorisms represented as "The Notebooks of Lazarus Long" in *Time Enough for Love* (1973); in this respect Heinlein differed sharply from another writer who played a key role in shaping genre science fiction, Isaac Asimov, who frequently argued against social Darwinist conceptions, especially their racist versions.

Social Darwinist arguments occasionally resurfaced in the context of stories anxious about the *population explosion—most obviously in Lester del Rey's *The Eleventh Commandment* (1962)—but the most obvious manifestation of social Darwinist thinking in late twentieth-century speculative fiction was in the subgenre of survivalist fiction, which reflected the attitudes and policies of American communities engaged in active preparation for the disintegration of society in the wake of an impending nuclear holocaust. The subgenre's principal contributors employed the by-lines Jerry Ahern and James Axler, whose produce became prolific in the 1990s, but key precedents had been set by Robert Heinlein's *Farnham's Freehold* (1964) and Dean Ing's *Pulling Through* (1983). The strong emotions aroused by the thesis were frequently expressed in scathing critical condemnations of survivalist fiction, and in such sceptical literary works as David Brin's *The Postman* (1985).

SOCIOBIOLOGY

A branch of speculative biology that originated from attempts to show how examples of apparent altruism in animal behaviour could be consistent with Charles *Darwin's theory of natural selection. It took its name from Edward O. Wilson's *Sociobiology: The New Synthesis* (1975), although the elaboration of its characteristic style of argument was begun by G. C. Williams' *Adaptation and Natural Selection* (1966) and its key concept of "kin selection" was first developed by W. D. Hamilton. The new discipline was popularised by Richard Dawkins in *The Selfish Gene* (1976).

Sociobiological explanations make much of the fact that the ultimate object of natural selection is the gene, and that genes associated with behaviour that protects or assists proliferation of other copies of the same gene will inevitably be favoured by selection. Genes promoting protective behaviour towards close biological relatives—especially offspring—would, therefore, be strongly favoured. Although Darwin had recognised the possibility of some such effect in *The Descent of Man* (1871), subsequent users of his theory had deemphasised it by comparison with the negative selective effects of the struggle for existence.

The great triumph of Wilsonian sociobiology was the clarification of the Darwinian logic of hive societies, in which sterile worker bees or ants seem altruistic in labouring to assist the queen's reproductive success at the expense of their own. Because female bees have two sex chromosomes (XX) while males have one that has no counterpart (X), a female bee shares more of her genetic inheritance with her sisters (half the maternal complement plus all the paternal complement) than with her mother. Any combination of genes promoting the production of sisters rather than daughters could therefore be favoured by natural selection; thus, the workers' "selfish genes" reproduce themselves more effectively by assisting the queen's reproduction than they could if the workers were fertile themselves, while the queen's genes make up for her lesser genetic commonality with her daughters by mass production.

Sociobiology remains a speculative science because no direct causal connection between genes and behaviour has yet been demonstrated; although it seems rationally plausible that the behaviour of insects is *neurologically "hard wired", that becomes increasingly difficult to believe as the complexity of behaviour increases, and ethological studies suggest that young birds and mammals learn the greater part of their behavioural repertoire by imitating parental models. Attempts to apply sociobiological logic to human behaviour in the speculative discipline of "evolutionary psychology" are problematic, in that there are rival theories to account for the fact that people generally behave in ways that favour their own interests and those of their close kin, and because people behaving in such ways have a vested interest in arguing that they are merely following biological imperatives rather than making blameworthy choices.

Sociobiological explanations can be seen as plausible anecdotes—and are sometimes dismissed by sceptics as "Just So stories", by analogy with Rudyard Kipling's humorous fabular accounts of how elephants acquired their trunks, leopards their spots, and so on—and they lend themselves to literary elaboration in *ecological puzzle stories set in *exobiological contexts; notable examples include Joseph L. Green and Patrice Milton's "Still Fall the Gentle Rains" (1981) and Gregory Benford's "World Vast, World Various" (1992). Literature—and the arts in general—provide a significant challenge to sociobiological explanation, which evolutionary psychologists have been enthusiastic to meet, and their opponents equally anxious to deny; both sides of the debate are represented in such anthologies as Brett Cooke and Jan Baptist Bedaux's *Sociobiology and the Arts* (1998) and Cooke and Frederick Turner's *Biopoetics: Evolutionary Explanations in the Arts* (1999).

SOCIOLOGY

The systematic study of society and social relationships. The French equivalent of the term was coined in 1838 by Auguste Comte, and rapidly taken up by other human scientists interested in large-scale generalisation—a kind of study that was beginning to emerge from political economics, assisted by the collection of empirical data in the form of social statistics, as in W. Cooke Taylor's *The Natural History of Society in the Barbarous and Civilized State* (1840). The term was popularised by Herbert Spencer's *The Study of Sociology* (1873), which is a capsule introduction to notions discussed at much greater length in *Principles of Sociology* (1876–1896).

The early evolution of sociology was closely connected with Comte's *positivist attempts to isolate scientific accounts of society from the dogmatic ethical and political presuppositions previously incorporated into social philosophy, although all such philosophy inevitably possesses an empirical dimension. *Ethnology is a form of sociology in which the societies under analysis are all external to the scientist's own, and it thus escapes some of the problems of objectivity generated when sociologists attempt to turn a clinical eye on the societies of which they are active members, in whose values they have been immersed since childhood.

The early development of sociology also involved attempts to establish a distinct set of "social facts" that were irresolvable into the data of individual psychology and separate from—or, at least, broader than—the data of economics and political science. The proposition that there is a distinct order of social facts was insistently put forward by Émile Durkheim, who tried to prove his case by arguing that different suicide rates recorded in various nations and social groups were the product of differences in social cohesion; this assisted the forging of a strong link between sociology and social statistics. On the other hand, some sociologists also made a bid to take over the theoretical aspects of *history, as in the thesis set out in Max Weber's *Die Protestantische Ethik und der*

Geist des Kapitalismus (1904-1905; trans. as *The Protestant Ethic and the Spirit of Capitalism*), which attempted to explain the origins of the central institutions of capitalism as by-products of patterns of behaviour encouraged by the attitudinal shifts inherent in the Reformation.

All naturalistic fiction, insofar as it attempts to represent and comprehend the social situations of characters, is implicitly sociological. In much the same way that literary attempts to depict the individual "stream of consciousness" parallel the development of scientific *psychology, so literary analyses of the social forces constraining individual behaviour parallel the development of sociological theory. Attempts to cultivate a quasi-scientific *naturalism in literature inevitably pay attention to both dimensions of human life, and the development of the novel provides very abundant proof of the sociological truism that "the self is a social product".

It is sometimes argued by literary critics that fiction provides a better insight into such sociological factors as customs, norms, and rituals than sociological theory, and some novelists have explicitly embarked on informal sociological analyses; Leo Tolstoy's *Anna Karenina* (1873–1877), Thomas Hardy's *Jude the Obscure* (1895), and Robert Tressell's *The Ragged-Trousered Philanthropists* (written 1914; abridged version published 1918; restored text, 1955) are cardinal examples. It is arguable that the first and second cast at least as much light on the social causes of suicide as Durkheim's deductions from his statistical analysis; indeed, one of the anomalies with which Durkheim's theory struggles to cope is the potential of literary works like J. W. Goethe's *Die Leiden des jungen Werther* (1774; trans. as *The Sorrows of Young Werther*) to become active suicidogenic forces.

All speculative fiction has a similar sociological dimension, which inevitably makes more use of informal theoretical analysis. This is obvious in respect of any fiction that involves the imaginative construction of hypothetical societies, but it is also true of intrusive fantasies in which the existing social order is subject to some kind of external stress. Although Isaac Asimov took some pains to identify a particular train of thought in speculative fiction—extending from *Utopian and *satirical traditions to science-fictional future histories—as "social science fiction", all fantastic fiction routinely makes use of sociological assumptions. The speculative fiction that is most interesting from a sociological viewpoint is that which deals directly and methodically with the construction of hypothetical societies, especially eutopian and euchronian designs, and sophisticated exercises in *xenology. Examples are very numerous; those attempting scrupulously to embrace a scientific method

of construction include H. G. Wells' *The First Men in the Moon* (1901), James Gunn's *The Joy Makers* (1961), and Samuel R. Delany's *Triton* (1976).

Notable narrative thought experiments in sociology include Philip Wylie's *The Disappearance* (1951), Katherine MacLean's "The Snowball Effect" (1952), the description of a factory run according to the principle of "from each according to his ability, to each according to his need" in Ayn Rand's *Atlas Shrugged* (1957), Michael Young's *The Rise of the Meritocracy* (1958), and Maya Kaathryn Bohnhoff's "Hand-Me-Down Town" (1989). Many exercises in *alternative history fit into this category, including a number that accept the logic of Max Weber's thesis regarding the complicity of Protestantism and capitalism; Keith Roberts' *Pavane* (1968) is a notable example.

Accounts of social responses to *disaster—especially those paying close attention to the forces implicit in social recovery—also tend in the direction of sociological thought experiments; notable examples include Leigh Brackett's *The Long Tomorrow* (1955) and Walter M. Miller's *A Canticle for Leibowitz* (1960). Stories in which social groups are isolated from their parent society for long periods of time, including Robinsonades, accounts of life aboard generation starships, and stories featuring "lost colonies", similarly acquire an experimental dimension, very obvious in such examples as W. L. George's *Children of the Morning* (1927), George Zebrowski's *Brute Orbits* (1998), and many stories in Ursula K. *Le Guin's Hainish series.

There is also a notable subgenre of works employing hypothetical viewpoint characters who are supposed to be sophisticated sociological analysts, including Grant Allen's *The British Barbarians* (1895), Eden Phillpotts' *Address Unknown* (1938), and Robert Heinlein's *Stranger in a Strange Land* (1961). In some such stories alien sociologists study humans in a methodologically disciplined fashion; examples include Somtow Sucharitkul's *Mallworld* (1981) and Karen Joy Fowler's "The Poplar Street Study" (1985) and "The View from Venus" (1986).

The most elaborate literary attempt to construct a hypothetical new branch of sociology is Isaac Asimov's "psychohistory", whose further deployments included Michael F. Flynn's "Eifelheim" (1986) and Donald Kingsbury's "Historical Crisis" (1995; exp. 2001 as *Psychohistorical Crisis*). Flynn's two-part article "An Introduction to Psychohistory" in the April and May 1988 issues of *Analog* cited Colin Renfrew and Kenneth Cooke's *Transformations: Mathematical Approaches to Cultural Change* (1979) and Paul Colinvaux's *The Fates of Nations: A Biological Theory of History* (1980) in arguing for the possibility of a fruitful combination of trend analysis and a version of social *Darwinism, proposing that some such combination might have been made in the nineteenth century by a "Babbage Society"—a possibility dramatised in his secret history story "The Steel Driver" (1988).

The category of sociological theory most relevant to this kind of speculative exercise—especially in its science-fictional versions—is *technological determinism, which attempts to account for social change as a series of responses to technological innovation. Another subcategory of sociology that attracts particular attention in speculative fiction is demography, which is implicit in all accounts of the *population principle, although demographers are rarely used as characters; Hilbert Schenck's A Rose for Armageddon (1982) is a notable exception.

Further subcategories of particular relevance to the subject matter of this book are the sociology of science, which developed in the wake of Thomas Kuhn's analysis of the role played by *paradigms in the scientific community, and the sociology of literature, which has a much longer history and more elaborate theoretical subdivisions. European sociologists of literature mostly attempt to account for the contents of literature in terms of the class-generated *ideologies of their authors, while American sociologists of literature are more likely to employ functionalist "uses and gratifications" analyses of audience demand. The sociology of science fiction summarised in Brian Stableford's The Sociology of Science Fiction (1987) attempts to strike an even-handed balance between the two. Speculative literary responses to the development of the sociology of science include Isaac Asimov's The Gods Themselves (1972) and Howard L. Myers' "Out, Wit!" (1972); responses to the sociology of literature are far more common in naturalistic fiction, although some observations of the sociology of science fiction are ironically reflected in Barry N. Malzberg's Galaxies (1975).

The representation of sociologists in naturalistic fiction is generally unflattering, often representing them as illicit appropriators of a licence to spy on or manipulate their neighbours. Notable examples can be found in Irving Wallace's The Chapman Report (1960; film, 1962), which includes a fictionalised version of Alfred Kinsey, J. B. Priestley's The Image Men (1968), and Alison Lurie's Imaginary Friends (1967), which includes a character based on Leon Festinger. Inquisitive sociologists in speculative fiction are more likely to stand in for the reader in pursuing their enquiries; examples include K. W. Jeter's Seeklight (1975), Jayge Carr's "The Icarus Epidemic" (1990), Connie Willis' Bellwether (1996), and Edward M. Lerner's "By the Rules" (2003). Sociologists have, however, been more enthusiastic to employ speculative

fiction as an educational instrument than many other scientific practitioners; Richard Ofshe's The Sociology of the Possible (1970) is a notable anthology with elaborate theoretical commentaries.

SPACE
The medium of extension. Early philosophical treatments of the idea of space hesitated over the question of whether space could be said to exist apart from the objects within it—in other words, whether it was to be conceived as a kind of receptacle or as an attribute of *matter.

The notion that space is a void—and that matter consists of particles arrayed therein—was accepted as a fundamental assumption by the Greek *atomists but rejected by *Aristotle, who considered the idea of empty space abhorrent, and asserted that space must be conceived as the extension of something, however rarefied. In the mundane world, this minimal role was assumed by air, but Aristotle felt obliged to introduce a fifth *element—a "quintessence"—to serve as the extensive quality of celestial space: the *ether. In Aristotelian *cosmology, however, celestial space was limited, thus generating the problem of trying to imagine—or, conversely, of trying not to imagine—what could be "beyond" it. Because of this difficulty, the void banished from within the Aristotelian universe continued to lurk without it.

The adoption of Aristotelian ideas rather than atomist ones by the Christian church had considerable consequences for the development of Renaissance science. It did, however, give rise to a *theological conundrum that exercised the minds of scholastic philosophers: the question of whether God could move the universe. If there were no void, then he could not, because there would be nowhere to move it to—which seemed to some theologians to be a slur on his omnipotence. If, on the other hand, he could move it, and there was a void within which it could be moved, then the Aristotelian "universe" could only be a sector of a much larger universe. In any case, it seemed odd to some theologians that God might be content with a small and compact Aristotelian cosmos when he was perfectly capable of creating an infinite one; the latter train of thought led Nicholas of Cusa to speculate that the universe might in fact be an infinite void, filled with a *plurality of worlds.

When the heliocentric theory began to displace the geocentric theory of the solar system, many of its supporters continued to abhor the idea of a void, preferring to modify and extend Aristotle's ether, but prejudice against the void declined as the concept of space expanded, as did corollary prejudice against atomism. Nature's supposed abhorrence of a void seemed far less obvious after 1620, when Otto von Guericke devised the first vacuum pump. Further seventeenth-century experiments on air pressure, routinely involving the creation of vacuums, by Evangelista Torricelli, Blaise Pascal, and Robert Boyle, revived interest in the notion of the void and helped pave the way for the revitalisation of atomic theory by Pierre Gassendi.

The notion that space is an objectively real void, functioning as a container for matter and describable in terms of the three dimensions of Euclidean *geometry, became fundamental to Isaac *Newton's cosmology; his notion of it is often described as "absolute space". On the other hand, René Descartes continued to conceive of space as the essence of substance, while idealists such as Gottfried Leibniz and George Berkeley insisted that it was a purely mental construction, employed to organise the sensory data of sight and motion. Immanuel *Kant attempted a compromise, holding to the idealist philosophy but stressing the necessity of the idea of space as an *a priori* assumption in the business of making sense of sensory data.

In the literary imagination the anxieties of idealist philosophers were often seen as mere quibbles; space was usually conceived as a Newtonian frame, though not necessarily as a void. It was in this context that the concept of *space travel evolved. The continued popularity of the ether in speculative accounts of space travel probably had more to do with its usefulness as a facilitating device than any innate abhorrence of the idea of void, but fictional representations of etheric space travel helped maintain the notion until James Clerk Maxwell reintroduced it as the medium of electromagnetic vibration.

The philosophical controversy regarding the nature of space was confused again when nineteenth-century mathematicians became interested in hypothetical spaces possessed of more or fewer than the three dimensions of Euclidean space. The notion that actual space might not be Euclidean—perhaps possessing an innate curvature in a *fourth dimension—seemed whimsical until the early twentieth-century revolution in physics prompted by Albert *Einstein's general theory of *relativity wrought a revolution in scientific thought. Einstein's theory abolished Newton's concept of absolute space in favour of the kind of "space-time continuum" suggested by Hermann Minkowski, and opened the way for modern atomic theorists to increase the number of potential dimensions dramatically in the search for a unifying theory that would bring gravity in line with the other fundamental *forces.

The literary imagery of space became much more elaborate in this period, in quality as well as quantity, as writers wrestled with the idea of a multiplicity of dimensions. This was an era in which literary *geography became much more refined, and in which new varieties of *microcosmic and *macrocosmic romance were developed in connection with analogical theories of the atom—but it was still the literature of space travel, illuminated by discoveries in *astronomy, that took centre stage in the development of popular conceptions of space.

The dominant twentieth-century conception of space was one in which the notions of void and infinity no longer seemed in the least strange, their thorough domestication reflected in numerous titles akin to Austin Hall's "Into the Infinite" (1919) and Leslie F. Stone's *Out of the Void* (1929; book, 1967). The increasingly common notion of the "spaceship", on the other hand, embodied an analogy in which space was a (tacitly etheric) ocean, and the worlds within it islands—an ocean that was navigable by "astronauts" and "space pilots", and whose problematic expanses might be avoided by taking short cuts through *hyperspace.

Given the circumstances of America's own "discovery" by the heroic navigator Christopher Columbus, and the legendary westward expansion of its population, it is not surprising that American science fiction made much of the notion of space travel, and of the notion of pioneering a new "space frontier" with a view to its eventual "conquest". This network of ideas—all of which came to seem perfectly natural to their users—became the foundation stone of the mythical representation of the future as the *Space Age.

A further complication in the use of the term "space", especially in speculative fiction, occurred after World War II, when it became commonplace to refer to the space beyond the atmosphere as "outer space"—a phrase whose fine ring made up for its pleonastic quality. The term became particularly fashionable in referring to the possible source of *flying saucers, as in Donald Keyhoe's *Flying Saucers from Outer Space* (1953) and the film *It Came from Outer Space* (1953). Its widespread use proved an irresistible temptation to neologists anxious to provide it with an antithesis by means of the notion of "inner space"—a term whose early popularisers included J. B. Priestley, in an article in the *New Statesman* entitled "They Came from Inner Space" (1954). Priestley argued that it was a mistake for speculative fiction to explore realms beyond the Earth's atmosphere rather than attempting to plumb the hidden "depths" of the human psyche.

Geometrical models of the mind—implicit in such analogies as "theatre of the mind"—were by no means new. The idea that thoughts, images, and the entire integral self might be considered as entities occupying some kind of receptacle, much as matter occupies space, could easily be related to Descartes' notion of "mental substance" inhabiting the brain—although Descartes, whose notion of space was Aristotelian rather than Newtonian, had not done so. The spaces of the imagination had, however, more often been conceived as *parallel spaces than inner ones: alternative universes accessed by portals such as the gates of ivory and horn.

The notion of the mind as a hierarchical organisation of internal spaces, equipped with mysterious "hidden depths", was popularised in the nineteenth century—most notably in the context of psychological theories of the unconscious—but such depths remained implicitly murky and tacitly unnavigable during the first half of the twentieth century. In the second half of the century, that situation changed, and the notion of a microcosmic inner space, contrasted with but analogous to the macrocosm of outer space, became much more commonplace.

Priestley's plea for more literary explorations of this inner space was reiterated and amplified in 1962 by J. G. *Ballard, laying significant groundwork for "new wave" science fiction, and a good deal of late twentieth-century fiction drawing ideas from psychology was formulated as a subgenre of inner-spatial odysseys. The phrase "inner space" continued to expand its range of meanings—it was often used with reference to the ocean depths, and in 2003 the University of Michigan launched an "inner space program" using nanoprobes to observe chemical activity in living cells—but its primary association was always with the depths of the human psyche.

Early fictional uses of the notion of inner space included Howard Koch's "Invasion from Inner Space" (1959), which expanded the notion to take in the habitations of *artificial intelligence, especially the "hidden depths" within *computers. This extension eventually gave birth to the notion of *cyberspace, similarly conceived as an analogical reflection of "outer space": a void within which information can be stored or transmitted, and in which entities of Cartesian mental substance can move about, sometimes embarking on exploratory odysseys.

The rapid establishment of the world wide web as a significant social space in which people could meet and interact, and its parallel mythologisation by contemporary science fiction, led some commentators to draw specific analogies with the Aristotelian "celestial space" that was integrated into Mediaeval Christian belief; Margaret Wertheim's *The Pearly Gates of Cyberspace: A History of Space from Dante to the Internet* (1999) constructs a history of space that begins with a dualistic separation of mundane and celestial

space, moves through a phase when "physical space" established a monopoly that banished "soul space" into the conceptual wilderness, and makes its way back via the complexities of relativistic space and hyperspace to a new dualism in which cyberspace becomes—at least potentially—"cyber-soul-space".

The fundamental philosophical dispute between void theorists, plenum theorists, and idealists as to the essential nature of space remains unsettled, and perhaps more vexed than ever before in consequence of the proliferation of hyperspaces in theoretical physics and the implications of various versions of inflation theory in cosmology. Literary representations continue to play upon the imaginative difficulties of conceiving space in other-than-Euclidean terms—Christopher Priest's *Inverted World* (1974) is a notable example—and of conceptualising fundamental alterations of its extensive capacity, as in Philip Latham's "The Rose Bowl-Pluto Hypothesis" (1969). In David Ira Cleary's "In the Squeeze" (2000), "space" is a drug combating the effects of a fundamental warp in the continuum—a representation of which an idealist would be bound to approve.

SPACE AGE, THE

A characterisation of the future based on the supposition that *rocket flights into *space, particularly the first landing on the *Moon, would constitute the early phases of an inexorable historical process, whose unfolding would see a gradual expansion of the human population throughout the solar system, and then throughout the galaxy. The future history thus mapped out follows the historical model of European *colonisation that resulted in the "discovery" and subsequent development of the New World, including the creation of the United States and that nation's spectacular ascent to world dominance.

Early images of space colonisation include John *Wilkins' speculations regarding the colonisation of the Moon in *The Discovery of a New World* (1638), further celebrated in Thomas Gray's "Luna Habitabilis" (1736)—whose translation by Sally Purcell includes the lines "A time will come that sees great hastening crowds / Of colonists leaving for the moon ..." and "... trade begins / Between the worlds, through now-familiar space. / Our England, that already rules the waves / And keeps the winds in awe, shall now extend / Her ancient triumphs over conquered air". The motif is echoed in numerous nineteenth-century works celebrating the triumphs of the British Empire, and also in the futuristic sections of Victor Hugo's *Légende des siècles* (1859–1885), but it could not become a consensus view of the likely shape of future history until there was a genre of futuristic fiction ready and willing to embrace it. The *Vernian genre of *voyages extraordinaires* did not do so, and neither did Wellsian *scientific romance, but American science fiction took it aboard wholeheartedly.

The development of some such centralising mythology was a natural response to the narrative problems associated with the use of the *future as a narrative space. In much the same way that folktales benefit from the use of the mythic past as a flexible but readily comprehensible setting in which their hearers and readers can readily orientate themselves, futuristic fiction stood to benefit from a vague consensus view of the broad shape future history is likely to take. The fact that the consensus view of British scientific romance was narrowly focused on the prospects of future *warfare caused considerable problems for its historical development during and after World War I, just as Vernian fiction ran into problems as the geographical exploration of the world was completed and tourism became commonplace.

The utility of the myth of the Space Age as an organising principle was the vastness of its range, both spatially and temporally; it converted the galaxy into a vast reservoir of imaginary worlds, including as many Earth clones as might be convenient, on which all kinds of societies and their supportive ecologies could be sited, whose exploration could be extended over centuries and millennia. It was also elastic; when the utility of the planets in the solar system as plausible settings for melodrama was drastically reduced by the progress of twentieth-century *astronomy, the acolytes of Space Age mythology only had to move into the wider spaces of the "galactic empire".

David Lasser, the first managing editor of Hugo *Gernsback's *Wonder Stories* and the president of the American Interplanetary Society, titled his pioneering popularisation of the possibility of space travel *The Conquest of Space* (1931)—a phrase that soon acquired an iconic significance in American science fiction. The first article written for *Astounding Stories* by exiled German rocket pioneer Willy *Ley advertised "The Dawn of the Conquest of Space" (1935), the notion of conquest having by then become fundamental to American science fiction's representations of *space travel. John W. *Campbell Jr. began a projected series of serial novels with *The Conquest of the Planets* in a rival magazine in the same year, although circumstances prevented him from continuing it.

Writers in the editorial stable Campbell built at *Astounding* soon began to produce works attempting a shrewd combination of the inspirational and the realistic; Lester del Rey's "The Stars Look Down" (1940) is an archetypal example. The introduction to the first hardcover showcase anthology of genre science fiction, *Adventures in Time and Space* (1946), blithely announced that the true significance of the explosion of the atom bomb was that "the universe is ours". The development of this mythology conferred an iconic significance on the spaceship, which became far more than a mere means of transport; its crucial blastoffs became symbolic of a "cosmic breakout" that might and must transform the nature and prospects of the human species. In competition with this infusion of meaning, attempts to stigmatise spaceship stories as "space opera" stood no chance of success; the term was swiftly shorn of its pejorative implications, imbued instead with a slightly patronising but warm affection.

It was this establishment of the myth of the Space Age as a general backcloth to American science fiction that placed the motif of space travel at the genre's core and equipped the subsidiary myth of cosmic breakout with sufficient emotional force to be routinely employed as a narrative climax, uplifting in more ways than one. The cosmic breakout motif readily lent itself to exaggeration in stories in which escape into space becomes the only exit available to humankind in the event of Earthly devastation—as in Edwin Balmer and Philip Wylie's *When Worlds Collide* (1933)—and such stories rapidly took on much of the symbolic load of the Biblical tale of Noah's Ark, including the implication of a new Covenant. By the 1940s, the myth was so well established that science fiction writers had begun to produce metafictional commentaries on it, celebrating the iconic significance of the space ship; Ray Bradbury's "King of the Gray Spaces" (1943; aka "R Is for Rocket") is one of the most expressive.

After World War II the idea of an imminent Space Age was popularised with unparalleled fervour, along with the phrase itself, by Arthur C. *Clarke, who claimed that reading Lasser's book had changed his life; his contribution to Reginald Bretnor's groundbreaking study of *Modern Science Fiction: Its Meaning and Its Future* (1953) was uncompromisingly titled "Science Fiction: Preparation for the Age of Space". Clarke's early fiction and nonfiction alike were conceived as propaganda for this cause, and he considered the prophetic case securely made by the time he wrote *Voices from the Sky: Previews of the Coming Space Age* (1965) and edited *The Coming of the Space Age* (1967). Willy Ley continued to lend enthusiastic support, recruiting Chesley Bonestell and the entire genre of space *art to the cause in *The Conquest of Space* (1949). Adherents of the myth dated the beginning of the "actual" Space Age as 4 October 1957, when Sputnik 1 was launched into orbit.

Fictional representations of Space Age imagery became acutely aware of their own mythical pretensions as rocket research entered its postwar phase; notable examples of such self-consciousness include Murray Leinster's "The Story of Rod Cantrell" (1949), Robert A. Heinlein's "The Man Who Sold the Moon" (1950), Arthur Clarke's *Prelude to Space* (1951), Fredric Brown's *The Lights in the Sky Are Stars* (1953; aka *Project Jupiter*), David Duncan's *Dark Dominion* (1954), and the components of Dean McLaughlin's mosaic *The Man Who Wanted Stars* (1956–1957; book, 1965). The mythic significance of the theme is very obvious in James Blish's "Surface Tension" (1952), whose "cosmic breakout" is a microcosmic journey in a tiny "spaceship". Future histories developed by science fiction writers often mapped out phases of the Space Age in terms of evolving technologies; A. Bertram Chandler's *Spartan Planet* (1969) specified the three stages of humankind's expansion into the universe described by earlier works in his Rim Worlds series (launched 1959), the first achieved by generation ships, the second by "gaussjammers" using the Ehrenhaft Drive (a magnetic tunnelling effect), and the third by "timejammers" using the more powerful superluminal Mannschenn Drive.

Edmond Hamilton's "The Pro" (1964), produced in the wake of the most extravagant celebrations of cosmic breakout, is the most explicit of all metafictional studies of science fiction's ambitions in this regard. A detailed prospectus for the Space Age was set out by one of the genre's most prolific paperback editors, Donald A. Wollheim, in *The Universe Makers* (1971), under the chapter title "The Cosmogony of the Future". Wollheim construed the consensus of support for the future history among science fiction writers as evidence that it is what their "mental computers" have calculated as the shape the future is bound to take—modestly downplaying his own influence as a gatekeeper, whose liking for Space Age fantasies was very well known to his suppliers.

The absence of the Space Age from the images of the future contained in British scientific romance did not go unnoticed, but the myth's American followers considered that a simple case of imaginative blindness; Charles Galton Darwin's *The Next Million Years* (1952) received a scathing review in *Galaxy*, because its failure to mention space travel seemed to Groff Conklin to disqualify it from having anything useful to say. Soviet science fiction, as might be expected, was always enthusiastic to endorse the indigenous space program, but was much less enthusiastic to see it as a step in the direction of colonialism and imperialism. Most Soviet authors avoided stories set on colony worlds; the notable exceptions—including several by the Strugatsky brothers—tended to take a gloomy view of their prospects. The Polish writer Stanislaw Lem wrote two space fiction series, one featuring the pioneering pilot Pirx and the other the far-ranging Ijon Tichy, but neither subscribes to Space Age mythology.

As the Apollo program brought the first step in the Space Age closer to actuality in the 1960s, the fantasies promoting it became more realistic in terms of the hardware, and more strident in proclaiming the significance of the impending moment. Notable examples included Jeff Sutton's *Beyond Apollo* (1966). Neil Armstrong endorsed the myth when he described his descent to the lunar surface as "one small step for a man, one giant leap for mankind". Subscribers to the myth within the genre often took it for granted, as Clarke did, that the primary social function of science fiction was to provide inspirational propaganda for the Space Age, thus assisting its progress. J. G. *Ballard was widely regarded as a traitor to this cause when he began to write stories in the 1960s suggesting that the first step into space might also prove to be the last, and that the Space Age might be rapidly aborted before the end of the twentieth century; his stories of this kind are sampled in *Memories of the Space Age* (1988).

Few other writers followed Ballard's lead, but when the first Moon landing in 1969 was followed by a gradual scaling down of the U.S. space program, it became increasingly probable that he was right. Propagandist Space Age science fiction took on a more defiant tone as time went by, the more extreme exhibiting a sense of betrayal and arguing for a heroic reaffirmation of the mythology's ideals; notable examples include Joseph Green's *Star Probe* (1976), G. C. Edmondson's *The Man Who Corrupted Earth* (1980), and Ben Bova's *Privateers* (1985). Propaganda did, however, continue to appear; one notable example is the fundraising anthology *Project Solar Sail* (1990) edited by Arthur C. Clarke and David Brin, compiled on behalf of the World Space Foundation.

Sceptical opposition to the likelihood of the Space Age future history was based on the proposition that there is no destination available in the solar system that could possibly justify the expense of sending a manned expedition there. The development of *computer technology made it much easier to design and build tiny machines much better equipped for extraterrestrial exploration than humans, by virtue of requiring no elaborate life support. Fictitious accounts of *artificial satellites were modified alongside actual plans, so that huge manned space stations were largely displaced by much smaller machine-operated entities.

Stories accepting the logic of this situation—sometimes reluctantly—include Charles L. Grant's "Abdication" (1973), in which an astronaut who wins the U.S. presidency then opposes the space program. The dangers of space travel were dramatically demonstrated by the explosion of the space shuttle *Challenger* in January 1986, which inspired such sober responses as Lucius Shepard's poem "*Challenger* as Viewed from the Westerbrook Bar" (1986). Paul Levinson's story series launched with "Loose Ends" (1997) acknowledged the force of the lesson by sending a time traveller back to 1963 with a specific mandate to prevent the *Challenger* disaster—although it transpires that the tragedy was far worse in his world than in ours.

Space Age enthusiasts never conceded that the argument was lost, and continued to regard science fiction as a key vehicle of their propaganda until the end of the twentieth century. The notion of space colonisation as a *rite de passage* for the species continued to echo in such works as John Ford's *Growing Up Weightless* (1993). The second man on the Moon, Buzz Aldrin, collaborated with John Barnes on two Space Age fantasies, *Encounter with Tiber* (1996) and *The Return* (2000). In spite of this propagandising, the mythical currency of the scheme had suffered a severe devaluation by the time the twenty-first century dawned. Images of space colonisation were shunted several centuries forward in most subsequent speculative maps of future history, usually to the far side of a technological *singularity, and the conquest of space came to be seen as an essentially *posthuman project.

SPACE TRAVEL

Flight beyond the Earth's atmosphere. Early accounts of space travel usually took the form of journeys to the *Moon, beginning with the satirical expeditions described by Lucian in the second century, of which the most widely read was the one ironically labelled the *True History*. That satirical tradition extended into the nineteenth century, gradually taking on a greater degree of realism in response to the evolution of scientific *cosmology. The practicalities of space travel were first addressed by John *Wilkins in the 1640 appendix to the third edition of *The Discovery of a New World*.

Most early accounts of space travel were perfectly content with supernatural or frankly preposterous means. The Greek god Mercury carries a soldier to Mars and Venus in Barnaby Rich's *A Right Excellent and Pleasaunt Dialogue Betwene Mercury and an English Souldier* (1574). John Kepler's dreamer in *Somnium* (written 1609; published 1634) is carried aloft by a daemon. Francis Godwin's *Man in the Moone* (1638) employs a flock of "gansas". Cyrano de Bergerac's *alter ego* Dyrcona tests several methods in *L'autre monde* (written ca. 1650) but eventually contrives to design a machine capable of doing the

job, thus issuing in a new era of interplanetary fantasy. John Dryden's "Annus Mirabilis" (1667), inspired by Wilkins, confidently stated that "Then, we upon our Globes last verge shall go, / And view the Ocean leaning on the sky: / From thence our rolling Neighbours we shall know, / And on the Lunar worlds securely pry".

The mechanics of space travel remained an awkward challenge to the literary imagination throughout the eighteenth century. The giant spring envisaged in David Russen's *Iter Lunare* (1703) made little appeal, but flying machines seemed equally fanciful in a pre-aeronautical era. The advent of balloons, however, had a considerable impact, and balloons became a favourite means of space travel in the nineteenth century, in such works as Willem Bilderdijk's *Kort verhaal van eene aanmerklijke luchtreis en nieuwe planeetontdekking* (1813; trans. as *A Short Account of a Remarkable Aerial Voyage and a Discovery of a New Planet*), Alfred Driou's *Aventures d'un aëronaute parisien dans les mondes inconnus* (1856), and the anonymous *The Narrative and Travels of Paul Aermont Among the Planets* (1873). George Tucker's satirical *Voyage to the Moon* (1827; by-lined Joseph Atterley) was among the first works to extrapolate the *gravity-defying tendencies of balloons to a more general antigravitational effect.

The idea of space travel was scathingly satirised in the anonymous "Anti-Humbug" (1840), which suggests giant condors endowed with intelligence by galvanic plates as an alternative to balloons, and features a railroad extending all the way to Jupiter. A revised version of Edgar Allan *Poe's "The Unparalleled Adventure of One Hans Pfaall" (first issued as "Hans Phaal" in 1835) appeared in the same year, the additions including a tongue-in-cheek preface calling for greater verisimilitude in accounts of space travel, and claiming (implausibly, given that Pfaall also uses a balloon) to have provided one. Poe's preface was, however, taken seriously by Jules Verne, who did make a serious attempt at verisimilitude in *De la terre à la lune* (1865; trans. as *From the Earth to the Moon*)—although his proposal that a missile might be accelerated to escape velocity by a gigantic gun gave insufficient consideration to the plight of the passengers within the missile, who could not have survived such abrupt impulsion.

Most of Verne's contemporaries remained content to fudge the issue by using some kind of antigravity device or some means of drawing propulsive energy from a hypothetical ether, or some combination of the two. Notable examples include *The History of a Voyage to the Moon* (1864) by "Chrysostom Trueman", Percy Greg's *Across the Zodiac* (1880), Robert Cromie's *A Plunge into Space* (1890), John Jacob

Astor's *A Journey in Other Worlds* (1894), H. G. Wells' *The First Men in the Moon* (1901), and Fenton Ash's *A Son of the Stars* (1907). Many such stories were equally content to believe in an interplanetary atmosphere or a breathable ether, which provides space travellers with basic life support as well as permitting the occasional propeller-driven craft—like the one in Charles Dixon's *Fifteen Hundred Miles an Hour* (1895)—to undertake interplanetary journeys.

When Verne complained that Wells' Cavorite was pure invention, while his space gun was technically feasible, Wells brushed off the complaint, but he subsequently employed a Vernian gun to provide the climactic image of his script for the Alexander Korda film *Things to Come* (1936). By then, however, a much better means had come clearly into imaginative view in the form of *rockets, first popularised as a means of space travel by John Munro in *A Trip to Venus* (1897) and the didactic fiction of Konstantin *Tsiolkovsky, and advocated as a practical endeavour by various ambitious experimenters in the 1930s. Rockets became the standard method of spaceship propulsion in twentieth-century speculative fiction, imported into the U.S. pulps from their inception. Atomic power, first adopted to the powering of space flight by Garrett P. Serviss' *A Columbus of Space* (1909), also became a frequent recourse of early pulp science fiction.

The establishment of the myth of the *Space Age in the 1930s enabled space travel to be represented as a crucial historical breakthrough, and it was entirely natural that the discovery of the expanding universe by Edwin Hubble and his collaborators should be reflected in genre science fiction by the expansion of science-fictional accounts of space travel into interstellar space. E. E. Smith's *The Skylark of Space* (1928; book, 1946) and Edmond Hamilton's "Crashing Suns" (1928) founded a subgenre of space opera that was greatly elaborated in the 1930s and 1940s, notable further contributors to the subgenre including John W. *Campbell Jr. and Jack Williamson. Space opera offered a Romantic vision of space travel, in which interstellar distances, however hazard strewn, became essentially irrelevant, and spaceships could engage in spectacular battles. The exuberant spirit of such stories was, however, countered by stories that took pains to represent local space travel as an unglamorous matter of futuristic routine. Notable examples included Otto Binder's Etherline series (1938–1942; all but the last by-lined Gordon Giles; book as *Puzzle of the Space Pyramids*, by-line Eando Binder, 1971), Lester del Rey's "Habit" (1939), and Cleve Cartmill's stories of *The Space Scavengers* (1949–1950; book, 1975).

The Romantic tradition usually employed space travel merely as a means of reaching interesting destinations, or to facilitate exotic space battles. Within the context of Space Age mythology, however, it was clearly desirable to equip accounts of interstellar travel with a smoother gloss of realism. This appearance was largely achieved by drawing on analogies likening the business of interstellar travel to the navigation of the Earth's oceans. The crews of many starships were likened to the crews of merchant navies, most explicitly in the long-running Rim Worlds series written in the latter half of the century by A. Bertram Chandler (who was an officer in an actual merchant navy), but the magnetism of glamour combined with the imperatives of melodrama in producing far more images of military navies translocated to the infinite void.

Although many early works of military science fiction focused on the role of "space marines" who did their actual fighting on planetary surfaces, a subgenre of "naval science fiction" became increasingly manifest in the 1940s, and increasingly sophisticated as Edmond Hamilton's Interstellar Patrol and E. E. Smith's Lensmen gave way to institutions more obviously modelled on the U.S. Navy. Ex–Navy officer Robert A. Heinlein was content to leave such matters in the background of his stories in the 1940s but brought them into much clearer focus in juvenile novels focusing on military training, from *Space Cadet* (1948) and *Starman Jones* (1953) to *Starship Troopers* (1959).

Naval glamour was by no means the extreme of the Romantic tradition, which inevitably sought other means of sophistication. Hyperspace became a significant source of existential strangeness as well as a means of dodging the limited velocity of light, and the experience of space travel increasingly tended towards the transcendental—or at least the *psychotropic—in the latter half of the century. Notable developments of the trend can be seen in the work of Cordwainer Smith, especially "The Game of Rat and Dragon" (1955), "The Lady Who Sailed the Soul" (1960), and "Think Blue, Count Two" (1963). It was in this context that stories began to appear in which spacefarers *became* *cyborg starships in order to experience space travel directly, as in Thomas N. Scortia's "Sea Change" (1956; aka "The Shores of Night"), Anne McCaffrey's "The Ship Who Sang" (1961), and Kevin O'Donnell Jr.'s *Mayflies* (1979).

The Romantic tradition's connections to the realistic tradition were more sturdily maintained by a subgenre of stories that respected the limiting velocity of light and accepted that interstellar travel would be a slow business—far too slow for such flights to be undertaken in a single lifetime. The notion that interstellar distances might be navigable in spite of this limitation gave rise to the notion of the "generation starship", first popularised in Don Wilcox's "The Voyage That Lasted 600 Years" (1940) and Robert A. Heinlein's "Universe" (1941). In such stories interstellar vessels become tiny worlds in their own right, and travel within them a way of life—whose possibilities were further explored in such stories as Clifford Simak's "Spacebred Generations" (1953; aka "Target Generation"), Milton Lesser's *The Star Seekers* (1953), Brian Aldiss' *Non-Stop* (1958), Edmund Cooper's *Seed of Light* (1959), and J. T. McIntosh's *200 Years to Christmas* (1961). This notion—a mordantly literal embodiment of the motto *per ardua ad astra*—was readily adaptable to the mythic motif of the extraterrestrial Ark, as in Leigh Brackett's "The Ark of Mars" (1953; exp. book 1963 as *Alpha Centauri—or Die!*), Roger Dixon's *Noah II* (1970), and James White's *The Dream Millennium* (1974). John W. MacVey's *Journey to Alpha Centauri* (1965) is a nonfiction treatment of the notion, although it concludes with a dramatised section.

Another compromise between the naturalistic and Romantic imagery of space travel was struck by space-set *disaster stories, such as Boyd Ellanby's "The Star Lord" (1953) and Murray Leinster's "The *Corianis* Disaster" (1960), and by accounts of starship-based cultures such as Robert A. Heinlein's *Citizen of the Galaxy* (1957) and Alexei Panshin's *Rite of Passage* (1963). A subset of the latter category features starfaring cultures isolated by time dilatation effects, as in L. Ron Hubbard's "To the Stars" (1950; book 1954 as *Return to Tomorrow*) and Poul Anderson's "Ghetto" (1954). Romantic and realistic imagery also overlapped in accounts of "yachts" borne by the solar wind sailing in local space; notable examples included Poul Anderson's "Sunjammer" (1964; by-lined Winston P. Sanders) and Arthur Clarke's "Sunjammer" (1965; aka "The Wind from the Sun"). A similar "sail" allows acceleration to near light speed in A. Bertram Chandler's "The Winds of If" (1963; book as *Catch the Star Winds*, 1969).

The standards of realism applicable to speculative accounts of local space travel became inexorably more demanding as rocket technology made swift progress after World War II, going into overdrive when the space race began after the launching of Sputnik in 1957. The U.S. National Aeronautics and Space Administration (NASA) was founded in 1958. Project Mercury (1959–1963) put pilots into Earth orbit, Project Gemini (1962–1966) developed orbital maneuvering, rendezvous, and docking, and Project Apollo completed the sequence, culminating in the Moon landings of 1969–1972. Apollo spacecraft were subsequently used in Skylab missions and in collaborative missions with the Russian Soyuz program.

Once Yuri Gagarin had orbited the Earth in a space capsule in 1961, stories of space travel moved to the margins of naturalistic fiction, and the first Moon landing served as a dramatic confirmation of John Wilkins' proposal that it would one day be possible to journey to the Moon.

Cautionary tales such as Hank Searls' *The Pilgrim Project* (1964) and burlesques such as Robert Buckner's *Starfire* (1960; aka *Moon Pilot*) were far outnumbered in this period by accounts in which the takeoff points of rockets were represented as the launchpads of a glorious New Era. Realism of a different sort was, however, maintained in such stories as Walter M. Miller's "The Lineman" (1957), in which the routines of extraterrestrial journeywork are interrupted by the arrival of a travelling whorehouse. In the meantime, accounts of travel to worlds beyond the solar system remained fundamentally Romantic, routinely employing fantastic devices—including *hyperspace and *matter transmitters—to facilitate faster-than-light travel. Such fiction usually made generally light of the problems of life support, casually equipping interstellar vessels with artificial gravity and endlessly recyclable air.

Works in the realistic tradition produced after the advent of the Apollo program are very numerous, but notable examples included Nigel Balchin's *Kings of Infinite Space* (1967), Martin Caidin's *Planetfall* (1974), Harry Harrison's *Skyfall* (1976), Gordon R. Dickson's *The Far Call* (1978), Lee Correy's *Shuttle Down* (1980–1981) and *Manna* (1984), J. B. Cather's "Pulsebeat" (1987), and Jack Dann and Jack C. Haldeman II's *High Steel* (1993). Within twenty years of that advent, however, the contraction of the actual space program had begun to force would-be realists to envisage heroic attempts of revitalisation, or to make use of alternative histories, as in Stephen Baxter's *Voyage* (1996). Missions credited to NASA had to be represented as the desperate last gasps of a dying institution, as in Baxter's *Titan* (1997). Almost as soon as the first Moon landing had occurred, fictional astronauts began to be haunted by an awareness that the myth of the Space Age was not working out as scheduled, that their *raison d'être* was questionable, and that their experiences might be more akin to delusions than everyday experiences; such anxieties afflict the protagonists of Barry Malzberg's *The Falling Astronauts* (1971), J. G. Ballard's "The Man Who Walked on the Moon" (1985), and Dan Simmons' *Phases of Gravity* (1989) with increasing discomfort.

One response to the disappointments of the actual space program and the discoveries made by its probes was an increased interest in the possibility of skipping over that phase of the Space Age. In spite of the conceptual and practical difficulties of interstellar travel, there was no shortage of engineers eager to produce designs for hypothetical starships. One such design, the Orion spacecraft—originated by one of the inventors of the H-bomb, Stanislaw Ulam, in the 1950s—used fusion bombs to supply thrust to a "pusher plate". Ulam originally proposed its use in interplanetary travel, but Freeman *Dyson adapted the notion to interstellar flight. Nuclear fusion and matter/antimatter collisions were employed in similar designs to produce plasma that might be ejected, in the manner of a rocket, to produce a continuous thrust. In 1960, Robert Bussard produced a speculative design for an interstellar "ramjet" that would scoop up fusible hydrogen from space rather than carrying its own stocks of fuel, although designing a vast but supremely lightweight scoop proved to be a challenge comparable to that of developing a controllable fusion reactor.

Other speculative starship designs employed power beamed from the vicinity of the Sun to sustain an engineless starship, usually imagining that the beam would be some sort of laser—although microwave radiation sometimes served instead, and some models employed pellets fired by an electromagnetic mass driver. Most of these systems were dramatised in fictional representations, although they were rarely placed centre stage in stories because they had relatively little dramatic potential in themselves, unless they suffered some drastic but remediable malfunction. Propulsion is, however, only one aspect of the problem of long-distance space travel.

Early representations of space travel tended to skip over the problem of life support (although Poe's Hans Pfaall was careful to ensure that his air supply would last for the duration of his trip) and the business of supplying starships with supportive "microeco-spheres" foresaw few serious problems prior to the 1960s. When attention was devoted to the problem, it usually seemed adequate to consign both food and air production aboard starships to plants grown by means of hydroponic technology (the plants being rooted in water rather than soil). Early experiments involving small-scale marine ecosystems sealed in glass jars in the late 1960s endorsed the view that something of this sort might be practicable; a version containing a single shrimp and numerous microorganisms was marketed as a curio in the 1980s, many examples enduring for considerably longer than the usual lifespan of the shrimp. Larger versions were sometimes incorporated into marine aquaria in various zoos. When experiments in human life support were carried out by space scientists in the 1970s, they suggested that the problems might not be so easily solved. The first difficulty to rear its head was the stink caused by the buildup of organic excreta,

and it became obvious that waste management would be a key problem in designing a sustainable microecosphere.

The problems of equipping spaceships with miniature ecospheres were further complicated by problems of "space medicine": maintaining the health of astronauts who would have to spend long periods in microgravity. The wasting of muscles and the weakening of bones were supplemented by a host of other awkward physiological and biochemical effects—as dramatised in such pulp science fiction stories as Ross Rocklynne's "Pressure" (1939), but largely ignored by subsequent writers. The Russian Bios-3 habitat, designed in 1972, laid the groundwork for the life support systems incorporated into the space station Mir, but the station benefited from the periodic renewal of its supplies and the regular exchange of crews who would otherwise have suffered serious medical problems as a result of their long sojourns in zero gravity.

The most ambitious experiment in microecospheric management so far carried out—without the further complication of microgravity—was undertaken by a group whose initial base was a commune at Synergia Ranch in New Mexico. Their projects culminated in the construction of the eight-person "ark" Biosphere 2, which was sealed for the first time in 1991–1993. The study illustrated the *ecological dictum that the stability of an ecosystem increases in proportion to its complexity, while always remaining vulnerable to chaotic disruption when one of its populations undergoes a dramatic increase or dwindles to extinction—a lesson difficult to apply in the confines of a spacecraft, although it is incorporated into the description of the space voyage featured in Kim Stanley Robinson's *Red Mars* (1992).

While the problems of designing vessels capable of reaching the stars at sublight speeds became more visible, arguments intensified as to whether the velocity of light really is an absolute limit, as decreed by *relativity theory. Isaac Asimov's robust declaration that faster-than-light travel is "Impossible, That's All!" in his column in *The Magazine of Fantasy and Science Fiction* (1967) prompted Arthur C. Clarke to pen a reply entitled "Possible, That's All!" (1972). The dispute was extrapolated in the theme anthology *Faster Than Light* (1976) edited by Jack Dann and George Zebrowski, with the addition of further essays by Keith Laumer, Ben Bova, and Poul Anderson as well as an illustrative selection of stories.

This discussion was complicated by the proposition that the mathematics of relativity permitted the existence of particles that could *only* travel faster than light, which were dubbed "tachyons". The early investigators of the notion included Gregory

*Benford in his role as a physicist, and "tachyonic drives" were immediately added to the lexicon of science fiction's facilitating devices. Notable examples of FTL drives supported by seemingly robust scientific argument include the one developed by Charles *Sheffield's McAndrew, whose early exploits were first collected in 1983, the Bussard ramjet that drives the "starcology" in Robert J. Sawyer's *Golden Fleece* (1990), and the antimatter drive featured in Charles R. Pellegrino's *Flying to Valhalla* (1993).

The assumption that some means of superluminal travel would ultimately be possible continued to support the Romantic science fiction tradition, which increasingly took the form of military science fiction —a subgenre whose *fin-de-siècle* writers, including David Weber, David Feintuch, and Lois McMaster Bujold, increasingly emphasised naval analogies, conducting many of their military maneuvers aboard ship as well as sending "marines" down to planetary surfaces to do their fighting. The transition was assisted by notable exemplars in the visual media, especially the various *Star Trek* TV series and the film series launched by *Star Wars* (1976), and by the increasing popularity and sophistication of computer games following the debut of *Space Invaders* in 1978.

This sophistication of space opera was supplemented by another as space travellers were increasing modified by cyborgisation and biotechnological modification, in order to equip them for the experience. Gradually but inexorably, space travel became an essentially *posthuman experience, especially in the margin where the realistic and Romantic traditions of space fiction overlapped. The dream of simple and inexpensive space travel—nostalgically preserved in such admittedly optimistic works as Reginald Bretnor's *Gilpin's Space* (1986)—faded into oblivion.

The effects of this sophistication were many and various. Spacefaring worldlets grew in size and scope, often taking up a suggestion—first made by J. D. Bernal in the 1920s—that asteroids might be hollowed out and equipped with drives so that they might depart from the solar system; notable examples are featured in R. W. Mackelworth's *Starflight 3000* (1972), George Zebrowski's *Macrolife* (1979), and Pamela Sargent's *Earthseed* (1983). Generation starships became more complex, both materially and culturally, as in Robert Reed's "Aeon's Child" (1995) and "Chrysalis" (1996), Richard Paul Russo's *Ship of Fools* (2002), Ursula K. Le Guin's "Paradises Lost" (2002), and Stephen Baxter's *Mayflower II* (2004). Vast "worldships" taking these trends to extremes are featured in Gene Wolfe's Long Sun series (1993–1996) and Robert Reed's *Marrow* (2000) and *The Well of Stars* (2005). When space vessels did not become larger, they often became much more exotic; notable

examples of such bizarrerie are featured in Eric Brown's *Engineman* (1994), Jack Williamson's *The Black Sun* (1997), and Alastair Reynolds' *Revelation Space* (2000).

The increasing awareness of the maladaptation of human anatomy and physiology for space travel also increased interest in the possibility that other species might be better fitted to the task, like the dolphins and chimpanzees in David *Brin's *Startide Rising* (1983) and *The Uplift War* (1987) or the squid in Stephen *Baxter's *Manifold* trilogy (1999–2002) and Ken Macleod's *Cosmonaut Keep* (2000).

The realistic tradition of local space fiction continued on its defiant path to the end of the twentieth century and beyond. The second man on the Moon, Buzz Aldrin, was recruited to the cause, writing two novels—*Encounter with Tiber* (1996) and *The Return* (2000)—in collaboration with John Barnes. Allen Steele produced an extensive series of space program thrillers, including *Orbital Decay* (1989), *Lunar Descent* (1991), *Labyrinth of Night* (1992), and numerous short stories. Michael F. Flynn's series comprising *Firestar* (1996), *Rogue Star* (1998), *Lodestar* (2000), and *Falling Stars* (2001) offered a minutely detailed account of a space program designed to protect Earth from asteroid strikes, but Flynn indulged a revealing nostalgia for the charismatic spaceships of old in *The Wreck of the River of Stars* (2003).

David Brin's "An Ever-Reddening Glow" (1997), in which members of an intergalactic Corps of Obligate Pragmatists beg human beings to stop polluting the universe with the noxious effluvia of their space drive, is framed as a joke—although it recalls earlier texts in which similar notions are developed as stark tragedy, such as Bob Shaw's *The Palace of Eternity* (1969)—but the wryness underlying the comedy reflects a considerable sullying of twentieth-century dreams of space travel.

SPECULATIVE NONFICTION

Speculation plays a key role in scientific thought, which overlaps that of *extrapolation but usually makes more use of imagination in proceeding far beyond matters of logical deduction. It is the process used to generate hypotheses, including specific *predictions, whose subsequent testing by observation and *experiment produces and refines scientific knowledge. Although modern practices of scientific *publication have attempted to normalise a situation in which publication does not occur until some relevant testing has been carried out, however tentatively, it remains the case that speculations are routinely published as suggestions, or even as confident claims, long before they can be put to rigorous proof.

Scientific predictions vary very widely in their scope, and it is often necessary or politic to publish predictions that are not readily amenable to testing, sometimes far in advance of their potential fulfilment. Even though scientific predictions always remain contingent and cannot function as prophecies, *futurological speculations can be useful. Speculations regarding new technologies can often function as a guide to profitable research and an inspiration to further *invention. There is also a purely inquisitive dimension to scientific speculation, which addresses significant issues in *philosophy and continually tests the boundary between the physical and the *metaphysical.

Speculation in cosmology, evolutionary biology, and the human sciences is rarely amenable to testing in the same manner as speculations in physics and chemistry, but it nevertheless plays a key role in building theories and attempting to harmonise those theories within the scientific worldview. In all these fields, fictional formats offer useful scope for the development of speculations and for thought experiments, which play a significant role in enabling scientists to visualise and grasp the implications of their theories.

The variety of narrative formats is such that the distinction between fiction and nonfiction can never be entirely clear. There are numerous examples of early endeavours in speculative science, from Plato's dialogues onwards, that combined elements of fictional and nonfictional presentation. The philosophical dialogue was still in use when the scientific revolution of the seventeenth century began, and John *Kepler's *Somnium* (written 1609; published 1634) is a strikingly chimerical work combining fictional and nonfictional modes of presentation.

The division between speculative fiction and speculative nonfiction became increasingly marked in the seventeenth and eighteenth centuries as ambiguous formats like the dialogue were abandoned by scientists and the notion of "fiction" became increasingly bound to the narrative techniques of the novel, but chimerical works were still being produced in the nineteenth century. Notable examples include Humphry *Davy's incorporation of a cosmic vision into his meditations on *Consolations in Travel* (1830), Edgar Allan *Poe's request that *Eureka* (1848) should be treated as a poem as well as an essay, Charles Renouvier's painstaking construction of an alternative *history in *Uchronie* (1857), and Camille *Flammarion's attempts to incarnate light and Halley's comet as literary characters in *Récits de l'infini* (1872). Esoteric as they were, such chimerical works had considerable utility, especially in the context of the *popularisation of science.

When a new generation of "middlebrow" magazines emerged in Britain at the end of the century, they opened up scope for the development of a new kind of scientific journalism—exemplified by the early essays of H. G. *Wells and the essays of C. H. *Hinton—as well as the development of *scientific romance. As the business of popularisation became increasingly challenging in the twentieth century, the potential utility of such journalistic essays in speculative nonfiction increased dramatically.

It is not surprising that some of the most successful popularisers of twentieth-century science—notably Isaac *Asimov and Arthur C. *Clarke—were equally successful in the fields of speculative fiction and nonfiction, routinely transferring skills between their short stories and their essays. The relatively brief items of speculative nonfiction that Wells contributed to popular periodicals were supplemented by more substantial essays by such writers as J. B. S. *Haldane and Julian Huxley, which helped to maintain a tradition of respectable scientific journalism until the last decades of the century, when it was largely displaced from periodicals into "popular science" books by such writers as Carl *Sagan and Clifford A. *Pickover.

Such popularising work is often lively in presentation and style even when it is entirely serious, but there is also a substantial body of speculative nonfiction that is anything but serious. This includes satirical works of a Swiftian inclination, such as Alan Sokal's hoax article calculated to expose the pretensions of *postmodernism, but it also has a purely comic component. The delight that scientists are capable of taking in parodies of their own endeavours is graphically illustrated by such publications as *The Worm Runner's Digest* founded in 1959 by James V. McConnell's Planaria Group, whose adventures in humorous speculative nonfiction were sampled in *The Worm Re-Turns* (1965) edited by McConnell.

The formats of speculative nonfiction were borrowed by writers whose purposes extended far beyond the educational. *Utopian descriptions of hypothetical societies often employ nonfictional formats, while writers of speculative fiction easily found scope for mock histories such as Olaf *Stapledon's *Last and First Men* (1930), mock biographies such as H. G. Wells' *The Holy Terror* (1939), mock scientific papers such as Isaac Asimov's "The Endochronic Properties of Resublimated Thiotimoline" (1948), mock academic studies such as Thomas M. Disch's "Thesis on Social Forms and Social Controls in the USA" (1964) and R. A. Lafferty's "Primary Education of the Camiroi" (1966), items of mock reportage such as Thomas M. Disch's "The Children's Fund to Save the

Dinosaurs: A Charity Appeal" (1997), and even reviews of imaginary books, as in Stanislaw Lem's *Doskonala proznia* (1971; trans. as *A Perfect Vacuum*).

It is often convenient within literary works of many kinds to introduce passages of prose framed as items of nonfiction—newspaper articles, quotations from histories or textbooks, and so on—and speculative fiction finds such devices especially convenient because of its need to supply explanations and equip entire worlds with "back stories". Isaac Asimov's use of chapter-heading quotations from the *Encyclopedia Galactica* in the Foundation series is a relatively brutal device, but one that has been widely imitated.

STAPLEDON, (WILLIAM) OLAF (1886–1950)

British philosopher and writer. He obtained an M.A. from Balliol College, Oxford, in 1909 before teaching for a year at Manchester Grammar School and then working briefly for a shipping company. In 1912, he found a more settled position as a lecturer in history and English for the Workers' Education Association, based at the University of Liverpool. He was a pacifist, but served for three years in the Friends' Ambulance Unit in France, commencing his literary activities as a war poet before resuming his teaching in Liverpool.

Stapledon continued to publish poetry after the war and also wrote *A Modern Theory of Ethics* (1929) before embarking on *Last and First Men* (1930), a future history of humankind extending over two billion years. The bare bones of the future history were appropriated from J. B. S. Haldane's "The Last Judgment" (1927), which pointed out that earlier accounts of the far future, including H. G. Wells' *The Time Machine* (1895) and S. Fowler Wright's *The Amphibians* (1925), had been based on an erroneous estimate of the Sun's lifespan made by Lord Kelvin, and that the human species had far more scope for future development than was allowed therein. Stapledon might also have been influenced by John Lionel Tayler's *The Last of My Race* (1924), in which a biologist set out a relatively modest prospectus for humankind's evolution over a similar timespan. *Last and First Men*, which details the evolutionary history of *Homo sapiens*' seventeen descendant species, was one of the key works of the 1930s revival of British scientific romance, immediately establishing Stapledon as the most important writer in that genre between the world wars. Its sequel, *Last Men in London* (1932), employs one of the eighteenth men as a hypothetical viewpoint for an exhaustive critical examination of contemporary society.

The examination carried out in *Last Men in London* formed the basis for a nonfictional account of a *Waking World* (1934), which set out to be optimistic but could not muster the conviction required to maintain its optimism. The same is true of *Odd John: A Story Between Jest and Earnest* (1935), a novel that revisits the theme of the last prewar classic of scientific romance, J. D. Beresford's *The Hampdenshire Wonder* (1911). Beresford had chronicled the brief career of a member of an advanced human species born before his time, favouring a model of the superman based on the evolutionary prospectus set out in Wells' account of "The Man of the Year Million" (1893); Stapledon preferred a model in which intellectual development involves the evolution of stereotyped *parapsychological powers. He allowed his protagonist to grow up and to discover others of his kind, but the development of the better world whose promise they represent is nevertheless nipped in the bud.

In the unprecedentedly bold *Star Maker* (1937), Stapledon set the history told in *Last and First Men* in a galactic context. A discarded first draft subsequently published as *Nebula Maker* (1976) reveals that he initially set out to track the evolutionary history of the universe in chronological order, but the form on which he finally settled was a visionary one in which the protagonist is able to place his own personal predicament and that of his world in a series of conceptual frames whose exponential expansion concludes with a climactic vision of the Creator at work. Far from justifying God's ways to man, however, Stapledon's protagonist deduces from man's imperfect nature and awkward historical situation that the Star Maker has not yet mastered his craft, and that the universe is an apprentice work far short of masterpiece standard.

Stapledon wrote five more philosophical works before returning to fiction, the most important being a didactic popularisation published as a Pelican paperback in two volumes, *Philosophy and Living* (1939). *Beyond the "Isms"* (1942) and *Darkness and the Light* (1942) are a companion pair, the former attempting to negotiate a middle way between various pairs of antithetical theses while the latter is an essay in speculative nonfiction offering two alternative future histories, one supposedly representing the worst choices his contemporaries might make in living according to their faiths and the other the best—the fact that the better of the two does not work out conspicuously well reflects the dark mood of the depths of World War II.

Sirius: A Fantasy of Love and Discord (1944) returned to an even more modest scale than *Odd John* in telling the story of the troubled but loving relationship between a dog with artificially enhanced intelligence and his creator's daughter. It was followed by the brief Utopian sketch *Old Man in New World* (1944) and another hybrid work in the overlapping margins of speculative fiction and nonfiction, *Death into Life* (1946). The latter is a visionary fantasy anticipating the future evolution of a collective spiritual entity not unlike the one imagined in Pierre Teilhard de Chardin's *Omega Point hypothesis. His other philosophical publications of this period were tentative and rather trivial, although the fragments posthumously gathered together by his widow as *The Opening of the Eyes* (1954) suggest that he might have made one last attempt at constructive synthesis had he lived long enough. His last two works of fiction, on the other hand, maintain a determined seriousness of purpose in spite of their deep pessimism.

The Flames (1947) is a relatively orthodox narrative, although its heart is a straightforward philosophical dialogue between a contemporary man and a refugee alien which requests temporary asylum for its species on Earth, although their natural habitat is the interior of a star. *A Man Divided* (1950) takes up where *Odd John* left off, but its protagonist is only superhuman during brief interludes, and his inability to sustain his better self against the corrosive influence of the merely human eventually drives him mad. A few further items of short fiction and exercises in speculative nonfiction were posthumously assembled in *Far Future Calling* (1980), edited by Sam Moskowitz.

Stapledon's influence is very obvious in subsequent scientific romance and in one significant strand of British science fiction, represented by the far-futuristic fantasies of Brian *Aldiss and Arthur C. *Clarke. It also echoes in the work of some American speculators, especially Freeman *Dyson and writers of Omega Point fantasy. The imagery of his work was a more significant consultation point for future writers than his experiments in literary method, but the extreme narrative distance of the "Stapledonian voice" of *Last and First Men* and *Star Maker* retains a certain utility in imaginatively ambitious science fiction, which occasionally makes unrepentant use of it in spite of its flagrant opposition to the intimate mimetic mode favoured by modern *narrative theory.

STAR

A term initially applied to all luminous entities visible in the night sky, subsequently restricted to the "fixed stars" forming a background across which the *planets moved. The significance of the term shifted again as it was generally realised that the *Sun was the same kind of object as the stars, and yet again as *astronomers became more sharply aware of the distinction that could be drawn between compact stellar bodies and more loosely organised nebular clouds, from which they were presumably formed. The notion that there might be similar bodies that were not luminous eventually gave rise to the notion of "dark stars".

The stars in the night sky always exerted a powerful fascination on the human mind, especially when the relationships between their apparent movement and the Earthly seasons were determined. The *pseudoscience of *astrology attempted to extrapolate the predictive capacity of calendrical calculations into other aspects of human life. Numerous cultures have woven the patterns of various constellations into their *myths, and the myths mapped by the constellations in the Greek system of naming continue to echo in modern astronomy.

Although *Aristotle's cosmology took it for granted that the heavens were unchangeable, the fact that the luminosity of certain stars varied was known in Classical times; the most obvious variable star, Beta Persei, was sometimes called the Demon Star, and its Arabic name Algol means "the ghoul". It was not until 1596, however, that David Fabricius published his observations of the variable star Mira. This discovery, coupled with the observation of a *nova by Tycho Brahe in 1572, challenged the Aristotelian notion of a sphere of fixed stars even before the invention of the *telescope brought about a sudden and very dramatic increase in the number of observable stars—a shift in perspective that struck *Galileo and other early users of the instrument very forcibly. The notion generated by the heliocentric theory of the solar system that the stars might have planetary systems of their own was easily integrated into the ongoing debate regarding the *plurality of worlds. Such discoveries altered the significance of literary references to the stars, but mostly in a subtle fashion, since they still had no literary function other than to serve as an existential backcloth and distant source of imaginative inspiration.

In 1718, Edmond Halley, having compared the positions of Sirius, Procyon, and Arcturus with the positions recorded by Greek astronomers, determined that the apparent positions of the stars were not, in fact, "fixed". Many astronomers then increased their efforts to measure the distances of stars by means of parallax: the shift in their apparent positions relative to the background when measured from different points in the Earth's orbit. Their attempts initially proved fruitless, although William Herschel's attempts to detect parallax shifts allowed him to demonstrate that binary stars—such as the two elements of Zeta Ursae Majoris distinguished by Johannes Riccioli in 1650—were pairs of stars orbiting one another rather than stars that simply happened to lie close to the same line of sight. Herschel and his son John went on to identify hundreds of such compound stars, including the Sun's near neighbour Alpha Centauri. Emanuel Swedenborg's *Arcana coelestia* (1749–1756) included voyages to other stars as well as other planets, but offers little sense of the different order of magnitude involved in such journeys.

It was not until the late 1830s that the first calculations of stellar distance were made, when Thomas Henderson measured the distance of Alpha Centauri, Friedrich von Struve the distance of Vega, and Friedrich Bessel the distance of 61 Cygni. Alpha Centauri, which proved to be 1.3 parsecs away, established a significant benchmark for interstellar distances that made the size of the universe and the scale of stellar distribution seem almost unimaginably immense. A parsec—that is, a parallax second [of arc]—is equal to approximately 31,000,000,000,000 kilometres (3.26 light years). There was, however, a further expansion of scale still to come when it was realised that the Milky Way is merely one *galaxy among many. Again, the new appreciation of the size scale of the universe made a difference to the significance of literary representations of the stars, but it was relatively slight because the distances involved are very difficult, if not impossible, for the imagination to grasp. Charles Defontenay's *Star ou Psi de Cassiopée* (1854; trans. as *Star: Psi Cassiopeia*) conveys no better sense of stellar distances than Swedenborg's visions, and although Camille *Flammarion's *Lumen* (1866–1869; exp. 1887) tries very hard, it is not obvious that it succeeds.

The development of *spectroscopy permitted a rapid sophistication of observations of stars; Pietro Secchi began the classification of stars into distinct spectral types in 1867. The measurement of stellar Doppler shifts was begun by William Huggins in 1868, adding a second dimension to observations of lateral motion and thus permitting the analysis of the actual motion of stars relative to the galactic center. Many binary stars that could not be discerned optically were identified by spectroscopic analysis of their light, and A. A. Michelson's interferometer, developed in 1881, made it possible to measure the sizes of stars by observing the interference of rays emitted at different points on its surface.

The system of classifying stars by spectral type was refined by Charles Pickering in 1900, using a system of letters ranging from A to O. The sun's category was designated G, and when the system was further refined it was consigned to the subclass G2. Measurements of the sizes of stars were able to add further

characterisations to the types, distinguishing between such groups as red giants and white dwarfs. The classification of stars became the basis of twentieth-century theories of stellar evolution, which accounted for such phenomena as novas and gave rise to such notions as neutron stars and *black holes.

This proliferation of types of stars provided a new incentive for writers actually to visit them. Tentative steps in that direction were made in Robert William Cole's *The Struggle for Empire* (1900) and Jean Delaire's *Around a Distant Star* (1904), and numerous stars were included in the extravagant cosmic tour described in the Rev. William S. Harris' *Life in a Thousand Worlds* (1905), but it was not until the development of pulp science fiction that interstellar tourism became commonplace. As soon as that genre gave birth to space opera, elaborate star systems like the dark star and the bizarre multiple that serve as the principal settings of E. E. Smith's *The Skylark of Space* (1928; book, 1946) immediately became popular. Giant stars, dwarf stars, and stars of every imaginable colour filled the pages of pulp science fiction, often in complex combinations like the one featured in Isaac Asimov's "Nightfall" (1941), written to John W. Campbell's instruction to contradict Ralph Waldo Emerson's assertion that "if the stars should appear one night in a thousand years, how would man believe and adore and preserve for many generations the remembrance of the city of God!"

The roles played by stars in twentieth-century speculative fiction were limited by the fact that there was relatively little scope for their variation beyond size and colour—the one shaped like a doughnut in Donald Malcolm's "Beyond the Reach of Storms" (1964) is a rare and relatively late exception. Nor was there much that stars could *do* in a story, except fade away, send out the occasional flare, and eventually go nova. They could, however, be credited with various kinds of life, or with a godlike intelligence of their own, as in such works as Ross Rocklynne's Darkness series (1940–1942; book as *The Sun Destroyers,* 1973), Olaf Stapledon's *Star Maker* (1937); Gérard Klein's *Le gambit des étoiles* (1958; trans. as *Starmaster's Gambit*), Frederik Pohl and Jack Williamson's *Starchild* (1965) and *Rogue Star* (1969), Frank Herbert's *Whipping Star* (1970), and Gordon Eklund and Gregory Benford's "If the Stars Are Gods" (1973; exp. book, 1977).

Alpha Centauri always occupied a special place in science fiction in consequence of its proximity, although the discovery of Proxima Centauri—which may be the third element of the same system—resulted in a partial displacement and it had to share its utility as a prime target with Barnard's Star, which is much more similar to the Sun. Leslie F. Stone's

"Across the Void" (1931), Murray Leinster's "Proxima Centauri" (1935), and R. Frederick Hester's "The Gypsies of Thos" (1935) are among the earliest depictions of interstellar pioneering, while William R. Barton and Michael Capobianco's *Alpha Centauri* (1997) offers one of the most sophisticated accounts of that system and a journey thereto.

Notable examples of exotic stars featured in science fiction of the second half of the twentieth century include the "dead stars" in Poul Anderson's *The Enemy Stars* (1959) and *World Without Stars* (1967) and Connie Willis' "The Sidon in the Mirror" (1983), and the neutron stars in Larry Niven's "Neutron Star" (1966) and Robert L. Forward's *Dragon's Egg* (1980). The stars of a dense globular cluster fill the night sky of the hypothetical planet of Poul Anderson's "Starfog" (1967). The Sun is gifted with two "black dwarf" companions—one of which is made of antimatter—in Joe W. Haldeman's "Tricentennial" (1976).

The power of fascination that the stars continue to exert, in spite of their demystification, is celebrated in such stories as Robert F. Young's "The Stars Are Calling, Mr. Keats" (1959) and Louise Lawrence's *The Power of Stars* (1972)—and, by virtue of their abrupt disappearance, in Robert Charles Wilson's *Spin* (2005). The "cold light of the stars", held to be symbolic of a "hypercosmical reality, with its crystal ecstasy", is the macrocosmic component of the paired sources of inspiration offered for human guidance at the end of Olaf Stapledon's *Star Maker* (1937).

STEAMPUNK

A term coined in the late 1980s, by analogy with cyberpunk, to describe science fiction stories that import a calculatedly irreverent sensibility into accounts of *alternative historical patterns of scientific discovery, usually involving fanciful technological *inventions. Such stories usually display a keen awareness of the triumphs and limitations of the various traditions of popular speculative fiction ancestral to science fiction, especially Vernian tales of *voyages extraordinaires*, Wellsian scientific romance, and early twentieth-century pulp fantasy. Such stories often employ obsolete narrative styles in order to create the impression that they might belong to genres of "alternative science fiction" written in worlds where the history of science and technology followed different paths, or in which writers responded with greater alacrity and acuity to such sources of inspiration.

Key exemplars of the kind of work that inspired the coinage of the term include two stories by Howard Waldrop and Stephen Utley: "Custer's Last Jump"

(1976), in which the battle of the Little Big Horn is transformed by the availability of aircraft, and "Black as the Pit, from Pole to Pole" (1977), a sequel to Mary Shelley's *Frankenstein* (1818) in which the monster wanders into the interior of the kind of hollow *Earth advertised by John Cleve Symmes. Waldrop went on to write many other works in the same vein, including "The World as We Know't" (1982), "The Night of the Cooters" (1987)—an account of the American South's response to a Wellsian Martian invasion—and "Fin de Cycle" (1990).

The sensibility exhibited by the Waldrop-Utley stories was partially anticipated in some of Avram Davidson's short fiction, notably "I Do Not Hear You Sir" (1958) and "What Strange Stars and Skies" (1963). It was also foreshadowed by Brian W. Aldiss' "The Saliva Tree" (1965), and by such early 1970s novels as Michael Moorcock's *The Warlord of the Air* (1971), Edmund Cooper's *The Overman Culture* (1971), Harry Harrison's *Tunnel Through the Deeps* (1972), and Richard Lupoff's *Into the Aether* (1974). A significant influence was also exerted by such metafictional exercises as Manly Wade and Wade Wellman's *Sherlock Holmes's War of the Worlds* (1975), Poul Anderson's Shakespearean fantasy *A Midsummer Tempest* (1974), and Arthur Byron Cover's *Autumn Angels* (1975). All these works, however, exhibited a tentativeness typical of pioneering endeavours; once the fundamental notion and narrative ambience of such works became familiar, the way was open for the development of a more exotic flamboyance.

Waldrop's *contes philosophiques* were supplemented by K. W. Jeter's *Morlock Night* (1979) and Patrick Moore's *How Britain Won the Space Race* (1982; with Desmond Leslie) before the first novellas and novels consciously written with the term in mind began to appear. These included James Blaylock's "Lord Kelvin's Machine" (1985; exp. book, 1992) and *Homunculus* (1986), K. W. Jeter's *Infernal Devices* (1987), William Gibson and Bruce Sterling's *The Difference Engine* (1990), Rudy Rucker's *The Hollow Earth* (1990), Stephen Baxter's *Anti-Ice* (1993), Paul Di Filippo's *The Steampunk Trilogy* (1995), John Barnes' Timeline Wars trilogy, comprising *Patton's Spaceship* (1997), *Washington's Dirigible* (1997), and *Caesar's Bicycle* (1997), Paul J. McAuley's series begun with "Naming the Dead" (1999), and Eric Brown's "The Blue Portal" (2002).

All of the above-cited examples qualify comfortably as science fiction, although the input of metafictions extended the blurred boundaries of the subgenre into rationalistically inclined fantasies and horror stories such as Esther Friesner's *Druid's Blood* (1988) and Kim Newman's *Anno Dracula* (1992). Such metafictional intrusions, especially when they involve significant speculative writers like Edgar Allan Poe, Verne, and Wells—as they often do—sometimes forge very intricate links between the anachronistic science and technologies featured in the stories and the literary representations of their primary world equivalents, giving the steampunk subgenre a special relevance to the topic of this book.

As futuristic narrative spaces were rendered less useful to speculative writers in the early twenty-first century by the decline of the myth of the *Space Age and the inevitability of the impending *ecocatastrophe, alternative pasts became much more attractive, and it seemed likely that the steampunk genre would continue its already spectacular proliferation.

STERLING, (MICHAEL) BRUCE (1954–)

U.S. writer. His father, a mechanical engineer, worked in the Far East from 1969 to 1972 and Sterling spent a good deal of time there before completing his formal education at the University of Texas, Austin, graduating in 1976 with a B.A. in journalism. He published his first science fiction story in the same year. His first novel, *Involution Ocean* (1978, but dated 1977), is a *Decadent fantasy set on a world whose only habitable region lies at the bottom of a crater containing an "ocean" of extremely fine dust, whose whalelike native life-forms are hunted for the psychotropic drug syncophine.

Although Sterling's subsequent works had near-future settings developed with an increasingly intense realism, they never wholly abandoned the colourful and ironic flamboyance of the Decadent sensibility. *The Artificial Kid* (1980), set on a world named Reverie, features a young "combat artist" whose adventures in a Decriminalized Zone are assiduously tracked by robot cameras for broadcasting as entertainment. Its hero and its climactic journey—which takes the characters into the symbolic heart of an alien Mass—is reminiscent of the work of Samuel R. *Delany, as were several items in Sterling's core contribution to the science fiction of the early 1980s, the Shaper-Mechanist series.

The earliest elements of the series, "Spider Rose" (1982), "Swarm" (1982), and "Cicada Queen" (1983)—initially collected in *Crystal Express* (1989)—appeared alongside William *Gibson's early cyberpunk stories, and the two sequences were subsequently identified as the core threads of that movement. Sterling read Gibson's *Neuromancer* (1985) in manuscript while he was guiding his own series towards the climax it eventually attained in *Schismatrix* (1985; reprinted with the short stories as *Schismatrix Plus*, 1996), which

incorporated some Gibsonian motifs into a dramatic vision of the early phases of a *posthuman diaspora. The adaptive radiation of the species is still simple enough to permit a rough division into Shapers (groups who have remade themselves primarily by genetic engineering) and Mechanists (groups who have remade themselves by extensive cyborgisation), but these main categories are elaborately subdivided into many splinter societies organised according to a wide range of political and religious creeds. The ultimate mechanists are immobile and immortal "wireheads" equipped with all manner of mechanical senses, while the most exotic reshaped individuals are stranger than the actual alien species whose presence within and without the solar system complicates the human expansion into space.

In 1984–1986, Sterling produced a fanzine, *Cheap Truth*, where he pontificated extensively—employing the polemical persona of "Vincent Omniaveritas"—about the nature and significance of the movement of which he and Gibson were a part, along with Lewis Shiner, John Shirley, and Rudy Rucker. The climax of this endeavour was *Mirrorshades: The Cyberpunk Anthology* (1986), which also featured Pat Cadigan, Tom Maddox, Greg Bear, James Patrick Kelly, Marc Laidlaw, and Paul Di Filippo. Sterling's introduction to the anthology paid homage to cyberpunk's precursors within the science fiction field and drew analogies to parallel cultural movements before providing a definitive explanation of the movement's nature and ambitions, proposing that "technical culture has gotten out of hand" and that "the traditional power structures, the traditional institutions, have lost control of the pace of change", as a result of which "a new alliance is becoming evident: an integration of technology and the Eighties counterculture".

Sterling attempted to practice what he preached in *Islands in the Net* (1988), which explored the political implications of the global integration of the world's computers into a vast network; he was enabled by his experience of the Far East—earlier displayed in the novella "Green Days in Brunei" (1985)—to take a more global view of development than most of his contemporaries in the United States.

In view of the publicity given to cyberpunk and the fact that its writers often worked in collaboration— Sterling had written "Red Star, Winter Orbit" (1983) with Gibson, "Storming the Cosmos" (1985) with Rudy Rucker, "Mozart in Mirrorshades" (1985) with Lewis Shiner, and "The Unfolding" (1985) with John Shirley—it is not surprising that Sterling and Gibson should be commissioned to write a novel together, although some commentators were surprised that what they elected to write was the *steampunk novel *The Difference Engine* (1990). Sterling had already written several stories in which people in times past obtain supernatural insights into the incredible transformations awaiting them, including "Telliamed" (1984), "Dinner in Audoghast" (1985), and "Flowers of Edo" (1987), but *The Difference Engine* (1990) takes a different tack. It investigates what might have happened if the revolution in information technology had taken place 150 years earlier than it actually did, when Charles Babbage and Ada Lovelace first attempted to build a programmable mechanical computer. Sterling followed it with a journalistic account of *The Hacker Crackdown: Law and Disorder on the Electronic Frontier* (1992), an analysis of the overreaction of law enforcement agencies to the rumour that clever PC users were engaged in conspiracies to invade and subvert the systems of large corporations and government agencies.

Heavy Weather (1994) is a near-future thriller extrapolating the exploits of the real-world meteorologists who chase "twisters" along the American Midwest's "tornado alley". *Holy Fire* (1996) is similarly limited in is temporal scope, and makes elaborate use of experience that Sterling had accumulated while carrying out journalistic assignments for *Wired* in various European locales, but its theme is more extravagant. It looks forward to a transition from the human to the posthuman condition, but not in the hectic manner of *Schismatrix*; it cleaves very closely to the viewpoint of its human protagonist as a host of new possibilities gradually opens up before her, while she is forced to leave behind the past in which she felt at home.

Distraction (1998) is a lively political satire set in a fragmented near-future United States of America afflicted by climatic change, elaborating a sarcastic tone and skewed morality that had come increasingly to the fore in Sterling's short fiction. *Zeitgeist* (2000) is a similar development whose satirical and picaresque elements are even more pronounced; its protagonist is Leggy Starlitz, an opportunist entrepreneur specialising in exotic traffic, who had been previously featured in "Hollywood Kremlin" (1990) and "Are You for 86?" (original to the 1992 collection *Globalhead*). Many of the shorter stories sharing the irreverent spirit of these novels were collected in *A Good Old-Fashioned Future* (1999), while the serious aspect of Sterling's endeavour was more assiduously channelled into nonfiction. He edited a special issue of the environmentalist periodical *Whole Earth* (June 2001) and produced the painstaking *futurological analysis *Tomorrow Now: Envisioning the Next Fifty Years* (2002). A darker note was, however, evident in his next novel, *The Zenith Angel* (2004), a technothriller responding to the terrorist demolition of the World Trade Center.

Although Gibson's tight focus on the transactions of computers and their users made his work more directly relevant to the interests of early participants in the emergent cyberculture, Sterling's complexity of vision and imaginative reach made him the more significant cultural commentator. When he declared the term cyberpunk "obsolete before it had been coined", he was not merely being flippant; from his viewpoint the movement always had much broader concerns. He was the first writer to envisage the consequences of simultaneous revolutions in biotechnology and information technology in terms of posthuman adaptive radiation, and to subject that notion to increasingly close and passionate analysis. Although the future history sketched out in *Schismatrix* contains nothing as tidy, mathematically speaking, as a *singularity, it casually takes for granted the fact that the old world can and will be swept away in the space of a single near-future lifetime, to be replaced by one that is infinitely stranger.

SUBMARINE

A vessel designed for navigation beneath the surface of a body of water. The first significant design for a submarine boat powered by oars and supplied with air by snorkels was produced by the Englishman William Bourne in 1578. Three devices of a similar kind were built for the Navy and tested in the Thames by the prolific Dutch inventor Cornelius Drebbel in 1620–1624. Further designs were published by Marin Mersenne in 1634, John Wilkins in *Mathematicall Magick* (1648), and Giovanni Borelli in 1680 before the next attempt at construction was made by Denis Papin in 1696. Nathaniel Symons' machine of 1729 was a diving bell rather than a submarine, but David Bushnell constructed a vessel in 1776, nicknamed the Turtle, that was used in the American Revolution to mount an unsuccessful attack on a British vessel.

In 1797, Robert Fulton—an American living in Paris—volunteered to build a vessel like Bushnell's for the French to use against the English, and constructed a vessel he called the *Nautilus* in 1800. Although it was tested successfully, its attacks on British vessels failed; the "torpedo" that Fulton invented for use in that cause was actually a mine, which the vessel merely towed into position, but the name was borrowed by Robert Whitehead for a self-propelled mine that he called an "automobile torpedo", and it became associated thereafter with the submarine's principal assault weapon. In 1815, an Englishman named Thomas Johnstone was rumoured to have been commissioned to construct a submarine for the purpose of rescuing the ex-Emperor Napoleon from his first exile on Elba; although the story is almost certainly apocryphal, it may have been the inspiration of the first significant literary work featuring a submarine—Théophile Gautier's *Les deux étoiles* (1848; trans. as *The Quartette*)—which features a conspiracy designed to that end.

Numerous submarines were constructed in the 1850s, the most successful being Wilhelm Bauer's *Diable Marin* [*Sea Devil*], constructed in Russia, and the American Civil War prompted the building of several such vessels, one of which—the Confederate *H. L. Huntley*— actually managed to sink a Union vessel, although it was lost with all its crew in the process. Jules Verne saw a French vessel built in 1863 by Charles Burn and Simon Bourgeois, *Le Plongeur*, at a technological exhibition in Paris and consulted with the French pioneers of diving suit design Benoit Rouquayrol and Auguste Denayrousse before penning the first great submarine romance in *Vingt mille lieues sous les mers* (1870; trans. as *Twenty Thousand Leagues Under the Sea*).

Verne's novel more or less ran the gamut of the marvels lurking in the undersea world; the discovery of the ruins of Atlantis, the attack of the giant *poulpe* (it is unclear whether the word signifies an octopus or a squid), and the danger of getting one's feet trapped by a giant clam became the staples of the subgenre of submarine romance. There was so little to add that Albert Robida borrowed the entire apparatus—including Captain Nemo and his diving suits—for redeployment in *Voyages très extraordinaires de Saturnin Farandoul dans les 5 ou 6 parties du monde et dans tous les pays connus et même inconnus de M. Jules Verne* (1879), while Pierre d'Ivoi, Captain Danrit, and many other contributors to the Vernian *Journal des Voyages* replayed the same melodramatic encounters endlessly. Further elaboration of the motifs—such as the still-thriving civilisation featured in André Laurie's *Atlantis* (1895; trans. as *The Crystal City Under the Sea*)—tended to shift the stories into the realms of pure fantasy.

Verne's advertisement was spectacularly successful; from then on the submarine was a common motif in futuristic fiction. It was imported into American dime novel fiction before attaining greater respectability in Frank Stockton's slightly more sophisticated *The Great Stone of Sardis* (1898), and into English Vernian fiction in such imitative dramas as Harry Collingwood's *The Log of the Flying Fish* (1887), but the restrictions imposed by diving suits and submarine observation decks meant that submarine adventure fiction could never match the flexibility, versatility, and intimacy of adventure set on land. Submarines played a significant but minor role in such extravagant

visions of future *war as George Griffith's *The Angel of the Revolution* (1893).

The race to construct viable vessels for use in warfare had begun in earnest before the boom in future war fiction; John Philip Holland, who began his experiments in the 1870s, eventually produced a model (the *Holland VI*) that was produced in quantity and sold to the U.S. and British navies in 1898–1900. By the time the first German U-boat [*unterzeeboat*] was launched in 1906, the British and French navies each had more than fifty submarines—but the Germans reaped the benefits of late entry in 1912, when the U-31 pioneered an advanced design; although they were outnumbered, it was the German submarines that made the biggest impact when World War I began. The threat they posed was more accurately estimated in fiction than in reality; when Arthur Conan Doyle's alarmist "Danger!!!" (1914) advertised the hazards to merchant shipping posed by the U-boats, the Admiralty issued hasty reassurances that the enemy would not stoop so low as to attack non-military targets; the assurances were proved wrong within weeks, as a new reign of submarine terror began.

The significance of submarines in warfare was reproduced in numerous naturalistic dramas, but their operations were subject to very little variation; the elements of the drama—diving to escape depth charges, periscopic targeting, launching the torpedo, and the fatal leak—quickly became familiar. In speculative fiction the utility of submarines as a means of transport was fatally limited by the fact that they had nowhere interesting to go—except various versions of Atlantis, which became increasingly implausible as the subgenre progressed through Arthur Conan Doyle's *The Maracot Deep* (1929) and Stanton A. Coblentz's *The Sunken World* (1928; book, 1949) to Dennis Wheatley's *They Found Atlantis* (1936).

The submarine still had significant roles to play in such *technothrillers as Frank Herbert's *The Dragon in the Sea* (1956), *Voyage to the Bottom of the Sea* (film, 1961; TV series, 1964–1966), Alan Gardner's *The Escalator* (1963), Rodney Quest's *Countdown to Doomsday* (1966), Martin Caidin's *The Last Fathom* (1967), Richard Cowper's black comedy *Profundis* (1979), and Tom Clancy's *The Hunt for Red October* (1984), but the claustrophobia that made such a powerful contribution to the dramatic tension in submarine fiction was reflected in the straitjacket confining their plots.

Science fiction stories occasionally draw analogies between submarines and spaceships—in Harry Harrison's *The Daleth Effect* (1970; aka *In our Hands, the Stars*) a submarine is actually adapted as a spaceship, while James White's *The Watch Below*

(1966) juxtaposes the problems of an alien spaceship with those of survivors in the hold of a submerged ship—but space offers far more potentially interesting destinations than the seabed. Isaac Asimov's "Waterclap" (1970), which deals with a conflict of interest between rival projects colonising the seabed and the Moon, dutifully points out that the two projects can only be seen as parallel if one ignores everything that lies beyond the Moon. The notion that a first contact with aliens might be made on the seabed, as in the film *The Abyss* (1989), is another idea whose potential extrapolative mileage is limited.

SUN, THE

The radiant object that lights the day sky and warms the Earth, rising in the east and setting in the west. The realisation that the movements of the planets* across the sky can be more elegantly explained by hypothesising that they and the Earth orbit the Sun—whose apparent movement about the Earth is due to the planet spinning on its axis—was the foundation stone of the scientific revolution precipitated by Nicolaus *Copernicus, *Galileo, and John *Kepler. Rather than merely substituting the Sun for the Earth as the hub of the universe, the revolution eventually established that the Sun is merely one star among a vast host, of no particular significance in universal terms. The further progress of this crucial shift in perspective revealed that the Sun is the energy source fuelling the Earth's biosphere and facilitating its local defiance of the principle of *entropy.

The prediction of solar eclipses was one of the key triumphs of astronomical observation, so inherently spectacular that the ability to predict an eclipse by virtue of possessing an almanac became a key method by which European explorers could impress superstitious native populations in adventure stories. The trick was employed in the first edition of H. Rider Haggard's *King Solomon's Mines* (1885), but later editions had to be revised because of the author's mistaken assumption that solar eclipses last for several hours (a lunar eclipse was substituted). The time traveller in Mark Twain's *A Connecticut Yankee in King Arthur's Court* (1889) used the trick to put Merlin's wizardry in the shade. Eclipses remained symbolically useful, but once the prediction trick had grown stale, they were of very limited use in speculative fiction; William Lemkin's "The Eclipse Special" (1930) has to go to implausible lengths to make their investigation interesting.

The principle of plenitude enshrined in the theological argument for the *plurality of worlds suggested that the Sun, like every other heavenly body,

ought to be inhabited, and this notion proved remarkably durable, though not quite as durable as the notion that the other planets ought to be inhabited. William Herschel considered it habitable as late as 1795, but it was rarely used thereafter as a setting in literary tours of the cosmos; notable exceptions include a brief supplementary visit in George Fowler's *A Flight to the Moon; or, The Vision of Randalthus* (1813) and an episode in the anonymous *Journeys into the Moon, Several Planets and the Sun* (1837) as well as more extended visits in Joel R. Peabody's *A World of Wonders* (1838) and Sydney Whiting's *Heliondé; or, Adventures in the Sun* (1855).

The nature of the Sun and the process by which it produced its radiation remained mysterious until the twentieth century. Galileo observed sunspots on its surface, whose particular mystery was compounded when an eleven-year cycle in their activity was identified by Heinrich Schwabe in 1844—a phenomenon hypothetically connected to Earthly events in various ways by numerous subsequent speculators, giving rise to such literary works as Clifford D. Simak's "Sunspot Purge" (1940) and Philip Latham's "N Day" (1946) and "Disturbing Sun" (1959). Richard Carrington observed a solar flare in 1859, and such phenomena were subsequently correlated with geomagnetic storms on Earth. Spectroscopic analysis revealed the existence of a previously unknown element—helium—in the Sun in 1868.

The temperature of the Sun's photosphere was measured by William E. Wilson and P. L. Gray in 1894 as 6,200°C, but a few unorthodox theorists persisted in hypothesising that it was a relatively cool body; John Mastin felt free to imagine a voyage *Through the Sun in an Airship* (1909), which presumably helped to inspire Donald Horner's *By Aeroplane to the Sun* (1910), similarly aimed at a juvenile audience. Similar imagery crops up occasionally in pulp science fiction; Henry J. Kostkos' "We of the Sun" (1936) and Nat Schachner's "The Sun-World of Soldus" (1935) feature habitable worlds within the Sun's photosphere. Hyman Kaner's *The Sun Queen* (1946) is set on a sunspot, visualised as a solid "island" floating on a photospheric ocean.

Attempts to account for the source of the Sun's heat inevitably began with the hypothesis that it was the product of combustion, but that notion became rationally implausible when spectroscopic analysis revealed that it was composed almost entirely of hydrogen. In 1862, Lord Kelvin proposed that the heat was produced by the energy of gravitational collapse, and on that basis concluded, rather vaguely, that the Sun could not endure "for many millions years longer". This thesis and its pessimistic estimate were accepted and illustrated by Camille Flammarion's

La fin du monde (1893; trans. as *Omega*), H. G. Wells' *The Time Machine* (1895), George C. Wallis' "The Last Days of Earth" (1901), and William Hope Hodgson's *The House on the Borderland* (1908) and *The Night Land* (1912). The visionary in *The House on the Borderland* sees the Sun's heat briefly reinvigorated as the planets fall into it one by one.

The latter notion was recapitulated in Clark Ashton Smith's "Phoenix" (written ca. 1935; published 1954), although Kelvin's theory had been rendered obsolete by then, Arthur Eddington having proposed in 1926 that the radiation was actually produced by a nuclear reaction in its core. Even so, Gene Wolfe's "Book of the New Sun" series (1980–1983) featured a more sophisticated revivification project. The implication of Eddington's hypothesis that the Sun's heat certainly would endure for many millions of years was swiftly reflected in such visionary fantasies as J. B. S. Haldane's "The Last Judgment" (1927) and Olaf Stapledon's *Last and First Men* (1930).

The dependence of Earthly life on the generosity of the Sun gave it a key role in apocalyptic disaster stories, although the magnitude of the disaster made it more useful in stories focusing on the psychological and social effects of the event's anticipation, such as Hugh Kingsmill's "The End of the World" (1924). A more limited disaster scenario in which the Sun becomes a "flaming variable" is featured in Arthur G. Stangland's "50th Century Revolt" (1932). The notion that humankind might survive the explosion of the Sun permitted a useful climactic flourish in Arthur C. Clarke's "Rescue Party" (1946), in which aliens arrive to save humankind from extinction by nova but find that their aid is unnecessary. The Sun's imminent demise also forces desperate measures in J. T. McIntosh's *One in Three Hundred* (1954). The hero of George O. Smith's *Troubled Star* (1953) discovers that aliens intend to make the Sun into a variable star, to serve as an interstellar lighthouse.

In Norman Spinrad's *The Solarians* (1966), the Sun is deliberately exploded to destroy an alien spacefleet, while the human race makes a spectacular escape. In Edward Wellen's "Hijack" (1970), disinformation regarding the Sun's imminent explosion tricks the mafia into hijacking a spacefleet and blasting off for the stars. Solar flares were employed as agents of disaster in such scientifically sophisticated melodramas as Larry Niven's "Inconstant Moon" (1971), Roger McBride Allen's "A Hole in the Sun" (1987), and Stephen Baxter and Arthur C. Clarke's *Time's Eye* (2004) and *Sunstorm* (2005), while Doug Beason's "Ben Franklin's Laser" (1990) found new melodramatic resources in the nova threat story. A different kind of postcatastrophic survival is featured in Connie Willis' "Daisy, in the Sun" (1979).

In twentieth-century stories of space travel the Sun became a useful source of danger in numerous accounts of uncomfortably close encounters; notable examples include Willy Ley's "At the Perihelion" (1937; by-lined Robert Willey), Charles L. Harness' *Flight into Yesterday* (1947; aka *The Paradox Men*), Hal Clement's "Sun Spot" (1960), Poul Anderson's "What'll You Give?" (1963; as by Winston P. Sanders), George Collyn's "In Passage of the Sun" (1966), David Brin's *Sundiver* (1980), Lucius Shepard's symbolically inclined "The Sun Spider" (1987), Jerry Oltion and Lee Goodloe's "Sunstat" (1988), and Geoffrey A. Landis' "Sundancer Falling" (1989). Brin's *Sundiver* includes an extensive and scrupulous summary of modern scientific knowledge, including detailed studies carried out by Skylab crews in 1973–1974, but not the results of the Solar Maximum Mission (1980–1989), whose endeavours were further extrapolated in the description of the solar probe featured in Stephen Baxter's *Ring* (1994).

The Sun becomes subject to technological control in such stories as Theodore L. Thomas's "The Weather Man" (1962), in which weather technicians skim across its surface in "sessile boats", and Philip E. High's *The Prodigal Sun* (1964). The idea that the "solar wind" of charged particles discovered by Ludwig Biermann in 1951 might be used as a means of spaceship propulsion gave rise to the notion of interplanetary sailing ships, as featured in such stories as Arthur C. Clarke's "Sunjammer" (1965; aka "The Wind from the Sun"). The notion that the Sun might still serve as an abode of exotic life was preserved in such stories as Olaf Stapledon's *The Flames* (1947), Arthur C. Clarke's "Out of the Sun" (1954), and Edmond Hamilton's "Sunfire!" (1962). The notion that the Sun's ultimate death might be mournfully observed by human-descended members of a galactic culture is extrapolated in such stories as Edmond Hamilton's "Requiem" (1962) and Terry Carr's "Virra" (1978).

SUPERMAN

A term that first achieved prominence as a translation of Friedrich Nietzsche's *übermensch*, extravagantly celebrated in the calculatedly poetic and fabular *Also Sprach Zarathustra* (1883–1892; trans. as *Thus Spake Zarathustra*). The term was more commonly translated "overman" to begin with, and that term was preferred in the parlance of British Nietzscheans in the 1890s—including that of the speculative writers John Davidson and M. P. Shiel—and in such American literary renderings as Upton Sinclair's "The Overman" (1906), but the replacement term became increasingly common thereafter and eventually displaced its rival. It was popularised by George Bernard Shaw's play *Man and Superman* (1903), in which Nietzschean ideas are touched upon in an intermediate section (usually performed separately as "Don Juan in Hell"), although the framing drama uses the term ironically.

Nietzsche conceived his *übermensch* as a clear-sighted philosopher whose "will to power" was exercised in artistic and intellectual creativity, but those unfamiliar with his works tended to assume that it implied a desire to exercise political and military power; this drastic misconception became closely associated with the political development of fascism. John Davidson's *A Full and Free Account of the Wonderful Mission of Earl Lavender, Which Leaked Out One Night and One Day; with a History of the Pursuit of Lord Lavender and Lord Brumm by Mrs. Scamler and Maud Emblem* (1895), Michael Georg Conrad's *In Purpurner Finsteriss* (1895), Karl Bleibtreu's *Die Vielzuvielen* (1909), and M. P. Shiel's *The Isle of Lies* (1911) are distinctively Nietzschean fantasies of superhumanity—as is H. G. Wells' *The Food of the Gods* (1904), although Wells otherwise showed little sympathy for Nietzschean ideas, which he misrepresented in *When the Sleeper Wakes* (1899). By the time Shiel revisited the theme of the overman in *The Young Men Are Coming!* (1937), however, Nietzsche's image had been blighted by the usurpation and deliberate misrepresentation of his ideas by the Nazis.

Nietzsche's ideas had closer affinities with the notion of "creative evolution" promoted by Henri Bergson—whose one-time pupil Alfred Jarry produced the comic-erotic fantasia *Le surmâle* (1902; trans. as *The Supermale*)—than with the Darwinian theory of natural selection, but writers conflating the Nietzschean *übermensch* with the idea that *Homo sapiens* was fated to be replaced some day by a "more advanced" species were more inclined to construe the notion of the superman in the light of Herbert Spencer's notion of "the survival of the fittest". Because humankind's own progress to ecospheric dominance had obviously been associated with mental development rather than physical development, most evolutionist speculators imagined that *Homo superior* would be even further advanced in mental prowess.

Most speculators also assumed that *Homo superior*'s attitude to *Homo sapiens* would mirror the naked contempt that permeated contemporary attitudes to animals and "savages"—and the similar contempt with which intellectuals, especially artists, habitually regarded the "lower orders" of society. George Bernard Shaw's *Back to Methuselah* (1921), whose extrapolations were defiantly based in neo-Lamarckian rather than Darwinian theory, did not dissent from the general opinion that our evolutionary successors would be exceedingly contemptuous of *Homo sapiens*.

Because the mental advances of *Homo sapiens* seemed to have been correlated with a loss of physical prowess, by comparison with such near relatives as the gorilla, many speculators assumed that further mental advancement would be correlated with further physical decay. H. G. Wells imagined "The Man of the Year Million" (1893) as a huge-brained weakling, an image echoed in numerous further representations—most notably J. D. Beresford's *The Hampdenshire Wonder* (1911)—and taken to rather absurd extremes in the imagery of the science fiction pulps, in such stories as Donald Wandrei's "The Red Brain" (1927) and Harry Bates' "Alas, All Thinking!" (1935). The antithetical image, in which superhumanity was a purely physical matter, remained rare in the early years of the twentieth century, although it too was adopted by the science fiction pulps once Philip Wylie's *Gladiator* (1930) had produced a significant exemplar.

John Russell Fearn gradually transformed the superhuman character introduced in "The Golden Amazon" (1939; by-lined Thornton Ayre) into a costumed "superhero", reflecting a process that was taking place simultaneously in the *comic book medium. Gardner F. Fox, who became a significant writer in the comic book medium, trained for the work in such pulp stories as "Man Nth" (1945) and "The Man the Sun Gods Made" (1946). The co-option of Superman ("the Man of Steel") as the name of the archetypal comic book superhero made the term vulnerable to a great deal of condescending humour, but did help to erase its lingering pejorative undertones. It is perhaps remarkable that the two contrasting images of superhumanity were so rarely combined, but the development of the image of the mental superman tended to set aside the requirement for conventional physical superhumanity by assuming that *Homo superior* would develop *parapsychological means of exercising power over other creatures and inanimate objects, thus obviating the need for the well-developed muscles that looked so good in comic book illustrations.

The idea that *Homo superior* would be so eager to see the back of *Homo sapiens* that hastening our extinction would be a matter of urgent policy resulted in supermen being used as figures of melodramatic menace in many early twentieth-century literary accounts, including Austin Hall's "Into the Infinite" (1919), Helen Pittard's *Le nouvel Adam* (1924, as Noëlle Roger; trans. by-lined *The New Adam*), Sophie Wenzel Ellis' "Creatures of the Light" (1930), A. H. Johnson's "The Superman" (1931), John Taine's *Seeds of Life* (1931; book, 1951), John Russell Fearn's *The Intelligence Gigantic* (1933; book, 1943), Horace

L. Gold's "The Avatar" (1935; by-lined Clyde Crane Campbell), and Stanley G. Weinbaum's "The Adaptive Ultimate" (1936). Such stories assumed that *Homo superior* would have no compunction about the extermination of his parent species, having put away such childish things as emotion and morality. This assumption was, however, challenged by the images of superhumanity offered in Olaf Stapledon's *Odd John* (1934), Claude Houghton's *This Was Ivor Trent* (1935), and Stanley Weinbaum's *The New Adam* (1939), which took the view that a superior species—especially one endowed with parapsychological talents capable of liberating its members from the toils of existential *angst*—ought to be able and willing to cultivate a superior morality.

The increasing popularity of the latter kind of story opened up an ideological battleground, whose problems were highlighted in such wryly ambivalent scientific romances as Guy Dent's *Emperor of the If* (1926), Howell Davies' *Minimum Man* (1938; by-lined Andrew Marvell), J. D. Beresford's *What Dreams May Come ...* (1941) and Olaf Stapledon's *A Man Divided* (1950), while writers in the American science fiction pulps became increasingly zealous in the defence of their parapsychologically talented supermen throughout the 1940s, spearheaded by A. E. van Vogt in such works as *Slan* (1940; book, 1948), the series comprising *The Weapon Shops of Isher* (1941–1949; book, 1951) and *The Weapon Makers* (1943; book, 1946), "Recruiting Station" (1942; aka *Masters of Time* and *Earth's Last Fortress*), "The Changeling" (1944), and—most extravagantly of all—in *The World of Null-A* (1945; book, 1948) and its sequel.

The parapsychological superman became one of the standard clichés of pulp science fiction in this era, carried forward in an entire subgenre of van Vogtian fantasies, whose most notable early manifestations included Robert A. Heinlein's "Lost Legacy" (1941) and "Gulf" (1949), C. L. Moore and Henry Kuttner's "The Children's Hour" (1944; by-lined Laurence O'Donnell), "When the Bough Breaks" (1944; by-lined Lewis Padgett), and the Baldy series (1945–1953, by-lined Lewis Padgett; book as *Mutant*, 1953), and Charles L. Harness' *Flight into Yesterday* (1949; book, 1953; aka *The Paradox Men*) and "The Rose" (1953). Van Vogt abandoned writing science fiction for some years at the end of the 1940s when he became involved with L. Ron Hubbard's Dianetics movement, which used the cliché as the basis of a *pseudoscience that was eventually transfigured into a religion. It had been conclusively demonstrated by 1950 that the audience for genre science fiction was not merely willing but very eager to identify with all manner of superhuman characters; "fans are slans" became briefly fashionable as a slogan.

Sympathy for superhumans reached a fervent climax in the decade following the end of World War II, when the case for superhuman morality was argued with remarkable polemical fervour by Theodore Sturgeon in such stories as "Maturity" (1947), *More than Human* (1953), and "... And My Fear Is Great" (1953). The proliferation of *mutant stories after the advent of the *atom bomb greatly assisted the production of stories featuring groups of innocent superhumans—often initially manifest as *wunderkinder*—misunderstood and cruelly persecuted by their envious cousins; notable examples included Wilmar H. Shiras' *Children of the Atom* (1948–1953; book, 1953), the early items in Zenna Henderson's "People" series (1952–1959; book as *Pilgrimage* 1961), and Wilson Tucker's *Wild Talent* (1954).

The basic pattern was complicated by melodramas in which virtuous supermen were also opposed by evil supermen, as in James Blish's *Jack of Eagles* (1951), Jack Vance's "Telek" (1951), Frank M. Robinson's *The Power* (1956), and George O. Smith's *Highways in Hiding* (1956), but virtuous superhumanity always prevailed. Stories of both sorts often employed a *deus ex machina* formula pioneered by van Vogt, in which the plot's denouement involved the abrupt climactic flourishing of previously latent superpowers among the ranks of the virtuous. Notable exceptions to the rule included Damon Knight's "Special Delivery" (1954), in which a superembryo is luckily normalised by the birth trauma, and Jerome Bixby's "It's a *Good* Life" (1955), which features the ultimate superbrat. The alien-implanted superchildren in John Wyndham's *The Midwich Cuckoos* (1957) are explicitly antihuman, but the two films adapted from the book, *Village of the Damned* (1950) and *Children of the Damned* (1963), were more ambivalent in their portrayal.

The attractiveness of fantasies of latent superhumanity to the teenagers who formed the core of the genre science fiction audience is easy to understand, and was calculatedly exaggerated by the rapid proliferation of comic book superheroes who had to conduct their everyday lives in the meek and downtrodden guise of their "secret identities". Nor were fantasies of latent superhumanity restricted to realms of fabulation; Hubbard was by no means the only cult creator to import them into a pseudoscientific or religious context. Throughout the latter half of the twentieth century, entrepreneurial enterprises offering parapsychological transcendence as a cure for existential dissatisfaction became increasingly common. In the comic books, however, the age of superheroic innocence did not last; its tarnishing was clearly reflected in the 1960s resurgence of Marvel Comics under the aegis of Stan Lee, whose superheroes were routinely afflicted by feelings of angst and *alienation exaggerated rather than ameliorated by their powers.

The literary reflection of this trend spread far beyond science fiction, but the genre inevitably provided the most extravagant and explicit exemplars. The imagery of superhuman transcendence had reached new extremes in Sturgeon's *More than Human*, Arthur C. Clarke's *Childhood's End* (1953), and Daniel F. Galouye's "Secret of the Immortals" (1954), but such secular apotheoses were soon cheapened by repetition. The van Vogtian *deus ex machina* was increasingly difficult to take seriously as its echoes gradually faded away in such works as Phyllis Gotlieb's *Sunburst* (1964), Arthur Sellings' *The Uncensored Man* (1964), Keith Laumer's *The Infinite Cage* (1972), Oscar Rossiter's *Tetrasomy Two* (1974), and Zach Hughes' *The Stork Factor* (1975). Postmetamorphic godlike supermen like the one featured in John Brunner's *Rites of Ohe* (1963) became a standard feature of the work of Roger Zelazny, as exemplified in *This Immortal* (1966) and *Lord of Light* (1967), but they no longer seemed awe inspiring.

In struggling for further effect, such fantasies attempted to draw new energy from images of metamorphic rebirth, as in Robert Silverberg's *To Open the Sky* (1967) and "Born with the Dead" (1974), Thomas M. Disch's *Camp Concentration* (1968), Robert Heinlein's *I Will Fear No Evil* (1971), Philip José Farmer's *Traitor to the Living* (1973), Alfred Bester's *The Computer Connection* (1974; aka *Extro*), and Ian Watson's *The Martian Inca* (1977), *Alien Embassy* (1977), and *Miracle Visitors* (1978), but they too exhibited a rapid diminution of effect. Existential fantasies attempting to examine the superhuman condition in more detail, such as Wyman Guin's *The Standing Joy* (1969) and Raymond Z. Gallun's *The Eden Cycle* (1974), also lacked conviction.

By the end of the 1970s, the science-fictional boom in images of superhumanity had run out of steam. The successful translocation of comic book imagery to the cinema and TV helped to maintain the fashionability of caped crusaders in those media, although they became increasing angst ridden. Examples in print made increasing use of the symbolic potential of the imagery in such works as Ian Watson's *The Gardens of Delight* (1980), Timothy Zahn's *A Coming of Age* (1985), and Jack Williamson's *Firechild* (1986).

The notion of superhumanity was complicated in the last decades of the twentieth century by the actual and speculative development of *biotechnology and *cyborgisation, as reflected in such otherwise orthodox superman stories as Raymond Z. Gallun's *Bioblast* (1985). It was quickly realised, however, that the variety of such technologies suggested that the idea of any linear evolution from *Homo sapiens* to *Homo superior* was now outdated, and the early 1980s also saw the widespread replacement of the idea of a single kind of preprogrammed superhumanity by diverse kinds of facultative *posthumanity.

As the end of the century approached, sufficient time had elapsed since the 1950s boom to permit careful revisitations of the wunderkind formula such as George Turner's *Brain Child* (1991), Nancy Kress' "Beggars in Spain" (1991) and its sequels and *Nothing Human* (2003), and Greg Bear's *Darwin's Radio* (1999) and *Darwin's Children* (2003), but the imaginative context of such works had shifted dramatically.

SUSPENDED ANIMATION

A biological phenomenon by means of which a living organism temporarily enters a dormant state. Sleep is a familiar form of suspended animation, but the term is usually reserved for much longer periods of inactivity during which an organism's metabolic activity is drastically reduced. The most common observed form is hibernation, by means of which many animals avoid the problem of reduced winter food supplies. Low winter temperatures facilitate hibernation, and much lower temperatures—the subject of *cryogenic science—permit the dramatic extension of suspended animation.

Suspended animation has a long folkloristic and literary history, featured in such Christian legends as the tale of the "seven sleepers of Ephesus" and the fairy tale recorded by Charles Perrault and the Brothers Grimm whose two versions are known in English as "The Sleeping Beauty" and "Briar Rose". The motif has played a significant role in futuristic fiction by virtue of its convenience as a means of transporting characters into the future, as in such euchronian romances as John Banim's *Revelations of the Dead-Alive* (1824), Mary Griffith's *Three Hundred Years Hence* (1836), Edward Bellamy's *Looking Backward, 2000–1887* (1888), Alvarado M. Fuller's *A.D. 2000* (1890), H. G. Wells' *When the Sleeper Wakes* (1899; rev. as *The Sleeper Awakes*), George Gordon Hastings' *The First American King* (1904), Herbert Gubbins' *The Elixir of Life; or, 2905 A.D.* (1914), and Kenneth S. Guthrie's *A Romance of Two Centuries* (1919).

Suspended animation is also employed in speculative fiction to bring characters from the distant past into the present—usually by virtue of accidental cryogenic storage, although this version of the notion was significantly complicated by the inspiration of the ancient Egyptian habit of mummifying the dead. The popularisation of *archaeological discoveries in Egypt in the nineteenth century gave rise to numerous fantasies featuring reanimated Egyptian princesses, including Edgar Lee's *Pharaoh's Daughter* (1889), Florence Carpenter Dieudonne's *Xartella* (1891), Clive Holland's *An Egyptian Coquette* (1898; rev. as *The Spell of Isis*), and George Griffith's *The Mummy and Miss Nitocris* (1906). The motif of carefully conserved beauty also recurs in other mildly erotic fantasies such as Stephen Chalmers' "The Frozen Beauty" (1914).

Visitors from the past preserved by more enterprising means of suspended animation are featured in Edmond About's *L'homme à l'oreille cassée* (1861; trans. as *The Man with the Broken Ear*), G. Firth Scott's *The Last Lemurian* (1898), Frank Barrett's *The Justification of Andrew Lebrun* (1894), E. Nesbit's *Dormant* (1911), and Erle Cox's *Out of the Silence* (1919; book, 1925). The invented means used in these stories require more careful discussion than the familiar stereotypes but are rarely discussed in much detail; the notion received more focused attention in *contes philosophiques* such as Edgar Allan Poe's "The Facts in the Case of M. Valdemar" (1845) and Grant Allen's "Pausodyne" (1881), and in F. E. Daniel's *The Strange Case of Dr. Bruno* (1906), an account of a chemical cocktail of natural substances—including wasp venom and curare—that slows down metabolism.

The adoption of suspended animation into pulp fiction initially continued the familiar traditions. It was employed as a facilitating device in such works as Stanton A. Coblentz's *After 12,000 Years* (1929; book, 1950), Laurence Manning's *The Man Who Awoke* (1933; book, 1975), Charles W. Diffin's "The Long Night" (1934), and Edgar Rice Burroughs' "The Resurrection of Jimber Jaw" (1937). The potential utility of suspended animation in interstellar travel was soon realised and similarly exploited; notable examples of its use in that context include J. Schlossel's "The Second Swarm" (1928), Aladra Septama's "Tani of Ekkis" (1930), A. E. van Vogt's "Far Centaurus" (1944), Stanley Kubrick's film *2001—A Space Odyssey* (1968), Michael Moorcock's *The Black Corridor* (1969; with Hilary Bailey), and James White's *The Dream Millennium* (1974). Alien space travellers in suspended animation are notably featured in Ed Earl Repp's "The Stellar Missile" (1929), Murray Leinster's "The Ethical Equations" (1945), Raymond F. Jones' *The Alien* (1951), Larry Niven's *World of Ptavvs* (1966), Arthur C. Clarke's *Rendezvous with Rama* (1973), and Colin Wilson's *The Space Vampires* (1976).

Suspended animation continued to be used occasionally as a convenient means of time travel, the device extending into the latter part of the twentieth century in such works as Richard Ben Sapir's *The Far Arena* (1978) and Richard Lupoff's *Sun's End* (1984), but the most enterprising uses of the motif in genre science fiction attempted to explore psychological and social consequences of the exploitation of technologies of artificial hibernation; notable examples included Abner J. Gelula's "Hibernation" (1933), L. Sprague de Camp's "The Stolen Dormouse" (1941), Roger Zelazny's "The Graveyard Heart" (1964), W. C. Francis' "To Sleep, Perchance to Dream ..." (1968), Orson Scott Card's *The Worthing Saga* (1978–1989; book 1990), Charles Sheffield's *Between the Strokes of Night* (1985), and Walter Jon Williams' "Elegy for Angels and Dogs" (1990).

Means of suspending animation that are more drastic than simulated hibernation include those employed in Brian Stableford's *The Walking Shadow* (1979) and Vernor Vinge's *The Peace War* (1984) and *Marooned in Real-Time* (1986). Other innovative variations on the theme included Vercors' *The Insurgents* (1957), an existential fantasy about the ability to suspend animation voluntarily, and John Collier's scathingly satirical fable "Sleeping Beauty" (1938).

SWEDENBORG, EMANUEL (1688–1772)

Swedish natural philosopher, mystic, and theologian. His father, Jasper Swedberg, who was a professor of theology at the University of Uppsala, modified the family name in 1719 when he was ennobled as the Bishop of Skara.

After graduating from Uppsala in 1709, Emanuel Swedberg—as he then was—spent several years travelling, visiting England, France, and Holland, in order to meet people involved in the rapid advancement of mathematics and natural science. When he returned to Sweden in 1715, he founded the country's first scientific periodical, *Daedalus Hyperboreus*, writing numerous accounts of his own researches and the mechanical inventions of Christopher Polhem. He was appointed Polhem's assistant on the Royal Board of Mines and continued to write treatises on such subjects as cosmology, optics, and human sensory perception. He also dabbled in Latin verse, but he fell out of favour after the death of Charles XII in 1718, and published nothing further for more than a decade.

Swedenborg undertook two further journeys abroad in 1721–1722 and 1733 before publishing a comprehensive three-volume summary of his endeavours in physical science, *Opera Philosophica et Mineralia* (1734), which was heavily influenced by the work of René Descartes. It includes an early version of the nebular theory of the solar system's origin, which was to be brought to maturity by

Immanuel Kant and Pierre Laplace, and an anticipation of Kant's hypothesis of island universes (that is, *galaxies).

Following the death of his father in 1735, Swedenborg set out on another trans-European expedition. He published a complement to his earlier summary of his philosophical endeavours, *Oeconomia Regni Animalis* (1740–1741; trans. as *The Economy of the Animal Kingdom*) in Amsterdam. Although it included sophisticated studies in anatomy, it was primarily an attempt to carry forward Descartes' attempts to clarify the relationship between the human body and soul. After returning to Stockholm in 1740, Swedenborg set out to extend this work into a seventeen-volume encyclopaedia of a new human science, but only published three volumes as *Regnum animale* (1743–1744). This work introduced a significant preoccupation with the notion of a universal language, which was subsequently transformed into a "doctrine of correspondence" based on the notion that there is a natural symmetry between propositions in natural science and propositions related to spiritual matters, determined by an innate symbolic aspect of Creation: a new version of *occult holism.

Swedenborg now began to take an intense interest in his dreams, which he began increasingly to consider as visions offering insight into these universal patterns of symbolic correspondence. In the wake of a vision of Christ he experienced in 1744, he began to turn away from his studies in natural philosophy, abandoning that kind of work for good after the publication of *De Cultu et Amore Dei* (1745; trans. as *On the Worship and Love of God*). He devoted himself thereafter to accounts of his visions, interpreted as communications from and with spirits, and to the interpretation of the Bible in the light of his occult theory. He published abundantly, though mostly anonymously, during the remainder of his life, eventually summarising his theological ideas in *Vera Christiana Religio* (1771; trans. as *True Christian Religion*).

Many of Swedenborg's visions, if considered as works of fiction or speculative nonfiction, are very striking and unprecedentedly far ranging, offering detailed accounts of expeditions to other planets within and without the solar system, whose descriptions are ingenuously informed by his early scientific training. The most interesting, from this viewpoint, are collected in *Arcana coelestia quae in Scriptura sacra seu verbo Domini sunt detecta, etc.* (1749–1756; trans. in 12 vols. as *Arcana Coelestia; or, Heavenly Mysteries Contained in the Sacred Scriptures, etc.*). His scientific work was frequently ignored by subsequent historians of science, embarrassed by its aftermath—Isaac *Newton's reputation was preserved by the opposite strategy of ignoring his mystical adventures—and the cosmic visions are usually omitted from histories of speculative fiction because of the manner of their presentation, but he was an important figure in both traditions.

The appropriation of Swedenborg's works by mystics and religious disciples began in the 1780s, when Swedenborgian societies began to form in some profusion, the first significant congregation of the Church of the New Jerusalem being founded in London. His visions and religious ideas became very influential in nineteenth-century literature, especially on the German and English *Romantic movements; Charles Augustus Tulk, the founder of the Swedenborg Society, was a close friend of William Blake and Samuel Taylor Coleridge, while Swedenborg's translator and biographer James John Garth Wilkinson was a friend of Thomas Carlyle, Nathaniel Hawthorne, Robert Browning, Ralph Waldo Emerson, Coventry Patmore, and George MacDonald.

Swedenborg's mystical theology was reflected in the work of such contrasting writers as Honoré de Balzac—most elaborately in *Séraphita* (1835)—Charles Baudelaire, William Butler Yeats, August Strindberg, Marie Corelli, and Jorge Luis Borges. Henry James, the father of Henry James the novelist and the psychologist William James, raised both his sons in the Swedenborgian faith; neither clung to it steadfastly, but it left an imprint on both of them. Carl *Jung also acknowledged a considerable debt to Swedenborg as both scientist and mystic.

Swedenborgian ideas took on a sinister aspect in such late Gothic fantasies as J. Sheridan le Fanu's *Uncle Silas* (1864) and served as a topic of enthusiastic debate in such naturalistic novels as James Spilling's *The Evening and the Morning* (1877) and Julian Hawthorne's *Garth* (1877), but their influence on speculative fiction is evident in such works as the Rev. W. S. Harris' *Life in a Thousand Worlds* (1905), which is modelled on the *Arcana Coelestia*, and Henry Francis Allen's *A Strange Voyage* (1891; by-lined Pruning Knife), in which the inhabitants of Venus are Swedenborgians. Cornelia Hinkley Hotson's *The Shining East* (1964) represents the afterlife as a Swedenborgian utopia.

T

TECHNOLOGICAL DETERMINISM

The hypothesis that the primary cause of social change is technological innovation, and that patterns of social evolution can be largely explained as adaptations to new technological resources. The term itself was first used by the sociologist Thorstein Veblen in *The Engineers and the Price System* (1921) but the idea is considerably older.

Western philosophers of *history were initially inclined to view the social evolution of their own ancestors as an essentially intellectual and political process: a matter of increasing knowledge and evolving ideas gradually leading European societies from reckless barbarism to increasingly orderly ages of Reason and Enlightenment. Antiquarian proto-*archaeologists, by contrast, inevitably saw prehistory—evidenced by its surviving artefacts—in terms of evolving technology: as a sequence of Stone, Bronze, and Iron ages, the first being further subdivided into palaeolithic and neolithic phases. These two modes of thought came together in the eighteenth-century philosophy of *progress, which proposed that moral and technological progress were inextricably linked.

The notion that social progress was the result rather than the cause of technological progress was significantly elaborated in the nineteenth century when Karl *Marx, objecting to the idealist history of G. W. F. Hegel, proposed that the motor of historical change was fundamentally material—a matter of technological means of production and the dynamic tension between social classes defined by their relationship to those means. Ideas, in this view, were "superstructural" by-products of economic relationships defined and remade by technological change. However, Marx's growing obsession with "correcting" the political ideologies generated by the contemporary material reality left the technological determinist aspects of his theory to be developed and varied by other writers.

Marxist technological determinism was elaborated and sophisticated by Lewis Mumford, whose *Technics and Civilization* (1934) divided the recent history of technology into three overlapping phases: the eotechnic (1000–1750), based on the use of wind, water, and wood as *power sources; the palaeotechnic (1700–1900), based on the exploitation of coal in association with iron and steam engines; and the neotechnic (begun in 1820), based on electricity. He conceived of the first phase as a relatively harmonious one, but represented the second as a brutal severance of humankind from Nature, indicting the new science of *Galileo and *Newton as the progenitor of factories run by the clock, which enslaved people to the demands of machinery and mechanised their slaughter in technologically sophisticated warfare. The third phase offered the hope of a new, but as-yet unrealised reharmonisation whose eventual realisation would depend on the rapidity of political reform.

The last part of this argument emphasised Mumford's recognition that causal relationships between technology and social order could not be unidirectional, but resembled a feedback loop. He attempted to analyse the social imperatives that had selectively generated rapid technological progress in the Western world, which had in turn generated new social imperatives. He concluded that warfare and political oppression had been the principal engines of palaeo-technic innovation, although the former conclusion was challenged by John U. Nef, who argued that war had almost invariably been harmful to technological progress, offering the suggestion that the force of demand that gave birth to modern metallurgy was not for better cannon but for louder church bells.

The role of warfare in driving technological change had been emphasised before Mumford's dramatisation in such arguments as Heinrich Brunner's contention (in 1887) that feudalism had been the social product of the development of the cavalry charge as a mode of warfare by the Franks. This particular opinion was challenged by the technological determinist historian Lynn T. White Jr. in a significant analysis of *Medieval Technology and Social Change* (1962), who suggested that both these phenomena had been the result of the introduction to Europe of the stirrup, which facilitated mounted combat with the "couched" lances made famous by knightly jousting. Orthodox historians—most notably Bernard Bachrach—attacked White's thesis on the grounds that there were virtually no documentary references to stirrups in the relevant period, but this might only be one more illustration of the historical invisibility of items of technology whose causal significance was not recognised by their users.

Mumford's hostile account of the driving forces that had generated and been dramatically amplified by palaeotechnic technology was carried forward in *The Myth of the Machine* (1967), which set individual inventions within a much broader framework of the "megamachine": organised labour tyrannically disposed. A similar attitude is reflected in the work of other Marxist technological determinists; Jacques Ellul's analysis of *La technique* (1954; trans. as *The Technological Society*) similarly represents technology as the basic framework of human society, remaking all social institutions—and the human mind itself—in its own mechanical image. Marxist sociologists of art and literature often extrapolated this kind of indictment into scathing attacks on the mechanising influences of the mass media.

Another variant of Marxist technological determinism was proposed by Harold Innis in *Empire and Communication* (1950), which argues that it was technologies of communication, rather than technologies of material production, that were the principal determinants of the forms adopted by social and political institutions in ancient times. Innis attempted to extrapolate the argument in *The Bias of Communication* (1951), which took in the produce of several studies of the influence of the invention of printing on European politics, but the thorough modernisation of his theory was left to his disciple Marshall McLuhan, whose ideas regarding the advent of new media technologies were widely popularised in the 1960s in such works as *The Gutenberg Galaxy* (1962) and *The Medium Is the Massage* (1967).

An unusually forthright version of technological determinism was developed outside a Marxist theoretical context by William Ogburn, who proposed in *On Culture and Social Change* (1964) that all social change could and ought to be seen as a series of adjustments to new technological opportunities, and that most social problems could be explained by the inertial resistance of existing institutions to their replacement by better-adapted ones. This resistance, he argued, amplified the effects of the inconvenient "cultural lag" to which social institutions were perennially subject as they struggled to adapt to new technologies.

Historians following up the work done by Lynn White tended to employ more subtle, sophisticated forms of technological determinism than Ogburn's, but nevertheless tended to place a heavier emphasis on new technologies as agents of change than on social factors prompting invention. Notable examples include several works by Carlo M. Cipolla, including *Guns, Sails and Empires: Technological Innovation and the Early Phases of European Expansion 1400–1700* (1965) and *Clocks and Culture 1300–1700* (1967) and Jean Gimpel's account of *La revolution industrielle du Moyen-Age* (1975; trans. as *The Medieval Machine: The Industrial Revolution of the Middle Ages*), which also cites climatic factors as significant enablers and inhibitors of social change.

When Isaac *Asimov defined the most significant fraction of 1940s science fiction as "social science fiction", he was tacitly assuming a broadly Ogburnian view of social change, although a good deal of Campbellian science fiction focuses on spurs to technological progress as well as the social effects of new technology. Like Lewis Mumford, but with more sustained optimism, hard science fiction almost invariably looks to neotechnic developments to solve the problems generated in the palaeotechnic era. The Innis thesis was imported into science fiction following McLuhan's popularisation, in such works as Dean R. Koontz's "A Mouse in the Walls of the Global Village" (1972) and Norman Spinrad's accounts of future media development, but consideration of its implications became much more widespread in the 1980s, when further elaborations and sophistications of communication technology left McLuhan's ideas looking conspicuously dated; the extrapolation of the train of thought Innis set in motion are intrinsic to fiction considering the social implications of information technology, such as the works of William *Gibson and *Paul Levinson.

A broader spectrum of considerations is, however, taken into account by the works of Bruce *Sterling and the prophets of the technological *singularity.

Theories of technological determinism play a considerable role in accounts of *alternative history, a highly significant model having been provided by L. Sprague de Camp's *Lest Darkness Fall* (1939; book, 1941), which explicitly champions the view that the Dark Ages might have been averted by relatively subtle technological development. Images of societies that might have emerged had the Reformation been suppressed or had the South won the American Civil War frequently focus on the supposed effects such variations would have had on the pace of technological progress, while the entire subgenre of *steampunk fiction focuses on disruptions of history occasioned by technological wild cards.

De Camp supplemented *Lest Darkness Fall* with the conscientiously sceptical "Aristotle and the Gun" (1958), in which history proves ironically resistant to an attempted acceleration of technological progress; a similar scepticism is more elaborately displayed in William Golding's "Envoy Extraordinary" (1956; dramatised as *The Brass Butterfly*), in which a Roman emperor fails to see the potential in gunpowder, Ronald W. Clark's *Queen Victoria's Bomb* (1967), in which the eponymous monarch finds the idea of the *atom bomb distinctly unamusing, and Gregory Feeley's "Arabian Wine" (2004), in which a seventeenth-century industrial revolution is nipped in the bud. On the whole, though, twentieth-century speculative fiction is strongly committed to the idea that new technologies have the capacity to bring about drastic transformations of society that are ultimately irresistible, and that characters who labour to reduce the duration or awkward side effects of Ogburnian cultural lag are doing heroic work.

This is, in fact, the kind of triumph that the majority of *hard science fiction's heroes strive for; the epiphanic rewards of conceptual breakthrough are usually subsidiary to some such practical accomplishment. When innovations are stifled by cultural conservatism—as, for instance, in E. C. Large's *Sugar in the Air* (1937)—a sense of tragedy is generated that is quite distinct from conventional representations of personal and social tragedy, in that it involves the frustration of moral as well as technological progress. When, on the other hand, the forces of cultural conservatism (or retreatism) are ingeniously defeated by the ingenuity of scientists and technologists—as they repeatedly are, for instance, in Isaac Asimov's archetypal Foundation series (1942–1950; books, 1951–1953)—the sense of triumphant closure attained by such narratives is equally distinct.

TECHNOLOGY

The application of science, especially in a *mechanical sense. The term is often used in a narrow sense to refer specifically to the design, construction, and use of machines, but its broader meaning takes in the whole range of applied knowledge; "technics" is sometimes preferred when emphasising that the reference includes agricultural methods and other biotechnologies. The term is derived from a Greek word whose ultimate signification was carpentry.

The cumulative evolution of technologies is a major component of the notion of *progress, and its influence on social change is the subject of theories of *technological determinism. The term is often coupled with science, reflecting the widespread view that the utility of science is measurable in its technological spin-off, but that coupling was a product of the scientific revolution; the dependence of technology on scientific knowledge was first clearly asserted by Francis *Bacon in the early seventeenth century—although hints can be seen retrospectively in the work of many Renaissance architects and engineers—and was not widely recognised for a further hundred years thereafter. In tribal societies the technological heritage tends to be elaborately divided, communicated via oral culture as a matter of tradition, and largely taken for granted—a process still enshrined in the artisan culture of seventeenth-century England. The general concept only becomes significant in situations where *invention becomes perceptible as a social activity and a social necessity; it was not until *engineering became a significant vocation in civil as well as military contexts that "technology" became historically visible.

The development of Greek philosophy was certainly paralleled by significant technological progress, but the latter was not recorded with the same assiduous concentration. This pattern was long maintained, with the result that the modern compilation of the story of technological progress, even with respect to recent periods, has owed as much to *archaeologists as to historians. The relative historical invisibility of patterns of technological change is reflected in the fact that they are often relegated in an academic context to the status of a subsidiary field of the hybrid discipline of "economic history". An understanding of the extent to which the recorded history of past eras had been influenced by unnoticed technological changes was very slow to emerge in the wake of the scientific revolution.

The historical invisibility of technological progress prior to the nineteenth century, and the lack of any substantial awareness of its importance as an agent of social change, is further exaggerated in literature. In spite of the significant precedents set by Bacon's *New Atlantis* (written ca. 1610; published 1627) and John Wilkins' *Mathematicall Magick* (1648), there was relatively little awareness in the subsequent *Utopian tradition of the significance of technology as an agent of social change.

It was not until the development of the philosophy of progress in the late eighteenth century that the idea of an intimate link between social and technological progress was widely popularised. The association of the philosophy of progress with the French Revolution of 1789 made the idea seem ominous to political conservatives—especially in Britain, where intellectual resistance to "Jacobin science" made a ready alloy with aesthetic objections to the changes brought to the landscape by the Industrial Revolution. William Thomson's *Mammuth* (1789; as by "The Man in the Moon") was an early strident assertion of the principle that *Nature is always superior to technology. In America, however—where Benjamin Franklin proposed by way of definition that "man is a tool-making animal"—the spectrum of attitudes was quite different, and the seeds were sown there that would bring the United States to the forefront of technological innovation and development within a hundred years.

This pattern of development ensured that the concepts of "technology" and "technological progress" were intimately associated in nineteenth-century literary rhetoric and imagery with a profound anxiety, readily exaggerated into fears of human enslavement to the demands and requirements of machinery. Even in the United States, literary culture remained far more conservative than the social forces prompting technological development—a disjunction that persisted throughout not only the nineteenth century but the twentieth century too. Miguel de Cervantes did not intend Don Quixote's famous assault upon the windmills he mistook for giants as an allegory of technology, but more than one modern critic has hailed his futile charge as a heroic endeavour rather than a farcical error, on the grounds that such semi-automated devices were indeed unrecognised monsters, inimical to all the values a true knight should work to uphold.

The priorities of melodrama have ensured that far more visionary endeavour has been devoted to quixotic "tilting at windmills" than to dreams of contrived perpetual motion, even though it is invariably conceded from the outset that the windmills will win. Samuel Butler presumably intended the "Book of the Machines" in *Erewhon* (1872)—which revises the story of evolution to make humankind a mere instrument in the inexorable progress of machinery—as a satire on Darwinism, but it lends itself readily enough to the same critical revaluation as Quixote's folly.

The development of the future as a narrative space in the wake of Louis-Sébastien Mercier's *L'an deux mille quatre cent quarante* (1771; trans. as *Memoirs of the Year 2500*) relied heavily on the notion of continued technological development, often signified by *aeronautical imagery, but the development was patchy for a further hundred years, until Jules *Verne moved new technological devices to centre stage in his more ambitious *voyages extraordinaires*. The idea of technological progress then became the principal focus of the new genres of *scientific romance and *science fiction—which were automatically relegated to the margins of a literary culture profoundly fearful of that idea, even in the United States.

By 1851, when the Great Exhibition was held in London's Crystal Palace, technology had become the apparent symbol and embodiment of humankind's new mastery of its destiny, but the literary celebrations of the event were almost entirely satirical. Luddism was dead by then in a literal sense, but its soul was marching on, and continued to do so in such explicitly Luddite literary works as Walter Doty Reynolds' *Mr. Jonnemacher's Machine* (1898) and Edmund Cooper's *The Cloud Walker* (1973).

The development of nineteenth-century technology was inevitably symbolised in thought and imagery by its hardware, especially the steam engine, in both its static and locomotive manifestations. As Adam Smith pointed out, however, the economics of technology were also dependent on the organisation of working practices: the efficient division and physical distribution of labour within factories for the purposes of "mass production". By the end of the century, this kind of process had been formalised by Frederick Winslow Taylor, whose findings—after some thirty years of practical experience—were summarised in *The Principles of Scientific Management* (1911). The adoption and application of such principles by Henry Ford on his assembly lines seemed to many observers to be an ongoing adaptation of human workers to the requirements of machinery, reducing them to mere technological devices in themselves.

The cinema provided ample scope for graphic representations of this notion; Fritz Lang's film *Metropolis* (1926) depicts human workers reduced to exhaustion by hopeless attempts to keep pace with indefatigable machinery, reduced by a symbolic dream sequence to the status of sacrifices marching into the maw of a mechanical Moloch. Lewis Mumford's argument that it was the clock, not the steam engine, that was the truly definitive machine of the "palaeotechnic era" is reflected in a great deal of literary and visual imagery of this period; Lang's workers are shown moving the hands on giant clock faces. The ultimate iconic symbol of technology, the multitoothed cogwheel, is an item whose most familiar setting during the preceding centuries had been clockwork; Charlie Chaplin's comic counterpart to Lang's *Metropolis, Modern Times* (1936), is similarly dominated by clockwork imagery. Elmer Rice's play *The Adding Machine* (1923) foregrounds the kinds of machines found in offices rather than factories, but is similarly obsessed with the temporal management and control of human action. Words on a printed page could not illustrate this kind of mechanisation process with the same immediacy, but they could attempt to get to grips with its psychological effects via studies of modern and metropolitan *alienation.

The difficulties of illustrating technology—conceived as a general phenomenon—on the printed page are reflected in a relative scarcity of allegorical representations, but notable examples from early scientific romance include H. G. Wells' "The Lord of the Dynamos" (1894), J. S. Fletcher's *Morrison's Machine* (1900), and E. M. Forster's "The Machine Stops" (1909). Wells' symbolic use of the dynamo was echoed by the American Henry Adams, reflecting on his visit to the Paris Exhibition of 1900 in *The Education of Henry Adams* (1918), when he began—very uneasily—to "feel the ... dynamos as a moral force, much as the early Christian felt the Cross", but it was in Britain that the effect was most penetrative. The case against technology made in Bertrand *Russell's *Icarus: or, The Future of Science* (1923) continued to haunt the entire genre of scientific romance until its demise in the 1950s.

A similar oppositional stance was incorporated into pulp science fiction at an early stage, when *Hugo Gernsback recruited the services of David H. Keller, whose deep suspicion of technological progress was manifest in most of his works, culminating in the considerable delight he took in the disintegration of technological society tracked in "The Metal Doom" (1932). Gernsback provided his own extravagant championship of technology in *Ralph 124C41+* (1911), and the science fiction pulps published many other stories with similarly gadget-laden backgrounds—to the extent that science fiction historian Everett F. Bleiler felt obliged to employ the term "Ralphism" as a category description—but Kellerian suspicion always had the upper hand in the currency of melodrama. Such hymns to technology as Arthur G. Stangland's "The Ancient Brain" (1929), the works of Henrik Dahl Juve, and imported German *zukunfstromans* such as Otfrid von Hanstein's *Ein Flug um die Welt und die Insel der Seltsamen Dingel* (1927; trans. as "Utopia Island") and *Elektropolis* (1928; trans. as "Electropolis") were always handicapped by their Utopianism in the development of narrative tension and climactic stress.

In spite of this limitation, the science fiction pulps did become a significant locus of propaganda for technocracy: the proposal that society ought to be run by a scientific elite exploiting technological means in the instrumentality of government. Nathan Schachner's series begun with "The Revolt of the Scientists" (1933) tracks the emergence and triumph of the Technocrats, and the same author's account of "The Robot Technocrat" (1933) may have been commissioned to supplement an advertisement for the launch of Gernsback's short-lived periodical *Technocracy Review*. Even the most ardent apologists for technology tended to have reservations about the notion of technocracy, however; although the science fiction pulps never produced a satire as scathing as Aldous Huxley's *Brave New World* (1932), they were entirely hospitable to cautionary tales in which government by technology turns sour.

John W. *Campbell Jr.'s anxieties about the relationship between humankind and technology, spelled out in such stories as "Twilight" (1934) and "The Machine" (1935), helped make *Astounding Science Fiction* as comfortable a home for the pastoral "post-technological nostalgia" of Clifford *Simak as it was for the technocratically inclined fantasies of Robert A. *Heinlein. On the global stage of international relations, meanwhile, a *de facto* technocracy was effortlessly established, the *politics of those relations being increasingly conceived in terms of "development"—or, more revealingly, in terms of problems of "underdevelopment".

By virtue of its keen appreciation of the role played by technology in facilitating social change, American genre science fiction played a significant part in the development of the modern imagery of technological potential. The illustration of the early specialist pulps was remarkably potent in this respect in spite of the technical crudity of artists like Frank R. Paul, who dominated the Gernsback pulps. The imagery of futuristic buildings and highways, the vehicles on and above them, and the clothing worn by their inhabitants cultivated a peculiar glamour of its own. William Gibson's subsequent dismissal of this imagery as a shallow folly in "The Gernsback Continuum" (1981) avoided mention of the difficulties faced by any illustrator endeavouring to replace it with anything other than images of desolate ruination.

Although the ideals of technocracy continued to excite suspicion in genre science fiction, cautions against it never reached the fever pitch of warnings issued against its antithesis: the establishment of anti-technological ideologies as a tyrannical imposition. Although science-fictional descriptions of revolt against technocracy almost always equip the rebels with their own "Jacobin science", it is in descriptions of revolt against antitechnocracy that paeans to the virtue of technology in general become most eloquent. Notable examples include Leigh Brackett's *The Day After Tomorrow* (1955), James E. Gunn's *The Burning* (1972), Norman Spinrad's *Songs from the Stars* (1980), and Poul Anderson's *Orion Shall Rise* (1983)—all of which, by no coincidence, are fantasies in which the legacy of the *atom bomb has created a traumatised society that lives in dire dread of the destructive power of science and technology. In the absence of some such destructive trauma, the universal assumption is that antitechnological ideology could never be more than a silly and rather hypocritical self-indulgence; after all, even Don Quixote's daily bread was presumably made from milled flour.

The advent of *computer technology and the promise of *artificial intelligence complicated the idea of human "mechanisation" in the latter half of the twentieth century, by laying the groundwork for images of fruitful *cyborgisation and the prospect of *cyberspatial afterlives. The advent of the notion of a technological *singularity suggested that technology might be the means by which a dramatic transcendence of the contemporary human condition might be achieved, facilitated by an intoxicating cocktail of biotechnology and *nanotechnology. In this view, technology no longer threatened humankind with a degradation to mere mechanism, but rather with an exaltation to a posthuman *Heaven—in which context it is not surprising that the pejorative description of the singularity as "the rapture of the nerds" was co-opted with pride.

The grounds of technological anxiety shifted significantly in the latter part of the century, anxiety about technological change *per se* being replaced by an inherently superficial anxiety about the *pace* of innovation in Alvin Toffler's best-selling *Future Shock* (1970). Although the possibility of a managed technological retreat did become a significant theme of *ecological science fiction, even giving rise to an Ecotopian movement, the main theme of such work was "sustainable development"—a more careful control of the pace of progress, and a more judicious selection of a forward route. Although such notions contrast strongly with the emphasis on rapid acceleration found in anticipations of a technological singularity, the difference is one of degree rather than kind—as might be expected given that, if any theory of technological determinism is even partly true, all government is fundamentally technocratic.

TECHNOTHRILLER

A term coined by reviewers to describe books structured according to the standard plot formula of thriller fiction that employ advanced technological devices—including science-fictional inventions—to heighten the threat posed by the plot's antagonist. Although a thriller plot is basically a quasi-gladiatorial contest of wits and strength between a hero and a villain, the melodramatic stakes determining the apparent value of the prize depend on the extent of the threat posed by the villain's machinations, and the equipment of the villain with superior *technology is a useful means of increasing his moral debit.

Although forced marriages, usurped inheritances, kidnappings, and armed robberies were perfectly adequate fuel for nineteenth-century thrillers, the effect of melodramatic inflation on the genre—and on particular series within it—ensured a continual drift towards larger-scale threats, which routinely reached apocalyptic dimensions by the end of the twentieth century. The narrative formula of the thriller demands that such threats are averted before taking full effect—hypothetical technologies usually remain in the background, often amounting to little more than an ominous label, as in Edgar Wallace's *The Green Rust* (1919), Edmund Snell's *The Z Ray* (1932), and Alastair Maclean's *The Satan Bug* (1962; by-lined Ian Stuart)—but the pressure to spell out what they *might* do increased steadily as the genre evolved, as did the pressure to display larger and larger samples of their gruesome potential. In the early part of the twentieth century, however, the more explicitly science-fictional such thrillers became—notable examples include John Taine's *The Gold Tooth* (1927) and *Quayle's Invention* (1927)—the more severely they tested the tolerance of the genre's followers.

The subgenres of thriller fiction that are most hospitable to technothrillers are spy stories—in which technological gadgets are often manifest in the form of "secret plans"—and medical melodramas, in which technological threats can be equipped with an exaggerated yuck factor. Significant late twentieth-century writers of technothrillers—who included Ian Fleming, Robin Cook, Ken Follett, Tom Clancy, Michael Crichton, Sharon Webb, and Dean Koontz—usually fell into one or other of these categories. Specialist technothriller writers who became so entranced with their inventions that they gave them too much scope to change the world—notable examples include Martin Caidin, D. F. Jones, and Dean Ing—inevitably found their work drifting into the science fiction genre, with a consequent loss of sales potential.

The converse temptation that led many science fiction writers to produce technothrillers in order to bid for the greater economic rewards available in the thriller genre bore increasingly abundant fruit as the century progressed. Notable examples include Kate

Wilhelm's *The Nevermore Affair* (1966) and *City of Cain* (1974), Gregory Benford's *Artifact* (1985) and *Chiller* (1993; by-lined Sterling Blake), Neal Stephenson's *The Big U* (1984) and *Zodiac: The Eco-Thriller* (1988), Allen Steele's *The Jericho Iteration* (1994) and *Oceanspace* (2000), Nancy Kress' *Oaths and Miracles* (1995) and *Stinger* (1998), Ian Watson's *Hard Questions* (1996) and *Oracle* (1997), and Paul J. McAuley's *Whole Wide World* (2001) and *White Devils* (2003). Because the necessity of providing psychopathic antagonists and normalising endings preys on the conscience of science fiction writers reluctant to pander to the *Frankenstein complex, however, such crossover exercises often lack conviction. Science-fictional crossovers into the neighbouring subgenre of *disaster fiction routinely suffer from the same problem.

TELEPHONE

A device for reproducing sounds, especially speech, at a distance. The principle was illustrated by the nineteenth-century development of the "string telephone", in which sounds are communicated mechanically from one vibrating diaphragm to another by a connecting string, so the possibility of developing an electrical telephone was easy to imagine long before the practical problems were solved. Philipp Reis built a limited working model as early as 1861, but the race to develop a system capable of efficient sound reproduction within a complex and far-ranging network was so close that Alexander Graham Bell beat Elisha Gray to the U.S. Patent Office by mere hours in 1876, and was immediately embroiled in a fierce developmental contest with Thomas Alva *Edison.

Although advanced communication systems are featured in numerous Utopian fictions, and Bell's device was swiftly taken up in such euchronias as Edward Bellamy's *Looking Backward, 2000–1887* (1888), the use of the telephone in futuristic fiction always tended to imagine something more extravagant than the actual machinery distributed throughout the world by Bell's company and its various competitors, often involving picture transmission and wireless transmission.

Such devices were rarely given much focused attention in speculative fiction, being seen as mere facilitating devices embodying the promise of more sophisticated communication. It is, therefore, rather ironic that no other technological device ever had such a profound influence on naturalistic fiction. It was not simply that the domestic telephone was integrated into the patterns of communication featured in novels, but that the mechanics of plotting were drastically altered by the fact that characters in contemporary novels could (and must) now use telephones in many instances where they had previously used the mail.

The literary letter had always been a highly significant narrative device, defining an entire subgenre of epistolary novels as well as providing—by means of its going astray—a vital method of creating and sustaining misunderstandings between characters. In novels, failures of communication are far more important than successful communications, and the advent of the telephone changed the spectrum of potential failure dramatically. Although the accidentally unposted letter had no ready equivalent in the telephonic world, the telephone compensated for the virtual eradication of that device from the literary armoury by greatly enhancing the possibilities of another favourite literary device: the overheard conversation.

Although the invention of the extension allowed some literary eavesdroppers to overhear both sides of a telephonic conversation, those not so equipped could only hear one, considerably enhancing the scope for misunderstanding. Cinematic narrative, born into the telephonic era, made even more use of its potential as a narrative device than popular fiction; the iconography of the telephone, and the etiquette of its use, profoundly influenced—and was in turn profoundly influenced by—its deployment in movies, especially when talking pictures displaced silent ones.

Although the telephone's effects on the communications taking place between major characters in fiction were profound, they were probably less significant than its effects on the orchestration of hazardous situations—the lifeblood of melodrama. Before the invention of the telephone, help usually arrived—when it did arrive—coincidentally; afterwards, the first impulse and priority of a character in danger had to be to telephone for help, using an iconic emergency number. This offered all kinds of new opportunities to writers, in frustrating access to telephones, interrupting emergency calls, and delaying the response to such calls—the sum of which brought a fundamental change to the choreography of plotting and the management of narrative suspense.

The adoption of the telephone into the genres of scientific romance and science fiction was remarkable in a strangely negative sense, in that it made almost exactly the same difference to plot development in those genres as it did in other fictional genres—with one surprisingly slight exception. The addition of pictures to telephonic communications in science fiction stories was merely an incidental detail, but the frequent representation of phones as portable wireless devices was more significant. The idea that everyone might one day have a device that facilitated instant person-to-person communication wherever the people in question happened to be was a commonplace of pulp science fiction from its inception, such devices often being conceived as an extrapolation of *radio technology rather than telephonic technology.

Such devices were often taken for granted in the context of *space travel, it being understood that people in space suits would have to communicate by that means. The utility of such devices in space opera was abundantly demonstrated by the "communicators" employed in the TV series *Star Trek*, which were widely (but falsely) rumoured to have exercised a powerful influence on the design of actual portable phones. On the other hand, science fiction stories frequently left such technologies entirely out of account in Earthbound plots modelled on conventional thrillers and mysteries, and thus largely failed to anticipate the dramatic upheaval visited upon naturalistic versions of such plots by the actual advent and rapid miniaturisation of the devices called cellphones in the United States and mobile phones in the United Kingdom. The goalposts were abruptly moved in the intricate game of managing and frustrating telephonic calls for help.

The majority of the situations of dire jeopardy in which the protagonists of naturalistic melodrama might find themselves were potentially defused by the ability to take a mobile phone from their pocket or purse and summon help. In addition to the problems of orchestration generated by this kind of problem, writers had also to deal with yet another dramatic transformation of telephone iconography and etiquette, which had already been recomplicated by such social innovations as cold call advertising and phone sex; the additional potential of texting added a whole new dimension to such complications.

For these reasons, the literary spin-off of telephone technology was far more noticeable in other popular genres than it was in speculative fiction throughout the twentieth century, and even more noticeably so in the twenty-first. The telephone played a particularly significant role as a source of psychological menace in horror fiction, whose extension into the realms of the supernatural began with Barry Pain's *An Exchange of Souls* (1911). Such fiction developed in parallel with the telephone's progress to become a significant medium of subtle intimidation in actuality, transforming the experiential significance of silence and the sound of breathing, although supernatural motifs provided a significant icing in such accounts of exotic connections as Richard Matheson's "Sorry, Right Number" (1953).

Science-fictional versions of the strange connection story include Henry Kuttner's "Line to Tomorrow" (1945; by-lined Lewis Padgett), Murray Leinster's "Sam, This Is You" (1955), Robert Silverberg's "Mugwump Four" (1959), Thomas N. Scortia's "When You Hear the Tone" (1971), Damien Broderick and Rory Barnes' *Zones* (1997), and Terry Bisson's "Lucy" (2000). Science fiction stories venturing significant hypotheses regarding the future evolution of the telephone system are, however, rare—especially if one sets aside such fantasies of acquired sentience as Arthur C. Clarke's "Dial F for Frankenstein" (1963). Notable exceptions include Jack Wodhams' "Stormy Bellwether" (1972), Rob Chilson and William F. Wu's "A Hog on Ice" (1987), and Charles Stross' *Festival of Fools* (2003; aka *Singularity Sky*). Even so, it seemed perfectly natural for the mobile phone company Nokia to commission the production of an anthology on the theme of communication, interleaving science fiction stories with futurological essays, to be used as a promotional device: *Future Histories* (1997), edited by Stephen McClelland.

TELESCOPE

An optical instrument that facilitates the observation of distant objects. The magnifying effects of glass lenses were observed long before such instruments came into common use, Roger *Bacon being one of the first persons to record that lenses could make the Moon and stars "descend hither in appearance". A copy of Bacon's text may have prompted Leonard Digges and John *Dee to begin experimenting with lenses. The results of their work were first published by Digges' son Thomas in the 1580s, although there is no evidence that Dee and Thomas Digges used one in the astronomical observations they were conducting at that time. Reflecting telescopes with a magnifying power of 11 or thereabouts were apparently constructed in England for military use in the late 1570s, and refracting telescopes not long thereafter, although the documentation is uncertain—probably because the instruments' users were attempting to keep them secret.

The bulk manufacture of standardised telescopes for military purposes was begun by Hans Lippershey in Holland in 1608, but he was refused a patent and such instruments were soon on sale elsewhere. *Galileo built his own instruments, using his theoretical understanding of *optics to combine the properties of a large convex objective lens with a smaller concave lens to achieve a magnifying power of 33, coupled with considerable light-gathering facility.

This newly powerful combination allowed him to make a series of pioneering *astronomical discoveries, including the moons of Jupiter, and made the telescope into an iconic instrument; images of men studying the stars with the aid of such objects became emblematic not only of the nature of scientific endeavour but of the power of technological devices to transform humankind's conception of the universe. Christian Huygens made further design improvements, facilitating his discovery of Saturn's largest moon, Titan.

The telescope became a crucial weapon in a war of ideas, demonstrating that received wisdom could not be trusted and that arguments from authority could not withstand the criticism of arguments from experience. Ironically, one of the earliest observatories established in Europe was the Vatican Observatory, founded in 1576—whose successor, refitted in 1888, continued to make a contribution to astronomical science in the twentieth century, in spite of the fact that Galileo had not yet been pardoned for his heresy.

The Galilean telescope was soon replaced by models employing a second convex lens placed beyond the focal point of the first—a type used by John *Kepler, although it produced an inverted image. The image could be reinverted by adding a third lens, but the cost in light intensity caused most astronomers to tolerate the inversion. The fact that two crossed wires could be placed at the common focal point of the two lenses facilitated measurement with the aid of the micrometer devised by William Gascoigne in 1640. This device had a considerable impact on the artistry of artillery fire as well as astronomy. (Thomas Digges combined his knowledge of telescopes with his mathematical work in ballistics to become an expert artillerist.)

Chromatic aberration was not as troublesome in telescopes as in *microscopes because it was easier to use lenses thin enough to minimise the problem, although the contrivance often made the lengths of telescopes unwieldy. Achromatic telescopes using complex lenses were developed in the second half of the eighteenth century, after which the principal limiting factor on their further development was the difficulty of casting large objective lenses. Reflecting telescopes lagged behind refracting telescopes for more than a century, although Isaac *Newton demonstrated one to the Royal Society in 1672. The production of large concave mirrors remained difficult until the mid-eighteenth century, when James Short began manufacturing reflecting telescopes in accordance with a standard design. Although these could not be fitted with micrometers, some observers preferred them because modestly sized instruments produced better images; many of William Herschel's discoveries were made with reflecting telescopes.

Although Samuel Butler's account of "The Elephant in the Moon" (1854) was conscientiously sceptical of telescopic discoveries, such instruments became a standard instrument of visionary fantasy, featured with particular effect in Richard Adams Locke's "Moon Hoax" of 1835, Robert Duncan Milne's three-part series begun with "A Dip into Space" (1881), the same author's "A Telescopic Marvel" (1886), Frederick Graves' "The Vision of Mars" (1910), Hugh Kingsmill's "The End of the World" (1924), and Charles C. Winn's "The Infinite Vision" (1926). Such fantasies became increasingly detached from the development of actual technology because the progress of *photography in the late nineteenth century usurped the human eye's role in astronomical discovery, distancing amateurs who actually looked through their telescopes from professionals who examined photographic plates. The telescope retained its iconic significance, but the visionary element of *hard science fiction stories featuring astronomers at work—such as those penned by Robert S. Richardson as Philip Latham—became increasingly abstract, especially when electromagnetic radiation outside the visual spectrum became a significant observational instrument.

Stanton A. Coblentz's pulp science fiction story "The Radio Telescope" (1929) featured a device for capturing and focusing dispersed light rays rather than an actual *radio telescope, but it was known by that date that the Earth's atmosphere has two transparent "windows" letting in electromagnetic radiation, and the possibility of building telescopes to exploit the "radio window" had already been broached. The radio engineer Karl Jansky was the first person to pick up extraterrestrial radio signals—from the direction of the galactic centre—in 1931. In 1937, Grote Reber constructed a parabolic reflector dish in his back yard in order to scan the sky for similar signals, publishing the first radio map of the Milky Way in 1940.

Although radio sources were weak and difficult to resolve, it was much easier to build large radio antennas than to make large lenses and mirrors, so bigger and better radio telescopes were soon constructed. The 250-foot dish at Jodrell Bank in Cheshire attained iconic significance in Britain as a symbol of scientific enterprise and engineering ingenuity. Radio antennas could also be combined in extensive arrays of variously ingenious design, but it was the gigantic dish that lent itself more readily to use as a symbol of modern science's ability to look into the depths of the universe with arcane sensory apparatus. The literary reflection of this symbolism was most obvious in *SETI fantasies, which overlapped a small subset of horror stories featuring invasions *via* radio telescope, including Frank Crisp's *The Ape of London* (1959).

As the power of optical telescopes increased, the effects of the atmosphere became increasingly significant factors in determining what could be discerned by surface-based instruments. The Hubble Space Telescope launched in 1990 was initially problematic because of a design flaw in its primary mirror, but once Space Shuttle astronauts had carried out a corrective repair in 1993, it launched a new era in optical astronomy, its photographs producing a plethora of memorable images, especially those produced in December 1995, when the instrument spent two weeks imaging a vacant region in Ursa Major to produce the Hubble Deep Field of remote galaxies. Science-fictional accounts of supertelescopes were still being produced on occasion, as in Robert Charles Wilson's *Blind Lake* (2003), but the vast majority of such works regarded the instruments as facilitating devices in the search for extraterrestrial intelligence.

Late twentieth-century attempts to put the romance back into observatory life—which reached their nadir in the absurdly misrepresentative Australian TV sitcom *Supernova* (2005)—had no means of recovering the talismanic significance the telescope possessed in the era that extended from Galileo to Camille *Flammarion, but Richardson's "The Dimple in Draco" (1967; by-lined Philip Latham), Gregory Benford's "Exposures" (1981), and Geoffrey A. Landis' "Impact Parameter" (1992) make the most of the available resources.

TELEVISION

The broadcasting of moving pictures and sound. The term is often abbreviated as TV, and is routinely used as a label for apparatus designed to receive such signals, TV being understood in that context as an abbreviation of "TV set".

The notion of scanning a sequence of pictures line by line and frame by frame in order that the information could be transmitted and the pictures reconstituted was broached in the 1880s. In 1884, Paul Nipkow obtained a patent for a TV system using a rotating disk with a spiral aperture, but the development of such systems was frustratingly slow. Even so, a literary version of such an apparatus was featured in Edward A. Robinson and George A. Wall's *The Disk* (1884). First contact with Mars is made via television in Erle Cox's "The Social Code" (1909).

The idea of using a cathode-ray tube as the receiver in a TV system was proposed by Boris Rising in 1907, and A. A. Campbell Swinton suggested soon afterwards that cathode-ray tubes might be used as

cameras as well as receivers. It was, however, the mechanical transmitter that was first successfully used to send signals, John Logie Baird making the first public demonstration in 1926. By this time, broadcast *radio was making rapid progress, but speculative writers tended to assume that a technology of visual reproduction and transmission was as likely to be developed as an adjunct to the *telephone, and used for person-to-person communication, as it was to become a significant medium of broadcasting. It is used in the former context in Hugo *Gernsback's *Ralph 124C41+* (1911), although Gernsback—dissenting from radio pioneer Lee De Forest's judgement that TV would be "commercially and financially ... an impossibility"—subsequently became an ardent propagandist for broadcast television. He launched the magazine *Television* in 1928, in hopeful anticipation of the day when his radio station WRNY would be able to pioneer TV transmission, and made some experimental pictorial broadcasts, but his plans were soon ruined by his bankruptcy.

Television became a common background feature of science-fictional images of the future, although few stories employed it as a specific subject matter because few anticipated the cultural impact it would make. A notable exception is George McLociard's "Television Hill" (1931), which grasped the potential of broadcast news as a window on the world. The notion of TV as a medium for alien contact was inevitably recycled in such stories as Theodore Sturgeon's "Ether Breather" (1939) and Murray Leinster's "Interference" (1945). Robert A. Heinlein's "Waldo" (1942), which featured artificial "arms" remotely controlled via TV screens, pioneered the notion of "telepresence"—although it did not use the term—that was eventually to be a key precursor of *virtual reality. Heinlein also anticipated the employment of TV as significant evangelical vehicle; it prompts the religious revival that leads to the dictatorship of "If This Goes On ..." (1940).

While Baird's system was being used for experimental broadcasts between 1929 and 1935, a patent was taken out by V. K. Zworykin in the United States for an electronic camera, and the first wholly electronic system was constructed by the Radio Corporation of the Americas (RCA) in 1932. Such systems were soon in development in Europe, a competition developing in Britain between Baird's mechanical system and an electronic system developed by Electric and Musical Industries (EMI). Progress was limited by the problem of definition, which required the maximisation of the number of scanning lines; RCA developed a system with 343 lines, but the 405-line EMI system was used for the first public service, launched by the British Broadcasting Corporation (BBC) in 1936. In spite of its progress in Britain, TV did not play a prominent role in 1930s scientific romance, although its potential as a voyeuristic medium was graphically illustrated in *Death Rocks the Cradle* (1933), by-lined Paul Martens (aka Neil Bell).

Development of TV was halted by the advent of World War II, although the United States managed to launch regular broadcasting in 1941 before getting involved and picked up the thread immediately when restrictions on the manufacture of receivers were lifted in 1946. From then on, the spread of the new technology was explosive; further progress in picture definition and colour transmission was rapid. TV replaced radio as the dominant medium of popular entertainment in the 1950s and had permeated the entire globe by the 1980s, with the exception of a few tiny regions where it was banned.

When the enormous potential of the TV medium was belatedly recognised, the prospect was initially viewed with horror; TV sets play key roles in such postwar dystopias as George Orwell's *Nineteen Eighty-Four* (1949) and Ray Bradbury's *Fahrenheit 451* (1953). Ironically, the 1955 BBC TV production *1984* was one of the medium's early artistic highlights, and Bradbury went on to have more of his literary work adapted for TV than any other living writer.

As with other technologies of communication, writers of speculative fiction were continually wrong-footed by the rapid development of the actual technology, but the intimacy that the medium acquired with the development of handheld and concealed cameras was anticipated, and dramatically exaggerated, in stories in which human eyes are adapted as cameras, such as D. G. Compton's *The Continuous Katherine Mortenhoe* (1974; aka *The Unsleeping Eye* and *Death Watch*) and Robert Charles Wilson's *Memory Wire* (1988)—a notion taken to an even further extreme in Wilhelmina Baird's *Crashcourse* (1993). TV's permeation of all aspects of everyday life was also extrapolated in such stories as Kit Reed's "At Central" (1967) and Robert Chilson's "Living on the Air" (1994).

Science-fictional treatments of TV's social instrumentality—even relatively sympathetic ones, such as Norman Spinrad's *Bug Jack Barron* (1969) and *A World Between* (1979)—routinely assumed that its potential to do harm is vast, and that its employment for good is likely to require heroic effort. The increasing power of the TV medium to grip its audience—exerting corollary pressure to keep the audience entertained at all costs—and to transform the audience's perceptions was subject to searching satirisation in such works as E. C. Tubb's "Sense of Proportion" (1958), Robert Sheckley's "The Prize of Peril" (1958) and its numerous sequels, Robert Silverberg's "The Pain Peddlers" (1963), Kate

Wilhelm's "Baby, You Were Great" (1967), Keith Laumer's "The Big Show" (1968), Glen L. Gillette's "Violence on TV" (1974), Joe Patrouch's "The Man Who Murdered Television" (1976), Orson Scott Card's "Lifeloop" (1978), Harlan Ellison's "Laugh Track" (1986), and Kim Stanley Robinson's "Remaking History" (1989). In Thomas Pynchon's *Vineland* (1990), addicted "tubefreeks" are pursued by the National Endowment for Video Education and Rehabilitation (NEVER).

Such literary antipathy made no difference to the near-universal avidity with which TV broadcasts were consumed, but it did have a colourative effect on attitudes to TV's displacement of paperback books as the primary medium of popular fiction—including genre science fiction—during the last decades of the twentieth century. This shift was significant because TV's dependence on regular scheduling made it much more dependent on genrification than theatre or cinema; making shows in batches strongly favoured the use of segmental series whose units employed normalising endings.

This narrative requirement, in combination with the fact that TV shows had to aim for large audiences, ensured considerable stereotypy in all kinds of TV drama. TV "sci-fi" inevitably became dominated by futuristic costume dramas employing the standard narrative formulas of crime fiction—especially *tech-nothrillers—although series that extended beyond a single season inevitably began to reproduce the narrative texture and standard plot devices of soap opera, making much of tensions inherent in the relationships between the chief characters.

Early TV science fiction continued traditions established in radio and the cinema, although its primitive special effects consigned its early adventures in space almost entirely to children's TV, and its adaptations of alien invasion stories worked best when the writers and directors were careful to keep the monsters off stage, as in Nigel Kneale's *The Quatermass Experiment* (BBC, 1953; book, 1959) and its two sequels (a strategy unfortunately discarded in the movie versions).

The only serious attempt to adapt *hard science fiction to the TV medium, *Men into Space* (CBS, 1959)—an exercise in dramatic propaganda for the space program—proved far less popular than the whimsical *Twilight Zone* (1959–1964), which presented moral tales and *contes cruels* that made no distinction at all between science-fictional and supernatural narrative apparatus. Although the medium was host to numerous exercises in the popularisation of science, including Carl *Sagan's *Cosmos* (1980), the limited appeal of such material resulted in concerted attempts to make it more dramatic and visually interesting, with the result that its content was often heavily distorted.

The principal innovation anticipated in speculative fiction that was slow to emerge in actuality was TV with three-dimensional images, often labelled "3-V" or "holovid" (the latter being a contraction of holographic video). It was usually employed as a background feature, although it moved to centre stage in Stanley Schmidt's "A Flash of Darkness" (1968). By the end of the century, the implicit hostility of satirical examinations of TV's evolving relationship with its audience had dwindled to wry resignation, and such end-of-century projections as David Marusek's "VTV" (2000) were more earnest.

By this time, the future roles of synthetic imagery and artificial intelligence had become a significant issue; the classic Turing Test is adapted as a game show in Brian Plante's "It's Only Human" (2002), while a future soap opera whose *dramatis personae* are all self-aware computer programs is featured in Robert Reed's "555" (2003). The sad demise of the mythology of the Space Age is eloquently symbolised in Alex Irvine's "Pictures from an Expedition" (2003), in which the first trip to Mars (sponsored by Bill Gates) is reduced to the humble status of one more reality TV show.

TERRAFORM

A verb coined by Jack Williamson in "Collision Orbit" (1942; by-lined Will Stewart) to describe the adaptation of asteroids for human life with the aid of "paragravity" generators and artificially generated atmospheres. It was later adapted—usually in the form of its present participle, terraforming—to the more general purpose of describing the adaptation of planetary biospheres to render them habitable, and thus amenable to *colonisation, by human beings. Williamson assumed that terraforming's extraterrestrial applications would be extensions of techniques of *ecological management initially applied on Earth; such techniques were given the general label "ecopoiesis" by Robert Haynes in 1984.

In terms of the mythology of the *Space Age, terraforming is a strategy antithetical to that defined in James Blish's "Pantropy" series, which suggested that colonisation of alien ecospheres would inevitably require the adaptive *genetic engineering of the colonists. Fictional terraforming projects envisaged in advance of the term's coinage include those carried out in Olaf Stapledon's *Last and First Men* (1930), in which Venus has to be carefully prepared for human habitation when the Sun cools, and Neptune has to be similarly adapted when the Sun expands again.

Laurence Manning's "The Living Galaxy" (1934) imagined the routinisation of such transformations as humankind expands to fill the universe.

As science fiction writers gradually came to terms with astronomical revelations about the utter inhospitability of the other planets in the solar system, the idea of terraforming inevitably became more important as a key element of the instrumentality of the Space Age. Because optimism was conserved in the case of Mars until the 1960s, the ecological transformation projects sited there in such works as Arthur C. Clarke's *The Sands of Mars* (1951) and Patrick Moore's *Mission to Mars* (1956) tended to be relatively modest, but terraforming Venus was seen as a more challenging prospect in such stories as Henry Kuttner's *Fury* (1950) and Poul Anderson's "The Big Rain" (1954).

The only other worlds in the solar system that seemed to be plausible candidates for terraforming in the 1950s were some of the satellites of *Jupiter and *Saturn, especially Ganymede and Titan. Jack Vance's "I'll Build Your Dream Castle" (1947), which follows Williamson's precedent in featuring custom-terraformed asteroids, is a tongue-in-cheek comedy. Walter M. Miller's "Crucifixus Etiam" (1953) argues that terraformers would inevitably transform themselves in the process, so that the ultimate mutual accommodation would be a compromise. Poul Anderson's "To Build a World" (1964) carefully considered the difficulty of terraforming the Moon—a project eventually carried to glorious completion in Gregory Benford's "The Clear Blue Seas of Luna" (2002).

The idea that terraforming might be reduced to a matter of businesslike routine in the building of a galactic empire became increasingly common in the 1960s and 1970s; Roger Zelazny represents "worldscaping" as an art form in *Isle of the Dead* (1969). Such projects are usually background features, only rarely edging into the narrative foreground in such novels as David Gerrold's *Moonstar Odyssey* (1977) and Andrew Weiner's *Station Gehenna* (1987). The resurgence of *ecological mysticism in this period increasingly complicated the practical questions investigated in stories of this kind with moral anxieties as the idea of terraforming other worlds—effectively destroying native ecospheres in order to substitute clones of Earth's—came to seem atrocious. Serial terraforming is represented as a galactic plague in Jayge Carr's "Child of the Wandering Sea" (1980). In Ian Stewart's "The Ape That Ate the Universe" (1993), serial worldforming by rival species becomes the ultimate medium of Darwinian selection.

This tendency eventually reached its extreme in Ernest Yanarella's *The Cross, the Plow and the*

Skyline: Contemporary Science Fiction and the Ecological Imagination (2001), which offers a horrified reaction to "The Specter of Terra (Terror)Forming". Observing that James *Lovelock had attempted to apply the lessons of the Gaia hypothesis to the possibility of *The Greening of Mars* (1984; with Michael Allaby), Yanarella described the ideology of the Space Age as a kind of terrorism, echoing the moral repugnance fell by many contemporary historians contemplating the exploits of European colonists (including the colonists of the Americas).

Although *The Greening of Mars* became a powerful influence on science fiction stories reconsidering the possibility of colonising Mars in the light of information provided by the Viking landers, a distinct note of moral scepticism sounded in many such works, especially those produced by the self-declared "ecotopian" Kim Stanley Robinson in "Green Mars" (1985) and the trilogy subsequently developed from it, comprising *Red Mars* (1992), *Green Mars* (1993), and *Blue Mars* (1996). Environmentalists protest against the terraforming of Mars in Daniel Hatch's "Intervention at Hellas" (1991).

Moral qualms regarding the propriety of terraforming worlds could easily be set aside in respect of worlds that were home to the organic precursors of life rather than life itself, as in Pamela Sargent's trilogy begun with *Venus of Dreams* (1986), or even in cases where indigenous life has not yet emerged from the sea, as in Alexis Glynn Latner's "The Life-Blood of the Land" (1997), but the scale of such transformations made them more difficult to contemplate. The grandiosity of the notion continued to override moral doubts in such lyrical celebrations of Martian terraforming as Frederick Turner's epic poem *Genesis* (1988) and Ian McDonald's picaresque *Desolation Road* (1988), but distant terraforming projects gone awkwardly or horribly awry became commonplace in such works as Dave Wolverton's *Serpent Catch* (1991), Kay Kenyon's *Rift* (1999), and Neal Asher's *Gridlinked* (2001), while would-be terraformers were featured as villains to be thwarted in such works as Monica Hughes' *The Golden Aquarians* (1994) and Joan Slonczewski's *The Children Star* (1998).

Terraforming projects were viewed in a more positive light in Jack C. Haldeman II's *The Fall of Winter* (1985), Robert L. Forward's *Martian Rainbow* (1991), William H. Keith Jr.'s "Fossils" (1999), Roger McBride Allen's Chronicles of Solace, comprising *The Depths of Time* (2000) and *The Ocean of Years* (2002), and Laura J. Mixon's "At Tide's Turning" (2001). Jack Williamson's calculatedly elegiac account of the ultimate restoration project, *Terraforming Earth* (2001), is conscientiously and appropriately ironic.

THEOLOGY

A term originated by *Plato—dismissively—to describe the exploration of the divine as practiced by *religious believers rather than *metaphysical philosophers. Because it is undertaken from a position of committed faith rather than one of noncommittal scepticism, theology is unscientific by definition, but that does not prevent theologians making use of scientific notions.

Although scientists who are also religious believers generally compartmentalise their knowledge and their faith, they can hardly help being interested in making connections between them. Scientist-theologians such as Nicolaus Copernicus, Isaac *Newton, Athanasius Kircher, and Emanuel *Swedenborg usually end up being decisively claimed by one camp or the other in terms of their historical significance, but that selective process can be seen as a distortion of their own purposes. The most crucial change of perspective involved in the scientific evolution of the seventeenth century had begun as a theological argument regarding the *plurality of worlds.

In opposition to science, which holds the logical analysis and extrapolation of empirical evidence to be the only source of true knowledge, theology credits two other sources: direct revelation from a divine source and authority based in previous revelation. It proposes that these are the only means by which answers can be obtained to questions that science considers meaningless; the most commonly quoted examples are those related to the purpose of the universe and human life.

The psychological impulse producing questions of this kind is presumably also responsible for the phenomena of psychological *probability, insistently searching for explanatory patterns where science sees only the mathematical vagaries of chance. The literature associated with the extrapolation of theology can be described as "theological fantasy", although that label has to be employed in the awareness that some of what seems manifestly to be "fantasy" from a scientific standpoint aspires to be accepted as revelation within its own context.

Although Western history tends to imply that philosophy triumphed over theology in ancient Greece, the intellectual supremacy of Plato, *Aristotle, and Epicurus probably did not seem so sweeping at the time, and it was largely erased once Christendom assumed its spiritual hegemony over the residue of the Roman Empire. When Greek philosophy was rediscovered in Renaissance Christendom, renewed and reinvigorated within the natural philosophy that became the parent of science, it was in a considerably disadvantaged position. Although the Church's attempts to silence Copernicus and *Galileo were unsuccessful, and its attempts to oppose the likes of Voltaire and Charles *Darwin were inhibited by the further weakening of its perceived authority, the fact remains that for much of its early history, Western science was politically subservient to Christian theology.

For this reason, the generalisations and conclusions of early Western science often had to be stated in ways that seemed to endorse—or at least not to dissent from—authoritative accounts of the Scriptural God. Ventures in speculative fiction were even more constrained; from Plato's story of Er to the early years of the twentieth century, imaginative fiction was primarily a branch of theological fantasy, its occasional interventions of freethought and premonitory echoes of science fiction being fraught with difficulty. Such elements were mixed in different proportions, afforded different degrees of allegiance, and confused according to various patterns of hybridisation and chimerisation, but were very rarely allowed to take a bold and openly defiant stance. Many early contributions to speculative fiction were made by clergymen—John *Wilkins was a bishop, as was Francis Godwin, author of the satirical lunar voyage *The Man in the Moone* (1638)—and freethinkers building on precedents they set, such as Cyrano de Bergerac and Voltaire, recognised in so doing that the existing agendas for imaginative fiction had been set by theology.

Theological fantasy's polemical attempts "to justify the ways of God to man"—in John Milton's phrase—were inevitably influenced, if not controlled, by the changes in the image of Creation brought about by increasing scientific knowledge. Milton's Adam is advised not to worry about recent changes in the conception of the cosmos, but wilful ignorance was not really an option. From the point of view of many theologians, new scientific ideas and speculations based therein could only be seen as additional items in a vast catalogue of dangerous heresies, and that view is reflected—even in literature that dissents from the opinion—in much pre-twentieth-century literature. On the other hand, a school of theological thought became established in the Renaissance that held scientific discovery virtuous, on the grounds that it was a continuing revelation of the glory and grandeur of God's creation: a testament to divine ingenuity, originality, and subtlety. In this view, the discovery of scientific *laws was the explication of divine methodology.

This kind of thinking was promoted in the eighteenth century by such works as Samuel Clarke's *A Demonstration of the Being and Attributes of God* (1705) and Bishop Joseph Butler's *The Analogy of Religion* (1736), and gave rise to such literary reflections as Joseph Addison's "An Ode" (1712), in which "the spacious firmament on high" proclaims "in reason's ear" the indubitability of its divine making. It reached its apogee in William Paley's *Natural Theology; or, Evidences of the Existence and Attributes of the Deity, Collected from the Appearances of Nature* (1802).

Paley argued that the ordering of Nature compels belief in a maker, just as the discovery of a watch would imply a watchmaker to a technologically unsophisticated observer—an analogy he borrowed from William Derham. This argument eventually came to be seen as a crucial challenge that had been defiantly answered by Charles Darwin—whose theory of natural selection thus becomes *The Blind Watchmaker* (1986) in Richard Dawkins' popularisation—although Darwin loved Paley's book when he read it. There is a certain irony in the twenty-first-century enmity that has developed between Darwinists and those who believe, in Derhamesque fashion, that the complexity of the natural world compels belief in "intelligent design".

Paley's most enthusiastic successor was William Whewell, whose significant contributions to the *history and *philosophy of science were supported by his faith in natural theology, as outlined in *Astronomy and General Physics Considered with Reference to Natural Theology* (1833) and *Indications of the Creator* (1845). The former was one of a famous set of eight propagandist tracts published in twelve volumes, commissioned in accordance with a bequest from Francis Henry Egerton, the eighth Earl of Bridgewater, which became known as the Bridgewater Treatises. The others included John Kidd's *On the Adaptation of External Nature to the Physical Condition of Man*, which proposed an early version of the *cosmological anthropic principle, Charles Bell's *The Hand: Its Mechanism and Vital Endowments as Evincing Design,* and William Buckland's *Geology and Mineralogy Considered with Reference to Natural Theology*. The computer pioneer Charles Babbage added *The Ninth Bridgewater Treatise* in 1838.

William Whewell was tutor—at Trinity College, Cambridge—to Alfred, Lord Tennyson, and his ideas echo in both "Locksley Hall" (1842) and *In Memoriam* (1850). Another significant believer in natural theology was Philip Gosse, who produced a distinctive account of the psychology of divine creativity in *Omphalos* (1857) and *The Romance of Natural History* (1860–1861)—but his friend Charles Kingsley deduced an alternative evolutionist God from the same data. The idea that natural history can be used as a means of insight into the mind of God was, however, extrapolated sarcastically in Robert Browning's

"Caliban upon Setebos, or, Natural Theology on the Island" (1864), in which Shakespeare's contemplative monster "discovers" a God, Setebos, who is his own mirror image. This procedural method was extrapolated to more radically unhuman observers in such essays as Julian Huxley's "Philosophic Ants" (1923) and J. B. S. Haldane's "Possible Worlds" (1927). Humans using the precepts of natural theology in searching for insight into the nature of God could come up with equally bizarre results. C. H. *Hinton's four-dimensional God and Marie Corelli's God of pure electric force, as glimpsed in *A Romance of Two Worlds* (1886), are notable examples.

The church's influence on education far outlasted its medieval monopoly on literacy, and a marked dissonance developed in Britain between the conservatism typical of schoolteachers—many of whom were paid by the Church of England—and the rapidly evolving knowledge they were required to teach. A similar dissonance was reflected in nineteenth-century generation gaps, and many writers of speculative fiction seem to have been drawn to such work in the course of rebellion against devout fathers; pioneering writers of *scientific romance who were freethinking sons of clergymen included Samuel Butler, Grant Allen, George Griffith, M. P. Shiel, J. D. Beresford, C. J. Cutcliffe Hyne, and William Hope Hodgson.

Natural theology had already passed the peak of its fashionability when Darwin published *The Origin of Species* (1859), but it continued to inspire such texts as Peter Guthrie Tait and Balfour Stewart's *The Unseen Universe* (1875), which cited recent developments in physics as evidence for the immortality of the soul. They followed it with *Paradoxical Philosophy* (1875), a conversation piece reminiscent of Thomas Love Peacock, which elaborated the argument of the earlier book. The theological elements of fictitious cosmic voyages remained conspicuous long after accounts based on the Aristotelian cosmos were superseded by the Copernican accounts of Emanuel *Swedenborg, Marie-Anne de Roumier, and Camille *Flammarion. A significant number of nineteenth- and twentieth-century works of that kind were produced by devout believers intent on reconciling theological and scientific viewpoints; notable examples include W. D. Lach-Szyrma's *Aleriel* (1886), John Jacob Astor's *A Journey in Other Worlds* (1894), James Cowan's *Daybreak* (1896), Jean Delaire's *Around a Distant Star* (1905), the Rev. W. S. Harris' *Life in a Thousand Worlds* (1905), and John Mastin's *Through the Sun in an Airship* (1909).

Although agnostic writers were less likely to discover proof of Scriptural authority in the course of such interplanetary and interstellar missions, that did not prevent them from searching their visions for keys to God's seemingly mysterious ways; the inevitably awkward confrontation with divine spokespersons in Edgar Fawcett's *The Ghost of Guy Thyrle* (1895) was echoed in other literary thought experiments in speculative theology, including Olaf Stapledon's *Star Maker* (1937). The realisation that devotion to natural theology could—and, in fact, almost certainly would—produce an image of God radically different from that of the Scriptures was much more injurious to its prospects than the Darwinian revolution.

It was the growing realisation of the treachery of natural theology, rather than the threat of evolutionism, that generated a rapidly increasing flow of "fundamentalist fantasies" whose primary purpose was to reassert the cardinal authority of the Scriptures, including such backlash works as Guy Thorne's *When It Was Dark* (1904) and Robert Hugh Benson's apocalyptic *Lord of the World* (1907). Benson supplemented the latter item with *The Dawn of All* (1911), which describes a Utopian future in which such heinous heresies as materialism, humanism, socialism, and Protestantism have all been set aside, but it was his apocalyptic fantasy that set a trend followed by such hybrid texts as Martin Hussingtree's *Konyetz* (1924) and Bernard MacLaren's *Day of Misjudgment* (1957). Thorne's *The Angel* (1908) helped to set another trend in motion, in which orthodox angels fought back against the heretical message brought from the Land of Dreams by the angel in H. G. Wells' *The Wonderful Visit* (1895).

The British tradition of scientific romance never severed its connections with theological fantasy, although many works in the genre can be collated into a tradition of "antitheological fantasy" whose conflation with its opposite mirrors the perceived conflation of antiscience fiction with science fiction. Wells was still prepared to dabble in the subgenre at the end of his career, as in *All Aboard for Ararat* (1940), and cryptotheological speculation remained central to the work of Olaf Stapledon, whose reconstructive work is similar in some respects to the unorthodox theology of Pierre Teilhard de Chardin, and is similarly echoed in *Omega Point fantasies. C. S. Lewis co-opted the methods and ideas of scientific romance for the inventive theological fantasy trilogy launched by *Out of the Silent Planet* (1938); Louis de Wohl's *The Second Conquest* (1954) is similar.

American science fiction was restrained for a long time by editorial diplomacy—no pulp magazine editor would publish Clifford D. Simak's account of "The Creator" (1935), although a similar natural theological argument shaped the alien creators featured in C. L. Moore's "Greater Glories" (1935)—but as soon as standards were relaxed in the late 1940s, a flood of theological fantasies in science-fictional form was unleashed. The way was led by Ray Bradbury's "The Man" (1949), in which Jesus pursues his interplanetary mission of salvation at a relentless pace, and "In This Sign ..." (1951; aka "The Fire Balloons"), in which priests encounter sinless beings on Mars. In Anthony Boucher's "The Quest for St. Aquin" (1951), a robot's perfect logic enables it to deduce the existence of God.

In James Blish's "A Case of Conscience" (1953; exp. book, 1958), a Jesuit is forced by his faith to infer that an alien world is the creation of the Devil. Walter M. Miller's "The Ties That Bind" (1954) offers a new take on the notion of original sin. In Lester del Rey's "For I Am a Jealous People" (1954), alien invaders take possession of the Earth after making their own covenant with God and becoming His new chosen people. In Arthur C. Clarke's "The Star" (1955), spacefarers discover the planets destroyed by the nova that shone over Bethlehem, and count the miracle's casualties. Philip José Farmer's "Father" (1955) began a series featuring the conscientious crises of a priest whose eventual mission was to serve as an alien "Prometheus" (1961). The protagonist of Richard Matheson's "The Traveler" (1962) tracks Jesus' mission of salvation across the galaxy, always one step behind. Ian Watson's *God's World* (1979) makes theological notions flamboyantly incarnate. In P. M. Fergusson's "Snapshot of the Soul" (1985), it is discovered that *atom bombs can destroy souls as well as bodies. In Norman Spinrad's *Deus X* (1993), the Vatican attempts to determine whether computer images of human minds are their souls.

The influence of the techniques and motifs of scientific romance and science fiction on twentieth-century theological fantasy is very obvious. Franz Werfel's futuristic fantasy *Stern der Ungeborenen* (1946; trans. as *Star of the Unborn*) features a faith-based society far more elaborate in its technological resources than Robert Hugh Benson's Roman Catholic Utopia. Romain Gary's *The Gasp* (1973) is a satirical account of the commercial and industrial exploitation of the energy of the soul. In E. E. Y. Hales' Dantean fantasy *Chariot of Fire* (1977), a damned engineer sets about restoring the Infernal railroad. In Pierre Boulle's *Les coulisses du ciel* (1979; trans. as *Trouble in Paradise*), the Virgin Mary's return to Earth offers her the opportunity to become a media star and prime minister of France. Bernard Malamud's *God's Grace* (1982) is formulated as a post-holocaust novel. In Jeremy Leven's *Satan* (1982), a psychoanalyst confronts the problem of evil incarnate in a computer.

This kind of influence is particularly obvious in revisionist Messianic fantasies such as Upton Sinclair's *They Call Me Carpenter* (1922), Philip José

Farmer's *Jesus on Mars* (1979), Michael Moorcock's *Behold the Man* (1966; exp. book, 1969), Barry N. Malzberg's *Cross of Fire* (1982), James Morrow's *Only Begotten Daughter* (1990), and Russell T. Davies' TV play *The Second Coming* (2003), in which awkward questions are raised regarding the existential predicament of a destined redeemer who cannot be perfectly certain of his (or, in the penultimate case, her) own divine status or eventual fate no matter how much psychological conviction is mustered in support.

Attempts to reconcile God with twentieth-century physics became increasingly problematic, many writers agreeing with Albert *Einstein that the notion of a God who "plays dice" encouraged by quantum mechanics was aesthetically unsatisfactory within the stern framework of Christian determinism. On the other hand, the uncertainties of quantum mechanics made a more reasonable fit with the ideas of other creeds—an idea variously expressed in Fritjof Capra's *The Tao of Physics* (1975), Heinz R. Pagels' *The Cosmic Code* (1982), Paul Davies' *God and the New Physics* (1990), and Trinh Xuan Thuan's *The Secret Melody* (1995). One mystical cult in Britain began to field candidates in various parliamentary elections under the name of the Natural Law Party.

The science fiction writer who dealt most prolifically with issues in speculative theology in the twentieth century was Philip K. Dick, whose long-standing fascination with such matters was brought to a head by the unusual experiences he underwent in the early months of 1974, which gave rise to *Radio Free Albemuth* (written 1976; published 1985; comprehensively rewritten as *VALIS*, 1981). The evolution of Dick's fascination with theology can be tracked through such works as "Faith of Our Fathers" (1967), *Galactic Pot-Healer* (1969), and *A Maze of Death* (1970), culminating in *The Divine Invasion* (1981) and *The Transmigration of Timothy Archer* (1982). Frank Herbert's similarly deep interest in theological issues was developed in such works as *The God Makers* (1960, as "The Priests of Psi"; exp. 1972), *Destination: Void* (1966), *The Eyes of Heisenberg* (1966), and *The Heaven Makers* (1968; rev. 1977).

Late twentieth-century science-fictional images of God sometimes echoed Setebos—as in George Zebrowski's "Heathen God" (1970)—but were often more enterprisingly innovative in His characterisation, as in Clifford D. Simak's *A Choice of Gods* (1972), Harlan Ellison's "The Deathbird" (1973), Michael Bishop's "The Gospel According to Gamaliel Crucis; or, The Astrogator's Testimony" (1983), R. M. Meluch's *The Queen's Squadron* (1992), and John Clute's *Appleseed* (2001). In Jamil Nasir's *Distance Haze* (2000), a science fiction writer joins a team of physicists in search of their God—an entirely appropriate millennial project.

TIME

The medium of duration. Like *space, it is a basic aspect of experience; early philosophical treatments of the idea hesitated in a similar fashion over the question of whether time could be said to exist apart from the objects manifesting its effects. The manner of time's experience is, however, markedly different from that of space; time appears to "flow" unidirectionally from the *past into the *future, bearing all existence with it, encapsulated in the momentary present.

The controversy as to whether time's flow is the very essence of reality or a mere illusion was already sharp in Classical times, Heraclitus holding to the former view while Parmenides and Zeno were convinced of the latter. *Plato and the Buddha, while not considering the temporal world illusory, considered it distinctly inferior to the time-cleansed perfection of the world of Ideas or Nirvana. Isaac *Newton's notion of time as an absolute, framing the processes of change affecting objects contained within space, was similarly contrasted with idealist notions locating time within perception, although Immanuel Kant tried to effect a compromise by regarding it as an *a priori* necessity of structured experience.

Another long-standing controversy developed regarding the question of whether time's flow is fundamentally cyclic or directional. The former view is intrinsic to Stoic, Hindu, Buddhist, and Chinese philosophy, numerous tribal religions, and F. W. Nietzsche's notion of eternal recurrence. It is echoed in various theories of cyclic *history. The latter is coupled in Christianity and Hegelian theories with the notion of an ultimate goal—echoed in *Omega Point hypotheses—but was conceived as infinite in Newtonian cosmology. The conceptual difficulties involved in imagining that time might have had a beginning, and might yet come to an end, were reintroduced into cosmology by the *Big Bang theory.

The qualitative difference between space and time is seemingly eliminated in graphical representations, in which time can be represented as an axis like any of the spatial dimensions. In this sort of representation the present loses its privileged status, becoming no more than a line on the map, and the irreversibility of time seems to become arbitrary. That arbitrariness is reproduced in algebraic formulas describing temporal transactions, so the descriptions of the world contained in laws of *physics tend to represent time in a manner that is markedly different from its experience, thus complicating the philosophical question of whether the asymmetry between past and future is necessary or merely contingent.

Such questions were further complicated by Albert *Einstein's establishment of the *relativity of space and time, which seemed to favour the mathematical interpretation of time over the experiential one. Popular expositions of the theory, however—including an oft-cited anecdotal summary credited to Einstein—often emphasise the similarity between relativistic accounts of the variability of duration and the subjective variation associated with the fact that pleasurable experiences seem to pass more quickly than painful ones.

The treatment of time as a dimension was strongly opposed on philosophical grounds by Henri Bergson and other "process philosophers", but the mathematical sophistication of science in the late nineteenth and early twentieth centuries made the contrary position—which holds that the experience of time is indeed subjective, and illusory—seem rationally plausible in spite of its counterintuitive implications. Bergson drew a distinction between "lived" time and "measured" or "socialised" time in *Essai sur les données immédiates de la conscience* (1889; trans. as *Time and Free Will: An Essay on the Immediate Data of Consciousness*), which began a debate whose consequences included the heavy emphasis lent to the concept of duration in the prefatory arguments of H. G. Wells' *The Time Machine* (1895).

The measurement of time's flow has always been a significant scientific and technological problem. The intimate connection of astronomical observation with the measurement of time—in terms of the day, the month, the seasons, and the year—motivated the extraordinary ingenuity devoted to the development of such instruments as sundials and astrolabes in advance of the crucial realisation that the Earth was not, after all, a central hub about which a complex of heavenly spheres rotated. The importance of calendars in agricultural society is reflected in the fact that almanacs outnumbered all other printed books in the seventeenth and eighteenth centuries, their basic calendrical information supplemented by detailed astronomical data (including phases of the moon, eclipses, and the positions of the planets).

The replacement of graduated candles and water clocks by mechanical clocks, and the subsequent regulation of spring-driven clocks by various kinds of escapement—assisted by *Galileo's discovery of the principle of the pendulum in the 1580s and its application to the principle to clockmaking by Christian Huygens in the 1650s—helped to lay the foundations of scientific measurement as well as those of modern industrial society. The development of chronometers sufficiently stable and accurate to permit calculation of longitudes aboard ships at sea was vital to the practicalities of navigation; its importance was recognised by the offer of a huge prize by the British Admiralty to the man who could solve the problem, although their reluctance to part with the cash ruined its eventual winner, John Harrington.

The irresistibility and irreversibility of time are perennial preoccupations of literature, featuring—almost without exception—as matters of deep regret. Examples are very numerous, but some of the most famously eloquent and aphoristic include Virgil's reference to the flight of time in the *Georgics*, Shakespeare's references to the "dark backward and abysm of time" and "the whirligig of time" and Macbeth's final speech, Andrew Marvell's reference to "Time's winged chariot", Edward Young's reference to procrastination as the "thief of time", several of the quatrains attributed by Edward Fitzgerald to Omar Khayyam, the "choric song" from Alfred, Lord Tennyson's *The Lotos Eaters,* and Henry Wadsworth Longfellow's reference to "footprints on the sands of time". Although Ecclesiastes informs us that there is "a time to every purpose under heaven" and proverbial wisdom assures us that "time heals all wounds", it is very common to link the passage of time with the inevitability of *death and the irrecoverability of the past, except in the limited and nostalgic sense languorously celebrated in Marcel Proust's *À la recherche du temps perdu* (1913–1927).

The irretrievability of the past is a problem for science, by virtue of the importance of *prediction in scientific proof. Although it seems perfectly sensible to describe archaeology and palaeontology as sciences, and to think of the reconstructions of the past produced by *geology and *cosmology as scientific, they do not lend themselves to predictive testing in the same fashion as the laws of *physics or the fundamental equations of *chemistry. Although Charles *Darwin's theory of *evolution by natural selection provides a powerful interpretation of past events, its inability to predict the future course of Earthly evolution (or, indeed, the course of any evolutionary sequence) has caused some anxiety regarding its entitlement to be reckoned as a scientific theory at all, let alone one that is proved. This problem is sharpened in the realms of human science by the fact that the immediate agents of historical action and change—human desires, intentions, and plans—leave no evidential traces save for dubious reportage, licensing the suspicion that the past reconstructed by *history is not as different from the mythical past as it aspires to be.

Although the present seems to be the moment in which we live, and hence the only aspect of time that seems to possess any tangible reality, it is intrinsically elusive, no sooner apprehended than transformed into the past, and hence irretrievably lost. Its seeming reality dissolves before the most elementary analysis into a mere margin, licensing Bergson's insistence that one should not even try to imagine it in terms of an instant capable of isolation, but should instead regard the essence of experience as a matter of constant transformative *becoming*. Literature, like graphical representation, may try to defy this fact of life with the linguistic artifice of the present tense, but it is at least arguable that the use of past tense in narrative is capable of creating a greater sense of immediacy than the use of the present tense—an observation no more paradoxical than the recognition that the future is far more easily graspable as a literary subject if it is reported in the past tense than it is in the very few experiments that use the future tense.

The literary management of time is a complex business, which extends far beyond the choice of tense. Past-tense narratives remain very flexible in terms of "narrative distance": the explicit or implicit lapse of time that has occurred between the event being reported and the moment of its reporting. Narrative also has to accommodate various kinds of "time gap" within its structure, moving from one relevant occurrence to another, while maintaining a seemingly smooth narrative flow—a task that has generated such conventions as the text break and that gives chapter breaks a manifest function. Stories are not bound by chronological order, so narratives can move back and forth along a story line by means of such devices as flashbacks and flashforwards. All these techniques are particularly relevant to the cinema, which has supplemented the standard textual devices with several of its own, including the use of a split screen to present simultaneous streams of action. Given the facility of print in accommodating chronology-defying devices, it is not surprising that writers and readers can accommodate themselves so readily to literary accounts of arbitrary timeslips.

Literary attempts to capture the transience of the present became more elaborate in the period when Einstein popularised the relativity of time and space and the consequent flexibility of the notion of "simultaneity". Interest in this concept was markedly increased by the global regulation of time instituted in the late nineteenth century, when international agreements created fixed "time zones". Standardisation of time within nations was closely associated with the development of railway timetables. The internationalisation of time was discussed at the International Geographical Conference held in Brussels 1876. The division of the world into twenty-four time zones was agreed, although the decision was not immediately implemented, by the International Meridian Conference of 1884 in Washington, D.C. By then "Standard Railway Time" had already come into effect in the United States, instituted in 1883—three years after Britain had instituted a standard national time.

Standardisation was facilitated by wireless telegraphy; the U.S. Navy began transmitting time signals in 1905 and the Eiffel Tower—which transmitted Paris time after 1910—sent the first signal transmitted around the world in 1913. The anarchist plot to blow up Greenwich Observatory featured in Joseph Conrad's *The Secret Agent* (1907) can be construed as a protest against the globalisation of time, but a more direct response was Henry Olerich's *A Cityless and Countryless World* (1893), which features a Martian society in which all clocks are synchronised and money is calculated in units of time. Stamped time cards invented so that workers could clock on and off had first been introduced in the United States in 1890. Daylight saving time—whose use had been facetiously suggested by Benjamin Franklin—was seriously proposed by William Willett in 1907, and was then implemented during World War I to save fuel.

The most direct literary reflection of contemporary concerns with the notion of simultaneity is to be found in the attempted development of "simultaneous *poetry" by such writers as Guillaume Apollinaire, but literary preoccupation with simultaneity is taken to its extreme in various passages in James Joyce's *Ulysses* (1922), whose final phase is the most celebrated example of an attempt to capture and map the Bergsonian movement of the "stream of consciousness" that constitutes subjective time. Similar ideas cropped up in Filippo Marinetti's futurist manifesto of 1909, which asserted that "Time and Space died yesterday. We already live in the absolute, because we have created eternal, omnipresent speed". Wyndham Lewis's Vorticist movement, incarnated in the short-lived periodical *Blast* (1914–1915) that he coedited with Ezra Pound, took a different view, favouring graphical representations against Bergsonian experiential ones.

Paul Cézanne had produced a famous image of a clock without hands in 1870, but Giorgio de Chirico used clock imagery more effectively in *Enigma of the Hour* (1912) and other paintings. Salvador Dali's melting watches in *The Persistence of Memory* (1931) and other paintings became notorious. The notion of time as an element of perception was dramatised by Max Ehrmann's *A Fearsome Riddle* (1901) and further illustrated by Marcel Duchamp's *Nude Descending a Staircase* (1912) and Umberto Boccioni's *Synthesis of Human Dynamism* (1912), *Unique Forms of Continuity in Space* (1913), and *Dynamism of a Cyclist* (1913).

The counterintuitive aspects of relativity theory helped to bring about a new intensity and eccentricity in philosophical and literary contemplation of the nature of time. J. W. Dunne's ruminations on *An Experiment with Time* (1927) and *The Serial Universe* (1934) were echoed in Clare Winger Harris' "The Fifth Dimension" (1928), J. B. Priestley's "time plays", most notably *Time and the Conways* and *I Have Been Here Before* (both 1937), and his novel *The Magicians* (1954), and John Lymington's *Froomb!* (1964).

Other notable literary examinations of time's essence and potential mutability include John Taine's *The Time Stream* (written ca. 1921; published 1931), Clark Ashton Smith's "The Eternal World" and "Flight into Super-Time" (both 1932), David R. Daniels' "The Branches of Time" (1935), Robert Nathan's *Portrait of Jennie* (1940), several *contes philosophiques* by Jorge Luis Borges, including "La noche cíclica" (1940; trans. as "The Cyclic Night"), "El jardin de senderos que se bifurcan" (1941; trans. as "The Garden of the Forking Paths"), and "Nueva refutación del tiempo" (1947; trans. as "New Refutation of Time"), Ralph L. Finn's *Time Marches Sideways* (1950), John Gloag's *Slow* (1954), David Duncan's *Occam's Razor* (1957), J. G. Ballard's "The Voices of Time" (1960), "Chronopolis" (1960), "The Garden of Time" (1962), and *The Crystal World* (1966), David I. Masson's "Traveller's Rest" (1965), Philip K. Dick's *Ubik* (1969), Michel Jeury's *Le temps incertain* (1973; trans. as *Chronolysis*), Gordon R. Dickson's *Time Storm* (1977), R. A. Lafferty's "Bank and Shoal of Time" (1981), Robert Holdstock's *When Time Winds Blow* (1982), David Bischoff's "Waterloo Sunset" (1982), Eliot Fintushel's "Ylem" (1994), and Richard Waldholm's "From Here You Can See the Sunquists" (2001).

Subjective distortions of temporal experience constitute an important subset of *psychotropic fantasy, which is particularly interesting because of its considerable overlap with accounts of objective distortion; notable texts that fall within this borderland include H. G. Wells' "The New Accelerator" (1901), Jack London's "The Shadow and the Flash" (1903), Arthur C. Clarke's "All the Time in the World" (1952), Brian W. Aldiss' "Man in His Time" (1965), Norman Spinrad's "The Weed of Time" (1970), Kate Wilhelm's "The Plastic Abyss" (1971), Kurt Vonnegut's *Slaughterhouse-5* (1979), Marc Stiegler's "Petals of Rose" (1981), David Brin's "Coexistence" (1982; aka "The River of Time"), Eric Brown's "The Time-Lapsed Man" (1988), Mike Jittlov's film *The Wizard of Space and Time* (1989), Molly Brown's "Bad Timing" (1991), Stephen Baxter's "PeriAndry's Quest" (2004) and "Climbing the Blue" (2005), and Robert Charles Wilson's *Spin* (2005).

The most important subgenre of fiction concerned with time consists of accounts of *time travel, but another significant subset comprises accounts of time's reversal, a theme tentatively broached in J. A. Froude's "The Lieutenant's Daughter" (1847, in *Shadows of the Clouds*, by-lined "Zeta") and developed more extravagantly in Albert Robida's *L'horloge des siècles* (1902), F. Scott Fitzgerald's "The Curious Case of Benjamin Button" (1922), Oliver Onions' *The Tower of Oblivion* (1921), Michael Maurice's *Not in Our Stars* (1923), M. C. Pease's "Reversion" (1949), Malcom Ross' *The Man Who Lived Backward* (1950), Damon Knight's "This Way to the Regress" (1956; aka "Backward, O Time"), Brian Aldiss' *An Age* (1967; aka *Cryptozoic!*), Philip K. Dick's *Counter-Clock World* (1967), Martin Amis' *Time's Arrow* (1991), and Lee Grimes' "Retro Lives" (1993).

Although many versions of the latter theme are trivial instances of literary game playing, some call attention to the point made by the eponymous spirit in Camille Flammarion's *Lumen* (1866–1869), while viewing the battle of Waterloo in reverse (because he is travelling faster than light), to the effect that the universe might seem more edifying if the dead really could rise up and be relieved of their wounds, then to grow younger instead of older, and never have to fear any cruel and arbitrary interruption on the road to birth.

TIME TRAVEL

Movement through *time in defiance of its innate flow. Time travellers may go into the *past or *future, but the two sorts of journeys are markedly different. In spite of its psychological *plausibility, time travel into the past seems to be a logical impossibility, because any alteration of *history is implicitly *paradoxical. Time travel into the past seems to be entirely absent from folklore and mythical fantasy, although movement into *parallel works where time flows at a different rate often permits displacements into the future.

The speculative notion of time travel can be seen as a derivative of the graphical representation of time as a sequence of moments arranged in a continuum— from Henri Bergson's philosophical standpoint, in which nothing exists but the momentary process of becoming, all that a "time machine" could do would be to stop the process of transformation, as in Alfred *Jarry's "Commentaire pour servir á la construction pratique de la machine á explorer le temps" (1900; trans. as "How to Construct a Time Machine"), which provided an ideative counterpart to H. G. Wells' famous account of *The Time Machine* (1895).

It can also be seen as an imaginative corollary of the mechanical possibility of winding the hands of a clock backwards, and narrative "flashbacks" are often represented in that fashion in the cinema.

The psychological plausibility of time travel reflects the ability of the memory to recover impressions of experienced moments in no particular order and the ability of the imagination to anticipate future moments. These faculties are reflected in narrative itself, which can refer back and jump ahead in the course of storytelling. Dreams often involve apparent reenactments of times past and apparent anticipations of events yet to come, and literary dreams offered a convenient means of visionary time travel long before the notion of employing a vehicle for that purpose occurred to anyone.

Dreams retained a virtual monopoly on literary time travel from Plato's "Story of Er" until the mid-nineteenth century, when their increasing versatility was demonstrated in such works as Charles Dickens' *A Christmas Carol* (1843) and Edgar Allan Poe's "A Tale of the Ragged Mountains" (1844). The use of dreams as a method of time travel encouraged their eroticisation, as in such accounts of time-crossed lovers as Théophile Gautier's "Omphale" (1834) and "Arria Marcella" (1852). The extra measure of plausibility introduced into such stories by the invocation of the erotic impulse helped sustain a significant subgenre of stories whose protagonists make voluntary leaps through time, which persisted long into the twentieth century in such sentimental fantasies as Jack Finney's *Time and Again* (1970), Richard Matheson's *Bid Time Return* (1975), and Erica Jong's *Serenissima* (1987).

The dream-driven time journey inevitably became a cliché crying out for variation as examples piled up; many nineteenth-century stories featuring arbitrary timeslips—including the anonymous "Missing Ones's Coach" (*The Story-Teller*, 1843), Mark Twain's *A Connecticut Yankee at King Arthur's Court* (1889), and Robert W. Chambers' "The Demoiselle d'Ys" (1895)—attempted to avoid or ameliorate the anticlimactic quality of the awakening. The device used in Chambers' story, whereby the dreamer is enabled to bring back a physical token as evidence that his experience was more than a dream, soon became a cliché in its turn.

Speculative writers used various strategies to sophisticate dream fantasy in such a way as to make its temporal visions more plausible; the tricks played with time in Camille *Flammarion's *Lumen* (1866–1869) prompted Eugène Mouton to invent "L'historioscope" (1884; trans. as "The Historioscope"), which pioneered a significant subgenre of "time-viewer" stories whose notable twentieth-century examples include Garret Smith's "On the Brink of 2000" (1910), "The Treasures of Tantalus" (1920–1921), and "You've Killed Privacy" (1928), Gardner Hunting's *The Vicarion* (1926), T. L. Sherred's "E for Effort" (1947), and Arthur C. Clarke and Stephen Baxter's *Light of Other Days* (2000), but windows into time were no substitute for actual travel.

Unlike the past, the future seemed physically accessible by the simple means of sleeping for a long time, as Washington Irving's "Rip van Winkle" (1820) did. As in dreams, it is only the protagonist's consciousness that "travels" by means of protracted sleep; the body remains bound by time. Writers of speculative fiction augmented this notion with various forms of artificial *suspended animation, including *cryogenic preservation and drugs such as Grant Allen's "Pausodyne" (1881), but the narrative use of such devices was limited by the fact that there was no obvious way to return travellers to their own time, or to convey their tales to contemporary tellers.

Because of these imitations, H. G. Wells' invention was a crucial breakthrough in "narrative technology", providing speculative fiction with one of its most significant facilitating devices. Wells never used the machine again, but many others did. The original model—or something indistinguishable therefrom—was borrowed by "A Disciple" in *The Coming Era; or, Leeds Beatified* (1900), Miles J. Breuer in "The Time Flight" (1931), and Ronald Wright in *A Scientific Romance* (1997), as well as many providers of belated sequels to Wells' own story, but most imitators customised their copies of the invention, as S. Fowler Wright did in *The Amphibians* (1925).

William Wallace Cook's *A Round Trip to the Year 2000* (1903; book, 1925) looked forward sarcastically to the accumulation of time travellers expectable in the Millennial year. The eponymous machine employed in H. S. MacKaye's *The Panchronicon* (1904) is unashamedly ludicrous and E. V. Odle's *The Clockwork Man* (1923) also affects lightheartedness—although that does not affect the story's profundity—but the machine in Guy Dent's *The Emperor of the If* (1926) is presented in earnest. In Vladimir Mayakovsky's futurist fantasy *Banya* [The Bathhouse] (1930), a time machine brings a phosphorescent woman from the future to serve as an allegory of revolution. Most European writers, however—including such devoted Wellsians as J. D. Beresford—continued to prefer visionary fantasy as a method of time exploration, so it was largely left to American writers of pulp science fiction to figure out what might be done with time machines if one had the imaginative daring to employ them in wholesale fashion.

Early pulp writers who took advantage of time machines included Ray Cummings, in *The Man Who*

Mastered Time (1924; book, 1929) and *The Shadow Girl* (1929; book, 1947), and Ralph Milne Farley, who began a sequence of experiments with "The Time Traveler" (1931) that was eventually collected in *The Omnibus of Time* (1950). The complications they introduced into the pattern of Wells' novel immediately began to expose the logical difficulties consequent upon the changeability of history. Other variations and complications soon began to appear. John Beynon Harris' "Wanderers of Time" (1933) images a trap being set to catch time travellers, while John Russell Fearn's *Liners of Time* (1935; book, 1947) attempted to imagine a situation in which time travel might be reduced to routine commuter traffic. Jack Williamson's *The Legion of Time* (1938; book, 1952) made significant tentative steps in imagining warfare fought with the aid of time machines.

The trickle of tales exploring the hectic complications that could be derived by the extrapolation of the time machine hypothesis soon became a flood. L. Sprague de Camp's *contes philosophiques* "The Isolinguals" (1937) pointed out the language difficulties that time travellers would encounter, and de Camp took the logical problems of time travel sufficiently seriously to declare all such stories fantasies, which could have no place in *hard science fiction. His *Lest Darkness Fall* (1939; book, 1941) appeared in John W. Campbell Jr.'s *Unknown* rather than *Astounding Science Fiction*, even though it set new standards of conscientiousness in examining what an arbitrarily timeslipped protagonist might achieve if he set his mind to it.

Time paradox stories soon became a subgenre in their own right, whose appearance in *Astounding* became commonplace in the 1940s, on the grounds that fans of hard science fiction were better placed than anyone else to appreciate the aesthetic delights provided by their elegant recomplications of the impossible. Many other science fiction writers, however, followed de Camp's example in preferring the careful extrapolation of single timeslips, whose disruptions to the time stream were minimal. Whereas writers outside the genre usually timeslipped their protagonists out of the present, science fiction writers became equally interested in objects timeslipped into the present, as in Henry Kuttner and C. L. Moore's "The Twonky" (1942; by-lined Lewis Padgett) and "Mimsy Were the Borogoves" (1943; by-lined Lewis Padgett), William Tenn's "Child's Play" (1947), and C. M. Kornbluth's "The Little Black Bag" (1950). A potential escape route from the logical paradoxes arising from time travel into the past was provided in this period by the suggestion that time travellers into the past merely create new "time lines", each of which consists of an *alternative history contained in a *parallel world—although this strategy could not explain the "*Fermi paradox of time travel", which argues that the absence of present evidence of time travellers from the future is proof enough of the impossibility of time travel into the past.

One consequence of the development of "time line" theory in science fiction was that the disruptive effects of time machines on history were countered by the invention of policing systems to protect time lines. Stories in which the universe automatically protects itself, such as Eando Binder's "The Time-Cheaters" (1940) and Fritz Leiber's "Try and Change the Past" (1958), were inevitably less interesting than accounts of active security measures like the one featured in Anthony Boucher's "Barrier" (1942). Organisations protecting entire manifolds of alternative histories against accidental or malevolent disruption by time travellers sprang up in some profusion, usually imagined as secret police attempting to minimise the disruptions caused by their own navigations; when they become formally organised armies, as in Fritz Leiber's Change War series (launched 1958), the series begun in Keith Laumer's Worlds of the Imperium (1962), Avram Davidson's Masters of the Maze (1965), Barrington J. Bayley's The Fall of Chronopolis (1974), John Barnes' Finity (1999), and Neal Asher's Cowl (2004), the conflicts in which they are engaged inevitably become eternal, individual historical sequences becoming islands of apparent stability temporarily suspended in infinite chaos.

Notable examples of time police series include the one launched by Sam Merwin's House of Many Worlds (1951), Poul *Anderson's Time Patrol series (launched 1955), H. Beam Piper's series launched with "Time Crime" (1955), and the stories collected in John Brunner's Times Without Number (1962). Variants in which agents strive to protect a unique historical sequence from perversion, as in Isaac Asimov's The End of Eternity (1955) or Diana Wynne Jones' A Tale of Time City (1987), are more amenable to closure, but cultivate a curiously exaggerated claustrophobia in consequence. Time-travelling vigilantes such as Doctor Who (launched 1963)—who became one of BBC TV's most cherished institutions, along with his iconic TARDIS—inevitably fall prey to delusions of grandeur as they become the only truly stable point in a universal history whose form increasingly reflects the effects of their interference.

Once the brief 1950s heyday of time police stories had passed, it was commonly accepted by many speculative users of time machines that multiversal chaos was the inevitable ultimate consequence of the premise, and that time travellers would simply have to become accustomed to that existential plight—a conclusion blithely accepted in such works as Robert

Silverberg's Up the Line (1969), Keith Laumer's "The Timesweepers" (1969; exp. as Dinosaur Beach), Spider Robinson's Callahan's Crosstime Saloon (1977), and John Crowley's Great Work of Time (1989; book, 1991). Fiction outside the genre remained resistant to such chaotic extrapolations for some time, but eventually began to exploit their potential in such works as Audrey Niffenegger's The Time Traveler's Wife (2003).

Certain periods of the past inevitably attract more time travellers than others. The *dinosaurs were the biggest prehistoric draw, even for mere onlookers like the users of the time viewer in John Taine's Before the Dawn (1934). The crucifixion, similarly viewed at a distance in Jean Delaire's Around a Distant Star (1904), also attracted visitors in the flesh in Michael Moorcock's Behold the Man (1966; exp. book, 1969), Brian Earnshaw's Planet in the Eye of Time (1968), and John Kessel's Corrupting Dr. Nice (1997).

The practical and moral implications of these kinds of time tourism were thrown into sharp relief by such contes philosophiques as C. L. Moore's "Vintage Season" (1946; initially by-lined Lawrence O'Donnell), Ray Bradbury's "A Sound of Thunder" (1954), Garry Kilworth's "Let's Go to Golgotha" (1975), Connie Willis's "Fire Watch" (1982), Robert Silverberg's "Sailing to Byzantium" (1985) and "In Another Country" (1989)—the latter is a sequel to "Vintage Season"—Geoffrey A. Landis' "Ripples in the Dirac Sea" (1988), S. N. Dyer's "Nostalginauts" (1997), and Christopher Evans' "Posterity" (2002).

As magnets drawing time travellers, famous individuals were as effective as eventful eras. Manly Wade Wellman's "Giants from Eternity" (1939) used a time machine to assemble a "dream team" of great scientists, while the same author's Twice in Time (1940; book, 1957) allowed a timeslipped protagonist to attain historical celebrity by the back door. Other notable examples of person-targeted time trips include Abraham Lincoln in Wilson Tucker's The Lincoln Hunters (1957) and Ludwig van Beethoven in H. G. Stratmann's "Symphony in a Minor Key" (1996). Robert Silverberg's anthology Time Gate (1989) employed a *computer-simulated time machine to set up interesting meetings between famous people, including Socrates and Pizarro in the editor's "Enter a Soldier. Later: Enter Another" and Voltaire and Joan of Arc in Gregory Benford's "The Rose and the Scalpel".

The one person the average time traveller was most interested in meeting, of course, was an earlier version of himself—in spite of the fact that this was the kind of meeting most likely to generate paradoxes and psychological traumas. Notable examples of such meetings are featured in Osbert Sitwell's The Man

Who Lost Himself (1929), Ralph Milne Farley's "The Man Who Met Himself" (1935), and Eliot Crawshay-Williams' "The Man Who Met Himself" (1947), while the possibility was taken to extremes in Barry N. Malzberg's "We're Coming Through the Window" (1967; by-lined K. M. O'Donnell) and David Gerrold's *The Man Who Folded Himself* (1973). Such meetings are equally difficult to handle when they involve no physical duplication, merely allowing minds to slip back to an earlier phase of existence, as in P. D. Ouspensky's *Kinemadrama* (1915; trans. as *Strange Life of Ivan Osokin*), Louis Marlow's *The Devil in Crystal* (1944), J. T. McIntosh's "Play Back" (1954), Ken Grimwood's *Replay* (1986), and Thomas Berger's *Changing the Past* (1989).

Although few twentieth-century designers of time machines followed H. G. Wells' example in using the bicycle as a model, most remained relatively conservative in mirroring other kinds of vehicles, especially diving bells. Most were careful in steering around the moments separating departure and arrival, thus avoiding the problem of continued presence that Wells fudged; Ian Watson's "The Very Slow Time Machine" (1978) is a notable exception. Serious attempts to explain the physics underlying the construction of time machines were also rare, although Robert L. Forward's *Timemaster* (1992) is a notable exception and Clifford A. Pickover's *Time: A Traveler's Guide* (1998) adds a fictitious scenario to a popularisation of the relevant science.

TRANSPORT

The process of moving people and property from one place to another. The necessity of transporting goods and people provided one of the primal challenges of *technology, supplying the motivation for the domestication of various beasts of burden and the development of various mechanical devices, especially the wheel. Transportation is even more vital to settled societies than to nomadic ones because the development of *civilisation is dependent on the ability to transport food into cities on a large scale and to elaborate systems of trade.

The building of nations and empires is dependent on the ability to move and sustain armies, and their maintenance is dependent on systems of communication that require elaborate means of transporting information, including *writing. Technologies of transportation are, therefore, fundamental enabling factors not merely in *politics and *economics but also in education, philosophy, and science. The most elementary form of sporting activity is racing, which has always been a significant cultural expression of

the motivation to improve technologies of transportation, from the selective breeding of horses to the refinement of the internal combustion engine.

Given this context, it is not surprising that speculative engineers and scientific visionaries very often fixed their attention on the possibility of making new means of transportation—as is evident in the drawings of *Leonardo da Vinci and such compendia of imaginary technologies as John Wilkins' *Mathematicall Magick* (1648), in the continual attempts to manufacture *submarines and *aeronautical devices that eventually gave birth to the heroic era of *engineering, and modern speculative fiction's romance with the idea of *space travel.

The literary reflection of transportation technology and its evolution is less vague than the reflection of many other aspects of technology, primarily because of the importance of journeys as narrative devices. There is a sense in which any story can be likened to a journey—just as life itself can be considered as one—but very many stories are formulated as journeys in a more literal sense. The fact that such journeys are often used merely as facilitating devices for moving protagonists from one place of temporary residence to another ensured that greater pressure was put on fictional means of transportation than actual ones to maximise speed and convenience.

Actual means of transportation such as horses and ships play even more important roles in fiction than in life; fictional examples are very often said to be the finest imaginable examples of their various kinds. It was in the development of imaginary means of transportation—including such airborne devices as flying horses, magic carpets, obliging djinn, and generous whirlwinds and such seagoing artefacts as giant fish, irresistible currents, and directional storm winds—that the early literary imagination was tempted to its most adventurous extremes. Tales of space travel formed a significant subgenre of imaginative fiction long before it was incorporated into speculative fiction, and the rapid nineteenth-century growth of speculative fiction was largely inspired and greatly encouraged by the application of steam power to the business of locomotion.

Given the heavy emphasis on their utility as facilitating devices, it is not surprising that the great majority of hypothetical technologies of transportation featured in fiction are arbitrary improvisations, scant attention being paid to issues of rational *plausibility. The ever-readiness of writers to employ admittedly impossible devices did not, however, prevent new advances in actual technology being adopted into imaginative literature with considerable alacrity.

The origins of generic speculative fiction are closely connected with the actual development of the steam locomotive, which made a far greater impact on the popular imagination than any other kind of steam engine when it was developed as a means of public transportation. The opening of the Stockton-to-Darlington railway in 1825 began a railway revolution that extended throughout Europe and across the burgeoning frontier of the United States in the following half-century. George Stephenson's *Rocket*, revealed to the public with much fanfare in 1829, became one of the key icons of the new era.

The advent of the railways in Britain is very evident in the Victorian novel, and the role played by the railroad in making the West accessible became a key feature of popular fiction in the United States. Nicholas Daly, in *Literature, Technology and Modernity, 1860–1900* (2004), argues that it also had a crucial influence on the development of popular theatre, where the "railway rescue" became a staple of stage melodrama, exemplified by Augustin Daly's New York production *Under the Gaslight* and Don Boucicault's London production *After Dark* (both 1868). (The motif was inherited and further enhanced by the cinema, where tying potential victims to railroad tracks became a cliché.) Nicholas Daly suggests that the pace and pitch of theatrical melodrama and the "sensation novel" can be seen as an echo of the speed and excitement of railway travel. William Gilpin's fictitious account of *The Cosmopolitan Railway* (1890) anticipated great economic and personal benefits flowing from the globalisation of the railway system.

The first distinct genre of speculative fiction, whose paradigm examples were provided by Jules *Verne, was described by its founder as a series of *voyages extraordinaires*. Even that description might be deemed derivative of Charles Garnier's thirty-six-volume anthology of *Voyages imaginaires, songes, visions, et romans cabalistiques* (1787–1789), which had gathered a complex set of Utopian satires and romances, Robinsonades, and visionary fantasies into a single proto-genre. The considerable inspiration that Jules Verne took from hot air balloons was echoed, perhaps a trifle bathetically, in the similar inspiration that H. G. Wells took from the bicycle; *The Wheels of Chance* (1895) is just as fascinated by the socially transformative possibilities of technology, in its own humble fashion, as *The Time Machine*, published in the same year. Nor was Wells the only speculative writer to take such inspiration; Maurice Leblanc's *Voici des ailes!* (1898) appeared with a striking and entirely appropriate cover illustration of a bicycle equipped with symbolic wings.

The significance of transportation in shaping and characterising cultures was explicitly recognised by such groundbreaking futuristic fantasies as the anonymous *The Reign of George VI, 1900–1925* (1763) and

Félix Bodin's *Le roman de l'avenir* (1834), both of which cultivate a "futuristic" ambience by means of the imagery of future transportation: a canal network in the former instance, aerial transport in the latter. This strategy was carried forward by many other futuristic writers, the same representative technique recurring in the early pulp science fiction magazines and in Fritz Lang's film *Metropolis* (1926). Magazines devoted to the popularisation of technology always made lavish use of cover imagery featuring futuristic vehicles. When a school of "futurist" art developed in the early twentieth century its central theme was *speed*—an ideative association sufficiently powerful at the end of the twentieth century to establish the running shoe as an iconic fashion accessory among the young.

Most speculative transport systems are sufficiently important to warrant separate entries in this book—including such fanciful extreme examples as *matter transmission—but the residue includes a significant subset of stories about tunnels. The Channel tunnel connecting England to France was occasionally featured in late nineteenth-century fiction—sometimes serving as a means of invasion, as in James Peddie's *The Capture of London* (1887)—but transatlantic tunnels are more dramatic, as featured in Bernhard Kellermann's *Der Tunnel* (1913; trans. as *The Tunnel*), Ray Nelson's "Turn Off the Sky" (1963), and Harry Harrison's *Tunnel Through the Deeps* (1972; aka *A Transatlantic Tunnel, Hurrah!*). A high-speed tunnel for transcontinental trains is stricken by disaster in Thomas N. Scortia and Frank M. Robinson's *Blowout!* (1987).

Moving walkways also became a common feature of futuristic imagery, although they rarely took centre stage. The most notable exception, Robert A. Heinlein's "The Roads Must Roll" (1940) describes an industrial dispute focused on the system's maintenance. A similar narrative device is employed in one of the most notable accounts of "maglev" (magnetic levitation) transportation, Dean Ing's *The Big Lifters* (1988); variants of the notion had earlier been featured in Stephen Nemeth and William Walling's "Earth. Air, Fire and Water" (1974) and P. M. Fergusson's "The Year the Indy Died" (1986).

Sailing vessels adapted for use on solid surfaces are also extensively featured, becoming highly significant in imaginary locales that are inhospitable to alternatives, such as the glaciated expanses of Michael Moorcock's *The Ice Schooner* (1969) and Alan Dean Foster's *Icerigger* (1974), the exotic surfaces of David Lake's *Walkers on the Sky* (1976) and Bruce Sterling's *Involution Ocean* (1977) and the deserts of Brian Herbert's *Sudanna, Sudanna* (1985), Terry Dowling's series whose early items are collected in *Rynosseros*

(1990), and William Nicholson's series begun with *The Wind Singer* (2000). The notion that space travel might be assisted by mechanical systems for elevating loads into orbit is extrapolated in Arthur C. Clarke's *The Fountains of Paradise* (1979) and Charles Sheffield's *The Web Between the Worlds* (1979).

The significance of mobility in modern civilisation, emphasised by descriptions of automobile-bound nomadic cultures, is more directly celebrated in images of mobile cities such as Christopher Priest's *The Inverted World* (1974), Drew Mendleson's *Pilgrimage* (1981), and Philip Reeve's *Mortal Engines* (2001). The essential romance of transportation is effectively preserved, in a classic vein, in accounts of extraterrestrial rail transport such as the Circum-Phobic Railway in John M. Ford's "The Wheels of Dream" (1980) and the Martian railroads in Ian McDonald's *Desolation Road* (1988) and Eric Vinicoff's "The Great Martian Railroad Race" (1988). A powerful compound beam of artificial laser light on an intercept path with Earth turns out to be the tracks of a transgalactic railway in Andrew J. Offutt and Richard Lyon's "Rails across the Galaxy" (1982).

TSIOLKOVSKY, KONSTANTIN (EDUARDOVICH) (1857–1935)

Russian scientist and writer. He was educated at home in Kaluga after becoming hard of hearing following a bout of scarlet fever, and subsequently worked in the town as a mathematics teacher until 1920. He was the first person to popularise the notion that *space travel would be possible using the principle of jet propulsion, publishing the results of research begun in 1878 in a monograph whose title translates as *Free Space* (1883), followed up by a paper on "How to Protect Fragile and Delicate Objects from Jolts and Shocks" (1891) and a then-definitive analysis of "The Probing of Space by Means of Jet Devices" (1903), which proposed the use of multi-stage liquid-fuelled *rockets.

Tsiolkovsky became a disciple of the futurist philosopher Nikolai Fyodorovich Fyodorov, a champion of radical life extension and the possibility of technological resurrection who believed that the colonisation of space was possible, and Fyodorov's optimism was built into Tsiolkovsky's own philosophy. Tsiolkovsky found a significant disciple of his own in Friedrich Zander, who published important works of his own on the theory of rocket travel and life support systems in 1908–1911. Tsiolkovsky, Zander, and Yuri Kondratyuk established a Soviet Society for Studies of Interplanetary Travel in 1924, when Tsiolkovsky obtained an appointment as a professor at a Military Air Academy. The Soviet government began sponsoring rocket tests in 1930, with Zander in charge of one of the programs.

Tsiolkovsky's fiction is all didactic, intended for the instruction and inspiration of children; it was reprinted when the Soviet space program got under way, along with exemplary nonfiction, in the showcase omnibus *Put'k zbezdam* (1963; trans. as *The Call of the Cosmos*), edited by V. Dutt. The items translated as "On the Moon" (1893) and "Dreams of Earth and Sky" (1895) are fictional exercises in the popularisation of science imitative of Camille *Flammarion. "On Vesta" (written 1896) is a more adventurously speculative account of a visit to the *asteroid, which turns out to be a watery world harbouring intelligent life.

The novel *Vne zemli* (written 1896–1920; trans. in *The Call of the Cosmos* as "Outside the Earth", having earlier appeared in a different translation as *Beyond the Planet Earth*) describes an epoch-making space journey and its Fyodorovian aftermath. Its account of the first stages in the *colonisation of the solar system entitles Tsiolkovsky to be retrospectively recognised as the originator of the myth of the *Space Age, although the original prospectus had been Fyodorov's. The story also imagines the inauguration of an international scientific fellowship whose anachronistically aggregated membership includes Isaac *Newton, Pierre Laplace, and Benjamin Franklin—all of whom are included in the crew of the pioneering space rocket.

Tsiolkovsky's contribution to space research was recognised by the placing of an obelisk over his grave, inscribed with a quotation that translates as "Man will not always stay on earth; the pursuit of light and space will lead him to penetrate the bounds of the atmosphere, timidly at first but in the end to conquer the whole of solar space". This illustrates the extent to which the Soviet version of the myth of the Space Age mirrored the American version.

U

UNCERTAINTY

In science, uncertainty may result from the inability to determine certain data, or from the inability to establish a crucial test to discriminate between rival theoretical explanations of existing data. A particular "uncertainty principle" relevant to quantum theory was formulated by Werner Heisenberg in 1927; it proposes that it is impossible simultaneously to determine the position and velocity of a subatomic particle.

Heisenberg's uncertainty principle is often illustrated by a thought experiment that imagines an observer attempting to recover such information, only able to do so by observing the interaction of the particle with others; any interaction sufficient to determine one of the properties would inevitably alter the other. The thought experiment seems to imply that the difficulty is a practical one, and that the uncertainty lies in the experimenter's means of discovery rather than objective reality, but that conclusion assumes a materialist philosophy. Heisenberg argued that the values of position and velocity could not be considered definite in themselves, but could only be represented as probability distributions. Niels Bohr, who supported Heisenberg's interpretation, preferred the stronger term "indeterminacy principle."

Another famous thought experiment that attempts to illustrate indeterminacy is Erwin Schrödinger's hypothesis of a cat sealed in a box, in the sights of a lethal weapon whose triggering depends on an uncertain subatomic event. Schrödinger preferred an idealist interpretation, which assumes that matter is the possibility of perception, arguing that the cat must be reckoned neither dead nor alive until the box is opened to observation, at which point the contending probabilities are finally "collapsed" into one reality or the other. Although materialist physicists like Albert *Einstein persisted in the conviction that the problem was merely one of measurement, others were content to accept that reality is intrinsically uncertain at "the quantum level"; this became known as the "Copenhagen interpretation" after a conference in that city at which Heisenberg, Schrödinger, and Bohr all argued for it. Indeterminacy/uncertainty vanishes with respect to larger objects—even whole atoms—because positional uncertainty is inversely proportional to mass.

The application of the uncertainty principle to energy and time has some peculiar consequences, allowing pairs of complementary particles, such as an electron and a positron, to materialise spontaneously, and permitting *black holes to "evaporate" in spite of the fact that nothing material can escape their event horizons. One significant extrapolation of the Copenhagen interpretation of uncertainty is Hugh Everett and John Wheeler's "many worlds" interpretation, which suggests that every time a probabilistic relationship collapses into certainty *both* potential collapse states are actually realised in different universes: an extreme variant of the hypothesis that *alternative histories might be held in *parallel worlds. The Everett-Wheeler hypothesis is ingeniously dramatised in such speculative fictions as Larry Niven's "All the Myriad Ways" (1968), John Gribbin's "Doomsday Device" (1985), Graham Dunstan Martin's *Time-Slip* (1986), Robert Charles Wilson's "Divided by

Infinity" (1998), Alastair Reynolds' "Everlasting" (2004), and Paul Meiko's "Ten Sigmas" (2004).

Early attempts to co-opt the notion of Heisenbergian uncertainty into pulp science fiction—John W. Campbell Jr.'s "Uncertainty" (1936; book as *The Ultimate Weapon*) is the most valiant—were not conspicuously successful, and the great majority of modern literary uses construe the term in a more general and symbolic sense, but notable attempts to extrapolate tangible consequences of the notion include Brian W. Aldiss' *Report on Probability A* (1968), Michel Jeury's *Le temps incertain* (1973; trans. as *Chronolysis*), Robert Anton Wilson's Schrödinger's Cat trilogy (1979–1981), Rudy Rucker's "Schrödinger's Cat" (1981), Greg Bear's "Schrödinger's Plague" (1982), Greg Egan's *Quarantine* (1992) and "Singleton" (2002), Liz Williams' "Quantum Anthropology" (2002), Gardner R. Dozois' "The Hanging Curve" (2002), Alex Irvine's "Agent Provocateur" (2002), and Eugene Mirabelli's "The Woman in Schrödinger's Wave Equation" (2005).

Heisenberg's principle can be broadened by analogy to refer to other situations in which the act of observation affects the phenomenon under observation in such a way as to prevent the desired information being ascertainable. Such situations are widespread in certain areas of biological and human science, a popular example being that of the naturalist wishing to observe the behaviour of nocturnal animals, who takes along a powerful torch in order that he can do so. This kind of uncertainty is magnified whenever a subject's awareness of being observed provokes behavioural modification, as invariably happens whenever humans are aware that they are being observed by their neighbours, let alone by scientists. A "feedback effect" corollary to the prediction-frustrating Oedipus effect occurs whenever awareness of a scientific theory leads to changes in the behaviour that the theory is supposed to explain, as often happens in *economic accounts of the logic of the marketplace.

Heisenbergian uncertainty has been construed by some onlookers as a legitimation of certain kinds of mysticism, as in Fritjof Capra's *The Tao of Physics* (1975), and by such speculators as Alfred Lotka, Evan Walker, and Roger Penrose as a margin in which such frustrating aspects of the mind/body relationship as the problems of consciousness and free will might somehow be settled. Thus far, however, that kind of intellectual exercise has produced more questions than answers—as reflected in such *contes philosophiques* as Frederik Pohl's "Redemption in the Quantum Realm" (1994), in which the Holy Church of Quantum Redemption attempts to figure out why wave functions don't collapse if God is an observer,

and Edd Vick's "First Principles" (2003)—in which Heisenberg is required to assist in the negotiation of the consequences his idea has wrought.

URANUS

The seventh planet in the solar system, discovered by William Herschel in 1781, who initially took it for a comet. It had already been observed by John Flamsteed and included on one of his star maps, but Flamsteed had taken it for a star; it was not until Herschel measured the object's motion more accurately that he was able to determine its true nature; he also identified two satellites, Titania and Oberon.

Uranus was the first new planet to be added to the complement known to the ancients, although talk of "the seven planets" had earlier been commonplace because the Sun and Moon were routinely counted in that company by *Aristotelian cosmologists, while the Earth was not. The discovery was celebrated in the pseudonymous political satire, *A Journey Lately Performed Through the Air, in an Aerostatic Globe, Commonly Called an Air Balloon, from this Terraqueous Globe to the Newly Discovered Planet, Georgium Sidus* (1784; by-lined "Monsieur Vivenair"). Uranus was, however, omitted from most nineteenth-century cosmic voyages of exploration.

Uranus' diameter is less than half Saturn's, but it still qualifies as a gas giant, although some theorists have suggested that it might have a solid silicate core covered by a deep liquid layer. Its axial rotation is highly eccentric, that axis being almost parallel to the plane of the ecliptic. Two further satellites, Umbriel and Ariel, were discovered by William Lassell in 1851 and a fifth, Miranda, by G. W. Kuiper in 1948. Thirteen more were added to the list by Voyager 2 in 1986 and two more by the Hubble Space Telescope.

The Shakespearean theme of the names allocated to the satellites was initially supplied by John Herschel, but the astronomers naming the satellites discovered by Voyager diverted from the scheme in order to insert some names taken from Alexander Pope's "The Rape of the Lock" (1712). In 1977, astronomers observing the occultation of a star by Uranus found observational anomalies, suggesting the existence of a ring system like Saturn's; the observation was confirmed by other observers before Voyager 2 transmitted photographs of the rings.

Uranus' remote location ensured that it was rarely featured in speculative fiction, although Stanley Weinbaum's "The Planet of Doubt" (1935) equipped it with an ecosphere broadly similar to those he fitted to other planets and satellites and it is also featured in R. R. Winterbotham's "Clouds over Uranus" (1937) and Raymond Z. Gallun's "The Long Winter" (1940). Ariel had earlier been featured in J. Harvey Haggard's "Evolution Satellite" (1933–1934), and the cult featured in Neil R. Jones' Durna Rangue series (launched 1936) hid on another Uranian satellite before returning to conquer Earth. The planet made a modest science-fictional comeback at the end of the century in such stories as Charles Sheffield's "Dies Irae" (1985), Geoffrey A. Landis' "Into the Blue Abyss" (1999), and G. David Nordley's "Into the Miranda Rift" (1993) and "Mustardseed" (1999).

UTOPIA

A term improvised from Greek for use by Thomas More as the title of his 1516 description of a hypothetical society favourably contrasted with his own. The influence of More's book—which was first translated into English in 1551—was such that it became the titular head of a long tradition of such descriptions, which was retrospectively extrapolated back to Plato's *Republic* and other works inspired thereby, including Euhemeros' account of Pachaea. Although *Utopia* is a *satire and does not represent More's view of an "ideal state", the label was often construed as if it were derived from "eutopia" (good place) rather than "outopia" (no place). The latter is what More intended, and many modern scholars insist on construing it in that fashion, but the ambiguity lingers, especially in the usage that contrasts utopias with *dystopias.

It is also useful to contrast Utopian images of *politically ordered civilisation with Arcadian notions of a life of pastoral ease, as reflected in such folkloristic notions as the land of Cokaygne or the Isles of the Blessed, and with transcendental notions of an ideal state of being, such as Nirvana or Heaven. In the Western literary imagination, Arcadian imagery is sometimes overlain by or confused with the imagery of chivalric romance, but that tendency is less obvious in its eutopian extensions than it is in other kinds of nostalgic fantasy.

Within the literary tradition, a further distinction needs to be made between the two overlapping traditions of Utopian satire and Utopian romance, although most of the classic Utopias have elements of both. In Utopian satire the primary emphasis of the reader's experience is the biting criticism of the text's native society; the more essential function of the hypothetical society is to provide a standard for comparison that exposes the shortcomings of the world the writer and reader actually share. In Utopian romance the primary emphasis of the reader's experience is to obtain a taste, however brief, of a better world; the more essential function of the hypothetical society is to act as a lure or inspiration.

Frank Manuel argues in his exemplary anthology *Utopias and Utopian Thought* (1966) that a crucial shift in Utopian thought took place when writers changed from talking about a better place (eutopia) to talking about a better time (euchronia), under the influence of the idea of *progress. He argues—following the example of Abraham Maslow, the champion of "self-actualisation"—that an equally significant shift had already begun, as many twentieth-century images of ideal society entered a "eupsychian" mode, reemphasising the individual ability to discover an idiosyncratic *modus vivendi* within a liberal social framework, rather than fitting all the members of society into a single stereotyped pattern. Of the three modes, eutopia is most easily adaptable to the satirical function of Utopias and eupsychia to the romantic function—although dystopian fiction is even more suited to satire and Arcadian fiction to romance.

When the first of these shifts occurred, Utopias ceased to be constructions with which contemporary society could only be compared and became speculative statements about actual historical possibilities and probabilities. This was the point when the scientific imagination became fundamental to Utopian thinking, more because of the necessity of extrapolating from the present into the future than the widespread recognition of the role played by *technological advancement in facilitating social change, although the latter factor became more important as time went by. Scientific thinking also became significant in other ways, most significantly in the founding of a rich tradition of *eugenic eutopias and dystopias, whose fundamental assumption was that euchronia would be achieved if, and only if, the people unfit to live in it could be eliminated from consideration—an assumption previously made, and far more extravagantly practised, by Christians enthusiastic to evangelise pagans and persecute heretics.

An awareness of the advancement of scientific knowledge, and of the role that technology might play in transforming society for the better, first became evident within the Utopian tradition in the seventeenth century, most obviously in Francis Bacon's *New Atlantis* (1627) but also in Tommaso Campanella's *La Città del Sole; Dialogo Poetico* (written 1602; published 1623 as *Civitas Solis*; trans. as *The City of the Sun*), J. V. Andreae's *Republicae Christianopolitanae Descriptio* (1619; trans. as *Christianopolis*), and *The Discovery of a New World, Called the Blazing World* (1668) by Margaret Cavendish, the Duchess of Newcastle. The last named is a remarkable account of a society based on the principle of Enlightenment, which includes a digest of the duchess' *Observations upon Experimental Philosophy* (1666) in the form of a passage in which the empress of the Blazing World interrogates her various subjects—hybrids of animals and men symbolising different branches of emergent science—as to the sum of their discoveries—but the text then goes on to champion *occult science against empirical science, much as Campanella had done, reflecting the eutopian (or eupsychian) aspirations of occultism.

Heliogenes de l'Epy's *A Voyage into Tartary* (1689) features a society (Heliopolis) explicitly based on principle of Reason, although advanced technology is mostly relegated to a museum, and a similar tendency is seen in many eighteenth-century Utopias impressed by the arguments of Jean-Jacques *Rousseau. The emphasis shifted again, however, in Louis Sébastien Mercier's pioneering euchronian novel *L'an deux mille quatre cent quarante* (1771; trans. as *Memoirs of the Year 2500*), which presents an image of a Utopia that has evolved from present society by means of technical discovery as well as wise political action. Nicolas Restif de la Bretonne's *La découverte australe par un homme volant, ou le Dédale français* (1781) followed it with an elaborate description of a conventional eutopian state based on the principles of natural philosophy and scientific advancement.

Euchronian optimism was dealt a hard blow in 1798 by Robert Malthus' objections, on the grounds that the tendency of the human *population to increase geometrically would prevent the amelioration of poverty and misery by technologically enhanced production. Although Malthusian criticism did not deter technological euchronians such as John Adolphus Etzler, author of *The Paradise Within Reach of All Men* (1833) and *The New World, or Mechanical System* (1841) and Mary Griffith, author of *Three Hundred Years Hence* (1836, in *Camperdown*), it did assist in the deflection of eutopian arguments towards discussions of how to achieve more equitable distribution rather than more abundant production—an argument that became increasingly intense in the context of socialist political movements. In the latter part of the century, the situation was further confused when Arcadian ideas began to resound in such British eutopias and euchronias as Edward Bulwer-Lytton's *The Coming Race* (1870), Samuel Butler's *Erewhon* (1872), Richard Jefferies' *After London; or, Wild England* (1885), and W. H. Hudson's *A Crystal Age* (1887).

Edward Bellamy's best-selling *Looking Backward, 2000–1887* (1888) took future technological advancement for granted, accommodating many modest technical improvements within its background. The book stimulated a great deal of debate, inspiring a special

"Twentieth Century" issue of *The Overland Monthly* (June 1890) that was one of the earliest serious ventures in *futurology. *Looking Backward* provoked a great many imitations and replies in kind; those paying most attention to the technological aspects of Bellamy's euchronianism included Alvarado M. Fuller's *A.D. 2000* (1890), Arthur Bird's *Looking Forward: A Dream of the United States of the Americas in 1999* (1899), Paul Devinne's *The Day of Prosperity* (1902), and Herman Hine Brinsmade's *Utopia Achieved* (1912). Most of the dissenting voices objected to Bellamy's socialism on political grounds but Ignatius Donnelly's *Caesar's Column* (1890; initially by-lined Edmund Boisgilbert) employed a *Social Darwinist argument. William Morris' *News from Nowhere* (1890) reflected the resurgence of British Arcadianism in objecting to the prospect of humankind living in idleness while machines supplied the necessities of life.

Bellamy's success assisted the development of a school of technically sophisticated euchronias and eutopias, the latter often using extraterrestrial settings. The one that makes most use of the notion of technological progress, Chauncey Thomas' *The Crystal Button* (written 1878; published 1891) had been written some time before but only achieved publication in Bellamy's wake. The most detailed and emphatic account of science generating technology, thus facilitating social progress, was offered in John MacMillan Brown's *Limanora: The Island of Progress* (1903; by-lined Godfrey Sweven); Brown, a New Zealander, framed the work as a sequel to a wider-ranging satirical critique of eutopian ideals, *Riallaro: The Archipelago of Exiles* (1901).

Stephen Leacock's "The Man in Asbestos" (1920) satirised technological euchronias, but the accelerated pace of technological change associated with applications of *electricity made it impossible to doubt that the future would indeed see dramatic technological development, for good or ill. European writers had now begun to produce technological euchronias, the British examples heavily influenced by the examples provided by H. G. *Wells, including *A Modern Utopia* (1905) and *In the Days of the Comet* (1906). The German statesman Walter Rathenau produced key examples in *Von kommenden Dingen* (1917; trans. as *In Days to Come*) and *Der neue Gesellschaft* (1919; trans. as *The New Society*). Visions of future technological development contained in such euchronias as Wells' *Men like Gods* (1923) and *The Shape of Things to Come* (1933) and Charles Elton Blanchard M.D.'s *A New Day Dawns: A Brief History of the Altruistic Era* (1932) grew steadily more extravagant.

The advent of eupsychian scepticism is evident in Anatole France's *Sur la pierre blanche* (1905; trans. as

The White Stone), in which a citizen of a future that has attained social equality, peace, and plenty judges them insufficient to ensure happiness, that being a problem of a different, innately psychological, kind. E. M. Forster's "The Machine Stops" (1909) objected that technological euchronianism was essentially sterile, and would lead to the stagnation of the human mind. Alexandr Moszkowski's *The Isles of Wisdom* (1924) set out to demonstrate the absurdity of all eutopian schemes, given the essential perversity of human nature. Thomas More's design—which seemed Arcadian by now—was nostalgically reproduced in Oliver Onions' *The New Moon* (1918) and Katherine Burdekin's *The Rebel Passion* (1929), anticipating the spirit of R. A. Lafferty's *Past Master* (1968), in which More is reincarnated as an expert consultant to explain the malaise that makes people persist in their misery even in a world designed on euchronian principles.

Although pulp science fiction made a determinedly euchronian start with Hugo *Gernsback's ultratechnological romance *Ralph 124C 41+* (1911; book, 1925), the notion that gadgetry would be sufficient to ensure the good life was swiftly challenged by such sceptical works as Miles J. Breuer's "Paradise and Iron" (1930), Laurence Manning and Fletcher Pratt's "City of the Living Dead" (1930), and John W. Campbell Jr.'s "Twilight" (1934; by-lined Don A. Stuart), all of which were fearful of the cultural *decadence that might result from overdependence on mechanical production. The science fiction pulps accommodated both eutopian satires such as Stanton A. Coblentz's *The Sunken World* (1928; book, 1949) and eutopian romances such as Lilith Lorraine's "Into the 28th Century" (1930)—Lorraine's "The Celestial Visitor" (1935) even features an asteroid named Eutopia—but it was not only the demands of melodrama that kept such works in a tiny minority.

Like contemporary writers of scientific romance such as S. Fowler Wright and J. Leslie Mitchell, many science fiction writers feared that the unchallenging life would not be worth living, and that the eutopia of comforts might be a dispiriting dead end. Whereas writers of scientific romance generally preferred quasi-Arcadian solutions, however, science fiction writers mostly adopted the thesis that the vital challenge would be provided by the imperatives of the *Space Age. This thesis was elaborately spelled out by one of the few British recruits to science fiction who could have written scientific romance instead, had he so wished: Arthur C. *Clarke, whose most graphic didactic fantasy in this vein was his first, *Against the Fall of Night* (1948; rev. as *The City and the Stars*).

As dystopian anxiety and eupsychian scepticism made rapid headway in the twentieth century,

Utopian fiction became increasingly escapist; eutopian fiction made a comeback because of, rather than in spite of, the fact that the *geography of the world no longer had any ready accommodation for undiscovered societies, as eutopias became secret enclaves to which the fortunate few might conceivably make their escape, leaving their unworthy neighbours to stew in self-inflicted dystopian misery. This kind of fugitive impulse is strongly associated with neo-Arcadian dreams in such works as James Hilton's *Lost Horizon* (1933), Austin Tappan Wright's *Islandia* (1942), Robert Graves' *Seven Days in New Crete* (1949; aka *Watch the North Wind Rise*), Aldous Huxley's *Island* (1962), and Richard Brautigan's *In Watermelon Sugar* (1968), although Arcadianism was subsequently diverted into the kind of *ecological euchronianism that took its lead from Ernest Callenbach's *Ecotopia* (1975).

As eupsychian philosophy gained ground, Utopian designs became increasingly idiosyncratic. Writers like "Godfrey Sweven" and Moszkowski had already complained that very few twentieth-century persons could have been content to live in any of the classical Utopias, but it seems even harder to believe that anyone but their authors could seriously want to live in Robert A. Heinlein's *For Us the Living* (written 1939; published 2004), Chalmers Kearney's *Erone* (1943), or B. F. Skinner's *Walden Two* (1948). Herman Hesse's *Das Glasperlenspiel* (1943; trans. as *Magister Ludi* and *The Glass Bead Game*) wonders whether its eutopian society is fit even for its architect and guiding hand.

Science fiction writers committed to the experimental method often became interested in trying eutopias and euchronias out for size, as in Paul Capon's *Into the Tenth Millennium* (1956), Theodore Sturgeon's *Venus Plus X* (1960), and James Blish and Norman L. Knight's *A Torrent of Faces* (1967), but such authors usually ended up turning the thumbs down on their own creations. Robert Sheckley's "A Ticket to Tranai" (1955) is a satirical joke about a eutopia that is exceedingly difficult to reach, and which then turns out to have a single fatal flaw. Stanley Zuber's *The Golden Promise* (1956) also tantalises only to deceive.

The Soviet science fiction writer Ivan Yefremov was obliged to try much harder than his U.S. counterparts to reflect the eutopian ideals of his native political culture in *Tumannost' Andromedy* (1958; trans. as *Andromeda*), but his inability to sustain his own optimism was too evident in its sequel, *Chas Byka* (1968), which was quickly suppressed. The only eutopian model that was given any significant endorsement during the first fifty years of American genre science fiction was one based in the responsible use of *parapsychological powers—a further endorsement of the now-standard supposition that anyone intent on Utopian design must first design the Utopians, since humans were so obviously ill fitted for a life of order and harmony.

The most sustained attempt at serious euchronian design carried out within genre science fiction was Mack Reynolds' calculated revisitation of Edward Bellamy's political ideals in *Looking Backward from the Year 2000* (1973) and its sequels. Like Bellamy, Reynolds took technological advancement for granted, and his central assumption is that future socialism will become possible, necessary, and unavoidable within an "economy of abundance" generated by *nuclear fusion. Economic equality is possible in Reynolds' future because everyone can be rich enough to meet all their material desires, and the only reward that will be difficult to attain is the esteem of one's fellow human beings. Even so, after penning the Bellamyesque sequel, *Equality in the Year 2000* (1977), Reynolds fell prey to accumulating doubts in *Perchance to Dream* (1977) and *After Utopia* (1977), when the old anxieties about leisure-induced decadence crept back, insidiously but insistently. Like his predecessors, Reynolds had only one answer to offer, and that was the extraterrestrial diaspora; having established euchronia, it would be necessary to leave it behind.

It was in this climate of thought that Ursula K. Le Guin subtitled *The Dispossessed* (1974) "An Ambiguous Utopia". Taking the opposite tack to Reynolds, Le Guin proposes that socialism might only be possible in circumstances of extreme scarcity, where survival depends on close collaboration and no one could ever entertain the thought of striking out alone. Perhaps, the novel argues, it is only in a society in which everyone *has* to love one another that everyone can—and even then, alternatives cannot be entirely excluded. Le Guin's subtitle was countered by Samuel R. Delany's *Triton* (1976), described as "An Ambiguous Heterotopia" in honour of the eupsychian dream of a society in which everyone is free to make exactly what they want of themselves, however eccentric their tastes might be. Like Reynolds' future Boston, Delany's Triton is founded in an economic abundance that sets everyone free—but like Le Guin's Anarres, it is not isolated from neighbouring political systems that are very different in kind and intent, and thus cannot avoid the threat of warfare.

The notion that human individuals are so different, and so changeable, that only a heterogeneous society could possibly provide appropriate opportunities for all became an orthodoxy of sorts, reflected in such science-fictional euchronias as Mack Reynolds' *Commune 2000* (1974) and R. Faraday Nelson's *Then Beggars Could Ride* (1976), but even its champions lacked conviction. Reynolds' *The Towers of Utopia* (1975) and Larry Niven and Jerry Pournelle's *Oath of Fealty* (1981) attempt to find Utopian potential in "vertical cities" representing the ultimate in urban design, but such imagery seemed more comfortably consonant with the surreal dystopian satire of Robert Silverberg's *The World Inside* (1971) and J. G. Ballard's *High-Rise* (1975).

Images of extraterrestrial eutopia, such as those contained in Arthur C. Clarke's *Imperial Earth* (1975) and *The Songs of Distant Earth* (1986) and James P. Hogan's *Voyage from Yesteryear* (1982), sometimes gained conviction in distance, but usually paid a penalty in apparent relevance. Galactic culture did, however, provide the most significant arena for eutopian experimentation, as in such works as Jayge Carr's "Mustard Seed" (1981). Somtow Sucharitkul's "The Thirteenth Utopia" (1979; incorporated into *The Utopia Hunters*, 1984) casts the extraterrestrial eutopia as an eternally elusive Holy Grail, worth searching for even though it can never be found. Gardner Dozois and Michael Swanwick's "The City of God" (1996), on the other hand, reduces it to an archaeological relic, confined in a layer of dirt immediately below the one in which post-eutopian relics are similarly entombed.

Alongside these various trains of thought some traditional images proved remarkably persistent. Eugenic eutopias and euchronias continued to thrive in spite of the bad odour into which the term had fallen, especially in the many feminist versions that take it for granted that the only requirement for the establishment of an ideal society is the elimination of the male of the species. Feminist eutopias often tended to the Arcadian, feminist and ecotopian ideas sometimes being fused into a hybrid philosophy making much of Gaian *ecological mysticism—a marriage scathingly satirised in such works as James Tiptree Jr.'s "All This and Heaven Too" (1985), which contrasts the harmonious society of Ecologia-Bella with its evil neighbour Pluvio-Acida, and Michael Swanwick's "Girls and Boys Come Out to Lay" (2005).

Increasing interest in *genetic engineering in the last decades of the twentieth century opened new scope for the designing of more ingenious Utopians than those featured in Aldous Huxley's *Brave New World* (1932), but an energy-rich high-tech world in which alphas could thrive without betas, gammas, and deltas, such as Gregory Benford's Brotherworld in "As Big as the Ritz" (1986; exp. 1987) still seemed extremely discomfiting when subject to thought-experimental development. Eutopian optimism did survive until the end of the twentieth century, in such works as Yorick Blumenfeld's *2099: A Eutopia*

(1999), and progressed into the twenty-first century in such stories as John Kessel's "The Juniper Tree" (2000) and "Stories for Men" (2002) and Walter Jon Williams' "The Green Leopard Plague" (2003), but the tradition was conspicuously enfeebled.

The enthusiastic prophets of the technological *singularity and the consequent advent of limitless *posthuman opportunity conserved their enthusiasm as well as their optimism, although many also retained a deeply ingrained cynicism. The majority of readers must have assumed that the titles of John C. Wright's trilogy, *The Golden Age* (2002), *The Phoenix Exultant* (2003), and *The Golden Transcendence* (2004)—which celebrate the postsingularity emergence of the euchronian Golden Oecumene—had a darkly ironic component, and they would not have been misled by that assumption.

V

VENUS

The second planet from the Sun. The brightest object in the sky after the Sun and Moon, it is often prominent after dusk and before dawn, in the former instance being reckoned "the evening star" and in the latter "the morning star". It is named after the Roman goddess of love, thus loading it with a metaphorical significance even greater than—and starkly contrasted with—that of *Mars. The identification of Venus with femininity has been perpetuated by mapmakers naming features identified by radar, all of which have been given female names except for the Maxwell Mountains, which had been named after James Clerk Maxwell before the decision was taken.

Although the implications of its Classical name were ignored by Emanuel *Swedenborg, whose description of it in the *Arcana Coelestia* (1749–1756) is mundane and dismissive, Achille Eyraud's *Voyage à Venus* (1865) contrasts it very favourably with Earth, and the visitor therefrom who featured in W. D. Lach-Szyrma's *A Voice from Another World* (1874) is effectively an angel. Lach-Szyrma's *Aleriel* (1886) has no hesitation in declaring Venus to be "The Queen of Beauty, or The Planet of Love", and lingers longer over its contemplation than any other world. It is similarly paradisal in James W. Barlow's *History of a Race of Immortals Without a God* (1891; by-lined Antares Skorpios; aka *The Immortals' Great Quest*), John Munro's *A Trip to Venus* (1897), and George Griffith's *A Honeymoon in Space* (1901), in which its quasi-angelic inhabitants communicate by means of music.

Because Venus presented a featureless face to early astronomers, it became something of a mystery planet; the ready inference that it was completely shrouded in cloud gave rise to the corollary hypothesis that it must be warm and wet, so the most popular images offered in the late nineteenth and early twentieth centuries were a planet of vast oceans—sometimes a "panthalassa" with no land at all—or of primeval swamps and jungles. The latter image was popularised by Svante Arrhenius in *Stjärnornas Öden* (1915; trans. as *The Destinies of the Stars*) and was incorporated into such interplanetary fantasies as Gustavus W. Pope's *Romances of the Planets, no 2: Journey to Venus* (1895) before becoming a staple of pulp science fiction imagery. The warm conditions produced gigantic vegetation, with appropriately massive insects, in Fred T. Jane's *To Venus in Five Seconds* (1897), Maurice Baring's "Venus" (1909), and Ludwig Anton's *Brücken über den Weltenraum* (1922; trans. as *Interplanetary Bridges*). In Garrett P. Serviss' *A Columbus of Space* (1911), it is imagined as a tide-locked world that keeps the same face perpetually turned towards the sun.

Two of the most enthusiastic imitators of Edgar Rice Burroughs' Martian series set their principal series of exotic romances on Venus. Ralph Milne Farley began his with *The Radio Man* (1924), while Otis Adalbert Kline began his with *The Planet of Peril* (1929). Burroughs launched his own Venerean series, perhaps by way of reprisal, with *Pirates of Venus* (1934). Homer Eon Flint's "The Queen of Life" (1919) also has Burroughsian aspects, but is more enterprising in its description of a *decadent anarchist native society. Images of Venus were much rarer in scientific romance, but tended to be equally romantic;

having been recommended as an appropriate home for humankind when Earth becomes uninhabitable in J. B. S. Haldane's "The Last Judgment" (1927), Venus is lovingly described in Olaf Stapledon's *Last and First Men* (1930), where the colonisers are adapted for life there as winged creatures inhabiting floating islands in a vast sea. The latter image was recapitulated in C. S. Lewis' *Perelandra* (1943; aka *Voyage to Venus*), where one such island serves as a new Garden of Eden.

The oceanic version of Venus was featured in Harl Vincent's "Venus Liberated" (1929) and Clifford D. Simak's "Rim of the Deep" (1940), but many stories in the science fiction pulps, including John W. Campbell's "Solarite" (1930), John Beynon Harris' "The Venus Adventure" (1932), and Stanton A. Coblentz's *The Blue Barbarians* (1931; book, 1958) and *The Planet of Youth* (1932; book, 1952), imagined Venus as fundamentally Earthlike but warmer and cloudier. More enterprising adventures in exobiology such as Clark Ashton Smith's "The Immeasurable Horror" (1931), P. Schuyler Miller's "Red Flame of Venus" (1932; aka "The Flame of Life"), C. L. Moore's "Black Thirst" (1934), Stanley G. Weinbaum's "The Lotus Eaters" (1935) and "Parasite Planet" (1935), Clifford D. Simak's "Hunger Death" (1938), and Lester del Rey's "The Luck of Ignatz" (1939) often retained a gaudy Burroughsian element, and this tradition was carried forward into the most garish of the action-adventure pulps, *Planet Stories*, when the Venus featured in Leigh Brackett's "Lorelei of the Red Mist" (1946; with Ray Bradbury), "The Moon That Vanished" (1948), and "The Enchantress of Venus" (1949) was much more colourfully exotic than her Barsoomian Mars.

John Campbell wrote an article in the January 1941 *Astounding* (by-lined Arthur McCann) observing that recent spectroscopic measurements of the quantity of carbon dioxide in the Venerean atmosphere implied that there could not be much plant life on the surface, but his writers continued to be more optimistic. Venus became a favourite target for *colonisation, although writers in Campbell's stable dutifully accepted that it would offer a sterner challenge than Mars—a challenge met with equally stern resolve in such stories as Robert A. Heinlein's "Logic of Empire" (1941), Clifford D. Simak's "Tools" (1942), and C. L. Moore's "There Shall Be Darkness" (1942), "Clash by Night" (1943; by-lined Laurence O'Donnell), and its sequel *Fury* (1947, with Henry Kuttner, by-lined O'Donnell; book 1950, by-lined Kuttner).

This kind of story overflowed from *Astounding* into other magazines and children's books in the 1950s, establishing a kind of orthodoxy in such works as

Ray Bradbury's "Death-by-Rain" (1950; aka "The Long Rain"), Robert Heinlein's *Between Planets* (1951), Philip Latham's *Five Against Venus* (1952), F. L. Wallace's "Tangle Hold" (1953), Bryan Berry's trilogy—by-lined Rolf Garner—comprising *Resurgent Dust* (1953), *The Immortals* (1953), and *The Indestructible* (1954), Isaac Asimov's *Lucky Starr and the Oceans of Venus* (1954; by-lined Paul French), Poul Anderson's "The Big Rain" (1954) and "Sister Planet" (1959), Chad Oliver's "Field Expedient" (1955), and Robert Sheckley's "Prospector's Special" (1959). In Frederik Pohl and C. M. Kornbluth's "Gravy Planet" (1952; book, 1953 as *The Space Merchants*), a blatantly uncolonisable Venus has to be sold to desperate would-be emigrants by high-pressure advertising, even though Earth itself is becoming intolerable.

Growing suspicions that Venus might be very much hotter and even more desolate than Campbell's 1941 editorial had supposed were finally confirmed in 1962, when the space probe Mariner 2 flew past the planet. In 1970, the Russian Venera 7 probe landed on the surface, and in 1975 Venera 9 sent back pictures of an arid landscape subject to an atmospheric pressure ninety times greater than that of Earth's surface, with mean temperatures in the region of 480°C. This information was further elaborated by data gathered by the Magellan probe in 1990–1993, but the fundamental picture remained the same. It was quickly realised that the difference between Venus and Earth has less to do with their relative distances from the Sun than with the effects of the *greenhouse effect that traps solar heat in the Venerean atmosphere.

Once the true nature of the Venerean surface was accepted, the interest of science fiction writers waned considerably. The realistic accounts pioneered by Larry Niven's "Becalmed in Hell" (1965) continued to be outnumbered, as well as outshone, by such calculatedly nostalgic farewells to Venerean Romanticism as Roger Zelazny's "The Doors of His Face, the Lamps of His Mouth" (1965) and Thomas M. Disch's "Come to Venus Melancholy" (1965). The strength of this feeling was reflected in Brian W. Aldiss and Harry Harrison's anthology *Farewell, Fantastic Venus!* (1968), and by anachronistic revisitations of earlier scenarios such as Frederik Pohl's *The Merchants' War* (1984)—although Pohl had offered a rather different image in "The Merchants of Venus" (1971)—and David Drake's *The Jungle* (1991), an "alternative sequel" to C. L. Moore's "Clash by Night", whose imagery had earlier been echoed in Drake's *Surface Action* (1990).

Hard science fiction writers who remained interested in the possibility of colonising Venus in the wake of the Venera probes—or exploiting its resources, as in

Brenda Pearce's "Crazy Oil" (1975)—had perforce to recognise that the conditions were challenging in the extreme, but some were still willing to rise to the challenge. Bob Buckley's "Chimera" (1976) and "World in the Clouds" (1980) started out on a path more conclusively beaten by Pamela Sargent's *Venus of Dreams* (1986) and *Venus of Shadows* (1988) and by Paul Preuss' novels—based on a scenario outlined by Arthur Clarke—*Maelstrom* (1988) and *Hide and Seek* (1989), G. David Nordley's "The Snows of Venus" (1991), and Ben Bova's *Venus* (2001). Raymond Harris' *Shadows of the White Sun* (1988) looks forward to a day when the difficult task of *terraforming the planet has been satisfactorily completed.

VERNE, JULES (GABRIEL) (1828–1905)

French writer. He was the son of a lawyer but rebelled against the expectation that he would follow in his father's footsteps by taking up residence in Paris and becoming a protégé of Alexandre Dumas. His attempts to build a career writing for the theatre in the 1850s did not make as much progress as he hoped, and he began to work more prolifically in prose. His most interesting early work was the allegorical "Maître Zacharius" (1854), in which a clockmaker is seduced by the Devil—a complaint about soulless technology that seems starkly at odds with his subsequent work. His career as a novelist might have developed differently had he been able to publish an exercise in futuristic fiction written in the early 1860s, but he was persuaded to set it aside; whether the text published as *Paris au XXe siècle* (1994; trans. as *Paris in the 20th Century*, 1996) is the work in question is open to doubt, but it is a fascinating development of the prospectus set out by Félix Bodin in *Le roman de l'avenir* (1834).

Verne's crucial breakthrough came when he offered a nonfiction piece on ballooning to P.-J. Hetzel, one of the great pioneers of children's literature—for whom Dumas had done a good deal of work before both of them had been exiled from Paris in the wake of Louis Napoléon's *coup d'état* of 1851. Hetzel persuaded Verne to use the material in a novel, which ultimately materialised as *Cinq semaines en ballon* (1863; trans. as *Five Weeks in a Balloon*). Verne followed it with *Voyage au centre de la terre* (1863; trans. as *Journey to the Centre of the Earth*), an account of an exploratory expedition in which scientific observations are continually made as a matter of course. The story conserves its realism conscientiously until it allows melodrama to overtake method in a series of brief but spectacular encounters in a subterranean world where species from remote prehistory still survive.

Hetzel founded *Le Magasin d'Éducation et de Récréation* in 1864. Wanting to ensure a steady supply of material, he offered Verne a commission to write three volumes (that is, about two hundred and fifty thousand words) a year for serialisation and subsequent book publication. Verne—not unnaturally—was glad to accept. Verne probably did not want Hetzel to market his works as children's books, and was certainly ambitious to make free use of his imagination, but he followed Hetzel's wishes in producing adventure stories of a relatively modest kind for the magazine, celebrating the transition from an age of heroic exploration to an age of tourism by means of exciting but plausible *voyages extraordinaires*, the first of which was *Les aventures du Capitaine Hatteras* (1864; trans. as *The English at the North Pole*).

In spite of this restraint placed upon him by his publisher, Verne continued to write speculative fiction, bringing an unprecedented verisimilitude to the description of the bolder exploratory ventures he constructed. The most important of these were *De la terre à la lune* (1865; trans. as *From the Earth to the Moon*), which described the building of a huge gun for the purpose of firing a manned missile into space, and the classic *Vingt mille lieues sous les mers* (1870: trans. as *Twenty Thousand Leagues Under the Sea*), which introduced the enigmatic Captain Nemo and his ultrasophisticated submarine *Nautilus*. It is possible that Verne made Nemo a shadowy figure in order to hide his plot away as an episode of secret history, but the character created a precedent at least as important as his vessel. In the same year Verne issued a sequel to his space gun story, *Autour de la lune* (1870; trans. as *Around the Moon*), in which the missile orbits the Moon before returning to Earth. The title novella of the collection *Une fantaisie du Docteur Ox* (1872; trans. as "Dr. Ox's Experiment") is a light-hearted story in which a project to bring gas lighting to a small town has unexpected side effects.

Alongside these adventure novels Verne wrote *Le désert de glace* (1866; trans. as *The Desert of Ice*), *Les enfants du Capitaine Grant* (1867–1868; trans. as *In Search of the Castaways*), the two novellas collected as *Une ville flottante suivi Les forceurs du blocus* (1871; trans. as *A Floating City* and *The Blockade Runners*), *Aventures de trois russes et de trois anglais dans l'Afrique australe* (1872; trans. as *The Adventures of Three Russians and Three Englishmen in South Africa* and *Measuring a Meridian*), and *Le pays des fourrures* (1873; trans. as *The Fur Country*), all of which were much more explicitly aimed at the audience of Hetzel's *Magasin*. He followed up with the two works that brought him to the peak of his celebrity, *Le tour du monde en quatre-vingt jours* (1873; trans. as *Around the World in Eighty Days*), and the languorous Robinsonade *L'île mystérieuse* (1874–1875; trans. as *The Mysterious Island*), in which Captain Nemo made a return appearance by popular demand.

All of these books were translated into English, but the translations were mostly execrable—especially the first translation of *Journey to the Centre of the Earth*, which was extensively and abominably rewritten. Much scientific exposition was cut out of the speculative novels, while the romances of exploration were often crudely carved up into multivolume works whose separate titles gave little indication of their connectedness Even so, the editions helped win Verne an international audience and reputation, and prompted numerous imitations, almost all of which were written for a juvenile audience.

Verne ventured into space again in *Hector Servadac* (1877), although its account of a fragment of the Earth's surface being dislodged by a cometary impact lacks plausibility in spite of the painstaking accounts of the scientific observations by which the characters analyse their predicament. He seems to have suffered a loss of imaginative impetus in the late 1870s, because Hetzel gave him a manuscript by a new writer named Paschal Grousset to rewrite for publication under his name. The book, which appeared as *Les cinq cents millions de la bégum* (1879: trans. as *The Begum's Fortune*), is an interesting account of two heirs to a vast fortune, who use the money to build two experimental cities based on their contrasted political beliefs: the republican Frankville and the totalitarian Stahlstadt. It is surprising that Hetzel allowed the latter name to stand, given that he published all his own fiction under the pseudonym P.-J. Stahl. Grousset supplied at least two other manuscripts for Verne to rewrite—one of which was credited as a collaboration—and went on to write many more books for Hetzel, including several speculative novels, under the pseudonym André Laurie.

Still struggling to recover his impetus, Verne reproduced the pattern of *Vingt mille lieues sous les mers* in *Robur le conquérant* (1886; trans. as *The Clipper of the Clouds*), substituting an airship for the submarine. He was more successfully innovative in *L'île à hélice* (1895; trans. as *Propellor Island*), in which the world's richest men construct a movable island as a tax-avoidance measure, and *Face au drapeau* (1896; trans. as *For the Flag*), a political fantasy about the development of an unprecedentedly powerful explosive. By this time he had renegotiated his contract with Hetzel so that he only had to deliver two volumes a year, although he seems to have kept well ahead of the required schedule. *Le village aérien* (1901; trans. as

The Village in the Tree Tops), is one of his most interesting speculative novels, offering a thoughtful account of the discovery of a new primate species. It clearly endorses evolutionism, even if it treats the issue diplomatically; although Verne had lapsed, his family was still devoutly religious.

The last significant speculative work that Verne completed himself was probably *Maître du monde* (1904; trans. as *Master of the World*), a lacklustre sequel to *Robur le conquérant*, but his career continued until and beyond his death with the active involvement of his son Michel (1861–1925), who published several works under his father's name that he had either rewritten from rough drafts or composed himself. These include *L'invasion de la mer* (1905; trans. as *The Invasion of the Sea*), about a project to flood the Sahara desert, *La chasse au météore* (1908; trans. as *The Chase of the Golden Meteor*), and an elegiac novella published in *Hier et demain* (1910; trans. as *Yesterday and Tomorrow*), "L'eternel Adam" (trans. as "The Eternal Adam"), in which a historian of the far future discovers a manuscript account of a twentieth-century world catastrophe.

Partly because of the brutal abridgement of his translated works and partly because of local marketing considerations, the vast majority of Vernian novels written in Britain and the United States are devoid of any significant speculative acumen or literary elegance. Most of those published in his native land also tended to be dully derivative, although the periodicals devoted to the genre, most notably the weekly *Journal des Voyages* (1885–1915) did provide a ready home for a good deal of adventurous and interesting speculative fiction. The widening influence of these derivatives in English boys' books and American dime novels laid vital groundwork for the subsequent development of scientific romance and pulp science fiction.

In 1958, I. O. Evans set out to prepare a comprehensive English edition of Verne's works, some of which he retranslated or translated for the first time. Many were split in two in order to be accommodated within a standardised format, however, and many of the new translations were abridged in much the same fashion as the nineteenth-century ones. The project was never completed. New translations of the most famous works made in the 1980s and 1990s helped redress the balance somewhat, but it was not until the early twenty-first century that a series of translations—many by Arthur B. Evans—issued by Wesleyan University Press began to bring some of the later works into English and to provide authoritative editions of some other texts.

Captain Nemo was borrowed by several contemporary writers, including Albert Robida, in the elaborate homage-cum-parody *Voyages très extraordinaires de Saturnin Farandoul dans les 5 ou 6 parties du monde et dans tous les pays connus et même inconnus de M. Jules Verne* (1879), issued as an illustrated part-work in more than a hundred parts. His modern replicas include those featured in Josef Nesvadba's "Posledni dobrodruzstvi kapitána Nemo" (1964; trans. as "Captain Nemo's Last Adventure") and Thomas F. Monteleone's *The Secret Sea* (1979). Philip José Farmer's *The Other Log of Phileas Fogg* (1973) is a sequel to *Around the World in Eighty Days* that follows Farmer's usual policy of reckless appropriation. The advent of *steampunk fiction prompted a new interest in Vernian fiction, the author being featured in David Brin and Gregory Benford's "Paris Conquers All" (1996), in which he responds pragmatically to the alien invasion featured in H. G. Wells' *The War of the Worlds*. Verne's cameo appearance in R. Garcia y Robertson's "Stuck Inside of Mobile" (2004) preceded a new wave sparked by the centenary of his death, which produced such projects as Mike Ashley and Eric Brown's *The Mammoth Book of New Jules Verne Adventures* (2005)—a volume of sequels and prequels—Eric Brown's novel *The Extraordinary Voyage of Jules Verne* (2005), and a series of adventures purporting to reveal Captain Nemo's true identity by Jean-Marc Ligny and Patrick Cothias, collectively entitled *Monsieur Nemo et l'éternité* and launched with *L'aiglon à deux têtes* and *La dame blanche* (both 2005).

VINGE, VERNOR (STEFFEN) (1944–)

U.S. mathematician and writer. He completed his education at the University of California, San Diego, where he obtained his M.A. in 1968 and his Ph.D. in 1971, having previously received his B.S. from Michigan State University, East Lansing. He stayed on at San Diego as an assistant professor of mathematics, and was promoted to associate professor in 1978. He began writing science fiction during his student days, publishing his first short story, "Apartness" (1965), in the British *New Worlds* before placing the more typical "Bookworm, Run!" (1966) in *Analog*.

Vinge's first novel, *Grimm's World* (1969; exp. as *Tatja Grimm's World*, 1987) was a colourfully elaborate planetary romance, but he stuck to shorter lengths for some time thereafter, including the novellas "Just Peace" (1971; with William Rupp) and "Original Sin" (1972); the work in question was collected in *True Names and Other Dangers* (1987) and *Threats ... and Other Promises* (1988), which were combined in *The Collected Stories of Vernor Vinge* (2001).

In 1972, Vinge married Joan Denison, who began publishing science fiction as Joan D. Vinge with "Tin Soldier" (1974). Although he published *The Witling* (1976)—another relatively lighthearted action-adventure story set on a colony world whose inhabitants have extraordinary *parapsychological, powers—before she published *The Outcasts of Heaven Belt* (1978), her career seemed set to overtake his when they divorced in 1979; she had won a Hugo Award in 1978 and won another with her epic science-fantasy *The Snow Queen* (1980). Shortly thereafter, however, Vinge published the novella "True Names" (1981; book, 1984), a groundbreaking work anticipating the central themes of cyberpunk fiction, including an elaborate account of a game played in virtual reality; it established Vinge as one of the leading writers of hard science fiction, and his work thereafter became increasingly ambitious.

The Peace War (1984) is an ingenious extrapolation of the aftermath of the development of a "stasis field", which can freeze time around an object for an indeterminate period. The plot concerns the difficult relationship between a female air force captain newly liberated from a period of stasis and her former lover, who has aged considerably while she has been in suspended animation, but the novel's strength lies in the intricately developed background, in which stasis technology is integrated into a general pattern of progress involving new developments in *biotechnology and information technology. In the sequel, *Marooned in Realtime* (1986), stasis fields are used for more ambitious ventures in exploratory *time travel, allowing the extrapolation of an elaborate future history whose crux—mentioned almost *en passant*—was a rapid acceleration of technological development described as a technological *singularity—a notion that Vinge had previously discussed in nonfiction. The two novels were reprinted in an omnibus edition as *Across Realtime* (1986), which was augmented in a 1991 edition with a further story, "The Ungoverned".

Vinge went on to develop the notion of a technological singularity much more elaborately in nonfiction, including a 1993 article presented at the NASA-sponsored VISION-21 symposium and reprinted in the *Whole Earth Review*. His next novel, *A Fire upon the Deep* (1992), was a sophisticated space opera based on the premise that the laws of physics vary markedly between the centre of the galaxy and intergalactic space. In the central Unthinking Depths the limitations on information transfer make thought processes impossible, while in the intergalactic Beyond—where the velocity of light is unlimited—thought is extremely rapid, permitting the development of superintelligence. The regions in between, where humans have evolved and have begun a gradual and halting expansion into the galaxy, constitute a Slowness whose transitional phases are gradual—and beyond the Beyond is the Transcendent, whose native Powers are godlike but transient.

This time, Vinge followed up his exploratory novel with a prequel, *A Deepness in the Sky* (1999), which fills in more of the historical background of humankind's belated discovery of cosmic variability, and the difficulty the species had in colonising local space. Like the earlier couplet, the two novels make ingenious use of time dilatation to lay out an expansive future history, this time on a galactic scale. He returned thereafter to the difficult task of analysing the progress of contemporary society towards the technological singularity, although the novella "Fair Times at Fairmont High" (2001) is relatively tentative in its anticipations of the development of computer networks, and is focused on sociological observations regarding the casual fashion in which new technologies are taken up by adolescents.

VIRTUAL REALITY

A term that became fashionable among computer engineers and science fiction writers in the 1980s, displacing "virtuality", which had been coined in 1980; an early use of the term can be found in Damien *Broderick's *The Judas Mandala* (1982), although its popularisation was largely due to Hans Moravec's *Mind Children: The Future of Robot and Human Intelligence* (1988). It describes artificially generated scenarios into which computer users can "project themselves", usually by using eyepieces that allow them to look into a synthesised "world" and gloves that allow them to control their movements therein and manipulate its native objects.

Virtual reality (VR) is, in effect, an extrapolation of telepresence, by which individuals using the same equipment can "project" themselves into a distant environment, cameras projecting an image into their eyepieces while their gloved hands operate mechanical manipulators. That idea had emerged as imaginative spin-off from the idea of *television in such stories as Robert A. Heinlein's "Waldo" (1942; by-lined Anson MacDonald), but had lain fallow for a long time while the technology caught up. Interest in it had been restimulated by such potential uses of telepresence as using robots to disarm bombs and carrying out delicate surgery with tiny instruments. The possible applications of telepresence in education also attracted a good deal of interest, reflected in such cautionary tales as Michael A. Burstein's "Teleabsence" (1995) and Rajnar Vajra's "Viewschool" (2004). Telepresence involving the use of android

bodies became a popular motif in late twentieth-century science fiction, as in Laura J. Mixon's *Proxies* (1998).

In essence, virtual reality simply substitutes a computer-synthesised environment for the one relayed by cameras in telepresence. In an article in the November 1990 *Analog* John Cramer described VR as the "technological twin of telepresence" and detailed early applications of the idea in the Human Interface Technology Laboratory at the University of Washington. The idea that VR might be developed as an entertainment medium soon became commonplace as a background item in near-future science fiction, and was foregrounded in such stories as Mick Farren's *The Feelies* (1990).

The notion of artificial sensory input had been explored in speculative fiction long before the first appearance of telepresence, in such stories as E. M. Forster's "The Machine Stops" (1909) and Laurence Manning and Fletcher Pratt's "City of the Living Dead" (1932), where information is fed directly into the nervous system for the brain to decode as sensory experience. Other significant anticipations of aspects of VR include William Hjortsberg's *Gray Matters* (1971).

A variant kind of "virtual reality" frequently featured in science fiction before the advent of personal computers involved various hypothetical means of synthesising dreams. Tailored dreams make the business of government easier in Clifford D. Simak's "Worlds Without End" (1956), and the marketing of dreams becomes commercially significant in such stories as Damon Knight's "Satisfaction" (1964; aka "Semper Fi"), William F. Temple's "The Legend of Ernie Deacon" (1965), and Lino Aldani's "Good Night, Sophie" (trans. 1973).

The rapid development of computer *games in the 1970s lent a sudden impetus to the notion that enhanced interactivity with gaming scenarios was not merely possible but inevitable and imminent. The kinds of active engagement implicit in games became common features of adventures in *cyberspace of the kinds promoted by such works as Vernor *Vinge's "True Names" (1981) and William *Gibson's *Neuromancer* (1984). The Manning-Pratt scenario is updated in the context of computer games in Rob Chilson's *Rounded with Sleep* (1990). Fictional extrapolations of these notions that bring VR and the possible extrapolation of its technologies into sharp focus include Ian Watson's *Whores of Babylon* (1988), Kim Newman's *The Night Mayor* (1989), Pete D. Manison's "The Golden Life" (1992), Jeff Noon's *Vurt* (1993), Maureen McHugh's "A Coney Island of the Mind" (1993), Alexander Besher's *RIM: A Novel of Virtual Reality* (1994) and *Mir* (1998),

David Brin's "Reality Check" (2000), Ian R. MacLeod's "Nevermore" (1998), and Dennis Danvers' *Circuit of Heaven* (1998) and *End of Days* (1999).

The development of multiuser computer role-playing games like Everquest (released 1999)—which reportedly had four hundred and fifty thousand participants by 2004—brought virtual reality close enough to realisation to make it a taken-for-granted feature of almost all early twenty-first-century science-fictional accounts of the near future. Tad Williams' Otherland series (1996–2001) is a straightforward extrapolation of such domains. More elaborate private worlds are designed, customised, and populated to suit the requirements of the rich in Robert Reed's "Like, Need, Deserve" (2003), while living in VR becomes a widely available lifestyle choice in Aaron A. Reed's "Shutdown/Retrovival" (2003). The "virtuals" abandon their obsolete kin, the "physicals", to inevitable extinction in Chris Beckett's "Piccadilly Circus" (2005).

WAR

Armed conflict between tribes, nations, or substantial factions therein, usually subject to formal declaration and eventual closure by peace treaty. The first significant analytical treatise on the subject was Sun Tzu's *The Art of War* (fifth century B.C.); its most famous modern counterpart is Carl von Clausewitz's *Vom Kriege* (1832; trans. as *On War*). War is usually regarded as an exceptional and undesirable state of affairs, and as a major affliction of human existence, but wars are so frequent that many ancient observers and some modern ones consider warfare to be the normal state of affairs and peace the anomaly.

The recording of warfare was a major factor in the development of *history—including the history contained in such scriptures as the Bible—and historians have always been preoccupied with its effects as a primary determinant of social change and celebrity. It is frequently seen in early written documents as a means to glory and political power; the *Iliad* describes and defines heroism in terms of conduct in battle—a notion carried forward into the tradition of epic poetry, although war is peripheral to the *Odyssey* and Virgil's *Aeneid*. It also tends to be peripheral in drama because of difficulties in staging; William Shakespeare's attempt to depict the battle of Agincourt in *Henry V* illustrates the problem well enough.

It is obvious to modern historians that the history of warfare and the history of technology are closely interrelated, and that most conflicts are settled by the superiority of technology, or superior skill in its use. This was not so obvious to ancient historians,

however, nor to the combatants in many battles. Ancient literature, reflecting this relative obliviousness, pays extravagant testimony to the powerful roles played by psychological *probability and *plausibility in mis-estimations of the likely outcomes of battles by generals and common soldiers alike. By the Renaissance, however, military commanders knew very well how useful technological superiority was, and often took care to recruit military engineers to their campaigns—although *Leonardo da Vinci is one of many such engineers to have felt direly underappreciated.

The representation of war in literature is heavily biased by its retrospective quality. Countless writers active between the era of Geoffrey Chaucer's knight and the American Revolution lived through wars, but few offered any substantial account of them. When litterateurs wrote about battles, they almost invariably did so from a distance, temporally as well as physically. Early literary works that take war as their subject matter, such as Barnaby Rich's *A Right Excellent and Pleasaunt Dialogue Betwene Mercury and an English Souldier* (1574), tend to discuss it in abstract rather than concrete terms. Hans Jacob Christoph von Grimmelshausen was one of the first to incorporate the legacy of his own experience—he was press-ganged into the Thirty Years War at the age of thirteen—into a major literary work, the satirical novel *Simplicissimus* (1669; trans. 1912), but he saw his duty as the demolition by mockery of the guiding myths of "aristocratic warfare"—duty, chivalry, and heroism—rather than description or analysis of the reality of warfare.

In theory, Grimmelshausen's complaints were out of date—Hugo Grotius' *De Jure Belli et Pacis* (1625; trans. as *The Rights of War and Peace*) had already laid foundations for the international regulation of the conduct of warfare on more businesslike lines, and Oliver Cromwell had demonstrated what a New Model Army might achieve against old-fashioned Cavaliers—but in practice war continued to be a game played by aristocrats with live cannon fodder for some time to come. Had Napoleon Bonaparte not inherited a French army from which the aristocrats had been rudely expelled, he might not have found it so easy to conquer Europe. Although it was the Russian winter of 1812 rather than Lord Nelson or the Duke of Wellington that eventually ruined Napoleon's ambitions, the English never stopped congratulating themselves for finishing him off and went into World War I with their aristocratic military hierarchy still in place, occasioning a famous aphorism regarding "lions led by donkeys".

The celebratory note struck by Thomas Campbell in such poems as "Hohenlinden" (1803) and "Ye Mariners of England" (1809) recurs in countless nineteenth-century works that exult in the expansion by force of the British Empire, which invariably give far more credit to British pluck than British arms and armour, even when they describe the mechanised slaughter of "savages" armed with nothing more than spears. The same curious bias is found in nineteenth-century American accounts of the conquest of the West, which gives the pioneer spirit far more credit for the achievement than grain alcohol, and rarely makes any reference to such ingenious devices as smallpox-infested blankets. It is, however, not surprising that fiction, in which psychological probability and plausibility play such a crucial role, should endorse and amplify the roles played in warfare by the same factors, at the expense of actual probability and actual plausibility.

The business and representation of war were irrevocably altered by the Crimean War of 1854–1856, which was the first to be extensively reported by newspapers. The highly critical running commentary provided by the London *Times*—which appointed Florence Nightingale as its only real hero and established the Charge of the Light Brigade as a key example of aristocratic imbecility—mobilised popular opinion so successfully that the public became intoxicated by its newly discovered right of censure and laid virtual siege to Parliament. The combatants in the Crimea included Leo Tolstoy, who preferred to look back to another conflict in compiling his massive pseudosociological study of *Voyna i mir* (1863–1869; trans. as *War and Peace*), and G. A. Henty, who became the archetypal author of jingoistic British

"boys' books" glorifying the use of extreme violence in imperialistic adventurism.

The American Civil War of 1861–1865 was reported even more conscientiously than the Crimean War, with the additional luxury of illustrative photography. That reportage provided the imaginative kindling for the genre of contemporary war poetry, although the vast majority of the works subsequently collected in such volumes as Herman Melville's *Battle-Pieces and Aspects of the War* (1866) and William Gilmore Simms' anthology *War Poetry of the South* (1867) were written by civilians reacting to the news rather than by combatants. Prose analysis of the war was belated, most of the classic works describing its course being written in the twentieth century. Stephen Crane's *The Red Badge of Courage* (1895), which represents battle as a uniquely challenging and self-revealing form of personal experience, has a Civil War setting, but its author was born in 1871. The technologies displayed during its course did have a significant effect on the course of speculative fiction, however.

Although the pseudonymous Herrmann Lang had been able to envisage radically new patterns of future combat in *The Air Battle* (1859), it was the technologies displayed and reported during the American Civil War—including ironclad ships, submarines, observation balloons, and the logistical employment of railways—together with the further examples provided by the Franco-Prussian War of 1870, that revealed the likely impact of new technologies on future warfare. The evident strength and firepower of the new German Army—whose observers had taken a keen interest in the armaments and tactics employed in the American Civil War—inspired an urgent campaign for the reform and rearmament of the British Army, whose case was cleverly dramatised by George Chesney's account of the hopeless attempt to repel a German invasion at *The Battle of Dorking* (1871). Future war stories continued to appear thereafter in some quantity, forming a distinct subgenre that became the first seed of *scientific romance—a process mapped by I. F. Clarke in *Voices Prophesying War 1763–1984* (1966; exp. 1992).

The realisation that new technologies would make wars much more destructive spread far and wide in the late nineteenth century. Chesney's second futuristic novella, *The New Ordeal* (1879), suggested that it ought to be possible to find alternatives to technologically sophisticated warfare, but hardly anyone believed it probable that trials by individual ordeal might be revived. Jean de Bloch argued at great length in *La guerre Future* (6 vols., 1898; abridged trans. as *Is War Now Impossible?*) that the deadliness of modern weaponry and the economic costs of modern warfare were sufficient to render future wars unthinkable, and hence impossible, but he too was in a tiny minority. The popularity of British future war fiction increased markedly in the 1890s. Such examples as W. Laird Clowes' *The Captain of the Mary Rose* (1892) and the account of *The Great War of 189–: A Forecast* (1893) compiled by P. H. Colomb and other military experts remained conscientiously moderate, but the latter, serialised in the periodical *Black & White,* encouraged the press magnate C. Arthur Pearson to go to an opposite extreme. He commissioned his employee George Griffith to produce an uninhibited account of a war fought with the aid of airships and submarines, using unprecedentedly powerful explosives and incendiary bombs.

Griffith's novel, serialised in *Pearson's Weekly* and reprinted as *The Angel of the Revolution* (1893), precipitated a boom in similar melodramas. Griffith's fellow Pearson employee Louis Tracy's key contribution was *The Final War* (1896), which helped seed the treacherous supposition that the next war might and ought to be a definitive settlement of world politics: a "war to end war" that would secure Anglo-Saxon global hegemony. Tracy's worldview was echoed in M. P. Shiel's early "yellow peril" novel—also written for Pearson—*The Yellow Danger* (1898), but Shiel repented of it in such later novels as the misleadingly retitled *The Dragon* (1913; rev. as *The Yellow Peril,* 1929). Pearson's rivals were initially outgunned, but William le Queux's account of *The Great War in England in 1897* (1894) prompted Alfred Harmsworth to hire him for a more determined counterattack; le Queux's *The Invasion of 1910* (1906) made a great impact when it was serialised in the newborn *Daily Mail.*

The flood of alarmist fiction continued until the eve of the actual Great War; its landmark works included Griffith's *Olga Romanoff* (1894) and the posthumous *The Lord of Labour* (1911), Fred T. Jane's *Blake of the Rattlesnake* (1895), H. G. Wells' "The Land Ironclads" (1903), *The War in the Air* (1908), and *The World Set Free* (1914), Erskine Childers' *The Riddle of the Sands* (1903), H. H. Munro's *When William Came* (1913), and Arthur Conan Doyle's "Danger!" (1914). Most of the writers involved branched out in the meantime into other kinds of scientific romance. The excesses of this kind of fiction were parodied by P. G. Wodehouse's first novel, *The Swoop!* (1909), and—retrospectively—by Michael Moorcock's *The Warlord of the Air* (1971) and *The Land Leviathan* (1974). Moorcock also edited a theme anthology of works from the period published in two volumes as *Before Armageddon* (1975) and *England Invaded* (1977). The craze was communicated to Germany—where Chesney's account of "The Battle of Dorking"

was also a best-seller—and to France, in such works as Wilhelm Lamszus' *Das Menschenschlachthaus* (1912; trans. 1913 as *The Human Slaughterhouse: Scenes from the War That Is to Come*) and Louis Gastine's *Les torpilleurs de l'air* (1913; trans. as *War in Space: A Grand Romance of Aircraft Warfare Between France and Germany*).

From their earliest inception, stories featuring future invasions displayed a paranoid anxiety that the invaders might already be lurking undetected in our midst; William le Queux was an indefatigable propagator of the notion that a "fifth column" of German agents was already in Britain, preparing to play their part in open conflict; such notions allowed le Queux to become the great pioneer of the spy story subgenre of thriller fiction. H. G. Wells' *The War of the Worlds* (1898) can also be seen as a logical extension of the nineteenth-century future war story, as was Robert William Cole's story of colonial war against Sirian aliens in *The Struggle for Empire* (1900).

Future war fiction spread to the United States, in such novels as Samuel Barton's *The Battle of the Swash and the Capture of Canada* (1888) and Frank R. Stockton's *The Great War Syndicate* (1889), but its context was very different. The United States had little fear of invasion, and the anxieties it did have concerned Asiatic invasions like those featured on a piecemeal basis in Lorelle's *The Battle of the Wabash* (1880) and more violently in Marsden Manson's *The Yellow Peril in Action* (1907), Parabellum's *Banzai!* (1909), Johnston McCulley's "When the World Stood Still" (1909), and Thomas Dixon's *The Fall of a Nation* (1916). Such fears of interracial conflict were also reflected in such accounts of future civil war as King Wallace's *The Next War* (1892). The body counts featured in such accounts of international conflict as Stanley Waterloo's *Armageddon* (1898) and James Barnes' *The Unpardonable War* (1904) were, however, conspicuously low by comparison with British works.

It was partly because the Great War of 1914–1918 was the first to have been loudly and lavishly advertised in advance that writers responded to its outbreak with such avidity; the poet laureate, William Watson, published sixteen war poems in the first three weeks. A bibliography compiled by Catherine Reilly lists 2,225 British war poets, 417 of whom were on active service; German writers reportedly produced more than a million poems in the first six months of hostilities. Novelists were, of necessity, slower off the mark, but the first classic account of trench warfare, Henri Barbusse's *Le feu* (trans. as *Under Fire*), appeared in 1916. The Great War was the first in which litterateurs were consulted as to how enemy propaganda might be countered. Within weeks of the outbreak, the British government had assembled a team that included Thomas Hardy, Arnold Bennett, H. G. Wells, G. K. Chesterton, John Galsworthy, Arthur Conan Doyle, and J. M. Barrie. Initially, war poetry was intended to boost morale, and the growing tide of antiwar sentiment was temporarily stemmed by censorship, but Siegfried Sassoon's public appeal for the war to be ended in 1917 proved a key inspiration to many writers, including Robert Graves and Wilfred Owen.

The impact that new technology would make on the fighting of the Great War had been anticipated, but not understood. When the experience of hi-tech warfare and such side effects as "battle neurosis" had been digested, the response to its horrors was extreme. The war left behind an exceedingly bitter legacy among the survivors on both sides, many of whom felt that their dead comrades and relatives had been betrayed by politicians and generals who had botched its termination as badly as its strategy. That acute sense of betrayal became both the cause and context of its sequel, World War II. The United States' reluctance to get involved in the Great War is reflected in the American literary response, whose most notable early produce came from members of the Ambulance Corps like Ernest Hemingway, John Dos Passos, and E. E. Cummings. Cummings' *The Enormous Room* (1922) was a study of valiant individual struggle against insane but relentless authority—an attitude subsequently echoed in such acrid black comedies as Joseph Heller's *Catch-22* (1961), Kurt Vonnegut's *Slaughterhouse-5* (1969), and Thomas Pynchon's *Gravity's Rainbow* (1973).

World War I was reflected in a different fashion in action-orientated pulp fiction, especially in the subgenre of *aeronautical adventures, but the historical sector of that subgenre was supplemented by anticipations of future war that were considerably darker. The pulps also played host to future war secret agent fiction and political fantasies such as Fred MacIsaac's "World Brigands" (1928), much of which continued in the "yellow peril" vein of earlier U.S. future war fiction, including most of the adventures of *Operator-5* (1934–1939).

Accounts of alien invasion antedated the advent of specialist science fiction pulps, notable examples including J. Schlossel's "Invaders from Outside" (1925), Nictzin Dyalhis' "When the Green Star Waned" (1925), and Edgar Rice Burroughs' *The Moon Maid* (1926), but the specialist pulps wasted no time in catching up. They imported yellow peril fiction in Philip Francis Nowlan's first Buck Rogers story, "Armageddon 2415 A.D." (1929) and soon standardised spectacular genocide as a standard response to alien contact in such stories as Edmond Hamilton's

"The Other Side of the Moon" (1929). Wars were waged across time as well as space once Jack Williamson's *The Legion of Time* (1938; book, 1952) had set a precedent. The translations from the German encouraged by Hugo Gernsback did, however, include Carl Spohr's bitter account of "The Final War" (1932)—a futuristic transfiguration of Erich Maria Remarque's *Im Westen nichts Neues* (1929; trans. as *All Quiet on the Western Front*)—and such antiwar stories as Miles J. Breuer's "The Gostaks and the Doshes" (1930) and Nathan Schachner's "World Gone Mad" (1935) helped preserve a semblance of balance. Murray Leinster's "Tanks" (1930), which described a war fought by tanks and aircraft in 1932, introduced a more realistic species of future war fiction.

Outside the pulp magazines future war stories were relatively sparse in the United States, but anxieties about race war were earnestly carried forward in Hector C. Bywater's *The Great Pacific War* (1925) and Floyd Gibbons' *The Red Napoleon* (1929). Again, the contrast with European future war stories produced between the two world wars is extreme. Like its predecessor, World War II was widely anticipated in Europe long before the outbreak of its prelude, the Spanish Civil War. British future war fiction of the 1930s was frankly apocalyptic, insisting that airfleets armed with poison gas, high explosives, and incendiaries could obliterate civilisation. Such representations may have encouraged Adolf Hitler's mistaken belief that *blitzkrieg* tactics would rapidly demolish British morale. Notable examples of apocalyptic future war stories include Edward Shanks' *The People of the Ruins* (1920), Cicely Hamilton's *Theodore Savage* (1922; rev. as *Lest Ye Die*), Shaw Desmond's *Ragnarok* (1926), Neil Bell's *The Gas War of 1940* (1931, by-lined Miles; aka *Valiant Clay*), John Gloag's *Tomorrow's Yesterday* (1932), Frank McIlraith and Roy Connolly's *Invasion from the Air* (1934), S. Fowler Wright's trilogy *Prelude in Prague* (1935), *Four Days War* (1936), and *Megiddo's Ridge* (1937), Joseph O'Neill's *Day of Wrath* (1936), and P. G. Chadwick's *The Death Guard* (1939).

British writers of popular fiction produced a handful of alien invasion stories, including G. McLeod Winsor's *Station X* (1919) and Bohun Lynch's *Menace from the Moon* (1925)—Olaf Stapledon's *Last and First Men* (1930) also includes a Martian invasion—but the domestic legacy of Wells' *War of the Worlds* was very thin by comparison with the prolific and increasingly varied produce of U.S. pulp science fiction. Another theme pioneered in early British future war fiction was also extrapolated to new extremes in the pulps when "fifth column" paranoia was taken to new extremes in respect of aliens able to masquerade as humans. It was not until World War II began that such fantasies began to appear in profusion—Joseph J. Millard's *The Gods Hate Kansas* (1941; filmed as *I Married a Monster from Outer Space*, 1958) was a notable early example—and not until the war was over that they found their ideal historical context. Murray Leinster's "The Man in the Iron Cap" (1947; book, 1954 as *The Brain Stealers*) and Ray Bradbury's "Zero Hour" (1947) laid the groundwork for an extravagant expansion in the McCarthy era, spearheaded by Robert Heinlein's *The Puppet Masters* (1951), Eric Frank Russell's *Three to Conquer* (1955), and Jack Finney's *The Body Snatchers* (1955; filmed as *Invasion of the Body Snatchers*, 1956) and taken up with great enthusiasm by low-budget filmmakers.

The outbreak of war in Europe in 1939 had brought a new seriousness to American future war fiction, reflected in Herbert Best's *The Twenty-Fifth Hour* (1940) and L. Ron Hubbard's seemingly derivative *Final Blackout* (1940; book, 1948), and pulp accounts of alien warfare had briefly taken on a more pragmatic complexion in such works as A. E. van Vogt's "Co-operate—Or Else!" (1940; incorporated into *The War Against the Rull*, 1959) and Ross Rocklynne's "Quietus" (1940), but the manner of World War II's ending brought about a dramatic and immediate transformation of the depiction of future wars. The spectre of the *atom bomb threw all previous anxieties into the shade, and almost obliterated the previously stark differences in attitude reflected in American and European fiction. The plausibility of fictional accounts of nuclear war was nourished by the Cold War confrontation of the United States and the Soviet Union, which also brought about dramatic transformations of espionage fiction and technothrillers.

Genre science fiction of the 1950s became much more hospitable to such antiwar parables as Eric Frank Russell's "Late Night Final" (1948) and "I Am Nothing" (1952) and Fritz Leiber's "The Foxholes of Mars" (1952) and "A Bad Day for Sales" (1953), such satirical treatments of institutionalised warfare as C. M. Kornbluth and Judith Merril's *Gunner Cade* (1952; by-lined Cyril Judd) and Mack Reynolds' "Mercenary" (1962; exp. as *Mercenary from Tomorrow,* 1968), and such sardonic anticipations as Philip K. Dick's "Second Variety" and "The Defenders" (both 1953), Michael Shaara's "Soldier Boy" (1953), and Murray Leinster's "Short History of World War Three" (1958).

The postwar years also saw the growth of a macabre interest in the subtleties of *psychological warfare, which sparked off many thrillers about "brainwashing". The explicitly pacifist science fiction writer James White—an Ulsterman by birth—added

a violent ending to the U.S. book version of his first novel, "Tourist Planet" (1956; book, as *The Secret Visitors* 1957), at the insistence of its publisher, but devoted much of his subsequent effort to ingenious accounts of activities at Sector General, a hospital catering to a wide variety of species with radically different life-support needs, whose wartime activities are described in "Field Hospital" (1962; incorporated into *Star Surgeon*, 1963).

One result of the globalisation of future war anxiety was that stories of interstellar war became a kind of safe haven for militaristic adventures, notable exemplars for a new genre of military science fiction being provided by Robert A. Heinlein's *Starship Troopers* (1959), Gordon R. Dickson's *Dorsai!* (1959; book, 1960, initially as *The Genetic General*), and Poul Anderson's *The Star Fox* (1965). The initial historical context of this fiction was provided by the Korean War, where the intervention of U.N. troops embodied a new philosophy of military action and responsibility, but doubts about the role played by U.S. forces were subsequently amplified by the progress of the war in Vietnam—in which context their loud expression prompted a backlash, resulting in a sharp polarisation of attitudes.

*Television involved every American in the Vietnam War as a spectator, and this immediacy was reflected in the promptness of the literary response. The war was the subject of fourteen novels published in 1966 and a further twenty-two in 1967. The commercial pace was set by Robin Moore's *The Green Berets* (1965), whose author was an advertising executive; it launched a new subgenre of machismo-soaked novels about elite forces (which eventually spread to Britain in post–Falklands War novels about the SAS). Many newspaper correspondents delegated to cover the Vietnam War—some of them, like Gustav Hasford, author of *The Short Timers* (1967; filmed as *Full Metal Jacket*), seconded from military units—subsequently wrote novels based in their reportage. The anonymous *Report from Iron Mountain on the Possibility and Desirability of Peace* (Dial Press, 1967)—a satirical analysis of possible substitutes for the "valorising" effects of war (valorisation is a term used in economics to describe the strategic destruction of stockpiled goods to stimulate demand for new production)—provided a striking example of the cynicism with which the war was observed.

The polarisation of the science fiction community by the Vietnam war was vividly illustrated by a pair of advertisements that appeared on pages 4 and 5 of the June 1968 issue of *Galaxy*, when the moral justification of war and the politics of militarism had already become matters of fervently ingenious debate—not only in the United States—in such works as Harry Harrison's *Bill the Galactic Hero* (1965), Keith Laumer's *A Plague of Demons* (1965) and its sequels, Norman Spinrad's *The Men in the Jungle* (1967), Barry Malzberg's "Final War" (1968; as by K. M. O'Donnell), Larry S. Todd's "The Warbots" (1968), David S. Garnett's *Mirror in the Sky* (1969), Kit Reed's *Armed Camps* (1969), Richard Meredith's *We All Died at Breakaway Station* (1969), Gérard Klein's *Les seigneurs de la guerre* (1971; trans. as *The Overlords of War*), Ralph E. Hamil's "The Vietnam War Centennial Celebration" (1972), Jerry Pournelle's *A Spaceship for the King* (1973) and *The Mercenary* (1977), and Joe Haldeman's *The Forever War* (1974). Spinrad went on to write *The Iron Dream* (1972), in which the Fascist fantasies of one Adolf Hitler, who emigrated to the United States in the early 1930s and became a minor science fiction writer, superimpose the clichés of pulp future war fantasies on the rise of the Third Reich, the fighting of World War II, and the "final solution" to the problem of the insidious "Dominators".

Memories of the Vietnam War continued to haunt science fiction—directly reflected in such works as *In the Field of Fire* (1987) edited by Jean Van Buren Dann and Jack Dann, Lewis Shiner's "Shades" (1987), Bruce McAllister's *Dream Baby* (1987; exp. book, 1989), and Elizabeth Scarborough's *The Healer's War* (1988) and indirectly in Lucius Shepard's *Life During Wartime* (1987)—although the subgenre of military science fiction flourished. It produced such theme anthologies as Reginald Bretnor's *The Future at War* (3 vols., 1979–1980), Jerry Pournelle and John F. Carr's series launched by *There Will Be War* (1983), and various shared-world series, as well as individual series such as those launched by Orson Scott Card's "Ender's Game" (1977), David Drake's *Hammer's Slammers* (1979), and Lois McMaster Bujold's *The Warrior's Apprentice* (1986). H. Bruce Franklin's *War Stars: The Superweapon and the American Imagination* (1988) suggested that the ideology of such fiction is deep rooted in American culture. In the meantime, the influence of the *Fermi paradox on accounts of alien life prompted representations of a galaxy riven by all-out war, perhaps in the context of an ultimate war between organic and inorganic intelligences, as in Gregory Benford's *Across the Sea of Suns* (1984).

While military strategists produced relatively modest scenarios such as *The Third World War* (1979) by General Sir John Hackett and others, David Langford—then an employee at the Nuclear Weapons Research Establishment at Aldermaston—produced the more wide-ranging *War in 2080* (1979). Langford dramatised some of his suggestions in *The*

Space Eater (1982), while other writers searched for subtler ways to fight wars in such works as Mack Reynolds' *Computer War* (1967), Robert Asprin's *The Cold Cash War* (1977), Charles Sheffield's "Fixed Price War" (1978), Stephen Goldin's *The Eternity Brigade* (1980), Frederik Pohl's *The Cool War* (1981), Vernor Vinge's *The Peace War* (1984), James Tiptree Jr.'s "Yanqui Doodle" (1987), and Connie Willis and Cynthia Felice's *Light Raid* (1989). Many writers who believed unlimited future war to be inevitable were sidetracked into a burgeoning subgenre of survivalist fiction, in which the fugitive heirs of a ruined world fight for scraps with all the residual viciousness they can muster—which is often considerable, as illustrated by the paradigm example of William L. Pierce's *The Turner Diaries* (1978; by-lined Andrew McDonald).

Such stories as these embodied the movement of future war fiction into a significant new phase, based on the conviction that warfare had reached one significant boundary with the development of the atom bomb and another with the polarisation of attitudes that attended the Vietnam conflict. Subsequent wars, including the Falklands conflict and the two Gulf Wars, were mere skirmishes by comparison with Vietnam, let alone World War II, and the ideological disputes surrounding them were thoroughly familiar—as they had to be, given the parameters of the new *status quo*. The aphoristic allegation by *postmodern critic Jean Baudrillard that the (first) Gulf War did not actually take place, being only a "simulacrum" contained in political rhetoric and media reportage—the logic of which is minutely explained in Chris Hables Gray's futurological *Postmodern War* (1997)—was an exaggerated but apt expression of the almost universal conviction that a present or future war to which the contending sides were fully committed would undoubtedly be apocalyptic, any wholehearted exchange of fire being followed by the kind of ecocatastrophic "nuclear winter" popularised by Carl *Sagan.

The logical consequence of this consciousness was that any wars actually fought in the present or future would have to be exceedingly halfhearted, if not blatantly fake, if anyone were to win anything thereby. This is one of the reasons for the late twentieth-century boom in *alternative history stories, a very large proportion of which deals with the imperatives and outcomes of wars fought when wars of total commitment still had the power to shape history rather than merely ending it. The notion of a "war on terror", used as a slogan in the wake of the demolition of the World Trade Center on 11 September 2001, was an extension of other metaphorical uses of the term such as "war on crime" and "war on drugs", in which the word "war" functions as an emphatic signifier of antipathy.

This was the context in which the future war fiction of the last years of the twentieth century and the early years of the twenty-first was produced, with all dreams of military glory banished to the far arenas of space opera and alternative history, while Earthbound conflicts situated in the foreseeable future became surreally as well as cynically unbalanced. Notable examples of surreal and cynical imbalance can be found in Tom Purdom's "Sergeant Mother Glory" (2000), Ian R. MacLeod's "Chitty Chitty Bang Bang" (2000), Lucius Shepard's "A Walk in the Garden" (2003), and Richard Morgan's *Market Forces* (2004).

WATER

One of the four Classical *elements, initially proposed as the primordial substance by Thales in the sixth century B.C. Its compound nature, as H_2O, was not discovered until the eighteenth century, as a result of work by Joseph Priestley and Antoine Lavoisier. Although its liquid state is regarded as primary, its solid state (ice) and gaseous state (steam) are equally familiar and significant—early temperature scales were calibrated using the freezing and boiling points of water as reference points. Water vapour—consisting of liquid droplets distributed in *air—also has considerable significance as the substance of clouds.

Water—which covers 71% of the Earth's surface area—has a special significance in *biology by virtue of being the suspension medium of biochemistry. Along with atmospheric carbon dioxide it is one of the raw materials of biological primary production, the two being combined by photosynthesis to make up all the organic compounds in the biosphere. Because water is the topmost item in the biological hierarchy of needs, thirst is the primal human appetite. The biological importance of water is confused by the fact that the oceans—which were the principal abode of life for a long period in advance of the land's "conquest"—contain dissolved salts, particularly sodium chloride, which render their water useless to land-based organisms; thirst can only be satisfied by fresh water derived from precipitation. The basic *meteorological cycle by which water that evaporates from the oceans and is distributed as atmospheric water vapour falls on land as rain, accumulating in lakes and rivers, is the fundamental determinant of the extent and nature of the biosphere and the most basic context of human life and culture.

The distinction between fresh water and sea water is reflected in two fundamental water sciences distinguished in the nineteenth century—hydrology is the science of continental surface water while oceanography is the study of the seas—although they soon began to spin off subsidiary disciples such as limnology (the study of lakes). Robert Hooke and Robert Boyle had conducted experiments to discover physical and chemical properties of seawater in the late seventeenth century, but while modern *chemistry remained undeveloped, the most significant knowledge in this area comprised accounts of tides and currents compiled in connection with navigation.

The oceans posed awkward technological problems to would-be navigators, whose solution was by no means easy, although the economic, cultural, and scientific rewards reaped by means of the technologies that facilitated the great navigations of the fifteenth and sixteenth centuries were tremendous. The sea has played a highly significant adversarial role in literature from the *Odyssey* onwards, its symbolism being very different from the equally significant symbolism of freshwater bodies such as lakes and rivers.

The power and pervasiveness of such symbolism far overshadows the influences exerted on fiction by the development of scientific knowledge; the technology of shipbuilding and sailmaking is almost always taken for granted in works of fiction, while the ocean itself continued to be invested with quasi-supernatural qualities while science made steady inroads into the understanding of its vagaries. The first practical steamboat, the *Charlotte Dundas*, was built in 1801—although it was not until the development of the screw propeller in 1840 for Isambard Kingdom Brunel's *Great Eastern* that the revolution in powered marine transport really began—but steamships had far less impact on the scope and tenor of sea stories than steam locomotives had on accounts of continental travel.

The account in the *Arabian Nights* of the career of Sinbad the Sailor was satirically transfigured in the nineteenth century by Captain Marryat, in the voyages of Huckaback featured in *The Pacha of Many Tales* (1835), but the intrusion of some speculative fiction and a more cynical outlook does not contrive any fundamental transformation of the essential wondrousness of the tales. Edgar Allan Poe's scrupulously scientific account of "A Descent into the Maëlstrom" (1841) and Jules Verne's description of the discoveries of Captain Nemo's *Nautilus* in *Vingt mille lieues sous les mers* (1870: trans. as *Twenty Thousand Leagues Under the Sea*) are more carefully distanced from previous models, but still contrive to reemphasise the overwhelming awesomeness of their subject matter. The extent to which the sea retained its power over steamships was dramatically underlined by the formation of one of the great legends of the twentieth century, the sinking of the *Titanic* on 14 April 1912, which had already been anticipated in literary form in Morgan Robertson's *Futility* (1898; aka *The Wreck of the Titan*).

Scientific romances dealing with exotic sea life, such as H. G. Wells' "In the Abyss" (1896) and "The Sea Raiders" (1896), Owen Oliver's "Out of the Deep" (1904), and Eden Phillpotts' *The Owl of Athene* (1936), and science fiction stories such as Raymond Z. Gallun's "Davy Jones' Ambassador" (1935), Frank Belknap Long's "The Great Cold" (1935), Robert A. Heinlein's "Goldfish Bowl" (1942; by-lined Anson MacDonald), and Hal Clement's *Ocean on Top* (1973), are markedly different in tone from similar stories of land-based discovery, reflecting the fact that the "world" beneath the sea remained almost entirely inaccessible to human observation—more so than the remote heavens—until the late nineteenth century. Its depths are still difficult to explore because of the effects of pressure on divers and various kinds of diving vessels, including *submarines.

Images of future colonisation and commercial exploitation of the oceans include Robert Ellis Dudgeon's *Columbia* (1873), Douglas Newton's "Sunken Cities" (1923), Norman L. Knight's "Crisis in Utopia" (1940), Arthur C. Clarke's *The Deep Range* (1954), Frederik Pohl and Jack Williamson's *Undersea Quest* (1954) and its sequels, Kenneth Bulmer's *City Under the Sea* (1957), Dean R. McLaughlin's "The Man on the Bottom" (1958; exp. as *Dome World*, 1962), Keith Roberts' "The Deeps" (1966), Carl L. Biemiller's *The Hydronauts* (1970), Bruce McAllister's *Humanity Prime* (1971), Thomas J. Bass' *The Godwhale* (1974), David Andreissen's *Star Seed* (1982), Peter Watts' *Starfish* (1990), and Maureen F. McHugh's series launched with "The Queen of Marincite" (1990). Such works invariably retain an impression of the essential indomitability of the ocean.

On the other hand, literary history also offers abundant testimony to the magnetic appeal of the sea, not merely as a route to distant fame and fortune but in itself; it is frequently represented as a "mistress" to mariners who can never feel entirely at home on land. The open sea often represents an escape from the strictures of life on land, taken to an extreme in romantic adventures of piracy and exotic travellers' tales of remote and wondrous islands. Islands provided useful settings in literature throughout its history, not just because they provided stages for Utopian and satirical experiments in social design and settings for exotic adventures stories, but also because they have a *microcosmic charm of their own closely associated with their watery setting. The

addictive loyalty of mariners and the essential fascination of islands are closer in spirit to the symbolic qualities of fresh water, although that has unique features connected with the benevolence of rain, the bounty of springs, the flow of rivers and the reflective qualities of pools.

The remarkable range of such symbolism is further increased when ice, water vapour, and steam are added to the spectrum; as with oceanographic phenomena, the power and versatility of the symbolism is easily sufficient to overshadow the disenchanting input of scientific knowledge even in the most determinedly materialistic speculative fiction. Hard science fiction stories anticipating future problems in maintaining supplies of fresh water to thirsty cities, including Rick Raphael's "The Thirst Quenchers" (1963) and "Guttersnipe" (1964), Charles Einstein's *The Day New York Went Dry* (1964), and Joe Poyer's "Pipeline" (1968), do not quite contrive to be exceptions to the rule.

The notion of adapting humans to "breathe" water is one of the simplest and most appealing imaginable applications of speculative biotechnology, as featured in such stories as Aleksandr Belayev's *Chelovek amfibiya* (1928; trans. as *The Amphibian*), L. Sprague de Camp "The Merman" (1938), Kobo Abe's *Inter Ice Age 4* (1959), Kenneth Bulmer's *Beyond the Silver Sky* (1961), Gordon R. Dickson's *The Space Swimmers* (1963; book, 1967), and Paul D. d'Entremont's "Waterbreathers, Inc." (1990). The attractions of such a way of life are, however, more clearly evident in the peculiar qualities of the fascination with dolphins that developed in both scientific and literary communities in the latter half of the twentieth century.

Scientists became intently interested in dolphins during the 1960s, inspired by the idea that they might possess high *intelligence—a notion that swiftly became invested with mystical qualities, often embodied in the lifestyle fantasy of "swimming with dolphins". The particular species of *ecological mysticism associated with the sea—exemplified in some of the stories collected in Hilbert Schenck's *Wave Rider* (1980) and taken to a curious extreme in *At the Eye of the Ocean* (1980)—invests the ocean with maternal properties of its own, distinct from those attached by James *Lovelock to the biospheric Gaia.

The art of water-divining, or "dowsing", attracted some attention from *parapsychologists as a possible psi power, especially in connection with Kenneth Roberts' attempts to promote his protégé Harry Gross, which culminated in *Water Unlimited* (1957), but its essential lack of melodrama reduced its impact on speculative fiction to negligibility. There is, however, a small but significant subgenre of scientific and science-fictional writings concerned with exotic types of water, initially inspired by the utility of "heavy water"—formed by the hydrogen isomers deuterium and tritium—in *nuclear power generation. David Duncan's *Beyond Eden* (1955; aka *Another Tree in Eden*) describes the discovery of such a substance, which seems at first to be lethal but holds the promise of a magical transformation. Kurt Vonnegut's *Cat's Cradle* (1963) features Ice-9, a voracious isomer capable of converting all the world's water into its own sterile substance. "Water II", an unusually dense variety "discovered" by Russian scientists, including Boris V. Derjagin, in 1962 became popularly known as polywater; its existence was endorsed in the United Kingdom and Belgium in the late 1960s, and in the United States by Ellis R. Lippincott, but it turned out to be illusory and Derjagin recanted the claim in 1973. The notion is echoed, but not slavishly replicated, in Theodore L. Thomas and Kate Wilhelm's *The Year of the Cloud* (1970). An old joke about the manufacture of "synthetic water" is co-opted into fiction in Edmundo Hamiltowne's "The Water Doctor" (1978).

WEAPON

A technological device intended to increase the effects of violent action. The invention and enhancement of lethal devices used in hunting was a key motive force in the early development of *technology; spearheads, arrowheads, and stone axes are among the most prolific artefacts found by *archaeologists and *palaeontologists. The notion that the discovery of such lethal devices—with the side effect of their being used in disputes between human beings—was a significant threshold in human evolution is commonplace in *anthropological fantasies of prehistory.

The use of weapons must have become a central fact of human social existence at an early stage, and the desire to develop better weapons of *war may have been an important driving force of technological *progress throughout history; such *technological determinists as Lewis Mumford consider it the most important causative factor. The history of the military use of weapons has, inevitably, been paralleled by the history of their private ownership and personal use.

In much the same way that war is routinely justified as a means of securing peace, the bearing of personal arms is routinely justified as a means of ensuring that people might go about their everyday business safely and securely. Weapons are second only to means of *transportation as objects of technofetishism, the mystique of the sword—illustrated by such celebrated examples as King Arthur's Excalibur—being easily displaced by objects of more effective phallic symbolism. The social significance of the handgun is encapsulated in the ironic nickname that deems it the quintessential "equaliser".

Literature has always taken a more intimate interest in personal weaponry than weapons of war, for obvious reasons; fiction thrives on personal confrontation, and hence on formal and informal duelling. The ideal climax of a formularised action-adventure story is a crucial personal confrontation, which is almost invariably settled by armed conflict. In crime fiction, weapons also function as agents of murder—an occurrence far more common in the world of fiction than in the world of experience. The extent of this permeation is most tellingly represented, however, by the orchestration of fiction in which literal weaponry is hardly featured at all—the domestic drama and the genre romance, for instance—but in which metaphorical weaponry is everywhere.

Technological determinists who are careful not to overestimate the causative force of warfare can cite such examples as the decorative impulse, expressed at the personal level and in the business of worship, and the communicative impulse, as represented in letter writing and the printing of books, but even the most superficial study of literature suggests that such devices can easily be considered as metaphorical weaponry, even more effective in its fashion than daggers and petards. Edward Bulwer-Lytton observed that the pen is mightier than the sword, but did not add that fine clothing is more effective armour than chain mail.

The general tendency of history to pay little regard to advances in technology is less marked with respect to weapons than other devices, although it is somewhat confused by a tendency to keep new ones secret for as long as possible. The formulas for Greek fire written down by Aeneas the Tactician in 350 B.C. and by Vegetius in *De Re Militari* (350 A.D.) cannot account for the seemingly liquid "wildfire" sometimes used in the interim, whose composition remains a matter for speculation. Although the formula for gunpowder was written down in several mid-thirteenth-century sources, the history of its subsequent application in making rockets, petards, and firearms is difficult to piece together. The gradual and extraordinarily complex evolution of firearms thereafter, however, encouraged speculators to see the future of weaponry in terms of guns that would hurl bigger bullets farther, and bombs that would make bigger bangs, with the occasional nod towards incendiary devices; thus, the catalogue of new technologies offered in Francis Bacon's *New Atlantis* (1627) mentions more powerful cannons, more powerful explosives, and "wildfires burning in water, unquenchable".

This pattern had not changed significantly when the nineteenth century drew towards its close. Albert

Robida offered spectacular images of future troop carriers in action in *La guerre au vingtième siècle* (1887; trans. as "War in the Twentieth Century"), but the actual business of killing was still a mere matter of making bigger bangs. Jules Verne's *Face au drapeau* (1896; trans. as *For the Flag*) equipped its "fulgurator" with a "boomerang" action, while the Comte de Villiers de l'Isle Adam provided an extraordinarily detailed description of a glass arrow charged with explosive chemicals in "Etna chez soi" (1886; trans. as "Etna in Your Own Home"), but all the devices actually do is explode. In the meantime, American dime novel writers were building a new commercial genre around the mystique of the Winchester rifle, the Gatling gun, and the Colt 45 revolver—but even the most accomplished gunslinger was, at the end of the day, merely a deliverer of bullets.

Chemical and biological weapons had been used far in advance of this period, but the rapid evolution of nineteenth-century chemistry—especially organic chemistry—and the establishment of the germ theory of disease promised and ensured that such weaponry would become more easily manipulable and more destructive in future. Tentative literary developments of the notion included T. Mullett Ellis's *Zalma* (1895), W. L. Alden's "The Purple Death" (1895), and M. P. Shiel's *The Yellow Danger* (1898). The scientific developments that seized the speculative imagination most powerfully as possible sources of new weaponry were, however, Röntgen's discovery of x-rays in 1895 and Becquerel's discovery of radioactivity in 1897. The imagination of writers immediately leaped ahead to imagine all kinds of destructive "rays" being used as weapons, as well as weapons that would make the biggest bangs imaginable by releasing the energy locked up in matter. The speculative weaponry of the twentieth-century imagination was abruptly revolutionised.

Although much British future war fiction remained focused on new ways of transporting guns and explosives, the genre's chief populariser, George Griffith, moved on in *The Lord of Labour* (written 1906; published 1911) to imagine a war fought with atomic missiles and disintegrator rays, and such rays became increasingly common thereafter. While the Great War was in progress, William le Queux attempted to raise morale with an account of the development of a new ray in *The Zeppelin Destroyer* (1916). Percy F. Westerman's *The War of the Wireless Waves* (1923)—in which the British ZZ ray counters the menace of the German Ultra-K ray—was one of countless thrillers featuring arms races of this kind. Pierrepont Noyes' *The Pallid Giant* (1927; aka *Gentlemen: You Are Mad!*) credits the "death ray" with the destruction of a technological civilisation.

Ray guns were rapidly taken to all conceivable extremes in pulp science fiction; E. E. Smith's *The Skylark of Space* (1928; book, 1946) features heat rays, infra-sound, ultraviolet rays, and "induction rays", while Irvin Lester and Fletcher Pratt looked forward to "The Reign of the Ray" (1929) and John W. Campbell's "Space Rays" (1932) provided examples so numerous and so extravagant that Hugo Gernsback advertised it as a "burlesque". The illustrative potential of ray guns recommended them strongly to cover artists, who made lavish use of "blasters" deluging their targets with spectacular radiance.

Similar radiance was a recurrent feature of weapons supposedly based on atomic radioactivity, as well as such revivifications of Greek fire as the "radiant inflammatol" featured in John Gloag's *Winter's Youth* (1934). Crime fiction was equally entranced with these new kinds of weaponry, which became the basis of a subgenre of "world blackmail" stories, including C. J. Cutcliffe Hyne's *Empire of the World* (1910), Victor MacClure's *The Ark of the Covenant* (1924; aka *Ultimatum*), Alexei Tolstoy's *Giperboloid inzhenera Garina* (1926; trans. as *The Deathbox* and *The Garin Death Ray*), Neil Bell's *The Lord of Life* (1933), and C. S. Forester's *The Peacemaker* (1934).

On the actual battlefields of World War I, the new weapons that made the greatest imaginative impact were chemical, and the rapid development of such weapons in the final year of the war suggested that they would play an even greater role in future conflicts. Poison gas became the major bugbear of British future war stories between the wars, deployed to bloodcurdling effect in Shaw Desmond's *Ragnarok* (1926), Neil Bell's *The Gas War of 1940* (1931; by-lined Miles; aka *Valiant Clay*), and Frank McIlraith and Roy Connolly's *Invasion from the Air* (1934), and featured as objects of dire anxiety in Norman Anglin's play *Poison Gas* (1928) and Sarah Campion's *Thirty Million Gas Masks* (1937). (It is perhaps surprising that the general pessimism about the likelihood of the Geneva Convention being observed in the next war proved unjustified.)

Chemical and biological weapons were also widely deployed by criminals; Sax Rohmer's Fu Manchu was an adept user of exotic poisons, while biological blights were used as blackmail threats in Edgar Wallace's *The Green Rust* (1919), William Le Queux's *The Terror of the Air* (1920), and Robert W. Service's *The Master of the Microbe* (1926), and these devices too became commonplaces of American pulp fiction. Poul Anderson's "The Perfect Weapon" (1950) is an ironic reflection on this alarmist tradition, featuring a gas that breaks down cellulose, thus destroying books—cancelling out the might of the pen as an instrument of dictatorship.

This pattern of evolution was so rapid that it ran into acute dramatic problems. Huge explosions, powerful ray guns, and poison gases threatened to eliminate the personal element of combat. Swordplay and rapidly drawn Colt 45s had melodramatic advantages that atom bombs, disintegrator rays, and biological weapons could never match. Space opera writers like Edmond Hamilton and Jack Williamson soon revealed the awful truth that blowing up stars at the push of a button became rather anticlimactic as soon as the trick was repeated. The development of hypothetical personal weaponry therefore took on a tendency to calculated restraint, reflected in the evolution of the "stun gun"; one of the archetypal weapons of mature futuristic melodrama is *Star Trek*'s "phaser", which can be set to stun or kill at the twist of a knob, according to melodramatic circumstance.

The actual development of *atom bombs, and the development of ray guns of a sort in the beams of coherent *light known as lasers, confirmed the central argument that early twentieth-century speculative writers had been developing for some time, but they remained blunt instruments. The significant developments in late twentieth-century imaginary weaponry were much more personal: the evolution of a spectacular array of intimate weapons in the technothriller subgenre, especially for use by secret agents, and the development of an extraordinarily rich subgenre of "martial arts" fiction, in which the subtleties of swordplay and gunplay were replaced by the use of hands and feet as lethal weapons, augmented by the hurling of all manner of exotic blades. Within genre science fiction, these trends were supplemented by *cyborgisation and *genetic engineering, whose use in virtuous causes very often involved the enhancement of fighting abilities.

As the issue of civilian disarmament became increasingly controversial in the American political arena, its futuristic extrapolations in such stories as A. E. van Vogt's series begun with "The Weapon Shop" (1942)—which makes much of the slogan "the right to bear weapons is the right to be free"—and Robert A. Heinlein's *Beyond This Horizon* (1942; by-lined Anson MacDonald; book, 1948) became increasingly technofetishistic—lending themselves to such parodies as William Tenn's "The Masculinist Revolt" (1965), Philip K. Dick's *The Zap Gun* (1967), and John Brunner's *The Jagged Orbit* (1969). The intimacy of the relationship between heroes and their weapons became a key feature of the success of commodified fantasy fiction in the 1970s, particularly in the sword-and-sorcery subgenre, which featured such carefully fetishised weapons as Michael Moorcock's Stormbringer. Poul Anderson supplemented his earlier account of "The Perfect Weapon"

with a similarly ironic account of the ultimate handgun in "The Inevitable Weapon" (1967).

The actual arms race between the United States and the Soviet Union reached a highly speculative climax in Ronald Reagan's Strategic Defense Initiative project, involving a series of heavily armed *artificial satellites. H. Bruce Franklin's *War Stars: The Superweapon and the American Imagination* (1988) argues that this was the end result of American foreign policy's long-term fetishistic fascination with "superweapons" capable of inducing shock and awe in any and all enemies; he cites the evolution of popular science fiction as a key manifestation of that *zeitgeist*.

WELLS, H[ERBERT] G[EORGE] (1866–1946)

British writer. At the time of his birth his father was a shopkeeper—having earlier been a gardener and cricketer—but the business failed and Wells' mother was forced to return to domestic service as housekeeper at Up-Park. Her desire to re-elevate the family to middle class status resulted in "Bertie", like his brothers before him, being apprenticed to a draper, but he decided to beat his own path to respectability. In 1883, he became a pupil/teacher at Midhurst Grammar School, obtaining a scholarship to the Normal School of Science in London, where he studied *biology under Thomas Henry Huxley—a vociferous proponent of Charles *Darwin's theory of evolution, who made a deep impression on him. Wells did not complete his course, but resumed teaching and took his degree externally.

Wells published the episodic "The Chronic Argonauts" (1888) in his own *Science Schools Journal* while working as a teacher, extrapolating ideas about future evolution he had absorbed from Huxley. He dabbled in scientific journalism, publishing an essay on "The Rediscovery of the Unique" in 1891, and soon began to sell speculative nonfiction regularly in the popular magazines that burst forth in some profusion in the early 1890s. He also wrote two textbooks while working for the University Correspondence College. The most ambitious of his early articles was "The Man of the Year Million" (1893), an evolutionary fantasy describing the ultimate human species as a creature with a huge head and eyes, delicate hands, and a much reduced body, permanently immersed in nutrient fluids, having been forced to retreat beneath the surface of the planet after the cooling of the Sun. In others he anticipated "The Advent of the Flying Man" and "The Extinction of Man", and described "An Excursion to the Sun" and

"The Living Things That May Be". His early short stories were less adventurous, most of the speculative items featuring encounters with strange life-forms, as in "The Stolen Bacillus" (1894), "In the Avu Observatory" (1894), "The Flowering of the Strange Orchid" (1894), and "Aepyornis Island" (1894).

Wells produced an elaborated version of "The Chronic Argonauts", serialised (sans title) in W. E. Henley's *National Observer* (1894), before producing the version serialised in Henley's *New Review* and reprinted—in slightly abridged form—as *The Time Machine: An Invention* (1895). The second version added a preliminary narrative—further elaborated in the final version—justifying the protagonist's invention of a time machine with an elaborate jargon borrowed from C. H. *Hinton. It injected more narrative verve into its account of a future human species subdivided into the gentle Eloi and the bestial Morlocks, both of which ultimately become extinct—as, eventually, does all life on Earth as the Sun is gradually extinguished. The novella became the paradigm example of the burgeoning genre of *scientific romance.

Wells' interest in social reform and socialist political ideas was reflected in the fantasy *The Wonderful Visit* (1895), in which an angel displaced from the Land of Dreams casts a critical eye upon late Victorian mores and folkways. *The Wheels of Chance* (1896) is a comedy drawing upon his own experiences, presenting the pretensions and predicaments of the aspiring lower middle class as occasion for amusement. The central themes of these early novels—the implications of Darwin's evolutionary theory and the inequities, injustices, and hypocrisies of contemporary society that were ripe for eradication—ran through all Wells' later work, although the ways in which he chose to develop them changed radically over time.

The Island of Dr. Moreau (1896) is an allegorical satire featuring animals surgically gifted with human form, partly inspired by Victor Hugo's *L'homme qui rit* (1869; trans. as *The Man Who Laughs*). It develops ideas from an earlier essay on "The Limits of Plasticity" (1895) into the story of a hubristic scientist populating a remote island with beasts surgically reshaped as men. The beast-men's veneer of civilisation—exemplified by their chanted "laws"—proves unfortunately thin. Wells' short stories grew bolder in conception at this time, as exemplified by the visionary fantasy "Under the Knife" (1896) and the cosmic disaster story "The Star" (1897). "A Story of the Stone Age" (1897) is a notable attempt to imagine the circumstances that allowed Man to evolve from his bestial ancestors in the remote past. The novella "A Story of the Days to Come" (1897) is an elaborate study of future society, imagining a technologically developed world where poverty and misery are needlessly maintained by class divisions.

The Invisible Man: A Grotesque Romance (1897) is a satirical thriller, which includes a study of scientific hubris brought to destruction. A similar moral is succinctly developed in the cautionary parable "The Man Who Could Work Miracles" (1898). Wells broke more important new ground, however, in *The War of the Worlds* (1898), which introduced *alien beings as competitors in a universal struggle for existence, determined to take possession of Earth when the exhausted biosphere of Mars can no longer support them. The novel set a precedent that was to loom large over twentieth-century Anglo-American science fiction, founding one of its guiding myths. Another narrative template of which science fiction writers would make prolific use was provided by *When the Sleeper Wakes* (1899: rev. as *The Sleeper Awakes*, 1910), a fantasy of future revolution against oppressive capitalism whose hero awakes from suspended animation to play a quasi-messianic role. Wells was never able to believe in proletarian socialism, always assuming that social justice would have to be imposed from above by a benevolent intelligentsia.

Wells' commitment to innovative scientific romance did not long survive the turn of the century. The articles collected in *Anticipations of the Reaction of Mechanical and Human Progress upon Human Life and Thought* (1901) pioneered the genre of speculative nonfiction nowadays called *futurology. He ceased thereafter to see the future as an infinite reservoir of possibilities, but dedicated himself to the much narrower task of figuring out what the near future would actually be like. His last great scientific romance, *The First Men in the Moon* (1901), employed antigravity as a facilitating device complementary to the time machine; such devices could have opened up all of space as well as all of time for exploration had Wells cared to make further use of them, but he left that work to others. The novel carried forward the satirical tradition of lunar voyages, describing the hyperorganised society of the Selenites.

Wells' works of this period were routinely labelled "scientific romances" by reviewers, and he had used the label himself in early interviews, but he now chose to lump them together in lists of his works with such moralistic fantasies as *The Sea Lady* (1902) as "fantastic and imaginative romances". He also decided to submit his imaginative power to the yoke of politically guided prophecy, persuading himself that the future could be anticipated by methods outlined in a lecture reprinted as *The Discovery of the Future* (1902). His futurological essays had brought him to the attention of Sidney and Beatrice Webb, and he joined their Fabian Society in 1903; he tried to assume command of the society in 1906, and withdrew in 1908 following his failure to do so, but he continued in his dedication to change the world rather than merely interpreting it. *The Food of the Gods and How It Came to Earth* (1904) set out as a scientific romance, but eventually turned into propaganda for Utopian socialism.

In developing his literary career in the early years of the twentieth century, Wells was afflicted by the knowledge that he would only acquire respectability by writing fiction of a more "literary" kind. His scientific romances were scathingly parodied in J. F. Sullivan's "The Island of Professor Menu" (1896), C. L. Graves and E. V. Lucas' *The War of the Weenuses* (1898), George Edward Farrow's *The Food of the Dogs* (1905), and Jules Castier's "The Finding of Laura" (1920), and it was obvious that such works would not be taken entirely seriously during his lifetime. Wells set out to make his reputation as a "real" novelist in such earnest studies as *Love and Mr. Lewisham* (1900) and such comedies as *Kipps* (1905) and *The History of Mr. Polly* (1910), arguing with Henry James in the meantime as to whether the literary world was large enough to admit "novels of ideas" as well as "novels of character". Wells conceded the point by desertion, but he was probably right to judge that he had no chance of winning, and that speculative fiction was doomed to suffer the contempt of literary snobs no matter what it might achieve in its own terms. When he eventually condescended to publish an omnibus of *The Scientific Romances of H. G. Wells* (1933), his introduction was vitriolically dismissive of his earlier ambitions.

Wells toyed with the traditional semifictional format of *A Modern Utopia* (1905) before deciding that his propaganda would benefit from a more novelistic method. *In the Days of the Comet* (1906) describes a wondrous change in human personality brought about by the gases in a comet's tail, deploying its facilitating device in an unapologetically casual manner, without any attempt to cultivate plausibility in the manner of the early scientific romances. His most determined early attempt to produce an all-out novel of ideas was *Tono-Bungay* (1909), about the marketing of a quack medicine; it was quickly followed by *Ann Veronica* (1909), a polemic on the situation of women in society, and the political novel *The New Machiavelli* (1911). *The Research Magnificent* (1915) attempted to focus on science as a social activity, but without much conviction.

Some of Wells' later novels of ideas incorporated fantastic twists for dramatic purposes although remaining basically naturalistic, as in the visionary fantasy that frames *The Dream* (1924), but the majority—including the longest and most ambitious, *The World of William Clissold* (1926)—remained determinedly naturalistic. For a long period in the early twentieth century, his speculative thought was almost entirely confined to nonfictional developments such as *Mankind in the Making* (1903), *New Worlds for Old* (1908), *The Outline of History* (1920), *The Salvaging of Civilization* (1921), *The Way the World Is Going: Guesses and Forecasts of the World Ahead* (1928), *The Open Conspiracy: Blue Prints for a World Revolution* (1928), *World Brain* (1938), *The Fate of Homo Sapiens* (1939), *The New World Order* (1939), and *The Conquest of Time* (1942).

The only element of scientific romance Wells took care to preserve in his work of his period was the continuation of a series of earnestly anxious future war stories that he had begun with "The Land Ironclads" (1903). *The War in the Air, and Particularly How Mr. Bert Smallways Fared While It Lasted* (1908) and *The World Set Free: A Story of Mankind* (1914) both made significant late contributions to the future war subgenre; the first revised Wells' earlier dismissive opinion of the likely impact of aircraft on he business of warfare, while the second features atom bombs whose "chain reactions" cause them to explode repeatedly.

Wells had initially taken a gloomier view of the prospect of a great war than such journalistic writers as George Griffith, Louis Tracy, and William le Queux, but his enthusiasm grew when he decided that socialist reconstruction could not begin in earnest until the old order had been comprehensively obliterated—a prospect he revisited with increasing relish in such didactic futuristic scenarios as *Men like Gods* (1923) and *The Shape of Things to Come* (1933). The latter was a fictional extrapolation of the comprehensive summary of his Utopian philosophy that he had published as *The Work, Wealth and Happiness of Mankind* (1931).

During the First World War, Wells had been active in the League of Nations movement, although he had published such morale-boosting endeavours as *Mr. Britling Sees It Through* (1916). Afterwards, he became increasingly active in that cause, visiting many countries on personal diplomatic missions. He addressed the Petrograd Soviet, the Sorbonne, and the Reichstag. In 1934, he had discussions with both Stalin and Roosevelt, attempting to recruit them to his world-saving schemes, but that only served to deepen his despair when the world became embroiled in war for a second time. He became increasingly impatient with the follies of his fellow men, and dubbed the post-1918 world "the Age of Frustration", elaborating the thesis in *The Anatomy of Frustration: A Modern Synthesis* (1936).

Frustration is the dominant mood of an extensive series of "sarcastic fantasies" begun with *The Undying Fire* (1919), an allegory in which the Book of Job is reenacted in contemporary England—reflecting a brief investment in religious faith explained in *God the Invisible King* (1917) and dramatised in *The Soul of a Bishop* (1917). The series and continued in the angry satires *Mr. Blettsworthy on Rampole Island* (1928), *The Autocracy of Mr. Parham* (1930), and *The Croquet Player: A Story* (1936). In the last named, a village is haunted by the brutal spectres of humankind's evolutionary heritage, and Wells became increasingly convinced that human nature was too innately brutal to be redeemable.

Wells continued to make use of fantastic devices in *The Camford Visitation* (1937), *Star-Begotten: a Biological Fantasia* (1937), and *All Aboard for Ararat* (1941), but used them as straightforward expressions of his resentments and hopes. *The Holy Terror* (1939), a fictional biography of a modern dictator based on the careers of Stalin, Mussolini, and Hitler, was a more significant endeavour in speculative psychology. Wells also expanded his endeavours into the cinema medium between the wars. He worked the future history of *The Shape of Things to Come* into a script for Alexander Korda's *Things to Come* (1935; book, 1935) and also scripted a film version of *The Man Who Could Work Miracles* (1936), but several other film scripts, including a Utopian account of *The King Who Was a King* (1929), never reached the screen.

Despite his defection from the cause, Wells remained the idol of twentieth-century scientific romance and science fiction—rightly so, given the astonishing measure of his achievements in the first seven years of his career. No other writer was ever so spectacularly innovative, and he was ahead of his time in his ability to provide his bolder innovations with a gloss of plausibility. He never managed to resolve the imaginative conflict between his Utopian dreams and his interpretation of Darwinian "natural law"—*Mind at the End of Its Tether* (1945) opines that mankind is doomed, because people cannot and will not adapt themselves to a sustainable way of life, and he imagined his own career as an analogue of that of the luckless sighted man in his classic allegory "The Country of the Blind" (1904)—but he may have been too hard on humankind, and on himself. He portrayed himself as a deluded idealist in *Christina Alberta's Father* (1925) and as a quirky eccentric in *Experiment in Autobiography: Discoveries and Conclusions of a Very Ordinary Brain (since 1866)* (1934), but he was a clearer and more adventurous thinker in his heyday than any of his contemporaries.

Notable literary works in which Wells appears as a character include Frederik Pohl and C. M. Kornbluth's "Nightmare with Zeppelins" (1958), Christopher Priest's *The Space Machine* (1976), Karl Alexander's *Time After Time* (1976), Eric Brown's "The Inheritors of Earth" (1990), John Kessel's "Buffalo" (1991), and Stephen Baxter's "The Adventure of the Inertial Adjustor" (1997). Explicit variants of his works and sequels by other hands are very numerous. Sequels to *The Time Machine* include Théo Varlet and André Blandin's *La Belle Valence* (1923), Richard A. Lupoff's "Nebogipfel at the End of Time" (1978), K. W. Jeter's *Morlock Night* (1979), David J. Lake's *The Man Who Loved Morlocks* (1981), Stephen Baxter's *The Time Ships* (1995), and John Morressy's "When Bertie Met Mary" (2002). Variants on the theme of *The Island of Dr. Moreau* include Joseph Nesvadba's "Doctor Moreau's Other Island" (trans. 1964), Brian W. Aldiss' *Moreau's Other Island* (1980), and Gwyneth Jones' *Dr. Franklin's Island* (2001). Elaborations of *The War of the Worlds* include Garrett P. Serviss' *Edison's Conquest of Mars* (1898; book, 1947), Will McMorrow's "The Sun-Makers" (1925) and "Venus or Earth?" (1927), Manly Wade and Wade Wellman's *Sherlock Holmes's War of the Worlds* (1975), Kevin J. Anderson's anthology *War of the Worlds: Global Dispatches* (1996), and Eric Brown's "Ulla, Ulla" (2002). Stephen Baxter's "The Ant-Men of Tibet" (1995) is a sequel to *The First Men in the Moon*.

WRITING

The symbolic representation of ideas by inscription. The earliest writing systems were pictorial, but the flexibility of its techniques took a considerable leap forward with the invention of phonetic scripts, in which the signs represent the sounds employed in spoken language. Alphabetical writing of this sort first appeared in Greece at the beginning of the first millennium B.C., although syllabic and hieroglyphic systems dated back much farther. The subsequent refinement of phonetic and numerical representation was a slow process, the latter lagging behind the former. The evolution of technologies of inscription—including such instruments as chisels, styli, quill pens, and steel nibs—the preparation of various kinds of ink, and the manufacture of such media as soft stone, clay, leather, sheet metal, papyrus, parchment, and paper provided the chief facilitating devices for the evolution of philosophy, financial accounting, legal codes, science, and literature.

The pace of all these evolutionary processes was primarily determined by the availability and efficiency of writing materials, and by the processes of duplication that allowed written texts to be widely distributed. The development of printing was a significant watershed in the technological history of Christendom, which precipitated both the Reformation and the scientific revolution, and accelerated the pace of European technological progress so rapidly that Western culture colonised and conquered the greater part of the globe, transforming the remainder by its example.

Socrates is said to have disapproved of writing, partly on the grounds that reliance on it would be deleterious to the development of the memory, but its encouragement of linear thought and complex argument transformed the nature and increased the scope of philosophy—as reflected in the development of *Plato's dialogues—and supplied the means of recording data that provided empirical science with its foundation. Because writing requires schooling, and therefore needs institutional support, teachers of writing inevitably became key custodians of culture and gatekeepers of a new kind of elitism.

These cultural developments routinely encouraged the establishment of a core of sacred documents—containing a mixture of myth and law—whose dictates were held to be unchallengeable, thus giving rise to book-based religions very different in kind from religions based in oral folklore and custom. This often created a situation in which the linear reasoning and empirical observations facilitated by writing were opposed by the cultural elites that the same technology tended to generate.

It is perhaps ironic that the evolution of writing technology should be as nearly invisible in the writings that constitute history as many other chains of development; the only surviving description of the manufacture of papyrus—the most important writing material of the ancient world—is second hand, given by Pliny the Elder in the first century A.D. Parchment and paper must have been invented at about that time, although paper—which originated in China—did not reach the West until the eighth century, when it entered into a fruitful combination with the knife-sharpened goose-quill pen and inks based (although their manufacturers were unaware of it) on ferrous salts. The development of printing in the fifteenth century required a remarkable convergence of different technologies, not merely in the manufacture of type and the construction of presses, but in the manufacture of new kinds of paper and ink. The humble pencil was developed about a hundred years thereafter.

The printing press became the disseminator of the New Learning and the agent of the scientific revolution, and maintained its cultural dominance until the twentieth century. According to the *technological determinist Harold Innis—whose position was supported by evidence supplied by such *ethnologists as Jack Goody and such historians as H. J. Chaytor—

the printing press was the foundation of political, religious, economic, and literary culture during that period, imposing the linearity of thought and argument typical of writing on a wide range of other cultural activities.

Although the principal difference between print and manuscript was the ease with which texts could be duplicated and distributed, the visual uniformity of print also allowed texts to be read "directly" or "silently" rather than being mentally translated into sounds, as was required by the idiosyncratic formulations of manuscript. One of the effects of this facilitation was the gradual displacement of poetry, which is designed to be read "aurally", by prose consumed at a much faster pace—specifically by the novel—and by the gradual displacement within that prose of diegetic narrative techniques mimicking the discourse of an oral teller by mimetic techniques that permitted readers to identify with viewpoint characters and experience the story in a more immediate and intimate fashion.

The extrapolation of Innis' argument suggested that the supplementation of print by new twentieth-century media, especially *radio and *television, might have profound effects on the evolving pattern of those cultural activities—effects that writers like Marshall McLuhan attempted to anticipate. McLuhan's most celebrated slogan, "the medium is the message" suggested that science and modern fiction, as parallel products of the print medium, might have more in common than was apparent, in terms of the basic formulation of their *rhetoric. It also implied that both might be due for a dramatic transformation and supersession as auditory and visual imagery increasingly intruded upon the conceptual world formulated by the specialised use of eyesight as a system for decoding a linear string of symbols. It is arguable, however, that neither Innis nor McLuhan took sufficient account of the versatility of print and the implications of its ability to function in different ways when read "aurally" and "silently"—a versatility that had complicated the message of the medium in such a way as to facilitate a sharp divergence of the rhetoric of science and the rhetoric of literature, and was itself further complicated by the conceptual distinctiveness of the "direct" consumption of mathematical information.

The substitution of pens by typewriters at the beginning of the century, and the subsequent substitution of typewriters by electronic word processors, attracted less attention from cultural theorists, although litterateurs were often keenly aware of changes in their patterns of creativity brought about by the new technologies. The sparse anticipations of speculative fiction in this field were sometimes spectacularly misconceived, as in David H. Keller's "Stenographer's Hands" (1928), which imagines the legs and bodies of future generations of typists atrophying while their hands become more adept, and often bizarre, as in such images of living books as those contained in S. Fowler Wright's *The World Below* (1929) and Paul Di Filippo's "The Reluctant Book" (2000).

The utility of late twentieth-century technologies in transcending the linearity of the printed text, in producing labyrinthine "HyperTexts", was initially explored in the context of computer *games, but the exploration of its potential in a literary context, begun with such endeavours as Geoff Ryman's *253* (1996; book version, 1998), was applied to the specific problems of speculative fiction in Paul Di Filippo and Bruce Sterling's "The Scab's Progress" (2000). The online version of the latter was published on December 29, as close to the eve of the twenty-first century as the authors could contrive.

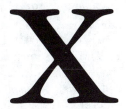

X

XENOLOGY

An associate concept of *exobiology, referring to a hypothetical science of extraterrestrial, especially *alien, society. Its analogical and extrapolative relationship to *ethnology is similar to that between exobiology and *biology. The term is not common, but its utility is argued in such popularising articles as David Brin's "Xenology: The New Science of Asking 'Who's Out There?'", which appeared in the 26 April 1983 issue of *Analog*.

Ethnological perspectives took over from theological ones in the further extrapolation of long-standing discussions of the *plurality of worlds, reconfiguring the notion of the inhabitants of other worlds as "alternative humankinds". In a sense, the move is an extrapolation of the generalising impulse of *anthropology, viewing cultural development as a universal phenomenon of which the currently available examples happen to be human ones.

Although many xenological fantasies may seem to be products of intellectual indolence—especially in the context of TV shows, which have little alternative but to represent aliens as human actors in fancy makeup—the subgenre also provided an ingenious method of side-stepping the intrinsic limitations of speculative ethnological fiction set in the past and present. Rather than decaying into seemingly inevitable extinction, the subgenre of ethnological speculative fiction contained in "lost race" stories was relocated in an extraterrestrial context, its form exactly mirrored in "lost colony" stories set within the framework of a galactic global society, where the possibilities of constructing hypothetical human societies became endless.

Ingenious users of xenological fantasy in this relatively narrow fashion include Poul *Anderson, Jack Vance—most notably in *Big Planet* (1952), *The Languages of Pao* (1958), and *The Blue World* (1966)—and Ursula K. *Le Guin, whose Hainish series and stories collected in *Changing Planes* (2003) brought it to a new level of sophistication. Other notable examples of exotic and technologically limited human societies contained within a galactic cultural framework include Joanna Russ's *And Chaos Died* (1970), Cherry Wilder's *Second Nature* (1982), Donald Kingsbury's *Courtship Rite* (1982; aka *Geta*), Ian Stewart's "Displaced Person" (1987), Helen Collins' *Mutagenesis* (1993), and Ruth Nestvold's "Looking Through Lace" (2003). The utility of this kind of fiction as speculative anthropology is neatly supported in Robert Silverberg's *conte philosophique* "Schwartz Between the Galaxies" (1974).

More adventurous exercises in xenology vary the pattern of "lost colony" stories by substituting alien societies for displaced human ones, and attempting to extrapolate differences in biology and ecology to a cultural level. The anthropologist Chad Oliver produced a considerable number of theoretically sophisticated exercises of this kind, in such stories as "Rite of Passage" (1954), "Field Expedient" (1955), "Between the Thunder and the Sun" (1957), and *Unearthly Neighbors* (1960; rev. 1984). His chief successor in this role was C. J. Cherryh, whose elaborate descriptions of alien culture include the Chanur series (1982–1992) and the series begun with *Foreigner* (1994). James Tiptree Jr.'s *conte philosophique* "And I Awoke and Found Me Here on the Cold Hill's Side" (1971) encapsulated the potential of the subgenre.

Other notable examples of ambitious xenological science fiction include Frank M. Robinson's "The Fire and the Sword" (1951) and "The Santa Claus Planet" (1955), Robert Silverberg's "Precedent" (1957), Richard McKenna's "Mine Own Ways" (1960), John Brunner's *The Long Result* (1965), Fred Saberhagen's *The Water of Thought* (1965; exp. 1981), Edmund Cooper's *A Far Sunset* (1967), Poul Anderson's "The Sharing of Flesh" (1968), Tom Godwin's *Beyond Another Sun* (1971), Michael Bishop's "Death and Designation Among the Asadi" (1973; exp. as *Transfigurations*), Stanley Schmidt's *The Sins of the Fathers* (1976) and *Lifeboat Earth* (1978), John Barnes' "The Limit of Vision" (1988), Deborah D. Ross' "Expression of the Past" (1990), Eleanor Arnason's numerous accounts of the hwarhath, including "The Lovers" (1994), "The Actors" (1999), and "The Potter of Bones" (2002), Philip C. Jennings' "Otherness" (1999), Keith Brooke and Eric Brown's "The Denebian Cycle" (2000), and Karen Traviss' *City of Pearl* (2004).

The alien societies deployed in these stories often display greater similarities to human tribal societies than the "human" examples accommodated within the lost colony framework, because the latter have to be assumed to have started from a situation of technological sophistication. The frequent invocation of *parapsychological powers in lost colony stories and more ambitious xenological fantasies—and in more complex examples that juxtapose hypothetical human and alien societies, such as Ian Watson's *The Embedding* (1973)—inevitably removes such stories to a greater or lesser degree from their ethnological foundations, but such extrapolations are often conducted in a very painstaking fashion.

Accounts of extraterrestrial societies often employ professional anthropologists or xenologists as viewpoint characters, as in Murray Leinster's "Anthropological Note" (1957), Gordon R. Dickson's *Wolfling* (1969), Phyllis Eisenstein's "Taboo" (1981), Eleanor Arnason's *A Woman of the Iron People* (1991), Maya Kaathryn Bohnhoff's "Shaman" (1990) and "Squatter's Rights" (1993), and Robert Reed's "Mere" (2004) and *The Well of Stars* (2005). Accounts of extraterrestrials undertaking xenological studies of humankind include Nancy Kress' *An Alien Light* (1988), Gillian Rubinstein's *Beyond the Labyrinth* (1988), and Sheila Finch's "Nor Unbuild the Cage" (2000). Like actual ethnologists, fictitious xenologists sometimes take the method of participant observation to extremes in "going native", as in Nicola Griffith's *Ammonite* (1993). Alien Rights activists kidnap a visitor from the Carl Sagan Institute for Xenology in James L. Cambias' "The Alien Abduction" (2000).

The great majority of xenological speculators assume, overtly or covertly, a "cultural entropic principle", according to which cultures in contact will always tend to homogenise in the direction of the "higher" level of technological development. Exceptions to this assumption almost invariably assume that heterogeneity can only be maintained in the long term by fervently determined separatism. Many xenological fantasies assume that attempts would be made to counter this tendency by the institution of laws forbidding advanced species to interfere with primitive ones—or at least to refrain from introducing new technologies thereto, as in L. Sprague *de Camp's Viagens series. The general assumption in accounts of human adventurism is that such strictures would prove ineffective because the temptation to meddle would be irresistible; believers in the interpretation of the *Fermi paradox that argues that humans are being protected from alien interference are obliged to hope that the inability to resist temptation is not universal.

Z

ZOOLOGY

The major branch of *biology dealing with the study of animals. The roots of the science extend back to observations made by *Aristotle, reported in *Historia animalium, De partibus animalium,* and *De generatione animalium.* The first deals with the diversity of animal life, the second with morphology, and the third with reproduction. The active nature of animals ensured that zoology would be more glamorous than its immediate counterpart within the larger science, *botany, but this did not inhibit the tendency of the speculative imagination to design creatures far more bizarre and aggressive than those provided by nature. This propensity is not merely manifest in fiction; it is clearly evident in the rich mythology of dragons, the embellishment of Pliny the Elder's *Naturalis Historia* (first century A.D.), mediaeval bestiaries, and the *pseudoscientific extensions of cryptozoology that deal with *Fortean accounts of fabulous creatures.

The fascination of exotic animals is reflected in the habit of collecting and displaying them in menageries, which first developed in Classical times. The particular fascination of large predators is further reflected in the use made of them in Roman circuses. For most of human prehistory, there must have been competition for food between human hunters and various large predators—some of which would also have stalked human prey—but the victory of humankind is clearly written in the *palaeontological record; the great majority of the large species contemporary with the ancestor species of humankind became extinct not long after the initial invasion of their natural territory.

Greek mythology abounds with monstrous animals, many of them chimerical, and such exotic creatures as the phoenix and the sphinx had sufficient allegorical potential to retain them permanent places of honour in the literary tradition. The original accounts were presumably based on travellers' tales, as are the accounts of the unicorn and manticore contained in Ctesias' report of his travels in India. *Plato was the first writer to attempt a methodical debunking of such stories, but his efforts did not dissuade Aristotle from including such creatures in the *Historia Animalium.* Alexander the Great took the trouble to send his former tutor an elephant while he was attempting to conquer India, although he neglected to provide funds for its upkeep.

Pliny's *Naturalis Historia* remained a definitive textbook for centuries, continually echoed in mediaeval texts while most of the legacy of Classical learning had been quite forgotten. It was supplemented in the following century by Aelian's imitative *De Natura Animalium* and the anonymous *Physiologus* but was not replaced as a primary source until the sixteenth century. Pliny showed less restraint than Aristotle, revelling in such dramatic descriptions as an account of a duel to the death between and Indian elephant and a giant python, and adding pegasi (winged horses), the catoblepas (a mammal possessed of a fatal stare), the basilisk (a deadly reptile), the yale (a mammal with movable horns), and various kinds of sea monsters to the traditional catalogue. Much of this material was reproduced in the pioneering encyclopaedia compiled by Isidore of Seville in the early seventh century, and in Albertus Magnus' *De Animalibus* (thirteenth century).

The fabulous beasts of the mediaeval bestiaries were routinely incorporated into romances, where dragons came to play a particularly significant role as adversaries to be defeated; they play a similar role in the legends of the saints collated by Jacobus de Voragine in the thirteenth century, whose account of St. George's dragon-slaying is a carbon copy of a chivalric romance. This kind of crossover became the basis of an elaborate system of "heraldic zoology" whereby shields and coats-of-arms routinely depicted actual and fabulous beasts equipped with all manner of allegorical overtones. A similar process of co-option resulted in the adaptation of the phoenix, the dragon, the unicorn, and the salamander to the symbolism of *alchemy.

Actual travellers did not hesitate to interpret their experiences in the context of the bestiaries with which they were familiar, so Marco Polo's account of his adventures, recorded in 1298, is careful to record that actual unicorns (rhinoceroses) and "gryphons" (flightless birds, also said to be responsible for the mythology of the rukh, or roc) are not what he had expected, and that actual salamanders are actually mineral artefacts (a crude form of asbestos). This did not prevent a roc-like creature, the Garuda bird, cropping up again in Antonio Pigafetta's account of Ferdinand Magellan's pioneering voyage around the world, along with such actual wonders as birds of paradise. When Ludovico Ariosto attempted to satirise the use of fabulous creatures in chivalric romance by inventing the hippogriff in Orlando Furioso (1532), he merely succeeded in adding yet another item to the catalogue. It was against this background that scientific zoologists had to work, and they were bound to be seen by many litterateurs as spoilsports; it is little wonder that the more extravagant discoveries of animal palaeontology—especially mammoths and *dinosaurs—were greeted with such enthusiasm as replacements for creatures banished to the realms of *myth.

More disciplined attempts at zoological classification are evident in such sixteenth-century texts as Conrad Gesner's Historia animalium and Edward Topsell's Historie of Foure-Footed Beasts (1607) and History of Serpents (1608). Topsell was much more expansive than his predecessors—his chapter on the horse ran to book length—and other detailed specialist texts began to proliferate, including Thomas Moffet's pioneering work in *entomology. Carolus Linneaus' attempt to produce a general classification of animals in the eighteenth century was unjustly attacked by the Comte du Buffon, whose own system of classification in the monumental Histoire naturelle des quadrupèdes (12 vols., 1775–1767) and Histoire naturelle des oiseaux (9 vols., 1770–1783) left much

to be desired. Buffon made up for that, however, with the sheer mass of empirical detail he included in his accounts of animal species—whose compilation was greatly assisted by Louis Daubenton, who carried out Buffon's dissections and prepared his specimens for display in the Jardin du Roi. In parallel with Buffon's studies of the higher vertebrates, other French naturalists catalogued the lower vertebrates and invertebrates with the same assiduity, culminating in such definitive studies as Jean-Baptiste de *Lamarck's massive survey of invertebrate species.

The accumulation of these data inevitably gave rise to theories of *evolution, in spite of the opposition mounted by such influential figures as Georges Cuvier. The painstaking work in comparative anatomy done by dissectors like Daubenton also laid the groundwork for the studies in physiology that subsequently became the cutting edge of biological research. Many of the collections of dead and living animals built up in the eighteenth-century era for the purposes of scientific study survived into the twenty first, the institutions maintaining them continuing to work at the forefront of zoological science. The literary reflection of the development of actual zoology, however, never contrived to displace or significantly transform literary reflections of imaginary zoology, which could be custom designed to delight and shock. Accounts of expeditionary zoology like Robert W. Chambers' In Search of the Unknown (1904) and Police!!! (1915) tread a fine line between naturalism and fantasy. Zoos do perform useful symbolic functions, though, in such works as David Garnett's A Man in the Zoo (1924) and Angus Wilson's The Old Men at the Zoo (1961).

The genre of animal fantasy descendant from allegorical and satirical beast fables—which extended into the nineteenth century in such works as Joel Chandler Harris' tales of Brer Rabbit, Rudyard Kipling's Jungle Books (1894–1895), and into the twentieth in the works of Manfred Kyber, Walter Wangerin, and Richard Bach, gradually branched out into naturalistic fictions of a kind pioneered by studies of social insects. Early fiction of this sort featuring higher animals was extensively developed by such writers as Charles G. D. Roberts, "F. St Mars" (Frank Atkins Jr.), and Henry Williamson. When the popularity of animal fantasy was significantly revitalised by Richard Adams' Watership Down (1972), the author made much of his reliance on scientific studies of rabbits, although he borrowed his plot from Virgil's Aeneid. Writers who followed in his footsteps, including William Horwood and Garry Kilworth, made similar attempts to adjust the attitudes and lifestyles of their animal protagonists to contemporary zoological, *ecological, and ethological data.

A distinctive kind of zoological fascination is reflected in the best-selling success of Gerald Durrell's accounts of collecting animals for zoos, including *The Bafut Beagles* (1954), and the manner in which the kind of "wildlife documentary" developed by David Attenborough became an important staple of British TV production. Autobiographical accounts of human interaction with animals like Joy Adamson's *Born Free* (1960), Jane Goodall's *In the Shadow of Man* (1971), and Diane Fossey's *Gorillas in the Mist* (1983) similarly captivated a large audience. The fictional reflections of this kind of fascination include a substantial subgenre of children's fiction featuring horses and a slightly broader subgenre of cat stories, although the most striking examples are fanciful extrapolations into animal fantasy such as the successful subgenre of dragon fantasy.

Extraterrestrial zoology remains the most Romantic branch of *exobiology, frequently giving rise to images of cute aliens reminiscent of Earthly pets and children's toys as well as to all manner of gargantuan and chimerical *monsters. Earth-set stories of exotic discovery informed by scientific perspectives are, however, rare; notable exceptions include the title story of Gerald Heard's *The Lost Cavern* (1948), Gerolf Steiner's account of the nose-walking "rhinogrades" in *Bau und Leben der Rhinogradentia* (1961; by-lined Harald Stümpke; trans. as *The Snouters*), and Rick Shelley's "Safari" (1997). Hilbert Schenck's "Send Me a Kiss by Wire" (1985), Robert Reed's "Blind" (1993), and Gregory Bennett's "Fish Tank" (1995) feature deep-sea life-forms, in recognition of the fact that few large animal species are likely to remain undiscovered on land. The opportunity presented by *genetic engineering to design and create new exotic species is reflected in such stories as Ian Watson's "Hyperzoo" (1987).

One area of zoology that has attracted intense speculative interest in futuristic fiction is the question of which of humankind's competitor species is best equipped to replace us as the planet's dominant species should we be unfortunate enough to become extinct. Apes have had the greatest popular exposure thanks to the film version of Pierre Boulle's *La Planète des singes* (1963; trans. as *Monkey Planet*; film 1968 as *Planet of the Apes*), but other favourite contenders include dogs, as in Clifford Simak's *City* series (1944–1951; book, 1952); rats, as in Hugh Sykes Davies' *The Papers of Andrew Melmoth* (1960) and A. Bertram Chandler's *The Hamelin Plague* (1963); and pigs, whose surprising popularity in this kind of story—reflected in Sylvie Denis' anthology *Histoires de cochons et de Science-Fiction* (1998)—was probably assisted by their key role in George Orwell's *Animal Farm* (1945).

Notable literary accounts of zoologists at work are relatively rare, but Kandis Elliot's series about a zoologist investigating the fauna of Dodge County, Wisconsin, begun with "Laddie of the Lake" (1994) is a notable exception; others include numerous accounts of specialist delphinologists and Robert R. Chase's "Seven Times Never" (2001). The language of elephants is belatedly decoded, although the independent state set up in recognition proves short-lived, in M. Shayne Bell's "Refugees from Nulongwe" (2001). All such representations have to work against a background in which the diversity of species is dwindling, and the loss is highly likely to accelerate sharply in the near future—an awareness ironically reflected in Robert Reed's "At the Corner of Darwin and Eternity" (1999).

Bibliography

I. Specialized bibliographical works containing details of numerous works to which reference is made in the articles

Bleiler, Everett F. *The Checklist of Fantastic Literature: A Bibliography of Fantasy, Weird and Science Fiction Books Published in the English Language.* Chicago: Shasta, 1948. Rev. as *The Checklist of Science-Fiction and Supernatural Fiction.* Glen Rock, N.J.: Firebell, 1978.

———. *Science-Fiction, the Early Years: A Full Description of More than 3000 Science-Fiction Stories from Earliest Times to the Appearance of the Genre Magazines in 1930, with Author, Title, and Motif Indexes.* Kent, Ohio: Kent State University Press, 1990.

Bleiler, Everett, F., and Richard Bleiler. *Science-Fiction: The Gernsback Years.* Kent, Ohio: Kent State University Press, 1998.

Brown, Charles N., and William G. Contento. *The Locus Index to Science Fiction (1984–1999),* combined with William G. Contento, *Index to Science Fiction Anthologies and Collections.* Oakland, Calif.: Locus Press, 2000. Available in a CD-ROM version or online at www.locusmag.com.

Clareson, Thomas. *Science Fiction in America, 1870s–1930s: An Annotated Bibliography.* Westport, Conn.: Greenwood, 1984.

Clarke, I. F. *The Tale of the Future from the Beginning to the Present Day: An Annotated Bibliography.* London: London Library, 3rd ed. 1978.

Hardy, Phil, ed. *Science Fiction: The Aurum Film Encyclopedia.* 2nd ed. London: Aurum Press, 1991.

Miller, Stephen T., and William G. Contento. *Science Fiction, Fantasy, & Weird Fiction Magazine Index (1890–1999).* Oakland, Calif.: Locus Press, 2000. Available in a CD-ROM version or online at www.locusmag.com.

Sargent, Lyman Tower. *British and American Utopian Literature 1516–1986.* 2nd ed. New York: Garland, 1988.

II. Works on the relationship between science, the history of ideas, and fiction

Amrine, Frederick, ed. *Literature and Science as Modes of Expression.* Boston: Kluwer, 1989.

Apollonio, Umbro, ed. *The Futurist Manifestos.* New York: Viking, 1973.

Arbold, Matthew. "Literature and Science". *The Nineteenth Century* (August 1882): 216–230.

Backscheider, Paula R., ed. *Probability, Time, and Space in Eighteenth Century Literature.* New York: AMS Press, 1979.

Barnes, Myra Edwards. *Linguistics and Language in Science Fiction-Fantasy.* New York: Arno Press, 1974.

Beer, Gillian. *Darwin's Plots: Evolutionary Narrative in Darwin, George Eliot and Nineteenth-Century Fiction.* 1983.

Benjamin, Marina, ed. *A Question of Identity: Women, Science, and Literature.* New Brunswick, N.J.: Rutgers University Press, 1993.

Blunden, Edmund. *English Scientists as Men of Letters.* Hong Kong: Hong Kong University Press, 1961.

Brown, Harcourt. *Science and the Human Comedy: Natural Philosophy in French Literature from Rabelais to Maupertuis.* Toronto: University of Toronto Press, 1976.

Bush, Douglas. *Science and English Poetry: A Historical Sketch, 1590–1950.* Oxford: Oxford University Press, 1950.

Cartwright, John H., and Brian Baker. *Literature and Science: Social Impact and Interaction.* Santa Barbara, Calif.: ABC-CLIO, 2005.

Chapple, J. A. V. *Science and Literature in the Nineteenth Century.* London: Macmillan, 1986.

Christie, John, and Sally Shuttleworth, eds. *Nature Transfigured: Science and Literature 1700–1900.* Manchester, England: Manchester University Press, 1989.

Cohen, John. *Human Robots in Myth and Science.* Cranbury, N.J.: Barnes, 1967.

Cosslett, Tess. *The Scientific Movement and Victorian Literature.* Brighton: Harvester Press, 1982.

Crowe, Michael J. *The Extraterrestrial Life Debate 1750–1900: The Idea of a Plurality of Worlds from Kant to Lowell.* Cambridge: Cambridge University Press, 1986.

Crum, Ralph Brinckerhoff. *Scientific Thought in Poetry.* New York: Columbia University Press, 1931.

Cunningham, Andrew, and Nicholas Jardine, eds. *Romanticism and the Sciences.* Cambridge: Cambridge University Press, 1990.

Czerneda, Julie. *No Limits: Developing Scientific Literacy Using Science Fiction.* Toronto: Trifolium, 1998.

Daly, Nicholas. *Literature, Technology and Modernity, 1860–1900.* Cambridge: Cambridge University Press, 2004.

Dann, Jack, and George Zebrowski, eds. *Faster than Light.* New York: Harper and Row, 1976.

De Camp, L. Sprague. "Language for Time Travelers". *Astounding Science Fiction* (July 1938): 63–72.

De Laurentis, Teresa, and Andreas Huyssen and Kathleen Woodward, eds. *The Technological Imagination: Theories and Fictions.* Madison, Wis.: Coda, 1980.

Duncan, Carson S. *The New Science and English Literature in the Classical Period.* Menasha, Wis.: George Banta, 1913.

Eastman, Max. *The Literary Mind: Its Place in an Age of Science.* New York: Scribner, 1935.

Eastwood, Winifred, ed. *Science and Literature.* London: Macmillan, 1957.

BIBLIOGRAPHY

———. *Science and Literature: Second Series*. London: Macmillan, 1960.

Edgerton, Samuel Y. *The Heritage of Giotto's Geometry: Art and Science on the Eve of the Scientific Revolution*. Ithaca, N.Y.: Cornell University Press, 1991.

Flammarion, Camille. *Les Mondes imaginaires et les mondes réels: voyage pittoresque dans le ciel et revue critique des théories humaines, scientifiques et romanesques, anciennes et modernes sur les habitants des astres*. Paris: Didier et cie, 1864; exp. Paris: Marpon et Flammarion, 1892.

Freeman, Michael. *Victorians and the Prehistoric: Tracks to a Lost World*. New Haven, Conn.: Yale University Press, 2004.

Freud, Sigmund. *The Uncanny*. London: Penguin, 2003 [1919].

Ginestier, Paul. *The Poet and the Machine*. Trans. by Martin B. Friedman. Chapel Hill: University of North Carolina Press, 1961.

Glicksberg, Charles I. "Science and the Literary Mind". *Scientific Monthly* 70, 1950.

Gossin, Pamela, ed. *Encyclopedia of Literature and Science*. Westport, Conn.: Greenwood Press, 2002.

Goswami, Amit and Maggie. *The Cosmic Dancers: Exploring the Physics of Science Fiction*. New York: Harper, 1983.

Green, Martin. *Science and the Shabby Curate of Poetry: Essays About the Two Cultures*. London: Longmans, 1964.

Guthke, Karl. *The Last Frontier: Imagining Other Worlds, from the Copernican Revolution to Modern Science Fiction*. Trans. by Helen Atkins. Ithaca, N.Y.: Cornell University Press, 1990.

Hardison, O. B., Jr. *Disappearing Through the Skylight: Culture and Technology in the Twentieth Century*. New York: Viking, 1989.

Harvie, Christopher, and Graham Martin and Aaron Scharf, eds. *Industrialisation and Culture 1830–1914*. London: Macmillan, 1970.

Hawley, Judith, ed. *Literature and Science, 1660–1834*. 8 vols. London: Pickering and Chatto, 2003–2004.

Hayles, N. Katherine. *The Cosmic Web: Scientific Field Models and Literary Strategies in the Twentieth Century*. Ithaca, N.Y.: Cornell University Press, 1984.

———. *Chaos Bound: Orderly Disorder in Contemporary Literature and Science*. Ithaca, N.Y.: Cornell University Press, 1990.

———, ed. *Chaos and Order: Complex Dynamics in Literature and Science*. Chicago: University of Chicago Press, 1991.

———. *How We Became Posthuman: Virtual Bodies in Cybernetics, Literature and Informatics*. Chicago: University of Chicago Press, 1999.

Hayter, Alethea. *Opium and the Romantic Imagination*. London: Faber, 1968.

Heath-Stubbs, John, and Salman Phillips, eds. *Poems of Science*. Harmondsworth, Middx., U.K.: Penguin, 1984.

Henderson, Linda Dalrymple. *The Fourth Dimension and Non-Euclidean Geometry in Modern Art*. Princeton, N.J.: Princeton University Press, 1983.

Heninger, S. K., Jr. *Touches of Sweet Harmony: Pythagorean Cosmology and Renaissance Poetics*. San Marino, Calif.: Huntington Library, 1974.

Henkin, Leo J. *Darwinism in the English Novel, 1860–1910: The Impact of Evolution on Victorian Fiction*. New York: Russell and Russell, 1940.

Hirsch, Walter. "The Image of the Scientist in Science Fiction". *American Journal of Sociology* 43 (1958): 506–512.

Hogan, Patrick Colm. *Cognitive Science, Literature and the Arts: A Guide for Humanists*. New York: Routledge, 2003.

Huxley, Aldous. *Literature and Science*. London: Chatto and Windus, 1963.

Hyman, Stanley Edgar. *The Tangled Bank: Darwin, Marx, Frazer and Freud as Imaginative Writers*. New York: Atheneum, 1962.

Isaacs, Leonard. *Darwin to Double Helix: The Biological Theme in Science Fiction*. Boston: Butterworth, 1977.

Jeffares, A. Norman. *Language, Literature and Science: An Inaugural Lecture*. Cambridge: Leeds University Press, 1959.

Jennings, Humphrey. *Pandaemonium: The Coming of the Machine as Seen by Contemporary Observers*, ed. Mary-Lou Jennings and Charles Madge. London: André Deutsch, 1985.

Johnson, Francis R. *Astronomical Thought in Renaissance English: A Study of Scientific Writing from 1500 to 1645*. Baltimore, Md.: Johns Hopkins Press, 1937.

Jones, William Powell. *The Rhetoric of Sciences: A Study of Scientific Ideas and Imagery in Eighteenth-Century English Poetry*. Berkeley: University of California Press, 1966.

Jordanova, L. J., ed. *Languages of Nature: Critical Essays on Science and Literature*. New Brunswick, N.J.: Rutgers University Press, 1986.

Kern, Stephen. *The Culture of Time and Space 1880–1918*. Cambridge, Mass.: Harvard University Press, 1983.

Klingender, Francis. *Art and the Industrial Revolution*. London: Noel Carrington, 1947.

Knoepflmacher, U. C. *Religious Humanism and the Victorian Novel*. Princeton, N.J.: Princeton University Press, 1965.

Lambourne, Robert, and Michael Shallis and Michael Shortland. *Close Encounters? Science and Science Fiction*. New York: Hilger, 1990.

Lem, Stanislaw. "Cosmology and Science Fiction". *Science Fiction Studies* 4 (July 1977): 107–110.

Levere, Trevor Harvey. *Poetry Realized in Nature: Samuel Taylor Coleridge and Early Nineteenth-Century Science*. Cambridge: Cambridge University Press, 1981.

Levine, George. *Darwin and the Novelists: Patterns of Science in Victorian Fiction*. Cambridge, Mass.: Harvard University Press, 1988.

———, ed. *One Culture: Essays in Science and Literature*. Madison: University of Wisconsin Press, 1990.

Lewis, Arthur O., Jr., ed. *Of Men and Machines*. New York: Dutton, 1963.

Livingston, Paisley. *Literary Knowledge: Humanistic Inquiry and the Philosophy of Science*. Ithaca, N.Y.: Cornell University Press, 1988.

———. *Literature and Rationality: Ideas of Agency in Theory and Fiction*. Cambridge: Cambridge University Press, 1991.

Ludwig, Arnold M. "Hypnosis in Fiction". *Journal of Clinical and Experimental Hypnosis* 11 (1963): 71–80.

Lutwack, Leonard. *Birds in Literature*. Pensacola: University Press of Florida Gainesville, 1994.

Marsh, Rosalind J. *Soviet Fiction Since Stalin: Science, Politics and Literature*. Totowa, N.J.: Barnes and Noble, 1986.

Marx, Leo. *The Machine in the Garden: Technology and the Pastoral Ideal in America.* Oxford: Oxford University Press, 1964.

McColley, Grant, ed. *Literature and Science: An Anthology from English and American Literature, 1600–1900.* Chicago: Packard, 1940.

McKean, Kevin. "Computers, Fiction and Poetry". *Byte* (July 1982): 50–53.

Meehan, James R. *The Metanovel: Writing Stories by Computer.* Yale University Research Report 74 (1976).

Meyers, Amy R. W. *Art and Science in America: Issues of Representation.* San Marino, Calif.: Huntington Library, 1998.

Meyers, Walter E. *Aliens and Linguists: Language Study and Science Fiction.* Athens: University of Georgia Press, 1980.

Millhauser, Milton. "Dr. Newton and Mr. Hyde: Scientists in Fiction from Swift to Stevenson". *Nineteenth-Century Fiction* 28 (1973–1974): 287–304.

Moore, Patrick. *Science and Fiction.* London: Harrap, 1957.

Morton, Peter. *The Vital Science: Biology and the Literary Imagination.* London: Allen and Unwin, 1985.

Mumford, Lewis. *Art and Technics.* New York: Columbia University Press, 1952.

Nadeau, Robert. *Readings from the New Book on Nature: Physics and Metaphysics in the Modern Novel.* Amherst: University of Massachusetts Press, 1981.

Nahin, Paul J. *Time Machines: Time Travel in Physics, Metaphysics and Science Fiction.* New York: Springer-Verlag (American Institute of Physics Press), 1999.

Nash, Christopher, ed. *Narrative in Culture: The Uses of Storytelling in the Sciences, Philosophy, and Literature.* London: Routledge, 1990.

Nicholls, Peter, and David Langford and Brian Stableford. *The Science in Science Fiction.* London: Michael Joseph, 1982.

Nicolson, Marjorie Hope. *Newton Demands the Muse: Newton's Opticks and Eighteenth Century Poets.* Princeton, N.J.: Princeton University Press, 1946.

———. *The Breaking of the Circle: Studies in the Effect of the "New Science" upon Seventeenth Century Poetry.* Evanston, Ill.: Northwestern University Press, 1950.

———. *Science and Imagination.* Ithaca, N.Y.: Cornell University Press, 1956.

Norford, Don Parry. "Microcosm and Macrocosm in Seventeenth-Century Literature". *Journal of the History of Ideas* 38 (1977): 409–428.

O'Brien, Edward J. *The Dance of the Machines: The American Short Story and the Industrial Age.* New York: Macaulay, 1929.

Ordway, Frederick I., and Randy Liebermann, eds. *Blueprint for Space: Science Fiction to Science Fact.* Washington, D.C.: Smithsonian Institution, 1992.

Otis, Laura, ed. *Literature and Science in the Nineteenth Century.* Oxford: Oxford University Press, 2002.

Paradis, James, and Thomas Postlewait, eds. *Victorian Science and Victorian Values: Literary Perspectives.* New York: New York Academy of Sciences, 1981.

Parrinder, Patrick. "Scientists in Science Fiction: Enlightenment and After". In *Science Fiction: Roots and Branches,* ed. Rhys Garnett and R. J. Ellis, pp. 57–78. London: Macmillan, 1990.

Pastourmatzi, Domna, ed. *Biotechnological and Medical Themes in Science Fiction.* Thessaloniki, Greece: Aristotle University, 2003.

Plotnisky, Arkady. *The Knowable and the Unknowable: Modern Science, Nonclassical Thought and the "Two Cultures".* Ann Arbor: University of Michigan Press, 2002.

Polak, Fred. *The Image of the Future.* Amsterdam: Elsevier, 1973.

Priestley, J. B. *Man and Time.* London: Aldus, 1964.

Read, Herbert. *Art and Industry.* London: Faber and Faber, 1934.

Richards, I. A. *Science and Poetry.* London: Kegan Paul, Trench, Trubner, 1926. (Reissued as *Poetries and Sciences,* New York: Norton, 1970.)

Roberts, Marie Mulvey, and Roy Porter, eds. *Literature and Medicine During the Eighteenth Century.* London: Routledge, 1993.

Rousseau, G. S., and Roy Porter, eds. *The Ferment of Knowledge: Studies in the Historiography of Eighteenth Century Science.* Cambridge: Cambridge University Press, 1980.

Russell, W. M. S. "Biology and Literature in Britain, 1500–1900. I: From the Renaissance to the Romantics". *Biology and Human Affairs* 44:1 (1979): 50–72.

———. "Biology and Literature in Britain, 1500–1900. II: The Victorians". *Biology and Human Affairs* 44:2 (1979): 114–133.

———. "Biology and Literature in Britain, 1500–1900. III: The Parting of the Ways". *Social Biology and Human Affairs* 45:1 (1980): 52–71.

Schenkel, Elmar, and Stefan Welz, eds. *Lost Worlds and Mad Elephants: Literature, Science and Technology, 1700–1900.* Leipzig, Germany: Galda + Witch Verlag, 1999.

Sewell, Elizabeth. *The Orphic Voice: Poetry and Natural History.* London: Routledge and Kegan Paul, 1961.

Slade, Joseph W., and Judith Yaross Lee, eds. *Beyond the Two Cultures: Essays on Science, Technology, and Literature.* Ames: Iowa State University Press, 1990.

Soltzberg, Leonard J. *Sing a Song of Software: Verse and Images for the Computer Literate.* Los Altos, Calif.: Kaufmann, 1984.

Soupel, Serge, and Roger A. Hambridge, eds. *Literature and Science and Medicine.* Los Angeles: Clark Memorial Library, University of California, 1982.

Stevenson, Lionel. *Darwin Among the Poets.* Chicago: Chicago University Press, 1932.

Stocker, Jack H., ed. *Chemistry and Science Fiction.* Washington, D.C.: American Chemical Society, 1998.

Street, Brian V. *The Savage in Literature: Representations of "Primitive" Society in English Fiction, 1858–1920.* London: Routledge and Kegan Paul, 1975.

Sussman, Herbert L. *Victorians and the Machine: The Literary Response to Technology.* Cambridge, Mass.: Harvard University Press, 1968.

Todd, Ruthven. *Tracks in the Snow: Studies in English Science and Art.* London: Grey Walls Press, 1946.

Vos Post, Jonathan, and Kirk L. Kroeker. "Writing the Future: Computers in Science Fiction". *Computer* 33:1 (January 2000): 29–37.

Wachhorst, Wyn. *The Dream of Spaceflight: Essays on the Near Edge of Infinity.* New York: Basic Books, 2000.

Warrick, Patricia S. *The Cybernetic Imagination in Science Fiction.* Cambridge, Mass: MIT Press, 1980.

Wilson, David L., and Zack Bowen. *Science and Literature: Bridging the Two Cultures.* Gainesville: University Press of Florida, 2001.

Wright, Hamilton, and Helen Wright and Samuel Rapport, eds. *To the Moon: A Distillation of the Great Writings from Ancient Legend to Space Exploration.* New York: Meredith Press, 1968.

Young, R. M. *Darwin's Metaphor: Nature's Place in Victorian Culture.* Cambridge: Cambridge University Press, 1985.

III. Works on science, pseudoscience, and the history of ideas that have particular relevance to the relationship of science and fiction

Achenbach, Joel. *Captured by Aliens: The Search for Life and Truth in a Very Large Universe.* New York: Simon & Schuster, 1999.

Anderson, Poul. *Is There Life on Other Worlds?* New York: Crowell-Collier, 1963.

Andreadis, Athena. *To Seek Out New Life: The Biology of Star Trek.* New York: Random House, 1998.

Arrhenius, Svante. *Worlds in the Making.* New York: Harper, 1908.

————. *The Life of the Universe as Conceived by Man from the Earliest Ages to the Present Time.* Trans. by H. Borns. New York: Harper, 1909.

Asimov, Isaac. "Not as We Know It". *The Magazine of Fantasy & Science Fiction* (September 1961): 82–92.

————. *Extraterrestrial Civilizations.* New York: Doubleday, 1979.

Bachelard, Gaston. *The Poetics of Space.* Trans. by Maria Jolas. Boston: Beacon Press, 1964.

Bannister, Robert C. *Social Darwinism: Science and Myth in Anglo-American Social Thought.* Philadelphia: Temple University Press, 1979.

Barrow, John D., and Frank Tipler. *The Anthropic Cosmological Principle.* Oxford: Oxford University Press, 1986.

Baudrillard, Jean. *Simulations.* New York: Semiotext[e], 1983.

Bazerman, Charles. *Shaping Written Knowledge: The Genre and Activity of the Experimental Article in Science.* Madison: University of Wisconsin Press, 1988.

Benford, Gregory. *Deep Time: How Humanity Communicates Across Millennia.* New York: Avon/Bard, 1999.

Bernal, J. D. *The World, the Flesh and the Devil: An Enquiry into the Future of the Three Enemies of the Rational Soul.* London: Kegan Paul, Trench and Trubner, 1929.

Berstein, Jeremy. *Cranks, Quarks, and the Cosmos.* New York: Basic Books, 1993.

Boden, Margaret. *Artificial Intelligence and Natural Man.* New York: Basic Books, 1977.

————. *The Creative Mind: Myths & Mechanisms.* New York: Basic Books, 1991.

Bolter, J. David. *Turing's Man: Western Culture in the Computer Age.* Chapel Hill: University of North Carolina Press, 1984.

Börner, Gerhard. *The Early Universe: Fact and Fiction.* Berlin: Springer-Verlag, 1992.

Brock, W. H., and A. J. Meadows. *The Lamp of Learning: Taylor & Francis and the Development of Science Publishing.* London: Taylor & Francis, 1984.

Broughton, Richard S. *Parapsychology: The Controversial Science.* New York: Ballantine, 1991.

Brown, Norman O. *Life Against Death: The Psychoanalytical Meaning of History.* London: Routledge and Kegan Paul, 1959.

Brush, Stephen G. *The Temperature of History: Phases of Science and Culture in the Nineteenth Century.* New York: Burt Franklin, 1978.

Burrow, J. W. *Evolution and Society: A Study in Victorian Social Theory.* Cambridge: Cambridge University Press, 1966.

Bury, J. B. *The Idea of Progress.* London: Macmillan, 1920.

Butler, Elizabeth M. *The Fortunes of Faust.* Cambridge: Cambridge University Press, 1952.

Carey, John, ed. *The Faber Book of Science.* London: Faber and Faber, 1995.

Chapuis, Alfred, and Edmond Droz. *Automata: A Historical and Technological Study.* New York: Griffon, 1958.

Cipolla, Carlo M. *Guns, Sails and Empires: Technological Innovation and the Early Phases of European Expansion 1400–1700.* New York: Minerva Press, 1965.

————. *Clocks and Culture 1300–1700.* New York: Walker, 1967.

Clarke, Arthur C. *The Exploration of Space.* London: Temple, 1951.

————. *The Challenge of the Spaceship.* New York, Harper, 1959.

————. *Profiles of the Future.* London: Gollancz, 1962.

————. *Voices from the Sky.* New York: Harper and Row, 1965.

————. *The Coming of the Space Age.* New York: Meredith, 1967.

Cleator, P. E. *Rockets Through Space: The Dawn of Interplanetary Travel.* New York: Simon and Schuster, 1936.

Cohen, Jack, and Ian Stewart. *The Collapse of Chaos: Discovering Simplicity in a Complex World.* Harmondsworth, Middx., U.K.: Penguin, 1994.

————. *Evolving the Alien: The Science of Extraterrestrial Life.* London: Ebury Press, 2002.

Cohen, John. *Psychological Probability; or, The Art of Doubt.* London: Allen and Unwin, 1972.

Cowley, Robert, ed. *What If? Eminent Historians Imagine What Might Have Been.* 2 vols. New York: Putnam, 1999–2001.

Darwin, Charles. *On the Origin of Species by Means of Natural Selection; or, The Preservation of Favoured Races in the Struggle for Life.* London: John Murray, 1859.

————. *The Descent of Man, and Selection in Relation to Sex.* London: John Murray, 1871.

————. *The Expression of the Emotions in Man and Animals.* London: John Murray, 1872.

Darwin, Erasmus. *The Botanic Garden, A Poem.* London: J. Johnson, 1791.

————. *Zoonomia; or, The Laws of Organic Life.* London: J. Johnson, 1801.

————. *The Temple of Nature; or, The Origin of Society.* London: J. Johnson, 1803.

Davies, Paul. *Are We Alone? Implications of the Discovery of Extraterrestrial Life.* New York: Basic Books, 1995.

De Camp, L. Sprague. "The Science of Whithering". *Astounding Science Fiction* (July–August 1940): 83–93, 108–116.

De Landa, Manuel. *War in the Age of Intelligent Machines.* New York: Zone, 1991.

Dennis, Geoffrey. *The End of the World.* London: Eyre and Spottiswoode, 1930.

Dery, Mark. *Escape Velocity: Cyberculture at the End of the Century.* London: Hodder and Stoughton, 1996.

Dick, Steven J. *Life on Other Worlds: The Twentieth Century Extraterrestrial Life Debate.* Cambridge: Cambridge University Press, 1998.

Diebold, John. *Man and the Computer: Technology as an Agent of Social Change*. New York: Avon, 1969.

Dixon, Bernard, ed. *From Creation to Chaos: Classic Writings in Science*. London: Blackwell, 1989.

Drexler, K. Eric. *Engines of Creation: The Coming Era of Nanotechnology*. New York: Doubleday, 1986.

Drexler, K. Eric, and Chris Peterson, with Gayle Pergamot. *Unbounding the Future: The Nanotechnology Revolution*. New York: Simon and Schuster, 1991.

Dunne, J. W. *An Experiment with Time*. London: A. & C. Black, 1926.

———. *The Serial Universe*. London: Faber, 1934.

Dyer, Frank, and Thomas C. Martin, with William Meadowcroft. *Edison: His Life and Inventions*. New York: Harper, 1910; rev. 1929.

Dyson, Freeman. "Time Without End: Physics and Biology in an Open Universe". *Reviews of Modern Physics* 51 (1979): 452–454.

———. *Disturbing the Universe*. New York: Basic Books 1981.

———. *Infinite in All Directions*. New York: Basic Books, 1988.

Dyson, George B. *Darwin Among the Machines: The Evolution of Global Intelligence*. Reading, Mass.: Addison-Wesley, 1997.

Ehrlich, Paul R. "Ecocatastrophe". *Ramparts* 8 (1969): 24–28.

Eiseley, Loren. *The Firmament of Time*. New York: Atheneum, 1960.

———. *The Unexpected Universe*. New York: Harcourt, Brace and World, 1969.

Ettinger, Robert C. W. *The Prospect of Immortality*. Author, 1963; exp. New York: Doubleday, 1964.

Famelo, Graham, ed. *It Must Be Beautiful: Great Equations of Modern Science*. London: Granta, 2002.

Febvre, Lucien, and Henri-Jean Martin. *The Coming of the Book: The Impact of Printing, 1450–1800*. London: Verso, 1976.

Fisher. Len. *Weighing the Soul: The Evolution of Scientific Beliefs*. London: Weidenfeld and Nicholson, 2004.

Fleck, L. *Genesis and Development of a Scientific Fact*. Chicago: Chicago University Press, 1935.

Flew, Antony. *A New Approach to Psychical Research*. London: C. A. Watts, 1953.

Fogg, Martin J. *Terraforming: Engineering Planetary Environments*. Warrendale, Penn.: SAE International, 1995.

Fort, Charles. *The Book of the Damned*. New York: Boni Liveright, 1919.

———. *New Lands*. New York: Boni Liveright, 1923.

———. *Lo!* New York: Kendall, 1931.

———. *Wild Talents*. New York: Kendall, 1932.

Foucault, Michel. *Madness and Civilization: A History of Insanity in the Age of Reason*. Trans. by Richard Howard. New York: Random House, 1965.

Fraser, J. T., ed. *The Voices of Time*. New York: Braziller, 1966.

Frazer, James G. *The Golden Bough: A Study in Comparative Religion*. 2 vols. London: Macmillan, 1890. Rev. as *The Golden Bough: A Study in Magic and Religion*. 13 vols. London: Macmillan, 1932.

Frazier, Kendrick. *Paranormal Borderlands of Science*. Buffalo: Prometheus, 1981.

Freitas, Robert A. "Xenobiology". *Analog* (30 March 1981): 30–41.

Freud, Sigmund. *The Interpretation of Dreams*. London: George Allen, 1913.

———. *Introductory Lectures in Psychoanalysis (Revised Edition)*. London: Allen and Unwin, 1929.

———. *Civilization and Its Discontents*. Trans. by J. Rivière. London: Hogarth Press, 1930.

Friedman, Louis. *Starsailing: Solar Sails and Interstellar Travel*. New York: Wiley, 1988.

Fuller, John G. *The Interrupted Journey*. New York: Dial Press, 1966.

Fuller, Robert C. *Mesmerism and the American Cure of Souls*. Philadelphia: University of Pennsylvania Press, 1982.

Galton, Francis. *Hereditary Genius: An Enquiry into Its Laws and Consequences*. London: Macmillan, 1869.

Gamow, George. *Mr. Tompkins in Wonderland*. Cambridge: Cambridge University Press, 1929.

———. *The Birth and Death of the Sun*. New York: Viking, 1940.

———. *Biography of the Earth*. New York: Viking, 1941.

———. *Mr. Tompkins Explores the Atom*. New York: Macmillan, 1944.

———. *1, 2, 3 ... Infinity*. New York: Viking, 1947.

Gee, Henry. *The Science of Middle-Earth*. London: Souvenir Press, 2005.

Gimpel, Jean. *The Medieval Machine: The Industrial Revolution of the Middle Ages*. London: Gollancz, 1977.

Glacken, Clarence. *Traces on the Rhodian Shore: Nature and Culture in Western Thought from Ancient Times to the End of the Eighteenth Century*. Berkeley: University of California Press, 1967.

Glassy, Mark C. *The Biology of Science Fiction Cinema*. Jefferson, N.C.: McFarland, 2001.

Gould, Stephen Jay. *Ever Since Darwin*. New York: Norton, 1977.

———. *The Mismeasure of Man*. New York: Norton, 1993.

Greene, John C. *The Death of Adam: Evolution and Its Impact on Western Thought*. Ames: Iowa State University Press, 1959.

Gribbin, John. *In Search of Schrödinger's Cat*. New York: Bantam, 1984.

Gribbin, John, and Mary Gribbin. *The Science of Philip Pullman's "His Dark Materials"*. London: Hodder and Stoughton, 2003.

Gross, Alan G. *The Rhetoric of Science*. Cambridge, Mass.: Harvard University Press, 1990.

Haldane, J. B. S. *Daedalus; or, Science and the Future*. London: Kegan Paul, Trench & Trubner, 1923.

———. *Possible Worlds and Other Essays*. London: Chatto & Windus, 1927.

———. *The Inequality of Man and Other Essays*. London: Chatto & Windus, 1932.

Hanley, Richard. *The Metaphysics of Star Trek; or, Is Data Human?* New York: Basic Books. 1997.

Hanlon, Michael. *The Science of The Hitchhiker's Guide to the Galaxy*. London: Palgrave Macmillan, 2005.

Hanson, Norwood Russell. *Patterns of Discovery: An Inquiry into the Conceptual Foundations of Science*. Cambridge: Cambridge University Press, 1958.

Hardin, Garrett. "The Tragedy of the Commons". *Science* 162 (1968): 1243–1248.

Harris, John. *Wonderwoman and Superman: The Ethics of Human Biotechnology*. Oxford: Oxford University Press, 1992.

Hawking, Stephen W. *A Brief History of Time*. London: Bantam, 1988.

Hinton, C. H. *Scientific Romances*. London: Swann Sonnenschein, 1886.

Hofstader, Douglas R. *Gödel, Escher, Bach: An Eternal Golden Braid*. New York: Basic Books, 1979.

Hostader, Douglas R., and Daniel C. Dennett. *The Mind's I: Fantasies and Reflections on Self and Soul*. New York: Bantam, 1982.

Hofsteader, Richard. *Social Darwinism in American Thought*. New York: Braziller, 1959.

Hoyle, Fred. *The Intelligent Universe: A New View of Creation and Evolution*. London: Michael Joseph, 1983.

Hoyle, Fred, and Chandra Wickramasinghe. *Lifecloud: The Origin of Life in the Universe*. London: Dent, 1978.

———. *Evolution from Space*. London: Dent, 1981.

Huizinga, Johan. *Homo Ludens: A Study of the Play-Element in Culture*. New York: Roy, 1950.

Huxley, Aldous. *The Doors of Perception*. London: Chatto and Windus, 1954.

———. *Brave New World Revisited*. New York: Harper, 1958.

———. *Heaven and Hell*. New York: Harper, 1966.

Huxley, Julian. *Essays of a Biologist*. London: Chatto and Windus, 1923.

Islam, Jamal N. *The Ultimate Fate of the Universe*. Cambridge: Cambridge University Press, 1983.

Israel, Paul. *Edison: A Life of Invention*. New York: Wiley, 1998.

James, Jamie. *The Universe Around Us*. Cambridge: Cambridge University Press, 1929.

———. *The Mysterious Universe*. Cambridge: Cambridge University Press, 1930.

———. *The Music of the Spheres: Music, Science and the Natural Order of the Universe*. New York: Grove Press, 1993.

Jenkins, Susan, and Robert Jenkins. *Life Signs: The Biology of Star Trek*. New York: HarperCollins, 1998.

Jones, Harold Spencer. *Life on Other Worlds*. New York: Macmillan, 1940.

Josephson, Eric, and Mary Josephson, eds. *Man Alone: Alienation in Modern Society*. New York: Dell, 1962.

Jung, Carl G. *Modern Man in Search of a Soul*. Trans. by Cary Baynes. London: Routledge and Kegan Paul, 1933.

———. *Flying Saucers: A Modern Myth of Things Seen in the Sky*. Trans. by R. F. C. Hull. London: Routledge and Kegan Paul, 1959.

Jung, Carl G., and M.-L. von Franz, Joseph L. Henderson, Jolande Jacobi, and Aniela Jaffé. *Man and His Symbols*. London: Aldus, 1964.

Kahn, Herman J., and Anthony J. Wiener. *The Year 2000*. New York: Macmillan, 1968.

Kaku, Michio. *Hyperspace: A Scientific Odyssey Through Parallel Universes, Time Warps, and the 10th Dimension*. New York: Anchor Books, 1995.

Kasner, Edward, and James Newman. *Mathematics and the Imagination*. New York: Simon and Schuster, 1940.

Keyhoe, Donald E. *The Flying Saucers Are Real*. New York: Gold Medal, 1950.

Kline, Morris. *Mathematics in Western Culture*. London: Allen and Unwin, 1954.

Knorr-Cetina, K. *The Manufacture of Knowledge*. Oxford: Pergamon, 1981.

Koestler, Arthur. *The Sleepwalkers: A History of Man's Changing Vision of the Universe*. London: Hutchinson, 1959.

Koyré, Alexander. *From the Closed World to the Infinite Universe*. Baltimore, Md.: Johns Hopkins University Press, 1991.

Kranzberg, Melvin, and William H. Davenport, eds. *Technology and Culture: An Anthology*. New York: Schocken Books, 1972.

Krauss, Lawrence N. *The Physics of Star Trek*. New York: Basic Books, 1995.

———. *Beyond Star Trek Physics: Physics from Alien Invasions to the End of Time*. New York: Basic Books, 1997.

Kuhn, Thomas. *The Structure of Scientific Revolutions*. Chicago: University of Chicago Press, 1962.

Kurzweil, Ray. *The Age of Spiritual Machines: How We Will Live, Work and Think in a New Age of Intelligent Machines*. London: Orion, 1999.

Landes, David S. *Revolution in Time: Clocks and the Making of the Modern World*. Cambridge, Mass.: Harvard University Press, 1983.

Langford, David. *War in 2080: The Future of Military Technology*. Newton Abbot, U.K.: Westbridge, 1979.

Larrain, Jorge. *The Concept of Ideology*. London: Hutchinson, 1979.

Lasser, David. *The Conquest of Space*. New York: Penguin, 1931.

Lawrence, D. H. *Fantasia of the Unconscious*. New York: Thomas Seltzer, 1922.

Ley, Willy. *The Conquest of Space*. New York: Viking, 1949.

———. *Dragons in Amber*. New York: Viking, 1951.

———. *Days of Creation*. New York: Viking, 1952.

———. *Engineers' Dreams*. New York: Viking, 1954.

———. *Beyond the Solar System*. New York: Viking, 1964.

———. *Rockets: The Future of Travel Beyond the Stratosphere*. New York: Viking, 1944. Rev. 2nd ed. as *Rockets and Space Travel*, 1947. Further rev. 3rd ed. as *Rockets, Missiles and Space Travel*, 1951.

———. *Watchers of the Skies: An Informal History of Astronomy from Babylon to the Space Age*. New York: Viking, 1963.

Ley, Willy, and Wernher von Braun. *The Exploration of Mars*. New York: Viking, 1956.

Lombroso, Cesare. *L'hommme criminel*. Paris: F. Alcan, 1887.

Lovelock, James. *Gaia: A New Look at Life on Earth*. Oxford: Oxford University Press, 1973.

———. *The Ages of Gaia; A Biography of Our Living Earth*. Oxford: Oxford University Press, 1988.

Lowell, Percival. *Mars as the Abode of Life*. New York: Macmillan, 1908.

Lowenthal, David. *The Past Is a Foreign Country*. Cambridge: Cambridge University Press, 1985.

Lucky, Robert W. *Silicon Dreams: Information, Man and Machine*. New York: St. Martin's Press, 1989.

Macey, Samuel L. *Clocks and the Cosmos: Time in Western Life and Thought*. Hamden, Conn.: Archon Books, 1980.

Mackay, Charles. *Memoirs of Extraordinary Popular Delusions and the Madness of Crowds*. London: Illustrated Library, 1852.

MacKenzie, W. J. M. *Biological Ideas in Politics*. Harmondsworth, U.K.: Penguin, 1978.

MacVey, John W. *Journey to Alpha Centauri*. New York: Macmillan, 1965.

Mandrou, Robert. *From Humanism to Science 1480–1700*. Trans. by Brian Pearce. Harmondsworth, Middx., U.K.: Penguin, 1978.

Manheim, Karl. *Ideology and Utopia*. Trans. by L. Worth and E. Shils. London: Routledge and Kegan Paul, 1972.

Manuel, Frank E., ed. *Utopias and Utopian Thought*. Boston: Houghton Mifflin, 1966.

Margulis, Lynn. *The Symbiotic Planet: A New Look at Evolution*. London: Weidenfeld and Nicholson, 1998.

Maslow, Abraham H. "Eupsychia: The Good Society". *Journal of Humanistic Psychology* 1.2 (1961): 1–11.

McClennon, James. *Deviant Science: The Case of Parapsychology*. Philadelphia: University of Pennsylvania Press, 1984.

McConnell, James V., ed. *The Worm Re-turns*. New York: Prentice-Hall, 1965.

McKenna, Terence. *Food of the Gods: The Search for the Original Tree of Knowledge*. London: Rider, 1992.

McLuhan, Marshall. *The Gutenberg Galaxy: The Making of Typographical Man*. Toronto: University of Toronto Press, 1962.

———. *Understanding Media: The Extension of Man*. New York: McGraw-Hill, 1964.

———. *The Medium Is the Massage: An Inventory of Effects*. New York: Bantam, 1967.

Minsky, Marvin. *The Society of Mind*. New York: Simon and Schuster, 1985.

Moravec, Hans. *Mind Children: The Future of Robot and Human Intelligence*. Cambridge, Mass.: Harvard University Press, 1988.

Mumford, Lewis. *Technics and Civilization*. New York: Harcourt Brace, 1934.

———. *The Myth of the Machine: Technics and Human Development*. New York: Harcourt Brace and World, 1967.

Murphy, Michael. *The Future of the Body: Explorations into the Further Evolution of Human Nature*. Los Angeles: Tarcher, 1992.

Nef, John U. *War and Human Progress*. Cambridge, Mass.: Harvard University Press, 1950.

Nietzsche, Friedrich W. *Thus Spake Zarathustra*. Trans. by Alexander Tille. London: H. Henry, 1896.

Nisbet, Robert. *History and the Idea of Progress*. New York: Basic Books, 1980.

Noble, David F. *The Religion of Technology: The Divinity of Man and the Spirit of Invention*. New York: Knopf, 1997.

Nye, David E. *American Technological Sublime*. Cambridge, Mass.: MIT Press, 1996.

Oelschlaeger, Max. *The Idea of Wilderness from Prehistory to the Age of Ecology*. New Haven, Conn.: Yale University Press, 1991.

Oldroyd, D. R. *Darwinian Impacts: An Introduction to the Darwinian Revolution*. Milton Keynes, England: Open University Press, 1980.

O'Neill, Gerard K. *The High Frontier*. New York: Morrow, 1977.

Owen, G. *The Universe of the Mind*. Baltimore, Md.: Johns Hopkins University Press, 1971.

Pais, Abraham. *"Subtle Is the Lord...": The Science and the Life of Albert Einstein*. Oxford: Oxford University Press, 1982.

Penrose, Roger. *The Emperor's New Mind: Concerning, Computers, Minds, and the Laws of Physics*. Oxford: Oxford University Press, 1989.

Pickover, Clifford A. *The Science of Aliens*. New York: Basic Books, 1998.

———. *Time: A Traveler's Guide*. New York: Oxford University Press, 1998.

———. *Surfing Through Hyperspace*. New York: Oxford University Press, 1999.

———. *The Mathematics of Oz*. Cambridge: Cambridge University Press, 2002.

———. *Sex, Drugs, Einstein, and Elves*. Petaluma, Calif.: Smart Publications, 2005.

Postman, Neil. *Technopoly: The Surrender of Culture to Technology*. New York: Knopf, 1992.

Pratchett, Terry, and Ian Stewart and Jack Cohen. *The Science of Discworld*. London: Ebury Press, 1999.

———. *The Science of Discworld II: The Globe*. London: Ebury Press, 2002.

———. *The Science of Discworld III: Darwin's Watch*. London: Ebury Press, 2005.

Press, Frank. *Science and Creationism: A View from the National Academy of Science*. Washington, D.C.: National Academy Press, 1984.

Pullman, Bernard. *The Atom in the History of Human Thought*. Trans. by Axel Resinger. Oxford: Oxford University Press, 1998.

Reichardt, Jasia. *Robots: Fact, Fiction and Prediction*. Harmondsworth, Middx., U.K.: Penguin, 1978.

Rheingold, Howard. *Virtual Reality*. New York: Summit, 1991.

Robin, Harry, and Daniel, J. Kevles. *The Scientific Image: From Cave to Computer*. New York: Abrams, 1992.

Ross, Andrew. *Strange Weather: Culture, Science and Technology in the Age of Limits*. New York: Verso, 1991.

Ross, Sydney. "Scientist: The Story of a Word". *Annals of Science* 18 (1962): 65–85.

Rucker, Rudy. *Infinity and the Mind: The Science and Philosophy of the Infinite*. Cambridge, Mass.: Birkhäuser, 1982.

———. *The Fourth Dimension*. London: Rider, 1985.

Russell, Bertrand. *Icarus; or, The Future of Science*. London: Kegan Paul, Trench & Trubner, 1923.

———. *The Scientific Outlook*. London: Allen and Unwin, 1931.

———. *The Impact of Science on Society*. London: Routledge, 1952.

Russell, Claire, and W. M. S. Russell. *Population Crises and Population Cycles*. London: Galton Institute, 1999.

Sagan, Carl. *The Cosmic Connection: An Extraterrestrial Perspective*. New York: Doubleday, 1973.

———. *The Dragons of Eden: Speculations on the Evolution of Human Intelligence*. New York: Ballantine, 1977.

———. *The Demon-Haunted World: Science as a Candle in the Dark*. New York: Random House, 1996.

Sekuler, Robert, and Randolph Blake. *Star Trek on the Brain: Alien Minds, Human Minds*. New York: W. H. Freeman, 1998.

Sheffield, Charles. *Borderlands of Science*. New York: Baen, 1999.

Silverstein, Alvin. *Conquest of Death: The Prospects for Emortality in Our Time*. New York: Macmillan, 1979.

Squire, J.C., ed. *If, or History Rewritten*. Viking: New York, 1931.

Stableford, Brian, and David Langford. *The Third Millennium: A History of the World, AD 2000–3000*. London: Sidgwick & Jackson, 1985.

Sterling, Bruce. *The Hacker Crackdown: Law and Disorder on the Electronic Frontier*. New York: Bantam, 1992; London: Viking, 1993.

———. *Tomorrow Now: Envisioning the Next Fifty Years*. New York: Random House, 2002.

Stock, Gregory. *Metaman: The Merging of Humans and Machines into a Global Superorganism.* New York: Simon and Schuster, 1993.

Teilhard de Chardin, Pierre. *The Phenomenon of Man.* London: Collins, 1959.

———. *The Future of Man.* London: Collins, 1964.

Thorndike, Lynn. *A History of Magic and Experimental Science During the First Thirteen Centuries of Our Era.* 8 vols. New York: Columbia University Press, 1923–1958.

Tillyard, E. M. W. *The Elizabethan World Picture.* New York: Vintage, 1942.

Tipler, Frank. *The Physics of Immortality: Modern Cosmology, God and the Resurrection of the Dead.* New York: Doubleday, 1994.

Toffler, Alvin. *Future Shock.* New York: Random House, 1970.

———. *Ecospasm.* New York: Bantam, 1975.

———. *The Third Wave.* New York: Bantam, 1980.

Uglow, Jenny. *The Lunar Men: The Friends Who Made the Future, 1730–1810.* London: Faber and Faber, 2002.

Vinge, Vernor. "Technological Singularity". *Whole Earth Review* 81 (Winter 1993).

Wacchorst, Wyn. *Thomas Alva Edison: An American Myth.* Cambridge, Mass.: MIT Press, 1981.

Walton, Stuart. *Out of It: A Cultural History of Intoxication.* London: Hamish Hamilton, 2001.

Warwick, Kevin. *March of the Machines: Why the New Race of Robots Will Rule the World.* London: Century, 1997.

Wells, H. G. *Anticipations of the Reaction of Mechanical and Scientific Progress upon Human Life and Thought.* London: Chapman and Hall, 1901.

———. *The Discovery of the Future.* London: Unwin, 1902.

Wertheim, Margaret. *The Pearly Gates of Cyberspace: A History of Space from Dante to the Internet.* London: Virago, 1999.

White, Andrew D. *A History of the Warfare of Science with Theology in Christendom.* New York: Appleton, 1896.

White, Lynn, Jr. *Medieval Technology and Social Change.* Oxford: Oxford University Press, 1962.

Whitehead, A. N. *Science and the Modern World.* Cambridge: Cambridge University Press, 1926.

Williams, Raymond. *Culture and Society, 1780–1950.* London: Chatto and Windus, 1958.

———. *The Long Revolution.* London: Chatto and Windus, 1961.

Worster, Donald. *Nature's Economy: A History of Ecological Ideas.* Cambridge: Cambridge University Press, 1985.

Wrobel, Arthur, ed. *Pseudo-Science and Society in Nineteenth-Century America.* Lexington: University of Kentucky Press, 1987.

Yates, Francis. *The Rosicrucian Enlightenment.* Boulder, Col.: Shambala Press, 1978.

———. *Giordano Bruno and the Hermetic Tradition.* Chicago: University of Chicago Press, 1979.

IV. Works on fiction that have particular relevance to its relationship with science

Aldiss, Brian W. *Billion Year Spree*, London: Gollancz, 1973. Rev., with David Wingrove, as *Trillion Year Spree*. London: Gollancz, 1986.

Alkon, Paul K. *Origins of Futuristic Fiction.* Athens: University of Georgia Press, 1987.

———. *Science Fiction Before 1900: Imagination Discovers Technology.* Studies in Literary Themes and Genres no. 3. Boston: Twayne, 1994.

Anisfield, Nancy, ed. *The Nightmare Considered: Critical Essays on Nuclear War Literature.* Bowling Green, Ohio: Bowling Green University Press, 1991.

Armytage, W. H. G. *Yesterday's Tomorrows: A Historical Survey of Future Societies.* London: Routledge and Kegan Paul, 1968.

Arnold, Matthew. *Culture and Anarchy: An Essay in Political and Social Criticism.* London: Smith Elder, 1869.

Ashley, Michael. *The History of the Science Fiction Magazines.* 4 vols. London: New English Library, 1974–1978.

———. *The Time Machines: The Story of the Science-Fiction Pulp Magazines from the Beginning to 1950.* Liverpool, U.K.: Liverpool University Press, 2001.

Asimov, Isaac. "Social Science Fiction". In *Modern Science Fiction: Its Meaning and Its Future*, ed. Reginald Bretnor, pp. 157–196. New York: Coward-McCann, 1953.

Bailey, J. O. *Pilgrims Through Space and Time: Trends and Patterns in Scientific and Utopian Fiction.* New York: Argus, 1947.

Bainbridge, William Sims. *Dimensions of Science Fiction.* Cambridge, Mass.: Harvard University Press, 1986.

Ballard, J. G. "Which Way to Inner Space?" *New Worlds* 118 (May 1962): 2–3, 116–118.

Balsamo, Anne. *Technologies of the Gendered Body: Reading Cyborg Women.* Durham, N.C.: Duke University Press, 1996.

Barron, Neil, ed. *Anatomy of Wonder: A Critical Guide to Science Fiction.* Westport, Conn.: Libraries Unlimited, 5th edition, 2005.

Bartter, Martha J. *The Way to Ground Zero: The Atomic Bomb in American Science Fiction.* Westport, Conn.: Greenwood, 1988.

Bate, Jonathan. *Romantic Ecology: Wordsworth and the Environmental Tradition.* London: Routledge, 1991.

———. *The Song of the Earth.* London: Picador, 2000.

Baxter, Stephen. "Martian Chronicles: Narratives of Mars in Science and SF". *Foundation* 68 (Autumn 1996): 5–15.

Berger, Albert I. *The Magic That Works: John W. Campbell and the American Response to Technology.* San Bernardino, Calif.: Borgo, 1993.

Berger, Harold. *Science Fiction and the New Dark Age.* Bowling Green, Ohio: Bowling Green University Press, 1976.

Bloomfield, P. *Imaginary Worlds; or, The Evolution of Utopia.* London: Hamish Hamilton, 1932.

Booker, Keith. *Monsters, Mushroom Clouds, and the Cold War: American Science Fiction and the Roots of Postmodernism, 1946–1964.* Westport, Conn.: Greenwood Press, 2001.

Botting, Fred. *Sex, Machines and Navels: Fiction, Fantasy and History in the Future Present.* Manchester, England: Manchester University Press, 1999.

Bretnor, Reginald, ed. *Science Fiction: Today and Tomorrow.* New York: Harper, 1974.

———, ed. *Modern Science Fiction: Its Meaning and Its Future,* New York: Coward-McCann, 1953; rev. Chicago: Advent, 1979.

Brians, Paul. *Nuclear Holocausts: Atomic War in Fiction, 1895–1984.* Kent, Ohio: Kent State University Press, 1987.

Broderick, Damien, ed. *Reading by Starlight: Postmodern Science Fiction.* New York: Routledge, 1995.

———. *Transrealist Fiction: Writing in the Slipstream of Science*. Westport, Conn.: Greenwood Press, 2000.

———. *Earth Is but a Star: Excursions Through Science Fiction to the Far Future*. Crawley, Australia: University of Western Australia Press, 2001.

Carter, Paul A. *The Creation of Tomorrow: Fifty Years of Magazine Science Fiction*. New York: Columbia University Press, 1977.

Clareson, Thomas. *Some Kind of Paradise: The Emergence of American Science Fiction*. Westport, Conn.: Greenwood Press, 1985.

———. *Understanding Contemporary American Science Fiction: The Formative Period (1926–1970)*. Columbia: University of South Carolina Press, 1990.

Clark, Stephen R. L. *How to Live Forever: Science Fiction and Philosophy*. London: Routledge, 1995.

Clarke, Arthur C. "Science Fiction: Preparation for the Age of Space". In *Modern Science Fiction: Its Meaning and Its Future*, ed. Reginald Bretnor, pp. 197–220. New York: Coward-McCann, 1953.

Clarke, I. F. *Voices Prophesying War: Future Wars 1763–3749*. Oxford: Oxford University Press, 1966; 2nd ed., 1992.

———. *The Pattern of Expectation: 1644–2001*. London: Cape, 1979.

Clute, John, and Peter Nicholls. *The Encyclopedia of Science Fiction*. London: Orbit, 2nd ed., 1993.

Davin, Eric Leif, and Norman Metcalf. "Presumption of Prejudice: Women Writers of the 1929–49 Science Fiction Magazines and Their Lost Legacy". *Fantasy Commentator* 53/54 (Winter 2001–2002): 24–74.

———. "Hidden From History: The Female Counterculture of the 1950–1960 Science-Fiction Magazines". *Fantasy Commentator* 55/56 (Spring 2003): 138–191.

Delany, Samuel R. *The Jewel-Hinged Jaw: Notes on the Language of Science Fiction*. Elizabethtown, N.Y.: Dragon Press, 1977.

———. *The American Shore: Meditations on a Tale of Science Fiction by Thomas M. Disch—"Angoulême"*. Elizabethtown, N.Y.: Dragon Press, 1978.

———. *Starboard Wine: More Notes on the Language of Science Fiction*. Pleasantville, N.Y.: Dragon Press, 1984.

———. *Silent Interviews: On Language, Race, Sex, Science Fiction, and Some Comics*. Hanover, N.H.: Wesleyan University Press, 1994.

Dissanayake, Ellen. *Homo Aestheticus: Where Art Comes From and Why*. New York: Free Press, 1992.

Dowling, David. *Fictions of Nuclear Disaster*. Iowa City: University of Iowa Press, 1987.

Dunn, Thomas P., and Richard D. Erlich, eds. *The Mechanical God: Machines in Science Fiction*. Westport, Conn.: Greenwood Press, 1982.

Emme, Eugene E., ed. *Science Fiction and Space Futures Past and Present*. San Diego, Calif.: American Astronautical Society, 1982.

Erlich, Richard D., and Thomas P. Dunn, eds. *Clockwork Worlds: Mechanical Environments in SF*. Westport, Conn.: Greenwood Press, 1983.

Fairchild, H. N. *The Noble Savage: A Study in Romantic Naturalism*. Oxford: Oxford University Press, 1928.

Featherstone, Mike, and Roger Burrows. *Cyberspace/Cyberbodies/Cyberpunk: Cultures of Technological Embodiment*. Thousand Oaks, Calif.: Sage, 1995.

Ferguson, John. *War and the Creative Arts: An Anthology*. London: Macmillan, 1972.

Fischer, William B. *The Empire Strikes Out: Kurd Lasswitz, Hans Dominik and the Development of German Science Fiction*. Bowling Green, Ohio: Popular Press, 1984.

Fisher, Peter S. *Fantasy and Politics: Visions of the Future in the Weimar Republic*. Madison: University of Wisconsin Press, 1991.

Fitting, Peter, ed. *Subterranean Worlds: A Critical Anthology*. Middletown, Conn.: Wesleyan University Press, 2004.

Foote, Bud. *The Connecticut Yankee in the Twentieth Century: Travels to the Past in Science Fiction*. Westport, Conn.: Greenwood Press, 1990.

Fortunati, Vita, and Raymond Trousson, eds. *Dictionary of Literary Utopias*. Paris: Honoré Champion, 2000.

Franklin, H. Bruce. *War Stars: The Superweapon and the American Imagination*. New York: Oxford University Press, 1988.

———. *Future Perfect: American Science Fiction of the Nineteenth Century—An Anthology*. New York: Oxford University Press, 1966; rev. 1970. Rev. as *Future Perfect: American Science Fiction in the Nineteenth Century—An Anthology*. New Brunswick, N.J.: Rutgers University Press, 1995.

Gerber, Richard. *Utopian Fantasy: A Study of English Utopian Fiction Since the End of the Nineteenth Century*. London: Routledge, 1955.

Glad, John. *Extrapolations from Dystopia: A Critical Study of Soviet Science Fiction*. Kingston, N.J.: Kingston Press, 1982.

Glotfelty, Cheryll, and Harold Fromm, eds. *The Ecocriticism Reader: Landmarks in Literary Ecology*. Athens: University of Georgia Press, 1996.

Gold, John Robert. "Under Darkened Skies: The City in Science-Fiction Film". *Geography* 86:4 (October 2001): 337–348.

Goodwin, Barbara, ed. *The Philosophy of Utopia*. London: Frank Cass, 2001.

Gottlieb, Erika. *Dystopian Fiction East and West: Universe of Terror and Trial*. Montreal: McGill-Queens University Press, 2001.

Gove, Philip Babcock. *The Imaginary Voyage in Prose Fiction*. New York: Columbia University Press, 1941.

Green, Roger Lancelyn. *Into Other Worlds: Space Flight in Fiction from Lucian to Lewis*. New York: Abelard-Schumann, 1958.

Green, Scott. *Contemporary Science Fiction, Fantasy and Horror Poetry: A Resource Guide and Biographical Dictionary*. New York: Greenwood Press, 1989.

Greven-Borde, Hélène. *Formes du roman utopique en Grande-Bretagne (1918–1970)*. Paris: Presses Universitaires de France, 1984.

Griffiths, John. *Three Tomorrows: American, British, and Soviet Science Fiction*. New York: Barnes and Noble, 1980.

Gunn, James E., ed. *The New Encyclopedia of Science Fiction*. New York: Viking, 1988.

Haraway, Donna J. "A Manifesto for Cyborgs: Science, Technology and Socialist Feminism in the 1980s". *Socialist Review* 80 (1985): 65–107. [Reprinted as "A Cyborg Manifesto: Science, Technology, and Socialist-Feminism in the Late Twentieth Century". In *Simians, Cyborgs, and Women: The Reinvention of Nature*, pp. 149–181. New York: Routledge, 1991.]

Hartwell, David J. *Age of Wonders: Exploring the World of Science Fiction*. 2nd ed. New York: Tor, 1996.

Harvey, A. D. *A Muse of Fire: Literature, Art and War*. London: Hambledon Press, 1998.

Hassler, Donald M., and Clyde Wilcox, eds. *Political Science Fiction*. Columbia: University of South Carolina Press, 1997.

Hellekson, Karen. *The Alternate History: Refiguring Historical Time*. Kent, Ohio: Kent State University Press, 2001.

Hillegas, Mark R. *The Future as Nightmare: H. G. Wells and the Anti-Utopians*. Oxford: Oxford University Press, 1967.

James, Edward, and Farah Mendlesohn, eds. *The Cambridge Companion to Science Fiction*. Cambridge: Cambridge University Press, 2003.

Ketterer, David. *New Worlds for Old: The Apocalyptic Imagination, Science Fiction, and American Literature*. Bloomington: Indiana University Press, 1974.

Kilgore, De Witt Douglas. *Astrofuturism: Science, Race, and Visions of Utopia in Space*. Philadelphia: University of Pennsylvania Press, 2003.

Kroeber, Karl. *Ecological Literary Criticism: Romantic Imagining and the Biology of Mind*. New York: Columbia University Press, 1994.

Kumar, Krishan. *Utopia and Anti-Utopia in Modern Times*. Oxford: Blackwell, 1987.

Landon, Brooks. *Science Fiction After 1900: From the Steam Man to the Stars*. Studies in Literary Themes and Genres no. 12. Boston: Twayne, 1997.

Larbalestier, Justine. *The Battle of the Sexes in Science Fiction*. Middletown, Conn.: Wesleyan University Press, 2001.

Lefanu, Sarah. *In the Chinks of the World Machine: Feminism and Science Fiction*. London: Women's Press, 1988.

Le Guin, Ursula K. *The Language of the Night: Essays on Fantasy and Science Fiction*. New York: Putnam, 1979. Rev. New York: HarperCollins, 1992.

———. *Dancing at the Edge of the World: Thoughts on Words, Women, Places*. New York: Grove, 1989.

Lem, Stanislaw. *Microworlds: Writings on Science Fiction and Fantasy*, ed. Franz Rottensteiner. New York: Harcourt, 1985.

Lofficier, Jean-Marc and Randy. *French Science Fiction, Fantasy, Horror and Pulp Fiction: A Guide to Cinema, Television, Radio, Animation, Comic Books and Literature from the Middle Ages to the Present*. Jefferson, N.C.: McFarland, 2000.

Magill, Frank N., ed. *Survey of Science Fiction Literature*. 5 vols. Englewood Cliffs, N.J.: Salem, 1979. Rev. in combination with *Survey of Modern Fantasy Literature, 1983* as *Magill's Guide to Science Fiction and Fantasy Literature*, ed. The Editors of Salem Press, 1996.

Malik, Rex, ed. *Future Imperfect: Science Fact and Science Fiction*. London: Francis Pinter, 1980.

Malmgren, Carl. *Worlds Apart: Narratology of Science Fiction*. Bloomington: Indiana University Press, 1991.

Manuel, Frank E., and P. Fritzie, eds. *Utopian Thought in the Western World*. Cambridge, Mass.: Belknap Press, 1980.

Martin, Graham Dunstan. *An Inquiry into the Purposes of Speculative Fiction—Fantasy and Truth*. Lewiston, N.Y.: Edwin Mellen, 2003.

McCaffery, Larry, ed. *Storming the Reality Studio: A Casebook of Cyberpunk and Postmodern Science Fiction*. Durham, N.C.: Duke University Press, 1991.

McGuire, Patrick L. *Red Stars: Political Aspects of Soviet Science Fiction*. Ann Arbor, Mich.: UMI Research Press, 1985.

Meeker, Joseph. *The Comedy of Survival: Studies in Literary Ecology*. New York: Scribner's, 1974.

Miller, Fred D., Jr., and Nicholas D. Smith, eds. *Thought Probes: Philosophy Through Science Fiction*. Englewood Cliffs, N.J.: Prentice Hall, 1981.

Motte, Warren F., ed. and trans. *Oulipo: A Primer of Potential Literature*. Lincoln: University of Nebraska Press, 1986.

Moylan, Tom. *Demand the Impossible: Science Fiction and the Utopian Imagination*. New York: Methuen, 1986.

———. *Scraps of the Untainted Sky: Science Fiction, Utopia, Dystopia*. Boulder, Colo.: Westview, 2000.

Moylan, Tom, and Raffaella Baccolini, eds. *Dark Horizons: Science Fiction and the Utopian Imagination*. London: Routledge, 2003.

Myers, Robert E., ed. *The Intersection of Science Fiction and Philosophy: Critical Studies*. Westport, Conn.: Greenwood Press, 1983.

Newman, John, and Michael Unsworth. *Future War Novels: An Annotated Bibliography of Works in English Published Since 1946*. Phoenix, Ariz.: Oryx Press, 1984.

Nicolson, Marjorie Hope. *Voyages to the Moon*. New York: Macmillan, 1948.

Nordau, Max Simon. *Degeneration*. London: Heinemann, 1895.

Panshin, Alexei and Cory. *The World Beyond the Hill: Science Fiction and the Quest for Transcendence*. Los Angeles: Tarcher, 1989.

Pence, Gregory E. "Putting 'Science' Back in Science Fiction: Cloning in Science Fiction". *Future Orbits* I:2 (January 2002).

Phillips, Michael, ed. *Philosophy and Science Fiction*. Buffalo, N.Y.: Prometheus, 1984.

Philmus, Robert M. *Into the Unknown: Science Fiction from Francis Godwin to H. G. Wells*. Berkeley: University of California Press, 1970.

Pierce, John J. *Foundations of Science Fiction: A Study in Imagination and Evolution*. Westport, Conn.: Greenwood Press, 1987.

———. *Great Themes of Science Fiction: A Study in Imagination and Evolution*. Westport, Conn.: Greenwood Press, 1987.

———. *When World Views Collide: A Study in Imagination and Evolution*. Westport, Conn.: Greenwood Press, 1989.

———. *Odd Genre: A Study in Imagination and Evolution*. Westport, Conn.: Greenwood Press, 1994.

Porush, David. *The Soft Machine: Cybernetic Fiction*. New York: Methuen, 1985.

Rabkin, Eric S., and Martin H. Greenberg and Joseph D, Olander, eds. *No Place Else: Explorations in Utopian and Dystopian Fiction*. Carbondale: Southern Illinois University Press, 1983.

Robu, Cornel. "A Key to Science Fiction: The Sublime". *Foundation* 42 (1988): 21–36.

———. *O cheie pentru science-fiction*. Bucharest: Cluj-Napoca, 2004.

Rucker, Rudy. *Seek!: Selected Nonfiction*. New York: Four Walls Eight Windows, 1999.

Russell, W. M. S. "Life and Afterlife on Other Worlds". *Foundation* 28 (1983): 34–56.

———. "Time in Folklore and Science Fiction". *Foundation* 43 (1988): 5–24.

———. "Time Before and After *The Time Machine*". *Foundation* 65 (1995): 24–40.

Samuelson, David. *Visions of Tomorrow: Six Journeys from Outer to Inner Space*. New York: Arno Press, 1975.

Sandison, Alan, and Robert Dingley, eds. *Histories of the Future: Studies in Fact, Fantasy, and Science Fiction.* New York: Palgrave, 2001.

Schaer, Roland, and Gregory Claes and Lyman Tower Sargent, eds. *Utopia: The Search for the Ideal Society in the Western World.* New York: Oxford University Press, 2000.

Scholes, Robert. *Structural Fabulation: An Essay on Fiction of the Future.* South Bend, Ind.: University of Notre Dame Press, 1975.

———. *The Fabulators.* New York: Oxford University Press, 1967. Rev. as *Fabulation and Metafiction.* Urbana: University of Illinois Press, 1979.

Scholes, Robert, and Robert Kellogg. *The Nature of Narrative.* New York: Oxford University Press, 1966.

Scholes, Robert, and Eric Rabkin. *Science Fiction: History/Science/Vision.* New York: Oxford University Press, 1977.

Shaw, Debra Benita. *Women, Science and Fiction: The Frankenstein Inheritance.* New York: Palgrave, 2001.

Shippey, Tom, ed. *Fictional Space: Essays on Contemporary Science Fiction.* Oxford: Blackwell, 1991.

Sibley, Mulford Q. *Technology and Utopian Thought.* Minneapolis: Burgess, 1973.

Silverberg, Robert. *Drug Themes in Science Fiction.* Rockville, Md.: National Institute on Drug Abuse, 1974.

Slusser, George, and Eric S. Rabkin, eds. *Hard Science Fiction.* Carbondale: Southern Illinois University Press, 1986.

———, eds. *Aliens: The Anthropology of Science Fiction.* Carbondale: Southern Illinois University Press, 1987.

———, eds. *Fights of Fancy: Armed Conflict in Science Fiction and Fantasy.* Athens: University of Georgia Press, 1993.

———, eds. *Styles of Creation: Aesthetic Technique and the Creation of Fictional Worlds.* Athens: University of Georgia Press, 1993.

Smith, Nicholas D., ed. *Philosophers Look at Science Fiction.* Chicago: Nelson Hall, 1982.

Stableford, Brian. *Scientific Romance in Britain, 1890–1950.* London: Fourth Estate, 1985.

———. *The Sociology of Science Fiction.* San Bernardino, Calif.: Borgo Press, 1987.

Sterling, Bruce. "Preface". In *Mirrorshades: The Cyberpunk Anthology,* pp. vii-xiv. New York: Arbor House, 1986.

Stockwell, Peter. *The Poetics of Science Fiction.* London: Longman, 2000.

Street, Brian V. *The Savage in Literature: Representations of "Primitive" Society in English Fiction 1858–1920.* London: Routledge and Kegan Paul, 1975.

Suvin, Darko. *Metamorphoses of Science Fiction: On the Poetics and History of a Literary Genre.* New Haven, Conn.: Yale University Press, 1979.

———. *Victorian Science Fiction in the U.K.: The Discourses of Knowledge and Power.* Boston: G. K. Hall, 1983.

———. *Positions and Presuppositions in Science Fiction.* Kent, Ohio: Kent State University Press, 1988.

Tuck, Donald H. *The Encyclopedia of Science Fiction and Fantasy Through 1968: A Bibliographic Survey of the Fields of Science Fiction, Fantasy, and Weird Fiction Through 1968.* 3 vols. Chicago: Advent, 1974, 1978, and 1982.

Versins, Pierre. *L'Encyclopédie de l'utopie, des voyages extraordinaire et de la science-fiction.* Lausanne, Switzerland: L'Age d'Homme, 1972.

Walsh, Chad. *From Utopia to Nightmare.* London: Bles, 1962.

Wendland, Albert. *Science, Myth, and the Fictional Creation of Alien Worlds.* Ann Arbor, Mich.: UMI Research Press, 1984.

Westfahl, Gary. *Cosmic Engineers: A Study of Hard Science Fiction.* Westport, Conn.: Greenwood Press, 1996.

———. *The Mechanics of Wonder: The Creation of the Idea of Science Fiction.* Liverpool, U.K.: Liverpool University Press, 1998.

———, ed. *Space and Beyond: The Frontier Theme in Science Fiction.* Westport, Conn.: Greenwood Press, 2000.

Westfahl, Gary, and George Slusser, eds. *No Cure for the Future: Disease and Medicine in Science Fiction and Fantasy.* Westport, Conn.: Greenwood Press, 2002.

Westfahl, Gary, and George Slusser and David Leiby. *Worlds Enough and Time: Explorations of Time in Science Fiction and Fantasy.* Westport, Conn.: Greenwood Press, 2002.

Wollheim, Donald A. *The Universe Makers: Science Fiction Today.* New York: Harper, 1971.

Wolmark, Jenny. *Aliens and Others: Science Fiction, Feminism, and Postmodernism.* Iowa City: University of Iowa Press, 1994.

———, ed. *Cybersexualities: A Reader on Feminist Theory, Cyborgs and Cyberspace.* Edinburgh, U.K.: Edinburgh University Press, 1999.

Yanarella, Ernest J. *The Cross, the Plow and the Skyline: Contemporary Science Fiction and the Ecological Imagination.* Parkland, Fla.: Brown Walker Press, 2001.

Yoke, Carl B., and Donald M. Hassler, eds. *Death and the Serpent: Immortality in Science Fiction and Fantasy.* Westport, Conn.: Greenwood Press, 1985.

———, eds. *Phoenix from the Ashes: The Literature of the Remade World.* Westport, Conn: Greenwood Press, 1987.

Zaki, Hoda M. *Phoenix Renewed: The Survival and Mutation of Utopian Thought in North American Science Fiction 1965–1982.* Mercer Island, Wash.: Starmont House, 1988. Rev. San Bernardino, Calif.: Borgo Press, 1993.

V. Studies of individual authors

Barbour, Douglas. *Worlds out of Words: The SF Novels of Samuel R. Delany.* Frome, Somerset, U.K.: Bran's Head, 1979.

Beresford, J. D. *H. G. Wells.* London: Nisbet, 1915.

Bergonzi, Bernard. *The Early H. G. Wells: A Study of the Scientific Romances.* Toronto: University of Toronto Press, 1961.

Bierman, Judah. "The New Atlantis, Bacon's Utopia of Science". *Papers on Language and Literature* 3 (1967): 99–110.

Bittner, James. *Approaches to the Fiction of Ursula K. Le Guin.* Ann Arbor, Mich.: UMI Research Press, 1984.

Bleiler, Everett F., and Richard Bleiler. *Science Fiction Writers: Critical Studies of the Major Authors from the Early Nineteenth Century to the Present Day.* 2nd ed. New York: Scribner, 1999.

Butcher, William. *Verne's Journey to the Centre of the Self: Space and Time in the Voyages Extraordinaires.* London: Macmillan, 1990.

Carrere, Emmanuel. *I Am Alive and You Are Dead: The Strange Life and Times of Philip K. Dick.* New York: Holt/Metropolitan, 2003.

Cavallaro, Dani. *Cyberpunk and Cyberculture: Science Fiction and the Work of William Gibson*. London: Athlone Press, 2000.

Clark, Cumberland. *Shakespeare and Science*. Birmingham, England: Cornish Brothers, 1929.

Cowart, David, and Thomas J. Wymer, eds. *Dictionary of Literary Biography, Volume 8: Twentieth-Century American Science-Fiction Writers*. Farmington Hills, Mich.: Gale, 2 vols., 1981.

Crossley, Robert. *Olaf Stapledon: Speaking for the Future*. Liverpool, U.K.: Liverpool University Press, 1994.

Curry, Walter Clyde. *Chaucer and the Medieval Sciences*. Oxford: Oxford University Press, 1926.

Evans, Arthur B. *Jules Verne Rediscovered: Didacticism and the Scientific Novel*. Westport, Conn.: Greenwood Press, 1988.

Forsström, Riikka. *Possible Worlds: The Idea of Happiness in the Utopian Vision of Louis-Sébastien Mercier*. Helsinki: Suomalisen Kirjallisuuden Seura, 2002.

Franklin, H. Bruce. *Robert A. Heinlein: America as Science Fiction*. New York: Oxford University Press, 1980.

Gill, Stephen. *The Scientific Romances of H. G. Wells*. Cornwall, Ontario, Canada: Vesta, 1975.

Grabo, Carl H. *A Newton Among Poets: Shelley's Use of Science in Prometheus Unbound*. Chapel Hill: University of North Carolina Press, 1930.

Grebens, G. V. *Ivan Efremov's Theory of Soviet Science Fiction*. New York: Vantage Press, 1978.

Griffin, Brian, and David Wingrove. *Apertures: A Study of the Writings of Brian Aldiss*. Westport, Conn.: Greenwood Press, 1984.

Gunn, James E. *Isaac Asimov: The Foundations of Science Fiction*. New York: Oxford University Press, 1982.

Hammond, John R. *H. G. Wells and the Short Story*. New York: St. Martin's Press, 1992.

Harris-Fain, Darren, ed. *Dictionary of Literary Biography, Volume 255: British Fantasy and Science-Fiction Writers, 1918–1960*. Farmington Hills, Mich.: Gale, 2003.

———, ed. *Dictionary of Literary Biography, Volume 261: British Fantasy and Science-Fiction Writers Since 1960*. Farmington Hills, Mich.: Gale, 2003.

Haynes, Roslynn D. *H. G. Wells, Discoverer of the Future: The Influence of Science on His Thought*. London, Macmillan, 1980.

Hollow, John. *Against the Night, the Stars: The Science Fiction of Arthur C. Clarke*. New York: Harcourt Brace, 1983. Rev. Athens: Ohio University Press, 1987.

Huntington, John. *The Logic of Fantasy: H. G. Wells and Science Fiction*. New York: Columbia University Press, 1982.

Kemp, Peter. *H. G. Wells and the Culminating Ape: Biological Themes and Imaginative Obsessions*. London: Macmillan, 1982.

Ketterer, David. *Imprisoned in a Tesseract: The Life and Work of James Blish*. Kent, Ohio: Kent State University Press, 1987.

King-Hele, Desmond. *Erasmus Darwin and the Romantic Poets*. London: Macmillan, 1985.

Lockyer, Norman L., and Winfred Lockyer. *Tennyson as a Student and Poet of Nature*. London: Macmillan, 1910.

Martin, Andrew. *The Mask of the Prophet: The Extraordinary Fictions of Jules Verne*. New York: Oxford University Press, 1990.

McConnell, Frank. *The Science Fiction of H. G. Wells*. New York: Oxford University Press, 1981.

Moskowitz, Sam. *Explorers of the Infinite: Shapers of Science Fiction*. Cleveland, Ohio: World, 1963.

———. *Seekers of Tomorrow: Masters of Modern Science Fiction*. Cleveland, Ohio: World, 1966.

Parrinder, Patrick. *Shadows of the Future: H. G. Wells, Science Fiction and Prophecy*. Liverpool, U.K.: Liverpool University Press, 1996.

Patrouch, Joseph F., Jr. *The Science Fiction of Isaac Asimov*. Garden City, N.Y.: Doubleday, 1974.

Robinson, Kim Stanley. *The Novels of Philip K. Dick*. Ann Arbor, Mich.: UMI Research Press, 1984.

Russell, W. M. S. "Voltaire, Science and Fiction: A Tercentenary Tribute". *Foundation* 62 (1994–1995): 31–46.

Slusser, George Edgar. *Asimov: The Foundations of His Science Fiction*. San Bernardino, Calif.: Borgo Press, 1980.

Stableford, Brian. *Algebraic Fantasies and Realistic Romances: More Masters of Science Fiction*. San Bernardino, Calif.: Borgo Press, 1995.

———. *Outside the Human Aquarium: Masters of Science Fiction*. San Bernardino, Calif.: Borgo Press, 1995.

Stephenson, Gregory. *Out of the Night and into the Dream: A Thematic Study of the Fiction of J. G. Ballard*. Westport, Conn.: Greenwood Press, 1991.

Tolley, Michael J., and Kirpal Singh, eds. *The Stellar Gauge: Essays on Science Fiction Authors*. Melbourne, Australia: Norstilia Press, 1980.

Touponce, William F. *Isaac Asimov*. Boston: Twayne, 1991.

Williamson, Jack. *H. G. Wells: Critic of Progress*. Baltimore, Md.: Mirage Press, 1973.

Wyatt, John. *Wordsworth and the Geologists*. Cambridge: Cambridge University Press, 1995.

VI. Websites

An Atlas of Cyberspace: www.cybergepgraphy.org/atlas

Dinosaurs in Science Fiction Literature: A Guide to Stories, Novels, Anthologies and Pulps. www.dinosauria.com/jdp/misc/fiction

International SF Database: www.isfdb.org

Locus On-Line: www.locusmag.com

Odenwald, Sten. "Hyperspace in Science Fiction". www.astronomycafe.net/anthol/scifi2

Prehistoric Fiction Bibliography: www.trussel.com/prehist

Science and Literature: www.britishcouncil.org/arts-literature-science-and-literature.htm

Science Fiction and Fantasy Research Database: http://library.tamu.edu/cushing/sffrd

Science Fiction Research Bibliography (including *Nuclear Holocausts Bibliography*): www.wsu.edu/#brians/sciencefiction/sfresearch.html

Science Fiction Stories with Good Astronomy & Physics: A Topical Index: www.astrosociety.org/education/resources/scifi.html

Society for Literature, Science, and the Arts: ssla.press.jhu.edu

Uchronia: The Alternate History List: www.uchronia.net

Ultimate Science Fiction Poetry Guide: www.magicdragon.com.

Watson, Ian. "Making Universes: Cosmology in Science Fiction". *The World & I Online* (1987): www.worldandi.com/public.

Index

A

Abbe, Ernst, 308
Abbott, Edwin, 217, 229, 451
ABC of Relativity, The (Russell), 372, 452
"Abdication" (Grant), 492
Abduction: The UFO Conspiracy (Bischoff), 184
Abe, Kobo, 208, 562
Abel, Franklin, 195
"Abercrombie Station" (Vance), 36
Abernathy, Robert, 141, 274
Ability Quotient (Reynolds), 247
"Ablest Man in the World, The" (Mitchell), 34
Abominable Earthman, The (Pohl), 387
About, Edmond, 288, 511
Abraham, legend of, 433
"Absent Friends" (Burstein), 372
Absent-Minded Professor, The (film), 85
Absolute at Large, The (Čapek), 404
"Absolute Zero" (Colter), 108
Absolute Zero (Tidyman), 108
Abyss, The (film), 506
"Abyss, The" (Keller), 254, 423
"A Capella Blues" (Popke), 25
Accelerando series (Stross), 402
Accelerating universe, 160
Acceptance, temporary, 190
"Accepting for Winkelmeyer" (Jacobs), 472
Account of a Meeting with Denizens of Another World, An (Langford), 184
Account of Life and Death, An (Bacon), 56
"Account of the Organs of Speech in the Orang Outan" (Camper), 24
Account of the Winds, An (Bacon), 56
"Accursed Galaxy, The" (Hamilton), 102
"Achilles and the Tortoise" (Gunther), 273, 290
Achilles' Choice (Niven & Barnes), 334
Achilles paradox, 353–354
Achromatic telescope, 521
Acker, Kathy, 403
Ackerman, Diane, 385, 459
Ackroyd, Peter, 28, 126
Acoustics, 1–3
Across the Sea of Suns (Benford), 60, 179, 560
Across the Space Frontier (Ryan), 36
"Across the Void" (Stone), 502
Across the Zodiac (Greg), 282, 404, 493
"Actors, The" (Arnason), 572
"Acts of Conscience" (Tourtelotte), 330
A.D. 2000 (Fuller), 510, 542
"AD 2380: *Homo sapiens* Declared Extinct" (Sterling), 402
Adam, Paul, 390
Adam M–1 (Anderson), 115
Adams, Albert, 295
Adams, Brooks, 122
Adams, Douglas, 139, 248, 271, 274, 458
Adams, Henry, 200, 517
Adams, John Couch, 328
Adams, John Quincy, 69
Adams, Richard, 574

Adamski, George, 182–183
Adamson, Joy, 575
Adaptation, evolutionary, 169. *See also* Evolution
"Adaptation" (Reynolds), 145
Adaptation and Natural Selection (Williams), 485
"Adapter" (Leinster), 164
Adaptive cyborgs, 115
"Adaptive Ultimate, The" (Weinbaum), 509
Adding Machine, The (play), 517
Addison, Joseph, 526
Additives, food, 185–186
Address Unknown (Phillpotts), 487
Adler, Alfred, 194, 413, 418
Adler, Allen, 2
Adler, Elizabeth, 240
Adrift in the Unknown (Cook), 299
"Advent of the Flying Man, The" (Wells), 565
"Adventure in Time, An" (Flagg), 477
"Adventure of the Dancing Men, The" (Conan Doyle), 110
"Adventure of the Devil's Foot, The" (Conan Doyle), 422
"Adventure of the Inertial Adjustor, The" (Baxter), 59, 568
"Adventure of the Laughing Clone, The" (Flynn), 92
Adventure of Wyndham Smith, The (Wright), 121
Adventures in Time and Space (anthology), 491
Adventures of a Micro-Man (Pallander), 159
Adventures of Captain Popanilla (Disraeli), 164
Adventures of John Daniel (Morris), 3
"Adventures of Professor Emmett, The" (Hecht), 158
Adventures of Terra Tarkington, The (Webb), 297
Adventures of Three Russians and Three Englishmen in South Africa (Verne), 549
Advertising
  automobile, 52
  dinosaurs in, 130
  in dystopian fiction, 134
  ecology and jargon of, 142–143
  radio and, 429
  reportable and, 437
  satire about, 387
  sex and, 478
  subliminal, 240
Aeneid (Virgil), 555
"Aeon's Child" (Reed), 497
"Aepyornis Island" (Wells), 346, 348, 566
Aerial Burglars, The (Blyth), 4
"Aerial Cone Deflector, The" (Milne), 344
Aerodrome, The (Warner), 5
Aeronautics, 3–6
  elements and, 154
  fictional use of, 250
  ornithology and, 346
  war and, 558
Aesthetic relativism, 431
Aesthetics, 6–9, 55
  aesthetic evaluation, 9
  Aristotelian, 29
  chaos and, 80
  of crystallisation, 111
  of detective fiction, 190
  extrapolation and, 175

B

E

F

I

J

Mach-1, 2
Mach, Ernst, 46, 161, 401
Mach 1: The Story of Planet Ionus (Adler), 2
Machen, Arthur, 341
Machiavelli, Niccolo, 389
"Machine, The" (Campbell), 517
"Machine-Man of Ardathia, The" (Flagg), 114
Machines, fear of, 292. *See also* Frankenstein complex; Luddites
"Machines of Living Grace" (Dozois), 276
Machine Stops, The (Bayley), 131
"Machine Stops, The" (Forster), 51, 87, 134, 517, 543, 552
Machine to Kill, The (Leroux), 443
"Machmen, The" (Schimtz), 115
MacIsaac, Fred, 251, 558
Mackay, Charles, 11–12, 126
Mackay, Minnie. *See* Corelli, Marie
MacKaye, H.S., 533
Mackelworth, R.W., 40, 217, 497
Mackenzie, Compton, 313
Mackenzie, Henry, 451
MacLaren, Bernard, 527
Maclean, Alastair, 365, 518
MacLean, Katherine, 121–122, 163, 208, 261, 288, 435, 487
MacLean, Paul, 330
MacLeod, Ian R., 140, 161, 179, 473, 479, 553, 561
MacLeod, Ken, 130, 392, 497
MacLeod, Sheila, 445
Macmillan's Magazine, 396
Macneice, Louis, 471
Macnie, John, 185
MacNish, Robert, 426
Macpherson, James, 448
Macrae, Norman, 201
Macrocosm, 102, 148, 279–280, 340
    occult science and, 339
Macroeconomics, 143
Macrolife (Zebrowski), 40–41, 497
Macroscope (Anthony), 42
Macroshift (Laszlo), 202
MacVey, John W., 495
Madam How and Lady Why (Kingsley), 395
"Made in USA" (McIntosh), 23
Mademoiselle de Maupin (Gautier), 30, 157
Mad Love (film), 85
"Mad Machines, The" (Arnold), 51
Mad Metropolis, The (High), 97
"Mad Moon, The" (Moore), 172
"Mad Moon, The" (Weinbaum), 254
Madness, 415–416, 421. *See also* Psychopathology
Madness and Civilization: A History of Insanity in the Age of Reason (Foucault), 416
"Madness Has Its Place" (Niven), 420
"Mad Planet, The" (Leinster), 159
"Mad Robot" (Gallun), 268
Mad Scientist, The (MacDonald & Leger), 110, 471
Maelstrom (Preuss), 549
Mäeterlinck, Maurice, 158, 345
Magazine of Fantasy & Science Fiction, The, 38–39, 60, 466, 496
Magazine of Speculative Poetry, The, 385
"Magic Camera, The" (Atkins), 370
Magic Goes Away, The (Niven), 333
Magician, John Dee as, 126
"Magician of Green Valley," 394
Magicians, The (Priestley), 531
Magic Mountain, The (Mann), 364

Magister Ludi (Hesse), 206, 543
Magnetic fields, 280
Magnetic poles, 281
Magnetism, 150, 187, 213, 280–281, 372
    animal, 280
    Anton Mesmer and, 299–300
    ether and, 161
    occult science and, 340
Magnetism's Fifth Winter (Enquist), 300
Magnetisörens Femte Vinter (Enquist), 300
Maiman, Theodore, 439
Maine, Charles Eric, 36, 131, 288, 313, 361, 415
Maine, Eric Frank, 430
Main Experiment, The (Hodder-Williams), 337
Maitland, Edward, 86
Maître du monde (Verne), 550
"Maître Zacharias; or, the Watch's Soul" (Verne), 292, 549
Make Room! Make Room! (Harrison), 135, 399
Makeshift Rocket, The (Anderson), 122
Make Us Happy (Herzog), 134
Making History (McAuley), 235
Making of a Moon, The: The Story of the Earth Satellite Program (Clarke), 89
Making of Religion, The (Lang), 433
Makropoulos Secret, The (Čapek), 275
Malamud, Bernard, 528
Malartre, Elisabeth, 172
Malcolm, Donald, 501
"Malice in Wonderland" (Hunter), 423
"Malignant Entity, The" (Kline), 306
Malinowski, Bronislaw, 165
Mallett, David, 332
Mallock, W.H., 396, 400
Mallot Diaries, The (Nathan), 25
Mallworld (Sucharikul), 487
Malthus, Robert, 117, 139, 144, 200, 287, 398, 409, 542
Malzberg, Barry N., 33, 65, 195, 207, 315, 360, 419, 488, 495, 528, 535, 560
Mammoth
    Jarkov, 349
    woolly, 348, 349
Mammoth (Thomson), 516
Mammoth Book of New Jules Verne Adventures, The (Ashley & Brown), 551
Mammoth trilogy (Baxter), 59, 92, 349
"Mammy Morgan Played the Organ, Her Daddy Beat the Drum" (Flynn), 361
"Man, Android, and Machine" (Dick), 23
"Man, The" (Bradbury), 528
Man Abroad (Bellamy), 144
Man Among the Monkeys, A (Gozlan), 25
Man and Dolphin (Lilly), 248
Man and His Mate (film), 130
Man and His Works (Herskovits), 431
Man and Materialism (Hoyle), 237
Man and Nature (Marsh), 139, 327
Man and Superman (Shaw), 508
Man and the Monster, The: The Fate of Frankenstein (Béraud et al.), 193
Man Changes the Weather (Bova), 72
Manchurian Candidate, The (Condon), 240
Mandeville, Bernard de, 106, 144, 380
Man Divided, A (Stapledon), 247, 500, 509
Mandrill (Gardner), 104
"Man-Eating Tree, The" (Robinson), 70

INDEX

INDEX

T

U

INDEX

"Vulcan's Forge" (Anderson), 299, 376
Vulcan's Hammer (Dick), 97
"Vulcan's Workshop" (Vincent), 375
Vurt (Noon), 424, 552
"Vybalez proti sobe" (Nesvadba), 52

W

Wacker, Watts, 202
Wagar, Warren, 201
"Wages of Synergy, The" (Sturgeon), 64
"Wages of Syntax, The" (Vukcevich), 272
"Waging Good" (Reed), 313
Wagnerbuch, 177
Wain, John, 385
"Waitabits, The" (Russell), 15, 457
"Waiting for the Iron Age" (Langford), 160
"Waiting Grounds, The" (Ballard), 18
"Wait It Out" (Niven), 382
"Wait Till Next Year" (Rowland), 473
Wakefield, H.R., 432
Waking the Dead (TV series), 189
Waking World (Stapledon), 499
Walden (Thoreau), 139, 327
Walden Two (Skinner), 413–414, 543
Waldholm, Richard, 531
"Waldo" (Heinlein), 156, 552
Waldrop, F.N., 316
Waldrop, Howard, 20, 28, 184, 193, 316, 346, 349, 393, 502
Walker, Adam, 304, 327
Walker, Evan, 540
Walker, John, 268
Walkers on the Sky (Lake), 536
Walking Shadow, The (Stableford), 511
"Walk in the Garden, A" (Shepard), 561
"Walk in the Sun, A" (Landis), 313
Walks, Charles Edmonds, 267
Walk to the End of the World (Charnas), 135
"Walk with Me" (Chilson), 16
Wall, George A., 522
Wall, Stone, Craft (Williams), 449
Wallace, Alfred Russel, 398
Wallace, Edgar, 376, 518, 564
Wallace, F.L., 173, 430, 548
Wallace, Ian, 66, 298
Wallace, Irving, 488
Wallace, King, 557
Wall Around a Star (Pohl & Williamson), 388
Wall at the Edge of the World, The (Aikin), 361
Walling, William, 47, 283, 536
Wallis, B. and G.C., 94
Wallis, G. McDonald, 345
Wallis, George C., 139, 376, 507
Wallis, George C. and B., 254
"Wall of Darkness" (Clarke), 218
Wall of Serpents (de Camp), 124
Walsh, Godwin, 2
Walsh, J.M., 312, 328
Waltari, Mika, 27
Walter, W. Gray, 330
Walters, Hugh, 299
Walton, Harry, 65, 356
Wanderer, The (Leiber), 133

"Wanderer of Infinity" (Vincent), 356
"Wanderers of Time" (Harris), 533
"Wanderer's Return, The" (Pratt), 320
Wanderground, The (Gearhart), 142, 479
Wandering Jew, The (Sué), 288, 365
Wanderings in the Crystal Palace (Franklin), 395
Wandflungen und Symbole der Libido (Jung), 253
"Wand of Creation, The" (Coblentz), 267
"Wand of Creation, The" (Gallun), 267
Wandrei, Donald, 26, 62, 154, 199, 269, 279, 328, 356, 508
War, 555–561. *See also* War stories; Weapons *and specific wars*
  alien invasion, 558
  alternative history, 560–561
  British fiction, 557
  engineering and, 154–155
  ethics and, 162
  Falklands, 559, 560
  future, 557, 567
  Gulf, 560
  Korean, 559
  as metaphor, 560–561
  poetry of, 557–558
  psychological warfare, 559
  rules of, 556
  Social Darwinism and, 484
  submarines in, 505
  technological change and, 513–514
  Vietnam War, 559–560
  weapons, 563–565
  weather and, 305
  World War I (Great War), 557–558. *See also* World War I
  World War II, 558, 559. *See also* Hitler, Adolf; Nazism; World War II
  yellow peril idea, 420, 557, 558, 564
War Against the Rull, The (van Vogt), 559
War and Peace (Tolstoy), 233, 556
War Birds magazine, 4
"Warbots, The" (O'Donnell), 560
Warbots series, 445
Ward, E.D., 121
Ward, Herbert D., 152
Ward, Mrs. Humphry, 170
War in Space: A Grand Romance of Aircraft Warfare Between France and Germany (Gastoine), 4, 557
War in the Air, The (Wells), 557, 567
"War in the Twentieth Century" (Robida), 32, 564
War in 2080 (Langford), 560
Warlord of the Air, The (Moorcock), 502, 557
War machines, 35
"Warm Space, The" (Brin), 239
Warner, Rex, 5
War of the Weenuses, The (Graves & Lucas), 567
War of the Wing-Men (Anderson), 3, 21
War of the Wireless Waves, The (Westerman), 564
War of the Worlds: Global Dispatches (Anderson), 568
War of the Worlds, The (radio), 313, 430
War of the Worlds, The (rock opera), 314–315
War of the Worlds, The (Wells), 14, 93, 172, 282, 446, 485, 551, 557, 566
Warped Passages: Unraveling the Universe's Hidden Dimensions (Randall), 357
War Poetry of the South (Simms, ed.), 556
Warren, Samuel, 395
Warriors of Day, The (Blish), 279
Warrior's Apprentice, The (Bujold), 560

722

X

Y

Z